the
beach

riverhead books

New York

1997

Alex Garland.

the
beach
alex garland

r i v e r h e a d   b o o k s

a division of G. P. Putnam's Sons
Publishers Since 1838
200 Madison Avenue
New York, NY 10016

Library of Congress Cataloging-in-Publication Data

Garland, Alex, date.
The beach / Alex Garland.
p.   cm.
ISBN 1-57322-048-5
I. Title.
PR6057.A639B4   1997   96-25033 CIP
823'.914—dc20

Printed in the United States of America

1   3   5   7   9   10   8   6   4   2

This book is printed on acid-free paper. ∞

Book design by Marysarah Quinn

For Suzy

the
beach

Boom-Boom

Vietnam, me love you long time. All day, all night, me love you long time.

"*Delta One-Niner, this is Alpha patrol. We are on the northeast face of hill Seven-Zero-Five and taking fire, I repeat, taking fire. Immediate air assistance required on the fucking double. Can you confirm?*"

Radio static.

"*I say again, this is Alpha patrol and we are taking fire. Immediate air assistance required. Can you confirm? We are taking fire. Please confirm. We are— Incoming, incoming!*"

Boom.

"*. . . Medic!*"

Dropping acid on the Mekong Delta, smoking grass through a rifle barrel, flying on a helicopter with opera blasting out of loudspeakers, tracer fire and paddy field scenery, the smell of napalm in the morning.

Long time.

Yea, though I walk through the valley of death I will fear no evil, for my name is Richard. I was born in 1974.

bangkok

Bitch

The first I heard of the beach was in Bangkok, on the Ko Sanh Road. The Ko Sanh Road was backpacker land. Almost all the buildings had been converted to guest houses, there were long-distance telephone booths with air-con, the cafés showed brand-new Hollywood films on video, and you couldn't walk ten feet without passing a bootleg tape stall. The main function of the street was as a decompression chamber for those about to leave or enter Thailand; a halfway house between the East and the West.

I'd landed at Bangkok in the late afternoon, and by the time I got to Ko Sanh it was dark. My taxi driver winked and told me that at one end of the street was a police station, so I asked him to drop me off at the other end. I wasn't planning on crime but I wanted to oblige his conspiratorial charm. Not that it made much difference at which end one stayed, because the police obviously weren't active. I caught the smell of grass as soon as I got out of the cab, and half the travelers weaving past me were stoned.

The driver left me outside a guest house with an eating area open to the street. As I studied it, checking the clientele to gauge what kind of place it was, a thin man at the table nearest me leaned over and touched my arm. I glanced down. He was, I guessed, one of the heroin hippies that float around India and Thailand. He'd probably come to Asia ten years ago and turned an occasional dabble into an addiction. His skin was old, though I'd have believed he was in his thirties. The way he was looking at me, I had the feeling I was being sized up as someone to rip off.

"What?" I said warily.

He pulled an expression of surprise and held up the palms of his hands. Then he curled his finger and thumb into the O-shaped perfection sign, and pointed into the guest house.

"It's a good place?"

He nodded.

I looked again at the people around the tables. They were mostly young and friendly-looking, some watching the TV and some chattering over their dinner.

"Okay." I smiled at him in case he wasn't a heroin addict but just a friendly mute. "I'm sold."

He returned the smile and turned back to the video screen.

Quarter of an hour later I was settling into a room that was a little larger than a double bed. I can be accurate about it because there was a double bed in the room, and on each of its four sides there was a foot of space. My bag could just slide into the gap.

One wall was concrete—the side of the building. The others were Formica and bare. They moved when I touched them. I had the feeling that if I leaned against one it would fall over and maybe hit another, and all the walls of the neighboring rooms would collapse like dominoes. Just short of the ceiling, the walls stopped, and across the space was a strip of metal mosquito netting. The netting almost upheld the illusion of being in a confined, personal area, until I lay down on my bed. As soon as I relaxed, I began to hear cockroaches scuttling around in the other rooms.

At my head end I had a French couple in their late teens—a beautiful, slim girl with a suitably handsome boy attached. They'd been leaving their room as I got to mine and we exchanged nods as we passed in the corridor. The other end was empty. Through the netting I could see that the light was off, and anyway, if it had been occupied I would have heard the person breathing. It was the last room on the corridor, so I presumed it faced the street and had a window.

On the ceiling was a fan, strong enough on full setting to stir the air. For a while I did nothing but lie on the bed and look up at it. It was calming, following the revolutions, and with the mixture of heat and soft breeze, I felt I could drift to sleep. That suited me. West to east is the worst for jet lag, and I wanted to fall into the right sleeping pattern on the first night.

I switched off the light. Enough of a glow from the corridor outside came through for me to still see the fan. Soon I was asleep.

Once or twice I was aware of people in the corridor, and I thought I heard the French couple coming back, then leaving again. But the noises never woke me fully and I was always able to slip back into the dream I'd been having before. Until I heard the man's footsteps. They were different, too creepy to doze through. They had no rhythm or weight and dragged on the floor.

A muttered stream of English swearwords floated into my room as he jiggled the padlock on his door. Then there was a loud sigh, the lock opened with a click, and his light came on. The mosquito netting cast a patterned shadow on my ceiling.

Frowning, I looked at my watch. It was two in the morning—late afternoon, English time. I wondered if I might get back to sleep.

The man slumped onto his bed, giving the wall between us an alarming shake. He coughed awhile, then I heard the crackle of a joint being rolled. Soon there was blue smoke caught in the light, rolling through the netting.

Aside from the occasional deep exhalation, he was silent. I drifted back to sleep, almost.

"Bitch," said a voice. I opened my eyes.

"Fucking bitch. We're both as good as . . ."

The voice paused for a coughing fit.

"Dead."

I was wide awake now, so I sat up in bed.

"Cancer in the corals, blue water, my bitch. Fucking Christ, did me in," the man continued.

He had an accent but at first my sleep-fogged head couldn't place it.

"Bitch," he said again, spitting out the word.

A Scottish accent. Beach.

There was a scrabbling sound on the wall. For a moment I thought he might be trying to push it over, and I had a vision of myself being sandwiched between the Formica board and the bed. Then his head appeared through the mosquito netting, silhouetted, facing me.

"Hey," he said.

I didn't move. I was sure he couldn't see into my room.

"Hey. I know you're listening. In there, I know you're awake."

He lifted up a finger and gave the netting an exploratory poke. It popped away from where it was stapled to the Formica. His hand stuck through.

"Here."

A glowing red object sailed through the darkness, landing on the bed in a little shower of sparks. The joint he'd been smoking. I grabbed it to stop it from burning the sheets.

"Yeah," said the man, and laughed quietly. "Got you now. I saw you take the butt."

For a few seconds I couldn't get a handle on the situation. I kept think-ing—what if I actually had been asleep? The sheets might have caught fire. I might have burned to death. The panic flipped into anger, but I sup-pressed it. The man was way too much of a random element for me to lose my temper. I could still only see his head and that was backlit, in shadow.

Holding up the joint, I asked, "Do you want this back?"

"You were listening," he replied, ignoring me. "Heard me talking about the beach."

". . . You've got a loud voice."

"Tell me what you heard."

"I didn't hear anything."

". . . Heard nothing?"

He paused for a moment, then pressed his face into the netting. "You're lying."

"No. I was asleep. You just woke me up . . . when you threw this joint at me."

"You were *listening*," he hissed.

"I don't care if you don't believe me."

"I don't believe you."

"Well . . . I don't care . . . Look." I stood on the bed so our heads were at the same level, and held up the joint to the hole he'd made. "If you want this, take it. All I want is to go to sleep."

As I lifted my hand he pulled back, moving out of the shadow. His face was flat like a boxer's, the nose busted too many times to have any form, and his lower jaw was too large for the top half of his skull. It would have been threatening if not for the body it was attached to. The large jaw ta-pered into a neck so thin it seemed incredible that it supported his head, and his T-shirt hung slackly on coat hanger shoulders.

Past him I saw into his room. There was a window, as I'd assumed, but he'd taped it up with pages from a newspaper. Apart from that it was bare.

His hand reached through the gap and plucked the butt from my fin-gers.

"Okay," I said, thinking I'd gained some kind of control. "Now leave me alone."

"No," he replied flatly.

". . . No?"

"No."

"Why not? What do you . . . Do you want something?"

"Yep." He grinned. "I want lots. And that's why"—again he pushed his face into the netting—"I won't leave you alone."

But as soon as he said it he seemed to change his mind. He ducked out of sight, obscured by the angle of the wall. I stayed standing for a couple of seconds, confused but wanting to reinforce my authority—like it wasn't me stepping down, just him. Then I heard him relight his joint. I let that mark the end of it and lay back down on the bed.

Even after he'd switched his light off, twenty or so minutes later, I still couldn't get back to sleep. I was too keyed up, too much stuff was running through my head. Beaches and bitches, exhaustion; jumpy with adrenaline. Perhaps, given an hour of silence, I might have relaxed, but soon after the man's light went out the French couple came back to their room and started having sex.

It was impossible, hearing their panting and feeling the vibrations of their shifting bed, not to visualize them. The brief glimpse of the girl's face I'd caught in the corridor was stuck in my head. An exquisite face. Dark skin and dark hair, brown eyes. Full lips.

After they'd finished I had a powerful urge for a cigarette, empathy maybe, but I stopped myself. I knew that if I did they'd hear me rustling the packet or lighting the match. The illusion of their privacy would be broken.

Instead I concentrated on lying as still as I could, for as long as I could. It turned out I could do it for quite a long while.

Geography

The Ko Sanh Road woke early. At five, muffled car horns began sounding off from the street outside, Bangkok's version of the dawn chorus. Then the water pipes under the floor started to rattle as the guest house staff took their showers. I could hear their conversations, the plaintive sound of Thai rising above the splashing water.

Lying on my bed, listening to the morning noises, I felt the tension of the previous night become unreal and distant. Although I couldn't understand what the staff were saying to each other, their chattering and occasional laughter conveyed a sense of normality. They were doing what they did every morning, their thoughts only connected to routine. I imagined they might be discussing who would go for kitchen supplies in the market that day or who would be sweeping the halls.

Around five-thirty a few door bolts clicked open as the early-bird travelers emerged and the die-hard partygoers from Patpong returned. Two German girls clattered up the wooden stairs at the far end of my corridor, apparently wearing clogs. I realized that the dreamless snatches of sleep I'd managed were finished, so I decided to have a cigarette, the one I'd denied myself a few hours before.

The early-morning smoke was a tonic. I gazed upward, an empty matchbox for an ashtray balanced on my stomach, and every puff I blew into the ceiling fan lifted my spirits a little higher. Before long my mind turned to thoughts of food. I left my room to see if there was any breakfast to be had in the eating area downstairs.

There were already a few travelers at the tables, dozily sipping glasses of black coffee. One of them, still sitting in the same chair as yesterday evening, was the helpful mute / heroin addict. He'd been there all night, judging by his glazed stare. As I sat down I gave him a friendly smile and he tilted his head in reply.

I began studying the menu, a once white sheet of paper with such an extensive list of dishes that I felt making a choice was beyond my ability. Then I was distracted by a delicious smell. A kitchen boy had wandered over with a tray of fruit pancakes. He distributed them to a group of

Americans, cutting off a good-natured argument about train times to Chiang Mai.

One of them noticed me eyeing their food and he pointed at his plate. "Banana pancakes," he said. "The business."

I nodded. "They smell pretty good."

"Taste better. English?"

"Uh-huh."

"Been here long?"

"Since yesterday evening. You?"

"A week," he replied, and popped a piece of pancake in his mouth, looking away as he did so. I guessed that signaled the end of the exchange.

The kitchen boy came over to my table and stood there, gazing at me expectantly through sleepy eyes.

"One banana pancake, please," I said, obliged into making a snap decision.

"You wan' order one banan' pancake?"

"Please."

"You wan' order drink?"

"Uh, a Coke. No, a Sprite."

"You wan' one banan' pancake, one Spri'."

"Please."

He strolled back toward the kitchen, and a sudden warm swell of happiness washed over me. The sun was bright on the road outside. A man was setting up his stall on the pavement, arranging bootleg tapes into rows. Next to him a small girl sliced pineapples, cutting the tough skin into neat, spiraling designs. Behind her an even smaller girl used a rag to keep the flies at bay.

I lit my second cigarette of the day, not wanting it, just feeling it was the right thing to do.

The French girl appeared without her boyfriend and without any shoes. Her legs were brown and slim, her skirt short. She padded delicately through the café. We all watched her. The heroin mute, the group of Americans, the Thai kitchen boys. We all saw the way she moved her hips to slide between the tables, and the silver bracelets on her wrists.

When her eyes glanced around the room we looked away, and when she turned to the street we looked back.

After breakfast I decided to have a wander around Bangkok, or at the very least, the streets around Ko Sanh. I paid for my food and headed for my room to get some more cash, thinking I might need to get a taxi somewhere.

There was an old woman at the top of the stairs, cleaning the windows with a mop. Water was pouring off the glass and down to the floor. The lady herself was completely soaked, and as the mop lurched around the windows it skimmed dangerously close to a bare light bulb hanging from the ceiling.

"Excuse me," I said, checking I wasn't about to be included in the puddle of potential death that was expanding on the floor. She turned around. "That light is dangerous with the water."

"Yes," she replied. Her teeth were either black and rotten or as yellow as mustard, and it looked like she had a mouth full of wasps. "Hot-hot." She deliberately brushed the light bulb with the edge of her mop. Water boiled angrily on the bulb and a curl of steam rose up to the ceiling.

I shuddered. "Careful! The electricity could kill you."

"Hot."

"Yes but . . ." I paused, seeing that I was onto a nonstarter language-wise, then decided to soldier on.

I glanced around. We were the only two people on the landing.

"Okay, look."

I began a short mime of mopping down the windows before sticking my imaginary mop into the light. Then I began jerking around, electrocuted.

She placed a shriveled hand on my arm to stop my convulsions.

"Hey, man," she drawled in a voice too high-pitched to describe as mellow. "It cool."

I raised my eyebrows, not sure I'd heard her words correctly.

"Chill," she added. "No worry."

"Right," I said, trying to accept the union of Thai crone and hippy jargon with grace. She'd clearly been working on the Ko Sanh Road a long time. Feeling chided, I started walking down the corridor to my room. "Hey," she called after me. "Le'er for you, man."

I stopped. "A what?"

"Le'er."

". . . Letter?"

"Le'er! On you door!"

I nodded my thanks, wondering how she knew which was my room, and continued down the corridor. Sure enough, taped to my door was an envelope. On it was written, "Here is a map," in labored joined-up writing. I was still so surprised at the old woman's strange vocabulary that I took the letter in my stride.

The woman watched me from down the corridor, leaning on her mop. I held up the envelope. "Got it. Thanks. Do you know who it's from?"

She frowned, not understanding the question.

"Did you see anybody put this here?"

I started another little mime and she shook her head.

"Well, anyway, thanks."

"No worry," she said, and returned to her windows.

A couple of minutes later I was sitting on my bed with the ceiling fan chilling the back of my neck and the map in my hands. Beside me the empty envelope rustled under the breeze. Outside the old woman clanked up the stairs with her mop and bucket to the next level.

The map was beautifully colored in. The islands' perimeters were drawn in green ink, and little blue pencil waves bobbed in the sea. A compass sat in the top right-hand corner, carefully segmented into sixteen points, each with an arrow tip and appropriate bearing. At the top of the map it read, "Gulf of Thailand," in thick red marker. A thinner red pen had been used for the island names.

It was so carefully drawn that I had to smile. It reminded me of geography homework and tracing paper. A brief memory surfaced of my teacher handing out exercise books and sarcastic quips.

"So who's it from?" I muttered, and checked the envelope once more for an accompanying note of explanation. It was empty.

Then on one of a cluster of small islands I noticed a black mark. An X mark. I looked closer. Written underneath in tiny letters was the word "Beach."

———

I wasn't sure exactly what I was going to say to him. I was curious, partly, just wanting to know what the deal was with this beach of his. Also I was pissed off. It seemed like the guy was set on invading my holiday, freaking me out by hissing through the mosquito netting in the middle of the night and leaving strange maps for me to find.

His door was unlocked, the padlock missing. I listened outside a minute before knocking, and when I did the door swung open.

In spite of the newspaper pages stuck over the windows, there was enough light coming in for me to see. The man was lying on the bed, looking up at the ceiling. I think he'd slit his wrists. Or it could have been his neck. In the gloom, with so much blood splashed about, it was hard to tell what he'd slit. But I knew he'd done the cutting. There was a knife in his hand.

I stood still, gazing at the body for a couple of moments. Then I went to get help.

Etienne

The policeman was perspiring, but not with the heat. The air-con in the room made it like a fridge. It was more to do with the exertion of speaking English. When he came to a difficult word or complicated sentence his brow would crease into a hundred lines. Then little beads of sweat would pop up like opals on his brown skin.

"But Mis'er Duck no you frien'," he said.

I shook my head. "I'd never met him before last night. And listen. The Duck name, it's not real. It's a joke name."

"Jo' name?" said the policeman.

"Not a true name." I pointed to where he'd written the name in his notebook. "Daffy Duck is a cartoon character."

"Ca'oon?"

"Yes."

"Mis'er Duck is Ca'oon?"

"Like Bugs Bunny. Uh, Mickey Mouse."

"Oh," said the policeman. "So, he give false name to gues' house."

"Definitely."

The policeman wiped his shirtsleeve over his face. Sweat sprinkled over his notebook, blurring the ink. He frowned and new droplets replaced the ones he'd just swept away.

"Now I wan' ask you abou' scene of crime."

"Okay."

"You en'er Mis'er Duck room, because wha'?"

I'd worked this out on the walk down the Ko Sanh Road to the police station.

"Because he'd been keeping me awake last night and I wanted to tell him not to do it again."

"Ah. Las' nigh' Mis'er Duck make a noise."

"Right."

"And wha' you fin' in room, hah?"

"Nothing. I just saw him dead and went to tell the guest house manager."

"Mis'er Duck already dead? How you know abou' tha'?"

"I didn't. I just thought he was. There was a lot of blood."

The policeman nodded sagely, then leaned back on his chair.

"I think you angry abou' so much noise las' nigh', hah?"

"Sure."

"How angry with Mis'er Duck?"

I held up my hands. "I spent the whole morning in the restaurant eating breakfast. From six until nine. A lot of people saw me there."

"Maybe he die before six."

I shrugged. I wasn't worried. There was a clear image in my head of the low light coming through the newspapered windows and the sparkling highlights on Mister Duck. The blood had been pretty wet.

The policeman sighed. "Okay," he said. "You tell me again abou' las' nigh'."

Why didn't I mention the map? Because I didn't want to get involved in some foreign police investigation and I didn't want my holiday fucked

up. Also I didn't care much about the guy's death. I saw it as, well . . .
Thailand's an exotic country with drugs and AIDS and a bit of danger, and
if Daffy Duck got too caught up, then it was his lookout.

I didn't get the impression that the policeman cared much about the
whole thing either. After another thirty minutes of ruthless interrogation
("Can you ve'ify you eat banan' pancake?") he let me go, asking me not to
leave Ko Sanh within twenty-four hours.

The French girl's boyfriend was sitting on the steps of the police station with his face angled up toward the sun. Obviously he'd been brought
in for questioning too. He glanced around as I walked down the steps,
maybe thinking I was the girl, then turned back.

Normally I'd have taken that as a sign someone doesn't want to chat. I
do a lot of my traveling alone, so sometimes I get starved of conversation
and company. It makes me alert to body language, because even if I'm
feeling a bit lonely I don't want to inflict myself on a person who isn't interested. But this time I ignored the sign. Despite my not wanting to get
involved with the police, the death had made for an unusual start to the
day and I had the urge to talk about it.

I sat down right beside him so he couldn't avoid me. As it turned out
I'd read the sign wrong anyway. He was very friendly.

"Hi," I said. "Speak English? Uh, *je parle français un petit peu mais mal-
heureusement je suis pas très bon.*"

He laughed. "I speak English," he replied in a gently accented voice.

"You're here about that guy who died, huh?"

"Yes. I heard you were the one to find him."

Fame.

"Yep," I replied, pulling my cigarettes out of my pocket. "Found him
this morning."

"It must have been bad for you."

"It was okay. Do you smoke?"

"No thank you."

I lit up.

"So I'm Richard," I said, exhaling.

"Etienne," said Etienne, and we shook hands.

Last night I'd put him at eighteen or so, but in the daylight he looked older. Twenty or twenty-one. He had a Mediterranean look about him— short dark hair and a slim build. I could see him in a few years' time, a couple of stone heavier, a glass of Ricard in one hand and a *boule* in the other.

"This is so weird," I said. "I only got to Thailand last night. I wanted to relax in Bangkok, if that's possible, and instead I got this."

"Oh, we have been here already four weeks, and it is weird for us, too."

"Well yeah, I suppose someone dying is always a bit strange. So where've you been for the last month? Not only Bangkok, surely."

"No, no." Etienne shook his head vigorously. "A few days in Bangkok is enough. We have been north."

"Chiang Rai?"

"Yes, we went on a trek. We rafted on a river. Very boring, no?" He sighed and leaned backward, resting his back on the stone step behind him.

"Boring?"

Etienne smiled. "Raft, trek. I want to do something different, and everybody wants to do something different. But we all do the same thing. There is no . . . ah . . ."

"Adventure."

"I think it is why we come here." He pointed around the corner of the police station, toward the Ko Sanh Road. "We come for an adventure, but we find this."

"Disappointing."

"Yes."

Etienne paused for a moment, frowning slightly; then he said, "This man who died. He was very strange. We would hear him late at night. He would talk and shout . . . The walls are so thin."

To my irritation I blushed, remembering the sound of Etienne and his girlfriend having sex. I took a deep drag on my cigarette and looked down at the steps we were sitting on. "Are they?" I said. "I was so tired last night I slept . . ."

"Yes. Sometimes we do not return to the guest house until late so he will already be asleep."

"It won't be a problem anymore."

"Often we could not understand him. I know he talked English, because I would recognize some words, but . . . it was not easy."

"It wasn't easy for me either. He was Scottish. Strong accent."

"Oh . . . You heard him last night?"

Now it was Etienne's turn to go red while I concentrated on my cigarette. My embarrassment was compounded by his. It was odd, but if his girlfriend had been ugly, then I'd only have been amused, but because she was so attractive it almost felt as if I'd had some kind of affair with her. Which of course I had. A mental affair.

We blushed at each other until the awkward silence became too oppressive.

"Yes," I said, far too loudly. "He had a thick Scottish accent."

"Ah," replied Etienne, also a little firmly. "Now I understand."

He stroked his chin thoughtfully as though he were smoothing down a beard, although I could see from his light stubble that he was a long way from being able to grow one. Then he said, "He would talk about a beach."

He looked straight at me as he said it. He was watching my face for a reaction—it was obvious. I nodded to make him continue.

"He would talk about it all night. I would lie on my bed awake, because I could not sleep with his shouting, and I would try to follow his words. Like a puzzle." Etienne laughed. "Fokkin' bitch," he said, approximating the man's voice pretty well. "It took me three nights to understand it was a beach. Just like a puzzle."

I took another drag on my cigarette, leaving a pause in the conversation, letting Etienne fill it.

"I like puzzles," he said, but not really to me. Then he let the silence grow.

A trip to India, seventeen years old, more dope than sense, me and one friend decided to take about an eighth of hash on a flight from Srinagar to Delhi. We each made our own plans as to how to take it. I wrapped mine up in plastic, swathed it in masking tape and deodorant to mask the smell, and tucked it into a bottle of malaria pills. The precautions were probably unnecessary. The customs officers were unlikely to be too interested in internal flights, but I did it anyway.

When we got to the airport I was shit scared. I mean I was *shit scared*—eyes popping, shaking, sweating like a pig. But in spite of my fear, I did the most extraordinary thing. I told a complete stranger, a guy I met in the waiting lounge, that I had some dope hidden in my backpack. It wasn't even like he'd winkled the information out of me. I volunteered it. I made the conversation move onto the subject of drugs, and then confessed that I was a smuggler.

I don't know why I did it. I knew it was a fantastically stupid thing to do, but I went right ahead and did it anyway. I simply needed to tell someone what I was doing.

"I know where the beach is," I said.

Etienne raised his eyebrows.

"I've got a map."

"A map of the beach?"

"The dead guy drew it for me. I found it stuck to my door this morning. It shows where the beach is, how to get there. I've got it in my room."

Etienne whistled. "You told the police?"

"Nope."

"Perhaps it is important. Maybe it is something to do with why he . . ."

"Maybe it is." I flicked away my cigarette. "But I don't want to get involved. Maybe they'd think I knew him or something, but I didn't. I never met him before last night."

"A map," said Etienne quietly.

"Cool, huh?"

Etienne stood up suddenly. "Can I see it? Would you mind?"

"Uh, not really," I replied. "But aren't you waiting for . . ."

"My girlfriend? Françoise? She knows the way back to the guest house. No, I would like to see the map." He rested a hand lightly on my shoulder. "If I may."

I was surprised by the intimacy of the gesture; my shoulder twitched and the hand dropped. "Yeah, sure," I said. "Let's go."

Mute

We didn't talk as we walked down the Ko Sanh Road toward the guest house. There was no point. Dodging through the hundreds of travelers made it impossible to have a conversation. Passing the bootleg tape stalls, moving through the music zones, picking up the walking pace for one beat, slowing it for another. Credence Clearwater told us to run through the jungle, as if we needed to be told. A Techno beat pumped out of fuzzy speakers, then Jimi Hendrix.

Platoon. Jimi Hendrix, dope, and rifle barrels.

I looked for the smell of grass to complete the connection, and found it through the stench of a hot gutter and sticky tarmac. I think it came from above—a balcony full of braided hair and dirty T-shirts, leaning on the guardrail, enjoying the scene below.

A brown hand flashed out and caught hold of me. A Thai trader sitting by his stall, a slim man with acne scars, was gripping my arm. I looked toward Etienne. He hadn't seen, was still walking down the road. I lost him behind bobbing heads and tanned necks.

The man began stroking my forearm with his free hand, smoothly and swiftly, not loosening his grip. I frowned and tried to pull away. He pulled me back, taking my hand toward his thigh. My fingers clenched to a fist and my knuckles pressed against his skin. People pushed past me on the pavement, knocking me with their shoulders. One caught my eye and smiled. The man stopped stroking my arm and started stroking my leg.

I looked at him. His face was passive and unreadable and his gaze was leveled at my waist. He gave my leg a final caress, turning his wrist so his thumb slipped briefly under the material of my shorts. Then he released my arm, patted me on the behind, and turned back to his stall.

I jogged after Etienne—he was standing on the pavement twenty yards ahead with his hands on his hips. As I approached he raised his eyebrows. I frowned and we continued walking.

———

At the guest house the silent heroin addict sat in his usual seat. When he saw us he drew a line with his finger over each wrist. "Sad, huh?" I tried to say, but my lips were sticky and barely opened. The sound that came from my throat was a sigh.

Françoise

Etienne gazed at the map for five minutes without speaking. Then he said, "Wait," and darted out of my room. I heard him rummaging around next door, then he came back holding a guidebook. "There." He pointed to an open page. "These are the islands in the map. A National Marine Park west of Koh Samui and Koh Phangan."

"Koh Samui?"

"Yes. Look. All the islands have protection. Tourists cannot visit, you see?"

I couldn't. The guidebook was written in French, but I nodded anyway.

Etienne paused, reading, then continued. "Ah. Tourists can go to . . ." He took the map and pointed to one of the bigger islands in the small archipelago, three islands down from where X marked the beach. "This one. Koh Angthong. Tourists can go to Koh Angthong on a special guided tour from Koh Samui, but . . . but they can only stay one night. And they cannot leave the island."

"So this beach is in a National Park?"

"Yes."

"How are people supposed to get there?"

"They cannot get there. It is a National Park."

I leaned back on the bed and lit a cigarette. "That's settled then. The map is bullshit."

Etienne shook his head. "No. Not bullshit. Really, why did the man give it to you? He went to so much trouble. See the little waves."

"He called himself Daffy Duck. He was mad."

"I do not think so. Listen." Etienne picked up his guidebook and began a halting translation. "The most adventurous travelers are . . . exploring the islands beyond Koh Samui to find . . . to find, ah, tranquillity, and Koh Phangan is a favorite . . . destination. But even Koh Phangan is . . ." He paused. "Okay, Richard. This says travelers try new islands beyond Koh Phangan, because Koh Phangan is now the same as Koh Samui."

"The same?"

"Spoiled. Too many tourists. But look, this book is three years old. Now maybe some travelers feel these islands past Koh Phangan are also spoiled. So they find a completely new island, in the National Park."

"But they aren't allowed in the National Park."

Etienne raised his eyes to the ceiling. "Exactly! This is why they go there. Because there will be no other tourists."

"The Thai authorities would just get rid of them."

"Look how many islands are there. How could they be found? Maybe if they hear a boat they can hide, and the only way to find them is if you know they are there—and we do. We have this." He slid the map across the bed at me. "You know, Richard, I think I want to find this beach."

I smiled.

"Really," said Etienne. "You can believe me. I do."

I did believe him. He had a look in his eye that I recognized. In my early adolescence I went through a stage of mild delinquency, along with two of my friends, Sean and Danny. During the early hours of the morning, weekends only because we had school to think of, we would patrol the streets around our area, smashing things. "Hot Bottle" was the favorite game. It involved stealing empty milk bottles from people's doorsteps. We would throw the bottles high into the air and try to catch them. Most of the fun came when bottles were dropped, seeing the silvery explosion of glass, feeling the shards flick against our jeans. Running from the scene of the crime was an extra kick, ideally with the shouts of enraged adults ringing in our ears.

The look I recognized in Etienne's eyes came from one particular experience when we graduated from smashing milk bottles to smashing a car. We'd been sitting in my kitchen, playfully discussing the idea, when Sean said, "Let's just do it." He said it casually, but his eyes said he was serious. Through them I could see he'd already moved beyond thoughts of practicality and consequence, and was hearing the sound of the windshield folding in.

Etienne, I imagined, was hearing the sound of the surf on this hidden beach, or hiding from the Marine Park wardens as he made his way to the island. The effect on me was the same as when Sean said, "Let's just do it." Abstract thoughts suddenly flipped into thoughts about reality. Following the path of the map had become something that could happen.

"I think," I said, "we could probably hire a fisherman to take us to the island."

Etienne nodded. "Yes. It might be difficult to get there, but not impossible."

"We'd have to go to Koh Samui first."

"Or Koh Phangan."

"Or maybe we could even do it from Surat Thani."

"Or Koh Angthong."

"We'd have to ask around a little . . ."

"But there would be someone to take us."

"Yes . . ."

At that moment Françoise appeared, having returned from the police station.

If Etienne was the one who turned the idea of finding the beach into a possibility, it was Françoise who made it happen. The odd thing was, she did it almost accidentally, simply by taking for granted that we were going to try.

I didn't want to seem impressed by her prettiness, so when she stuck her head round the door, I looked up, said "Hi," then went back to studying the map.

Etienne shifted over on my bed and patted the space he had made. Françoise stayed in the doorway. "I did not wait for you," he said, presumably speaking in English for my sake. "I met Richard." She didn't follow the language lead and began rattling away in French. I couldn't follow their conversation past recognizing the odd word, including my own name, but the speed and forcefulness of the exchange made me think that either she was pissed off that he'd left without her, or she was just keen to fill him in on what happened at the police station.

After some minutes the tone of their voices relaxed. Then Françoise said in English, "May I have a cigarette, Richard?"

"Sure." I gave her one and held out a light. As she cupped her hands to cover the flame from the ceiling fan, I noticed a tiny dolphin tattoo half hidden beneath her watch strap. It seemed like a strange place for a tattoo and I nearly commented on it, but to do so seemed too familiar. Scars and tattoos. You need to know someone fairly well before asking questions.

"So what is this map from the dead man?" Françoise asked.

"I found it on my door this morning," I started to explain, but she cut me off.

"Yes, Etienne has told me already. I want to see it."

I passed the map to her and Etienne pointed out the beach.

"Oh," she said. "Near Koh Samui."

Etienne nodded enthusiastically. "Yes. Just a little ride on a boat. Maybe first to Koh Angthong, because the tourists can go there for one day."

Françoise put her finger on the X-marked island. "How can we know what we will find here?"

"We can't," I replied.

"And if there is nothing, how do we get back to Koh Samui?"

"We get back to Koh Angthong," said Etienne. "We wait for a tourist boat. We say we were lost. It doesn't matter."

Françoise took a delicate puff on her cigarette, barely taking the smoke into her lungs. "I see . . . Yes . . . When are we leaving?"

I looked at Etienne and he looked back at me.

"I am tired of Bangkok," Françoise continued. "We can get the night train south tonight."

"Well, uh," I stammered, thrown by the speed at which events were developing. "The thing is, we've got to wait a bit. This guy who committed suicide . . . I'm not supposed to leave the guest house for twenty-four hours."

Françoise sighed. "Go to the police station and explain you have to leave. They have your passport number, yes?"

"Yeah, but . . ."

"So they will let you go."

She stubbed out her cigarette on the floor as if to say, end of discussion. Which it was.

Local Color

That afternoon I went back to the police station, and as Françoise predicted I didn't get any hassle. The detailed excuse I'd worked out, about how I had to meet a friend at Surat Thani, was brushed aside. Their only concern was that Mister Duck had been without ID, so they didn't know which embassy to inform. I said I'd thought he was Scottish, and they were pleased about that.

As I walked back to the guest house, I found myself thinking what would happen to Mister Duck's body. Amidst all the business of the map, I'd forgotten that someone had actually died. Without ID, the police would have nowhere to send him. Perhaps he'd lie in a Bangkok deep freeze for a year or two, or perhaps he'd be incinerated. An image came into my head of his mother back in Europe, unaware that she was just about to start several dark months of trying to find out why her son had stopped contacting her. It seemed wrong that I could have such an important piece of information while she remained ignorant. If she existed.

These thoughts unsettled me. I decided not to continue directly to the guest house, where Etienne and Françoise would be wanting to talk about the beach and the map. I felt like a bit of time alone. We'd arranged to catch the eight-thirty train south, so there was no need for me to get back for at least two hours.

I took a left off the Ko Sanh Road, went down an alley, ducked under the scaffolding of a half-finished building, and came out on a busy main street. I suddenly found myself surrounded by Thais. I'd half forgotten which country I was in, stuck in backpacker land, and it took me a few minutes to adjust to the change.

Before long I came to a low bridge over a canal. It was hardly picturesque but I stopped there to find my reflection and follow the swirls of petrol color. Along the canal banks, squatters' shacks leaned dangerously. The sun, hazy throughout the morning, now shone hard and hot. Around the shacks a gang of kids cooled off, dive-bombing each other and playing splashing games.

One of them noticed me. I suppose that a pale face would once have had some interest for him, but not now. He held my gaze for a few seconds, either insolent or bored, then leapt into the black water. He achieved an ambitious somersault and his friends shouted their appreciation.

When the kid surfaced, he looked at me again, treading water. The motion of his arms cleared a circle in the floating litter. Shredded polystyrene that, for a moment, looked like soapsuds.

I tugged at the back of my shirt. Sweat was making it stick to my skin.

All in all, I probably walked two miles from the Ko Sanh Road. After the canal, I ate some noodle soup from a roadside stall, wove through some traffic jams, passed by a couple of small temples that were tucked discreetly between stained concrete buildings. Not sights that made me regret leaving Bangkok so soon. I'm not much for sight-seeing, anyway. If I'd stayed a few more days, I doubt I'd have explored any further than the strip joints in Patpong.

Eventually I'd wandered so far I didn't have a clue how to get back to the guest house, so I caught a *tuk-tuk*. In a way it was the best part of the excursion, chugging along in a haze of blue exhaust fumes, spotting the kind of details you miss when you're on foot. Can't think what they are now. I just remember that the ride was more interesting than the walk.

Etienne and Françoise were in the eating area, their bags beside them.

"Hey," said Etienne. "We thought you have changed your mind."

I said I hadn't and he looked relieved.

"So maybe you should pack soon. I think we should arrive early for the train."

I went upstairs to get my bag. On the landing of my level I passed the heroin mute on his way down. A double surprise, partly to see him moved from his usual seat and partly because it turned out he wasn't mute after all.

"You off?" he said as we neared each other.

I nodded.

"Heading for white sands and blue water?"

"Uh-huh."

"Well, have a safe trip."

"I'll try."

He smiled. "Of course you'll *try* to have a safe trip. I'm saying, actually have one."

It's Life, Jim, But Not as We Know It

We took the night train south from Bangkok, first-class. In first class you get a waiter come to your table, a cheap meal of good food, and an hour later the table is flipped up to reveal spotless bunk beds. At Surat Thani we got off the train and took a bus to Donsak. From there we caught the Songserm ferry, straight to the pier at Na Thon.

That was how we got to Koh Samui.

I only felt able to relax once I'd shut the curtains on my bunk bed and cut myself off from the rest of the train. More to the point, cut myself off from Etienne and Françoise. Things had been awkward since leaving the guest house. It wasn't that they were getting on my nerves, just that the reality of our undertaking was sinking in. Also, I was remembering that we were virtual strangers—something I'd forgotten in the excitement of our quick decision. I'm sure they were feeling the same, which is why their attempts at conversation were as limited as mine.

I lay on my back with my hands behind my head, content in the knowledge that the muffled sound of the wheels on the tracks and the rocking movement of the carriage would soon send me to sleep.

While I waited, I studied the clever design of my bunk. The carriage had been dimmed, but enough light came through the gap around my curtain for me to see. There was a whole array of useful pouches and compartments which I'd done my best to employ. My T-shirt and trousers were tucked into a little box at my foot end, and I'd put my shoes in an elastic net above my waist. Above my head was an adjustable reading lamp, switched off, but beside it a tiny red bulb gave a reassuring glow.

As I became sleepy I started to fantasize. I imagined the train was a spaceship and I was en route to some distant planet.

I don't know if I'm alone in doing this kind of thing. It isn't something I've ever talked about. The fact is, I've never grown out of playing pretend, and so far there are no signs that I ever will. I have one quite carefully worked-out nighttime fantasy that I'm in a kind of high-tech race. The race takes place over several days, even a week, and is nonstop. While I sleep my vehicle continues on autopilot, speeding me toward the finish line. The autopilot thing is the rationalization of how I can be in bed while I'm having the fantasy. Making it work in such a logical way is important—it would be no good fantasizing that the race was in a Formula One car, because how could I go to sleep in that? Get real.

Sometimes I'm winning the race, other times I'm losing. But on those occasions I also fantasize that I have a little trick up my sleeve. A shortcut perhaps, or just a reliance on my ability to take corners quicker than the other competitors. Either way, I fall asleep quietly confident.

I think the catalyst for this particular fantasy was the little red bulb beside the reading lamp. As everyone knows, spaceships aren't spaceships without little red bulbs. Everything else—the clever compartments, the rushing noise of the train's engine/warp drive, the sense of adventure— was a happy complement.

By the time I fell asleep, my scanners were detecting life forms on the surface of a distant planet. Could have been Jupiter. It had the same kind of cloud patterns, like a tie-dye T-shirt.

The warm security of my spaceship capsule slipped away. I was back on my bed on the Ko Sanh Road, looking up at the ceiling fan. A mosquito was buzzing in the room. I couldn't see it but its wings pulsed like a helicopter when it flew near. Sitting beside me was Mister Duck, the sheets around him red and wet.

"Would you sort this out for me, Rich?" Mister Duck said, passing me a half-rolled joint. "I can't do it. My hands are too sticky. The rizla . . . The rizla keeps falling apart."

He laughed apologetically as I took the joint.

"It's my wrists. Slit them all over and now they won't stop bleeding." He lifted up his arm and a squirt of blood arced across the Formica wall. "See what I mean? What a fucking mess."

I rolled the joint but didn't lick it. On the strip of gum was a red fingerprint.

"Oh. You don't want to worry about that, Rich. I'm clean." Mister Duck looked down at his sodden clothes. "Well, not clean . . ."

I licked the rizla.

"So spark it up. I'll only make it wet."

He held out a light and I sat up on the bed. My weight sank the mattress and a stream of blood ran down the slope, soaking into my shorts.

"Now how's that? Hits the fucking spot, huh? But you want to try it through a rifle barrel. That's a serious hit, Rich."

"Blow my mind."

"Yeah," said Mister Duck. "That's the boy. That's the kid . . ."

He lay back on the bed with his hands above his head, wrists facing upward. I took another drag. Blood ran along the blades of the fan and fell around me like rain.

koh samui

R & R

The journey from the train station at Surat Thani to Koh Samui passed in a sleep-fogged blur. I vaguely remember following Etienne and Françoise onto the bus to Donsak, and my only memory of the ferry ride is of Etienne shouting in my ear over the noise of the boat's engines. "There, Richard!" he yelled, pointing toward the horizon. "That's the Marine Park!" A cluster of blue-green shapes was just visible in the distance. I nodded obligingly. I was more interested in finding a soft spot on my backpack to use as a pillow.

Our Jeep from the Koh Samui port to the Chaweng beach resort was a big open-top Isuzu. On the left the sea lay blue between rows of coconut palms, and on the right a jungle-covered slope rose steeply. Ten travelers sat behind the driver's cabin, our bags clamped between our knees, our heads rolling with the corners. One had a baseball bat resting against his shoulder, another held a camera on his lap. Brown faces flashed past us through the green.

"Delta One-Niner," I muttered, "this is Alpha patrol."

The Jeep left us outside a decent-looking bunch of beach huts, but backpacker protocol demanded we check out the competition. After half an hour of slogging across the hot sand, we returned to the huts we'd first seen.

Private showers, a bedside fan, a nice restaurant that looked onto the sea. Our huts faced each other over a gravel path lined with flowers. It was *très beau*, Françoise said with a happy sigh, and I agreed.

The first thing I did after shutting the door behind me was to go to the bathroom mirror and examine my face. I hadn't seen my reflection for a couple of days and wanted to check that I was looking okay.

It was a bit of a shock. Having been around lots of tanned skin, I'd somehow assumed I was also tanned, but the ghost in the mirror corrected me. My whiteness was accentuated by my stubble, which, like my hair, is jet-black. UV deprivation aside, I was in bad need of a shower. My T-shirt had the salty stiffness of material that has been sweated in, sun-dried, then sweated in again. I decided to head straight to the beach for a swim. I could kill two birds with one stone—soak up a few rays and get clean.

Chaweng was a travel brochure photo. Hammocks slung in the shade of curving palm trees, sand too bright to look at, Jet Skis tracing white patterns like jet planes in a clear sky. I ran down to the surf, partly because the sand was so hot and partly because I always run into the sea. When the water began to drag on my legs I jumped up and the momentum somersaulted me forward. I landed on my back and sank to the bottom, exhaling. On the seabed I let myself rest, head tilted slightly forward to keep the air trapped in my nose, and listened to the soft clicks and rushes of underwater noise.

I'd been splashing around in the water for fifteen minutes or so when Etienne came down to join me. He also ran across the sand and somersaulted into the sea, but then he leapt up with a yelp.

"What's up?" I called.

Etienne shook his head, pushing backward through the water away from where he'd landed. "This! This animal! This . . . fish!"

I began wading toward him. "What fish?"

"I do not know the English. Aaah! Aaah! There are more! Aaah! Stinging!"

"Oh," I said as I reached him. "Jellyfish. Great!"

I was pleased to see the pale shapes, floating in the water like drops of silvery oil. I loved their straightforward weirdness, the strange area they occupied between plant and animal life.

I learned an interesting thing about jellyfish from a Filipino guy. He was one of the only people my age on an island where I'd once stayed, so we became pals. We spent many happy weeks together playing Frisbee on the beach, then diving into the South China Sea. He taught me that if you pick up a jellyfish with the palm of your hand, you don't get hurt—although then you had to be careful to scrub your hands, because if you rubbed your eyes or scratched your back the poison would lift off and sting like mad. We used to have jellyfish fights, hurling the tennis-ball-sized globs at each other. On a calm day you could skim them over the sea like flat pebbles, although if you chucked them too hard they tended to explode. He also told me that you can eat them raw, like sushi. He was right. Literally speaking, you can, as long as you don't mind a few days of stomach cramps and vomiting.

I looked at the jellyfish around us. They looked the same as the ones in the Philippines, so I decided it was worth the risk. The gamble paid off. Etienne's eyes opened wide as I plucked one of the quivering blobs from the sea.

"Mon Dieu!" he exclaimed.

I smiled. I didn't realize French people actually said *"Mon Dieu."* I always thought it was the same thing as English people supposedly saying "what" at the end of every sentence.

"It is not hurting, Richard?"

"Nope. It's about how you hold it, like stinging nettles. You try."

I held out the jellyfish.

"No, I do not want to."

"It's fine. Go on."

"Really?"

"Yeah, sure. Hold your hands like mine."

I slid the jellyfish into his cupped hands.

"Oooh," he said, a big grin spreading over his face.

"But you can only touch it with your palms. If you touch it anywhere else it'll sting."

"Only the palm? Why is that?"

I shrugged. "Don't know. That's the rule."

"I think maybe the skin is more thick there."

"Maybe." I picked another one out of the water. "They're weird, aren't they? Look, you can see right through them. They don't have any brains."

Etienne nodded enthusiastically.

We peered at our jellyfish in silence for a few moments, then I noticed Françoise. She was on the beach, walking toward the water in a one-piece white swimsuit. She saw us and waved. As her arm lifted, her swimsuit drew tightly over her chest and shadows from the one o'clock sun defined her breasts, the dip under the rib cage, a groove of muscle down her stomach.

I glanced at Etienne. He was still examining his jellyfish, pulling its tentacles outward from the bell so it sat on his palm like a glass flower. Perhaps familiarity had blunted him to Françoise's beauty.

When she reached us she was unimpressed by our catch. "I do not like them," she said curtly. "Will you come for a swim?"

I pointed at the chest-deep water, shoulder-deep for Françoise. "We are swimming, aren't we?"

"No," said Etienne, finally looking up. "She means a swim." He gestured to the open sea. "Out there."

We played a game as we swam out. Every thirty feet we would each dive to the bottom and return with a handful of sand.

I found the game strangely unpleasant. A meter below the surface, the warmth of the tropical sea would turn cold, so abruptly that by treading water one could pinpoint the dividing line. Diving down, the chill would start at the fingertips, then swiftly envelope the length of the body.

The further we swam, the blacker and finer the sand became. Soon the water at the bottom became too dark for me to see in, and I could only kick out blindly with my legs, arms outstretched, until my hands sank into the silt.

I began dreading the cold area. I would hurry to catch my fistful, pushing up hard from the seabed though my lungs were still full of air. During the times I waited at the surface, while Etienne or Françoise swam down, I would keep my legs bunched up beneath me, using my arms to stay afloat.

"How far out do we go?" I said when the sunbathers on the beach behind us had turned into ants.

Etienne smiled. "You would like to go back now? Are you tired? We can go back."

Françoise held up her hand clear of the water and unclenched her fingers. A lump of sand rolled out and dropped into the sea, where it sank, leaving a cloudy trail behind. "You are tired, Richard?" she said, eyebrows arched.

"I'm fine," I replied. "Let's swim further."

Suckered

At five that afternoon the temperature cooled, the
sky turned black, and it rained. Unexpectedly, loudly—heavy droplets,
cratering and recratering the beach. I sat on the small porch outside my
hut and watched a miniature Sea of Tranquillity form in the sand. Across
the way Etienne appeared briefly, snatching the swimming shorts he'd left
out to dry. He called something to me but it was lost in a roll of thunder;
then he ducked back inside.

I had a tiny lizard on my hand. It was about three inches long, with
enormous eyes and translucent skin. The lizard had been sitting on my cigarette packet for ten minutes and when I'd got bored with watching it,
waiting for a tongue to lash out and lasso a fly, I'd reached out and picked
it up. Instead of wriggling away, as I'd expected, the lizard had casually re-
arranged itself on my hand. Surprised by its audacity, I let it sit there—
even though it meant keeping my hand in an unnatural position, palm
facing upward, which made my arm ache.

My attention was distracted by two guys running up the beach,
whooping and shouting as they came. As they reached my hut they turned
off the beach and leapt athletically onto the porch next to mine.

"Man!" whooped one of them, white-blond with a goatee.

"That's some fuckin' storm!" replied the other, yellow-blond and
clean-shaven. "Whoop!"

"Americans," I whispered to the lizard.

They rattled at their door, then ran back into the rain toward the beach
restaurant, weaving around, trying to dodge the rain. A couple of minutes
later they came speeding back. Again they rattled at their door—then
white-blond saw me, apparently for the first time. "Lost our fuckin' key!"
he said, and jabbed a thumb toward the restaurant. "They lost theirs too!
Can't get in!"

"Stuck out here!" said yellow-blond. "In the rain!"

I nodded. "Bad luck. Where did you lose it?"

White-blond shrugged. "Miles down the fuckin' beach, man! Miles
and miles!" Then he walked up to the wooden guardrail that separated our

two porches and peered over. "What you got in your hand there?" he asked.

I held up the lizard.

"Wow! Is it, like, dead?"

"Nope."

"Excellent! Hey, can I come over? You know, meet the neighbors!"

"Sure."

"You want to smoke a joint?"

"Sure."

"Excellent!"

The two of them vaulted over the guardrail and introduced themselves. White-blond was Sammy, yellow-blond was Zeph.

"Zeph's a strange name, right?" said Zeph as he shook my left hand, not wanting to disturb the lizard. "Can you guess what it's short for?"

"Zephania," I answered confidently.

"Wrong, dude! It isn't short for anything! I was christened Zeph, and everyone thinks it's short for Zephania, but it isn't! Cool, huh?"

"Definitely."

Sammy started rolling up, pulling the dope and papers out of a waterproof plastic bag in his pocket. "You're English, huh?" he said as he flattened out a rizla with his fingers. "English people always put tobacco in joints. You see, we never do. Are you addicted to smoking?"

"Afraid so," I replied.

"I'm not. But if I put tobacco in joints I would be. I smoke all day, like that song. How's that song go, Zeph?"

Zeph started singing a lyric that said, "Don't bogart that joint, my friend," but Sammy cut him off.

"No, dude. The other one."

"What, 'I smoke two joints in the morning'? That one?"

"Yeah."

Zeph cleared his throat. "Uh, it goes, 'I smoke two joints in the morning, and I smoke two joints at night, and I smoke two joints in the afternoon, and then I feel all right . . .' And then it goes, 'I smoke two joints in times of peace, and two in times of war. I smoke two joints before I smoke two joints, then I smoke two more.' I can't remember the rest." He shook his head.

"No matter, dude," said Sammy. "You get the idea, Ricardo? I smoke a lot."

"Sounds like it."

"Uh-huh."

Sammy had finished rolling the joint while Zeph had been singing. He lit it up and passed it straight to me. "That's another thing about English dudes," he wheezed, smoke coming out of his mouth in short bursts. "You hang on to the joint for ages. Us Americans take a toke or two and pass it on."

"It's true," I replied, sucking in.

I was going to apologize for the poor manners of my countrymen but I collapsed into a coughing fit.

"Rickster!" said Zeph, patting me on the back. "You gotta cough to get off."

A couple of seconds later a blistering bolt of lightning crackled over the sea. After it was gone, Sammy said in an awestruck voice, "Most totally excellent, dude!" Zeph quickly followed it up with, "Like, utterly outrageous, compadre!"

I opened my mouth, then hesitated. "Excellent, dude," I muttered thoughtfully.

"Most excellent," Sammy repeated.

I groaned.

"A problem, Ricardo?"

"You're winding me up."

Sammy and Zeph looked at each other, then at me.

"Winding you up?"

"Having me on."

Sammy frowned. "Speak in English, my man."

"This . . . Keanu Reeves thing. It's a joke, right? You don't really talk like that . . . do you?"

There was a brief silence, then Zeph swore. "We're rumbled, Sammy."

"Yeah," Sammy replied. "We overplayed our hand."

They were Harvard students. Sammy was studying law, Zeph was studying Afro-American literature. Their surf act was a reaction to the condescending Europeans they kept meeting in Asia. "It's a protest against bigotry," Zeph explained, pulling knots out of his tangled blond locks. "Europeans think all Americans are stupid, so we act stupid to confirm your prejudices. Then we reveal ourselves as intelligent, and by doing so, subvert the prejudice more effectively than an immediate barrage of intellect—which only causes confusion and, ultimately, resentment."

"Really?" I said, genuinely impressed. "That's so elaborate."

Zeph laughed. "No, not really. We just do it for fun."

They had other acts they liked to do. Zeph's favorite was the surf dude, but Sammy had another—he called it the nigger-lover. As its name implies, it was a bit more risqué than the surf dude.

"One time I got punched doing the nigger-lover," Sammy said, as he began to roll another joint. "Knocked flat on my fuckin' back."

I wasn't at all surprised. The act involved Sammy starting violent arguments with total strangers, insisting that because there's a country in Africa called Niger, all people from Niger were niggers—regardless of whether they were black or white.

"Aren't they called Nigerians?" I asked, bristling slightly, despite knowing I was being suckered.

Sammy shook his head. "That's what everyone says, but I don't think so. Think about it. Nigeria is right below Niger. They border each other, so if they were both called Nigerians it would cause chaos."

"Well, I still doubt they're called niggers."

"Oh, sure. Me too. I only say it to make a point. . . . Fuck knows what the point is, but . . ." He drew on the joint and passed it on. "It's like my granddad taught me. He was a colonel in the U.S. Marines. Sammy, he'd say, the ends *always* justify the means. And you know what, Richard? He was right."

I was about to disagree, but I realized he was winding me up again. Instead I replied, "You can't make an omelette without breaking some eggs."

Sammy smiled and turned to look at the sea.

"That's the boy," I thought I heard him say.

Lightning silhouetted the line of palm trees on the beach into a line of claws with pencil arms. The lizard scuttled out of my hand, startled by the flash.

"That's the kid."

I frowned. "Sorry? What was that?"

He turned back, also frowning, but with the smile still not faded from his lips. "What was what?"

"Didn't you just say something?"

"Nope."

I looked at Zeph. "Didn't you hear him say something?"

Zeph shrugged. "I was watching the lightning."

"Oh."

Just the dope talking, I guessed.

The rain continued as night fell. Etienne and Françoise stayed in their hut, and Zeph, Sammy, and I stayed on the porch until we were too stoned to do anything but sit in silence, passing the odd comment between us if there was an impressive roll of thunder.

An hour or two after dark a tiny Thai woman came over to our porch from the restaurant, almost hidden under a giant beach parasol. She looked at the dope paraphernalia strewn about us with a wan smile, then handed Zeph a spare key to their room. I took that as my cue to crawl into bed. As I said good night, Sammy croaked, "Hey, nice meeting you. Catch you tomorrow, dude."

He seemed to say it without a trace of irony. I couldn't work out whether it was a continuation of his surfer joke, or the grass had regressed his Harvard mind. It seemed too complicated to ask, so I said, "Sure," and shut the door behind me.

At around three in the morning I woke up for a short while, dry-mouthed, still high, and listened. I could hear cicadas and waves sucking down the beach. The storm had blown itself out.

Spaced Invaders

The next morning the sky was still clouded over. As I walked out onto the porch, scattered with rain-soaked joint butts, I had the bizarre sensation that I was back in England. There was a slight chill in the air and I could smell wet earth and leaves. Rubbing the sleep from my eyes, I padded over the cool sand to Etienne and Françoise's hut. There was no answer from their door, so I tried the restaurant and found them eating breakfast. I ordered a mango salad, thinking an exotic taste might compensate for the feeling of being in England, and sat down with them.

"Who did you meet last night?" said Etienne as I pulled up a chair. "We saw you talking outside your room."

"We watched you from our window," Françoise added.

I pulled out a cigarette to kill time before breakfast arrived. "I met a couple of Americans. Zeph and Sammy."

Françoise nodded. "Did you tell them about our beach?"

"No." I lit up. "I didn't."

"You shouldn't tell people about our beach."

"I didn't tell them."

"It should be a secret."

I exhaled strongly. "And that's why I didn't tell them, Françoise."

Etienne interrupted. "She was worried you might have . . ." The sentence trailed off into a nervous smile.

"It didn't even cross my mind," I replied irritably, and stubbed out my cigarette hard. It was tasting like shit.

When the mango salad arrived I made an effort to relax. I told them about how the Americans had fooled me with their surfer act. Françoise thought the story was extremely funny. Her laughter partially diffused the tension and we began making plans for the day ahead.

We decided that we had to hire a boat. The normal tour agencies wouldn't do because they'd be too organized and we doubted we'd be able to slip away from their supervision. Instead we would need to find a fisherman who was unaware of or unconcerned about the rules concerning tourists in the Marine Park.

After breakfast we split up to optimize our chances. I went north, toward Koh Matlang, and the other two went south, aiming for a small town we'd passed on the Jeep ride. Our rendezvous was in three hours' time, back at our huts.

The sun came out as I set off down Chaweng, but it did little to improve my mood. Flies buzzed around my head, smelling the sweat, and the walking became increasingly laborious as the night's rain dried off the sand.

I began counting the guest houses I passed along the shoreline. After twenty minutes I'd counted seventeen, and they were still showing no signs of thinning out. If anything, the palm trees were more cluttered with Ray-Bans and concrete patios than before.

In 1984 I sat in my livingroom, playing on my Atari, and listened to the baby-sitter talk about Koh Samui. As I mopped the screen clear of space invaders, names and places stuck in my head.

Pattaya was a hellhole. Chiang Mai was rainy and cold. Koh Samui was hot and beautiful. Koh Samui was where she had stayed with her boyfriend for five months, hanging out on the beach and doing strange things she was both reluctant and keen to talk about.

Exams out of the way, my friends and I scattered ourselves around the globe. The next August we started coming back, and I learned that my baby-sitter's paradise was yesterday's news. Koh Phangan, the next island along, was Thailand's new Mecca.

A few years later, as I checked my passport and confirmed my flight to Bangkok, a friend telephoned with advice. "Give Koh Phangan a miss, Rich," she said. "Hat Rin's a long way past its sell-by date. They do printed flyers for the full-moon parties. Koh Tao. That's where it's at."

After an hour of walking I gave up trying to find a fisherman. The only Thais I met were selling gemstones and baseball caps. By the time I got back to my beach hut I was exhausted, sunburned, and pissed off. I went straight to the restaurant and bought a packet of cigarettes. Then I chain-smoked in the shade of a palm tree, looking out for Etienne and Françoise, hoping they'd had better luck.

TV Heaven

Thais, or Southeast Asians in general, make eerily convincing transvestites. Their slight builds and smooth faces are a recipe for success.

I saw a particularly stunning transvestite as I waited under the palm tree. His silicon breasts were perfectly formed and he had hips to die for. The only thing to betray his gender was his gold lamé dress—a bit too showy to be worn by a Thai girl on a stroll down Chaweng.

He was carrying a backgammon set under his arm, and as he slunk past he asked if I wanted to play a game.

"No thanks," I replied with neurotic haste.

"Why?" he wanted to know. "I think maybe you afrai' I win."

I nodded.

"Okay. Maybe you wan' to play in bed?" He tugged at the long slit up the side of his dress, revealing fabulous legs. "Maybe in bed I le' you win . . ."

"No thanks," I said again, blushing slightly.

He shrugged and continued walking along the beach. A couple of beach huts down someone took him up on the backgammon offer. Curious, I tried to see who, but they were blocked by the trunk of a leaning coconut tree. A few minutes later I looked back and he was gone. I guessed he'd found his punter.

Etienne appeared not long after, beaming.

"Hey, Richard," he said. "Did you see you see the girl walking this way?"

"With a lamé dress?"

"Yes! My God, she was so beautiful!"

"She was."

"Anyway, Richard. Come to the restaurant." He reached out a hand and hauled me up. "I think we have a boat to take us into the Marine Park."

The man was a Thai version of a spiv. Instead of being lean and weasel-like, with a pencil mustache and a flash suit, he was short, fat, and wore drainpipe marbled jeans tucked into giant Reebok trainers.

"Tha' can be arrange'," he said, quoting from the universal phrase book of the entrepreneur. "Of course, yes." He grinned and made an expansive gesture with his arms. Gold sparkled in his mouth. "No' difficul' for me to do tha'."

Etienne nodded. So far he'd done all the bargaining, which was fine as far as I was concerned. I don't like dealing with money transactions in poor countries. I get confused between feeling that I shouldn't haggle with poverty and hating getting ripped off.

"Actually, my frien', your gui'book is no' correc'. You can stay Koh Angthong one nigh', two nigh'—is okay. Bu' this island you can only stay one nigh'." He took Etienne's book and laid a chubby finger on an island close to Angthong.

Etienne looked at me and winked. From my memory of Mister Duck's map, which was back in the beach hut, our island was the next one along.

"Okay," said Etienne, and lowered his voice conspiratorially, even though there was no one around the restaurant to hear. "This is the island we want to see. But we want to stay more than one night. That is possible?"

The spiv furtively looked over his shoulder at the empty tables.

"Yes," he whispered, leaning forward, then looked around again. "Bu' is mo' money, you un'erstan'."

The deal was eventually struck at 1,450 baht, diligently knocked down from 2,000 by Etienne. At six the next morning we were to meet the spiv in the restaurant and he would take us to his boat. Only then would we pay him the money, a point Etienne wisely insisted upon, and he would take us to the island. Three nights later he would come back to pick us up—our contingency plan in case we got stuck there.

That left us with only a couple of problems.

If we successfully made it to the next island along, we would be missing when the spiv came to collect us. To deal with this, Etienne invented a story about some other friends we were going to meet there, so we might come back early—no cause for alarm.

Another difficulty was how to get from the drop-off island to the beach island. We could have asked the boat to take us directly there, but not knowing exactly what we were going to find on the beach, we didn't want to blunder in on a motorboat. Anyway, as the beach island was out of bounds to tourists, we thought it better to start from one where technically we were allowed to stay—if only for one night.

Etienne and Françoise seemed far less concerned about this last step of the journey than I was. They had a simple solution—we would swim. By examining Mister Duck's map and the map in their guidebook, they'd decided that the islands were roughly a kilometer apart. According to them, that was a manageable distance. I wasn't so confident, and remembered the diving game from the day before. The tide had pulled us a long way down Chaweng beach as we swam. If the same thing happened between the islands, the length of the swim could effectively double as we corrected and recorrected our course.

The final problem was what we would do with our bags. Again, Etienne and Françoise had worked out a solution. Apparently they'd done a lot of planning last night while I was getting stoned. Later that day, sitting in the shallows with the wash collecting sand around our feet, they explained.

"The backpacks will not be a problem, Richard," said Françoise. "Actually, maybe they will help us to swim."

I raised my eyebrows. "How's that?"

"We need some plastic bags," said Etienne. "If we have some plastic bags we can tie them so water does not enter. Then . . . they float. The air inside."

"Uh-huh. You think it'll work?"

Etienne shrugged. "I think it will. I saw it on television."

"On TV?"

"It was the A-Team."

"The A-Team? Oh, that's great. We'll be fine, then."

I lay back in the water, propping myself up on my elbows.

"I think you are very lucky to have met us, Richard." Etienne laughed. "I think without us you could not reach this beach."

"Yes," Françoise said. "But also we are lucky to meet him."

"Oh of course. Without your map we could not find the beach either."

Françoise frowned, then smiled at me. "Etienne! We are lucky to meet him anyway."

I smiled back, noticing as I did so that the bad mood I'd been carrying all morning had completely lifted. "We're all lucky," I said happily.

Etienne nodded. "Yes. We are."

We sat in silence for a few minutes, basking in our luckiness. Then I stood up, clapping my hands together. "Right. Why don't we go for a long swim now? It could be a practice."

"It is a very good idea, Richard," Etienne replied, also standing. "Come on, Françoise."

She shook her head and pouted. "I think I will stay in the sun. I shall watch you two strong men from here. I will see who can swim the furthest."

Doubt flickered in my mind. I looked at her, trying to see if her words were as loaded as they appeared. She was watching Etienne as he made his way into the sea, giving nothing away.

That's it then, I thought. Just wishful thinking.

But I failed to convince myself. As I waded after Etienne, I couldn't help wondering if Françoise's eyes were now on my back. Just before the water became deep enough to swim I needed to know, and glanced behind me. She had moved up the beach to dry sand and was lying on her front, facing the land.

Just wishful thinking after all.

Eden

Sunset was spectacular. Red sky gently faded to deep blue, where a few bright stars already shone, and orange light threw elastic shadows down the beach as people strolled back to their huts.

I was stoned. I'd been dozing on the sand with Françoise and Etienne, recovering from our epic swim, when Sammy and Zeph had turned up with half an ounce of grass wrapped in newspaper. They'd spent the day at Lamai hunting for their lost room key and found it hanging on a piece of driftwood, stuck in the sand. They'd bought the grass to celebrate.

"Someone must have put it there knowing we'd come looking," Zeph had said as he sat down beside us. "Isn't that such a decent thing to do?"

"Maybe it was a stupid thing to do," Françoise replied. "Someone could have taken this key and robbed your room."

"Well, uh, yeah, I suppose." Then he'd looked at Françoise, obviously taking her in for the first time, and given his head a little shake. I think he was clearing a mental image that had just appeared. "No, definitely. You're right."

The sun had begun its rapid descent to the horizon line as the grass began to take hold. Now we all sat, watching the colors in the sky as intently as if we were watching television.

"Hey," said Sammy loudly, breaking us out of our reverie. "Has anyone ever noticed that if you look up at the sky, you can start to see animals and faces in the clouds?"

Etienne looked round. "Have we ever noticed?" he said.

"Yeah," Sammy continued. "It's amazing. Hey, there's a little duck right above us, and that one looks like a man with a huge nose."

"Actually, I have noticed this since I was a small child." ·

"A small child?"

"Yes. Certainly."

Sammy whistled. "Shit. I only just noticed it. Mind you, that's mainly to do with where I grew up."

"Oh?" said Etienne.

"See, I grew up in Idaho."

"Ah . . ." Etienne nodded. Then he looked confused. "Yes, Idaho. I have heard of Idaho, but . . ."

"Well, you know about Idaho, huh? There's no clouds in Idaho."

"No clouds?"

"Sure. Chicago, the windy city. Idaho, the cloudless state. Some weird weather thing to do with atmospheric pressure, I don't know."

"There are no clouds at all?"

"Not one." Sammy sat up on the sand. "I can remember the first time I saw a cloud. It was in upstate New York, the summer of '79. I saw this vast fluffy thing in the sky, and I reached and tried to grab it . . . but it was too high." Sammy smiled sadly. "I turned to my mom and said, 'Why can't I have the cotton candy, Mommy? Why?'" Sammy choked and looked away. "I'm sorry. It's just a stupid memory."

Zeph leaned over and patted him on the back. "Hey, man," he murmured, just loud enough to hear. "It's okay. Let it out. We're all friends here."

"Yes," said Etienne. "We don't mind. Of course, everybody has a sad memory."

Sammy spun around, his face all screwed up. "You, Etienne? You have a sad memory too?"

"Oh yes. I used to have a little red bicycle, but it was stolen by some thieves."

Sammy's expression darkened. "The bicycle thieves? They stole your little red bike?"

"Yes. I was seven."

"Seven!" Sammy shouted and thumped the ground with his fist, spraying everyone with sand. "Jesus! That makes me so fucking mad!"

There was a shocked silence. Then Sammy grabbed the rizlas and started furiously rolling up, and Zeph changed the topic of conversation.

The outburst was probably a clever move. Etienne's response had been so charming that it would have been cruel to reveal the truth. Sammy's only way out was to follow the bluff to its natural conclusion.

By the time we'd smoked the joint, the sun had almost disappeared. Just the slightest curve of yellow shimmered over the sea. A slight breeze picked up, sending a few loose rizlas skimming along the sand. With the breeze came the smell of cooking, lemongrass and fried shellfish, from the restaurant behind us.

"I'm hungry," I muttered.

"Smells good, huh?" said Zeph. "I could do with a big plate of chicken noodles."

"Or dog noodles," said Sammy. He turned to Françoise. "We had dog noodles in Chiang Mai. Tasted like chicken. All those things, dog, lizard, frog, snake. They always taste like chicken."

"How about rat?" I asked.

"Uh-huh, rat too. Distinctly chickenlike."

Zeph picked up a handful of sand and let it run through his fingers, trailing patterns between his legs. Then he coughed, almost in a formal way, as if he wanted everyone to pay attention. "Hey," he said. "Do you know about Kentucky Fried Rat?"

I frowned. It sounded like another wind-up, and I felt that if Etienne was going to fall for it in the same kind of way, I might start crying. I still had a picture in my head of his concerned face as he explained about his little red bike.

"No. What is it?" I said warily.

"It's one of those stories that gets around."

"Urban myths," said Sammy. "Like someone got a small bone stuck in his throat. Then he got it analyzed and it was a rat bone."

"Yeah, and the guy it happened to was a friend's aunt's cousin. It never happened to the person you're talking to."

"Oh," I said. "I know."

"Right. So there's a Kentucky Fried Rat doing the rounds at the moment. You heard it?"

I shook my head.

"About a beach. This amazing beach hidden somewhere, but no one knows where it is."

I turned my head away. Down by the sea a Thai boy was playing with a piece of coconut husk, keeping it in the air using his knees and the sides of his feet. He timed a flick badly and the husk flew into the water. For a few moments he stood there with his hands on his hips, perhaps wondering if it was worth getting wet to retrieve it. Then he started jogging up the sand toward the guest house.

"No," I said. "I haven't heard about that. Fill us in."

"Okay," said Zeph. "I'll paint you a picture." He lay back on the sand. "Close your eyes and think about a lagoon."

Think about a lagoon, hidden from the sea and passing boats by a high curving wall of rock. Then imagine white sands and coral gardens never damaged by dynamite fishing or trawling nets. Freshwater falls scatter the island, surrounded by jungle—not the forests of inland Thailand, but jungle. Canopies three levels deep, plants untouched for a thousand years, strangely colored birds and monkeys in the trees.

On the white sands, fishing in the coral gardens, a select community of travelers pass the months. They leave if they want to, they return, the beach never changes.

"Select?" I asked quietly, as if talking through a dream. Zeph's vision had entirely consumed me.

"Select," he replied. "Word of mouth passes on the location to a lucky few."

"It's paradise," Sammy murmured. "It's Eden."

"Eden," Zeph agreed, "is how it sounds."

Françoise was completely thrown by hearing that Sammy and Zeph also knew about the beach. She couldn't have acted more suspicious if she'd tried.

She stood up suddenly. "Now then," she said, dusting sand off her legs. "We leave early tomorrow morning for, ah, for Koh Phangan. So I think we shall go to bed now. Etienne? Richard? Come."

"Huh?" I said, disoriented as the image of the beach splintered. "Françoise, it's seven-thirty in the evening."

"We leave early in the morning," she repeated.

"But . . . I haven't eaten any dinner. I'm starving."

"Good. So we shall eat now. Good night, Sammy and Zeph," she said, before I could ask them to join us. "It was very nice meeting you. And really, your beach, what a silly story." She laughed gaily.

Etienne sat upright, looking at her as if she'd lost her mind, but she ignored his appalled expression and began marching toward the restaurant.

"Look," I said to Sammy and Zeph. "I think she's . . . If you want to eat with us . . ."

"Yes," said Etienne. "You are very welcome. Please."

"It's cool," Sammy replied, smiling slightly. "We'll hang out here a bit longer. But listen, have a good time in Koh Phangan. Are you coming back this way?"

I nodded.

"Okay, so we'll catch up later on. We're here for a while. A week at least."

We all shook hands, then Etienne and I followed after Françoise.

Dinner was laden with heavy silences, sometimes broken by a terse exchange in French. But Françoise knew she'd acted foolishly and was apologetic as we said good night.

"I do not know," she explained. "I was suddenly frightened they would want to come with us. Zeph made it sound so . . . I only want it to be us . . ." She frowned, frustrated by her inability to express herself. "Do you think they have realized we know about the beach?"

I shrugged. "Hard to say. Everyone was pretty stoned."

Etienne nodded. "Yes," he said, and put his arm around her shoulder. "Everyone was stoned. We should not worry."

It took me a long time to get to sleep that night. It wasn't just because I was anxious about what might happen tomorrow, although that was part of it. I was also troubled by the hurried way I'd said good-bye to Zeph and Sammy. I'd enjoyed their company and knew it was unlikely I'd find them again, if I did come back to Koh Samui. Our parting had been too quick and awkward, too confused by dope and secrets. I felt there was something I'd left unsaid.

A Safe Bet

I wouldn't call it a dream. Nothing with Mister Duck was like a dream. In this case, it was more like a movie. Or news footage, swaying on a hand-held camera.

Mister Duck was sprinting toward me across the embassy lawn, his wrists still freshly slit, blood looping out from the cuts as he pumped his arms. I was reeling from the noise of the screaming crowds and helicopters, watching a snowfall of shredded files. Classified snow, swirling in the backdraft from the rotor blades, settling on the manicured grass.

"Born twenty years too late?" shouted Mister Duck, belting past me and flipping into a cartwheel. "Fuck that!" His blood echoed the movement, briefly hanging in the air like the trace from a firework.

"See up there!"

I looked where he pointed. A hovering insect shape was lifting off the roof with people clinging to the landing skids. It dipped as it pulled away, struggling with the heavy load, and clipped a tree outside the embassy walls.

I shouted with excitement.

"That's the boy!" Mister Duck yelled, ruffling my hair with a wet hand, soaking the collar of my shirt. "That's the kid!"

"Do we get to escape from the embassy roof?" I yelled back. "I always wanted to do that!"

"Escape from the embassy roof?"

"Do we get to?"

"You bet," he laughed. "You fucking bet."

Leaving

I drew quickly, sweating despite the early-morning chill. There wasn't time to take the same kind of care over the map as Mister Duck. The islands were rough circles, the curving shoreline of Thailand a series of jagged lines, and there were only three labels. Koh Samui, Koh Angthong, and Eden

At the bottom of the page I wrote, "Wait on Chaweng for three days. If we haven't come back by then it means we made it to the beach. See you there? Richard."

I crept outside. A light already shone in Françoise and Etienne's hut. Shivering, I stole along the porch and slipped the map under Zeph and Sammy's door. Then I collected my bag, locked up my room, and went to the restaurant to wait for the others.

The Thai boy who'd been kicking the coconut husk was sweeping the floor. As I arrived he glanced outside, to check it was as early as he thought it was.

"You wan' banan' pancake?" he asked cautiously.

I shook my head. "No thanks. But I would like to buy four hundred cigarettes."

getting there

Littering

The spiv's motorboat was painted white down to the watermark strip, and below that it was yellow—or yellow when it lifted clear of the sea, pale green when it sank back down. At one time his boat must have been red. The white was blistered or scraped away in places, leaving crimson streaks that looked like cuts. That, with the rolling movement and growling engine, was enough to make me feel the boat was alive. It knew which way I expected it to lurch and routinely surprised me.

Beside us, where the water was disturbed, the morning sun played tricks in the sea. Gold shapes like a shoal of fish spun beneath the surface, matching our speed. I reached down and trailed my hand, catching a fish on my palm. It swam there, flickering over my life line, until I balled my fist. The fish slipped out and swam on my closed fingers.

"You should not look down," said Françoise, leaning over from the other side of the boat. "If you look down, you will feel sick. Watch the island. The island does not move."

I looked where she pointed. Strangely, Koh Samui seemed miles behind us but the drop-off island still appeared as distant as it had an hour ago.

"I'm not feeling sick," I said, and sank my head back over the side.

Hypnotized by the gold fish, I didn't move again until the water turned blue and I saw a coral bed loom beneath me. The spiv cut the engine. I put a hand up to my ears, surprised by the silence, half thinking I might have gone deaf. "Now you pay," said the spiv reassuringly, and we slid toward the shore.

The sand was more gray than white and strewn with dried seaweed, laid out in overlapping arcs by the tide. I sat on the trunk of a fallen coconut tree, watching our ride chug into the distance. Soon it was hard to find, a white speck occasionally appearing on the ridge of a high swell. When five minutes passed without a sighting I realized that it had gone and our isolation was complete.

A few meters away, Etienne and Françoise leaned against their ruck-sacks. Etienne was studying the maps, working out which of the several is-lands near us we had to swim to. He didn't need my help, so I called to him that I was going to take a walk. I'd never been on a real desert island before—a deserted desert island—and I felt I ought to explore.

"Where?" he said, looking up and squinting against the sun.

"Just around. I won't be long."

"Half an hour?"

"An hour."

"Yes, but we should leave after lunch. We should not spend the night here."

I waved in reply, already walking away from them.

I stuck to the coast for half a mile, looking for a place to turn inland, and eventually found a bush whose canopy made a dark tunnel into the treeline. Through it I could see green leaves and sunlight, so I crawled in-side, brushing spiderwebs from my face. I came out into a glade of waist-high ferns. Above me was a circle of sky, broken by a branch that jutted out like the hand of a clock. On the far side of the glade the forest began again, but my impulse to continue was checked by a fear of getting lost. The tunnel I'd crawled through was harder to make out from this end, dis-guised by the tall grasses, and I could only orientate myself by the sound of breaking waves. I gave up my token exploration and waded through the ferns to the middle of the glade. Then I sat down and smoked a cigarette.

Thinking about Thailand tends to make me angry, and until I started writing this book, I tried not to do it. I preferred it to stay tucked away in the back of my mind. But I do think about Thailand sometimes. Usually late at night, when I've been awake long enough to see the curtain pat-terns through the darkness and the shapes of the books on my shelves.

At those times I make an effort to remember sitting in the glade with the shadow of the clock-hand branch lying across the ferns, smoking my cigarette. I choose this moment because it was the last time I could pin-point that I was me being myself. Being normal, with nothing much going through my head apart from how pretty the island was, and how quiet.

It isn't that from then on every second in Thailand was bad. Good things happened. Loads of good things. And mundane things, too: washing my face in the morning, swimming, fixing some food, whatever. But in retrospect, all those instances are colored by what was going on around them. Sometimes it feels to me that I walked into the glade and lit the cigarette, and someone else came along and finished it. Finished it, stubbed it out, flicked it into the bushes, then went to find Etienne and Françoise. It's a cop-out, because it's another thing that distances me from what happened, but that's how it feels.

This other person did things I wouldn't do. It wasn't just our morals that were at odds, there were little character differences, too. The cigarette butt—the other guy flicked it into the bushes. I'd have done something else. Buried it maybe. I hate littering, let alone littering in a protected Marine park.

It's hard to explain. I don't believe in possession or the supernatural. I know that in real terms it was me who flicked the cigarette butt.

Fuck it.

I've been relying on an idea that these things would become clear to me as I wrote them down, but it isn't turning out that way.

When I got back to the beach, I found Etienne crouched over a little Calor gas camping stove. Laid out beside him were three piles of Magi-Noodle packets—yellow, brown, and pink.

"Great," I said. "I'm starving. What's on the menu?"

"You may have chicken, beef, or . . ." He held up a pink packet. "What is this?"

"Shrimp. I'll go for chicken."

Etienne smiled. "Me also. And we can have chocolate for dessert. You have it?"

"Sure." I unclipped my rucksack and pulled out three bars. The ones closest to the top had melted and remolded themselves around the shape of my water bottle, but the foil hadn't split.

"Did you find anything interesting on your walk?" asked Etienne, cutting open one of the yellow packs with a penknife.

"Nothing in particular. I stuck to the coastline mainly." I looked around. "Where's Françoise? Isn't she eating with us?"

"She has already eaten." He pointed down the beach. "She went to see if it is a big swim to our island."

"You worked out which one it is?"

"I think so. I'm not sure. There are many differences between the map in my guidebook and your friend's map."

"Which one did you go for?"

"Your friend."

I nodded. "Good choice."

"I hope so," said Etienne, hooking a noodle from the boiling water with his penknife. It hung limply on the blade. "Okay. We can eat now."

Thai-Die

Françoise said it was one kilometer away and Etienne said two. I can't judge distances over water, but I said one and a half. Mainly it just looked like a long swim.

The island across the sea was wide, with tall peaks at each end that were joined by a pass about half their height. I guessed it had once been two volcanoes, close enough together to be connected by their lava flow. Whatever its origins, it was at least five times the size of the one we were on, and gaps in the green showed rock faces which I hoped we wouldn't need to climb.

"Are you sure we can do this?" I said, more to myself than anyone else.

"We can," said Françoise.

"We can try," Etienne corrected, and went to get the backpack he'd prepared with plastic garbage bag liners, bought from the restaurant that morning.

The A-Team: a television series that was a hit when I was around fourteen years old. They were B. A. Barracus, "Faceman," Murdock, and "Hannibal"—four Vietnam veterans accused of a crime they didn't commit, who now worked as mercenaries, taking on the bad guys the law couldn't touch.

They let us down. For a moment it had looked as if Etienne's contraption would float. It dipped underwater and held its level, the top quarter bobbing above the surface like an iceberg. But then the bags collapsed and the pack sank like a stone. Three other attempts failed in exactly the same way.

"This will never work," said Françoise, who had rolled her swimming costume down to her waist to get an even tan and was not catching my eye.

"There's no way," I agreed. "The rucksacks are far too heavy. You know, we really should have tried this out on Koh Samui."

"Yes," Etienne sighed. "I do know."

We stood in the water, silently considering the situation. Then Françoise said, "Okay. We take one plastic bag each. We only take some important things."

I shook my head. "I don't want to do that. I need my rucksack."

"What choice? We give up?"

"Well . . ."

"We need some food, some clothes, only for three days. Then if we do not find the beach, we swim back and wait for the boat."

"Passports, tickets, traveler's checks, cash, malaria pills."

"There is no malaria here," said Etienne.

"Anyway," Françoise added. "We do not need a passport to go to this is-land." She smiled and absently brushed a hand between her breasts. "Come on, Richard. We are too close, huh?"

I frowned, not understanding, a list of possibilities appearing in my mind.

"Too close to give up."

"Oh," I said. "Yes, I suppose we are."

We hid our rucksacks under a thick patch of shrubs near a distinctive palm tree—it had two trunks growing from a single stem. In my garbage bag I packed puri-tabs, the chocolate, spare shorts, a T-shirt, Converse shoes, Mister Duck's map, my water bottle, and two hundred cigarettes. I wanted to take all four hundred, but there wasn't room. We also had to leave the Calor gas stove. It meant that we'd have to eat cold noodles, soaked long enough to make them soft, but at least we wouldn't starve. And I left the malaria pills, too.

After tying the bags with as many knots as the plastic would allow and then sealing them again inside a second one, we tested their seaworthiness. Without the weight of the rucksacks they floated better than we could have hoped. They were even strong enough to lean on, so we only had to swim with our legs.

At a quarter to four we waded into the sea, finally ready to leave. "Maybe more than one kilometer," I heard Françoise say behind me. Etienne said something in reply, but it was lost as a wave broke.

The swim passed in stages. At first we were full of confidence, chatting as we found a kicking rhythm and making jokes about sharks. Then, as our legs began to ache and the water no longer felt cold enough to cool us down, we stopped talking. By this time, as on the boat ride from Koh Samui, the beach behind us seemed as far away as the island ahead. The jokes about sharks became fears, and I started to doubt that I had the strength to finish the swim. We were about halfway between the two points. Not being able to finish the swim would mean dying.

If Etienne and Françoise were also worried they didn't show it. In any case, it wasn't like there was anything we could do to make things easier. We'd put ourselves into the situation. All we could do was deal with it.

And then, strangely, things did become easier. Although my legs still ached like crazy, they'd developed a kind of reflex kick, something like a heartbeat. It kept me moving and allowed my mind to drift beyond the pain. One idea that kept me distracted for ages was composing the newspaper headlines that would inform people back home of my fate. "Young Adventurers in Thai-Die Death Swim—Europe Mourns," covered the necessary angles. Writing my obituary was harder, as I'd never done anything of much importance, but my funeral was a pleasant surprise. I drafted some good speeches, and a lot of people came to hear them.

I'd moved on to thinking that I should try to pass my driving test if I got back to England, when I saw driftwood on the beach ahead and realized we were nearly there. We'd been careful to stick together over most of the swim, but in the last hundred meters Etienne pulled away. When he reached the beach he did a cartwheel, achieved with a last reserve of energy, because then he collapsed and didn't move again until I joined him.

"Show me the map," he said, trying to sit up.

"Etienne," I replied between gasps for breath, and pushed him back down. "We've done enough. We're staying here tonight."

"But the beach may be close, no? Maybe it is only a short way down the island."

"Enough."

"But—"

"Shh."

I lay down, pressing the side of my face into the wet sand, my gasps becoming sighs as the aching drained from my muscles. Etienne had a strand of seaweed caught in his hair, a single green dreadlock. "What is this?" he muttered, tugging at it weakly. Down by the sea Françoise splashed out of the water, dragging her bag behind her.

"I hope this beach exists," she said as she flopped beside us. "I am not sure I can do the swim again." I was too exhausted to agree.

All These Things

There are one hundred glow-stars on my bedroom ceiling. I've got crescent moons, gibbous moons, planets with Saturn's rings, accurate constellations, meteor showers, and a whirlpool galaxy with a flying saucer caught in its tail. They were given to me by a girlfriend who was surprised that I often lay awake after she went to sleep. She discovered it one night when she woke to go to the bathroom, and bought me the glow-stars the next day.

Glow-stars are strange. They make the ceiling disappear.

"Look," Françoise whispered, keeping her voice low so Etienne wouldn't wake. "Do you see?"

I followed the path of her arm, past the delicate wrist, up her finger to the million flecks of light. "I don't," I whispered back. "Where?"

"There . . . Moving. You can see the bright one?"

"Uh-huh."

"Now look down, then left, and . . ."

"Got it. Amazing . . ."

A satellite, reflecting what—the moon or earth? Sliding quickly and smoothly through the stars, tonight its orbit passing the Gulf of Thailand, and maybe later the skies of Dakar or Oxford.

Etienne stirred and turned in his sleep, rustling the plastic bag he'd stretched out beneath him on the sand. In the forest behind us some hidden night bird chattered briefly.

"Hey," I whispered, propping myself up on my elbows. "Do you want me to tell you something funny?"

"What about?"

"Infinity. But it isn't that complicated. I mean, you don't need a degree in—"

Françoise waved a hand in the air, tracing a red pattern with the tip of her cigarette.

"Is that a yes?" I whispered.

"Yes."

"Okay." I coughed quietly. "If you accept that the universe is infinite, then that means there's an infinite amount of chances for things to happen, right?"

She nodded and sucked on the red coal floating by her fingertips.

"Well, if there's an infinite amount of chances for something to happen, then eventually it will happen—no matter how small the likelihood."

"Ah."

"That means somewhere in space there's another planet that, by an incredible series of coincidences, developed exactly the same way as ours. Right down to the smallest detail."

"Is there?"

"Definitely. And there's another which is exactly the same, except that palm tree over there is two feet to the right. And there's another where the tree is two feet to the left. In fact, there're infinite planets with infinite variations on that tree alone . . ."

Silence. I wondered if she was asleep. "So how about that?" I prompted.

"Interesting," she whispered. "In these planets, everything that can happen will happen."

"Exactly."

"Then in one planet, maybe I am a movie star."

"There's no maybe about it. You live in Beverly Hills and swept last year's Oscars."

"That's good."

"Yeah, but don't forget, somewhere else your film was a flop."

"Oh?"

"It bombed. The critics turned on you, the studio lost a fortune, and you got into booze and Valium. It was pretty ugly."

Françoise rolled on to her side and looked at me. "Tell me about some other worlds," she whispered. In the moonlight her teeth flashed silver as she smiled.

"Well," I replied. "That's a lot to tell."

Etienne stirred and turned over again.

I leaned over and kissed Françoise. She pulled away, or laughed, or shook her head, or closed her eyes and kissed me back. Etienne woke, clasping his mouth in disbelief. Etienne slept. I slept while Françoise kissed Etienne.

Light-years above our garbage bag beds and the steady rush of the surf, all these things happened.

After Françoise had shut her eyes and her breathing had eased into a sleeping rhythm, I crept off my plastic sheet and walked down to the sea. I stood in the shallows, slowly sinking as the tide pulled away the sand around my feet. The lights of Koh Samui glowed on the horizon like a trace of sunset. The spread of stars stretched as far as my ceiling back home.

In Country

We set off immediately after breakfast: half a bar of chocolate each and cold noodles, soaked in most of the water from our canteens. There wasn't any point in hanging around. We needed to find a freshwater source, and according to Mister Duck's map, the beach was on the other side of the island.

At first we walked along the beach, hoping to circle the coast, but the sand soon turned to jagged rocks, which turned to impassable cliffs and gorges. Then we tried the other end, wasting precious time while the sun rose in the sky, and found the same barrier. We were left with no choice but to try inland. The pass between the peaks was the obvious goal, so we slung our plastic bags over our shoulders and picked our way into the jungle.

The first two or three hundred meters from the shore were the hardest. The spaces between the palm trees were covered in strange rambling bushes with tiny leaves that sliced like razors, and the only way past them was to push through. But as we got further inland and the ground began to rise, the palms became less common than another kind of tree—trees like rusted, ivy-choked space rockets, with ten-foot roots that fanned from the trunk like stabilizer fins. With less sunlight coming through the canopy, the vegetation on the forest floor thinned out. Occasionally we were stopped by a dense spray of bamboo, but a short search would find an animal track or a path cleared by a fallen branch.

After Zeph's description of the jungle, with Jurassic plants and strangely colored birds, I was vaguely disappointed by the reality. In many ways I felt like I was walking through an English forest, I'd just shrunk to a tenth of my normal size. But there were some things that felt suitably exotic. Several times we saw tiny brown monkeys scurrying up the trees, Tarzan-style lianas hung above us like stalactites, and there was the water—it dripped on our necks, flattened our hair, and stuck our T-shirts to our chests. There was so much of it that our half-empty canteens stopped being a worry. Standing under a branch and giving it a shake provided a couple of good gulps, as well as a quick shower. The irony of having kept my clothes dry during the swim, only to have them soaked when we turned inland, didn't escape me.

After two hours of walking we found ourselves at the bottom of a particularly steep stretch of slope. We had to pull ourselves up on the tough fern stems to keep from slipping down on the mud and dead leaves. Etienne was the first to get to the top and he disappeared over the ridge, then reappeared a few seconds later, beckoning enthusiastically.

"Hurry up!" he called. "Really, it is amazing!"

"What is it?" I called back, but he'd disappeared again.

I redoubled my efforts, leaving Françoise behind.

The slope led to a soccer-field-sized shelf on the mountainside, so flat and neat that it seemed unnatural in the tangle of the surrounding jungle. Above us the slope rose again to what appeared to be a second shelf, and above that it continued straight up to the pass.

Etienne had gone further into the plateau and was standing in some bushy plants, gazing around with his hands on his hips.

"What do you think?" he said. I looked behind me. Far below I could see the beach we had come from, the island where our hidden rucksacks lay, and the many other islands beyond it.

"I didn't know the Marine Park was this big," I replied.

"Yes. Very big. But that is not what I mean."

I turned back to the plateau, putting a cigarette in my mouth. Then, as I patted down my pockets looking for my lighter, I noticed something strange. All the plants in the plateau looked vaguely familiar.

"Wow," I said, and the cigarette dropped from my lips, forgotten.

"Yes."

". . . Dope?"

Etienne grinned. "Have you ever seen so much?"

"Never . . ." I pulled a few leaves from the nearest bush and rubbed them in my hands.

Etienne waded further into the plateau. "We should pick some, Richard," he said. "We can dry it in the sun and . . ." Then he stopped. "Wait a moment, there is something funny here."

"What?"

"Well, it is just so . . . These plants . . ." He crouched down, then looked round at me quickly. His lips had begun to curve into a smile, but his eyes were wide and I could literally see color draining from his face. "This is a field," he said.

I froze. "A field?"

"Yes. Look at the plants."

"But it can't be a field. I mean, these islands are . . ."

"The plants are in rows."

"Rows . . ."

We stared at each other. "Jesus Christ," I said slowly. "Then we're in deep shit."

Etienne started running back toward me.

"Françoise?"

"She's . . ." My mind was filling with too many thoughts to answer the question. "Coming," I eventually replied, but he had already passed me and was crouching over the slope.

"She's not there!"

"But she was just behind me." I jogged to the ridge and looked over. "Maybe she slipped."

Etienne stood up. "I will go down. You look here."

"Yes . . . Right."

He began slithering down the mud, then I saw the yellow flash of her T-shirt in some trees further along the edge of the plateau. Etienne had already slid halfway down the slope and I threw a pebble at him to get his attention. He swore and began making his way back up.

Françoise had come out into the plateau, tucking her T-shirt into her shorts. "I needed the bathroom," she called.

I waved my hands frantically, mouthing at her to keep her voice down. She cupped a hand by her ear. "What? Hey! I have seen some people further up the mountain. They are coming this way. Maybe they are from the beach, no?"

Hearing her, Etienne called from down the slope, "Richard! Make her be quiet!"

I sprinted toward her. "What are you doing?" she asked, and then I'd reached her and was pushing her to the ground.

"Shut up!" I said, clamping my hand to her mouth.

She tried to squirm out of my grip and I pressed harder, bending her head back on her shoulders. "This is a dope field," I hissed, carefully enunciating each word. "Do you understand?"

Her eyes bulged wide and she started snorting through her nose. "Do you understand?" I hissed again. "It's a fucking field."

Then Etienne was behind me, pulling at my arms. I dropped Françoise, and for a reason I still don't understand, I lunged for his neck. He twisted behind me and wrapped his arms around my chest.

I tried to struggle but he was too strong. "You idiot! Let me go! There are people coming!"

"Where are the people?"

"On the mountain," Françoise whispered, rubbing her mouth. "Higher."

He looked up to the second plateau. "I can't see anyone," he said, easing his hold on me. "Listen. What is that?"

We all went silent but I couldn't hear anything except blood pounding in my ears.

"Voices," said Etienne quietly. "You can hear it?"

I strained to listen again. This time I found it, distant but getting clearer.

"It's Thai."

I choked. "Fuck! We've got to run!" I clambered to my feet but Etienne dragged me back down.

"Richard," he said, and through my fear some part of me registered surprise at the calm expression on his face. "If we run we will be seen."

"So what do we do?"

He pointed to a dark copse. "We hide in there."

Lying flat against the earth, peering through the mesh of leaves, we waited for the people to appear.

At first it seemed that they would pass us out of sight, but then a branch cracked and a man stepped into the field, close to where Etienne and I had been standing a few minutes before. He was young, maybe twenty, with a kick-boxer's build. His chest was bare and etched with muscle, and he wore military trousers—dark green and baggy with pouches sewn into the legs. In his hand was a long machete. Slung over his shoulder was an automatic rifle.

I could feel Françoise's body pressed against mine—she was trembling.

I looked round, somehow thinking I might calm her, but I could feel the tightness in my face. She stared at me, eyebrows raised as if she wanted me to explain. I shook my head helplessly.

A second man appeared, older, also armed. They stopped and exchanged a few words. Though they stood more than twenty meters away, the curious looping sound of their language carried perfectly over the distance. Then another man called out from within the jungle and they set off again, vanishing over the ridge, down the slope we'd originally come from.

Two or three minutes after their singsong chatter had faded away, Françoise suddenly burst into tears. Then Etienne started crying too. He lay on his back and covered his eyes, his hands bunched into fists.

I watched the two of them blankly. I felt in limbo. The shock of discovering the fields and the tension while we'd been hiding had left me empty. I just kneeled on the ground, sweat running from my hairline and down the side of my face, and thought of nothing.

Finally I managed to gather my wits. "Okay," I said. "Etienne was right. They didn't know we were here, but they might find out soon." I reached for my bag. "We've got to leave."

Françoise sat up, wiping her eyes on her mud-streaked T-shirt. "Yes," she muttered. "Come, Etienne."

Etienne nodded. "Richard," he said firmly. "I do not want to die here."

I opened my mouth to speak but couldn't think what to say.

"I do not want to die here," he repeated. "You must get us out."

Falling Down

I must get them out? Me? I couldn't believe my ears. He'd been the one who'd kept his head when the dope guards were coming. I'd lost my shit. I felt like saying, *"You* fucking get us out!"

But just by looking at him I could tell he wasn't about to take control of the situation. And neither was Françoise. She was gazing at me with the same scared, expectant expression as Etienne.

So, not having a choice, I ended up being the one who made the decision to go on. In one direction there were gunmen, walking along the tracks we had ignorantly assumed were made by animals. Perhaps they were even on the way to the beach and might find a chocolate wrapper or footprints that would betray our presence. In the other direction we didn't know what we might find. Maybe more fields, maybe more gunmen, maybe a beach full of Westerners, and maybe nothing at all.

Better the devil you know is a cliché I now despise. Hidden in the bushes, shivering with fright, I learned that if the devil you know is the guard of a drug plantation, then all other devils pale in comparison.

I have almost no recollection of the few hours after we left the plateau. I think I was concentrating so hard on the immediate that my mind couldn't afford space for anything else. Maybe to have a memory, you need time for reflection, however brief, just to let the memory find a place to settle.

What I do have is a couple of snapshot images: the view from the pass looking back on the dope fields below us, and a more surreal one—surreal because it's a sight I could never have seen, but if I close my eyes I can see it as clearly as I can see any image in my mind.

It's the three of us making our way down the mountain on the far side of the pass. I'm looking from behind, so I can only see our backs, and the image is elevated slightly as if I'm standing further up the slope. We don't have our garbage bags. My arms are empty and outstretched, like I'm trying to steady myself, and Etienne is holding one of Françoise's hands.

The other strange thing is that beyond us I can see the lagoon and a white smear of sand over the treetops. But that isn't possible. We never saw the lagoon until we reached the waterfall.

It was the height of a four-story building—the kind of height that I hate to stand upright near. To gauge the drop I had to crawl to the cliff edge on my belly, afraid that the sense of balance which allows me to stand on a chair would desert me and I would lunge drunkenly forward to my death.

On either side the cliff continued, eventually curving around into the sea, then, unbroken, rejoining the land on the far side. It was as if a giant circle had been cut out of the island to enclose the lagoon in a wall of rock—just as Zeph had described. From where we sat, we could see that the sea-locked cliffs were no more than twenty meters thick, but a passing boat could never guess what lay behind them. They would only see a continuous jungle-topped coastline. The lagoon was presumably supplied by underwater caves and channels.

The falls dropped into a pool from which a quick-flowing stream ran into the trees. The highest trees were more than equal to our height. If they'd been a little closer to the precipice, we could have used them to get down—and getting down was the big problem. The drop was too sheer and too far to consider climbing.

"What do you think?" I said, crawling back from the cliff edge toward Etienne and Françoise.

"What do *you* think?" Etienne replied, apparently not yet ready to let control pass from my hands.

I sighed. "I think we've definitely found the right place. It's where Mister Duck's map says it is, and it fits Zeph's description perfectly."

"So near and so far."

"So near and yet so far," I corrected vacantly. "That's about it."

Françoise stood up and stared over the lagoon toward the seaward rock face. "Perhaps we should walk around there," she suggested. "It may be easier to climb."

"It's higher than here. You can see where the land rises."

"We could jump into the sea. It is not too high to jump."

"We'd never clear the rocks."

She looked irritated and tired. "Okay, Richard, but there must be a way down, no? If people go to this beach, there must be a way."

"If people go to this beach," I echoed. We hadn't seen any sign that people were down there. I'd been carrying an idea that when we reached the beach we'd see groups of friendly travelers with sun-kissed faces, hanging out, coral-diving, playing Frisbee. All that stuff. As it was, from what we could see the beach looked beautiful but completely deserted.

"Maybe we can jump from this waterfall," said Etienne. "It is not so high as the cliff in the sea."

I thought for a moment. "Possibly," I replied, and rubbed my eyes. The adrenaline that had kept me going over the pass had faded and now I was exhausted; so exhausted I couldn't even feel relief at having found the beach. I was also dying for a cigarette. I'd thought of lighting up several times but was still too jumpy about who might smell the smoke.

Françoise seemed to read my mind. "If you want a cigarette, you should have one," she said, smiling. I think it was the first time one of us had smiled since leaving the plateau. "We saw no fields on this side of the pass."

"Yes," Etienne added. "And maybe it can help . . . The nicotine . . . It helps."

"Good point."

I lit up and crawled back to the cliff edge.

If, I reasoned, the waterfall had been pounding down into the pool below for a thousand years, then it was likely that a basin had been eroded into the rock. A basin deep enough to accommodate my leaping into it. But if the island had been created relatively recently, maybe the result of volcanic activity two hundred years ago, then there might not have been time for a deep enough pool to have formed.

"But what do I know?" I said, exhaling slowly, and Françoise looked up to see if I was talking to her.

The pebbles in the water were smooth. The trees below were tall and old.

"Okay," I whispered.

I stood up cautiously, one foot an inch from the cliff, the other set back at a stabilizing angle. A memory appeared of making Airfix airplanes, filling them with cotton wool, covering them in lighter fuel, setting fire to them, and dropping them from the top window of my house.

"Are you jumping?" called Etienne nervously.

"Just taking a better look."

As the planes fell they would arc outward, then appear to curve back toward the wall. The point where they landed, exploding into sticky burning pieces, always seemed to be nearer to the edge of the house than I expected. The distance was difficult to judge; the model planes always needed a harder shove than seemed necessary if they were to clear the doorstep, as well as the head of anyone coming to investigate the patches of flame around the yard.

I was turning this memory over when something happened. An overwhelming sensation washed over me, almost boredom, a strange listlessness. I was suddenly sick of how difficult this journey had become. There was too much effort, too many shocks and dilemmas to dissect. And this sickness had an effect. For a vital few seconds it liberated me from a fear of consequences. I'd had enough. I just wanted it over with.

So near and so far.

"So jump," I heard my voice say.

I paused, wondering if I'd heard myself correctly, and then I did. I jumped.

Everything happened as things are supposed to happen while one falls. I had time to think. Stupid things flashed through my head, such as how my cat slipped off the kitchen table one time and landed on its head, and how once I misjudged a dive from a springboard and the water felt like wood—not concrete or metal but wood.

Then I hit the pool. My T-shirt shot up my chest and jammed under my neck and seconds later I bobbed to the surface. The basin was so deep I never even touched the bottom.

"Ha!" I shouted, thrashing the water around me with my arms, not caring who might hear. "I'm alive!"

I looked up and saw Etienne's and Françoise's heads poking over the cliff.

"You are okay?" called Etienne.

"I'm fine! I'm brilliant!" Then I felt something in my hand. I was still holding my cigarette—the tobacco part had been torn away but the brown filter sat in my palm, soggy and nicotine stained. I started laughing. "Fucking brilliant! Chuck down the bags!"

I sat on the pool's grassy shore, my feet dangling in the water, and waited for Etienne and Françoise to jump. Etienne was having some difficulty psyching himself up, and Françoise didn't want to jump first and leave him up there on his own.

The man appeared just as I was lighting another cigarette to make up for the one I'd ruined. He walked out of the trees a few meters away from me. If it hadn't been for his features and his full beard I could hardly have told he was a Caucasian. His skin was as dark as an Asian's, although a slightly bronze color hinted it had once been white. All he had on was a pair of tattered blue shorts and a necklace made of seashells. With the beard it was hard to tell his age, but I didn't think he was much older than me.

"Hey," he said, cocking his head to one side. "Pretty quick, for an FNG. You did the jump in twenty-three minutes." His accent was English and regionless. "It took me over an hour, but I was alone, so it was harder."

FNG

I covered my eyes with an arm and lay back. Over the sound of the waterfall, Etienne's disembodied voice called to me, saying he was about to jump. From his angle, he wouldn't have been able to see the man. I didn't bother to answer him.

"You okay?" I heard the man ask, and the grass rustled as he took a few steps toward me. "I'm sorry, I should have . . . You must be really freaked out."

Freaked out? I thought. "Not really. I feel quite relaxed."

Extremely relaxed. Floaty. Between my fingers I could feel the cigarette warming my skin, burning closer to my hand.

"Who are you calling an FNG?" I murmured.

A shadow passed across my face as the man bent over to check that I hadn't fainted. "Did you say something?"

"Yeah. I did."

Etienne shrieked as he fell, and the noise of his splash merged into the pounding of the water, and the pounding of the water sounded like the pounding of a helicopter.

"I said, who are you calling an FNG?"

The man paused. "You've been here before? I don't recognize you."

I smiled. "Sure I've been here before," I replied. "In my dreams."

Fragging. Bagging. Klicks. Grunts. Gooks. Charlie. MIA. KIA. LZ. DMZ. FNG.

FNG. Someone who's just starting his first tour in Vietnam. A Fucking New Guy.

Where do I learn these things?

I saw *84 Charlie Mopic* in 1989. I saw *Platoon* in 1986. My friend Tom said, "Rich, you want to see *Platoon?*" "Okay," I said, and he grinned. "Then you'd better find someone to go with." He was always making jokes like that—it was as natural to him as breathing. We went to see it that night at the Swiss Cottage Odeon, screen one, 1986.

In 1991, standing in an airport lounge, looking for something to pass the hours over a long flight to Jakarta. "Eric Van Lustbader?" suggested Sean, and I shook my head. I'd seen Michael Herr sending dispatches. The hours flew by.

Fucking New Guy? Yea, though I walk through the valley of death I will fear no evil, for I am the evilest motherfucker in the valley.

New to what?

We followed the man through the trees. Sometimes we crossed the stream from the pool as it meandered through the jungle, and sometimes we passed glades—one with a smoldering campfire and charred fish heads strewn around it.

We didn't talk much as we walked. The only thing that the man would tell us was his name—Jed. The rest of our questions he waved aside. "Simpler to deal with the talking at the camp," he explained. "We've got as many questions for you as you've got for us."

At first glance the camp was close to how I'd imagined it might be. There was a large dusty clearing surrounded by the rocket ship trees and dotted with makeshift bamboo huts. A few canvas tents looked incongruous, but otherwise it was very like a kind of Southeast Asian village I'd seen many times before. At the far end was a larger construction, a longhouse, and beside it the stream from the waterfall reemerged, bending around to run along the edge of the clearing. From the straightness of its banks, it had obviously been deliberately diverted.

It was only after taking all this in that I noticed there was something strange about the light. The forest had been both dark and bright by turns, but here everything was lit in an unchanging twilight, more like dusk than midday. I looked up, following the trunk of one of the giant trees. The height of the tree alone was breathtaking, accentuated by the fact that the lower branches had been cut away, so it was possible to appreciate its size. Higher up the branches began to grow again, curving upward across the clearing like gables until they joined with the branches from the other side. But their point of joining seemed too dense and thick, and as I looked harder I began to see that they were coiled around each other, intertwining to form a cavernous ceiling of wood and leaves, hanging with the stalactite vines that now became magically appropriate.

"Camouflage," said Jed, behind me. "We don't want to be seen from the air. Planes sometimes fly over. Not often, but sometimes." He pointed upward. "Originally the branches were tied together with ropes but now they just grow that way. Every so often we have to cut them back a bit, or it gets too gloomy. Impressive, huh?"

"Stunning," I agreed, and was so captivated by this sight that I didn't even register that people had begun to emerge from the longhouse and were walking across the clearing toward us. Three people to be exact. Two women and a man.

"Sal, Cassie, and Bugs," said one of the women as they reached us. "I'm Sal, but don't try to remember our names." She smiled warmly. "You'll only get confused when you meet the others, and you'll learn them all eventually."

I'm not likely to forget Bugs, I thought to myself, just managing to suppress a laugh. I frowned and put a hand up to my temples. Since I'd jumped off the waterfall my head had been feeling increasingly light. Now it had started to feel like it might float off my shoulders.

Françoise stepped up to the woman and said, "Françoise, Etienne, and Richard."

"You're French! Lovely! We've only got one other French person here."

"Richard is English." Françoise gestured to me and I tried to nod politely, but I overran the motion forward and the nod turned into a little bow.

"Lovely!" exclaimed the woman again, watching me curiously out of the corner of her eye. ". . . Well, let's get you some food, because I know you're all hungry." She turned to the man. "Bugs, you want to fix some stew? Then we can all have a good long chat and get to know each other. Does that sound good?"

"It sounds great, Sal," I said loudly. "You know, you're quite right. I do feel hungry." The laugh I'd suppressed before suddenly worked its way out. "We've only eaten these cold Magi-Noodles and chocolate. We couldn't take the Calor gas stove . . . Etienne's stove . . . And . . ."

Jed lunged to catch me as I fainted, but too late. His alarmed face spun out of view as I toppled backward. The last thing I saw was a blue pinprick of sky through the canopy ceiling, before darkness rushed in and engulfed it.

Batman

I waited patiently for Mister Duck to show up. I knew he was near, because in the candlelight I could see blood scattered in the dust around my bed and there was a red handprint on the sheets. I guessed he was in the shadows at the other end of the longhouse, waiting to loom out and surprise me. But he was the one who was going to be surprised. This time I was expecting him.

Minutes passed. I sweated and sighed. Wax ran down the candle, balling in the dust. A lizard fell from a beam above and landed between my legs.

The lizard from the rainstorm, come back to visit me.

"Aah," I said. "Hello there." I reached to pick him up but he wriggled free, leaving a centimeter of pink tail behind.

One of Mister Duck's games.

I swore and held up the tail, and it flopped around on my palm. "Very clever, Duck. Don't know what it means, but it's very clever." I sank back on the pillow. "Hey, Duck! That's the kid, huh? That's the boy!"

"Who are you talking to?" said a sleepy voice from deep in the shadows.

I sat up again. "That you, Duck? You sound different."

". . . It's Bugs."

"Bugs. I remember. Hey, let me guess. Bugs Bunny, right?"

There was a long pause. "Yes," said the voice. "That is right."

I scratched my head. Sticky clumps were matted into my hair. "Yeah, thought so. So you've taken over from Duck now. Who's next?" I giggled. "Road Runner?"

Two people muttered in the darkness.

"Porky Pig? Yosemite Sam? No, wait, I've got it . . . Wile E. Coyote. It's Wile E. Coyote, isn't it?"

In the orange candlelight I saw a movement down the longhouse, a figure padding toward me. As it moved closer I recognized the slim shape.

"Françoise! Hey, Françoise, this is a better dream than the last one."

"Shh," she whispered, kneeling beside me, her long white T-shirt drawing up around her thighs. "You are not dreaming."

I shook my head. "No, Françoise, I am. Trust me. Look at the blood on the floor. That's Mister Duck, from his wrists. They never stop bleeding. You should have seen what happened to my room in Bangkok."

She looked around, then back at me. "The blood is from your head, Richard."

"But . . ."

"You hurt it when you fell."

". . . Mister Duck."

"Shh. There are people asleep in here. Please."

I lay back, feeling puzzled, and she rested her hand on my forehead.

"You have a little temperature. Do you think you can go back to sleep?"

". . . I don't know."

"Will you try?"

". . . Okay."

She tucked the sheets over my shoulders, smiling slightly. "There now. Close your eyes."

I closed them.

The pillow shifted as she leaned over. She kissed me gently on the cheek.

"I am dreaming," I murmured as her footsteps padded away down longhouse. "I knew it."

Mister Duck hung above me like a wingless bat, his legs gripping the beam, the curve under his rib cage stretched into a grotesque cavity, his swinging arms dripping steadily.

"I knew it," I said. "I knew you were near." A pulse of blood splashed onto my chest. "Cold like a fucking reptile."

Mister Duck scowled. "It's as hot as yours. It's only cold because of the fever. And you should put the covers back. You'll catch your death."

"Too hot."

"Mmm. Too hot, too cold . . ."

I wiped my mouth with a wet hand. "Is it malaria?"

"Malaria? Nervous exhaustion, more like."

"So how come Françoise doesn't have it?"

"She wasn't as nervous as you." His outsized jaw jutted out and split his face into a mischievous grin. "She's been very attentive, you know. Very attentive indeed. Checked on you twice when you were asleep."

"I am asleep."

"Sure . . . Fast asleep."

The candle flame faltered as melting wax began to flood the wick. Cicadas chirped outside. Blood like icy water dripped, made me shiver and twist the sheets.

"What was the deal with the lizard, Duck?"

"Lizard?"

"It ran away. In the rainstorm I could hold it in my hand. But here it ran away."

"I seem to remember it running in the rainstorm, Rich."

"I held it in my hand."

"Is that what you remember, Rich?"

The pool of wax grew too large for the candle to contain. Suddenly it drained away and the wick flared brightly, throwing a crisp shadow on the longhouse ceiling. A silhouette. A wingless bat with hanging claws and pencil arms.

"Lightning," I whispered.

The jaw jutted out. "That's the boy . . ."

"Fuck . . ."

". . . That's the kid."

". . . you."

Minutes passed.

Talk

Late morning, I reckoned. Only from the heat. In the darkness of the longhouse and the steady glow of the candle, there was nothing else to reveal the time.

A Buddha sat cross-legged at the foot of my bed, palms resting flat on ocher knees. An unusual Buddha, female, with an American accent, heavy breasts clearly outlined through a saffron T-shirt, and long hair tied back from her perfectly round face. Around her neck was a necklace of seashells. Beside her, incense sticks burned, sending tiny spirals of perfumed smoke up to the ceiling.

"Finish it, Richard," said the Buddha, looking pointedly at the bowl I held in my hands—half a freshly cut coconut, now nearly drained of a sugary fish soup. "Finish all of it."

I lifted the bowl to my mouth, and the smell of the incense mixed with the fish and sweetness.

I put it down again. "I can't, Sal."

"You must, Richard."

"I'll throw up."

"Richard, you must."

She had the American habit of frequently using one's name. It had the strange effect of being both disarmingly familiar and unnaturally forced.

"Honestly. I can't."

"It's good for you."

"I've finished most of it. Look."

I held up the bowl for her to see and we stared at each other across my bloodstained sheets.

"Okay," she sighed. "I guess that'll have to do." Then she folded her arms and narrowed her eyes and said, "Richard, we need to talk."

We were alone. Occasionally people would enter and leave but I never saw them. I'd hear the door at the far end of the longhouse bang open and a small rectangle of light would hover in the darkness until the door swung shut.

When I reached the part about finding Mister Duck's body, Sal looked sad. It wasn't a strong reaction; her eyebrows flicked downward and her lower lip tensed. I guessed she'd already heard about Duck's death from Etienne and Françoise, so the news wasn't as shocking as it could have been. Her reaction was pretty hard to read. It seemed more directed at me than anything else, like she was sorry that I'd had to witness something so horrible.

Aside from that one moment, Sal made no other signs. She didn't interrupt me, frown, smile, or nod. She just sat in her lotus position, motionless, and listened. At first her blankness was disconcerting and I paused after key events to give her time to comment, but she'd only wait for me to continue. Soon I found myself slipping into a stream of consciousness, talking to her as if she were a tape recorder or a priest.

Very like a priest. I began to feel as if I was in confession, describing my panic on the plateau with embarrassment and trying to justify why I'd lied to the Thai police; and the silent way she absorbed these things was like absolution. I even made an obscure reference to my attraction to Françoise, just to get it off my chest. Probably too oblique for her to pick up, but the intention was there.

The only thing I held back was that I'd given two other people directions to the island. I knew I should tell her about Zeph and Sammy, but I also thought she might be pissed off if she knew I'd spread their secret. Better to wait until I knew more about the setup on the island.

I also didn't tell her about my dreams with Mister Duck, but that was different. There wasn't any reason why I should.

I punctuated the end of the story, leading right up to the point where I'd walked into the camp and collapsed, by leaning out of bed and pulling the carton of two hundred cigarettes out of my plastic bag. Sal smiled and the confessional atmosphere was broken, abruptly flipped back to the semifamiliarity of before.

"Hey," she said, stretching out the word in her North American drawl. "You sure came prepared."

"Mmm," I replied, all I could say as I sucked the candle flame onto the tip. "I'm the addict's addict."

She laughed. "I see that."

"You want one?"

"No thanks. I'd really better not."

"Giving up?"

"Given up. You should try too, Richard. It's easy to give up here."

I took a few quick drags without inhaling, to burn the waxy taste out of the cigarette. "I'll give up when I'm thirty or something. When I have kids."

Sal shrugged. "Whatever," she said, smiling, then brushed a finger over each eyebrow, smoothing out the sweat. "Well, Richard, it sounds like you had quite an adventure getting here. In normal circumstances, new guests are brought here under supervision. Your circumstances were very unusual."

I waited for her to elaborate but she didn't. Instead she uncrossed her legs as if she was about to leave.

"Uh, now can I ask you some questions, Sal?" I said quickly.

Her eyes flicked down to her wrist. She wasn't wearing any watch; it was a motion of pure instinct.

"I have some things to do, Richard."

"Please, Sal. There's so much I've got to ask you."

"Sure there is, but you'll learn everything in time. There's no particular hurry."

"Just a few questions."

She crossed her legs again. "Five minutes."

"Okay, uh, well, first I'd just like to know something about the setup. I mean, what is this place?"

"It's a beach resort."

I frowned. "A beach resort?"

"A place to come to for vacations."

I frowned harder. By the look in Sal's eyes, I could see she found my expression amusing.

"Holidays?" I tried to say, but the word caught in my throat. It seemed so belittling. I had ambiguous feelings about the differences between tourists and travelers—the problem being that the more I traveled, the smaller the differences became. But the one difference I could still latch onto was that tourists went on holidays while travelers did something else. They *traveled*.

"What did you think this place was?" Sal asked.

"I don't know. I didn't think anything really." I exhaled slowly. "But I certainly didn't think of a beach resort."

She waved a chubby hand in the air. "Okay. I'm kind of teasing you, Richard. Of course this is more than a beach resort. But at the same time, it is just a beach resort. We come here to relax by a beautiful beach, but it isn't a beach resort because we're trying to get away from beach resorts. Or we're trying to make a place that won't turn into a beach resort. See?"

"No."

Sal shrugged. "You will see, Richard. It's not so complicated."

Actually, I did see what she meant but I didn't want to admit it. I wanted her to describe Zeph's island commune of free spirits. A holiday resort seemed like a poor reward for the difficulties we'd had to overcome, and a rush of bitterness ran through me as I remembered the swim and the terror of hiding on the plateau.

"Don't look so disappointed, Richard."

"No, I'm not . . . I'm . . ."

Sal reached over and squeezed my hand. "After a little while you'll see that this is a wonderful place, as long as you appreciate it for what it is."

I nodded. "I'm sorry, Sal. I didn't mean to look disappointed. I'm not disappointed. I mean, this longhouse and the trees outside . . . It's all amazing." I laughed. "It's silly really. I think I was expecting an . . . an ideology or something. A purpose."

I paused while I finished the cigarette. Sal made no movement to leave. "How about the gunmen in the dope fields?" I asked, conscientiously tucking the dead butt back into the packet. "Are they anything to do with you?"

Sal shook her head.

"They're drug lords?"

"I think drug lords is a bit dramatic. I have a feeling the fields are owned by ex-fishermen from Koh Samui, but I could be wrong. They turned up a couple of years ago and pretty much took over that half of the island. We can't go there now."

"How do they get around the Marine Park authorities?"

"Same as us. They keep quiet. And half of the wardens are probably in on it, so they make sure the tourist boats don't come near."

"But they know you're here."

"Of course, but there isn't much they can do. It's not like they can re-port us. If we got raided, then they'd get raided too."

"So there's no trouble between you?"

Sal's hand flicked to the seashell necklace around her neck. "They stick to their half. We stick to ours," she said briskly, then suddenly stood up, patting the dust from her skirt with pointless attention. "Enough talk, Richard. I really do have to go now and you're still running a fever. You need some rest."

I didn't bother protesting and Sal began walking away, her T-shirt catching the candlelight a little longer than her skin and skirt.

"One more question," I called after her, and she looked round. "The man in Bangkok. You knew him?"

"Yes," she said quietly, then she began walking again.

"Who was he?"

"He was a friend."

"He lived here?"

"He was a friend," she repeated.

"But . . . Okay, just one more question."

Sal didn't stop, and now only her saffron T-shirt was visible, bobbing in the darkness.

"One more!"

"What?" her voice floated back.

"Where's the toilet?"

"Outside, second hut down by the edge of the camp."

The bright sliver of light through the longhouse door slid back to blackness.

Exploring

The toilet, a small bamboo hut on the edge of the clearing, was a good example of how well the camp had been organized. Inside the hut was a low bench with a football-sized hole, through which I could see running water—a tributary from the diverted waterfall stream.

There was a second hole cut into the roof, to let in what little light filtered past the canopy ceiling.

All in all, it was a lot more agreeable than many of the bathrooms one finds outside the Westernized world. There wasn't, however, any toilet paper. Not a surprise in itself, but I'd thought there might be some leaves or something. Instead, by the water channel, there was a plastic pitcher.

You find plastic pitchers all around provincial Asia and their purpose has confounded me for years. I refuse to believe that Asians wipe themselves with their hands—it's a ridiculous idea—but aside from washing digits, I can't see what other use the pitcher has. I'm sure they don't splash themselves down. Apart from being ineffective it would make an incredible mess, and they emerge from their ablutions as dry as a bone.

Of the various mysteries of the Orient this should be the easiest to unravel, but the subject matter appears to be veiled in a conspiracy of silence. A Manilan friend once came with me on a trip to a small island off the coast of Luzon. One day I found him standing on a mud dike, peering into the mangrove swamps with obvious concern. When I asked him what the matter was he blushed furiously, which made his brown skin go almost purple, and pointed to some bits of toilet paper that were floating in the water. The tide was leading the toilet paper toward some houses, and this prospect had thrown him into a panic. Not for reasons of hygiene but because it would betray his Western toilet habits—habits the locals would find unacceptably disgusting. In his shame, he was considering wading into the swamps to hoick the pieces out and hide them elsewhere.

We managed to solve the problem by bombarding the water with stones until the paper shredded or sank. As we slunk away from the scene of the crime I asked him to describe the locals' acceptable alternative, but he refused to tell me. He just hinted darkly that I'd find it as disgusting as they found our way. This was as close as I ever got to finding out the truth.

Luckily I only needed to piss, so I was spared having to experiment. When the time came for solids, I decided, I'd slip into the jungle.

I left the toilet and began walking back across the clearing. I was still feeling slightly feverish but I didn't want to spend any more hours breathing stuffy air and watching flickering candle flames. Instead I continued past the longhouse, thinking I might explore. I also hoped that I might find

Etienne and Françoise, who'd been missing since I woke up. I imagined they were exploring too.

I counted nine tents in the clearing and five huts, not including the longhouse. The tents were only used for sleeping— inside the flaps I could see backpacks and clothes, and in one I even saw a Nintendo Gameboy— but the huts all seemed to have functional uses. Apart from the toilet, there was a kitchen and a washing area, also fed by tributaries. The other huts were for storage. One contained carpentry tools and another some boxes of tinned food. It made me wonder how long the camp had existed. Sal had said that the dope fields had appeared a couple of years ago, which implied that the travelers had been around for some time before that.

Tents, tools, tinned food, Nintendo. The more I saw, the more I marveled. It wasn't just how organized the camp was, it was *how* it had been organized. None of the huts looked newer than the others. The tents' guy-lines were held with rocks, and the rocks were molded into the ground. Nothing seemed random, everything seemed calculated: designed as opposed to evolved.

As I wandered around the clearing, peering through tent flaps and studying the canopy ceiling until my neck ached, my sense of awe was only matched by a sense of frustration. Questions kept appearing in my mind, and each question raised another. It was clear that, at some point, the people who'd set up the camp had needed a boat. This suggested the help of Thais, which in turn suggested a certain kind of Thai. A Koh Samui spiv might bend the rules to let backpackers stay on a Marine Park island for a few nights, but it was harder to imagine them ferrying crates of food and carpentry tools.

I also found it strange that the camp was so deserted. It apparently supported a large number of people, and a couple of times I thought I heard voices nearby, but no one ever appeared.

After a while, the quietness and occasional distant voices began to get to me. At first I just felt a little lonely and sorry for myself. I didn't think Sal should have left me on my own, especially when I was ill and new to the camp. And Etienne and Françoise were supposed to be my friends. Shouldn't friends have hung around to make sure I was okay?

But soon loneliness turned into paranoia. I found that I was starting when I heard jungle noises, my shuffling footsteps in the dirt sounded oddly loud, and I caught myself acting with an affected casualness, aimed at the eyes I suspected were watching me from the trees. Even the absence of Etienne and Françoise became a reason to worry.

Maybe it was partly to do with my fever, or maybe it was a normal reaction under abnormal circumstances. Either way, the eerie quietness was freaking me out. I decided I had to get out of the clearing. I went back to the longhouse to pick up my cigarettes and some shoes, but when I saw the long avenue of shadow that lay between the door and my candlelit bed, I changed my mind.

There were several paths that ran from the clearing. I chose the nearest.

By good luck, the path I chose led directly to the beach. The sand was too hot for bare feet, so I jogged down to the water's edge, and after making a mental note of where I'd come out of the jungle, I flipped a mental coin and took a left.

Getting out from the claustrophobic cavern of trees calmed me. There was plenty to distract me as I walked through the shallows.

From the waterfall, I'd seen the vast circle of granite cliffs as a barrier to getting down, but now they were a barrier to getting back up. A prison could hardly have been built with more formidable walls, although it was hard to think of such a place as prisonlike. Aside from the lagoon's beauty, there was a sense that the cliffs were protective—the walls of an inverse castle, sunk instead of raised. Sal hadn't given me the impression of being very threatened by the dope farmers, but the knowledge that the cliffs lay between me and them was still comforting.

The lagoon itself was almost perfectly divided between land and sea. I estimated its diameter at a mile, though I wouldn't rely on the accuracy of this guess. Now, nearer to the seaward cliffs than on the waterfall, I could make out features in the rock face I hadn't seen before. Along the watermark were black hollows and caves. They looked as if they penetrated the cliff deeply—perhaps deeply enough to provide a passage for a small boat. The sea itself was punctuated by protruding boulders, slick where the waves lapped against them, flattened into slabs by centuries of tropical rain.

I'd walked a few hundred meters down the beach when I noticed some shapes splashing around one of the larger boulders. Bizarrely, my first thought was that they were seals, until I realized there couldn't possibly be seals in Thailand. Then, looking harder, I realized they were people. At last I'd found someone.

I checked the urge to call out, for no particular reason other than a vague instinct to be cautious. Instead I jogged back over the sand to the treeline, where I could sit in the shade and wait until the swimmers returned. There I found footprints, T-shirts, and to my delight, an open packet of Marlboros. After a millisecond of debate I stole one.

Contented for the moment, I blew smoke rings into the still air, discovering that when they floated over the beach they would rise quickly and, without dissipating, drift into the overhanging palm leaves. It took me several baffled puffs to work out that it was due to heat rising from the sunbaked sand.

The swimmers were less confusing. They were spearfishing. Every so often they'd all get out of the sea and gaze intently at the water around them, spears poised. Then they'd all throw their spears at once, dive back in, splash around a bit, and repeat the process. They seemed to catch a lot of fish.

Exocet

Neutralized by wet hair and dark skin, each of the six swimmers looked like a carbon copy of the others. I didn't recognize Etienne and Françoise until they'd crossed the hot sands and were laying out their catch on the grass.

Something made me hesitate before I stepped out from behind the treeline. Seeing my two traveling companions on such friendly terms with the other swimmers felt strange. They were all laughing and calling each other by name. It made me realize how much I'd been left out by sleeping through the first night and day in the camp. And then, when I did step out, none of the group noticed me. I had to stand there a few moments, a grin frozen on my face, waiting for one of them to look up.

Eventually, not knowing what else to do, I coughed. Six heads turned in unison.

"Hi," I said uncertainly. There was a silence. Françoise was frowning slightly, as if she couldn't quite place me. Then Etienne's face split into a huge smile.

"Richard! You are better!" He bounded over and embraced me. "Everybody," he said, tightly gripping me with one wet arm and making an expansive gesture with the other. "This is our friend who was sick."

"Hi, Richard," the swimmers chorused.

"Hi . . ."

Etienne hugged me again. "I am so happy you are better!"

"I'm happy too."

I looked over Etienne's shoulder at Françoise. She was still standing with the group and I smiled at her. She returned the smile but in a lopsided way. Or a knowing way. I suddenly wondered what kinds of things I might have blurted out to her in my delirious state.

As if to panic me further she walked over and lightly brushed a hand against my arm. "It is good to see you better, Richard," she said flatly; then as I opened my mouth to reply she turned away.

"I caught a fish!" said Etienne. "This is my first time fishing, and I caught a big fish!" He pointed to the catch. "You see this big blue fish?"

"Uh-huh," I replied, only half listening as cold thoughts flooded my head.

"Mine!"

I was introduced to the other swimmers.

Moshe was a tall Israeli with an earsplitting laugh. He used it in the same way as a madman uses a gun, spraying it around with bewildering randomness. Hearing the laugh made me blink instinctively, like hearing a hammer pound on brick or metal. Our conversation was impeded by having to watch him through the strobe effect of my convulsing eyes.

Then there were two haughty Yugoslavian girls whose names I could never pronounce and certainly never spell, and who made a big deal about being from Sarejevo. They said, "We are from Sarejevo," then paused meaningfully like they expected me to faint or congratulate them.

And there was Gregorio. Gregorio I warmed to at once. He had a kind face and a soft Latin lisp, and when we were introduced he said, "I am very pleathed to meet you." Then he dried his hand on his T-shirt before offering it to shake, adding, "We are all very pleathed to meet you."

I can't remember one thing about what Etienne said to me as we walked back along the shallows. I remember he was talking about what I'd missed while I was asleep, and I have a vision of the way he cradled his catch, smothering his brown chest with silver scales, but everything else is a blank. It's a measure of how disturbed I was by what I might have said to Françoise.

I realized I had to find out the truth or it would drive me crazy. Françoise was walking a few paces behind the group, so I lagged behind Etienne, pretending to find an interesting seashell. But as soon as I did so, she picked up her pace. Then when I caught up with her she seemed to deliberately drop behind again.

Seemed. It was impossible for me to tell. When she slowed she was apparently distracted by something in the trees, but that might have been no more real than my interesting seashell.

It was enough for me. By now I felt sure my suspicions were correct and, rational or otherwise, I decided I had to clear the air without any delay.

When I lagged behind the next time, I caught her by the arm.

"Françoise," I asked, trying to find the right balance between firm and casual, "is there something funny going on?"

"Funny?" she replied, wide-eyed. "Oh, well, everything here is so strange. Of course, I am not used to it yet."

"No, I didn't mean here. . . . Look, maybe it's just me, but it feels like there's something funny going on between us."

"Us?"

"Me and you," I said, and instantly began to blush. I coughed and pointed my head at the ground. "I thought that, while I was ill, maybe I said something that . . ."

"Oh." She looked at me. "What are you afraid you said?"

"I don't know what I said. I'm asking you."

"Yes. And I am asking what you are afraid you said."

Fuck, I thought. Rewind.

"Nothing. I'm not afraid I said anything."

"So . . . ?"

"So I don't know. I just thought you were acting funny. It's just me. Forget it."

Françoise stopped. "Okay," she said. The rest of the group began drawing away from us. "Let me say it, Richard. You are worried you said you loved me, yes?"

"What?" I exclaimed, momentarily thrown by her Exocet-like bluntness. Then I gathered my wits and lowered my voice. "Jesus Christ, Françoise! Of course not!"

"Richard . . ."

"I mean, that's a ridiculous idea."

"Richard, please. It is not ridiculous. It was what you were afraid of."

"No. Not at all. I was . . ."

"Richard!"

I paused. She was staring straight at me. "Yes," I said slowly. "It's what I was afraid of."

She sighed.

"Françoise," I began, but she interrupted me.

"It does not matter, Richard. You had this fever, and in a fever people can say strange things, no? Things they do not mean. So you are afraid you said something strange. It means nothing. I understand."

"You aren't angry?"

"Of course not."

"And . . . did I say anything? Anything like that?"

"No."

"Really?"

She looked away. "Yes, really. You are very sweet to worry, but it is nothing. Do not think of this again." Then she pointed to the others, who were now fifty feet down the beach. "Come. We should go."

"Okay," I said quietly.

"Okay."

We caught up with the group, neither of us talking. Françoise walked up to Etienne and started chatting with him in French, and I walked a little aside from the others. As we neared the turning to the campsite, Gregorio sidled over.

"You feel like the new boy in school?"

"Oh, uh . . . Yeah. A bit."

"These first days are difficult, of course, but do not worry. You will find friends quickly, Richard."

I smiled. The way he emphasized the "you" made it sound personal, like he thought there was something particular about me that would make it easy to find friends. I knew it was just the way he spoke English, but it made me feel better all the same.

Game Over, Man

While we'd been on the beach, the camp had filled up with people. I could see Bugs and Sal by the entrance to the longhouse, talking to a group who all carried ropes. A fat guy was busy gutting fish outside the kitchen hut, stacking the hollowed bodies on broad leaves and emptying the innards into a blood-smeared plastic bucket. Beside him a girl blew on a wood fire and fed the flames with kindling.

The center of the clearing seemed like a focus point. Most of the people were there, just milling around and chatting. At the furthest end a girl was carefully laying wet clothes over tent guylines.

Gregorio was right. I did feel like the new boy in school. I scanned the clearing as if it were the playground on my first day's lunch break, wondering what divisions and hierarchies would have to be learned, and which of the thirty or so faces would end up as friends.

One face stuck out. It belonged to a black guy sitting alone, his back against a storeroom hut. He looked around twenty, he had a shaved head, and his eyes were fixed intently on a small gray box in his hands—the Nintendo Gameboy I'd spotted earlier.

Etienne and Françoise followed Moshe to deposit their catch with the fish gutters. I nearly trailed after them. The schoolyard atmosphere was telling me to stick with the people I knew, but then I looked back at the Nintendo guy. His face suddenly screwed up and over the murmur of talking I heard him hiss, "Game Over."

I began walking toward him.

I once read that the most widely understood word in the whole world is "okay," followed by "Coke," as in cola. I think they should do the survey again, this time checking for "Game Over."

Game Over is my favorite thing about playing video games. Actually, I should qualify that. It's the split second before Game Over that's my favorite thing.

Streetfighter Two—an oldie but goldie—with my friend Leo controlling Ryu. Ryu's his preferred character because he's a good all-rounder—great defensive moves, pretty quick, and once he's on an offensive roll he's unstoppable. My brother Theo's controlling Blanka. Blanka's faster than Ryu, but he's only really good on attack. The way to win with Blanka is to get in the other player's face and just never let up. Flying kick, leg sweep, spin attack, head bite. Daze them into submission.

Both players are down to the end of their energy bars. One more hit and they're down, so they're both being cagey. They're hanging back at opposite ends of the screen, waiting for the other guy to make the first move. Leo takes the initiative. He sends off a fireball to force Theo into blocking, then jumps in with a flying kick to knock Blanka's green head off. But as he's moving through the air he hears a soft tapping. Theo's tapping the punch button on his control pad. He's charging up an electricity defense so when Ryu's foot makes contact with Blanka's head it's going to be Ryu who gets KO'd with 10,000 volts charging through his system.

This is the split second before Game Over.

Leo's heard the noise. He knows he's fucked. He has time to blurt, "I'm toast," before Ryu is lit up and thrown backward across the screen, flashing like a Christmas tree, a charred skeleton. Toast.

The split second is the moment you comprehend you're just about to die. Different people react to it in different ways. Some swear and rage. Some sigh or gasp. Some scream. I've heard a lot of screams over the twelve years I've been addicted to video games.

I'm sure that this moment provides a rare insight into the way people react just before they really do die. The game taps into something pure and beyond affectations. As Leo hears the tapping he blurts, "I'm toast." He says it quickly, with resignation and understanding. If he were driving down the highway and saw a car spinning into his path I think he'd react in the same way.

Personally, I'm a rager. I fling my joypad across the floor, clench my eyes shut, throw back my head, and yell abuse at anything within abusing distance.

A few years ago I had a game called Alien 3. It had a great feature. When you ran out of lives you'd get a photo-realistic picture of the Alien with saliva dripping from its jaws, and a digitized voice would bleat, "Game Over, man!"

I really used to love that.

"Hi," I said.
The guy looked up. "Hi."
"How many lines did you make?"
"One-four-four."
"Uh-huh. Pretty good."
"I can do one-seven-seven."
"One-seven-seven?"
He nodded. "How about you?"
"Uh, about a hundred and fifty is my best."
He nodded again. "You're one of the three FNGs, huh?"
"Yep."
"Where are you from?"
"London."
"Me too. Want a game?"
"Sure."
"Okay." He gestured to the dirt. "Pull up a chair."

beach
life

Assimilation, Rice

A few years ago I was going through the process of splitting up with my first serious girlfriend. She went away to Greece for the summer and when she came back she'd had a holiday romance with some Belgian guy. As if that wasn't bad enough, it seemed that the guy in question was going to show up in London sometime over the next few weeks. After three hellish days and nights, I realized that I was dangerously close to losing my head. I biked over to my dad's flat and emotionally blackmailed him into lending me enough cash to leave the country.

On that trip I learned something very important. Escape through travel works. Almost from the moment I boarded my flight, life in England became meaningless. Seat belt signs lit up, problems switched off. Broken armrests took precedence over broken hearts. By the time the plane was airborne I'd forgotten England even existed.

After that first day, wandering around the clearing, I didn't really question a single thing about the beach.

The rice: Over thirty people, two meals every day, eating rice. Rice paddies need acres of flat, irrigated land which we simply didn't have, so I knew we couldn't be growing it. If the situation hadn't come up with the Rice Run, I might never have known where it all came from. Unremarked, I would have let it pass.

Assimilation: From day one we were working, everybody knew our names, we had beds allocated in the longhouse. I felt like I'd been living there all my life.

It was the same thing that had happened on the airplane; my memory began shutting down. Koh Samui became a hazy, dreamlike place, and Bangkok became little more than a familiar word. On the third or fourth day I remember thinking that Zeph and Sammy might turn up soon, and wondering how people would react. Then I realized I couldn't quite recall Zeph's and Sammy's faces. A couple of days later I'd forgotten they might be coming at all.

There's this saying: In an all-blue world, color doesn't exist. It makes a lot of sense to me. If something seems strange, you question it, but if the outside world is too distant to use as a comparison, then nothing seems strange.

Why would I question it, anyway? Assimilating myself was the most natural thing in the world. I'd been doing it ever since I became a traveler. Another saying: When in Rome, do as the Romans. In the traveler's ten commandments, that's commandment number one. You don't march into Hindu temples and start saying, "Why are you worshiping a cow?" You look around, take on board, adjust, accept.

Assimilation and rice. These were just things to accept—new aspects of a new life.

But even now, I'm not asking the right questions.

It doesn't matter why I found it so easy to assimilate myself into the beach life. The question is why the beach life found it so easy to assimilate me.

Over the first two or three weeks there was a song that I couldn't get out of my head. Actually it wasn't even a song. It was just a couple of lines from a song. And I don't know the song's name but I suspect it's called "Street Life," because the only lyric I could remember went, "Street life, it's the only life I know, street life, dah dah-dah dah dah dah dah-da-dah." Except the way I sang it went, "beach life," instead of, "street life," and all I could do was repeat that little bit over and over.

It used to drive Keaty crazy. He'd say, "Richard, you've got to stop singing that fucking song," and I'd have to shrug and say, "Keaty, I can't get it out of my head." Then I'd make an effort not to sing it for a while, but without meaning to I'd start again a couple of hours later. I'd only realize I'd started again when Keaty would smack his forehead and hiss, "I asked you not to fucking sing it! *Jesus*, Richard!" Then I'd have to shrug again. Eventually I got Keaty singing it too, and when I pointed this out he said, "Aaargh!" and wouldn't let me play on his Nintendo for the rest of the day.

Night, Jim-Bob

I quickly fell into a routine.

I'd wake around seven, seven-thirty, then head straight down to the beach with Etienne and Keaty. Usually Françoise wouldn't swim because it was too much hassle getting the salt out of her long hair every day, but sometimes she would. Then we'd go back to the camp and rinse off in the shower hut.

Breakfast was at eight. Every morning the kitchen crew would boil up a load of rice and it was up to the individual to sort out anything else. Most had their rice plain but a few made the effort to boil up some fish or vegetables. I never bothered. For the first three days we mixed in our Magi-Noodles for a bit of flavor, but when the Magi-Noodles ran out we settled for the rice.

After breakfast people would begin to disperse. Mornings were for working and everybody had their job to do. By nine the camp was always empty.

There were four main areas of work: fishing, gardening, cooking, and carpentry.

Etienne, Françoise, and I were on the fishing detail. Before we'd arrived there'd been two fishing groups, but we made it three. Gregorio and us made up one group, Moshe and the two Yugoslavian girls made up another, and a bunch of Swedish guys were the third. They were very serious about their fishing and every day they'd swim through the cliff caves to the open sea. Sometimes they'd come back with fish as big as your leg and everybody would make a fuss over them.

Workwise, I felt pretty lucky. If it hadn't been for Etienne and Françoise volunteering to go fishing on that first day, we wouldn't have met Gregorio, and I might have ended up on the gardening detail. Keaty was on the gardening detail and complained about it all the time. He had to work over half an hour from the clearing, up by the waterfall. The head gardener was Jean, a farmer's son from southwestern France who pronounced his name like he was clearing his throat, and he ran his garden with an iron fist. The problem was, once you'd taken on a job it was pretty hard to change. It wasn't like there were rules, but everybody worked in groups, so if you changed jobs you had to leave one group and break into another.

If I hadn't been a fisher, I probably would have tried to get in with the carpenters. Kitchen duties didn't appeal at all. Aside from the hellish chore of cooking dinner for thirty people every day, the three cooks all carried a lingering odor of fish innards. The head cook, whose nickname was Unhygienix, had his own private store of soap in his tent. He seemed to get through a bar a week, but it didn't do any good.

The carpenters were run by Bugs. Bugs was Sal's boyfriend, and he was a carpenter by trade. He'd been responsible for the longhouse and all the huts, and he'd had the idea of tying the branches together to make the canopy ceiling. From the way people treated him, it was obvious that Bugs was much respected. It was partly that everybody relied on the things he made, but it was also because he was Sal's boyfriend.

If there was a leader, it was Sal. When she talked, people listened. She spent her days wandering around the lagoon, checking on the different work details and making sure things were running smoothly. At first she devoted a lot of time to making sure we were settling in okay. She often joined us when we swam down to the boulders, but after the first week she seemed satisfied and we rarely saw her during the work period.

The only person who didn't have a clear working detail was Jed. He spent his days alone and was usually the first person to leave in the mornings and the last person to come back. Keaty said that Jed spent a lot of time near the waterfall and above the cliffs. Every now and then he would disappear and spend the night somewhere on the island. When he turned up again he usually had fresh grass, clearly taken from the dope fields.

Around two-thirty, people would start drifting back to camp. The kitchen crew and the fishers would always be first so the food could be prepared. Then the garden detail would arrive with their vegetables and fruit, and by three the clearing would be full again.

Breakfast and dinner were the only meals of the day. We didn't really need more. Dinner was at four o'clock and usually people went to bed about nine. There wasn't much to be done after dark, apart from get stoned. Nighttime campfires weren't allowed because fires were too conspicuous to low planes, even through the canopy ceiling. There were a lot of low planes around, flying to and from the airstrip on Koh Samui.

Apart from those with tents, everybody slept in the longhouse. It took me a while to get used to sleeping with twenty-one other people, but soon I started to enjoy it. There was a strong sense of closeness which Keaty and the others with tents missed out on. There was also the ritual. It didn't happen every night, but it happened often, and every time it made me smile.

The origin of the ritual was *The Waltons* TV series. At the end of each episode you'd see a shot of the Waltons' house and hear all of them saying good night to each other.

The way it worked in the longhouse was like this.

Just as people were drifting off, a sleepy voice from somewhere in the darkness would say, "Night, Jim-Bob." Then there'd be a short pause while we waited for the cue to be picked up, and eventually you'd hear someone say, "Night, Jesse," or "Sal," or "Gregorio," or "Bugs," or anyone they felt like saying good night to. Then the named person would have to say good night to someone different, and it would go around the whole longhouse until everyone had been mentioned.

Anybody could start the game off and there was no order to the names called out. When there were only a few names left it got difficult remembering which people had been mentioned and which hadn't, but that was part of the game. If you screwed it up, then there'd be loud tuts and exaggerated sighs until you got it right.

Although the ritual was sort of taking the piss, in another way it wasn't. No one's name was ever passed over and right from the first time, Etienne, Françoise, and I were included.

The nicest thing was when you heard your name but couldn't recognize the voice. I always found it comforting that someone unexpected would think to choose me. I'd fall asleep wondering who it could have been, and who I'd choose the next time.

Negative

On the morning of my fourth Sunday, all the camp was down on the beach. Nobody worked on Sundays.

The tide was out, so there was forty feet of sand between the treeline and the sea. Sal had organized a huge game of soccer and just about everyone was taking part, but not me and Keaty. We were sitting out on one of the boulders, listening to the shouts of the players drifting over the water. Along with video games and movies, an indifference to soccer was something we shared.

A flash of silver slipped past my feet. "Gotcha," I muttered, flicking an imaginary spear at the fish, and Keaty scowled.

"Easy life," he said.

"Fishing?"

"Fishing."

I nodded. Fishing was easy. I'd had the idea that as a city-softened Westerner I wouldn't be able to manage such ancient skills, but actually it was as simple as anything. All you had to do was stand on a rock, wait until a fish swam by, then skewer it. The only trick was in snapping the wrist, the same as throwing a Frisbee. That way it spun in the water and didn't lose momentum.

Keaty ran a hand backward over his head. He hadn't shaved it since I'd arrived and now his scalp was covered in a few weeks' worth of stubble.

"I'll tell you what it is," he said.

"Mmm?"

"It's the heat. Fishing you can cool off anytime, but in the garden you just bake."

"How about the waterfall?"

"Ten minutes away. You go there, swim, and by the time you get back you're hot again."

"Have you talked to Sal?"

"Yesterday. She said I can transfer if I find someone to swap with, but who wants to work on the garden detail?"

"Jean does."

"Yeah. Jean does." Keaty sighed. "Jean de fucking Florette."

"Jean le Frogette," I said, and he laughed.

A cheer erupted from the beach. Etienne appeared to have scored a goal. He was running around in circles with his hands in the air and Bugs, captain of the other side, was yelling at his goalkeeper. Up by the trees I could see Françoise. She was sitting with a small group of spectators, applauding.

I stood up. "Feel like a swim?"

"Sure."

"We could swim over to the corals. I haven't really checked them out yet. I've been meaning to."

"Great, but let's get Greg's mask first. There's no point swimming to the corals without the mask."

I glanced back to the beach. The game had started again. Bugs had the ball and was weaving down the sand, looking to make up the deficit, and Etienne was hot on his tail.

"You want to get it? I'll wait here."

"Okay."

Keaty dived off the boulder. For a few strokes he stayed underwater, and I followed his shape along the seabed until he was lost from view. He finally resurfaced an impressive distance away.

"I'll get some grass, too," he called.

I gave him the thumbs up and he ducked back under again.

I turned away from the beach, toward the seaward cliffs. I was looking for a split in the rock face that Gregorio had pointed out a few days before. According to him, the most spectacular of the coral gardens lay in the waters directly beneath it.

At first I was confused. I was sure I was looking in the right place. Gregorio had indicated the split by making me follow a line of boulders that stretched across the lagoon like stepping stones. The boulders were still there, but the fissure had vanished.

Then I found it. Gregorio had shown me the spot in late afternoon. The cliffs had been in full shadow, and the split had been dark. But now, caught in the low morning sun, the jagged edge of the fissure glowed white against the black granite.

"Like a negative," I said out loud, smiling at my mistake.

Corals

Under the weight of two grapefruit-sized stones, I drifted down to the seabed and sat, cross-legged, on the sand. Then I rested the stones on my lap so I wouldn't float back up again.

Around me were banks of coral: brightly colored pagodas, melted and sprawling in the hot tropical waters. In the recesses of their fans, something recoiled at my presence. It was almost imperceptible—a slight ripple of light spreading across the colors. I gazed harder, trying to pinpoint the strange effect, but once the change had happened the corals looked no different from before.

A strange creature was lying in front of me. A name popped into my head—sea cucumber—but only because I'd heard that such things existed. It could have been a sea marrow for all I knew. The creature was just over a foot in length and about the thickness of my forearm, and at the end nearest to me it had a nest of tiny tentacles. Using a snapped finger from one of the coral fans, I gave it an exploratory poke. The cucumber didn't move or flinch, so, emboldened, I touched it with my own finger. It was the softest thing I'd ever felt. Only the barest sensation of resistance was offered by the silky flesh, and I pulled back for fear of tearing its skin.

Curiouser and curiouser, I thought, smiling. Holding my breath was getting me high. From the blood humming in my ears and the mounting pressure in my lungs, I guessed I had less than twenty seconds of air remaining.

I looked up. Six or seven feet above me, perched on an overhanging rock shelf, I could see Keaty's disembodied legs. He was swinging them gently, like a kid on a high chair, and had attracted the attention of a little blue fish. The fish was mainly interested in his ankles. Every time they swung near, it would dart forward as if to take a bite, but stop abruptly an inch or so away. Then, as his ankles swung back, the fish would flick its fins and retreat, perhaps cursing itself for its lack of courage.

A cold trickle of water eased past the hollow of my temples. With my head pointed upward, the trapped air was pulling the mask away from my face. I looked down quickly, pushing at the glass to reestablish the seal, but it was no use. Too much water had worked its way in. I rolled the stones off my lap and let myself float back to the surface.

On impulse, I nipped Keaty's ankle as I passed it by, using my bunched fingernails like a row of teeth.

"What did you do that for?"

I rubbed at the itch from where the mask had been gripping my face. Keaty was rubbing his ankle.

"There was this little fish," I began, then started laughing.

"What little fish?"

"It wanted to bite you but didn't have the nerve."

Keaty shook his head. "I thought it was a shark."

"There's sharks here?"

"Millions." He jabbed a finger at the cliffs behind him, indicating the open sea, then shook his head again. "You made me jump."

"Sorry."

I hauled myself out of the water and sat next to Keaty on the rock shelf. "It's amazing down there. It would be so good to have Aqua-Lungs or something. A minute isn't really long enough."

"Or a hosepipe," Keaty said. He pulled a plastic film carton from his pocket. Inside were loose rizlas and grass. "I went to Ujung Kulon two years ago. You been there?"

"Charita."

"Well, in Ujung Kulon there were some corals and these guys there used a hosepipe. You could stay under for a while, but you couldn't really move around. Still . . ."

"I don't suppose we've got a hosepipe here?"

"Nope."

I waited while Keaty finished rolling the joint.

". . . So you've done a lot of traveling."

"Sure. Thailand, Indonesia, Mexico, Guatemala, Colombia, Turkey, India, and Nepal. Oh, also Pakistan. Sort of. I was in Karachi for three days on a stopover. You count that?"

"Uh-uh."

"Me neither. How about you?"

I shrugged. "I've never done any of the Americas stuff, nor Africa. Just around Asia really. Europe too, I suppose. How about Europe? Does Europe count?"

"Not if you won't count Karachi." He lit up. "Got a favorite?"

I thought for a couple of moments. "It's a toss-up between Indonesia and the Philippines."

"And your worst?"

"Probably China. I had a lousy time in China. I went for five days without talking to one person except when I ordered food in restaurants. Terrible food too."

Keaty laughed. "My worst was Turkey. I was supposed to stay for two months but I left after two weeks."

"And the best?"

Keaty looked around, inhaling deeply, then passed me the joint. "Thailand. This place, I mean. It isn't really Thailand, considering there's no Thais, but . . . yeah. This place."

"This place is unique. . . . How long have you been here?"

"Two years. Just over. I met Sal in Chiang Rai and we got friendly. Hiked around a bit. Then she told me about this place and took me along."

I flicked the dead joint butt into the water. "Tell me about Daffy. No one talks about him."

"Yeah. People were shocked when they heard." Keaty scratched at his stubble thoughtfully. "I'm not a good person to ask. I barely knew the guy. He was a bit distant, to me anyway. I mean, I knew who he was, but we didn't talk much."

"So who was he?"

"Are you kidding?"

"No. Like I said, nobody mentions him, so . . ."

Keaty frowned. "You haven't seen the tree yet? The tree by the waterfall?"

"I don't think so."

"Shit! You don't know anything, do you, Rich? You've been here, what? A month?"

"Just over."

"Man." Keaty smiled. "I'll take you to the tree tomorrow. Then you'll see."

"How about now?"

"I want to swim. Especially now I'm stoned. And it's my turn with the mask."

"I'd really like to . . ."

Keaty slipped into the water. "Tomorrow. What's the hurry? You waited four weeks." He snapped the strap tight over the back of his head and ducked under, end of discussion.

"Okay," I said to the flat water, allowing dope and beach life to cloud my curiosity. "Tomorrow then."

On my next turn with Gregorio's mask I looked out for any shifting colors in the corals, but the strange effect refused to repeat itself. The coral-dwellers were still hidden in their pagoda homes. Either that, or my presence no longer scared them.

Bugged

That night, just as the light was starting to fade, we were given our seashell necklaces. It wasn't a big deal, no ceremony or anything. Sal and Bugs just wandered over to where we were sitting and handed them over. Still, it was quite a big deal for me. However friendly everyone was, being the only ones without necklaces drew attention to our new arrival status. Now that we'd got them, it was like our acceptance had been made official.

"Which is for me?" said Françoise, carefully examining each one in turn.

"Whichever you like, Françoise," Sal replied.

"I think I will have this one. I like this color on the big shell." She looked at me and Etienne, challenging us to make a rival claim.

"Which do you want, Etienne?" I said.

"You."

"I don't mind."

"I also do not mind."

"So . . ."

We shrugged at each other and laughed. Then Sal leaned forward and plucked the two remaining necklaces from Françoise's hands. "Here," she said, and made the choice for us. They were both much the same, but mine had a centerpiece, the snapped arm of a red starfish.

I slipped it over my head. "Well, thanks a lot, Sal."

"Thank Bugs. He made yours."

"Okay. Thanks, Bugs. It's a really nice necklace."

He nodded, accepting the compliment silently, then began walking back across the clearing to the longhouse.

I couldn't make up my mind about Bugs. It was weird, because he was exactly the kind of guy I felt I ought to like, almost out of obligation. He was broader and more muscular than me; as head of the carpentry detail, he had obvious skills; I also suspected he was pretty intelligent. This was harder to gauge because he didn't speak much, but when he did speak it seemed to be things worth saying. But despite all these fine characteristics, there was something about him that left me a little cold.

One example was the way he accepted my thanks for the necklace. His silent nod belonged in Clint Eastwood land; it didn't feel like it had a place in the real world. Another time we were going to eat some soup. Gregorio said he was going to wait until the soup cooled down—it was bubbling and still over the flame. Bugs immediately made a point of taking a spoonful straight from the saucepan. He didn't say anything, just took the spoonful. It was such a small thing that repeating it now, I'm almost embarrassed by how petty it sounds.

Maybe this stands up to repeating. On the Monday of my second week, I saw Bugs struggling to fit a swinging door on the entrance to one of the storeroom huts. He was having trouble because he only had two hands, and he needed three: two to keep the door in place and a third to hammer a peg into the hinge. I watched him for a while, wondering whether to offer any help, and as I began walking over, the hammer slipped from his grip. Instinctively, he moved to catch it and the door also fell, bashing against his leg.

"Shit," I said, breaking into a jog. "You okay?"

Bugs glanced down. Blood was dripping from a nasty graze on his shins. "I'm fine," he said, then bent to pick up his hammer.

"Do you need a hand holding the door?"

Bugs shook his head.

I went back to where I'd been sitting, slicing the tops off bamboo sticks to make spears for fishing, and about five minutes later I misjudged a swipe and cut open my thumb.

"Ow!" I shouted.

Bugs didn't look round, and as Françoise ran over, her face even prettier for being alarmed, I could sense his satisfaction—stoically tapping the peg into place while blood collected in dusty pools around his feet.

"That really hurt," I said when Françoise reached me, and made sure I said it loud enough for Bugs to hear.

While I'm on a roll, I might as well add that there was one more thing that bothered me about Bugs. His name.

The way I saw it, calling himself Bugs was like, "I'm taciturn and stoical, but I don't take myself too seriously! I call myself Bugs Bunny!" As with my other gripes, it wasn't a reason to dislike him; it was just something that grated. The whole point was that Bugs took himself extremely seriously.

Over the two weeks I was getting to know Bugs, I spent some time wondering where his name had come from. If, like Sal, he'd been American, I could have imagined that Bugs Bunny was how he'd been christened. No disrespect to Americans—they just come up with some odd names. But Bugs was South African, and I couldn't see Warner Brothers as having that strong an influence over Pretoria. Then again, I once met a South African called Goose, so you never know.

Anyway. Back to the night I received my necklace.

"Night, Jim-Bob."

Silence . . . Panic.

Had I said it loudly enough? Was there a rule of etiquette that I hadn't picked up on? Getting the necklace had given me the courage, but maybe only group leaders were allowed to start it off, or people who'd been coming to the beach more than three years. . . .

My heart began to pound. Sweat sprung. Well, that's it, I thought to myself. It's all over. I'll leave tomorrow morning before dawn. I'll just have to swim the twenty miles back to Koh Samui, and I'll probably be eaten by sharks, but that's okay. I deserve it. I—

"Night, Ella," said a dozy voice in the darkness.

I froze.

"Night, Jesse," said another.

"Night, Sal."

"Night, Moshe."

"Night, Cassie."

"Night, Greg."

"Night . . ."

Zero

Colorwise, progress was good. The sky had been mainly cloudy over the first few days, and by the time it had cleared I had enough of a base tan to avoid burning. Now I was getting close to my darkest shade. I peeked under the waistband of my shorts to check I was as dark as I hoped.

"Wow," I said, seeing the creamy skin beneath.

Etienne looked round. He was sitting by the edge of the boulder, cooling his legs in the water. His tan was rich and golden, I noticed enviously. I never went golden. At best I went the color of a recently plowed field. Walnut brown, I would sometimes describe it, but much more like earth.

"What is it?"

"Just my tan. I'm getting dark."

Etienne nodded, tugging absently at his necklace. "I thought maybe you were thinking of this place."

"The beach?"

"You said, 'Wow,' so I thought you were thinking how good it is here."

"Oh, well, I often think that . . . I mean, it was worth the trouble, wasn't it? That swim, and the dope fields."

"Worth the trouble."

"You fish, swim, eat, laze around, and everyone's so friendly. It's such simple stuff, but . . . If I could stop the world and restart life, put the clock back, I think I'd restart it like this. For everyone." I shook my head to stop myself rambling. "You know what I mean."

"All these thoughts are the same as mine."

"They are?"

"Of course. The same as everybody's."

I stood up and gazed around me. Gregorio and Françoise were climbing out of the water a few boulders over, and past them, near the sea-locked cliffs, three dots of color described Moshe and the two Yugoslavians. From the land I could hear a steady tapping—Bugs and the carpenters working on some new project—and walking along the beach, I could see a single figure. Ella, I thought, until I squinted against the bright white sands and recognized Sal.

I remembered the way Sal had teased me to realign my expectations. "You'll see that this is a wonderful place, as long as you appreciate it for what it is," she'd said. I pushed my shoulders back and closed my eyes against the hot sun, and thought how right she was.

I was broken out of my reverie by a sudden cold splash of water against my legs. I opened my eyes and looked down. It was the fish in the bucket, getting close to the split second before Game Over. I watched them for a while, impressed by their tenacity. It often surprised me how long it took for fish to die. Even speared right through their bodies, they still flapped about for as long as an hour, working up a bloody lather in the water around them.

"How many do we have?" said Etienne.

"Seven. A couple are big ones. That's enough, isn't it?"

Etienne shrugged. "If Gregorio and Françoise also have seven, it is enough."

"They'll have seven at least." I checked my watch. It was exactly midday. "I think I might go back early today. I'm meeting up with Keaty and he's going to show me this tree."

"Tree?"

"Some tree by the waterfall. Want to come? We could leave the bucket here."

He shook his head and pointed to Gregorio and Françoise. Gregorio had his mask pushed up onto his forehead. "I want to see the corals. They sound very beautiful."

"Yeah, they are. Maybe I'll come and find you after this tree thing."

"Good."

"Tell the others for me."

"Yes."

I dived into the water, shooting down at a steep angle, then leveling out to skim over the seabed. The salt stung my eyes but I kept them open. Even without Gregorio's mask, the blurred colors and scattering fish were a sight to see.

There were two ways I could get to the garden. The first was the direct route that Keaty walked every morning. It was the quickest way, but I'd only done it a couple of times, and that was with Keaty. I knew if I tried to do it alone I'd only get lost; once you were in the jungle, there wasn't much to orientate yourself by, apart from distinctive trees and plants. Instead I chose the second route, which was to follow the waterfall stream to its source. Once there, I could turn left and walk along the base of the cliff, which eventually led to the garden.

After about ten minutes of walking I began to empathize with Keaty's complaints about his work detail. Without a sea breeze or cool water, the heat was incredible. By the time I reached the waterfall my whole body was prickling with sweat.

Since arriving at the beach, I'd only been to the waterfall a couple of times, and never on my own. It was partly because I had no reason to go there, but also, I now understood, because the area made me feel uneasy. It represented a link between the lagoon and the outside world, the world I'd all but forgotten, and as I stood by the pool I realized that I didn't want to be reminded. Looking up through the fine mist of water vapor I could see the spot where I'd crouched before jumping. The memories it brought back were uncomfortable. I didn't even pause to cool my face. I found the path that led toward the garden and headed straight down it.

Quarter of an hour later I found Keaty on the outskirts of the vegetable patch, disconsolately poking at weeds with a Bugs-made trowel.

"Hey," he said, perking up. "What are you doing down here?"

"You were going to show me a tree. I got off work early."

"Right. I forgot." He looked over to where Jean was growling at one of the other gardeners. "Jean!"

Jean looked round.

"Gottataketimeoff."

"Heugh?" Jean replied.

"Backlaterifthere'stimeokay?"

Keaty waved and Jean waved back uncertainly. Then Keaty propelled me out of the garden. "If you talk quickly he can't understand," he explained. "Otherwise he would have tried to make you wait until the detail stopped work."

"Smart."

"Uh-huh."

It was a rocket ship tree about twenty meters to the right of the pool. I'd noticed it before when I'd been wondering how to get down from the waterfall. Some of its branches grew near to the cliff, and I'd considered an Indiana Jones–style leap into its lower canopy. Standing at its base, I was glad I'd had the sense not to try. I'd have jumped onto a deceptively thin layer of leaves and fallen forty feet to the ground.

It was, like all the other rocket ship trees, an impressive sight, but that wasn't why Keaty had brought me to see it. He'd brought me to see the markings cut into one of its twelve-foot stabilizer fins. Three names and four numbers. Bugs, Sylvester, and Daffy. The numbers were all zeros.

"Sylvester?"

"Salvester."

I shook my head. "Sal."

"I tawt I taw a puddy," said Keaty.

"So they were the first?"

"The first—1989. The three of them hired a boat from Koh Phangan."

"They knew about this place already, or . . ."

"Depends who you talk to. Bugs said he'd heard about a hidden lagoon from some fisherman on Koh Phalui, but Daffy used to say they were just island-hopping. Found the place by chance."

"Chance."

"But all the camp and stuff. That didn't start until '90. They spent the second half of '89 doing the Goa thing, then came back to Koh Phangan for the new year."

"And what, Koh Phangan was on the way out?"

Keaty nodded. "Well on the way. That's when it clicked. The thing was, those three had been going to Koh Samui since it was a secret, so when they saw Koh Phangan had maybe a year left . . ."

"A year left at best. I heard by '91 it was already fucked up."

"Right, so they'd seen it all before. Especially Daffy. Daffy was completely obsessed. You know he wouldn't ever go to Indonesia?"

"I don't know anything about Daffy."

"Boycotted because of Bali. He went there only once in the late eighties and wouldn't ever go back. Used to talk all the time about how sick it made him."

We sat down with our backs against the slab of root and shared a cigarette.

"I mean," said Keaty, exhaling hard, "you've got to hand it to them."

"Definitely."

"They really knew what they were doing. Most things were set up by the time Sal took me here, which was . . . uh . . . '93. The longhouse was up and the ceiling was sorted out."

"Two years."

"Uh-huh." He passed me the cigarette.

"So when you came, were there this many people?"

Keaty paused. "Well . . . Pretty much . . ."

I looked at him, sensing that he was being cagey. "How do you mean, pretty much?"

". . . Everyone apart from the Swedes."

"In two years, the only new people were the Swedes?"

". . . And Jed. The Swedes and Jed."

"That's not many. Well-kept secret."

"Mmm."

I stubbed out the cigarette. "And the zeros. What are they about?"

Keaty smiled. "That was Daffy's idea. It's a date."

"A date? The date of what?"

"The date they first arrived."

"I thought that was '89."

"It was." Keaty stood up and patted the stabilizer fin. "But Daffy used to call it year zero."

Revelations

Set up in Bali, Koh Phangan, Koh Tao, Boracay, and the hordes are bound to follow. There's no way you can keep it out of the Lonely Planet, and once that happens it's countdown to doomsday. But set up in a Marine park, where you aren't even supposed to be . . .

The more I thought about it, the more the idea grew on me. Not just a Marine park but a Marine park in Thailand. Of all places, backpacker central, land of the beaten track. The only thing sweeter than the irony was the logic. The Philippines is an archipelago of seven thousand islands, but even in that huge fractured landscape, an equivalent secret would be impossible to contain. But with the legions of travelers passing through Bangkok and the southern islands, who'd notice when a few slipped away?

Strangely, the thing that least intrigued me was how they'd actually managed to get it all done. I suppose I sort of knew. If I'd learned one thing from traveling, it was that the way to get things done was to go ahead and do them. Don't talk about going to Borneo. Book a ticket, get a visa, pack a bag, and it just happens.

From Keaty's few words, I pictured the scene. January 1990, maybe New Year's Eve, Koh Phangan, maybe Hadrin. Daffy, Bugs, and Sal, talking as the sun comes up. Sal's found a boat to hire or even buy, Bugs has some tools in his backpack, Daffy's got a sack of rice and thirty packs of Magi-Noodles. Perhaps bars of chocolate have melted and molded around the shape of his water bottle.

By seven that morning they're walking down the beach. Behind them they can hear the rumble of a portable generator through the thump of a sound system. They don't look back, they just push off from the sand and head for the hidden paradise they found a year before.

As I walked back toward the camp, on the way to find Etienne at the coral garden, I found myself almost hoping for another meeting with Mister Duck. I wanted to shake him by the hand.

I never did find Etienne and Françoise. I bumped into Gregorio on the beach. He was carrying our catch back to camp, and when I told him I was going to the corals, he looked doubtful.

"I think you should wait," he said. "Wait for . . . maybe one hour."

"How come?"

"Etienne and Françoise . . ."

"They're having sex?"

"Well . . . I do not know, but . . ."

"Uh-huh. An hour, you reckon?"

"Oh . . ." Gregorio smiled awkwardly. "Maybe I am too generous to Etienne."

I shook my head, remembering my first night in Bangkok. "No," I replied, irritated to hear a sudden tightness in my voice. "Spot on, I'd say."

So I went back to the camp with Gregorio.

There was nothing much to do there except compare fish sizes with the other details. The three Swedes, as usual, had caught the biggest and were swaggering about, telling the cooks about their fishing technique. I got pretty pissed off listening to them, but even more annoying were the images of Françoise and Etienne that kept popping into my head. Eventually, craving something to occupy my mind, I went to Keaty's tent and dug out his Nintendo.

Most bosses have a pattern; crack the pattern, kill the boss. A typical pattern is illustrated by Dr. Robotnik during his first incarnation in Sonic One, Megadrive version, Greenhills Zone. As he descends from the top of the screen, you jump at him from the left platform. Then, as he starts swinging toward you, you duck under and jump at him from the right. As he swings back, you repeat the process in reverse until, eight hits later, he explodes and runs away.

That's an easy boss. Others require much more manual dexterity and effort. The last boss on Teken 2, for example, is a relentless fist-swinging nightmare.

The boss that distracted me from Etienne and Françoise was none other than Wario, nemesis of Mario. The problem was that to reach him, I had to struggle through several tortuous stages. By the time I arrived at his lair I'd taken too many hits and had lost the vital power-ups I needed to finish him off.

Every now and then, Unhygienix would take a break from cooking and wander over to inspect my progress. He and Keaty were the only two people in the camp who'd ever completed the game. He'd say things like, "Don'ta pausa on thata platforma." (I'm abandoning his Italian accent from now on.)

I'd scowl in frustration. "If I don't pause I get spiked by the falling block."

"Si. So you jump more quickly. Like this."

He'd take the Gameboy, guiding Mario with amazing skill considering the size of his fat hands, and show me how the trick was done. Then he'd wander back to his cooking, fingers drumming a rhythm on his giant belly. The Gameboy was always slippery after he'd used it, and smelled of fish, but I considered that a fair price to pay for his expertise.

It took an hour and a half, but eventually I was able to reach Wario with a full complement of power-ups. Finally I could start trying to crack his pattern. Or so I thought, because at that moment the monochrome screen began fading away.

"Evereadys!" I yelped.

Keaty, who'd returned from the garden while I'd been playing, poked his head out of his tent.

"That was the last batch, Rich."

"There's none left?"

"None at all."

"But I've nearly cracked Wario!"

"Well . . ." He shrugged apologetically. "Leave it alone awhile. If you turn it off for twenty minutes you might get another five minutes' playing time."

I groaned. Five minutes wasn't nearly enough.

It was a bitter blow, running out of batteries. I could live without completing the Mario game, but Tetris was another matter entirely. Since Keaty had told me his record of 177 lines, I'd been trying hard to beat him. The closest I'd made was 161 but I was improving every day.

"This is ridiculous," I said. "Walkmans. What about them?"

Keaty sighed. "Forget Walkmans."

"Why?"

"Give, and gifts will be given to you, for whatever measure you deal out to others will be dealt to you in return."

I paused for a moment. "What?"

"I went to church every Sunday until I was fifteen."

"You're quoting the Bible?"

"Luke, six, thirty-eight."

I shook my head incredulously. "What's the bloody Bible got to do with anything?"

"There's only five people with Walkmans in the camp, and I've refused all of them batteries in the past."

"Then we're fucked."

"Mmm," Keaty agreed. "Looks like it."

Invisible Wires

But, as fate turned out, we weren't fucked. Help ar-rived from an unexpected source.

We went over to the cooking hut to tell Unhygienix about the batteries, and as I began to explain he turned from the fire, his face an angry red and shining with sweat. I took an instinctive step backward, amazed he was taking the news so hard.

"Batteries?" he said, in an alarmingly quiet voice.

"Uh . . . yes . . ."

"What about the rice?"

"The rice?"

Unhygienix began swiftly marching to one of the storeroom huts, so we followed behind.

"There!"

We looked inside. I could see three empty canvas sacks and two more, full.

"What's the problem?" said Keaty.

Unhygienix tore open the top of the nearest full sack and rice poured out, black and green, puffed up into fat clods of fungus, completely rotten.

"Jesus," I muttered, covering my nose and mouth to block the appalling smell. "That's horrible."

Unhygienix pointed to the roof.

"It leaked?"

He nodded, too furious to speak. Then marched back to his cooking.

"Well," said Keaty as we walked back to his tent. "It isn't all bad news about the rice. You should be glad, Rich."

"How's that?"

"No more rice means a Rice Run. Now we get some new batteries."

Keaty lay on his back, smoking one of my cigarettes. I was down to one hundred, but seeing as I'd finished up his Evereadys, I couldn't really refuse him.

"I think," he said, "there's two main reasons people don't like doing the Rice Run. Number one, it's a complete hassle. Number two, it means visiting the world."

"The world?"

"The world. It's another Daffy thing. The world is everything outside the beach."

I smiled. I knew exactly where Daffy had picked up the term; the same place I had. Keaty noticed and propped himself up on his elbows. "What's so funny?"

"Nothing. Just . . . The GIs used that word in the same way, to describe America . . . I don't know. I just thought it was funny."

Keaty nodded slowly. "Hysterical."

"So what happens on the Rice Run?"

"A couple of people take the boat and head for Koh Phangan. Then they pick up some rice, and head back here."

"We've got a boat?"

"Of course. Not all of us are such good swimmers as you, Rich."

"I didn't realize . . . I didn't think about that . . . Well, a quick trip to Koh Phangan doesn't sound too bad."

"Yeah." Now Keaty was grinning. "But you haven't seen the boat yet."

An hour later the entire camp sat in a circle, all except Etienne and Françoise, who still weren't back from the corals. The news about the rice had been spread quickly, and Sal had called a meeting.

Keaty nudged me while we waited for the talking to start. "I bet you Jed volunteers," he whispered.

"Jed?"

"He loves taking on missions. Just watch him."

I was about to reply when Sal clapped her hands and stood up. "Okay," she said briskly. "As everyone knows, we've got a problem."

"Too fuckin' right," drawled an Australian voice from the other side of the circle.

"We thought we had another seven weeks of rice, but it turns out we've only got enough for two days. Now, this isn't a major catastrophe, nobody's going to be starving to death, but it is a minor one." Sal paused. "Well, you know what's coming. We need to go on a Rice Run."

Several people booed, mainly, I guessed, out of a sense of duty.

"So . . . who's volunteering?"

Jed's hand shot up.

"What did I tell you?" hissed Keaty.

"Thank you, Jed. So okay . . . that's one . . . Who else?" Sal scanned the faces, most of which had noticeably downcast eyes. "Come on . . . We all know Jed can't do it alone . . ."

Just as when I jumped from the waterfall, I only really realized what I was doing after I'd started doing it. An invisible wire seemed to have attached itself to my wrist and was pulling it upward.

Sal noticed, then glanced at Bugs. Out of the corner of my eye I saw him shrug. "Are you volunteering too, Richard?"

"Yeah," I answered, still a little surprised to find that I was. "I mean . . . Yeah. I'm volunteering."

Sal smiled. "Good. That's settled then. You'll leave tomorrow morning."

There wasn't much preparation to be done. All we needed was money and the clothes on our backs, and Sal produced the money. I spent the rest of the afternoon fielding Keaty's accusations about my sanity.

Etienne and Françoise finally returned from the corals as it was getting dark. They were also surprised I'd volunteered.

"I hope you are not bored with life here," Françoise said as we chatted outside the longhouse entrance.

I laughed. "No way. I just thought it might be interesting. Anyway, I haven't seen Koh Phangan yet."

"Good. It would be sad to be bored of Eden, no? If you are bored of Eden, what is left?"

"Eden?"

"Yes, you remember. Zeph called this place Eden."

"Zeph . . ." I frowned, because, of course, I hadn't remembered. "Yeah, that's right . . . he did."

'Toon Time

I stared hard at the water. I needed to stare hard. The image under the surface kept shifting and I had to concentrate to work out what I was seeing.

One moment I was looking at coral. Red corals with curving white fingers. The next moment I was looking at bare ribs poking out of bloody corpses. Ten or twenty ruined bodies, or as many bodies as there were coral beds.

"Rorschach," said Mister Duck.

"Mmm."

"Is it a cloud of butterflies? Is it a bed of flowers? No. It's a pile of dead Cambodians." He laughed quietly. "That's a test I don't see you passing."

"I don't see you passing it either."

"Well said, Rich. A salient point."

Mister Duck looked down at his wrists. Large black scabs had formed around his hands and lower arms. It seemed he'd finally stopped bleeding.

"I tell you, Rich," he said. "Getting these bastards to close up has been a nightmare. . . . A total fucking nightmare, I'm not kidding."

"How did you do it?"

"Well, I tied a cloth around the top of each arm, really tight, and that slowed the blood enough to let me clot. Clever, huh?"

"That's the boy . . ." I began, seeing my chance, but he interrupted me.

"All right, Rich. That'll do." He rocked on his heels like a kid with some good news to tell. "So, ah . . . do you want to know why I did it?"

"Healed the cut?"

"Yes."

"Okay."

Mister Duck smiled proudly. "I did it because you wanted to shake me by the hand."

I raised my eyebrows.

"Remember? You were walking back from the carved tree and you decided you wanted to shake me by the hand. So I said to myself, I'm not going to let Rich shake my hand if I'm bleeding all over the place! No fucking way!" He emphasized his words with a jabbing finger. "Rich is going to get a clean hand to shake! A dry hand! The kind of hand he deserves!"

I wondered how to respond. Actually, I'd completely forgotten about shaking his hand and wasn't even sure I still wanted to.

"Well . . ."

"Put it there, Rich!" A darkly stained palm shot out.

"I . . ."

"Come on, Rich! You wouldn't refuse to shake a guy's hand, would you?"

He was right. I never could turn down an extended hand, even from enemies. "No. Of course not . . ." I replied, and added, "Daffy," as an afterthought.

I reached out.

His wrists exploded. They burst apart into two red fountains, spraying like high-pressure garden hoses, soaking me and blinding me, filling my mouth.

"Stop it!" I yelled, spitting and spinning away from the jets.

"I can't, Rich!"

"Just fucking stop it!"

"I—!"

"Jesus!"

"Wait! Wait, wait . . . They're getting back to normal . . ."

The sound of the fountains dropped away to a steady splashing. Cautiously I looked around. Mister Duck was standing with his hands on his hips, still bleeding profusely, examining the mess and shaking his head.

"Christ," he mumbled. "How awkward."

I stared at him incredulously.

"Really, Rich, I can't apologize enough."

"You stupid bastard! You knew that was going to happen!"

"No . . . Well, yes, but . . ."

"You fucking planned it!"

"It was supposed to be a joke."

"A jo—" I hesitated. The taste of iron and salt in my mouth was making me feel sick. "Idiot!"

Mister Duck's shoulders slumped. "I'm really sorry," he said unhappily. "Maybe it wasn't a very good joke. . . . Perhaps I'd better go." Then he walked past me and straight off the edge of the rock shelf, but instead of falling the few feet down to the water, he simply hovered in midair.

"Could you just answer one thing, Rich?"

"What?" I snapped.

"Who are you planning to bring back?"

"Back from where?"

"The world. Aren't you and Jed . . ."

Mister Duck paused, suddenly frowning. Then he looked down at the empty space beneath him as if noticing it for the first time.

"Oh damn," he groaned, and dropped like a stone.

I looked over the shelf. When the ripples cleared, the water was cloudy and I couldn't make him out. I waited awhile, watching to see if he'd resurface, but he never did.

the
rice run

Jed

Jed wouldn't let me wake Etienne and Françoise.
They'd asked me to say good-bye before I left, but Jed shook his head
and said, "Unnecessary." I stood over their sleeping bodies, wondering
what he meant. He'd woken me five minutes earlier by putting his hand
over my mouth and whispering, "Shh," so close to my ear that his beard
had brushed my cheek. I'd thought that had been pretty unnecessary myself.

I thought his knife was unnecessary too. It appeared as we stood on the
beach, getting ready for the swim to the seaward cliffs, a green handled
lock-knife with a Teflon-coated blade.

"What's that for?" I asked.

"It's a tool," he replied, matter of factly. Then he winked and added,
"Sinister, huh?" before wading into the water with the knife between his
teeth.

Until the Rice Run, Jed was a mystery to me. The most time we'd ever
spent together had been on my first day, when he escorted us from the waterfall. After that we'd had almost no contact. Sometimes I saw him in the
evenings—never earlier because he returned to the camp so late—and
small talk had always been the extent of our conversations. Normally,
small talk is enough for me to form an opinion of someone. I make quick
judgments, often completely wrong, and then stick by them rigidly. But
with Jed I'd made an exception and kept an open mind. This was mainly
due to conflicting accounts about his character. Unhygienix liked him, and
Keaty thought he was an idiot.

"We were sitting on the beach," Keaty had once said, his forehead
creased up with irritation, "and there was this noise from the jungle. A coconut falling off a tree or something. A crack. So Jed suddenly stiffened up
and did this little glance over his shoulder, like he was some finely tuned
commando. Like he couldn't help his own reflexes."

I nodded. "He wanted you to notice."

"Exactly. He wanted us to notice how fucking alert he is." Keaty laughed and shook his head, then launched into a familiar diatribe about what crap it was to work in the garden.

But Unhygienix liked Jed. Sometimes I'd needed the toilet late at night and found them still awake, sitting by the kitchen hut, getting stoned on grass nicked from the dope plantations. And if Unhygienix liked Jed, he couldn't be all bad.

There were three caves that led into the seaward cliffs. One was at the base of the jagged fissure, by the coral gardens, another was maybe two hundred meters to the right of the fissure, and the last was maybe fifty meters to the left. That was the one we swam for.

It was a good swim. The water was cool and cleared the morning haze out of my head. I spent most of the time underwater, watching fish scatter, wondering which ones might end up as today's lunch. It was strange that there were always so many fish in the lagoon. We must have been pulling out thirty a day, but the numbers never seemed to go down.

Dawn was breaking by the time we reached the cave. We couldn't see the sun yet—the east was blocked by the cliffs as they curved around to rejoin the island—but the sky was bright.

"You know this place?" Jed asked.

"I've seen it while I've been working."

"But you've never been through."

"No. I went up to the coral gardens once and saw the cave there . . . beneath the fissure."

"But you've never been through," he repeated.

"No."

He looked disapproving. "You should have. Golden rule, first thing to do when you arrive someplace is find out how you can get out again. These caves are the only ways out of the lagoon."

I shrugged. "Oh . . . So is that how you get above the waterfall?"

"See here." He walked into the entrance of the cave and pointed directly upward. Bizarrely, in the blackness, I could see a fist-sized circle of blue, and as my eyes adjusted to the light I made out a rope, hanging the length of the shaft.

"It's a chimney. You can climb it without the rope, but the rope makes it easier."

"And then you can walk around the cliff tops, back to the island."

"Exactly. Want to try?"

"Sure," I said quickly. I had the idea he was testing me.

Jed raised his eyebrows. "Uh-huh. An adventurous type. I had you down for something else."

That annoyed me. "I found this place, and what's the big deal about climbing up the—"

He cut me off. "Maybe this place found you," he said, looking at me out of the corner of his eye. Then suddenly he smiled. "I'm taking the piss, Richard. Sorry. Anyway, we don't have time now. The journey will take four hours at least."

I checked my watch. It was almost seven. "So our ETA is eleven hundred hours."

"Eleven hundred hours . . ." He chuckled and patted me on the arm, lapsing into an American accent. "ETAs, FNGs. You're my kinda guy."

Keaty had met Sal and Bugs in Chiang Rai. They'd gone on an illegal trek together over the Burmese border, and after the trek was over, Sal had asked him if he was interested in being taken to paradise.

Gregorio had met Daffy in Sumatra. Gregorio had been beaten up and robbed, and when Daffy found him he was trying to hitch his way to Jakarta so he could contact the Spanish embassy. Daffy had offered him cash to get to Java. Gregorio had been reluctant to accept, because he could see Daffy was short of money himself. Daffy had said, "Fuck Java," and told him about the beach.

Sal had been on an eighteen-hour bus ride with Ella. Ella had a portable backgammon set.

Daffy had heard Cassie asking for a job in a Patpong bar.

Unhygienix had cooked Bugs a six-course meal on a houseboat in Srinagar, starting with hot coconut soup and ending with a mango split.

Moshe had caught a Manilan pickpocket trying to razor Daffy's backpack.

Bugs had worked with Jean, grape picking in Blenheim, New Zealand.

Jed . . .

Jed had just turned up. Jumped from the waterfall, walked into the camp with a canvas overnight bag and a soaking-wet bushel of grass under his arm.

Keaty said the camp had been thrown into instant panic. Was he alone, how had he learned about the beach, were there more with him, more coming? Everyone ran around going crazy; then Sal, Bugs, and Daffy turned up. They took him into the longhouse to talk while everyone waited outside. People heard Daffy shouting and Bugs trying to calm him down.

The cliffs were about twenty meters thick, but you couldn't see through them to the open sea because, not far in, the roof of the cave dropped below the water level. I wasn't happy about swimming into the blackness but Jed assured me the roof rose up again quickly. "It's a piece of piss," he said. "You're up again before you know it."

"Really?"

"Yeah. It's low tide, so we only have to swim half the cave. When it's high tide you have to swim the whole cave in one go, and even that's easy." Then he took a deep breath and slipped under, leaving me alone.

I waited a minute, treading water and listening to my splashes echo round the walls. My feet and shins were cold, kicking in the chilled area, reminding me of the diving game on Koh Samui. "Put me down as the adventurous type," I said loudly. It was supposed to be a joke, something to give me courage, and in a way I suppose it worked. The echo spooked me so much that the inky water seemed less scary than hanging around.

Jed had worked on an official work detail, carpentry, for only six days. Then he'd been taken off and started doing his 'missions crap,' as Keaty put it, above the waterfall.

People talked about it at first. They thought he ought to be working and were irritated that Sal, Bugs, and Daffy refused to explain why he was allowed to do his own thing. But time passed, and as Jed's face became more familiar they stopped asking questions. The main thing was that no other travelers appeared immediately after him, which had been everyone's fear, and he brought in a steady supply of grass, previously a luxury in short supply.

Keaty had a theory. Because Jed hadn't been recruited he was an unknown quantity, and therefore, if he decided to leave, a danger to the camp's secrecy. So when Sal had realized that Jed was the type who was into missions, she created one just to keep him happy.

Personally, I thought the theory was unlikely. Whatever Jed was doing, it was what Sal wanted him to be doing. Diplomacy wouldn't have entered into it.

Unusually for me, I kept my eyes shut as I swam, feeling my way along the cave roof with outstretched hands and only using my legs for propulsion. I guessed that each kick made a meter and carefully counted my strokes to give me a sense of distance. After I'd counted ten I began to feel worried. An ache was building in my lungs and Jed had been adamant that the underwater passage was no more than a forty-second swim. At fifteen I realized I had to make a decision about whether to turn back. I gave myself a limit of three more kicks; then my fingertips broke surface.

I knew there was something wrong as soon as I took a breath. The air was foul. So bad that even though I was bursting for oxygen, I could only manage short breaths before I started gagging. Instinctively, pointlessly, I looked around me, but the absence of light was so absolute that I couldn't see my fingers an inch from my face.

"Jed!" I called.

Not even an echo.

I reached up and my hand sank deep into something wet, with freezing tendrils that clung to my skin. A jolt of adrenaline rushed through my body and I snatched my hand back.

"It's seaweed," I whispered after my heart had stopped smashing into my eardrums. Seaweed, coating the rock, absorbing the noise.

I gagged again. Then I retched, pushing up a mouthful of vomit.

"Jed . . ."

Self-Help

Once I'd started, I kept throwing up for several min-
utes. Every time my stomach contracted I couldn't help doubling up and
I'd vomit with my head underwater, then have to straighten up quickly to
snatch a breath before the next heave. The vomiting finally stopped, although it took three dry retches before my stomach would concede it was
empty. Then I was left floating in blackness and amino acids, wondering
what the fuck I should do next.

My first thought was that I should continue down the passage—I was
assuming that I'd surfaced too soon, tricked by an air pocket left over from
some extra-low tide. But that was easier said than done. While I'd been
throwing up I'd twisted and turned twenty times and was now completely
disoriented. That led me to my second thought: that I should work out the
dimensions of the air pocket. This, at least, was something I could accom-
plish. Steeling myself, I reached up again and pushed my hand into the
seaweed. I flinched but this time I didn't pull my hand back, and through
the slimy growth I felt rock an arm's length above my head.

Several fumbling minutes later I'd created a good mental image of my
surroundings. The pocket was about two meters wide and three meters
long. On one side there was a narrow shelf, big enough to sit on, and
everywhere else the walls curved straight down from the ceiling and ran
into the water. There, the mental image began to fall apart. By groping
around with my hands and feet, I seemed to find four passages leading into
the rock, but it was hard to judge underwater. There could even have been
more.

It was a grim discovery. If there'd been only two passages, then
whichever direction I chose to swim, I'd come up in either the lagoon or
the ocean. But these other passages could lead to nowhere. I could find
myself swimming into a maze.

"Two out of four," I heard myself muttering. "One in two. Fifty-fifty."
But it didn't matter how I put it. The odds sounded bad.

The alternative was to stay put and hope Jed came to find me, but it
wasn't very appealing. I felt like I'd lose the plot if I waited in the pitch-

blackness, swimming around in my own sick, and I hadn't the faintest how long it would be before I started breathing carbon dioxide. This was an idea I found particularly frightening. I could see myself huddled up on the small rock shelf, gradually succumbing to a sinister sleepiness.

For a minute I stayed relatively still, treading water and going over my options. Then I started to panic. I splashed around wildly, bumping into the walls, choking, whimpering. I snatched at the seaweed above my head and pulled it down in great clumps. I lashed out, smashed my elbow on the rock shelf, felt my skin tear and hot blood run over my arm. I shouted, "Help."

"Help."

My voice sounded pathetic, like I was crying. It was a shocking noise and it jolted me into a second of silence. A second later, my fear was swamped by a sudden tidal wave of disgust. Ignoring the foul taste, I took a huge gulp of air and ducked underwater. I didn't count the strokes this time, or worry about feeling my way. I took whichever of the four passages I found first and swam as hard as I could.

The List

I was in a bad way. My legs and hands were knocking painfully against the passage walls and there was a pressure deep inside my chest, something the size of a grapefruit trying to drive itself upward through my neck. After perhaps fifty seconds I began to see red through the darkness. It means I'm dying, I thought as the color grew brighter and the grapefruit reached my Adam's apple. In the middle of the redness a spot of light started to form. It was yellow, but I expected it to turn white. I was remembering a TV program about how dying people see light at the end of tunnels as their brain cells shut down. Suddenly resigned, I felt my kicks grow weaker. My powerful breaststroke became an erratic underwater doggy paddle. When I felt rock scraping along the length of my stomach I realized I was no longer aware if I was facing up or down.

To say that this pissed me off sounds flippant, but that's the best way I can describe it. I think that a part of my mind, however bewildered, resented being wrong about the split-second theory in video games. I wasn't raging or fighting in the way I'd always imagined I would. I was just fading away. The resentment provided a new burst of energy, and with it came the realization that the redness might not be death after all. It might be light. Sunlight, passing through the water and the lids of my tightly shut eyes. Drawing from my last reserve of strength, I forced myself to make one more hard kick.

I came straight up into brightness and fresh air. I blinked the glare out of my eyes, gasping like a speared fish, and slowly Jed came into focus. He was sitting on a rock. Beside him was a long boat, painted the same blue green as the sea.

"Hey," he said, not looking round. "You took your time."

I couldn't answer at first because I was hyperventilating.

"What were you doing back there? You've been ages."

"Drowning," I finally managed to say.

"Yeah? You know anything about engines? I've tried to get this going but I can't."

I splashed over to him and tried to haul myself onto the rock, but I was too weak and I slipped back into the water. "Didn't you hear me?" I panted.

"Sure." He started absently running the blade of his knife against his beard, as if he were shaving. "Now, I know it's got enough gas because the tank's full, and I know the Swedes said they had it running the other day."

"Jed! I got stuck in some air pocket with more exits than . . ." I couldn't think of anything famous with a large number of exits. "I nearly drowned!"

For the first time Jed looked at me. "An air pocket?" he said, lowering the knife. "Are you sure?"

"Of course I'm fucking sure!"

"Where?"

"I don't know, do I? Somewhere . . . in there." I turned back to the black entrance of the cave and shivered.

Jed frowned. "Well . . . that's pretty weird. I've been through there a hundred times and I've never found any air pocket."

"You think I'm lying?"

"No. . . . And there were several exits?"

"Four at least. I could feel them and I didn't know which one I should take. It was a fucking nightmare."

"So you must have strayed down a split off the main passage. Shit, Richard, I'm sorry. I honestly didn't know that could happen. I must have been through there so many times that I automatically follow the same route." He tutted. "But it's amazing. Everybody on the beach has swum through that cave and no one's ever got lost."

I sighed. "That's my fucking luck."

"Bad luck all right." He held out a hand and pulled me onto the rock.

"I might have died."

Jed nodded. "You might have. I'm sorry."

A voice in my head was telling me that I ought to lose my temper, but there didn't seem anything to lose my temper at. Instead I lay back and looked up at the clouds. A silver speck was threading a vapor trail across the sky and I imagined people inside peering out of the windows, watching the Gulf of Thailand unfold, wondering what things could be happening on the islands beneath them. One or two of them, I was sure, must be looking at my island.

They'd never have guessed what was happening in a million years. Thinking this, I managed a dizzy smile.

Jed brought me back to earth by saying, "You smell of sick."

"I've been swimming in the stuff," I replied.

"Your elbow's bleeding too."

I glanced down and at once my arm began to sting.

"Jesus. I'm a wreck."

"No." Jed shook his head. "It's the boat that's the wreck."

The boat was twenty feet long and four feet wide, with a single bamboo outrigger on the right-hand side. On the left side it was lying flat against the rocks, tied up, protected by a line of buffers made of tightly rolled palm leaves. It was also protected, and hidden, by the mini-harbor formed by the entrance to the cave.

Inside the boat were some of the Swedes' fishing implements. Their spears were cut longer than ours and they had a landing net, I noticed enviously. Not that we needed a landing net inside the lagoon, but it would have been nice to have one all the same. They had lines and hooks, too, which explained why they always caught the biggest fish.

Despite what Jed had said, I took to the boat immediately. I liked its Southeast Asian shape, the painted flourishes on its prow, the strong odor of grease and salt-soaked wood. Most of all I liked the fact that all this stuff was familiar to me, remembered from other island trips in other places. I felt pleased to have a store of memories which enabled me to feel nostalgic about such exotic things.

Collecting memories, or experiences, was my primary goal when I first started traveling. I went about it in the same way as a stamp collector goes about collecting stamps, carrying around with me a mental list of all the things I had yet to see or do. Most of the list was pretty banal. I wanted to see the Taj Mahal, Borobudur, the Rice Terraces in Banave, Angkor Wat. Less banal, or maybe more so, was that I wanted to witness extreme poverty. I saw it as a necessary experience for anyone who wanted to appear worldly and interesting.

Of course witnessing poverty was the first to be ticked off the list. Then I had to graduate to the more obscure stuff. Being in a riot was something I pursued with a truly obsessive zeal, along with being tear-gassed and hearing gunshots fired in anger.

Another list item was having a brush with my own death. In Hong Kong, aged eighteen, I'd met an old Asia hand who'd told me a story about having being held up at gunpoint in Vietnam. The story ended with him having the gun shoved in his chest and being told he was going to be shot. "The funny thing about facing death," he'd said, "is that you find you aren't afraid. If anything, you're calm. Alert, naturally, but calm."

I'd nodded vigorously. I wasn't agreeing with him out of personal experience. I was just too thrilled to do anything but move my head.

The dope fields had fitted neatly into this category of the list, and so did the air pocket. The only downside was that I wasn't able to claim being alert (naturally) but calm, which was a line I fully intended to use one day.

Twenty minutes later I was ready to get going.

"Right," I said, sitting up. "Let's start up the engine."

"The engine's fucked. You can't start it. I think we might have to go back and get the Swedes to sort it out."

"Sure I can start it. I've been on this kind of banka loads of times."

Jed looked doubtful but gestured for me to give it a try.

I crawled into the boat and slid down to the stern end, and to my great delight I recognized the engine type. It was started like a lawn mower, by winding a rope around a flywheel and giving it a hard tug. A closer look revealed a knot at one end of the rope and a groove in the wheel for it to fit into.

"I've tried that fifty times," Jed muttered as I put the knot in place.

"It's in the wrist," I replied with deliberate cheerfulness. "You have to start slowly, then snap it back."

"Uh-huh?"

When I was ready to pull I gave the engine a last cursory check. I wasn't looking for anything in particular but I wanted to give the impression that I was, and my shallowness paid off. Almost obscured by layers of grease and dirt was a small metal switch with "on/off" written beneath it. I glanced backward over my shoulder and discreetly flicked it to the correct setting.

"Here we go!" I shouted, and gave the rope a yank. Without even a splutter the engine roared into life.

Westmoreland

When we finally set out, noisily chugging away from the mini-harbor in a cloud of petrol fumes, I was keen to get to Koh Phangan. Although I'd been told it was past its best, Hadrin still had a somewhat legendary reputation. As with Patpong Road or the opium treks in the Golden Triangle, I wanted to know what all the fuss was about. I was also pleased to be doing something important for the beach. I knew that Sal appreciated my volunteering for such an obviously unpopular task, and I felt like I was involved in something serious and worthwhile.

But an hour later, as the shape of Koh Phangan was forming on the horizon, I began to feel anxious. It was the same feeling I'd had under the waterfall. I was suddenly aware that encountering the world would bring back all the things I'd been doing such a good job of forgetting. I wasn't exactly sure what those things were, because I'd forgotten them, but I was pretty convinced that I didn't want to be reminded. Also, although we couldn't really talk over the noise of the engine, I sensed Jed was thinking along the same lines. He was sitting as rigidly as the choppy motion of the boat would allow, one hand gripping the tiller, keeping his eyes absolutely fixed on the island ahead.

I reached into my shorts pocket for a cigarette. I'd taken a new packet—hoping the seal would keep them waterproof—and matches. They were in the plastic film carton that Keaty used to keep his rizlas dry. "This is the most precious possession I have," he'd said before handing it over. "Guard it with your life." "Count on it," I'd replied earnestly, imagining a three-hour boat trip without nicotine.

Lighting up turned into a bit of a drama because the matches were a crappy Thai brand and they splintered if you pushed them too hard. The first three broke and the next four blew out in the wind. I'd only taken ten in the film can and was beginning to lose my cool when I finally managed to get the cigarette lit. Jed lit one too, off the end of mine; then we both went back to gazing at Koh Phangan. Between the blue and the green I could now make out a strip of white sand.

To avoid thinking about the world, I started thinking about Françoise.

A few days earlier, near the coral garden, Etienne and I had been having a diving competition to see who could make the smallest splash. When we asked Françoise to judge it, she watched us both and then shrugged, saying, "You are both very good." Etienne looked surprised. "Yes," he said impatiently. "But who is better?" Françoise shrugged again. "What shall I say?" She laughed. "Really. You are both as good as the other." Then she gave us both a little kiss on the cheek.

Her reaction had surprised me, too. The truth is, Etienne was a much better diver than I was. I knew that without a shadow of a doubt. He could do effortless backward dives, swan dives, jackknifes, weird twists without names, all sorts of things. I, however, could only manage a backward dive with a violent jerk that usually flipped me right back onto my feet. As for who could make the smallest splash, Etienne entered the water as straight

as a bamboo spear. I didn't need to see myself to know that I was more like
a tree trunk, branches and all.

So when Françoise said that we were both as good as the other, she was
lying. A funny sort of lie. Not malicious, apparently diplomatic, but
vaguely puzzling in a way I found hard to pin down.

"West . . . more . . . land . . ." I heard over the noise of the engine. Jed
was calling to me, snapping me out of my daydreaming.

I looked round and cupped my hand to my ear. "What?" I yelled.

"I'm heading west! There's more open beach to land! Less beach
huts!"

I gave him the thumbs-up and turned back to the prow. While I'd been
thinking about Françoise, Koh Phangan had got much closer. I could now
see the trunks and leaves of the coconut trees, and the midday shadows
beneath them.

Reentry

A hundred or so meters from the shore, Jed cut the
engine so we could paddle the rest of the way in. The idea was to look like
day-trippers, but we needn't have bothered. The stretch of beach we
landed on was empty apart from a few beat-up old beach huts, and they
looked like no one had stayed in them for quite a while.

We jumped out and waded to the sand, dragging the boat by the outrigger. "Are we going to leave the boat here?" I asked when we were clear
of the water.

"No, we'll have to hide it." Jed pointed to the treeline. "Maybe up
there. Go and check it out. Make sure this area is as empty as it seems."

"Okay."

I started jogging up the beach, then slowed to a walk almost immediately. My sense of balance still thought I was at sea and I was swaying

drunkenly from side to side. It passed quickly, but for a couple of minutes I actually had to concentrate to keep from falling over.

Not far from where we'd landed I found two palms that were far enough apart to let the outrigger through and close enough together to look inconspicuous. Between them was a bush with a large canopy that would cover the boat completely, especially with the help of a few well placed branches, and the nearest of the ramshackle beach huts was a good fifty meters away.

"Here seems fine," I called to Jed.

"Right. Give us a hand then."

Everything would have been much easier if there'd been a third person to help us. With the weight of the engine, it took both of us to lift the stern—we had to keep the propeller up to stop it from getting damaged—so the front end kept sliding away from us. It was hard enough on the sand, but getting it over the small grass verge was a nightmare. We had to shunt it in short backbreaking bursts, none of which seemed to move it more than a foot.

"Bloody hell," I panted, after the boat had swiveled away from the treeline for the twentieth time. "Is it always this hard?"

"Is what always this hard?"

"Rice Running."

"Of course," Jed replied, smoothing the sweat out of his beard. A stream of oily drops ran down his wrist and dripped off his elbow. "Why do you think nobody wants to do it?"

Eventually we managed to maneuver the boat between the trees and under the bush. After we'd knocked up some camouflage, there was no way anyone would have spotted it unless they were going out of their way to look. We were even worried that we'd have trouble finding it again ourselves, so we marked the spot by pushing a forked stick into the sand.

We were completely exhausted, but there were two consolations. One was that it would be easier getting the boat back to the water, because it would be downhill and the ocean made for a bigger target than the space between two palm trees. The other was that we could treat ourselves to a big meal as soon as we got to Hadrin.

We set off in high spirits, discussing which soft drinks we were going to order and whether Sprite had the edge on Coke. Jed noticed the couple first, but we were already a fair distance from the boat, so we didn't worry too much. As we passed them I looked straight at their faces, not for any reason except to be ready with a smile if they said hello.

They didn't. They kept their eyes pointed at the ground, and by their expressions I could see they were putting the same concentration into walking as I had earlier.

"Did you see them?" I said when they were out of earshot. "Wasted by lunchtime."

"Liquid lunch."

"Powdered lunch."

Jed nodded, then hawked up and spat on the sand. "Fucking freaks."

An hour later we were walking past rows of busy beach huts and weaving between sunbathers and Frisbee games. I was surprised that people weren't taking more notice of us. Everyone looked so strange to me that I couldn't believe I didn't look equally strange to them.

"Let's eat," said Jed when we were about halfway down Hadrin, so we walked into the nearest café and sat down. Jed looked over the menu while I continued to marvel at our surroundings. The concrete under my toes felt particularly weird, as did the plastic chair. It was just a standard chair—the same kind as I used to have at school; curved seat with a hole in the back, V-shaped metal legs—but I found it bizarrely uncomfortable. I couldn't work out the right way to sit on it: either I was slithering down or I was perched on the edge.

"How the hell do you do this?" I muttered.

Jed looked up from the menu.

"I can't seem to sit . . ."

He started laughing. "Does your head in, doesn't it? All this."

"It sure does."

"What about your reflection?"

". . . How do you mean?"

"When was the last time you saw your reflection?"

I shrugged. There was a makeup mirror outside near the shower hut which the men used for shaving, but it only showed a tiny area of your face at any one time. Apart from that, I hadn't seen myself since Koh Samui.

"There's a sink and mirror over there. Go and have a look. You'll get a real shock."

I frowned, suddenly worried. "Why? Has something happened to my face?"

"No. Just go and have a look. You'll see."

Shock was right. The person who gazed back at me over the sink was a stranger. My skin was darker than I'd imagined it could possibly get, my black hair had been sun-bleached almost brown and matted into curls, and my teeth were so white they seemed to jump out of my face. I also looked old—twenty-six or twenty-seven—and there were some freckles on my nose. The freckles were a particular shock. I never get freckles.

I stared at my reflection for five minutes at least, transfixed. I could have stared for an hour if Jed hadn't called me back to order some food.

"What did you think?" he asked as I wandered back to the table, grinning like an idiot.

"Really weird. Why don't you have a look too? It's great."

"No. . . . I haven't seen myself for six months now. I'm saving up to completely freak myself out."

"Six months!"

"Uh-huh. Maybe more." He tossed me the menu. "Come on. What'll it be? I'm starving."

I glanced down the enormous list, pausing on banana pancakes but thinking the better of it.

"I believe I'd like a couple of cheeseburgers."

"Cheeseburgers. Anything else?"

"Uh . . . okay. Spicy chicken noodles too. We're in Thailand, after all."

Jed stood up, glancing over his shoulder toward the sunbathers on the beach. "I'll take your word for it," he said dryly, then went to place our order.

While we waited for our food we watched TV. There was a video at the far end of the café and it was playing *Schindler's List*. Schindler was on a horse watching the ghettos being emptied, and he'd noticed a little girl in a red coat.

"How about that coat?" Jed asked, sipping his Coke.

I sipped my Sprite. "What about it?"

"Do you reckon they painted it on the film with a brush?"

"On each frame? Like animation?"

"Yeah."

"No way. They would have done it with a computer, like *Jurassic Park*."

"Oh . . ." Jed drained the bottle and smacked his lips. "It's the real thing."

I frowned. *"Schindler's List?"*

"No, you jerk. Coke."

The food must have taken ages, because by the time it arrived, Schindler was looking at the red coat again. If you've seen the film you'll know that's an hour after he first sees it, if not more. Luckily I discovered that the café had an old Space Invaders machine, so for me the waiting wasn't so bad.

Kampuchea

Jed gave me a choice. I could go with him to sort out the rice or I could stay on the beach and meet him later. He didn't really need my help so I decided to stay. In any case, I had my own shopping to do. I wanted to restock my supply of cigarettes and get more batteries for Keaty's Gameboy.

In one of the other Hadrin cafés I found a shop—or a glass counter with a few goods beneath it—and after buying the batteries and cigarettes it turned out I still had plenty of money left to get a few presents.

First of all I bought some soap for Unhygienix. This was tricky because they had several varieties, some Western, some Thai, but none of them the brand I'd seen Unhygienix using. I rummaged through the bars for a while before finding one called Luxume. It said it was "luxuriant yet perfumed." The "yet" turned my head and the "perfumed" clinched it, since I knew how important this was to him.

Then I bought a load of razors, which I thought I'd share with Etienne,

Gregorio, and Keaty. Then I bought a tube of Colgate for Françoise. Nobody used toothpaste on the beach; there were ten toothbrushes, which were shared by everyone, although many couldn't be bothered and just chewed a twig each morning. Françoise didn't mind sharing a toothbrush but she did miss the toothpaste, so I knew she'd appreciate the gift.

The next purchase was several packets of boiled sweets—I didn't want anybody to go empty-handed—and finally I bought a pair of shorts. Mine were getting ragged and I couldn't see them lasting more than a month or two.

With my shopping done I had nothing left to do. I had another Sprite, which didn't last long, so I decided to pass time by walking the length of Hadrin. After only a few hundred meters I gave up. There was nothing much to see apart from beach huts. Instead I sat on the sand and paddled my feet in the water, imagining the warm reactions I'd get when I handed out my presents. I envisaged an *Asterix*-style scene, returning from the adventure to a huge feast. We'd have to do without wild boars and Gaulish wine, but we'd have plenty of dope and more rice than you could shake a stick at.

"Saigon," said a male voice, and broke me straight out of my daydreaming. "Mad."

"Sounds it," said another voice, female.

"We were there two months. The place is like Bangkok ten fuckin' years ago. Probably better."

I looked round and saw four sunbathers. Two girls, English, and two boys, Australians. All of them were talking very loudly; so loudly it was like their conversation was aimed more at passersby than each other.

"Yeah, but if Saigon was mad, then Kampuchea was fuckin' unreal." This was the second Aussie speaking—a skinny guy with very cropped hair, long sideburns, and a tiny patch of beard on his chin.

"We were there for six weeks. Would have stayed longer but we ran out of cash. Had to get back to Thailand to pick up a fuckin' wire."

"Good scene," the first agreed. "Could have stayed six months."

"Could have stayed six years."

I looked back into the sea. It was a familiar enough exchange, I thought to myself, and not worth tuning in to. But then I found that I couldn't tune it out. It wasn't the volume of their chattering; I was intrigued that the guy had been talking about Kampuchea. I wondered if this was the new term for Cambodia.

Without thinking it over any more than that, I leaned toward them. "Hey," I said. "Out of interest, why do you call Cambodia Kampuchea?"

All four faces looked at me.

"I mean," I continued, "it's Cambodia, right?"

The second Aussie shook his head, not like he was disagreeing with me; like he was trying to figure out who I was.

"It's Cambodia, right?" I repeated, in case he hadn't heard me.

"Kampuchea. I've just been there."

I got up and walked over. "But called Kampuchea by who?"

"Cambodians."

"Not Kampucheans, then."

He frowned. "What?"

"I'm just interested to hear how you picked up the word Kampuchea."

"Mate," the first Aussie interrupted, "why does it matter what we call Kampuchea?"

"It isn't that it matters. I was just interested because I thought Kampuchea was a Khmer Rouge name. I mean, I'm probably wrong. Maybe it's just the old-fashioned name for Cambodia, but . . ."

The sentence trailed off. I was suddenly aware that all four of them were looking at me as though they thought I was insane. I smiled uncertainly. "It isn't a big deal . . . I was interested, that's all. . . . Kampuchea . . . It sounded strange . . ."

Silence.

I began to feel myself blushing. I knew I'd made some kind of faux pas but I didn't know what it might be. With my smile getting increasingly desperate, I tried to explain myself better, but my confusion and nervousness only made things worse. "I was just sitting over there and you said 'Kampuchea,' which I thought was a Khmer Rouge name, but you also used the old name of Ho Chi Minh City . . . Saigon . . . Not that I'm making a parallel between the VC and the Khmer Rouge, obviously . . . but . . ."

"So what?"

This was a fair point. I considered it for a couple of seconds, then said, "So nothing, I guess . . ."

"Then why are you bothering us, mate?"

I couldn't think what to say. I shrugged awkwardly and turned to walk back to my shopping bag, and behind me I heard one of them mutter, "Another fuckin' spacehead. Can't move for them, man." The comment made my ears burn and the tips of my fingers tingle. I hadn't had that feeling since I was a little kid.

When I sat back down I felt terrible. My good mood was completely gone. I couldn't understand what I'd said that was so wrong. All I'd been doing was joining in their conversation, which didn't seem like such a terrible thing to do. It was the beach and the world, I decided coldly. My beach, where you could walk into a conversation at any time between anybody, and the world, where you couldn't.

A few minutes later I got up to go. I'd noticed that their talking was quieter, and I had the miserable feeling that they were talking about me. I found a suitably secluded palm tree a short way up the beach and settled beneath it. I'd arranged to meet Jed at seven, back at the café where we'd eaten lunch, so I still had a few hours to kill. Too many hours. The wait was beginning to feel like it might be an ordeal.

I chain-smoked two and a half cigarettes. I wanted to chain-smoke three, or even more, but the third gave me a five-minute coughing fit. Reluctantly I stubbed it out and pushed it into the sand.

My embarrassment had turned quickly to anger. Before, I'd been looking at Hadrin with a detached curiosity, and now I was looking at it with hatred. I could sense shit all around me, Thais smiling like sharks and careless hedonism, too diligently pursued to ring true. Most of all, I could pick up the scent of decay. It hung over Hadrin like the sand flies that hung over the sunbathers, zoning in on the smell of sweat and sweet tanning lotion. The serious travelers had already moved on to the next island in the chain, the intermediary travelers were wondering where all the life had gone, and the tourist hordes were ready to descend on their freshly beaten track.

For the first time I understood the true preciousness of our hidden beach. To imagine Hadrin's fate unfolding in the lagoon made my blood run cold. I began scanning the dark bodies that lounged around me as if

I were photographing the enemy, familiarizing myself with the images, filing them away. Occasionally couples walked near me and I caught snatches of their conversations. I must have heard twenty different accents and languages. Most I didn't understand, but they all sounded like threats.

Time dragged with only these thoughts for company, so when my eyes grew heavy I let them close. The heat and the day's early start had caught up with me. An afternoon siesta would be a welcome retreat.

Blame

The music started up at eight, which was lucky or I might have slept until midnight. Up and down the beach, four or five different sound systems blasted out, each with its own agenda. I could only hear two clearly, the ones on either side of me, but all the bass lines seemed to be vibrating through my head. Swearing and rubbing the daze out of my eyes, I jumped up and ran back down the beach to the café.

The café was now packed with people but I spotted Jed immediately. He was at the same table we'd sat at earlier. He had a bottle of beer in his hands and was looking extremely pissed off.

"Where the fuck have you been?" he said angrily when I sat down beside him. "I've been waiting."

"I'm sorry," I replied. "I fell asleep . . . I've had a bad day."

"You did, huh? Well, I'll just bet it wasn't a patch on mine."

"Why, what happened? Didn't you get the rice?"

"I got the rice, Richard. Don't worry about that."

I looked at him hard. There was a worrying note of menace in his voice. "What then?"

"You tell me."

"Tell you . . . ?"

"About two Yanks."

"Two Yanks?"

Jed took a huge gulp of beer. "Two Yanks I heard talking about a place called Eden in the Marine Park."

". . . Oh shit."

"They know you, Richard. They used your name. And they've got a map." He squeezed his eyes shut like he was fighting to keep control of his temper. "A fucking map, Richard! They were showing it to some Germans! And who knows who else has seen it."

I shook my head. I was feeling dazed. "I'd forgotten . . . I'd . . ."

"Who are they?"

"Jed, wait. You don't understand. I didn't tell them about the beach. They told me. They already knew about it."

He put his bottle on the table with a thump. *"Who are they!"*

". . . Zeph and Sammy. I met them on Koh Samui."

"Go on."

"They were just these two guys in the hut next to mine. We spent some time together, and the night before we were going to leave for Angthong, they started talking about the beach."

"Unprompted?"

"Yes! Of course!"

"So you drew them a map."

"No! I didn't say a thing, Jed! None of us did."

"Then where did the map come from?"

"The next morning . . . I drew it and pushed it under their door . . ." I pulled out a cigarette and tried to light it. My hands shook badly and it took me three attempts.

"Why?"

"I was worried!"

"You just drew them the map? They didn't even ask for it!"

"I didn't know if the beach really existed. We could have been aiming at nowhere. I had to tell someone where we going in case something went wrong."

"What could go wrong?"

"I don't know! We didn't know anything! I just didn't want us disappearing with nobody knowing where we'd gone!"

Jed put his head in his hands. "This could be bad, Richard."

"We could have disappeared into the Marine Park and no one would have . . ."

He nodded slowly. "I understand that."

We sat in silence for several minutes, Jed staring at the table and me looking anywhere but at him. Over by the Space Invaders machine a tubby black girl with cornrows was trying to hit the last invader. It was moving so fast it was a blur. She missed it on every pass, and just before it reached the bottom line she turned away, disgusted. The sound of talking and music was too loud for me to hear her exploding spaceship, but I saw it on her face.

Eventually Jed lifted up his head. "These two Yanks. Do you think they'll make the trip?"

". . . They might do, Jed. I don't know them well enough."

"*Fuck*. This could be so bad." Then suddenly he reached over and laid his hand on my forearm. "Listen," he said. "Are you blaming yourself?"

I nodded.

"Don't. I'm serious. Whatever happens with these Yanks, it isn't your fault. If I'd been in your shoes I might have done the same thing."

"How do you mean, 'whatever happens'?" I said warily.

"I mean . . . I mean whatever happens I don't want you to blame yourself. It's important, Richard. If you really want someone to blame, blame Daffy." He sighed deeply. "Or me."

"You?"

"Me."

I opened my mouth to ask him to explain, but he held up a hand. "There's no point talking about it."

"Okay," I said quietly.

"Look, we might not even have a problem. In a few weeks the Yanks will probably be flying off home and the map should go with them. Even if they stay in Thailand there's a good chance they won't bother trying to reach us. They seemed like a couple of airheads, and the trip isn't easy."

"I hope you're right," I said hollowly, remembering how skilled they were at their surfer act.

"Hoping's about all we can do. That and wait . . ." He finished his beer. "We've got to get the rice back to the boat tonight because I don't want to be carrying those sacks in broad daylight. Are you ready to go?"

"Yes."

He stood up. "Good. Then let's get to it."

Around the back of the café was a thin passage between two beach huts, and under a tarpaulin were our rice sacks. We put them on the tarpaulin so we could drag them along the sand, and, holding a corner each, we set off on the long trek back to the boat.

Just after leaving Hadrin, we had a fag break and ate a few of the boiled sweets from my bag of presents.

"I'm sorry if I flew off at you," Jed said as I passed him the packet.

"It's all right."

"No. I'm sorry. You didn't deserve it."

I shrugged. I felt like I did.

"I didn't ask you why your day was so bad."

"Oh. It's nothing . . . It was just Hadrin. The place, or the people . . . They gave me the creeps."

"Me too. Fucked up, isn't it?"

"Fucked up . . . Yeah. It is."

"Richard?"

"Yes?"

"When we get back to the camp, don't mention this thing with the Yanks."

"But . . ."

"Sal and Bugs. I don't think they'll understand."

I looked at him but he was busy trying to get the wrapper off one of the sweets.

"If you think that's the right thing to do."

"Yeah. I do."

It took us another three hours to get back to the marker. The forked stick showed up clearly in the bright moonlight, and we left the sacks beside it. Then I went to check on the boat while Jed moved the sacks off the tarpaulin and spread it across the sand. It was pitch-black under the bushes but I could feel the curved prow. That was enough for me. As long as we had our means of escape, I could relax.

Jed was already asleep by the time I got back to the marker. I lay beside him and looked at the stars, remembering the way I'd looked at the stars with Françoise. Somewhere amongst them was a parallel world where I'd kept the map to myself, I thought, and wished it could have been this one.

Through Early-Morning Fog I See

Mister Duck sat in his box room on the Ko Sanh Road. He'd pulled back one of the newspapers that covered the window and was peering down to the street. Behind him, strewn across his bed, were colored pencils. Obviously the ones he'd used to draw the map. The map was nowhere in sight, so maybe he'd already tacked it to my door.

I saw that his shoulders were shaking.

"Mister Duck?" I said cautiously.

He turned, scanned the room with a puzzled frown, then spotted me through the strip of mosquito netting.

"Rich . . . Hi."

"Hi. Are you all right?"

"No." A tear rolled down his grubby cheek. "I'm going to kill myself pretty soon. I'm feeling really bad."

". . . I'm sorry. Is there anything I can do?"

He sighed. "Thank you, Rich. You're a good friend, but it's too late now. I've been in a Bangkok morgue for the last eleven weeks."

"There's no one to collect you?"

"No one. The Thai police contacted the British embassy. They found my parents in Glasgow but my folks didn't want to come out here to sign the release papers. They don't care about me." Another tear trickled out. "Their only son."

"But that's awful."

"And I'm going to be incinerated in another four weeks if no one signs my release papers. The embassy won't cover the cost of returning my body."

"You . . . wanted to be buried."

"I don't mind being incinerated, but if my parents won't come to collect me, then I don't want to be sent. I'd rather have my ashes left out here." Mister Duck's voice began to crack. "A small ceremony, nothing fancy, and my ashes scattered into the South China Sea." Then he collapsed into uncontrollable sobbing.

I pressed my face and hands against the netting. I wished I were in the room with him. "Hey, come on, Mister Duck. It isn't so bad."

He shook his head angrily, and through his sobbing I noticed he'd started to sing the theme song from *M*A*S*H*.

I waited until he'd finished, not knowing where to look; then I said, "You've got a good voice," mainly because I didn't know what else to say.

He shrugged, wiping his face with his filthy T-shirt. His face ended up dirtier than it had been before. "It's a small voice but it can carry a tune."

"No, Mister Duck. It's a good voice . . . I always liked *M*A*S*H*."

He appeared to brighten up slightly. "So did I. The helicopters at the beginning."

"The helicopters were great."

"It was about Vietnam. Did you know that, Rich?"

"Korea, wasn't it?"

"Vietnam. Korea was the excuse."

"Oh . . ."

Mister Duck turned back to peek between the newspapers again. He didn't seem like he was about to speak, so to keep the conversation going, I asked him what he was looking at.

"Nothing," he replied softly. "A *tuk-tuk* driver asleep in his cab . . . A stray dog sifting through litter . . . You take these things for granted when you're alive, Rich, but when they're the last things you're ever going to see . . ." His voice began to quaver again and he bunched up his fists. "It's time I got this over with."

". . . Killing yourself?"

"Yes," he said. Then he said it again, more firmly. "Yes."

He walked briskly over to the bed, sat down, and pulled a knife from under the pillow.

"Don't, Mister Duck! Don't do it!"

"My mind's made up."

"There's time to change your mind!"

"I won't turn back now."

"Mister Duck!" I cried out feebly.

Too late. He'd already started to cut.

I didn't watch him die because I thought it would be disrespectful, but I checked on him five minutes later to see how he was getting on. He was still alive, jerking around on the sheets and spraying the walls. I waited another fifteen minutes before checking again, wanting to be sure. This time he was still, lying in the position I'd first found him. His torso was twisted so that his legs were off the edge of the bed—a detail I hadn't noticed previously. Maybe he'd tried to stand up just before he died.

"I'll sort your ashes out, Mister Duck," I whispered through the netting. "You don't have to worry about that."

Messed Up

I woke up at the first glimmer of dawn. The sun was still under the horizon and the beach was lit with a strange blue light, both dark and bright at the same time. It was very beautiful and calm. Even the waves seemed to be breaking more quietly than usual.

I didn't wake Jed because I like being awake when other people are asleep. It makes me feel like pottering around, fixing breakfast if there's anything to be fixed, and in this case, wandering aimlessly up the shore. While I walked I looked out for pretty shells. The necklace that Bugs had made me was okay, but many of the shells were a bit drab. I got the feeling that he hadn't been too bothered to make them nice. Even Françoise's necklace, which was the best of the three, wasn't as good as most of the others in the camp. It didn't take long before I'd worked up a collection and was having to make hard choices about which shells to discard. The prettiest I found was flecked with blue, red, and green—the back of a tiny crab. I decided that this would make the centerpiece of my new necklace and looked forward to restringing it when I got home.

I found the couple lying fast asleep on the grass verge, about two hundred meters further on from where we'd hidden the boat. It was the same couple that Jed and I had passed yesterday. My first instinct was to turn back, but curiosity stopped me. They'd chosen an oddly remote beach hut to stay in, miles from Hadrin, and I was intrigued to see what kind of people they were. I pocketed my shells and padded across the sand toward them.

Now that I had a chance to see the couple from close up, they made an ugly sight. The girl had nasty sores around her mouth and was covered in fat black mosquitoes. At least thirty or forty were clustered on her legs and arms, and when I waved my hand over them they didn't budge an inch. There were no mosquitoes on the guy. "No surprise," I thought, because he wouldn't have made much of a meal. Judging by his height, I reckoned he should have been eleven stone, but he couldn't have weighed more than eight. His body was like an anatomical diagram. Every bone was clearly visible, as was every pitiful muscle. Beside him was a pill bottle, marked with the address of some dubious pharmacy in Surat Thani. I checked inside but it was empty.

I'd been studying the guy for a while before I noticed that his eyes were slightly open. Just little slits, easy to miss at first glance. I waited to see him blink. He didn't, or didn't seem to, so I waited to see him breathe. He didn't do that, either. Then I bent down and touched his chest. He was warm enough, but the air was pretty warm too, so that didn't mean anything. I pressed my hand down harder. My fingers sank deeply between his ribs and the skin moved slackly against the bone. No pulse. I started counting, carefully marking the seconds with elephants, and by the time I reached sixty I knew he was dead.

I frowned and looked around me. Apart from the silhouette of Jed and the rice sacks, the beach was completely deserted. Then I looked back at the girl. I knew she was alive because of the mosquitoes, and anyway, her chest was rising and falling.

This unsettled me. I wasn't bothered about the guy, because he'd come to Thailand and messed up, so that was his lookout. But the girl was another matter entirely. As soon as her opiate slumber wore off she'd wake up to an empty beach and a corpse. I thought that would be a terrible thing to happen, and seeing as I'd been the one to find her, I felt I had some responsibility for her. I lit up a cigarette and wondered how I might help.

Waking the girl up was out of the question. Even if I managed to bring her round, she'd only freak out. Then the authorities on Koh Phangan would get involved and it would be a disaster. Another option was to wake Jed up and ask his advice, but I decided against it. I knew what he'd say. He'd say it was none of our business and we should leave the couple as we found them, and I already knew I didn't want to do that.

Eventually I hit on a good idea. I would drag the guy's body away to the bushes and hide it. Then, when she woke up, she'd just think he'd gone for a walk. After a day or so she'd realize he was missing and might worry about what had happened to him, but at least she wouldn't know he was dead. By that time he would probably have been eaten by ants and beetles, and no one but me would be any the wiser.

I busied myself with the task at hand, keeping half an eye on my watch. Jed would be awake soon and then it would be time to leave.

"Jed!" I said softly.

He stirred and waved a hand over his face, like he was brushing away a fly.

"Jed! Wake up!"

"What?" he mumbled.

"We should go. It's getting light."

He sat up and looked up at the sky. The sun was fully above the horizon line. "Shit, yeah, we should. Overslept. Sorry. Let's get cracking."

When we were halfway between Koh Phangan and our island I told him what had happened with the corpse and how I'd dealt with it.

"Jesus fucking Christ, Richard!" he shouted—only because the engine was so loud. "What the flying fuck did you do that for?"

"Well, what should I have done?"

"You should have left him there, you bloody idiot! What did it have to do with us? Nothing!"

"I knew you'd say that," I said happily. "I knew it."

prisoners of the sun

Bible Bashing

No one was even slightly interested. A few asked, "How was it?" out of politeness, but as soon as I began to answer, their eyes glazed over or their attention became diverted by something over my shoulder.

At first I found this attitude pretty frustrating. I wanted to talk at length about how fucked up Koh Phangan was, and the frustration was compounded by the unenthusiastic response I got when I handed out my little presents. Françoise took one taste of the toothpaste and spat it out, saying, "Ugh, I did not remember the way it burns," and Keaty said I shouldn't have bought Thai-brand batteries because they run out so fast. The only person who seemed at all grateful was Unhygienix. He went straight off for a shower after I gave him the bars, and later he gave me a glowing report on the thick lather they produced.

But my frustration only lasted while Koh Phangan was fresh in my mind, which wasn't long. Just as when I'd first arrived at the beach, my memory began to shut itself down. Steadily, quickly, so that within a week nothing much existed beyond the lagoon and its circle of protective cliffs. Nothing except the world, that is, and that had returned to its previous condition, a name to something faceless and indistinct.

My worries about Zeph and Sammy were the last things to go. As late as the fifth night I was kept awake fretting about what plans they and the mysterious Germans might be making. But it became hard to maintain that level of worry as the days passed, and still no one had turned up. Having said that, the day after the fretful fifth night I did ask Jed whether he'd also been thinking about the Zeph and Sammy problem, and he made a seesaw motion with his hands. "I've been thinking about it a little," he said. "But I think we're okay."

"You do?" I replied, already sensing the weight of the problem lifting.

"Yeah. Those two were on the pilgrim's route. They had guidebook written all over them. If not, like I already said, we'll deal with it when it happens." He pulled a knot of hair out of his beard. "You know, Richard, one of these days I'm going to find one of those Lonely Planet writers and I'm going to ask him, what's so fucking lonely about the Ko Sanh Road?"

I smiled. "Just before you punch his lights out, right?"

The smile wasn't returned.

Jaws One

A few weeks after the Rice Run, I woke up to the noise of rain on the longhouse roof. It had rained only three or four times since I'd arrived at the beach, and those had just been showers. This was a tropical storm, even heavier than the one on Koh Samui.

A few of us huddled around the longhouse entrance, looking out across the clearing. The canopy ceiling was channeling the water into thick streams that dropped like lasers and cut muddy holes into the earth. Keaty was standing under one of them, his top half obscured by the silver umbrella that exploded off his head. I only recognized him from his black legs and the faint sound of his laughter. Bugs was also standing outside. He had his head tilted so that one cheek was angled upward, his arms were held slightly away from his body, and his palms were ready to catch the rain.

"Thinks he's Christ," muttered a voice behind me. I turned around and saw Jesse, a compact New Zealander who worked in the garden detail with Keaty. Jesse was one of the people I'd never had much cause to speak to, but I'd always suspected that he'd been the one to pick up my first Jim-Bob cue.

I looked back at Bugs and smiled, because there *was* something piously Christlike about his pose. Either the pose or the beatific expression on his face.

"Know what I mean?" Jesse said.

I smiled.

"Maybe the carpentry's gone to his head," said Cassie, who was also standing near, and we all chuckled. I would have added something but Jesse nudged me. Sal had emerged from the far end of the longhouse and was walking toward us. Gregorio was beside her, looking a little hassled.

"What's the delay?" asked Sal as she approached.

Nobody answered her, so I said, "Delay about what?"

"Fishing, gardening, work."

Jesse shrugged. "Not much gardening to be done in the rain, Sal."

"The plants can be protected, Jesse. You can rig up a shelter."

"Plants need rain."

"They don't need rain like this."

Jesse shrugged again.

"And you, Richard? What will we eat with your rice if you don't go fishing?"

"I was waiting for Greg."

"Greg's ready now."

"Yes," said Gregorio, and Etienne and Françoise also appeared. "We are ready now."

We jogged down to the beach, sliding around in the mud. I don't know why we were jogging because we were soaked within seconds, and in any case, we were going to spend the next three hours in the sea. I suppose there was a general feeling that we wanted to get the fishing done as quickly as possible.

While we jogged, I thought over the brief exchange under the longhouse entrance. I'd never mentioned the way Bugs irritated me, not even to Keaty. It hadn't seemed like a wise idea, considering Bugs's standing in the camp, and my criticisms seemed so petty. But from the way Jesse and Cassie had been talking, I began to wonder if others felt the same way. Although they hadn't said anything nasty they'd certainly been taking the piss, and until that moment it hadn't occurred to me that people took the piss out of Bugs.

The thing that most struck me was the way they'd hushed up when Sal came over. If not for that, the joking would have seemed far less telling. As it was, I felt like I'd witnessed some kind of division—however slight—and had possibly been included in it. I wondered if I ought to find out more about Jesse and Cassie, if only to get to know them better. I'd have asked Gregorio but I knew I'd get a uselessly diplomatic answer. Keaty or Jed were the ones to talk to.

———

The sea was covered in a thick low mist of vaporized raindrops. Under the shelter of a palm tree, we leaned against our spears and shook our heads.

"This is too stupid," said Françoise. "We cannot kill fish if we do not see them."

Etienne grunted his agreement. "We cannot even see the water."

"Yes, we use the mask," Gregorio replied, holding it up, and I groaned.

"Is that what you normally do when it rains?"

"Of course."

"But that means only one person can fish at a time. It's going to take forever."

"It will take a long time, Richard."

"How about Moshe and the Yugoslavian girls, and the Swedes? They don't have masks."

"They will try to catch fish but they will kill only a few. . . . When it rains like this, we can get very hungry on the beach."

"And if it rains for five days?" said Françoise. "It can rain for five days, no?"

Gregorio shrugged and glanced at the sky. From the look of it, the rain wouldn't ease up for at least another twenty-four hours. "We can get very hungry on the beach," he repeated, and dug his spear further into the wet earth.

We lapsed into silence, each of us apparently waiting for someone else to take the first go on the mask. I wanted to stand under the palm tree all day, ignoring the enormity of the work ahead, because as soon as the work was begun we'd all be committed to finishing it.

Five minutes passed, then another five, and then Etienne slung his spear over his shoulder.

"No," I said, sighing. "I'll go first."

"Are you sure, Richard? We can throw a coin."

"You've got a coin?"

Etienne smiled. "We can throw . . . the mask. Facedown, I will go first."

"I don't mind going first."

"Okay," he said, patting my arm. "So I shall go next."

"Okay."

Gregorio passed me the mask and I set off for the water. "Swim deeply and look under the boulders," he called after me. "The fish will be hiding."

It was a buzz swimming through the thick vapor. I couldn't wear the mask because the spray was too dense to let me breathe through my mouth, which meant I was constantly blinking to clear the water from my eyes. With nothing to see but a blurred foot of sea on either side of me, and each breath requiring a manageable amount of labor, I felt agreeably cocooned by a mildly dangerous world.

I stopped at the first boulder I came to. It was one of the smaller ones, sixty or so meters from the shore. We rarely used it as there was only room for one person to sit on it at a time, but seeing as I was alone it didn't make much difference. When I stood up my top half cleared the layer of mist. Etienne was standing on the sand, holding his hands like a peaked cap to ward off the rain. I waved my spear in the air and he spotted me, then turned to walk back to the treeline.

The first thing I needed to do was to find a heavy stone so I could rest on the bottom with a decent lungful of air. I put on the mask and slipped into the water, kicking out for the sea floor. The light was dark gray, deadened by the black sky and the mist, but the visibility was good. There weren't, however, any fish to be seen. Not even the clouds of tiny fry that usually wheeled around the corals.

I took my time hunting for the stone, making myself move slowly. If there were any fish around I didn't want to scare them off. Eventually I spotted a stone that looked like the right size and weight. I'd run out of air by that time, so I stuck my spear beside it, to make it easy to find again, and rose up to the surface.

On the way back down a few milkfish appeared, coming to inspect the new arrival to their storm shelter. I settled at the bottom with the stone on my lap and waited for their curiosity to bring them within range.

I saw the shark on my third dive. I'd just killed my first milkfish, so it must have been attracted by the smell of the blood. It wasn't much of a shark, about a foot longer than my leg and much the same width, but it gave me a hell of a shock. I didn't know what to do. Despite its small size it made me nervous, but I didn't want to swim back with only one fish. I'd have to explain why I'd given up so soon, and it would also be embarrassing if the shark was seen later. It was probably only a baby.

I decided I'd have to resurface and hang around on the boulder, hoping it would go away. I did this and spent the next ten minutes shivering in the mist and rain, crouched down because I didn't want the others to see that I wasn't fishing. Every so often I peered underwater to check if it was still there. It always was, circling slowly near the spot where I'd been sitting, watching me—I reckoned—with its inky eyes.

A brilliant idea coincided with a blistering peal of thunder. I put my milkfish, which was still in the twitching stage of death, on the tip of my spear. Then I rolled onto my front so I could dip my head and arms into the water, and held the spear ahead of me. The shark responded at once, breaking out of its leisured pace with a crisp snap of its tail. It headed toward me at an angle that would have carried it past the boulder, but six feet away it turned abruptly and lunged at the milkfish.

Out of sheer instinct I pulled the spear back. The lunge had been so quick and threatening that my reflexes had gotten the better of my common sense. The shark whipped past me and vanished behind a bank of corals. It didn't reappear within ten seconds, so I pulled myself out of the water to get some air.

I swore at myself, took a few deep breaths, then dipped back in.

The next time the shark appeared, it was more cautious, swimming near but showing little interest. The milkfish was dead by now and floating limply, so I tried jerking the spear to approximate life. The shark's enthusiasm was revived. Again it began its angled approach, but this time I took care to tense my arms. As it lunged, I pushed. The point of the spear caught momentarily on its teeth or gums, then sank into its mouth.

With a mighty wrench I pulled myself upward, stupidly thinking I'd hoist the shark onto the boulder behind me, but the spear simply snapped. I looked blankly at my broken spear for a couple of seconds, then shoved myself completely off the rock.

Underwater, the grayness was already hanging with curiously static strings of blood. Close by, the shark wildly thrashed and twisted, champing at the splintered bamboo between its teeth, sometimes diving directly downward and ramming its snout on the seabed.

Watching it, I realized I'd never killed anything as large before, or anything that fought so violently for its survival. As if to complement my thought, the shark increased the intensity of its thrashing so that it became obscured behind a cloud of disturbed sand and shredded seaweed. Occasionally, like in a comic book fight, its tail or head would appear out of the cloud before darting back inside again. The sight made me grin and salt water eased through the sides of my mouth. I resurfaced. I needed to spit and I needed some air. Then, with no intention of going near it while it was in that frantic state, I floated facedown and waited for it to die.

Hi, Man

I don't keep a travel diary. I did keep a travel diary once, and it was a big mistake. All I remember of that trip is what I bothered to write down. Everything else slipped away, as if my mind felt jilted by my reliance on pen and paper. For exactly the same reason, I don't travel with a camera. My holiday becomes the snapshots, and anything I forget to record is lost. Apart from that, photographs never seem to be very evocative. When I look through the albums of old traveling companions I'm always surprised by how little I'm reminded of the trip.

If only there was a camera that captured smell. Smells are far more vivid than images. I've often been walking in London on a hot day, caught the smell of hot refuse or melting tarmac, and suddenly been transported to a Delhi side street. Likewise, if I'm walking past a fishmonger I think instantly of Unhygienix, and if I smell sweat and cut grass (the lawn kind) I think of Keaty. I doubt either of them would appreciate being remembered in such a way, especially Unhygienix, but that's how it is.

All that said, I wish there'd been someone with a camera when I sauntered out of the mist with a dead shark over my shoulder. I must have looked so cool.

That afternoon, I was the toast of the camp. The shark was grilled and cut into strips so everyone would get a proper taste, and Keaty made me stand up and repeat my story to the whole camp. When I got to the part about the shark's first lunge, everyone gasped like they were watching fireworks, and when I told how I tensed my arms for the death blow, everyone cheered.

For the remainder of that day and night I had people constantly coming up to me to give their congratulations. Jed was the nicest. He walked over to where I was smoking with Etienne, Françoise, and Keaty, and said, "Well done, Richard. That was really something. I think we ought to rename you Tarzan." That made Keaty giggle like crazy, mainly because he was so stoned, so Jed sat down with us and we all got wasted together.

It was doubly nice because Keaty and Jed got on so well. After the Rice Run I'd been trying to persuade Keaty that Jed was okay, and now I felt like I'd had some success. It also turned out they had something in common, one of those weird coincidences that could easily never have been realized. Six years ago they'd both stayed at the same guest house in Yogyakarta, on the very same night. They were able to work this out because on that night the guest house had mysteriously burned down—or not so mysteriously, as it turned out. Keaty had been tripping and the mosquitoes in his room were driving him mad. Knowing that mosquitoes were driven away by smoke, he lit a small fire, and the next thing he knew, the room was completely ablaze. Jed explained that he'd had to escape the guest house by jumping from a third-story window and that all his money had been burned, and Keaty apologized, and everyone rolled around laughing.

If there was a sour note to the evening, it was Bugs, but ironically even that turned out okay. He came over while we were in the middle of another laughing fit, this one about the moment when Etienne had realized we were standing in a dope field.

"Hi, man," he said, flicking his head back to clear the hair from his eyes.

At first I didn't answer, because I was out of breath, and then I said, "What?" It wasn't a good choice of words. I'd honestly meant it in a friendly way, but it came out sounding like a confrontation.

If Bugs was taken aback he didn't show it—then again, he wouldn't have.

"I just came over to say congratulations. About the shark."

"Oh, yeah. Thanks. I . . . uh . . . I'm glad I caught it . . ." Again, my stoned head seemed to be putting the most inappropriate words into my mouth. "I've never caught a shark before."

"We're all glad you caught it. . . . Actually, I've caught a shark before."

"Oh?" I said, now trying extremely hard to concentrate on what I was saying. "Really? That's amazing. . . . You should certainly . . . uh . . . certainly tell us about it."

"Certainly," Keaty echoed, then coughed in a way that sounded suspiciously like a suppressed giggle.

Bugs paused. "It was in Australia."

"Australia . . . Gosh."

"Must be about five years ago now."

"Five years? Was it as long ago as that . . . uh . . ."

"A tiger shark, twelve-footer."

"How very . . . huge."

Suddenly Keaty dissolved into hysterics, and he set off Jed, who set off the others.

Bugs smiled thinly. "Maybe I'll save it for another time."

"It sounds like a great story," I managed to say before he turned to go. Then Keaty gasped, "Certainly," and I collapsed as well.

"My God, Richard," said Françoise a couple of minutes later. Her face was shining from tears. "What were you saying to Bugs? Everything you said . . ."

"Was wrong. I know. I couldn't help it."

Etienne nudged me. "You do not like Bugs, huh?"

"It isn't that. I'm just wasted. I'm not thinking straight."

"That's bullshit, Rich," said Keaty, grinning slyly.

Jed nodded. "Admit it. I've seen the way you look at him."

There was a silence while everyone looked at me, waiting for an answer. Eventually I shrugged. "All right then, you've got me. I think he's a prat."

This time we laughed so long and so helplessly that people started peering at us to find out what was going on.

Cab!

"Night, Jim-Bob," said a voice. Bugs's voice, loud and firm.

"Night, Rich," came the immediate reply—hard to recognize, but I guessed Moshe.

I grinned at the darkness. I knew Bugs had been pissed off by the way we'd laughed at him, and knew this was his way of regaining—what? Authority or respect. And now his cue had been chucked directly back to me, the person who had caused the laughter. That must have grated.

My grin widened and I let the silence hang for a few seconds, then I said, "'Night, Jesse."

Jesse passed it to Ella, who passed it to an Aussie carpenter, who passed it to one of the Yugoslavian girls, and I tuned out the rest of the game.

There was a question that needed answering, I realized as I lay awake that night and listened to the laser beams hammering on the longhouse roof. Why did Bugs get on my nerves so much? Because he really did. I hadn't even realized how much until Jed had made me admit it.

I mean, it wasn't like he'd done anything bad to me or said anything rude. In fact I barely ever talked to him. Not *talk* talked. Our exchanges were all about work, arranging the carpentry detail to knock up some new spears, passing on a message from Gregorio or Unhygienix, stuff like that.

To answer the question I made a mental list of all the things he'd done to piss me off. There'd been his stupid stoicism when he hurt his leg, the thing with the soup, his almost wacky name. He also had an irritating competitive streak. If you'd watched the sun rise over Borobudur, he'd tell you that you should have seen the sun set, or if you knew of a good place to eat in Singapore, he'd know of one better. Or if you'd caught a shark with your bare hands . . .

I decided to deny him the chance to talk me through his tiger shark experience.

But anyway, these weren't big enough reasons. There had to be something else.

"Just a hunch then," I muttered, and rolled over to go to sleep, but it didn't satisfy me as an answer.

It would have been useful if Mister Duck had dropped by that night, because I could have asked him to fill me in more about Bugs's character. Unfortunately he didn't. He was a bit like taxis in that respect. Taxis and night buses.

Seeing Red

The rain continued to pour all through that week and half the next, but in the early hours of a Thursday morning it stopped. Everyone was relieved, and no one more than the fishing details. Sitting on the seabed for one-minute bursts, occasionally spotting a fish and usually missing it, had gotten old pretty fast. When we woke to see that the blue skies were back, we couldn't get down to the water quick enough. Something of a killing frenzy ensued—we caught our entire quota within an hour and a half—and after that, the only thing left to kill was time.

Gregorio and Etienne swam off to the coral gardens, and Françoise and I swam back to the beach to sunbathe. We lay in silence at first, me watching how much sweat could collect in my belly button before it spilled out, and Françoise on her front, sifting sand through her fingers. A few meters away, in the shade of the trees, our catch splashed in their buckets. Considering its source, the sound was strangely soothing. It complemented the moment—the sea breeze and the sunshine—and I missed it when the fish were all dead.

Not long after the last splash Françoise sat up, twisting gracefully out of her recline so that she was kneeling with her hands on her hips and her slim brown legs tucked neatly to the side. Then she rolled the top of her swimsuit down to her waist and stretched her arms up toward the blue sky. She held that pose for several seconds before relaxing again and dropping her hands into her lap.

Without thinking I sighed, and Françoise glanced at me. "What is the matter?" she said.

I blinked. "Nothing."

"You sighed."

"Oh . . . I was just thinking"—my mind ran through a quick list of options: the return of the sunshine, the stillness of the lagoon, the whiteness of the sand—"how easy it would be to stay here."

"Ah yes." Françoise nodded. "To stay on the beach forever. Very easy . . ."

I paused for a moment, then sat up too, spilling my sweat reservoir into the waistband of my shorts. "Do you ever think about home?"

"Paris?"

"Paris, family, friends . . . All that."

"Uh . . . no, Richard. I do not."

"I don't either. But don't you think that's a bit strange? I mean, I've got a whole life back in England that I can hardly remember, let alone miss. I haven't telephoned or written to my parents since arriving in Thailand, and I suppose I know they'll be worried about me, but I don't feel the urge to do anything about it. When I was in Koh Phangan, it didn't even cross my mind . . . Don't you think that's strange?"

"Parents . . ." Françoise frowned as if she were struggling to remember the word. "Yes, it is strange, but . . ."

"When did _you_ last contact them?"

"I do not know. . . . It was . . . That road. The road we met you."

"Ko Sanh."

"I called them from there . . ."

"Three months ago."

"Three months . . . Yes . . ."

We both lay back down on the hot sand. The mention of our parents was slightly disquieting and neither of us wanted to dwell on the subject.

But I did find it interesting that I wasn't the only one to experience the amnesiac effect of the beach. I wondered where the effect came from, and whether it was to do with the beach itself or the people on it. It suddenly occurred to me that I knew nothing about the past lives of my companions, except their place of origin. I'd spent countless hours talking to Keaty, and the only thing I knew about his background was that he used to go to Sunday school. I didn't know if he had brothers or sisters, or what his parents did, or which area of London he grew up in. We might have had a thousand shared experiences that we'd never made an effort to uncover.

The only talking topic that stretched beyond the circle of cliffs was travel. That was something we talked about a lot. Even now, I can still reel off the list of countries that my friends had visited. In a way it wasn't so surprising, considering that (apart from our ages) an interest in travel was the only thing we all had in common. And actually, travel conversation was a pretty good substitute for conversation about home. You could tell plenty about someone from the places they'd chosen to visit, and which of those places were their favorites.

Unhygienix, for example, reserved his deepest affection for Kenya, which somehow complemented his taciturn nature. It was easy to imagine him on safari, quietly absorbing the vastness of the landscape around him. Keaty, livelier and more prone to enthusiastic outbursts, was much more suited to Thailand. Etienne had an unfulfilled yearning to go to Bhutan, quietly good-natured fellow that he was, and Sal often talked about Ladakh—the northern province of India, laid-back in some ways and hard-edged in others. I knew my affection for the Philippines was equally as telling: a democracy on paper, apparently well ordered, regularly subverted by irrational chaos. A place where I'd felt instantly at home.

Amongst some of the others, Greg went for gentle southern India, Françoise for beautiful Indonesia. Moshe for Borneo (which I took as connected to the junglelike growth of his body hair), and the two Yugoslavian girls chose their own country, appropriately nationalistic and off the wall. Daffy, I didn't need to be told, would have chosen Vietnam.

Of course, I know that there's an element of pop psychology about how much you can read into people's favorite travel locations. You can choose which aspects of a nation's character you want to accept or ignore. In the case of Keaty, I chose liveliness and enthusiasm because mercenary and calculating didn't fit the bill, and in the case of Françoise I ignored dictatorship and mass murder in East Timor. But nonetheless, I have faith in the principle.

"I'm going to take the catch back," I said, standing up.
Françoise pushed herself up on to her elbows. "Now?"

"Unhygienix might be ready."

"He will not be ready."

"Well, no . . . but I fancy a walk. You want to come?"

"Where will you go?"

"Uh, don't know. I was thinking about heading for the waterfall or into the jungle somewhere . . . maybe to find that pool."

"No, I think I will stay here. Or maybe I will swim to the corals."

"Okay."

I walked to the buckets, and as I bent to lift them up I saw my face reflected in the bloody water. I paused to study myself, almost a silhouette with two bright eyes, and then I heard Françoise padding over the beach toward me. Her dark face appeared behind my shoulders and I felt her hand on my back.

"You do not want to come to the corals?"

"No." My fingers squeezed around the handles but I didn't straighten, knowing that if I did her hand would drop. "I'd rather go for a walk. . . . Are you sure you don't want to come?"

"Yes." Her red reflection shrugged. "It is too hot to walk today."

I didn't reply, and a couple of seconds later I heard her footsteps padding back across the sand. When I looked around she was wading into the water. I watched her until the water reached her torso, then started the walk back to camp.

Naturism

Facing in the direction of the mainland, the jungle to the left was familiar because the carpentry detail used it for their lumber. The area was crisscrossed with paths, some of which led to Jean's garden and the waterfall, some of which led down to the beach. To the right, however, the jungle was still virgin, so this was the direction I chose to explore.

The only path that led into it stopped after fifty meters. It had originally been cleared because a freshwater pool lay further along, and Sal had thought it could be converted as a larger substitute for the shower hut. The idea was abandoned when Cassie discovered that monkeys used the pool for drinking, and now the path was only used by people who, like me, were uncomfortable with the plastic pitcher option in the toilet. Judging from the faces I'd passed on the path, I'd say that accounted for at least three quarters of the camp. It was used commonly enough to have acquired a nickname—the Khyber Pass—and the regular tramping of our feet kept the weeds under control.

It took me half an hour to find my way to the pool, which turned out to be a slight disappointment. As I picked my way through the undergrowth, I'd been imagining a cool glade where I could bathe whilest watching monkeys swinging in the trees. Instead I found a muddy puddle and a cloud of flies. Flies that bit, I should add. I stayed by the pool for less than a minute. Then I pressed on into the jungle with the sound of primate laughter ringing in my ears.

Apart from the sharp grasses that occasionally nicked my legs, the walking wasn't taxing. Weeks without shoes had hardened the soles of my feet and left them almost numb. A few days before, I'd pulled a thorn from my heel, half a centimeter long. Its base had been covered in a crust of dirt and I guessed I'd been strolling around with it for quite some time, never feeling a thing.

The hardest part about walking was that my progress was so slow. I was constantly detouring around thickets and bamboo clusters, and I was never completely sure about which direction I was heading. This didn't worry me too much, because I was sure that sooner or later I'd reach the beach or the wall of cliffs. Unfortunately my confidence also meant I didn't make an effort to remember my route, so when I came across the papaya orchard, over an hour later, I didn't have a clue as to how I could ever find it again.

I call it an orchard for want of a better word. The papayas were random in size and spacing, so they hadn't been planted. Possibly the soil in that patch was particularly suitable or the limited room on the forest floor had kept them all together. Whatever, they made a wonderful sight. Much of the fruit was ripe, bright orange and as big as marrows, and the air was filled with sweetness.

I pulled one down with an easy twist of the stalk and split it open on a tree trunk. The fluorescent flesh tasted like melon and perfume—not, perhaps, as nice as it sounds, but pretty good all the same. Then I pulled out the joint I'd rolled before leaving the camp, found a clear area to sit, and settled down to watch smoke collect beneath the papaya leaves.

After a while, monkeys began to appear. I couldn't name their species but they were small and brown, with long tails and oddly catlike faces. At first they kept their distance. They didn't study me or register my presence in any way, beyond giving me a wide berth. But then a mother monkey with a tiny baby clinging to her stomach ambled over and took a piece of papaya from my hand. I hadn't even been holding it out to her—I'd been saving it until I finished the joint—but clearly she had other ideas. She casually helped herself, and I was too surprised to do anything but gape.

It didn't take long before another monkey followed the mother monkey's cue. Then another, and another. Within a couple of minutes the papaya was being pulled out of my hands as quickly as I could tear it from the fruit. My body was covered in sticky juice, my eyes were watering because I didn't have time to pull the joint from my lips, and little black fingers were pawing at me from all directions. Eventually all of them managed to get a chunk, and I was left sitting cross-legged in a sea of munching monkeys. I felt like David Attenborough.

It was the distinctive sound of falling water that finally led me out of the jungle. I heard it fifteen minutes after leaving the orchard, and then it was just a matter of zoning in on the noise.

I came out by the carved tree and immediately dived into the waterfall pool, keen to wash the sweat and papaya juice off my body. It was only when I came up that I realized I wasn't alone. Sal and Bugs were kissing, naked, in the penumbra of the spray.

Damn, I thought, and was about to swim discreetly back to the bank when Sal noticed me.

"Richard?"

"Hi, Sal. Sorry. I didn't see you there."

Bugs looked at me and smirked. It seemed to me that he was saying my apology was prurient. Gauche next to his relaxed but frank sexuality.

The prick. I held his gaze and his smile twisted into an inane sneer, the expression he should have started with.

"Don't be silly, Richard," Sal said, detaching herself from Bugs's embrace. "Where have you come from?"

"I went for a walk down the Khyber Pass and found a bunch of papaya trees, then ended up here."

"Papayas? How many?"

"Oh, loads."

"You should tell Jean, Richard. He's always interested in that sort of thing."

I shrugged. "The problem is, I doubt I could find them again. It's hard to keep your bearings in there."

Bugs revived the sneer. "It takes practice."

"Practice with a compass."

Smirk. "I spend so much time in the trees, I suppose I've got an instinct . . . almost animal, man . . ." He pushed his wet hair back with both hands. "Maybe I'll find them tomorrow."

"Good luck." I turned to go, adding, "Don't get lost," quietly.

I ducked under and swam back to the shore, surfacing only when the water was too shallow to cover me. But I hadn't escaped quite yet.

"Richard," Sal called as I hauled myself out. "Hang on."

I looked round.

"Are you heading back to the camp?"

"I was going to."

"Well . . . wait." She began to swim over, looking slightly like a turtle with her chin jutting up clear of the water. I waited until she reached me.

"Will you walk with me to the garden? I've got to go down there and Bugs has to go to the longhouse. I'd like some company, and we haven't talked for a while."

I nodded. "Okay, sure."

"Good."

She smiled and went to get her clothes.

The Good News

The walking pace Sal set was slow. Sometimes she paused to look at flowers or to pull a weed from the path. Sometimes she stopped for no apparent reason, aimlessly drawing dust circles with her toes.

"Richard," she began, "I want to tell you how pleased we all are that you found our secret beach."

"Thanks, Sal," I replied, already understanding that this conversation had a point beyond a casual chat.

"Can I be blunt, Richard? When you three arrived, we were all a little worried. Perhaps you can understand why . . ."

"Of course."

"But you all fitted in so *well*. You really entered into the spirit of what we have here, better than we could have hoped . . . You mustn't think we didn't appreciate you doing the Rice Run, Richard, and catching that lovely shark."

"Oh, well." I tried to look modest. "The shark was a fluke."

"Garbage, Richard. The shark gave everyone something to feel good about, and morale does get low during rainstorms. I still feel a little guilty about the way I spoke to you that wet morning, but sometimes I need to be . . . pushy. I don't consider myself to be the leader here, but . . ."

"We all understand that."

"Thank you, Richard."

"And you *are* the leader really, Sal."

"Oh, maybe in some ways I am. Reluctantly." She laughed. "People come to me with their problems and I try to sort them out . . . Keaty, for example. I know you and Keaty are close, so I presume you know about his problem."

"He wants to leave the garden detail."

"That's right. Such a headache. It isn't easy moving people around. Someone has to provide the space before he can move, and the fishing detail is already full. . . . He wants the fishing detail, you know."

"Uh-huh."

"For months now I've been telling him it isn't possible. You see, he was

about to start fishing when your little group arrived. He was terribly disappointed, Richard, but he took it very well. Others might have . . . I
don't know . . . held it against you."

"Sure. Three people turning up out of the blue, taking his job."

"Exactly, Richard. I was so grateful to him, and so pleased when you
became friends. I was only sorry I couldn't do anything to improve his situation . . ." A weed caught Sal's eye and she pulled it out, tutting at its
stubborn grip on the dirt. "But my hands were tied without a vacancy in
the fishing detail. And now I've realized that one isn't going to appear unless I make it. . . ."

I gulped. "Uh, no one wants to move, I suppose. What about one of the
Swedes?"

"One of the Swedes?" Sal chuckled. "You couldn't break up their trio
without a gun, and even then you'd have a job. No, they're together to the
death. The Three Blond Musketeers."

"Moshe?"

"Mmm . . . I don't think I'd want him to move. He's rather good with
those Yugoslavian girls."

"Who then?" I asked, and obviously failed to keep a note of anxiousness out of my voice.

"Yes, Richard. I'm sorry. I don't have a choice."

I groaned. "Oh no, Sal. Please, I really don't want to move. I love the
fishing detail, and I'm good at it."

"I *know* you are, Richard. I *know.* But do try to see it from my position.
Keaty needs to move out of the garden, I can't separate Etienne and
Françoise, Gregorio has been fishing for two years, the Yugoslavians . . ."
Sal shook her head. "Well I shouldn't really tell you this, Richard, but they
haven't the wit to do anything else. Jean can't bear them and they could
never cope with carpentry. I regret bringing them here at all. I'm a
pushover for refugees. . . . Truly, Richard, if I had a choice . . ."

"Yeah," I muttered.

". . . And it isn't like I'm going to put you in the garden detail."

I paused. "You aren't?"

"God, no. I don't think I'd be able to do that after the things Keaty
must have been telling you."

A terrible thought crossed my mind. Given a choice between the garden detail and working with Bugs in carpentry, I'd have taken Jean's iron

discipline anytime. "Well," I began to say, not bothering to disguise my nervousness. "He hasn't said that much . . ."

"I'm sure he's said plenty, Richard. No need to be diplomatic."

"No, Sal, honestly . . ."

She waved her hand. "It doesn't matter anyway. You won't be working in the garden detail . . ."

I closed my eyes, waiting for my sentence.

". . . you'll be working with Jed."

I opened my eyes again. *"Jed?"*

"Yes. He wants a partner on his excursions, and he suggested you."

"Wow," I said, genuinely. It had never occurred to me that Jed might want someone with him. Although we'd become friendly, he still struck me as a loner.

"I know, he never seemed the team type," Sal continued, apparently reading my mind. "I was just as surprised. You must have made a good impression on the Rice Run."

"But what does Jed need help with? Doesn't he just . . . steal grass?"

"He does that, yes, but other things besides. He'll explain."

". . . I see."

Sal beamed. "Richard, I'm so glad we've sorted it all out. I've been worried about telling you this for days . . . Now then, all that remains is to find Keaty. Would you like to give him the good news or shall I?"

Ich Bin Ein Beacher

When we reached the garden, Jean told us that Keaty had already started out back to the camp, so I jogged off to catch up to him and Sal stayed behind, explaining to Jean that he'd have to make do with one less worker.

I found Keaty a few hundred meters down the track, and when I told him the news he was very sympathetic, despite the fact that it was good news for him.

"I feel shit about this, Rich," he said after I'd finished explaining. "I didn't mean for Sal to take you off fishing, I swear."

I nodded. "My guess is, it has more to do with Jed than you. You've been asking to leave the garden detail since I got here, and it's only now that something's happened."

"Maybe . . . You're pissed off, right?"

". . . Well . . ."

"I'm sorry."

"No, it isn't your fault. It's just bad . . . luck. Or something. But not your fault."

"Well, I hope not, Rich . . . and I'm sorry anyway."

We walked in silence for a few moments, then Keaty said, "Do you know why Jed's suddenly decided he needs help?"

"I don't even know what he needs help with. We still don't know what he does up there."

"At least now we'll find out."

"I will, you mean. If I were to tell you what goes on I'd have to kill you straight after."

Keaty smiled. "You know what? I bet you're secretly pleased about all this. I bet you're looking forward to prowling around up there."

I shrugged. "Ask not what your beach can do for you."

"That's the spirit."

"Yeah . . ." I paused. "I suppose if I've got to leave the fishing detail, then I'd rather I was working with Jed than anyone else."

"Uh-huh. I wouldn't wish the garden detail on you."

"And the other option was carpentry. For a moment I thought that's what Sal was suggesting and I nearly had a fucking heart attack. I got this sudden flash of working with Bugs all day, so when Sal said it was with Jed . . . I don't know . . . I had to feel relieved."

"If you say so, Rich."

"I think I do."

We turned a corner on the path and saw the longhouse through the trees. There were figures around the kitchen hut, so I guessed the other fishers were back with their catch. I couldn't see any of my detail. They probably weren't back from the corals yet.

Just as we were about to enter the clearing, someone behind us called our names. We both turned round and saw Jesse jogging along the track with a bag of vegetables from the garden.

"Hey, man," he said to Keaty as he reached us. "Hear you're leaving the Jar Dan." It took me a couple of seconds to translate his Kiwi accent to *jardin*.

"Yep. I'm moved to the fishing."

"I heard, you lucky bastard." Jesse looked at me. "Not you though, mate. You must be pissed off, losing that cushy number. You'll be sweating with us now."

"I'm not going to the garden."

Jesse grinned. "Carpentry! With Jesus!"

"No. Jed."

"Jed?"

"Uh-huh."

"Blow me. What's all that about? Not enough weed to go round?"

"Maybe. I'll find out soon, anyway."

"Yeah . . . You will." He nodded thoughtfully, then he patted Keaty on the back. "You'll be all right, anyhow. Get to watch Françoise swimming all day. I could do with a bit of that."

Keaty shot me a quick glance, which puzzled me, and said, "Watch it, Jesse. You don't want Cassie to hear you."

Jesse laughed. "Too right. Skin me alive." He winked at no one in particular, then looked into the clearing. "So. Looks like the cooks have got food on the way. Better get the veg down there."

"Sure," said Keaty, and Jesse jogged off. Keaty watched him go, then turned to me. "He's the one person I'll really miss from the garden detail."

"Seems like a decent guy."

"He is. You'd like him and Cassie a lot. Especially as they aren't exactly Bugs's biggest fans."

"Oh?"

"I used to bitch about Jean being a tough boss, but Bugs . . . he drives Cassie nuts."

"I'd picked up on that before."

". . . I guess you'll miss working with your detail too."

"Mmm." I took a deep breath and exhaled slowly. Probably too deeply and too slowly, because I noticed Keaty giving me another curious glance. "I'm sure I will."

Dislocation

It was a long walk from where I entered the clearing to where Etienne, Françoise, and Gregorio stood talking. I had plenty of time to think about how much the change of work detail would affect my life on the beach. Mainly I thought in rapid slide-show images, different shots of the four of us chatting and having fun: diving off our favorite fishing boulder, taking bets on who would catch the biggest fish, swimming for spears that had missed their mark or found their mark, or reenacting throws that were comically bad. The image I lingered on the longest was, unsurprisingly, of Françoise. Françoise as an Amazon, frozen with a spear poised above her head, concentrating fiercely on the shapes beneath the water. Even now it's a picture I can clearly recall.

It seemed to me, as I got nearer, that they must have heard the news. They paused in their conversation and all turned, watching me with quiet and serious expressions. But it was simply that they'd read the look on my face. That and my posture, and the speed I was walking. If someone walks unhurriedly toward you, head bowed, you have to know that something's up.

There was a strange moment when I reached them. They remained silent, waiting for me to speak, but I felt like I'd already been isolated from their group. It reminded me of the first morning after my fever, discovering that Etienne and Françoise had made themselves a part of the new world while I had been asleep. When no words came I frowned and put a hand on the back of my neck, then shrugged helplessly.

"What is it, Richard?" said Etienne apprehensively. "There is something the matter?"

I nodded.

"What? Tell us."

". . . I'm off the fishing detail."

"Off?"

"Moving to another detail. Sal . . . She just told me."

Françoise gasped. "But why? How can she do that?"

"Something to do with Jed. He needs a work partner. Keaty's going to replace me."

Gregorio shook his head. "But wait, Richard. You do not want to move, yes?"

"I like the fishing detail . . ."

"Then okay. You will stay. I will find Sal and talk to her now." Then he marched off toward the longhouse.

"Gregorio will stop this," said Etienne a few moments later. "Do not worry, Richard. You will not have to move."

"You will not have to move," Françoise echoed. "We are a good team, Richard. Of course you will stay with us."

I nodded, pleased by my friends' display of solidarity, but at the same time I was entirely unconvinced. I knew that Sal's decision would be final, and, as if to force the point home, the sound of her low voice began to drift across the clearing, telling Gregorio that this was the only way it could be.

Although I was feeling sorry for myself, unsure of the sudden way in which things had developed, as the day went on I felt more sorry for Keaty. After Gregorio's failure to change Sal's mind, the four of us spent the rest of the afternoon sitting in a circle, getting stoned and bitching about the way things had turned out. Keaty, however, sat by the entrance of his tent. He was apparently engrossed in his Gameboy, but he looked miserable. I think he felt responsible for everything, and it must have been depressing to feel that his new workmates were so unhappy with the circumstances of his arrival.

Eventually, Keaty's obvious discomfort became intolerable. Sensing that the onus was on me, I called over to him and suggested he join us. He sheepishly put down his Nintendo and came over, immediately launching into an apology for the situation he felt he'd caused. All of us protested at once but it did nothing to cheer him up. He also told us that he'd spoken to Sal himself, insisting that he didn't mind remaining in the garden detail, to no effect. This, at least, provided a topic of discussion that didn't make Keaty's discomfort any more acute, because it raised the underlying reason for the job switch.

"Perhaps," Françoise said, "there is something happening on the island. Something to do with the drug farmers."

Keaty muttered his agreement, but Gregorio looked doubtful. "So maybe the Thais are putting new fields on this side of the island. It would be a problem, but why would Jed need a partner? If he had ten or fifty partners, he could not stop them. There is no difference."

"Is there ever any talking with the Thais?" Etienne asked.

Gregorio shook his head. "Daffy spoke to them when they first came, but he is the only one. He said they knew we were here already, and they were not interested in us if we did not move from the lagoon. Since then, nothing."

"Maybe they've got pissed off with Jed nicking grass," I suggested.

"Yes, but it is the same thing. If they are angry or not angry, what difference if Jed has a partner?"

"So what else could it be?"

Gregorio looked down at his hands, then back at me. "I do not know, Richard . . . I really do not know."

We continued chatting until late evening, but only going round in circles. Without Jed or Sal, there was no way our questions could be answered, but Jed was still absent by the time we went to bed, and no one felt like talking to Sal.

It took me over two hours to get to sleep that night, and the thoughts that kept me awake were as unusual as the rest of the day had been. For the first time since arriving on the beach, I started thinking about home. Almost, in fact, wishing I could return. Not to leave the beach permanently; just to contact a few important people and let them know I was still alive and okay. My family particularly, and a few of my friends.

I suppose it may have had as much to do with my earlier conversation with Françoise as with the subsequent unsettling events. The mention of parents had hovered in the back of my mind, reluctant to fall under the beach's amnesiac spell.

The Decisive Moment

"Hi," said a voice, and I turned round. A small boy was standing in the gateway of the house behind me. He grinned and marched over the pavement. "Would you like a drink?"

I looked at him blankly. Mister Duck was fair-haired and close to tubby as a child. It surprised me that this well-fed kid would become the scrawny figure I'd meet on the Ko Sanh Road.

"That is you, isn't it?" I said, to make certain.

"It's me." His chubby arms stretched out and clapped me on the shoulders. "Would you like a drink?"

"Well . . ." I rubbed my throat. "What have you got?"

"Orange squash or water."

"Orange squash is good."

"Okay. Wait here."

Mister Duck went inside the house, waddling slightly as he walked. I wondered if that was where his nickname had originally come from. A minute later he came back out, holding a cup in both hands.

"I'm afraid it's not really very cold. It takes ages for the tap to run cold."

"That's okay."

He gave me the cup and watched me closely while I drank it.

"Is it all right? Maybe I should've put some ice in it."

"It's very nice."

"I can get some ice for you."

"No." I drained the remainder. "It was just right."

"Great!" He smiled radiantly. "You want to see my room?"

Mister Duck's bedroom was a lot like mine had been: clothes in heaps, dog-eared posters on the walls, duvet scrunched up at the bottom of the mattress, battered matchbox cars on the shelves, marbles and toy soldiers everywhere else. The main difference was that I'd shared my room with my younger brother, so the mess was doubled.

In the middle of the floor was a collapsed pile of Tintin and Asterix books.

"Shit," I said admiringly, as I spotted them. "That's a good collection."

Mister Duck's eyes opened wide, then he ran to his bedroom door and peered nervously out. "Richard," he hissed, turning back to me with a sternly raised finger, "you mustn't say that!"

". . . Shit?"

His tiny face went bright red and he waved his arms. "Shh! Someone will hear you!"

"But . . ."

"No buts!" He dropped his voice to a whisper. "Swearing carries a twopence fine in this house!"

"Oh . . . right. I won't swear anymore."

"Good," he said gravely. "I should ask you for some money, but you didn't know the rule, so we'll leave it at that."

"Thanks . . ." I walked over to the pile of books and picked one up— *Cigars of the Pharaoh*. "So you like Tintin, huh?"

"I *love* Tintin! Do you? I've got every Tintin book except one."

"I've got every Tintin book except none."

"Including *The Blue Lotus?*"

"Only in French."

"Exactly! That's why I haven't got it. It really annoys me."

"You should get someone to talk you through it. My mum went through it with me. It's pretty good."

Mister Duck shrugged. "My mum can't speak French."

"Oh."

"So which is your favorite one?"

"Hmm. Tricky question." I thought for a couple of seconds. "It isn't *Tintin in America*."

"No. And it isn't *The Castafiore Emerald*."

"No way. It might be *Tintin in Tibet* . . . or *The Crab with the Golden Claws*. I can't decide."

"Do you want to know what my favorite is?"

"Sure."

"*Prisoners of the Sun.*"

I nodded. "That's a good choice."

"Yes. Would you like to know another book I like?"

"Okay."

Mister Duck walked over to his bed and crouched down, feeling around underneath. Then he dragged out a large hardback, coffee table size. Its cover was plain red and stamped with gold-leaf writing. It read: *Time. A Decade in Photographs: 1960–1970.*

"This book is my dad's," he said airily, squatting down and beckoning me to sit beside him. "I'm not even supposed to have it in my room. You know what?"

"What."

"In this book"—he paused for dramatic effect—"there's a picture of a girl."

I snorted. "Big deal."

"A naked girl!"

"Naked?"

"Uh-huh. You want to see it?"

"Sure."

"Okay . . . hold on." Mister Duck started flicking through the pages. "It's somewhere near the middle . . . Ah! Here it is!"

I pulled the book onto my lap.

The girl was indeed naked, and aged between ten and twelve, I guessed. She was running down a country road.

Mister Duck leaned over and put his mouth to my ear. "You can see *everything!*" he whispered excitedly.

"You certainly can," I agreed.

"Everything! All her bits!" He started giggling and rolled forward with his hands over his mouth. "Everything!"

"Yes," I said, but I was suddenly feeling uncertain. There was something puzzling about the photo.

I noticed the fields that surrounded the country road; they were strangely flat and alien. Then I noticed the collection of indistinct buildings behind the girl, either out of focus or made fuzzy through clouds of smoke. And the girl was upset, holding her arms away from her sides. Other kids ran beside her. A few soldiers, apparently indifferent, watched them as they passed.

I frowned. My gaze flicked quickly from the girl to the soldiers, back to the girl again. It was as if my eyes had become confused, unsure of where to settle. I wasn't even sure what they were settling on.

"Fuck," I muttered, and shut the book with a snap.

Mister Duck sat up. "I'm sorry, Rich," he said. "But I've already warned you once about swearing. This time it's going to cost you."

in country

Aspect One

Jed's eyes were a little wider apart than mine, so it took some adjustment before I was seeing one crisp circle instead of two hazy ones. Then I had to scan slowly across the sea, steadying myself on my elbows as the tiniest movement sent the image a mile off track. It took me several seconds to find the strip of sand and line of green palms, but once there, I located the five familiar figures almost immediately. They were in the same place they'd been yesterday morning, and nearly every morning for the past nine days. The only exception had been four days ago when the beach was completely empty. That had caused us a bit of concern, until they reappeared from the treeline a couple of hours later.

"They're still there," I said.

"Up to anything?"

"Uh-uh."

"Just lying there."

"Looks like one is standing, but he isn't moving."

"And you can count all five."

I paused. "Five, yeah. They're all there."

"Good." Jed coughed quietly into his hand. We had to be careful about noise, this close to the dope fields, and we couldn't smoke either, which didn't do much for my nerves.

My first day with Jed had started off badly. I'd woken up in a shit mood, the previous night's dream still clinging to me, faintly depressed about leaving the fishing detail. But as soon as he'd explained about the people, I'd understood. Then I'd been thrown into a panic, saying, "It's the worst-case scenario," over and over like a mantra, while Jed patiently waited for me to calm down. It took some time but eventually I stopped jittering long enough for him to get a word in edgeways, and I was able to take in the exact nature of the situation.

The good news was that Sal still didn't know about my indiscretion with the map. Jed had only told her that we had new guests on the neighboring island, but not that they might have a connection with me. As far as Sal was concerned, the reason I was working with Jed was because he'd gotten fed up with being alone and wanted a partner. The other good news was that the people had been hanging around on the island for two days before Sal had agreed to move me. So if they were aiming for our beach, they were obviously finding it difficult to reach us.

On the downside, we had to assume that the people *were* aiming for the beach. We also had to assume that two of them were Zeph and Sammy, and the other three were the Germans that Jed had seen on Koh Phangan. We couldn't be sure about this because the people were too small to make out clearly, even to see a flash of blond hair, but it seemed likely.

I'd spent the rest of that day in a state of shock, sitting with Jed's binoculars clamped to my face, convinced—every time one of them appeared to move—that they were about to start swimming toward us. But they didn't. In fact they barely budged from their patch of sand, occasionally taking a brief dip or disappearing into the jungle for a couple of hours. After three or four similar days had passed, my initial level of panic became impossible to sustain. It faded, mellowing into anxiousness, finally settling as a generalized tension. With the tension I was able to think more clearly and, in a manner of speaking, relax. That was when the other aspects of my new detail begin to emerge.

The first was getting to know Jed. We spent every hour until nightfall sitting on a rocky outcrop at the highest point of our island, and aside from the spying, all we could do was talk. Mostly we talked about plan B, which was what we were going to do when they finally got here. The only problem with plan B was that, like most plan B's, it didn't exist. We had several options but could never agree on which one to take. The option I favored was that Jed would go down to intercept them and explain that they weren't welcome on the beach, but he didn't want to do that. Although he was sure he'd be able to make them leave, he was also sure that they'd go straight back to Koh Phangan and tell everyone what they'd found. Instead Jed wanted to rely on the island's natural barriers. There was the swim, they had to get past the dope fields, find the lagoon, and then find a way of getting down to it. Jed was confident that this obstacle course would put them off, apparently unconcerned that it had failed to deter me, Etienne, Françoise, the Swedes, and himself.

It was during one of our endless plan B discussions that I discovered Jed had once watched me in exactly the same way as we were now watching Zeph and Sammy. He'd seen the spiv drop us off and when we made the swim he'd told Sal—which was why she, Bugs, and Cassie had been ready to greet us when we reached the camp. This was the main function of his detail, as a lookout, and the dope collecting had been more of a sideline. He went on to tell me that since his arrival, there had been three groups that had tried to find the lagoon. Two had given up at one or another of the obstacles. The ones to get through had been the Swedes.

Knowing this made me feel marginally less guilty about having given out a copy of the map, because people were managing to find us anyway. Jed explained that they'd heard about the beach as the Eden rumor Zeph had described. Jed himself had heard it from a guy in Vientiane, and "with nothing better to do," he'd decided to follow the rumor up. He'd had to check out six other islands in the Marine Park before finding the right one. The Swedes had gone on more concrete information. They'd overheard Sal talking with Jean on a Chaweng Rice Run.

It came as a surprise to me to hear that acting as a lookout was the primary function of my new detail. I couldn't understand why the job needed to be clouded in so much mystery, and Jed, in turn, was a little surprised to hear that the mystery existed. He admitted that Sal didn't want it talked about, as she felt it would be bad for the morale, but as far as he was concerned, the main reason he didn't talk about it was because nobody ever asked him.

This had led to the most interesting revelation about Jed, connected to Daffy's reaction to his uninvited arrival on the beach. I remembered Keaty telling me that the camp had listened outside the longhouse while Daffy shouted and Sal tried to calm him down. What I didn't know was that Daffy had refused to speak to Jed from that day on. For thirteen months, until Daffy left the island, he and Jed had never exchanged a single word. It had been the original reason for the creation of Jed's detail: to keep him away from the rest of the camp for most of the day.

I felt a great deal of pity for Jed when he told me this. It explained why he'd always seemed so distant from the rest of us. His apparent aloofness was only because he felt he ought to keep out of people's way, even now that a year and a half had passed. It also explained why he so conspicuously accepted unpopular tasks, such as the Rice Run.

But Jed didn't appear to feel any pity for himself. When I suggested to him that it must have been hard to face such a cold reaction, he shrugged and said he could understand it.

"Something's bothering me," I said, putting down Jed's binoculars.

Jed frowned. "You and me both."

"I'm afraid they'll find my rucksack."

". . . Your rucksack?"

"I hid my rucksack there, and so did Etienne and Françoise. We couldn't swim with them . . . and if they find our bags they'll know they're on the right track."

"How well did you hide them?"

"Pretty well. The thing is, I'm starting to think I might have copied the map down wrong. I drew it in a real hurry and there were a lot of islands to fill in. I remember there were differences between Daffy's map and the map in Etienne's guidebook too. I easily could have missed out an island between Koh Angthong and here."

Jed nodded. "It's possible."

"So if they reckon they're on the right island, that explains why they haven't moved for the last nine days. They're checking the place out, looking for the beach . . . which they won't find, but they might find the rucksacks."

"It's possible," Jed repeated. "But they might also have spent the last nine days wondering how the fuck they're going to get back to Koh Phangan."

"And wondering how they could have been so stupid as to believe in a map that someone slid under their door."

"That would make them about as stupid as you then."

"Stupid as me . . . Yeah."

Jed scowled and ran his hands over his face. "What I want to know is what they're doing for food and water."

"Magi-Noodles and chocolate. That's what we did."

"And water? They'd have needed to take a barrel of the stuff to've lasted this long."

"Maybe there's a source on the island. It's high enough."

"Must be . . . I'll tell you what, though, you're wrong about that map. Look at them. They sit in that one spot all fucking day. It faces us, right? So they *know* this is the right island. They're sitting there and trying to work out how to reach us . . ."

I sighed. "You know what we should do?"

"No."

"We should take the boat and head round to them. Then we get them on board, set a course for the open sea, and make them walk the plank. Problem solved."

Jed tilted his head at the sky. "Okay, Richard, let's do it."

"Okay. Let's."

"Okay."

"Okay."

We looked at each other briefly, then I went back to staring through the binoculars.

White Lies

We'd stay on our lookout post until the bottom curve of the sun was just about to hit the horizon line, then we'd head back. There wasn't much point in spying if it was too dark to see, and anyway, Jed said it wasn't safe to be up on the island after nightfall. You didn't know what or who you might walk into. Back at camp, Jed would go and talk to Sal, filling her in on the day's nonevents, and I'd get some dinner. Then, carrying my bowl of leftovers, I'd look for my old fishing detail. Usually I'd find them near the kitchen hut, having a smoke before bedtime.

Lying to Sal and Bugs was easy, but I hated lying to my old detail, and

I hated lying to Keaty even more. The truth was that I didn't have a choice. Until we knew whether Zeph and Sammy would make it to the beach, there was no sense in stirring. The best I could do was to satisfy Keaty's curiosity about the exact nature of Jed's work, and when I told him, he wasn't as surprised as I'd expected him to be.

"It's a good idea," he said, matter of factly. "Since the Swedes, people have been worried about who might turn up."

"What about since me?"

"Daffy told you. It's different."

"Were people angry about the Swedes then?"

". . . Daffy mainly."

"Jed said Daffy didn't like him much, either."

Keaty started cleaning his Gameboy screen against his shorts. "He didn't make it very easy for any of them, but once they were here . . . you know . . . what could he do?"

"Is that why he left the beach?"

My question hung in the air while Keaty carefully inspected the tiny glass panel.

I asked him again.

"Basically," he said eventually. "Yeah." He pushed in the Mario cart and switched on the machine. "You completed this yet?"

"About twenty times."

"I was wondering where the batteries were going . . ." He gazed at the Nintendo but didn't begin playing. "So what do you do if you find someone coming?" he asked casually.

". . . Just watch them, I guess."

Keaty grinned. "You mean you take them out, right? Terminate with extreme prejudice."

"I'll tell you when it happens," I replied, laughing uncomfortably, and was spared any further questions by the arrival of Jesse, looking for some rizlas.

After that conversation I'd more or less managed to avoid the subject of my detail. It wasn't difficult. Keaty had taken to his work in a big way and it only needed a small nudge to get him talking about it. To my relief, the same applied with my other ex-colleagues, so I could always steer the conversation toward fishing. From their point of view, I suppose they were trying to emphasize my inclusion in the group by sticking to topics of shared experience. From my point of view, I was happy to talk about anything that upheld a sense of normality.

For the first few days, during my panicky stage, this was a bit of an effort. Given the way I was feeling, a calm exterior required constant concentration. When I let my guard drop I would drift off into my own anxious thoughts while people were talking to me. I could only use the excuse of being stoned or tired up to a point.

But there was a helpful side to the constant concentration: I never had time to feel jealous of the ease with which Keaty had replaced me, or sad that the secrets I was keeping were creating unexpected barriers between me and my friends. Unexpected because I'd been worried that the detail would distance me from them, but soon I understood that it actually distanced them from me. I was still involved in their lives. I knew what was going on. I knew when they'd caught a strange fish, and that Jean was trying to lure Keaty back to the garden, and that Cassie was trying to arrange a move from carpentry so she could work with Jesse, and that Bugs wasn't having any of it.

I no longer had to struggle to maintain a calm appearance. In theory, perhaps then I should have started to feel jealous of Keaty and sad about the lies. But I didn't. I realized that I had been given one less problem to worry about, because if I was the one creating the distance, then I had equal power to remove it. And if Zeph and Sammy failed in their attempt to reach us, I would be able to bring my friends closer without any effort. It would simply be a matter of not lying to them anymore, which would be easy, as there'd be nothing to lie about. Obviously, this was only a comfort if Zeph and Sammy failed to reach us, but if they didn't fail, then Sal would certainly get to hear about the map, and I'd be fucked anyway.

It was in this frame of mind—alert but calm or something close—that the second aspect of my new detail emerged. I think I first noticed it on the fifth day, when I woke half an hour before Jed and impatiently counted the minutes until it was time to go. Or maybe it was the sixth day, when the figures were missing from their beach and we scanned the sea for three silent hours, coolly professional, nothing to be said, until they reappeared. Most accurately, Keaty noticed it first, although he didn't realize it at the time. "I bet you're secretly looking forward to prowling around up there," he'd joked when I told him about the switch in details, but my mood had been too sour to see that he was right.

There was nothing strange about it. Jed and I were on a covert mission. We had binoculars, jungle, a quarry, a threat, the hidden presence of AK-47s and slanted eyes. The only missing element was a Doors sound track.

Too familiar to be strange, and too exciting to dread. Before long, impossible not to enjoy.

Ol' Blue

At the end of the tenth day we were, as usual, hurry-ing to get back to the lagoon before nightfall. The sun was already below the western curve of the seaward cliffs and the orange light of early evening was turning blue. Whenever we were on the move we wouldn't talk, so all our communication was made by way of hand signals. A clenched fist meant stop and stay still, a flat palm held horizontally to the ground meant hide, a pointing gesture with all fingers together meant move forward cautiously. We'd never discussed the meanings of these signs; neither had we discussed the new words we'd started using. We'd say, "I'll take point," instead of, "I'll walk first," and we described distances in terms of Klicks. I don't actually remember how or when these things had been adopted. I think they'd simply felt like the most appropriate vocabulary for the circumstance.

That evening, Jed had taken point. He always did if the light was failing, because he knew the island so much better than I did. I was having a little difficulty keeping up with him, unable to find his easy compromise between speed and stealth, and when he gave the clenched fist signal I missed it and walked straight into his back. The fact that he didn't frown or swear made me aware that something serious was up. I eased myself away from him and stood still.

Just ahead of us the jungle became patchy and broke into a wide area of grasses and shrubs, so at first I assumed that Jed had seen someone in the clearing. Then I noticed that his gaze was pointed almost directly at his feet. For a couple of moments we both remained motionless. I still couldn't tell what the problem was because his body was obscuring my view. After a long minute of silence, I cautiously reached out and tapped him on the shoulder. He didn't react and it suddenly struck me that there could be a poisonous snake on the ground in front of him. I glanced around for a stick but I couldn't see one; then I inched to the side in order to get a better view.

I would have gasped if my jaw and chest muscles hadn't seized up. Lying less than a meter from Jed's feet was a Thai. He was flat on his back, eyes closed, and he had an automatic rifle lightly resting in the crook of his arm. Jed slowly moved his head to face me, as if he was afraid that by disturbing the air he might wake the man up. "What now?" he mouthed. I jabbed a finger in the direction we'd come, but he shook his head. I nodded vigorously, and Jed shook his head again, glowering. Then he pointed at his foot. He was standing on the barrel of the rifle. The pressure had lifted the butt several inches above the Thai's bare arm. As soon as he moved his foot away, the butt would drop.

"Shit," I mouthed, and Jed rolled his eyes desperately.

I thought for a minute. Then I started to creep backward along the track. Jed stared at me, as if to say, "Where the fuck are you going?" but I raised a hand to tell him not to worry. I knew what to do because I'd seen it done on *Tour of Duty*.

I can never remember the names on *Tour of Duty*. That's partly because the series is so terrible, but it's also because the characters come from the same school as *NYPD Blue* (black lieutenant, unorthodox cops who get results). So in *Tour of Duty* you have the tough sergeant who knows all the tricks, the green lieutenant who learns all the tricks, the simple southern hick who learns to make friends with the sassy blacks, the Hispanic whom you can rely on in a firefight, and the East Coaster who wears glasses and probably reads books. The names really aren't important.

The main thing is the scenes that these characters play out. These would include tending for the orphan who's been wounded by shrapnel, stopping a rival platoon from doing a Zippo raid, leaping from helicopters into a whirlpool of flattened grass, hugging comrades as they cough and die, and dealing with mines.

The platoon is walking through the jungle when suddenly there is a barely audible click. Everyone hits the dirt except one man, an FNG, who stands rigid with fear. "I don't wanna die, Sarge!" he blurts, and starts to recite the Lord's Prayer. Sarge crawls over on his belly. "You hang on in there, soldier," he mutters. He knows what to do. He had the same thing happen in Korea, '53.

Bizarrely, Sarge starts to tell the soldier about an apparently unrelated incident that happened when he was a kid, working on his daddy's farm. Sarge had a hound dog that he loved dearly, name of Ol' Blue, and the soldier listens, distracted by the clever ploy. Meanwhile, Sarge is easing his knife under the soldier's boot and sweat is cutting a line through the dirt on his brow.

Ol' Blue was caught in a rabbit snare, Sarge explains, and every time he struggled the snare grew tighter. The soldier nods, still not grasping the connection. "What happened to Ol' Blue?" the soldier asks. "Did ya get him out, Sarge?" "Sure we did, soldier," Sarge replies. Then he tells the soldier to lift his foot, nice and easy now. The soldier is confused, frightened, but he trusts Sarge. He does as he is told, and Sarge slips a rock on to the knife blade, maintaining the pressure on the mine. Sarge chuckles. "Son, all Ol' Blue had to do was relax."

I wasn't going to start blathering on to Jed about 'Ol Blue. As I gently laid the stone on the rifle barrel, even the noise of rock scraping against metal sounded like someone hammering on a petrol drum. When the stone was positioned I looked up at Jed. He shrugged calmly and motioned for me to get up. I suppose he wanted me to be ready to start running if the gun dropped.

Inch by inch, Jed eased up his foot. The butt shifted downward a fraction and I heard him draw in a quick breath, but it didn't contact the Thai's arm. We exchanged a glance, stepped gingerly over the man's legs, and continued quietly down the island.

It took us another forty-five minutes to reach the top of the waterfall, and I grinned continuously every step of the way. I was grinning so much my jaws were aching, and if we hadn't needed to keep silent I would have been laughing out loud.

Credit

I dove off the waterfall that day, much to Jed's sur-prise, and much to my surprise too. I hadn't been planning on it. We were standing on the cliff edge looking at the sunset, which was cloudless and very beautiful and deserved a moment's reflection. Sometimes, with these cloudless evenings, the light played a strange trick. Instead of beams of brightness radiating out from the horizon, there were beams of darkness—in other words, the polarized image of a traditional sunset. At first glance you accepted the image, only vaguely aware that something about it was wrong. Then, as with Escher's endless staircase, you suddenly realized it made no logical sense at all. Each time I saw this effect it intrigued me and I could always pass twenty quiet minutes pleasantly confounded.

Jed had no better answers for the phenomenon than I did, but he always gave it a try. "Shadows, cast by clouds hidden behind the horizon line," he was arguing that night, when I tapped him on the arm and said, "Watch this." Then I toppled forward. The next instant I was watching the cliff face rushing past me and feeling a distant sense of alarm that my legs were bent. Their displaced weight was turning me in the air, and I was in danger of landing on my back. I tried to straighten them and a moment later I hit the pool, where I spun through several violent underwater revolutions, lost all the air from my lungs, and drifted back to the surface.

Up on the cliff top I could see Jed watching me with his hands on his hips. He didn't say anything but I knew he disapproved. A little while later he snapped at me as we made our way from the waterfall pool to the camp, although it may also have had something to do with the song I was singing.

It was: "I saw a mouse! Where? There on the stair. Where on the stair? Right there! A little mouse with clogs on, well I declare, going *clip-clippity-clop* on the stair, *right there!*"

"Jesus, Richard!" he said as I looped the tune and began the chorus again. "What's got into you?"

"I'm singing," I replied breezily.

"I know you are. Cut it out."

"You don't know that song?"

"No."

"You must know it. It's famous."

"It's the stupidest song I ever heard."

I shrugged. I couldn't deny it was a stupid song.

We walked in silence for a few minutes, me turning the tune over in my head and humming under my breath; then Jed said, "You know, you want to watch yourself, Richard." I didn't know what he meant so I kept quiet, and a couple of seconds later he added, "You're high."

". . . High?"

"Dope. High."

"I haven't smoked a joint since last night."

"Exactly," he said with emphasis.

". . . You're saying I should cut down on smoking dope?"

"I'm saying dope's got nothing to do with it." A branch was blocking our path and he held it aside until I passed him, then let the branch snap back. "That's why you should watch yourself."

I snorted dismissively. The way he was talking reminded me of his obscure references to blame on Koh Phangan. Sometimes Jed could be willfully cryptic, and uncharitably I decided that his attitude had probably led to his alienated position in the beach life just as much as the awkward circumstances of his arrival. That, in turn, made me think of my own budding alienation.

"Jed," I said, after a pause. "Do you think it would be okay if I told people about our run-in with the dope guard? It doesn't involve Zeph and Sammy . . ."

"Mmm."

". . . See, I'm constantly being coy about what we're doing up on the island. I sort of feel like this would be a chance for me to—"

"Tell them," he interrupted. "No harm. It's probably a good idea."

"Uh-huh?"

"We don't want it to seem like we're hiding stuff from people."

"Great," I said, and started to whistle the first bars of the mouse song before catching myself.

It was pitch-black back at the camp. What color remained in the sky was entirely blocked by the canopy ceiling. The only light came from candles through the open door of the longhouse and spatterings of red cigarette and joint butts, glowing in clusters around the clearing.

Although I was looking forward to telling my ex-detail about the sleeping guard, my first thought was food, so I aimed straight for the kitchen hut. Every day Unhygienix wrapped a couple of portions in banana leaf for me and Jed, and made sure we got some of the choicest bits of fish. It was cold by the time we'd get to it, but I was usually too hungry to mind. That night I noticed Unhygienix had added papaya to the stew, which irritated me slightly as it meant Bugs had succeeded in tracking down my orchard.

After getting my dinner portion I walked around the clearing, joining the dots between the clusters of smokers, looking for my friends. Unusually, they were nowhere to be found, and nobody seemed to know where they were. Confused, I checked Keaty's tent and then the longhouse, where I found Unhygienix, Cassie, and Ella playing blackjack, and, further up, Jesse writing in his diary.

"Ah!" said Unhygienix when he saw me, and pointed to my food. "What do you think?"

"Of the stew?"

"Yes. You notice the fruit? A good taste?"

"Sure. Sweet and savory. Very Thai."

Unhygienix beamed. "You know what I did? I made some papaya juice and stewed it with the fish, but I only put in the flesh in the last two minutes, or it falls apart in the heat. So this way you have the taste and the texture."

"Ah."

"And Richard, we can have this again, because Jean will plant the seeds and we will grow papaya in the garden. I am very pleased with this dish."

"You should be. It tastes really good. Well done."

Unhygienix shook his head modestly. "You should be thanking Bugs."

". . . Why is that?" I said suspiciously.

"He discovered these papayas in the jungle."

I choked on a fish bone. "Bugs did what?"

"In the jungle, he found a whole orchard of papayas and monkeys."

"No he didn't!"

"Yes. Yesterday, he found this orchard."

"I found the fucking orchard! I found it a couple of weeks ago!"

". . . Really?"

"Was Bugs saying he found it?"

". . . Uh . . ."

Cassie smiled. "Yes, he was."

"That *prick!*" In my temper I squeezed the banana leaf and some of the stew spilled onto the ground.

"Careful," said Ella.

I frowned, suddenly aware that I was making a scene. "Well, anyway . . . he's lying."

"Don't worry," Cassie chuckled, laying down a long run from threes to picture cards. "We don't doubt it."

"Good."

They went back to their game and I continued up the longhouse toward Jesse.

"I heard," he said dryly, as I approached. "Congratulations on finding the papayas."

"Yes, well, it isn't a big thing. It just . . ."

"Got on your nerves," he finished for me, and lowered his diary. "Course it did. Understood. Are you looking for Keaty?"

"Yeah." I nodded morosely. As a consequence of the papayas my mood had gone bad. "And the others. I can't find them. I think they've all gone off together somewhere."

"Right. He left me a message to give you."

"Oh," I said, perking up a bit. "Let's hear it."

"It was a note. I put it on your bed."

I thanked him and jogged the rest of the way up the longhouse, keen to find out what was going on.

The note was folded on my pillow, and beside it was a rolled joint. It read: "Smoke this quick! Phosphorescence! Keaty!"

I frowned. "Hey, Jesse," I called. "What does the note mean?"

I waited while he completed his sentence; then he looked up. "Dunno, mate. Didn't read it. What's it say?"

"Phosphorescence. And it's got a joint."

"Ah." Jesse waggled his pencil at me. "Phosphorescence!"

"What is it?"

"You don't know?"

". . . No."

He smiled. "Go down to the beach. You'll see. And make sure you smoke that joint on the way."

Phosphorescence

I walked along the path to the beach as fast as I could, which wasn't that fast because I didn't want to bump into any tree trunks or stub my foot on a root. At the same time, I smoked the joint, practically hit-and-running it even though I was alone, because I felt like getting wasted and because Keaty had told me to smoke it quick.

Meanwhile I seethed about the papayas, and pretty soon I was very stoned and deeply involved in a fantasy about beating up Bugs. In its earliest form the fantasy started off as just me and him, but soon I decided I needed an audience to bear witness to his humiliation. I added Françoise, then Jed and Keaty, then Etienne and Greg, and eventually the whole camp.

———

It was a Sunday. It had to be a Sunday, because that was the only time you got the whole camp in one place. Most people were kicking a ball around, a few were swimming, and a few were playing Frisbee. I was standing with Françoise. We were sharing a joke when Bugs appeared from the treeline with Sal, and three big papayas cradled in his arms.

"Got some more papayas," he called. "Enough for everyone."

"Excuse me," I said quietly to Françoise. "Won't be a moment."

He caught my eye as I strode toward him and did a double take, recognizing the purposeful nature of my step and the grim set of my mouth. First he looked alarmed, then arrogant. He was going to bluff it out, I realized.

"Yes," he said loudly, holding up the fruit for all to see, still watching me from the corner of his eye. "Here are some more papayas that *I found.*"

I stopped a meter away from him. "Papayas that *you* found, Bugs?"

"That's what I said."

"Uh-huh. Then how about we take a walk down to the orchard . . . right now."

His eyebrows flicked upward. ". . . Now?"

"Now. And I'll show you the joint butt I left . . . when I found the orchard less than *two weeks ago!*"

Everyone gasped, including Sal. A crowd had formed a circle around us and Françoise had come running over to stand by my side. "Is this true?" she demanded angrily.

Bugs scoffed. "Of course not! He's lying! I found the orchard!"

"So how about that walk?"

"I don't have to prove myself to you!"

"I think you do."

"Up yours. I found the orchard. End of story."

I smiled. "You know what, Bugs?" The silence was deathly, aside from the gentle lapping of the waves on the shore. "You're kinda *buggin'* me!"

The crowd laughed and Bugs's face twisted with rage. "Is that right?" he sneered. "Well, take this!" A papaya hurtled toward my head but I ducked and it flew past me into the crowd.

"Hey!" someone yelled. "Watch it!"

Bugs swore and made like he was about to throw another, but quick as a flash I grabbed the Frisbee from Cassie, who was standing beside me, and hurled it with lethal accuracy. The papaya exploded at the impact. The remaining chunks slithered from his hand and fell to the sand, harmless.

"Why you . . ." he started to say, but I was already on him. I faked with a left and floored him with a right. He dropped like a sack of potatoes.

"I'm thorry," he yelped, holding a hand up to cup the blood splashing from his busted lips. "It'th true! I didn't find the papayath! Richard did!"

Slowly I bent down and picked the Frisbee up again, pausing to wipe away a few shreds of pulped papaya flesh. "Too late for that, Bugs," I muttered softly, almost kindly. "Too late . . ."

The Frisbee shot down and connected squarely with the bridge of his nose, shattering the bone. Then he rolled onto his side and scrabbled weakly at the sand, trying to crawl away. I kicked him on the back of the head and gave him four hard punches in the kidney.

He whimpered. "Pleathe," he said. "Don't."

A bad choice of words. My temper rose. Looking around me, I spotted a fishing spear.

"Rewind," I said, taking the last drag from the joint. "Can't do that."

I sucked until the tips of my fingers burned, then threw away the roach and rewound back to my first punch.

I faked with a left and floored him with a right. He dropped like a sack of potatoes.

"I'm thorry," he yelped. "It'th true! I didn't find the papayath!"

"Say that again!" I shouted, looming over him with the Frisbee poised.

"I didn't find them! You did! I'm thorry!"

"Louder!"

"You found the papayath!"

I nodded curtly, and turned to Françoise. "Just wanted to set the record straight."

She glanced down at Bugs's twitching figure. "Of course," she said briefly. "You want to swim out to the coral garden?"

"Yes, Richard," she breathed, interlocking her arm with mine. "I would love to."

———————

The fantasy might have happily continued from there, but the dead leaves and dirt under my feet had become sand. I'd reached the beach.

It took me ages to find Keaty and the others. Even with the moonlight I couldn't see them, and their laughter seemed to come from everywhere, spread evenly over the water and faintly echoing off the cliffs. But after twenty minutes of stoned wandering along the shore I finally pinned them down to a group of small boulders, one hundred meters out.

As I couldn't see them and they couldn't see me, I decided there wasn't much sense in calling out, so I slipped off my T-shirt and began swimming toward them. Gradually their figures became discernible in the darkness. They were all standing and bending over to look downward into the water. Then—at roughly the moment I must have become visible to them—their laughter abruptly ceased, and as I got closer I saw that they had all turned to face in my direction. "Hey!" I said, finding their watchful silence a little eerie. "What's up?" They didn't answer. I continued swimming and repeated the question, irrationally thinking they might not have heard me. When they didn't answer again, I stopped, treading water ten feet from the boulder. "Why aren't you answering me?" I asked, puzzled.

"Look down," Keaty replied after a moment or two.

I paused, then did so. The water was as black as ink, except for where the moonlight caught the ripples. ". . . What's to see?"

"He is too close," I heard Etienne say.

"No," said Keaty. "Richard, move your hands, just under the surface."

I did as he said. From the boulder I heard Françoise sigh, but I still couldn't see anything past the blackness. "I don't get it. . . . What's this about?"

"Too close," Etienne repeated.

Keaty's silhouette scratched its head. "Yeah, you're right. . . . Come up onto the boulder, Richard. Watch me dive. We'll show you . . ."

At first I could see nothing but the disturbed water and reflected moonlight from where Keaty had vanished. Then, as the water settled, I began to see light below the surface. A milky glow at first that separated into a thousand tiny stars, next becoming a slowly moving meteor trail behind the brightest cluster. The cluster rose and turned back on itself, and turned again to form a glittering figure eight. Then it sank downward, disappearing for several seconds.

"What . . . ?" I said, baffled and astonished and unable to think of anything better to say.

Françoise put her hand on my arm. "Wait," she whispered. "Look now."

Deep in the blackness the glow returned, but this time it quickly divided into seven or eight clusters, brighter than before. They flickered and darted, dissolving and shedding light, but somehow replenishing themselves and becoming more intense. I took an instinctive step backward, suddenly aware that the miniature fireballs were traveling up toward me at an increasing speed. The next instant the surface broke into a flurry of bubbles and Keaty appeared, gasping for air.

"What did you think," he spluttered between lungfuls. "Did you ever see anything like it?"

"No . . ." I replied, still stupidly dazed. "Never."

"Phosphorescence. Minute creatures or algae or something. They glow when you make a movement." He hauled himself onto the boulder. "Phew! What an effort! We've been practicing that all night. Trying to get the best display."

"It looked incredible. . . . But . . . where do the creatures come from?"

"Daffy would say they come from the corals," said Gregorio. "It only happens on some nights. Not often. But now it is here, it will stay for the next few days. Maybe three or four."

I shook my head. "Amazing . . . Just amazing . . ."

"Ah-ha!" Etienne slapped me on the back and pushed Gregorio's diving mask into my hands. "But there is still the best to see!"

"Underwater?"

"Yes! Put this on and follow me! I will show you something you could never imagine!"

"It'll blow your mind," Keaty agreed. "It's indescribable."

The DMZ

I returned Jed's binoculars to him and lay on my back.
My head was still bleary from all the dope I'd smoked the night before, despite the brisk morning trek up the island, and I couldn't seem to focus on the tiny figures. "Basically," I said, folding my hands behind my head, "it was like being in space. Floating with loads of stars and comets around you. One of the most amazing things was disturbing a shoal of fish . . ."

Jed readjusted the binoculars to suit him. "I've seen phosphorescence before."

"But not underwater."

"No. Underwater sounds good."

"Yeah. Really good . . ." I sighed. "Did I tell you about Bugs and the papayas?"

"Nope."

"I found a papaya orchard a couple of weeks ago, and now Bugs is making out like he found it. Granted, I couldn't remember the orchard's exact location, but it was me that found it first." I sat up to see how Jed was reacting. He didn't appear to be reacting at all. "I suppose it isn't that big a deal. What do you think?"

"Mmm," Jed replied absently.

"Mmm, it is a big deal, or mmm, it isn't?"

"Oh . . . probably . . ."

I gave up. This was, after all, the precise problem with Bugs. Unless you were tuned into the subtleties of his character, you couldn't appreciate how irritating he was. I lay back down again and looked up at the clouds, feeling frustrated.

Actually, I'd been feeling frustrated for quite some time. It had started when we'd arrived at our lookout post two hours earlier to find, yet again, that Zeph and Sammy were still on their same patch of beach. I was aware that this should have been cause for relief, but instead it had gotten on my nerves, and as the morning passed I'd thought carefully about this paradox. My first guess was that it was connected to the uncertainty of the situation. I'd become tired of the waiting and I wanted some kind of resolution to occur. Even if it was the worst-case scenario and they set off toward us, at least the situation would become tangible. It would be something that was in our power to affect.

But it didn't take long for me to realize that my first guess was wrong. In the process of working through the worst-case scenario, I inevitably worked through the best-case. I imagined Zeph and Sammy disappearing, going back to Koh Phangan or Angthong; and never seeing them again. It was at that point I realized my mistake, because what I registered, while entertaining this optimistic thought, was disappointment. The strange truth was that I didn't want them to leave. Neither, as the root of my frustration, did I want them to stay put. And that left only one possibility; the worst-case scenario was the best-case scenario. I wanted them to come.

"Bored," I murmured carelessly, and Jed laughed.

"Bored is good, Richard," he said. "Bored is safe."

I paused. I hadn't mentioned my thoughts about Zeph and Sammy yet, assuming that Jed wouldn't take them too well. But I wasn't sure. It was possible that he felt the same way. I knew he took pleasure from evading the dope guards, part of which had to be a danger buzz, and I hadn't forgotten the way Keaty used to talk about him. I decided to obliquely test the water.

"Jed," I said, yawning to reinforce the casual nature of the question. "You remember the Gulf War?"

"Course."

"I was just wondering . . . You remember the buildup? When we were saying get out of Kuwait or we cream you, and Saddam was saying whatever he was saying."

"He was saying no, wasn't he?"

"Right." I leaned on my elbows. "So I was just wondering, how were you feeling at the time?"

"Feeling?"

"About the buildup to the Gulf War."

Jed lowered the binoculars and rubbed his beard. "I was feeling that it was all a load of hypocritical bullshit, if I remember correctly."

"No, I meant about the possibility of there being a war. Did it bother you much?"

"Uh . . . not really."

"You weren't sort of . . . looking forward to it?"

"Looking forward to it?"

"Yeah. . . . Speaking personally"—I took a deep breath—"I was kind of hoping Saddam wouldn't back down. You know, just to see what would happen."

Jed narrowed his eyes. "Now, Richard," he said dryly. "I can't imagine why you've suddenly brought this up."

I felt my cheeks flush. "I can't either. It popped into my head for some reason."

"Uh-huh. Well, I suppose I was looking forward to the Gulf War in a way. It was all dramatic and exciting, and like you said, I wanted to see what would happen. But when I saw the pictures of the Basra road and that civilian shelter that got hit, I felt pretty bad. I felt like I'd missed the point, and only got it too late. Does that answer your question?"

"Oh yes," I said quickly. "Absolutely."

"Good." Jed chuckled. "So, Richard, you're bored."

"Not bored . . ."

"Listless."

"Maybe."

"Whatever. You want some excitement. Fine. Perhaps we should go and nick some grass."

"We?" I said, stammering slightly because I was both eager and surprised. Since I'd begun working with Jed he'd only gone dope collecting once, and he'd left me behind on our lookout spot. "You mean both of us?"

"Sure. We've got plenty of time to come back here later, and we can risk them not doing anything while we're away. Anyway, I noticed camp supplies are getting low."

"I think it's a great idea!"

"Okay." He stood up. "Come on then."

The pass between the island's two peaks was the one position from which you could clearly make out the location of the dope fields, although the fields themselves were obscured behind trees. The only thing you could see were sudden dips in the canopy where one terrace dropped down to another. From higher up, the terraces seemed to merge into a single slope with natural-looking breaks in the canopy, an illusion caused by the elevated angle. I guess it prevented them from getting spotted from the air.

Once we reached the pass, Jed made the closed-fingers-pointing gesture and we began our descent into the DMZ—as I'd decided to call it. While we walked, I watched Jed's feet closely. I'd noticed he was able to walk much more quietly than me, even though we were both treading on the same mixture of dead leaves and twigs, and I was determined to discover how he did it. One thing was that he used the flat of his foot instead of the ball. I'd been doing the opposite, simply because of my instinct to walk on tiptoe when trying to move without noise. But after watching him, I realized that my way lacked common sense. By spreading the pressure across his whole foot he put less weight on twigs and flattened an area of leaves instead of just one or two. When I switched to his method, I heard the change immediately. The other thing he did was to lift his feet quite high, so that they weren't skimming just above the surface of the ground and catching loose material.

In order to press these lessons home, I played a private game as we crept through the DMZ. If I snapped a twig, then I'd triggered a land mine, and if I rustled a leaf above a particular volume—a rustle that couldn't pass as a regular jungle sound—then I'd been shot by a sniper. I also decided that the spiderweb strands which occasionally stretched across the path were Claymores, and took care to step over them if they hadn't already been broken by Jed. In deference to video games I gave myself three lives, allowing an extra life if I saw any animal larger than a beetle before it saw me. The only flaw to the game was that there was no punishment if I lost all my lives—as I did several times. But the shame was punishment enough, and that one flaw aside, the game proved to be excellent.

I was enjoying myself so much that I was a bit pissed off when we reached a dope field. At the edge we crouched in silence for several minutes, checking that the coast was clear. Then Jed turned to me. "Okay," he mouthed, pointing at me. "You go."

I raised my eyebrows and touched my chest, and he nodded. I grinned and gave him the thumbs-up. Then I hunched down as low as I could go without being on all fours and scuttled forward.

Between the trees and the start of the dope field was a space of at least
three meters, well beaten down where the guards made their patrol. Once
clear of the trees, I looked both ways and sped across the gap. I was mind-
ful that a guard might appear on my perimeter at any moment, so I wasted
no time in trying to pull off a few good-sized branches. But I immediately
ran into difficulty. The stems of the marijuana were remarkably tough. I
twisted and ripped, as quietly as I could, but was completely unable to get
them free of the main stalk. Worse, my hands were sweating like mad and
infuriatingly slippery, and I couldn't get a proper grip. I looked back at Jed,
who had a hand clamped to his head in despair.

"What do I do?" I mouthed.

He held up his knife, waving the point sarcastically. I realized I'd scuttled off before he'd had a chance to give it to me. Cursing my haste, I
cupped my hands, indicating that he should throw it. The knife came sailing through the air and finally I was able to sever the troublesome stems.
In order to compensate for the fuckup I hung around a minute longer than
I had to, so I could return with a particularly daring-sized bunch.

"What's the matter, Richard?" said Jed when we'd got back to the
safety of our lookout position. "I thought you'd be happy after all that excitement." He patted me affectionately on the back. "I thought you'd be
singing that ridiculous mouse song."

I shook my head and laid out my bushel. "I'm fine, Jed."

"It wasn't that thing with the knife, was it? That was my fault, you
know, not yours. I told you to go before I'd given it to you."

"No, no. The knife thing didn't bother me . . . not much anyway . . .
and it wasn't your fault. I should have stopped to think. But I'm fine, really."

Jed seemed unconvinced. "I know what it is. You wanted to spot some
of the guards, right?"

"Well . . ." I shrugged. "It would have been interesting."

"I don't know, Richard. You get disappointed by all the wrong things.
Listen, take it from me, you're glad we didn't run into anyone."

"Sure . . ." I thought for a moment, idly plucking at a couple of
buds. "Out of curiosity, what do you think would happen if they were to
find us?"

"Mmm . . . don't know. Rather not find out."

"Do you think they'd kill us?"

"It's possible. In a way I doubt it though, because there'd be no sense to it. They know we're here and vice versa, and neither of us want our secrets to get discovered, so . . ."

"I heard that Daffy once talked to them."

Jed looked surprised. "Who told you that?"

"Uh . . . Greg I think."

"I think maybe Greg has that wrong. Sal would have told me if there'd been any contact with them, and she never has."

"So what if they caught Zeph and Sammy? That would be different, because they're not connected to us."

"Yeah. They might kill Zeph and Sammy."

"That would solve our problem at least," I suggested cautiously, waiting for Jed to say something disapproving, but he didn't. He just nodded.

"Yep," he said bluntly. "It would."

Zombie Fish Eaters

It was dark by the time we got our act together. We had to jump into pitch blackness, unable to see the edges of the pool or even the white foam where the waterfall landed. Then we had to find our way through the forest, something I'd have found difficult without Jed to guide me.

My plan was to eat some food quickly and spend the rest of the evening swimming in the phosphorescence. I also wanted to tell my friends about the sleeping dope guard, which had slipped my mind in the excitement of the previous night. But when I got to the kitchen hut, I discovered that our banana-leaf food parcels were missing. All I found was a cold pile of boiled rice. Next, I hunted for the big cooking pot, assuming that Unhygienix had just forgotten to lay the fish and vegetables out, but the pot was empty too. That was strange because usually the cooks kept some dregs for the next morning's breakfast. Pensively, I patted my empty stomach and looked around me. Then I noticed something else even stranger. Apart from Jed, who was sitting a few meters away, the clearing seemed to be completely empty. I couldn't see any joint butts glowing in the darkness, or flashlights inside the tents.

I walked over to Jed. "You notice anything weird?" I said.

He shrugged. "Only that I can't see my food."

"Well . . . exactly. There isn't any food. And there aren't any people, either."

"People?" Jed shone his Maglite around him.

"See what I mean?"

". . . Yeah." He stood up. "That is weird . . ."

We gazed about us for a few seconds, following the yellow beam. Then, from somewhere close by, there was a loud moan, clearly the sound of someone in pain.

"Jesus!" Jed whispered, and switched off the light. "Did you hear that?"

"Of course I did!"

"Who was it?"

"How should I know?"

We paused, listening carefully. Then we heard the moan again and the hairs on the back of my neck stood up.

"Christ, Jed! Put the torch back on! This is making me nervous!"

"If you're nervous, why are you smiling?"

". . . How did you know I was smiling?"

"I could hear it in your voice."

"Just put the bloody light back on!"

"No," he hissed, "we don't know what's going on yet."

We listened some more. I remembered my first morning on the beach, waking up after my fever to an empty clearing. I'd found it pretty freaky in broad daylight. There was something unsettling about an empty place that you knew should be full of people. In the blackness with the eerie moans it was ten times as bad.

"This is like a zombie film," I muttered darkly, and giggled. *"Zombie Flesh Eaters."* Jed didn't reply.

The next time we heard the moan we were able to place it. It was coming from our left, around where most of the tents were pitched.

"Okay," said Jed. "We'll investigate. You take point."

"Me? You've got the torch!"

"I need to hold it so you've got both your hands free."

"Free for what?"

"Fighting off the zombies."

Jed put the beam on and illuminated Unhygienix's tent, so I mumbled a swearword and began slowly walking toward it.

I'd only gone a few feet when the flap opened and Ella's head poked out. "Jed?" she said, squinting against the glare.

"Richard."

"And Jed. What's going on, Ella?"

She shook her head. "Come inside. It's a disaster."

"It was Keaty," Ella explained, mopping at Unhygienix's forehead. It had been Unhygienix who was moaning, and he continued to do so while we were talking. His eyes were closed and he was clutching his great brown belly in both hands. I don't think he was even aware we were in the tent. "That idiot."

I raised my eyebrows. "Why? What did he do?"

"He put a squid in one of the fishing buckets, and we chopped it up and chucked it in with everything else."

"So?"

"The squid was already dead when he speared it."

Jed sucked in his breath sharply.

"Most of the camp is sick. The bathroom hut is clogged with vomit and you don't want to go near the Khyber Pass."

"What about you?" I asked. "You seem okay."

"Five or six of us are all right. I've got a few pains, but it looks like I've been lucky."

"And why did Keaty spear a dead squid?"

Ella narrowed her eyes. "I'd like to ask him that myself. We'd all like to ask him that."

"Yeah . . . Where is he? In his tent?"

"Maybe."

"Okay. Well, I'll go and see him . . ."

I chose the right moment to leave, because as I was backing out, Unhygienix sat bolt upright and vomited everywhere. I vanished quickly into the darkness with Ella's exasperated cries ringing in my ears.

It took me ages to find Keaty. He wasn't in his tent and there was no response in the clearing when I called his name. Eventually I decided to check the beach, where I spotted him, sitting in a patch of moonlight a little way down the shore.

When he saw me coming toward him he made a movement, as if he was half considering running away. Then he relaxed and his shoulders slumped. "Hi," he said in a low voice.

I nodded and sat beside him.

"I'm not flavor of the month, Rich."

". . . Neither is squid."

He didn't laugh.

"So what happened?"

"Don't you know? I poisoned the camp."

"Yeah, but—"

"I was using Greg's mask, I saw this squid, we've eaten squid a hundred times before, so I speared it and chucked it in the bucket. How was I supposed to know it was already dead?"

"Because it wasn't moving."

He glared at me. "Well, I know that now! But I thought . . . I thought squid were like jellyfish. They just floated around and . . . and its arms looked like they were moving . . ."

"So it was a mistake. It wasn't your fault."

"Yes, Rich. That's right. It was Jean's fault." He paused to punch the sand between his legs. "Of course it was my fucking fault! *Jesus!*"

"Okay . . . it was your fault, but you shouldn't—"

"Rich," he interrupted. "Please."

I shrugged and looked away. Across the lagoon, the moonlight was catching the jagged fissure that ran down the cliffs to the coral garden. "Kapow," I said quietly.

Keaty leaned forward. "What?"

"Kapow."

". . . Why?"

"Just because that's the sound lightning makes." I pointed at the fissure. "See?"

Bedlam

I only stayed with Keaty a short while because I wanted to check on Etienne and Françoise. He wouldn't come with me because he said he wasn't ready to face people yet, the poor guy. It was rough to have fought for so long to get into the fishing detail and then to be responsible for such a fuckup. He felt especially guilty that he'd been one of the few unaffected by the squid. I tried to tell him not to be so daft, because he could hardly blame himself for having a good immune system, but it didn't do any good.

When I saw what was happening at the longhouse, I was glad Keaty had decided to stay behind. The scene inside would only have made him feel worse. I'd had no idea that the effects of the food poisoning had been so severe, and actually I doubted that Keaty had realized it either or he'd have been back at the camp helping.

Running all the way down the center of the room were candles, placed there, I guessed, to keep them from being kicked over by the writhing figures on the beds. Through the burning wax fumes was the sour smell of vomit. Everybody was moaning—probably not constantly, but there were enough moans to overlap and keep the noise at a steady level. And everybody seemed to have reverted to their own language. Picking out recognizable words in the meaningless babble made it all the more surreal. People needed water or wanted sick to be wiped off their chests. When I passed Jesse he lunged for my foot and asked me to carry him to the bathroom hut. "I've got shit all over my fucking legs!" he gasped incredulously. "All over! Look!"

I spotted Cassie and Moshe darting between the beds, hopelessly trying to attend to all the different requests. When Cassie saw me she made a despairing motion with her arms and said, "Are they dying?"

I shook my head.

"How do you know, Richard?"

"They're not dying."

"How do you *know?*"

"I don't." I shook my head again. "Jesse's calling for you."

Cassie ran to check on her boyfriend and I continued down the long-house toward Françoise and Etienne.

Françoise was the worse off, I think. Etienne was asleep, so I suppose he might have been unconscious, but he was breathing steadily and his forehead didn't feel too hot. Françoise, however, was awake and in a great deal of pain. The cramps seemed to come in regular waves about sixty seconds apart. She didn't cry out like everybody else, but she bit her bottom lip and all over her stomach were marks from where she'd been digging in her fingernails.

"Stop doing that," I said firmly, after she'd nearly drawn blood from biting so hard.

She looked at me through dull eyes. "Richard?"

"Yes. You're chewing your mouth to pieces . . . You shouldn't."

"It hurts."

"I can see, but . . . Here." I reached into my pocket and pulled out my cigarettes. Then I ripped off the top of the box and pressed it flat. "You can bite on that instead."

"It still hurts."

I smoothed her damp hair away from her face. "I know it does, but this way you get to keep your lips."

"Oh." She managed to look faintly amused. She might even have managed a smile if another pain wave hadn't followed.

"What is happening, Richard?" she asked when her muscles had relaxed.

"You've got food poisoning."

"I mean, what is happening now?"

"Well . . ." I looked down the longhouse. I wasn't sure how to answer. I didn't want to frighten her. "People are chucking up, and . . . Moshe and Cassie are here helping . . ."

"Do you think this is serious for us?"

"No, no," I replied, laughing encouragingly. "You'll all be much better tomorrow. You'll all be fine."

"Richard . . ."

"Uh-huh?"

"When Etienne and I were in Sumatra, someone died from eating bad shellfish."

I nodded slowly. "Yes, but they probably ate the whole thing. You would have only had a tiny little bit, so you'll be okay."

"Really?"

"Sure."

She sighed. "Good . . . Richard, I need some water . . . Please will you bring me some?"

"Of course. I'll be back in two minutes."

As I stood up her cramps came back again. I watched her for a moment, uncertain of whether I should go or wait with her until the pain had passed; then I jogged down the longhouse, ignoring the pleas I passed on the way.

Incubus

Unexpectedly, I found Jed sitting outside the kitchen hut, eating plain rice with his Maglite upended in front of him like an electric candle. He held out his bowl as I approached, and mumbled, "You should eat."

"I'm not hungry. Have you seen inside the longhouse?"

He swallowed. "Stuck my head round the door, saw enough not to go in. Got plenty to deal with in the tents."

"What's happening in the tents?"

"Same as the longhouse. The Swedes seem okay, but the others are fucked."

"Are you worried?"

"Are you?"

"I'm not sure. Françoise said people can die from this stuff."

"Mmm. They can." He took another mouthful and chewed carefully. "We need to keep them tanked up with loads of water. Can't let them get dehydrated. And we need to keep ourselves fit so we can look after them. That's why you should eat some food. You haven't eaten since this morning."

"Later," I said, thinking of Françoise, and scooped a pitcher into the drinking water barrel. "And if the Swedes are okay, then tell them to come and help."

Jed nodded, his cheeks too puffed up to speak, and I set off back across the clearing.

Back inside the longhouse, Bugs was metaphorically and literally losing his shit. He was squatting alongside the line of candles, eyes bulging like cue balls, while a pool of feces collected around his feet. Moshe was standing a few feet away, gagging, and when he saw me he hurriedly moved away, as if having seen Bugs, I'd been tagged with the responsibility of dealing with him.

Bugs groaned. A string of drool looped out of his mouth and swung crazily from his chin. "Richard," he spluttered. "Get me outside."

I looked around. Cassie was several beds away and Moshe was bent over one of the Yugoslavian girls. "I'm in a hurry," I replied, covering my nose and mouth with the crook of my arm.

"What?"

"I'm in a hurry. I've got to get this water to Françoise."

"I've got to get outside! She can wait!"

I shook my head, then grimaced. The smell was so bad it was making me feel giddy. "She already *has* waited," I said.

His face contorted as though he was going to yell at me. I looked at him impassively while he held the expression, then he gurgled and another stream of shit splashed onto the ground. "No!" he wailed, then his legs buckled and he slipped backward.

I took a step sideways to keep clear of the spreading dark puddle. "Jesus, Bugs. Can't you hold on?"

Bugs whimpered and doubled up into the fetus position, tried to straighten, and doubled up again.

I continued watching him, still breathing into my elbow though it did nothing to block the stench. The giddy feeling was getting stronger, mixing with intense rushes of irritation. It seemed to me, through the pulse that had developed behind my eyes, that there was something self-indulgent about his debasement. How could he not have had the strength to drag himself to the door? He'd distracted me from bringing the water to Françoise, and he was making a terrible mess that someone else would have to clean up. I remembered his stoicism when he'd bashed his leg, and the memory nearly made me laugh out loud.

"I've got to get this water to Françoise," I said coldly, but didn't move. "I said I'd only be two minutes. I've already been longer." Bugs opened his mouth, maybe to reply, and a slimy bubble of spit popped over his lips. This time I did laugh. "Look at yourself," I heard myself say. "Who the fuck do you think's going to clean that mess up?"

Suddenly a hand grabbed my shoulder.

"My God, Richard! What's the matter with you? Why aren't you helping him?"

I turned and saw Cassie staring at me. She looked very angry, but when our eyes met the anger quickly changed to something else. Something like concern, I noted vacantly, or alarm.

"Richard?"

"Yes?"

"Are you okay?"

"I'm fine."

"You . . ." She paused. "Come on. We've got to get him outside at once."

"I need to take this water to—"

"You need to get Bugs outside."

I rubbed my eyes and wished they would stop throbbing.

"Now, Richard."

"Yes . . . Right." I put the pitcher down, a safe distance from the puddle, and went to help her lift Bugs.

He was heavy, being so broad, and he made no effort to walk, so we practically had to drag him along the ground. Luckily one of the Swedes, Sten, arrived before we'd got halfway to the door. With his assistance we got Bugs outside and over to one of the diverted streams, where we dropped him so the current could wash him down.

Sten agreed to stay with Bugs—probably a relief after seeing what was going on in the longhouse—and Cassie and I headed back. I wanted to jog but she made me stop so she could feel my forehead.

"What's the matter?" I asked testily.

". . . I thought you might have a temperature."

"Do I?"

"You're a little hot . . . but no, thank God. We can't have anyone else getting ill." She gave my hand a squeeze. "We've got to be strong."

"Uh-huh."

"We've got to keep calm."

"Sure, Cassie. I know."

"Okay . . ."

"I've got to get the water to Françoise."

"Yes," she said, and I thought she might be frowning, but in the darkness it was impossible to tell. We started walking again. "Of course."

During the time I'd been away, Françoise's condition had gotten worse. She was still talking but she'd deteriorated into a dreamy, feverish state, and her cheeks were burning up. I had to prop her up against my lap so I could feed the water into her mouth without her choking, and even then she lost most of the liquid down her chest.

"Sorry I took so long," I said as I dried her down with one of her T-shirts. "Bugs was all over the place. Had to deal with him."

"Richard," she whispered, then said something in French that I couldn't understand.

I made a guess at the meaning. ". . . I'm fine. I missed out on the squid."

"Etienne . . ."

"He's here, right next to you . . . sleeping it off."

Her head twitched to the side. "I love you," she muttered drowsily.

I blinked, thinking for the slightest second that she might be talking to me. Then I caught myself, seeing the direction that her head had pointed, and realized her words were for Etienne. But in a way it didn't matter. It felt nice just to have heard her say them. I smiled and stroked her hair, and her hand reached up and closed weakly around mine.

For the next five minutes I stayed as still as I could, supporting her shoulders on my crossed legs. Then, when her breathing had become slower and heavier, I eased myself backward and gently lowered her onto the sheets. They were a little damp from where the water had spilled, but it couldn't be helped.

It isn't something I feel I ought to justify, but I'll justify it anyway. I was thinking about the time I'd had a fever. Françoise had given me a kiss, so I gave her one too, in exactly the same affectionate spirit. And I wouldn't have called it a kiss that was open to interpretation. It was straightforward; on the cheek, not the lips, unambiguous.

Technically, if you can get technical about such things, maybe I did hold it for a couple of seconds too long. I do remember noticing how soft and smooth her skin was. In the middle of that hellish night, with all the vomiting and groaning and flickering candle flames, I wasn't expecting to find sweetness. It took me by surprise, the little oasis. I dropped my guard and closed my eyes, drifting a few moments, just for the chance to block the bad stuff out.

But when I pulled back from the kiss and saw the way Etienne was staring at me, I knew he hadn't seen it the same way.

There was a short silence, as you might imagine, then he said, "What were you doing?"

". . . Nothing."

"You were kissing Françoise."

I shrugged. "So?"

"What do you mean, so?"

"I mean, so?" If I sounded irritable, it was nothing more than exhaustion, and maybe a hangover from the business with Bugs. "I gave her a kiss on the cheek. You've seen me do that before, and you've seen her kiss me too."

"She has never kissed you like that."

"On the cheek?"

"For so long."

"You've got this wrong."

He sat up in bed. "So what should I think?"

I sighed. The pulsing behind my eyes was starting again, turning into a sharp ache. "I'm very tired," I said. "You're very ill. It's affecting you."

"What should I think?" he repeated.

"I don't know. Anything. I kissed her because I was worried, and because I care about her . . . Just the same as I'm worried about you."

He didn't say anything.

I tried a joke. "If I give you a kiss, will that even things up?"

Etienne paused a bit longer, and finally nodded. "I am sorry, Richard," he said, but his voice was flat and I knew he didn't mean it. "You are right. I am ill and it is affecting me. But I can look after her now. Maybe some others can use your help."

"Yeah. I'm sure they can." I stood up. "If you need anything, give me a shout."

"Yes."

I glanced back at Françoise, who, thankfully, was still fast asleep. Then I began walking back down the longhouse, keeping to the side so I didn't get roped into helping Moshe as he shoveled away Bugs's shit.

Good Morning

I slept in the clearing. I would have slept there even if I hadn't thought it best to stay away from Etienne. I'd lost my sense of smell and become selective about which moans I chose to hear, but I couldn't stand the candles. Their accumulated heat was so strong that the ceiling was wet with condensation. The drips fell like a light rain through clouds of waxy fumes, and by midnight there wasn't a dry square inch in the longhouse. That aside, Gregorio was in my bed. I'd moved him there so he could get away from Jesse, who'd had the same incontinence problem as Bugs.

The last thing I remember before falling asleep was Sal's voice. She'd recovered enough to walk around and was calling Keaty's name. I could have told her he was down on the beach, but I decided not to. There was something ominously controlled about her tone. It was the way a parent might call for a kid, trying to draw them out of their hiding place in order to tell them off. After a few minutes I felt her flashlight shining through my eyelids and she asked me if I knew where he was. I didn't move, and eventually she moved away.

The only other disruption that night was the sound of someone crying nearby. I tried to make myself get up and check on who it was, but it turned out I was too tired to care.

Jed woke me around six-thirty, with a bowl of rice and a boiled sweet, one of the last from Koh Phangan.

"Good morning," he said, violently shaking my shoulders. "Have you eaten yet?"

"No," I mumbled.

"What did I tell you last night?"

"Eat."

"So." He hauled me to a sitting position and put the bowl in my lap. The single sweet, a lurid chemical green, looked ridiculous perched on the mound of sticky grains. "Eat this now."

"I'm half asleep."

"Eat it, Richard."

I pressed a rice ball with my fingers and dutifully began to chew it, but my mouth was too dry to swallow. "Water," I croaked. Jed went to get me some, and I poured it straight into the bowl. Actually it didn't taste so bad, if only because it didn't taste of anything.

While I ate Jed talked, but I didn't listen to him. I was looking at the bone-white rice and thinking about the dead freak on Koh Phangan. I was sure the ants would have stripped him down by now. They work fast, ants. He probably never even got to the rotting stage. I pictured the freak on his back, a clean skeleton grinning through his loose covering of leaves, dappled in a few pinpricks of sunlight. In fact I'd left him on his front, lying on his arms, but there wasn't much sense in picturing the back of his head, so I revised the image to make it more aesthetic. The dappled effect was another revision. As I remember his shallow grave, no light filtered past the thick foliage above him. I just liked the idea that it did.

"Pretty," I said, putting the sweet in my mouth. "Maybe a monkey exploring the rib cage."

Jed looked at me. "Huh?"

"Or maybe a monkey would be too . . . kitsch . . ."

"Kitsch?"

"Monkeys."

"Have you listened to a word I've been saying?"

"No." I crunched the sweet and my tongue tingled with the sudden flood of lime. "I've been thinking about the freak on Koh Phangan."

"The dead guy you hid?"

"Yeah. Do you think he's been found yet?"

"Well . . ." Jed started to say, looking perplexed. "I suppose he might have been found if the girl was . . ." Then he slapped his head. "Jesus Christ! What the fuck am I talking about? Who cares about the dead freak? You should have left him where he was, and we've got much more important stuff to deal with right here!"

"I was only interested. And he's bound to get found one of these days."

"Shut up! Now listen! One of us has to get up to the island to check on Zeph and Sammy!"

"Oh, okay . . . Why not both of us?"

Jed made an exasperated sobbing sound. "Why do you think, you dozy fool? Someone has to stay here to look after the sick people, and almost all the fishing detail is out of action. Only the Swedes and Keaty are healthy, and Keaty's still missing."

I nodded. "I guess that means me."

"No. It means me. I need to stay here because I know some stuff about first aid, so you'll be going up to the island alone. Are you up to that?"

"You bet!" I said brightly. "No sweat at all!"

"Good. Now before you go I want you to find Keaty. There's about fifteen who are well enough to eat, so we need food. But I won't have time to go fishing, so he'll have to do it."

"Okay. And what should I do if Zeph and Sammy are on their way?"

"They won't be."

"But what if they are?"

Jed paused. "I'm trying not to think about it, but if they are, then get back here as fast as you can and tell me."

"And if there's no time?"

"Plan B."

". . . Which one?"

"You wait and see what happens. I'm positive they'll turn back at the dope fields, but if they don't, then follow them to the waterfall. Then, if they get down, intercept them and make fucking sure they know not to start talking about your map."

Across the clearing, Jesse appeared out of the longhouse. He wobbled toward the bathroom hut, got about a quarter of the way there, and threw up.

"Right," I said, suddenly feeling immensely cheerful. After last night I hadn't expected the next day to start so well. "I'd better find Keaty then."

There was only one bad note to the morning. On the way to the beach I passed Sal sitting outside the longhouse and she called me over. It turned out that Bugs—who was sitting next to her and giving me the evil eye— had told her what I'd done to him. Sal wanted an explanation.

I was slick. I said that I'd been exhausted and was only catching my breath before I gave him a hand outside, and if Bugs remembered it differently I was truly sorry but maybe his sickness had warped his memory of the incident. Then I suggested we shake on it, and that pleased Sal a lot. She was so hassled, what with everything else she had to deal with, that she was more than ready to get the distraction out of the way.

Bugs wasn't though. When I set off again for the beach he hobbled after me and called me a bastard. He was really angry, poking his finger in my chest and saying what he'd do to me if only he was well enough. I waited until he'd finished, then told him to fuck off. I wasn't going to let him spoil my good mood.

Epitaph

Keaty was sleeping in the same spot I'd left him. High tide was well on its way and it wasn't going to be long before the wash reached his feet, so rather than wake him I decided to smoke a cigarette. I assumed he'd had a rough night and could do with the extra fifteen minutes. I was just getting down to the filter when the Swedes appeared. I put my finger to my lips, pointing at Keaty, and we walked out of earshot.

Karl, Sten, Christo. Considering that two of them ended up dead and the other ended up nuts, I feel bad that their names mean so little to me.

Like Jed, the Swedes had arrived at the beach uninvited, and although they'd probably found it easier to get accepted—having arrived second—it partly explained why they chose to fish outside the lagoon. They'd never been as involved in beach life as everyone else. They were around but they kept mainly to themselves, all sharing a single tent and often eating away from the crowd. The only times I ever saw them participate socially was on Sundays. They were good soccer players and everyone wanted them for their team.

If they had found integration difficult, it couldn't have helped that only one of them, Sten, could speak fluent English. Christo could just about muddle along but Karl was hopeless. As far as I knew, his vocabulary was limited to a few words based around fishing, like "fish" and "spear," and a couple of pleasantries. He would greet me with an uncertain "Hulloo Ruchard," and would bid me good morning even if he was just about to go to bed.

"So," I said when we were a safe distance from Keaty. "You've got your work cut out for you today."

Sten nodded. "But there is only half the camp to fish for, no? We only need to catch fifteen fishes. Not so difficult, I think . . . Would you like to fish with us?"

"No. I'll be staying here."

"You are sure? There is room for four in the boat, and you may be lonely working alone."

I smiled. "Thanks, but Keaty will wake up soon."

"Ah yes, Keaty. Is he sick?"

"No, he's fine. A bit down, but he didn't get food poisoning."

"That is good. Well, we should be going. We will see you later, Richard."

"Okay."

Sten said something to the other two in Swedish. Then they walked down to the shore and began swimming for the caves.

It was a short, bland conversation. Not the sort of conversation you'd want to be remembered by. I've tried to think of ways to jazz it up a bit, to make it more poignant or more of an epitaph, but the best I could think of was some kind of pun based around Sten saying, "See you later." Something along the lines of, I didn't see him later but I did see him late. Dead late. Late/dead. "I saw him later, though not in the way I expected . . . I saw him late!" It doesn't even make sense.

I also looked for extra information to provide about their characters, aside from their similarities with Jed and soccer skills, but our relationship had revolved entirely around a vague rivalry based on fish sizes. I barely knew them. If two of them hadn't died I doubt I'd have given them a second thought.

So, if I'm going to be honest, I suppose their epitaph must be this: If you've ever sat down with an old school friend and tried to remember all the kids that used to be in your class, the Swedes were the kids you remembered last.

The only thing I'd tag on the end was that they seemed like decent guys, and they shouldn't have had to die that way. Especially Sten.

Eventually I got bored with waiting for the tide to reach Keaty's feet, so I scooped some water in my hands and poured it on his head.

"Hi," I said after he'd recovered from the shock. "Did you sleep all right?"

He shook his head.

"Me neither." I squatted beside him. "I got about four hours."

". . . Are things bad in the camp?"

"They were last night. It's better now, but people are still pretty sick."

Keaty sat up and rubbed the sand off his legs and arms. "I should get back. Got to help."

"Then don't go back. You'll only have to come back here. They want you to do some fishing."

"They want *me* to go fishing?"

"That's what Jed said. All the fishers are ill except for the Swedes and Moshe, and Moshe's busy looking after people in the longhouse. That leaves you."

"It leaves you, too."

"Uh, yeah . . . but . . ." I thought for a moment. "I really need some sleep. I mean, when I said I got four hours, it was more like three. Or two and a half. I'm going to collapse if I don't get some rest." Keaty still didn't look convinced, so I added, "Also, if you turn up with food instead of empty-handed, it might calm Sal down a bit. She's pretty pissed off that you haven't been around to help."

"Yeah, I heard her calling for me last night. That's why I didn't go back to my tent." He shrugged wearily. "But I've got to go back sometime, and . . . I don't know if it's such a good idea, me going fishing. I mean, that's what caused all this."

"I haven't talked to anyone who sees it that way."

"I could help at the camp."

I shrugged. "The camp needs fish."

"You really think I should do the fishing?"

"Uh-huh. I was specifically told to find you and give that message."

Keaty frowned and twirled his fingers in his hair. He hadn't shaved it for so long that he was getting tiny dreads. ". . . All right then. If you're sure."

"Great." I patted his shoulder. "So I'll catch some sleep in the trees."

"Should I come and find you before I head back?"

I didn't answer. I was looking across the lagoon at the circle of cliffs, wondering how I'd swim over without him seeing.

Keaty repeated the question.

"Uh . . . No . . ."

If Keaty chose the main boulder to fish from, I could just manage an underwater leapfrog between the smaller boulders, hiding behind them when I needed air.

"What if you oversleep? Then Sal will get pissed off with you, too."

"I won't oversleep. I only need a few hours."

"Okay. And how many fish should I catch?"

"Ten or so. The Swedes will be fishing too, and most people won't be eating." I started toward the trees. "I'll see you back at the camp."

"Back at the camp. Sure."

I could feel his eyes on my back, so I dropped my shoulders and dragged my feet to show how tired I was. As I reached the grasses he called after me, "Hey, Rich, I'm sorry you got kept awake. I feel like it's my—"

I waved a hand. "No trouble," I called back. Then I slipped into the bushes.

It was easy to hide from Keaty as I swam across the lagoon, but it was infuriatingly slow. It took over twenty-five minutes just to make it to the caves, and it shouldn't have taken half that. The slowness gave me a nasty feeling inside. It was like I wanted to take a deep breath, but however hard I sucked I could never fill the bottom of my lungs. I didn't shake the feeling until I'd climbed the chimney and worked my way around the cliff tops to the mainland.

The VC, the DMZ, and Me

I paused for a few minutes at the pass, looking down at the DMZ. There was no need, I knew, for me to descend the terraced slope, but at the same time I knew I would. I might never be alone on the island again and the opportunity was too big to miss. But I also had to check on Zeph and Sammy, so I continued upward toward our lookout point.

"Delta-One-Niner," I murmured as I located the figures. I could see two of them, one in the normal spot and the other about thirty meters to the right, standing down by the shore. The other three were obviously exploring, or busy doing whatever it was they did behind the treeline. "This is Alpha patrol. We confirm we have a positive ID, repeat, positive ID. Request further orders." In the back of my head I heard the fuzz of radio static. "Orders acknowledged. Will continue recon as advised."

I dropped the binoculars and sighed, feeling the familiar frustration well up in me again. Their apparent inactivity no longer held any interest for me and had started to seem like a complicated insult. Part of me wanted to yell at them to get a fucking move on. If I'd thought it would work I'd have probably done it.

In that frame of mind, the time went slowly. I felt duty-bound to stick around for at least two hours, even though I was sure that nothing would happen. So every ten minutes I checked to see if they were up to anything new, and when I saw that they weren't—occasionally another would appear or two would disappear—I went back to daydreaming about what I'd do in the DMZ.

I had only one goal, because there was no sense in getting more grass. All I wanted to do was to see one of the dope guards. Not napping on a jungle path but active and armed and patrolling. That alone would satisfy me. It would be a proper engagement, a fair fight on equal terms. Him looking out for trespassers, and me trespassing.

The more I daydreamed, the harder it became to stay at my lookout post. Over the last half hour of my two-hour tour of duty, I counted the minutes like a kid waiting for Christmas morning. When the minute finally came—12:17—I made one last check on Zeph and Sammy. Typically, for the first time that day, none of the figures were visible, but I only hesitated for an instant. I made a quick check of the sea to make sure they hadn't started swimming, then said, "Fuck it" out loud and set off down the hill.

My daydream came true not far from the field that Jed and I had visited the previous day. I'd chosen to go there because it seemed logical that the best place to find a dope guard would be at a dope field, and also because it meant I was traveling on a route I'd taken before, if only once.

The contact came about three hundred meters above the terrace. I'd been just about to step around a thick copse of bamboo when I saw a flash of brown through the leaves, too golden to be anything but Southeast Asian skin. I froze, of course, holding the awkward position of three quarters of the way through a step. Then the brown vanished, and I heard the sound of rustling footsteps heading away from me.

I debated my options swiftly. To follow the guard was a serious risk, but a glimpsed impression was not what I'd had in mind, and the longer I delayed the less chance I'd have of seeing him again. Also, I knew that if I didn't follow him at once I'd probably lose my nerve and have to head back. This, I suppose, was what clinched it. I didn't even wait for the footsteps to get out of earshot before creeping around the thicket in pursuit.

The next ten minutes are vague in my memory. I was listening and looking so intently that, as when I made my original descent down to the waterfall, I was incapable of storing anything past the immediate. My memory returned when I heard his footsteps stop—making me stop too—and I spotted him less than fifteen feet away, taking a breather between two tall trees.

Gradually I crouched down and eased my head around a branch to get a better view. The first thing I registered was his markings: a black-blue dragon tattoo crawling up a densely muscled back, with a claw on one shoulder blade and flames on the other. Then I saw that he was the same guard I'd seen with Etienne and Françoise, the guy with the kick-boxer build. Recognizing him, I had to concentrate hard to control my breathing. At first it was from an adrenaline rush and a throwback to the fear I'd had on the plateau, but then it became awe.

The man was facing away from me in three-quarter angle, with one arm resting on his rifle and the other on his hips. Across his tattoo, running from his neck to the left side of his rib cage, was a deep, pale scar. Another scar cut a white line across the cropped hair on his head. A crumpled packet of Krong Thip was tied to his upper arm with a filthy blue bandanna. He held his AK as casually as a snake charmer holding a cobra. He was perfect.

I knew he'd probably be gone in a minute or less, and my mind was frantic trying to record each aspect of his form. It was all I could do to stop myself from crawling nearer. If only I could have frozen him I'd have circled him like a statue in a museum, taking my time, noting his posture and listing the items he carried, studying his eyes to read what was happening behind them.

Just before he walked away he turned to face in my direction. Maybe he'd sensed someone watching him. He opened his mouth as he turned and I saw he had his top two front teeth missing. It was the final touch, a dangerous complement to the broken butt of his AK and the torn pouches on his baggy green combat trousers. At that moment, if I'd tried to slip further into the bushes he would have seen me. I could tell from his expression that he wasn't looking hard, just absently scanning, but he'd have noticed a movement. I stayed still. I was hypnotized. Even if he had seen me I doubt I'd have tried to run.

I didn't move for quite some time after the guard had gone. I realized that to leave at once would be the wrong thing to do, not so much because he might be near and out of sight, but because I needed a moment to collect my thoughts. I was dimly thinking of road accidents, of the drivers who crash soon after a narrow escape.

Hours later, on the way home after spending the afternoon at the lookout point, I paused for a second time at the pass. This time, the sight of the terraces and steamy evening jungle made me clench my fists. I was shaken by a powerful surge of jealousy toward Jed. He'd had the DMZ for over a year, all to himself. I couldn't begin to imagine what it would feel like, such extended private access, and the briefness of my own encounter only seemed to make it worse. I felt like I'd been damned by a glimpse of paradise.

Split

The clearing was empty apart from Ella, who was gut-
ting fish outside the kitchen hut, and Jed, who was chatting to her. Jed
stood as I approached and I answered his inquisitive look with a subtle
nod. He returned it, then excused himself and set off for the tents.

"Haven't you brought any fish?" Ella asked briskly. "I was hoping you'd
be bringing some more."

"Oh . . ." I glanced at her bucket, which held less than ten small milkfish. "No, Ella. Sorry, I haven't. . . . Is that all there is?"

"Yes. It's pathetic. I can't see how I'm supposed to make this stretch to
half the camp. Was this the best you and Keaty could do?"

"Uh, yeah . . . but it's my fault. Last night caught up on me and I had
to get some sleep. Keaty was working alone really. . . . But what about the
Swedes? Haven't they brought any?"

"No," she replied irritably, gouging out a handful of guts and tossing
them into the dirt. "They bloody well haven't. The only person who's
brought me anything is Keaty. What time is it, anyway?"

"Six-thirty."

"Six-thirty! I've waited over two hours for them to show up. But most
people are feeling much better than yesterday and that means they're getting hungry, so I can't wait any longer."

"I wonder what could be taking them so long."

"I haven't a clue. It's so stupid of them. Of all the possible days they
might have gotten delayed, I can't believe they decided to pick this one."

I frowned. "Come on, Ella. That's ridiculous. I'm sure they didn't
choose to get delayed. They know what's going on. . . . Maybe their engine broke down or they ran out of petrol."

Ella clucked her tongue as she sank her knife into the belly of the last
fish. "Maybe," she said, with an expert snap of her wrist. "Maybe you're
right. . . . But if you stop to think about it, they could have swum back by
now."

———

I brooded on this last comment of Ella's as I walked toward the long-house, because she was absolutely right. The Swedes could easily have swum back in two hours, even dragging the boat behind them. I knew from previous conversations that they never fished more than two hundred meters out to sea, a safety precaution in case they spotted another boat and had to get to cover in a hurry.

In a way then, I was already aware that something serious had happened. Logically, it was the only explanation. But I didn't act on my sense of foreboding, probably for the same reasons that no one else had. There were too many problems at hand to start worrying about new ones. For the others, perhaps it was a call for water that distracted them, or a need for sleep, or a puddle of sick that had to be cleaned up. For me, it was the prospect of seeing Etienne again. I'd been having second thoughts about the kiss. I still didn't think I'd been at fault, but I could see why Etienne had thought I was, and I was sure that our next meeting would be awkward. So as I pushed open the longhouse, I also pushed thoughts of the Swedes to the back of my head, with no more consideration than a vague decision to worry about it later.

My immediate impression inside the longhouse was that some kind of division had occurred while I was away. A tense silence greeted my arrival, shortly followed by a low buzz of noise. At the near end was my old fishing detail, along with Jesse, Cassie, and Leah, another member of the gardening detail. At the far end, in the area of my bed, were Sal, Bugs, and the remainder of the gardening and carpentry details. Moshe and the two Yugoslavian girls were sitting between the two groups, apparently neutral.

I assessed the situation. Then I shrugged. If a division had occurred, choosing sides wasn't going to be an issue. I closed the door behind me and went over to my old detail.

Nobody spoke for a couple of seconds after I sat down—which gave me a brief scare, since I automatically assumed that the split was related to me. A chain of events quickly began to form in my mind, connected to the kiss. Perhaps Etienne had told Françoise, and Françoise was furious, and everyone had heard, and the tension was nothing to do with divisions in the camp but an embarrassed reaction to my arrival. Fortunately, I was way off track, as was shown when Françoise leaned forward and took my hand. "There has been trouble," she said in a hushed voice.

"Trouble?" I withdrew my hand slightly clumsily, glancing at Etienne, who was watching me with a completely unreadable expression. "What kind of trouble?"

Keaty coughed and pointed to his left eye. It was badly puffed up. "Bugs hit me," he said simply.

"Bugs *hit* you?"

"Uh-huh."

I was too shocked to speak, so Keaty continued.

"I turned up with the fish around four and hung around with Jed in the tents. Then I came to the longhouse about half an hour ago, and as soon as Bugs saw me he jumped up and threw a punch."

"What happened then?" I eventually said.

"Jean pulled him off, and then there was a massive argument between that lot"—he gestured to the group at the far end—"and this lot. Personally, I stayed out of it. I was trying to stop my nosebleed."

"He hit you because of the squid?"

"He said it was because I wasn't around to help last night."

"No!" I shook my head angrily. "I know why he hit you. It had nothing to do with being missing last night. It was because he shat himself."

Keaty smiled without humor. "That makes a lot of sense, Rich."

I struggled to keep my voice steady. My tongue felt thick and I was suddenly in such a rage that I could actually see blackness around the edge of my vision. "It makes sense to *me*, Keaty," I said tightly. "I know the way his head works. It was the knock to his pride, slipping around in his own shit. That's why he hit you."

I stood up, and Gregorio caught my arm.

"Richard, what are you doing?"

"I'm going to kick his head in."

"At *last*," Jesse said, rising. "That's *exactly* what I've been saying we should do. I'll help."

"No!"

I looked around. Françoise had also stood up.

"This is too stupid! Both of you sit down now!"

At that moment there was a jeer from the far end of the longhouse. Bugs was calling to us. "Oh, let me guess! The cavalry's arrived!"

"I'm going to stick a spear in your fucking *neck!*" I yelled back.

"I'm worried!"

Jesse howled. "You'd better be fuckin' worried! You'd better be very fuckin' worried!"

"Is that right, you kiwi cunt?"

"You've got no fuckin' idea how right it is!"

Then Sal was standing too. *"That's enough!"* she screamed. *"Both of you! All of you! Enough!"*

Silence.

The two groups stared at each other for a long thirty seconds. Then Françoise stabbed a finger at the ground.

"Sit!" she hissed. So we sat.

Ten minutes later I was crawling up the walls. I wanted a cigarette so severely I thought my chest was going to cave in, but my supply was at the other end of the longhouse and there was no way I could get them. In an effort to help, Cassie rolled a joint, but it didn't do much good. It was nicotine I needed. The dope only made the craving worse.

Not long after, Ella brought in the food she'd cooked, but she'd burned the rice and without Unhygienix's magic touch the fish stew tasted like seawater. Plus she had to hand it round in the most uncomfortable atmosphere imaginable, which baffled her and made her think it was her cooking. No one bothered to explain, so she left the longhouse nearly in tears.

Jed stuck his head through the door at eight-fifteen, gazed around curiously, then disappeared.

So that's how the time passed, a succession of tense episodes, all serving to distract us from the fact that the Swedes still hadn't returned from fishing.

At a quarter to nine the longhouse door banged open.

"Oh there you are . . . " Keaty started to say, but the words dried up in his throat.

Karl was half bent over, barely illuminated by the candles. It was the expression on his face that instantly informed us there was something badly wrong, but I think it was his arms that had choked Keaty. They seemed to be absurdly dislocated, jutting out from the top of his shoulders. And there was what looked like a tear in his right hand. Between his thumb and forefinger the split continued down to his wrist, so that the two halves hung like a limp lobster claw.

"Jesus Christ," said Jesse loudly, and all over the longhouse I heard movement as people rose to get a better look.

Karl took a single heavy step toward us, moving into the brighter candlelight. That was when we realized that the mutilated arms belonged to the person he was carrying on his back—Sten. Abruptly Karl collapsed, toppling forward without making any effort to break his fall. Sten slipped off him, balancing for a moment on his side, then rolling over. There was a ragged semicircle of flesh as large as a basketball missing from his side, and the remainder of his stomach area had been flattened to no more than four inches thick.

Etienne was the first to move. He barged past me, almost knocking me to the ground.

When I looked up he was bending over Sten, trying to give him mouth-to-mouth resuscitation. Then I heard Sal call behind me, "What's happened?" and at once Karl began yelling at the top of his lungs. For a minute he yelled nonstop, filling the longhouse with a high, frantic sound that made some people cover their ears or yell equally loudly, for no apparent reason other than to block him out. It was only after Keaty had grabbed him, shouting at him to shut up, that he managed to form an intelligible word. "Shark."

The Third Man

The stunned quiet after Karl said "shark" only lasted a heartbeat. Then we all started jabbering again as abruptly as we'd all shut up. A circle quickly formed around Karl and Sten—the same kind of circle you get in a schoolyard fight, jostling for position while keeping a safe distance—and suggestions started flying thick and fast. It was a crisis after all. Whatever else a crisis causes, it causes a buzz, so everyone wanted to be in on the act. Etienne and Keaty, tending to Sten and Karl, respectively, were instructed, "He needs water!" and, "Put him in the recovery position!" and, "Hold his nose!"

"Hold his nose" was directed at Etienne by one of the Yugo girls, because you have to hold a victim's nose when giving mouth-to-mouth to stop the air from escaping. I thought it was a stupid thing to say. You could see the air bubbling out of the hole in Sten's side, so his lungs were obviously fucked, and anyway, you couldn't imagine anyone looking more dead. His eyes were open but showing the whites, he was as limp as rags, and there was no blood coming out of his wounds. In fact, just about all the advice was stupid. Karl could hardly be put in the recovery position while he was jerking around and screaming, and I didn't have a clue what use he'd have for water. Morphine yes, water no. The only person talking sense was Sal, who was yelling at everyone to get back and shut up. No one took any notice though. Her role as leader had been temporarily suspended, so her good suggestions were about as useful as the bad ones.

The whole scene left me feeling flustered. I was telling myself, "Alert but calm," and waiting for my head to come up with the kind of suggestion that was needed. Something that would cut through the chaos, creating a stern efficiency that was appropriate to the gravity of the situation. Specifically, something like the way Etienne had acted on the plateau. With that in mind, I considered pushing my way through to Sten and saying, "Leave him, Etienne. He's dead." But I couldn't shake the idea that it would sound like a line from a bad movie, and I wanted a line from a good movie. Instead I pushed my way backward through the crowd, which was easy as most people were trying to get closer.

As soon as I was out of the circle I began thinking a great deal more objectively. Two realizations hit me at once. Number one was that I now had a chance to get my cigarettes. Number two was Christo. Nobody had even mentioned the third Swede, who might have been on the beach, wounded and waiting for help to arrive. Possibly even dead like Sten.

I dithered for a couple of moments like a cartoon character, first looking one way, next the other. Then I made my decision and ran down the longhouse, passing the few squid-sufferers who were still too sick to see what was going on. I lit up on the run back, taking two matches to catch the flare of the phosphorus. Just before I ducked out of the long-house door, I shouted, "Christo!" but I didn't wait to see if anyone had heard me.

Through the jungle, I cursed myself for not having also grabbed a torch. I couldn't see much apart from the red glow of my cigarette, occasionally brightening as it burned through a spider's web. But having recently walked the path in darkness, en route to seeing the phosphorescence a couple of nights before, I didn't have too much trouble. My only mishap was walking straight into a bamboo thicket which had been recently cut for spears. My tough feet were okay. It was my shins and calves that got cut, which bothered me because I knew they'd sting if I had to go into the salt water.

On the beach, however, there was enough moonlight to see clearly. Across the sand were deep tracks where Karl had dragged Sten. He seemed to have reached the beach about twenty meters from the path to the clearing, come down, missed the entrance to the path, and doubled back. Christo, I noted as I dropped the butt, couldn't have made it as far as the shore. In the light from the moon, the sand was silver. The odd coconut husks and fallen palm branches were black. If he'd been there, I'd have seen him.

I took a deep breath and sat down a few feet from the water, juggling options and ideas. Christo wasn't on the beach and I hadn't passed him on the path—unless I'd walked over him unawares—so he was either in the lagoon, in the open sea, at the cave that led to the sea. If he was in the open sea, he was probably dead. If he was in the lagoon, he was either on a boulder or floating facedown. If he was at the cave, he had to be at one of its two entrances, maybe too tired to swim the lagoon or too injured to get through the underwater passage.

That was the Christo angle. The shark angle was more straightforward. It, or they, could be anywhere. I had no way of knowing any more than that, short of spotting a silhouette fin weaving across the lagoon, so I figured I'd be better off if I ignored the shark angle altogether.

"I bet he's in the caves," I said, and lit another cigarette to help me think. Then I heard a noise behind me, a padding footstep on the sand.

"Christo?" I called, and heard myself in stereo. The other person had called Christo at the exact same moment.

"No," we both answered together.

A pause.

I waited a few seconds, looking in all directions, unable to spot the figure. "Who then?"

No answer.

"Who then?" I repeated, standing. ". . . Is that . . . Is that you, Mister Duck?"

Still no answer.

A swell swept up the sand and tugged at my feet. I had to take a quick step forward to keep my balance. The following swell was just as strong and I had to take another step. The next thing I knew, the water was up to my knees and my cuts were smarting at the salt. The second cigarette, which I'd forgotten about, fizzled out as my hand hit the water.

I tried to swim along the route Christo would most likely have taken between the cave and the beach, pausing every so often to climb a boulder and scan around me. By the time I'd crossed three quarters of the lagoon, I could see flashlights on the beach. The others had arrived, but I didn't call to them. I wasn't decided whether their distant presence was a reassurance or a drag.

Shadowed

Christo's name was being called. Low-pitched and high-pitched, boys' voices and girls' voices, floating across the lagoon. I didn't like the sound. From my position, resting on a boulder by the entrance to the cave, the call was always answered by an echo. It gave me the creeps, so I swam into the cave to cut the sound out. Then, once started, I didn't stop. I swam straight ahead until I bumped blindly against the rock face where the passage ducked below the water level, took a lungful, and dived.

It was very exciting underwater. The rock walls, never warmed by sunlight, cooled and deadened the water. I felt as if I'd dared to enter a forbidden area; the zone I'd shied away from with Etienne and Françoise, diving for sand on Koh Samui. Braver now, I thought dreamily, relaxing my legs and slowing my arm strokes. I wasn't hurried. Christo and the shark seemed rather distant concerns. I was almost enjoying myself, and I knew my lungs were practiced enough to keep me under for over a minute and a half without serious discomfort.

Every few feet I stopped and groped around to make sure I wasn't accidentally heading down the side passage to the air pocket. In the process, I discovered that the central passage was far wider than I'd previously imagined. At full arms' length I couldn't touch either of its sides, only the barnacle-covered ceiling and floor. I realized, with a reproachful grimace, that to have ended up in the air pocket I must have strayed quite a way off course.

I grimaced harder when I came up on the seaward side of the cliffs. A strong night swell gave me a harsh reality check, pulling me out of my otherwordly stupor by knocking me against the rocks. I had to clamber awkwardly out of the water, slipping on algae and cutting my legs yet again. When I'd found my balance I looked around for Christo and yelled his name, without a lot of hope because the moonlight was bright enough for me to see he wasn't there. I could, however, see the boat. It was floating freely in the small cove that served as its port and hiding place, untied. I made my way over and scooped the rope out of the sea, securing the boat with as many granny knots as the rope's length would allow, not very nautical but the best I knew how. Then I perched on a small rock shelf and wondered what I should do next.

The problem was, I could easily have missed Christo on several stages of my search, the boulders particularly. It was possible that he'd already been found and was back at camp. But I also had a powerful sense that I hadn't missed him. The untied boat told me that the Swedes had gotten as far as the entrance to the cave. If Christo hadn't been injured, he'd have made the swim with Karl. If he had been injured, however, Karl would have left him where I was sitting, intending to come back for him later.

"Unless . . ." I muttered, clicking my fingers and shivering in the sea breeze.

Unless he'd been killed outright at sea, in which case it was a safe bet he'd never be found.

"Or . . ."

Or he'd only been injured a little. He'd been fit enough to make the swim through the underwater passage. He'd swum under with Karl, helping him with Sten, but something had happened. Swimming three men wide. Slightly hurt. Had to be scared and confused.

"That's it," I said firmly.

Karl wouldn't have realized Christo had gone until he came up in the lagoon. With Sten to deal with, maybe still alive, he couldn't go back. Maybe he waited for as long as a man could last without breathing. One or two desperate minutes extra to be sure. Maybe then he gave up.

"That's it. Christo's in the air pocket."

I stood up, filled my lungs, and dived back into the water. I found the side passage to the air pocket on my third attempt.

I surfaced, incredibly, into stars. I wondered if I'd missed the turning a fourth time, got disorientated, come up in the open sea or the lagoon. But the stars were beside and ahead of me. The stars were everywhere, unnaturally dense, within reaching distance and a thousand miles away.

Lack of oxygen, I thought, and took a tentative breath. The air tasted better than the last time in the air pocket, maybe freshened by an extra-low tide, but the stars didn't go away. I took another breath, shut my eyes, waited, opened them again. The stars remained, twinkling away, even a little brighter. "Impossible," I whispered. "This makes no—"

A murmur cut me off, coming from somewhere in the thick constellation. I paused, treading water slowly.

"Here . . ." said a quiet voice.

I pushed my hands out and felt a rock ledge, then I ran my hands along and felt skin. "Christo! Thank God! I've been—"

"Richard?"

"Yes."

"Help me."

"Yes. I'm here to help."

I continued feeling along the skin, working out which part of the body I was touching. It was surprisingly difficult to tell. What I first took to be an arm turned out to be a leg, and what I took to be a mouth turned out to be a wound.

Christo groaned loudly.

I shook my head. "I'm sorry . . . Are you badly hurt?"

". . . I have . . . some injury . . ."

"Okay. Do you think you're able to swim?"

"I do not know . . ."

"Because you have to swim. We have to get out of here."

"Out?"

"We've got to get out of the air pocket."

"Air . . . pocket . . . ?" he repeated, forming the sounds uncertainly.

"Air pocket. Uh . . . this little cave. We need to get out of this cave."

"But sky," he muttered. "Stars."

I frowned, surprised that he could see the stars, too. "No. They aren't stars. They're . . ." I hesitated. Then I reached up and my hand sank into cold strands of hanging seaweed. "Not stars," I finished, managing a short laugh, and pulled down a glittering strand.

"Not stars?" He sounded upset.

"Phosphorescence."

There was a small space left on the ledge, so I hauled myself out of the water and sat beside him. "Listen, Christo, I'm afraid we're going to have to try for this swim. There's no choice."

No reply.

"Hey, did you get that?"

". . . Yes."

"So what we'll do is, I'll swim ahead using my arms, and you'll have to hold on to my legs and try to kick. Are your legs injured?"

". . . Not legs. It is my . . . my . . ." He felt for my hand and put it someplace on his torso.

"So you can kick. We'll be fine. No sweat."

"Yes."

His voice sounded like it was getting fainter, so I talked my plans out loud to keep him awake. "Now our only problem is going to be finding the right passage out of here. If I remember right, there are four passages to choose from, and we don't want to get the wrong one. You understand?"

". . . I understand."

"Good. Let's do it, then." I leaned forward to drop back into the water, but stopped myself just as I was about to slip off the ledge.

"What?" asked Christo feebly, sensing that something had happened.

I didn't answer. I was transfixed by a chilling and beautiful sight, a slender comet cruising through the blackness beneath my feet.

"What happens, Richard?"

"Nothing . . . There's just . . . uh . . . something down there."

"The shark?" Christo's voice instantly rose to a frightened sob. "Is it this shark?"

"No, no. Definitely not. Don't worry." I watched the comet carefully. Actually, when I'd first seen it I had thought it was the shark, which is why I'd hesitated before answering Christo. But now I was sure it wasn't. Something about the way it moved wasn't right; it wasn't gliding and it was too jerky. It was more like a person.

"It's probably me," I said with a drunken smile.

"You?"

"My wake . . ." I giggled. "My shadow."

"What? I do not . . ."

I patted Christo's leg gently. "It's probably a shoal of fish."

The comet continued on its leisurely path and then, curiously, began to shorten. It took me a moment to realize it was passing into one of the passageways leading out.

"Okay, Christo," I said, putting a cautious hand on the back of my head. I'd suddenly felt as if part of my skull had fallen away and its contents were streaming out or expanding like vapor. Relieved to find hard bone and wet, matted hair, I allowed myself to slip into the water. "I think I know which direction to take."

Within a few strokes I understood that the passage was not the one leading back to the original cave. It twisted almost immediately to the right, whereas the other passage was virtually straight. But I was also confident, so I didn't attempt to turn back. Ten or so meters along we found a second air pocket, and ten meters further we found another. At the last air pocket we came up into fresh air. Ahead was the exit, circled by darkness. Through it I could see real stars and the real sky, just bright enough to pick out the faint black shapes of palm trees. Claws on pencil arms, running along the cliff top as it curved around to the mainland.

I laid the exhausted Christo out on the flat shelf beneath the lightning-bolt fissure and walked forward a couple of steps so I was looking over the coral gardens.

"Mister Duck?" I hissed softly. "Daffy? It was you, wasn't it? You're here."

"Yeah," Mister Duck replied, from so nearby it made me jump. "I'm here."

incoming

Politics

"Damn," I said, spotting Cassie. She was standing near the kitchen hut, talking to Ella. It meant I had no choice but to pass her. My only other options were to walk directly across the center of the clearing or to skirt around and come from behind the longhouse. In other words, passing Bugs or passing Sal. Not really options at all.

I sighed. Getting from one side of the clearing to the other had become like an eye-contact obstacle course. It was true that the shark attack had diverted attention away from the flare-up in the longhouse, but although an unspoken truce had been agreed, the tensions behind the incident were still there. Tactically, I had to hand it to Bugs. His group—basically the carpenters and gardeners minus Cassie and Jesse—had taken over the center of the clearing. Starting from the first afternoon after the shark attack, I'd come back from the island to find them all sitting there in a loose circle, smoking dope and chatting quietly. So as well as the commanding vantage point they had over the camp, there was a psychological aspect. It was like they represented the establishment, making the rest of us feel like dissenters.

Our dissenters' role was accentuated by the fact that, unlike the Bugs group, we had no sense of unity. In effect we were several subgroups. There was my old fishing detail and Keaty, which I included myself in, but there was also Jed, and I included myself with him as well. Then there was Moshe's detail, who seemed uncertain of where their affiliations lay, and there were the cooks. The cooks, as a result of Ella, partly included Jesse and Cassie. But you could also partly include Jesse and Cassie with my old fishing detail, because of their friendship with Keaty.

Finally, there were Sal and Karl. Karl was a law unto himself, drifting somewhere in outer space, and Sal was trying extremely hard to appear neutral—though we all knew where her loyalties would lie if push came to shove.

If it sounds complicated, that's because it was.

This, then, was the politics involved in crossing the clearing, and we all had to deal with it to the same degree. Except me, that is, who had an extra burden to deal with in the form of Cassie. Ever since the incident where Bugs had shat himself, she'd been treating me like I was mentally unstable, talking slowly, carefully enunciating each word, using an evenly modulated tone, as if she thought a sudden noise would scare me. It was really getting on my nerves. But I'd have shinned up a rocket ship tree to avoid passing Bugs, and Sal would make me give her a troublesome report on our guests on the neighboring island, so Cassie it had to be. Biting my lip and looking intently at the ground, I moved out from behind the foliage and set off in her direction. Out of the corner of my eye I could see that she was deep in conversation with Ella. I'm going to make it, I thought optimistically, but I was wrong.

"Richard," she said, just as I was about to move out of her range.

I looked up with a studiously blank expression.

"How are you?"

"Fine," I replied quickly. "On my way to see the patient."

She smiled. "No, Richard. I mean, how *are* you?"

"Fine," I repeated.

"I think this has been harder for you than anyone."

"Oh, well, not really."

"Finding Christo . . ."

"It wasn't so bad . . ."

"And now you have to work up on the island without company, without . . . support."

I shrugged helplessly. It would have been quite impossible to explain that from my point of view, the three days since Sten's death had been great. Jed's knowledge of first aid meant he was spending all his time looking after Christo, and that meant I got to spend my days alone in the DMZ.

Alone in a manner of speaking, anyway.

"But maybe being without company is a good thing, Cassie. It gives me time to think and come to terms with what's happened." From similar encounters, I knew this was the right thing to say.

Cassie widened her eyes as if she hadn't considered this, but now that she had, yes, it was a good idea and she was impressed I'd thought of it. "That's a *positive* attitude," she said warmly. "Well done."

I felt that this exchange was enough for me to disappear without appearing rude, so I made my excuses and continued on my way.

I was aiming for the hospital tent. More accurately, the Swedes' tent, but seeing as Sten was dead and Karl had started living on the beach, I'd begun calling it the hospital tent. Disappointingly, no one else did. Even though I'd made a point of using the new name at every opportunity, it had stubbornly refused to catch on.

"Back early today," said Jed when I climbed in. "It's still light." He sounded very tired and was sweating like a pig. It was baking under the canvas, even with the flap pegged open.

"Got hungry, needed a fag. Nothing much going on."

"No developments then."

I looked at Christo.

"He's asleep. It's okay."

"Oh . . . well yeah, no developments," I lied. There had been a very particular development, but not one I could go into. "Just the same as always."

"So we're lucky again. I wonder how long it will last."

"Mmm . . . I got some more grass, by the way."

"More? Richard, you . . ." Jed shook his head. "We've got grass coming out of our ears. Every day you've brought some back."

"People are smoking a lot at the moment."

"We'd need all the hippies in Goa to smoke through your supplies, and if you take too much the guards might notice."

I nodded. The same thought had crossed my mind, though with a different slant. I'd been hoping that my regular expeditions would get the guards on their toes. They were so pathetically easy to avoid that it made you wonder why they were there in the first place.

"So what about Christo?" I asked, changing the subject. "Any developments with him?"

Jed rubbed his eyes. "Yes. He's getting worse."

"Delirious?"

"No, just in pain. If he's awake. He spends most of the time unconscious and he's running a bad fever. Without a thermometer it's hard to tell, but I'm sure it's higher than yesterday . . . To tell you the truth"—Jed lowered his voice—"I'm getting seriously worried about him."

I frowned. Christo looked okay to me. When I'd seen him in the day-

light the morning after rescuing him, I'd felt slightly let down by the un-
dramatic nature of his injuries. Apart from a single cut on his arm—the
cut I'd mistaken for a mouth—his only wound was a large bruise on his
stomach from where the shark had rammed him. The injuries were so superficial that he'd walked around on the first day, trying to find Karl. He'd
only collapsed on the second day, which we'd thought was a result of
stress or possibly a relapse of the food poisoning.

"I mean," Jed continued, "the bruise should be going down, shouldn't
it?"

"You're the doctor, Jed."

"I'm not a fucking doctor. That's the point."

I leaned over to take a look. "Well, it's blacker than it was. Not so purple. I think that means it's healing."

"Do you know that for a fact?"

"Not for a fact, no." I paused. "I'm sure it'll just be the food poisoning
that's keeping him low. Jesse is still getting gripes."

"Uh-huh."

"And so is Bugs . . . unfortunately!" I added, with a mischievous wink
that Jed either missed or ignored. "Well, I'm going to get some food and
catch up with Françoise and the others."

"Okay. Leave a cigarette, will you? And come back later. Nobody
comes in to check on me apart from you and Unhygienix. I think they're
avoiding having to see Christo . . . Pretending it hasn't happened maybe."

"Pretty hard," I said, chucking him the packet. "Sten's still lying in that
sleeping bag around the back of the longhouse. It's right on the other side
from where I sleep, and I can smell him through the walls."

Jed glanced at me. There was obviously something he wanted to say, so
I nodded, to say, "Go on," but he only sighed. "Tomorrow morning," he said
sadly. "Sal said she's given up on trying to persuade Karl to be there, so
he'll be buried by the waterfall tomorrow morning."

Dissent

Sal had been sitting in her usual spot outside the longhouse entrance, which, if one wanted to get to the beach, was unavoidable without an exhaustingly roundabout route via the Khyber Pass. But to my relief she'd moved by the time I left the hospital tent. I assumed she'd gone to the center of the clearing to talk to Bugs; something I could have confirmed with a simple turn of the head, but I didn't want to look in the enemy's direction so I took it on faith. My mistake. I should have confirmed. Just like with Cassie, I was sprung as I thought I was leaving the danger zone—in this case past the longhouse, about to join the path from the clearing to the beach.

"Richard," said a stern voice.

Sal was standing chest-deep in the shrubs beside the track. She'd clearly been hiding there in order to ambush me. "You were hiding," I blurted, surprised into speaking the truth.

"Yes, Richard. I was." She stepped forward, delicately parting the ferns with a pudgy hand. "I didn't want to force you into one of your ludicrously transparent evasion exercises."

"Evasion? I haven't been evad—"

"You have."

"No, really."

"Save it, Richard."

This was the third time she'd used my name, so I knew she meant business. I gave up the pretense with a feeble grin.

"Wipe that smirk off your face," she said immediately. "Have you got any idea what trouble you've been causing me?"

"Sorry, Sal."

"Sorry doesn't cut it. You're a pain in the ass. How simple were your instructions?"

"Very simple, Sal."

"*Very* simple. But you've forgotten them already."

"No, I—"

"Repeat them."

"... The instructions?"

"Yes."

I had to make an effort to keep a schoolboy's insolence out of my voice. "While Jed is looking after Christo, it's my responsibility to keep you up to date on ..." I stammered and a cold flush pricked my neck. I'd nearly said Zeph's and Sammy's names.

"On?" Sal demanded.

"... on our potential new arrivals."

"Exactly. Now perhaps you can tell me why you're finding that one little task so difficult."

"There was nothing to tell today. No developments, same as always."

"Wrong." Sal shook a finger at me. I watched the little hammocks of fat under her upper arm wobble indignantly. "Wrong, wrong, wrong. If there's nothing to tell, I want to hear it. Otherwise I worry, and I've got a *lot* to worry about at the moment, so I don't need you making things worse. Get it?"

"Yes."

"Good." She lowered her finger and took a breath to compose herself. "I don't mean to be tough on you, but I just can't deal with extra hassles at the moment. Morale is ... well, morale is bad."

"We'll pull through."

"I know we will, Richard," she said curtly. "I have no doubt of it. But to make certain, I want you to pass on a message to all your friends."

"... Sure."

"Yes. I want you to tell them that for the past three days, for obvious reasons, I've been tolerating this absurd rift that has blown up in the camp."

I made a rather foolish attempt at appearing innocent. "Rift?"

"Rift! As in half the camp not talking to the other half! As in people threatening to stick spears in other people's necks!"

I reddened.

"Now you may or may not know that tomorrow morning we're going to be burying Sten. I want that burial to mark the end of the tension so that some good can come out of this appalling tragedy. I also want you to know that I'm giving the same message to Bugs. I don't want you guys thinking he's getting preferential treatment because he's my man. Okay?"

"Okay."

Sal nodded. Then she put the base of her palm flat on her forehead, and held it there silently for several seconds.

Poor Sal, I thought. I hadn't been very understanding of the stress she was under, and I made a resolution to be a good deal more understanding in the future. I wasn't even sure why I'd been avoiding her. My problem was with Bugs. I'd unfairly allowed my dislike of him to spill over to her.

"So," she said eventually, "where were you going before I nabbed you?"

"To the beach. Looking for Françoise . . . and checking up on Karl."

"Karl . . ." Sal muttered something indistinct and looked up at the canopy. When she looked down she seemed surprised to find me still with her. "Go on then," she said, ushering me away. "What are you waiting for? Get lost."

It was getting close to six o'clock when I reached the beach, cool enough to walk slowly on the dry sand if I'd wanted to. But I didn't. I was playing one of my games, and it required walking in the damp sand by the shore.

The aim was to leave the perfect footprint, and it was a lot harder and more preoccupying than it might sound. If the sand was the dry side of damp, the footprint crumbled; the moist side and it melted as the squeezed-out water seeped back in. Then there was the application of pressure. The toes sank too deeply with a normal step and flawed the imprint. The alternative, taking an artificial step with even pressure, created a good imprint at the cost of ethics. This was the compromise I wrestled with.

In this way I made my way along the beach, hopping, pausing, groaning, mashing up bad prints in frustration. My eyes were always pointed downward, so I didn't realize that I'd reached my friends until I was within a couple of meters of them.

"Are you going insane, Rich?" I heard Keaty say. "If you are, tell us. It might mean you'll have better luck getting through to Karl."

"I'm trying to make the perfect footprint," I replied without raising my head. "It's really difficult."

Keaty laughed in a way that told me he was stoned. "The perfect footprint, huh? Yeah, that's getting pretty close to insane. And more original than trying to draw the perfect circle."

"Circle?"

"It's what mad people do."

"Oh." I stamped out my last effort and trudged over, disappointed to see that Françoise wasn't with them. "Is that what Karl is doing?"

"Nope. He's too mad even for circles."

"Actually," Etienne interrupted, not about to join in with Keaty's flippant appraisal, "Karl is not mad. He is *dans un état de choque.*"

Keaty arched his eyebrows. "Uh-huh. Just what I figured . . . Now maybe you could tell us what it means."

"I do not know the correct English. It is why I said it in French."

"That's helpful."

"If you had been interested to help, you would be taking Karl to Koh Phangan," said Etienne stiffly, and stood up. "And I am tired of arguing this with you. Excuse me, Richard. I am going back to camp. You will tell Françoise when she returns?"

"Okay," I replied uncomfortably. I'd obviously turned up in the middle of something, and I wasn't at all happy with the idea that my friends had been arguing. We had to stick together, even if Sal was going to be calling for a truce tomorrow.

Etienne began walking away. A couple of seconds later, Keaty turned to Gregorio and hissed, "Why the fuck weren't you backing me up?"

Gregorio looked at his hands pensively. "I do not know . . . I thought perhaps he was right."

"He isn't right. How can he be right?"

"Hold on," I said, first checking behind me to make sure that Etienne was out of earshot. "Was Etienne being serious about Koh Phangan?"

Keaty nodded. His tiny dreadlocks were still short enough to stand bolt upright and they seemed to accentuate his expression of incredulity. "Dead serious. He's been saying it all day. Says he's going to bring it up with Sal."

"But he *must* know we can't take him to Koh Phangan. What would we say? 'Here's a friend of ours who's been attacked by a shark and had a nervous breakdown on our secret beach. Well, we'll be off then. See you . . .'"

"He thinks we could take him there and drop him off near Hadrin."

"That's ridiculous. Even if he didn't give everything away, how would we know he got looked after? There's a million fucked-up freaks over there. If someone saw him wasting away on the sand, they'd just ignore him." I shook my head. "No way. The best thing for Karl is for him to be here."

"I've been telling that to Etienne all day. But wait, it gets worse. He wants to drop Sten off on Koh Phangan as well."

"*Sten?*"

"Yep."

"But he's dead! What would be the point of . . ."

"His family. Etienne thinks we have to let them know what's happened to their son. See, if we left them both on the beach, then Karl would definitely be noticed and Sten's family would be contacted."

I smiled in disbelief. "Yeah, and meanwhile we'd definitely get discovered. We'd be finished. It's the worst idea I ever heard."

"Tell me about it," said Keaty. "And while you're at it," he added, pointing at Gregorio, "tell him."

Gregorio lay on his back to avoid our accusing stares. "I only think we should think about what Etienne says. If Karl is not talking to any people here, maybe he will not talk to any people on Koh Phangan."

"No," said Keaty. "He'll talk, eventually. And when he does, I'd rather he did it to us. Not some fucking Thai cop or Swedish shrink."

I couldn't have put it better myself.

Whoosh, Boom, Zzz

After all the discussion about Karl, I decided I ought to go and see him myself. Or that's what I told Keaty and Gregorio. Really I was just interested in catching up with Françoise, whom I'd barely seen over the past few days. The main reasons were our different work details and the hectic circumstances, though I hadn't been very active in seeking her out. Following the misunderstood kiss, I'd been slightly wary of giving Etienne any reasons to be suspicious.

I found Françoise by Karl's hole, about four hundred meters further on from Keaty and Gregorio. Karl had dug the hole when he'd decamped to the beach. It wasn't much of a hole: thigh-high if he stood up, chest-deep if he sat down. More impressive was the shelter which Etienne and Keaty had rigged up. Because Karl refused to budge from his hole all through the day, they'd been worried about him getting sunstroke. They'd found three long palm branches and tied them against each other like a teepee. The gaps in the fronds wouldn't have stopped rain but they kept him in the shade.

I was expecting Françoise to be in a bad mood, as everyone else seemed to be, so I was happily surprised when she ran over and gave me a hug.

"Richard!" she said. "Thank you! I have not thanked you yet! So, thank you!"

I paused. "What for?"

"For helping me when I was sick. Really, you were so kind. I wanted to tell you before, but there was never a good chance. Always so much to do. We have to catch all the extra fish now and then I stay with Karl, and often you are not back until late."

"Françoise, don't give it another thought. It was nothing. Anyway, you did the same for me once."

"Yes, with your fever." She smiled, then looked at me straight in the eyes, and suddenly the smile turned into a sly chuckle. "You kissed me!"

My eyes flicked away. "I thought you were sleeping . . ."

"I was. Etienne told me the next day."

"Oh," I said, mentally unleashing a stream of curses at Etienne's big mouth. "Well . . . I hope you don't mind . . . It was sort of complicated . . ."

"Of course I do not mind! You know, when you were ill I also kissed you."

"I was never completely sure if I dreamed that or not."

"You did not dream it. And remember the next morning! You were so worried!"

I nodded, remembering my awkwardness and Françoise's Exocet-style questions extremely clearly.

"So tell me," she said. "Why do you say it was complicated?"

"Well . . . complicated is probably the wrong, uh . . . It wasn't like the kiss was . . . The kiss wasn't . . ." I stopped myself and started again. "I'm not sure what Etienne told you, but he took the kiss the wrong way. I was kissing you because you were so sick, and there was so much other sickness around that once I'd started . . . it was kind of hard to stop."

"How was Etienne taking it?"

Whoosh, I thought. Boom.

". . . Well, I guess he thought it was . . . you know . . ."

"A sexy kiss."

"Mmm."

Françoise laughed again. Then she leaned over and planted a little kiss on my cheek.

"Was that a sexy kiss?"

"No," I replied; only a small fib. "Of course not."

"So there is no problem. Not complicated."

"I'm glad you understand."

"Always," she said. "I always understand."

For a moment we held each other's gaze, just long enough for it to acquire a mild resonance. It reminded me of other moments from months back, loaded exchanges on Koh Samui, our midnight conversation about the parallel worlds in the Milky Way. Then the moment was over, broken by Françoise as she turned to look at Karl.

"He does not push down the shelter anymore," she said a few seconds later.

"Yeah. I saw it was up. Maybe it's a good sign. An improvement or something."

She sighed. "No. It means nothing. We discovered he only pushed the shelter down because of the leaves . . . He could not see the caves. He likes to watch them. When we left a space for him to watch through, he left the shelter alone."

"Ah . . ."

"But maybe he is improving . . . He eats the food I give him now."

"That's something, I guess. Not much though."

Françoise nodded. "Yes . . . Poor Karl . . . Not much."

Sal cornered me a final time that day. I'd stayed with Françoise until long after the sun went down, and Sal got me just as I was about to enter the longhouse on my way to bed.

"Did you pass on my message?" she asked.

I slapped my forehead. "Shit, Sal, it totally slipped my mind. I'm really sorry. I got distracted because people were talking about Karl and then . . ."

Sal shook her head dismissively. "Okay, okay. I know what happened because I've had a chat with Etienne this evening. It seems like there'll be a lot of ground to cover at the funeral tomorrow morning and . . . Please don't tell me you've forgotten about the funeral."

"Sal!" I said, probably overdoing the outrage. "Of course not!"

"Well, it's hard to tell with you . . . Anyway, following the talk with Etienne, I've had a slight change of plan. I've decided to be a bit blunter with the camp than I'd originally planned to be. Desperate times and desperate measures, or something like it . . ." She hesitated. "Funerals have a way of drawing people together, don't you think, Richard?"

"They can," I said doubtfully.

"They can, yes. . . . So the point is, don't lose any sleep over not passing on the message."

I nodded. "I won't."

"Good. I'll see you tomorrow then."

"Sure. Tomorrow."

Moshe was the last to bed, so he blew out the last candle. The Jim-Bob game, obviously, was out of the question, but it crossed my mind to try it. I was interested to know what would happen. Probably we'd have labored through it, only calling out the names of our friends until some poor sap was stuck and had to pass it over to the Bugs side. Probably via the Yugo girls, I imagined, or maybe Sal.

I moved on to thinking about Françoise, a train of thought that, once started, could occupy me almost indefinitely. Indefinitely turned out to be at least an hour. That was how long I'd been lying awake before I realized that everyone else in the longhouse was lying awake too. It was a revelation I found annoying. As there was no light in the longhouse for one's eyes to become accustomed to, normally one felt snugly cocooned by the insulating wall of blackness. Paradoxically, it was the snores and sounds of others sleeping that reinforced this cocoon, the sleepers distanced by their unconsciousness.

Once I was alerted to the lack of heavy breathing, the cocoon illusion was ruined. Ruined and, worst of all, replaced by a nagging puzzle. I was awake because I had Françoise to mull over, but why was everyone else awake? It took me another half hour to deduce that it had to be because they were fretting about Sten's funeral.

Five minutes later, the puzzle solved, I fell fast asleep.

Ashes to Dust

Despite the stench of rotten Sten (a sudden hot blast erupted when his feet slipped out of his sleeping bag), the funeral had some dignity. We all circled the grave that Jean had dug the day before, close enough to the waterfall to make a pleasant spot, far enough to stop our drinking water from being spoiled. Then Sal said a few words, talking of his unfailing commitment to the camp and the extent to which we'd all miss him. Unhygienix, as head cook, said a few more. He talked about how Sten always caught big fish, which weren't necessarily tastier than the smaller ones from the lagoon, but went further in terms of keeping people's stomach's full. He also pointed out that although Sten hadn't played the most active social role in the camp, he was always ready to join in if a Sunday soccer game was organized and had never been known to foul. This last point drew a couple of murmurs of agreement from the crowd.

No one was visibly upset until we started filling in the grave. Then several of the girls started crying. Ella particularly—like all the cooks, she'd had more contact with him than the rest of us had. Anyway, I could understand the tears because there was something poignant about watching the sleeping bag shroud become slowly covered with earth. It brought home how absolute Sten's absence from the world had become.

Finally, Bugs planted a wooden headstone. To his credit, he'd made a real effort with the carving, putting little flourishes around Sten's name and the date. If I had to niggle, I'd mention that the headstone was missing Sten's second name and date of birth. The trouble was, Christo wasn't able to answer questions about Sten, and Karl wasn't willing, so there was nothing that anyone could do about it. But perhaps it was more appropriate that way. Second names felt connected to the world, maybe because they were a link to family and home, so they were never used or asked. It's a funny thought that if today—for some inexplicable reason—I wanted to track down any of the people I once knew on the beach, I'd have no better clue to work from than a nationality and a fading memory of a face.

Throughout the proceedings, I was wondering at which point Sal would address us about the tensions in the camp. I'd assumed it would be when she spoke at graveside, and I think she'd assumed the same thing, but the smell had probably changed her mind. It was distracting. Although we all listened attentively to her and Unhygienix, I think there was a quiet sense of relief when the earth sealed the head hole of Sten's sleeping bag.

Sal eventually made her move when we thought it was over. Jed turned to head off back to camp—he was in a hurry because he didn't want to leave Christo unattended for too long—but Sal stopped him.

"Hold on, Jed," she called over our heads, standing on tiptoe. "I don't want anyone leaving yet. There's something important I want to say, and I want everyone around to hear it."

Jed frowned but stayed put. Among the others I noticed several more puzzled frowns. I also noticed some expectant expressions among Bugs's crew, and to my dismay, something in those expressions which appeared worryingly close to smugness. More worrying was that Bugs had maneuvered himself so that he was standing right by Sal's side. This wouldn't have been surprising in normal circumstances, but when Sal had called to Jed she'd taken a couple of steps forward. Bugs had matched these steps to remain with her, nudging Cassie aside in the process. I kicked myself for having forgotten to pass on Sal's message. "Forewarned," I muttered to myself, "is forearmed," which made Keaty glance at me.

"Okay!" Sal clapped her hands. "I'd like to start by asking everyone to sit down so you can all see me . . . and so I can be reassured that there are still a few things, funerals excluded, that we can all do together."

With a good many exchanged looks we arranged ourselves on the grass, Bugs, predictably, remaining standing longer than everyone else.

Sal surveyed us until we were settled, then nodded. "In case anyone hasn't realized or heard," she began, "I'm going to talk about the atmosphere in the camp. I'm going to talk about it because I have no choice. I'm going to talk about it because no one else seems willing to do so, except in painfully indiscreet huddles."

Here, to my astonishment, she stared directly at Bugs. But my astonishment was nothing to his, and a broad grin leapt to my face as I saw his cheeks flush. She'd kept her word about being evenhanded, I thought approvingly, and suddenly wondered if there were unknown strains in their relationship. Delighted, I imagined the nosedive his position in the camp would take if Sal chucked him. The grin vanished, however, when she directed her next comment straight at me.

"I'll add that matters have not been helped by certain individuals who have hardly tried to patch things up. In fact, I might say they've deliberately made things worse. And yes, Richard, before you even dream of denying it, I mean you. I don't want to repeat anything that was said in the longhouse a few nights ago, but I will say that if anything like it ever happens again, the one who'll be chucking spears is me. Clear?"

She didn't wait for an answer.

"Not that Richard should be singled out. As far as I'm concerned, with *very* few exceptions, everybody here is guilty of having acted like a fucking idiot over this whole mess. Between the two sides of the split, I haven't seen anyone making an effort to cool things down, so I don't see Richard's behavior as any worse than the ones who sit around in sullen gangs."

By now the exchanged glances had stopped and we were all picking at loose threads on our shorts or looking rather intently at the leaves above us. Anywhere but at Sal.

"So the way I see things is like this. We've had two severe disasters over the past week. First there was the food poisoning and then we had the unspeakable tragedy that has collected us here now. For these reasons, the atmosphere in the camp has been understandably bad. If we weren't all in a

state of shock with tempers fraying, we wouldn't be human. . . . *But*"—
Sal punched a fist in her palm—"it ends *here!* It ends with the burial of a
friend, so that something positive will come of his otherwise senseless
death.

"Now, dates don't mean much on the beach, but I keep a calendar. And
it may interest you to know that the date is September the eleventh."

As a matter of fact, it interested me a lot to hear that the date was September 11, because it meant it was close to five months since I'd left England. But I was surprised that it interested everyone else to the extent
that it did. There was a ripple of exclamations around me and someone
whistled.

"For the sake of our newest arrivals, it means that the Tet festival is in
three days' time. The Tet festival, named by another absent friend, Daffy,
is our yearly birthday. It was the date we first spent a night on the beach,
and we celebrate it accordingly."

As she said this, the fire dropped from Sal's eyes and she looked rather
sad. "To be honest, I haven't been much looking forward to this year's Tet.
Without Daffy, I don't mind telling you, it will feel very strange. But after
the trouble we've been through, particularly losing Sten, I now feel that
the festival is exactly what we need. It will remind us what we are and
why we're here. As it marks our birthday, it will mark a fresh start."

Sal paused for a moment, clearly lost in thought. Then her face hardened and she snapped back into business mode. "Obviously, this means a
trip to Koh Phangan to get party supplies. Normally I'd ask for volunteers,
but this time I won't. Bugs and Keaty, as you two were the catalyst for the
split, I want you to make the trip together."

I instantly checked to see how Keaty was taking this bit of news, and
he looked completely appalled. Bugs I couldn't see anymore because he'd
slumped over slightly, but I was pretty sure he would have known about
Sal's decision already. I doubted he'd have been happy with it, but he
wouldn't have been as shocked as Keaty.

"You can see it as a symbolic gesture if you like. I see it as practical. . . .
And Etienne," she said as an afterthought, "I've been thinking about your
suggestion to take Karl to Koh Phangan, but for the reasons we discussed
I simply don't think it's possible."

Suddenly I felt a finger jab into my ribs. I turned around and saw Jed leaning toward me. "Hey," he whispered. "I didn't know Etienne wanted to take Karl to Koh Phangan."

I nodded. "Yeah. He went to see Sal about it yesterday. Why?"

Jed's eyes flicked down. "Just interested," he muttered.

I shrugged and looked back at Sal, but while I'd been turned away she'd obviously made a gesture to show that her sermon was over. People were stirring and starting to rise.

"Okay," she said. "So that's it. I hope you all listened hard. For today, details as normal. Tomorrow Keaty and Bugs leave for Koh Phangan."

I tried to catch Jed as we all filed out of the waterfall clearing, but he'd run on ahead to get back to Christo. Instead I walked with Keaty and Gregorio.

The conversation, as we made our way through the jungle, was amusingly surreal. It was blindingly obvious that we were all dying to swap opinions about Sal's speech, but we had to limit ourselves to small talk for fear of our insights being overheard. So ahead of me I had Jean conferring with Ella about whether the tomatoes were ready for the pot, and behind me I had Cassie saying that her machete needed sharpening.

But this facade of geniality aside, it was also apparent that Sal's speech had had its desired effect. The mood was curiously upbeat, our walking pace fast. Already the funeral seemed as if it had been consigned to the past. If it hadn't been for Jed hurrying off to look after Christo, I could almost have forgotten that the Swedes had been the main reason for the meeting by the waterfall.

Neither did the mood change when we reached camp. I was half expecting us to fall back into our factional huddles and begin the analysis of the morning's events. But within a few minutes the different details had separated out and the clearing was empty. Apart from me, that is, and Sal.

"Was I fair?" she said, walking over.

"Fair . . ." I scratched my head and dropped the cigarette I was smoking, stubbing it out with my toe. "Yeah, you were fair. I think it all worked out pretty well. I was even surprised you let me off so light . . . seeing as Bugs is your boyfriend and all."

"Favoritism isn't my scene, Richard. I'd have hoped you knew that by now. Anyway, I think you redeemed yourself when you rescued Christo. That was a brave thing you did . . . not to mention dumb."

I smiled. "Thanks."

"Well." She smiled back. "So shouldn't you be going? Our neighbors might be up to something, and I'm looking forward to my evening report."

"Right."

I started to walk toward the path to the beach, then, on instinct, I stopped and glanced around. Sal was still looking at me.

"You like me, don't you, Sal?" I said.

She was just close enough for me to see her eyebrows rise. "Excuse me, Richard?"

"You like me. I mean . . . you tell me off when I do something wrong, but you never stay angry for long."

". . . I don't hold mistakes against anyone."

"And you trusted me with the Rice Run and the Jed detail. You could have easily refused his request, especially with me being one of the newest arrivals. And you chose me to pass on the message about your meeting, even though you knew I couldn't be relied on."

"Good Lord, Richard. You do say the strangest things."

"But I'm right, aren't I?"

Sal sighed. "I suppose you are. But that isn't to say . . ."

"I know. Favoritism isn't your scene." I paused. "Shall I tell you why you like me?"

"Go on then."

"It's because I remind you of Daffy, isn't it?"

". . . Yes. But how could you . . ." She shook her head. "Yes, you do remind me of Daffy. Very much."

"I thought that was it," I said. Then I continued on my way.

My Lost Shit

Mister Duck was waiting for me at the lookout post, as he had done every morning since the shark attack.

I'd had a shock the first time I found him up there, and we'd promptly had an argument. I felt it had been reasonable for him to appear while I was helping Christo in the caves. With or without the phosphorescence, the caves had the qualities of a nightmare—exactly where you'd imagine Mister Duck might show up. But to see him in crisp sunshine, sitting with an unlit joint clamped between his teeth like a cowboy's cheroot, was hard to take.

For as long as the initial bewilderment gripped me, I'd stood gaping while he grinned and tilted his head from side to side. Then I said, "It's *broad daylight*, Mister Duck!"

I said it angrily because I felt obscurely insulted by the brazen nature of his apparition.

"Broad daylight," he'd replied evenly, "is what it is."

I paused. ". . . I'm not dreaming."

"True."

"Then I'm going insane."

"Do you want an honest answer?"

"Yes."

He shrugged. "I'd only query the tense. But I'm not a professional, so, you know, seek out a second opinion."

I threw up my arms, threw them down again, and sat heavily on the ground. Then I reached out and touched his shoulder. It was as dry and warm and solid as my own.

Mister Duck frowned when I shuddered. "You have a problem?"

I shook my head. "Yes, I have a problem. I'm mad."

"So? Are you complaining?"

"Complaining?"

"Is that what you're doing? Complaining?"

"I'm—"

He cut me off. "If you're complaining, buddy, I'm going to tell you right now, I don't want to hear it."

"I'm just—"

"I'm just, I'm just," he mimicked. "You're just what?"

"I'm very fucking shocked! Seeing you and . . . being mad!"

Mister Duck's face screwed up in disgust. "Where's the shock in being mad?"

"Everywhere!" I said furiously. "I don't want to be mad!"

"You don't *want* to be mad? Well, well. Mind if I pick you up on that?"

I pulled out a cigarette with slightly shaking hands, then put it back, remembering I couldn't smoke on the island. "Yes. I mind. I want you to go away."

"Tough. Answer this. Where are you?"

"Leave me alone!"

"Where are you?" he repeated.

I covered my face with my hands. "I'm in Thailand."

"Where?"

"Thaila—"

"Where?"

Through the cracks between my fingers, I stole a glance down to the DMZ. My shoulders slumped as I got the gist. "Vietnam."

"Vietnam!" A great crowing grin spread across his features. "You said it! You *wanted* it! And now these are the breaks! In country, losing your shit comes with the territory!" He whooped and slapped his thigh. "Fuck it, man, you should be welcoming me! I'm the proof you made it! Rich, I *am* your lost shit! Viet-fuckin'-*nam!*"

By the end of that day, I was already feeling pretty comfortable with Mister Duck's presence. And by the end of the second, I realized I was quite pleased about it. He was good company, in his way, and he knew how to make me laugh. Also, as we were spending hours with each other, a lot of our conversation was about commonplace stuff, like places we'd both been to or films we'd both seen. It was hard to stay shocked by someone while you were talking about *Star Wars*.

After the burial I was very keen to get to the lookout post. I had lots of questions for Mister Duck about Tet and I wanted to tell him about Sal's speech to the camp, so I jogged almost all the way up to the pass.

I found him with Jed's binoculars clamped to his eyes.

"I've got loads to tell you," I panted as I sat down beside him, breathless from my haste. "We buried Sten, and Sal made a long speech to the camp. She talked about Tet. You haven't told me about Tet. And she talked about you, too."

An odd look passed over Mister Duck's face. "Sal talked about me? What did she say?"

"She said Tet would be different this year because you were gone."

". . . Is that all she said?"

"That's all she said about you. But she also talked about Tet and camp morale."

Mister Duck nodded. "Very nice," he muttered disinterestedly.

"Don't you want to hear about it? It was really impressive the way she spoke. I think she had a real effect on—"

"No," he interrupted. "I don't."

"You don't want to hear about it?"

"Nope."

"Oh . . . Why not?"

"Because, Rich . . . Because . . ."

He seemed to drift off for a moment, lowering the binoculars, raising them to have another look, and then lowering them again.

"Because I want to talk about Airfix models."

To Those Who Wait

"Airfix models."

"Or Matchbox models. Either."

"Any particular reason?"

"Curiosity."

"Mister Duck, we just buried Sten today. Sal made an amazing speech. There's some celebration called Tet coming up, which you've never mentioned, and—"

"Spitfires," he said patiently, sliding himself round to face me. "Messerschmitts. Did you ever make them?"

I looked at him. "Yes."

"Hurricanes?"

"Hurricanes too."

"Lancaster bombers? Lysander bombers? Mosquitoes?"

". . . I think I made a Lysander once."

"Hmm. Any jets?"

I resigned myself to the unlikely topic. "No. I never liked making jets."

"Me neither. How about that? No jets . . . Or boats, tanks, trucks . . ."

"Or helicopters. They were such a pain, which was a shame because I loved the way they looked."

"Naturally."

"It was the rotor blades . . ."

"Those bloody rotor blades. They'd keep falling off before the glue was dry."

I didn't reply for a moment. A gentle tickling had alerted me to an ant that had found its way onto my stomach. After a couple of seconds I found it, trapped in the line of hair that ran from my belly button. I picked it up by licking my finger so the ant stuck to the spit. "Very difficult," I finally said, and blew the ant away.

Mister Duck's eyes gleamed mischievously. "So you weren't very good at making models then."

"I didn't say that."

"Well, were you any good?"

"Uh . . ." I hesitated. "I was okay."

"You didn't used to mess them up? Too much polyester cement, the pieces not fitting together properly, annoying gaps where the wings met the body, or where the two halves of the undercarriage met. Be honest now."

"Oh, well . . . Yeah. That used to happen all the time."

"Same. It used to drive me nuts. I'd start the model with the best intentions, trying so hard to do a perfect job, but it would almost never work out." Mister Duck chuckled. "And at the end, I always got left with the same problem."

"Which was?"

"What to do with the messed-up model once it was finished. I knew a guy who made perfect models and he'd hang them from his ceiling with bits of thread. But I didn't want to do that with the planes I made. Not with their gluey fingerprints all over the place. It would have been embarrassing."

"I know what you mean."

"I thought you would."

Mister Duck lay back on the grass contentedly, using his folded arms as a pillow. As he did so a butterfly passed near him. A big one, with long strips on each wing that ended in a bright blue circle, like tiny peacock feathers. He reached up a finger, hoping for the butterfly to land, but it ignored him and fluttered off down the slope toward the DMZ.

"So, Rich," he said lazily. "Tell me what you used to do with the messed-up models."

I smiled. "Oh, I used to have the best laugh with them."

"Yeah? It didn't drive you nuts then."

"Sure. At first I'd be kicking chairs around and swearing. But then I'd go out and buy some lighter fuel and I'd drop them out of windows. And also I'd cut holes in the bodies and slide in a firecracker to blow them up."

"Good fun."

"Great fun."

"Burning the bad models."

"So you used to do the same thing?"

"Sort of." Mister Duck closed his eyes against the hot sun. "I burned the good ones, too."

It must have gone midday before I checked on Zeph and Sammy. Our chat had distracted me from the job at hand, which may have been its intent. I'd sunbathed and dozed for a couple of hours, remembering melting Focke-Wulfs and plastic burns from being careless. I might have forgotten about them altogether if Mister Duck, with careful timing, hadn't reminded me.

"Sal's not going to be happy," he said.

I sat up. "Huh?"

"Sal's not going to be happy. In fact, she's going to be seriously pissed off. She'll do her funny little frown . . . You ever notice her funny little frown?"

"No. But how come she isn't going to be happy?"

"I can't believe you've never noticed her frown. I always used to think she looked so pretty when she was pissed off. Her eyes would glow and . . . Do you think Sal's pretty?"

"Uh . . ."

"I think she is."

I looked at him for a couple of moments, then burst out laughing. "Well, well! You had a crush on her, didn't you?"

"A crush?" He went red. "I wouldn't call it a crush. We were very close, that's all."

"You mean she didn't fancy you."

"I just told you, we were very close."

I laughed harder. "Nothing ever happened, did it?"

Mister Duck shot me an annoyed look. Then he said, "Nothing physical happened. But some relationships, *close* relationships, don't need a physical connection. A spiritual bond can be more than enough."

"Unrequited love," I groaned, wiping tears from my eyes. "Now I understand why you put up with Bugs all that time."

"Well, you'd be the expert on unrequited love."

"Excuse me?"

"Does the name Françoise ring a bell?"

I stopped laughing.

"Ding dong!" Mister Duck chimed. "How's that for a fucking bell?"

"Do me a favor. It's completely different. For a start, Françoise actually does fancy me. And whereas Bugs is a prick, Etienne is a great guy. Which, I should point out, is the only reason nothing happens. Neither of us wants to hurt his feelings."

"Mmm."

I glowered at him. "Anyway. Do you think we could get back to the point?"

"What point?"

"You said Sal was going to be seriously pissed off about something."

"Oh . . . Yeah." Mister Duck chucked me the binoculars. "Because of the raft."

". . . *Raft?*" I scrambled over to the edge of the lookout point and slammed the binoculars to my face. Quickly I scanned along their beach. It was empty. "I don't see anything," I said. "What are you talking about?"

"Where are you looking?" Mister Duck replied languidly.

"Their beach!"

"Find the split palm."

". . . Got it."

"Okay. Now go to six o'clock. Six or seven."

I eased the binoculars downward, leaving the sand behind, moving into the blue water.

"There yet?"

"*Where* yet? I still can't see anythi—" I gulped. "Oh fuck."

"Impressive, huh? They may have taken their time, but they sure put it to good use." He sighed while I hyperventilated. "Tell the truth, Rich. No bullshit. Do you think Sal ever thinks about me?"

Fine, Thanks

Discovering that Zeph and Sammy were on their way left me a lot more anxious and a lot less excited than I'd expected. I found this confusing, and was still trying to make sense of my reaction when I arrived back at camp. Whereupon, immediately, I became even more confused.

There was nothing in the clearing to suggest we'd buried Sten that morning. The atmosphere was more like a Sunday than a wake. A few people were kicking a soccer ball beside the longhouse, Jesse and Cassie were whistling as they laid out some washing to dry, Unhygienix was playing the Gameboy with Keaty watching over his shoulder. Françoise was the

biggest surprise. She was sitting with Etienne and Gregorio in the spot occupied by the Bugs faction until only yesterday. I'd expected her to be
keeping an eye on Karl until sundown, as she had every day since the attack. In fact, a quick look around didn't show up any missing faces, so I
guessed Karl had been left alone.

In a way, it was reassuring to learn that whatever my own state of
mind, I was sane enough to recognize this as abnormal behavior. And to
make sure that my companions' behavior was as inappropriate as it appeared, when I passed Cassie I asked her how she was feeling. I chose her
partly because she was on my route, but also because this was the question she'd nagged me with in the days following the food poisoning. "Um,"
she said, not pausing from hanging up the washing. "I've been worse."

". . . You aren't feeling sad?"

"About Sten? Oh yes, I am, of course. But I believe the burial helped.
It puts it in the past, I think. In perspective, wouldn't you say?"

". . . Sure."

"It was so difficult to find perspective while his body was lying
around." She laughed, looking puzzled. "What an awful thing to say."

"But it's true."

"Yes. I think the burial was the release we needed. Just look how it relieved the tension around here. . . . Shorts, Jesse."

Jesse handed her a pair of shorts.

"And Sal's speech was a great help too. We needed her to bring us together. We've been talking a lot about Sal's speech. We thought it was very
good, didn't we?"

Jesse's face was hidden by the heap of damp T-shirts he held in his
arms, but I saw his scalp nod.

"Yes," Cassie continued, in her vague and cheerful monologue. "She's
good at that kind of thing. . . . Charisma and . . . And what about you,
Richard? How are you feeling?"

"I'm feeling fine."

"Mmm," she said absently. "Of course. You always are, aren't you?"

I left Cassie and Jesse a few minutes later, after some small talk that
wouldn't bear mentioning if it wasn't that the small talk was another rea-

son why everything felt so strange. The only time I got close to unsettling Cassie was when I asked after Karl and Christo. She dropped the T-shirt she was holding at the time—not the dramatic response it might seem but an inconsequential slip of the hand. Less inconsequential was her reaction. "Fuck it!" she snapped, which was unusual in itself because Cassie rarely swore, and her face darkened with a sudden flush. Then she held the shirt up, glowering at where the dirt had stuck to the damp material, and threw it back at the ground. "Fuck it!" she said again. A strand of spit that had been linking her lips broke with the force of the words, and the top half swung upward and clung to her cheek. I didn't bother to repeat the question.

Cabin Fever

On my way across the clearing, I briefly debated who I should tell first about the raft, Jed or Sal. Going by the book, it should have been Sal. But we didn't have a book, so I went with my instincts and told Jed.

I noticed the bad smell as soon as I climbed into the hospital tent. It was sweet and sour, vomit for the sour and something less distinct for the sweet.

"You get used to it," Jed said quickly. He hadn't even turned round, so he couldn't have seen me wince. Maybe he'd heard me cut my breathing. "In a couple of minutes you won't smell a thing. Don't go."

I pulled up the neck of my T-shirt to cover my nose and mouth. "I wasn't going to go."

"Not one person has come in all day. Can you believe it? Not one person." Now he did turn to look at me, and I frowned with concern when I saw his face. Spending almost all his time in the tent had taken a toll. Although his tan was still deep—it would have needed more than five days to wash that out—it seemed underlaid by gray, as if his blood had lost its color. "I've been listening to them out there since two," he muttered. "They came back at two. Even the carpenters. They've been playing soccer."

"I saw."

"Playing soccer! None of them thinking to check up on Christo!"

"Well, I think after Sal's speech everyone's trying to get back to—"

"Even before Sal's speech they were staying away . . . But if it was Sal in here . . . if it was anyone else . . . apart from me . . ." He hesitated, looking blankly at Christo, then laughed. "I don't know. Maybe I'm being paranoid . . . It's just that it's so weird. Hearing them outside, wondering why they don't come to check up . . ."

I nodded, although actually I was only half listening. His confinement with Christo was obviously getting to him and he clearly wanted to talk about it, but I had to bring up the subject of the raft. Sammy and Zeph would have covered the sea between the two islands before nightfall—a conservative estimate I'd worked out with Mister Duck by halving the time it had taken us to make the swim. At the earliest, that meant they could start the journey across the island tomorrow morning, and could conceivably reach the beach by tomorrow afternoon.

Christo stirred, distracting us both. For a second his eyes opened, clearly not focusing on anything, and a line of dark bile ran out of the corner of his mouth. Then his chest heaved and he appeared to slip back into unconsciousness.

Jed wiped away the line with Christo's sheet. "I try to keep him on his side but he always rolls back . . . It's impossible. I can't tell what I should be doing."

"How long will he be like this?"

"Two days at best . . . It might coincide with Tet."

"Well, that's perfect. It'll be the perfect birthday present for the camp, and maybe it will help Karl snap out of his—"

"Help Karl?" Jed looked at me curiously.

"Sure. I think half the problem is that no one can talk to him in his language. I think if Christo was talking to him, then—"

Jed shook his head. "No," he said quietly. "You don't understand. Christo's not getting better."

"You just said, in two days—"

"In two days Christo will be dead."

I paused. "He's dying?"

"Yes."

"But . . . How do you know?"

Jed reached out and took hold of my hand. Confused, I thought he was trying to console me or something, which got on my nerves and I pulled my hand back. "How do you know, Jed?"

"Keep your voice down. Sal doesn't want people to find out yet." He reached out again to take hold of my hand, and this time he held it tightly, drawing it toward Christo's stomach.

"What the fuck are you doing?" I exclaimed.

"Shh. I want you to see."

Jed pulled back the sheet. The entire area of Christo's stomach was almost jet-black, as black as Keaty's.

"Feel there."

I stared at the skin. "Why?"

"Just feel."

"I don't want to," I protested, but at the same time I felt my arm relax. Outside I heard the soccer ball bouncing near the entrance of the tent, a regular thumping that rose and faded like passing rotor blades. Someone cheered, or screamed, and someone else chuckled. Through the canvas, short bursts of conversation sounded singsong and foreign.

Gently Jed guided my hand until it rested on Christo's torso.

"What can you feel?" he asked.

"It's hard . . ." I muttered. "It's like rock."

"He's been bleeding inside. Bleeding badly. I couldn't be sure until last night. Or I knew . . . I think I knew, but—"

"That thing . . . it's a hemorrhage?"

"Uh-huh."

I nodded respectfully. I'd never seen a hemorrhage before. "Who else knows?"

"Just you and Sal . . . and Bugs too, probably. I talked to Sal today. She said nobody can find out. Not after we've started to get things back to normal. I think she's mainly worried about Etienne hearing."

"Because he wanted to take Karl to Hadrin."

"Yes. And she's right to worry. Etienne would insist we take Christo to Koh Phangan, and it would be for nothing."

"You know that for sure?"

"If we'd taken him the day after the attack, maybe two days after, he might have been okay. And I'd have taken that chance, even if it meant losing the beach. I think Sal would have too . . . But now . . . what would be the point?"

"No point . . ."

Jed sighed and stroked Christo's shoulder before pulling back the sheet. "No point at all."

We sat in silence for a minute or two, watching Christo's shallow and irregular breathing. It was strange that, once explained, it was obvious to me he was dying. The smell I'd noticed on entering the tent was the smell of encroaching death, and the waxy appearance of Jed's flesh was from living in death's proximity.

This thought jolted me and I broke the silence bluntly. "Zeph and Sammy built a raft. It was what they were doing behind the treeline. They're on their way."

Jed didn't even blink. "If they make it to the beach," he said, "they'll see Christo die. Everything here will fall apart." And that was all.

Secrets

I walked close to the longhouse entrance, past where Sal sat talking with Bugs and Jean, and continued along to the beach path. At the first corner I stopped, leaning against the fin of a rocket ship tree, and lit up. Sal appeared when I was about an inch from the filter.

"Something is up," she said immediately. "What is it?"

I raised my eyebrows.

"By the way you walked, by the look in your eye. How do you think I know? So spit it out, Richard. Tell me what's happened."

I opened my mouth to reply but she beat me to it.

"They're on their way, aren't they?"

". . . Yes."

"Fuck." Sal stared into middle distance for a few seconds. Then she snapped back into sharp focus mode. "What's their ETA?"

"Sometime tomorrow afternoon, if they don't get scared off by the dope guards."

"Or the waterfall."

"Or the waterfall. Yeah."

"Their timing is unbelievable," Sal muttered. "Absolutely unbelievable."

"It turns out they were building a raft."

"Building a raft. Of course they were. They had to be doing something . . ." She clutched her forehead. "I'm taking it for granted you know about Christo."

I thought for a moment, then nodded. I didn't want to get Jed in trouble, but when Sal was in this mood it was dangerous to lie. "You don't mind me knowing?" I said nervously.

"No. The thing about secrets is, you can't keep them unless you tell at least one other person. It's too much pressure. So I knew he had to tell someone, and I was fairly sure it would be you . . ." She shrugged. "Seeing as you have your own secrets to keep, I figured that this way we'd keep all the secrets together in one little bunch."

"Oh."

"Yes. It is clever, isn't it? Unless . . ."

I waited.

"Unless the person you told about our guests wasn't Jed. After all, Jed already knew, so it was hardly telling him a secret . . ."

". . . Hardly relieving the pressure."

"Quite," she said casually, but watching me pretty close. "So did you tell anyone apart from Jed? Keaty maybe . . . or Françoise? I certainly hope it wasn't Françoise, Richard. I'll be extremely upset if you told Françoise."

I shook my head. "I didn't tell a living soul," I said firmly, thereby excluding Mister Duck.

"Good." Sal looked away, satisfied. "To tell the truth, I was worried you might have told Françoise. She'd tell Etienne, you see . . . And you haven't told Françoise about Christo, either?"

"I only found out about Christo twenty minutes ago."

"If Etienne finds out about Christo . . ."

"I know. Don't worry. I won't tell anyone."

"Fine." Her gaze lapsed back into middle distance. "Okay, Richard . . . It looks like we have a slight problem with these rafters . . . But you don't think they can possibly get here until tomorrow?"

"No way."

"Absolutely sure?"

"Yes."

"Then I'm going to sleep on this. I need time to think. I'll give you my decision on what we do about them in the morning."

"Right . . ."

I hung around, unsure as to whether I'd been dismissed or not. But a full minute later, Sal was still gazing into nothingness, so I slipped away.

Black Cloud

I felt I could use some time to think myself, so instead of going back to the clearing I headed down to the beach. I had complicated thoughts about the way things had developed over the course of the day, and I wanted to clear them up in my head.

The way I saw it, there was something that both Sal and Jed hadn't picked up on. Whether the rafters reached the beach or not, there was still the question of Karl.

I'll put it another way. Sal and Jed were stuck on the worst-case scenario. They were thinking in terms of what would happen if the rafters reached us. Zeph and Sammy would arrive, probably during Tet. Everyone would go crazy and freak out about the secrecy of the beach being compromised, and unless I got to Zeph and Sammy first, I'd be in a lot of trouble too. The morale that had been revived by Sal's stirring speech would be completely destroyed. Not only that, there'd be the difficulty of explaining to outsiders why we had one insane and one dying Swede with us. It would be a catastrophe.

I, however, was thinking in terms of the rafters not reaching us. In the back of my mind, the reason I'd been half looking forward to Zeph and Sammy's arrival was the challenge of stopping them. And, I was fairly confident, the challenge would somehow be met. The point was that it *had* to be met. The consequences of them succeeding were far too serious. I didn't know how we'd manage it, but with Sal on the case my instincts were that we wouldn't fail.

So this left not a worst-case scenario to consider, but a medium-case one.

The rafters never reach us. The beach is never aware they even tried. The Tet celebration gives us a fresh start for the new year, and we cope with Christo's death the same way we coped with Sten's. But what about Karl? Karl wasn't about to die. He was going to stick around indefinitely, a constant reminder of our troubles, an albatross around our necks.

This bothered me a great deal.

I bent over, peering at Karl's yellow face through the palm tree fronds of his shelter. He was painfully thin. Even though he'd accepted food recently, flesh had fallen off him over the past week. Already his collarbone stuck out so far it looked like a suitcase handle, as if you could pick him up by it. He'd probably have been light enough if I'd wanted to try.

Lying by the gap in his shelter—the one that gave him a clear view over the lagoon to the caves—was a coconut shell, half full of water, and a banana-leaf parcel of rice. What was left of the rice, I noticed, was browning. From this I guessed it was the parcel Françoise had left him yesterday, dried out from a day in the sun. It suggested that Françoise hadn't replenished the supply. I contemplated the possibility that this was a new therapy tactic—ignoring him so he'd be goaded into signs of life—but I doubted it. It was more likely that, gripped by the camp's sudden upbeat brand of madness, Françoise had simply forgotten. I remembered my conversation with her the day before. She'd seemed concerned about him then. It was interesting how quickly Sten's funeral had turned everything around.

"Karl," I said.

Maybe it was hearing his name, or maybe I was tricked by a breeze disturbing the palm fronds and playing the shadow slits across his head, but I thought I saw him move. I chose to take this as a reaction.

"Karl, you're a fucking albatross."

I wasn't much bothered that he couldn't understand me. In a way, for Karl's sake, it was probably a good thing.

"You're a black cloud."

This time Karl did move. No doubt about it. He made a little jerky movement forward, like he was stiff from having sat still so long. Then slowly he reached out of the shelter and picked up the coconut shell.

"Hey," I said. "Drinking. That's good." I rubbed my stomach. "Mmm."

He took a tiny sip—it couldn't have done more than wet his mouth—and put the shell back in its place. I glanced over. There was still a gulp of water left in the bottom.

"You left some. Aren't you going to finish it up?" I rubbed my stomach again. "Mmm-mm. Very delicious. Aren't you going to have a little more?"

He didn't move. I watched him for a short while before shaking my head.

"No, Karl. You aren't. And that's my point. You're going to keep going like this for days. You'll get so thin and weak that you won't be able to drink even if you want to. Then we'll have to force-feed you or something and this shark business will end up hanging over us for weeks. . . . Maybe more!"

I sighed and, as an afterthought, kicked down his shelter.

"Get sane, Karl. Do it in a hurry. Because Christo's going to be dead soon."

Shh

To confirm my fears about the black cloud, when I did return to the clearing I found it causing trouble. Françoise, Etienne, and Keaty were sitting in a circle, and Etienne and Keaty were repeating the argument I'd heard them have before.

"What's the big deal?" Keaty was saying, at the same time as he played his Gameboy. "He's taking water. That's good, isn't it?"

"Good?" Etienne scoffed. "Why is it good for him to take a little water? Nothing is *good* about his condition. Karl should not be here. This is obvious to me, and I cannot believe it is not obvious for everybody else."

"Give it a fucking rest, Etienne. We've been over this a hundred ti— Oops." He paused, frowning in intense concentration. Then his body slumped and he let the Nintendo drop to his lap. "One-five-three lines. I was going fine until you distracted me."

Etienne spat in the dust. "So sorry. How could I distract you from a computer game because our friend is in need of help?"

"Wasn't my friend. Hardly spoke to him."

"Does that mean you do not care about his problems?"

"Sure I do. I just care about the beach more. And you should too. Okay. Now this time I'm going for the record, so I don't want any more of these bullshit distractions."

Etienne got to his feet. "What would be a real distraction for you, Keaty? Please tell me. Then I will pray I never have to see it."

The question went unanswered.

"Sit down, Etienne," I said in an attempt to lower the temperature. "Remember what Sal was saying at the funeral. We've got to get over all the difficulties we've had."

"Difficulties," he echoed coldly.

"Everyone else is making an effort."

"Really? I am surprised to hear that you find it an effort."

"What's that supposed to mean?"

"It means maybe I do not know you anymore, Richard. I recognize your face when you walk toward me, but when you are close I recognize nothing in your eyes."

I took this as some French saying he'd translated. "Come on, Etienne. This is stupid. Remember Sal's—"

"Sal," he interrupted, "can fuck herself." Then he marched away in the direction of the waterfall path.

"Actually," Keaty muttered thoughtfully, not looking up from the tiny monochrome screen, "I doubt even Sal could manage that."

A couple of minutes later Françoise also left. She seemed annoyed, so I guessed she didn't feel the same way as Etienne.

———

When Keaty had finished his Tetris high-score attempt, I finally got the chance to ask him how he felt about doing the Rice Run with Bugs. He said he was pretty relaxed about it. He also said it had been a bit of a shock at first, but he'd come round to the idea if it was for the benefit of the camp. Aside from its being a decent conciliatory gesture, he wanted to make sure we had some good stuff brought in for the Tet festival.

I wanted to talk more about Tet, but Sal wanted the Rice Run over in one day, so they were getting a very early start and he needed to turn in. I sat alone for twenty minutes or so, polishing off a bedtime joint, then I decided to turn in too. With Zeph and Sammy on their way, Keaty wasn't the only one with a heavy day ahead.

I stuck my head into the hospital tent on the way back to the longhouse, thinking Jed would appreciate another look in. But as soon as I saw inside, I wished I'd stayed away.

Jed was fast asleep, lying next to Christo. Christo, however, was semi-awake. He even recognized me.

"Richard," he whispered, then muttered something in Swedish and made a gurgling noise.

I hesitated a moment, unsure of whether I should be talking to him.

"Richard."

"Yes," I whispered back. "How are you feeling?"

"I feel very bad, Richard. I feel very bad."

"I know. But you'll be better soon."

"Stars . . ."

"You see them?"

"Phos . . . phos . . ."

". . . phorescence," I finished. "You can see it?"

"I feel very bad."

"You need some sleep."

"Sten . . ."

"You'll see him in the morning."

"My chest . . ."

"Close your eyes."

". . . hurts . . ."

"I know. Close your eyes."

". . . very bad . . ."

"Shh now."

Beside him, Jed stirred, and Christo turned his head a fraction. "Karl?"

"Right there next to you. Don't move or you'll wake him."

He nodded and at last his eyes shut.

"Have good dreams," I said, maybe too quietly for him to hear.

I pegged the tent flap open behind me as I left. I wanted to keep Jed from breathing too much of that dying air.

fng, kia

Fuckin' A

Bugs and Keaty left just after five thirty. Sal gave me my instructions at a quarter to six.

I liked being up while everyone else was asleep. I almost always was, since I'd started working up on the island, but usually there were a few signs of stirring: a spot of movement in one of the tents or someone padding their way across the clearing to the Khyber Pass. That morning the camp was as still and quiet and cool as it could ever be. It made everything more exciting. While I talked with Sal and Jed outside the hospital tent, I was so keyed up for the day ahead that I had to keep hopping from one foot to the other. I could tell it was pissing Sal off, but I couldn't stop myself. If I hadn't channeled my energy somewhere, I'd have started shouting or running around in little circles.

Sal and Jed were arguing. They both agreed that I should head into the DMZ and track Zeph and Sammy's progress across the island. The disagreement was over the interception point. Sal said not until they reached the top of the waterfall, putting some faith in the obstacle course. Jed said earlier, as early as possible, although he seemed reluctant to explain why. Personally, I was siding with Sal, although I kept my mouth shut.

Interception point aside, they both agreed on what to do next. I was to tell the rafters that they weren't welcome and that they should leave at once. That failing, I was to keep them from descending the waterfall. Any way I saw fit to delay them was acceptable, in Sal's words. If necessary I would stay up there with them, missing Tet. It could be explained to the rest of the beach later. Nothing was more important than making sure they didn't arrive at camp until Christo was dead. After that, we would work out whether to let them down or keep them out.

By the way Sal was talking, I was sure she had a fallback plan that she wasn't telling us. I knew the way her head worked, and she wasn't the type to say, "We'll cross that bridge when we come to it." Especially with something so important. The thing I particularly didn't understand was the idea of turning Zeph and Sammy's group back. If we got to the point where I was forced to intercept them, turning them back seemed as problematic as letting them stay. You could as good as guarantee they would talk back on Koh Phangan or Koh Samui, about what they'd found, and we'd have lost our secret status.

If it had been anyone else but Sal, I'd have pointed this out, but with her I didn't feel it was worth bothering. I felt sure that if I'd been able to think of it, she would have too. I don't think I remember her asking my opinion about anything, unless it was to lead me into something by making it seem like my idea. Come to think of it, I don't remember her asking anyone's opinion. Not even Bugs's.

If it needs saying, the argument about the interception point was eventually won by Sal. A big surprise. I honestly don't know why Jed even tried.

Mister Duck was waiting for me at the pass. He was dressed in full combat fatigues with an M16 over his shoulder and his face all painted up with green and black camouflage stripes.

"What's with the gun?" I said when I saw him.

"Just making sure I fit the bill," he replied flatly.

"Does it work?"

"Works for me."

"Guess that's a yes . . ." I walked past him so I could see down the pass to the DMZ. "So how you feeling? Nervous?"

"I feel good. I feel ready."

"Ready for the recon?"

"Well . . ." He smiled. "Just ready, that's all."

"Just ready," I muttered. I always felt suspicious of his lopsided grin. "Daffy, there'd better not be something going on here that I don't know about."

"Mmm."

"Mmm what?"

"Mmm let's get going."

"I'm serious. Don't start any of your shit. Not today."

"Time is ticking, Rich. We've got an RV to keep."

I hesitated, then nodded. "Okay . . . If you're all set."

"All set."

"Then let's do it."

"Fuckin' A."

Their Big Mistake

By setting off so early, I was hoping that Zeph and Sammy would still be with their raft. Finding them would be a lot harder if they'd already entered the jungle. I was also trusting that they'd have landed on the same stretch of beach where Etienne, Françoise, and I had first come ashore. I was fairly confident they would have, but you never knew. They might have tried to circle the island, not realizing they'd passed the only open stretch of sand. Either way, the more time I gave myself to play with, the better.

At least dodging the guards wasn't a problem. They were dozy enough at the best of times, but at seven a.m. they'd definitely still be sleeping off their dope hangovers. In a way, my biggest problem was Mister Duck. He was badly out of shape, wheezing like an old coal miner, frequently pausing to lean against trees and catch his breath. I tried to tell myself that his ghostly status made it unlikely that anyone else could hear him, but all the same, each time he barked a swearword my heart would miss a beat. I'd turn and glare at him, and he'd raise his hands apologetically. "Sorry," he muttered after a stream of abuse at a razor-leaf thicket. "I'm not as good at jungle warfare as I'd imagined." A few minutes later he tripped and fell on his gun, letting off a round into the bushes. He didn't have his safety catch on, the idiot, and he'd been walking with his finger on the trigger. After that we decided the gun was more trouble than it was worth—seeing as it couldn't kill anything real—and we left it hidden in the undergrowth.

About thirty meters before the treeline along the beach, I made him wait behind. Even though I was sure that no one else could see or hear him, he distracted me. If I wanted to get close to the rafting group, I couldn't afford to be compromised.

Unexpectedly—though clearly hurt—he took it in good grace.

"I understand, Richie," he said gamely. "You hate me."

"I don't hate you," I sighed. "But like I said, this is serious."

"I know, I know. You go ahead. Anyway . . ." His eyes became slits and flicked to the side. "In my experience these types of jobs are one-man affairs."

"Exactly."

I left him under a coconut tree, using a serrated bowie knife to pick the dirt from under his nails.

The early-morning effort paid off. The rafters were still on the beach.

Even though I'd been watching them for months, it was a shock to see the group close up. It confirmed that it actually *was* Zeph and Sammy we'd been watching; that our assumption had been correct and that the blame for their presence could only come down to me. It was also curious because I'd been anticipating this moment for what seemed like ages, but the reality of their presence left me feeling cold. I'd anticipated something more dramatic than the bedraggled figures who sat huddled around their raft. Something a lot more sinister, considering that—as outsiders—they represented a threat to the secrecy of the camp and a threat to me. I still hadn't worked out what I was going to say to Sal about the map. I didn't have the nerve to countermand her orders, so I just had to rely on the island's obstacle course. That failing, my only hope was that I could explain the situation to Zeph and Sammy while I kept them delayed above the waterfall.

From my spy point—about twenty meters from where they sat, lying flat under the shelter of some ferns—I could see only four of them. The fifth was obscured behind their raft. Of the two visible Germans, one was a boy and one was a girl. With some satisfaction, I saw that the girl was pretty but not as pretty as Françoise. No one on the beach was as pretty as Françoise and I didn't want her usurped by a stranger. The girl would have been prettier if it wasn't for her nose, which was tiny and turned up so she looked like a tanned skull. The guy, however, was a different matter. Even though he was clearly exhausted, weakly hauling his (pink pastel) backpack off the raft, he had the same build and appearance as Bugs. They could have been brothers, even down to the long hair, which he kept having to flick out of his eyes. I took a comfortably instant dislike to him.

Eventually the fifth popped up to finish off the team. Another girl, and, annoyingly, I was unable to find anything to hold against her. She was short and curvy, and she had an attractive quiet laugh that rolled cleanly across the sand to where I lay. She also had very long brown hair that at one point, for a reason I couldn't fathom, she wrapped around her neck like a scarf. It was a surreal sight and it made me smile, until I remembered I should be scowling.

I was mildly put out that the rafters didn't make the same mistake as I had with Etienne and Françoise—walking to each end of the arrival beach before realizing that the only way to get around the island was to go across it. But this was more than compensated by another, far more serious mistake they made.

Actually, I knew they were about to make the mistake even before it happened. Firstly, they hadn't properly hidden their raft—only dragging it up beyond the high-tide mark—and secondly, they chatted loudly as they walked. In German, I noticed with grudging respect. (Grudging respect for Zeph and Sammy rather than the Germans, obviously.) To me, this clearly suggested one thing: they were entirely unaware of any need for caution. Mister Duck, who had rejoined me when the group turned inland, noticed it too.

"Not very perceptive," he said, just under an hour into the trek.

I nodded, putting a warning finger to my lips. I didn't want to talk because we were following them so closely. Not closely enough to see them through the thick foliage, but always close enough to hear.

"If they carry on like that they'll get caught," he continued, undeterred.

I nodded.

"Maybe you should do something, don't you think?"

"No," I whispered. "Now shut up."

I was a bit perplexed by Mister Duck's concern, but no more than that. The next time he opened his mouth I put the warning finger to his lips instead of mine, and he got the message.

So anyway. That was the rafters' big mistake: not being very perceptive. When they came to the first plateau, not one of them realized they were in a field.

I Know Abou' Tha'

Sammy whooped, just as he'd whooped six months ago, running through the rain on Koh Samui. And he shouted, "This is way outa fuckin' line, man! I've never seen so much fuckin' weed! This is more weed than I've ever fuckin' seen!" Then he started ripping up big handfuls of leaves and throwing them in the air, and the other four started whooping and throwing leaves in the air too. They looked like million-dollar bank robbers throwing their loot around. Completely out of control. Completely dead meat. It was ten a.m. The guards would have been patrolling for two hours at least and if they hadn't heard them crashing through the jungle, they'd heard them now.

By a twist of fate, nothing intentional about it, Mister Duck and I were hiding in the same bush that I'd hidden in with Etienne and Françoise. It certainly gave the scene an extra edge. Watching Zeph and Sammy was like watching myself—what could have come to pass six months ago if not for Etienne's cool head—and I felt a peculiarly vivid blast of empathy for Scrooge. Perhaps Mister Duck is my Ghost of Christmas Future, I remember thinking as my stomach knotted with the memories of my fear. But I was also buzzing. It looked like the problem with our uninvited guests was about to be solved, and as if that wasn't enough, I was also going to find out what happened when the dope guards caught someone. Better than that, I was actually going to see it.

Not that I'd want anyone thinking I was without pity for them. I didn't want Zeph and Sammy on the island and I knew it would be convenient if they were to disappear, but it didn't have to be this way. Ideal scenario: They arrived, I had a couple of days tracking them as they found their way across the island, then they gave up at the waterfall and went back home. I would have had my fun and there'd have been no spilt tears and no spilt blood.

Zeph bled like a stuck pig. When the guards had appeared, he'd begun walking straight over toward them like they were old friends. To my mind an inexplicable thing to do, but that's what he did. He *still* didn't seem to realize what was going on, even though the guards all had their guns off their shoulders and were jabbering in Thai. Maybe he thought they were part of the Eden community, or maybe he was so shocked that it just didn't click how much trouble he was in. Either way, as soon as he got close, one of the guards smashed him in the face with the butt of his rifle. I wasn't surprised. The guard looked very nervous, and just as confused by Zeph's strange behavior as I was.

After that there were a few seconds of silent staring across the heads of the dope plants, Zeph taking little backward steps while he cupped the blood spilling out of his nose. It seemed as if each of the two groups was as bewildered as the other. The rafters were having to make a considerable mental adjustment, Eden to hell in the space of a few seconds. The dope guards seemed stunned that anyone could be so stupid as to walk into their plantation and start ripping it to pieces.

It occurred to me—during this brief interlude—that most of the guards were more like country boys than experienced mercenaries, with scars from sharp corals rather than from knife fights. A bit like the real VC. But I'm sure these observations would have been of small interest to Zeph and Sammy, and in this case I think it made the guards more dangerous than they might otherwise have been. Maybe someone more experienced wouldn't have panicked and smashed Zeph's face in. Isn't there a saying that the only thing more dangerous than a man with a gun is a nervous man with a gun? If there isn't, there should be. Once the short period of staring was over, the guards flipped. I read it as a panicky reaction to the situation. They just waded in and began beating the shit out of what were now their uninvited guests, and not mine.

I suppose the rafters might have been battered to death right there and then, but just as I was beginning to feel that the scene was getting too unpleasant to watch, another bunch of guards arrived, and this lot appeared to have a boss. I'd never seen him before. He was older than the others and had no automatic rifle; only a pistol, still in its holster. Traditionally a mark of power among gunmen. One word from him and the beating stopped.

Beside me, Mister Duck reached over and clutched my arm. "Rich, I think they're going to be killed."

I frowned at him and mouthed, "Quiet."

"No, listen," he persisted. "I don't want them killed."

This time I shut him up not just with my finger but my whole hand. The guards' boss had started talking.

———

He spoke in English. Not flawlessly by any means. Not like a Nazi POW camp commandant who appreciates English poetry and says to his prisoners, "You know, we are much alike, you and I." But good enough.

"Who are you?" he said, very loud and clear.

A deceptively tricky question. What do you say? Do you formally introduce yourself, do you say, "No one," do you beg for your life? I thought Sammy handled it very well, considering he'd just had his front teeth knocked out.

"We're travelers from Koh Phangan," he replied between tight gasps for air, involuntarily dribbling as he spoke. "We were looking for some other travelers. We made a mistake. We didn't know this was your island."

The boss nodded, not unkindly. "Ve'y big mistake."

"Please, we're very . . ." Gasp. "Sorry."

"You alone now? Any frien' here now?"

"We're alone. We were looking for a friend. We thought he was here, and we know we made a mis—"

"Why you look for frien' here?"

"Our friend gave us a map."

The boss cocked his head to the side. "Wha' map?"

"I can sh—"

"You can show me tha' map. La'er."

"Please. We're very sorry."

"Yes. I know abou' you bein' sorry."

"We'd like to go. We could leave your island now and we wouldn't tell anyone about anything."

"Yes. You tell no one. I know abou' tha'."

Sammy tried to smile. All his remaining teeth were bright red. "Will you let us go? Please?"

"Ah." The boss smiled back. "You can go."

". . . We can go?"

"Yes."

"Thank you." With an effort, Sammy raised himself onto his knees. "Sir, thank you. I promise you, we won't tell any—"

"You can go wit' us."

". . . With you?"

"You go wit' us now."

"No," Sammy began to protest. "Please, wait, we made a mistake! We're *very* sorry! We won't tell *anyone!*"

One of the German guys started to get up, holding his arms in the air. "We will not speak!" he blurted. "We will not speak!"

The boss gazed at the German impassively, then spoke quickly to the guards. Three of them moved forward and tried to lift Zeph by the arms. He began to struggle. Another guard stepped forward and jabbed the barrel of his rifle into Zeph's stomach.

"Richard," said Mister Duck, who had squirmed from under my grip. "Listen to me. They're definitely going to be killed."

I took no notice.

"Do something, Richard."

Again I didn't respond, and this time he poked me hard in the ribs with his finger. Luckily, my yelp was drowned out by the sounds of the rafters screaming.

"Jesus fucking Christ!" I whispered incredulously. "What's your problem?"

"Do something to help them!"

"Like what?"

"Like . . ." He considered this question while over in the field the guards piled onto the German girl. She'd tried to run away and had been brought down after only a couple of stumbling meters. "I don't know!"

"Well neither do I, so belt up! You'll get me killed too!"

"But—"

Resisting the urge to shout at him, I grabbed him by the lapels of his combat jacket and put my mouth right up against his ear. *"For the last time, shut the fuck up!"*

Mister Duck covered his face with his hands and the guards began dragging their terrified captives away.

Cheap Shots

The cries and howls were gradually replaced by jungle noises. Commonplace sounds I'd never normally have registered, but which now seemed unnatural. Worse, obscurely facetious: twittering bird-song like twittering bad jokes, jangling my nerves and my temper. I stood up without a word to Mister Duck and set off on my way back up to the pass. It wasn't an easy trek. My head ached with a fading adrenaline rush, my legs felt unsteady, and I was giving far too little thought to stealth. Twice I tripped and more than twice I pushed through a thicket without pausing to see who might be on the other side.

Looking back, it seems obvious that I was shaken by what I'd seen and in a hurry to leave an area which still felt heavy with screams. But that wasn't how I saw it at the time. I only thought about the importance of getting back to camp and filling in Sal about the morning's developments. I was also furious with Mister Duck. From the moment we'd started tracking the rafters, his wires seemed to have gotten severely crossed. Not only had he asked me to intercept Zeph and Sammy before the plateau, his blathering had put me in jeopardy. As far as I was concerned, that was a serious offense. The DMZ was way too dangerous a place if you couldn't rely on your company.

I think Mister Duck sensed this anger, because, rarely for him, he made no attempt at conversation. Until we reached the pass. Then he stopped me with a firm shove and said, "We need to talk."

"Fuck you," I replied, shoving him back. "You could have got me killed."

"The rafters probably *are* being killed!"

"You don't know that. And I didn't want that beating shit to happen any more than you, so don't get on some fucking moral high horse. We *knew* they might be caught. That was understood when we made the decision to make no contact with them unless they got to the waterfall, so what do you want from me?"

"Decisions? I didn't make any decisions! I wanted you to help them!"

"Steaming in like Rambo, waving an M16 that doesn't even exist?"

"You could have done something!"

"Like what? You live in a dream world! There was *nothing* I could have done!"

"You could have warned them before they got to the plateau!"

"I had clear orders *not* to warn them!"

"You could have broken the orders!"

"I didn't want to fucking break them!"

"You . . . didn't?"

"Not for one second!"

Mister Duck frowned and opened his mouth to reply, then appeared to check himself.

"What?" I snapped.

He shook his head, his features calming. When he eventually spoke I knew he wasn't saying what was on his mind. "That was a cheap shot, Richard," he said quietly. "About me living in a dream world."

"You could have got me killed, but I hurt your feelings. God forgive me. I'm a monster."

"It's your world I live in."

"That must be a comfort, considering you were the one who pointed out that I'm—"

I cut myself off. While I'd been talking, I'd heard a sharp crack from somewhere in the DMZ.

"Did you hear that?"

Mister Duck hesitated, his eyes narrowing, and suddenly he looked extremely worried. "Yes. I heard something."

"You sure?"

"Definite."

We both waited.

Within five or six seconds the silence was exploded by a burst of gunfire. It was entirely unambiguous, somehow managing to ripple through the trees like a quick breeze and tear through them with shocking loudness. A single burst, but a long one. Long enough for me to blink and hunch my shoulders, and then be aware that the shooting was still going on.

When it finally did stop, the next thing I heard was Mister Duck taking a deep breath and exhaling slowly.

"Jesus . . ." I muttered. "Jesus Christ . . . It's happened. They've actually . . ."

"Been shot," he finished vacantly.

To my surprise, I nearly threw up. Out of nowhere, my stomach knotted and my throat tensed up. An image jumped into my head: the rafters'
bodies, their shirts scattered with spreading stains, limbs twisted. Swallowing hard, I turned to the DMZ. I suppose I was looking for a corrobo-
rating sign, maybe a vague blue smoke in the distance. But there was
nothing.

"Been shot," I heard once more, and then, very faintly, "Damn."

A moment later I turned back to Mister Duck. He was gone.

Mama-San

It had all gone wrong or it had all gone right. I
couldn't decide which.

On the one hand, just like on the plateau, when it came down to it I'd
lost my nerve. I hadn't been alert but calm; I'd been alert but queasy. But
on the other hand, maybe that was how it should be. Right to panic on the
plateau, right to feel sick when I heard the gunshots. I've read about it
enough times, seen it in enough films: the first day on your first tour,
you're supposed to lose your shit in a contact. Later, more experienced,
jaded, you are caught unawares one day that death still has the capacity to
appall you. It is something you dwell on, and through it you gain strength.

I ran this second interpretation over and over as I made my way down
to the waterfall. I also tried to look on other bright sides. Mainly that our
problem with the new arrivals was over, and my part in compromising the
beach's secrecy was irreversibly closed. But they didn't make a dent in the
way I was feeling. Still battling with my contracting stomach, struggling to
focus on the terrain ahead of me, trying to work through my urge to yell.
I wanted to yell a lot. Not an Iron John, exorcising kind of yell. More this
kind: running down a road at top speed to catch a bus, and bashing your

knee straight into a concrete bollard. Just like you'd done it deliberately, as hard as you possibly could. It isn't a yell born from pain, because at that moment nothing hurts. It's a yell that comes from a brain on overload, refusing to concede what has just happened, and refusing to try.

Sal was waiting for me beneath the waterfall. "What the hell happened?" she said, more angry than anxious, before I'd even finished swimming to the shore. "Why did I hear gunshots?"

I didn't answer until I'd reached the shallows and was wading toward her. "The rafters," I puffed. The impact on hitting the water always knocked the air out of me, and this time it had been worse than usual.

"They've been killed?"

"Yes. I saw them get caught by the guards and then later I heard the firing."

"You didn't see it?"

"No."

"What happened when they were caught?"

"They were beaten."

"Badly?"

"Yes."

"Badly enough to scare them? Maybe just a message?"

"Worse."

"Then?"

"They got taken away somewhere. Dragged."

"Dragged . . . You didn't follow."

"No."

"What next?"

"The shooting . . . when I reached the pass."

"I see . . ." Sal's eyes bored holes into my head. "Badly beaten, you say . . ."

"Very badly."

"You feel responsible for their deaths."

I thought about this before replying, not wanting to give away my connection to Zeph and Sammy at this late stage. "It was their decision to come here," I said eventually, shifting my weight from my left foot to my right. I was still standing knee-deep in the pool and my feet were sinking slightly into the mud. "They made a lot of noise in the jungle. It was their fault."

Sal nodded. "Others may have heard the shooting. What will you tell them?"

"Nothing."

"I think Etienne might know about Christo. He's being difficult again—"

"I won't tell Etienne," I interrupted. "I won't tell Françoise or Keaty or anyone . . . Except Jed . . . You know I'll tell Jed."

"Of course I do, Richard," she said crisply. "But it's nice of you to ask permission." Then she spun on her heel and began walking away. She didn't even wait for me to climb out of the pool, or to hear me whisper, "I wasn't asking your fucking permission."

Reanimator

I didn't follow Sal back to camp because I didn't want to see everyone yet. In fact, I didn't want to do anything much. Except maybe sleep. It was the idea of oblivion that appealed; nothing to do with tiredness. I wanted to get away from the brain that was still making me want to yell. The problem was, of the various benefits sleep might provide, oblivion wasn't in the cards. If I slept I'd dream and I knew dreams were not the place to avoid these things.

I ended up talking to myself. Walking around the pool, treating my mind as if it were a separate but reasonable entity, I asked it to leave me alone for a while. Or at least turn down the volume.

This wasn't the deranged caricature it might sound, full of expressive gestures and wild looks. It was an earnest attempt for some peace and quiet that happened not to work. My mind deflected reason like Superman deflecting bullets, chest puffed out, completely unfazed. So I tried a few different tacks, like attempting to get interested in a pretty flower or the bark patterns on the carved tree. But all these techniques failed equally. If they achieved anything, it was that my failure compounded my frustration and made me feel worse.

My last attempt was to dive back into the pool. Underwater had always had the qualities of a refuge for me. Calming, blinding, deafening; a perfect escape. It worked too, enveloping me in anonymous coolness, but in an unavoidably temporary way. Without gills I had to keep surfacing, and as soon as I surfaced my mind resumed its circular debates.

No place to avoid these things. I realized this eventually, hammered into breathless submission. I climbed out of the pool and headed straight into the jungle. I didn't follow the gardeners' path. I followed the network of carpentry paths, which I could use to reach the beach without crossing the clearing.

I'll keep this brief. Absolutely limited to what I remember, with no filling in the blanks. Not that I've been filling in the blanks up until now; it just so happens that my memory of the next few minutes is patchy. No doubt a result of the traumatic morning and the previously described frame of mind.

"The rafters are dead," I said. "Christo will be dead within forty-eight hours. All our problems are over except you. It's time you got sane."

Karl looked at me through his waxy eyes. Or he looked through me, or he wasn't looking at anything at all. Whatever. I didn't really care. I took a step toward him, and as I did so he lashed out viciously at my legs. Maybe revenge for having kicked down his shelter. The blow hurt, so I hit him back.

I sat on his chest, my knees against his upper arms, trying to push a handful of rice into his mouth. His skin reminded me a lot of the dead freak on Koh Phangan, slack to the touch, moving loosely over the muscle. Touching it wasn't a pleasant sensation at all. Especially when he began to writhe.

———

He made sounds, probably words. "That's the boy!" I shouted. "Guess I'm curing you now!" His fingers clawed at my neck. I pushed them away. I think I may have lost the rice in the struggle. I think I may have been holding sand.

I assume I closed my eyes. Instead of Karl's face with bugging eyes, I have a mental picture of a reddish-brown blanket. Nothingness, so closed eyes seem like a logical explanation. They would also explain the next image I have in my memory slide show: a blue blanket, reopening my eyes for a split second as I fell backward and glimpsed a cloudless sky. And the next image, returning to the red-brown blanket again.

I sat up. Karl was twenty or more meters down the beach, running like crazy. Amazed that he could still have so much strength after days of virtual starvation, I leapt to my feet and sprinted after him.

Reasonable Doubt

Down the beach, through the treeline, up the path, into the clearing. I'd nearly caught him. I was just about to get a hand to his hair. Then I tripped over a guyline on one of the tents and went flying, and Karl made a beeline for the Khyber Pass.

I scrambled up. Several people were standing directly in his way. "Catch him!" I shouted. "Jesse, Greg, for fuck's sake! Bring him down!" But they were too shocked to react and Karl whizzed by. "You idiots! He's getting away!" A few seconds later he'd reached the pass. In the baffled quiet that followed we listened to him crashing through the undergrowth, and then the silence was complete.

"Fuck!" I shouted, sinking to my knees, and started banging my fist on the ground.

A light hand touched my shoulder. I looked round to see Françoise leaning over me, and behind her a semicircle of curious people. "Richard?" she said anxiously.

Another hand, Jesse's, reached under my arms and hauled me up. "You okay, mate?"

"Yes . . ." I began, and then stopped, trying to remember what had happened. ". . . I think Karl's out of his coma thing."

"So I saw. What happened?"

". . . He attacked me," I said doubtfully, and everyone gasped.

"You are hurt?" said Françoise, peering at my face to check for damage.

". . . I managed to fight him off. I'm fine . . ."

"Why did he do it?"

"I . . . I really don't know . . ." I shook my head in desperation. I didn't feel at all ready to cope with these questions. "Maybe . . . Maybe he thought I was a fish. He was a fisher and . . . he's mad . . ."

Sal saved me from this shit I was coming out with. The crowd parted and she came striding through.

"Karl attacked you, Richard?"

"Just now. On the beach."

The second confirmation of Karl's assault brought a second gasp from the crowd and they all started to talk at once.

"It should have been me to catch him!" said Unhygienix furiously. "He ran so close!"

"I saw the look in his eye!" added Cassie. "He looked right at me! It was terrifying!"

"And the foam in his mouth!" said someone else. "Like rabies! We should catch him and tie him up!"

Only one voice went against the flow: Etienne's. "This is impossible," he shouted above the racket. "I do not believe Karl would attack Richard! I do not believe it! I was with him this morning!"

The din began to die down.

"This morning I was with him for one hour! One hour, and he ate rice with me! He was getting better! I know he would not attack anyone!"

I got myself together enough to frown in disbelief. "Are you saying I'm a liar?"

Etienne hesitated, then turned away from me, addressing the others.

"For one hour I was with him! He said my *name!* For the first time in a week he talked! I *know* he was getting better!"

Quickly I began to backtrack, not caring about this argument, just wanting to get away. "Yes, Etienne's right. It may have been my fault. I could have frightened him—"

"No!" Sal interrupted sharply. "I'm afraid that Karl has become dangerous. This morning I also went to see him, and he made a lunge at me, too."

Startled but not about to contradict her, I studied her expression hard and wished I had her capacity for sniffing out a lie. She was acting like she was telling the truth, but I knew that meant fuck-all.

"Luckily Bugs was there to pull him off. We were down on the beach, just before he left for Koh Phangan with Keaty. I should have warned you all already, but I was trying to work out the best way to deal with him . . ." She sighed with apparent and entirely uncharacteristic regret. "I was stupid. I didn't want to bring down the Tet celebration with more bad news. It was irresponsible, but things had been going so well . . . I didn't want to ruin morale."

Jesse shook his head. "Tet's all very well, Sal, but we can't have someone that dangerous just roaming around."

Everyone nodded, and for some strange reason, I felt they were all nodding at me.

"Richard, I hope you can accept my apologies. You shouldn't have been put in that situation."

"No need for that, Sal," I replied immediately. Even in the context of a lie—and by now I was sure she was lying—I felt extremely uncomfortable having her apologize to me. "I understand."

"But I do not!" said Etienne desperately. "Please! Please, everybody *must* listen! Karl is not dangerous! He needs help! I think maybe we could take him to Koh Pha—"

This time it was Françoise who cut him off, by doing nothing more than walking away. His voice failed him as he watched her march across the clearing. Then he started after her, still not able to speak, holding his arms ahead of him, paralyzed in midplea.

Upended

Almost as soon as Etienne and Françoise walked off,
the rest of us began to wander across the clearing. There was no further
discussion about Karl. As far as the others were concerned, I think they
were all aware that the calm since Sten's funeral was in jeopardy, and that
a huge exercise in denial was under way. Instant, informal, an intuitive
consensus, so that talking about anything remotely contentious was out of
bounds. No problem for me. It meant that no one asked me to elaborate
on Karl or brought up the topic of the gunshots. The only downside was
having to labor through a few contrived conversations, which seemed a
fair trade-off.

The strangest of these exchanges was with Jean, not least because he
almost never spoke to me. He came over with a shy smile and asked the
kind of stupid question that can only come from uneasiness. "You are
working, Richard?" he said.

At the time I was having a smoke outside the kitchen hut, trying to reconstruct my splintered nerves. "No, Jean," I managed to reply, relatively
steadily. "Not at this exact moment. I'm smoking a cigarette."

"Ah."

"Would you like one?"

"Oh no!" he said hurriedly, looking quite alarmed. "I do not want to
take your cigarette."

"Go ahead. Keaty's bringing me some back from Hadrin."

"No, no. I can smoke grass."

". . . Okay." I returned his smile, willing him to fuck off with all my
heart.

But he didn't. He scratched his head and shuffled his feet a bit. I had
the impression that if he'd owned a cap he'd have been holding it in his
hands. "You know, Richard, I was thinking."

"Mmm?"

"Perhaps you would like to see the garden one day. Sometimes you
would come to see Keaty, but now it has changed. After Keaty was fishing,
I made the garden even larger. Now it has seven areas."

"Seven?" I said tightly. "Great."

"So one day you will come to see it?"

"It's a date."

"A date! Yes!" He let out a roar of laughter, so theatrical that for a few seconds I thought he was taking the piss. "A date! Then we will see a film!"

I nodded.

"A date," he repeated. "See you on our date, Richard!"

"See you then," I replied, and mercifully he backed away.

I avoided visiting Jed until darkness was beginning to set in. I didn't want to be seen entering the hospital tent. I knew that this would be a tacit acknowledgment of Christo's existence—which, under our consensus, was perhaps the most important of the Things to Ignore.

If possible, conditions were even worse inside the tent than they had been before. Stenchwise it was the same deal, but the trapped heat inside seemed more intense and there were puddles of dried and drying black liquid everywhere. Blood from Christo's stomach, soaking in the sheets, collecting in the folds of the canvas floor, and smeared across Jed's arms and chest.

"Jesus Christ," I said, feeling sweat begin to prickle my back. "What the fuck's been going on in here?"

Jed turned toward me. He was lit from below by his upended Maglite. It made the stray hairs of his beard glow like light bulb filaments and hid his eyes in absolute darkness. "Do you have good news for me?" he murmured. "I'm tired of bad news now. I only want to hear good news."

I paused, squinting at the shadows in his eye sockets, looking to see some form inside them. Something about his manner was threatening and his demonic glow made me wonder if I was having a hallucination. So much so that I felt I should confirm his realness if I was going to stick around. Eventually I reached for the Maglite and shone it directly at his face. His hand flicked up to shield the glare, but I saw enough flesh to reassure me.

I rested the torch back on the floor. "I've got news. Zeph and Sammy are dead."

"Dead," Jed said without emotion.

"Shot by the dope guards."

"You saw it?"

"No."

He cocked his head to the side. "Disappointed?"

"No. I saw them get beaten and . . ."

"That was enough for you."

". . . it made me feel sick," I finished. "I didn't expect it to, but it did."

"Oh." The bright filaments of Jed's beard twitched as some invisible expression passed across his features.

". . . Aren't you pleased? Not pleased, I mean relieved . . . In a way."

"I'm not relieved at all."

". . . You aren't?"

"No."

"But it means the beach is safe. Tet and morale . . . and our secrecy . . ."

"I don't care about the beach anymore, Richard."

"You . . . You don't care about the beach?"

"Would you like to hear my news?"

I shifted my weight to disguise my unease. ". . . Okay."

"Today's news is that there isn't any."

". . . No visitors."

"That's right, Richard. No visitors. Again." He cleared his throat. "I haven't seen a single soul, except his and maybe mine . . . Can't stop thinking about why that might be . . . Why do you think it is, Richard? Me and Christo, waiting here all day long, with no visitors . . ."

"Jed . . . We've been over this before."

"Are you in a hurry?"

". . . No."

"So we can go over it again."

". . . Okay. It's just like you said, people are trying to get back to normal. They don't want to be reminded."

"And it would be the same if it was Sal in here."

"It might be different if it was Sal. She's the boss. But I don't think—"

"What if it was you?" he interrupted.

"In here?"

"In here dying. What if it was you?"

"Some people would come, I guess. Françoise and Etienne. Keaty . . ."

"Me?"

"Yeah. You'd come." I laughed weakly. "I hope."

Jed let the laughter hang in the air, making it sound unpleasant and alien. Then he shook his head. "No, Richard. I meant what if it was me in here."

". . . You?"

"Me."

"Well . . . people would come to see you."

"Would they?"

"Of course."

"Would they?"

". . . Yes."

"But I *am* in here, Richard." He leaned toward me, blocking the Maglite, throwing the whole of his upper body into shadow. I pulled back at once, unsure of how close he was. When he spoke, hissed, he couldn't have been more than five or six inches away. "I'm in here all fucking day and all fucking night. And nobody comes to visit."

"I come to visit."

"But no one else."

"I . . . I'm sorry."

"Yes. I'm sorry too . . ."

"But . . ."

"Sure."

A couple of seconds later he sat back, and we watched each other across Christo's stained body. Then his head dropped and he absently began rubbing flakes of dried blood off his forearms.

"Jed," I said quietly. "Do me a favor."

"Mmm."

"Get out of the tent for a while. I'll stay here with Christo and . . ."

He waved a hand dismissively. "I think you miss the point."

"You really should . . ."

"I don't want to see those fuckers outside."

"You wouldn't have to. You could go down to the beach."

"Why?" he said, suddenly sounding very clear and definite. "To clear my head? To get me thinking straight and keep me sane?"

". . . If you like."

"As sane as everyone else?"

"It would help you get some perspective."

"It would help nothing. It doesn't matter where I am. I'm still in this tent. I've been in this tent since the day I got here, just like Christo. Just like Karl and Sten. The tent, the open sea, the DMZ. Out of sight and out of . . ."

Just for the briefest moment I heard a thickness in his voice. I held my breath, oddly panicked by the prospect of him in tears, but he appeared to regain control and continued.

"When the Swedes arrived and Daffy freaked . . . Daffy vanished . . . I really thought it would change . . . With him gone, I thought it would change . . . But he was so sly . . . He came back . . . so sly . . ."

Jed's voice faded to an indistinct whisper. Then he rocked forward and touched his temples with his fingertips.

"Jed," I said, after a pause. "What do you mean, he came back?"

"Killed himself," he replied. ". . . Came back."

I frowned, dislodging the buildup of sweat in my eyebrows. It ran down my face and stung the corners of my mouth. "You've seen him?"

"Seen him . . . yes . . ."

"When?"

"Koh Phangan, first . . . Should have seen him earlier . . ."

"You saw Daffy on Koh Phangan?"

"With your friends. Your dead friends . . ."

"With Zeph and Sammy?"

"He gave them the map."

I hesitated. "Jed, I gave them the map."

"No . . ."

"I'm telling you, I gave them the map. I remember doing it clearly."

"No, Richard." He shook his head. "Daffy gave them the map."

"You mean . . . they had the map before I gave it to them?"

"I mean he gave them the map when he gave it to you." Jed sat upright again. The movement drew the canvas floor tight and unbalanced the up-ended Maglite. As it fell it briefly dazzled me, then rolled to rest as a single beam. "He gave the map to Etienne," he said, carefully replacing the torch. "And to Françoise, and Zeph, and Sammy, and the Germans, and all the others . . ."

"The others?"

"The ones we haven't seen yet. The ones that will arrive next month, or week, and the ones that will arrive after them."

I sighed. "Then . . . you see Daffy when you see me."

"Not so much before . . . But now, yes." Jed nodded sadly. "Every time I see you . . . Every time . . ."

Same-Same, but Different

As I got into bed, the first into the longhouse that night, I heard the sound of Bugs and Keaty returning with the Tet supplies. There was a lot of excited chatter when people saw what they had brought for the celebration, and later I heard Keaty calling my name. Later still, Françoise joined him. I didn't answer either of them. I was lying on my back with a T-shirt draped over my head, waiting for sleep. Surprisingly I didn't have to wait too long.

The clearing had always been a clearing. It had almost doubled in size as the camp grew, but had existed in some form since the rocket ship trees were saplings. Two hundred years ago? Maybe more. The only way I know how to date a tree is to cut it down, but it wasn't hard to imagine those rocket ship trees having seen a few centuries through.

"A Herculean task," said Mister Duck thoughtfully. He was standing in the spot where the longhouse now stood, thigh-deep in ferns. "Diverting the stream. We only attempted it in the second year, when there were fourteen of us living here. Couldn't have done it without Jean, of course. Not just the know-how. He worked like an ox . . . kept us going . . . I wish you could have been with us, Rich. I wish you could have been with us from the very beginning. Me, Sal, and Bugs . . . The mood, you can't imagine . . ."

I pushed carefully through the shrubs, pacing out the distance from the longhouse door to where I estimated my bed must be. It was curious to be in the position where I knew, at that moment, I was also sleeping. "I can imagine the mood," I said, stepping sideways, disconcerted by the idea that I was standing on my head. "I can imagine it easily."

Mister Duck waggled a finger at me. "If I didn't know you better, Rich, I'd take offense at that. There's no way you can imagine the way we felt. Apart from anything, you're too young. On and off, I'd been traveling with Sal and Bugs for over eleven years. Eleven years, Rich! How can you imagine what it's like, living with cancer for eleven years?"

". . . Cancer?"

"Sure, cancer. Or AIDS. What do you want to call it?"

"Call what?"

"Living with death. Time limits on everything you enjoy. Sitting on a beautiful beach, waiting for a fucking time limit to come up. Affecting the way you look at the sand and the sunsets and the way you taste the rice. Then moving on and waiting for it to happen all over again. For eleven years!" Mister Duck shivered. ". . . Then to have that cancer lifted. To think you've found a cure . . . That's what you can't imagine, Rich."

The waterfall and its pool, at least, were exactly the same. A few shrubs different, I suppose, and doubtless a few invisible branches had broken in the trees, but not enough differences to warrant a double take.

One major difference perhaps, but one that would have taken me a while to notice. The carved tree hadn't been carved, and as soon as we arrived by the pool, Mister Duck produced a pocketknife and set about cutting in the names.

I watched him for a while, interested by the concentration on his usually restless face. Then, as he began to write the zero calendar, I asked, "Why me?"

He smiled. "I liked the way you talked when I threw the joint at you. You were so indignant and funny. But mainly, I chose you because you were a traveler. Any traveler would have done the job. Spreading the news is in our nature."

"Our?"

"I'm no better than you. I'm just the same."

"Maybe worse . . ."

Mister Duck completed the last zero with a twist of his wrist, and an oval of bark dropped cleanly onto his lap. "Hey," he said happily. "I'd forgotten I did that. How amazing."

"Maybe worse," I repeated. "If I had a part in destroying the beach, I did it unwittingly. You did it on purpose."

"Who says I destroyed this place? Not me, pal. Not from where I'm standing." He glanced at his crossed legs. "Sitting."

"Who was it then?"

Mister Duck shrugged. "No one. Stop looking for some big crime, Rich. You have to see, with these places, with all these places, you can't protect them. We thought you could, but we were wrong. I realized it when Jed arrived. The word was out, somehow out, and after that it was just a matter of time . . . Not that I acted on it at first. I waited, hoping he was a one-off, I guess. But then the Swedes arrived and I knew for sure. Cancer back, no cure, malignant as fuck . . ." He stood up, dusted the earth off his legs, and flicked his bark zero into the waterfall pool. "Terminal."

I punched him as hard as I could, square on his solar plexus. Then, when he doubled up, I pushed him on the floor and kicked him in the face.

He took it all without any attempt to fight back. He let me lay into him until my knuckles were cut and my ankle was twisted. Then, when I'd run out of breath and had collapsed on the grass beside him, he uncurled, pulled himself up, and started to laugh.

"Shut the fuck up!" I panted. "Shut your fucking mouth!"

"Cripes," he chuckled, spitting out a broken tooth. "What's got into you?"

"You tricked me!"

"How? What did I ever offer you? What did I ever say I'd provide?"

"You . . ."

"I never offered you anything but Vietnam, and only because you asked for it. It so happens you wanted the beach, too. But if you could have had Vietnam and kept the beach, it wouldn't have been Vietnam."

"I didn't know that! You never told me!"

"Exactly." Mister Duck beamed. "That was the beauty of it. You not knowing was Vietnam too. Not knowing what was going on, not knowing when to give up, stuck in a struggle that was lost before it started. It's incredible really. It all works out."

"But I didn't want that Vietnam!" I began. "I didn't want that kind! I wan—" Then I stopped. "All? . . . Wait, you're saying it *all* works out?"

"All. Right to the bitter end." He rubbed his hands together. "You know, Rich, I always thought euthanasia was a kindness. But I never dreamed it could be so much fun."

beaucoup
bad
shit

Spud Bashing

I watched Sal from just inside the longhouse door.
Everyone was standing in a big circle and she was in the middle, glowing, marching round, dishing out orders like they were birthday presents. For Greg's and Moshe's teams, special fish quotas to achieve; for Bugs and the carpenters, an eating area to construct; for Unhygienix and the gardeners, a feast to prepare; for Ella, seven whole chickens to pluck.

"Meat!" I heard one of the Yugoslavian girls say. "I have not eaten meat since . . . since . . ."

Since the last Tet celebration, it was generally agreed. Nine or ten months ago, a few had eaten a monkey that Jean had killed. Monkey, which tasted more like lamb than chicken, Jesse reported. Something Sammy might have found interesting, as an exception to his rule of exotic food.

Watching Sal's skillful organizing, I wondered how she'd react if I explained that our respite with the rafters was temporary in the extreme, and that all our efforts to protect the beach would come to nothing. I wondered if this news would frighten her as much as it frightened me.

When everyone had woken that morning and the longhouse had begun to buzz, I'd pretended to be asleep. Difficult, when Françoise tried to rouse me, but Sal soon called her off.

"Leave him be," she'd said, doubtless realizing I was faking. "Richard had a tough day yesterday, collecting all the dope for tonight."

Thankfully it didn't take long for the longhouse to empty and I was able to remove the sheets from over my head, light a candle, and light a cigarette. I'd actually been awake for a good two hours before the others, itching for nicotine all that time. I should have crept out when I had the chance. It would have meant I wasn't trapped in the longhouse. But at five a.m. I knew it would still be dark outside, and darkness was something I didn't feel ready for. I didn't know what it might be hiding. So instead I had two hours of my imagination running riot, trying to second-guess Mister Duck.

The only thing I could be sure of was that if Vietnam was heading for a bitter end, I was too. Past that, I couldn't be sure of anything. Working through the possibilities, the areas in which the end might come were as good as infinite. As an infantryman, all it might take was an ill-advised command from my CO. One that pushed my luck in the DMZ, one I accepted against my better instincts. Equally it might come from random bad luck. The same luck that jammed a soldier's M16 at the wrong time could make me slip as I jumped from the waterfall.

But knowing Mister Duck the way I did, I realized that these were not the threats that scared me the most. They were real enough, but they didn't have his nightmare hallmark. When he spoke about the bitter end, deep down I knew he only meant one thing. The VC. The fall of Saigon.

I was fortunate that, in her attempt to wake me, Françoise hadn't tried to pull the sheets from my head. If she had done, she'd have discovered that they were soaking wet and cold with sweat.

By eight, all the camp had been given their duties for the day's preparations and were busy working around the clearing. Worried about being seen and asked to join in, I went back to sit on my bed. It was a waste of time, knowing that someone would come to find me sooner or later, but I wanted to put it off as long as possible.

It was past eight thirty when a plump silhouette appeared in the longhouse doorframe. "You're being missed," Sal said, walking through the shadows until she was caught in the light from my candle. "Greg's asked if you can work on his detail today. Keaty wants to swap notes on Koh Phangan." She smiled. "And Françoise, I know you'll be glad to hear, has asked me to make certain you join them as soon as you wake up."

"What about Jed?" I asked quickly.

"Jed?" Sal frowned as she settled into a lotus position beside my bed. "I haven't seen him yet. But I'm sure he'd like to see you too."

". . . I'll go to see him later."

"Fine." She nodded. "Actually, just a thought, but maybe leave it for a while. There's quite a few people near the tent at the moment, and I have a feeling that things are getting extremely delicate with Christo. Jed might prefer not to be disturbed, and I think we should respect that."

"But he might prefer me to—"

"I'll check on him myself in a little while if it's worrying you. And anyway . . ." The barest suggestion of apprehension appeared on Sal's face. So slight that if I'd looked away as it happened, I'd never have noticed a change. "There was something else I was hoping you might do."

I tried to keep my expression as steady as hers.

"You see, Richard, I know it may feel like with our rafters gone, our troubles are as good as over. But I'm afraid that isn't quite the case. We still have the problem of the Swedes, and having gotten this far, I'm extremely reluctant to risk anything else going wrong. Now . . ." She paused to tuck a stray curl of hair back over her ears. "If Christo dies during Tet, no one has to know. People aren't exactly begging for news, so I can hold it back until the time feels right. No, our real problem, to my mind, is . . ."

"Karl . . ."

". . . Karl. That's right. And I'm afraid the responsibility for him must lie with you."

Unconsciously I squeezed the sheets with my fists. "With me?"

"Yes, you're quite right to look so guilty."

"Guilty?"

"If you hadn't disturbed him, he'd have stayed in his hole all through today and tonight, and maybe through the next week as well. Of course, we'd have had to deal with him at some point, but I was planning to leave that matter until after Tet . . . thanks to you, a luxury that has gone." She gestured vaguely in the direction of the longhouse door. "Take a look out there. You can see how important Tet is to everyone here. It's vital we make sure it goes smoothly. I can't really stress that enough . . ."

With a jolt, I realized the direction she was taking. She might have been a long way from delivering the bottom line, but I suddenly understood exactly what it would be.

"So," she said, and now I could clearly hear the controlled tension in her voice. "Let me spell the problem out. With Karl running around like a headless chicken, who's to say he won't suddenly appear during—"

"Sal," I interrupted. "I won't do it."

There was a short silence.

Although her composure remained fixed, I could sense the level of calculation at which Sal's mind was working. With a chess player's vacant gaze she was running through lists of responses, possible responses to the responses, and beyond. Four or five moves in advance, the variables becoming more complex at each step.

Eventually she crossed her arms. "You won't do what, Richard?"

"I won't, Sal. I won't do it."

"Do what?"

"Don't ask me, please . . ."

"Don't ask you to . . ."

I looked at her carefully, wondering if it was possible I'd read the signals wrong. But as my eyes moved to her face, hers dipped, and I knew for certain I was right.

And Sal saw this too. Immediately the pretense dropped, and with a slight shrug she said, "I'm afraid I *am* asking you, Richard."

I shook my head. "Sal, please . . ."

"I'm going to leave the longhouse now. In half an hour I'll come back and you will be gone. By tonight, all of our troubles will be behind us. The last month will be concluded. We'll never have to even think about it ever again."

She stood up to go, drawing in a deep breath as she rose.

"The beach is my life, Richard, but it's yours, too. Don't forget that. You can't afford to let me down."

I nodded miserably.

"Good." She returned the nod, turned around, and walked away.

Outside, everyone apart from the fishing details was busy in the clearing. Most were outside the kitchen hut, helping to peel an enormous mound of vegetables, at least four times our usual ration. Unhygienix had stuck some of the chicken feathers in his hair. The carpenters were in the middle, marking out the dimension of the seating area. Bugs and Cassie had started to lay down palm leaves, loosely meshed together, as a carpet.

All engrossed in their work and laughter. I easily ducked around the jungle side of the longhouse without being seen.

Is It Safe?

I thought of the caves after I'd checked around the waterfall and the far end of the Khyber Pass. If I'd been thinking more clearly, I would have checked the caves first. Not that it would have made much difference. The boat had probably been gone since sunup.

These days I can find comfort in the idea that, weirdly, my deranged assault had cured Karl after all. I often picture him, trying to guess what he's doing at this moment or that. All the images revolve around him having a normal life, and a loose impression of what a normal life might be in Sweden. Skiing, eating, working in an office, drinking with friends in a bar. An oak-paneled bar with moose heads and hunting trophies on the walls, for some reason. The more mundane the picture, the more comfort it gives me.

But at the time, my reaction wasn't so straightforward. Part of me was relieved that killing Karl was now an impossibility. I doubt I'd have killed him if he had been in the caves, despite the inflexibility of Sal's order, but I'm glad I never had the chance to find out. Most of me, however, was numb with shock. For the first few minutes after seeing the empty cove, I didn't even have the will to climb out of the water. All I could manage was to hang on to the rocks, and let myself be scraped up and down by the swell. I couldn't begin to imagine how Sal would react to this development. Karl turning up during Tet was of almost zero consequence compared to losing the boat, let alone the possible consequences of his arrival on Koh Phangan.

Eventually one of the larger swells as good as threw me onto the shelf where the gasoline can was usually tied down. Once there I dragged myself a little further in and didn't move again until, a short while later, I saw someone surface near the underwater passage.

Instinctively I ducked down, not recognizing the dark bobbing head at first. An instant paranoid scenario had formed: since I was someone who knew too much, Sal had sent Bugs after me in the same way that I'd been sent after Karl. Maybe this was what she'd meant by saying I couldn't afford to let her down.

"Richard?" the head called over the sound of the waves. It was Etienne. He was treading water, looking around, apparently having spotted neither me nor the missing boat. "Are you here, Richard?"

Of all the people I might fear on the beach, Etienne was the least likely candidate. Warily I stood up and waved him over.

I only noticed how cold he was when he'd swum over to the shelf and hauled himself up. I could hear his teeth chattering. The sun was still too low in the sky to reach inside the cave entrance, and the sea wind chilled the spray. "I followed you," he said, rubbing goose bumps off his arms. "I wanted to talk."

I paused, wondering why he hadn't noticed that the boat was gone. Then it dawned on me that there was a good chance he'd never been on this side of the caves. In which case he'd also never been through the underwater passage before. Very brave, I commented to myself. Or just as crazy as everyone else.

"I know there has been some difficulty between us," he continued. "Some difficulty between us, yes?"

I shrugged.

"Please, Richard. I would be very happy if we could talk about this. We should not be this way. Not at this time . . ."

"What time is that?"

"Before . . ." Etienne swallowed awkwardly. "Before Tet. Sal wants all difficulties to be over for Tet. A new start for the new year . . . Everybody else in the camp has forgotten their arguments. Keaty and Bugs even. So . . . I thought we should talk about our problem and make friends again . . . I thought we should talk about when you kissed Françoise . . ."

It was funny. My world was falling to pieces, everything in my life revolved around threat, and my nerves were shot to shit. But hearing that Etienne was still worried about the kiss with Françoise made me feel like laughing out loud.

"That is the problem, no? It is because of my reaction. My stupid reaction. Really, it was all my fault. I am very sorry that—"

"Etienne, what the hell are you talking about?"

". . . The kiss."

"The kiss." I glanced up at the sky. "Fuck the kiss. And fuck all that crap about Tet and Sal too. I know how much you care about Tet."

"I care about Tet!" he exclaimed, very alarmed. "Of course, I care very much! I am working very hard to make sure tha—"

"Bullshit," I interrupted.

Etienne stood up, making as if he was going to dive back into the water. "I have to get back to the fishing detail now. I only wanted to apologize so that now we can be friends and—"

I caught his elbow and dragged him back down. "Jesus! What's the matter with you?"

"Nothing! Richard, I only wanted to apologize! Please, now I must get back to—"

"Etienne, will you cut it out? You're acting like I'm the fucking Gestapo!"

He went very silent.

"What?" I shouted. "What is it?"

He still wouldn't reply, but looked extremely worried.

"Say something!"

After at least half a minute, Etienne cleared his throat. "Richard, I want to speak to you, but . . . I do not know . . ."

"You don't know what?"

He took a deep breath. "I do not know if it is . . . safe."

"*Safe?*"

"I . . . I understand Sal has not been happy with me . . ."

I dropped my head into my hands. "Christ," I muttered. "You do think I'm the Gestapo."

"I think you . . . do things. You do things for Sal. Everybody knows . . ."

"Everybody knows?"

"Today, you were looking for Karl . . ."

"What does everybody know?"

"Where is Karl, Richard? Did you catch him?"

I closed my eyes against a wave of nausea.

"Is he dead now?"

Everyone knew I did things for Sal. Everyone talked about it. They just didn't talk about it in front of me.

Etienne might have continued speaking, asking about what I'd done with Karl, but I can't be sure because I wasn't really listening. My head was filling up. I was remembering the way Cassie had looked at me when I'd let Bugs slip and slide in his shit. And the way a consensus of silence could drop as fast as an Asian rainstorm, and Jean nervously asking me on a date, and unmentioned gunshots. Unnoticed Christo dying in the death tent, Sten's funeral forgotten in half a day, Karl forgotten on a beach.

Except now, suddenly, not forgotten on a beach after all. Deliberately avoided to provide me with a discreet window of opportunity. A space for me to do the things I did for Sal.

God knows what those days since the food poisoning had been like for Etienne. It's impossible for me to put myself in his shoes, working through how he must have interpreted the events around him. I know because I've tried. The nearest I got was while I was sitting with him in the empty cove, and I've never been close since.

Ultimately, I've only got one reliable touchstone to his experience. The scene that followed Karl running through the clearing with me on his tail. The moment when Françoise strode away from Etienne, distancing herself from the liability that he'd become, ignoring his outstretched arms. I'd give a lot to know what she'd said to him later. But obviously it was enough for him to realize that once Karl was out of the way, he might be next.

"Etienne," I said, hearing my voice from far away. "Would you like to go home?"

He didn't seem to reply for a long time. "You mean . . . the camp?"

"I mean home."

". . . Not the camp?"

"Not the camp."

"Not . . ."

"Leaving the beach. France for you and Françoise, England for me."

I turned to face him, and was immediately hit by a second rush of sickness. It was the expression on his face, hiding his hope so badly. "It's all

right," I murmured, and reached out, intending to pat his shoulder for reassurance. But as soon as I moved, he recoiled.

"Don't worry," I said. "Everything will be okay. We're going to leave
tonight."

Efforts

I was a fool. I was kidding myself. As the idea of
leaving had come into my head, another idea had sneaked inside with it.
That maybe this was the way it could all end up. Not in some VC dope
guard attack and a panic-stricken evacuation from the clearing, but with a
simple demobilization of forces. After all, this was the way Vietnam ended
for a lot of American soldiers. Most American soldiers. Statistics were on
my side, I'd have played by Mister Duck's rules, and I'd be out in one
piece.

I could not have been more wrong, but that was the way I was thinking. Full of hasty schemes and plans, and the fucked-up optimism that
comes from desperation.

I wasn't bothered by the practicalities of leaving. It would have been
easier if Karl hadn't taken the boat, but we still had the raft. If that was
gone, we'd swim. We were all much fitter than we had been and I had no
doubt we could do it again. So with transportation out of the way, the only
other complication was food and water. But water could be solved with
water bottles, and catching fish was our specialty. All in all, the practicalities weren't worth more than passing consideration. I had much more serious things on my mind, like who we'd take with us.

Françoise was the first to sort out. She was standing two boulders over
from mine, one hand loosely resting on her thigh and the other pressed to
her lips. Etienne stood in front of her, talking rapidly, too quiet for the
sound to carry.

Their conversation became increasingly animated. Intense enough for me to start worrying that Gregorio would notice there was some kind of problem. He was in the water, closer to me than to them, diving with Keaty. But just as I began to contemplate ways I might distract Greg's attention, the exchange abruptly ended. Françoise looked over at me with wide eyes. Etienne said something urgent and she quickly turned back. Then Etienne threw a quick nod in my direction, and that was that. I knew she'd agreed to leave.

It was a big relief. I'd been completely unable to predict how she'd react, and, worryingly, so had Etienne. He'd said that it would all depend on whether she put the beach above her love for him. A close call, judging by the way things had been going, and we both knew it.

But however close the Françoise call was, it was a lot more straightforward than the other two names on our list: Jed and Keaty. Or my list, I should say, because Etienne didn't want to take either of them. I could see his point—if we only had to take Françoise, we could almost have left at once. We could have been above the cliffs and on our way to the raft within sixty minutes. But over the months of my beach life, I'd done enough to keep me in nightmares for the next twenty years. I didn't want to add to my sentence now. Jed and Keaty had been my best two friends on the beach, and even if it was risky—particularly with Keaty—I couldn't disappear without offering them the chance to come too.

The nightmares I couldn't avoid were Gregorio, Ella, Unhygienix, Jesse, and Cassie. Even if they agreed to come—which they wouldn't—and we managed to keep it secret from Sal—which would be impossible—we'd never all fit on the raft. So they had to be left behind. And I accepted that without any internal debate. It was irrelevant how it made me feel.

Soon after Etienne had finished talking to Françoise, she swam over to where I sat and pulled herself halfway out of the water. I waited for her to say something, but she kept quiet. She didn't even look at me.

"Is there a problem?" I whispered, keeping one eye over her shoulder. Gregorio and Keaty were still diving nearby. ". . . You understand why we have to go?"

"Maybe," she replied after a pause. "I understand that Etienne wants to leave because he is frightened of Sal."

"He's right to be frightened of her."

"Is he?"

"Yes."

"But I do not think that is why you are leaving. . . . For you, there is something else."

". . . Something else?"

"You would not leave if it was only because Etienne is frightened of Sal."

"I would. I am."

"No." She shook her head. "Will you tell me why you want to leave?"

"It's just like Etienne told you . . ."

"Richard. I am asking you. Please tell me why."

"There's nothing to tell. I think if we stay Etienne may be in danger."

"You do not think it can get better after Tet? Everyone says life will be better after Tet. You do not think maybe we should stay? We can wait for a few more days, and then, if you are still afraid . . ."

"Tet will change nothing, Françoise. Life will only get worse."

"Worse . . . Worse than we have had."

"Yes."

"But you will not tell me why."

". . . I don't know how I could."

"But you are sure."

"Yes. I'm sure."

She slipped back into the water. "We will never be able to come back," she said just before her head submerged, and sighed. "So sad . . ."

"Perhaps," I replied to the stream of bubbles she left behind her on the surface. "If there was anything to come back to."

Ten minutes later, Gregorio held up his fishing spear. A milkfish flapped on its point, sliding itself further down the shaft with its efforts to get free, the last fish needed for the extra quota.

Françoise, Etienne, and Gregorio began to make their way back toward the beach, jumping between the boulders where possible, swimming where necessary. Keaty and I stayed back.

"Hang on," I said when the others had set off. "I want to show you something."

He frowned. "We've got to get the catch back."

"It can wait. Twenty minutes. Twenty-five. It's important."

"Well," he said, and shrugged. "If it's important . . ."

Show, Don't Tell

I had imagined that, of the three, Keaty would be the hardest to persuade. He'd lived on the beach longer than the rest of us, he didn't have Françoise's attachment to Etienne, or Jed's bleak disillusionment. But it turned out he was the easiest. All I had to do was to show him where the boat had been and he virtually came up with the idea himself.

"It can't be gone," Keaty said, and leaned over, trailing his arms in the water as if hoping to find its sunken prow. "It just can't be. It's not possible."

"But it is."

"It *can't* be."

"You can see for yourself."

"Don't tell me what I can see!"

". . . I don't know what Sal's going to say . . ."

"I do! She's going to fucking flip! She's going to lose her mind! She's going to—" He rose up with a jerk and clapped both hands to his head. "Oh my God, Rich . . ."

I frowned with what I imagine looked like innocent concern. ". . . What is it?"

"I was the one who tied it up . . . I was the one who . . . Jesus *Christ!*"

"What? Tell me!"

"I'm dead!" he almost screamed. "I'm a fucking dead man!"

". . . Dead? Why?"

"The food poisoning! And now losing the boat! *Shit! Fuck!* Of all things, losing the . . . Don't you get it? She'll do for me like she did for . . . for . . . Oh *no!*" He leapt to his feet and started quickly backing away. "This is why you got me here, isn't it? She already knows! *She already fucking knows!*"

I stood up too.

"You stay where you are!"

"Keaty . . ."

He drew back a fist. *"Stay where you are!"*

"Keaty . . ."

"I swear, if you make one fucking move I'll . . ."

"Keaty!" I yelled, suddenly feeling angry myself. "Shut the fuck up! I'm not going to attack you, for Christ's sake!"

"Back off!"

"Okay, okay!" I took several steps away from him. "I'm backing off!"

"Further! Get right back against the rock!"

I did I as was told. "There! Satisfied?"

He stayed frozen with his fist raised. "If you make one move . . ."

"You'll pulverize me. I know."

"I will do it! I'm not Karl! I'm telling you, you won't have a fucking prayer!"

"I *know*. I'll be creamed. But you've *got* to believe me, I've got no intention of attacking you. I can't even believe you think I would! You're one of my best friends!"

His fist lowered, but no more than an inch.

"Does Sal know about the boat?"

"No."

"You *promise?*"

"On my life. The whole reason I brought you here is so you could find out before she did. And think about it, Keaty. How could she know? You only got back last night, so when could she have had a chance to find out?"

He thought about this a few seconds, then lowered his fist completely. "Yes," he murmured blankly. "That's true . . . She couldn't know . . ."

"Right."

" But . . . she'll find out soon . . . She'll have to . . ."

"She'll find out very soon."

"Fuck!" he blurted, his panic rising again. "And then what will I do? I won't be able to sleep at nights! I won't be able to go anywhere alone! I'll have to . . ."

"Leave?"

"I'll have to leave! Yes! Jesus! I should leave right now! I'll take the—"

He whirled around and stared at the cove. "Oh God," he whispered. "But I can't. I'm trapped here . . . trapped . . ."

"No," I replied, raising a hand to my temples as if formulating a rapid and brilliant scheme. "There just might be another option."

Spiked

Now I was on a roll. Getting on top of things. The two hardest converts were converted and all I had to do was get to Jed, fill him in, and wait for our chance to slip away. I was feeling so good that I started humming my mouse song as Keaty and I reentered the clearing. The only problem was, Keaty joined in too. Joined in with manic gusto, hitting the wrong notes, turning heads. "What are you doing?" I hissed. "You sound like a swarm of bees."

"I can't help it," he hissed back through a rigid ventriloquist's smile. "I'm freaking out. I feel like everybody's watching us."

"You've got to act normal."

"I don't know if I'll be able to handle this, Rich."

"The Gameboy. Go and play the Gameboy. And if Sal asks you to join in with the preparations, just try to be calm."

"Got it," he whispered, and walked off to his tent, arms stiffly swinging by his sides.

Etienne and Françoise were coping a lot more successfully, but they did have each other for support. They sat close to the kitchen hut, apparently chatting idly, busy helping to gut the enormous catch of fish.

Sal, meanwhile, was nowhere to be seen. I wanted to locate her before I tried to get to the hospital tent—remembering that she'd told me to stay away from Jed—so I moved to the center of the clearing, expecting to spot her with Bugs and the carpenters.

The seating area had progressed swiftly over the time I'd been away. Our bedsheets and one or two unzipped sleeping bags had been suspended between bamboo poles, making a flat marquee about twenty-five feet in diameter. Bugs had Cassie on his shoulders, who was giggling and laying palm leaves above the sheets. I guessed the canopy needed to be thick enough to block out the glow from our candles and barbecue, in case any planes happened to pass over us tonight.

But Sal wasn't with the carpenters, either. Which meant there was a strong possibility she was in the hospital tent with Jed.

"Shit," I said.

"Not impressed?" said a crisp voice, directly behind me.

I delayed for a second in order to compose myself and do some rapid thinking, then turned around. ". . . Impressed, Sal?"

"With our construction."

"Oh, I'm very impressed with that. *Very* impressed. It's amazing. No, I was thinking about something else."

"Mmm?"

"My cigarettes. I left half a packet on the beach."

"Oh."

"No big deal. I've just got a feeling they were at the low-tide mark, and the water's coming in. Stupid of me."

"Doesn't seem too serious."

"No, no." I shook my head. "Not at all serious."

"Good . . . I'm glad to see you've cheered up since this morning."

"I feel much better."

"I assume that means I shouldn't worry about any unexpected problems tonight."

". . . That's right. No problems. You can . . . forget about him."

"Forget?" Sal said, not missing a beat. "Forget about who?"

". . . Karl."

She gave me an odd look. "Who?"

"Karl."

"Who's Karl?"

"Karl's . . ." I began, then the penny dropped. "Nobody."

"I thought you were talking about someone here."

"No."

"Fine." Sal nodded fractionally. "Well, I'd better get back to work. Still lots to do."

"Sure."

"If you get stuck for a chore, let me know. We'll soon find something."

"Right."

"Lovely."

A few moments later Sal was standing under the marquee and pointing out gaps in the sheets to Bugs, although he didn't appear to be paying attention. He still had Cassie on his broad shoulders, and he kept breaking into a little jog to make her squeal.

It was past four o'clock before I had a chance to get to the hospital tent, and a chance to do something else as well. A piece of inspired opportunism, I thought at the time.

At four, all of the preparations for the evening were as good as finished. The marquee was complete, the stews were bubbling, the chickens were ready to barbecue, and the vegetable peelings, feathers, and fish guts had been taken down the Khyber Pass and thrown away. So Sal, sensing a lull, suggested a huge game of soccer down on the beach. "Let's work up an appetite!" she'd called out. "A serious appetite!"

This was excellent news. As Keaty and I never joined in the soccer, we had an excuse to remain behind. Plus we could offer to tend the cooking pots, meaning Unhygienix could leave with the others. By ten past, the clearing was empty.

"He's going to notice," said Keaty nervously, watching me sprinkle huge handfuls of grass into the stew. "It's going to taste really strange."

"If he notices I'll just admit it was me. I'll say it was for the atmosphere."

"He hates people fucking with his food."

"Yeah, well, if we don't do something the party will go on all night." I paused, picking up roughly half an ounce, and chucked it into the biggest pot. Then I chucked in another half. "Anyway, after an hour he'll be too messed up to give a shit."

"He'll be tripping. Everyone will."

"Whatever. Just make sure you don't eat any of this. Stick to the

chicken and rice. And make sure Etienne and Françoise get the same message."

"It won't be easy to avoid eating the stew."

"We'll manage." I dusted my hands off and surveyed my handiwork.
After a couple of turns with a stick there was no evidence of the new in-
gredient. "You reckon we should chuck in some magic mushrooms or
something?"

"No."

"Okay. So how much do you reckon is in there now?"

"In total? All the pots?"

"In total."

"A lot. Way too much. You're a fucking lunatic."

"A lunatic!" I laughed. "Hold the front page."

Don't Mean Nothing

The atmosphere in the hospital tent was the kind
where you feel uncomfortable if you cough or make a hurried movement—contemplative, detached. I felt like I was in a temple. Even more so
because I was praying.

"Die," went the prayer. "Make this breath the last one."

But every time, Christo would breathe again. Despite all the odds, despite the achingly long gaps, his chest would suddenly inflate and deflate.
He'd still be alive, and the waiting would start all over again.

For much of the time, I studied Jed. He looked strange because his hair
and beard were completely slick, flattened down with blood and sweat. I
could see the shape of his head in a way I never had before. It was more
angular than I'd imagined. Smaller and, where his scalp showed between
the wet curls, shockingly white.

He didn't look at me once; neither had he acknowledged my presence
when I climbed in. His eyes were set on Christo's calm face, and weren't
going to budge until they were good and ready. Christo's face, I noticed,

was just about the only clean thing in the tent. Under his chin you could see the dark smear marks where Jed had wiped him down, and by the time you reached his neck you couldn't see past the dirt to his skin.

Another thing that caught my attention was that a little bag—which had been sitting just to the right of Jed until yesterday—was now gone. Karl's bag. I'd known it was his because peeking out of its top flap had been the Nike swim shorts he sometimes wore. Although the missing bag was my only evidence, and remains my only evidence, I felt sure that Karl must have visited Christo before he left. I liked that idea. Visiting his friend, taking his bag, stealing the boat. Cured, all right.

Time passed much faster than I estimated. When I looked at my watch I was expecting it to read four-thirty, but instead it read ten after five. I'd been in there for a whole hour. But watching Christo was absorbing. It set my mind thinking about stuff like the afterlife, because there was something about the way Christo was dying that made an afterlife seem particularly unlikely. It's hard to explain what the something was. His eyes maybe, which were slightly open even though he was obviously unconscious. The two glittering slits made him look so nonfunctional. Just a machine that, for whatever reason, happened to be packing in.

When I saw my watch, I realized I had to go. The rest of the camp would be returning soon, so I decided that I had no choice but to break the temple atmosphere.

"Jed," I said in a soothing, priestly manner. "There's something we should talk about."

"You're leaving," he said bluntly.

". . . Yes."

"When?"

"Tonight . . . Tonight, when everyone's crashed out after Tet. Will you come?"

"If Christo is dead."

". . . And if he isn't."

"I'll stay."

I bit the inside of my lip. "You understand that unless you come tonight, there'll be no way off the island."

"Mmm."

"You'll be stuck here with whatever's coming. And the problem isn't going to be more travelers turning up. Karl's taken the boat. If he contacts his family or Sten's and Christo's families . . ."

"It isn't the Thai police that are coming."

"And when Sal finds out we're gone tomorrow, the shit's going to—"

"It's already hit."

"I won't be able to wait for you."

"I don't expect you to."

"I want you to come."

"I know."

"And do you know that it makes zero difference to Christo if you're here or not? Do you know that, too? With the amount of oxygen he's taking in, most of his brain has already shut down."

"He isn't dead until he stops breathing."

"Okay . . ." I thought hard for a couple of seconds. "So what if we stop him breathing? We could cover up his mouth. It would only take five minutes."

"No."

"You don't have to do it. I'll do it for you. You could hold his hand or something. It would be a nice way for him to go. It would be very tranquil and—"

"Fuck it, Richard!" Jed snapped, spinning his head round and looking at me for the first time. But as soon as he did so, his expression softened. I was biting my lip again. I didn't like Jed shouting at me.

"Look," he said. "Christo should be dead by tonight, so I should be able to come with you."

"But . . ."

"Now why don't you go? I don't think Sal would like it if you were in here."

"No, but . . ."

"You'll check on me before you leave."

I sighed. Jed turned back to Christo. I stuck around for a minute or so, then backed out of the tent.

———

Outside, I saw Keaty scurrying off toward the Khyber Pass with an armful of something soggy and unrecognizable. When he came back I asked him what he was doing.

"I took the dope out of the cooking pots," he explained, drying his sticky chest with a T-shirt. He smelled of lemongrass and his hands were shaking.

"What?"

"I had to. It kept floating to the surface. Unhygienix would have seen it immediately. But it was in there for an hour so . . ."

"Your shorts," I said.

"Shorts?"

"They're covered in stew. Go and change them."

His eyes flicked down. "Shit!"

"Just go and change them. It's no big deal."

"Change them. Right."

Before he'd returned, the rest of the camp began pouring into the clearing. Singing, laughing, arm in arm. Tet was about to kick off.

Potchentong

Take a green coconut, still up in the tree, and cut a small incision in its base. Under the incision, hang a flask to catch the dripping milk. Then leave it for a few hours. When you come back, you'll find that the milk has fermented and that if you drink it you'll get pissed. A neat trick. It tastes okay; a bit sugary but okay. I was surprised I'd never seen it done before.

Thanks to the gardeners, we all had coconut-shell cups filled with the moonshine beer. "Down in one!" Bugs was shouting. "Down the hatch!" And people had fizzy juice running over their chins and chests. Françoise was eyeing Keaty, and Etienne was eyeing me, and we had more running over our chins than anyone else.

Bugs finished his cup first and kicked it into the jungle like it was a soccer ball. It must have fucking hurt, like kicking a lump of wood. But the idea caught on and just about everyone had a crack, and soon the clearing was filled with people hopping around, clutching a foot, giggling like crazy. "Hopping mad," I said to Keaty, but he didn't get the joke.

"Sal keeps staring at me," he whispered. "She *knows* something. Should I kick the coconut? What if I break my foot? Would you leave me behi—" He interrupted himself by dropping the shell and punting it. His face screwed up with the pain and he let out a yell louder than all the others. "Did it," he gasped. "Is she still looking?" I shook my head. She never had been looking anyway.

When Jean began to produce a second round of drinks, I maneuvered myself around to where Françoise and Etienne were standing. I did it partly to get away from Keaty, whose jumpiness didn't seem helped by my presence. I think it reminded him of what was going on.

Françoise was giving a great performance. If she was feeling the tension, I'd never have guessed it. Externally, she seemed to be in the party spirit one hundred percent. When I walked up she gave me a flamboyant hug and a kiss on each cheek, and loudly said, "This is all so wonderful!"

I mentally congratulated her. She was even taking the performance through to slightly slurring her words, and not overdoing it either. Getting it exactly right.

"Can I have a kiss too?" said Jesse, nudging one of the carpenters.

"No," Françoise replied with a dizzy smile. "You are too ugly."

Jesse clasped one hand to his heart and the other to his forehead. "I'm too ugly! I'm too ugly for a kiss!"

"That's right," said Cassie. "You are." She gave him her beer. "Here. You'd better drown your sorrows."

"I think I should!" Tipping his head back, he drained the liquid in one slurp and tossed the empty vessel behind him. "But you still love me, don't you, Caz?"

"Not when you call me Caz, Jez."

"Caz!" he howled. "Caz! Jez! Caz!" Then he scooped her up in his arms and began staggering off toward the longhouse.

A couple of minutes later, Etienne was called over to help carry the food to the eating area, and Françoise and I were left alone. She said something to me, but I didn't catch it because I was concentrating on something else. By the kitchen hut I'd seen Unhygienix tasting some of the stew with a puzzled frown.

"You are not listening to me," Françoise said.

Unhygienix shrugged and began organizing the cooking pot carriers.

"You never listen to me anymore. Before, if I was talking to you, you would always listen. But now you have no time to even talk to me."

"Yeah . . . Has Keaty told you not to eat the stew?"

"Richard!"

I frowned. "What?"

"You are not listening to me!"

". . . Oh. Well I'm sorry. I've got a lot on my mind."

"Not me."

"Huh?"

"I am not on your mind."

"Uh . . . Of course you are."

"I am not." She poked me in the ribs. "I think you do not love me anymore."

I looked at her in astonishment. ". . . Are you serious?"

"Very serious," she said petulantly.

"You can't be."

"I am! For so many weeks you have not even talked to me. Not even *looked* at me. In fact, I think you are only interested in Sal."

"*Sal?*"

"Yes! You remember how it was with us before? Always, we were . . ." Françoise hesitated. ". . . You *know* how we were."

"Yes. I mean, no. But . . . Jesus! Do we have to talk about this right now? Of all times, does it have to be *right* now?"

"Of course, it must be now. Etienne is not here, and maybe soon I will never see you again!"

"Françoise!" I hissed. "Keep it down!"

"Maybe I should keep it down, but maybe I should not. In the dope field, when I would not be quiet, you pushed me to the ground and held me tightly." She giggled. "It was very exciting."

With a quick look around, I linked my arm in her elbow and began propelling her away toward the edge of the clearing. Once we were out of sight of the others I turned her round, held her head between my hands, and looked carefully at her pupils. They were all over the place. "Oh my God," I said furiously. "You're drunk."

"Yes," she admitted. "I am. It was this potchentong."

"Potchentong? What the fuck are you talking about?"

"Jean calls the drink potchentong. It is not the real potchentong, but—"

"How much have you had?"

"Three cups."

"Three? When?"

"With the football. The game."

"You *idiot!*"

"I had no choice! They were passing around the shell, and you had to drink it all. They were watching and clapping, so what could I do?"

"Christ! Did Etienne drink some too?"

"Yes. Three cups."

I closed my eyes and counted to 10. Or meant to. That stuff never works. I stopped when I was on about 4.

"Right," I said. "Come with me."

"Where are we going?"

"Over here."

Françoise gasped as I pulled her behind a tree.

"Open your mouth," I instructed.

"Are you going to kiss me?"

The infuriating thing is, I'm sure that if I had tried to kiss her, she'd have let me. She was that drunk. But I had to shake my head.

"No, Françoise," I replied. "Not exactly."

She bit my fingers really hard when I stuck them down her throat. And she struggled and squirmed like a snake. But I was holding her with a vise grip around her neck, and once the fingers were in, there wasn't a lot she could do about it.

After she'd finished throwing up, she slapped me in the face, which I accepted. Then she said, "I could have done that myself."

I shrugged. "I didn't have time for an argument. Are you feeling more sober now?"

She spat. ". . . Yes."

"Good. Now go and wash yourself down in the waterfall stream and then discreetly make your way back to the clearing. And don't touch a drop of potchentong." I paused. "Or the stew."

When I returned to the party, Etienne had finished helping carry the food and was standing alone, probably looking for Françoise. I walked straight up to him. "Hi," I said. "Are you drunk?"

He nodded unhappily. "The potchentong . . . They made me drink it and—"

"I heard," I said, and tutted with sympathy. "Strong stuff, huh?"

"Very strong."

"Well, no worries. Just come with me."

A Loose End

The layout was simple. Concentric circles under the marquee, the first a ring of candles, the second our banana leaf plates, the third our seated selves, and the fourth a final ring of candles. It looked spectacular and terrifying. Orange faces, flickering light, diffused through clouds of dope smoke. And such a level of noise. People weren't talking, they were shouting. Sometimes screaming. Nothing more than jokes or requests to pass the rice pot, but it sounded like screaming.

I'd made us all sit together. Keeping us together made it easier all round. We were able to get rid of our stew more easily and it kept Keaty and Françoise contained between me and Etienne. It also meant that our relative temperance was less likely to be noticed, something that was fast turning into a problem. Keaty had picked up on it first, a little under an hour after we'd started to eat.

"I told you they'd trip," he said. With the racket as a backdrop, he didn't even have to whisper. "You put way too much in."

"You think they're actually tripping?"

"Maybe not seeing stuff, but . . ."

I looked over at Sal, who was directly opposite me in the circle. Strangely, despite the din, she looked like someone in an old silent movie. Sepia-toned, flickering, twisted lips with no discernible sounds coming out. Frozen lips. Arched eyebrows. She must have been laughing.

"But yeah, they're tripping," Keaty finished. "Either that or I am."

Unhygienix appeared behind us. "More stew!" he shouted.

I raised a hand. "So full! Can't eat more!"

"Yes! Eat more!" He reached over and ladled a huge dollop in front of me. It poured over the edges of my banana leaf like a lava flow, smothering rice grains, taking them with it. Little people in the lava, I thought, and suddenly felt like I was tripping too. I gave Unhygienix the thumbs-up, and he continued on his rounds.

A half hour later, around a quarter to nine, I excused myself on the pretext of a piss. I did need a piss as it happened, but mainly I wanted to check up on Jed. With the way things were going, I couldn't see the manic level being sustained later than midnight, so I wanted to know if our problem was resolved yet.

I relieved myself outside the hospital tent. Bad form in normal circumstances, but civic responsibility wasn't high on my list of priorities anymore. Then I stuck my head inside the flaps. To my amazement, Jed was asleep. He was in the same spot he'd been in earlier that day, but keeled over on his side. He'd probably been awake all the previous night.

Even more amazing was that Christo was still alive, doing his pitiful inflate-deflate thing. So slight I'd be hard put to call it a genuine breath.

"Jed," I said, and he didn't stir. I said it louder, again with no response. Next a huge cheer came from the marquee. It lasted for a pretty long time, and when Jed still hadn't stirred I knew I had a golden opportunity in front of me.

I reached Christo's head by sliding around the left-hand side of the tent. Then, just as I'd suggested earlier, I pinched his nose and covered his mouth. There was no twitching, no resistance. A few minutes later I took my hands away, counted to 120, and slid back to the cool outdoors. And that was it. It really was that simple.

As I returned across the clearing, clicking my fingers in time with my footsteps, I saw the reason for the cheering I'd heard. Both the Yugoslavian girls were in the central circle of candles, heads resting on each other's shoulders, slow-dancing to the buzz of noise.

Something Happening Here

By the time I'd retaken my seat, the Yugoslavian girls had inspired some of the others. Sal and Bugs started dancing too, then Unhygienix and Ella, then Jesse and Cassie.

I may have had a few screws loose, but I was able to recognize this as a nice moment. Watching the four couples revolving around each other reminded me of the way things used to be on the beach. Even Sal seemed at peace, all her plans and manipulations pushed aside for the time being, aware of nothing more than straightforward affection for her lover. In fact, Sal looked like a completely different person. None of her confidence was apparent in her dancing. Her steps were tentative and slow, and she clung to Bugs with both arms, head pressed flat against his chest.

"You do not recognize her," Gregorio said to me, having followed the direction of my gaze. While I'd been killing Christo, he'd taken my place so he could chat with Keaty. "You have never seen her like this."

"No . . . I haven't."

"You know why?"

"No."

"Because tonight it is Tet, and Sal will only smoke or drink on Tet. The rest of the year, her mind is always clear, all hours in the day. We get high, but she keeps her mind clear for us."

"She cares very much about the beach."

"Very much," Greg echoed. "Of course." He smiled and stood up. "I will get us more coconut beer. You would like some?"

Both Keaty and I said no.

"Just for me then?"

"Just for you."

He ambled off toward the fishing buckets, which held the last of Jean's moonshine.

Ten o'clock. The dancing had stopped. Moshe was standing where the dancers had been, holding a candle up in one hand, the other hand touching the side of his face. I didn't know if anyone else was taking an interest in him, but I was. "This flame," he said as hot wax ran onto his wrist and down the length of his arm, forming a slim stalactite on his elbow. "Look."

"Look," said Etienne, gesturing to Cassie. She was also studying the candle flames, crouched over with an expression of rapt pleasure. Jesse was next to her, muttering something in her ear that made her jaw drop. Behind them, Jean sat with his back to one of the bamboo poles, covering his eyes with his fingers, removing them and blinking like a baby kitten.

"Night, Jim-Bob," called one of the Australian carpenters.

Six or seven people provided names, all at once. A ripple of laughter spread beneath the marquee. "Night, Sal," Ella called, above the competing voices. "Night Sal, night Sal, night Sal."

Soon Ella's cue became a soft chant that lasted as long as the cigarette I was smoking. Then Sal replied, "Thank you, children," and the ripple of laughter spread again.

A few minutes later the carpenter that had called out Jim-Bob said, "Is anyone else seeing shit?" When no one answered he added, "I'm seeing all kinds of shit over here."

"Potchentong," sang Jean like a tolling bell.

Moshe dropped the candle.

"Seriously, guys, I'm seeing all kinds of shit."

"Potchentong."

"Did you put mushrooms in the potchentong?"

"This flame," said Moshe. "This flame burned me." He began pulling the line of wax from his arm.

"Moshe's losing his fucking skin . . ."

"I am losing my skin?"

"Losing his skin!"

"Potchen-fucking-tong . . ."

I leaned over to Keaty. "This *can't* be just the dope," I whispered. "Even eating it, dope wouldn't do this, would it?"

He wiped beads of sweat off the back of his neck. "They're all crazy. It's worse being straight. It's doing my fucking head in just watching them."

"Yes," said Etienne. "Really, I do not like this. When can we go?"

I checked my watch for the fifteenth time in as many minutes. To the extent that I'd thought it out, I'd imagined leaving at around two or three a.m., when there'd be a bit of light creeping into the sky. But Etienne was right. I didn't like the way things were either, and at a pinch, we could probably set off while it was still dark.

"Give it an hour," I said. "I think we might be able to leave in an hour."

What It Is
Ain't Exactly Clear

But an hour was no good. At ten-thirty, things started to go wrong.

Up until then I'd felt I was in control of the situation. Perhaps I even *was* in control of the situation. A number of difficulties—Françoise drunk, Christo breathing—had been solved; we'd gotten through the meal without anyone noticing that we were throwing our stew away; aside from Jed, there were no further loose ends to be tied; Tet was winding down. All we had to do was to bide our time and then make our move.

But at ten-thirty Mister Duck appeared in the marquee, and I knew I had a problem.

He appeared out of the shadows, stepping over the outer ring of candles. Then he walked over to Sal and Bugs and, after acknowledging me with a vague grin, sat down beside them.

"Where are you going?" said Françoise as I stood up. It was the first thing she'd said in a while. Since the dancing she'd been lying with her head in Etienne's lap, staring intently at the sheets on the marquee. From her color I'd assumed she was feeling the effects of her afternoon boozing, but when she spoke I realized that she was also scared. Obviously, considering the circumstances, but I wasn't in a very empathic frame of mind. Neither was I in the right frame of mind to reassure anyone.

"We could be fucked," I said, stupidly speaking my thoughts out loud.

Etienne began looking around. "What? What is it?"

". . . I've got to check something out. The three of you don't move from this spot. Clear?"

"Not fucking clear." Keaty caught me by the leg. "What's going on, Richard?"

"I've got to do something."

"You're going nowhere unless you tell me what's going on."

"Let go of my leg. Greg is watching us."

Keaty squeezed tighter. "I don't care. You tell us what the fuck—"

I bent down and clamped my fingers on the soft underside of Keaty's wrist, blocking the blood. A couple of seconds later his hand fell away.

"Hi," I said to Sal.

"Richard," she replied happily. "Richard, my right-hand man. How are you, right-hand man?"

"Left-handed. I've started seeing fucked-up stuff." The last words were directed at Mister Duck, who seemed amused.

"Sit down with us."

"I need to get some cigarettes from the longhouse."

"If you were sitting with us . . ." Sal drifted off briefly, then picked up the thread. "I'd know that you and Bugs were friends again."

"We are friends."

Mister Duck guffawed, but Bugs nodded, full of dreamy goodwill. "Yeah, man," he said. "All friends here."

"It was . . . This was the last thing I was worried about . . . I needed you two to be friends . . ."

I patted Sal's shoulder. "There's nothing more for you to worry about. Things are back to normal, just how you wanted."

"Yes . . . We did it, Richard."

"You did it."

"I'm sorry for shouting at you, Richard. All those times . . . I'm sorry."

I smiled. "I need to get the cigarettes. We'll talk later."

"And you'll sit with us."

"Sure."

When Mister Duck walked through the longhouse door, I grabbed him by the neck and slammed him against the inside wall. "Right," I said. "Tell me what you're doing here."

He stared with a slightly baffled, innocent expression, then chuckled.

"Are you here to stop us?"

No answer.

"Tell me why you're here!"

"The horror," he said.

". . . What?"

"The horror."

"What horror?"

"*The* horror!"

"*What horror?*"

He sighed, and with a quick movement, twisted out of my grip. "The horror," he said a final time, ducked through the doorway, and was gone.

For a few seconds I stayed where I was, my arms still pointlessly raised in the position where they'd been holding Mister Duck. Then I came to my senses and started jogging back to the marquee, making only the most cursory attempt at casualness in my haste.

"Okay," I whispered when I reached Keaty and the other two. "Get ready. We're going."

"Right now?"

"Yes."

"But . . . it's still pitch black out there!"

"We'll manage. I'll go first so I can get Jed and pick up the water bottles, then Etienne and Françoise, you leave five minutes later, then Keaty. We'll meet by the beach path in . . ."

That Sound

At the exact moment I said "path," Bugs jumped to his feet. His dreamy goodwill was out the window. His eyes were wide and his teeth were bared. "What the *fuck* was that noise?" he hissed.

Everyone turned to look at him.

"What was that fucking *noise?*"

Unhygienix laughed sleepily. "Can you hear noises, Bugs?"

"It was . . . a branch being pushed. It was somebody pushing through branches."

Sal pulled herself out of the lotus position to sit on her knees. ". . . Are we all here?" she said, scanning around the sprawled figures.

"I'm not really *here*," drawled Jesse. "I'm not really anywhere."

Bugs took a step away from the blackness outside the marquee. "Somebody is definitely out there."

"Maybe it's Karl . . ." someone offered.

Several heads turned to me.

"It isn't Karl."

"Jed?"

"Jed's in the hospital tent."

"Well, if it isn't Karl or Jed . . ."

"Wait!" Cassie was standing too. "I heard something! . . . There!"

We all strained our ears.

"It's nothing," Jesse began to say. "Will you all relax? It's just this strange trip—"

"This is no fucking trip," Bugs interrupted. "Everyone, get your heads together. I'm telling you there's people coming."

"*People?*"

And suddenly we were all rising to our feet, because we could all hear the noise. It was unmistakable. People, pushing through branches, walking on leaves, coming our way from the waterfall path.

"Run!" Sal shouted. "Everyone run! Now!"

————

Too late.

A figure materialized within four meters of us, picked out by the oily flames around the marquee. Within seconds, more appeared by his side. They all had their guns up, leveled straight at us. None seemed wet, so they couldn't have jumped from the waterfall. Maybe they knew a secret route into the lagoon or had used ropes to abseil the cliffs, or maybe they had simply floated down. The way they hovered in the darkness, it didn't seem unlikely.

I turned to look at my companions. Apart from Etienne and Françoise, I doubt any of them had seen the VC before and I was interested to see their reaction. It was suitably awed. Moshe and one of the gardeners had dropped to their knees, and the others were frozen in a perfect tableau of fright. Slack jaws, tensed jaws, arms bunched up to chests. I almost envied them. For a first encounter, it took some beating.

Apocalypse

Escape was not an option. We were all about to get killed. I accepted the realization without bitterness. There wasn't anything I could do to stop it from happening and I felt I'd be dying with a clear conscience. Although I'd known that Vietnam might end this way, I hadn't run. I'd selflessly stuck around until I was sure that my friends would be able to run with me. For once, I'd done the right thing.

And this is why I was furious that the VC weren't doing the right thing. They weren't doing the right thing at all, and I was outraged.

As I turned back from looking at my companions, I saw the dope guard boss jab a finger at me. The next moment, one of his men dragged me out of the marquee and forced me to the ground. Appalled, it dawned on me that I was going to get shot first.

First! If I had to get shot, then tenth, eleventh, twelfth would be fine. But *first*. I couldn't believe it. I'd miss out on everything.

The guard rested the muzzle of his AK against my forehead. "You're making a big mistake," I said angrily. "You're *really* screwing up." I tilted my head at Moshe. "Why don't you do him instead? What difference does it make to you? Do him."

His sleek face gazed down at me indifferently.

"Him, for Christ's sake! That ape!"

". . . Aape."

"*Ape*, you fucking slope! You dink motherfucker! That gorilla! *Him* over there!"

I pointed at Moshe, who moaned feebly. Then the guard behind kicked me in the back.

"Oh shit," I gasped as red pain burned into my kidneys.

Unable to stop myself, I rolled over onto my side. The tableau didn't seem to have shifted, apart from Etienne, who had covered his eyes.

"Okay." With an effort, I got back onto my knees. "At least let me choose who does it."

I didn't make the mistake of pointing again. Instead I swiveled around so that it was the kick-boxer's gun that was aiming at my head.

"I want this guy. Fair enough, right? Get him to do it."

Kick-boxer frowned, then glanced over at the boss. The boss shrugged.

"Yes, you. You with the dragon tattoo." I paused, then had a look at his mouth. It was closed, pouting slightly with his puzzled expression. "Guess what? I know you don't have any front teeth!" I showed him mine and gave them a tap. "Missing, huh?"

He lifted a wary finger and touched between his lips.

"That's right!" I yelled. "You don't have any front teeth! And I already knew that!"

The kick-boxer kept his finger in his mouth a few moments, exploring his gums. Then he said something to the boss in Thai.

"Ah." The boss nodded. "You the boy always come to see us . . . Every day, ha? You li' to come see us."

I glared at him. Then, to my surprise, he squatted beside me and ruffled my hair.

"Funny boy in trees, every day. We li' you too. Take some Mary Jane, ha? Okay Mary Jane. Some Mary Jane, for you frien's."

"Hurry up and kill me," I said bravely.

"Kill you? Ah, funny boy . . . I no' kill you now." He ruffled my hair again and rose. "I no' kill anyone now," he said to the huddled figures under the marquee. "I give you warning. You people here, tha' okay for me. One year, two year, three year, no problem, ha?"

If he was waiting for a reply, none came. This seemed to piss him off. He took a slow lungful of air, then flew into a hysteria of rage. *"Bu' now, you makin' problem! You makin' bad fucking problem!"*

There was complete silence as he reached into his pockets and pulled out a piece of paper. Even the cicadas seemed to have got the message. *"You making maps!"* he screamed. Half the next sentence was lost on me, drowned out by a pounding in my ears. ". . . *Bu' why you wan' do tha'? Maps bring new people! New people here! New people are danger for me! Tha' is bad fucking danger for you!"*

He hesitated, and with the same bewildering abruptness, became calm again. "Okeydokey," he muttered. Then he dropped the map on the dirt, unholstered his pistol, and fired a shot into it. The shot missed but was close enough to send the paper fluttering into the air. For the second time I was deafened. The muzzle had only been a foot away from my head.

When my hearing began to return, the boss was chatting away in an eerily conversational tone of voice. "So, my frien's. I li' you all ve'y much. Ve'y good. One year, two years, no problem. So you lis'en to my warning. Nex' time I will kill you all."

This final remark didn't have time to sink in, because for a third time my senses were put out of action. The boss punctuated his sentence by whipping his gun on the top of my head. Out of shock, I tried to stand up, and he hit me again. I dropped straight back down to my knees. The next thing I knew, he was holding on to the back of my T-shirt, keeping me steady.

"Wait," I said thickly. My bravado was entirely gone. I was afraid. Having had a little taste of what it might be like, I was absolutely certain I didn't want to be beaten to death. "Wait a moment please."

No use. The boss hit me incredibly hard. For a few seconds I was conscious, staring at his shoes. Reeboks, like the Koh Samui spiv. Then I blacked out.

I didn't know what was going on. A few things registered: footsteps, rustling, some hushed Thai voices, a couple of kicks that rolled me over.

But none of these things felt connected to any of the others. They were arbitrary and baffling.

When I was finally able to get up and stay up, which must have been at least ten minutes later, the VC had gone. I began crawling back to the marquee, where I could still see the blurred shapes of my companions, and while I crawled I abstractly wondered why I'd been chosen as the punching bag. In fact, why have a punching bag at all? If they hadn't been planning on shooting us, it seemed unfair to have put me through all that pain.

Now

There was another question that I should have been asking myself, but wasn't. In my now considerable experience, it's part of the strange way the brain works when reeling from a severe knock. You get hung up on the inconsequential mysteries and not the important ones.

The question I should have been asking was, why wasn't anyone coming to help me? If I'd been out for ten minutes, as I suspected I had, then they'd have had plenty of time to get their act together. But there they were, cowering behind the circle of candles, as much use as a bunch of waxworks.

"Help me," I slurred. "What's the matter with you?"

I tried to scowl at them, which was extremely difficult. Apart from being out of focus, I was seeing double, so I wasn't sure where the scowl should be directed.

"Keaty . . . help."

Hearing his name seemed to spur him into life. He took a few steps toward me, but even through my fucked-up eyes I could tell there was something weird about the way he was moving. It was as if he was scared of something over my shoulder.

My elbows gave way and my chin hit the ground. I dribbled to get the dust off my mouth. "Hurry, Keaty."

Then he was next to me, with someone else. Françoise, by the smell. They picked me up and pulled me back to the marquee, only strong enough to raise my arms and shoulders. When I passed over the candles, they were extinguished by my stomach. It was an extra bit of pain I really didn't need, but at least it startled me into thinking a bit more clearly. And a gulp of coconut beer was a boost too. It goes to vinegar pretty fast, and the stuff I gulped down was already on the turn. Sharp enough to make me wince and shut my eyes, and when I reopened them, my sight was back to normal.

At last I was able to see why everyone had turned into statues. Using Etienne and one of the bamboo poles that supported the canopy of sheets, I hauled myself up to a standing position. The VC hadn't felt that beating me up was a severe enough warning. They'd left us with a reminder, just to ram the point home.

Bullets had done nasty things to the rafters. Big holes, smashed skulls. All the bodies were naked, suggesting they'd been stripped before they were killed. Rigor mortis had given them strange positions. Sammy was lying on his back, but he must have been on his front when the stiffness set in, so he looked as if he were pushing upward against the weight of the sky. The German girl with the pretty laugh and long hair was on her side. She looked as if she were asking for a hug.

I don't see any need to describe them further than that. I've only described them as far as I have because it's relevant to what happened next.

To be confronted with such a sight would have been bad at the best of times. Directly following the scene with the dope guards would have made it worse. But to have been through all that while you were tripping—it would make anyone crazy.

"Right," Sal said, coming out of her trance, and she began to walk toward the heap of bodies. "I think we should get this cleaned up. It won't take long if we all . . ."

She paused. Her shoulders twitched as if she were slipping off a jacket, and she sat down with a thump.

"It won't take long. Come on, everyone. Let's get this mess cleaned up."

She stood up again.

"This mess. Such a mess."

The German guy was trapped beneath Zeph's chest, and his rigid arms were hooking the two of them together. Sal couldn't make him budge. We all watched in silence as she yanked uselessly at the German's legs.

"What a mess," Sal panted, and gave another hard tug.

Her grip slipped.

She fell backward, twisting as she fell, and landed on Sammy's corpse. "Clumsy," she exclaimed brightly.

Then she started screaming and clawing at her cheeks. Sal's and Sammy's faces had made contact as she rolled off him, and Sammy had no lower jaw.

She screamed the way some people cry. People who never normally cry, so you know that the tears are coming from somewhere unthinkably deep inside. It was a sound that made my skin crawl, but for Bugs, it seemed to blow his mind.

I've thought a lot about what he did, and I've got two explanations. One is that he was angry with Sammy for having kissed Sal. The other is that he saw Sammy as the cause of Sal's misery, and he wanted to make the misery stop. Both explanations rely on Bugs being insane, but that's okay. He was.

He called Sal's name. Then he sobbed, only once, not loudly. Then he went over to the seating area and picked up one of Unhygienix's stubby cooking knives. Then he went over to Sammy and attacked him.

It began with kicking, which quickly became stabbing. In the chest, the groin, the arms, everywhere. Next he straddled the corpse and began tugging at the neck. Or that's what I thought he was doing. It wasn't completely clear through the shadows, and most of the view was blocked by Bugs's broad back. I only saw when he rose up. He'd cut Sammy's head off. Cut it off, and was swinging it by the hair.

And suddenly Jean had a knife and was cutting at the thin German girl, slicing into her belly and pulling out her insides. Then Cassie joined them, hunched over Zeph, working on his thighs. Etienne vomited, and within seconds the corpses were swarmed.

Looking back, I know that we could have left at that moment. There were still people under the marquee—all the cooks, Jesse, Gregorio, and a few of the gardeners—but they wouldn't have tried to stop us. And I was physically able to leave. The scene in front of me had sent so much adrenaline pumping through my system that my battering was forgotten. I could have run a marathon if necessary, let alone crept into the darkness.

But we stayed put. We were transfixed by the dissection of the rafters. Every severed limb seemed to root me further to the spot.

Friendly Fire

I don't know how long the frenzy lasted. It could have been as long as half an hour. The cutters had to fret and struggle with some of the joints, twisting arms around until tendons gave way. But at some point, I noticed that the crowd had dispersed, sitting exhausted beside their handiwork or milling in the darkness. Only Moshe remained. He was concentrating on something small, a finger perhaps. It was while I was watching Moshe that I heard Sal's voice.

"Wait on Chaweng for three days," she read with numbing coldness. "If we haven't come back by then it means we made it to the beach. See you there? Richard."

The words took time for me to comprehend. Several seconds passed in which they meant nothing beyond random noises. But then, with a flash of understanding so tangible I almost saw it, their relevance became clear.

I turned. Sal was standing beside me, holding the piece of paper that the VC boss had left behind. It had passed me by, that piece of paper. Deafened, pistol-whipped, I had missed its importance.

". . . See you there," she repeated flatly. ". . . Richard."

Outside the marquee, the surgeons stirred. Some appeared, nudging past Keaty, who was staring at me with a peculiarly blank expression.

"Richard?" one of them whispered. "Richard brought the people here?" It was a girl, but she was so stained with red and black that I couldn't place her.

More arrived, quietly surrounding me, shutting off Keaty and

Françoise. Desperately I began to search for a face I knew. I wanted to appeal to someone, plead a case. But the more cutters that arrived, the more anonymous they became. Under their shifting feet, candles were kicked over. Darkness spread, features melted. When Etienne vanished, I was alone with strangers.

"Jean!" I shouted.

The strangers laughed.

"Moshe! Cassie! I know you're here! . . . Sal! *Sal!*"

But even she had gone. Where she'd been, a squat creature hissed at me. "After Tet, life will be back to normal."

"Sal, *please*," I said, and a needle jabbed into my leg. I looked down. I'd been stabbed. Not deeply, but somehow that scared me more. I cried out and was stabbed again. The same pressure. Half an inch into the skin, this time my arm, the next time my chest.

For a moment I was too shocked to do anything but stupidly wipe at the blood running down my stomach. Then terror bubbled up in me, and when it reached my throat I started screaming. I also tried to fight. I threw a punch at the nearest face but it landed poorly and glanced harmlessly off the person's cheekbone. The next punch I threw was blocked, and my wrists were held.

I pleaded, "Don't," and began spinning. Fear gave me strength and I managed to wrench myself free of the hold. But every time I spun away from the knives, I was simply cut from behind. I could feel by the impact of the blows that the stabs were getting worse. No longer piercing but slicing. A different pain, less acute. Infinitely more alien and alarming.

"Not like that," I sobbed.

Something slippery was wrapped around my neck. Intestines. Mine, I thought, my brain convulsing with fright, and tore them off. The strangers laughed and more objects were thrust at me. A ragged hand that pawed my chest. An ear clamped to the side of my head.

Feeling my knees about to buckle, I bunched up my arms. A last time, I looked up at the howling figures and their knives. I called for Sal again. I asked her to make them stop. I told her that I was very sorry for whatever I'd done, but I didn't know what it was anymore. I only knew that I'd never wanted to do anything bad.

Finally I called out for Daffy Duck.

Suddenly, in the whirling faces, I saw one I recognized.

But Nothing

The stabbing continued, but no longer hurt. The faces continued whirling, but the face I knew remained constant. I could talk to it calmly, and it could talk back.

"Daffy," I said. "This is fucked."

"Yeah, GI." He smiled. "Beaucoup bad shit."

"Fragged by my own side."

"Happens all the time."

A blade punctured my top lip. "It doesn't mean anything, right?"

"Doesn't mean much."

"Never should have been here. That's all." I sighed as my legs collapsed and I fell down to the palm-leaf carpet. "Jesus, this is a nasty way to die. At least it's ending."

"Ending?" Daffy shook his head. "It can't end now."

"Can't?"

"Come on, Rich. Think. Think how it ought to end."

"Ought to . . ."

"A flat roof, a panicking crowd, not enough room on the . . ."

". . . Last chopper out."

"That's the boy."

"Evacuation."

"Every time."

Daffy was gone. The knives had stopped. One of the cutters had started twisting, fumbling at her belly, and another was toppling sideways, flailing out with his arms.

I looked around and saw Jed standing beside me. And beside him, Keaty, Etienne, and Françoise. The four of them carried fishing spears, points fanning outward. On the ground, Bugs sat with his arms crossed, fresh blood streaming into his lap. Moshe leaned against one of the bamboo posts, also bleeding, sucking air through clenched teeth, and clutching his ribs.

"You all keep back!" Jed yelled. He reached down, lifted my arm over his shoulders, and dragged me up. *"Keep back!"*

Bugs closed his eyes and slumped forward.

"But," said Sal. "But . . ." She took a step in our direction and Jed pushed his spear deep into her stomach. Immediately he pulled it back. Sal remained standing, swaying as the point exited.

"Back!" Jed yelled again. *"All of you keep back!"*

And amazingly, they all did. Though we were outnumbered and they could have easily prevented us if they'd wanted to, they let us go. I don't think it was because of Sal, who had closed her eyes and couldn't seem to catch her breath. It was because they were tired. Their slack arms and glazed eyes told me as much. Tired of everything. Beaucoup bad shit, too beaucoup.

game over

Strange but True

I feel I should provide an account of how we all got back home. But it's going to be a brief account because the story is over. This is just an epilogue.

We talked a lot. That's what I remember most about the journey; the talking. It's stuck in my memory because it seems so unexpected. You'd imagine silence, all of us withdrawn into our private horrors. And the first part of the journey, the nighttime trek to the raft, *was* silent. But it was only because we were afraid of being heard by the guards. As soon as we'd pushed off and were on our way, we opened our mouths and never shut them. The funny thing is, I can't really remember what we talked about. Maybe because we talked about everything, maybe because we talked about nothing.

Because of my condition, I wasn't much help, but the others took a paddling-and-swimming rotation in pairs. I kept getting shivering attacks. When they hit, all I could do was curl up and shake. They'd only last a couple of minutes, but Jed thought it better to keep me out of the sea in case I drowned. I'd already nearly drowned once, when we were swimming across the lagoon on the way to the caves and the chimney. In any case, the salt water was murder on my stab wounds, superficial as they were.

We didn't have to paddle for long. A few hours after dawn broke, a fishing boat came to check us out. And after a bit of banter, they towed us back to Koh Samui. It was extraordinary. They didn't seem more than cheerfully curious about who we were and what we were doing on a raft in the Gulf of Thailand. The only thing that raised an eyebrow was me and my cuts. By which I mean, a raised eyebrow was the full extent of their reaction. We were just another bunch of weird *falang*, doing the weird kind of things that *falang* do.

On Koh Samui, we ran into a couple of problems because we had no money. But we were travelers, so it wasn't that big a deal. Keaty and I sold our watches. Then, to everyone's surprise, Etienne stole a wallet. Bit of a dark horse, Etienne. Some dickhead had left his room key under his T-shirt while he went for a dip. We stole a long-sleeved shirt and a pair of trousers, which I needed to hide my cuts. The cash was enough to get us all back to the mainland, eat, *and* buy Keaty's watch back.

From Koh Samui to Surat Thani, and the bus ride to Bangkok, for which Keaty had to resell his watch. And still we were talking, irritating our fellow passengers, keeping them awake.

Back in the city, the only thing left to do was to call home. We all took turns in an air-con phone booth on the Koh Sanh Road. The last thing I want to do is lapse into sentimentality at this late stage, but we were all crying by the time we'd hung up. We must have made a pretty stupid sight, me in my blood-flecked new shirt, and the others in their rags, all in floods of tears.

Seventy-two hours later we had airline tickets and replacement passports from our respective embassies. I had my last shivering attack getting cigarettes in the Bangkok duty-free. As soon as we boarded the plane, I felt okay.

At this exact moment, I'm sitting in front of a word processor. At this exact moment, I'm typing this sentence. At this exact moment, it's a year and a month since I flew out of Thailand.

I never saw Etienne and Françoise again. One day I will. It's going to be by chance but I know it's going to happen, because the world is a small place, and Europe is even smaller.

I see Keaty and Jed all the time. Like the talking, it's another thing you wouldn't expect. By rights we should have drifted apart, unable to deal with our shared history. But we didn't. We're good friends.

So I see Keaty and Jed all the time, and they see each other even more. This is strange but true: they both work at the same place. Different firms, same building. Stranger still, they got the jobs without knowing the other was there. And even stranger still, it sort of ties in with the way they stayed at the same Indonesian guest house all those years ago; the one that Keaty burned down. They haven't burned down their office yet, which would be the icing on the cake.

Actually Keaty hates the job (admin shit), so it might actually happen. I won't mention the name of the firm in case it does.

What else.

About three months ago, maybe four, I was flicking through Ceefax when I read, "Briton caught smuggling in Malaysia." A few nights later, I saw Cassie on the news. She was sitting in the back of an Isuzu van, flanked by policemen in khaki uniforms. The van was outside a crummy-looking courthouse. She'd been busted at Kuala Lumpur airport with over a pound of heroin, and the word is, she's going to be the first Western smuggler to be executed in *six years*. The BBC reporter managed to get a microphone to her before she was driven away, and she said, "Tell my parents I'm sorry I haven't written in a while."

Poor Cassie. She was probably trying to fund her flight home. Her mum and dad, who look like decent types, are appealing for clemency and appearing on TV. But they're wasting their time. She's dead meat. Or toast.

But the point is that Cassie got off the island, so at least some of the others must have too. I'm curious to know which ones. I like to think that Gregorio and Jesse made it, and Unhygienix and Ella. I'm sure they did. I'm also sure that Bugs died, and I'd like to think Sal died with him. Not out of maliciousness. I just can't stand the idea that she might turn up on my doorstep someday.

As for me . . .

I'm fine. I have bad dreams, but I never saw Mister Duck again. I play video games. I smoke a little dope. I got my thousand-yard stare. I carry a lot of scars.

I like the way that sounds.

I carry a *lot* of scars.

Youngblood Hawke

BY HERMAN WOUK

NOVELS:
Youngblood Hawke
Marjorie Morningstar
The Caine Mutiny
The City Boy
Aurora Dawn

PLAYS:
Nature's Way
The Caine Mutiny Court-Martial
The Traitor

NON-FICTION:
This Is My God

YOUNGBLOOD HAWKE

a novel by HERMAN WOUK

1962

DOUBLEDAY & COMPANY, INC., GARDEN CITY, NEW YORK

NOTE:

The accidental use of the names of living people in a long novel is virtually inevitable nowadays, when literary manners shut out unrealistic coined names. Moreover the author in naming scores of characters, now and then pulls a name from the air, and then finds imbedded in his printed book the first or second names of people he has known. Any such inadvertences in this work are wholly without meaning. If there are actual people in the land bearing the full names of any of the phantoms in this work of fiction, they are unknown to me, and no reference is intended. In this novel there are no attempted portraits of any actual people, living or dead. Finally, the various industries which capitalize literature in the United States have seen many minor changes since the end of the second world war. Some business details of this story, in the earlier passages, are not the same as they would be today. They are accurate for the years in which they are represented as occurring. The general picture presented by the novel is, I believe, a true one as of the present hour.

THE AUTHOR

This novel is dedicated
to my wife,
with all my love

Part One
1946

CHAPTER ONE

1

HAVE you ever known a famous man before he became famous? It may be an irritating thing to remember, because chances are he seemed like anybody else to you.

The manuscript loomed on the desk between the two men, a high pile of torn and dented blue typing-paper cartons. The yellow labels on the boxes had been scrawled over with thick red crayon, *Alms for Oblivion, Part 1, Part 2, Part 3*. Two of the boxes, overstuffed with manuscript, had split open. Dog-eared dirty sheets of typewritten manuscript showed through, mostly white, with sprinklings of yellow and green. Waldo Fipps had never seen a larger or more untidy manuscript—or for that matter, a larger and more untidy author.

He stared at the young man with peculiarly stirred feelings. The young man, who looked more like a truck driver than a writer, stared back. He had big piercing brown eyes, and the lower lip of his full wide mouth was curled and pressed tight over the upper, as though to say, "Try and stop me!" This part of Hawke's attitude was unconscious. He presented the usual agitated surface of the new author, bashfulness and fear struggling with pride, hope, and greed for praise, all this covered by stammering modesty and awkward shifts in the hard yellow chair. Young authors were all afraid of Fipps. Under the business-like smiles of the editor lay the fishy chill of a man who had read too many novels, and criticized too many. The odd thing was that Fipps felt a little afraid of Hawke, this hulking sloven of twenty-six who had written an ugly bellowing dinosaur of a novel, amateurish as it could be, full of imitation, crude, slopped-over, a horror of an editing task, the kind of writing Fipps least admired.

"Cigarette?" Fipps leaned toward Hawke, offering him the pack.

"Mand ef Ah smoke uh see-gaw?" said Hawke. It was the thickest Southern accent Fipps had ever heard.

He said, "Not at all. I'm sorry I don't have any. But I think Mr. Prince —" he broke off, seeing Hawke draw a glossy leather cigar case from the breast pocket of his shabby wrinkled blue suit.

"Ma one vass," said Hawke. It took Fipps a few seconds to realize that what Hawke had said was, "My one vice." Removing the cedar wrapping from an enormous cocoa-brown cigar, Hawke held a flaming match to the

end until it was well scorched, then lit it up with expert puffs. A wisp of blue drifted to the nostrils of Fipps, reminding him unpleasantly of his employer, Jason Prince. This preposterous pauper, this scribbling hillbilly, smokes dollar cigars, he thought. He decided then and there that he did not like Youngblood Hawke. "Well, first things first," Fipps said amiably. "Everybody in the house likes the book. Or at least is impressed."

Hawke's attempt to be impassive was pitiable. The big cigar shook in his fingers. The joy that crossed his face was like a wave of powerful heat; Fipps almost felt it. Perhaps it was real animal heat given off by the blood that rushed into the broad thick-featured rustic face. Hawke stammered a little, trying to say lightly, "It's a—a little too long, isn't it?"

Fipps said, "Well, you are a very exuberant writer. I'm reminded of Dickens, of Dreiser. Perhaps a bit of Dostoevsky?" He paused, smiling.

Gloom, joy, fear, uncertainty: Hawke's look changed almost with every word Fipps uttered. "Mr. Fipps, you've nailed me. My three gods. The three D's."

"Yes. Well," Fipps said in a dry cutting tone, stabbing two fingers at the manuscript, "I think possibly we want a good strong dose of Flaubert. The art of leaving out, you know! From the first page to the last. Practically in every paragraph. Whole sections would have to go."

He savored the quenched, the staggered look of Hawke. No determination in the big mouth now; the open hanging pain of a man punched in the stomach. Fipps' mood improved, and he was ready to forgive this big, possibly profitable oaf for his power of tumbling out exciting scenes and vivid portraits in a muddy torrent of verbiage, full of recognizable flotsam and jetsam from standard authors. "We want to publish your book, Mr. Hawke," he said. "We're really enthusiastic. Providing, of course, that you'll meet us in the matter of revising."

Hawke stood. "You—you want to *publish* mah book? You *goin'* to publish it?"

Fipps was drawn to his feet by the fierce excitement in the young man's voice. "Of course we want to publish it. We expect to have a lot of fun with it, and we think—"

Youngblood Hawke put down his cigar, strode around the desk, and folded the elegant Waldo Fipps in a crushing hug. He bawled like a bull, pounding the editor's back. "Mr. Fipps, god damn it, you're a brilliant goddamn bastard. I've read about you, heard about you, read your books, you know everything about novels, everything, and you want to publish *mah novel!*" Fipps was astonished and not at all pleased to find himself being hugged and pounded, his face jammed against rough blue serge reeking of cigar smoke. Hawke was half a head taller than Fipps, and half again as broad. He was pasty-faced, he needed a haircut; there were flecks of dandruff on his suit; he had cut himself near his ear shaving, and dried blood stood on the gash. Fipps was skinny, brown, his suit was tweedy

brown, he was immaculate to the last hair of his sandy little mustache.

"My dear fellow—" murmured Fipps.

Hawke shook him like a doll. "I'll write forty books, Mr. Fipps, forty goddamn wonderful truthful books and every one better than the last, and you'll publish them all. And we'll make millions. You'll see. I'm not just talking. I'm a goddamn genius, Mr. Fipps, or I'm nothing. God, I'm so happy! *ee*-yowww!"

Throughout the busy halls of Prince House, stenographers looked up from their typing, and shipping clerks halted in their tracks, and editors glanced at their secretaries, as the male bellow echoed down the sound-proofed corridors.

Fipps disengaged himself from Hawke with a thin embarrassed smile. "Well, I'm glad you're pleased. I'd like to take you to lunch. We have a lot to talk about. First come and meet Jason." He added, at Hawke's puzzled look, in a humorous tone, "Mister Prince."

"Mr. Prince? I get to meet Mr. Prince?" said Hawke, retrieving his cigar and following Fipps humbly into the corridor. Fipps led the big clumsy young man through corridors and offices full of talk and typing clatter, a cut-up maze of partitions and desks, to a heavy door made of pearly wood, the only closed door Hawke had seen in the place. A girl at a desk by the door said to Fipps, "Mr. Prince is waiting for you."

Fipps opened the pearly door.

2

Take an ostrich egg, color it fleshy-gray, ink small shrewd features on it, attach a pair of large ears, and you have a fair likeness of what confronted Youngblood Hawke from behind the desk of Jason Prince. The egg hung between broad gray-clad shoulders, peering suspiciously upward. Very long powerful arms clutched a typewritten contract on an otherwise empty desk, the more strikingly empty because the desk top was a slab of glass, allowing a view of a huge empty leather wastebasket underneath, and of Mr. Prince's lolling legs. The office was very long and very wide. The windows were open, and the air was cold. Bare bleak modern furniture, and bookshelves too-smoothly lined with too-clean books from ceiling to floor on two walls, added to the cold emptiness. The other walls were mostly glass, looking out on downtown New York, the jagged skyscrapers in a gray midday haze under a low black sky that threatened snow, and the far muddy rivers, sloshing away the great city's dirt.

"This is Youngblood Hawke, Jay," said Fipps.

The suspicious egg changed into the face of a warm friendly man of fifty or so who happened to be very bald, whose pale blue eyes were not at all shrewd and veiled, but gay and candid. "*Alms for Oblivion*, eh?" he said

in a strong throaty voice, all different from Fipps' controlled pipe. He stood and offered his hand. "No oblivion for you, my young friend. Quite an explosion of talent, that book. And only the beginning."

The long arms of the two men—Hawke's was a little longer—met in a powerful clasp over the desk; the two tall men looked straight into each other's eyes. There was a silence. To Fipps it seemed a long silence, and he was a bit surprised at the way Hawke met the glance of Prince. Then a blush spread over the young author's face, he shuffled his feet, and awkwardly dropped Prince's hand.

"Hope you get back the price of the printing job, sir," he said. "It's my first try."

"We'll get back more than that," said Prince. "And we're going to do a lot of printing, too." He pressed a button, and said into a voice box, "Bring me a box of cigars and the Hawke contract." He pulled a chair beside his desk, and motioned Hawke into it, ignoring Fipps, who lounged into a settee behind the publisher. "Long experience with artists," Prince said, "has convinced me that I can best minister to your sensitive spirits by discussing dough." Hawke laughed uproariously. The publisher smiled and went on, "Advances for a first novel generally run about five hundred to a thousand dollars. I've advanced fifteen hundred for a sure-fire first book." He named a best-seller of a few years back. "Turned out to be right. Been spectacularly wrong on occasion. Right often enough to stay in this chair and keep the rent paid. Why haven't you got an agent?"

"Should I have one?" Hawke said. "I don't know anything about all this."

Prince shrugged. "I can't advise you to give away ten percent of your bloodstained earnings to an agent. I can't advise you to trust yourself to my tender mercies, either." A girl came in with a box of cigars and a contract, put them on the publisher's desk, and left. Prince thrust the cigars toward Hawke. "I get these sent up to me from Havana. Try them."

Hawke opened the plain wooden box, and saw an array of unbanded brownish-green cigars, longer and thicker than his Romeos. He took one, slid the box to Prince, and found it abruptly pushed back at him. "All for you," Prince said. "The contract's ready. It's our standard form. The only blank in it is the amount of the advance. Take it away with you and have a lawyer or an agent look over the fine print. Or sign it and take our check away instead. Suit yourself. It's a good contract."

Hawke looked at the publisher for a long moment, his lower lip pressed over the upper one. Then he pursed his mouth like an old lady, and shrugged. "I'll sign it. Your business isn't to skin authors."

"No it isn't. Our business is to make them rich and pay our bills in the process. How about the advance?"

"I'd like five thousand dollars," Hawke said.

The suspicious egg briefly reappeared where Prince's affable head had

been. It turned and glanced at Fipps, but by the time the glance came back to Hawke the egg was gone and there was a pleasant face again, wryly surprised.

"I'm sure you would like five thousand dollars," Prince said. "But it's ten times the going advance for a first novel. The chances against your earning that much in royalties are slim, in fact prohibitive. You'd better get an agent. He'll explain all that to you."

The young man said, "The thing is, Mr. Prince, I'm halfway into my second novel, a war book. It's called *Chain of Command*. It's much better than *Alms for Oblivion*. But I'm wasting time working on a construction job by day. I only get to write a few hours at night, and I'm tired." He spoke reasonably and winningly, with no hesitation, the soft Southern cadences giving his speech almost the beat of poetry. (Ah only git to *rat* a few ahrs at *nat*, an' Ah'm *tahd*.) "I figure I can finish it and start on a third—which I've got all blocked out in my head, a political novel—inside of a year if I do nothing else. You feel like gambling on me, fine. Otherwise let me try another publisher. Though I sure would like my first book coming out with the imprint of Prince House. To me that's always been a magic name."

Prince looked over his shoulder at Fipps again, his glance uncertain and amused. "Waldo, move around here where I don't have to break my neck to talk to you."

Fipps picked up a chair, brought it forward of the desk, and sat. Prince said, "What do you make of all this?"

The editor pressed his fingertips together, appraising Hawke like a dean looking at a delinquent college boy. "If I understand Mr. Hawke, he's actually asking for an advance on three books. But even at that the figure is absurd, Jay." He turned to Hawke. "Look here, it's always better to be candid. Mr. Prince cast the deciding vote for your novel. Several of us had strong reservations, though we all of us, myself included, admire your promise. You'll get your book published elsewhere—though they'll want you to work on it just as we do—but I very much doubt that anyone else will give you a bigger advance than a thousand, if that much. We're not the movies."

Hawke said with sudden boyish good humor, odd in a big man with such an intense look, "Well, look, Mr. Fipps, why don't I just try another publisher? I'm mighty encouraged by your interest, and grateful to you, and there's no reason to—"

Jason Prince had been sitting hunched over his desk, large knobby fingers interlaced, the knuckles blue-white. Now he sat up. "Hawke, five-thousand advance against three novels. Is that what you want?"

"I want five thousand advanced against this one."

"Suppose this one doesn't earn back the advance? If it does it'll be a real freak of a first novel. Do you want us to lose money on you? Your

price is fantastic. You wouldn't ask for it if you weren't so inexperienced. Now look here. I'll give you five hundred dollars a month for the next ten months. That's meeting your terms. But for that I want the second novel delivered and an outline of the third before the period is up."

"Okay," said Youngblood Hawke, as casually as if he were agreeing to go for a walk.

Fipps said severely, "You'll sign a contract to that effect?"

"Sure."

"But what is this optimism based on?" the editor said. "Can you show us the outlines of your next two novels?"

"I don't work from outlines, Mr. Fipps, I just sort of go along."

"Well, can we see what you've written so far on this war book?"

Hawke said, "The thing is it's in a big mess and it's simpler just to finish it."

Fipps rolled his eyes at the publisher in exasperation.

Prince said, "All right, Waldo." He pressed a button, and through the voice box asked for a check book. "The usual thing, Hawke," he said, "is for the check to be handed over when the contract is signed, but this contract will have to be revised. Meantime would you like to see the color of our money? Sort of an earnest of good faith? If you take the check you're tying up three novels."

"I'll take it."

The book came. Prince wrote a check for five hundred dollars, and handed it to Hawke. "The first of ten," he said.

Hawke stared at the stiff orange slip of paper. "Well, doggone. I've been paid for writing prose," he said. "I've been paid for English prose."

Fipps said, "Haven't you sold anything before?"

"Nothing."

"The wrong kind of prose isn't worth the paper it's written on," said Prince. "The right kind is worth its weight in diamonds. Remember that, as you pound the typewriter. It's a great era for writers. There has never been such an era."

"Dickens and Balzac did all right," Hawke said. "Adjust your currency and I bet Dickens did better than Sinclair Lewis. No taxes. I'd like to phone my mother. My mother's in Kentucky. Can I use the phone in your office?" he said to Fipps.

Fipps, who was having a little trouble catching his breath, nodded. Hawke walked out. He came back instantly, picked up the box of cigars Prince had given him, grinned at the two men, and left.

The editor and the publisher stared at each other. Waldo Fipps, in a lifetime of writing, had never received five thousand dollars, or half that much, for a piece of work. At forty-five, at the top of his reputation, he had once drawn an advance of twenty-five hundred dollars for a clever but tenuous play which had remained unproduced. He said testily, "What

on earth is this, Jay? So far as I'm concerned the main thing this man
has is enormous energy. He has no style, no wit, just coarse humor, he's
crude, imitative, in fact he frequently shades off into plagiarism. Possibly
he has a good narrative sense, and a serviceable knack of caricature. You're
being strangely generous with him."

Prince leaned back, cradling his head against interlocked fingers, his
elbows spread out, one long leg crooked over a knee. "The thing is,
Waldo," he said, "I think Youngblood Hawke is money."

3

The cigar box under his arm, Hawke strode happily down the long
narrow corridor to Fipps' office, peeking into each open door that he
passed, taking automatic note of what he saw. He had been keeping this
mental inventory of every passing detail around him all his life, and
was scarcely aware of the habit. It was the reason for his strange obtuseness
to some things and his overkeen awareness of others. He had noticed, for
instance, Waldo Fipps' way of blinking his eyes half a dozen times and
then opening them wide before saying anything to Prince. But he was
unaware that he himself had just scored a historic victory over one of the
closest bargainers in the publishing trade.

Jay Prince was notorious for his meager advances. The most hard-
bitten literary agent in New York in 1946 would not have tried to extract
five thousand dollars from Prince for a first book, with a wild story of a
second big novel coming in September and a third one the following
year. But Hawke had experienced few business interviews. The entire
process of testing for pressure, interest and advantage, the cautious hard
game of words by which men of affairs came to grips over money, was
unknown to him. While talking to Prince he had gone on with his
inventory, noting the coldness of the room, the whiteness of Prince's
knuckles as he clasped them on the desk, Waldo Fipps' quick change in
attitude from acidly confident critic to hangdog employee, marked by an
apprehensive stare at his boss and a wary tightness of the mouth. He had
made the offer to go to another publisher in all innocence, not realizing
that this was the shot across the bow. Prince had scornfully told agents
dozens of times to go down the street by all means, when they had
ventured this warning shot. But to Youngblood Hawke he had meekly
run up the white flag. Such is sometimes the power, or the luck, of
ignorance.

A girl in a plain white shirtwaist sat hunched in Waldo Fipps' armchair, reading *Alms for Oblivion* and laughing out loud. A box of
manuscript was in her lap and she was holding some sheets high in her
left hand, scanning the top page in the box.

"Sit up straight," Hawke said as he came in. "Fellows don't like a girl who slumps."

She sat up, blinking at him through round black glasses like a startled owl. She had a lot of glossy reddish hair piled on her head, and she was very pale. "Gad, that's just what my mother says. I haven't heard it in years."

"What are you laughing at? There's nothing funny in the first chapter."

"Are you Mr. Hawke?" She put the papers back in the box, coughed in a grating convulsion, and lit a cigarette. "You have a comical way of putting things. I was reading the description of the aunt. It's sort of like O. Henry."

"O. Henry?" Hawke scowled horribly, turning his back on her, and picked up the telephone.

The girl said in a contralto rasp, "I meant that as a compliment. I admire O. Henry."

"Long distance, please."

"It's the finest beginning of a story that I've read in a long time," croaked the girl. "My name is Jeanne Green. I'm in the copy editing department."

"I see," Hawke said. "Operator, I want to call Kentucky."

The girl regarded his broad back despairingly, shrugged, and went out, coughing.

Waiting for his call to go through, Hawke sat in the editor's chair and read all the papers on the desk. He was a pryer and snooper without conscience. He read business letters, sales reports, office memoranda, advertising proofs, and a note about shopping to be done for Mrs. Fipps. He flicked through the editor's appointment calendar. Fipps had had lunch with John Marquand in November; two weeks ago he had gone to the theatre with Evelyn Waugh! And Hawke was going to lunch with the man who knew these luminaries! He was dizzy with exaltation. He began reading his novel at page one, this marvellous scrappy heap of paper that had become his passport into the golden world. He wanted to admire himself. He also wanted to see what on earth the idiotic girl could have meant, comparing him to O. Henry.

Fipps came in, and noted with displeasure that his papers had been moved about. Hawke was sitting with one big shoe in a lower desk drawer, reading his own work intently. The air in the cubicle was gray with cigar smoke. Fipps said, "Congratulations on your contract. I hope you know how remarkable it is."

"Well, it was sure nice of Mr. Prince to give me what I asked for."

"Nice! It's unique in this house. You should be glad we went in to see him. You'd never have gotten it from me, and Jay is supposed to be the tough man here. I'm delighted, of course. I haven't the latitude to pay such advances. How about lunch?"

"Haven't gotten through to mama yet. There was a girl reading my manuscript when I came in here. Can anybody in this place read a manuscript who wants to?"

"I expect that was the stylist."

"Stylist?"

"Well, you know, we have staff people who see to grammar, punctuation, and all that. Some houses call them copy editors."

Hawke said instantly, "My grammar and my punctuation will stay as they are. Punctuation! My punctuation! That girl!"

Fipps laughed again, and stabbed two fingers at the manuscript. "My dear Hawke, you take terrific liberties with semicolons and you slop all over the place, if you'll forgive me, when you get into the subjunctive. Of course you have a veto over the stylist. You'll be very grateful to her, you'll see."

"But this girl looked like a file clerk. Stoop-shouldered, glasses, a kid!"

"That's Jeanne Green. Young, yes, but sharp. Since Jay is so hot on you, I think maybe we'll be using our head stylist instead."

"Let's not use this girl," Hawke said. "She said my writing reminded her of O. Henry."

A cruel pleased smile wisped over the editor's face. "Did Jeanie say that? Well, stylists aren't supposed to be critics."

"*Vare* is ze young genius? Vare is Youngblood Hoke?" It was a high voice with a European accent, and its owner swept into the office in a black fur coat, a tiny hat and nose veil, and a rolling wave of very sweet perfume.

"Right here, Fanny," Fipps said. "Mr. Hawke, this is Mrs. Prince."

The woman seized Hawke's hand. "Ve are going to be very good friends. You don't know me yet, but already I know you so well from *zis!*" She tapped the manuscript with one black-gloved little hand. "I am your discoverer! Ask Jay. Did he read it first or did I? Such an enormous blurry manuscript, and my poor eyes! It was sitting on the desk in the library. I felt it was sending out little sparkles. Like a lump of radium. Don't ask me how I knew. I knew! Immense! How does a young man like you know already so much about life?"

Hawke started to answer, but Mrs. Prince went right on. "There are two kinds of novelists, Mr. Hoke, life-enrichers and life-impoverishers. You are a life-enricher. I read your book and I was taller, and cleaner, and younger, and sadder, and happier. I was still Me. But I was more Me than before. Vat else is a novel for?" she said, turning on Fipps with sudden immense indignation.

Fipps, reaching for his hat and coat, said, "That's very well put, Fanny. Uh, I'm taking Mr. Hawke to lunch. If you'd care to join us—"

"Ah, Waldo, I can't. Mr. Hoke! Come tomorrow for cocktails at our

home. Christmas Eve, it's our custom, a few friends—quiet, a fire, a smell of warm evergreen, a little eggnog, a little snack, some charming ladies, some good talk—"

Hawke said, "I'm sorry, Mrs. Prince, I'm having dinner with a friend of mine, and—"

"You have friends in New York already?"

"Yes, ma'am. Maybe you know him. Karl Fry."

"Karl Fry?" Mrs. Prince's pretty face briefly took on her husband's suspicious egg look. "Yes. Of course. Charming man. Fantastically talented," she said as though reciting a telephone number. Karl Fry was a nearly forgotten failure, a satiric poet of the twenties who had rapidly burned out, now a mystery story writer and a communist. Prince House published his mysteries.

Fipps said, "Fact is, Karl brought in the Hawke manuscript."

"Oh? Well, bless his heart! Mr. Hoke! For years I try to get Karl to come to our Christmas party. Once he did, now no more. A snob. You come tomorrow night, hah? If you can drag Karl along, drag him. We count on you! Hah?" She swooped out before Hawke could say anything. Her perfume remained behind like a large solid object.

"Fanny's a superb human being," Fipps said. "She just takes a little getting used to."

"Everything in New York takes a little getting used to," Hawke said.

"That's the truth. Come along and start getting used to a very good restaurant. We'll have your Kentucky call transferred there."

"Gee, can you do that?"

"Nothing simpler."

Going down in the elevator, Hawke seemed dull and preoccupied to Fipps. Actually he was numbed by the swarm of new sensations. He had been in New York less than a year, and he had been working night and day. The fifty-story drop of the elevator, which to Fipps and the other people meant nothing at all, was a roller-coaster ride. Hawke was pleased as a child by the blinking change of the little red lights over the door— 48, 47, 46, 45, X—and then the speedy express plunge caught pleasurably at his insides, scaring and tickling him. His ears popped from the change in pressure.

"Taxi, or walk?" Fipps said as the revolving door spun them out into the cold windy street in a bubble of warm air, which instantly blew away.

"Walk, of course," Hawke said. "I can't understand why anybody drives anywhere in this town. Where are we going?"

"Number One," said Fipps, glumly tucking his chin down and striding into the wind.

"*Number One?* I'm not dressed for that! Isn't it the fanciest restaurant in New York?"

"You're an artist. You're privileged. Come along," said Fipps. He was acting under orders, which he did not like. He had planned to take the slovenly author to a hotel grill. But Prince, finding this out, had picked up the telephone and reserved a table at Number One.

4

The small wood-panelled foyer of the fabled restaurant was jammed with elegant women and sharply groomed men. Hawke felt ridiculous in his old duffle coat with the dirty sheepskin collar. The jackets of all the men fitted beautifully around neck and shoulders. Their shirt collars all seemed peculiarly small and tight, and their faces were all either bright pink or very brown. Hawke made a mental note to buy shirts with small tight collars; the one he had on was big, loose, and frayed. But there was nothing he could think to do about his pallor, except possibly get a sun lamp.

A man in a brown suit, with the tightest shirt collar and pinkest face of all, greeted Fipps by name. His eyes paused on Hawke's duffle coat, flicked to Hawke's face and to Fipps'; and Hawke realized he had been sized up and forgiven as a young author. The man passed them with a courtly gesture to the custody of a fat silvery-haired man in black formal clothes, who conducted them up a flight of stairs and through two crowded rooms, alternating pleasant conversation with Fipps, and savage hisses and barks in a foreign language at waiters scurrying past with copper dishes that flamed. Still another man in black, with an armful of brown menus big as posters, pulled a narrow table away from the wall, saying "Yes, sair," to Hawke. Hawke backed into the wall seat and sat, elbow to elbow with two strangers busily eating. The man slid the table back into place, sealing Hawke where he sat as effectually as a pilot in a fighter cockpit. Fipps took the chair opposite him.

Now another man appeared, all in maroon velvet and dangling brass chains, and offered them an immense leather-bound wine list, like an old Bible. Fipps selected a vintage champagne, and the second man in black noted their orders for food (the prices of which staggered Hawke—three dollars for a side dish of fresh asparagus!) on a slip of paper, which he passed to a man in a gold-trimmed red coat. Another man, in a white-trimmed red coat poured water for them. Yet another man in a plain white coat offered them hot rolls from a portable tin warmer with a sliding roll top. This parade of functionaries was as novel to Hawke as a Chinese wedding. He had been subsisting for a year in automats and delicatessens, which seemed the best places to eat in New York for little money. He said, peering around at the chattering crowd, and at the parti-colored array of old armor and regiment flags set along the

walls, and at the flaming saucepans everywhere—the place seemed full of talk, silver, lovely women, perfume, diamonds and flames—"Could I have gotten in here without you?"

"Possibly not," Fipps said. "It's all by reservation, you know. We're upstairs in the middle room because publishing is not the same thing as the theatre, banking, or the movies. If you should ever write a hit play or win the Pulitzer Prize, you'll be elevated to downstairs. Let's hope it happens with your first novel."

Hawke said, "Do these people care about such distinctions, really? It seems hard to believe."

The velvet-clad man brought champagne in a silver bucket; a bottle of Coca-Cola was also thrust in the ice.

"I think you'll find that a pleasant wine," Fipps said, watching the pale golden stream swirl into the glass set before Hawke.

"Come now, what's this?" Hawke said. "Coca-Cola?"

"I'm on the wagon. Bit of liver trouble. Here's to *Alms for Oblivion*." The editor raised his glass of Coca-Cola in bony trembling fingers.

"Well, shucks, I'm not going to kill a bottle of champagne by myself, Mr. Fipps. Come on, this is an occasion."

"Of course it is. Now drink up and stop fussing." An edge in the editor's voice caused Hawke to drink up silently.

Fipps said, "Well, now. I'll need some facts for our publicity release. I take it your book is mainly autobiographical?"

"Well, the story's all made up. The background is pretty much Hovey and Letchworth County, where I've lived all my life. Except in the war."

"What did you do in the war?"

"Machinist's mate in the Seabees. Three years in the South Pacific. Trucks, bulldozers, graders, and like that—I can run them and maintain them, sort of."

"You've been to college, haven't you?"

"Three years."

"Why weren't you an officer?"

Hawke shrugged. "Flunked the physical." He added, as the editor glanced with slight surprise at his huge shoulders and thick arms, "Busted arm and head injuries in my medical record, so the Navy said no stripes. I was plenty sore about it then, but now I wouldn't have had it any other way. The enlisted man sees the war."

"When did you get *Alms for Oblivion* written? In the Pacific?"

"No, just the first two parts. Then Sopac boiled up with all these emergency airstrip jobs, Saipan, Tinian, Iwo Jima, day and night. There just wasn't time to do much. I wrote most of it right here on Eleventh Street. Came here as soon as I got out."

"And what have you been living on?"

"That's been the trouble. When my separation pay ran out I had to

get a job running a bulldozer. I'd work by day and then write all night. I got in with one of these non-union builders on Long Island. I don't like a dozer, the bouncing bothers my head and wears me out, but I can make it do what I want. Whenever I could get a few dollars ahead I'd quit and just write. If not for this advance I'd be going back on the dozer in January, so I'm damned grateful for it."

Fipps said, after a moment, "These injuries . . . do you mind talking about them?"

"Not at all. Kid stuff. Summers I used to drive a coal truck to pay my way through college. There's this wild road from Edgefield down to Hovey, see, my home town, where the railroad is. Edgefield is about a hundred miles up in the mountains, a real one-horse town, nothing at all, but the coal sticks right out of the side of the hills. You can see it, black seams in the dirt two, three feet thick. But of course coal is worth nothing in itself, Mr. Fipps. It's just a funny kind of black stone that you can burn, unless it's near a railroad or a river where there's transportation. There's billions of tons of worthless coal all over the world, and, this Edgefield stuff is like that. But early on in the war, see, when the price of coal went way up, a few operators took a gamble and started running it down to Hovey in trucks. I went partners in an old truck and just ran day and night. It was good money. I did one run too many one night, and I'd had a few beers—you don't have too much sense at nineteen— and I didn't make it round the double turn at Little Bear Creek, rolled over down the mountainside, truck, coal and all—"

"Ye gods."

"Broke an arm and my collarbone and was unconscious for two days. I guess I'd be dead except nobody dies in the Youngblood family, that's my mother's side, till they're ninety-seven, and everyone agrees I'm a Youngblood. So, I came out of it, but the head injury does bother me a bit, now and then."

Fipps said, "Coal-hauled your way through college. Interesting."

Hawke said impatiently, "What's wrong with that? It's honest work."

"My dear fellow, it's colorful. A bit unusual for a literary gent." Fipps now noticed the dirt rimmed under Hawke's nails, and seamed into his knuckles. Hawke had a concealing way of clasping his fingers inward, but he had momentarily lost awareness of his hands, and they lay loose, big, and soiled on the white cloth. "I daresay you're the only coal driver off the Edgefield-Hovey run that's taken to writing novels."

"Them?" said Hawke. "Some of them can't sign their names. Or couldn't, till the army taught them. They're damned good guys, only ignorant, you just can't picture the ignorance, Mr. Fipps. Real hillbillies." Hawke shifted uneasily under the editor's amused look, and burst out, with a thrust of a clenched fist and rigid thumb, "But see here, Mr. Fipps, don't go working up this angle. My people are not mountaineers. My

mother was born in Hovey but her people are from South Carolina. My father came over from West Virginia, he went to college, he published a newspaper in Hovey for a while. My sister's one of the most intelligent people I've ever known, she works in the bank. We always had books in the house, piles of books, my father's taste was old-fashioned but by God he knew his Dickens and Mark Twain backwards and forwards. He'd read them to us, and half the time he wouldn't even be looking at the book. We never lived in a rented house, always owned the roof over our heads. There was one bad time in the depression when for two years we were in what was practically a mountain cabin—and I thought it was a fine home, four of us sleeping in one room and the other room kitchen, parlor, laundry, potato bin and everything else, privy and vegetable garden out back—but I tell you we owned that place too. We're good stock Americans, and I think pretty cultivated for the mountains of Kentucky, or maybe by any other standard. My Uncle Will, my father's brother, was the wealthiest man in Hovey, put up the Methodist church there practically out of his own pocket, and his family's one of the leading families in the town. Hawke Brothers is still the biggest coal operation in Hovey. They're the rich Hawkes."

This tirade in a swooping Southern singsong was broken off when the wine waiter with a flourish poured more champagne. Hawke blinked, seeming to become aware of where he was. He clasped his hands so that the fingers disappeared, and grinned sheepishly at Fipps. "My conversation seems to need the touch of Flaubert too."

"Waldo Fipps! How are you, you dear ghoul?" A man appeared behind the editor and uttered these words in a soft tone, almost a whisper, softly placing a hand on Fipps' shoulder. He had black alert eyes, black slick hair that needed cutting, and a peculiar upcurving smile that showed all his teeth without conveying any mirth. He peered curiously at Hawke.

"Hello, Jock," said Fipps. "This is Youngblood Hawke—Jock Maas."

"One of your new authors, Waldo?"

"Yes. We're celebrating the signing of his contract."

"Playwright, too, perhaps?" The toothed smile Maas turned on Hawke, with the serious stare of the sharp black eyes, gave him a hungry appearance.

"Not yet. First I'd better make sure I'm a novelist."

Maas cocked his head comically at the accent. "Well! From the South, eh? Splendid. Everything decent that's being written today comes from the South. The North's a sterile ant-heap. If there's a play in your novel I'd like to know about it, Mr. Hawke."

"There may well be, Jock," said Fipps, "with a tremendous editing job. We'll send you an advance copy."

"Good. With all due respect to you, Waldo, I am, as you know, the

best editor on earth." The intent gloomy face creased for an instant at Hawke with the disturbing smile, and Maas left.

Fipps said wryly, "You've heard of Jock?"

"Well, sure, I'm not that much of an ignoramus. He's a famous producer, isn't he?"

"Moderately famous. And moderately mad. A little gone to seed now. Every young author should have Jock Maas once, like the measles. Have you ever tried writing a play?"

"I've written seven . . . Why do you look so stunned? It was when I came on Maugham's plays, in the Pago-Pago base library. I read them all. I felt maybe that was what I should try to do. So I tried. Maugham says that a play should take three weeks to write. That was all I allowed for each one. I wrote seven plays in a year, but all I learned was that I can't stuff my ideas into stage form. Not straight off, anyway."

Fipps was distinctly irritated. His life fantasy was that he was a diverted and harassed Shaw, waiting for the leisure to explode a dazzling shower of plays on the world. So far he had written one. Alcohol had blurred the gap between the dream and the plain facts until his fiftieth year, when a doctor had warned him that the next drinking bout might prevent his celebrating his fifty-first birthday. Too pleasantly, he said, "We'd like very much to see your seven plays."

"They were no good. I burned them." (This was a lie. Hawke never discarded a sheet with a single mark of his handwriting on it.) "But it was practice, and the plot for my novel comes from one of them."

Hawke now committed the barbarism of pulling the wine out of the ice bucket and pouring himself more. The wine waiter sprang like a mother to a child in front of a bus, and wrested the bottle from his hand. But the deed was done. Reproachfully, with a despairing glance at Fipps, the waiter poured a ritual last splash into the glass, and flounced away with a mutter in French, his brass chain tinkling angrily. All oblivious, Hawke gulped wine and stuffed roast duck into his mouth. "This is marvellous food. I've never eaten anything like it."

Fipps said, "I take it then, writing plays forms no part of your ambitions?"

"I didn't say that. See, it's all a question of time, Mr. Fipps. How much time have I got? I figure I should do five or six novels in order to learn how to write them, and then get at the job in earnest. I know Alms for Oblivion is full of faults, but you have to make a start, don't you?" He reached for his empty wineglass, then looked at the bottle. The wine waiter fell on the ice bucket and poured the champagne with frigid gravity. "My gosh, one bottle holds a lot of wine," said Hawke. "I'll probably tumble down the stairs on the way out. Damn good wine. Not as sweet as some."

"No, not as sweet. Get at what job, Mr. Hawke?"

The young man's square, thick-featured face took on a look of sly cunning. After a moment he said, "Well, all right, you're my editor. Let's say it's the champagne talking from here on. All right?"

Fipps said through a thin smile, "Understood."

Hawke resumed his greedy eating, and talked as he ate. "I want to do the grand job, Mr. Fipps—the job that Cervantes and Balzac did, that Proust and Dos Passos did. The permanent picture of my time. I know right now it must sound like megalomania. I know I have a mountain of reading, a tremendous amount of travelling and living to do. I know all that! Meanwhile I can learn my trade and become financially independent. I hope I can do that in about ten years. Then I can get to work.

"Mr. Fipps, I may have acted a little strange when you said you were going to publish my book. But it was like being let out of an insane asylum, don't you see, suddenly released and told I wasn't crazy after all? In the Seabees I was regarded as a harmless lunatic, always reading or scribbling. My mother *knows* I'm out of my head, for wanting to be a writer. She calls me 'the big money maker.' To her, writers are all dead and famous. I'm alive and her son. That proves I can't write. That's how her mind works, and I tell you, most people's. But I can write. *Alms for Oblivion* proves that. There's no point trying to fix it, really. Please don't ask me to, Mr. Fipps. And don't make me cut it, not too much. Just let it go. You can't plane an elephant down to a Siamese cat. From an artistic viewpoint, from a money viewpoint, the thing is for me to just bulldoze ahead and get the next book out, and the next. Each one will be better than the last, I promise you. I learn very fast. The critics are going to compare me to Thomas Wolfe, I suppose, because I'm from the South and I write long books. Please don't think I'm crazy, but I think I can do better than Wolfe did. See, I can't touch his poetry, but I tell stories. All he did was write his memoirs. Beautiful, lyric, American, colossal, immortal memoirs, but Mr. Fipps, you *know* Thomas Wolfe never had the mortgage, the old folks going to the poorhouse, the lovely helpless girl tied to the railroad track, now did he? Ah me, let's save that poor girl, Mr. Fipps! Look at her lying there, all beautiful and trussed up, the wind blowing her skirts up around those pretty legs! And that train thundering down the mountain pass back there, whoo-whoo! Whooo! Whooo! Look, you can see the smoke! It's coming fast! WOO-WOO!"

On both sides of Hawke the diners had laid down their silver and were frankly staring at him. Fipps did not know whether to laugh, or frown, or curtly order the author—who was obviously much too elated by the quart of champagne he had consumed in fifteen minutes—to shut up. Hawke went right on, his Southern accent thickening comically, "Yes suh, Mistuh Fipps, we got to save that girl. Lookit huh lyin' thayuh helpless on huh back, look at them lovely titties strainin' against them croo-el, croo-el ropes! The train's out of the pass! It's a-thunderin' to'd huh! It

ain't a mahl away, not . . . one . . . MAHL! Mr. Fipps, whut's a-goin' to happen? *Whut?*"

More to choke off this maniacal outburst than anything else, Fipps said, "Obviously the hero's going to come galloping over the hill, cut the ropes, and whisk her out of the way just in time. Now if you'll—"

"*Mistuh* Fipps, the hero? The hero's in Japan with Perry, openin' up the forbidden land. No, Mr. Fipps, but don't you heah that rumble, way up high on the mountain? It's an avalanche, by God! Yes suh, a white roarin' slidin' avalanche, gettin' bigger an' bigger every second! Will it bury our girl? Will it bury the train? Here comes that train! There goes the avalanche! Roar, scream, crash, BANG!! Train ploughs into pile of snow, everybody shook up, nobody killed. Girl saved! Engineer jumps down, cuts the ropes, and you know what, Mr. Fipps? *She's his own sister,* by the Christ! That foul villain wanted her killed by her own brother, the fiend, the horrible feeend! Now Tom Wolfe was one great writer, Mr. Fipps, but where was that pretty girl on her back? Where was that avalanche?"

"Possibly Thomas Wolfe wasn't interested in stale Hollywood effects. Wouldn't you like some coffee? It's getting late, and—"

"*Mistuh* Fipps, Dostoevsky tied that girl on the tracks in the first fifty pages of every book he ever wrote, and in the last fifty he brought in that avalanche! Naturally in his books the avalanche buries the girl. Serious writer. Henry James had the girl and the avalanche, why he never wrote about anything else, hardly. Dickens had two avalanches coming down from both sides. Joyce didn't, no. That's why only English teachers read him, though maybe he was the best writer since Shakespeare. No avalanche, Mr. Fipps, no avalanche—"

The man in black had been standing behind Fipps with a telephone on a long cord in his hand. Now he struck in hurriedly, "Meestair Arthur Hawke? With Meestair Feeps?"

"I'm Arthur Hawke," the author said, looking up blankly. Then he exclaimed, "My Kentucky call. By gosh, it went through! Magic! In a restaurant!" He stretched out an immense arm for the telephone. "Mr. Fipps, this town is like Baghdad! Hello, hello! Mama? . . . What? Yes, operator. That's me. . . . What? Edgefield? Look, I called *Hovey.* . . . She is? Well, sure, I'll talk to her in Edgefield. . . . Hello? Hello? Mama? This is the Big Money Maker! What are you doing in Edgefield?"

What Mrs. Hawke was doing in Edgefield was looking into the possibility—obviously a remote one, but in her own mind a near certainty—that villainous people had done her wrong, and owed her more than a million dollars. Like her son, Mrs. Hawke was a visionary. But his visions took the form of tales. Hers involved only money—vast sums of it.

There was a dream-market in Letchworth County, such as you will find

in many places like it; a dream-market that traded in parcels of inaccessible mountain landscape containing coal. Because of the prohibitive cost of mining the coal and bringing it to a railroad or a navigable river, these parcels were worth next to nothing, but the trading was no less brisk and lively for all that. Mrs. Hawke had long been a speculator in that market. She knew only one thing: there was the coal, it stared at you from the hillside when you climbed up into the forested ravines on muleback; why, coal was valuable! She was continually buying and selling, in terms of pennies, land which would indeed have been valuable, if industry ever had pushed up into the area for the coal.

A more sober process went on at the same time in those counties: the buying of land and mineral rights by skilled and hard-eyed investors, who risked the sums needed to tie up gigantic tracts of wilderness, on the long chance that some sharp change in events would make the coal marketable. Such changes did occur—a war, a coal strike—but they were glacially slow in coming, and usually short-lived. Decade after decade the coal lay untouched in the hills, and then the big companies would lose interest and sell off the almost worthless acreage.

Hawke's mother had been in the thick of the dream-market as far back as Hawke could remember. The earliest squabbles he had heard between his parents were over her land dealings. His father had encountered his life's failure in coal, but whatever his weaknesses as a business man he understood coal mining, he knew by heart all the coal deposit maps of the state, and he was familiar with the laws of mineral rights and land ownership. He could tell the stories of a few famous lawsuits over land titles in which millions of dollars had swung one way or another. Hawke had heard him explain to the mother a hundred times, in a tired exasperated way, the economic logic that made the Edgefield deposits valueless. He also had heard his father repeat to weariness that for every lawsuit that had resulted in a money award there were thousands that sputtered and died emptily every year. Hovey and Edgefield had their law-crazed paupers. The father had often predicted, at the end of a squabble, in a raised and angry voice, that Mrs. Hawke would end as one of these lunatics.

They had not been grindingly poor except for one stretch in the depression that nobody in the family cared to think about. Ira Hawke had worked in a WPA project for a year, before giving in and accepting a humiliating loan from his brother to open a drugstore. There he had drudged, growing grayer and sadder, until he died when Hawke was fifteen. Mrs. Hawke was a resourceful and tough widow. She owned a small share in some coal royalties, an inheritance from an aunt; and the modest sums, once the worst of the depression passed, were enough to enable her to maintain her family in a decent way.

Probably Mrs. Hawke's real trouble was that she had these royalties.

To her coal in the ground meant money, if not today then tomorrow, in Edgefield as in Hovey. Her own grandfather had sold the mineral rights in his acreage around Hovey to professional speculators, at a time when Hovey had been little more than a trading post in the woods, at the end of long rutted mud roads. Then the railroad spur had thrust up the valley, and the yard where her mother had played with her dog as a child had become the mouth of one of the best producing pits in all of eastern Kentucky. There was no use telling Mrs. Hawke that the railroads of America were built, that it would not happen again, that no rail spur would ever climb up the steep ridge to a dead end in tiny Edgefield, that oil had nearly replaced coal as the nation's fuel. It had happened. In some form it would happen again!

Yet Mrs. Hawke was not a fool. In the dream-market of Edgefield coal land she was a sort of tycoon. She was brighter than most of the misfits and failures who traded the parcels back and forth. Over the years she had made a little money in Edgefield land, just by smart trading.

Her conversation was mainly about money. Hawke had grown up hearing money, money, money in the household. *Alms for Oblivion* was the story of the tugs and feuds in a family over the fortune of a rich dying aunt. It was the kind of fantasy Mrs. Hawke herself might have composed if she had undertaken a novel. Its value lay not so much in the story, which was worked out in crude melodrama, as in the real picture of Hovey and its inhabitants, and especially of his rich uncle's family. But Hawke's first novel was about money, all the same, where most first novels are about thwarted love, or boiling sex, or military service, or about a misunderstood sensitive young person in a crass world. He owed this peculiar interest to his mother.

Mrs. Hawke had sent him to college with some scrimping because she wanted a lawyer in the family. She was utterly sure, and she had said it a thousand times, that if there had been a lawyer in her mother's family, she and her children would be dwelling on an estate-farm near Lexington, owning horses, moving in high society, and living on interest. A lawyer who had put one smart clause in the sale of her mother's play yard, one little note about royalties—three percent, two percent—would have turned them from middle-class strugglers to gilded aristocrats. Knowledge of the law was the secret of secrets. She was religiously certain that if she ever got a lawyer in the family she would die worth millions. Hawke's writing was therefore a deep annoyance to her. The dreamy boy was going off the track. She never stopped hoping he would give up the scribbling and go to law school. When Hawke came home with the dirty incomplete manuscript it struck her as a disaster. She leafed through its pages uncomprehending and uncaring. The book did not seem good or salable literature like Mark Twain; it was a lot of

untidy gossip about Hovey and her own family, and certainly not worth publishing. So she thought.

Her literary judgment was faulty because, unlike her husband, she had never been a reader. She loved listening to the radio; she never quite got over the fact that it was free entertainment. She had what amounted to a crush on one news analyst because, as she said, he sounded like such a nice man. Listening to his syrupy singsong for fifteen minutes every night was a ritual, and very few Sunday evenings passed when she did not say, at his usual time, that it was a shame he didn't broadcast seven days a week. This was the mother of the young man who proposed to perform in American fiction the tasks of Balzac and Proust.

"Who? Who is it?" Hawke heard her say. Her voice was quite loud.

"The Big Money Maker! It's Art, ma! How are you?"

"Art! For heaven's sake, where are you calling from? Are you all right?"

"Mama, I'm just fine. I'm in the fanciest restaurant in New York. I sold my book, mama. Sold it to Prince House."

"New York! My, and you sound so close, but it's a bad connection, Art, I can't hardly understand you. Are you coming home? I have to see you. Something important has happened. That's why I'm up here in Edgefield with Judge Crain. It's business, Art, you have to come home."

"Ma, didn't you hear what I told you?"

"Yes, you said you're in a New York restaurant. Art, somebody's been mining our land at Frenchman's Ridge. You've got to come down here and see what's what. You're the man of the family, and—"

"Mama, I've *sold my book*, I tell you. Don't you understand? Sold it to a New York publisher! They're going to print my book. They're paying me five thousand dollars. That's why I'm calling you, ma. Aren't you glad to hear it?"

"Five thousand dollars? What for? I haven't got five thousand dollars, Art, don't be a fool. And speak up, I can't hardly hear you."

Dizzied as he was by champagne, Hawke was well aware of the open amusement of the strangers at his elbows. He was beginning his literary career by making an ass of himself amid the fashionable elite of New York. He would gladly have cut short the call and written his mother a letter, but he had been anxious to impress her with his achievement, and now here he was. He painfully repeated his news to her, undergoing agonies at Fipps' ill-concealed grin and the frank sneer of the wine waiter.

This time Mrs. Hawke heard him. "Why, Art, that's just fine! Why, that's wonderful. God bless you, my son, you'll be famous! I've always known you had it in you, I did my best to encourage you, you know that. My, you've really sold that book! Art, have you got a good lawyer? You

make sure you get your contract looked over by a smart lawyer. Maybe you should bring it down here to Judge Crain."

"These calls cost money, ma. Goodbye. Give my love to Nancy."

"Son, I'm so proud of you. One second. Are you coming home?"

"I don't know. This is a big new development, I'll be busy."

"Don't ever be too busy for your old mother, son. No really great man ever was. Don't let fame go to your head."

"Mama, I'm not famous, for Christ's sake, I've just been lucky enough to sell a book, and—"

"You ought to come home, Art. We ought to celebrate. It'll be Christmas, and all. Anyway, dear, the business on Frenchman's Ridge is serious. I was out walking on the land last week, and there was this big tunnel, see—"

"Look, ma, you're always seeing big tunnels when somebody digs a hole on a piece of land of yours and takes a little coal that's worth no more than the labor to haul it away—"

"It's your land, too. This was a big hole, I tell you."

"Goodbye, ma."

"Will you call Judge Crain?"

"When I get a chance."

"When will I see you?"

"Goodbye, ma. I'll let you know."

"I'm proud of you, son. My, what fine news! Thanks for thinking of your old mother."

"Goodbye, ma. Goodbye." He hung up and thrust the telephone at the wine waiter, who shrank from the profane thing. The man in black darted forward and took it.

Fipps said, covering his mouth with hand and cigarette, "It's very thoughtful of you to want to share your good news with your mother. Old-fashioned, and decidedly pleasant."

"Don't give me any credit for it," Hawke said, glaring around at the people who had been eavesdropping. "Just allow me my mean little triumph. The one thing that impresses my mother is the five thousand. Money is serious. Mind you, mama isn't avaricious, not what you'd *call* avaricious. Mama just knows that money is all that matters. Most of the world agrees with her, so as between us she's nearer normal, I guess."

"Ah, on our brief acquaintance, Mr. Hawke, I'd say you had a healthy regard for money."

Hawke drank coffee, narrowing his eyes at the editor. "Look, Mr. Fipps—and say, how long does the mister business go on? They call me Art back home."

"Good. And they call me Waldo. I'm glad you have a nickname, Art. Youngblood would be rather a jawbreaker, all the time."

"Well, there I'm imitating Somerset Maugham again, using my middle name. What do people call him—Bill?"

"Willie. Your name happens to be superb. You'd have to write very bad novels not to sell them, with a name like Youngblood Hawke."

Hawke became very red again. Brandy came, and he took a gulp that emptied the glass. He said, "A high regard for money? Yes indeed! I intend to make money and I know I will, but not for my mother's reasons. I want to be living on interest at the age of thirty-five, Waldo, when I expect my serious work to start. I want an adequate amount of invested money, a quarter million, a half million, a million dollars, whatever it takes"— Fipps opened his eyes very wide, and stared—"judiciously selected and balanced across the face of the economy, so that nothing after that can ever interfere with my work. Living on interest is the big open secret of the rich, Waldo. A writer who spends his income as he makes it is eating out his own bowels. I know all that. I've made a study of these things. I'm going to live on interest, and in the not too distant future."

Fipps said, his eyes still showing white all around the pupils, "Isn't that a curious goal for—well, for an artist?"

"It's not my goal, don't you see that? It's the start toward my goal."

"Well, it's a dream that most people have and few reach."

"I'll reach it."

5

Checkroom attendants were helping them into their coats when Hawke noticed Jock Maas regarding him from an armchair. Maas smiled the disturbing smile, stood, and came toward them. He needed a haircut worse than Hawke did; little dark whorls of hair disappeared down the back of his neck into his shirt collar. "Well, well, the editor and his gifted prey. Where are you gentlemen heading?"

The editor glanced at his watch. "Unfortunately, I have a sales conference now, Art. Can you come in tomorrow morning about ten? That is, if it won't interfere with your work on your new novel." The three men went through doors held open for them by attendants, out into a whirling snowfall that was faintly violet colored.

"I'll have my day's quota done by then," Hawke said, his breath smoking. "I get up late at night and work straight through."

Fipps said, "Splendid work habits. We'd better talk some more tomorrow about revisions, since you seem reluctant to make them." Fipps smiled and walked off a step or two. Then he stopped and turned. "Oh—once again—congratulations." He went off in a lurching stiff gait, like a walking skeleton, hands jammed in pockets, chin sunken.

Maas took Hawke's arm. He smiled at the young author, uncovering his

separated stained teeth, and wrinkling his whole face upward. The corners of his mouth seemed to move near his eyes. "Hawke, have you been to the top of the Empire State Building?"

"Not yet. I've been meaning to go, but—"

"Everybody means, nobody goes. Come along."

"Sure."

They trudged in slush to Fifth Avenue, and turned downtown. Neither spoke for a long time. Hawke found it more than a little odd to be walking silently arm in arm in a snowfall with this queer celebrity, but he waited for what would happen next. Maas said very abruptly, snatching his arm away from Hawke's elbow, "I have a feeling that I suggested the completely wrong thing, that you're bored, that the last thing you want to do on your day of triumph is to go with a stranger on a hayseed excursion to the top of the Empire State Building."

"Ye gods no," Hawke said. "Come on. I'm too excited to do anything more sensible. Am I wrong, or does New York really have the most beautiful women in the world? And they all seem to pour into this street, this one street, Fifth Avenue, between Fifty-ninth and Forty-second, and walk it in the daytime. Look at the way they walk. You'd think they were all movie stars."

Maas looked up—he was much shorter than Hawke—and the pale yellow light of a street lamp fell on his smiling face, the heavy black brows flecked with snow. He was hatless, like Hawke; snow was caking on his thin black hair. "Are you married?"

"It doesn't even occur to me. I have too much work."

"Do you have a girl?"

"No."

"Don't you get, well, hungry now and then?"

"Damned hungry."

"What do you do?"

"Hunger, mostly."

Maas uttered a short barking laugh. "My dear lad. Big and strong, and if I may say so, winning as you are?"

"I'd rather be hungry than involved. My trouble is I don't know how to be casual. Even if it's a waitress, I have to make a goddess of her in my own mind, I don't know why."

"Because you propose to mate her with a god," Maas said in his velvety voice, that somehow penetrated through the street noise.

Hawke halted in his tracks, stared at Maas, threw back his head and bellowed with laughter. He took the producer's arm and started striding along so fast that Maas had to trot a little. "By the Christ, Mr. Maas, I'm enjoying this. Where are those carols coming from, anyway? They seem to be floating in the air, like the music on Prospero's island. I swear this goddamn avenue is a Christmas card come to life, these lamps burning

in the middle of the day and the air sort of purplish and full of snow, and these big windows like fairy houses, with gorgeous immovable creatures in them smiling and flirting and wearing Arabian Nights clothes. Good God, will you look at that diamond necklace? Is that real? Just lying there behind a pane of glass? It must be worth half a million dollars."

"It's real," said the producer. "That's thick glass, and if it breaks it shrieks like an air raid siren. Do you mind telling me the plot of your novel?"

"Gosh, no." Hawke was still pretty drunk, and the flattering interest of a Broadway producer dissolved his usual caution. He spilled the story while they walked down Fifth Avenue, hurrying the plot to its climax as the Empire State Building loomed near, vague in the snowfall, its top disappearing into purple mist. Maas made no comment when the author finished.

The two men shot skyward in an elevator crowded with damp bundled-up tourists, most of whom stayed in the steam-heated glass observation room. Maas led Hawke out on a terrace bounded by a shoulder-high parapet of stone. The wind was screeching, and snowflakes stung Hawke's cheek, but there were only a few. The main body of the storm was rolling in a white cloud across the Hudson, uncovering the downtown skyscrapers and the black river. "See that? The view's opening up just for you. Good omen!" shouted Maas.

Hawke was staring out at the city, tears standing in his eyes from the force of the wind. He shook his head in wonder.

"Think you can lick it?" yelled Maas. And when Hawke did not reply he went on, "Just remember this. Franklin Roosevelt wasn't as tall as you are. This town can be had. This country can be had. Men are just men, even the best ones. Balzac wouldn't have come up to your shoulder, Hawke. Just a little fat Frenchman with thick lips and a garlic breath."

"I love this city. I'll never leave it," roared Hawke. "And I'll lick it!"

Maas shrilled, in his weak voice that somehow carried through all noise, "That book of yours sounds like a play. In three weeks, maybe two, working with me, you could edit that book down into a hit. Why don't we do it? It'll be fun, sheer fun. We can go to Mexico, or Bermuda, wherever you want."

Hawke was breathless: from the wind, or the height, or the amazing sudden offer, or all those things. The rich lunch was not sitting well. He felt uneasy in his middle, and a little dizzy, and his heart was thumping, but he was wildly exhilarated. "Jesus, Mr. Maas, all you know is a plot I just told you on the sidewalk. Maybe I can't write plays at all. Maybe I can't write novels either. Who knows?"

Maas laughed wildly, and shook snow out of his hair and eyes. "Maybe ah cain't ra-a-at plays. Maybe ah cain't ra-a-at novels!" He mim-

icked Hawke's accent precisely. "My lad, Waldo Fipps does not make a habit of wining and dining boys with first novels at Number One. You're red hot, obviously. But you're innocent. Write this play, I tell you. Do you know how much money there is in a hit play? They just sold that wretched comedy *The Rabbit Foot* to the movies for a million dollars. One million dollars in cash, *do you hear?*" Maas screamed over the howls of the wind. "Fifty thousand a year for twenty years! Come on, boy! Tomorrow morning! The nine-eighteen plane to Mexico City, and come as you are, we'll buy shirts and toothbrushes as we go. Have you ever been to Cuernavaca? A friend of mine has a villa there, marvellous servants, a pool, there's fresh linen on the beds, and by God, young man, it's a divorce mill for the rich, you've never seen such luscious blonde lonesome women—"

"Look, it's wonderful that you're interested in me, but I have this other work to do. I've been paid an advance—"

A look of the blackest gloom came over the producer's face, and he darted off the terrace. Hawke followed him, very disconcerted. In the elevator the man's face suddenly cleared into a charming smile. "What are you doing tomorrow night? I know several very agreeable ways we can pass Christmas Eve."

"Well, I've been invited to the Princes', and—"

"Dear old Fanny, eh? Well, that's always a pleasant do. Maybe I'll see you there."

On the sidewalk Maas hailed a cab, and Hawke found himself handed inside it, not knowing where he was going next. Maas muttered an address and slouched in a corner of the seat, his face sulky. The cab stopped at a dirty little building in the west forties, tucked between theatres where hit shows boasted of their success in garishly painted quotations from the critics. Maas said suddenly, "Hawke, I'll give you an advance, too. I'll give you an advance of twenty-five hundred dollars if you'll start work on this play within the next three days. Otherwise forget it. I have to go into rehearsal with *The Doctor's Dilemma* in mid-January."

Hawke knew that he should not make any decision. He was hearing words. His senses were numb, his vitality was sagging. He had taken in too much in one day. He had gone from the total obscurity of a scribbling construction worker to a contract for three novels, and lunch at Number One, and now this weird man wanted to give him money to dramatize his book! Things didn't happen this way. He had a pounding headache, a vivid smell of sharpened pencils was haunting him—a warning sign of exhaustion—and Jock Maas was beginning to seem like a ghost in a dream.

"Mr. Maas, your confidence in me staggers me. I'm sort of dimming out, I haven't been to bed in thirty-six hours. Let me phone you tomorrow."

"Phone me tonight. Any time. Here's my private number." Maas wrote a scrawl on a slip of paper. "You work all night, don't you? Call me four in the morning, or whenever you please. I don't sleep. I read." With this the producer got out of the cab and walked off, making no gesture to pay the fare, and vanished into the building.

Hawke directed the driver to take him to the loft building in the wholesale furniture district where he had his lair. He stumbled up three flights of deeply gouged heavy stone stairs, unlocked his door, and all but fell inside. The bed was as he had left it, unmade, a mere mattress on the floor with tumbled sheets and blankets. The room, bare and unfurnished except for an old armchair and an older refrigerator, was a chaos of books and clothes and luggage and stacked papers. In the middle of the mess was the desk, cleared and waiting, and beside it the coffeepot on its little electric grill on the floor. Hawke took three aspirins. The pounding at his temples was making him wince, and the pencil smell scared him, it was so strong; this was a queer thing that had been happening to him off and on since his truck accident, whenever he went over the edge of total fatigue.

He ranged on the desk the three bits of tangible evidence that this unbelievable day had not been a hallucination—the scrap of paper with Maas's telephone number, the box of cigars Prince had given him, which he had been carrying everywhere under his arm, and the orange Prince House check for five hundred dollars. The check seemed to have a hazy rainbow around it, like a street lamp in the rain. Hawke collapsed upon the bed with his clothes on, dragging the blanket over him. His eyes closed, then he forced them open. He reached for a tin alarm clock near his pillow, wound it, and set it to allow himself four hours of sleep.

CHAPTER TWO

1

Now Fanny Prince's eggnog party on Christmas Eve was not exactly the quiet little gathering she liked to call it. It was an institution that even the second World War had not shaken, a turbulent massive crush of celebrities and their satellites, powered by one of the most extravagant buffet dinners seen in New York from one year to the next.

It was a revel with a reason. Publishers are not socially important in

New York unless their companies date well back into the nineteenth century, and unless they themselves have a reasonable pedigree. Picture then, the position of people like the Princes, both of whom were parvenus: Fanny a wealthy refugee from Hungary, Jay a Chicago book salesman who had pushed his way upward and eastward and had brashly started his own house shortly before the 1929 collapse. Where many of the staid old houses had gone under, Prince House had flourished, using loud jocular advertising hitherto unknown to the book trade, printing books of jokes and comic strips and picking up star authors cast adrift by sinking publishers. Hawke thought the Princes were exalted New York aristocrats, and they were (relatively speaking) nobody at all. But Fanny was energetic, and in ten years of strenuous entertainment, charity work, and cultivation of useful people, she had made a place in what might be called the open or second layer of upper-class New York. The circle of the elect was beyond her: the nearly invisible group into which one must be born, where talent gives one nothing more than a passport to amuse now and then, and enough new-gained money can earn one an invitation to work on a charity committee, and occasional formal entry into otherwise closed homes. Fanny was fond of referring to this innermost circle as stuffy and dowdy. Indeed it is, for the most part, though it can outdazzle people like Fanny without half trying when it chooses. It seldom so chooses. Brilliance and display in a democracy are mostly for those who are on the climb, not for those who hold the citadel. It was not likely that the defenders would ever see the whites of Fanny's eyes.

But what did she care? Fanny knew and entertained senators, governors, foreign ambassadors, artists, movie stars, writers, scientists, and even European nobility, who might have looked down on her in their home ground, but who—looking down on all Americans as they did—found our own intramural distinctions a little amusing. Anywhere in the world, you can go far with a good table; and when Fanny spread a feast, celebrated men and beautiful women came to eat it, and behaved like children at a birthday.

As soon as Youngblood Hawke walked into the crowded lobby of the Prince home, a four-story mansion on East Sixty-seventh Street, he realized that his dress was wrong, and he wondered angrily why Karl Fry had said nothing to him about it. The line of men giving their black overcoats and white scarves to a smiling Negro butler, were all dressed in dinner jackets, or else black or very dark gray suits; nothing else. Fry, a small bitter-faced lean man with bad teeth, was dressed in brown like himself; not only that, he wore a blue shirt and red tie. Even Hawke, knowing nothing of New York manners, had thought Fry was outlandishly gotten up. By contrast his own outfit had seemed to him suave and knowing. It was his "novelist's suit," bought in a fit of exaltation the

day he finished *Alms for Oblivion,* with a sense when he wrote "The End" that he had licked the world. Brown tweed, heavy purplish-brown shoes, a white grainy button-down shirt, and a dark maroon tie with dark blue figures on it—and even a rough briar pipe, and a tobacco pouch and some tobacco—this was the costume Hawke had bought himself weeks ago out of a small hoard, for occasions of state. Tonight, obviously, he should have left it laid away, and had his blue suit cleaned and pressed; at least it was dark.

"Two sad hicks in brown," he muttered to Fry as he gave the impassively jolly butler his begrimed duffle coat.

"I haven't got the money to dress differently. I probably wouldn't if I had," Fry said. "It's economical to get an early reputation as a slob. I recommend that you start working at it." He led Hawke up a sweeping curved marble staircase, where some of the men were ascending. The others mingled with gaily chattering women to wait for a small elevator.

"To hell with that. This is the last time I go to a New York party at night in anything but black, ace-of-spades black, inside-of-a-brunette-cow black. What's so hard about that? Black, that's all. Black."

"Stop raging at yourself, you look exactly like a young Arnold Bennett, or William Faulkner, or whoever that rig is supposed to suggest. There's one touch of extraordinary sophistication about you, you don't have a pipe. Where did you get the wisdom to avoid that?"

Hawke, after a moment's hesitation, took the pipe out of his pocket and clenched it in his teeth. Then he burst out laughing, and Fry said "Huh, huh," through a twisted smile, the nearest to mirth he ever came. At the top of the staircase they slowed in the pile-up of the welcoming line, which was fed by the stairs and the discharging elevator.

Fanny and Jay Prince were briskly shaking hands with guests, standing against the wall under a painting which glowed richly in a beam of white light from a hole in the ceiling. Hawke knew little about painting, but this was a Renoir. He remembered seeing reproductions of it. Hung on a wall covered with dull white figured fabric, the painting smote the eye of the newcomer to the Princes' home. Hawke stared at the costly trophy, and his lower lip curled over the upper, as though he were about to get into a fight. It was very noisy in the high-ceilinged foyer: a general buzz of talk, trills of women, laughter breaking out, all this over a solid steady base of sound, a Christmas carol booming distantly from a phonograph. Through the inevitable New York fog of cigarette smoke, the perfume of women came to Hawke's nostrils one moment, and barber-shop smells of men the next, and now and then the smell of warm evergreen that Fanny had promised, and of burning logs; and more enticing than the rest was a rolling spicy smell of hot roasted meats.

"Karl Fry, you old misanthrope, so! Ve get you out of your cave one night, ha?" Fanny gave him her hand and a brilliant smile, then turned to

Hawke, the smile disappearing like a flashlight beam turned off. "So, Mr. Hoke, you came and you brought him." Fanny's expression was serious and tender. She pressed his hand. "You're very kind. You do oss honor."

"Well, I'm a bull in your china shop. I'll try not to break anything too valuable," Hawke said, aware that he was forcing for wit and attaining feeble facetiousness.

But Fanny Prince evidently didn't think so. She laughed, not a gay loud laugh but a low intimate one. "You're enchanting. Ve get off in a corner tonight, ha, maybe in the library later, and just talk." She turned to the next newcomer, with a little reluctant pressure on Hawke's hand as she released it, and he felt that he was without question one of the few guests Fanny Prince really was glad to see—and at the same time he noted the feeling and began to wonder how she had conveyed it. Jay Prince said —the publisher was magnificent, tall and red-faced, his dinner jacket smooth as a seal's coat, his white shirt oddly and beautifully frilled—"Well, Hawke, what's this? Why aren't you working on that new book you owe us?"

"I did my pages last night," Hawke said, "and I'll do them tonight, no matter what time I leave."

The publisher's jovial look passed for an instant to the business face, and his smile was small and approving. "By God I believe you. You look as though you've been working. Glad you came." He brightened again. "Have some eggnog before the food starts." He held out two hands to two other arrivals.

Karl Fry said as they were carried by the eddy of new guests into a crowd of drinking and gossiping people in the living room, "You don't want eggnog, do you? Slimy stuff, and so damned full of food! The booze corner is upstairs in the library. Let's go."

"Sure I want some eggnog," Hawke said. "You're supposed to drink eggnog on Christmas Eve."

"Okay, okay. Look for me in the booze corner when you want another brown suit to huddle against." Fry looked up at the broad-shouldered young author, bulky and shaggy in tweed, his haggard face pink from a too-close shave. "How do you manage, at six foot two, to look like a little lost boy? A little lost Christian among the lions?"

Hawke said, "Don't worry, my friend. This Christian is going to eat a few lions, tonight, if they start anything."

Fry uttered his huh-huh laugh, showing his stained teeth. "Well, thanks for getting me into Fanny's party this year. I love free drinks, and I have no prejudice against free food."

Hawke said, "What are you talking about? She said she keeps inviting you and you keep turning her down."

Fry looked at him from under half-closed lids, smiled, and turned to twist his way through the oncoming guests, a small brown figure bucking

the tide of men in black, women in black, and here and there the bold splash of a woman in color.

Left alone, Hawke did have a lost-boy feeling among these self-assured New Yorkers, talking and laughing in little knots, always glancing restlessly about, nearly always pausing for a brief stare when their eyes flitted to him. He saw some whispering and head gestures that obviously referred to himself, the big bulky boob in brown, and he became aware of his hands and feet, and seemed able to strike no natural pose. So he made for one of the tables where maids were serving eggnog out of ornate silver bowls. The maid darted the dipper down through heavy nutmeg-speckled yellow foam, and filled a silver cup for him. He retreated with it to a window seat, where he intended to keep the whole staring crowd in front of him.

His self-consciousness was unnecessary. He was really making an excellent impression, indeed a small sensation. You wear a brown suit in fashionable New York after dark for one of four possible reasons: ignorance, defiance, poverty, or calculated eccentricity; but he knew nothing of this. Most of the time he didn't think of clothes; then he had short tearing agonies, looking at a magazine or seeing a well-dressed young man on the street, when it seemed to him he would die if he couldn't walk into a Fifth Avenue shop at once and emerge with a five-thousand-dollar wardrobe that marked him a man of elegance. In one of these spells, after studying a picture of the author John Marquand on the front page of The New York Times Book Review, he had bought this suit. Big as he was, the tweed made him look twice as bulky; coarse as he was, it made him look coarser. He appeared so formidably out of place that the costume actually worked. For his face was full of life, and his eyes burned with sharp zestful curiosity, and he radiated the physical strength he had. These things gave him the authority to carry off his abominable dress. He succeeded by the outrageousness of his failure.

Not knowing this, he was trying to bury his embarrassment by taking inventory of the Prince living room.

But, beyond the mere size of the green-papered room, and the marble fireplace with its blazing logs, and the clumps of guests, and the tallest Christmas tree he had ever seen indoors, all tinsel and lights and red and green baubles, he would not have been able to describe the scene. His ignorance prevented him from being able to classify what he saw. The decoration of the room was of some period, he didn't know which; the pieces were antiques and probably French, since the wood was delicate and curlycued, and painted creamy or greenish. The pictures on the walls looked old, authentic, and important, glowing in their spotlights; he thought one was a Van Ruysdael because of the clouds, but he wasn't sure. He much admired the thick creamy drapes he was leaning against, almost two stories high, but he could not have named the material. Into his

mental notebook, as he peered about the room, went the admonition to buy books on interior decorating, painting, and furniture, and to haunt the fashionable auction galleries.

"Rich, isn't it?"

Hawke turned and saw a pretty girl in black standing beside him with a glass of eggnog in her hand, wrinkling her nose at the drink with comic distaste.

He said, "The drink, or the room?"

"Well, both."

"Rich, yes. Not too rich for me." He cocked his head to glance down at her, then said, "Why, you're the wretched girl at Prince House that compared my writing to O. Henry. What do they call you? The styler?"

"Stylist," she said. Her voice was much less hoarse. "I'm glad I said such a terrible thing, since it enabled you to remember me."

Hawke said, "Well, you look different." At first glance she had struck him as very smart in the strange feathered tricorne hat and long black gloves, almost like a window mannequin. But her manner, especially the direct bright look of her eyes, and a small smile that came and went in the corners of a wide full mouth, appealed to him more than her clothes.

"I hope I look a little better than I did yesterday."

"Well, you're not slouching, you're not coughing, you're not staring through glasses like two portholes. You look fine. Your name is Jeanie Green."

She smiled at him in gratitude. She had even white teeth, and her eyes shone. It was one of the pleasantest smiles he had seen in a long time. He said, "Where does a snip of a girl like you get off editing novels?"

She said with sudden pugnacity, "Where does a snip of a boy like you get off writing them?" A look of dismay passed over her face. "Oh Gawd now why did I say that? Well, I guess that plus O. Henry finishes me." Hawke had the grace to laugh. She went on, "I don't care. If you want to know my qualifications, Mr. Hawke, they include graduating from Berkeley magna cum, English major, M.A., then various secretarial jobs in government, since I'd decided I'd rather die than live the academic life, then getting fired from a good job in State because some Senator was rowing with my boss and found out that a snip of a girl not quite twenty-two was his administrative assistant. The requirements for styling a novel are an IQ of say 105, habits of honest work, fair knowledge of English, and a style book which you can buy for a couple of dollars. Okay?" Hawke was looking at her with a young man's admiring frank appetite. She stammered, "I mean—anyway, even if it's a man's world, won't you let me finish styling your novel?"

"Well, I don't know. I resent the whole idea. Who says I can't punctuate?"

"I do. That is, you're not true to your own punctuation scheme. You can

punctuate any strange way you want to, even like Joyce or Faulkner, but then you must be consistent, and you're not."

"Maybe my scheme is just that, Jeanie, inconsistency."

"How does the reader tell that from sloppiness?" Hawke burst out laughing. Jeanne said, "Moreover, and this is important, you've got some bad chronology slips. Birthdays and time lapses don't add up, and all that. Look, what I can do is the lowest menial cleaning-up, but I enjoy it when it's a book like yours. Are you going to take it away from me because I'm a girl?"

Hawke saw two men looking at him and talking with their heads close together. They were both small, both dressed in sculptured black, and both looked rather like birds: one a dark sparrow with quick-moving eyes, and swift hand gestures like the beat of wings, the other a fat parrot with a yellow top of hair, and a blinking sleepy manner. They came toward him now, the dark man leading.

"You're Mr. Youngblood Hawke, I think," he said, with a downward chop of a wing that became a hand extended to shake. "My name is Phil York."

Hawke's nerves tensed, and he automatically took an ingratiating tone, shaking the hand. "How do you do? I've enjoyed your columns very much."

"Thank you. I hear I'm going to be enjoying your novels. This is Mr. Lax, Mr. Ferdie Lax of Hollywood. If you don't recognize the name you ought to. Whenever a novel sells to pictures for more than fifty thousand, Ferdie usually is responsible. Naturally Ferdie is curious about this smashing new book that you've written, and that everybody in this room's talking about while you're chatting with this beautiful girl."

The blond man blinked and shook hands. "Is it your first novel, and has Jay given you an unprecedented contract, as the talk goes?"

"It's my first book. As to the contract, I don't know what the precedents are, you see."

"Your agent does."

"I don't have one."

The blinking eyes of Ferdie Lax opened very wide, he stared at Hawke, then he smiled and almost seemed to fall asleep where he stood. "Sometimes a man does just as well or better without an agent," he murmured. "I don't imagine you're interested in a Hollywood job. You're probably hard at work on a new novel."

"Yes, I am."

"Fine. There are plenty of good Hollywood writers, and very few good novelists."

York said sharply, "What's the novel about?"

Hawke felt as though he were defying the police, but he said, "I'm sorry, I can't discuss it yet."

"Got a title?" The columnist spoke in an offended tone, implying that

revealing the title might serve as an apology for Hawke's rudeness. The author was groping for a way to parry this question, when Fanny swooped in.

"Vell, Phil, Ferdie, you don't drink my eggnog, ha? Mr. Hoke, watch out zese are two dangerous men. . . . Jeanie, people are going opp in the library, maybe you take a look everything is okay there, enough hors d'oeuvres, ha? Thank you, darling."

"Certainly, Fanny." This was why Jeanne, with a few of the other pretty girls in the publisher's staff, were asked to the party. They were quasi-hostesses, rather like grown daughters, of which Fanny had none; and like daughters she ordered them about. Jeanne left, with one quick glance at the author.

"Mr. Hoke, somebody is dying to meet you, maybe you submit this once? A marvellous human being, not a monster like everybody says, Quentin Judd."

Hawke recognized the name of the most fearsome critic in America, a cobra who struck every few weeks in a comic magazine called *The Dandy*, now at a book, now at a play, now at a symphony conductor, now at a new fashionable painter. Judd belonged to no school of criticism. Indeed other critics were often his victims. His favorite game was to lie back until most of the other critics had committed themselves on a book or play or exhibit —either for or against—and then to sail in and assert the opposite view with skill and ferocity, thus making his colleagues look sick. He loved to affect ignorance, and to barb his stinging sentences with coarse slang; but he was better informed than most of the professorial critics, whom he sometimes slashed up with as much gusto as if they were authors. Hawke had read *The Dandy* for years, in college and in the Seabees. Quentin Judd had grown in his mind to the foe he would some day have to vanquish to take his place in literature. Often as he wrote he wondered how Judd would go about demolishing his work.

Ferdie Lax said, "Fanny, is that a good idea? Quent is best left alone, most of the time."

"Nonsense, he's a charming man. You Hollywood people hate him because he says movies are all awful, which they are."

Hawke said, "I'd be glad to meet him, if he's really interested."

"He asked, he *asked*, dear. Come along." Fanny took his hand and zig-zagged with him across the room toward the flaming fire.

2

Quentin Judd was sitting alone on an upholstered bench in front of the fire, a glass in his hand. Possibly because he was so totally different from anything Hawke had expected—for the author had never seen a picture

of the critic—he had a strange effect on Hawke. It seemed that the man was misty, or transparent, or not exactly there, like a phantom or a projected image. What Hawke saw as Judd rose to his feet was a person hardly more than five feet tall with a pudding body, thin arms and legs, and a large head which sloped away to a small pursed mouth, almost no chin, and a narrow neck. The man had scanty hair and thick square glasses which somehow gave him a benign look. This grotesque figure, clad in a rusty wrinkled dinner jacket, was so unlike the Quentin Judd of Hawke's imagination—the polished handsome New Yorker of commanding masculine presence and cold urbane charm—that he was stunned. His stupefaction deepened when Judd acknowledged their introduction with a high nervous giggle. "Well, Prince House's new author. How do you do?" He held his fingers in a strange stiff way as Hawke shook hands. It was like shaking the hand of a dummy. Judd said, "Fanny, I'd like another drink."

"Immediately, dear." Fanny disappeared among the guests. Judd slumped down on the bench again, and Hawke, not knowing what else to do, sat beside him. The critic's body was very short. Hawke's chin was now well above the top of Judd's head. The critic turned, looked upward, and gave Hawke a single measuring look. His eyeballs were opaque and yellowish, and the pupils were spots of startling ice-blue. He giggled, and Hawke almost jumped. "Been in New York long?" Judd said.

"About a year."

"Then you're getting used to these things."

"Well, no, I've been working pretty hard. If it doesn't bore you, I ought to tell you how much I admire your work. I've read you for years and years."

Judd said, with a smile in which only his upper lip moved, "Thank you very much. From what Fanny says I have a treat in store, in your new novel."

"Don't judge me by this one. I don't think it's up to your standards. I think the next one will be better."

"My standards? My standards aren't high. I'm starved for a good story written in an unaffected way . . . Thank you, Fanny." The hostess thrust a new drink in his hand.

Fanny said to Hawke, "You see? He didn't chop you to pieces, he didn't drink your blood."

Judd sighed. "I don't know why people take criticism so seriously. One good creator is worth all the critics who ever lived."

"Criticism is necessary to literature," Hawke said, and felt a fierce disgust with himself. It was as though he were trying to soothe a homicidal lunatic.

Judd said, "Nonsense, criticism is a minor form of entertainment, a sort of piggy-back writing that rides on other men's work. All that people really like in criticism is malice and destruction. I've done my best to

praise artists I've admired, and to point out where their merit lies. My editors never fail to complain at the dullness of such pieces. Nevertheless when I like work I praise it. And when I hate something, I say I hate it." He looked up at Hawke, the blue eyes sparkling frostily, and bent his head toward the center of the room. "People inevitably take it personally, though I can hate a book a man's written and still want him as my bosom friend. Somehow they never understand that. There's Jock Maas, Fanny, he won't even look my way. I'm one of the few people who really appreciates what Jock can do at his best. He produced a bad play, I said I hated it, and now he's my enemy."

"I'll bring him over," Fanny said. "You make friends again on Christmas Eve."

"Don't waste your time."

Hawke said, "Who's that woman with him? Is she an actress?"

He caught the swift amused look that passed between Fanny and the critic. She said, "No, dear. That's Frieda Winter."

"What does she do?" He wanted to get off the explosive subject of literary criticism. He was afraid he would say a wrong word and turn Judd against him forever. The woman with Maas looked about thirty or so. She wore a blue-gray dress, simply cut, with a black sash; she was of medium height and quite pale. In a room full of interesting-looking women she caught the eye, for no reason Hawke could define. She was peering here and there in a nearsighted way, her head bent down.

Fanny said, "Oh, a little of this and a little of that. Come, I introduce you to some more people. Quent, you like Youngblood? I think maybe I adopt him for a son."

The critic smiled at Hawke with his upper lip. "Your publishers are all for you. That helps. Good luck."

Fanny hissed as she led Hawke away, "Don't ask who people are or what they do, for God's sake. Don't be a boy." She glanced at her watch. "Vot's keeping them in the kitchen? People will start to leave. That was very good, you and Quentin. He sees you. You're somebody. You're a pleasant young man, not a face on a jacket. It makes a difference."

Jock Maas came darting at Hawke. Barbered and dressed in a black street suit of elegant cut, Maas looked a lot less seedy than he had in the restaurant. "Hawke! Don't you have a telephone? I spent the day trying to track you down." The woman in blue-gray walked up beside Maas, smiling a little at the impetuousness of his plunge away from her.

Fanny said, "Hello, Jock. Frieda, this is our new author, Youngblood Hoke. Frieda Winter. Mr. Hoke, I leave you in fine hands." She vanished in the crowd.

Maas took Hawke's arm. "Frieda is my associate in producing *The Doctor's Dilemma*. She wants to join me in doing *Alms for Oblivion* too.

I adore that title, by the way. I kept saying it out loud all night. Why didn't you call me?"

"I was working. I'm sorry."

Frieda Winter said, "Jock tells me that you write straight through the night." Her voice was low, with a warm timbre, and something seemed to be amusing her, for a smile hovered in her eyes and lips.

"I do."

"You're a determined man."

"Yes, ma'am, I am."

"Yes, ma'am, ah *am*." She repeated his intonations, and her imitation was graceful light flattery, rather than mockery. "That's good."

She was looking at him intently from under her eyebrows, her head bent far down. Hawke had the sensation that he knew Frieda Winter, that he had seen her before. Her manner, her voice, were peculiarly recognizable. Yet he was aware that this was almost impossible, if she was not an actress, for what New York women did he know, beside a couple of Greenwich Village tramps and the waitress whom he had briefly and idiotically worshipped?

Maas said, "I had the most frustrating morning you can imagine. I went up to Prince House to have a look at your manuscript, just to get a sense of your dialogue powers—which I'm sure are superb—and it was utter chaos there, they were preparing the Christmas party. Waldo had stayed in Connecticut, and Jay wasn't around, nor anybody else who knew me. I finally located your manuscript, a dreary little girl in some office had it in her desk, and do you know she wouldn't let me see it? Not even for ten minutes, not for five, not for one glance? I tried everything short of throwing her out of the window, and I'd have done that if I'd stayed another second, so I left. Who is that little idiot? A redhead who keeps coughing like a seal."

Hawke laughed. "That's Jeanie Green. She's here tonight. I guess she thought she was doing her job."

"Is Miss Green your editor?" Frieda Winter said softly.

"Good Christ, Frieda, Waldo Fipps is his editor," Maas exclaimed. "This is some file clerk. If I run into her here I'll kill her."

A maid came by announcing that the buffet dinner was being served. Maas said, "Ye gods, about time. Another minute and I'd have gnawed my own arm off." He dashed into the thick of the guests funneling through the foyer to the dining room. Hawke and Frieda Winter followed more slowly, moving with the crowd.

"Are you hungry?" she said.

"I don't know. I guess I am. I filled up on bread and cheese when I got out of bed. I've been too busy taking all this in. I'm nervous as hell. I guess I'll eat."

"When did you get out of bed?"

"Today? About three or four in the afternoon, I guess. I worked later than usual, far into the morning."

She was walking along by his side. She wore no jewelry but a curious pin on one shoulder, a large blue-enamelled flower like a morning glory; and on her left hand was a wedding band, and a ring with a blue stone. Her brown hair was arranged in a soft unpretentious way. She moved like a girl, with an easy swaying lightness, and her wide-eyed look, with the mannerism of holding her head down, gave her a shy innocent air. He wondered how old she was. She caught him staring at her, and as the quick smile came and went he said, just to say something, "You're not my idea of a theatrical producer."

"Me? I'm just a housewife. I'm putting some money in Jock's show. A friend of mine"—she named a prominent actress—"wanted to play Mrs. Dubedat, and I thought it might be fun, so I sort of helped the thing get rolling. You've read *The Doctor's Dilemma?*"

"I read everything Shaw wrote, in about two months, out in the Pacific. I came on an old dusty set in the library of a girl I knew in Honolulu, it was her father's library. I read one play and I never stopped till I'd read everything, the letters, the novels, the music criticism, everything except that Intelligent Woman's Guide to Communism, or whatever. I bogged down in that."

"Everyone does. Wasn't that too much Shaw all at once?"

"Well, sure, it got repetitious, but that's the way I read. You come on a body of work and crack it open like a nut and get the meat. You get everything that was in the man's mind, and then you have him."

They passed into the dining room, a place of blue and white; elaborate wallpaper of blue with white Greek figures painted on it to look like bas-relief, and thick drapes of white, and a blue carpet. The table had been extended so that it was about twenty feet long, and from what Hawke could see through the eager throng of guests—and over their heads as he drew close—every inch of it was laden with food. He saw a huge roast turkey, and several giant lobsters, and beef tongues in jelly, and whole brown hams, and two enormous boiled salmon parallel to each other; and great wooden bowls of lettuce, and silver bowls of celery and olives in ice; and platters of vegetables of every kind, some steaming and some cold; and at the far end of the table a man in a chef's hat cutting thick slabs of red roast beef from a long chunk of carcass on a platter over two spirit flames, and at the end near Hawke another chef passing out curry from a chafing dish a yard wide, with a silver tub of white rice and a wheeled table of condiments flanking him. Bowls of roses and ferns, flaming red candles, decorated the table from end to end. A sideboard was laden with a dozen different cakes, creamy, or chocolate, or pink. The guests were slashing at this panorama of food like sharks at a dead whale, and they had already gouged away much of it. The chatter, and the clanking of silver and

china, and the laughter, and "Silent Night, Holy Night" pouring from a loudspeaker, added up to a noise like a waterfall. Frieda Winter said something to Hawke and he merely saw her lips move. He shrugged, and bent down to her. Her perfume was like the scent of primroses, faint and wild and sweet. He had never smelled a perfume like it. She said in his ear, with a touch of warm breath, "Do we fight or wait?"

Hawke roared, "Fight!"

"Done!" She slipped into a crevice in the wall of guests, and he was able to follow her. She whisked plates and silver for both of them from piles on the table. As she glanced around at the food her eyes gleamed, and her tongue moved slowly across her upper lip, in an unconscious childish gesture. Then she plunged in. Following her lead, he was able to load his plate almost at once; he took things as she pointed to them. They broke out of the crowd, laughing at each other. She said in the foyer, "Look, there are two peaceful places where we can eat all this, Fanny's bedroom or the library. Where to?"

"The library." He remembered that Jeanne Green was there.

"This way." Frieda Winter went tripping up a narrow staircase, with a decent display of charming legs. When they came to the landing Hawke made a remark that sounded idiotic as it issued from his mouth. "Is Mr. Winter here?"

"He's in Jamaica with the children. I had to stay in town on business, damn it. But it isn't so bad. We've been avoiding Christmas in town for years. It's a mess but I find it's gay, after all."

"How many children do you have?"

"Four," Frieda Winter said brightly, and she led him into the library.

3

There was nobody in the long quiet room but Jeanne Green, Karl Fry, and a bartender.

It was the kind of room that usually made Hawke feel a little drunk, so stacked was it with books; books, his other better world, his food, his blood bank, his narcotic. But at the moment he was well caught in this world. He had scarcely a glance for the long rows of leather-bound classics mounting from the floor higher than his head, nor did he scan, as he ordinarily would have, the ranks of best sellers in fiction and non-fiction of twenty years, prim in their first paper jackets, nor the special section of Prince House books. He made straight for Jeanne Green with long strides. "Hi, why aren't you eating? It's a Roman feast down there."

The girl was standing at the bar in her very smart hat, picking at the upper arm of one of her black gloves. "Hi. Oh, I will . . . Damn, I bor-

rowed my roommate's white fox just to look elegant enough for this carnival, and see how it shed! I look as though I'd been tarred and feathered."

Hawke hadn't noticed the white hairs all over the girl before, but now he did. He laughed, and so did Jeanne. He said, "Here, take this plate and eat."

"Why? I can get my own. Thanks anyway. I have a drink to finish." Jeanie swept a highball off the bar and ducked her head into it.

"I have a drink to begin," Fry said from the depths of an armchair beside a big brownish globe of the world, holding out a glass to Hawke. "Be a good boy."

Hawke passed the squat glass to the bartender, who put one ice cube into it and filled it to the brim with twenty-year-old Scotch.

"Hello, Frieda," said Fry. "How wags the world?"

Mrs. Winter, perching herself on an ottoman near him, said, "Hello, Karl. Am I wrong, or have you lost weight?"

"Bachelors either get fat, cooking for themselves, or they wither, eating out of cans," Fry said. "Since my divorce I've lost twenty pounds."

"Eat this," said Hawke.

"Sure I will." Fry accepted the plate, put aside his drink and began eating quickly.

Jeanne said to Hawke, "I'll get plates for both of us. Let's see, what did you take? Roast beef, lobster, artichoke . . ."

"I'd better come. You'll be trampled," Hawke said.

"I ate for a year and a half in Washington cafeterias. I can carry a full tray of food through a lynch mob going the other way."

Frieda Winter was peering attentively at her. She said, "You're Miss Green, aren't you? You wouldn't let Jock Maas read Mr. Hawke's manuscript."

Jeanne said with some wariness, "That's right."

"Don't you two know each other?" Fry said. "Jeanie Green, Frieda Winter."

Mrs. Winter said, "It's a pleasure to meet someone who can stand up to Jock."

"He did whirl and howl some," Jeanne said. "Of course I knew who he was, but a novel manuscript isn't a newborn hippo in the zoo for all to see. It's a property."

"I'm sure Mr. Hawke's script is a valuable property."

"It's extremely valuable," Jeanne said. In a slight silence the two women inspected each other, with Hawke lounging between them against the bar. The only sound was the scrape of Karl Fry's knife and fork.

"Mrs. Winter is producing a Shaw play with Mr. Maas," Hawke said.

"I read about it," Jeanne said. "I'm looking forward to seeing it, if Mr. Maas will let me into the theatre."

"You'll come to opening night as my guest," Frieda Winter said, smiling at the girl. "It's the least you deserve for facing Jock down. Besides we do want to make a play of *Alms for Oblivion*, at least Jock's convinced me we do, and you seem to have custody of it."

"Anybody can take it away from me if Mr. Hawke says so."

Hawke said, "I'm beginning to think it's in pretty safe stowage."

Mrs. Winter said to Jeanne Green, "I like your hat." She said it with total sincerity, looking at the girl with obvious admiration. Hawke could not understand why, at that exact moment, the hat dissolved from an odd only slightly extravagant article into a coarse and comic absurdity. Suddenly it seemed that Jeanne Green was wearing a slice of blueberry pie on her head, with a long feather in it.

"Thank you, Mrs. Winter." Jeanne turned to Hawke. "I'm going to get my food."

"Bring me more," said Fry. "And bring me curry. I smelled curry when we came in."

In the hallway outside the library Jeanne ripped the hat from her head and in quick gestures stripped the long gloves from her pretty white arms. Hawke said, "Now what?" Jeanne stalked into a pink bedroom where women's furs were heaped on two beds, and viciously poked gloves and hat inside a white fox stole. "What's the matter?" Hawke said, following her.

"I got hot," Jeanne said. "Let's go eat."

In the library Frieda Winter was asking Fry how he knew Hawke. Fry told the story: a faulty chimney in one of Greenwich Village's worst old houses had poured smoke from his fireplace into the fireplace of Hawke's room upstairs. "He came down coughing and raging. It was three in the morning, and truth to tell I was entertaining a babe who admires my poetry but is otherwise a horror, but female, and we were both in bed. But after some yelling the three of us got drunk on beer and we toasted cheese and hot dogs in the fire, and that was it. Eventually he moved to a loft room in the furniture district for which he pays virtually nothing. We've remained friendly. I've been reading the book right along and criticizing it, not that he listens much. He's a torrential writer, and a wholesome egomaniac, all in all."

"Is his book good?"

"Good?" Fry put aside the well-cleaned plate, and drank half his Scotch. "What do you mean?" Frieda Winter said nothing, her eyes fixed on the poet. His chin was sunk to his chest. "Will it sell? I'm not sure. I think he may be a genius, a sort of ignorant empty-headed genius, one of these divine harps the wind blows on and they make music without knowing what the hell they're doing. Like Dickens, like Balzac, like Twain, to a certain extent like Sinclair Lewis. Every one of them was an arrant idiot,

you know. No real ideas. Maybe Shakespeare was too, who can say? In the case of those other birds we have their considered pronouncements on matters of the day, and it's the babble of bright children. I think you have to have something invincibly childlike in you to be an artist. So that you always see things fresh, as they are, as they happen, instead of abstracting and analyzing like a man of reason."

"Let me translate this into English," Mrs. Winter said. "Hawke isn't a communist, though you've done your best to talk him into it."

Fry said, "Huh huh" through a half smile. "He doesn't know that the science of economics exists. But that's all right, it may even be an advantage."

Mrs. Winter put her plate aside. "Do you think there's a play in the book?"

"Yes, because there's a strong story, and characters with thick greasepaint colors. Mind you I don't *like* Hawke's book, but then all novelizing seems crude and sloppy writing to me, and I include their precious Flaubert." He finished his drink. "Anything can happen to Hawke. He carries a very high charge. He can fizzle out, the way they all do nowadays, or he can sweep up all the marbles, if he somehow continues on. There's no competition today for a real ignorant-savage genius, if that's what Artie is."

"Artie?"

"Mr. Youngblood Hawke's name is Arthur. Art, actually. Artie annoys him."

Frieda Winter slowly said, "Arthur Hawke . . . That's more like it. Arthur . . ."

"Frieda, I've had a lot of Scotch, but I've also had some food now. I should be seeing fairly clearly. You're very beautiful tonight. Rather blindingly beautiful, to tell the truth." The sarcasm faded out of his voice. He spoke humbly.

Frieda said, her eyes lighting with pleasure, "Well, I'm holding it off, Karl, holding it off. I'm a soufflé that's barely standing up. One day somebody'll make a loud noise near me and I'll flatten into a fat old lady."

"Never. I felt sorry for little Jeanie," Karl said. "No contest."

"Contest? What are you talking about? What does she do exactly?"

Karl told her, adding, "She styles my books, and she's very able at it. Of course, knowing she's there, I've become a total slob. I never even look at the pages once I've typed them."

"Your poetry, too?"

"My poetry!" The slumping little figure in brown suddenly straightened as though air had been blown into a rubber doll. "D'you suppose I *type* my poetry, Frieda, for God's sake?" Then he sank back. "What poetry? My mysteries, dear. The Case of the Leper's Missing Nose."

4

The good-natured combat around the buffet dinner was still going strong; guests two and three deep were clustered around the table, scooping and stabbing away. "Noël, Noël, born is the King of Israel," a chorus of strong male voices chanted over the din.

"Aren't all these people rich? Why are they swarming at this food like cannibals?" Hawke said. "They can all go out to the best restaurants and eat themselves insensible in comfort, can't they?"

"It's free. Free food does something to people," Jeanne said. "I noticed that at church suppers when I was a little girl. Put out anything for free, just some old frankfurters and fried potatoes, and the most dignified grownups, yes, and the richest man in town, and even the minister and his prissy wife, turned into panic-stricken hogs."

"Well, let's dive at the trough," Hawke said, and they did.

Jeanne said, when her plate was piled high, "Come with me." She slipped around a Chinese screen, through the swinging door into the steamy odorous kitchen, and Hawke followed. He caught a glimpse of a large white-tiled room full of clamoring maidservants and men in kitchen garb, and then Jeanne slid through another door, and they were in a quiet little room furnished like a parlor in Hovey with worn commonplace chairs, lamps, and tables.

"Imagine a way of life where servants had sitting rooms," Jeanne said. "Fanny's lucky to have bought this old house while the buying was good."

"Is that mob in the kitchen all her servants?"

"Of course not. That's the caterer's staff." She sank into a chair. "Let Karl wait. I hate eating in a mob."

It occurred to Hawke that there was not much of a mob in the library. "Who is Frieda Winter, exactly?" he said, beginning to eat thick lobster chunks in a light cheese sauce. He was startled by the exquisite taste.

"Mrs. Winter is quite a celebrity," Jeanne said. "She runs a concert bureau, invests in plays, does lots of things. Culture is her line. She was a concert pianist, and during the war she was on ever so many committees, and all that. It's just a name you keep seeing in the papers."

"This food, Jeanie! It's unbelievable. At least for an automat denizen like me."

"Well, you'll soon get to where you can eat like this all the time."

"You think so?"

"Yes." They looked into each other's eyes, and they were alone in the dingy room, and Hawke felt a stir of desire for this small girl with the red hair.

He discounted the feeling. He was in a fevered state about sex, and he

knew it. A few months ago he had almost proposed to a waitress in a coffee shop, a vulgar blonde with big breasts and swelling hips, who for a few weeks had seemed to him a bruised and charming angel of the lower world whom he was going to lift with himself to exalted heights. He had taken her to plays; he had read Swinburne and Yeats to her. His skin crawled every time he remembered any detail of the episode, down to the denouement when he had spent a whole insane night in the rain outside her apartment house and had seen her enter at three in the morning with a greasy-looking man of forty, both laughing drunkenly. At dawn the man had not come out, and Hawke had never gone back to the coffee shop.

He had had several such experiences since his sixteenth year. He had never leaned his trust upon a girl without her breaking in some way and making him bleed. Hawke was desperately lonesome for a woman; but who was this Jeanne Green? Just a girl he had stumbled upon in a publisher's office. A little while ago he had been feeling much the same instant and upsetting attraction toward a woman who had four children. He was far off balance, steady was the word.

"In other words," he said, "you think my book will sell."

"If not this one, the next."

"Karl Fry and Waldo Fipps both want me to cut the guts out of it. What do you think?"

Jeanne took a long time to answer. "I know what they mean. I could suggest cuts, but that's not my job. Unless you cut very, very carefully, I think it's best to leave your book as it is. Don't tell Waldo I said so. I'm not paid to think."

"Have you begun—ah, styling my book?"

"Yes. The order came down this morning, straight from Jay Prince. He wants to get the book out by June. I have it at home so I can work on it over the holiday."

"I call that devotion to duty."

"Well, I'm interested."

"Don't you have a fellow, and dates, and all that?"

"At the moment, no," Jeanne said. "Nothing that would interfere with anything." So, with an unpremeditated and not quite truthful word, ended her current romance. The lawyer she had thought last week she might marry was in Denver with his family. She knew nothing yet about Hawke, but she knew that the lawyer, for all she cared at this moment, could stay forever in Denver.

"Where do you live?"

"About six blocks from here, in a furnished hole off Third Avenue, where fashionable people aren't found dead."

"Can we go to your place when we leave here, and have a look at what you're doing with the book?"

"Why not?" Jeanne said, and her head swam a little, and her throat

closed against the food. She stood, brushing her dress. "I'm feeling guilty about Karl Fry. Let's bring him his seconds."

At the table Hawke found himself next to Ferdie Lax, the Hollywood agent, who was getting more curry. "Enjoying yourself?" Lax said. The crowd had much lessened in the room. The feast was demolished. The dead heads of the two salmons stared from their clean-picked skeletons at the wreckage up and down the long table, and the red candles were dripping and running in long winding sheets. The roses drooped in the hot room, their petals scattering.

"Wonderful party," Hawke said.

"A little more rice, please," Lax said to the waiter. "Yes, Fanny does these things well. What kind of contract did you sign with Jay, Mr. Hawke? Standard Prince House form?"

"I think so."

"You have a copy?"

"Yes."

"What does the movie rights clause provide, do you recall?"

"I don't know. Mr. Prince said it was a good contract. He suggested I show it to a lawyer or agent, but I thought I could take his word for it." Lax blinked. A little uneasy, Hawke added, "He gave me a five-thousand-dollar advance."

"That's a fine advance for a first novel. You ought to check the movie rights clause before you sign a contract. It can be important." Lax smiled sleepily, nodding. "I'm sure Jay gave you a fine contract. Have fun."

Hawke said to Jeanne when Lax strolled away, "Do you know him?"

"No. Did you sign a contract without an agent or a lawyer?"

"Sure. Jay Prince doesn't strike me as a crook."

"He's a business man. He looks out for himself, and you're supposed to look out for yourself."

"All right, I'll check the contract tomorrow. If he's slipped something over on me then he's made a crude mistake, and he'll be sorry for it."

"I daresay it's all right," Jeanne said.

5

The tide of the party had flowed into the library. There were dozens of people in the smoky book-lined room, gossiping in small groups, or singing carols in a cluster around the baby grand piano. Most of them held shimmering bell-glasses of brandy. Frieda Winter was playing, her face alight with amusement as she added her voice to the shaky harmonies; but while she sang, and made faces at false notes, and cracked jokes, her hands like the hands of another person struck out the music with strength and

accuracy. Hawke lingered at the piano, watching those controlled and business-like white hands and the laughing face.

Jeanne brought Karl Fry his food. Fry looked up at her with an alcoholic bob of the head. "What? Did I ask for that?" He held a full glass of Scotch rather limply in a hand resting on the chair arm.

"Yes, and maybe you'd better eat it."

"Jeanie, my dear, I recently shed a wife who used those tones to me. I may have to get myself another stylist." He waved a soft hand weakly at her.

The round-faced tall man sitting on the other arm of his chair said, "She's quite right, Karl, eat it. You'll enjoy the booze more, and longer." He was Ross Hodge, a publisher by inheritance, head of the old strong house called Hodge Hathaway.

Fry took the plate of curry and ate. Jeanne looked around for Hawke and saw his head and a brown shoulder towering over the black huddle at the piano. She made for him.

Fry said to Hodge, "She's styling the Hawke manuscript. Why don't you waylay her and ask her a few questions?"

"Look, Karl, I've never stolen an author or a manuscript and I've never suborned someone else's employees."

"Then why are you climbing all over me?"

"I'm not climbing on you."

"Ross, you've all but got an elbow down my throat this minute."

Hodge was indeed leaning very close to Fry. He drew back a little. "I think I have a right to express surprise, that's all. If Jay publishes your mysteries, we've published your poetry, and I rather thought you set more store by that."

"I set store by nothing I write. It just didn't occur to me to send Hawke to you, Ross. It's a crude book, not the Hodge Hathaway kind of thing. It's a natural for Prince."

"Why?"

"Well, for one thing, it may just sell like hell if he puts on the old Prince House jazzeroo campaign."

"We're very interested in books that sell like hell. I hear the book's an exciting literary discovery, and that this man is a new major writer."

"Who says so? Nobody's read it yet but a few people at Prince. Naturally they're all beating tin pans."

"Has he signed, or is there a chance to bid still?"

"Ross, you don't even know what the book is about."

"There's a smell to these things. Everybody at this party is talking Youngblood Hawke, Youngblood Hawke."

"He upstaged the whole precious mob of you by showing up in a brown suit, that's all."

"Well, *is* the book available?"

"I truly don't know, Ross. From the look of things here you'd be snatching it out of Jay's jaws, at best."

"He's snatched a thing or two out of my jaws," Ross Hodge said, and he walked to the piano. Hawke was well hemmed in among the singers. Jock Maas and Jay Prince had each thrown an arm around him. Jock's other arm enfolded the slim shoulders of Jeanne Green, their feud having been dissolved with a greeting and a joke. Ferdie Lax was snuggled up to Jay Prince, his blond head hooked into the publisher's large elbow, and Fanny was leaning amiably on Lax, her own waist in the grip of a large brutal-looking dark man, Roberto Luzzatto, a European film producer who lived in constantly shifting states of affluence or bankruptcy. Luzzatto had been pumping Fanny industriously about the Hawke novel, and he knew the plot. To him, too, it smelled like money.

> *"The hopes and fears*
> *Of all the years*
> *Are met in thee tonight,"*

chanted some twenty people clustering around the massive young writer in brown. The only hole Ross Hodge could find was in the space above Ferdie Lax's head, so he threw his arms around Jay and Fanny and added his voice to the song. Hawke glanced around at him, and Hodge grinned almost flirtatiously.

Hawke knew that Ross Hodge was a publisher. He saw that something was happening around him, that he was becoming the center of a mild unacknowledged stampede. He was puzzled in the midst of his soaring exhilaration; after all, he had met a United States Senator tonight, and a successful playwright, as well as people like Quentin Judd and Frieda Winter. By comparison, who was he? He sensed the answer; these people all knew each other, but he was a novelty, and there might be money in him. What surprised him was that people as famous and as well-to-do as these could care so much about novelty and money; it was something like the odd discovery that they could act like a Sunday school picnic crowd over a buffet of rich food.

Frieda Winter looked up and laughed into his eyes as she played and sang. The glances of Frieda Winter cut into Youngblood Hawke like a cold wind that makes one brace and glow. She banged the last chords of the song, and jumped up. "I quit. I want my brandy. Who plays? Ross, come on."

Hodge said, "I'm not following a professional," but he was cried down, and went not unwillingly to the piano stool. Mrs. Winter stood passing her hands over a slightly moist white brow, and over her soft curled hair.

"Let me get you your brandy, Mrs. Winter," Hawke said.

"Well, thank you. I guess you can fight through, with those broad shoulders."

The two swift speeches caught the attention of the people around the piano; the talking and laughing faded down for a moment as though a dial had been turned, and glances went from the woman to the young man, and then the moment passed and the chattering flared up. Someone began to sing "Good King Wenceslas," and Hodge at the piano picked up the melody, and all joined in.

As Hawke broke out of the circle Prince came with him, saying, "Frieda deserves something special." He pulled a dusty bottle from a lower drawer of the bar, and told the bartender to pour three glasses. "Did the contract come in the mail?"

"Yes."

"Good. I thought it might have gotten swamped in the Christmas rush."

"I signed a copy and mailed it back to you, and kept the other one," Hawke said. The publisher merely nodded, looking not in the least pleased, or relieved, or concerned. Hawke added, "I didn't look it over too carefully. Should I have? There was a lot of small print."

"Well, it always pays to read anything you sign, Hawke. The small print is mostly warranties against plagiarism and such."

"What happens with the movie rights?"

The publisher gave him two glasses of brandy. "You'll find those in the long clause on the third page about subsidiary rights—book clubs, reprints, phonograph records, and all the various devices known to man for exploiting a book. We share all those equally."

"Is that standard?"

"On a first novel, I'd say so. Some publishers want more to minimize the risks of launching a new writer. Fifty-fifty seems a fair shake to me."

"Sounds okay," Hawke said.

Mrs. Winter accepted the brandy with a convivial laugh, and raised the glass. "Your novel, Mr. Hawke."

"Merry Christmas, Mrs. Winter."

Hawke went to the immense silver coffee urn, where Ferdie Lax was helping himself. The agent poured coffee for him, and said, "Roberto Luzzatto is hot about your novel."

"I hope he remains hot after he reads it."

"My advice to you is to sell it to pictures before publication if you can. Don't gamble on the first one. You'll make less money if it turns out a hit, but it'll be sure money. I'll try if you like."

"Thanks, I'll think about it." The very word agent had an unsavory odor to Hawke, and he thought this man pretty pushing and crude.

Lax said, as though Hawke's thoughts were running across his forehead like a news bulletin on the Times Building, "Of course you think I'm pushing. My business is representing writers. Take your time. Some day you may want my advice."

"I checked on my movie rights. The publishers and I share them fifty-fifty."

"Fifty-fifty," Lax repeated slowly and drowsily. He closed his eyes, and held them closed so long that Hawke thought the man might collapse. Then Lax reached into a breast pocket and gave him a card. "I'm at the St. Regis. I'm sailing for Europe tomorrow night. I'll be back in Hollywood in February. Maybe we can talk then."

Hawke took the card. "Well, are those standard terms?"

"Have you signed the contract?"

"Yes."

"For one book?"

"Well, for one, yes, but sort of for three, in a way."

Lax nodded, and walked off sipping coffee, without another word. Hawke saw Frieda Winter sitting alone, her eyes meditatively on him. She smiled and beckoned. "Is Ferdie laying his snares for you?"

"It's hardly subtle enough to be called laying snares, Mrs. Winter."

"Call me Frieda, for heaven's sake. Don't be a boy."

"That's the third time I've been called a boy this evening. A boy! I'm losing my hair, do you know that?"

"Ah'm losin' mah hayuh . . . you don't say. That thick mop? Let me hear you say 'house.'"

"Hass?" Hawke said, puzzled.

"Hass . . . I thought so. West Virginia?"

"Kentucky. Letchworth County where I come from is almost on the border."

"Are you going to put this party in a book some day, and show us all up cruelly?"

Hawke looked around the room. "My ignorance is beginning to bother me."

"Why?"

"This place is full of things I can't even name, let alone describe. That's the key to the whole place, isn't it? The things. A clutter of costly possessions to make something out of nothing in a hurry. I don't know what it is, but the things haven't weathered together. Do you know what I mean, Mrs. Winter? Not bad taste, not even a lack of blending, the blending is just fine, the colors and all. But there's no weathering, no *age*, for all the antiques. This apartment is a stage set, isn't it? Is that why New Yorkers prize antiques, because they give a stage touch of permanence to what's really a tent for the night?" None of this speech was premeditated. Hawke had not even been aware of these thoughts. They burst from him as paragraphs sometimes spurted from his pen on to the yellow paper.

Frieda Winter stared at him. "I wonder whether I should be offended. I decorated this apartment."

Hawke said uneasily, "I'm sorry."

"Don't apologize, you fool. Never, never apologize. I'll say this for myself, Fanny was breathing down my neck all the time, and it's really her doing as much as mine." She looked around at the room, head down, as though she had just walked into it.

"Mind you, Mrs. Winter, I think it's lovely, really stunning—"

She said slowly, "I believe I'd like to read your *Alms for Oblivion*."

"I'd like you to read it. Are you an interior decorator?"

"I decorate. I do a lot of things. I decorate very well, but it's only fun doing it for friends."

"I'm desperate to find out something about decorating. What should I read? Where shall I begin? Where are the books?"

"Well, as good a place as any is 935 Fifth Avenue."

"What's that, a library?"

"It's my home. I think I have as complete a collection of books on decoration, and architecture, and all that, as anybody does. You're welcome to come any time and make free with our books."

"That's very kind of you. When can I come without inconveniencing you? I'm about to write a scene in a rich man's house in Virginia. I don't know how to furnish it."

"Shouldn't a writer only write about what he knows?"

"I know the truth of what will happen in my story. I need external details."

"Well, why don't you come in tomorrow, noonish, and I'll give you coffee and turn you loose in the library? That is, if you intend to work Christmas Day."

"I intend to work." Hawke was thinking that if he did his night's writing, as he rigidly meant to do, a noon appointment would leave him little time for sleep. But the Winter library struck him as a find, and the prospect of coffee with Mrs. Winter had a glitter too. "I'll come with pleasure."

"Good. I have to leave for the country about one, so you'll be able to dig around undisturbed."

Hawke now felt his waist circled and gripped in a heavy hug and he smelled a strong leathery perfume. Roberto Luzzatto said to Mrs. Winter, squeezing Hawke in a hard friendly way, "Frieda, introduce me please to this talented young man." Mrs. Winter did, and Luzzatto went on, "From what I hear about your book, I am excited. It sounds like a picture. Can I read it?"

"I'm afraid not. I'm editing it, and there's only one complete manuscript."

"I come and look at it in your office, or wherever it is. I don't disturb you. I read fast."

Mrs. Winter said, "Oh, Roberto, wait for galleys like everybody else."

"Galleys will be weeks, maybe months. I'm stalled on my Russian

movie, the Soviet officials find new excuses every day to do nothing, hm? I can go to work tomorrow on a good property. What do you say, Mr. Hawke, a quick deal, a good deal? Cash and a percentage, hm? Where can I see your manuscript? When?"

All the lights in the room went out. There was sudden silence and then a babble of questioning voices in the dark which changed to laughter and shouts of pleasure. Floating through the darkness in the orange-and-blue flames of burning brandy, barely lighting the face of the waiter carrying it, came an immense round plum pudding, decorated with branches of holly.

"Hurrah! The pudding," Frieda Winter cried like a child. She jumped up and seized Hawke's hand. "Come on, I'm mad for it! Aren't you?"

The pudding was set on a coffee table, and everyone in the room gathered around, shadowy figures in the light of the flames. Hawke heard Quentin Judd's unforgettable giggle, and then his high voice, "The wise ones stick around, don't they, Fanny?"

"For the inner circle, the real friends, ve give something extra," Fanny said. "Christmas is Christmas, no?"

"Who cuts it?" somebody said. "Jay, Jay," said one voice, and another "No, Fanny."

Fanny Prince pushed up to the pudding, holding a long knife that glinted orange in the flames. "No, this year is something special. This year I think ve give the honor to a young man, so some day you all say you ate a piece of cake he cut for you. Vare is Mr. Youngblood Hoke? Mr. Hoke!"

A chorus of laughter showed the choice was popular. Hawke said, "I'll make a real mess of it."

"No you won't. Come on!"

Hawke stepped forward, took the knife, and made a deep gash in the soft flaming ball. There was a cheer, and then Fanny's excited voice, "All right, lights! Turn on the lights!"

The library was flooded with electric light again, and the guests blinked at each other and chattered with animation. Karl Fry was standing at Hawke's elbow, weaving a little. He said loudly, in a drunken declamatory voice, slapping Hawke on the shoulder,

> *"Now first, my boy, a slice for Fanny,*
> *Every author's favorite nanny."*

"Oh, good. Marvellous. Rhymes, like you used to do, Karl! Like the old days," Fanny exclaimed, clapping her hands, and accepting the first piece from the waiter.

Fry said,

> *"And now a slice for ol' Jay Prince,*
> *If Ross Hodge steals you, Jay will wince."*

There was a roar of laughter, and Fry went on, his eyes glittering,

"But give a meager slice to Hodge,
While he cooks up some artful dodge."

Ross Hodge said in confusion, accepting the pudding amid laughter, "I protest. He's all yours, Jay, and congratulations."

"Cut it real thick for Quentin Judd,
Offend him, lad, and your name is mud."

The guests, none of whom were sober, greeted the rhymes with appreciative laughs, and poked and slapped at each other. Mrs. Winter cried, "Karl, this is your old form. Keep it up, keep it up!"

"For Frieda Winter, cut it hot—"

Fry paused. Everyone looked at him in suspense. He grinned crookedly and said,

"Her name is cold, but she is not."

It was the biggest laugh yet, a ribald yell that puzzled Hawke and that sent Mrs. Winter and Fanny Prince into wild guffawing. Fanny said, "Oh vy did everybody go away? Now the party first gets good."
Karl said,

"No pudding, please, for Ferdie Lax,
Just give him the knife for Hollywood backs."

Lax threw back his head and laughed with huge enjoyment.
So Fry went around the circle of guests, rapping out the rhymes as fast as Hawke could cut slices. When the last slice was cut and Hawke himself took it, Fry said,

"My boy, your main job's still to do,
Now cut us all a piece of you."

Rhyming without forethought at a party is always a successful coup, providing the jingles come quickly and with point. The shabby little man in the brown suit and the blue shirt was now in command of the evening. Applause rippled when he finished, and men slapped his back, and women giggled and repeated his rhymes. He had moved to the bar and was leaning on it, and the guests were all facing him.

He said, "Well, thank you, thank you, one and all. I aim to please. It isn't often I'm invited these days to the running of a stag, and I thought I ought to show my appreciation."

"The running of a stag, Karl?" Fanny said, still laughing as she doled out great gobs of hard sauce on each guest's pudding.

"A stag of warrant, a stag, a stag,
A runnable stag, a kingly crop,
Brow, bay, and tray, and three on top,
A stag, a runnable stag,"

said Fry. "Davidson's not a great poet, but that one I envy him. Of course you have to know stag hunting to write such a poem. I've only read about it in books. They all gathered on horseback in great excitement, the gentlemen of the county, you know, when they heard that someone had started a runnable stag. What made a stag runnable I don't know. Much the same qualities I would guess that make a bull brave—it had to be big, male, full of fight, and worthy of being harried to death. It wasn't vermin, like a fox. It was a stag, a stag, a runnable stag, a royal beast, and running it to death was a pleasure for rich men. It was a long and wonderful pleasure. The ladies loved it, too, running the big male thing to death. The hunters ran it all over the countryside, they ran it with hounds and with horns, they lost it in riverbeds and found it in forests, they surrounded it and closed in on it and wore out even the fierce and marvellous energy of a stag, and at last its fuel burned out, it slowed and it stumbled, and it went down under the jumping dogs, and the party roared up all around the fallen beast. It lay there sobbing, the book says, looking at you with tragic eyes under the snarling, snapping triumphant pack of dogs. And a gamekeeper pulled its head back by its branching horns, took out a sharp knife and offered the loveliest lady in the party the cutting of the stag's throat. And that was the end of the stag."

Nobody talked when Fry stopped to drink. Hawke at last said, "Karl, didn't the stag ever outrun his pursuers and live to a ripe and royal old age?"

"I don't know anything about stag hunting. I believe he occasionally did. But you won't, Youngblood Hawke."

Then a thick silence fell. Fanny Prince said, "Karl, it's far from funny, we're all having a good time. I don't know why you—"

"Fanny, I'm being a miserable bastard after drinking nearly a whole bottle of the best Scotch I've had in years. The unsuccessful should stay away from such gatherings. They get self-conscious and mean. They want to shout dirty words and break mirrors. I am jealous of watching everybody clustering around young Hawke tonight, you see. I'm leaving now. Merry Christmas to all, and to all a good night." He walked down the long room. Nobody said a word until he was out, and his steps were heard on the stairs. Then Fanny stood uncertainly, looking around. "Poor Karl. A genius, a fabulous talent. I get the man to put him in a taxicab."

When she came back to the library people were shaking hands, saying goodbyes, moving toward the door. Only half a dozen or so remained at the bar, drinking with Jay Prince. Hawke assured her that he had had a superb evening, and that Karl Fry's sourness was an old joke to him. Jock Maas and Frieda Winter tried to take him with them to another party, but he declined. Mrs. Winter said nothing about their appointment next day. He wondered whether she had forgotten. Jeanne Green had disappeared from the library; had she too forgotten that they were going to her apartment? Hawke made his farewells and went downstairs, after glancing into the pink bedroom and observing that Jeanne's white fur was gone.

In the lobby below, the butler was helping Ferdie Lax with his black coat; no sign of Jeanne Green. It occurred to Hawke to wonder at the quiet way Lax managed to be in his path every so often, available for a question if he wanted to ask one—as he did. "Mr. Lax, I'm glad we met tonight. I know very little about contracts, I don't know whether I want an agent, but I sure would like to get some solid information."

Lax said, "Look, I'm a human being and you're a human being. Let's walk down Fifth Avenue and talk, if you're not doing anything else."

"I thought I had a date but it seems I don't." Lax smiled at the sight of his duffle coat. "Well, it keeps me warm."

"Have no fear, you'll be able to buy good clothes pretty soon."

"There's the first thing I want to ask you. How do you know? More people at this party seem sure I'm the new Sinclair Lewis, or something, but nobody's read my book, how can they *know*?"

"Hawke, these people can smell talent. Of course they make mistakes. Anyway talk is cheap. Nobody'll give you a quarter till they see your script. I'd like very much to read it, by the way."

They walked out into a frosty night. In the black band of sky over the lamplit gray façades of the houses, there were a few sharp blue points of stars. "Damn clear night," Lax said. "Good air. Seems like I've been in Fanny's house for a week."

Jeanne Green was there after all, leaning against the iron grillwork in front of the Prince house—funny hat, long gloves, white fox stole. She waved hesitantly to him. Hawke said, "There's my date."

Lax looked at the girl, and nodded. "Well, shall we talk some more tomorrow? My boat doesn't sail until midnight."

"You'll be busy."

"Nonsense," Lax murmured sleepily. "Come to the St. Regis at six. We'll have dinner."

"Thanks."

Swift as a striking cat's paw, Lax's hand shot up and stopped a cab going by.

CHAPTER THREE

1

JEANNE stood in a light blue silk slip, regarding herself in the narrow closet mirror of her tiny bedroom. In the next room Hawke was flopped on the sofa in front of the fire, his jacket, tie, and shoes off, drinking brandy and looking at her corrections to his manuscript. Jeanne was shifting from her evening dress to a housecoat, and the decision in two words was, business or romance? She owned a green silk robe that clung and flattered and revealed, and several sturdy opaque ones. Jeanne had a fairly sure touch with clothes, but Youngblood Hawke upset and confused her. She was still smarting over the disaster of the hat, a hideously costly thing on which she had splurged her entire Christmas bonus, simply because she had known she would be seeing Hawke at the Prince party. She had slipped into the error of trying too hard, a mistake that she scorned in other women; and she had laid herself open to Mrs. Winter's destructive little compliment.

It is hardly an exaggeration to say that Jeanne had all but fallen in love with the author on reading the first seven pages of his manuscript. She had been styling dull trash for months. Hawke's headlong narrative attack, his vivid character strokes, his coarse but strong humor, had awakened an instant and growing excitement in her; and then the man himself had walked into Fipps' office. He was not good-looking, but what did that matter? He was big and broad-shouldered, and he exuded the crude power that was in his manuscript. Jeanne had once hoped to be a writer herself. She had abandoned the dream, but to her a man who could create was godlike. An occasional glimpse of a famous writer at Prince House had made any day bearable. Now here was one of these demigods in her living room: unknown, young, lonesome, attractive to her. She was certain that he was destined for a great career. She suspected that he liked her. Well, then? What to wear?

All one's life goes into any decision, small or big. Jeanne chose a housecoat which she wore for comfort, a flowered yellow linen print, cheerful and unadventurous. She had been in and out of love since her fourteenth year; she had been engaged twice. She had never had an illicit love affair; her grand unlucky passion had involved a married man and she had been quite incapable of going to bed with him. Yet there was little she did

not know about the manners of men. She wanted to captivate Hawke more than she had ever wanted anything in her life; but though her judgment had deserted her in the matter of the hat, it now took hold again.

Jeanne was extremely pretty; she had confidence in her good looks, but her chief point in her own judgment was her brain. She was the only daughter of a drab dentist and a very ordinary mother, and she had grown up in a small town near Los Angeles. By some freak of heredity she had been born with intelligence that had carried her through school days at the very top of her class, with such trophies of energetic brightness as presidencies, editorships, and a Phi Beta Kappa key. She chose the opaque housecoat because Hawke had come to her apartment for a business conference. Though it was nearly midnight of Christmas Eve she was going to stick to business. It was up to Hawke to shift the ground. "The hell with him," was the way she put it to herself. Out into the living room she marched. "Well, have I marred your masterpiece? Am I fired?"

Hawke, of course, was not unaware of the possibilities of being alone with a pretty girl in her apartment on Christmas Eve, at the end of an exciting evening that had included a lot of alcohol. When Jeanne had withdrawn to take off her party dress, he had experienced the heart-thumping hope that she would return in a seductive negligee; for he did find this small red-headed girl enormously fetching. But meantime he had begun to look at his manuscript. He laid aside some manuscript sheets and sat up. "I was damned annoyed with you there for a while, especially at your suggestions that I change words. But I'm beginning to think I should be grateful. You're doing the last polish I thought I had to do. I've been putting it off because it's such a disgusting chore."

"Not to me it isn't."

"I'll argue with you about some of those words, Jeanne, but not many. Most of the time you're right."

"Well, all I do is check and check and check the dictionary and thesaurus. I don't believe in le mot juste, but I'm all for exact meaning."

"So am I. What's this big red X at the beginning of Chapter Five?"

"Oh, that." She sat beside him on the sofa, smiling nervously. "That may be the end of me."

"Never mind. Out with it."

She wanted him to cut the entire chapter. It disclosed information which emerged again later in the story. Dropping the chapter gave the later scene dramatic surprise, she said, and lost nothing but some colorful descriptions. The author bridled and argued. He said crossly at one point, "Well, why didn't Waldo or Karl suggest that, then? They're all for cuts, and they're free enough with their criticisms—clumsy transitions, derivative rhetoric, and on and on."

Jeanne said, "Such comments on this book are stupid. It's full of faults,

but it's alive from the first page to the last. That's why I think it should be left almost as it is. This suggestion has to do with storytelling. Judging by the way you attack a story, I think the chapter should come out."

Hawke slouched back on the sofa and glared at her. She said at last, "All right, what's the matter? Just shut me up, that's all. Don't stare like that."

"It's the first time," Hawke said, "that anybody's said anything I can use. My family and my shipmates just made meaningless remarks. Waldo Fipps wants me to write like *The New Yorker*, and Karl Fry wants me to write, as near as I can gather, like a communist Hemingway." He fell silent, still staring at her, his eyes rather unfocussed, as though his mind were far off. Suddenly he slapped his knee loudly. "You know what? I'll cut that chapter."

"Okay," Jeanne said, concealing the relief coursing through her body. "Now in this next chapter, there's a question of paragraphing that—"

"Hold on." Hawke stood and paced, a big young man in stocking feet, with hanging hair, a broad rough flushed face with reddened excited eyes, and a mouth compressed to a black line. "Put the manuscript away." She silently obeyed, slipping the sheets into the big envelope. He went on, "Here's what you do. From now on you have my authority to change punctuation and paragraphing without asking me. As for word changes, plot alterations, and cutting, I want you to keep a written record of your ideas and go over them with me, say every three or four days, as you plough through the book. I may not use your suggestions but I want them. Understood?"

"Understood."

The sternness vanished, the awkward boyishness came back, he dropped in an armchair beside the fire and lolled. "Well, all right. Now, Jeanie Green, what did you mean comparing me to O. Henry?"

"I stick to it," she said. "I mean his ability to bring people to life with a stroke. He had little to say and he leaned too much on magazine tricks, but I don't think we ever had a better storyteller."

He held out his brandy glass. "Hm. That's not too offensive, I guess. The fact is I know most of O. Henry by heart, but I thought it was a vice. He's supposed to be beneath contempt."

She refilled his glass. "Oh, what the devil, I'm going to have brandy too. I was going to work after you left." She poured a glass for herself. "To hell with it. A girl's entitled to take Christmas Eve off." She threw a sofa cushion in front of the fire and sat near his feet. They both sipped brandy, and she looked at the flames, and he looked at her.

"I'm enjoying myself," he said, "but this isn't much of a Christmas Eve, is it? For either of us."

"I miss my family," Jeanne said drowsily. "But there's no place I'd

rather be right now. I made my choice. New York is a terrible meat-grinder of a city, but it's the place where things happen."

"You talk like a career girl," Hawke said, "and you obviously have ability, but you don't look like one."

The heat, and the opiate in her cough medicine—she had taken a large dose upon coming home—and the flames, and the release from the fierce tension of the party, and the nearness of this man, all worked a strange effect on Jeanne. She felt herself softly unfolding, opening like a flower in a speeded-up nature movie, uncurling petals and beginning to be her natural self, too fast, and alarmingly. "What do I look like, Mr. Hawke?" she murmured.

Hawke slid out of the armchair and sat on the floor beside her. "Let's see," he said, and he took her by her shoulders. The soft yielding of the girl's frame in his touch was exciting. Flowing into his arms and through his body was a sense of her vulnerability.

A spasm of coughing shook Jeanne. She coughed and coughed, and she was in his arms, coughing hard, leaning against his chest. He held her, worried. "Are you all right?"

"Perfectly, I assure you," she gasped. "The fire's smoking a little." She coughed some more, then became quiet. She sat up, freeing herself shyly from his arms. "Well, so much for act three of *La Traviata*. I'll have to learn that dying aria if this keeps up. Sorry." With a poker, she thrust far back in the fireplace a broken log that was leaking smoke into the room. "I've had every X-ray and test known to man. All I've got is a chronic New York cough not helped by cigarettes. Once I was sort of engaged to a doctor. He chased me to a psychoanalyst to find out why I was such a slave to tobacco. The analyst turned out to be a chain-smoker. We had a high old time smoking and talking, and he ended up dating me a few times. He said it was all undoubtedly true about the death wish and oral satisfaction, and all that, but it was also true that cigarettes taste just great." Jeanne took the pack from the low table and lit one with gusto.

"What happened to the doctor?"

"Oh, him. He was in California. When I came to Washington it petered out. That's probably why I went to Washington. I preferred cigarettes to him."

Hawke said, "What puzzles me is that a girl like you is still at large. Seems to me you'd have been speared at sixteen."

Jeanne smiled at him. "Well I'll plead the usual defense. I've had lousy luck."

"Such as?"

Whereupon Jeanne told him the kind of story that many girls had to tell in the days right after the war: of the handsome and clever officer stationed at an Air Force base near her home; of the quick-blazing romance and the discovery that he was married; of his pledge to get a divorce and

his long stalling, coupled with persistent efforts to take her to bed; of a year and a half of futile passionate letter-writing when he was overseas, and his return to his wife and children after the war. "Some girls have said I was crazy not to sleep with him. They say that would have made the difference. I never believed it and besides the beautiful bastard *was* married, you know? I'm not all that enlightened. Or maybe I'm just a cold fish, as I've sometimes been told, and deserved the jilting. Anyway no other guy has really mattered before or since, and so, with this long heart-rending answer to your short question, here I am at large."

"Yes. Spending Christmas Eve with a stranger, catching up on your office work."

"It doesn't seem so bad. At the moment I'm not feeling in the least abused. Quite the contrary."

"Well, I've enjoyed it too." He stood, and so did the girl. They confronted each other, not an arm's length apart. He said, "I guess I have to go and write my fifteen pages."

"It's probably a good idea," Jeanne said. "Have I been talking stupidly? I don't know when I've felt so languid. No bones, and not much cartilage, just a heap of warm protoplasm."

"Protoplasm in a lovely shape," Hawke said. "Versatile stuff. No, you haven't been talking stupidly at all."

"Thank you, Mr. Hawke. I admire your book beyond words, as you may have gathered."

Hawke took her in his arms and kissed her. Hers was a brief wistful answer, but it was a kiss, and a sharply sweet one.

"Merry Christmas, Jeanie Green," he whispered.

"Merry Christmas, Youngblood Hawke. Here's hoping the stag outruns his pursuers. You're off to a good head start."

They stood so, the girl held loosely in the young man's arms, her body pliant, her face turned up to him, her forearms resting on his. Holding Jeanne so was a delicious sensation for Hawke. He pulled her powerfully to him. Her arms slipped around him.

The doorbell rang, a long nervous on-and-off ringing. Jeanne by instinct leaned back. Hawke said, "Expecting anyone?"

"No, my roommate's out for the night."

Another series of rings, impatient and loud; then a pounding of knuckles. "Come on Iris, for Christ's sake, open up the goddamn door." The voice was hoarse, male, slow, and drunken. "Come on, Iris. Iris! Let's go."

"Oh, hell," Jeanne said.

"Iris! What the Christ, Iris, it's Frank." Ringing and pounding. "Open up, baby."

Jeanne said in a low tone, "Iris is a professional lady, so to speak,

who lives on the next floor up. Some drunk or other makes this mistake every few days. A special charm of living in New York."

"I'll get rid of him," Hawke said.

Her hands tightened on his arms. "No! It's simplest to ignore them."

The man's voice became ugly. He beat with both fists on the door. "Iris, goddammit, if some guy's in there getting his I don't mind, I'll come in and wait my goddamn turn. Just open up the goddamn door." There was a short silence and then the man began to shout a stream of obscenities, kicking and pounding.

Hawke tore from Jeanne, strode to the door and flung it open. The man was big, swaying—a gray lean drunken face, a dirty gray hat, a thick nose—a man of fifty or so.

Hawke said, "You're in the wrong place. Shut up and get out of here."

The man looked foggily past him at Jeanne, standing frightened in the middle of the room. He said, "Hey, that stuff looks better than Iris. New girl? I'll take a piece of it too, mister. First I got to go to the can."

He put his hand on Hawke as though to push him aside. Hawke took him by the lapels of his coat, thrust him backwards into the dim-lit hall, and threw him down the stairs. Jeanne, coming to the doorway, uttered a shriek. The man, fortunately, did not go down head first, but caught the bannister with one hand and toppled and stumbled noisily down all the steps, yelling, "Hey! Hey!" and losing his balance only near the bottom, where he fell on his hands and knees on the landing. He crawled around, whimpering and cursing, found his hat, and they could hear him trampling down the last flight of stairs to the street. Hawke came back into the apartment and shut the door.

"That was an insane thing to do," Jeanne said shakily. "You might have killed him."

His arms and legs were trembling. He still felt the explosion of anger in him. He would have enjoyed smashing all the furniture. There was a side of New York he hated, the gray stupid-faced shoving horde of the sidewalks and subways, and the drunk at the door had been all that horde in one dirty malodorous apparition. He said in a thick tone, "Sorry," walked to the brandy bottle, and took a deep drink from it. Then he clasped her in his arms again. But the incident that had just passed made their kisses clumsy and lifeless, and they stopped.

"You have a wild temper," she whispered, looking up at him with a mischievous, somewhat scared smile. "I wouldn't have guessed that."

"Only now and then. What else do you do with such vermin?"

She put her hand briefly to his face. "A new year is starting in a few days. By the time it's over your book will be out, and you'll probably be famous."

"Unless you wreck my masterpiece with your punctuation," Hawke said, "and with your silly suggestions for cutting my best chapters. Thanks for the brandy, Jeanie, and for everything else. Where's that rag-picker's coat of mine? I'd better go back to work."

2

He walked downtown with tremendous strides, almost at a run. The two-mile walk down the lamplit canyon of Fifth Avenue in dry freezing air worked off his fit of anger. The vanity fair of the department store windows always amused and delighted him. He loved the improbable skyscrapers black against the stars, with enough patches of light in them to show that they were webs of power and life, not monuments; and the huge Christmas tree of Rockefeller Center, its colored globes big as basketballs, an extravagance worthy of the extravagant city, a giant dragged with the greatest pains from some remote wilderness to grace the city's revel briefly and then to die; and the stream of beautiful automobiles, and the sweet college girls, escorted by gawky boys, dashing in yellow, pink, and white flounced dresses under dark velvet wraps from one party to another, their faces shining, their hair bright with flowers, their laughter and talk like music played on glass instruments. The air was clean. No air in the world can be more gummy and choking than New York's; but every few days in the winter a keen wind comes from Canada or from the gray Atlantic, and the murk is swept away and the city stands in crystal icy air, the lines of its buildings sharp as though ruled in ink. This was such a night. Hawke walked so fast that the pure cold air came cutting into his lungs, and this sensation, with the universal murmur of the carols from car radios and public loudspeakers, made him think of Hovey, and of his sister and his mother, and of their small house on High Street where a scrawny tree with the battered ornaments his mother saved from year to year undoubtedly stood in the same corner of the parlor, by the old upright piano piled with yellowing popular songs of Nancy's high school days. How far, how far he was from home!

A letter from his mother lay in the unlit hallway of the old building where his loft room was; the street lamp threw a feeble yellow glare on the floor, and there it was, the usual cheap airmail envelope, bordered red, white, and blue, and her large unsteady scrawl slanting downward across it, and a ragged string of stamps for special delivery. A sentimental bleat about Christmas, no doubt, he thought, possibly an appeal to come home for the New Year. The envelope was thick; clippings from the Hovey *Gazette*? He went up the three flights of worn stairs, feeling his way in darkness. In his freezing room he turned on three electric switches— light, heater, coffee—and read the letter without taking off his duffle coat.

Dearest Art:

Well son it surely was good to hear your voice and to hear all the wonderful news about your book when will it be published? I want to start boasting to my friends (smile). You are a wonderful boy God bless you and I have always thought you would be a great man although I sort of thought you would be a judge well a famous author is good enough! I only wish your father was still with us to rejoice over this great news. Nancy of course is in seventh heaven she can't wait she says to go to the rental library and just offhand-like ask for the book by her own brother, the big money maker is right!

Honestly it is wonderful and I hope you've had a good lawyer look over the contract before you sign anything. I don't mean all people are out to skin you although there are plenty of rotten apples in every barrel but from what I've seen nobody looks out for you if you don't yourself and when you don't know the ropes you have to pay somebody who does. I wish my own grandmother had gotten this advice we would all be on easy street today.

Speaking of that Art and this is the real reason I'm writing special delivery, and I hope the U.S. mail has some conscience and will deliver, even though it's Christmas, you really should come home. The business in Edgefield is serious. I know you're like your father and just close your ears when your crazy mother gets started on coal land but Nancy will write a P.S. before I mail this and you'll see she agrees with me this time. I hate to intrude on your valuable time and I know you're working hard on your writing and this first success, did they really pay you five thousand dollars, have you got the cash yet? We'll need some money to fight this thing and if you won't fight even though it's your land I will. Art there may be millions of dollars in this and it's not my imagination Nancy will tell you so.

This is the piece of land I've told you about half a dozen times but it just goes in one ear and out the other, the piece I bought in your name way back when you were a baby. You have a little better than ninety-seven acres I got it cheap enough because it's all mountain wilderness, a big long ridge, in those days you had to go a whole day by mule to get to it. I figured some day when I was dead and buried your children or grandchildren would thank God they once had this crazy grandmother but it looks like you'll be thanking me yourself instead.

Somebody has been mining your land. It was *not* just a pit for household use that I saw, I'm not the fool you think I am. Exactly who would climb down a valley and up a ridge seven miles from the nearest decent road to get coal to burn? There is a tunnel mouth there, caved-in but it can't be anything but a tunnel, and to prove it I got a man with a pick and shovel to come up from Edgefield and dig around and he found timbers and roof bolts in the rubbish, so there you are. It will cost money to go in there and really see what's what so I do hope you've got some cash from this book. It was just luck that I found it, there's been talk here about a state mental hospital that's going to be built and they say the state is looking for land around Edgefield and so I went out and just walked some of our land to look for sites. It's easier now to get in and out with jeep and the trails that have been cut for power lines and all, give me jeep instead of mule any day.

I have an idea what's been happening in this land of yours but it's nothing I can put in a letter if it's as serious as I think, and if I'm right you don't have to write books any more if you don't want to you're rich or you will be if you get what's coming to you. Nuff said. You will have to come home and look into this Art your book can be finished a week later, this affects the whole family after all and we have to talk things over and decide what to do and then do it. I think we will want a big Lexington lawyer for this, Judge Crain is fine but this may involve fighting some big opponents and I'm not going to take this lying down and I hope you will show some fight too. I've always thought you were a fighter like me and I hope you are.

Well this is all and I've got to get back to cooking and all, and the washing machine broke down and so I've got to do a washing by hand. It will be a lonesome Christmas without you. We had too many of those during the war, but I still remember our wonderful Christmas last year. We are having the Bartletts again, she's almost blind by now and can't really do for herself let alone him and your uncle Harvey showed up in town with that three-hundred pound wife of his and there was nothing to do but ask him, so Nance and I have our work cut out, but after all there's something to be said for family and old friends, though not much to tell the truth (smile). I suppose our Christmas strikes you as a bore as you read this and you're glad you're in New York, and I hope you'll have a quiet dinner with some nice people and think of your mother and sister a little bit. I'm very happy you're flying so far and going so fast, I guess you always were a little too big for Hovey. Papa had very high hopes for you. So have I. If you meet a nice girl that can make all the difference, you need steadying down, you're a little crazy like me, but I'm not crazy about that White Branch section, that's your piece on Frenchman's Ridge, that is serious business and please come home, Art.

Love,
MAMA.

After his mother's spiky ill-slanted scrawl, with words scrunched and crowded and bent inward at the end of each line, his sister's dainty regular backhand was a relief, though in its flattened loops and curves all letters tended to look alike, and it was not easy to read.

Dear Art:

I'm not endorsing mama's current obsession all the way by any means. It does seem to me that possibly you ought to look into the matter. I talked on the phone to Crain and there's very little doubt that what mama found was a tunnel. It may prove expensive and time-consuming to get to the bottom of this business, but you should come, I think, as soon as you can, and have a look. Men talk differently to men than they do to women, and anyway you know mama.

Well, so you're an author, after all! I guess I can speak freely now about *Alms for Oblivion*. Honestly, I felt like such an utter idiot when you asked me what I thought of it. What could I say? I couldn't trust myself to speak. What do I know? I think it's a wonderful beginning, but you have so much

more to say! All I know is I read that big manuscript in three days, darn near read myself blind, and I didn't skip a word. I—well, I could go on for pages, but maybe the next time I see you the cat won't have my tongue.

I'm so proud I'm afraid I'll pop. Again, I'm drivelling, I can't find words. Why are you so articulate and why am I such a dumbbell, above all when I talk to you or write to you? Some people find me intelligent.

Love,
NANCY.

P.S.—One thing I hope I've made clear. You *should* come, right away. It'll be clearer to you why, once you're here.

N.

Hawke dropped the letter on the desk, and rested his face in his hands for several minutes, overpowered by the loss of energy that came on him at times, a blankness of will and idea as though there were a short-circuit in his vital battery. At last attention and interest flowed sluggishly back into his brain. He took an airlines schedule from a desk drawer. There were planes to Lexington at noon and at six P.M. He was going to visit Frieda Winter at noon. Did he have an appointment at six? Nothing he could remember, though a vague notion stuck like grit in his mind that he had promised to meet somebody or do something at six the next evening. He took his alarm clock from the floor and set it to ring in an hour and a half; then he dropped his head on his arms on the desk, and fell asleep with his desk lamp shining full in his eyes.

When the alarm went off he was sure he had made a mistake in setting it, for he knew he had scarcely shut his eyes. But there were the hands pointing to ten minutes past four. The room was warmer, and a wakening odor of coffee came from the percolator, which had shut itself down to minimum setting. He roused himself, drank coffee, and went about his working ritual: thick socks on his feet, the sweater, the crimson dressing gown, the huge cigar.

There was nothing on the desk but the yellow pad, a cigar humidor, a dictionary, a thesaurus, the desk pen, and beside it a cheap old watch. All around him was a littered mess of clothes, books, newspapers, luggage, and bedding, but in the pool of yellow light under the desk lamp there was an island of rectilinear order. The pad, the humidor, the books, were placed parallel to the edges of the desk. Only the moving arm and hand of the writer broke into the square lines. Hawke wrote slowly at first, with long pauses. Then the pen began to race, and he covered page after page.

While he wrote everything in his life faded from his consciousness. The world around him was a shadowy fable, which could not claim his attention against the strong colors and pressing events of the real world streaming from his pen to the yellow pages. The spell broke about five hours later when his coffee ran out. He counted the pages he had

written; five less than the quota. The warehouse across the street was turning gray in the dawn.

"Hell, it's Christmas, isn't it?" he said aloud, his voice sounding queerly hollow in the big empty room. "Holiday routine." He stood and stretched, with a long growling yawn, changed into pajamas, set the alarm for eleven, and crawled into his bed on the floor. It occurred to him that with five hundred dollars in hand he could buy a cot now, or possibly even rent an apartment like Jeanne's. But he was going to go slow in spending that money, very, very slow.

When he closed his eyes Jeanne Green came to mind again, the moment before the fireplace, the sweet feel of her flesh in his arms, the poignant charm of her brief kiss, and her wit and good sense, quite remarkable for a girl, and her acuteness about his work. His brain slowed, he relaxed, and he thought that it was too bad he wasn't ready for marriage; Jeanne would make quite a wife, probably. A last blink at the phosphorescent hands of the clock, paling as daylight began to water down the darkness in the room. Five hours to his meeting with Frieda Winter.

3

When Hawke rang the doorbell of Mrs. Winter's Fifth Avenue home he was expecting nothing more than a glimpse into the lives and the manners of the New York upper class. He was aware that Mrs. Winter had been pleasant to him, perhaps had even found him attractive. He had found her so. But this was nothing new.

From the age of sixteen Hawke had been at his ease with older women, especially married women. The odious element of competition with other young men was absent. The woman had a husband, and that was that. In college Hawke had endured repeated tortures, falling for girls and then seeing them taken out of his reach by absolute nincompoops, thin pimply fops a head shorter than himself, who danced well or dressed in style or talked collegiate gibberish with ease, or whose fathers allowed them to drive a convertible. He was utterly intolerant of the ordinary limits of ordinary people. He expected every girl who happened to attract him to see in him Youngblood Hawke, the future great author (this dream had been with him since the age of eleven); whereas the girls saw only what there was to see—Art Hawke, an overgrown ill-dressed sullen boy from a small mountain town, given to queer emotional outbursts, unbearably conceited as soon as he ventured any confidences, usually in bad need of a haircut, and wholly without the graces of adolescent society.

For older women, of course, collegiate talk and smooth dancing and papa's convertible were nonsense. They valued male force, they sensed Hawke's high charge of passion and drive, and the rude awkward pride

that frightened off the college girls they found pathetic and appealing. Hawke had had something very like a platonic love affair with an English teacher in high school. For a year at the state college he had been the lovesick slave of the wife of his favorite philosophy professor, with the professor's amiable pipe-chewing approval, now and then shaded with annoyance that pleased Hawke's soul. There is no use in dwelling on the wild fantasies he had harbored of going out into the world, becoming a rich and famous writer in three years, and returning to sweep his Candida with her two children away from her husband in a sensational divorce. These are things many young men have gone through, and all women can readily imagine. There is nobody more vulnerable, and more given to riotous mental folly, than a powerful young man who has not found himself, and who is displaced among those of his own age like a European among Zulus.

Mrs. Winter was a long time answering the doorbell. Hawke was turning away from the entrance in anger and humiliation when she appeared. Her breathless explanation—that she had had to run down three floors, because all the servants were off for the day—was probably true enough, but it only indicated more strongly to Hawke that he was an unawaited guest, if not an unwanted one.

But Mrs. Winter recovered from her embarrassment—if she was embarrassed. She gave him her hand, her eyes flashing from puzzlement to pleasure as soon as she saw who was ringing the bell. Confused and upset though he was, he felt the touch as something more than a handshake. The woman's hand was firm and small and cool, and her clasp was hard, and she drew his hand ever so slightly toward her before she let him go.

"Well! What's the situation?" she said, walking with him into a narrow red marble foyer, with a sweeping marble staircase running up one side. She took his duffle coat and hung it in a closet. "Have you eaten anything at all? Shall we have a lot or a little bit?"

"I've had my coffee. I don't want to put you out. If you'll just show me where the books are, I can get right to work. I'm not hungry."

"Ah kin git rat to wuk. Ah'm not hongry," she said. "Of course you're not. You've just come to my hass to work quietly, like a little mass."

"Okay, Mrs. Winter. I can't help where I was born." He wasn't offended. Mrs. Winter's mockery was harmless, even a compliment. You interested her and you pleased her, and she was signalling this by making fun of you; that was the effect.

"All the same," she said, taking him up the stairs, "I'm starved, if you're not, so you can watch me eat before you see my books. I've been holding off lunch, waiting for you."

He was not sure this was true, but what did it matter? "Look, Mrs. Winter, I'll eat."

"I'll bet you will, my boy," she said, "and I told you once before, my name is Frieda. What do they call you anyway? Youngie? Or Bloody?" Her laughter pealed out; she had a rich merry laugh, in curious contrast to the rather slow ironic gravity of her manner.

"Bloody! Ye gods. Nobody's ever thought of *that*," he said, laughing even louder. "My name's Arthur."

She had stopped on the stairs and was leaning against the shiny red marble balustrade, laughing and laughing, looking down at him on a lower step. "Well, you're Bloody to me from now on, and a bloody good name, I'd say. Now let me hear you say Frieda, and no nonsense."

"Frieda," he said.

"Let's eat something," she said, and she bounded up the stairs. She was wearing a gray sweater and a blue tweed skirt.

Mrs. Winter's face in the daylight at the doorway had been the face of a woman not his contemporary. The years had drawn the lines of her flesh faintly downward, against all her care and massage and diet. Her tissues had yielded to the beginnings of blurry lines here and there; nothing obvious, nothing unattractive, simply showing her as she was. Evening light was kinder; it had made her seem a freak when she said she had four children. There was nothing freakish about Frieda Winter in the daytime. She was a woman of thirty-nine, and Hawke saw this clearly when she first opened her door to him. But she was pretty, and full of life.

He walked with her past a large painting of her family in an opulent dining room, and she fondly told him the names of all of them, and he wondered a little at the elderly look of her husband. They passed into a large old-fashioned pantry, which unlike the rest of the house was brightly sunny, and she threw on a blue apron and went to work. The pantry had a small refrigerator and a two-burner electric grill in one corner.

She was sorry, she said, that she would have to leave him right after lunch; she was driving up to Connecticut to meet with some people who wanted to start an annual summer Shakespeare festival. Most of them were friends of hers; they were consulting her because for several years she had been chairman of a successful music festival, held in the football stadium of a Massachusetts college. But the theatre did not particularly interest her; too many brilliant spoiled children in it, too few reliable adults. "They say musicians are temperamental, but God's teeth, theatre people make musicians seem like a lot of grocery clerks. By the way, if you ever do make a play of *Alms for Oblivion* I can think of several people you should show it to before Jock Maas. He's a lunatic and rather passé."

"But you're associated with him."

"Well, Bloody my boy, the Shaw revival just fell together this way. Mainly I put in money. I'm co-producer so that I can watch what Jock

does with my cash. He has a great way of living up the capital investment of a show with trips to Venice for inspiration, and to Hollywood for casting, and champagne and caviar parties at the Waldorf for public relations, and all that kind of *hazzarai*. But he can be sat on, and I'm doing it."

"What's *hazzarai*, Frieda?"

She laughed. "It's a Jewish word. It means—I'm damned if I know what it means. *Hazzarai*, that's all, faking, foolishness, trash. A show business word."

"You're not Jewish, are you?"

"No, German on my father's side and mixed-up Polish-Swedish on mama's side, she was a singer. If you have any prejudices about Jews, my hillbilly friend, you'd better get rid of them. In the arts people are people."

"Well, I haven't known many Jews."

She had whipped together a batter and poured a can of corn into it. Now she jabbed fat gray pork sausages full of holes with a fork, and began to fry them. The smell made his nostrils flare. "Corn fritters and maple syrup with sausages is the menu, my boy. You don't like it, the hell with you."

"Mrs. Winter—Frieda—at the risk of calling myself a liar, I am so hungry I could die, and I'd rather eat corn fritters and sausages than get the Nobel Prize. Right now, anyway."

She laughed and pushed a wisp of hair off her face, ruddy from the stove heat and her rapid moving. "Happily you don't have to choose between them, you can have both. Except that I can't give you the prize here and now on a plate."

"Well, it wouldn't be good if you did. I shouldn't get the Nobel before I'm fifty or so."

"I swear you're serious."

"A little more than half. Why not shoot for the moon? I can always get killed crossing the street this afternoon too."

Frieda Winter shook her head, smiling to herself, and went about her work. "We'll eat here in the pantry, do you mind?" she said, as he hungrily watched her pile smoking brown fritters and a dozen hissing sausages on a plate.

"Frieda, I belong to the race of kitchen-eaters. I really don't know anything else."

"Well, you'll learn. Although the polite life is almost getting too troublesome to keep up. The servant class is vanishing from the earth. This house was built with a huge kitchen downstairs. The food's supposed to come up on a dumbwaiter and all that, and half the time we end by sloshing together a meal in this pantry. That's why I had the icebox and this grill put in. You'd be amazed how handy they've been. The staffs peo-

ple used to have . . . Go ahead and eat, do you stand on ceremony in
your mother's kitchen? My sausages will take a minute . . . Use more
maple syrup, there's another jug. That's better."

Eating voraciously, he managed to mumble "Wonderful" between great
mouthfuls.

She laughed, sitting opposite him with her plate, in sunlight streaming
through a tall window that looked out on a yard, a couple of barren gray
trees and a rear view of tall apartment houses. "Hunger is the best cook.
No lobster au gratin or Roman artichokes like Fanny's party, but it's a
breakfast. Or a lunch." She ate with appetite.

"Frieda, I'm terribly green at all this. How many servants do you need
to keep up a house like this in New York? Or a house like Fanny's?"

"Well, Fanny's is smaller. She gets by with three. I hate to admit
it, but I have five. That counts Paul's chauffeur, who does nothing but
drive him downtown in the morning and back at night, and eat like a
forest fire and periodically get my upstairs maids pregnant—and a laundress,
four children means a lot of laundry. Fanny and Jay are just the two of
them."

"Why did she need a caterer, with three servants?"

"Darling, don't you know she had more than a hundred fifty people
going in and out of that house?" It startled him to be called "darling"
by Mrs. Winter, but she tossed it off with complete absent-mindedness.
She jumped up and took his empty plate. "Good lad. I like a man to
eat. Paul's been watching his calories for years and years. Of course he has
to. . . . This book, the one you need to read up on furniture for, is it
contemporary?"

"Well, World War II. The idea of this scene is a furlough, and the
boy coming back with a shipmate and getting a glimpse of this different
world, still sort of surviving in Virginia. I'm after the contrast between
modern navy fighting and the living vestige of the life of Washington
and Jefferson—if I can bring it off."

"That's good." She looked at him with appreciation. "And true enough.
You can still find it in Virginia if anywhere, though today of course it's
all self-conscious and anemic and falling apart there too. Old people
try to keep it up and the youngsters go off to the suburbs and build
themselves flat ranch houses of glass and redwood. Anyway it's no problem.
I have books that are nothing but colored picture albums of classic Virginia
homes, with full inventories of the furniture."

"Perfect . . . no, Mrs. Winter, Frieda, no more sausages, gosh, thanks.
I'm doing a pretty good imitation of a forest fire here myself."

"Sorry I can't provide the upstairs maid, too," she said, and again they
laughed in great and growing mutual pleasure.

She insisted on washing the dishes; greasy dishes lying in the sink would
haunt her all day, she said. They had a brief wrestle over a dish towel.

He took it off a rack to help with the drying, and she got it away from him, putting one hand on his forearm and yanking the towel with surprising strength, then holding it behind her as he reached for it, so that he inadvertently embraced her for a moment. She shook him off, laughing. "Never let it be said that a Nobel Prize author, or even a candidate, dried dishes while Frieda Winter was around. Sit there in the sun and talk to me. You need some sun, Bloody my boy. You're pale as a maggot. All that night work, hey?"

"Jock Maas wants to take me to Mexico for a couple of weeks. Maybe I should go."

"Yes, on my money for *Doctor's Dilemma!* The hell with Jock."

"I owe him something. He introduced me to you."

She smiled slyly. "He sure did. Do you know that wild baboon dragged me to Fanny's house especially to meet you? He said you told him the plot of your book and it sounded like a great play. I had a ticket for a show, and I swear I don't know why I went with him. That Christmas brawl of hers is a great bore to me. Jock's idea was that I should get hold of your script by using my fatal charm. Imagine his nerve!"

"You can have the script," Hawke said. "I'm fatally charmed."

"I don't want it, thank you. You finish this navy book, it sounds good. If you want to adapt one of your books some day into a play, you let me know. I'll see to it that you talk to the right people. Not Jock Maas."

"Who, for instance?"

She began to tell him about producers and directors. It was obvious that she knew them all; not because she wielded their names casually but because of the sure, almost absent-minded way she ticked off their main business traits and artistic skills. The remote stars of the gossip columns were Frieda Winter's old friends. "Now, my lad, you can put these dishes in the top cupboard, I hate reaching up, half the time I pop my underwear."

In a bright haze of animal satisfaction and pleased ego he rose, yawned luxuriantly, and put away the dishes. She said, "Just like that. How tall are you?"

"Six one and a half."

"You look taller. That's strange, when you have such broad shoulders."

"Another inch and a half of hair that needs cutting."

"Well, a trim maybe, but leave it long like that, it looks well. I hate young men in crew cuts, they look alike as herrings." She glanced at her watch. "Let's get at your books."

They passed through the dining room again. He stopped in front of the painting and looked around. "This is a truly beautiful room. I can't say why. Nothing hits you in the eye as in Fanny Prince's house."

"Good boy, I'm proud of this room. Some day I'll tell you what goes into the effect. It's not simple to make a simple picture. For one thing there's

the use of plain empty space, which Fanny knows nothing about and never will know. If there's a square foot of empty space in her house she's afraid people will think she doesn't have the money to fill it with an object."

"Your children are all handsome, and so is your husband."

"I looked much better four years ago, I'm afraid, than I do now. It's a mistake maybe to hang up a portrait like that. You become your own worst rival."

He glanced from the picture to her. "Are you fishing, Frieda? I'd say the reverse has been happening, a Dorian Gray process."

Frieda said, radiating pleasure, "I was fishing, and you get a kiss." She stood on tiptoe to kiss him playfully on the lips, and took his hand. "Come on, I'll turn you loose among my books and I'm off."

The Winters' living room faced the park. It was a room that Hawke would remember for the rest of his life, but at the moment it was a rich brownish blur, a tall-ceilinged grand room with high shuttered bay windows, through which he could see the tangle of the park's bare trees, and patches of gray snow. That much he observed, but his faculties of observation were dulled, or rather they had narrowed to one object, Mrs. Winter. The crudest sexual desire was coming over him, a dizzying downhill-rushing sensation. He was appalled.

There was nothing to account for this sudden impulse, certainly not the kiss in front of the picture of her family; that had been nothing at all. This room was dim and huge and silent, and it was somehow like a hilltop in spring, and he was alone in it, in the big empty house, with this beautiful woman of thirty-nine in a gray sweater and a blue skirt, with a single strand of pearls around her neck. Everything about her was beginning to seem as tormentingly and provokingly lovely as the limbs and the movements of a young ballet dancer; and like a dancer she seemed to be moving slowly to some unheard music. Her attitude as she crouched, pulling large art books from a low shelf, was graceful and exciting; the turns of her hands as she took the books and opened them were exciting too; her two white hands might have been naked breasts, so strongly did they attract him. When she dropped naturally to a sitting position on the floor, leaning on one hand, her legs tucked under her, and began leafing through a book, he had to fight off the urge to throw himself down beside her and start kissing her. She seemed to be sitting in an amber spotlight, in an aureole, with the hair falling around her face, and all the time chattering amiably, "No, this isn't quite it, damn, where's the Satterthwaite house? That's what we want. Where is that section again? Could it be a different book? No, here it is." And he stood looking down on her in a rack of pleasant pain.

She looked up at him, and remained fixed so, holding the book open, leaning with one hand on the floor. After a terrible and exquisite moment

she said, in another voice, "What is it, my dear? What's the matter?" Then he dropped beside her.

She never lost her self-possession, though her excitement soon more than matched his, and even scared him. She remembered to whisper, "Stop," and she went and pulled the Venetian blinds, darkening the room to a faint glow of gray winter light. The picture of her as she put her hand to the hook of the skirt burned into his brain, and the vision of her in the pearls and sweater still, and the curious indecent modesty of her white laced slip, was a burst of revealed wonder that the young man thought he could not endure. Tumbling and drowning as he was in ecstasy in the minutes that followed, there was a steady small nag in his mind that what was happening was a dream, a mistake, a disaster.

She lay on the wide green couch, in a crushed attitude, in the sweater and slip, her head down on her arms, her knees drawn up, as though she had been whipped or run over. And she was still unspeakably beautiful, still desirable as before, more desirable. He sat apart, groping for a proper word or gesture; he was fearfully afraid that he had brutalized her, and he dared not say anything. But she lay without moving for such a long time that he kneeled on the floor beside her head on the couch, and he touched her, and whispered, "Frieda. I'm sorry."

She turned her head slowly, her eyes still closed. After a moment she opened them, and they were lively, a little sad, a little ironic. She said hoarsely, "Practically the first thing I ever told you was never, never apologize." She moved an arm lazily and loosely before her eyes, and looked at her wrist watch. "God's teeth. Poor Shakespeare." She sat up, and touched his hair. "You're right, it does need cutting, Bloody. Samson's hair. Shall I cut it and yell for the Philistines?" She took his head in her hands and kissed him. "What was all this?"

"Good God, I don't know," Hawke said.

"Well, don't let it worry you. I imagine the earth is still turning," she said, passing a light hand over his furrowed forehead. She left him, after a few quiet delicious endearments. "Be right back. Those two books on the floor will do for a starter—if you're still interested in Virginia homes," she added with a wonderful low mocking laugh, whisking herself from his sight.

Hawke sat in an armchair, staring at the empty couch, reliving the minutes so recently passed, already a milestone in his life, a tremendous irreversible occurrence, like the first gunfire in a war. It had all gone by so quickly, so quickly, this yielding to him of a grand New York woman, this plunge into the rainbow, and now he was himself again, in the everyday world of the senses, and time was whirling the event further and further away as the loud mantel clock ticked in the silent room, and the Fifth Avenue traffic murmured past the closed blinds.

He did not want to let in the light; he did not want to think of what was to come; in gray gloom he waited for her to return.

And there was her step, and he jumped up, and here she was, dressed for the street, a blue tweed jacket over her sweater, a casual dark blue felt hat jammed on her brown hair, a camel's hair coat slung over her shoulders, a bunch of keys jingling in her hand. "Darling, I have to go to those damned people. I just telephoned and there's no help for it. Are you very angry?"

"What right have I to be angry?"

She was holding out her left hand to him. He took it and without thinking crushed it to his mouth, bowing his head. She said, "My dear, I'm supposed to have dinner with them. Oh hell, hell. I can get back to town about ten or eleven. Where will you be? Where can I find you? Stay here. Work, sleep, there's food in the refrigerator, anything you want to drink in the bar here. Don't go away. The place is yours. The help won't be back till morning."

"Frieda, I'm flying to Kentucky at six tonight. I have to go home."

It pleased him to see that she looked sad at this. He had as yet not the faintest notion of her true feelings about him, or about their encounter. "Must you?"

"My mother wrote me, apparently it's urgent, or she thinks so."

"Your mother. . . . I don't know anything about her, and so little about you . . . Well. When will you be back?"

"I don't know. I thought I'd stay over the New Year."

Frieda paced, gnawing the end of her thumb. "Paul and the children have been hounding me to come down for New Year's. It's only a puddle jump by plane to Jamaica. Maybe I'll go. I guess I will." She looked brightly at him. "Then, when we both get back here, why—well. Are you all set? I have to roar off. God knows I'd like to take you with me. Game for a drive to Stamford?"

"Frieda, I'd never make my plane. There's nothing I'd rather do than stay with you, but—"

"Of course. Well." She came to him. She had cleansed her mouth and had not put on lipstick, and her pale natural lips seemed far lovelier than they had been before, a short thin upper lip over a fuller bow of flesh, the mouth of a child moving in fleeting lines of humor and passion. Frieda stood on tiptoe and kissed him, her lips rough and dry, and this kiss sent flares of pleasure and longing through him. She said, her hand on the back of his neck, caressing him, "This is terrible, I can't imagine what you think of me. Call me when you come back from Kentucky. You will, won't you? Promise!"

"Of course I will, Frieda."

She looked up at him. "My Nobel Prize winner." The darkly amused

look flashed across her face. "So far as I'm concerned, Bloody, it's all yours. Now goodbye. Stay here as long as you please. Take away any books you want. Merry Christmas!"

He heard her swift heels clicking down the marble staircase, and then the opening and closing of the front door. At the window, peering through the slats, he watched her get into her car, an oddly shaped red foreign machine, and drive off.

"Well, there you are," he thought. "Youngblood Hawke has committed adultery."

He went into the dining room, and stood before the family picture. He studied the face of Paul Winter, the man he had just cuckolded— and how queer it felt to have these literary terms applying to his own conduct!—a sedate long face, highly intelligent, rather jowly, with more than a little self-satisfaction in the set of the mouth, the hair scanty and graying, the mustache gray and full. And he studied the children: an older boy, two girls, a charming sad little boy on Frieda's knee, Frieda herself in a plum-colored dress, the center of the picture, sombrely beautiful even in this flat and—he thought—not very competent picture. The boy sitting on her knee was about three; the girls were ten or eleven. Here was a solid, superior American family, a family that sat for its portrait in elegant clothes. Frieda Winter had obviously loved this man, or certainly gone through the act of loving him, for many years. The fruit of her body was ranged around her. The painting declared a clear believable state of things; but this state of things had so little to do with what had just happened, at least as Hawke was trained to put facts together, that he felt dizzily hung between two worlds, as when one is just waking. Which was true, the rainbow vision in the living room, or the painted truth of this picture? He put his fingers to the canvas and felt the harsh surface of the paint.

On an odd impulse he dashed to the stairs and ran straight to the very top of the house; then he began prowling his way downward. In the garret the servants' quarters were squeezed under an irregular roof, three cubbyhole bedrooms with sloping ceilings, plainly furnished; meaningless photographs of unknown people stood on bureaus and bedside tables, Negro in two of the rooms, and a crucifix and colored religious pictures hung in one. Coming down one flight he entered the life of the wealthy, the bedrooms of the children. The toys in the youngest child's room were stacked on shelves, enough fire engines and stuffed animals and boxed games to equip an orphanage, and in the other two rooms books were neatly stowed and desks were clear, except for orderly stacks of school texts. These rooms were far larger than any in his own home in Hovey, and the maple furnishings, soft brightly colored bedspreads, and picturesque wallpaper would have seemed to him, in his childhood, the appointments of a Hollywood dream life; above all the incredible luxury

of two glittering clean-scrubbed bathrooms, one tiled in purple and one in red-and-white.

On the floor below, Paul Winter and his wife had separate bedrooms. The man's room was wood-panelled and full of books. The fireplace, trimmed with dark wood molding, screened by a loose brass curtain that moved on a pull chain, had heavy brass andirons. The desk was a large English antique, dark brown with a rich green leather top, and an elaborate old brass double lamp shaded in green glass. There was a lovely, somewhat feline portrait of Frieda on the desk, a photograph full of flattering shadow. All the furniture was thick, solid, and costly to the eye; the high drapes were made of woven greenish tapestry with hunting scenes on it. The two paintings on the wall had the technique and authority of museum pieces, one a still life of fruit and game and one a Dutch kitchen painted in strong side light. The rug was a thick Oriental, the high bed was covered with a rich brown spread, and on the bed table were three leather-bound volumes between brass book-ends: Marcus Aurelius, Shakespeare, and Montaigne's essays in French. Hawke suspiciously opened these books; all three were well-worn and copiously marked in pencil. This was the touch that Hawke could least forgive. He did not mind the fact that Paul Winter, the gray-mustached elderly phantom who owned Frieda and had begotten four solid children on her, was very rich; that seemed to be the nature of things. It cut his ego to the quick to think that Winter might also be a man of intelligence.

He came to Frieda's room last. Her perfume breathed at him as he opened the double doors on the grand oval of pink and blue, the strange clean light primrose-like odor which he had never smelled on any other woman. The rug, which looked like a vast piece of petit point embroidery, and the bed, a wide royal affair upholstered in blue silk, with a dust-pink canopy of silk towering nearly to the ceiling in a recess of the wall, sufficiently smote him with a sense that this was the boudoir of a very rich woman. But he was too ignorant then to appreciate the details, the very fact that an oval room had been constructed in a rectangular space, the wonderful curved walls of an old armoire which Frieda had built into the curves of her room; he barely noticed the silk coverings of the walls. He made for the closets and opened them, and stared hungrily at the array of her dresses and coats. Here the perfume was strong. He buried his face among the dresses, crushing them against his skin. A little delirious, he pulled open the drawers of her bureau and gloated and fretted over the silken piles of her lingerie. What on earth had happened between him and the woman who lived like this? From a swift sure determination to have just such a house, and a wife to go with a boudoir just like this, he swung in a few moments to black dejection. He was Art Hawke from Hovey, a mad hulking vulgarian who could write stories—maybe; but if he wrote the greatest stories the world had ever known, if

he wrote as powerfully as Tolstoy, as voluminously as Balzac, as trium-
phantly as Dickens, would it enable him to own such a home and such a
wife? Was there enough money in literature to drive up to this height—
book clubs, movie rights and all?

And it was there, in Frieda Winter's boudoir, as he stood with his
profane big hands plunged ridiculously to the wrists in her masses of
exquisite underclothes, that he remembered Ferdie Lax. *That* was what he
was supposed to do at six this evening! He had made a dinner appointment with the little Hollywood agent who looked like a parrot.

Out on the street, he paused to look up at the façade of the Winter
home, the grimy grayish stone rising to a tiled roof, and especially at the
rounded windows of Frieda's bedroom. Then he strode off down Fifth
Avenue, a huge hatless young man in a soiled duffle coat, hands thrust in
slash pockets, two big books under his arm. The bitter north wind sweeping down the avenue drove him along amid flying newspapers and whirls
of dry snow and dust.

4

Ferdie Lax climbed into the taxicab in front of the St. Regis, and
settled back comfortably, with his short plump legs perched on Hawke's
cracking old leather suitcase. "Hi. Sorry about dinner. Next time."

"Look, Mr. Lax, you don't have to ride out to the airport with me.
I have time for a drink here at the bar."

"I don't mind. More privacy this way. Newark Airport, you said? Go
ahead, driver. How's Frieda, Hawke?"

Alarm stung Hawke; he had the conscience of a mountain boy still. He
said stupidly, "Frieda?"

"You called me from her number. Remember? I couldn't talk and
you left the number for me to call back."

"Oh. She's up in Stamford, talking to some people about a Shakespeare
festival. She let me do some research on interior decorating in her library."

Lax uttered a grunt. "Well, let's see. Have you got your contract
with you?"

Hawke drew the thick papers out of his breast pocket. The agent unfolded them with practiced flips of his fingers: four long white closely
printed pages, with here and there a typed insertion. He studied the
contract for a couple of minutes, while the taxicab swayed and jerked
through heavy traffic. "How many people have read your book?"

"Maybe a half a dozen people at Prince House."

Lax pulled two wrinkled sheets of onion-skin paper from his overcoat pocket. "Here's a synopsis that a movie producer got hold of. Any
resemblance?"

Anger mounted in Hawke as he scanned the pages. "This is garbled foolishness, why it's disgusting, it's butchery!"

"Well, somebody talked to somebody in Prince House and pumped that version out of him or her. Maybe a few hundred bucks changed hands, who knows? The goddamnedest things go on in this business. But it's all a lot of nothing. In the end it boils down to whether a property will make a movie. And with the finest property you can get robbed. *Gone with the Wind* went for fifty thousand."

Hawke said, "Maybe I'm naïve. I'd jump at fifty thousand for my book."

"That's how Margaret Mitchell figured. That picture all came out of her brain. The movie makers grossed fifty million. Did she get her fair share?"

"I guess not."

"It's disgusting," Lax said amiably, "but it's the usual thing, especially with a new writer. Okay, if that outline murders your book, why don't you tell the plot to me the way you see it?"

Hawke glanced out at rows of sooty apartment houses. "What? Between here and the airport?"

"Well, make a try. It might be important."

When the taxi rolled up to the air terminal Hawke was in the middle of his story, and nervous and angry. "This is idiotic. I shouldn't have tried telling it. I've rushed it and mixed it up—"

"We've got plenty of time. I'm flying to Lexington with you." Lax stepped out of the cab and, brushing aside Hawke's astonished protests, paid off the driver. They were met at the ticket counter by a deferential woman who checked Hawke's bag, led them through a side gate, and put them aboard before the other passengers were called. Hawke said in bafflement, "What's this? Have you cancelled your trip to Europe?"

"No, I've got plenty of time before the boat sails. My bags are all aboard."

"You're flying to Lexington and back just to keep me company?"

"A plane's a good place to talk. I'm not doing anything else. Well, go on with your story. The aunt unexpectedly shows up at the wedding."

Hawke said, glancing around the silent empty plane, which smelled of fresh-sprayed pine deodorant, "Gosh, I feel like a president or something."

Lax said, "These passenger agents get to know you when you fly all the time. All right, continue. So far you've got me good and interested."

Hawke warmed to his story again; he went on with it as people streamed into the plane and dived for seats. He was at the climax when the plane started to take off, and he shouted most of the last scene over the full roar of four climbing engines. Lax listened with his eyes closed, now and then nodding. The plane levelled off; the warning signs went dark. Lax flipped open his seat belt with one hand and put a

cigarette in his mouth with the other. "That synopsis had the main points."

"Well, sure, it's not a synopsis of *Huckleberry Finn*, if that's what you mean."

"Movie people look for essentials, Hawke. Of course you make it sound a hell of a lot better."

"What are its prospects for pictures?" Hawke asked the question in what he thought was a casual tone. But he was hoping to hear that he was halfway to a house on Fifth Avenue like Frieda Winter's.

Lax folded his fingers across his little pot belly and slumped, looking at Hawke through half-closed eyes. All his limbs were short, and he moved them in a muscleless easy way. "There's no going price for a novel. Off-hand you've got two avenues here—try to sell it for sure money before publication, or wait and gamble for success."

"Well, can you give me an idea of prices?"

"All right. Just to get the range here, are you interested in twenty-five thousand dollars?"

Disappointed, Hawke said, "Not particularly."

"You just said you'd jump at fifty."

"That's twice as much."

"Well, I'll tell you, Hawke, I think your ideas have been climbing upward ever since we started talking."

This was true enough, and Hawke grinned, "Look, Mr. Lax. I always believed, when I started to write, that breaking into the literary field was the world's hardest job. Years of frustration, snowstorms of rejection slips, all that. That's what they told us in a creative writing course at college. That's what I read in books, and in writers' magazines, and that's what I heard young writers telling each other in Greenwich Village beer joints. Two weeks ago I still believed it. I'd sent plays to New York from the Pacific and they'd bounced back with polite letters or printed slips. I'd written this big novel and I didn't know where to turn with it. Luckily Karl Fry's fireplace smoked. So we became acquainted, and he took my book to Prince House, and I got a big contract. I feel as though I've leaned on a stone wall and it's collapsed, it's turned out to be painted cardboard."

Lax laughed, and asked the passing stewardess for coffee. "Okay. How much money from this book have you got in hand?"

"Five thousand dollars."

"A check for five thousand?"

Hawke said, with a little annoyance, "You read the contract. I got five hundred as the first payment."

"Exactly. For five hundred dollars paid, Jay Prince is going to publish your book, which you've worked on for a year or two. That's all you've got so far. He has to pay you nine more installments on a hell of an

iffy basis. Maybe he will, maybe he won't. How closely did you read that contract? What does 'satisfactory progress on a new book' mean? That's a nauseating clause. And don't you realize you've tied up three books, not one? For five hundred dollars Jay Prince has bought himself half the movie rights of three novels by a man who we hope is an important new writer. As for all that stuff about how hard it is to break in, sure, it's almost impossible to break in. A lot of people want to be writers, and very few can write. You've leapfrogged the obstacles the only way anybody can, by appearing with a new piece of goods that looks like it may sell. Your contract with Prince is very faulty. If it can be torn up you should tear it up, but you've signed it. It's too damned bad—obviously Jay's impressed with you, your bargaining position was fine for a new writer, but he practically made you an indentured servant before he parted with five hundred dollars. Why were you in such a hurry to sign? Why didn't you show it to a lawyer, at least? Are you proud, or something? It makes no sense."

"I'm not convinced that it's a bad contract. All that iffy stuff is meaningless, I'll make progress on my new novel such as they've never seen. Now as to the movie rights, that was a printed clause. It hadn't been typed in. I assumed that it was the usual thing."

"For crying out loud, Hawke, you're over twenty-one, aren't you? How much does it cost to print a contract form? Five dollars? The movie companies have a hundred different printed contracts with the most horrible clauses in them. The first thing I do on any deal is strike out about half of that horsemanure. Prince pulled out form J-2 for ignorant new writers and gave it to you, that's all, and you signed it."

"If that's true I'll return his check and his contract. I'll tell him I don't like it and I want out."

The plane took a sudden nasty dive, then straightened up. Hawke instinctively grasped the arm rests, but he saw that Lax rode out the bump like a baby in its cradle. The agent held out his hand and wriggled his fingers. "Let's see that goddamned thing again."

Hawke got his long legs out from under the seat before him with some difficulty and walked up and down the aisle of the plane while Lax studied the contract, holding it in a little cone of light from an overhead aperture. The young author's mind was whirling with perfumed recollections of the astounding Mrs. Winter, anger at having been gulled by Jay Prince—if he had been gulled!—and a mountaineer's suspicion of this cagey, bizarre, smooth little man who was obviously trying to prove that he needed an agent. When Lax laid the papers aside Hawke dropped into his seat.

Lax made a birdlike forward thrust with his head, a mannerism that punctuated his talk at key points. "Look, I'm a Hollywood man. You usually need an east coast agent to deal with publishers. But I know

Jay Prince. I'm as good a man as any to try to get this contract torn up and a decent one negotiated. It should be done immediately, Monday in fact, or even tomorrow. Those movie rights should be cut down to ten percent or to nothing. This is a situation that shouldn't be allowed to harden. Right now you'd be pulling out of wet cement, messy enough but possible. Two weeks from now you'll be hardened in like stone. That's the way Jay's mind will work, and that's how a court will look at it. Want me to try?"

Hawke felt that he was being rushed. He had no way of knowing whether Lax's criticisms of the contract were accurate, or mere salesmanship. He said uneasily, "But you're going to Europe tonight."

"I can get my bags off the *Elizabeth* and take the next boat."

"That's extremely accommodating of you. What would you get out of it?"

"Ten percent of all you earn from *Alms for Oblivion*." Seeing Hawke hesitate he said, "Well, leave that aside for the moment. Next thing. Want to sell the book to pictures right now? I have an offer for you."

"Yes! What is it, and who makes it?" Hawke said, his heart beating faster. He was beginning to see why Ferdie was riding with him to Lexington.

The agent leaned far forward, his elbows on his knees. "Roberto Luzzatto has a star under contract but he's got to start work on a picture in two weeks or he loses her. Buying a book is a step that binds her for another eight weeks. He offers you five thousand down, payable now. Ten thousand more when they start shooting. A final ten thousand when the picture is released. Twenty-five thousand is the total offer."

"Do you recommend that I take it?"

"Recommend? How desperately do you want money? I don't know you."

"I want money as badly as anybody you know, maybe more than most. I don't want to sell my work short."

"Well, look Hawke, I've brought you an offer. I couldn't tell Luzzatto to go climb a tree. I don't know your financial thinking. You're a peculiar fellow. I happen to be a bird-in-hand man. I don't think you can go wrong taking this. Your story is mature and dramatic, but frankly it's kind of downbeat for films."

"Suppose this man never makes the picture? Then all I get is five thousand dollars."

"True, but the book will revert to you in three years and you'll be the five thousand ahead."

Hawke stared down at the little man, and Lax sat blinking like a bird on a perch. The young author was depressed and obscurely offended. At the back of his mind the movie rights to his books had always loomed as the secret ladder to riches, the new element in writers' lives, a resource

Scott and Dickens and Twain had not known. The offer seemed paltry. It seemed a trap like the printed Prince House contract, and he did not want to play the same fool twice. "Would I have to sign up with you or something?"

"A handshake is good enough. You're an exciting new writer and I'd like to represent you. If you like the way I manage this matter we'll go on together, otherwise we can call it off with another handshake. If I find I need an east coast agent to handle publishing details I'll make my own arrangement and it won't cost you any more."

"Let me think about this."

"All the time in the world. I want to add just one thing. I'm going to Europe to see, among other people, Hemingway, Huxley, and Thornton Wilder. I don't represent actors. Writers are my business. I think I know them, and I think you have a fine future." Lax closed his eyes and settled back in his chair. If he did not fall asleep at once, he made a good pretense of it.

Hawke sat in the cramped airplane seat, confronted with the first important business decision of his life, and quite at a loss. Whom could he trust? Where could he turn? If Lax was telling the truth, his publisher Prince had already fleeced him. But did anybody from Hollywood ever tell the truth, especially an agent? All this talk of famous writers sounded like the clumsiest possible effort to impress him. His own family were naïve back-country people, their opinions would be no better than his. Five thousand dollars was a lot of money to him, and it was his now for the taking; none of these installments! And yet—a movie sale, and only twenty-five thousand dollars at most—how far it was from the big money! He had worked long and hard on *Alms for Oblivion*, and he loved the book.

It crossed his mind that he wished he could ask Jeanne Green for her advice. Jeanne, not Mrs. Winter; Mrs. Winter was an enigmatic woman from the high realms of New York, and his petty concerns would probably bore her. Jeanne was his kind of person, and she had a peculiar sympathy for his writing. However, neither Jeanne nor Mrs. Winter were at hand. The agent wanted to bring an answer back to Luzzatto before he sailed to Europe. This chance to get some movie money for the novel might slip out of his hands for good. Lax had said the story was too "downbeat," a word that made Hawke furious. The problem rolled round and round in his mind, obscured sometimes by hallucinatory flashes of his unbelievable afternoon with Mrs. Winter.

The stewardess's voice croaked through the plane, "We are approaching Washington D.C., and we will be on the ground in approximately fifteen minutes. Kindly fasten your seat belts."

Lax opened his eyes. "Already? Bat out of hell— Well, maybe I can get

off here and go back. Planes leave Washington for New York like subways."

Hawke blew out his cheeks in exasperation and tension. His time for making several major decisions was now sliced to minutes. He said, "Nothing's been settled."

"Take your time. I can go on to Lexington too."

The plane careened and wheeled, a carpet of lights swept past the black window and Hawke glimpsed the floodlit Capitol dome, tiny as a toy.

He said, making up his mind on the instant, "Well, here it is. I'm turning down the offer."

The agent blinked at him. "You are?"

"All I see in it for sure is five thousand dollars. It's plenty for an unknown scribbler from the Kentucky hills, maybe. I don't think it's enough for my *Alms for Oblivion*."

Lax smiled in a lazy, peculiar way, almost fatherly. "Well, good enough. I'll quote you to Luzzatto word for word."

Hawke said, "I'm going to talk to Jay Prince myself about the contract. I appreciate your advice. I think he'll change it any way I say, within reason."

The agent nodded, the same half-approving, half-patronizing smile on his face. "You're sure you want to undertake that yourself. You don't want me to do it."

"Yes. I'd feel odd—over-obligated, if you want to call it that—asking you to put off a European trip."

"I wouldn't offer to do it if it interfered with my business, Hawke."

"I understand that, and I'm grateful. All the same, that's how I feel."

"Well, good luck with Jay," said the agent, without the slightest rancor.

The plane bumped to earth. When it pivoted to a stop at the terminal Lax slid out into the aisle and offered a handshake. The agent's little hand was soft and his grip loose. "Okay, I've enjoyed this."

Hawke said, "You've wasted a trip. Sorry."

"Not at all. Paths cross in this business. I don't think your judgment is bad. I just hope you can handle Jay. When you see Frieda again, give her my best."

"Thanks. Enjoy Europe. Give my best to Hemingway. Tell him Art Hawke, from Hovey, Kentucky, is getting to work."

"I'd better not. I don't want to give him sleepless nights. Goodbye, Hawke."

CHAPTER FOUR

1

ARTHUR HAWKE knew the town of Hovey as a prisoner knows his cell.

Hovey's small buildings and houses of wood or red brick straggled along the east bank of a fork of the Kentucky River for about a mile, at a bend where there was some flat land. Across the muddy river there was the railroad and MacDougall Hill, which swelled almost straight up for twelve hundred feet, solid green in summer and solid brown in winter. There were wooded mountains to the north and to the south, and the town itself only climbed a little way up the steep eastern side of the valley before petering out into woods and a cemetery. The sun rose late and set early over Hovey, when it shone. Most often the weather was cloudy or rainy. The pervading smell of Hawke's boyhood, the smell that could always bring his earliest days to mind, was that of wet rotting leaves.

Education stopped at high school in this town. Youngsters who went on to the University of Kentucky in Lexington less than three hours away by car were exceptional: rich men's children, or else freaks like himself, marked queer since boyhood by his schoolmates for his unhealthy interest in books. If Art Hawke had not been a blazing basketball player, though moody and unreliable, and if he had not in his freshman year twice won bloody fist fights with Harry Tombs, his high school career would have been hell. He had acquired in high school the habit of walking alone, of giving his friendship and his confidence to nobody; and he had developed to a morbid degree the sharp defensive pride which was a general trait of the people of these hills.

Coal mining was the preoccupation of Hovey. There seemed to be almost nothing else to talk about except high school sports, local gossip, and violent death. Shotgun settlement of arguments still made routine news in the Hovey *Gazette*. The men who owned the stores, the automobile agencies, the filling stations—even the judges who sat in the courthouse, for Hovey was the county seat—often preferred the corn liquor brewed by the hill people to packaged whiskey from the outside.

The only time the outside heard of Hovey was when violence erupted in labor disputes. Letchworth was one of the last non-union counties in America. The Hovey chamber of commerce said it was because of the rugged American character of Letchworth miners. In fact they were all

native stock going back to Revolutionary times; few of the later immigrants had cared to come up into these gloomy hills. Union organizers retorted that the real reason was the feudal mentality of the operators, and the fact that the law was in their pockets. The truth was that Letchworth mining was far behind other coal areas in the use of machines. It was a marginal field, and the union wage would have exposed the uneconomic nature of mining in the county, and closed the pits. So neither the miners nor the operators especially wanted the union. The union organizers found this hard to believe, and occasionally the Letchworth people—sometimes the operators, sometimes the miners—sought to convince them by shooting them dead. This kind of oversimplification was a mark of Hovey character. Hawke's mother was strongly given to it, and in a way Hawke was too.

But these highly individual traits of Hovey were beginning to blur, even in 1946 chain stores and supermarkets were coming in. The movies, the radio, the national magazines had held a mirror up to the rest of the United States. The town was beginning to see how different it was. The younger business men had formed a chamber of commerce dedicated to making Hovey more like other American towns. The defiant signs that the chamber had posted around the main street said it all: WE LIKE LIVING IN HOVEY.

"The hell you do," Hawke muttered, stepping off the bus at the courthouse where one of the chamber's signs, decorated with holly and red plastic bells, stood on the lawn under the old trees. He was weary and out of sorts, having dozed only a few fitful hours at the Lexington bus terminal, waiting for his connection to Hovey. He dodged into Morgan's Diner because it was raining, and read a *Gazette* over a cup of coffee.

Nothing much had changed in the eight-page *Gazette* since a year ago. A better grade of paper, and big advertisements of some new stores, indicated that the post-war boom was trickling into the town. The news was still coal, religion, sports, and shooting in taverns. Half the reading matter was stories about revivals, or serialized articles on churchgoing, or reprinted sermons, or congregation gossip. Hawke skimmed Reverend Yeager's latest sermon, smiling wryly: *The Unchurched Are the Half-Alive.* There was the minister's picture, the aged round innocent face, the friendly eyes. He had once thought Yeager a great man. Now he knew he was a bright well-meaning weakling ruled by a hard wife and six frisky daughters.

Hawke had been a boy of intense if intermittent religiosity, much given to rushing up and being saved at revival meetings. Great upsurges of feeling had struck him as floods of grace, and he had highly enjoyed them. At college he had read books and thought thoughts which had split him away from the old-time religion of Hovey. All the same, the words that had come to his tongue when he saw Frieda Winter drive off in her car

had been, "Well, Youngblood Hawke has committed adultery." That was the thought in his Hovey-bred mind. He could be ironical about his morality, but he could not easily get rid of it. It was this morality that was bringing him back to see his mother. He had no relish for the visit, he was sure he was on a fool's errand, he had no belief in the millions she had prattled about, he could not wait to flee back to New York—yet here he was. His mother had sent for him.

The rain was not so heavy now, so he walked across Main Street and under the viaduct, and began to climb High Street. Two blocks up, passing the high school he had an impulse to go in. School was shut for Christmas, but the door was not locked. The main corridor, silent and empty, was hung with tinsel and Christmas baubles. His heels clicked loudly on the old green tile floor. He peered into the doorway of Room 107, where he had studied French, seeking he knew not what; the ghost of his younger self, more than anything. The shades were drawn and the spread-arm chairs were neatly lined up in brown gloom. Questions of a sociology test were still chalked on the board, in a firm woman's hand. The teacher had written into her last question an irritation with life in Hovey that indicated she would not last there long:

(D.) *High school students in mountain areas show scholastic perform-ance distinctly below the national average because of*
(1) *Poor heredity and bad nutrition.*
(2) *Prejudices and ingrained ideas of a backward society.*
(3) *Low valuation of education in communities isolated from urban civilization.*
(4) *Large percentage of morons and imbeciles in underdeveloped areas.*

Under this a student had written in a large boyish scrawl:

(5) *Inferior Instruction.*

Hawke laughed aloud when he saw this. Goal for Hovey High, he thought.

His home was two blocks further up the steepest part of High Street, where the street turned, and the houses became smaller and dingier, and the tiny front gardens tended to be choked with withered weeds. Mama had postponed the paint job yet again; what a weathered, flaky look the place had, and how small it was! He halted outside, annoyed to see that the newsboy was up to his old trick of flinging the *Gazette* on the porch roof. Three rolled-up papers lay sodden and moldy on the red asphalt shingles. The house was set back and low, and a careless toss by the boy as he bicycled past could land the paper on top of the porch instead of at the door. Hawke had climbed the porch countless times for the paper, and had had one historic fist fight with a huge newsboy named Froggy,

which—he recalled now with a satisfying grind of the teeth, as he stood on the porch rail to sweep down the papers—he had won. *That* moron had never thrown the paper on the roof again!

"Art! Lord have mercy, what are you doing climbing the roof in the rain? Don't you have any sense, big as you are? Come inside, boy."

His mother was wearing her good black dress, of course, and she was wiping her hands on an apron, peering up at him through her square steel-rimmed glasses and wrinkling her nose. With a heavy sigh, like a man about to hoist a piano on his back, Hawke jumped down to the porch, dutifully hugged his mother, and went into the house—the gloomy house, the tiny house, which seemed to get smaller each time he came back to it, with all the old furniture; except no, a screaming green new couch stood in the parlor, mail-order modern in style, with a green armchair to match.

"New furniture, mom. Nice."

"Well, you know, that old couch was just coming to pieces, I reup-holstered it four times, there's just so much good you can get out of a couch—"

His sister Nancy came running down the stairs and without a word threw herself at him. She was sallow, past thirty, heavy in hip and ankle, and apparently doomed not to marry. She had Arthur's broad thick features, except that her mouth was small and pretty, and her chin did not jut like his. She worshipped Art, and they both knew it, and not a word to acknowledge the fact had ever passed the lips of either. "Let's look at you. Heavens, you're fat!"

Inevitably, Mrs. Hawke marched him into the dining room, and in-evitably she produced a huge steaming plate of thick soup, a plate from the "good set," the purple willow pattern. He was glad enough to have the soup, and he fell to with appetite. This was probably the high point of the trip home; he might as well enjoy it.

"Take some bread, boy. Don't just gulp soup."

He cut into the fresh loaf, with the bone-handled knife his mother had sharpened so often that the middle of the blade arched high and thin. The bread was from Wertz's bakery, with a wrinkled ridge along one side, the bread he had grown up on.

"That's it, boy. Have more bread, that's good bread, you don't get bread like that in New York."

"It's good bread, mama."

Her eyes were bright, and the lines of her square face were strong, and above all she looked very alive, smiling and ready for a joke, a business talk or an argument. He thought her smile was beautiful. He had always thought so.

But he was not glad to be home. A crushing depression seeped from the very walls and furniture of this house. The heavy black dining-room set, stronger and uglier than pig-iron, which had followed the family every-

where, was crammed in a tiny room. He had found it close quarters as a skinny boy; he could slide himself into a chair today only at the end open to the kitchen. How mean and shabby it all was, compared to the Prince home and the Winter home! He could see in the parlor the scrawny Christmas tree with its meager ornaments, shoved out of shape against the old piano. The hideous new couch and chair somehow made the room look like a junk shop. The bookshelves still held the mildewy best sellers of his father's reading days—*Story of Philosophy, Kristin Lavransdatter, All Quiet on the Western Front, Sunset Gun,* and forty others, for his mother threw out nothing—and the cracking sets of classics which his father had bought from book agents when he saw his son was a reader. The boy had eaten through them like a fire. He had reread volumes like *Huckleberry Finn, The Count of Monte Cristo,* and *David Copperfield* until they had fallen to pieces; the broken volumes still stood ragged and backless on the shelves. Compare this to Jay Prince's library!

"You're so quiet, Art," Nancy said.

"Let him eat. He's tired and hungry."

Hawke tried to shake off his gloom. "Nancy's right, let's talk."

The mother said, "Art, I don't like to see good food get cold. I bet that's the first decent soup you've had since you left home. They don't know how to cook up north."

"You've never been north. How do you know? The fact is they cook a lot better than they do in the south."

"Ha! I bet!" The mother watched with pride and pleasure as he ate, wrinkling her nose each time he put the spoon into his mouth, as she had done when he was four years old. It was perhaps the earliest detail of observed life in his enormous catalogue of memory: his mother wrinkled her nose as she watched food go into his mouth. Here he was nearing thirty, and she was still doing it.

"Don't tell me you can get such soup up north, because I know you can't," Sarah Hawke said. "Look at him eat that soup, Nancy! Yes sir, it pays to come home once in a while, don't it, son, and get a plate of soup that's got some meat in it, real soup. You've got to be willing to use meat in soup, that's the whole secret of soup, you can't be stingy, and a lot of different vegetables, fresh out of the garden, I tell you you've got to know how to make soup."

These were the opening lines of one of his mother's major orations, known to him since boyhood, and to cut it off he said hastily, turning to his sister, "Come on Nancy, let's get at it. What's been going on up in Edgefield?"

"Let him eat," Mrs. Hawke said to Nancy. "Art, can't you just sit and eat a lunch any more and just kind of talk to the family?"

"I want to talk about your book, Art," his sister said, staring at him with

glad hunger, as she had been doing ever since his arrival. "Tell us everything. What's Prince House like? Did you meet any famous authors?"

"Nance, authors don't hang around publishing houses, they're all off working, or they ought to be."

"Does Hovey seem like a terrible hole after New York?"

"It isn't only Hovey." Hawke carved himself a huge chunk of bread. It was quite true that there was no such bread in New York. "Nancy, when I got off the plane in Lexington and heard the accents and *smelled* Kentucky, if you know what I mean—the air here has a smell, you know, a nice smell, you could bring a tank of it to New York and let it loose in my room and I'd tell you what it was—I tell you my heart went down in the bottom of my shoes. New York's horrible in its own way, but it's alive, you feel good, you feel you're in the world—"

"Ha!" his mother said. "I bet your nerves are unwinding by the minute. That's what you need, boy, a few weeks of good air and good food and a little quiet. Get some color in your cheeks, why you look like you've been working in a flour mill, did you ever see him looking so white, Nancy? And you've got such a strained face too. I bet that's how everybody looks in New York. More soup?"

"Coffee, mom, please." Hawke drew out his cigar case, and lit one self-consciously.

"Lord have mercy!" said Mrs. Hawke, wrinkling her nose. "Since when did you start on those? Why, that looks like a club you could beat a horse to death with. What does that cost?"

"Seventy-eight cents apiece exactly, mama."

Mrs. Hawke went to the kitchen, saying, "Well, I guess if you've got money to spend you're going to spend it, just like your daddy, though I sure don't see burning up a dollar bill just for a smoke, it can't taste that good, it sure smells ripe."

"It smells wonderful," Nancy said. "Rich. It has a rich smell."

From the kitchen Mrs. Hawke called, "Art, did you sure enough get five thousand dollars for that book of yours?"

"Yes, mom. That's just an advance on royalties."

"I understand all that," Mrs. Hawke said in an injured tone, bringing him steaming coffee. "I probably know a lot more about royalties than you do. Book royalties, coal royalties, they're all the same. What did you do with the money? Did you put it in a bank?"

"I haven't. I will."

"You mean you've got a check for five thousand dollars just lying around? Now Art, that's kind of simple."

"I got it Christmas Eve, mom."

"The whole five thousand, or are they paying it in installments?"

"Installments."

"What kind of installments?"

"Five hundred a month."

"Well, in your case that's a good thing, I'm surprised you were so sensible. You'll have money for ten months instead of spending it all in a month on dollar cigars and whatnot. Only it's not good business, generally speaking. If the price is five thousand get the cash paid down, boy, none of this installment business, I've been through enough of those. Cash in hand, boy, that's the thing, cash in hand." Mrs. Hawke smiled, and put her arm around her son's broad shoulders. "Art, I just can't tell you how proud I am. You do look peaked, boy, you're strong as an ox I know but you did have that accident and you should watch yourself, just a bit."

Hawke was both exasperated and pleased by his mother's solicitude, and by the touch of her cheek on his. He loved her, though he could not stand her. "Mama, I've been working nights, trying to get a second book done. I feel fine."

His mother sighed, and hugged him. "Well at least you've got some push to you. I'm sure glad you've got that money coming in, we're going to need it. We've got a big fight on our hands, Art."

"All right, mom. Now suppose you tell me what it's all about."

"Well, I'll give you Judge Crain's memorandum. That explains everything better than I can. You better study it up, Art, because we have to go to the Hawke Brothers office this afternoon." The mother went into the parlor, and fetched a legal-size manila folder.

"Oh, no!" he groaned. "Hawke Brothers! Mama, this isn't another one of those goddamned family fights! You didn't get me down here for one of those. Good lord, after all these years—"

Mrs. Hawke dropped the folder on the dining-room table in front of him. "Will you just read that first, before you start using foul language and carrying on? You just read what Harry Crain said. And just remember too that what he says isn't necessarily the whole truth. There isn't a lawyer in this town who isn't scared of Hawke Brothers, but even so he has to admit I've got a case. I made him put it in plain language, too. He was talking to me about things like adverse possession and estoppel and I don't know what all and I finally said, 'Harry, my son Art's coming down from New York to fight this, and he's a busy author and he has no time for all these four-dollar legal words, I want you to write out what it's all about in plain English on one sheet of paper.' Well, he took three sheets and it's still too legal, but I can understand it and so I reckon you can, too, being a college man and a writer. You just read that now. We have to go up there at one o'clock." She rumpled his thick hair. "I'm going to wash up. You either have to get a haircut, boy, or buy a violin. Aha ha ha!" She kissed him and went out.

Nancy said in a voice like a conspirator's, as the mother's firm tread sounded on the stairs, "Mama doesn't believe in changing her jokes, does she?"

"Nothing about mama changes." Hawke picked up the folder. "Have you read this?"

"I tried to. You know how I am about those things, Art."

She poured more coffee for him, and cleared away the dishes. With considerable reluctance, Hawke forced himself to open the folder and start reading.

MEMORANDUM ON
WHITE BRANCH SECTION, FRENCHMAN'S RIDGE

This summarizes a dispute about the mineral rights to a parcel of some 93 acres held by Sarah Hawke, trustee, in trust for Arthur Youngblood Hawke, her son. Fee simple deed on record in county clerk's office shows parcel was purchased May 27, 1921, from John Crewes.

On January 8, 1914, seven years earlier, John Crewes sold the mineral rights to this parcel to the Battle Coal Company. Battle in turn sold these rights on August 27, 1935, to Hawke Brothers Coal Company.

However, no notation of a restriction as to mineral rights appears in the deed of sale to Sarah Hawke. Perhaps due to senility John Crewes did not inform Mrs. Hawke that he had previously sold the mineral rights. At that time he was ninety-seven years old. Mrs. Hawke made no title search and was never aware that she did not own the mineral rights.

In 1941, due to the advance of the price of coal in wartime, the mining of coal in the Edgefield area became economically feasible. Hawke Brothers conducted extensive mining in Frenchman's Ridge, where it owned and still owns mineral and surface rights to some three thousand acres besides the parcel in dispute. Hawke Brothers took several hundred thousand tons of coal from that area including the land in dispute, exact figure unknown, but lost money, due to high trucking costs, problems of water, black damp, road washouts, and so forth. Mining was stopped in 1943.

Mrs. Hawke, walking the land in December of 1946, came upon a tunnel punched in her land from these workings, and determined on investigation that this tunnel was from a coal mine. She therefore is seeking legal redress.

It is clear that on the basis of the deed from Crewes she has no claim. In September 1927, Mrs. Hawke also bought a pro forma quitclaim on a dormant patent, bought in by the Pine Mountain Timber Company to quiet its own title on extensive holdings in the region. Mrs. Hawke's purchase was a legal formality recommended by me at the time, and it cost no more than the price of the registry stamps and stenographic work, about five dollars. There is an arguable case that since this was a senior patent Mrs. Hawke thereby acquired some further color of title. However, it must be said that considerations of adverse possession and estoppel tend to cancel this claim.

Essentially this is a situation where the purchaser, Mrs. Hawke, was deceived by the seller, Crewes, and for twenty-five years labored under the misapprehension that she owned coal rights (in trust for her son Arthur) which she did not own. A lawsuit is not recommended. In view of the family relationship involved, the peculiar circumstances, and the fact that Mrs.

Hawke does have some arguable ground, the proper course here is undoubtedly some kind of reasonable settlement paid to Mrs. Hawke by Hawke Brothers for a complete release.

HAROLD CRAIN.

Hawke closed the folder with an impatient slap. "Christ, mama hasn't got a goddamned thing here, Nancy. She was skinned by some old mountaineer twenty-five years ago, that's the long and short of it! All Harry Crain says is that Glenn Hawke should give her something out of charity." Hawke ran up the stairs two at a time with heavy thuds, brandishing the folder. "For crying out loud, ma!" She stood in her bedroom in an old bathrobe, combing her long grizzled hair. "Did you have this memorandum when you wrote me to come down here?"

"No, Judge Crain just sent it over this morning. I asked him for it yesterday."

"Mama, you've got absolutely nothing. This old fellow Crewes cheated you, that's all."

The mother said, "I don't know what all that means about adverse possession and whatnot. Do you?"

"No, but Judge Crain does."

"Harry Crain is as yellow as this comb," Mrs. Hawke said, waving the big plastic comb at him. "Don't fool yourself, we're going to have to get a lawyer from the outside, and that's where the money is going to come in. Why, Crain won't even come to the meeting today, he says he's in bed with laryngitis. He's just yellow."

"Mama, Harry Crain's been handling land law in Hovey for forty years. The plain fact is you thought you bought mineral rights and you didn't. Don't you understand that?"

"Ha! Coal was going at better than four dollars a ton at the mine head in wartime, boy. That was my coal and I want my rights. I mean it was your coal, of course. Now don't you be a quitter, Art. That was the trouble with your father, he would never fight, just drink beer and read books."

Hawke remembered that word "quitter"; it had been the goad that often sent his father shouting out of the house, and he felt the same sick surge of anger now that his father must have felt, hundreds of times. He realized how useless it was to argue with his mother. He had never known her to change her mind on any subject once it was made up. He dropped the folder on her dresser, and trampled down the stairs. "Goddamn wild goose chase," he said to Nancy, who was in the hallway putting on her coat.

She said, "Well, it got you home, didn't it? I'm satisfied."

He swept her into a bearhug. "Okay, Nancy. I'm satisfied, too."

His sister gave him a strange, almost flirtatious look. "I have to go back

to the bank. No time off for entertaining brothers. Let me ask you something. Do you object to a person who wears a wig?"

This was such a startling remark that Hawke blinked stupidly. "A wig? It's kind of an eighteenth-century thing to do. I guess I don't object. Why?"

"Oh, nothing, nothing. There's just this new man in the bank, he's nice enough but he wears this horrible brown wig. I never could have anything to do with a man like that. Well, have fun at Hawke Brothers. Better take along a sack to bring home the million in." She giggled in an old-maidish way and trotted out of the house.

"You, Art!" the mother called down from above. "Change your shirt and shave. I don't want people taking you for one of these tramp writers from Greenwich Village."

Hawke trudged upstairs, thinking what a long long way he was from Prince House, and Frieda Winter, and Jeanne Green. He was back in the gray trap; but not for long! He had a foothold in the realms of gold, and as soon as he could he would flee there again.

2

He had not been inside the Hawke Brothers building since his tenth or eleventh year, and it felt very queer to be mounting the cracked old cement steps again.

His father, Ira Hawke, had been the older brother, Will Hawke two years younger. They had both come over from West Virginia in their early twenties, to try their luck in the new fields opened up by the railroad spur. Will was the mining engineer, Ira presumably the man of business acumen. The partnership had broken up on the hard fact, emerging in bad times like a jagged rock at low water, that Will was a strong man, and Ira a good-natured weakling. Will had bought out his older brother, and Ira had been glad at the time to take the cash and try again on his own, away from the frustrating domination of the brother he had once patronized. Will had gone on to become the richest man in Hovey, before his death in 1940. Ira had drifted from one coal venture to another, always downward, and had left the mining business in the end to run a drugstore. Mrs. Hawke's version of this family history was that Mr. Will (as everyone in Hovey called him) was a cruel, heartless schemer, and that if Ira had only had a little more push *he* would have been Hovey's first citizen, though God knew she had pushed him as hard as she could. Indeed she had.

The front office of the grimy cement building had not changed much since those days. The old Underwood on which Hawke had pecked out a school newspaper at the age of nine still stood on a corner desk under a dusty cover. The smell of mimeographing ink, the stacks of mining maga-

zines and business forms, the yellowing maps of mine workings on the wall, closed a circuit in Hawke's mind. He saw his father's face more vividly than he had since his death, the long jowly cheeks, the broad humorous mouth, thick glasses—Dad, Ira Hawke, the sweet-tempered failure. And all the humiliation came back to him of being one of the poor Hawkes at the high school, while his cousins Glenn and Eleanor ran with the wealthier kids, and got into the secret societies, and wholly outshone the big lout who read books and wrote poetry.

The inner office was all new: knotty pine panelling, red leather furniture, a huge mahogany desk, and a large bad oil painting of Mr. Will— frills that Uncle Will would have scorned. Three men were in the room. He recognized two: his cousin Glenn, much older and heavier, pouchy-eyed, with the battered good looks and weak, sullen expression of the bourbon soaker and woman chaser all of Hovey knew him to be; and one of Hawke's college friends, Scotty Hoag. Scott was an officer of this corporation now, having met Eleanor Hawke at the university and married her. The third man was short and white-headed, neatly dressed in gray, with a round merry face and twinkling blue eyes.

Scott Hoag was sitting on the desk top when Hawke and his mother came in. He jumped down and strode toward them. "Hey, Art! Talk of the devil. We just been arguing whether you would really make the trip down from New York for this. How the hell are you? What's all this about you getting a book published? Hi, Aunt Sarah, you must be right proud of this boy, he gonna put Hovey on the map."

Scott shook hands with Hawke. He looked very much the same as he had at the university, especially since he still wore the horsy clothes he had always favored. Scott was middle-sized, with a wiry body, small handsome sunburned features, a peculiarly long upper lip and a thread-thin mouth. He radiated the same good cheer which had made him a campus leader: the infectious grin, the warm voice, the gay eyes. Only his curly black hair, Hawke noticed, was going rather quickly; you could see glints of smooth pink on Scotty's head.

Glenn Hawke, slouching in the swivel chair behind the big desk, did not rise. He said with no trace of Scotty's cordiality. "Hello, Aunt Sarah. Hi, Art."

Scotty introduced the little white-headed man as his Lexington attorney, Urban Webber. "Don't get scared, Aunt Sarah, Urban's not the lawyer for Hawke Brothers in this little binness of yours. He and I are up here on real estate binness, and Glenn asked us to sit in on this meeting, if it's all right with you."

"I don't mind," said Mrs. Hawke. "Art and I have no lawyer with us, Harry Crain's laid up, but mainly we just want to know what Hawke Brothers intends to do. Plenty of time for lawyers later if it comes to that."

Scotty laughed. Mrs. Hawke sat stiffly on a red couch, without having

been asked to sit down, and Hawke dropped beside her. There was a moment's silence, as the five people looked around at each other.

"Well, suppose I start," said Glenn with a squeak of his swivel chair, leaning forward and glowering at his aunt. "This shouldn't take long, Art, especially if you know the facts. I needn't tell you how shocked I was to get this call from Judge Crain. That Frenchman's Ridge mine was an old forgotten business, and we had damned poor luck with it, but good lord, aside from the implied accusation, how can anyone in his right mind think that we would go into an expensive operation like that if there was the slightest risk of trespass? It would have been insane. We had a certificate of title, naturally, in fact Urban Webber's office prepared it, as I recall. Anyway we've checked through everything. Maybe Harry Crain has too, by this time. Aunt Sarah, that old man Crewes sold you land in which the mineral rights were already gone. He sold them to the Battle Coal Company years before you bought the parcel, and we bought them in 1935, years before we went into Frenchman's Ridge. We checked your deed in the county office and it seems he didn't put in the restriction of the mineral rights. The old man was either falling apart or he just plain cheated you. We're sorry, but we're completely in the clear. You own the surface rights, the timber and all that. It's all pretty trashy. There isn't a doubt in the world that we had and still have the mineral rights. We don't owe you anything, Aunt Sarah, that's all there is to it. You've just found out twenty-five years late that the old fellow sold you a bill of goods."

Mrs. Hawke glanced at her son, who could think of nothing to say, since Glenn was telling the plain truth. She laughed. "Well, all I know is it's been my land for twenty-five years and now all of a sudden it turns out that it was all mined and nobody ever told me, and I had to find it out by myself stumbling over a tunnel."

Urban Webber said kindly, "It's just a lot of wilderness, Mrs. Hawke, and this firm owns the mineral rights to many thousands of acres out there."

"Which anybody can buy who'll make us a decent offer," Scott Hoag said. "Art, that stuff's all withering on the vine. You can't get the coal down to the railroad economically. I tell you, I feel funny in this binness, because the Frenchman's Ridge mine was my idea. It was just after I married Ellie. I suggested it to Mr. Will, and he thought it wouldn't work. I was still trying to talk him into it when he died. Well, I convinced Glenn to let me go ahead with it after that"—here Glenn Hawke laughed shortly and grumpily—"and that about finished me in the coal binness. I lost Hawke Brothers about a quarter of a million dollars."

Hawke said, "Scotty, the price of coal was way up in wartime. Hell, I was running a coal truck down from Edgefield in the summer of 1941, when I damn near killed myself. Trucks were going night and day. How could you lose?"

"Everything went wrong, Art, everything old Mr. Will warned me about. A long approach road, poorly graded, it kept washing out after every heavy rain, and I misfigured costs on truck transport by about twelve cents a ton, a few dumb things like that. About the only good thing was that I learned I wasn't a coal operator, and I got into another binness. I'm just on the board now, I show up once a year to air my wisdom." He turned to Mrs. Hawke. "Aunt Sarah, you ought to look at the books to satisfy yourself that we lost a fortune on that ridge. You're welcome to any time. I wish you had owned the mineral rights and kept us out of there, that's all I can say."

"Amen to that," said Glenn.

"Well, I wouldn't mind seeing those books," said Mrs. Hawke.

The white-haired Lexington lawyer said, "May I make a suggestion? Of course Mrs. Hawke should look at the books if she wishes. But it's irrelevant. She paid money a quarter of a century ago for what she thought was coal land, and she now finds the coal wasn't hers. She's very disappointed. This kind of grantor's fraud crops up all the time, especially in mountain areas. In similar cases I often recommend that the defrauded party be repaid what was originally paid for the land, plus expenses. That would be a reasonable and decent thing to do here."

Glenn Hawke was leaning forward holding up a finger. "It would not, and let me tell you why, Urban. Ordinarily I would say yes, sure, let's do that. But I know Aunt Sarah. We have a difficult family situation. Now Art, forgive me for putting this bluntly, but if we acknowledge we owe your mother anything, by giving her even a hundred fifty dollars—which is what she's on record as paying for the land in 1921—you know very well, all too well, that we'll never hear the last of it, and the town of Hovey won't, either. Once Hawke Brothers acknowledges an obligation of any kind the story'll be that we defrauded Aunt Sarah of millions of dollars. That's more or less the story anyway."

Mrs. Hawke said, "Ha! Don't worry, Glenn, I'm not selling all that coal for a hundred fifty dollars."

Scotty Hoag said cheerfully, "Look, Aunt Sarah, I think you'll only satisfy your mind by suing us. You're welcome to do that. It'll cost a lot of money, and you'll lose. It'll cost us money too. But you may as well go ahead and do it."

Mrs. Hawke said, "Well, the last thing I want to do is go to law, if I don't have to. I know the lawyers end up with all the money."

Urban Webber laughed, unoffended. Scotty said, "All right, Aunt Sarah, if you mean that, then how about this? I'll take the responsibility here to offer you one thousand dollars for a release. I'm doing it out of regard for your feelings, which I understand, and to avoid a lawsuit which nobody wants. It's the best you'll get, unless—"

Glenn Hawke said, "Hold on, just how are you taking the responsibility, Scott? A thousand dollars is money. Who pays this?"

Scotty said with a shade of impatience, "Glenn, I'm undertaking to recommend this to the board and to get it through. I know you've got this emotional family involvement, but it isn't sensible, Glenn, it isn't binness."

At this point Hawke intervened. "Scott, you're offering my mother a thousand dollars. You're also offering to let her examine your books if she wishes, to convince herself that the mining was a failure. Right?"

"That's it, Art, I just don't see a lot of bitterness and lawing over an absurd situation like this, where there's no money in it for anybody, it's all down the drain anyway."

Urban Webber smoothed his white hair, smiling. "I think Scotty is being Santa Claus, but it's in the spirit of the season."

"Mama, let's telephone Judge Crain," Hawke said. "Glenn, is there another office we can use?"

Without a word, Glenn Hawke got up and threw open a door into a room which Hawke recognized as his father's old office. Mine maps and blue topographical surveys were piled high on the two small desks. Hawke and his mother went in, and Glenn closed the door on them.

Hawke telephoned the old family lawyer and reported what had happened at the meeting. There was nothing fake about Judge Crain's laryngitis, he could hardly talk. "My God, a thousand dollars?" he rasped thickly. "Grab it. How did you talk them into it? Your mother has no claim, no claim at all."

When Hawke repeated this to his mother she said, "Well, how about that other thing, that quitclaim he says he bought for me?"

Hawke asked Judge Crain the question. The old man choked out, "Doesn't mean a damned thing. Crewes occupied that land and secured his title by undisputed adverse possession even if that patent still held good after it was forfeited to the state, which I doubt. You take the thousand. Get them to dictate and sign an agreement now if you can."

But Mrs. Hawke still hung back, when Hawke went to open the door. "Wait, wait, Art. Listen to me. They could have gotten to Harry Crain and bribed him, you know?"

Hawke was sickened by this, more because of what it revealed of his mother's mentality than because of the reflection on Judge Crain. "How long have you known him, mama? Thirty years? Forty years? He was co-executor of papa's will, for Christ's sake! If the whole world is in a criminal conspiracy against you, it's too goddamned bad, mama." He detected in his own voice the timbre of his father's exasperated tirades; a spooky effect, here in his father's office.

"Don't you swear at me, Arthur. It's your land. I'm doing this for you. Don't ever forget that." A wise grin crossed her face. "A thousand dollars

would still be about nine hundred percent on my money, you know? All right. I guess there's nothing else to do."

The three men in the other room showed no surprise when Hawke said the proposition was acceptable. Glenn Hawke gave Scotty a sour, unfriendly grin like a sneer. Webber said a little drily, smoothing his hair, "I guess Harry Crain has looked into the law of this matter."

But when Hawke suggested executing an agreement then and there, Scotty Hoag shook his head. "There's no rush, Art, I'm not going back on my word. Urban and I have binness up in town now." He held out his hand to Mrs. Hawke. "Well, Aunt Sarah, we've got a deal, have we?"

She hesitated noticeably, then took the outstretched brown hand. "Well, it being Christmas and all I guess the best thing is to forget about lawsuits and settle up. I don't bear grudges, whatever anybody else thinks." She glanced at Glenn, who heaved an exasperated sigh.

Hawke's mother was unusually silent as they drove away from the coal company building. Hawke thought she might be sulking, or reliving old times, and he did not break in on her reverie. Finally with a little laugh she said, "It seems pretty shabby, dragging you down from New York just for this, Art. Just for a thousand dollars."

"I'm glad you did, ma. I should have come home for Christmas, anyway. And listen, a thousand dollars is money, like Glenn said."

"Not for the big money maker." She put her hand on his thick forearm, and they both laughed. She said, "It's just that by rights we should own half that company, Art, you know that. Uncle Will took advantage of his own brother at a bad time and bought papa out for a song. I thought I'd get our own back for sure this time. I thought I had them at last." She sighed. "I tell you, if you were a lawyer, I'd never take this settlement. Or if I knew a good lawyer. But I guess it's all for the best."

3

When they got home he climbed up to his old bedroom and went to work. He had brought his manuscript with him, and there was nothing else to do really, but listen to his mother talk. The treasure trove of millions had gone up in smoke; the talk about it, however, would continue for years, dwindling at last to one more episode in the grand oral epic of the world's persecution of his mother. There would be enough of that at dinner.

At first he could not get his mind on his novel. The dislocation, the abrupt change from Manhattan to Hovey distracted him. Had he actually grown up in this tiny attic room with one dormer window, with a roof so steeply sloped that he could only stand up straight in one place near the door? Had he managed to hunch himself day after day at this little desk when he was a high school boy six feet tall, and had he slept for ten years

in that old iron bedstead, with black paint more than half flaked off in bubbles of rust? The bed took up nearly all the floor. A bureau, the desk, and the chair filled the rest. One corner of the bureau still rested on three of his old schoolbooks. He had shoved the furniture around in some forgotten fury, broken off a bureau leg, and propped the wretched thing up so. Cigarette burns notched the edge of the desk, and a broad inkstain covered one side and streaked down a leg. Gougings and carvings of a penknife mutely welcomed Youngblood Hawke, the author, on behalf of Art Hawke, the pimpled boy half out of his mind with frustrated ambition and bottled-up sex longing.

He lit a cigar, dismissed these thoughts, and took up his pen. Soon his miserable surroundings dissolved, he knew nothing but the world of his story, and he piled up an exceptional page count in a couple of hours. When he ventured downstairs Nancy had not yet come home, and his mother was out on her sick calls. Mrs. Hawke always had half a dozen invalided people whose lives she tried to lighten. For some reason she had worked out her time long ago so that she made her calls before dinner. He was glad the womenfolk weren't home. He could escape for a couple of beers before dinner. That had been his father's habit; the one thing Ira Hawke had held to in the face of his wife's perpetual nagging. Hawke had acquired the same taste at nineteen, and though in New York he hardly drank beer any more, he found himself now with a raging thirst for it.

He put on his duffle coat and all but ran down High Street, stepping springily and far with each stride. Along Main Street lights burned in store windows, and trucks were thundering through, but otherwise the quiet of suppertime lay on the town. When he reached the American Legion hall he went to the bar and poured three icy beers down his throat as though he were putting out a fire. Then all at once he felt absolutely wonderful. He was Sinclair Lewis, Thomas Mann, Honoré de Balzac, the home on Fifth Avenue was his already, and this visit to Hovey was but a touching comic interlude, the return of the great man to his humble origins. Some day he would put it all in a book, in one of the later novels, the row of twelve or fifteen panel-works which would capture twentieth-century America as enduringly as failing Athens had been caught in the plays of Euripides, the books he would write on the income from a million dollars—

"Hey Art, you ole sumbitch! How long you been here? Art! Come on over and join us."

The hall's red lights were so dim that for a moment he did not see the arm waving from a far booth, on the other side of the empty dance floor. Then he called uncertainly, "Scotty?"

"Doggone right! Come on, have a drink with the common people." As Hawke drew near, Scott Hoag added to the young man sitting with him, "Here's the sumbitch you want to interview, not me . . . Art, this here is

Bert Crawley of the *Gazette*. He don't know Hovey's got itself a celebrity. He thinks this supermarket I'm putting up in Low Bend is news, for Chrissakes." Scotty pushed aside an enormous role of blueprints that lay on the table before him. "To hell with this. Art, what'll you have?"

Hawke said, "Old Crow, beer chaser."

"Holy cow," Scott said, waving to a waiter.

"What's the matter?"

"Nothing, Art, only that's a man's drink. You a sensitive artist, I thought."

"Let's match drink for drink, Scott, for a few rounds," Hawke said.

Scotty laughed. "No, thanks. I remember you from college, fella."

Hawke had been friendly with only a few people at the University of Kentucky. Scott had been one of them. But then, Scotty Hoag had been almost everybody's friend. Nobody had known much about him; rumor said he was the son of a Louisville horse trainer. There was something coarse in his speech, but his geniality and energy were irresistible, and he had been top man in school politics. About the time he started dating Ellie Hawke, he had taken up with her big uncouth cousin who edited the literary journal, and Scott had often asserted at school that one day they would all be goddamn proud that they had known Art Hawke. Once Scott had gotten an extra appropriation out of the school council's funds for a special all-poetry issue of Arthur's magazine. That was the kind of thing he could do with ease.

Hawke said, "I seem to remember you held your own pretty good, Scott."

"I reckon we both got a hollow leg, Art, you got longer legs, is all."

The reporter, a scrawny young man of twenty-two in a badly fitting suit, pulled out a pencil and notebook. "Well, Mr. Hawke, is that true? You've had a book accepted?"

"That's right."

"And they're going to publish it in New York? Really?"

"Yes. Scotty, is that what you're doing, building supermarkets?"

"That and other things."

The reporter pestered Hawke for facts, any facts at all, about the book, but the author had an instinctive wariness about uncovering anything to the press. To shut him up Hawke at last told him the title and the publisher. The reporter thanked him sarcastically, said he hoped the book would sell a million copies, and walked off to the bar. Scott said, "Us binness men have to stay friendly with these small-time sumbitches, but what do you care? You just got to worry about the New York *Times* and *Time* magazine and like that. Here's to you, Art, and to your career. I know it's going to be great. You, the only distinguished man I've ever known, or maybe ever will."

They drank. The bourbon glowed exquisitely in Hawke's beer-cooled stomach, as Scott's praise did in his brain. "Scott, I always thought you

were going to be the distinguished one. I saw you going step by step in that easy way of yours—law office, county judge, state senator, maybe governor, maybe even U. S. Senator."

"So did I, Art, so did I, but a man's got to be realistic about himself or he'll fall on his sumbitchin' face. I haven't got it. My first year law school I knew I didn't, that's why I got married and quit. I'm no student, I never was. I can't hardly concentrate on a book any more at all, dunno now how I made it through college. I got into this building binness, Art, and builders are an ignorant lot. But I love it. So I guess I've found my niche. See, this lousy road up to the Frenchman's Ridge mine that we had to keep repairing, I couldn't get any contractor to do it right. Finally I studied up on the sumbitch and rebuilt the road myself. I did a good job, but by then the mine was a bust. Then, one thing and another, I got into contracting and building, and Ellie and I moved to Lexington—the schools are better there, Art, let's face it—and I've done pretty good. Say, Art, I feel bad about your mother. That's a hell of a note, you know?"

"Scott, I hope you're not paying that thousand out of your pocket. That's ridiculous."

"Hell, that's Glenn's talk, Art. The other directors will go for it. Ole Urb Webber sure made me laugh with that Santa Claus stuff. It's damn bad public relations, a widow suing a company for trespass, Art, especially in a place like Hovey, it's a black eye for us whether we win or lose. I'm glad your mom took the thousand. Art, how about another little soup's on here?"

"Well, one more Scott. I pay for this one."

"You pay for nothing, you pay when I come to New York and I visit the famous novelist, you old sumbitch . . . Goddamn, you really getting a book published! *Alms for Oblivion!* Prince House! What's it about?"

Hawke was feeling most pleasantly disposed to Scott Hoag. "Well, if it goes no further than you, Scotty—I don't want the whole town talking about it—" Hawke told him about *Alms for Oblivion*, and then, enjoying Scott's wide-eyed attention—also two more rounds of boiler-makers having come along while he talked—he described the new navy book he was writing.

Hoag stared at him and shook his head in admiration. "Art, I'm no authority on literature, Christ knows. But that first book is going to sell. Because it's the truth. That's how things happen in these hills. And boy, I think that navy sumbitch is going to be a barn-burner. *That* one sounds like a million dollars. In *hand.*"

Hawke laughed. "I wish it were in hand. I've got three hundred pages written, out of two thousand, first draft."

"Art, you want to know something?" Hoag's speech was becoming decidedly furry, and his head was drooping, but he stared at Hawke through the reddish gloom with alert eyes. "You make me feel ashamed that I

never went to the war. Ashamed and stupid. See, I married Ellie, and she had the twins right off the bat and I was goddamned if I was gonna volunteer to tote a goddamn gun. And I got a big head start in binness in wartime, don't think I didn't, but that story you were telling me just there gave me the chills, and I realized how much I missed. That's the power you have, to make a man see things." He sipped at his beer. "Art, you gonna make money on those books. Especially on that navy one. What you figuring on doing, blowing it in on high living like all artists?"

With some pride and not a little furriness of tongue on his own part, Hawke described to Hoag his plan for hoarding a million and then living on the income while he wrote great books. He told about the works on investment he had read, and about his careful following of the Wall Street magazines. He spoke of blue chips, convertible bonds, commodity futures, soft goods, dollar-cost averaging, and so forth; he had absorbed the jargon well. Hoag listened, resting his chin on a fist on the table, keeping his eyes on Hawke. "Well, what do you think, Scotty? You're the business man here."

Hoag said slowly, "You want the truth?"

"Sure I do."

"Art, you still thinking like a scholar. Goddamn it, boy, you think those sumbitches up there study magazines and books, the professionals that *make* the money? I've read a lot more than you. All I'm interested in is making money. Those books and charts and magazines are nothing but a lot of second-guessing on what happened yesterday and last year and ten years ago. You listen to me, Art. You put your goddamn money in *guvment bonds*. Nothing else."

"Scotty, bonds pay two, three percent."

"But they *pay*. You put 'em away and forget about 'em. I tell you, Art, you get into the stock market, and instead of writing the great books that are in you, you'll end up doing nothing but reading those sumbitchin' financial magazines and stock services that I wouldn't use to wipe my behind."

"Scotty, stocks have been going up ever since 1880, on the long pull. Whereas bonds—"

"The *long* pull! Sure, and in the *short* pull the unprofessional sumbitches like you and me get shook out every five or ten years, and the big boys pick up our marbles. *That's* what's been happening since 1880. You want to know what really appreciates? *Land*, boy. Good land appreciates. Buildings appreciate. You want to give up writing and go in the real estate binness, you let me know, I can tell you plenty. But stay away from Wall Street, boy. And stay away from real estate, too, unless you want to do nothing else. That's no binness for sissies. Look here!" Scotty seized the loose roll of blueprints and spread them out on the table with a crackle. The details were hard to discern in the dim light, but Hawke could see that

this was an ambitious project, a center for a dozen shops, on the highway at the bottom of MacDougall Hill on the other side of the filling stations, just before Main Street began. Scotty described how he was planning to finance the center—he was actually in Hovey with Urban Webber to negotiate with the two local banks—and then he launched into a mock-modest account of how he worked as a builder. He was obviously proud of his early success and eager to impress his literary friend. He described his dealings with banks, he outlined the ways of getting a project started with the least possible cash, and talked about limited partnerships, general partnerships, syndicates, and corporations; about the inside position and the outside position, the fee position and the lease position; about the importance of leases in hand before construction began. Hawke was indeed impressed by Hoag, and interested in the glimpse into the interior world of money-making. "Scotty, will a town of five thousand support a big thing like that?"

"Art, we got four times as many stores in Hovey as the town can support right now, don't you know that? This is the shopping hub of Letchworth County. With the new U.S. highway that's coming through here—and I know that's for real, boy—this sumbitch looks real good. We got a ten-year lease in hand from A & P, and with that we can get a good seventy-five percent of our construction money from an insurance company if these banks here won't talk sense. They a little slow understanding the possibilities in their own town. They afraid the stores on Main Street will get hurt. Christ, Main Street's going to be busting out of its britches and choking to death with traffic in five years if somebody don't build a thing like this. These fellas don't look beyond the next quarter."

"Scotty, a center like this one you're building—what does that pay you as an investment?"

"That's a speculation, boy. On paper we get our money out in four years and from then on we getting twenty-five percent a year—or we sell out when it's looking good, and we should double our money at least."

Mental arithmetic was a little hard after all the beer and bourbon, but Hawke foggily calculated that twenty-five percent of twenty-five thousand dollars was better than six thousand dollars a year. Six thousand! He could live royally on just that much, in a nice little apartment, say on Bank Street in the village. He could be independent at a stroke. Of course he didn't have twenty-five thousand dollars. But Lax's offer for his movie rights had at least held out the lure of that sum. Was it too wild to hope that *Alms for Oblivion* would finally sell to Hollywood for that much?

He said, "Would you be interested in a partner, Scott—say for fifteen or twenty thousand?"

"Who, Art—you?"

"Why not?"

Scott laughed. "I'll tell you why not. Come on, let's walk uptown, I've got to meet ole Urban again, we having dinner with these bank fellas." He slid out of the booth and rolled up the blue prints. "I'm gonna give you a little lecture, Art, maybe make a contribution to a great career."

Snow was falling in enormous flakes outside, but the air was warm. "Now listen, Art." Scott took Hawke's arm as they walked up Main Street, "I been giving you the rosy picture. Let me tell you what can go wrong. I been burned plenty, but that's my trade, it's not yours." He described the hazards of construction, the difficulty of controlling costs, the escape clauses that big firms like A & P insisted on, the sudden drying up of bank credit when a man needed it most. "I tell you, Art, it's a sickening thing to see your venture capital wiped out in a refinancing. It's happened to me more than once. You just got to take it on the chin, cut your losses, and get on with the next deal. When it's your trade, you do it, that's all. A fella like you can't take such risks." He glanced up at Hawke in the light of a street-lamp. "Anyway, you got that kind of cash, Art? Just lying around?"

"I think I may end up with a movie sale for that much. I've had nibbles."

"Well, that's great. You buy guvment bonds. You pile yourself up a good couple of hundred thousand dollars in guvment bonds, you gonna make that kind of money, mark my word, Art. Get yourself a *base*. After that you want to talk to ole Scott Hoag back in the hills about real estate, fine. Just stay out of Wall Street, Art. You a brilliant fella but brilliance isn't enough, you gotta *know*."

They halted under the viaduct to part company, both slipping a little in the slush and feeling very good indeed. Scott still held Hawke's arm. Hawke said, "Well, meantime, Scott, maybe I'll write a book about a real estate plunger and you'll give me all the dope."

"That I'll be glad to do. I'm goddamn proud of knowing you, Art. All I can say is I spotted you way back in school, didn't I?"

"I guess you did."

"Next time you in Lexington you give me a call, hear?" Scott released him and reached up to slap his shoulder. "Guvment bonds, y'ole sumbitch. That's tonight's sermon in two words. Guvment bonds."

"Guvment bonds, Scotty."

Somehow the phrase struck them both as funny and they burst out laughing. When Hawke was half a block away he heard Scotty call, "Guvment bonds, hear?"

Hawke turned and roared down the hill. "Guvment bonds, y'ole sumbitch!"

4

Mrs. Hawke wrinkled her nose at him fiercely, just as she had done at his father for years, and muttered about spoiled food, and people who brought the smell of a brewery into a decent house. Then she said, "There's been two calls waiting for you from New York this past hour. Don't be too long about them, dinner's all dried up as it is."

Hawke hurried to the telephone pad on the hallway table. Jeanne Green had called, and Roberto Luzzatto; the golden world was not forgetting him! He rang the operator and asked her to try to get Jeanne. He sat and waited for the clumsy mountain operators to clear a circuit to New York, meantime picturing Jeanne Green with a certain sexual excitement, undoubtedly augmented by the large amount of alcohol he had just drunk. How pretty and bright that hoarse little redhead was! There was a girl for him; he would be a fool to carry things any further with that strange and immoral Mrs. Winter, when a girl like Jeanne was within reach. He knew she liked him. He was hungering all at once to hear her odd grainy voice, and it was a real disappointment when the operator got through to New York and her number did not answer. He told the operator to keep trying Jeanne every hour; then he put the call in for Luzzatto, and reached him at once at the Waldorf-Astoria Hotel. The producer's voice, deep and harsh, sounded quite foreign on the telephone. "Hollo, Youngblood? What the hell are you doing in Kentucky? Why aren't you up here working?" A bass laugh, and he went right on. "Youngblood, I talked to Ferdie Lax before he left. So you turned down my offer."

"I'm afraid I did."

"That's quite all right. Now listen, I am excited about your book. To me, just from that outline, it's a work of art and it has a great chance as a movie. Now, I've got a problem, and let me tell you what it is. I've got a commitment with Anne Karen, you know who she is, I hope— Hollo, Youngblood, you still there?"

"I'm here, Mr. Luzzatto. I know who Anne Karen is," Hawke said, with what he hoped was quiet irony. Anne Karen!

"Okay. She's the greatest, as you know. She hasn't made a picture for years because she doesn't have to, she's one of the richest women in Hollywood and tremendously independent, but she's never stopped looking for a script. Now I think *Alms for Oblivion* would be fabulous for her, a complete change of pace. I think that part of the aunt is a sure Academy Award for Anne. I've told her so. She's here in New York, in fact she's right here in this hotel. The trouble is she suddenly doesn't like the New York weather. She wants to go to Hawaii for a month, she owns a house there and she's booked to sail next week. Youngblood, if I don't wrap

this up with her before she goes, the whole thing will fall through. She's leaving New York in a couple of days. Now she read the outline of your book and I have to tell you she hates it, she doesn't see anything in it."

"Mr. Luzzatto, that outline is disgusting, I never authorized it."

"Look, Youngblood, you don't have to sell me on your book. I can see values in an outline that an actress can't. Youngblood, I need the script. Anne has got to read your manuscript. At least enough of it to see the possibilities like I do. Now I spent all today at Prince House almost, trying to get that script. There's a girl there named Green. She won't let it out of her hands. She's some kind of a nut. Why, I got Jay Prince to tell her to give it to me, and she still wouldn't! She says you put it in her custody and she won't release it until you tell her to. Youngblood, can you hear me? What's all this noise on the line?"

"I hear you."

The producer said, "I'm trying to say I'm prepared to improve my offer. I can improve it substantially, but first I must get Anne Karen interested in your book. Do you understand?"

Hawke tried to keep his voice calm. Turning down the offer had been the right move, after all! He could see Nancy in the parlor, peeping at him over the *Gazette*. "What do you mean by improving the offer?"

"Youngblood, there's no sense talking money until we interest Karen. I want you to call that crazy Green girl and tell her to let me have the script tomorrow. What am I going to do, burn it, eat it? I want to show it to Anne Karen, I just want it for forty-eight hours! I think we can make a real deal, a fast deal."

Hawke's natural suspiciousness warned him that this might be a farrago of lies, that this man might be using the dazzling name of Anne Karen just to get ahead of other Hollywood people in reading his novel. "Well, now, Mr. Luzzatto, Jeanne Green's worried about that manuscript because I am. There's no carbon copy. How would it be if I call Jeanne and tell her to deliver it personally to Anne Karen at the Waldorf tomorrow, and then pick it up from Miss Karen forty-eight hours later? That way I don't see how we could lose track of it."

Luzzatto bellowed, "That's great! That's perfect! Will you do that Youngblood? Can I count on it? Can I tell Anne? Youngblood, I think we'll have a deal here, and I think we're going to make a fine film."

"I'll do it, Mr. Luzzatto." Hawke was convinced, and he began to envision the possibilities of having Anne Karen as the star in the movie of *Alms for Oblivion*.

"Youngblood, we're going to do business. I feel it. I am excited. I am calling Anne the minute I hang up. You're all right, Youngblood. Goodbye."

After that, dinner was a strained affair.

The Hawke household was one where deep enormous reticences could

be carried along for years, so long as a subject was not broached. After that the floodgates were down and his mother could unloose deluges of words. There had been a time years earlier when Nancy, by all the signs, was having an affair or was at least passionately involved with a married cashier at the bank; there had been plenty of talk about it in Hovey; but Nancy had sat white and haggard and silent at the dinner table night after night for half a year, and the topic had never been opened once. So tonight, though the name of Anne Karen had burst like a huge firework in this drab little home in the back hills of Kentucky—for of course there was no privacy in telephoning—though nobody could think of much else, the conversation was as inane and desultory as if Arthur had never mentioned the star on the telephone. Mrs. Hawke told Nancy about the settlement with Hawke Brothers, trying with half a heart to present it as a victory. Then she dropped into her old lines of talk: the inconsiderateness of the neighbors and their lack of good breeding, and the various machinations and villainies of her rivals in the Elizabeth Kilburn Circle of the Methodist church. Mrs. Hawke had held various posts in the Circle over the years but had never been elected president, and besides the treachery of Hawke Brothers this was the main grievance of her days. She clacked on and on, while Nancy threw inquisitive glances at her brother. Hawke had learned long ago that listening to his mother was not necessary; a smile and a nod now and then kept her going happily. He did not want to talk of the movie offer unless something came of it, so he let his mother fill the time with her usual noise while he devoured vast platefuls of beef and noodles, one of her best dishes. Then he went upstairs, thoroughly sobered by the food, and put himself to work in the tiny bedroom. It was hard to force thoughts of Anne Karen out of his mind, and also calculations of what various sums would fetch at twenty-five percent—fifty thousand dollars, eighty thousand dollars—but once he drove himself to write half a dozen lines the story seized his imagination and next thing he knew it was past eleven o'clock and Nancy was yelling at him from downstairs.

"Here's your other New York call, Art."

Jeanne's voice was just as he remembered it, very low in timbre and deeply stirring to him. She had waited a long time for him to return her call, she said, and finally had gone out to dinner. "With Karl Fry, as a matter of fact, Mr. Hawke. We talked a lot about your book. Karl said I was right not to give it to this man Luzzatto until you told me to."

"You were. I approve."

"Well, that's a relief! I had quite a little argument with Mr. Prince, you know. For all I know I'll be fired, but I don't much care."

"Jeanne, I appreciate your loyalty. I've talked to Luzzatto meantime. Now here's what you do." He gave her the instructions for bringing the manuscript to the actress at the Waldorf.

"What? Are you sure you want me to do that?" She sounded dismayed. "Suppose something happens to it?"

"Nothing will happen."

"Mr. Hawke, I realize selling the film rights can be important to you but—look, can't I get it duplicated first at least? I checked into microfilming, it wouldn't cost much."

"I promised to let her have it tomorrow, Jeanne."

She said obstinately, "Don't you have another copy? In any form, however crude?"

"Just scraps of drafts."

"Then I think it's too risky a thing to do. The book itself takes precedence over everything, even movie money."

He said a bit shortly, "Jeanne, that script survived four invasions, it'll survive two days in the Waldorf-Astoria Hotel."

She said even more shortly, "All right, Mr. Hawke. It's your novel."

"How are you doing on the styling?"

"I'm halfway through Part Two. Of course I'll lose these two days now."

"Any more sublime chapters you want to throw out?"

"Well, yes, to tell the truth. If I'm still employed at Prince House next week."

He was enjoying her brisk tart answers, and he found himself faintly puzzled and jealous at her having dined with a derelict divorced man like Karl Fry. "Jeanne, I miss you. I enjoyed our Christmas Eve."

"Oh? Did you? Why, thank you, I enjoyed it too." The modulation of the firm business voice into the tentative tones of an unmarried girl was amusing and delightful. "Am I really forgiven for O. Henry, then?"

"I've decided to be pleased with you about that."

"Well, good." Then the girl said impulsively, "As a matter of fact I miss you, too, though it's quite absurd considering that I hardly know you. Having your work in front of me all the time, well, it's a little as though you were here." She paused and then said, "Not enough, though. I shall now shut up."

"How's Karl, Jeanie?"

"Rather sad, but he's always witty, you know. We had a big blowup over the ending of his new mystery."

"I imagine you won."

She laughed in a very pleasant way. "As a matter of fact, I did."

"You'll give Anne Karen my script tomorrow?"

"Yes, sir. What a thrill! I may ask for her autograph."

"You lack reverence, Jeanne."

"Not for your book. For movie stars, yes. She's to have forty-eight hours, right?"

"Yes."

"She won't have forty-nine. Goodbye, Mr. Hawke."

"My name's Arthur, Jeanne."

"Oh, is it? Goodbye, Arthur."

Hawke walked into the parlor, where Nancy was curled on the couch very intent on a magazine. He dropped into the poisonous green armchair. "There's the kind of girl I may marry one of these days."

Nancy dropped the magazine instantly and sat up. "Really? Let's hear about her."

Hawke told the sister of his evening with Jeanne, and tried to give a physical description of the young stylist, but felt he was failing to do her justice. "All I can say is, she's not only pretty, she's smart and sweet and decent. Marriage is written all over her in huge red letters, that's the trouble. Nothing but marriage. I mean this girl is very sharp but she's not an emancipated type, if you understand me."

"I do." Nancy sat with her arms folded, eyes alive with interest. "Sounds to me like you ought to grab her."

"I've spent two hours with her in all, Nancy."

"That's all it takes to decide, sometimes." The sister's broad face showed some secret irony or amusement.

"Well, I'll say this, Nancy, it's damned reassuring to know that such girls do exist after all—competent girls, girls who don't drawl, and giggle, and tease, and talk silly rot in honey tones, and only want to know who your family is and have you got a convertible, these necking mindless Southern rabbits with one consuming urge, to marry a fellow with money, especially old family money, but in a pinch any kind of money."

"Don't carry on so, Art. Girls are girls, south or north. A girl wants a provider and there's nothing wrong with that." Again there was that secret, amused look. "It appears that you're going to be quite a provider yourself, so all these rabbits just guessed wrong and you've got the laugh on them. And this Jeanne Green girl is in luck."

"I'm a million miles from getting married, Nancy."

His sister said with a complete change of tone, "Are you? Why? I think you need looking after. How do you feel these days, Art? Tell me the truth. Does your head ever bother you?"

"No—well, truthfully, when I overwork, or I go too long without sleep, I fall into a kind of black hole, and various queer symptoms do begin to crop up—"

"What kind of symptoms?"

"It doesn't matter. A night's rest is all I ever need, Nancy, to clear them away."

"Working at night can't be good for you, Art. I was scared when I first saw you today. You look like the devil."

"Well, maybe now that I've got some money I can start going by human time again."

In another abrupt change she said, grinning, "Would you go out with me New Year's Eve?"

"Why, I guess so. What would we do, Nancy?"

"Who knows? Drive down to Tombs to the Green Frog, or something." The sister's sallow face was turning very red. "You see, there's this peculiar man in the bank. He's been there for months. He's the new assistant manager and he's very capable but he's insanely shy. He's never said anything to anybody, except for business. Well, yesterday he came up to me and said he heard my brother was having a book published, and I said yes, and he said he wanted to congratulate me, and would I go out with him New Year's Eve? Just like that!"

Hawke laughed. "I'm glad I brought you together. The thing is, three's a crowd."

"Well, but this man! He's sort of a German, Art, he has a queer heavy way of talking, and he has this ridiculous, really unbelievable brown wig. There isn't a single real hair on his head. I—well, somehow I don't dislike him, but—"

"But you want a chaperon."

"Well, I want to know what you think of him. I'm sure he'll just give mama the horrors."

"It's a date, Nancy."

"Now I've warned you, Art, he's an absolute fright. But I don't know, I don't exactly dislike him." The sister made her way out of the room, scarlet-faced and laughing. Hawke went back to work.

"I can't sleep. Phew! It's smoky in here. You could cut this air with a knife."

Hawke's desk clock read a quarter past four. He emerged from the visions of his story with a shake of the head, and turned to his mother. Her hair was in a gray gauzy cap. The quilted Japanese bathrobe which he had brought her from Hawaii enveloped her shapelessly. She blinked and peered at him, her face seeming as always many years younger without glasses.

"Sit down, mama. Want some of this coffee?"

"Mercy no, that's the last thing I need. My eyes popped open two hours ago like they were on springs, and I've been tossing and thinking ever since." She perched on the edge of his bed. "I reckon this room's getting a little on the small side for a famous writer. And it's so chilly! I'm going to have to put in an oil burner, Art, that coal furnace just doesn't throw any heat up into this front room. It never did and it never will. My room's warm as toast."

Hawke tried not to smile. He had frozen in this room through a dozen winters, and each winter his mother had talked about putting in an oil

burner. He wondered what subject she was circling around; he guessed it was Anne Karen. "I like writing in a cold room, mama, it keeps me waked up."

"Art, the more I think of it the more I don't want to take that thousand dollars."

Oh, lord, Hawke thought. "Why not, mom?"

The question might have been a mistake, but probably there was no escaping the flood that came. Mrs. Hawke reviewed her grievances against his dead Uncle Will, and the Hawke Brothers corporation, and against her husband for his lack of spine. She told him once again of her grandfather's fatal mistake in selling coal land outright instead of insisting on royalties. She reiterated her defiant faith that all the little parcels of wilderness she owned would some day prove to be treasures. They would make Art's children rich if not herself. The mine at Frenchman's Ridge was the best proof of this. Why, they had taken out hundreds of thousands of tons, they admitted it!

"Mama, anybody can mine coal up at Edgefield and lose money. That proves nothing."

"But that coal came out of our land, Art. It was worth a fortune and it's gone. What kind of payment is a thousand dollars for a thing like that?"

"Mom," said Hawke wearily, "you didn't own the mineral rights. Won't you ever see that? They made you a fair offer to settle a claim that can't hold up in a court."

"Art, that Hawke Brothers crowd wouldn't part with a thousand bottle caps, let alone a thousand dollars, unless they saw double their money out of it or better. *Why* do they want to give me a thousand dollars? That's what sticks in my craw."

"It was Scotty's idea. Glenn was against it."

"Ha! They were just putting on a show, all of them."

"Mama, I knew Scotty quite well at the university. He's a decent, responsible fellow."

"That was school. This is business. He's just like the rest of them, and that's why your cousin Eleanor married him, don't fool yourself. They're birds of a feather, that crowd. All money-mad."

"Let me understand you," Hawke said with exaggerated slow kindness. "You believe that the meeting yesterday was all rehearsed, correct? Glenn was only making believe he was grumpy. It was arranged for Scotty to offer the settlement and Glenn was supposed to object though really he was dying to have us fall in the trap and take a thousand dollars. The lawyers had their parts assigned too, that man from Lexington and Judge Crain. Or do you think old Harry Crain was in on the conspiracy? Let's get that clear."

"All right, Art, that was your father's way, making me out a fool. He was very good at that and in the end he ran a drugstore. Harry Crain's just an old lady. What we need is a lawyer."

"Scott Hoag offered to let you see the books of the mine, mom."

"Yes, I know, and that's something I want to take them up on, believe you me, before I accept their Santa Claus money. What's more you've got to do it, Art, not me. I can't read a company's books."

"I'm not an accountant."

"You're a man. It's a man's job to do these things. You can hire an accountant."

"An audit like that can take months."

"There's all the time in the world. The coal's gone."

"It could cost five hundred, a thousand dollars easily."

"You've got five thousand coming in. I don't have the money to spend myself, Art," whined the mother.

Hawke was not at all sure this was so. Devious secrecy about money came naturally to his mother. He knew that she was drawing some rental from the drugstore, and that she did receive a small coal royalty from her share in the estate of an aunt. His guess was that in this old house, especially with Nancy's earnings, his mother was living within her means, and probably buying more worthless coal land on remote cliffs. There was always plenty of excellent food in the house, and his mother and sister dressed well.

He said, more to dismiss his mother and get some sleep than anything else, "I'll phone Scott in the morning about the books, if that's what you want."

"That's just what I want. You're a good boy." She came to him and patted his head, a gesture which maddened him. He ground his teeth in silence. "Now I can sleep. I feel terrible, bothering a great writer with all this business talk, but some day you'll thank me." She gave him an irritating kiss on his forehead, and left. Hawke glanced mechanically at the last paragraph on the page before him. It seemed a jumble of words scrawled by an idiot. But this was a familiar effect, not necessarily accurate. Time to quit.

When he woke at noon the same paragraphs looked brilliant. The sun was blazing outside, and white snow mantled the yard. He had had seven straight hours of sleep. His first thought on waking was that at this very moment Anne Karen was reading his *Alms for Oblivion*; Anne Karen, whose luminous shadow he had adored as a boy of seventeen! The radio next door was blasting

> "*Jerusalem, Jerusalem,*
> *Open your gates and sing,*
> *Hosannah in the highest!*"

and for once the music from next door was a sound track made for his mood. He was picturing billboard signs all over the country and an electric display atop the Astor Theatre in New York:

ANNE KAREN
in
YOUNGBLOOD HAWKE'S
ALMS FOR OBLIVION

He looked at himself this way and that in the bathroom mirror singing. "Jerusalem, Je–roo–salem!" Yes, sir, that pasty young man with the broad square jaw, and the straight heavy nose, and that wide underlip curled over the upper one, was the author of that book! Yes indeed, he had seen his face in this same darkening spotty mirror the first time he had shaved, he had despaired over his pimples at this very mirror, and now he was looking at the face of YOUNGBLOOD HAWKE, by God! He came bawling into the kitchen, "Jeroosalem, Jer–oooo–salem!" flung himself into a chair with a crash, and ferociously attacked the ham and eggs his mother set smoking before him.

She said, "Well, you seem full of beans today."

"Mountain air, mama. Home cooking. The sight of my loved ones. Hey! Biscuits and honey, by God!"

What a marvellous breakfast! After all, there was something to being home. This was the only room in the house that Hawke liked. In fact he loved the kitchen. It was the biggest room, and it had the biggest windows. He didn't mind the familiar laundry smell from the foam-brimming washtub. This was the room where all the good things had happened, the eating, the family small talk, the giggling fits with Nancy. It was the real living room. The dining room and the parlor were both dingy gestures at polite life. The Hawkes had been a kitchen family, and he always felt good in a kitchen. If only it were spring, so that the lilacs at the window would be blooming, and warm perfumed air would be blowing in! There were worse places than home, and worse mothers than the woman who now put another slab of sizzling red ham before him, and poured his coffee. Mom was a problem, but she had a charming smile, and she was nobody's fool. A trifle paranoid; but then, he himself needed a streak of obstinate lunacy to be an artist, and no doubt he owed his ample endowment to his mother.

He blurted, in this wave of good feeling, "Mom, you know what? Now don't tell anybody, and don't ask me a lot of questions, nothing's definite, but I may sell my book to the movies."

"Really? My, that's nice, Art." She smiled uncertainly. "Very nice. How much would they pay you?"

"None of that's settled. It's all very complicated, a movie negotiation."

"But I mean, you can become a millionaire, can't you? Gracious! A movie!"

"Not with a first book."

"Don't sell it cheap, boy. I have a feeling it's good."

"Mom, you couldn't stand it when you read it."

"Well, I don't like these sordid stories, Art, everybody so greedy for money and all. Why, that book is all about money, and how mean people are. I'm not saying everybody's lily-white and altruistic but there's such a thing as loving your fellow man and serving him, and that's my creed. I think there should be more stories about wholesome people. You ought to write one. It would be a big money maker. But I'm only thinking with you selling this thing to a publisher right off like that, even if they only gave you five hundred down, and these phone calls from New York and all, why I think it must be worth money."

"Don't worry, I won't give it away."

"I hope not. Art, you won't forget to call Scott Hoag about examining those books, will you?"

Some of Hawke's elation departed, but he nodded, and wiped his mouth. "No time like the present." He went straight to the telephone.

Scotty said, "Boy, you really timed it. I had my hand on the doorknob, I'm all set to drive up to Lexington . . . Hey, boy, you see the *Gazette* yet this morning? You splashed all over the front page."

Hawke told him what his mother wanted. Scott's tone changed at once, still pleasant but serious. "That's a reasonable request, Art. She wants every last thing that's coming to her but by the Christ that's how you gotta be in this world."

"Is it all right?"

"I think so . . . Hell, sure it's all right, they couldn't stop her by law, I don't think, if she insisted. I'm not saying it won't be messy. You know, Art, your mother's antagonized that family over the years."

"I know."

"I had trouble last night over this thousand dollars. I don't want to bore you with all this, but ole Mister Will put the family's holdings in a trust fund, and every time we have to do something we end up discussing it with the ladies. Well, you know how women are in binness. I got them calmed down and it's all set. This might kick over the crock again. She definitely won't take the thousand?"

"After she's looked at the books, she says."

"Art, she shoulda been a binness man. Look, I gotta get down to Lexington like a bat out of hell. I'll do some phoning from there, and I'll call you on this tonight. Okay?"

"Thanks, Scott."

"Take a look at the *Gazette*, boy. You a goddamn local hero. Bye."

Hawke picked up the *Gazette* on the porch, surprised by the balminess of the air outside. He opened the paper with undignified speed:

HOVEY AUTHOR
SELLS NOVEL
'ARMS TO OBLIVION' TITLE
OF ARTHUR HAWKE'S BOOK

It was the leading story, in the right-hand corner. The photograph jolted him. What idiots, using a high school picture! Badly reproduced, it showed him with a growth of black hair all the way down on his forehead like a gorilla. Had he lost that much hair? His cheeks in the picture were hollow, his face mournfully long, sensitive, and innocent. The story was three short paragraphs, clumsily written and snide.

. . . Mr. Hawke steadfastly refused to tell the newspaperman, when interviewed in a bar, what his book was about. He seemed more interested in getting his drink refilled. Though he is living in New York now the author still likes bourbon, with a beer chaser, so he has not entirely deserted the South in his tastes. But Hovey is going to have to wait with baited breath until his book appears to find out the subject. First novels seldom sell, but Mr. Hawke exudes confidence about this one.

His mother scanned the newspaper with delight, holding it by the edges in her dripping hands, but her face fell when she read this last paragraph. "Mercy, this makes you sound like a barfly! Now why on earth would they write a thing like that? I declare, it must be some whippersnapper who's sick jealous of you. Well, he can just stew in his own bile." She put the paper down carefully. "What did Scott Hoag say?"

Hawke told her. The mother wrinkled her nose and pursed her lips. "He's stalling."

"Mom, he just has to get the consent of the trustees."

"Ha! We'll see."

He decided to walk down the hill to observe how his home town was taking the news about the book. Melting snow lay white on the street and the lawns, and MacDougall Hill, far across the river, was a great wall of white, but the air was so warm that he wore no hat or coat. The steep gutters gurgled with swift running water. Exaltation buoyed his steps as he walked down the street of his long anonymity, in his new identity of professional novelist. He saw High Street with peculiar clarity, as though it were an imaginary scene in a book he was writing. It was no longer quite real, or it was more than real. It lacked ordinariness. This strange light lay on all of Hovey, and on the people he talked to.

He talked to many neighbors and old school friends; and he met Reverend Yeager too, on Main Street. Their varying reactions—curiosity, effusiveness, skepticism, hostility, feigned casualness, genuine pleasure—

had one note in common, indeed one word. The word was "sell." They hoped it would sell, or they wondered whether it would sell, or did his publishers think it would sell, or nowadays novels didn't seem to sell. Even Reverend Yeager said with devilish worldliness, "I'm sure anything you write, Arthur, will ah, *sell*." And the Reverend mentioned that the church was building a new community room, and that it would be a fitting memorial for a loved one like, say, Ira Hawke. A plaque over the door could be arranged.

As he walked along Main Street, a car honked at him and drew up to the curb. It was Scotty Hoag, in a long new station wagon, the varnished yellow wood shining in the sun. "Hey Art, I tried to call you back. I'm off to Lexington. Think I'll make it with all that snow out there?"

"Hell, Scott, it's just mush, the trucks'll have it all smashed up by now."

"Well, boy, they all bowing down to you in this town?"

"Not at all. The question remains, will it sell? Most of them seem to think not, or hope not."

Scott laughed. "Human nature, boy. You a writer, you know all about that. Don't worry, it'll sell. Say, Art." He turned off the motor and slid away from the wheel to the window. "I thought I'd better get on the ball on this binness of your mother's, so I talked to them all. It's okay. You can look at the books up at the Hawke Brothers office today, or anytime, or send in an accountant."

"Thanks, Scott. You know this is all my mother's idea."

"Sure. What your ma wants most here is peace of mind, a sense that she wasn't cheated. Sleeping nights is more important than a thousand dollars to her, Art, and I think she should examine the books. In the long run that'll save you trouble too, won't it? These trips back to Hovey for legal conferences and all. Your work shouldn't be disturbed with this kind of thing. Frankly, Art, I don't know about the thousand any more, those old biddies are furious, but maybe they'll simmer down."

"Well, mama will want both, of course. The books and the thousand."

Scott shrugged, blew out his cheeks, and lit a cigarette with the dashboard lighter, blue puffs from a bright orange coil. "Well, let's see how it goes. It's all pretty small potatoes, Art. For me, and I reckon for you too." He slid across the seat, started the motor, and grinned at Hawke. "You still remember the sermon?"

"Guvment bonds, Scotty."

"That's the word. Now next time you in Lexington you call me, hear? Let's hope I don't get killed on this sumbitchin' road. Good luck with that book."

When Hawke got home and told his mother the decision, Mrs. Hawke smiled slightly, and nodded. "Fine. Will you hire the accountant, or do you want me to, or what?"

He and his mother argued about dividing the cost of an accountant. His mother made so much trouble about it, and began to whine so piteously—it was really Art's duty as the man of the family to look into those books, not hers, he was the one who was going to benefit, she only had a few more years to live anyway, and on and on—that he finally said he would bear the cost, providing his mother did the rest and he heard no more of it. Mrs. Hawke brightened as though the sun had just come out and shone on her, and said he was a good boy and always did the right thing in the end.

He was starting up the stairs to return to work when the telephone burst out with the long wavering ring of the long-distance operator. He heard Luzzatto's voice as soon as he picked up the receiver, "Hollo, hollo, Youngblood? Hollo? Operator, what's the matter?" Then the producer faded out, and a sugary Southern voice said, "One moment, please, fo' New Yoke."

Several minutes of exasperating foolishness followed among four different operators, two with thick Southern accents and two with screeching New York voices like rusty files. At last he heard again, "Hollo, Youngblood? What's wrong with those operators down there?"

"These are the back woods, Mr. Luzzatto. Our operator here in Hovey is a bear. Makes things a bit awkward. What can I do for you?"

Luzzatto roared with laughter, and said to somebody, "He says that down in the Kentucky mountains the telephone operators are bears." Hawke heard tinkling laughter of at least two women. "Youngblood, for a hillbilly you're all right. Say, Youngblood, that goddamn script of yours is two thousand pages long."

"I never said it was shorter."

"I've got Anne right here, I'm in her apartment. She took one look at the script and blew her top. She has eyestrain anyway, and half of the pages are faint carbon copies, and ten different colored papers, couldn't you get it typed up by a decent service?"

"Mr. Luzzatto, I wrote a lot of that book out in the Pacific. I'm sorry it isn't up to Hollywood standards of neatness. I'm just going to work on my new novel, and you've interrupted me. If there's anything I can do—"

"Hold your horses, Youngblood, we have a deal here that I'm trying to hold together, that's all. Now I just spoke to Ferdie Lax."

"Lax? Isn't he out at sea on the *Queen Elizabeth?*"

"Of course. What is that? I spoke to him ship-to-shore. He says you told him the story and it gave him goosepimples. Youngblood, why don't you come up here and tell your story to Anne?"

"When?"

"When? Now, this afternoon. Grab a plane. I want you here by tonight."

Standing at the telephone table, Hawke straightened up. His lower lip curled over the upper one, covering it tightly. He said nothing.

"Hey Youngblood, are you still there?"

"I'm here. Mr. Luzzatto, I'm up in the mountains. There are no planes here. I'm visiting my mother. I just came down from New York. I don't feel like going back up there. Anne Karen is welcome to read my book, as I said. It will be called for in forty-eight hours."

"Hawke, this is a deal. Don't be so goddamn independent, the whole thing will fall apart."

"Let it."

"Hm? Ha? Did you say *let it?*"

"That's right. Let it."

"One second." He heard a dim murmur, Luzzatto's voice and a woman's. Luzzatto spoke again: "Youngblood, I respect a man's privacy. I'm sorry I broke in on your work. We're in an emergency situation here. Look here—please—come up tonight. If Anne likes your story I'll pay you the twenty-five thousand dollars, all of it, right away. Now how is that?"

Hawke had been carrying on this conversation almost without thinking; rasped nerves and bristling pride had been dictating his answers. This sudden offer disconcerted him. He said nothing.

"Hollo, Youngblood? Are you still there?"

"I'm here. Let me think about that. I'll call you back."

"No, no, please. With those bears you got for operators who knows when we'll make another connection? Listen, Youngblood, this is my best offer. I'll pay you a bonus of *five thousand dollars* for the inconvenience of leaving your mother's home and making a special trip to New York. The same minute I shake hands with Anne Karen, I'll write you a check for thirty thousand dollars. Now that's the deal. That's for a first novel that hasn't even been published yet, that I haven't even read! I've never made such a deal before. I never *heard* of such a deal."

Twenty-five percent of thirty thousand dollars, Hawke swiftly figured, was more than seven thousand a year. As he hesitated the producer said, "Look, will you talk to Anne? Here she is."

The voice was unmistakable: husky, commanding yet gentle, rich with sexuality, faintly tinged by her Austrian accent, yet racy American in its tones, the wonderful voice of Anne Karen: "Hello, Mr. Hawke. I think we are being very dreadful to you. It's all my fault and I beg your pardon."

"There's nothing to apologize for, Miss Karen."

"Mr. Hawke, I have heard such marvellous things about you and your book, and that outline is such a wretched disappointment! I've read the first eight or nine pages of your book, I'm holding them in my hand this very second, and they're electrifying, Mr. Hawke. I'd sit up all night and read the book straight through if my eyes would stand it. But they won't.

They're getting worse by the day, I have to put drops in them to see my hand in front of my face. That's why I have to go to Hawaii. It's all nerves, when my nerves go bad my eyes dim out. What are we going to do? I simply must know a little more about your book, and I think you're the only one in the world who can tell me."

It was dizzying to hear such nervous business-like chatter in the grand-opera voice of Anne Karen. Until this moment he had heard that voice speaking only well-rehearsed sonorous lines of screen plays. This talk in her own identity was strangely flat and at the same time more exciting than any movie performance. He said, "Miss Karen, you're very kind, and —maybe I'm being ungracious, I just came home to see my mother, that's all. It's been a year since I've seen her and—"

"Please, Mr. Hawke, ungracious? We are the ones who are behaving terribly. This is an impossible profession, and we all become like animals. Look, I will cancel my booking to Hawaii. Boats leave every week. When can you come to New York? I will wait here for you."

Hawke said instantly, "Miss Karen, when must you leave New York? What day? What time?"

"One moment, —Honor, dear, he wants to know exactly when we leave —Just a moment, Mr. Hawke."

He heard a young woman's voice clearly say, "Well, mother, if we're to get on that boat Thursday we have to take the train Sunday night at eleven—unless you want to fly."

Anne Karen told this schedule to Hawke, adding, "I have an utter horror of flying. I'm sorry, I can't help it."

Hawke said, "All right. I can't make the plane from Lexington today. The next one leaves tomorrow around noon. I can be in New York late tomorrow, Saturday night. We can meet Sunday morning. Say ten o'clock?"

The movie star said, "No, no it's no good. You're only making me feel more ashamed of myself. I meant what I said about cancelling my boat tickets. I feel ghastly about breaking up your Christmas at home."

"Miss Karen, I daresay you've spent Christmas at home now and then. It's no great hardship to leave."

The woman burst into a glorious laugh, a golden shower of tone, and repeated what he had said to the others. He heard Luzzatto's rough laughter, and dimly, "Well, is he coming?"

She said, "Mr. Hawke, I leave it up to you. Either way."

"We have an appointment, Miss Karen. Ten o'clock Sunday morning in New York. Where?"

"Here at the Waldorf. Just come up to my suite, we'll have breakfast and we'll talk. You must be a marvellous young man. I'm very impatient to meet you."

"I'll be there, ma'am. Goodbye."

His mother and sister never questioned the inevitability of his going at once. Clearly they would have regarded even momentary balking as an insane act. Anne Karen! He had received a summons from on high, a telegram from the White House. Of course he would go. The women's part was to say goodbye bravely, smiling through not wholly unhappy tears. His mother said at dinner, "We'll miss you, Art, but anyway you accomplished what you came for. We're getting into the books of that mine. You mark my word, those robbers will pay us a fortune yet."

Hawke was too pleased at the prospect of leaving Hovey to argue. Let his mother comfort herself with her delusions; one needed something to give a spark to life in this dank, gloomy valley town cut off from the real world.

Nancy came into his bedroom late at night when he was packing, and embraced him and kissed him violently. "It's only the beginning. You'll go through New York and Hollywood like a hot knife through butter. Then you'll be all finished with that foolishness and you'll sit on a mountain top like Nietzsche and write books that will last forever." His sister was staring at him with glistening eyes.

"Nancy, I'm sorry I won't be here New Year's Eve."

"Oh, well, I guess I can handle my man with the wig. In fact he seems harmless as a sheep. But nice. He was actually glad when I said you'd come along on the date! He seemed relieved."

"I wish I could meet him."

"You will when you come back." Then the sister laughed, or rather giggled as she had used to years and years ago in their tickling fights. "That is, maybe you will. Who knows? Anyway, thanks."

"For what?"

"Just thanks." She kissed him again. "I guess this is goodbye for another long while."

"I'll see you at breakfast."

"I know, but—Art, take care of your health. You're terribly strong but you're not indestructible."

"Okay."

"I wish I could go to New York with you. Just to have a look at this Jeanne Green. But you see, I can't. It seems I've got this date." She looked at him, her eyes filling with tears, and she dashed a fist at her eyes, grinning. "Oh hell. Goodbye, Youngblood Hawke, till next time."

5

Hawke did not arrive at the Waldorf on ten o'clock Sunday morning. By then nobody was expecting him. A savage blizzard, rolling in from Canada early on Saturday, had grounded planes, delayed trains from twelve to twenty-four hours, and halted automobile traffic everywhere in the eastern part of the country. On Sunday morning the storm was still dumping snow in New York City. The deserted sidewalks were white, the streets were white where fresh tire tracks had not scarred them, the mournfully clanking snow removers were making no headway even on the main avenues, and parked cars, hydrants, and lamp posts were capped with tall, growing sugar loaves of clean snow. Roberto Luzzatto had not heard from the young author since their conversation on Friday. He had checked the airlines, buses, and railroads late Saturday night and had ascertained that there was no way Hawke could possibly get out of the Allegheny Mountains to New York at any time on Sunday, unless there was a sudden and unexpected let-up in the blizzard; in which case conceivably a plane might get out of Lexington and bring him to town about eleven-thirty at night. By then Anne Karen would already have boarded the train for the west coast; it was scheduled to depart on time, despite the snow. The blizzard was racking her taut nerves; she would not hear of a delay; she was not that interested in Hawke's book or in anything else. Luzzatto was known in the industry for his ability to digest bad luck. This was an ill turn of the wheel, that was all. Anne Karen's commitment to him would evaporate, since he now had no property with which to tie her down. A hundred things like this had happened to him over the years, sometimes bringing him heavy loss and even bankruptcy. He had notified the actress on Saturday night that the meeting could not take place. He had then proceeded to his usual midnight pleasures around the town, snow or no snow, misfortune or no misfortune, and had gone to sleep without a worry in the world, though the loss of the Anne Karen film threatened to throw down his entire shaky structure of interlocking loans and projects. Luzzatto had the right temperament for his trade.

At four o'clock Sunday afternoon when the snow was still falling heavily, and the great actress was soaking in a hot tub to relieve her nervousness, the telephone in her suite rang several times. A pudgy young woman came out of the bedroom carrying a gold lamé evening dress. She picked up the telephone with a disgusted glance at two maids who were yammering in a Scandinavian tongue over half a dozen open trunks and suitcases full of tumbled clothes. The operator said, "Mr. Youngblood Hawke is calling."

The young woman's face brightened. "Oh, yes. Put him on. Hello, Mr.

Hawke. No, I'm her daughter, my name is Honor Lesser— It's quite all right. The weather was impossible, we realized that. Mother hopes to see you when she returns, it'll only be a month or so— What? I beg your pardon? Mr. Hawke, aren't you calling from Kentucky?" A look of supreme astonishment came over her face. "You *are*? Well, how in heaven's name did you do it? One moment, Mr. Hawke."

She put down the telephone, went to the door of the master bathroom, and rapped. "Mother, that writer from Kentucky is here!"

"*What?*"

"Youngblood Hawke. He's calling from the lobby."

"It's impossible, dear. Roberto called the airlines and the railroad. There's no way he could have gotten here."

"He drove, mother. He rented a car and drove up from Kentucky. He's *here*," Honor Lesser said impatiently. "He's downstairs."

"Well, good God, he's another Lindbergh or something. Well, good God. Honor, call Roberto right away. And send Else in here. Tell her I want the green robe, I hope she hasn't packed it."

Hawke came into Anne Karen's suite like an ape let loose by a bored king in a French drawing room. His hair was wild and matted, black bristles stood on his face, his eyes were completely bloodshot, his trousers were out of press and his old duffle coat was grease-smeared. He said to Honor Lesser in a rasp—he had caught a fulminating cold and suspected his temperature was about a hundred and three—"I'm sorry, ma'am, I know I look like holy hell. I had to change two tires. It's a wonder they let me come up. I realize I'm a few hours late, but—"

"Mr. Hawke, it's amazing that you came at all. Hilda, bring some Scotch and glasses."

He fumbled the old leather toilet kit, a companion from navy days, in his big grease-blackened hands. "If I could shave and wash up a bit, ma'am—"

"Of course. But have a drink."

The whiskey went down his throat like warm water. He grinned in apology for tossing off such a large hooker. The young woman instantly poured him another, saying, "How on earth did you drive through that blizzard?"

"Well, it wasn't too bad, ma'am. You see I didn't go the short way through West Virginia, those mountains would be impassable in this weather. I just struck up along the Ohio Valley to U.S. 22. I knew the big trucks would keep the snow smashed on 22. Then it was straight across to New York, no strain, except I drove right through the night and I reckon I could use a little sleep." He grinned dolefully.

She said, "Good lord, I think you risked your life." Once more she re-filled his glass. He was babbling a bit, but she could scarcely blame him.

"Oh, nothing like that. It just didn't seem right to disappoint a lady."

They both laughed. "It was kind of interesting, you know, and beautiful. There wasn't much traffic. The accents of the disk jockeys keep changing every couple of hundred miles, it's something I never realized. But they all have the same feeble mind. Honestly, ma'am, you listen to the radio twenty hours straight in a car and you'll think this country's rotting into imbecility. I was right on the old track of the pioneers over the Alleghenies you know, the Ohio Valley and Route 22, only going the other way. I wonder what in hell the pioneers would make of the radio, and I swear to God, ma'am, I also wonder how we won two world wars. No, no more booze, thanks. That was just right, my blood's circulating again. Where can I wash?"

"Right in here. You know, I've managed to read about half your book, Mr. Hawke. I think it's a distinguished first novel, truly I do."

He smiled at her gratefully. "I sure look like a distinguished novelist, don't I? Just let me mess up a few Waldorf towels."

The daughter saw at once, coming into her mother's dressing room, that the actress was concerned about the meeting with Hawke. Nobody could be more slovenly than Anne Karen. She was incapable of looking really bad, even at fifty-one, and disorder often gave her a wonderful chance charm. But she was at her dressing table, polishing herself with care. "What is he like?"

"Sort of savage."

"Savage?"

"Well, he's huge, and hairy, and he's dressed like a truck driver. And I guess he hasn't shaved or slept for days. He looks frightful. Very young, and rather gentle."

The actress lifted one eyebrow. "Somehow you make him sound attractive."

"He has a pleasant smile. It's remarkable the way he got here."

"Thirty thousand dollars looks big to a young writer."

"He only agreed to come after you turned on the tears about going blind."

Anne Karen laughed. "I gave him a way to climb down off his high horse. Roberto offended him."

"Well, I don't know. He has a refreshing manner. Very genuine."

Anne Karen said with a slant glance at her daughter, "I'm sure he's genuine. He's new."

Hawke emerged from the bathroom looking remarkably better; indeed quite handsome in a brutish way, Honor Lesser thought. He had put off the queer duffle coat. He was wearing his brown tweed "novelist's suit," so the lack of press didn't matter much, and apparently he had had a new shirt somewhere on him, for his linen was very white. His eyes burned, and his face was ashen, but a ready smile of good humor and

will power cancelled any sickly appearance. He had gulped several aspirins, and he was not feeling badly at all.

"More Scotch?" she said.

"Well, yes, ma'am. Although this story I'll tell may not resemble the book I wrote very much if I keep slugging down the firewater."

"Nonsense. It's just what you need."

Roberto Luzzatto arrived and enfolded Hawke in a bearhug, and said if Hollywood writers had half his gumption, making movies would be simple. Then the bedroom door opened and out sailed Anne Karen in a loose green silk robe, her black hair falling to her shoulders, her great blue eyes sparkling like ice in sunshine. She apologized for her appearance, for her delay in coming out, for the horrid mess in the suite, and all the time Hawke stared at her as though the Mona Lisa had walked out of its frame and started talking. The daughter was not bad-looking, though much too plump; she had the actress's hair and a faint echo of her charm. But he felt sorry for any woman who had to live within range of Anne Karen. The actress was supernaturally beautiful. She did not seem more than thirty.

When he began to tell the story she slid off the sofa to the floor, and curled there with one arm on her daughter's knee, in a pose of delicious balance and charm. "I'm sorry, this is the only way I can think. I do all my reading on the floor—that is when my poor eyes are working." Sitting so, she somehow pulled all the lines in the room to converge on her. The brilliant green of her robe was like a jewel in the gold, pink, and cream of the room. Her beauty distracted Hawke like a blazing naked lamp, and he found it hard to get going in his tale. Anne Karen fiddled with the cord of her robe as he talked, and she seemed disappointed and bored, though she kept smiling sweetly.

But then he took hold of them. Hawke was himself not without some of the equipment of an actor—magnetic vitality, almost maniacal bursts of self-confidence, and natural expressive gesture. He had what the actors lack, and this lack makes them dumb prisoners until a script frees them to shine —command of words. He could not only write them, he could at moments like these pour them from his tongue. Anne Karen took her elbow from her daughter's knee. She sat up straight, hugging her knees, her lovely face hardening. She lit one cigarette and another, staring off to the wall, looking at him only now and then. Hawke's story took new possession of him, as he saw it beginning to grip his three listeners. Feverish thrills ran along his spine as he worked up to the climax; he knew he was quite sick, but it didn't matter. He paced as he talked. His voice faded to a scraping whisper. He finished the story, and sank in an armchair. It had taken him twenty minutes to tell it. He knew he had left out all the subtleties and some of the best scenes, but he also knew he had impressed

these people. He took the whiskey that Honor Lesser thrust in his hand and drank it down.

With a heavy sigh, Anne Karen turned to Luzzatto. "Roberto, come inside for a moment. Thank you, Mr. Hawke." They disappeared into the bedroom, the actress beckoning to her daughter.

Honor Lesser said to Hawke, "You told that story remarkably, but you look as though you have a fever, and good heavens, your voice!"

"Few hours sleep all I need," Hawke croaked. She left him.

His eyes dropped shut almost at once, and he was back at the wheel of the rented Plymouth, ploughing along a snowy highway that swooped back and forth before him in the dark and he was roaring past trucks on slippery upgrades, taking his life in his hands, and trucks were booming at him and past him with headlights that hurt his eyes, and he was bawling at the top of his lungs all the obscene songs from navy days that he could think of, to keep himself awake, and figuring over and over what twenty-five percent of five thousand dollars was, or ten thousand, or fifteen, it wouldn't do to gamble all of it at first—then he heard a door open and he snapped out of it, shivering, shocked for an instant to find himself in the ornate hot hotel room. Luzzatto and the actress were approaching. The actress said, "Mr. Hawke, can we talk about your wonderful, wonderful story for just a minute or two? Then I'll let you go, I know you're exhausted."

"All you want," Hawke grated. "I feel fine."

She was on the floor again, in a pool of green silk, leaning against an armchair, looking up at him. She said it was a splendid film story, and she was fascinated by the idea of playing the old aunt, a tremendous part, almost a female King Lear. "I have faced it long ago, Mr. Hawke, my days of playing silly love stories are over, these are the parts I must look for." It was five years since she had made a picture, and if ever she was to make one again *Alms for Oblivion* was the perfect vehicle. She talked so fluently that he had nothing to do but nod now and then. The dark burly producer sat on the edge of the sofa, biting his nails. Anne Karen was talking about the aunt, analyzing her character. Her comments were intelligent though flowery, and too much laced with Freudian cant. She spoke of the aunt's youth as she imagined it, of the love affairs that might have turned her into the queer tough spinster of the book. He nodded and nodded. What the woman was driving at soon became clear. She wanted scenes in the film of the aunt's youth, and a new subplot about her tragic first love. "It may be horribly presumptuous of me, Mr. Hawke. But films are a different medium, and I feel this would give the part a density, a range, it doesn't have now. The part would become one any actress would give her life to play. I don't think it would do violence to your book, on the contrary don't you think it

might make the story—purely from an audience standpoint—more emotional, more understandable?"

Hawke said, "I'm sure it would. Probably the novel would have been better if I'd thought of doing it that way in the first place."

"You really think that? You truly do?" The actress looked at Luzzatto, her eyes lighting.

"Oh yes."

"You wouldn't object to such an approach in the screenplay?"

"Not at all."

The actress stood, and both the men did too. "Talk to this wonderful young man for a while," the actress said to Luzzatto. "I want to call Roy."

When the bedroom door closed and the two men were alone together, Luzzatto charged at Hawke and pounded his back. "She's calling her agent. We are in, you brilliant bastard. We are in. We make the picture."

"I hope so." Hawke poured himself Scotch. It was not having the slightest effect on him except to keep him going.

"You are a goddamn salesman, not only a writer," Luzzatto said. "*The novel would be better if I'd thought of doing it that way in the first place!* Do you realize what that did to her ego? That was inspired. You closed the deal right there."

"Well, I meant it," Hawke said. "There are a hundred ways to tell a story."

Luzzatto's eyelids dropped lazily over his eyes, and he squinted at Hawke in silence. Then he too took Scotch.

A bottle of iced champagne arrived at the suite in a few minutes. The actress with her daughter reappeared from the bedroom, flushed and laughing, to drink toasts to *Alms for Oblivion*. Hawke felt no elation, only a slight relief. That barrier was crossed. He sensed that his own reactions were abnormal, that an unknown mountain boy who had just sold a novel to motion pictures should be in an ecstasy of pride and delight. But his last energy was waning, and all he wanted was a good excuse to get out of the suite. Luzzatto rescued him; they had a little business to discuss, he said, before he put this young man to bed. Honor Lesser brought out the dilapidated duffle coat.

He said hoarsely as he took it, "Sorry I drank up all your whiskey. I guess I'll be able to buy myself an overcoat now."

"Oh, don't," she said. "Anybody can wear an overcoat. I'll never forget how you looked when you burst in here."

Then one of the maids carried in the five battered boxes of manuscript, and Hawke took them. Anne Karen accompanied him to the elevator, transfixing with astonishment a couple of guests in the corridor. She said goodbye to him as though it were the end of a love scene.

Luzzatto sat him at a table in the wood-panelled men's bar. "Well, Hawke, this was one hell of a day's work. How about closing it with a

golden fastener, hm? Want to write the screenplay, too? I want to get going. Nobody knows this book better than you."

"I don't know, Mr. Luzzatto. Let me think about it. I'm pretty well played out."

Luzzatto took a check book from an inside pocket. "I make a deal with you for the screenplay right here in this bar. You know how long a movie script is? About ten thousand words. What do you say I give you a five thousand advance now, on top of the thirty you've got coming, and ten thousand more when you finish? Forty-five thousand instead of thirty. Why should some mediocrity in Hollywood get paid for writing your story over again, hm?"

An obscure alarm was sounding in Hawke's fevered mind. "It sounds good. We'll talk about it."

Luzzatto shrugged. "Well, meantime I owe you thirty." He began to write a check, then stopped. "Should I write this to Ferdie Lax? He made the deal or at least the contact. I suppose he gets ten percent."

"I don't know," Hawke said in confusion. "I guess I have to thrash that out with him."

"And does your publisher participate? Sometimes they do, in first novels."

Like a bee sting, the words brought Hawke angrily alert. He had forgotten that too, utterly forgotten it; Prince got half! Rapidly he calculated; unless he was out of his mind he was going to get from Luzzatto not thirty thousand but something like eleven or twelve thousand! How could he have blacked the publisher and the agent out of his mind? How could he ever have consented to these vampire percentages? He would have to fight for his money, right away! "Mr. Luzzatto," he said thickly and unsteadily, "Give me that check. I'll handle it."

"Of course." Luzzatto completed the check, ripped it free, and handed it to Hawke. "You brought this off fabulously, Hawke. I'm excited about you. You're a big talent. Maybe you're *the* big talent we're all looking for. I'll talk to you tomorrow."

There was no telephone in his cold lair in the loft building. He called Frieda Winter from the telephone booth in the candy store at the corner, shivering despite the choking radiator heat that filled the little store. Here came another shock. The maid who answered said that Mrs. Winter was out of the country.

"Is she still in Jamaica?"

"Nossuh, she gone to Europe."

"*Europe?* Did she leave a message for me?" Then, stammering, "Uh, I mean—my name is Youngblood Hawke. I borrowed some valuable books of hers."

There was a tinge of amusement in the voice of the young Negress.

"Nossuh. No message, I guess you better keep those books until she gets back, suh."

"When will that be?"

"Some time in February, suh."

But Jeanne Green was in. He talked to her briefly, then went up to his room, which surprised him with its barren squalor, its immense bare pipes along the ceiling, its grime-crusted windows, its streaky whitewashed walls. Quite a change from the Waldorf! Yet he felt safe and good, through his fever; the animal back in its hole. More aspirin, two scribbled notes, a long fiery gulp from a bottle of bourbon in his suitcase; then blackness.

Jeanne arrived half an hour later and climbed the twilit stairs. A note in Hawke's strong clear hand was taped to the dented rusty metal door. *"Come in, Jeanie. It's on the desk."* In the icy room a round electric heater gleamed coppery red on the floor, the only light. It enabled her to find and switch on the desk lamp. Hawke was breathing quickly and heavily on the mattress on the floor, covered with blankets, the duffle coat piled on top. *Alms for Oblivion* was stacked on the desk, with a note on it, *"Sold, by God, as a starring vehicle for Anne Karen. So be careful with it, and thanks. What are you doing New Year's Eve?"*

He was muttering in his sleep. She crouched beside him, slipped off a black glove, and put her cool hand on his hot, sweat-beaded forehead. He turned this way and that, opened his eyes, and smiled wearily. "Hi, Nancy," he said. He rolled over, his head pillowed on an arm. The girl sat in the chair at the desk, not moving, not taking off her coat, for an hour or so. Now and then she put her hand to his brow, but it did not disturb him. He became quieter, and began breathing more easily.

Jeanne Green took the manuscript, and staggered downstairs in the darkness with the heavy precious burden. She had written under his inquiry about New Year's Eve, *"Nothing. Got any ideas?"*

It was incredible to her that she had first met this strange man seven days ago. Her life seemed to have begun when he walked into the office of Waldo Fipps and found her reading his book; and that seemed to have happened in the far past.

Part Two
1947

CHAPTER FIVE

1

No MAN can know what it is like to be a woman taking her firstborn in her arms for the first time; but a writer who holds a freshly printed copy of his first book must have a fair idea of what the woman feels. It lies rectangular and spotless in his hands, with his name on the jacket. It is his pass to the company of the great. Fielding, Stendhal, Melville, Tolstoy wrote books. Now he has written one. It does not matter that the dust lies brown and thick on millions of books in libraries everywhere, it does not matter that most new books fall dead, it does not matter that of the thousands of books published each year only a half dozen will survive the season. All that may be. Meantime he has written a book! The exaltation does not last. It cannot. It is too piercing. It is gone before he has drawn twenty breaths. But in those twenty breaths he has smelled the sweetest of all savors, the savor of total fulfillment. After that, no matter what success he may achieve, he is just another writer, with a writer's trials and pleasures. That joy never comes again in all its first purity.

Hawke's first copy of *Alms for Oblivion* arrived in the mail on a morning in June, a few weeks before publication day. The volume seemed to fill his hot squalid loft room with light. He sat at his desk, staring and staring at it, enjoying his once-in-a-lifetime thrill. Then the question arose, what to do with the book? Hovey morality called on him to send it to his mother. Rationally, the person entitled to the book was Jeanne Green. She had been of the greatest help in preparing the manuscript for the press. Now she was working steadily on the chapters of *Chain of Command* as they came from his pen.

He and Jeanne had become warm comrades. He was in love with her, or he thought he was. He found her magnetically appealing. Yet he never tried to make love to her. The best reason he could discern for this was his knowledge that she would yield, and he would find himself a married man; married to a clever, lovely, but somewhat forbidding young woman. Jeanne's strictness seemed less a matter of conventional morality than of her own nature. She allowed no fooling around in her work, she tolerated nothing loose or second-rate in his manuscripts, and in the same way, he knew, she would require that he be a faithful husband. He was

willing to be a faithful husband—indeed a faithful husband to Jeanne Green, he believed; only not quite yet!

The real trouble was that the incredible Christmas Day episode with Mrs. Winter haunted him. He had not heard from her again. He knew from the gossip columns that she had returned to New York months ago. She had made no effort to track him down. At first he had told himself that she was being discreet, that in due course a letter or a wire would come to his telephoneless lair. None came. His pride became irked. He could not bring himself to call her, yet he felt balked of an exciting experience. How could a woman make love to him once in that wild way, and then ignore his existence? He was determined that somehow or other she would acknowledge his existence again, and that the suspense in his mind would be resolved, even if it took only one more innocuous meeting.

So when the volume of *Alms for Oblivion* came to his hand, what he did in the end was to send it to Mrs. Winter. He wasted half a day writing and rewriting a letter to go with it: a letter that defied his efforts to edit out an injured, high-flown note. He knew he was doing an ill-considered thing; and because of Jeanne, an unjust thing; and perhaps for that reason he could not get the letter to sound right. Also, there was the problem that her husband might read it! Finally he typed it up and mailed it off with his precious volume.

Mrs. Winter had quite definite ideas about what she wanted in life, and about how things should be done for her. For instance, she loved to be awakened about ten in the morning, and no earlier. At ten her husband was gone to his Broad Street office; at ten the chauffeur had taken the two girls off to their private school, and little Paul to his school; at ten the mail had arrived; and at ten the sun had risen far enough over the midtown towers of New York, even in the dead of winter, to dapple the treetops of the park, which she could see when she sat propped in bed. At ten, moreover, fresh flowers had come from the florist, so that the maid would bring them in with the newspapers, the mail, and the tea. Mrs. Winter had an acute sense of the sweetness of life and the preciousness of the passing moment. Her existence was ordered so that each moment, day by day, was as pleasant as possible. Fresh flowers in one's bedroom in the morning was a slight pleasure, but an easy and unfailing one.

It was early in June, so the flowers were lilacs, huge fragrant bunches. The day was sunny. The mail was heavy and looked interesting. She had had a good weekend of tennis and talk at her home in Connecticut. Last night the opening of the play she had attended had been a failure; a special treat, since the producer was a woman she disliked, a mannish bore who tended to wax theological about the drama. She had had her semi-annual physical checkup a few days ago, and the doctor—who, old as he was,

treated her with a debonair goatishness that she rather liked—had said that she was in the best shape ever, a real wonder. That too, was not randomly achieved. Mrs. Winter worked at staying healthy. People who dissipated, who burned the candle at both ends, she considered fools. The candle was invaluable, it was one's single sure possession. Properly trimmed and cared for it gave plenty of charming light from one end, for a long long time.

The package that came from Youngblood Hawke did not catch her attention at first. The shape was a familiar one, a cardboard book carton. Publishers were always sending new books to Mrs. Winter. She knew most of them, and she was a free member of the inner circle of New York celebrities whose talk could get a book started like nothing else. As usual, she telephoned her office while she drank her first cup of tea. The wistful, soft, bald young bachelor who had been her secretary for half a dozen years had only one bit of news; *The Doctor's Dilemma* had played the night before to a house of twenty-three hundred dollars. She knew without checking that this was a fall-off of two hundred odd dollars from the previous Monday. The show was slipping, and at this rate would not break even, unless the actors' contracts were renegotiated. "Call Jock Maas. Keep calling him till you get him. You know how he is in the morning. Tell him that I want him to meet me at four at the office," she said.

She opened the newspapers to the theatrical pages and glanced at the first and last paragraphs of the reviews, to be sure that the play had failed. (It had, most satisfyingly.) Then she noticed that the book package was addressed by hand. That was unusual. She picked it off the blue silk quilt and held it close to her nearsighted eyes: *From A. Youngblood Hawke, 345 W. 28th St.* She opened it quickly, pulled out the book, and a folded letter fell on the quilt.

Dear Mrs. Winter:

I send you herewith the first copy off the press of my first novel, *Alms for Oblivion*. I could make this letter one long string of apologies: for the crudity of my book, for my presumption in sending it to you, for certain things which you may or may not remember. I am not even sure you remember me! You were kind enough to make your library available to me on Christmas Day last year. Unlike you, I remember our encounter well. I am half in the business of remembering. And I recall that you said to me, on two different occasions, "Never, never apologize." So I won't.

Why do I select you for the doubtful honor of receiving this book, which means so much in my life, and can mean so little in yours? Why do I burden you with a favor which to you may be no favor, but an embarrassment and a bore? Because you were once kind to a young man alone in New York, and because kindness is not an outstanding trait of the people in the city.

I came to the city as so many young men have done before me, in order to

make my way. You called me a determined young man, and I think I am one. I wish I could believe that, with this book, I have broken into the identity that I believe will be mine some day. But looking at it now, at the first copy off the press, a month or so before the critics will pass judgment, I find my work not up to the mark. It is no use listing my mistakes; a woman of taste like yourself will see them all too clearly. But I will say this. As long as I live I do not think I will be ashamed of *Alms for Oblivion* as a first effort. So I send you this gift, faulty as it is, with a good conscience.

I am not seeking to renew our acquaintance, or to force myself on you. That would be a paltry use of a volume which may be meaningless to anyone else, but which looked to me, when I first drew it out of the box it came in, like the Holy Grail. You live in a world to which I will always be a stranger. In time I think I will be a welcome and respected stranger, an Othello in your Venice. Until your world seeks me out, whether to reward me for this young and botched first novel, or to acknowledge my gifts when I have made a better demonstration of them—as I shall—I am content to drudge along in obscurity. I have not even moved from the room without a telephone, though I have a little money now.

So please accept this tribute, dear Mrs. Winter, in the spirit in which I send it And as for this stilted and inarticulate letter, understand it for what it is. I allow myself two luxuries that I have not yet earned—Havana cigars, and the excessive pride of an artist.

I cannot forget the breakfast you gave me, out of your kindness, on Christmas Day in your grand home on Fifth Avenue. I have been a little delayed in thanking you properly. Now here is *Alms for Oblivion*.

Sincerely yours,
ARTHUR HAWKE.

It is not given to many women to get such a letter. Mrs. Winter did not even glance at the book until she had picked up the telephone and fired off a telegram to Youngblood Hawke. Then she did examine it curiously, especially the picture of the young man on the back of the jacket, a broad-shouldered fellow who needed a haircut, scowling ferociously into the camera, his chin resting on a clenched fist. A small smile came and went on Mrs. Winter's face.

2

When he caught his first glimpse of her, coming toward him through the warm-weather strollers in the zoo—the old ladies, the nurses with baby carriages, the college boys and girls holding hands in snatched lunch-hour idylls—he was disappointed. There was nothing very feminine in her walk, it was a swingy no-nonsense stride, purse tucked under one arm and the other arm pumping back and forth. And she was so obviously an older woman! There wasn't a trace of girlishness in the blue-gray

suit, the severe blue hat, the big plain blue leather purse. He was lounging against the rail before the lion's cage, where they had agreed to meet,
when he noticed her. She saw him almost at the same instant. Her free
hand shot up in a characteristic movement, a bend at the elbow and a brief
sharp wriggle of her blue-gloved fingers. "Hello!" She shook hands firmly.
"Gad, you're not half as tall as I remembered you. That's good. I thought
of you as a sort of man mountain."

She was looking up at him with the nearsighted peer out of large
gray eyes, with the downward tilt of the head, as though somehow she
could see better out of the top part of her pupils. He had never felt so
awkward, so empty of words. "We picked a nice day for it," he said,
stammering on *picked*.

"Yes, didn't we? One of the few days of the year when the town isn't
smelling like the inside of an old garage. . . . Good heavens, what's that,
and why?" He had taken the florist's box from behind his back, where he
had been holding it like a high school boy. She accepted the box and
opened it at once. "Well! God knows how many years it's been since
somebody gave me a flower! I mean when I wasn't chairlady of a committee
or something—a white camellia! Bless your heart, I'm putting it on this
minute. I should be giving you a flower, or some kind of a present anyway, for sending me that book." She pinned the camellia deftly to the
lapel of her suit. "You're overwhelming me. There. How's that? Where
shall we go?"

She was so completely at her ease, he thought; but he found himself
cutting off every sentence that came to his tongue because it seemed to
have a double meaning. He was looking silently at her, a big helpless
yokel. She took his hand and pressed it, smiling. "Shall we just walk?
Have you had your look at your *larn?*" When he had telephoned her, in
response to her wire, and had suggested this meeting place, she had made
a great joke of the way he said "lion." "He's not much to look at now,
poor sleepy *larn*." The lion was curled in a corner of the cage. "I know
where there are trees in bloom. Come! Then we'll go to the Margrave for
lunch, okay? I eat there all the time. It's good."

"Any place is all right, Mrs. Winter."

As they strolled uptown through the park she said, "You're very
thoughtful, aren't you? I looked in my library this morning and found
you'd returned the books while I was in Europe. I hadn't forgotten you,
Mr. Hawke, but I'd forgotten the books."

He could not find his tongue. What was the matter with him? "They
were useful," he forced himself to say. "I was a little taken aback when I
learned you'd gone to Europe."

"Well, you recall, I said I'd try to get some English actors for that
Shakespeare festival. Which is coming along beautifully, by the way. It's
no good writing to actors, they give the letters to their agents. No fine

actor really gives a damn about business. They want heaps of money, sure, but mostly they want a part, and they want to be told they'll be marvellous in it. You have to talk to an actor. So there was nothing to do but get on the boat. . . . I've heard wonderful things about your book. Roberto Luzzatto bought it for Anne Karen, didn't he?"

"Yes. Luzzatto wanted me to write the screenplay, too, but I thought I'd better write another book. I'm more than halfway through."

"Another book already? My, you're a fast worker," she said.

At that moment he was looking down at her, and her eyes met his. It seemed they both thought at once of the double meaning. An uncertain embarrassed smile flickered on her face. Then they both broke into laughter, rollicking laughter, laughter that filled him with excitement, it acknowledged so much and promised so much. The intervening months dissolved; the spell of Mrs. Winter blazed up as it had on that amazing afternoon, and she looked as desirable, all at once, as she had in his fantasies. She was older than he, and that was beautiful; see the college girl sitting on the bench they were walking past, the lumpy adolescent with the unlined pretty face, the inexpert paint, holding hands with an empty-faced boy! This woman was his equal, free and strong as a man, yet radiant with allure. Her stride in the daylight was purposeful, headlong, and that was lovely; where was the charm in the languishing dawdling steps of a girl? There were no eyes in the world like Frieda Winter's, gray, huge, sometimes merry and sometimes sharply alert, but always disturbing as they peered up under the very high arch of her dark brows. As for Jeanne —well, he was having an adventure, why the hell not? He was only twenty-seven, and he was free.

It was delicious to walk with Frieda Winter along a lane of flowering trees. He told her that Luzzatto was after him again to do the screenplay, because Anne Karen had rejected a scenario prepared by a Hollywood writer; but that he intended to decline. "Why? Are you afraid Hollywood will corrupt you?" she said with amused irony.

"Not at all. It's a question of time. My feeling is that if I work every day as though I were being shot at sunrise tomorrow, I may barely get my main jobs done in twenty or thirty years. There's no room in the scheme for writing movies."

"There's the question of money."

"My needs are few."

"But an artist shouldn't live like a hermit or a beggar. I don't believe in that. It's cramping. And it cuts you off from the experiences you ought to have."

"I won't always live this way. I have an investment program that will slowly but surely make me independent."

Mrs. Winter looked up at him keenly, then laughed. "I see. Very fine, very fine!"

He was more at ease in elegant restaurants now. Often he took Jeanne to the places he read about in the columns, and now and then he went himself, and read a book, ignoring the waiters' stares, while he ate complicated and exquisite French dishes alone. He thought he gave a fair account of himself ordering the food and wine, though the deference of the captain was aimed at Mrs. Winter. The captain had greeted her by name, with a more than routine bow.

She said, "Tell me about this investment program of yours. That sounds decidedly long-headed for a young writer."

When he began describing Scotty Hoag she wrinkled her nose, very much like his mother. "Real estate is not for somebody like you."

"Well, all I can tell you is, I invested ten thousand dollars with him in January. In the middle of May he sold the property, before it was even completed, and returned twenty-two thousand dollars to me."

"You were lucky. What did you do with that money?"

"I invested half of it in another project of Scotty's, a housing development that has Federal support. I wanted to put all the money into it, but he insisted that I salt away half in government bonds."

"Did you?"

Hawke toyed with the stem of his martini glass, and looked at her with a sidewise grin. "No. I told him I did, but I bought some stocks, and some commodity futures." He laughed as she shook her head. "I knew you wouldn't like that. All the same I've made eleven hundred dollars on onions and lard contracts, if you'll believe me, in a few weeks of fooling around. Before I made a move I studied up on the subject. I made theoretical purchases and sales for a few months. If you watch yourself you go in and out fast and you can't really get hurt. It's interesting. What's more, it's fun."

"But why should you put your mind to that kind of thing? Onions and lard, indeed."

"Mrs. Winter, I sold the movie rights in *Alms for Oblivion* for thirty thousand dollars. When all the bites came out—agent, publisher, taxes—I was left with about eight or so. Eight thousand instead of thirty is quite a cut! If I'm to achieve independence by my own efforts—without living like a hermit which, I agree with you, is not for me—I'm going to have to manage my money."

Frieda Winter said with a few quick raps of her cigarette lighter, "Look here, if you want your money managed there are people who do that too, reliable people who make it their business."

"Sure. You come to them with half a million dollars and they'll do all kinds of smart things with it. They're not going to build eight thousand back up to thirty."

"My husband is as good an investment manager as any in the business. He's really good. He's written a book, and all that, and he's done pretty well for a couple of musicians and writers I've sent to him over the years. He won't put you in commodity futures, but whatever money you make and give to him you'll have, and it'll yield you something too."

Hawke said, sitting up, "Wait, is he the Winter of Willis and Winter? *Rational Investing?*"

"Yes."

"Why, I've read that book. It's very good. Aside from everything else, he can write, and he has a sense of humor. And he's your husband! Why didn't that occur to me?"

Mrs. Winter's smile was strange, a mere wrinkling of her mouth. "Paul is quite a person. You'll have to meet him. I think he could help you, and keep you out of a lot of trouble."

"Well, right now nearly all my surplus money is with Scotty Hoag, Mrs. Winter."

"Why don't you call me Frieda? I shouldn't be Mrs. Winter to you, should I?"

They were looking in each other's eyes, and her business-like glance changed into quite another look. Hawke cleared his throat. "I suppose not, Frieda."

"Now what will I call you? It seems to me I had a name for you, a pretty good one."

Hawke said, with considerable embarrassment, "I remember, if you don't. Bloody."

Frieda Winter laughed, a low quiet laugh, and glanced mechanically around at the other tables. "Well that sounds like the Christmas spirit, doesn't it? Sausages and corn fritters in a shut-up house and all that. No, it won't do for an ordinary weekday, will it? What shall it be? Not Youngblood."

"No, only strangers trying to get friendly in a hurry call me that. And Hollywood people. For some reason they love it. My name is Arthur, Frieda."

"Then Arthur it is. Now tell me, this man Hoag down in Kentucky—why is he bothering to manage your money for you?"

"I think it flatters his vanity to be associated with a live novelist. He's an old college classmate of mine. I think too he enjoys patronizing me with his superior wisdom about real estate. Besides, on however small a scale, I'm supplying him with venture capital."

Frieda spun her lighter swiftly. "By and large people like that are out for themselves. It might not be a bad thing, somewhere along the line, if Paul looked into your Mr. Hoag. There are painless and effective ways of checking on business men."

Hawke didn't like the idea, but he realized the prudence of it. "That would be very kind of him."

The food came: cold poached salmon for both of them, garnished with garden vegetables. The captain poured a sip of white wine into Hawke's glass, gravely keeping up the New York fiction that an American can tell one wine from another. Hawke just as gravely sipped, and nodded. He had simply ordered the most expensive number in the white Burgundies, and its taste was excellent.

Frieda said, "Well, what do we drink to? Shall we say to literature, and to hell with onions, lard, and real estate?"

"To money, so long as it's honestly earned," Hawke said.

"Nothing doing. I won't drink to money, and I'm damned if you will. Here's to your book, Arthur, and here's to my book—for which I'm more grateful than I can say."

"The book, then," Hawke said, and they drank.

For a few minutes they ate eagerly, laughing at each other.

"Now, a couple of questions," Frieda said. "You lost me, cutting thirty thousand dollars down to eight. Where did all that money go, again?"

"For one thing Prince House took half."

"*Half!*"

"Jay maintains stoutly that it's standard for a first novel."

"Arthur, Jay Prince drives hard bargains, everybody knows that. But that's robbery."

"He gave me a printed form contract and I signed it. What's more I tied up two more books on that formula."

"Christ! Didn't you have an agent or a lawyer?"

"No. Being fresh down out of the hills, still full of my last meal of fried squirrels, as you might say, I naturally was playing the suave man of the world. I've had two arguments with Jay about that contract since. One last Christmas, right after Ferdie Lax told me something about movie percentages. Jay put me off with that heavy joviality of his—we wouldn't have any trouble, men of good will could always get together, let's get the book published and then we'll see—that kind of thing. Then three days ago, when they sent me that first book off the press, I went down and talked to him again. I lost that argument too. You see he's so damned *pleasant* about it. So I'm pleasant and nothing gets changed, nothing on paper. Just cheerful chatter about the future. Meantime he's collected my thirteen-plus thousand dollars. I owed it to him, and I was honor bound to give it to him. In return I got vague talk of a new contract, and maybe a refund if the book is a hit. It's more than he advanced me on all three books. And the contract says I owe him half the movie rights of two more books."

Frieda's arched brows contracted in a fierce way, emphasizing the slant of her eyes. She looked almost Chinese. "You'll have to get ugly with Jay."

"I'm becoming aware of that."

"Get an agent to do your arguing for you. Their business is getting ugly when necessary. I can recommend several."

"Well, I thought maybe I'd get hold of Ferdie Lax."

Frieda ate in silence for a little while. "That's all right. Ferdie can be as jovial a thug as Jay and then some. Of course you need an Eastern agent for magazine rights and that kind of thing, but Ferdie can arrange that. You'll have to give him ten percent of everything you earn."

"I know."

"And Ferdie is no Mahatma Gandhi, you understand. All he wants is money. He makes money by being on your side. Ferdie Lax is okay, Arthur."

The captain was filling her glass. "Everything all right, Mrs. Winter?"

"Fine. Fred, this young man is a new and important novelist, Young-blood Hawke."

The captain, with a sidewise dip of the head, and a small bow, said, "Yes, sair, Mr. Hawke," and refilled his glass too. When he left Frieda said, "It helps when they know your name. Sometimes you want a reservation at the last minute."

"Seems to me all I'd have to say is I'm a friend of Mrs. Winter."

"Oh well. This is around the corner from home. I use it a lot for lunch." She drank wine and laughed. "I must say I've fallen into quite a different vein than I intended. Sitting here in my old business corner and all. We haven't talked about anything but money, have we?"

"No. It's been all onions and lard, so far."

"You might as well be having lunch with Paul. Let's beat it. I want my coffee, and then I want to see where you work. The room without a telephone."

"Frieda, it's a hole, it's almost stagey it's so squalid. It's hot and it smells and I left it in a disgusting mess. I wouldn't take a dog up there, let alone Frieda Winter of Fifth Avenue."

"Oh, damn that Frieda Winter of Fifth Avenue, will you? I won't be patronized just because you don't have money, you're goddamn anxious for money, yourself, Bloody my boy." She was glaring at him from under her brows like an offended cat, the gray eyes wide and menacing. It was a droll, delightful effect.

Grinning, he said, "So I'm Bloody again."

Her anger, real or assumed, dissolved into amusement. What a face this woman had! She said, "It just came out. I guess because you were being a bloody bore. We'll have our coffee and then we're going to look at young Balzac's garret, do you hear?"

"Yes, Mrs. Winter," Hawke said.

She put her fingers for a moment on his clasped hands on the table. "Okay," she said. "That's settled."

When the captain brought the check he laid it unhesitatingly beside Frieda. She started to sign, but Hawke whisked the check from under her pen, saying, "Are you out of your mind?"

She said, "Look, Bloody, I'm not going to play snatch-the-check with you. But don't be a fool. I run an account here. It's all expenses for me. I eat on the government and I'm damn well entitled to do so with the taxes I pay. Give me the check."

"Where I come from men still pay if they take a lady to lunch."

"Oh, look, this is a business lunch, I exploit every writer I know, one way or another, and all I'm really after is the dramatic rights to your next novel. Don't you know that? Please give me the check and stop being a bully."

He gave her the check; it seemed the least ridiculous thing to do, though the little incident was not pleasant. At bottom he was enough of a Hovey boy still to be relieved at saving twenty-seven dollars, the price he had seen scrawled on the back of the check. "So much for the honor of Southern manhood," he muttered.

She signed the check cheerfully. "The Civil War didn't kill it, but the income tax did," she said. "Let's get on to your garret."

3

Going up the stairs he was conscious as never before of the grime, the gloom, the broken steps, the grooves worn by the feet of sweatshop workers in other days. "Don't say I didn't warn you, Frieda. Just remember I pay seventeen dollars a month for this."

"I'll remember."

The wide metal door came open with its usual horrible rasp, after a few tugs. Frieda hesitated in the doorway, head down, glancing around with dilated eyes. "I can't see anything."

He went in and switched on the overhead light, a fiercely glaring two-hundred watt bulb hanging on a long cord and shaded with a cone of green tin.

She came in with slow, uncertain steps, shading her eyes with a gloved hand. "What the devil do you have that floodlight for?"

"Spite. My landlord supplied a twenty-five watt bulb. I get electricity thrown in. I don't think he's making a nickel on me. He wants me to leave, but he's afraid I'd throw him down the stairs, so he doesn't press it. I talk real Southern when he comes around. He thinks I distill moonshine here and have a shotgun hidden away." He was talking with nervous haste while the elegant woman stood with her feet together, her purse under her arm, in the middle of the room, looking at the tumbled mattress-bed on the floor, the cardboard box half full of empty cans and bottles, the

open wooden footlocker which was bureau, closet, and laundry hamper, the books scattered pell mell, the old newspapers and magazines. Her eyes came to a stop on the clothes line stretching from an overhead pipe to the hasp on a window, strung with shirts, underwear and socks. "Ye gods, Bloody, you do your own washing?"

"Why should I waste five or ten dollars a week to get my shirts so starched they rub my neck raw? Seen enough, Frieda?" He turned on the desk lamp and switched off the overhead blaze. "Sit down. That's the chair in which I write. It's an honorable chair."

She sat, taking off her gloves and the jacket of her suit. It was stifling in the room. "Arthur, I've known many bachelors and various bizarre characters. There's nothing new about this to me. If it suits you, all right."

"It suits my present income."

"Couldn't you spend a little of the money you're speculating on onions and lard to rent a little furnished apartment, say over on Third Avenue? Want me to dig something up for you?"

"I know those places. Jeanie Green has one on Third and Sixty-fifth. I'll tell you, Frieda, that seems worse to me than this. Here I'm frankly holing up. I can bide my time."

"The prince disguised as a beggar."

"If you will. The prince disguised as a beggar."

Frieda said, "You keep your desk neat, at least. Remarkably so." She was peering with open curiosity at the squared-off files, the dictionary and the thesaurus, the yellow pad centered on the desk with the pen upright in the middle of it, and the cheap watch centered on the base of the pen holder.

"That's my gun mount."

"Jeanne Green . . . that's the girl at Prince House, isn't it? The one who corrects manuscripts?"

"Yes."

"She seemed extremely bright."

"She's brilliant. She's a find. I'm using her instead of Karl Fry to read this book as I go along."

"I thought she was very pretty."

"She is. Moody, severe, fits of acute melancholia, but damned attractive."

"Maybe you should marry her." With a swift charming gesture of one hand Frieda seemed to sweep the abominable loft room clean.

"I don't want a wife and children just yet. I have work to do. In this hole I get it done."

"Is Jeanie Green in love with you?"

"You can be pretty direct, Frieda."

"So I've been told."

"Well, every man knows he's irresistible and every woman he meets is

in love with him, unless there's something wrong with her. If Jeanie isn't in love with me she should be, obviously."

"And so should I, eh?"

This knocked him off balance. He was enjoying this turn of the conversation, it was thrilling, and he was afraid of it too. It was as though he were in a roller-coaster car, clanking slowly up to the high point for the plunge. "You're a happily married woman. That's different."

Frieda Winter stood, straightened her skirt, and came to him. He was leaning against the desk. She faced him, standing very close, and looked at him, from under her brows. "You're quite right, Bloody, I'm a happily married woman. Accidents don't count, and Christmas comes but once a year." She put both hands on the back of his neck, without moving closer. "All the same I think we can be friends, and I think I can do you some good, maybe."

"You can? What good?" He could scarcely get out the words. His hands went to her waist, to the silken frilled shirt under her open jacket. He held her lightly. She was a thin woman; he could feel the ridges of her ribs. Mrs. Winter had slight breasts, and a small figure that could hardly be called sexy. There was a fascination in her bony pretty face, and in the great sombre eyes full of intelligence and zest.

She said, "Well, I'll tell you, Othello my lad, Venice is a devious town with crooked streets and canals and byways, and it's pretty easy to get lost, or garrotted, or drowned. I think I can guide you around a bit, until you get the hang of it."

He tried to pull her toward him. She resisted, and her firm arched resistance—the thin body taut in his hands, the big gray eyes looking straight into his—was more pleasing than a slovenly yielding would have been. Frieda said, "We've got things to do. Let's get out of this place. I've seen it. I don't like it." She put her strong hands on his forearms and broke free. "Where's the nearest telephone?"

Hawke had eaten a couple of expensive dinners in the grill room of The Park Tower, where Frieda now took him, after making a long phone call in which she seemed to be talking French most of the time. The Park Tower was one of the grand apartment hotels that lined Central Park South, thrusting thirty stories and more into the air. "What are we going in here for?" Hawke said as he paid the taxidriver.

"Just come along," Frieda said, "and mind your manners. This man you're going to meet is awesome at first, but he's really a darling. Just be yourself. He can see through any pose. He posed all the poses before you were born."

"Who is it?"

"You'll know him." She was obviously enjoying the little mystification. The elevator took them up twenty-five floors. Hawke was staggered,

literally so, when Frieda rang a bell and the door was opened by Georges Feydal. The actor was in maroon silk pajamas and his long brown hair, streaked thickly with gray, stood in a mussed tangle on his head, a few straight locks falling into his eyes. "Frieda, I look horrible. Hello," he said to Hawke, drawing aside to let the young man in. His big belly showed naked and hairy through carelessly tied pajama bottoms. He was even fatter than he looked in the movies; but his church organ voice, with the slight French accent, was as unmistakable, as familiar to Hawke, as his own mother's. This was possibly the most recognizable person, and the most recognizable voice in the world: the great French actor, son of another great French actor and a British actress; Georges Feydal, first a star in the Comedie Française, then a Parisian actor-manager, then a Hollywood movie star; with a face of unforgettable gargoyle ugliness, he had yet played in love movies in his younger years opposite Garbo, and Dietrich, and Shearer and Karen; then he had been thin; now a fat man, a player of character parts, he was no less famous, no less admired. Feydal was in a Broadway play that was about to close, one of the catastrophes of the spring season, a translated French whimsy about Socrates.

The actor picked up a telephone lying off its hook, motioning Frieda and Hawke to chairs with a light kingly gesture. "Yes, now what else is there? No, no, this is my breakfast. Do you have some bouillabaisse? Very good. Bouillabaisse, and two double dry martinis, and—" he looked to Frieda and Hawke. Frieda shook her head. "That's all. Thank you." He sank in an armchair, and closed his eyes. Hawke became aware of a typewriter clicking behind the closed bedroom door.

Frieda said, "I suppose I was a beast to wake you up, but really, Georges, it's three in the afternoon."

Feydal opened his eyes, shrugged, and smiled at Hawke. "I was up till dawn, a ridiculous party. Unwinding after a performance to a hundred empty rows—so. You are the young man who wrote *Alms for Oblivion*. I hear great things about it."

Frieda said, "From whom?"

"Roberto came backstage last week. He's very high on it. Imagine, Anne's going to play an old woman."

"It's about time," Frieda said.

He turned to Hawke. "Is there a part in it for me? The kind old uncle, the villainous banker? Roberto said there isn't, but I never know when he's bargaining or telling the truth. Have you read it, Frieda?"

"Not yet. I just got an advance copy today." She glanced at Hawke, who could not help smiling at her. He saw the Frenchman look from his face to Frieda's, and he felt that Feydal could at this moment write a short memorandum describing how things stood between him and Frieda, exact to a hair.

His slight embarrassment prompted him to talk. "I think there are many

good parts in my book, but I don't think there is a part for Georges Feydal."

The actor laughed shortly, his thick lips hardly opening, and he blinked heavy lids over his bloodshot twinkling eyes. "My dear Mr. Hawke, Georges Feydal as of eleven-fifteen tomorrow night will be an out-of-work actor looking for a job, and not at all proud or hard to get."

"Poor fellow," Frieda said, "with only a four-month platform tour booked solid, and what average take per night?"

"Frieda, my darling, I'm deeply grateful to you for booking me into the concert circuit, it fills in for the summer, but then what happens? And by the time I pay your commissions and expenses all along the line you know what it boils down to."

"Yes, a goddamned fortune," Frieda said.

"Pennies," Feydal said, his eyes twinkling at Hawke. "Pennies thrown in my hat at the street corner."

The typewriter had stopped clicking. A tall young man came out of the bedroom, carrying a few yellow sheets of paper. He had a mass of wavy black hair, manly features like a statue's, healthy brown skin, a small waist, a stomach flat as a wall, and perfectly cut clothes: fawn-colored jacket, dove-colored slacks, gray suède shoes, and the thick doubled cuffs of his white shirt were fastened with huge black stone links. He would have seemed unreal, a walking dummy, so perfectly was he formed and turned out, except for an unpleasant pout on his full mouth, a puffy look about his brilliant blue eyes, and a grossness in his jaw.

"Already?" Feydal said. "You know Frieda. Youngblood Hawke— Pierce Carmian." He took the sheets. "Excuse me," he said to Hawke, putting on thick glasses and beginning to read, pencil in hand. Silence ensued. Feydal now and then emitted a groan, drawing his pencil through some lines and scrawling notes in the margins. Carmian lit and smoked a cigarette, making a show of long bony brown fingers, lounging on the arm of Feydal's chair. The waiter came. Carmian admitted him, told him where to put the table, signed the check, and handed Feydal one of the brimming double martinis in a wide shallow glass. The actor drained it absent-mindedly. "Pierce, this is much, much better, I think now you have a second act curtain." Feydal took off the glasses and handed the sheets to the playwright, who displayed gleaming teeth in a pleased smile.

"Well, if so, it's thanks to you, Georges."

Frieda said, "Is this the play about the little boy who commits murders?"

Carmian said bleakly, "Oh, you've read my play?"

"When Jock Maas was considering it. Terribly funny things in it, but I wonder whether death is a subject for comedy."

"The greatest, Frieda," Feydal said, hauling himself out of the armchair and proceeding to drink the second martini. He stood with his feet planted far apart, his belly bulging, the maroon pajamas drooping around his

ankles. "But it must be treated with unerring taste. *Le Malade Imaginaire*, or that marvellous *Mikado* of Gilbert, a comic oratorio about death two hours long, and maybe the only indestructible stage piece in English after Shakespeare. And Falstaff. 'Who hath honor? He who died o' Wednesday.' And Chaplin, Chaplin was greatly funny only about death. On the verge of starvation eating a shoe, or walking down a Klondike trail with death close behind in the shape of a bear—" All at once Feydal put down the martini, imitated a waddling bear, and then impersonated Chaplin hurrying along. Hawke did not know how Feydal achieved it, but first he could see the bear, and then it seemed that the fat man melted into Chaplin, baggy pants, cane and all, and then became himself again. It was something he did with his eyes, mouth and hands. "Pierce now has two acts of a wildly funny play."

"I'll have three acts in a couple of weeks," Carmian said, with a spiteful glance at Hawke—and this was, Hawke realized, the first and only notice Pierce Carmian had taken of him—"providing I can find a place to work." The playwright hitched himself off into the bedroom, and the typewriter began clacking again.

Feydal said comfortably, lifting whole small fish out of the tureen of bouillabaisse into a plate, and pouring the rich brown soup over them, "Pierce is annoyed about the apartment. He's a spoiled child. I feel much better about letting you have it," he said to Hawke. "I gather you really need decent surroundings. Pierce has a perfectly good little flat in the village."

"This apartment?" Hawke blurted. "Me? It's impossible. I can't pay for it." He looked at Frieda in amazement. She only smiled.

"It's paid for, alas, I lease it by the year," Feydal said, greedily attacking the bouillabaisse, dripping soup on his pajamas. "You like the place, eh? High, quiet, airy even in July, I promise you."

Hawke surveyed the room, seeing it now as a place for himself to live. Before he had had only a vague impression of comfort and wealth. But now he became aware of paintings which must be costly originals—mostly moderns, a Seurat and a black-and-white sketch by Picasso, but there were old things, a gold-haloed stiff saint on gray wood, a circular painting of a Madonna and child, somehow not incongruous—and every piece of furniture was handsome, none of it was bland hotel fittings. The view of Central Park, newly green, and its flanking tall buildings, was wonderful. "I can't possibly accept such a favor. If I could sub-lease a place like this I'd give an arm to be able to afford it, but—"

"But my dear Mr. Hawke I cannot sublease it. Nobody will lease an apartment in New York through the summer heat. Frieda tells me you need a place to lay your head for a month or two. My humble abode is yours. I expect a very high price. I expect a first exclusive look at the first play you write."

Hawke began to say, "I'm not planning any plays—" but Frieda struck in, speaking with a smile, but in a brisk tone. "Now Georges, none of that. That wasn't what we said on the telephone. You don't want this young man tying up a play he hasn't written yet."

Feydal bent over the bouillabaisse, his eyes winking sidewise at Hawke. "Tie it up? Curiosity, my darling, curiosity, based wholly on what I hear of his talents."

"You can have first look at any play I write whether I take your apartment or not," Hawke said, noticing that Frieda turned her Chinese frown on him but ignoring it. "I'd consider it an honor. But that's hardly compensation for the use of this palatial apartment."

The actor lunged out of his chair at him, making the bouillabaisse slosh on the white cloth as he jostled the table. "Done!" he said, holding out his small manicured hand, and Hawke shook it. "An honest bargain, I call that," Feydal said cheerfully to the frowning Frieda.

They talked about keys, and mail, and the maid service, and the delivery of newspapers—Hawke still only half-believing what was going on—and soon he was in the elevator with Frieda again, and Feydal was waving a roguish farewell through a partly opened door.

They were out on the street before Frieda spoke. Then she said, glaring at him from under her brows, "You're still full of fried squirrels."

"What's the matter?"

"A first look at a literary property is worth money. You don't just give it away to prove you're as debonair as Georges Feydal. You're not. You won't be if you live to be a hundred."

They were standing in bright sunlight on the street, and the lines in her face were plain, the two determined scores on either side of her mouth and the furrows on her forehead, but it didn't matter, she was lovely to him. "Frieda, he gave me his apartment. I'm a total stranger. I've never encountered such generosity."

"Oh, yes, it was generous of him, but I'd arranged all that on the telephone, and what becomes of his generosity if it turns into a literary transaction? However—" the cloud passed from her face. She took his hand. "We've got you out of that horrible hole on Twenty-eighth Street, anyway, haven't we? If you have to entertain a lady now you can do so, and she won't have to brush wet laundry aside to sit down. That's done." She glanced at her watch. "I have an appointment with Jock Maas. What do you say, shall we go to Georges's closing tomorrow night? There'll be a sad champagne party backstage, and he's flying to the coast at one in the morning, so you can take over the keys right there."

"Sure."

"Get yourself a haircut. Not too close, no college boy stuff, but you need one."

"Yes, Mrs. Winter."

"Go to hell," she said, touching his face with a gloved hand.

"Thanks for lunch."

"Oh, that. Write a bread-and-butter note to the Treasury, if you must. Bye." She stepped quickly into the first cab in the line outside the hotel.

4

At about a quarter past five that afternoon Jeanne was moiling through a difficult chapter of Hawke's book. The pages were scarred with changes and cuts in differently colored inks; the margins were choked with insertions written sideways, in little balloons at the end of long lines. The narrative itself contained time lapses that didn't add up and characters whose names had changed since the start of the story. She was drudging on while other girls in the office were closing their desks, because *Chain of Command* had the surge of a smash hit under its disorderly surface, and the work was continuously exciting. But it was a taxing job; her eyes ached, and her nerves were raw. The telephone, jangling unexpectedly, made her start. It was the mystery book editor down the hall, saying that Karl Fry had walked in half an hour ago, and was now coming to see her.

This was a surprise. Early in January Fry had had a heart attack, and after his discharge from the hospital he had gone to his home town, St. Louis, to recuperate. She had not seen him since the night he had taken her to dinner, the same night Hawke had called her from Kentucky; but she had had several funny and cheerful letters from him.

Jeanne worked in an unchanging fluorescent glare, in a large windowless room devoted to art work and publicity, where the stylists too had their cubicles. Through a couple of panels of partition glass she saw him coming. For a second or two she was not quite sure it was Fry. His clothes were different now. His manner of walking was different. The bizarre colors and the Bohemian shabbiness had given way to the correct grayish look of a college teacher or an editor. He even wore a vest, of the same stuff as his suit. His collar was white, his tie dull green, and nothing was new, but all was easy and neat. When he came into her cubicle she saw his shoes were freshly shined. The really astonishing thing was his smile. His teeth seemed whiter, the crookedness and the stains were gone, and a couple of black gaps had been filled. This improved his looks amazingly; made him indeed rather handsome.

He was brief with her. Would she have cocktails with him, and dinner? She shook off her surprise and declined dinner. She had a script session with Hawke that was supposed to begin at eight, though she did not tell this to Fry; cocktails, yes, with pleasure. "I'm not dressed for any place that's fancy," she said, stacking away her manuscript sheets and reference

books. "You pick up a working girl without warning and you're stuck with a working girl."

"That's all right. Are you game for a merry-go-round ride? That's a working girl amusement . . . don't look so puzzled, Jeanie, I mean it. The carousel in the park. It's a warm, lovely, daylight-saving kind of June afternoon out there."

"I'd love a merry-go-round ride, thank you. It'll be a pleasant change from this tomb."

So they walked uptown to the park and strolled along the same path through the zoo that Hawke and Frieda had traversed a few hours earlier. Jeanne had been feeling like the very devil all day, for no reason she could define; as though some mortal calamity were breaking on her, somewhere beyond her sight. It was a symptom of gloom, of worn nerves, and she had had it often in New York, but seldom so strongly. The walk in the park cheered her up a little.

When they were on the turning merry-go-round, facing each other on two horses, Fry moving up as Jeanne went down, he shouted over the clang and and whoop of *The Blue Danube*, "How do you like my teeth?"

"Hey?"

"How do you like the job they did on my teeth in St. Louis? Caps."

"Fine. Makes you look years younger."

"Glad you think so, Jeanne."

There were sailors on the carousel, some with girls and some alone, and mothers with children, and a few young couples, and the music was loud and thumpy, and the cymbals clashed in waltz time. Jeanne would have loved to throw back her head as the carousel turned faster, and laugh, and teeter and show her legs a bit, as some of the girls were doing; it was the thing to do on a carousel. But Fry seemed so odd, and the whole excursion had such an outlandish feeling, that she could not do the happy flirting girl, and she just rode up and down on the painted wooden horse.

"Fun?" Fry said as they walked away.

"Wonderful idea. Spun off all my blue devils. Thanks, Karl."

"I did that on the first date I had with the girl who became my wife. Depths of the depression. Those two dimes loomed larger then than two fifty-dollar bills today. What do you say, one of the hotels for cocktails, or my place?"

This kind of decision Jeanne was used to, and the standard answer was not to go to "my place." "My place" too often meant wrestlings and arguments. A pretty girl's sexual charm generated continual trouble, like carrying around a few thousand dollars in cash; always precaution, always suspicion. Yet, like the possessor of the cash, she had to be glad she had it. "Oh, hell, Karl, your place," she said. Karl seemed all right. Capped teeth or not, he was past forty, and a skirt and blouse were terrible for a hotel.

He had a new apartment not far from hers, on a side street to the west of

Third Avenue in one of the well-renovated buildings. His apartment, three small rooms, seemed all books; the furniture was new. He gave her a big cold martini, which she drank thirstily. As it turned out she was perfectly safe, Fry wanted to talk. Jeanne had a good instinct for knowing when only talk was in prospect. Youngblood Hawke was the world's most infernal talker, at least with her.

He talked of his illness with detached good humor. "Every man in his forties should spend a week on his back in an oxygen tent, Jeanie," Karl said, sipping ginger ale. "That is, if he makes it back to the sunlight. I guess most people nowadays need such a sharp arrest, people like myself who can't go to churches to stop and add up the score from time to time. I added it all up in the oxygen tent, Jeanie, I really did. When I got well I acted. Did you know that Hodge Hathaway's mystery editor was leaving them to join the story department at Metro?" Jeanne shook her head. "Well, he is. I heard about it shortly after I got out of the hospital and I called Ross Hodge long distance. I believe I'm going to get the job."

"Why, that's grand, Karl."

Jeanne had never had any particular feelings about Karl Fry, beyond a certain pity, in his derelict days—which certainly seemed over, or at least suspended—and some admiration for his intelligence. The fact that he was a communist had been enough to remove him from the range of normal people. She had known communists in college, in Washington, and in New York. Once she had been interested enough—when a very good-looking economist in the government who was paying court to her had fed her the usual books and pamphlets—to read up on Marxism. It had attracted her for a while with its vision of a perfect world realizable with a change in the laws of property. The idea of a worker's revolution led by a devoted band of brilliant insiders had been romantically exciting too. Still, she had never quite been able to picture Russia's October Revolution occurring in the United States of filling stations and Sears Roebuck catalogues and easy living. She had attended a few parlor meetings with the economist; it had been a novel kind of dating. But the people had repelled her. Jeanne had a candid eye, and she saw them for petty egotists, mostly of inferior ability and manners, seizing on the great dream to inflate their own importance; the cleverest ones, the leaders, had the ugly assurance of religious fanatics, peculiarly mixed with the bland toughness of professional politicians. The economist's shy charm and slender good looks had begun to dim when she saw him shrill and excited in arguments. At last when the note of clandestine planning had become clear to her, she had suddenly and finally decided that this business was not for her. Giving up the economist was not hard; he talked too much, after all, and she perceived that most of his brilliance was second-hand. Thereafter she had reacted to communists like someone who has been vaccinated.

She said, "I'm a little surprised at Ross Hodge."

"Why?"

"Well, isn't he the original stuffed-shirt from Boston, Republican right through to his liver and all that?"

"I've left the party, Jeanne."

"Well! That's news."

"It made no headlines but it's so. I told it to Ross, and he took my word. Ross isn't a stuffed shirt. He's a gentleman. A vanishing sort of animal like the prairie dog, but there are some."

"You don't believe in communism any more?"

Fry rose. "I want more ginger ale. You know, I'm really getting to like the stuff. How's your martini?"

"Well, one refill."

She followed him to his kitchenette. He said, "Believe in *what?* In the party? In Marxism? Or in myself as a crusader? I still think Marxism is the truth that used to be called God's truth. You take God out of the world, Jeanne—and he evaporated in the nineteenth century, and can no more be recalled than yesterday's rain—and I think the one possible line for the continuation of human history is the principle that for one man to live by the sweat of another man's brow is wrong. Here's your drink— Cheers." He kept talking as they walked back into the sitting room, and now he sounded more like the old Fry, and there was the sarcastic sidewise twist to his mouth as the words poured out. "I probably would give a great deal to be talked out of Marxism. It's cost me a lot, it's damned near killed me. But I don't think there's any other answer. Marx was a prophet. Everything's going the way that that sick lonely old bearded man in the British Museum foresaw that it would, a hundred years ago. There have been just a few unimportant variations in detail and timing. The wars, the overthrows, the changes in art, in industry, and in ideas, have reeled themselves off like episodes in a movie which Marx wrote, directed, and produced." He drank, and grinned at her, making the huh-huh sound that was his only laughter. "I ought to stop talking, but this is the first chance I've had in some time, and you're a good listener. I don't mean to give you a short course on Marx-Leninism, and anyway I can't, it all rests on a granite basis of economic science that must be mastered. Nobody who has mastered it has ever been able to believe anything else. Just as nobody who saw Jupiter's moons through Galileo's telescope could ever again believe that the earth was the center of the universe, and that man was the center of creation. The American economists make vague anti-Marx noises, and wish things could go on forever as they did in George Washington's day. But America is a freak, darling, an unbelievable island of riches. While communism emerges all over the world we'll go on plundering and squandering our natural wealth and keeping up the old George Washington way of life for a while. But it's not a serious program, Jeanie. It's a binge. There is no room on earth for the self-indulgent individual living of the Virginia

planter, not in the long range. Look, I'd like nothing better myself than to be carried back to old Virginny and hear them darkies singing in the moonlight while I sit on the veranda of my mansion sipping a mint julep, but that isn't the way the world is going to be. Not for anybody, not for long. Too many people, too little to go around. I think the communist party program is correct, Jeanie. I know everything that's wrong with it. There are horrible people in the movement and there are personal conflicts, inner conflicts, that tear you to pieces. But that's true of any activity of any magnitude. It's true of a publishing house, for Christ's sake."

Jeanne laughed. Karl grinned, grateful for the reaction. "What I've decided is that communism will probably not come in the United States in my lifetime, since we've got this mountainous wealth to burn away staving it off. I'm not going to give my remaining energy to making it come. I'm a dreadful flop as a member of a disciplined group. My sense of humor keeps breaking in. Three years ago they forced me to write a public recantation of a review in which I made wonderful fun, if I do say so, of a very lousy proletarian novel. That came closer to killing me than this heart attack. I did it, but something happened to me. In an obscure way my divorce stemmed from it. I haven't been worth a damn to the party since."

A church clock outside struck the quarter hour. Jeanne tried to be surreptitious about glancing at her watch, but Karl saw. He said hastily, "This will teach you to go to a man's apartment with him. I'm sure you'd have preferred a ravishing to this lecture."

"No, no, Karl, lecture me any time."

He grunted. "But that wasn't my reason for luring you here, I mean neither the ravishing nor the boring. How happy are you at Prince House?"

"Oh, acutely miserable but getting along," Jeanne said, surprised, "like most working girls. Why?"

Fry looked at her for a long moment and she began to feel uncomfortable. "Jeanne, the new mystery editor at Hodge Hathaway is going to rate an assistant. A hundred and ten a week to start with, I'd guess. No shorthand, there'll be a girl for that. The Hathaway family has decided, after a conservative twenty-year look at the situation, that they may be passing up a bet in mysteries. Ross wants me to try to build up the department."

Jeanne now broke a five-week stretch of abstinence by reaching for one of Karl's cigarettes. He swiftly lit it for her, an unexpected gallantry from Karl Fry. Jeanne had given up cigarettes after Hawke had teased and nagged at her for months, saying that he didn't want her to cough herself to death in the middle of the first useful work she'd done in her life. Of course the cough had promptly disappeared, and Hawke had been so triumphant, and so pleased with himself, that he had taken her to dinner at the Waldorf. But she had never stopped craving to smoke, and con-

fronted with a possible business decision she suddenly figured to hell with Youngblood Hawke. The first puff tasted atrocious. "Well, gosh, Karl, this is terribly kind of you. I haven't had any experience with mysteries."

"What does that matter? What's needed here is a little intelligence, the ability to see the good and the bad in a manuscript, and the tact to handle these womanish goofs called authors. Really, Jeanne, as long as you're in it you may as well do something better than styling. That's drudgery for a clerk."

Jeanne said, puffing away—the cigarette was tasting better—"Well, it's awfully tempting, and you're flattering me to little pieces, I must say."

She was certainly tempted. Jeanne's situation was bad at Prince House. The head copy editor was a woman in her forties, rather dull-witted and vinegarish. She hated Jeanne, and had managed to make Jay Prince and most of the editors believe that Jeanne was rebellious and hard to handle; the truth was that Jeanne had been rebellious enough toward her, having a natural inability to suffer fools. If not for Youngblood Hawke Jeanne would have been looking for work elsewhere. But that was it. Youngblood Hawke was at Prince House.

Karl spoke into her meditative silence. "Jeanne, I'll try to get you a hundred twenty-five. I want you as my assistant. I want you to do all the work while I draw a fat salary and try to start writing poetry again."

"Spoken like a man," Jeanne said, laughing. She stood. "I'm grateful as I can be, Karl. Whether it comes through or not, or whether I can take it or not, you've made me feel remarkably good. It's nice to be wanted."

"There's nothing nicer," Fry said with sudden intensity, and with a touching, almost frankly appealing look. "But you must live in a constant aura of that feeling."

"Not at Prince House. I got off on the wrong foot. My own fault, I have a mean streak. I've got to go. Thanks for everything. A wonderful afternoon, cheered me up no end."

He walked with her to the door, put his hand on the knob, and then didn't open it. "I spend a lot of evenings alone. Maybe we could take a few more dinners together. You make me feel very good, Jeanne, you always have. Some people improve life just by existing."

"I'd like to do that, Karl, some time." She took a little step toward the door, so that he was forced in politeness to turn the knob and open it. But still he barred her way.

"Tomorrow night, Jeanne?"

Though she was free she said, "Sorry, Karl, not tomorrow night." They sparred a bit and it ended in a dinner date for the following week. Jeanne did not at all mind the prospect of dining with Karl. But a quick acceptance would have shown him a pleasure in his attentions that she did not feel. She did not want to be courted by Karl Fry. She did not want to be courted by anyone, just now.

Karl walked with her to the elevator. "How's our young mountaineer friend?"

"You mean Youngblood Hawke?" she said, blushing a bit at the hollow note, the forced innocence.

"Yes, I mean Youngblood Hawke," Karl said with a sad little ghost of a grin.

"Well, he's an egomaniac, but at least he's a good writer."

"I hear you're working on the new one as he goes along."

"Yes, he requested that from Waldo Fipps and they assigned me to the job."

"Give Artie my best," Karl said as she stepped into the elevator.

"I will when I see him."

"Huh-huh," Karl grunted, and the door closed. Again she had made a fool of herself, she thought. Karl knew she was going to see Hawke now; it was written on her, and the pretense that she wasn't had betrayed her if her previous conduct hadn't. Good God, was the gossip all over Prince House that she had lost her head over Youngblood Hawke?

5

The doorbell rang at eight. Hawke was always prompt. She went to the door, swallowing nervously, and opened it. She was wearing a dark blue silk dress, and her hair, her nails, her face were done. Sometimes after a work session he offered to take her out. She was expected to clap on her hat and come along at once.

The red paper portfolio was under his arm; so he had new material to read to her. "Hi. How's it going?" he said, coming in without ceremony.

"Fine. The typist sent back the last four chapters yesterday. I'm pretty well caught up on it."

Without asking him, she served coffee. That was the rule: coffee when he came, and coffee straight through the work session. Then maybe a drink; but Hawke was reluctant to drink in her apartment. Jeanne would have had good grounds for believing that he found her repulsive, except that she knew otherwise. He acted exactly as though she were a married woman, and he was going to be honorable when alone with her, if it killed him.

When they settled down for his reading of the new pages—she curled on the couch, he in the armchair, minus jacket, tie and shoes—she lit a cigarette with pathetic defiance. "What's this?" he growled.

"Let's face it, I'm no good," she said. "I tried but I have no character."

"You have all kinds of character."

"All right, I have. I'd rather smoke and cough and die young. I love to smoke. I've searched my soul and that's how it stands. What's it to you?"

"It's nothing to me," Hawke said, "except that it's going to take me a while to break in another girl when they cart you off in a bag."

"You just won't have all those nagging queries to slow you up, when they cart me off in a bag."

"I can hardly wait." He opened the folder.

Some evenings are fated to go wrong. The new scenes he read to her were bad. Usually she could shrug off a patch of faulty work, knowing that his own instinct would cause him to change it in time; and then she could cheerfully do what he really wanted of her, and tell him that the book was going well. But now and then his very speed of composition took him far along a false path. She had to say what she thought, much as she dreaded to. He did not like criticism. "How is it?" he said, closing the folder.

She nodded. "All right."

"Why? What's the matter?" When Jeanne liked his work Hawke knew it, and he also knew when she didn't. He was the angrier with her because he didn't like the scenes himself. He had just written them. He had come back to his hole on Twenty-eighth Street in a turmoil, after the lunch with Mrs. Winter and the strange visit to Georges Feydal; he had hurled himself at his desk and scribbled off a great task. Even his handwriting looked different on this big batch of pages—hasty, spread-out, slanted. He had the usual symptoms of working too hard and too fast—racing pulse, shaky arms and legs. He had tried to sleep, instead of eating dinner, but had only tossed, so he was hungry too.

When Jeanne said nothing, but just looked at him and smoked, he said gently, "Look, I'm not satisfied either. What bothers you?"

She made her criticisms.

He said grouchily, "I'll look at it again after I've had some sleep. I dashed it off this afternoon. If you're right I'll be obliged to you. Let's get on to your queries."

"Maybe we'd better postpone them."

He looked at his watch. "Why? Are you tired?"

"Not in the least, but they usually irritate you, and I've annoyed you enough for one night."

"Don't be foolish. I may act irritated but you know I'm grateful, or I wouldn't pay attention to you."

But when they were halfway through the queries he jumped out of the armchair, and strode at her in his stocking feet, throwing his arms in the air. "Please, that's too much. This is a novel, Jeanie. That means it's an invention. A piece of fiction. It's a lie, you see. It never happened. I'm making it up. It's not naval history. It's a yarn."

"I know that," she said, looking up at him uncowed. On a point of fact it was impossible to bully her. "All I'm saying is that a jeep carrier couldn't have steamed from Eniwetok to Iwo Jima in that length of time. I've

checked the distances and the maximum speed of those ships. It couldn't happen."

"I want it to happen, so it does. That's known as a fictional liberty. Shakespeare foreshortened whole decades in his plays, turned history inside out—times, places, events—when he wanted to, and somehow the sloppy lazy bastard got away with it and people even pay to see his plays to this day."

"He wasn't writing in the convention of realism. You are. Anyway, I admire you, as I guess you know, but I'm not sure you can yet use the free hand of Shakespeare."

"That one stays as it is, Jeanne. What's next?"

He returned to the armchair and sank into it. He tried hard to be gracious through the remaining queries, but Jeanne found herself skipping the troublesome ones. She did not know what was causing the strain. They had had acrid exchanges before, but the tension tonight was new. When he said, after the last query, that he would like a Scotch and soda, she leaped to the buffet corner that served as a bar, and mixed two strong drinks quickly. He gloomily gulped the drink, said he would take another, and lit a cigar. Jeanne reflected that there would be no going out tonight, the silk dress and all the rest had been to no purpose; she could have received him in a housecoat. But she never knew.

He said, "You've made me feel odd tonight."

"Odd?"

"The correct word is guilty, I guess."

"But why, for heaven's sake?" She was coughing badly. "Excuse me, time for the opium. Sorry your effort to reform me failed." She took a spoonful from the brown bottle. "Maybe what I really want is the opium, and smoking is just a devious way to get at it."

Hawke said, leaning forward, resting his elbows on his knees and looking earnestly at her, "I'm suddenly aware that I'm imposing on you. Jeanne, do you think you'd enjoy working with me in a fancy suite in The Park Tower on the twenty-fifth floor, with a gorgeous view of the park, and all the room service we want, drinks and coffee and a seven course supper at midnight if we feel like it, served out of those big portable warming things by a couple of bowing waiters in gold and green uniforms?"

She said with a puzzled smile, "I suppose I could bear it. Why?"

"That's what we're going to be doing from now on for a while. I couldn't have you coming to that pigsty of mine on Twenty-eighth Street, but that's all over with. From now on I can be a bit less of a burden to you, stomping in on you at all hours, ordering you around—"

"You're not a burden," she started to say, but he kept talking.

"If you'll believe me," he said, "Georges Feydal is our benefactor, Georges Feydal in the flesh. I happened to meet him today, and he's

letting me have his apartment in The Park Tower for the summer. I'm moving in there lock, stock, and barrel, day after tomorrow, I really am, and that's where we'll have these sessions from now on. Nice?"

"Amazing. It's wonderful," Jeanne said slowly and cautiously. "What will you do after the summer?"

"Who knows? I haven't really thought about it, this all just happened a few hours ago."

"How on earth did you meet Georges Feydal?"

Having no ready lie, for all this was unpremeditated, Hawke said, "Frieda Winter took me up to his place. You remember Mrs. Winter."

"Yes, I remember Mrs. Winter. The lady who liked my hat at the Christmas party. How did she happen to pop up?"

"I sent her a copy of *Alms for Oblivion*. She was very helpful to me on the research for the Virginia scenes in the new book."

"Oh? Is she from an old Virginia family? I wouldn't have thought that."

"Of course not. Her mother's Swedish and her father's German or the other way around or something. Anyway she's an old friend of Feydal and she sort of manages him. She's booked him out on this summer lecture tour, and it was her idea to ask him for the apartment. He couldn't have been more gracious about it. We arranged it in a few minutes."

"You're not paying *anything?*"

"Well, he asked me for a first exclusive look at the next play I write, which seemed a pretty tenuous payment to me, but we shook hands on it. So, Jeanie, our headquarters transfer to The Park Tower day after tomorrow."

"Mrs. Winter went to a lot of trouble for you."

"She's an energetic woman. She insisted on seeing the place where I worked, and then she threw a fit when she saw it and marched right out and telephoned Feydal. She thinks my loft isn't a fit human habitation."

"Well, it's very bachelorish, but that was your own choice, I thought. You've done fine work there and you don't owe anybody anything."

"I won't owe anybody anything in The Park Tower."

"It seems to me you'll owe something to Mrs. Winter. You didn't know Georges Feydal. She did. He's doing her a terrific favor, it seems to me."

"Are you saying I shouldn't have accepted it?"

"That's hardly for me to say. But a furnished apartment in The Park Tower is probably worth a thousand dollars a month, don't you think?"

"He said it's impossible to sublease in the summertime."

"Try it. Ask a renting agent what he can get you for the place."

He began to put on his shoes. "You seem a bit annoyed about Mrs. Winter. She's a happily married woman of forty with four children."

"Yes, I know, a toothless bent old hag whose nose rests on her chin, but a great soul and a patron of the arts." Jeanne went to her desk and snatched

a copy of *Alms for Oblivion* from it. "I trust you autographed Mrs. Winter's book?"

"I autographed it, of course."

"Would you sign a copy for me?"

He looked up; he was tying his shoelaces. "What's all this?"

She stood over him, brandishing the book and a pen at him. Her eyes were wide open, glittering in the reddish light of the floor lamp. "I think it would be nice if I had a signed copy. I don't, you know. Not yet."

He took the book and pen, with a grin. He wrote, *For Jeanne Green, editor and collaborator, but for whom this first effort of mine would be a great deal worse than it is—or better, I'll never know—with affection and gratitude, Arthur Youngblood Hawke*. She stood looking at him, arms tightly folded, one leg out to a side, her weight on a hip. The attitude threw the feminine lines of the slight girl into relief. Having scrawled the inscription he now wished he had made it less facetious. Written out, it was coarse. Nevertheless he gave her the book.

She glanced at the inscription. "Thanks." She turned away and went to her desk. There she sat and coughed and shuffled papers while he put on his tie and coat. He said, "Come out and have a bite with me. I'm famished. That's one reason I'm surly, I daresay. I skipped dinner."

"Where to?" she said. "The Park Tower?"

"Any place."

"I don't think I'm hungry. Thanks, anyhow." Her back was to him. She was lighting another cigarette. The match fumes caught in her throat and she coughed in deep grating spasms. Hawke strode to her, yanked the cigarette out of her fingers, and crushed it in an ashtray. Then he pulled Jeanne from her chair by the hands. She came unwillingly. She said, "The reason I wanted the book is that I don't know whether I'll be seeing you any more, that's all. I think I'm quitting Prince House." Hoarsely, she told him of Karl Fry's offer.

He said, "Well, I suppose I should congratulate you, but this is upsetting. Couldn't you continue with me anyway, evenings?"

"I don't see how."

"It could be something you're doing on the side. I would pay you, of course."

Jeanne passed the back of her hand across her eyes. "Look, I don't like to put you out, but I'm really not feeling too good, the opium or whatever. You'd better go and eat without me. Thanks anyway. I'm going to bed."

"Well, what do we do? Just drop the arrangement here and now? It's absurd, Jeanne."

She said desperately, "Can't we talk about it tomorrow? I don't feel good, truly I don't."

He clumsily embraced her. She uttered a weak "No, no," but he pulled

her to the couch and began to make love to her. She was crying. The cool feel of the tears on her cheeks aroused him in a bitter very strong way. She kissed him with shy tentative excitement, with cutting sweetness. Her body in his arms was angelic. He said, "Don't cry. For God's sake, why cry?"

"Do you know what you're doing?" she said.

He released her.

She took a cigarette from the coffee table. "Don't you dare nag me, I'm going to smoke this one." She lit it and smoked and said nothing. He took her hand and held it, playing with her fingers.

If this was not love, he thought, what was it? Frieda was quite right. He ought to marry Jeanne Green. She was everything he wanted. He could hear himself saying, "Jeanie, let's get married." His lips half moved in the words, as he sat there not saying anything.

He was hanging on to his freedom, that was all, as a young man will. He wanted to play out the adventure with Mrs. Winter; it couldn't last long! He wanted to gamble on commodity futures for a while if he felt like it. This girl would wither his speculating with her cool skepticism. She would veto The Park Tower. She would put up with no adventures of the Frieda Winter variety.

Like every man who finds himself with almost no way out of proposing to a virtuous and lovely girl, Hawke was a bit appalled by the threatening closing-in of the walls of domesticity. But unlike the men who go through with it and—for the most part—live happily ever after, Hawke did have another ready and enticing alternative: Mrs. Winter and The Park Tower. If he could have put his best offer to Jeanne in words it would have gone something like this: "I love you. Be loyal to me, keep your heart intact, let me be a fool for a little while, work with me, I'll come around very soon." But no man can say such words, so he said nothing, but clung to her hand. A very little thing, a slight extra impulse, some lucky thing she said, and he might have asked her to marry him, then and there.

But Jeanne, in her own way, now did something wrong. She said, unable to fight down the fatal remark, and annoyed and troubled by his silence and by the thought of the sexual freedoms she had just allowed him and herself—and possibly feeling that combat was her one chance at this point—"I think Frieda Winter's paying Feydal for the apartment."

He left the couch and walked up and down the room. Then he faced her angrily. "That's an interesting thought, Jeanie. Why do you suppose she would do that?"

She answered up just as sharply, "Well, as I said, she's a patron of the arts. She probably had the whim and she acted on it. God knows the money would mean nothing to her."

"You are mistaken. Money means much more to rich people than it

does to you and me. That's one of the reasons they get rich and stay rich. Jeanie, I'm a little tired of my loft, can't you understand that? I think a sojourn in The Park Tower is an experience I ought to have. It's been offered to me, and I'm taking it. I don't believe Mrs. Winter is paying. I'm sorry that you do, because the opinion of me that you imply isn't pleasant."

She said, standing, "My opinion of you is a little too obvious. I'm not going to talk about that. I doubt very much that we could go on working together anyway. I'm glad I've been of use to you so far. You don't need me, you never have. Nothing can stop you from becoming an important novelist, a very successful one, possibly a great one, though I think the word 'great' can only be used after a writer is dead."

He said, in an irrelevant burst, "Does Karl Fry mean anything to you?"

This sudden inquiry stopped even Jeanne Green's facile tongue. She could not imagine what had given Hawke this preposterous impression. Sometimes she had quoted Karl's letters to him, especially jokes about Hawke himself, and she had always spoken kindly of Karl, but that was all. She looked at Hawke in round-eyed wonder, with an inquiring tilt of the head like an animal. "Hm?" It was a mere defensive noise.

And Hawke blundered on, "I mean if we have to discontinue our work because you and Karl, I mean because you like him or something, that's one thing, but I think it's ridiculous for you to leave me and Prince House just to take another job. I can go to Jay Prince and tell him you should have an editorial position, and more money—"

"Christ, did you say money didn't mean anything to you? Is there anything else that does?" she shrilled, in a tone he had never heard from her, a voice with no trace of girlishness in it, the hard scolding voice of an angry woman. "*Will you stop talking about money to me?* In fact, will you please get out of my apartment, Arthur Hawke?"

They glared at each other, almost toe to toe, the big heavy-shouldered man and the slender girl. And though she was lovely, she was infuriating, he thought; too quick by half, selfish, proud, clever, too clever, trying to pin him down. Marry this moody sharp-clawed pretty nobody? "You're throwing me out," he said.

"You can call it that. I want to go to bed. I told you that long ago. Stay if you want only let's work, then, or something."

He picked up the portfolio and put away his manuscript. In the few seconds this took he gained a trace of calm. "This has all been my fault. It was a bad night."

She managed to say without a break in her voice, by the strongest effort of the will, "Oh, look, nothing's decided. We'll talk tomorrow. Good night."

They confronted each other across three feet of brown-carpeted space

as wide as an ocean. He said gruffly, "Don't smoke. It isn't good for you, Jeanne."

"Don't go to The Park Tower. It won't be good for you," she said.

"Good night," he said, and he walked out.

6

The theatre was almost filled with Feydal's admirers for the closing performance, and the show went with a roar from start to finish. Hawke couldn't understand why the play had failed. It was light, but brilliant and amiable, or at least he thought so. So it was easy for him to be pleasant to Feydal when Frieda took him backstage. The Frenchman sat at a mirror framed in light bulbs, smearing cream on his painted fat face, slumped in an enormous coarse brown dressing gown like a monk's robe. There were several other chattering people in the room, including Pierce Carmian. "Hello, there," Feydal said, not turning around, with a tired smile at Hawke's image appearing behind his in the mirror.

Hawke said, "It's a wonderful show, every minute of it, and you were absolutely superb. They're all idiots."

Because he meant it, and spoke with his natural energy, the words struck home to the actor. Feydal turned around and held out his hand, sharp eyes beaming. "I'm so glad. It is an amusing little thing, isn't it? In the theatre you take the good with the bad, and get on with the next job." He wiped red-brown smears from his face on a fresh towel handed him by a Negro valet, uncovering swathes of pale pink jowl. "Maybe you and I will have a success one day soon, eh! What do you say, my young friend, will you write me a play in that inspiring apartment of mine?"

"Well, if I get an idea I'll certainly try."

"The apartment's cleaned and ready for you," Feydal said. "I left strict orders. We'll go there together later."

The party on stage was a crowded and buzzing affair, for the play had had a large cast. Hawke was astonished at the flatness, the shallowness, the crudely smeared paint of the setting. The curtain was up; the rows of seats stretched off into gloom. Frieda was chatting with some actors. He wandered away and stood alone at the footlights, his back to the party, staring out at the empty theatre.

"New worlds to conquer?" Pierce Carmian said, coming up to him with a bottle of champagne in one hand and paper cup in the other. Hawke laughed. The young playwright, streamlined as a shark, in a black suit, white shirt and oyster-colored silk tie, poured wine into both their cups, and put the empty bottle into the well of the footlights. "This, I warn you, is the theatre," he said. "A paper cupful of champagne. The excitement, the elegance, the poetry of champagne, all contained in the tawdry,

trivial impermanence of a paper cup. You're better off with the novel form."

"I'm sure of that."

They were like two strange dogs bristling at each other, Hawke thought, yet he wished Carmian no ill, and rather envied his fantastic handsomeness and his exquisite getups. Carmian was groomed like a woman, though there was nothing else effeminate about him, in fact his voice was resonantly deep and his gestures were hearty. Carmian said, after sipping champagne, "If I had to be dispossessed, I'm glad it was by a hardworking writer like yourself. I'm told you write all day and all night. I hope you'll take a little time off to enjoy the place."

"I wasn't aware I was dispossessing you. And that's really an exaggeration, I work by night because it's quiet then, that's all."

"Why, I'm told you wrote this perfectly enormous book in three or four months."

"It took me a year."

"That's still marvellous. Anyway, you're not exactly dispossessing me," Carmian said with a manly sweep of a flaring lighter to the end of his cigarette, "since I was just going to inherit the place by default, if Georges couldn't sublet it. But he's a Frenchman, and how could he resist all that cash? Of course I can't compete when it comes to money. I haven't sold a book to the movies recently."

Though Hawke was dumfounded, he had to say something under Carmian's appraising glance. "I can't afford it any more than you can. If I'd known you were supposed to have it, I'd have let it alone."

"I doubt that Frieda Winter would have allowed you to. She's a managerial soul, especially with promising young men. Once she made up her mind that you were going to have Georges's place, brother, you were going to have it. Of course, Georges thinks the world of her. So does everybody. You're lucky." Carmian smiled at him, raised his eyebrows knowingly, and turned his back and walked off.

There was a space of three or four seconds when Hawke had trouble keeping himself from springing at Carmian, spinning him around, and hitting him. But he had the sense to know how impossible that was. He stood in his tracks.

Frieda was peering around now, her head bent down, and when she saw him she made for him. "There you are. I can't see anything in this light. Georges suddenly realized he barely has time to pick up his bags and make the plane. We have to pile in his limousine this minute. Having fun?"

"Not much."

"I know. There's nobody more boring than actors, except to other actors. Of course Georges is different, he's brilliant. Let's go." She slipped an arm in his and tugged.

There was nothing to do but go along, and he went. In ten minutes they were in Feydal's gorgeous suite, all orderly and put to rights except for a stack of calfskin luggage in the center of the living room, with some folding bags for suits. In ten minutes more a parade of bellboys had carted all that away, and Feydal had given him keys and made him a present of the remaining liquor in the round little rolling bar decorated with red and gold Japanese figures; and they had drunk a toast in twenty-year-old brandy, and Feydal had made one phone call in the closed bedroom, and taken a preoccupied farewell and lumbered out, enormous in a black raincoat; and Hawke and Mrs. Winter were left in the suite together.

It seemed less glamorous to Hawke on this second visit, much smaller and disconcertingly familiar. He realized that the rooms were not large at all—the living room was only a fraction of the size of his loft, and cluttered with beautiful furniture, and there would be no chance for the headlong pacing that had been part of his work habits—and he found he was oppressed by the thought of living with, and using, another man's things. Yet it was a lush place, no doubt of that, and New York lay far below him, a conquered web of lights, the golden city at his feet.

"Frieda," he said rather miserably, "are you paying Feydal for this apartment?"

"What? Of course I'm not. Pay that monster, after all I've done for him? Why do you ask?"

He glumly told her of his conversation with Carmian. Her big gray eyes were fixed on his face. She was leaning, arms folded, against a smoky-tinted wall mirror. She heaved a long sigh. "Are you going to take Pierce Carmian's word against mine?"

"I'm asking, that's all."

"I have not paid Georges Feydal one cent. He told me on the telephone that you could have it, because I built you up as a potential major playwright. He reneged on me when he asked you for the exclusive reading of your next play. He's getting more than he deserves, and I'm a little angry at him. And I'm not pleased to death with you, either, making me swear on a stack of Bibles that a catty little lie of Pierce Carmian's isn't the truth. I'll be running along. Enjoy the apartment, Bloody."

She started to walk out, and of course he caught her arm. That she should be lying was beyond belief. Carmian had sunk a little poison sting in him to ruin his pleasure in the apartment; and he had almost succeeded. "Frieda, hold on. You're dealing with a clod from the mountains. I don't understand people like Carmian. The thing is I'm not dumb, and I promise you I'll catch on fast."

She turned willingly enough, and put a hand up to his face. Frieda was about Jeanne's size, or perhaps an inch taller. "I wonder whether you ever will. However, you'll make out. You can write, and we need writers."

"I've made an ugly mess of this. I don't know how to thank you."

"Don't you?" she said softly, and with a certain sliding movement that he remembered as long as he lived she was in his arms.

A man has only one honeymoon night. There may be women before it and women after it, it may come early in life or late, it may be with a true love or a false one, but one night one woman unlocks the sweet secret of the best delight the physical world holds—a questionable transient delight, some say, but the best—and for good or ill, his life rolls on and shapes itself on the far side of his honeymoon night. It is over. Arthur Hawke had his night with Mrs. Paul Winter, the mother of four children, in The Park Tower, on the wide lilac silk-sheeted bed of Georges Feydal, at the age of twenty-seven. What other events had occurred in that bed he did not know, but it was not his own wedding bed, and it was a decidedly unusual honeymoon bed. No beggar boy in the Arabian Nights, led by mysterious veiled messengers into the golden boudoir of a lovely queen, ever had a more enthralling night of it. And the night passed, the dawn was gray over New York, gray as his love's eyes, and she dressed and left him to sleep on for a while in The Park Tower. It was one of the few nights when he failed to write his regular quota of pages.

7

And he found out the truth about a week later, in an absurd and somewhat dishonorable way. Among the letters in his box was one in a long white business envelope from Frieda Winter's office, addressed to Georges Feydal. The hotel clerk was always forgetting to readdress Feydal's mail, there was no great mischance in that, and Hawke usually struck out the address himself and wrote in the address of the actor's attorney. But Hawke got his hands on the letter, and with a sickness in his stomach he guessed at the contents. He dropped into a chair in the marble-walled hotel lobby and opened it. It was a letter agreement about the apartment between Frieda and Feydal, a single typed page, and clipped to it was a check for eight hundred dollars, the first month's rent.

They had a battle over the letter that night. Frieda flew directly on the offensive and stayed there. She put him in the wrong for opening the letter, and she raged at Feydal for telling Carmian, and at Carmian for telling Hawke; and she raged at him for being a proud, suspicious, childish hillbilly, creating difficulties where there were none.

"But why did you lie to me, Frieda? That's all I'm asking you. Why did you lie?"

"Oh, please, lied! I was protecting your preposterous Southern vanity, I wasn't hiding anything mean, anything wrong, anything I was or am the slightest bit ashamed of."

"I believe that, Frieda. But my point is that—"

"What was my crime, what was the enormous deed I committed that I had to lie about? *You* sent me that book of yours! *I* didn't ask for it, *you* sent it to me, and we met at the lion cage and we had lunch, and before that lunch was over I was gone, my life fell apart like a house of cards, I knew I was hopelessly in love with a mad oversized young scribbler from Kentucky with a head like a Michelangelo, and I knew that that crazy Christmas afternoon I'd tried to forget was no accident but the beginning of my life when I thought it was all over. I loved you. I wanted to be with you. I made it possible. Did you want to make love to me on the floor of your goddamned loft, under your hanging wet socks, between the box of empty tin cans and the floor heater? Hey? Is that how you wanted to make love to me? Or didn't you want to make love to me? Answer me!"

"I wanted to make love to you all right. I want to make love to you right now. You know that, so don't confuse the issue."

"That *is* the issue, and get your hands off me. We'll talk this out, I will not be called a liar, and if I'm a liar why do you want to have anything to do with me? Let me go."

"Frieda, you should have told me, that's all I say. You should have told me the truth. You shouldn't have treated me like a baby."

"The truth! The truth is that I love you, that's the truth. You'd never be in this apartment if I'd told you I'd paid for it. Not you! I saw how you acted about that lunch check that day, why you sulked for an hour afterward. Southern pride, suh, mountaineer independence, old Dan'l Boone in the log cabin, that's you, Bloody my boy! Only the days of the log cabin are over. It takes money to live decently. You're going to have a ton of it, you fool, you're a brilliant writer—"

"I've got money now. I've torn up your check. I sent a check for eight hundred dollars to Feydal's attorney."

"What! You did *what*? Oh, Christ, you make me sick. I can afford it. You can't, you *can't*, that's all."

"Sure I can."

"Oh, yes. What are you going to do, draw another one of those stupid advances from Jay Prince and mortgage a valuable property you haven't written yet, and give it away for two cents on the dollar? If it offends your Southern manhood to stay here, why, move the hell out. We'll postpone our love affair for a couple of years, isn't that sensible? You see I can be sensible. Or I have a better idea. We'll make love in my house. But it'll have to be only once a year, when all the family and the servants are gone, on Christmas afternoon, complete with corn fritters. Okay?"

Her hand shot up, with wriggling spread fingers, and he had to laugh.

"Frieda, it's just that much less I'll be betting on onions and lard. That's all."

Frieda also laughed, coarsely and wildly. "Onions and lard! I'd forgotten them, by God. All right, pay for the apartment by all means, Daniel Boone, and be damned to onions and lard. Now come here, you big lunatic."

And so to love-making again, in the dim pleasant luxury of Feydal's suite, twenty-five stories above the busy streets of New York, where the traffic streamed in yellow rivulets of light.

He was appeased. He had asserted his manhood. And now that he was in The Park Tower, he liked it. All the same, he had found out Frieda's amazing ability to lie when it suited her.

CHAPTER SIX

1

PUBLICATION day of *Alms for Oblivion* was drawing closer. In the offices of Prince House Hawke had seen proofs of the first advertisements, and there was little doubt that Jay Prince was planning what Karl Fry called "the old jazzeroo campaign." The opening gun for *Alms for Oblivion* was to be a full page in the Sunday book section of the New York *Times*, with the novelist's name spread across the top in solid black letters two inches high:

HAWKE

A major new name in American fiction

followed by a delirious description of the book and of its coal-truck-driving author.

Prince was full of hopes for the novel. The failure of the book clubs to pick it up had not dampened him. "They'll hop on the bandwagon, Hawke, when we pass our first hundred thousand. They'll make it a special selection or something. They're always doing that. We've got a big goddamn doorstopper of a book here and it's going to sell like hell. You just get on with that next book as fast as you can."

Hawke was not wholly flattered by the description of his first novel as a big goddamned doorstopper. But the publisher's belief in the book

was exciting. Moreover Prince had infected his salesmen with this belief. They had pushed out an advance sale to the bookstores of thirty thousand copies. Prince House was money ahead on a first novel before publication, something that rarely happens. The air at the publishing company's offices was charged with favor for Youngblood Hawke, and he liked to drop in and collect the smiling deference of secretaries and sub-editors.

Jeanne Green was gone from her desk. She had taken the job at Hodge Hathaway, and in her place was a fat girl with a spotty skin, and that was saddening. Hawke missed Jeanne very much. The new chapters of *Chain of Command* seemed to him overstuffed and lacking in sharpness, and he would have given much to restore their working comradeship. But he had not been willing to give her a wedding ring, which had begun to seem the price, and that was that. He was riding very high, triumphant in the conquest of Frieda Winter, triumphant in the feeling of success at Prince House. He telephoned his mother, inviting her to come with Nancy to New York for publication. And when his sister got on the telephone and shyly started to talk about John Weltmann, the man with the wig, he told her by all means to bring him along, since that was what she seemed to be driving at.

Ten days before publication day, the telephone woke him in The Park Tower. It rang and rang and rang and rang, and at last the young man sat up heavily, blinking, and reached for the receiver. It was still a delicious novelty to have a telephone at his bedside, to be confronted on waking by a small Monet on the wall, and to see the Hudson River glittering far off through the western windows. "Hello?"

"Arthur, it's Waldo Fipps. I hope I didn't disturb you. Knowing your nocturnal habits I waited till eleven to call."

"Perfectly all right, Waldo. What is it?"

"We've got the first review. An advance proof. *The Saturday Review of Literature.*"

Hawke gripped the phone. "Yes? Is it all right?"

"It's an absolute stinker."

"Oh? I'm sorry to hear that . . . Nothing good in it at all?"

"Not much. Want me to read it to you? It isn't long."

"I guess so. Who wrote it?"

"A fellow named Phil Gebble. I know Phil, he's a ham writer, a frustrated novelist. We turned down a manuscript of his a few weeks ago. His opinion is utterly meaningless. Just a vomiting of spleen. Unfortunately that's the kind of fellow they sometimes get to do book reviews."

"Well, let's hear it, Waldo."

He sat there in the broad bed, telephone to ear, with the faint perfume of Mrs. Winter rising from the bedclothes when he stirred restlessly under the stream of abuse. Fipps read the review slowly and distinctly from start to finish. "Well, Arthur, that's it. Just half a column or so.

One mercy is they usually bury a panning like this in the back of the magazine."

"Is Jay upset?"

"He hasn't seen it yet. Why should it upset him? It couldn't mean less."

"But the *Saturday Review* is important, isn't it?"

"One notice is never of any consequence. You'll get plenty of raves to balance this."

"Let's hope so."

"You sound dismayed. I hope I haven't spoiled your morning or anything. Really, Phil Gebble is an idiot, and nobody can possibly take him seriously. I just thought you'd like to know about it."

"Of course. Thanks, Waldo. I may drop in later."

"By all means, do that. Goodbye."

Hawke hung up, and that was his welcome to the green pastures of American literature.

It seemed to him that he could repeat the whole review by heart. The phrases had sunk into him as though planted with a hot iron. *"Having gotten this pile of coal-heaving prose off his chest, Mr. Hawke will perhaps return now to his former occupation, unless he makes the fatal mistake of taking his publisher's claims seriously. To this reviewer, Dostoevsky and Faulkner remain untoppled, indeed unshaken, by Mr. Prince's literary discovery from the Kentucky coal country."*

Most of the review had attacked the extravagant boasts on the jacket. The book itself Gebble had dismissed as "a laboring mountain that never even brings forth its mouse." Hawke's writing was amateurish, his plot was a melodrama that would have done well in the nineteenth century, his aunt was a synthetic monster out of Dickens or possibly Dick Tracy. There had been one brief grudging sentence of praise: "The atmosphere of the town is well enough conveyed, and one somehow reads on and on in Mr. Hawke's interminable book to the very end, staying up to the late hours to do so, wanting to know how it will all come out and yet ashamed of oneself for this curiosity, as when one cannot get up and walk out of a bad movie."

Feeling a good deal as though his head had been chopped off, Hawke dragged his bleeding trunk out of bed, set his head back on his neck—as one might say—and went about showering, shaving, and dressing. The sight of Frieda's gray night dress in the bathroom was reassuring; he buried his face for a moment in the silken folds. He called room service and ordered a mighty breakfast, and when it came he ate all of it. With a double order of ham and eggs and half a dozen rolls under his belt, and the caffeine from two full coffee jugs coursing through his system, he brightened up, and combativeness began to flow from his heart to his brain and out along his limbs. It wouldn't do, of course, to find out where this Gebble lived, and go to him, and beat him senseless or throw

him through a window. That was exactly what Hawke wanted to do, and it really seemed the only thing to do to a stranger who had insulted him in this way. But he was able to laugh at himself for these feelings; a real mountaineer reaction! He was in the big city. City people didn't act like that. Under the city rules he had written a book, hoping for fame and money; once the book came to light, any man who thought he wasn't entitled to fame and money was privileged to say so in print in the most venomous terms. There was nothing he could do to Gebble, nothing at all.

And yet sickness throbbed in him at the thought of the rancor, the hatred, the urge to destroy, that his book had aroused in this faceless stranger. Another thing bothered him almost as much, though it was so queer that he had not quite grasped it at first, and awareness of it only nagged to the surface as he sat smoking his first cigar, on Feydal's soft couch upholstered in yellow-and-black striped satin—and this was the relish with which Fipps had told him the bad news. The phone had rung at the stroke of eleven, as though the editor had been holding himself in and had plunged to call him. He could hear that dry voice yet, enunciating the poisonous sentences with clarity and care. Why? Why had Fipps done this so eagerly, and with so much circumstance—why, come to think of it, had he called him at all? Had he been in Fipps' place he would have waited for some good reviews. It seemed the only sensible, the only kind thing to do; authors had feelings, even a truck driver from Letchworth County had them. Wasn't Fipps the editor of this book, and wasn't he bound to hope for its success and to suffer at any reverse, as much as the author? If there had been suffering in Fipps' heart, it had not come into his telephone voice; he had never sounded gayer and more full of life. Hawke finished dressing and went to Prince House.

Fipps greeted him with the same gaiety as he came into the office. "Hi. Recovered from the Gebble yet? Here's something to counteract it." He tossed across the desk a newspaper cutting with the pink tag of a press-clipping service on it. Hawke read it with hunger. It was a review in the Summit, Nebraska *Sentinel* praising the book wildly. The only trouble with it was that the whole review consisted of the advertising copy on the book jacket, word for word. He pointed this out to the editor. Fipps grinned. "Oh sure. The out-of-town papers are always doing that. Saves them the trouble of reading the book. But it's a straw in the wind, anyway. How are you feeling?" The editor stared at him, and Hawke imagined that he was looking hard for the red scar where his head had been chopped off.

"I'm feeling great," he said. "My new book's rolling fast now." As a matter of fact he was feeling wretched. He had arrived at the publishing office at lunch time, and perhaps a dozen employees had passed him on

his way to the editor's office. Unless it was a trick of morbid imagination, there had been a marked shading-off in the cordiality of their smiles, a sort of new politeness in their greetings, as though the Gebble review of *Alms for Oblivion* had been posted in every cubicle in Prince House.

The business face of Jason Prince now materialized, leaning into the doorway. "Waldo, we'd better try—oh, hello there, Youngblood," he said, walking in and slapping the author on the back. "Sitting around gossiping instead of working, hey? Bad business."

"I've just been commiserating with him over the Gebble," Fipps said.

"Phil Gebble? I would be seriously alarmed if that squirt liked the book. Look at the advance, Youngblood, not at one silly notice. We've passed thirty-one thousand."

"It just occurs to me," Hawke said, "that the jacket copy, and possibly the advertisements too, are a bit strong. I really don't think I've knocked out Dostoevsky. I may have to land a few more blows."

"My boy," said Jay Prince in a heavy jocose tone, "you just leave the bookselling to us and write up those two books you owe us. Waldo, come with me a minute."

Fipps should have looked at his desk before walking out, but he didn't. Hawke's prying eyes ran over manuscripts, letters, notes, and came on a green office memorandum clipped to several proof sheets of advertisements for *Alms for Oblivion*. In Jay Prince's quick spiky scrawl were these words: "In view of Gebble, etc. hold off any further advertising commitments on Hawke." This was an unpleasant turn. What did "etc." mean? What other bad news had come in? He heard the voice of Fipps in the hall, and made a show of looking out of the window.

"Arthur, still here? Anything else I can do for you?"

Hawke said, "I think I'd like to tell you about my new novel."

"Oh? Splendid." The bony, spruce editor glanced at his wrist watch, and sat behind his desk. "You've been awfully secretive about it."

"Yes, I know." Hawke was sinking into a black quicksand of despair, a deep certainty that *Alms for Oblivion* was a catastrophe, perhaps the most egregious failure in the history of American bookselling. He now wanted reassurance, and he wanted it so badly, he was so shaken, that he impulsively threw aside his reserve to get it from Waldo Fipps.

He told the editor the whole story of *Chain of Command*. He thought he told it well enough. Fipps smoked a couple of cigarettes in his elongated rather shaky fingers, rocked back and forth in his swivel chair, now and then touched his wispy mustache, and mostly stared out of the window, though once or twice his reddish eyes shifted to Hawke. When the author finished, Fipps clasped his hands behind his head, leaned back, and laughed. "It's a funny thing. It sounds like a novel that we turned down last week."

Hawke managed to say, "I don't believe you'll turn down this one."

"Oh certainly not. We've already bought it. Arthur, Jay and I have this lunch date. Jay's waiting for me." Fipps swept up the papers on his desk, dropped them in a drawer, locked the desk, and left.

Hawke had not seen or talked to Jeanne since their break-off. He telephoned her now without thinking, but the operator at Hodge Hathaway said she had gone to lunch. He hung up sadly; after this ghastly talk with Fipps he needed the assurance Jeanne, and only Jeanne, gave him. Most of the time a crest tide of self-confidence carried Hawke headlong through the days, but he could fall into suicidal troughs, and he had always suffered through these alone until he had encountered Jeanne. Frieda was different; Frieda made him feel virile and conquering. But he was not sure she really liked Alms for Oblivion, for all her frequent loving talk about his coming greatness; and he had told her little about Chain of Command. He now called Frieda at her office, despite their understanding that she was the one to call him. Her male secretary drily said, "Oh yes, Mr. Hawke, I'm sorry, Frieda is out."

2

She was lunching with Fanny Prince.

A woman needs not only a man to complete her, as the books say, she usually needs at least one other woman to talk with on pretty frank terms. Fanny Prince had discarded a husband and three small sons in her time, to take up with Jay. The two women were more or less of the same voltage. They knew the same people. Each had a good reason for looking down on the other. Frieda thought Fanny was devoid of taste, except for what she could pick up by quick imitation. Fanny thought Frieda was immoral, and what was worse, careless. Frieda's husband had more money, but the Prince money came from the creative field of publishing, whereas Paul Winter was only a wise dealer in bonds. It was a nice balance. They were good friends, as friendships go in the rapid circulation of well-to-do New York people.

They fenced around for a while on other topics before Fanny brought up Hawke. They were in the Commons Room of the Ritz Hotel, an expensive restaurant walled in gloomy wainscotting and stained glass to simulate a refectory in an old British university; it was the lunchtime haunt of the publishing trade at the moment.

Fanny said, "I talked to Jay on the phone just before I came. They're getting vorried about the Hoke book, a little bit."

"Oh?" Frieda sipped wine. "I thought it was a roaring smash before publication."

"Ve didn't mind about the Booksellers Bulletin. They can be wrong, God knows, they've missed some of the biggest ones. But they made it

class four. That really hurt. Some of the retailers who gave us big orders are cutting them in half, or even cancelling to 'vait and see.' The book clubs, Jay checked and not one of them sent it up to the judges, it got knocked out in the screening. Now the notices are starting to come in. The *Saturday Review* is horrible. The Sunday *Times* gave it to Todd Fenney to review, can you imagine, another young Southern novelist, and a homosexual at that! He hates it, naturally."

"Well, a good book can survive bad notices."

"Jay's going to push it, don't vorry."

"I'm not worried. Well, no, I'm a little worried about him, the way he'll take it. He doesn't look it, Fanny, but he's thin-skinned."

"How is everything?" Fanny took the woman-to-woman tone.

Frieda spun her cigarette lighter on one corner, and glanced demurely at Mrs. Prince. "Everything? Everything is divine, thank you."

"How is he taking to The Park Tower?"

"As though he'd been born there."

"But is it such a good idea? I mean, have you thought about it? The Park Tower! Vy didn't you put him in Macy's window, Frieda?"

"I know a lot of people in The Park Tower."

"That's my point, darling."

"Well, my point is that I'm in and out of there all the time, and always have been. Anyway, I didn't plan this, it all just happened, I wanted to get him out of the revolting hole he was in and I knew Georges was going on tour and I just went and did it. He can't stay there long. And if you want to know the truth, I plain don't care. I feel as though I've just been born. I'm not doing anything wrong. He's going to be a great man, but right now he's a lamb among wolves, and I think I'm good for him. I know I am. If I'd known him a year ago Jay wouldn't have gotten him to sign that contract."

"It was a very fine contract for an unknown writer," Fanny said coldly.

Frieda said with a drop in her voice, "There he is."

Fanny turned around, and saw Hawke talking to the head waiter. He came edging through the tables, in his bulky "novelist's suit" of brown; huge, clumsy, following the head waiter like a bull led by the nose. Frieda decided to take him to a tailor tomorrow; and why did he always seem to need a haircut? His hair grew like a little boy's. He walked past them with an awkward, shamefaced, "Hello," and Frieda lifted her arm and barely moved her fingers.

Fanny called, "Youngblood, you're alone? Come eat vith us." He looked over his shoulder at her with an embarrassed smile and shook his head, his pale face suddenly crimson. Fanny said, "Ach, Harry's putting him at that tiny table by the post. That's disgusting. Let me go get him. What's wrong if he has lunch with his publisher's wife?" She moved as though to get up.

"Let him alone," Frieda said in a razor voice.

Fanny looked at her, a smile curving her heavily painted lips, and shrugged. "Yes, darling."

Across the room, in a far dim corner booth that held six people, Jeanne was having lunch with Karl Fry and Ross Hodge; they were entertaining a new mystery writer and his agent. The writer was a shy man about Hawke's age, not much more than five feet tall, gotten up in the over-collegiate style favored by New York writers: bristly short haircut, thin black knitted tie, sport-cut dark gray jacket. His manuscripts—he had submitted two—were as violent and sexy as he was peaceful and sexless. Jeanne had been comparing him in her mind with Hawke when Hawke walked into the grill. The girl stopped eating, and watched Hawke walk toward Mrs. Winter's table. Had he stopped to chat with the two women, had he sat down to lunch with them, she would have been jealous, but she would have felt that the situation was not hopeless. Mrs. Winter's small wave of the fingers, Hawke's blush and his boorish hurry to get past her said too much; said everything. Jeanne had had some bad moments in the past weeks. This trivial instant, unperceived in all its nuance by anyone but herself, was the lowest. She endured it, and even managed to answer with relevance, and in a steady voice, a question about one of the manuscripts that Fry tossed at her.

Hawke didn't see Jeanne. He sat with his back to that corner, in a frame of mind as low as hers. He had never before come into this den of publishing people alone. He felt self-conscious, ridiculous, humiliated, perched at the tiny table by the post in the middle of the room. People on all sides were glancing at him and leaning toward each other to make remarks. Some of them were laughing. He was in the pillory! All eyes were on the big boob in the brown suit, sitting there with his face spattered with the Gebble review.

He had no friend in this man-eating city, not one. A waiter hurrying past struck his head with a hard elbow. "Sorry, sair." Anger rushed out in a palpable wave through his arms and legs. He tensed to perform some wonderful relieving violence: to throw over the table with a crash of glass and silverware, then to catch the waiter and knock him on his backside. What did he care about these people? Who said he had to write books? He was actually rising out of his chair when a hand was laid on his arm.

"Christ, you're a talented bastard." Ferdie Lax stood blinking at him through enormous black glasses on his parrot beak, his blond hair stiff and short in a new ludicrous crew cut.

"Hello, Mr. Lax." Still possessed by the wave of rage, Hawke could hardly speak.

He did not know whether to class Lax as a friend or enemy. The agent had steered him to his first movie sale. When Hawke had offered him a

ten percent fee he had at first declined it. But Jay Prince had told the young author that common business practice required them to pay Lax, and had added acidly that hereafter Hawke had better leave all marketing of rights to Prince House. Lax in the end had taken the money.

The agent said, "I pride myself on not reading new properties, Hawke. That way I can remain impartial, and talk about how good they are without lying. I glanced at the first page of that Mack truck of a book of yours, just to get the style, and I never stopped reading till I finished the goddamn thing. You killed two whole business days for me."

The words were like a sedative drug. Hawke didn't know whether they were true and hardly cared. The violence ebbed out of his muscles. "You really did like it?"

Lax said, "Come on over and eat with me." He led the big dazed author to a booth where a girl was sitting, a girl almost a head taller than the agent, one of the most beautiful Hawke had ever seen. "This is Anne," Lax said. "Anne, this is Youngblood Hawke." The exquisitely groomed brunette looked up at Hawke and her flawless features moved into a pleasant smile. Lax ordered a lunch of oysters and steak for all of them, and a bottle of champagne. He told Hawke of his adventures on another recent junket to Europe. He had acquired the film rights to a novel by André Gide, and had talked Gide into writing the screenplay in French. "Hell, translating it won't be a problem. Maybe you can do it. How's your French?" Lax talked as though the girl weren't there, or as though she were a water jug.

"Not so good. Anyway, I've got this book to finish, and then one other book to write before I get out of my bondage to Jay Prince."

Lax's head fell to one side, and he looked at Hawke with his tongue lolling. After a moment he said, "Why, what happened to that knockdown drag-out fight you were going to have with Jay?"

"I guess you were right about that. I can't handle him. He's so affable! He's like my father, but I can't get him to change anything. Not on paper."

Lax sat up and clasped his hands on the table. His lips vanished in a tight scowl. "Hawke, I just arrived in town yesterday from the coast. The word is getting around very fast here that your book is a louse."

Hawke said, swallowing his shock, "I seem to be the last one to be finding it out. I've had my first inkling today."

"Now listen," Lax said, "the thing to do is keep your head. This book business is disgusting, they're as bad as Hollywood. A lot of sheep, first they all run one way, then they all run the other as soon as they hear a twig snap. You take my word for it, you wrote a good book. I read the goddamn thing straight through and that's a miracle. Maybe you'll get solid bad notices. Maybe it won't sell. It's full of faults, you know, it's overwritten. Why did you put in those long chapters of arguments about

Kentucky politics? And what was the point of those long dreams that kept cropping up?"

"Please pass the salt," the girl said to Hawke, smiling like a sunrise. These were the first words she had spoken. She was eating an enormous steak with the quiet sure absorptive power of a boa constrictor.

"From now on I hope you'll just tell your stories and not horse around. Fancy writing just gets the English teachers, the people don't give a good goddamn about it, they want to know what happens next."

"I'm glad I ran into you," Hawke said. "I'm about ready to take on Jay Prince again. This time I'd like you with me."

Lax's briskness disappeared; he slumped slowly. "I caught Georges Feydal's one-man show in Chicago," he murmured. "It gets to be an awful lot of Feydal, but he had the place filled with tittering old ladies, a whole opera house full of them. He says you've got his apartment here."

"Yes."

"I gave him my copy of *Alms for Oblivion*. He claims he read it in one night."

"Did he like it?"

"He says there's a play in it."

"I have enough on my mind without that."

"I guess so. How's Frieda?"

Lax's conversational technique—these quick thrusts after sleepy maundering—was beginning to annoy Hawke. "Frieda who?" he said, glancing despite himself over at Mrs. Winter, and then at the oblivious Anne, eating away at the steak.

"Frieda McManus, of course," Lax said. "I heard you were engaged to her."

"Oh her. She went up to Cape Cod for a couple of weeks, and there was this singer in a bar there. She married him."

Anne looked up and said with genteel sympathy, "That's terrible, Mr. Hawke. I'm sorry."

Lax said, "That's all right, honey. This Frieda girl was no good. She had a studio in the village and all she did was make big plaster heads of colored men."

"Oh, one of those," Anne said, nodding wisely. "You're well out of it, Mr. Hawke."

"But I loved her," Hawke said. "I didn't care about those plaster heads. We had a marvellous fight one night. I broke six of them. I've never had such satisfaction in my life. I only wanted her to make more and more and more."

"Well, but she sounds abnormal to me," Anne said.

"All right, quiet, Anne," Lax said. "Hawke, the way things are going this may be just the time to talk to Jay. When's publication?"

"July 15. Tuesday."

"I'll call him up and make an appointment for the following week."

"Do I sign a contract with you?" Hawke said.

Lax held out his hand. "Here's the contract. Ten percent across the board." Hawke hesitated, then shook it.

"I knew a girl who had a studio in the village. She made statues out of sheet iron with a blowtorch," Anne said. "She set fire to herself."

"Quiet, Anne," Lax said.

3

Naked except for earrings and her wedding ring, Frieda Winter sat on the bed, smoking a cigarette. Hawke stood at the window in a scarlet dressing gown with a black satin collar which she had bought him that afternoon. He felt ridiculous in it, but he had put it on to avoid an argument. The sun was setting over the Hudson in a great splash of red and blue, and lights in the purple towers were beginning to twinkle.

"Yes, what's all this, now?" Frieda said.

"What's all what?" he said without turning.

"The deep gloom, the silent pensive stare out of the window. Aren't you having fun? Or are you worrying about tomorrow's reviews?"

"I was thinking of my mother, if you want to know," Hawke said. "She's coming here tomorrow with my sister."

"Oh? That's nice, I'd love to meet her." With a lazy motion she took up the gray gown and slipped it over her head.

"I rented a suite for them here in the hotel."

"Well, of course." Frieda looked hard at him and laughed. "Don't worry, they're not going to come in here and find me like this, if that's what you're thinking." Hawke grinned somewhat foolishly and she added, "Your mother's going to love me, my boy, just you wait and see."

Hawke hadn't been planning a meeting between the two women; in fact he had been wondering how to avoid it. This bland remark of Frieda's astonished him. "You don't mind meeting her?"

"Why, I'd love to. I'm infinitely grateful to her, didn't she bring you into the world?"

She was lounging comfortably against the pillow, her head turned to him at an angle that brought out the strong line of her jaw. When this happened she looked her age, but that no longer mattered to him. He came to the bed, sat beside her, and cupped a big hand over both her eyes. "Owl. The way you stare and peer."

"I could hardly make you out at that distance. Aren't you hungry?"

"Sure."

"Then take your hand off my eyes and let's go eat."

He said, freeing her eyes, "Have you always been so nearsighted?"

"Always. In this French convent school I went to, the doctor gave me big horrible greenish glasses to wear. The girls called me Crocodile."

"Frieda, I wish you'd write out a memoir of your life some time for me, and put in everything, every little detail that you remember. Like that about Crocodile."

"Oh yes, catch me doing that, just so's you can put me in a big nasty novel ten years from now, and make me the villain. You do your own dirty work."

"I'll never make you the villain, Frieda."

"Won't you? Why should you be different from the others?" She left the bed and began dressing with quick, spare gestures that he loved to watch. She seemed dearest to him not in their moments of passion— then she was too near, a wild stranger closer to him than anybody had been in his life, intoxicating but always a little alarming and saddening— but rather at this time, when she was receding from her nudity into her name and her usual appearance, Frieda Winter, the city woman whom he had won. She was at the mirror, saying, "Isn't it sickening, these novelists who strike out with a woman and instead of taking their defeat gracefully, rush to their typewriters and hammer away like mad, telling the world what a mean thing she was? Can you think of anything more cowardly?"

"That is known as catharsis," Hawke said.

"It's the revenge of a weakling," Frieda said. "The only thing I like less is these perfect women some others dream up, all sex and no logistics. Honestly, I think novelists are repulsive. God knows how I ever fell in with one. Get dressed, we're going to eat Chinese tonight."

"Does he like Chinese food?" Hawke said absently-mindedly.

"Who?"

"Your husband." Hawke was experiencing a recurring bitterness, watching her dress: the knowledge that she was another man's wife.

She stopped and turned to look at him. "What made you ask that? No, Paul hates to eat out. No matter what I'm doing he gets his hot dinner at home, carefully worked out as to calories."

Hawke remembered that she had often called her home from his apartment, sometimes from the bed, to talk to her cook about her family's dinner. He said, "I'd like to meet him some time."

Frieda said, "How very odd. Paul said almost the same thing last night. It's queer you two haven't met yet. You'll have to come up for dinner soon."

"Does he know about us?" Hawke said, instinctively alarmed.

"Does he know *what?*" Frieda said acridly. "What's there to know? Paul is a wonderful man, and you'd like him. He's much more intelligent than these publishing people you've met, believe me."

"Do you love him?"

"Of course I do."

"Then what are we doing here?"

She said, looking at the mirror, shaking her dress into neat folds, "What are you trying to do, start a fight? You *are* brooding about the reviews. Don't worry, whatever they are they'll come and they'll go, and you'll be the same size you were, with the same talent or genius, whatever that wonderful blaze is that's in you. What do you care?"

He said, "I'm not starting a fight, and for the first time all day I've forgotten the reviews. Do you think it's so peculiar of me to wonder about your husband, Frieda, the man you live with, the man whose name you sign, the man for all I know that you sleep with? Do you?"

"Shut up. What manners! Get dressed, I'm hungry, I say."

He strode to her, whirled her by the shoulders, and threw her on the bed. She landed on an elbow and stayed so, propped up. "You answer my question," Hawke said, "as long as I've asked it."

Her eyes became huge and tears welled in them. "You're mistreating me. What started this? Do you want to stop seeing me? That's easily arranged."

"Don't order me around, Mrs. Winter, that's all. 'Get dressed, we're going to eat Chinese.' I love you, Frieda, but I want to be answered like a human being when I ask a question."

"Stop shouting, you idiot, these hotels have paper walls. What do you want to know? About Paul? Paul is sixty-two. He was forty-four when I married him. He came after two horrible love affairs I had, one worse than the next, and when I married him it was like falling on a feather bed. I have a wonderful family and I love them all. I love Paul, he's good and he's clever. I'm not in love with him, that's not possible any more, but those things don't matter. Look at you! Staring at me with that big farm boy face of yours, pulling down the corners of your mouth! You're a boy, that's all you are."

"Well, you've answered my question, or at least I'm going to take it as answered, Frieda. Now I'll ask you one more and we can go get that Chinese food. Am I the only one there's been?" She only glared at him, still on one elbow, unmoving as a reptile. "Well, have there been two? Speak up! Four? Seventy-nine? A platoon, a division?"

She stood. "Good night. The hell with this. I'm going to get some dinner."

He caught her arm. "I want to know you, that's all. You're an utter stranger, a woman who phones me at five o'clock on the days when she feels like it."

"You know me. All there is of me is standing up in this dress. There was a woman with my name and she had a life and a husband and children and she dissolved into me and I'm yours, don't you know that? What more can I do to prove it? I looked for you all my life and I thought

you were one man and then I thought you were another and they all turned out to be impostors. How was I to know? How could I guess that you were dragging your heels in high school and in college while I was becoming twenty-five and then thirty and then thirty-five? There have been others. Why do you remind me of them? They're forgotten dreams. I've had a wonderful life and I'm not complaining, but it's been a damned strange one. I met my girlhood sweetheart for the first time when I was thirty-nine. I didn't remain a virgin till then. If that makes me immoral I'm immoral, and don't introduce me to your mother. Now take me to Mi Fong Chan's."

She ate with appetite, but he did not. He kept glancing at his watch, when he wasn't looking around uneasily at the other people, in the dim cellar on Pell Street that was supposed to be the best Chinese restaurant in New York. Hawke had done a lot of eating in cheap chop suey places, and he liked that food mainly because of the huge heaps of rice. The dishes in this restaurant seemed overflavored to him, and the rice was scanty. But Mi Fong Chan, the little proprietor, who called Mrs. Winter "Frieda," and sometimes sat at the table without being asked, scornfully referred to all Chinese food in New York outside his own as "coolie cooking." Frieda kept urging Hawke to eat.

"Look, you fool," she said at last, "the morning papers will be on the streets uptown in an hour. What's an hour in your life? Eat something. Maybe they won't review your book. Sometimes they wait a day or a week after publication. Eat, I say."

He did his best.

They made the cab driver stop at three news stands on the way uptown before they found one with bales of fresh newspapers piled beside it on the sidewalk. Hawke asked the wizened newspaperman for the *Times* and the *Herald Tribune*; he gave the man a dollar bill and told him to keep the change. It seemed to him that the weather had never been hotter. He was drenched inside his clothes. Simultaneously they opened the two newspapers, sitting in the back of the cab straining their eyes at the pages by the weak yellow light of a street lamp. Hawke found the book column; there was a photograph of another author, a review of a book about the Spanish-American War. His book was second on the alphabetical list of other books published that day.

Frieda was intently reading her paper through thick glasses. He leaned over her shoulder. There was his picture! He took in the first paragraphs of the review in a glance that might have lasted two seconds. Then he sank back in a corner of the cab.

"Where to now, sir?" said the driver.

"Brooklyn Bridge. I want to jump off," Hawke said.

"Don't be an imbecile. This isn't bad," Frieda said. "Listen." She read a few kindly sentences at the end. "What's in the *Times?*"

"The Spanish-American War," he said, passing her the paper. "Park Tower, driver."

She said when he got out of the taxicab, "I'd better come up and stay with you."

"No. Good night."

"I'm worried about you."

He leaned back into the cab and kissed her. "Wait till you meet my mother. They make us out of hard clay in Letchworth County. I love you, Frieda. Good night."

She clung to his hand. "Listen. If you haven't got anything else planned, bring your mother and sister to dinner at my house tomorrow night. Okay?"

"Tomorrow night? No, I have nothing planned. That's short notice for you, isn't it?"

"Nonsense. I want you to meet Paul. And I want to meet your family."

"All right, Frieda. I know they'll like that."

He went up to the ornate apartment, settled down on the couch with a yellow pad—somehow he was unable to work at Feydal's fine antique desk—and he wrote his night's quota of *Chain of Command.*

4

The alarm clock roused him at eleven; his mother's train was due at noon. He was turning on the shower when the telephone rang. For a moment he hesitated to answer it, then he picked up the receiver. "Hello. It's me," said the voice of Jeanne Green. "I'm just calling to wish you luck."

"Jeanne! That's sweet of you. Thanks."

"Do you know about the Boston *Globe?*" she said. Her voice was rough and warm.

"No. What about it?"

"I've got it here. Like me to read it?"

"If it's good."

"It's good."

"God, yes." He flopped on the bed.

It was the kind of notice he had dreamed about; the kind he had written dozens of in his head, pacing the loft in the icy winter nights. He was an important discovery, a sort of Jack London come to life, with some of the social observation and pile-driving force of Theodore Dreiser. *Alms for Oblivion* was a first testing of young powers by a major American

storyteller. Inexperience was written all over it, but as it stood it was the most interesting novel of 1947, and Youngblood Hawke was the first new writer of the year worth paying attention to. Sentence after sentence passed over his spirit like a healing hand.

"Who wrote that, Jeanne?" he said with forced lightness. "You?"

"No. Mildred Canaday. One of the most important reviewers outside New York. I'm the girl who thinks you're O. Henry, have you forgotten?"

"I've forgotten nothing. Not a thing. How are you, Jeanne?"

"Oh, fine. Drudging along, making money, which is lovely. The point is how are you?"

"Why, wonderful. Considerably better than I was a few minutes ago."

"I can imagine. That's why I called with the *Globe*."

"I haven't stopped working, Jeanne. I read the *Tribune* last night and then I wrote fourteen pages. I don't know how good they are but I wrote them. Right here in The Park Tower. How's Karl?"

"Just fine. Aren't you glad to be rid of my queries?"

"Any time you want to start querying again I've got a hundred and fifty new pages, Jeanie."

There was a little silence. He said, "Well all right. Bless you for calling. You've really lightened a heavy heart."

"That should be Mrs. Winter's job."

"I wish I had you here. I'd shake the teeth out of your head."

Jeanne said, her voice almost as husky as a man's, "Why don't you take me to lunch at the Commons Room and talk me back into doing your queries? If you have a girl with you they won't put you at the table by the post."

He laughed, embarrassed. "You saw me that day?"

"You still look like a Martian in a New York restaurant. With antennae and six eyes."

"Jeanie, I'd love to take you to lunch. Any time but today. Any time at all. I'm leaving in ten minutes to meet my mother and sister at Grand Central. Let's do it tomorrow."

"No, no forget it. Temporary insanity. The last thing I want to do in this life is see one of your manuscripts again. Or you. Goodbye. Happy publication day."

"I want to see you, Jeanne."

"Call me the day you move out of The Park Tower."

5

Coming out of the hotel, he made straight for the nearest bookstore on Fifty-seventh Street. At first he didn't see his book in the window, but then there it was off in a corner, a single copy, well in the shadow of

a big pyramid of the sensational new war novel full of dirty words. He paced in front of the store like a man about to enter a doctor's office with what he fears is a cancer; then he forced himself to go in. Nobody was in sight. On a table near the door were some of the successful books of the moment, but no sign of *Alms for Oblivion*. He was skulking here and there, looking for it on the shelves, when the proprietor came out of a back room. "Yes, sir, can I help you?"

Hawke could not have felt more startled, more guilty, had he had his hand in the man's cash register.

"Why, uh," he said, absolutely at a loss for words, and then he wildly asked for a copy of the new war book, though he had read it. The man nodded and took a fat volume off the huge stack on the center table of the store, and Hawke gave him five dollars with angry reluctance. "Uh, now what about this book about the Southern town that's just come out, have you got that?"

"What book about a Southern town? We usually have about fourteen." The man looked at him with a suspicious leer.

"Well, I mean *Alms for Oblivion*," Hawke said.

"Are you the author?"

Hawke wondered how this abominable little devil, this spidery horror with hairy ears and pince-nez glasses, could tell. It never occurred to him that his accent gave him away, if his face and his ridiculous furtive manner did not. "Yaas, ah'm the proud othah," he said with gruesome cheerfulness.

"I see you got murdered in the *Herald Tribune* and the *Saturday Review*," the man said. "Have you had any good reviews?"

"Plenty," Hawke said. "Do you have the book?"

"I'm not sure," said the man. "There's such a flood of first novels these days, but I think she ordered a copy."

"There's one in the window," said Hawke.

"I guess that's where she put it. We ought to have one in the lending library, too. The central office sends out a copy of almost every novel. Yes, there it is." He pointed to a high shelf, where *Alms for Oblivion* stood in a glistening virgin-clean cellophane wrapper in a long long row of novels, under which were several equally long rows of novels, right down to the floor, seemingly about five hundred different novels.

"Has anybody asked for it yet?"

"No. Everybody wants this new war book now, and of course the Marquand novel."

"Thanks," Hawke said, and he shuffled his feet, and added, "Well, I hope you do some business with my book," and hurled himself toward the door to the street, which seemed to be a mile away. He did not quite make it before the man called after him, "Better luck on the next one."

Then he was out in the hot sunshine, hurrying away downtown amid the crowds on the sidewalk, swearing to himself that for the rest of his life, if he won every literary prize known to mankind, he would never enter another bookstore. Two blocks down on Seventh Avenue he came upon another bookstore. He went in. The same humiliating scene repeated itself, with the slight variation that a sweet old lady was in charge of this store and she kept clucking at him in sympathy, and telling him that she admired books like his without all this filth in it. She would try to recommend it to people, but unfortunately all they wanted right now was this dreadful war novel. Stacks of the dreadful war novel were piled waist-high on the floor beside her cash register.

He walked all the way to Grand Central, and he did not go into any more bookstores, but he stopped at the window of every one he saw, crossing streets back and forth again and again. Sometimes there was a copy of his book on display, sometimes there wasn't; one large store, whose unknown proprietor he felt he would always love, had a sad little pyramid of three *Alms for Oblivions* in its window, next to a veritable cathedral of the war novel. By the time he reached the terminal, he had walked a road to Calvary that all authors walk at one time or another, and he knew that his book was a disregarded failure.

His mother and sister flew at him from the train in the sweltering gloom of the waiting platform, and embraced him from both sides. "I declare, it's hotter here than in Lexington, why, it's a furnace," Mrs. Hawke said. "Whew! It's a wonder people can live in this place, Art."

Nancy had a new copy of *Alms for Oblivion* under her arm. "I bought this in Lexington," she bubbled. "I told the man I was your sister. I couldn't resist. He said it's selling like hotcakes."

"That's good," Hawke said.

Mrs. Hawke was standing back, sizing him up. "Well, you've spruced up some, but you still look like the wrath of God."

A man appeared beside Nancy, followed by a porter with bags on a wheeled cart. He was fat, and he walked in a shambling way with his toes turned out, and he was stooped, and he had bulging eyes and a wide froggy mouth, and a thick brown wig sat on a melon-bald head; altogether one of the most grotesque people Hawke had ever seen. The sister put an arm through the man's elbow and turned to Hawke. "Art, this is John Weltmann."

Hawke shook hands with Weltmann, who smiled and ducked his big head and said nothing. "Well, let's get on to the hotel," Hawke said. "Then we're having lunch with my publisher." This arrangement had been made weeks ago at the height of Prince's enthusiasm. Now there was nothing to do but go through with it.

"With your publisher! Glory be!" Nancy said.

Mrs. Hawke and Nancy were not surprised at being installed in a handsome suite in The Park Tower. Nor did Feydal's apartment, which they visited briefly before going on to Prince House, especially impress them. They expected all this. They expected even more. Their minds had shifted from ordinary values to the childlike expectation of garish marvels with which one settles down in the gloom of a movie house.

Hawke had feared they would look like hicks, but there was nothing to apologize for in their appearance, not a trace of mail-order style. The mother had dug into her unguessable resources and bought clothes in Lexington. She had gone a bit too far, perhaps, in the lively purple of her dress and little jacket, and the bright grapes on her straw hat, but the effect was not bad. He had always thought his mother was pretty, and now she looked almost beautiful to him, despite the inevitable steel-rimmed square glasses. Nancy in a rust-colored shantung suit, tailored in spare lines, could well have passed for a New Yorker.

When they arrived at Prince House—without Weltmann, he had told Nancy he refused to "intrude"—the lunch hour was on. The place was almost deserted. The girl at the reception desk worked up a smile when she saw Hawke, and announced his arrival over the telephone. Prince's secretary soon appeared, wearing a similar smile as though she had just hung it on and was afraid it might fall off. She conducted them to the pearly door, which stood open. Prince and Fipps were waiting, all happiness and jocularity, in the big barren room, where the glass desk was as empty as ever, and the air, despite the heat of the day, somehow had a chill in it. The publisher heartily led off Mrs. Hawke and Nancy to show them the establishment. Hawke took the free moment to ask Fipps about reviews. Fipps said, "The afternoon papers are ignoring you. Perhaps it's just as well."

"I guess so. They don't seem to like me in New York. Any better luck out of town?"

"Well, yes, quite a few good ones. They're written by reporters as a rule, not critics. They're less sophisticated, and let's hope in this case more accurate."

"The Boston *Globe* was pretty good," Hawke said. "That Mildred Canaday."

"Yes, grand. As it happens the Associated Press is no good at all—we just had it read to us on the phone—and that gets printed in about seven hundred papers. Mostly about the jacket copy and Dostoevsky again. Really quite unreasonable."

"The jacket was a sad mistake, Waldo."

The editor shrugged. "I've tried for years to get a calmer tone here at Prince House, but I'm bucking the current. This ought to comfort you some." He picked up from a chair an advance copy of the Sunday *Times* book section, and turned it to the full-page advertisement:

HAWKE

A major new name in American fiction.

But of course the hollow praise in the copy only sickened the author. "I'd give a lot to suppress this," he muttered. "Is there a review?"

"Fortunately not. It was crowded out. When it comes next week it's going to be awful."

"How are sales?"

"Nil. That's always the risk when you push a book hard. They'll order if you insist, but then comes the backlash. By the way, I have to beg off from lunch. I have to have a milkshake in my office and keep working. You'll excuse me."

Hawke was glad enough to be rid of the editor, who was becoming a death's head to him. A few minutes later, when he walked down the long main corridor with Prince, Nancy, and his mother, he saw Fipps bent over his desk, making notes on galley sheets. They were almost at the exit door when he heard Fipps behind him call, "Oh, Arthur!"

He turned. "Yes?"

The editor was leaning out of his office, his head and shoulders showing. "Congratulations," he said gaily, and he disappeared.

Prince took them to the Commons Room. He displayed cordial interest in the mother's drivelling about the heat and dirt of New York, which Hawke tried in vain to cut off. He ordered champagne cocktails, and toasted *Alms for Oblivion,* as if he had a smash hit instead of a major miscalculation. Mrs. Hawke talked on, about the champagne—she didn't believe in drinking except on an occasion, but she reckoned this was an occasion, and my, did the bubbles always go up your nose like that— and about the food, the arrival of the minestrone soup setting off the monologue about her own famous soup. She obviously loved having a new audience for her old phonograph records. Nancy kept stealing glances at Hawke and grinning. Prince said to Hawke when the ladies left them for a while at the table after lunch, "Quite a gal, your mother."

"Now you know where I get my flow of words," Hawke said.

"A good thing," Prince said. "What does Ferdie Lax want to see me about?"

"I guess he wants to talk about our contract."

Prince said cheerfully, "I'm wondering what there is to discuss."

"There's some question about that contract in my mind, Jay. You know that."

Prince took out his cigar case. Hawke had forgotten to bring cigars and he wished the publisher would offer him one. But Prince helped himself, slid the case back into his pocket and lit the cigar with relish. "Of course, Youngblood, to me a contract is a man's word. I'm not talking

about legalities. The hell with them. You came into my office and made a bargain with me. I gave you what you asked for. Out in Hollywood a man's word is nothing. Ferdie Lax operates on fear of lawsuits alone, the way they all do. I like Ferdie, and I'll talk to him, there's nothing personal in all this, but business ethics are a little different here in the east. You ought to understand that."

"Jay, I didn't know much when I signed that contract."

"All I ask, Hawke, is that you look at the facts. I committed ten thousand dollars for advertising your book, practically our whole share of the movie rights. I ran off a large first edition. I had faith in your book. Now it looks like a failure. That's okay. The point is that unless we stop publishing first novels, or else throw them out to die in a printing of a couple of thousand copies with no advertising, we've got to get protection by sharing in your other rights. . . . Ah, the ladies," he said, as Hawke's mother and sister returned. Prince got to his feet and signalled for the check, saying in the jovial tone he had maintained throughout, "Well, this has been just grand, and we're all seeing each other again at Paul Winter's home for dinner tonight, aren't we? At this rate we'll be old friends very quickly."

CHAPTER SEVEN

1

HAWKE put on his new black suit for the first time that evening. Frieda had supervised the making of the suit through four fittings. He had himself gone out and bought a shirt with lavish French cuffs, and a pair of big black stone cuff links, and an oyster-gray silk tie. He arrayed himself in this finery, his thick fingers fumbling at the cuff links for several minutes. Then he went to examine himself in Feydal's smoky full-length mirror in the living room. He took one look and burst out laughing. Out of this flawlessly urbane clothing, out of the rich white cuffs and the columnar black jacket and the snowy collar—there poked the same old suspiciously squinting face, broad nose and big dangling hands. What was the use? He had hoped to see one of the distinguished New York men of the magazine advertisements, pictured standing in the lamplit gloom outside a hit play, helping an equally glittering and impossibly beautiful New York girl into a limousine like a battleship. But there in the mirror was old Art Hawke of Hovey, showing through the fancy costume; clumsy,

barrel-chested, with a trace of new fat at his middle, and black marks of dissipation around his eyes.

His mother came into the suite; they had agreed to meet and "talk a teeny bit of business," as Mrs. Hawke put it, before going to the Winters' dinner party. "My, aren't you the man about town!" she exclaimed, looking him up and down with real admiration. "Why, I wouldn't hardly know you in that getup, Art. I'm going to start believing you're a famous writer after all, aha ha ha! Only what's that on your ear, blood? You cut yourself shaving again! Art, it's a mercy you don't slice an ear off."

Mrs. Hawke almost never used lipstick, but her lips were red with paint tonight, and her graying hair was done in an unaccustomed way, and she had a necklace of opaque green stones he had not seen before; and with an orchid on the shoulder of her black frock, and the animated look in her eye that any woman gets when she is dressed up, Mrs. Hawke quite surprised her son with her presentability. He said, "You look wonderful. How's Nancy doing?"

"She'll be ready soon. You'd think she was going to her Junior Prom, the way she's fussing and fuming." Mrs. Hawke was carrying a blue accounting folder rolled up in her hand. She held it out to her son. "Well, here's the story, Art. Read it and weep. It won't take you long."

The white label pasted on the folder read:

SUMMARY ACCOUNT
HAWKE BROTHERS COAL COMPANY PIT 7 OPERATION
"FRENCHMAN'S RIDGE," EDGEFIELD

He riffled the folder, a smudgy carbon copy on onion skin paper, eighteen pages of columns and columns of figures. "What does the accountant say, mama? Did they make or lose money on that mine?"

"The accountant says they lost a quarter of a million dollars."

Hawke glanced at the last page, and dropped the folder on the desk. "Well, that sort of settles it. Or does it? Are you satisfied?"

The mother said, sitting and folding her hands primly, "I hope you feel I've done my best."

"Of course."

"I know I spent a lot of your money, Art, but I figured we needed an accountant from Lexington, a real outsider. It was a real mess, you know, with Harry Crain going and dying the week before this accountant came to work. If you believe those books, they lost money, and I don't know, you can go to jail for having fake books, can't you, Art? I mean the income tax men won't stand for that, will they?" The mother was clearly trying to cling to a hope that this might not be the end.

"They sure won't. Anyway, those books are prepared by certified public accountants, mom, probably by Wade Griffith's office in Hovey."

Mrs. Hawke heaved a heavy sigh. "Well, at least we made the effort, and I'm not sorry. I guess I'll take the thousand dollars."

"I don't know if it's still available, mama."

"Tripe! You call this fellow Hoag tomorrow and tell him I'm taking the money. He'll pay it fast enough."

Hawke said, "I'll call him."

Mrs. Hawke had the folder in her hands again and was rolling and unrolling it. "Art, frankly now, what do you make of this John Weltmann?"

"I don't know. He's hardly said two words to me so far. He's an awfully ugly devil."

Mrs. Hawke said, "Isn't he, though? I can't get used to that wig. It's really a sad story. His mother came from a family where everybody was bald. She was bald, she lived in a wig, slept in it. She had two normal children and then when John came along and was bald she turned queer and killed herself. He told all this to Nancy, but not before they'd been going together for months. The man's all pulled inside of himself like a turtle. Of course Nancy's no age to be choosy but—and he sort of talks like a foreigner, Art, but she says he was born in Cincinnati."

The subject of this discussion, when Hawke came out of the hotel a half hour later with his mother and sister, was sitting in a taxicab at the door, waiting for them. A summer thundershower was flooding the streets. No unoccupied taxis were in view, doormen's whistles were cawing and shrieking all over Central Park South, and perhaps twenty couples in evening dress were piled up at the hotel entrance, gloomily waiting for transportation. The Hawkes did not have to wait at all. John Weltmann had seen to that.

2

Hawke had not been in Frieda Winter's home since the Christmas afternoon which had changed the course of his life as a dam alters a riverbed beyond it for a thousand miles and more. Now here he was in that living room again, and his mother and sister were sitting with Fanny Prince on the very couch where he and Mrs. Winter had made love. Mrs. Hawke was talking a mile a minute, and Fanny was nodding and smiling while her eyes shifted every few seconds around the room. Frieda herself, in a prudish blue-gray dress with long sleeves, and a collar closed up to the throat, stood at the wheeled bar talking to Quentin Judd, refilling his martini glass every minute or two. When Hawke had greeted the critic, upon coming into the room, Judd had looked at him over the rim of his glass as at a stranger jostling him on the street, and had uttered an unfriendly growl. But he had been drinking ever since, and he now looked more cheerful. Mr. Winter sat on one of the two petit-point covered seats

near the red marble fireplace, in conversation with Jay Prince, Ross Hodge, and John Weltmann; though the wigged man appeared to be merely sitting and listening with a silly grin. The young author sat alone in an armchair, smoking a cigar and downing his third Scotch and soda though he did not want it.

He had been keyed up for some kind of debonair double game. He had imagined himself fencing with Mr. Winter, covering up for Frieda, protecting her honor, shielding his mother and sister from any suspicion of what was going on with a flow of brilliant talk. Nothing of the kind was happening. Nobody was paying much attention to him, and there was not a trace of drama or tension in the air. Yet the dinner party seemed to him the most transparent possible betrayal of his affair with Frieda. Why had he been invited to this luxurious home with his dowdy mother and sister —and they were dowdy, he knew, the moment he saw Fanny and Frieda again—if not because he was Mrs. Winter's lover? But none of the guests acted even faintly suspicious or ironic or puzzled; they were, so to say, unnaturally natural about the whole thing.

Frieda herself was unbelievable. On being presented to his mother she had put her arm around his waist and said, "You have a wonderful boy here. I wish he were mine." Mrs. Hawke had answered that he had always seemed more trouble than he was worth, but now she wasn't sure, and the two women had had a merry little exchange about raising children, while he stood in Frieda's loose embrace, paralyzed with embarrassment. And then Mr. Winter had come up, while Frieda still held him so, had shaken hands and told him he was halfway through *Alms for Oblivion* and for once he was inclined to agree with Frieda's taste, Hawke had remarkable talent. That was all. The husband had led Nancy and Weltmann off to the bar, and the confrontation was over!

Frieda left Judd hovering over the martini pitcher, and dropped on the ottoman in front of Hawke's chair. "Hi. Everybody's neglecting the guest of honor." Hawke looked to the husband. Winter sat facing them and clearly saw Frieda's move, but he went on chatting as though she had gone to a table to pick up a cigarette. "You seem sad, my boy. The purpose of all this is to cheer you up. Pretend it's working, at least. I love your mother."

"She sure likes you. Just as you predicted."

"Did I? Well, why shouldn't she? I'm very lovable. I have good news. Brace yourself. Quentin Judd likes your book! Likes it enormously."

Hawke sat up. "*Judd?* What is this, your doing?" He glanced toward the critic, who had dropped into a chair with a martini pitcher on a small table beside him, and was now feeding himself peanuts from a large fistful, blinking around with Pickwickian benevolence.

"Don't be an idiot. You're a great writer, that's all. What great writer was ever recognized at first by the hacks who write reviews? It takes a

Quentin Judd to spot you. . . . Here are my girls. Emily! Charlotte! Come and meet Youngblood Hawke."

Neither of them looked like Frieda. They were sallow girls in their early teens, both dumpy and ill-favored, wearing their expensive clothes awkwardly. "Is Paul in bed?" Frieda said.

Emily, the older and fatter one, shook her head. "He keeps asking for you."

"Tina thinks maybe he's sick," Charlotte piped.

"Nonsense," Frieda said, but she got off the ottoman. "This is his standard act for dinner party nights. Arthur, want to come and meet my youngest? He's a terrible monster, but sweet."

"Sure," Hawke said.

"Is your name Arthur?" the younger girl said. "I thought it was Youngblood."

The older one said with huge disgust, "That's just a pen name, silly."

Frieda went up two flights of stairs with Hawke. Before they got to the boy's room they heard him crying. He stood with his back against the bright wallpaper figured with circus designs, under a huge grinning clown face, a slight boy of six in yellow pajamas, with thick tumbled brown hair, Frieda's gray eyes, Frieda's face, a little male Frieda, complete to the determined slant-eyed scowl, his cheeks drenched with tears. Crouching before him, holding out a glass of milk, was a stout Negress in a green starched uniform, and she was crying too. "You cain' *have* no chocolate syrup, Paul, doan' blame me, you ma say not."

"Then I *won't drink it*—mama! Mama!" He rushed to Frieda and threw his arms around her legs.

The Negress stood and dashed tears from her eyes. "He call me a big ole black thing, Miz Winter."

Frieda dropped beside Paul on the floor, in a single motion that spread her skirt charmingly around her. She talked to the boy, and had him laughing through his tears in half a minute.

"This is my friend Arthur," she said. "He writes stories. Maybe he'll write one about you."

Hawke said, "If you drink that milk I will."

The boy turned wise, tired gray eyes on him. "No, tell me a story."

"Will you drink the milk?"

Paul hesitated, then held out a little curved hand to the Negress, and accepted the glass. He took a noisy formal sip, and Hawke began a tale about the big clown on the wall; he had been a real clown in a real circus, but he had offended a witch who had flattened him and put him into the wallpaper. The boy listened and drank, emptying the glass. He was very pale, and his eyes were heavily shadowed. Hawke broke off in the middle of his story. "Next time I'll tell you how he got out of the wallpaper."

"But he didn't," said Paul. "He's still there." He pointed with a thumb and forefinger, pistol fashion, at the clown.

"Well, he did get out," Hawke said, "and then the best part is how he got put back in."

"By the witch?"

"No," Hawke said, "by God."

The boy looked at the Negress. "Well, then, he'll never get out."

"He may," Hawke said. "You may be able to help him." He picked up Paul, and swung him—the boy was feather-light—and gave him a brief hug. "You smell soapy. Good night." He put him into the Negress' outstretched arms.

"Come back and tell me about God and the clown after dinner," the boy said.

On the stairs Frieda caught Hawke's hand in hers, and pressed it against her soft hip. "You were very nice to him. His father's forgotten how to tell stories."

"I like the boy," Hawke said, stirred as always by contact with Frieda's flesh, yet feeling a distaste for touching her here and now. "What's Ross Hodge doing here, Frieda?"

"Oh, I thought he would keep Jay and Fanny on their toes. They're such rabbits, I'm sure they're ready to panic away from your book."

Hawke had been fearing that his mother would gabble all through the dinner. But Mrs. Hawke behaved remarkably well, speaking only when spoken to, and then answering up usually with rough wit. Possibly she was overawed by the gold-trimmed scarlet china service for twelve, the immense mahogany table left bare and gleaming except for place mats, candles and a huge centerpiece of roses, and the procession of the butler and two maids, passing in and out of the high-ceilinged room with silver serving platters. Nancy and her grotesque suitor sat mum, far apart from each other, seemingly stupefied by the grand company.

It was Ross Hodge who lifted his glass of white wine that came with the crabmeat, and said, "Well, here's to *Alms for Oblivion*, a book I wish I'd published, and the start of an important career." His gestures were formal, and his speech had a New England precision, with a marked flat A.

Hawke, responding to the raising of glasses along the table, and a chorus of "*Alms for Oblivion!*" picked up his glass and said, "Death to all critics, present company excepted—until he reviews me."

There was a generous laugh. Quentin Judd said, speaking with austere clarity despite the martini pitcher which he had emptied, "You wrote a good book. I'm going to say as much."

Jay Prince looked amazed and delighted.

"Where will you review it, Quentin?" Frieda said. "The *Dandy*?"

"No. In *Midchannel*. Circulation about twelve hundred, unfortunately."

"And a quarterly, at that," Prince said, his elated look fading. "It won't be out till Thanksgiving. The life of a novel is only ninety days. It won't help much, Quent, but thanks anyway."

"Never thank or blame a critic," Judd said.

"*Alms for Oblivion* will live longer than ninety days," said Paul Winter from the head of the table, patting his white mustache with a napkin.

Prince said, "Paul, if a new novel doesn't become visible in the first three months that's it. It's buried. Fifty years later it may be exhumed and acquire a vogue, like *Moby Dick*. That doesn't do much good to the stockholders."

"I don't think the returns are in on *Oblivion*," Hodge said. "A few stupid notices—"

"Of course not," Prince said. "We're going to go right on pushing it like mad, and as a matter of fact sales right now are absolutely amazing."

"I read it. I liked it," the stout girl Emily spoke up. "In fact I'm writing a book report on it. It's the longest book I ever got through. It has a good story."

"That's almost precisely what I'm going to say in my notice," Judd said, baring his upper teeth at the girl. "I'm getting a little tired of this cult of college professors who keep writing and reviewing novels for each other and about each other, just passing back and forth their own slightly damp gray laundry. *Alms for Oblivion* isn't all it should be, by any means. It's a readable narrative, which removes it from the category of university laundry. It offers some diverting invention, a bit forced here and there. There's a concern in it with the psychology of the old, and some accurate reporting of the way people act in the presence of money. It's not a marshmallow about sex or high society, and it's not a bleat about adolescent problems or the military life. It's distinctly possible that our friend here can write serious fiction. In fact I think he has started to." He turned to Hawke, who was sitting to his right on the other side of Nancy, and he craned his neck forward and looked up at him with the scary ice-blue eyes set in eyeballs almost wholly bloodshot—and he added, "So as not to allow you to rest on your oars, I'm going to be very difficult about your overwriting and some of the coincidences. The day of Dickens is over, Mr. Hawke. The comic strips have pre-empted those freehand tricks. You have to be cleaner and more honest in your plotting. The Russians made that change. It's permanent. But all in all, I'm for you."

"That's marvellous, Quent," Prince said. "I wish you were saying all that in the *Times* next Sunday, instead of in *Midchannel* next November, that's all."

John Weltmann, speaking at the table for the first time, said, "Are any facts known about the relationship between reviews and the sales of

a novel?" He addressed Prince in a heavy way, German in manner rather than accent, and swung his big head around when Hodge spoke up from the other end of the table.

"There's no relationship. It's not like the theatre. Critics can't get people to read a dull book, and they can't stop them from reading a good book."

Weltmann said to Prince, "If that's so, why do you pay attention to the notices?"

"Well, it's better to have them with you than against you."

Hawke said, "Not to mention that a writer wants to be admired as well as rich.

Weltmann said, "Would you settle for being rich?"

"Yes," Hawke said instantly.

"That's because you get all the admiration you need from the one person who matters," Frieda said.

"His mother?" Judd said.

"Himself," Frieda said, winning a laugh.

Mrs. Hawke said, "I took Art to see Henry Clay's tomb in Lexington when he was twelve. The Youngbloods, that's my family, we're kin to the Clay family through the Hunt connection. Well, Art looked at this column about eighty feet high they've got over Clay's tomb and he said, 'My column's going to be a good twenty feet higher than that.'"

In the laugh that followed Hawke said, "It was before I knew that pillars are only for politicians."

"It's not too late for you to take up politics," Paul Winter said.

"I'm not that talented at fiction," Hawke said. He drank off his wine, feeling better and bolder in the laughter. The ice was broken. Everybody had faced the fact that the reviews of his book were wretched. Judd's unexpected support was heartwarming. His adultery with Frieda, which for him ran like a red diagonal across the table from himself to her, evidently was not visible to anyone else.

Ross Hodge said, "Hawke, the new girl in our mystery department, Jeanne Green, edited *Oblivion*, didn't she?"

"Edited it? She all but rewrote it," Hawke said. "She would have if I'd allowed her to. A strong-minded girl."

"A good girl. We hated to lose her," Prince said.

"A pretty girl," Fanny said.

"Very pretty," Frieda said.

Hodge said, "She's convinced you're the coming American novelist, Hawke. She says your new one is better than the first."

"Did she tell you anything about it?"

"Not a word more than that. She gave us the clear impression that thumbscrews wouldn't get more out of her."

Hawke said, "I'm fond of her and I'm sorry you stole her away."

"Just offered her more money than she was getting."

Prince said to Hawke, "Would the new one be the war novel you outlined to Waldo the other day?"

"Yes."

Hodge said, "Is Fipps as enthusiastic about it as Jeanne is?"

"Oh, he's enthusiastic," Prince said. "In his fashion. Waldo seldom runs a temperature, you know, about writers who are above the ground."

"Jeanne says it's a masterpiece."

Fanny Prince said, eating her soup daintily, "I think she also admires, a little bit, Mr. Hoke's broad shoulders."

Hawke quickly spoke into the titter, "Maybe Jeanie likes the book because she had a hand in it from the first. She was invaluable. I miss her."

He saw Quentin Judd make an odd motion in his chair, a restless weaving back and forth. Then the critic shot his head forward to speak to him across Nancy. "In what way was she invaluable?"

"In every way."

"Does she have a plot sense? I've fooled with a novel for years and I've always felt an editor with a plot sense could get me to finish it," Judd said.

"Many of her comments amounted to plot ideas. She'd probably be terrified of you. Otherwise I'd say you could hardly do better."

"What's terrifying about me?" Judd said plaintively to Mrs. Hawke.

"Why, I'm sure I don't know," Hawke's mother said. "You sort of look like Reverend Yeager back home, and he's the most henpecked man in Hovey."

Judd joined in the laughter as though she had paid him a compliment. Hawke laughed louder than anyone, because the critic really did look like Yeager. The wine was taking hold, and Hawke was beginning to feel exhilarated at the manner in which he was getting away with murder. There sat Frieda, about six feet away from him, demure, elegant, softly beautiful. In his first months in the city, in the lobbies of theatres and concert halls, he had seen many such remote jewel-like New York women, dressed with the exquisite finish of European noblewomen in old paintings, but with the added American sparkle of informality. More than once he had followed such a woman at a distance, with no thought in his mind except to keep looking at her as long as he could. And now he had won one of the best of them, a woman as clever as she was lovely; and here he was dining in her own home with her husband, and his mother and sister, and it was all going off smooth as water!

When the company moved into the living room for brandy and coffee, a lively conversation was going on about Hawke's picture of Hovey life in his book. Both Hodge and Judd came from small towns; they were baiting Mrs. Hawke in a good-natured way, and she was holding her own surprisingly well. The party grew very convivial. It was an extraor-

dinary success, considering its queer components; and Hawke was surprised to note that it was past midnight when Jay and Fanny Prince made the move to leave which swiftly broke it up.

Mr. Winter shook his hand with great cordiality when he was leaving. "About your notices, Arthur, just remember that the criticism an artist gets is the shadow he casts. You're starting out with a long shadow. It's the ones who make a debut to universal acclaim who usually turn out to be runts."

"That's very good of you," Hawke said, "but it's a little hard for me to be philosophic, at least right now. I have the feeling that nobody loves me."

"I wouldn't say that," Winter answered with a lopsided smile. "I hope I'll see you again. I daresay I will."

3

In the taxi returning to the hotel, Nancy Hawke babbled like one in delirium, making up for the long silence in which she had consumed an impressive amount of wine and brandy. The Winter home was beyond words. All the people she had met were superhumanly charming, Mrs. Winter most of all. New York was the only fit human habitation on earth. Everybody who lived outside it lived like pigs. She would live in New York some day if she had to bankrupt four husbands in a row to do it; this last remark she made with a flirtatious laugh at Weltmann, who grinned like a frog.

Mrs. Hawke, too, was elevated by her own success. "Well, it's a nice way to live, I must say, if you can afford it. If only everybody didn't drink so much!" (This with a wrinkle of the nose at Nancy.) "Drinking at lunch, drinking before dinner, drinking during dinner, drinking after dinner, I declare if that little fat man with the bloodshot eyes that sat next to me stood near an open flame he'd have gone pfft like a celluloid collar. Why, a body could have canned that man's breath and sold it. And him a critic! Why how can the poor man ever tell what he's reading?"

Nancy said, "Mama, Quentin Judd is one of the most famous critics in the United States. Imagine sitting around talking to a man like that!"

Mrs. Hawke said, "That Mrs. Winter, there's a lady, you just have to look at her and you know it. I'm not so sure about that Mrs. Prince, is she Jewish or something, the way she talks?"

"Hungarian, I think," Hawke said.

Weltmann said, "Are you satisfied with your publisher?"

"I guess so."

"Mr. Hodge is also a publisher."

"Yes."

"His house is more substantial than Prince's."

Hawke stared at his sister's peculiar fiancé, who sat hunched on a folding seat of the cab. Weltmann smiled foolishly. "I read an analysis of book publishing in a stock service report. Hodge Hathaway has a textbook department that was built up over fifty years."

"Yes. But Prince House tends to make more of a splash with new books."

"Is that a good thing? Maybe the critics are like fish you're trying to catch. Splashing could scare them and make them mad."

"I'm beginning to think so," Hawke said. He was also beginning to think that Weltmann had a vestige of intelligence after all.

"Mercy on us!" said Mrs. Hawke, as the cab driver jammed on his brakes at a red light, and all of them lurched forward. "These New York drivers are plumb crazy, every one of them!"

Nancy was giggling; she had almost toppled into Weltmann's lap. "That Mrs. Winter, now," she chirruped, "unless I'm totally mistaken, she also rather likes *Meestair Hoke's brudd shuldairs*, as the lady said." Whereupon she giggled again, and nudged Weltmann violently with her arm.

Weltmann said, "Never mind, Nancy."

"Well, I don't blame her a bit if it's so," Nancy said. "It got us a lovely dinner, anyway."

Mrs. Hawke laughed and said complacently, "I think it's fine for a nice older woman like that to take an interest in Art, maybe polish him up a bit."

"Providing she doesn't get carried away and want to run off with him," Nancy said.

"Ha! Catch a woman with all *that* leaving it behind for this big lunkhead," Mrs. Hawke said. "She's a lady every inch of her, and her head is screwed on right too. Just don't you go falling in love with her, Art, and mooning around like a darn fool the way you did over that high school teacher, Mrs. Krantenberg or whatever. You're too big for that now."

"Oh, *he's* not going to fall for *her*," Nancy said. "Why, she's all wrinkled. Didn't you see her eyes and her hands? She must dye her hair too. Does she, Art?"

"I don't know her that well, Nancy."

"She's well preserved," said Mrs. Hawke, "but I would be too if I had that kind of money and all those servants waiting on me. Why, my hands are in better shape than hers, for all the thousands of shirts I've ironed and dishes I've washed. Her hands are all bones and strings."

"She's a pianist, mama," Hawke said. "I guess their hands get that way." He did not, for a fact, much care for Frieda's rather talon-like hands, to look at; but the secret caresses of those hands were another matter. This conversation was like walking a tight-rope. He did not dare to cut

it off, and on the whole he was relieved by the innocence it disclosed in his mother and sister.

Nancy said, "How old is this Jeanne Green, Art?"

"Why, I don't know."

"Oh, come off it. You turned all colors at dinner when they started talking about her. Look at you, your ears are getting red right now. That's his girl friend, mama. When are we going to meet her, Art?"

"Nancy, I haven't seen Jeanne since she left Prince House."

"Did you have a fight or something?"

Mrs. Hawke said, "This is all news to me. Where's she from, Art? What's her family?"

"Mom, she's nothing but a nice girl who did some work for me."

"Green. Is she Jewish?"

"Christ, you're seeing Jews under the bed tonight. No, she isn't."

"Don't swear, Art. You know perfectly well that Abe Ittleman down at the dry goods store is an old friend of mine. I just don't think you ought to go marrying a Jew."

"I'm not marrying anybody right now. I have too much work to do."

Nancy said with a yawn, and a rather inebriated swing of her head, "I want to meet Jeanne Green and I'm not leaving New York until I do."

"I think Nancy's a little tired," Weltmann said, as the cab drew up at The Park Tower.

"I am not tired," said Nancy, whereupon she almost fell down stepping out of the cab. Weltmann caught her elbow and supported her gently and effectively. She said, "I am not leaving New York till I meet Jeanne Green. Is that clear, Art?"

Hawke said, "Okay, I'll try to arrange it. But you won't be meeting my future wife, or anything like that."

"Of course, of course," Nancy giggled. "Just friends."

A few minutes later, as Hawke was settling down in Feydal's apartment to try to write, his doorbell rang, and to his astonishment John Weltmann came shambling in. "I shouldn't intrude at this hour. But I have to go back to Hovey tomorrow. I actually came to New York to talk to you. I can make it brief."

"Certainly. Drink?"

Weltmann held up a fat hand, palm outward. "I'm like your mother. Though I don't think they drink any more in New York than in Hovey, per capita, probably less." He stood lumpishly in the middle of the room.

"Please sit down," Hawke said.

"Thank you." Weltmann bobbed his head and sat. "Nancy has no father. You're the man in the family. I think I have to talk to you."

Hawke said uncomfortably, "Nancy's old enough to do as she thinks best."

The man bumbled on, "I am not rich, but I'm able to provide for Nancy. My father is a small private banker in Cincinnati. He is from Switzerland. He and I had a sort of separation. I expect nothing from him. He gave me seventy-five thousand dollars. I manage that money as well as I can. It brings in between twenty-five hundred and three thousand a year. My position in the Hovey Bank and Trust Company brings in thirty-five hundred. My mother left me a trust fund that may be worth forty thousand. It has been badly invested, it was once worth more. I'll get the principal when I'm thirty-five. I'm thirty-one." He looked at Hawke, narrowing his puffy eyes until they almost closed, and he grinned. "You're surprised. You thought I was older."

Hawke said, increasingly embarrassed, "I wasn't sure."

"In my mother's family there was this affliction of congenital baldness. It may not strike you as a great affliction but my mother's family looked on it as a curse. My mother developed melancholia after my birth and killed herself. This is not a promising background, in my judgment, and I'm not sure I have any right to think of marriage."

"Mr. Weltmann, or I guess I'd better call you John, if you and Nancy love each other and want to get married, I think you should."

Weltmann again executed his slow curious nod several times, a ducking of his shoulders and head together rather than an up-and-down movement of his face. "You may be interested in how I came to Hovey. My father was looking into coal investments at one time. I made field trips for him when I first got out of college. I passed through Hovey once. It seemed so cut off from the world. MacDougall's Hill is like a big wall, and then the hills and mountains all around. I liked it. Later on I remembered it and came there."

"That's what I hate about Hovey," Hawke said, "and that's why I'll never go back."

Weltmann smiled in his face-cracking way. "The young artist needs the city. I think literature shows that." He glanced around at Feydal's apartment. "You have had an early success. These furnishings are beautiful."

"This place is rented. I don't own a stick in it."

Weltmann said, "There seems to be a contradiction between your publisher Mr. Prince's statement that the sales of your book are amazing, and his discouraged attitude about the criticisms."

"Well, you needn't tell Nancy or Mom, but the sales are not so hot. My book looks like a failure."

"And you're not discouraged."

"Not in the least. I've almost finished a new book. I think it will be a success."

"On what do you base that judgment?"

Hawke shrugged and laughed. Weltmann's plodding questions did not annoy him; they seemed rather comical. Weltmann laughed too. "I have the habit of asking stupid questions. I always try to spell things out if I can. You expect it to be a success because an artist should be an optimist. Is that it?"

"More or less."

"I think you're right to be an optimist," Weltmann said, "as long as you don't spend money on that basis." He put his fat hands decisively on his knees, and stood. "I'm taking up too much of your time. I'll say good night. My train leaves at seven. I appreciate everything you've said. Nancy and I have agreed not to settle anything until September."

"Frankly, on Nancy's side it seems to be settled. Why wait?"

Weltmann looked at him in silence, then he grinned. "Well, you see, I have to get used to believing that Nancy isn't sorry for me. That isn't a good basis for getting married." He held out his hand. "Good night. I have to thank you for the privilege of dinner at the home of Mr. and Mrs. Paul Winter. Mrs. Winter is a very striking woman. In a strange way she reminds me of your mother."

With this, Hawke's prospective brother-in-law took his leave.

4

Ross Hodge was a New England gentleman, to be sure, but his forebears had been Boston shipping men and merchants. Hodge's round placid face and quiet manner were the surface of a man who knew what a dollar was worth. Something like two billion dollars changes hands every year in the United States through the making and selling of books; and year by year Ross Hodge's firm got a solid slice of that large melon. Hodge admired literary art. He had published his share of prize-winning novelists and poets. But his interest in Youngblood Hawke was not primarily literary.

From the start, seeing him at a party, the publisher had had a hunch that Hawke was a major novelist; his definition of a major novelist being, quite simply an author whose books would sell over fifty thousand copies each in bookstores, and a few hundred thousand more at a cut rate through book clubs, and perhaps half a million more at a still cheaper rate in paperback reprintings. Reading *Alms for Oblivion* had reinforced this hunch, and had awakened the suspicion in him that Hawke might be a good novelist as well as a major one. Hodge thought that Hawke might well produce in time one or two of the giant best-sellers that are the gold strikes of American publishing, that run over a quarter of a million

copies in bookstore sales, that gross better than a million dollars to the publisher when all the receipts are counted, and that enable him to go on publishing serious biographies, experimental poetry, and fine difficult novels which by the strongest exertions cannot be pushed above a sale of ten thousand copies, with no hope of revenue from subsidiary rights.

When Hodge came to his office the morning after the dinner party, he sent for Jeanne Green. "Jeanie, your friend Hawke's book is beginning to look like a disaster." He had the *Saturday Review* spread open on his desk.

Jeanne glanced at the short frightful review on a back page and made a face. "I read a manuscript by that fellow. It was all about an introverted genius growing up in Newark."

"That's beside the point," Hodge said, "as you know very well. A good umpire is not supposed to be able to hit home runs."

"I just think men are bitchier than women, that's all. If you call writers men. It's an open question."

"Hawke struck me as a man," Hodge said, pulling at his ear.

"Yes, he's a man. A rather ape-like man, but a man. He's hardly a writer, in the ordinary sense."

Hodge said, "A freak."

"I have a mystery writer in my office, Mr. Hodge. Did you want me for something?"

"Sit down, please, Jeanne. I had dinner at Paul Winter's home last night. You know the Winters."

"I've met Mrs. Winter," Jeanne said, looking down at her nails.

"Youngblood Hawke was there with his mother and sister, and there were the Princes, and Quentin Judd. Judd, by the way, likes the Hawke book, with some reservations."

"Well, good for him. He's a horror, but a clever horror."

"You're not in a very good mood this morning."

Jeanne picked a paper clip off his desk and untwisted it to a straight bit of wire, looking at Hodge with bright wary eyes. She was dressed in a gauzy white shirtwaist and a full blue cotton skirt. Hodge had a charming wife, and his conduct toward the girls in the office over the years was unmarred. It occurred to him now, all the same, that this was quite a girl, and that Hawke must be a fool to take so little notice of her. He had half an idea that Frieda Winter might be the problem, but in his gentlemanly way he had shut from his mind, at the dinner party, the thought that had crossed it. Life among the artists often struck Hodge, a church-going Episcopalian, as an incessant tangled writhing of intelligent worms.

After a moment he said, "I think Jay Prince is getting cold on Hawke."

Jeanne nodded. "The weather at Prince House is changeable."

"Well, that's characteristic of people in a hurry. Is it a smash? Is it

a flop? That's all they want to know at Prince House, and they want to know it on publication day. They publish books, not authors. Hawke is an author, Jeanne. I think we can do a good job for him."

Jeanne's mouth curled in a suspicious smile. "But the notices on Hawke are so dreadful, Mr. Hodge."

Hodge laughed. "We have a sizable list here of major authors who started with bad notices. For that matter, Faulkner and Wolfe never did get many decent notices. *Alms for Oblivion* is a little amateurish, long-winded and all that, but Hawke is a major, or I'm crazy. I think even that book may eventually sell. Jay Prince said it's selling like mad. I wonder why he bothers. We know the stores are burying it. Jeanne, Hawke expressed admiration for your editorial talents last night."

"Oh, did he?" Jeanne said, and the paper clip fell out of her hand. "Damn, I left my cigarettes in my office."

Hodge quickly gave her one, and lit it. She said with a tremor in her voice, "Whatever made him mention my talents at such a distinguished gathering?"

"Well, he did. He advised Quent Judd to give you that famous invisible novel of his to edit."

"Good lord. I'd rather become a nurse in a home for the criminally insane."

"Jeanne, assuming that Hawke is turned loose by Prince, I'd like to have him here."

"He owes Prince House two more books."

"So I've heard. We can buy the contract, if Prince goes sour on him. I'd certainly like a chance at it. If you'd bring Hawke in, Jeanne, you'd probably be his editor."

In a daze, all Jeanne could think of to say was, "Youngblood Hawke doesn't write mysteries."

"I'm aware of that."

Jeanne stood. "Let me get back to my author. His ego must be leaking out fast. I'll think about Youngblood Hawke. Offhand I can't think of any way I can help. I'm sorry."

"There's no hurry."

Midway through the morning she returned to his office blushing, and she stammered around, all her briskness gone. "It's kind of spooky, but— I mean, after we were just talking about him and all—he called a little while ago, he's an absolute idiot, he knows nothing about business. I'm to take the day off, if you please, and come with him and his mother and sister for a boat ride around Manhattan! Honestly! The answer is no, isn't it? I'm a week behind on my work."

Hodge said, "You've got the day off."

"But I don't want it. Karl will kill me."

"Karl can do some work for a change instead of writing poetry on our time."

"Mr. Hodge, I won't be able to discuss business with Hawke. I'm hopelessly inept at that kind of thing."

"That's understood. Go ahead, Jeanne."

5

Hawke had long ago noticed Jeanne Green's habit of tossing her head when she first saw him. It was an unconscious gesture, a quick lift of the chin, and with it went a gay smile. As Jeanne came into the lobby of The Park Tower, she smiled, tossed her head, and her big beige picture hat fell off. She picked it up in confusion as he came hurrying to her. "Hi," she said, "I have more trouble with hats, don't I? Where's your family?"

"They just got back from shopping. They're upstairs. Come along. God, I'm glad to see you."

Her dress was beige crepe silk, with a loose flowing skirt and a green leather belt. She had her hair down to her shoulders, instead of piled up on her head. It changed her appearance; the business-like young woman was now the marriageable girl, and delicious to the eye, Hawke thought, yet he liked better the bright and somewhat tart Jeanne with the piled-up hair. She hung back as the elevator door opened. "Where are we going? Georges Feydal's apartment? I don't want to go there."

"We're going to a suite I parked mama in. Come along and stop making trouble."

Nancy and his mother were unwrapping packages like children on Christmas morning. They drew Jeanne into a discussion of New York stores, and the rules for returning purchases. Soon the three women were gabbling away and this went on all during the taxi ride to the boat dock. Jeanne still had the viewpoint of an out-of-towner, so she could agree readily with Mrs. Hawke about the rudeness of the crowds, and the supercilious ignorance of the sales girls, and she had some acid anecdotes to tell about these things. She charmed Hawke's family without the slightest effort. At the dock an old woman was selling bunches of violets from a basket. Hawke bought three; they were wilted by the noonday heat, but one bunch was larger and fresher than the rest, and Nancy pressed it on Jeanne. "You're the girl with the date," she said.

Jeanne said, "What date? I'm here on publishing business." Nancy took this as a wonderful joke, laughing and laughing.

Hawke also bought box lunches and beer aboard the excursion boat, an old tub painted white, with a green canvas awning running along the deck. Soon the boat backed off into the East River, hooting crankily. Hawke and Jeanne went to the rail at the bow, watching the Manhattan

buildings rise into view beyond the sheds of the wharf. The wind came sweeping along the river, carrying the fishy, oily smells of the tidewater, and blowing away the sticky city heat. All at once it was cool, and the deck was a bit unsteady underfoot, and Hawke felt the old elation of his Seabee days at getting under way on a ship, spurious though the sensation was at the start of a mere sightseeing ride. Far up in the midtown cluster of skyscrapers, the electric sign of The Park Tower made a black skeleton against the sunny day. He threw his bottle into the river. "More beer, Jeanie?"

"Not now. I'm loopy. I drank it like water."

He looked hard at her. She kept her gaze on the city, twirling the violets in her hands over the water. Hawke was trying to find something wrong with Jeanne's looks; trying to mitigate his overwhelming sudden feeling that he had taken a very wrong turn in New York. Yes, her mouth was too wide. Did he prefer red hair or brown? He did not know, but Jeanne's skin was smooth, and her hands were the rosy well-fleshed hands of a girl, thin but full of grace. The boat turned north and churned up the river. She said at last, "I'm under orders from Ross Hodge to steal you away from Prince House."

"Oh. Are you?"

"Yes. That's how I got the afternoon off."

"All right. Get to work," he said, looking at her sidewise, and raising his brows high. She had noticed these roguish mannerisms in many Southerners. "Ah'm listenin', stee-ul away."

"Don't make fun of me. Hodge is serious. He thinks you and Prince may be near a parting of the ways. If so, he's interested in you."

"But *wha* is he intrusted? Hasn't he read mah notices? *Ah* should be hung fo' mah *cramm* against the English language in *rahtin'* that book." Jeanne didn't know whether he was exaggerating his accent or whether she was more aware of it because of his mischievous sidewise glances, but she could hardly follow his meaning for listening to the sounds. She was resisting the impulse to laugh at him; not because she thought him ridiculous, exactly; he filled her with a warmth that wanted to spill out in laughter.

She said severely, "The point is if it's all moonshine about you and Prince just tell me so. I'll tell Hodge and that'll be the end of it."

"Jeanie, you know both houses. Where do you think I'd be better off?"

"Oh, no, you're not going to put me in that spot," she said, struggling with her skirt. As the boat drew to the middle of the river and the wind freshened, the beige silk was billowing all around her, and with one hand permanently clapped to her hat she was rather in trouble, though the legs thus uncovered in nacreous glimpses were lovely. "Let's go and sit down," she said. "Free shows for the tourists aren't included on the ticket."

They passed Nancy and Mrs. Hawke sitting on a bench at the rail. Nancy waved. "This is just wonderful, a front seat in Heaven," she called.

Mrs. Hawke said, "Well, it's quite a sight, but did you ever smell anything like this river? And the things that *float* in it. It's a wonder everybody in New York doesn't have the plague."

"Be right with you. We're talking business," Hawke said.

"Yes, monkey business," said Mrs. Hawke, and she was almost overcome with laughter.

Hawke bought more beer and they sat in the lee of the refreshment booth, well out of the wind. "Jeanne, I'm meeting with Jay Prince and my agent next week. It's helpful to know Hodge is interested. If I do leave Jay, the fact that you're at Hodge Hathaway would be decisive. If you're willing to work with me again, that is."

Jeanne said, "This is mighty unladylike, drinking beer from the bottle. Is your mother looking?" She took a long pull at the bottle.

"Mama's out of sight."

Jeanne said, "I don't know how I could refuse to work with you. Hodge was even making strange noises about my being your editor if you come over to us."

Hawke did not answer at once. He lit a cigar, struggling with the small eddies of wind, using up several matches. "Frieda Winter was paying for that apartment, all right. I found out, and now I'm paying."

Jeanne said in a weakening voice, "That's all water over the dam."

"I'd rather trust my manuscripts to you than to anybody else I can think of."

"If Jay Prince meets your agent's demands you'll stay there, won't you?"

"I'll have to."

"Well, I doubt that Prince will be foolish enough to let you go."

"How's Karl Fry?" Hawke said after a silence. "I haven't seen him for ever."

"Wonderful. Karl's been transformed. A soul crisis during a heart attack, is his story. Anyway he's out of the communist party. He's starting to write poetry again, and he's also doing a good job on mysteries for Hodge. You never saw such a man of the world. All hand-tailored tweed and tropical worsted by day, and black silk suits by night. He even had his teeth capped."

"Black silk suits by night?" Hawke said.

"Yes indeed. He seems to have discovered how much fun it is to have dates, and send flowers with comic doggerel that he writes on the cards, and dinners at Chambord and so forth. He enjoys it. He says the bourgeoisie seems to have had the right idea all along. I guess I'm the handiest girl to do it with."

"Let's face it, Jeanne, you're a fatal woman."

"Depending on the man's blood type, I suppose. I haven't caused any widespread damage."

"The only thing is, Jeanne, and it's none of my business, Karl is almost twenty years older than you."

"Oh? Do you find that gap too much for romance?"

This shut Hawke up for several thoughtful puffs at his cigar. Then with vast dignity he said, "For anything serious, yes."

"I told you Karl and I were just having fun. Karl's a sparkling conversationalist providing you keep him off communism, or even if you don't. He's very even-tempered, he takes no advantage of being my boss, and he's so considerate he makes me feel pampered. We both smoke cigarettes like fiends all the time. It couldn't be more convivial. Well, I'm to report to Hodge that we'll hear from you after you and your agent meet with Jay Prince. Right?"

"That's about it."

"Okay. Now I'll go talk to your sister and mother. That's why I was invited along, as I recall." Jeanne stood, flourishing her violets, and walked off, the slight roll of the deck accentuating the sway of her hips, her skirt blowing out wildly as she rounded the corner of the refreshment booth.

Hawke sat smoking his cigar, almost equally amused and annoyed. He thought Jeanne had axed him rather handsomely with the remark about the twenty-year gap; yet it might be better for both of them if she were not quite so quick with her tongue! A man did not enjoy being on the short end of repartee. Still, Jeanne had looked mighty appetizing, passing out of sight with beige silk swirling around her legs. A difficult creature. He sat where he was, enjoying the unexpected look of Manhattan at the north tip; green fields to the water's edge, ragged stone cliffs hiding the apartment houses: a brief illusion that Manhattan remained the wild green island it had once been. He began to think of the possibilities of a move to Hodge Hathaway. Ross Hodge had the reputation of giving the largest advances of any publisher in the trade. Hawke decided to forgive Jeanne her little thrust and talk some more business.

But he couldn't get her away from his family. She was not interested in going for a walk around the deck; no, the view was perfect from this bench. He had to sit and listen to more babble about Bonwit's and Saks and Bergdorf's. Then he had to hear for perhaps the fortieth time his mother's opinion of all the stores in Lexington, Kentucky, one of her really major soliloquies, and also one of the longest. Jeanne listened to this masterpiece with smiling attention, but Hawke observed after a while that her smile was becoming rigid, and her eyes rather glassy. At one point the beer bottle almost slipped out of her limp hand. He took it and threw it over the side. Nancy stood and hauled Mrs. Hawke off for a stroll, though all the mother wanted to do, she said, was sit and talk a bit

with Jeanne, who seemed like a home town girl, real refreshing, even if California was right far from Kentucky.

"Isn't it terrible? I almost fell asleep. It's the beer," Jeanne said, blinking and weaving. "The beer and the heat. It's hot. Isn't it hot?" Her voice was trailing off.

"Jeanne Green, don't you go to sleep now. I want to talk to you."

She tucked her skirt securely under her legs. "Sure. Let's talk." She covered a big yawn, and leaned her head lightly against his shoulder. "D'you mind? Just for a minute, while we talk? Your mother won't get ideas, will she? After all I may be your editor one of these days. Here, hold my hat. Don't let it blow away, I just bought it. Every time I buy a dumb hat it's because I'm going to meet you," she murmured, nestling against him as though he were the corner of a sofa. "I've never been so sleepy in my life. The beer . . . the rolling of the boat . . . but it's fun . . ." She was asleep almost instantly. He put his arm around her to steady her as the boat rocked. After a while Nancy and his mother came walking by. "Well, I declare, Art, you've bored the girl insensible," Mrs. Hawke said.

Nancy said almost in a whisper, looking down at the slumbering Jeanne in her brother's clumsy hold, "Yum. There is a girl."

Mrs. Hawke said, "She must be Jewish, she has that quick way of talking, but—"

Hawke exclaimed, "Ye gods, mama, Mrs. Yeager back home talks faster than Jeanne. You run on pretty goddamn fast yourself—"

"Look, you never let me finish," said the mother. "I think she's a fine girl, Jewish or not. I don't believe in this barring people on account of race or creed. It isn't as though she's colored."

"Nancy, go buy mama some ice cream," said Hawke.

6

It was after four when he got back to the hotel. Jeanne had taken herself off, absolutely declining cocktails. She had had more than enough beer, she said, and anyway, she had a dinner date with Karl Fry.

Frieda called, as usual, when the clock on the Paramount tower, seen from his bedroom window, showed about seven minutes after five. She never called before five; that was when her secretary left the office. If she didn't call by half past, it was not one of her days to see Hawke. That angle on that far high clock—the long hand a little past the hour, the short hand pointed at five—had come to spell for Hawke the sweet magic of promised sex. Today, however, after his refreshing afternoon with Jeanne, after holding her asleep in his arms, he could have foregone Frieda's visit. But she called, and she came, and he plunged at the door with all the

appetite of a man in his twenties when he heard her soft insistent rap—she never rang—and she was inside the door and in his arms, kissing him in her strange way, shy brushes of his face here and there. She wore a very light summer suit, a sleeveless brown silk jacket and skirt, unornamented, clinging to her figure. Frieda almost never wore brown. She said it was a librarian's color. But this suit was becoming, not to say enticing. "Hot, hot hot. What a boiling day! . . . Say, what's all this? Champagne! Bless your heart, Bloody, you're a mind reader. Open it, quick!" She licked her lips and her eyes shone as he pulled the bottle dripping from the ice bucket. "What's the celebration? Birthday? Good news?"

"You and me at quarter past five. The best possible news." Hawke popped the cork; the wine foamed crisply in the glasses. He had ordered it when she called because of a tinge of uneasiness generated by his afternoon with Jeanne.

"I'll drink to that," she said. She gulped her glass, put aside her wisp of a brown straw hat and drew close to him. "I thought I wouldn't be able to see you today. I thought you'd be all involved with your mother and sister."

"Not till seven. Then dinner and a show."

"Seven," she said. "Cinq à sept, as the Frenchies say. A long time." They drank more wine, and forthwith began making love eagerly, with gestures that were no less thrilling because they were coming to be familiar. Soon it was time to go to the bed. She went with him, and then held back. "I have to call home. Wait. Please. I must. Call the number." She handed him the telephone by the bedside and he gave the number to the hotel operator. Frieda took off her jacket, uncovering a thin white silk slip. Her naked arms and shoulders were rosy in the late afternoon sunlight. She said, "I called three times from the office. The number was busy, busy . . . Thanks . . . Hello, Tina? How was he when he woke up?" Her expression became serious. She sat on the bed, her nude shoulders drooping, her brow furrowed. "Are you sure? Why didn't you call me? Well, did you get Dr. Korvan?— That's good. When is he coming up?"

Hawke said, "Is it Paul?"

Frieda gave him a worried glance, and nodded. "All right. I'll be there right away. Is he trembling? . . . Give him an alcohol rub. Oh, fine . . . No, that's enough aspirin. Keep him quiet, and wrap him warmly." She hung up. "He has over a hundred and five. He was normal at noon. Normal!" She passed her hand over her brow. "I don't know what it is. One of these damnable viruses. They come and go. They're just hell, but the kids always throw them off." She stood. "I'll have to go home, my dear."

"Of course, Frieda. Poor Paul."

"There's *nothing* to worry about. Don't you go fretting now, my husband frets enough for everybody." She picked up her jacket and went to the

mirror. Her face was flushed, her hair in disorder. "Lord, look at me. Why are you so rough?" She tossed the jacket aside and began combing her hair, smiling at him in the mirror. He came and stood behind her. "Sorry, Frieda."

She said, "I'm the one who's sorry. This is a terrible thing to do to a man." She turned and took his chin in her hand, peering up at him from under her eyebrows. "You do believe I'm sorry? When will you be home tonight? One o'clock? Maybe I'll pay you a little late visit."

"I wish you would." His hands were resting lightly on the cool skin of her shoulders.

She said, "The doctor won't be there until six. Paul's perfectly all right, I swear he is."

"I hope he is."

"You're so sweet about this. I do love you, Arthur."

She left an hour later, dressing, combing, and painting herself with the speed of a chorus girl making a change between scenes, and chattering gaily as she always did during these chores. "Shall I get out the beard and dark glasses anyway, tonight, and sneak up here?" she said at the door.

"I'll be here," he said. "If you don't come I'll just scrawl for a few hours. Depends how Paul is, I suppose."

She looked at him wisely. "Okay. I think I'll let you write. Paul will be fine, but the march of American literature mustn't be slowed." She took his hand, pressed it to her bosom, and kissed his palm. "Enjoy the show. I haven't said a word to you about your mother and sister. I liked them so much!"

He threw himself on the disarrayed bed, weary and upset. Fifteen childhood years of fairly steady if elementary churchgoing had left their mark on him. He half feared that retribution was striking at Frieda through the little boy. Though he knew how foolish the idea was—because for one thing it gave the avenging deity the character of a cowardly sneak—the anxiety would not leave him. He had felt a strong attraction to the boy. He marvelled at Frieda's ability to go on making love, knowing that her child was so ill. Now that it was over and he was in the nervous trough that followed sex, the thought of what had passed disgusted him, his part as well as hers.

It was at this moment that Hawke felt the first stirrings of a conscious decision to break off with Frieda Winter as soon as possible. Enough was enough. She was forty, and married, and she had four children. The thing was impossible; and even by the most progressive standards, hardly decent. She had granted him love-making that he would never forget; but it was time to get out.

CHAPTER EIGHT

1

THE CLASH between Jay Prince and Ferdie Lax took place on schedule in the publisher's big bleak office, the following Monday morning at eleven o'clock. Both contestants were in fine fettle, and Hawke found the spectacle so interesting, merely as a sample of how business people behaved, that he sometimes forgot his own fortunes were at stake. He kept making mental notes on the battle, and he was almost as pleased when Prince scored as when Lax did. He also observed his own odd attitude, and he thought that perhaps he was being a damned fool; but to him the conduct of men under stress was more interesting than a question of money. He was a novelist. Of course he did want Ferdie Lax to win.

But the agent had his hands full. The two men exchanged pleasantry for pleasantry, angry outburst for angry outburst, then they turned pleasant again in a moment; it was a simulacrum of an emotional scene, without any actual emotion in it, and this was the new thing to Hawke. He had a naïve attitude toward the spoken word; he usually meant what he said, or thought he did when he was talking; and while a certain shading of truth sometimes went into politeness, or love-making, or disinclination to answer impertinent questions, that was as far as he departed, by nature, from candor. These men took positions and held them, displaying different emotions as they seemed useful to drive home one point or another. It was a game played with words and feelings, and both men seemed equally good at it; and Hawke saw that he had a lot to learn if he ever hoped to conduct his own business deals. But he thought he could learn this game, like any other.

The genial tones were used, he noted, to stake out one's own position. The angry or incredulous or injured attitudes were for knocking away the opponent's points. But there were fine small variations. For instance, at one juncture Lax flew into a picturesque rage and burst forth with a stream of obscene language. Instead of replying in kind, Jay Prince turned to Hawke with a pleasant smile and said, "Hollywood pidgin, Youngblood. We don't hear much of it in the east." Lax was caught off balance by this; and though he soon recovered, he did not use this particular means of communication again.

The positions of the two bargainers soon became clear through the

badinage and histrionics. Lax wanted a new negotiation for Hawke's future work, and a cancellation of the existing contract; he even drew a laugh from Prince by stating that the proper thing was for Prince House to return to Hawke the movie money it had already extorted from him. Prince held that the contract was a generous one, the most generous his firm had ever given a first novelist; that Prince House received a dozen manuscripts a week from new novelists, any one of whom would kiss his hand to get such a contract, let alone to get a book published on any terms.

Lax said, "You're talking about untalented nobodies. I'm talking about Youngblood Hawke. You misrepresented that contract to him, Jay, and you know it."

"Just a minute," Prince shouted, and this time his face grew so red that Hawke wondered whether the publisher really was having an emotion. "That kind of talk may be routine in Hollywood, Ferdie, but if we're going to have accusations of bad faith let's just stop this talk here and now. I don't need it. I've got a contract. My definition of bad faith is trying to crawl out of a contract!"

Lax shouted back, "Now goddamn it, Jay, you told this boy that a fifty-fifty split of movie money was standard. Standard! You fed this inexperienced author out of the back hills a lot of horsemanure, and so he signed a phony contract form you pulled out of your files, which you keep for just such situations. That's the truth here, and let's not have any more of this horsemanure about Hollywood." (Lax was still permitting himself the word horsemanure.)

Prince turned genial, and his face went back to its normal healthy color. "Ferdie, my boy, no first novel gets an advance of five thousand dollars, unless some well-known professional writer, or some celebrity, turns out a novel. Now you know that. A special price, such as I gave Youngblood, meant special terms."

Lax purred with equal amiability, "Jay, I'm taking Hawke away from you."

"There's no place he can go," Prince chortled. "We have a publisher's council, and unlike Hollywood, if you'll forgive me, we have little or no talent-stealing here. No reputable house will publish him."

Hawke had told Lax about the approach from Hodge Hathaway; he was interested to see whether Lax would use this lever. The agent made a different move. "I'll tell you, Jay," he said, "Hawke here has been working his goddamned head off, as you well know. He has a bad case of creative fatigue. Why, this young fellow has written about three quarters of a million words in two years. I don't think he can go ahead on this new book for a while. Certainly while he's tangled in an unjust and ridiculous contract, his emotional state will not enable him to continue writing serious fiction."

Jay Prince nodded, smiling broadly. "That's perfectly reasonable, and under the contract we'll just suspend our monthly payments until he resumes writing."

Hawke did not like this at all. Since moving into The Park Tower his expenses had increased almost tenfold, and he was decidedly short of cash. He interposed, "Jay, you assured me over and over that we'd discuss revising the contract after my novel came out."

"We are discussing it, Youngblood," said Prince kindly. "Nobody's sorrier than I am that the performance of *Oblivion* doesn't warrant a revision at this time. Do you dispute that?"

Lax looked at his watch. "My plane takes off in two hours. Listen, Jay, this is a stupid way to leave things. Hawke's not going to write any more, and you're not going to pay any more."

"Now, now, Youngblood isn't going to stop writing. Not for long."

"The hell he isn't, under this contract. Look, Jay, Hawke's first book is a hell of a disappointment to you. He told the plot of this second novel to your editor, what's his name—"

"Waldo Fipps—"

"Yes, Fipps, and Fipps as much as said it's no better than a dog you just turned down. There's no enthusiasm for Hawke at Prince House any more, and that's the simple truth. Let him go. Or at least let me try to peddle him elsewhere. If another house buys out the contract you might recover your whole advance, as well as the movie dough you've got in the bag."

For the first time, Prince's business face appeared in place of the jovial or angry countenances he had been presenting. He said, "Do you have an offer for his contract?"

"Are you interested in one?"

Prince paused, looked at Hawke, and laughed. "Absolutely not."

Lax stood, and said pleasantly, "Well, okay. This young man is doing no further work on his book until you talk sense, Jay. I guess we have to leave it at that."

The publisher pulled his gangling legs from under the glass desk and stood, holding out his hand to the little agent, whom he towered over by a head and a half. "Fine. He's entitled to a rest. I'll notify the treasurer to suspend payments for the time being. That is," he said, turning to Hawke, "if Ferdie is really speaking for you."

Hawke answered, "He is."

The publisher bade them both goodbye with the utmost good cheer. Going down in the elevator, Lax said to Hawke, "You don't mind about the five hundred a month, do you? That's spit. We're playing for potential big money here."

"I guess I can manage."

The agent's parrot-like face was wrinkled in thought. "Now we've got a problem," he said. "We run into it all the time on the coast. Jay has lost faith in you. That's obvious. But as soon as we disclose Hodge Hathaway's interest he'll get alarmed, figuring that Ross Hodge must have a reason for wanting you, and he'll decide to hang on to his goddamned contract. The dog-in-the-manger idea. It's going to take a little doing."

They walked out of the air-conditioned building into a bright muggy noonday. Lax offered Hawke his limp fat paw. "I think we've made a good start. I'll call you from the coast in a couple of days. You feel all right about this, don't you?"

Hawke said, "Well, it was sort of interesting, being bargained over like a horse. But I'm not going to stop writing."

"Naturally not. Just don't let Prince House see any copy and don't tell them about Hodge Hathaway." The agent's hand shot up and stopped a passing taxicab, while he was still blinking amiably at Hawke. "To Jay Prince you are a horse, you must realize that. A horse that didn't come in. That's why I think we can swing this, sooner or later. Then you can spend the rest of your life galloping off with all the big purses and making him feel like a dope. So long. I'm quite satisfied with the way this went."

2

Hawke was back in his apartment that afternoon, scrawling energetically at *Chain of Command*, when the doorbell rang. He thought it must be his mother or sister, and went to open the door. There stood a tall paunchy man in black with thin hair and a pink fat smiling face. He held a long yellow pencil in two hands, just under his chin, exactly parallel to the floor. He said through the smile, without altering it, "So sorry to trouble you, Mr. Hawke. George Macy, assistant manager of the hotel."

"Come in."

The man marched in, holding the pencil before him. He turned in the middle of the living room. "I hope I'm not disturbing you too much. Mr. Thompson, he's our manager, told me to be sure to express regret at disturbing you. I understand you have just had a novel published?"

"That's right."

"I trust it's selling well?"

"Fairly well," Hawke said, more and more puzzled.

"Mr. Hawke, a check of yours for one hundred dollars, which you cashed the other day, has been returned to the hotel marked *No Funds*. Oh, Mr. Thompson knows perfectly well it must be an oversight," he said, wagging the pencil frantically, "and we're not the least bit concerned."

Hawke said, sick with embarrassment, "Just put it through again. It'll clear." He had no idea he had run so low of cash.

The man said, "I took the liberty of calling the bank just now to see whether there was some error. They report your account still overdrawn. I presume your deposits are in the mail, or—or something." He shrugged, waved the pencil, and giggled. "Would you like us to hold the check a day or two? We'd be glad to extend the courtesy."

"That won't be necessary," Hawke said, in what he intended as a final tone.

But the man lowered himself into a chair smiling, looking at him hard, the pencil still horizontal under his chin. "Mr. Hawke, we find you haven't filled out our standard credit form for guests in residence. Would you be kind enough to stop at the cashier's desk and do that? It's just a formality."

"I'll be glad to."

"Mr. Hawke, it's our impression that you are using Mr. Feydal's suite in his absence as his guest. You are occupying the premises alone?"

"Certainly."

The man's entire face exploded with pleasure—raised eyebrows, popping eyes, huge open-mouthed grin. "You *are!*"

Hawke thought of a few of Frieda's accoutrements in the bedroom, which the chambermaids saw daily. "Look here," he barked. "I'm sorry that check came back. It won't happen again. I'm not occupying this place as a guest, I've sub-leased it. Now if that's all, I'd like to get back to my work."

The pencil man said with a giggle of glee, "Mr. Hawke, I do apologize, this is all very irritating, especially to an artist, I know. But if it's a sub-lease you should bring a copy of the agreement to Mr. Thompson's office, and just give him a few little routine details. It's really for your protection, you know, as well as the hotel's. Shall we say tomorrow at ten?"

"I guess so."

"Fine! Mr. Thompson will look forward to seeing you tomorrow morning at ten." He rose, pencil under chin as before, and marched to the door. "I don't read as much as I should, or I'd have read your novel. But I've read this new war book they're all talking about. Don't you think all those vulgar sex passages are unnecessary?"

"Not at all. I think an artist is entitled to any literary freedom he can handle."

"Oh, of course. And then there's always the matter of that little cash register, isn't there?" He punched an imaginary register with the end of his pencil, his eyes gleaming knowingly. "Ding, ding, deeeng, eh, Mr. Hawke?" he sang. "Jingle, jingle, jeengle!" And he danced backwards out of the door.

Here was a mess, Hawke thought. How could he be running through money so fast? He had sold off all his commodity contracts and put the

cash in the bank; it had been more than three thousand dollars, and it was all melted away! There remained his few stocks and bonds, and the eleven thousand dollars he had invested with Scott Hoag. Scott had often assured him that if ever he wanted to draw his money out of the housing venture, he had only to say so. Perhaps this was as good a time as any to test Scotty's probity. He was going to need a lot of cash to carry him through the next months, even if he moved out of The Park Tower. He could only hope Ferdie Lax knew what he was doing.

It seemed to Hawke that he would have to move out of the hotel, for more reasons than one. Certainly he was not going to report to the manager's office and submit himself to questioning, especially after the pencil man's broad hints that there was another occupant of the room; he didn't have a sub-lease agreement to show, and he couldn't show Frieda's! It was news to him that New York hotels pried at all into what went on behind the doors of their apartments. He had thought they were all rabbit warrens of unchallenged fornication. Frieda was a well-known woman. Appalling possibilities presented themselves to Hawke, that could result from his talking to the hotel manager. He picked up the telephone, and put in a long-distance call to Scott Hoag in Lexington.

Scotty came on the line with a roar. "Hey, Art! I be goddamn if I wasn't saying to Ellie ten minutes ago—we just sitting around having a toddy before dinner, Art, and it wasn't ten minutes ago I said to Ellie I ought to call up ole Art in New York and tell him how much we enjoying that book. Art, we so proud of that autographed copy and the inscription I can't begin to tell you. How the hell are you, boy?"

"Just great. I have my mom and sister up here."

"Say, I know that! Boy, you don't know how much you talked about down here. You a goddamn famous man. They was a piece in the Lexington papers about your folks going to visit you. Art, that *Alms for Oblivion* is one sumbitch of a book. You busting up my marital felicity, boy. I sat up three nights reading it and now it's got Ellie hooked. They just no action around here these nights. Look, she's laughing fit to bust. I'm serious! Say, that Clinton Road thing is looking pretty good, Art. We got all the foundations in and we're within budget. We sold forty percent of the houses from the blueprints. And I mean we got down payments. From here on it's simple. Put on the roofs and finish them off. About five six months from now we gonna sit down and have a mighty pleasant conversation, boy, the way it looks now."

Hawke wavered, hearing this news. But his reasons for getting out his cash were compelling. He said, "I'm calling to talk to you about that, Scott. I'm sorry, but I think I'll want my money out of Clinton Road now, if it's available. I need it."

There was a little pause. Then Hoag said, "Why, sure, Art. It's kind of a shame, because it looks awful good at this point, it looks like a hundred

percent profit again easy. Say, if I can loan you a couple of thousand for a few months, would that help?"

Hawke was tempted, but he had a Hovey-bred horror of being in debt. "That's damned nice of you, Scott. If it's all the same I'd rather have the money. It's a hell of a thing, I know, to pull out in the middle like this."

"Nothing simpler, Art. I'll buy your partnership, and glad to do it. I'll put a check and the papers in the mail tomorrow."

Hawke said, "I'll probably be very sorry."

"Art, I told you many times that cash money's the most valuable thing they is. You want it back, you got it. That's the basis we started on. Just don't go blowing it in on them New York showgirls, y'ole sumbitch. How about that, Art? You got a string of models you makin' scores with? Look at Ellie, she's laughing, I'm serious."

Hawke said, "One more thing, Scott, if you've got a minute." Hoag protested that he had all the time in the world. Hawke told him of the accountant's report to his mother, and of her readiness to take the thousand dollars.

Scott's tone became more sober. "Art, I got in a hell of a lot of hot water with the family, you know, letting your mom poke into those books. Especially with a Lexington accountant and all. I never thought she'd really do it."

Hawke said, "Mama's a tenacious woman."

"Boy, you know it. Glenn was fit to be tied, he said the plain implication was that we were all crooks, and those old ladies up in Hovey, they were even madder. They really got it in for your mother now."

"I can understand that, Scott. You'd better just pay the thousand and forget it, while she's in the mood to take it."

"Look, Art, I can't get the thousand out of Hawke Brothers any more. That's out of the question. I swear I'd pay the thousand out of my own pocket, it don't mean nothing, but—"

"Don't be ridiculous, Scott. I'm not asking for that."

Scott said, "The thing is I'm beginning to understand Glenn's viewpoint. If we offer her a thousand again, she'll begin to suspect all over again that we owe her fifty thousand, won't she? It's sort of a vicious circle, you know?"

"Scotty, if you don't pay her, mama's liable to sue you."

"Don't she ever listen to you, Art?"

"My mother's never listened to anybody in her life, once she's got an idea in her head."

Scott said, "I meant that offer kindly but I guess it was a mistake. It gave her an idea she had something. *Would* she be happy with a thousand? As much as anything I'd like to get her off your neck, boy."

Hawke said, "Well, you can try."

A little silence. Then a new hard note rang through Scott's habitual good cheer. "I tell you, Art. If your mom wants to sue over a defunct operation where the assets are a big goddamn hole in the ground and a loss of more than a quarter of a million dollars, I guess we better let her go ahead and do it."

"She can't have the thousand?"

"No. It's a mistake to offer it, Art. It always was. Sorry."

"Okay, Scott."

"Don't let it worry you, boy. You keep writing those books. If your mom wants to play around with lawyers it's expensive fun, but let her have it. Just don't get involved yourself. It's been great talking to you, y'ole sumbitch. How's about I come up to New York and you share a few of them models with me? Haw haw. I'll put that check in the mail tomorrow, Art. We'll do something else together real soon, hear? Things are sure booming around Lexington. So long, boy."

The mother and sister went back to Hovey next morning. Nancy, who had been afraid to fly coming up, was the one who insisted on returning by plane. Her lovesickness both amused and irritated Hawke. Nancy was thirty, but she might as well have been sixteen. He wondered at the power of love to turn a man like John Weltmann, ugly as a pig, into the object of such adoration. But the thing had clearly happened.

In the taxicab on the way to Newark Airport Hawke reported to his mother what Scotty had told him. She was neither surprised nor downcast. Her reaction was a loud sniff. "He really said they wouldn't pay?"

"That's it, ma."

"Ha! I bet he calls you up in a day or so and offers you five hundred. That's how they work. A bunch of old clothes peddlers."

"Well, mama, I don't want to argue about it, but if you'll take my word, it's definite and final. You looked at the books and you wore out your privilege, or your welcome, or whatever you had there. They're not going to offer you a cent."

"All right," said Mrs. Hawke with lively good humor, "then we'll sue them."

"Maybe you will. I paid for the accountant. I'm satisfied with the report. I'm not paying for a lawyer."

"I'll pay for the lawyer," said his mother. "Just let's find a good one."

Nancy said, "Let's talk it over with John first. John is very smart about such things. About everything."

Hawke and his mother exchanged an ironic glance, and dropped the topic.

A wave of loneliness swept him as his mother and sister left him at the plane gate in the airport, and walked the few yards to the stairway. The two nondescript Hawke women, one old and one not quite young, laden

with parcels and hand luggage, wearing last night's wilted orchids, looked back at him from the top of the stairway, waved, and disappeared into the dark oval mouth of the plane. Hawke went back to the island of sky-scrapers alone.

3

During the next few days the man with the yellow pencil seemed to be coming at him down every corridor and around every corner of The Park Tower, pencil held high and horizontal under his double chin be-tween two plump pink hands, smile unchanging as a rubber mask. "Mr. Thompson hopes you'll be able to see him today . . . Mr. Thompson is counting on you this afternoon . . . Mr. Thompson waited straight through the lunch hour for you . . ." and every now and then, by way of softening the nagging, a few stabs of the pencil at the imaginary cash register, "Ding ding deeng, how goes the new novel, Mr. Hawke? Jingle jingle jeengle!" It was impossible for Hawke to face the unseen ogre Thompson with the facts about the sub-lease, so there was nothing to do but endure this nuisance. Meantime Scotty's check had come. Instead of having no ready money he suddenly had eleven thousand four hundred dollars, so there was no question of any more overdrafts. Hawke was impressed by Scott's speedy return of the money, and a little sorry that he had pulled out of the venture. But it was pleasant to be under no fear of running short of cash.

Ferdie Lax, true to his word, called Hawke three days after the meeting with Prince. "One moment for Hollywood," the long distance operator said, "Is Mr. Lax there, operator? Ready with Mr. Hawke."

Then Lax, his voice clear, chirpy, and familiar across three thousand miles: "Hello, Hawke? When can you come out here?"

"What for?"

"The screenplay of *Oblivion*. It's all set."

Hawke's momentary excitement faded. "Ferdie, I said no to that six months ago. I've finished with that book. The thought of going back to it depresses me."

"It's all that's available, Hawke. They're having a hell of a retrench-ment out here. They have these panics every few years but this one is like the French Revolution, the way heads are rolling. Of course everybody gets hired again after a while, but that's how it goes. The thing is I've been talking to this Hodge fellow and Jay Prince. Hodge Hathaway is the place for you. That Hodge is a business man. But Jay isn't going to budge as long as you're sitting up in that flossy apartment on Central Park South. He knows you're working, what the hell else are you doing? How much time can a man spend in the hay, even a young man fresh out of the

hills? You come out here. Get him used to the idea that the new book's actually not getting written and he's not going to see any copy till dooms-day."

"What will I get paid if I come out?"

"I've got Luzzatto up to eight hundred a week. Frankly, that's not because of you, your book looks like a dog and so you're a dog. These ignorant bastards out here don't read, they look at best-seller lists. Fortunately Anne Karen has it in her head that you're the man to write the movie. You apparently wowed her. She keeps saying, 'I want the exact movie that young man described in the Waldorf during the blizzard.'"

Hawke was thinking that flight across the continent was the perfect quiet way to break with Frieda. "Ferdie, are you recommending that I come out?"

"I am. Frankly, Hawke, and this is none of my business, you're doing yourself no good in that goddamn Park Tower. You're a young man, a coming major writer, you have new words to sell, you're fresh and exciting. The lady in question is a fascinating woman, I know her well, but there are a lot of women in California too. In fact I'm going to tell you something. Half of the human race is women. There are so goddamn many women that it's frightening to think about. You come out here."

"What's today, Thursday?" Hawke said. "Suppose I come next Mon-day?"

"Perfect. Wire me your flight number. I'll meet you. We'll put you up at the Beverly Hills Hotel till we figure something out. How are your mother and sister? Enjoying New York?"

"They went home."

"They're smart. New York's a great town if you're a psychoanalyst or a head waiter. Not otherwise. Get on out here."

4

Frieda took the news with astonishing cheerfulness, hardly pausing in the brushing of her hair. She stood half-dressed before the bureau. "Well, you scoundrel. You waited until you'd had your will of me, eh? Instead of telling me like a gentleman when I got here, so we could have had a dignified farewell. Use me and then discard me, hey? Very masculine, very mature."

"Frieda, it's only for a couple of months. I'll be back."

"Ha! I'll bet." She startled him with his mother's phrase and tone. "No, this is it, my love, and decidedly the thing for both of us, before matters get out of hand. Fun's fun, and all that, as they say, but we may as well quit while everything's wonderful. I mean for me, at any rate. What goes on in your mind I've never been able to discern."

So he said some uncouth romantic things, to the effect that he adored her, and that giving her up was the last thing in his mind. She looked at him with fondness and growing amusement, and at last came and sat on the arm of his chair. "In other words, you've never been more relieved in your life. What a head you have, all the same!" She took his face in her hands, one firm cool palm on each jaw, and turned his head up to her, and kissed him coolly. "I think you're going just in time, myself. I could conceivably get to like you. That could become very messy. One favor, and we'll part the best of friends."

"What is it, Frieda?"

"Paul keeps asking for you. He's in bed all day, driving everybody mad —kids are always at their worst convalescing—and he wants to hear the rest of the story about the clown. Will you come and tell it to him?"

"Of course. I love that kid."

"Tomorrow morning about eleven, okay? And then we'll have lunch, and we'll drink a cup of kindness, and you'll be off to your grand destiny."

The boy smiled and held out both hands to Hawke. He looked better. His smile was mischievous instead of wistful, and his eyes were bright. "Hello! What did God do to the clown?" Frieda left them. Hawke spun the story out for about half an hour. The boy listened in an ecstasy of contentment, resting on huge pillows, never taking his gray eyes off Hawke. "Now tell me another story," he said as soon as Hawke had run out of improvisation, and had flattened the clown into the wallpaper to all eternity.

"What about?" Hawke said. "Hansel and Gretel? Jack the Giant Killer?"

"No, none of those old ones. Mama said you make up stories. Make up another one."

"I get paid for making up stories. Will you pay me?"

"Pay you what?"

"Well, how about a kiss?"

The boy looked embarrassed. "That's not paying. I get a dollar for taking my yellow medicine. It's horrible. I'll give you the dollar."

"All right," said Hawke, laughing. He started a story about a kitten who was born invisible, and its attempts to acquire solid form and color so that it could attract its mother's attention. Paul kept pestering Hawke for the creature's name. "Paul, he had no name, don't you understand? His mother couldn't see him to name him. He was the No-cat."

"The No-cat," said Paul. "He was the No-cat. That's the name of the story. The No-cat."

The fat colored maid appeared. "Miz Winter say you to come down to lunch, sah."

"No, no, no fair," the boy cried. "He's in the middle of a story."

"I'll finish it later, Paul."

"No you won't. I'll never know what happened to the No-cat. Never. Did he ever become visible? Did his mother ever see him? Just tell me that."

"Well, that's the whole story, I'm not going to give it away. I'll be back, Paul."

As he went down the stairs he heard the boy excitedly telling the start of the No-cat story to the maid. Hawke had no idea how to end it. Frieda was humming over the small range in the pantry, turning corn fritters and pushing sausages about in bubbling grease. "Hi there," she said, waving a fork at the food. "This is where we came in, isn't it? I'm a sentimental slob, in case you don't know it. One thing though, I'm not a weeper, so don't panic."

"That smells marvellous. Get it on the table."

"Yes, lord and master. Do you suppose champagne goes with sausages and corn fritters? Whether it does or not there's a bottle in that freezing compartment, and we're going to have it. Get it out."

After a while they were on the famous sofa in the living room again, finishing the wine. But it was nothing like Christmas Day. The windows were open, the warmth was open-air warmth fragrant with the smell of green leaves, not dry steam heat, and the park outside was a mottle of green and yellow instead of gray and brown. "Well," she said in a dramatic whisper, her eyes dancing with mockery over the rim of her glass, "what else can I do to entertain you?"

"Something seems to have been left out of the program," Hawke said.

"It sure has, and it's jolly well going to stay left out, Bloody. Ah memories, memories . . ."

He wanted to keep his promise to Paul; but when he went up to the bedroom with Frieda the little boy was fast asleep, his brow beaded with sweat. His mother tenderly wiped his face. "It's good," she said. "He's sweating out that damned virus, whatever it is."

Frieda's resolute cheerfulness broke only at the last moment, as they walked together down the red marble stairway to the foyer. All at once, at the bottom of the stairs, she turned in her curious sinuous way and clung to him. "It's only been eight weeks, do you realize that? Good God. Maybe I shouldn't have wired you when you sent me that book," she said, muffling the words against his chest.

"That's what I was asking for, Frieda," he said.

"I knew that. You looked so funny in that picture on the back of the jacket." She put her fist under her chin and glowered at him. He had to laugh. "Ah, Arthur," she said, clinging to him again. "It's a mess, after all."

He held her. She nestled against him, her hair brushing his face.

"Arthur, we'll see each other again, won't we? I mean there's no need to be melodramatic, is there? I like you. You behaved well under the bad notices. I've never said this before, but the way you drag yourself to your desk day after day no matter what is fine. It's the main thing. If I had had that quality I might have been a good pianist. It also helps to be inspired, which I believe you are. I don't think I was. You'll never be wholly civilized, but then an artist shouldn't be. You'll learn the motions." She drew away, and looked up at him, and now he saw her eyes were wet. "You don't really hate me, do you? There's no reason you should. I haven't hurt you. I've tried to be sweet to you. It hasn't been hard."

He pulled her close, and kissed her. She said, "This goddamn house is full of servants," and broke away. "Can I drive you somewhere? I have the car."

"I just want to walk down through the park to the hotel. Then I'm going to pack."

"And you prefer to walk alone."

"Come along, by all means."

She hesitated in the doorway, then shook her head. "No, the hell with that." She held out her hand. "Goodbye, Arthur."

"Goodbye, Frieda." They were shaking hands across the doorstep, exactly as they had done on Christmas Day. She said, "There's no harm in writing a letter once in a while, is there? Write and tell me how Hollywood strikes a hillbilly. I'm curious."

"Of course I will."

They stood looking at each other. "Well, go away," she said. "Take your walk."

"I'm in no hurry," he said. "I always have liked looking at you."

"Well, I'm a busy woman, and so I'm going to close this door. Don't write me any letters. Your last letter led to a hell of a mess, now that I think of it. Run along, I say." The door closed, and he could hear her heels clicking away on the marble floor.

He walked through the park in a high state of well being. Not only was he full of food and champagne, but he thought he had done a masterly job of the parting. Mrs. Winter had given him an instructive and risky adventure. He was out of it, and moving on.

5

Ross Hodge said, next day, leaning back in his swivel chair, taking off his glasses, and chewing one end of them, "Jeanie, there's news about your friend Hawke. He's going to Hollywood, leaving Monday."

"Is he? How nice for him," Jeanne said, with the greatest unconcern.

"Have you talked to Hawke since that day you went on the boat?"

"No. I guess I offended him. I fell asleep."

"On the contrary you must have done very well. I heard from his agent, a Hollywood fellow named Lax, the next day."

"Oh, yes. Sleepy parrot with X-ray eyes."

"That's him. Now this fellow Lax has a head full of movie figures. I want Youngblood Hawke and I'm willing to pay a lot for him, but— much more than anyone else in the business would right now, by the way. *Publisher's Weekly* just called *Alms for Oblivion* the disappointment of the year."

"I saw that. Idiots."

"Yes, well, stacks of unsold books are discouraging, Jeanne. However, I've never had any luck except when I was faithful to my own tastes, completely disregarding sales, critics, and all the rest. I was impressed by Hawke when I first met him. I was more impressed by his novel. You say this navy book of his is better."

"There's no comparison. If it isn't a smash hit I'll go into some other kind of work, and so should Hawke."

Hodge leaned forward. "I sort of felt Jay out yesterday at the Commons Room, just a few words as I walked by his table. Lax hasn't told him we're the ones who are interested. But Jay's no fool. He thinks I'm crazy, but he's going to hold me up for a sizable sum to let go of Hawke. Add to that the figures Lax is demanding for an advance, and the thing becomes hard to do. Do you suppose you could persuade Hawke to make our parrot friend talk more reasonably?"

The telephone rang. Hodge said, "Yes, Ruth, she's in my office. Who's calling? Really? Hang on." He turned to Jeanne and held out the telephone. "For you."

The too-casual gesture was not lost on Jeanne. "Oh, yes? Who is it?"

"It seems to be Youngblood Hawke."

"I can't talk to him now. I'll call him back."

Hodge grinned, and laid the telephone softly on the desk beside her. "I'll leave."

"Don't be absurd," she snapped. She put a cigarette in her mouth; Hodge held a flaming lighter to it; she picked up the receiver.

Hawke told her about his Hollywood job. She briskly wished him success. He wanted to have dinner with her. No, sorry, impossible; she was having dinner with Karl. Well, could he see her after dinner? Sorry, they were going out to a Long Island restaurant and wouldn't be back until very late. Hawke pleaded that he had something urgent to discuss with her. She sat silent, red, the receiver to her ear. Hodge lounged in his chair, staring out at the Chrysler Building, blowing smoke rings.

"Look here," she said, "I'll be tired as the devil when I come home. I'm getting a little old for late dates. Can't this wait until you return from the coast? Or can't you write me about it?"

Hawke said, "It's simple enough. I've got about two hundred new pages piled up. I want you to go back to work on them, Jeanne. Really, you must, and let's cut out the nonsense. I don't want to offend you by talking money. You just suggest any arrangement and I'll accept it. There are things in the script I want to discuss with you before I leave."

"Arthur, I thought all that was settled. I can't do it." She glanced at Hodge.

"You told me to try you again when I left The Park Tower. I'm leaving The Park Tower."

"Yes? Who's going with you to the coast?"

"Nobody. I'm leaving everything and everybody behind. When I return it will be as though I were coming here for the first time."

"Wait a minute." She put her hand over the receiver. "He wants me to go back to work on his manuscript."

"Do it!" Hodge said, swivelling around.

"But it'll cut into my work here. I'm all piled up. He's not one of our authors. It makes no sense."

"Jeanne, the best service you can render me is to take on the Hawke manuscript. That's the official word. From there on, and I mean it, suit yourself."

Jeanne hesitated another moment. "Look," she said into the telephone, "I have to go to a sales conference at four o'clock. How would it be if I met you right away, say in fifteen minutes, at The Park Tower? I'm jammed up, I can't stay more than half an hour, and this is about the only time today or tomorrow that I can manage."

"Why, that's absolutely marvellous," Hawke said. "That's perfect. That's great, Jeanne. Get yourself over here."

He let her into the apartment, and she sidled in with suspicious glances all around her, like a cat venturing into a new house. "How do you like it?" he said.

"I hate it. Give me the script and I'll get out of here."

"You sounded queer on the telephone. What was the matter?"

"Ross Hodge was sitting two feet from me. That's why I'm taking on your book. He ordered me to."

Jeanne was producing a dry calm tone with difficulty. She was in a great turmoil, finding herself suddenly in Feydal's luxurious suite, alone with Hawke, haunted by pictures of what had been happening here.

Hawke said, "Well, bless Ross Hodge then," and he began hauling great sheaves of yellow paper out of the desk drawers, and piling them into a red paper portfolio. She sat stiffly on the edge of the silk-covered couch. He talked about the work he had done, the way the story had advanced, certain problems he wanted her to examine. He felt he might have scrawled a whole superfluous section about a shore leave in Australia; also, was he

overwriting the battle of Iwo Jima? He wanted to talk to her by telephone from Hollywood early next week.

Jeanne said, looking at the overstuffed portfolio, "Well, you haven't been exactly idle here, anyway, have you? That's something."

"I've never stopped working."

He mixed a couple of highballs, despite her protest that she would have to leave in a few minutes. Jeanne's spirit was soaring, for all her wounded pride and her anger at Hawke, which this rich and perfumed apartment exacerbated. She could not help herself. Being with this man, discussing his work, feeling that she was useful to him, was as close to heaven as she expected to come in this world. She did not delude herself about these feelings. She had all but given up Hawke. She remained extremely wary of daring to hope again. The agony of rejection she had endured was not an experience she intended to repeat, or even to risk repeating.

She said, accepting the highball, "I'll never finish this. A couple of swallows and I'm off." She took a sip and added, "What does Mrs. Winter think of your Hollywood dash?"

"She's all for it, I gather. She has a strong belief that making money is never a mistake."

"Well, there I agree with her."

"You do? Don't you think that Ah may end up selling mah soul to Hollywood?" he said with heavy Southern archness, looking at her sidewise.

"If Hollywood can afford to buy it then that's where you belong. I think writing films must be wonderful work. But I imagine you'd be bored once you solved the technical problems."

"But suppose Ah become enSLAVED ba the *lucre?*"

"How? Successful novelists make more money than movie writers. Quite aside from the fact which we both know, that no power on earth short of death can stop you from writing your books, so what's all this foolishness about?"

He laughed. "I can stand some reassurance. I'm all agog over going to movieland."

"I'd be agog too. I wish I were going with you."

"Come along, by God, Jeanne! Ross Hodge'll give you a leave of absence. He's just using you as bait for me these days."

"Well, thanks, but it wouldn't be decent exactly, not to mention that I'm waist-deep in mystery writers. I'll work on your book here. That's all you want of me."

"Not at all. I'd love to have you there. Under honest circumstances, I promise you. We'll stay at different hotels and so forth. Come on."

"I'm afraid Mrs. Winter might not approve."

"Jeanne, will you get Mrs. Winter off your brain? She's off mine."

"Is she?" Jeanne looked straight at him.

"Yes."

"Does she know that?"

"Of course. She's an extremely clever woman, and I'm sure she's miles ahead of me."

"That's the exact truth," Jeanne said. "Well, we'll see. It's charming of you to want me to come to Hollywood with you. Once you get out there, please keep urging me. I really have very little character. Just enough to say no right now. I'm off." She put down the nearly full glass and picked up the portfolio. "Wow. Heavy."

"I'll take it down to a taxicab for you."

"Don't be absurd. Mostly what I do these days is haul around manuscripts. Not many like *Chain of Command,* I grant you."

He went with her to the door. "Seeing that you're helpless with your hands full," he said, "I'm going to kiss you."

"Not in this goddamned place," she said, but he embraced her and kissed her mouth.

"All right," she said, "I guess that comes under the heading of buttering up an author. Heaven knows Hodge has the butter order out on Hawke. It's quite smart of him, at this stage of your fortunes, but he'll be glad of it. Open that door, Arthur."

He obeyed, and walked with her to the elevator. "Well, you've got it again, Jeanne," he said.

"So it seems. This time I'll try to hang on to it. Call me from Hollywood, and easy on the starlets."

6

The plane dived out of clear late-afternoon sunshine into a heavy brown mist that lay in tufts and rolls on the earth, in a vast pan of mountains, like a dirty meringue. The ground came vaguely in sight. Hawke began to make out screaming colors of huge neon signs jigging and darting in the dim daylight all over the broad flat valley. Rectilinear streets, lined with palm trees and white or pink houses, stretched in every direction, fading off into the brown gloom. The sun hung low, a smudged orange ball. The plane settled to earth, coughing as though the brown cloud had gotten into its engines. "We have arrived in Los Angeles," croaked the stewardess.

Lax stood at the gateway, weeping into a fluttering silk handkerchief. He took Hawke's baggage checks and told him to meet him at a white convertible Cadillac in front of the terminal. "We're going straight to Travis Jablock's office. Travis is leaving for Palm Springs tonight. He wants to talk to you first."

Hawke said, "Travis Jablock? Why do I get to see such a potentate?"

"Bob Luzzatto is behind the eight-ball for financing."

There were four white convertible Cadillacs in the press of cars at the airport entrance. One of them had a chauffeur at the wheel, and a tall beautiful brunette in the back seat, whom Hawke recognized as the girl he had seen with Lax in the Commons Room. He said to the girl, "Hello, I'm Youngblood Hawke. Ferdie's corralling my bags. You're Anne, aren't you?"

"Why no," said the girl with a slight frown. "I'm with Ferdie, but I'm Fay. Fay Pulver."

Lax, displaying his usual airport wizardry, appeared almost at once, leading a porter with Hawke's bags. The Cadillac wheeled in rich silence out of the airport and down a highway thick with cars buzzing in two directions, almost bumper to bumper, two rivers of cars extending out of sight into brown haze. Hawke's eyes stung; he kept blinking.

Lax chirruped gaily on about the financing of the *Oblivion* movie, all the time weeping and dabbing at his eyes as though he were describing the death of his mother. Hawke was amazed at the sight of oil derricks bristling on empty brown hills near the airport. "I never knew this was oil country."

Lax said, "You didn't? Half of Los Angeles floats on a goddamn lake of oil. They're pumping it out from under us and cooking it down, and our air is darkening and turning to poison smog and we're slowly sinking, sinking. They say the end of it is the whole county breaks off from the continent and slides into the goddamn sea, when there isn't enough oil left to hold it up. —Now listen, Hawke, I know Travis very well. He's a strange guy. The thing to do is listen to him respectfully and then write what you please. If it's good he'll like it. What he says now doesn't mean anything. Just don't contradict him."

"Okay," Hawke said.

The girl said, "I don't think the government will allow them to pump out so much oil that Los Angeles will break off and fall in the ocean. There's too much valuable property here."

"All right, Fay," Lax said. "The Beverly Hills was full up, by the way, and so was the Beverly Wilshire. I've put you in Rainbow's End, which is better, you've got your own villa with a kitchen."

Fay said, "I know a girl who goes out with a geologist from the Sun Oil Company. I'm going to ask her to ask him about Los Angeles sinking into the sea."

"The other thing," Lax said, "is that Jablock has only one good ear, the left one. It's easy to remember, it's the side he holds the cigar on. If you want him to hear something make sure you're over on his left side."

The film studio had a barred gateway with a gray-haired sentinel on guard in a glass booth. The gate opened to Lax. The car crawled through narrow streets among immense concrete structures like airplane hangars,

labelled with towering numbers. These were the sound stages, Lax said. They rounded a corner and drove along West Forty-fifth Street in New York, then over a drawbridge through a Norman castle, then the car turned again and they were traversing a ghost town of the Wild West. They stopped on a plaza surrounded by pink stucco buildings, with large square lawns, a splashing fountain, and a festooning of flamboyant flowering vines, purple, yellow, and red. The entrance to the largest building had locked doors and another fat gray sentinel behind glass. The doors opened with a buzz and a click before Ferdie Lax. Fay was left in the car, smoking sulkily, with her long beautiful legs crossed.

Lax and Hawke passed through more guarded gates, and through corridors lined with immense ikons of movie stars, through offices full of pretty stenographers, into a small anteroom staffed by one stout ugly woman with shrewd little eyes. Roberto Luzzatto sat here on a sofa, and he fell on Hawke with a roar and a hug. The producer was a shiny nut brown and burlier than ever, dressed in dark sleek gray and barbered to a gleam. He could not have been in better spirits, though Lax had just explained to Hawke that Luzzatto owed about four million dollars here and there. Everybody agreed that Luzzatto could make pictures. He had mistakenly produced a gigantic war movie at precisely the time when Americans had turned their backs on war pictures and he was still reeling under the blow —financially speaking. There was nothing of this in his aspect. He looked like a man who never missed a night's sleep unless there was something pleasanter to do than sleep.

The innermost secretary said in tones just above a whisper to Luzzatto and Lax, quite ignoring Hawke, "Travis is ready." With this she opened a door. The three men passed into a room perhaps twenty feet high and sixty feet long, the windows tall and curved in Moorish arches with spiralling center columns, the floor heavily carpeted in dark green, the walls and ceilings painted light green. There was no furniture in the room but a great brown desk far at the other end, a few hard chairs, and a throne-like seat behind the desk. Back of this high chair and a little to the right, was a heavily carved wooden door in a Gothic-arched frame. The men walked in silence down the long room to the hard chairs and sat. Lax and Luzzatto exchanged glances, not untinged with apprehension. There was a pause of several minutes. Nobody said anything.

The Gothic door opened, and out of it emerged first of all a cigar, quite the most enormous that Hawke had ever seen. After the cigar came a man holding it in his mouth, and the anticlimax was so preposterous that Hawke almost burst out laughing. The man was Mr. Begg, his history teacher in Hovey High School; Mr. Begg, or his living double, except that he was dressed in a crimson sport shirt, and natty white slacks. He had the little mustache, the little spread-apart teeth, the jaunty little smile, and even the bouncy little walk of Mr. Begg, and though Hawke could not

see his feet he would have sworn that they had the Chaplinesque turn-out of Mr. Begg's. Jablock carried a portable radio which was blaring the plays of a baseball game. "Extra innings," he said, sitting in the throne and perching the radio on the desk opposite his good ear.

"This is Youngblood Hawke, Travis," the agent yelled.

The studio head made no acknowledgment at all. He sat staring at the ceiling for a couple of minutes, smoking and listening to the ball game. When the inning ended he turned down the volume, puffed on his cigar, and burst out, "*Alms for Oblivion* is Madame Bovary. This is the story of a woman whose strong thwarted natural impulses of love turn into an adulterous obsessive lust for money. That lust destroys her. Aunt Bertha is therefore a figure of tragic passion. We must see her passions. Without her passionate nature in mind the audience cannot possibly understand the exciting money climax. It will be melodrama, not tragedy. Tragedy can be box-office because of its emotional catharsis." Jablock delivered this speech with jerky gestures of the gigantic cigar, bouncing up and down in his chair. He turned up the radio, and when he heard the gibbering gaiety of a commercial he turned it down again.

"The story lacks *curves*. It says people care mainly about money, and that is not true, that is neither entertaining nor attractive, and very banal. There are great scenes, great characters. *Alms for Oblivion* needs work. It is Madame Bovary lusting for money in the Kentucky Hills." He turned on the radio, which was reporting baseball again, and leaned back in his chair, smoking.

The three men looked at each other. Luzzatto bawled, "That's a hell of an approach, Travis, and I know Youngblood here is going to come up with a hell of a screenplay."

For the first time Jablock looked at Hawke. "Do you feel you can execute that approach?"

Hawke stood, reached a long arm across the desk, and snapped off the radio. "I'm afraid I can't discuss my book with a ball game going," he said, talking straight at the good ear. "I'm more interested in baseball than novels any day."

Jablock looked astounded, then he burst out laughing and said to Luzzatto, "He's all right."

Hawke went on, "I think I know how to make my book into a movie, though I've never written a movie before—"

"That's an advantage," Jablock said. "We need freshness here. When can we see something on paper?"

Lax put in, "Youngblood figures he can have a rough draft in ten or twelve weeks."

"Well, that's goddamn fast if he delivers. Of course all these eastern writers know how to work . . . Get him a room in the old writers' build-

ing, and a decent secretary," he said to Luzzatto. He turned on the radio, picked it off the desk, and disappeared behind the Gothic door.

Luzzatto lunged at Hawke and pounded his back. "You son of a bitch, you're terrific. Ferdie, you see the way he turned off that radio?"

Fay was sitting in the Cadillac with her legs crossed as before. She said when she saw Lax, "I'm dying for a drink."

"Sure, honey. Rainbow's End, Harry." Lax now told Hawke, as the car threaded out of the studio grounds, that the entire project had hinged on this brief meeting with Jablock, who had a heavy schedule of pictures in production, and had been hesitating over *Oblivion*. He had said at last that if Hawke was as impressive as Luzzatto claimed, the studio would venture the writer's salary and some preliminary costs. "You impressed hell out of Travis," Lax said.

"How? He did all the talking, and he talked nonsense."

"Listen, Travis is a moviemaker. He gets the money, he gets the stars, he gets the directors, he throws them all into the pot and stirs them, and movies come out. Most of his movies earn a profit. He's the world's idiot when he talks about stories. He has his own methods for sizing up people. He liked the way you turned off the radio."

Rainbow's End was a cluster of white stucco cottages around an amoeba-shaped blue pool on the broad avenue called Sunset Boulevard. It was dark when the Cadillac pulled up in front of the neon sign, a half-rainbow flashing into an unblinking golden pot. To Hawke's surprise Fay got out of the car with him. "I have an apartment here, too," she said. "Just until I find something more permanent."

Soon Hawke found himself alone with his luggage in Villa 4: a spacious bedroom, a very large beige and tan living room, featureless hotel furnishings. He was weary; the airplane trip had been a rocky one, and the encounter with Jablock an unexpected added strain. But he had made up his mind to pass no day in Hollywood without writing some pages on his book. So he unpacked the smallest bag, which had his manuscript and other tools of his work, including a bottle of Barbados rum. Resolution and rum drove his pen through nine pages; then he went to bed without dinner, his head reeling, and fell asleep to the crashing of a thunderstorm, and a noise of rain on his roof like a dumping of gravel.

He had breakfast at a table by the side of the pool, in a cloudless morning. The sky was clear blue, the sun beat white and hard on the cottage walls, and the breeze smelled of flowers. Hibiscus and bougainvillea splashed raw color all around the courtyard. He was halfway through an oversized omelette with chicken livers when Fay Pulver emerged from a villa across the pool in a loose blue robe. She waved to him and dropped the robe on the lawn, uncovering a luscious body in a brief white bathing suit. She dived into the water, and cavorted around, treating him to a long twisting display of her charms while he finished his breakfast. He went off

to the studio in the rented Ford convertible Lax had provided for him, much perked up by the response of his endocrine system to Fay Pulver.

It gave him a not quite pleasant twinge to see the white card with YOUNGBLOOD HAWKE typed on it, in a brass holder on the door of Room 227 in the "old writers' building." Other doors with other cards lined the corridor: Mel Robbins, Phil Glick, William Murphy, Art Einstein, Sy Goodhand, Milton Ransom: writers all, of whom he had never heard. But his secretary, a pale bulging woman in tweed, told him that the rooms on the floor, except for Murphy's and Goodhand's were empty: retrenchment. She had stacked three new copies of *Alms for Oblivion* on his desk, and had prepared dozens of sheets of typing paper with carbons already interspersed. Pens, blue pencils, red pencils, and a whole bowl of freshly sharpened plain pencils, were ranged on the desk with full bowls of clips and rubber bands, a dictionary, a thesaurus, a book called *Bancroft's Twenty-One Basic Plots*, a stapler, a paper knife, a ruler, a pot of glue, a scissors, and a magnifying glass. She appeared from her anteroom armed with a dictation pad and she seemed much cast down when he had nothing to dictate.

Alone in the room, sipping coffee at the broad desk so amply furnished for creativity, Hawke had seldom felt less like writing. His room looked out on a brilliantly green golf course, where the small jerky figures of a few players were sharp and clear in the sunlight. He idly wondered what had become of the smog; the air today was translucent, and Hollywood as he drove to the studio had been one broad tropical garden, all spice, flower scents, and heavy greenery.

But here he was, and carving a movie out of his book was the task in hand. Now that he was faced with it, the problem was interesting. His boyhood had been a feast of reading and of movies. Even now there was hardly a movie he saw that he failed to enjoy, however bad the reviews were. He had learned in college, of course, that movies were contemptible, and he had observed in New York that the more literate magazines either ignored movies or had a critic on the staff whose main qualification was a large stock of caustic phrases. For all that, he still loved movies. He had read almost all the important plays and novels in the world; compared to them, the new plays and books seemed thin. But movies seldom disappointed him; moreover he liked the despised Hollywood pictures. Their repetitiousness, their total emptiness of intellectual content, their copybook moralities, their large implausible lying, their naïve licentiousness, did not bother him at all; in these childlike qualities they exactly resembled the Arabian Nights, and like the Arabian Nights, Hollywood pictures seemed to him part of one ever-running endlessly involuted rainbow-hued dream. He was not sure he could chop up his novel so as to add a satisfying episode to this epic of the assembly-line Scheherazade, but he was willing to try.

He lit a cigar and went at the task. He had hoped and half expected to be put to work with a director, because it seemed to him that the director was the true master of a film. But here he was, alone in a factory room, so he did the best he could. He scrawled a few new love scenes for Aunt Bertha's early life; he marked up a copy of his book, isolating a sequence of scenes to recount his main story in a clear and simple pictorial way; and to clarify the job for the secretary, he typed a twenty-five page step-by-step narrative outline of the sequence. Once warmed to it he worked hard, not pausing for lunch. Soon it was four o'clock. Now he was a little embarrassed, because it seemed to him that he had written the movie. He called the secretary in. "I guess you ought to type this stuff up smoothly," he said, "then we'll see where we're at."

The woman looked at the written pages, and the typed pages, and she thumbed through the marked book. She sank into a chair, staring at him. Then she broke into a wild laugh. "Excuse me, sir, but when did you do this?"

"Well, I'd thought about it some before, but I hadn't had a chance to put anything down until today."

"Mr. Hawke, do you know what we call this? This is the first master-scene draft."

"Is there anything wrong with my procedure?"

Giggling hysterically the woman said, "Wrong? No, there's nothing wrong, exactly." She picked up the ringing telephone. "Yes, Mr. Hawke's office? I'll see if he's here . . . Sir, it's Mr. Lax's secretary. He wants to talk to you."

Lax said, "How are you doing, mountain boy? Utterly baffled?"

"Well, sort of. I worked the thing out in the book and wrote the new love scenes and a narrative sequence and all that. Now my secretary says I've done the first master-scene draft, whatever that is."

"Holy Christ! Don't give it to her!" Lax exclaimed.

"I already have."

"Take it back. Put it in a drawer and lock it up. Stop working. Just sit and read a book. Don't do anything more. I'll be there within half an hour. You just do what I tell you, do you hear?"

"Sure." Hawke retrieved the material from the secretary, who backed out of the room, still staring at him.

Lax burst in about ten minutes later. "Let's see what you've done." He was breathing hard. Hawke showed him the work. Lax looked through it, shook his head over it, rolled his eyes to heaven, dropped in a chair, and seemed to fall asleep or to die. In a minute or so the agent lolled his head to one side as though his neck were broken, and languidly opened his eyes. "You're on salary week to week, Hawke," he said. "This is not a flat deal. Your daily salary comes to about sixty dollars, after taxes and

withholding. Do you really want to give a master-scene draft of *Alms for Oblivion* to Travis Jablock for sixty dollars?"

"No," Hawke said. "But I don't know anything about this place. What am I supposed to do?"

Lax scratched his head, picked up the telephone, and asked for Travis Jablock. "Trav, it's Ferdie. Now I'm in Hawke's office here. The boy is completely at sea. He can't come down out of the Tennessee hills and just start knocking off moving pictures."

"Kentucky," Hawke said, but Lax ignored him.

"Well, I want an experienced hand put on with him . . . I'd say try it for eight, ten weeks and see how far we get . . . maybe they'll do a master-scene draft . . . I know that's usually your policy, Trav, and frankly I think you're wise . . . Sy Goodhand is just finishing on Crosby, isn't he? Let's throw him in with Sy Goodhand. Great, Trav. Great. Fabulous." He hung up and turned to Hawke. "Goodhand is an old workhorse around here. You'll like him and he'll give you a lot of ideas. Take that stuff," he waved a little limp hand at the day's work on the desk, "and file it away back at Rainbow's End. Don't keep it here. Don't show it to Goodhand. Don't show it to anybody."

"I don't like this. I'll get paid less."

"What? Why should you be?"

"You're dividing the same job among two people."

Lax sighed. "Goodhand is a *staff* writer, don't you see? Whether he works with you, or polishes somebody else's seventh draft, or writes an original story, or just sits in his office and masturbates, it makes no difference. He gets paid." Lax put on his hat, a soft blue corduroy blob. "Next time I'll make a flat deal for you, since you're such a fireball, and you can write a master-scene draft in half an hour if the frenzy comes on you. The usual period is three to six months."

7

At midnight there came a tapping at Hawke's window. He sat in the dark living room in the yellow light of the desk lamp, drudging away at his novel. The dim outside light showed a woman at his window. He opened the door and Fay Pulver said, "My, you're the hard worker, aren't you? Don't you want to relax a bit and have a nightcap with me?"

The twenty-seven-year-old male in Hawke sprang to the alert. He was out of the door on the instant, walking with Fay to her villa. She gave him one drink and another, and changed to a clinging negligee, and all the time kept telling her life story. She had divorced her husband in San Francisco, a man in the electrical supply business, and she had come to Hollywood to act. Many men had promised to find her work, and some

were just out for no good, but she really did have some promising leads. Meantime however she had fallen in love with a married radio gagman, and he had gone to New York to divorce his wife. She liked Ferdie Lax because he was so clever and so generous, in fact she loved him, but she wasn't *in love* with him, if Hawke could understand that. At about two o'clock Hawke decided that sex was no more in the air than theosophy was; this girl was actually being sociable, despite her diaphanous dress, and her nymph-like pouts, laughs, and tongue-flickers, which were automatic. He left.

Fay must have enjoyed the little visit, because the next night she tapped at his window again. This time she came into his villa, and they sat around drinking. She began to question him about his love life. He had had nobody to confide in since the start of his New York adventures, and Fay was rather like a shipboard acquaintance. After a little prodding he came out with the whole tale: his involvement with "Mrs. X," and the unlucky zigzag of his romance with Jeanne. Fay's opinion was that he had been both fortunate and wise. His affair with "Mrs. X" had given him an emotional yardstick. Everybody needed an emotional yardstick, Fay said; she would never have married her husband if she had had an emotional yardstick. She had learned this important concept, she said, from a psychoanalyst in San Francisco. He was a most wonderful man, and she had had an affair with him, but then his wife had made trouble and she had had to break off the analysis; but meantime the affair had given her an emotional yardstick. As for Jeanne Green, Fay's opinion was that the world was full of girls eager to marry a glamorous person like a novelist, and Hawke could take his time.

They had several such evenings of mutual confession and gossip, and Hawke got so he rather enjoyed talking to Fay and listening to her cheery imbecilities. She showed him the letters the gagman sent her from New York, poetic epistles long on passion but short on news about the progress of his divorce. One night the beauty of the latest letter reduced Fay to tears, and Hawke put an arm around her to comfort her, and without many words he found himself in bed with the magnificent girl, whose sexual manners were athletic, intricate, and coarse. Afterward she yawned and said, "Well! Now I feel better." She staggered around sleepily to mix another drink, and continued to talk about her plans for marrying the gagman, as though the interruption had been a telephone call. Hawke left as soon as he could, and went back to his villa in a slump of revulsion. He could not sleep. He thought for hours about the contrast between this kind of savorless carrying-on and the terrible excitement and sweetness of his hours with Frieda. With something like dismay he began to understand that what he had experienced with Mrs. Winter in eight brief weeks had been precious, perhaps unique, perhaps unrecapturable in a lifetime. His resolution to maintain silence toward her gave way. He wrote her a long

letter, which he did not finish until the dawn was pale outside; and after an hour or so of restless sleep and a cup of coffee, he mailed it.

Frieda promptly fired back a wonderful letter—witty, articulate, long, and good-humored to the last page, when she allowed herself a fiery paragraph. Meantime Hawke had had two letters from Jeanne, cooler and briefer, dealing mainly with business, but redolent with her peculiar austere charm. The mood in which he had written Frieda had passed away. But of course he had to answer her, and so he found himself corresponding with Mrs. Winter, quite against his first intention.

CHAPTER NINE

1

HAWKE had been in Hollywood about three weeks when Lax decided it was time to strike for the shift from Prince House to Hodge Hathaway. The agent said as they sat at lunch in a garden restaurant, a gorgeous bower of tropical plants, its polychrome charm somewhat dimmed by swirling clouds of smog and insecticide, "For one thing, Hawke, I'm goddamned if your book isn't beginning to sell. I've been checking at the Pickwick Shop and the department stores. They've moved a few copies lately, they say."

"I have the figures from New York, Ferdie. Sales are zero."

The agent shrugged. "That book business is a horse and buggy game. Nobody knows what's going on. Let's shake loose from Jay today. He doesn't believe in you and he's a cheapskate. Hodge's outfit is the nearest thing to a real merchandiser in that tinpot business . . . Good lord, man, you've had Scotch broth and a broiled lobster. Are you really going to eat that chocolate pie?"

"I'm not used to rich feeding yet. Give me time." Hawke wolfed the pie, a fat velvety brown wedge heavily curlycued with whipped cream. He loved the food in Hollywood. One restaurant seemed better than the next. All his clothes were getting tight, but he didn't care. He had never eaten luxurious food until he had come to New York; and the taste for it was growing on him.

"Well, you're big and you're young," Lax said. "You're going to get fat, though."

In his office Lax told his secretary to telephone Jay Prince and Ross

Hodge. There were a couple of calls waiting for him. He immediately got on the telephone and began a violent argument with a producer at Warner Brothers over the terms of sale of a novel. While he barked and shouted, he calmly inspected a pile of mail, signed some letters, and made a few corrective notes. A second phone on his desk rang. Now Hawke, sprawled on a couch with a cigar, digesting his heavy lunch, saw a spectacle he found hard to believe. Lax took the other telephone and—turning the first phone up so that he was still listening, but shutting the mouthpiece with his hand—he started a cooing conversation with a female star about a new Broadway play he was trying to sell her. He talked to her for a minute or two in this sugary way. Then evidently the man on the other telephone paused. Lax asked the actress a question, rotated her telephone upward, rolled down the first one, and answered the producer with a howling stream of dirty language. He then turned the phone up again, and responded to the woman in tones of dulcet cajolery. A few moments later he was bellowing obscenely at the producer again. As he went on juggling these two conversations, he glanced at Hawke with a grin. Hawke rose, picked up Lax's latest headgear, a hairy plaid cap, put it on, and took it off with a low bow. Lax dipped his head. Then, frankly showing off, he lit a cigar while keeping both conversations going. He concluded both talks at about the same time, and hung up the two telephones with a flourish. "This is an insane business," he sighed.

The secretary announced through the talk box that Prince House and Hodge Hathaway were waiting on the line. Lax dropped his hands on the two telephones, wrists relaxed, like a pianist about to launch into a concerto. "Okay, here we go. From Jay we want out, right? From Hodge we want a ten-thousand advance on the navy book, and no participation in the movie rights. Correct?"

"You're in charge," Hawke said. "Go ahead."

Lax now repeated his two-telephone stunt, with Jay Prince on one line and Ross Hodge on the other. In a way the feat was more spectacular this time, because both conversations dealt with the same topic, and as the talk went on the situation kept changing. Yet the agent never made a slip that Hawke could observe. He maintained wholly different tones with the two publishers: a reasonable astringent manner with Hodge, and his former mixture of banter and bullying with Prince. It soon became clear to Hawke that Jay Prince was weakening, and probably would give in if enough money were forthcoming from Hodge to buy off the contract. Lax's task was to work Hodge up to the highest possible price for ransoming the author from Prince House, at the same time getting Hawke a large advance for *Chain of Command*. The double-barrelled negotiation must have gone on for ten minutes. Lax at no point disclosed to one publisher that he had the other on the line. His ability to give each one the impression that an ordinary conversation was going forward struck Hawke as

some kind of high water mark in this bizarre virtuosity. The most impressive moments, he thought, were when Lax was silent and both men were evidently talking at once; how on earth could the agent sort out the diverse information pouring into his two ears? But Lax never seemed to be in the least trouble.

At last he said, "One moment, Jay, I've got Hawke here and I want to talk to him . . . Look, Mr. Hodge, I understand the position, and if you'll give me a moment I want to consult with our author here."

Lax dropped the two receivers in his lap, his palms over the mouthpieces. "Well, this seems to be it. Jay's mouth is watering. Hodge is ready to give him four thousand, which is more than what Jay has already advanced you. But we're not going to get any ten thousand for *Chain of Command* from Hodge on top of that, Hawke. He says he won't budge from five."

Hawke said, "That's not bad. The main thing is I want out of Prince House."

The agent said, "I don't know. I've played this a little sloppily here. Jay's getting away with murder. Shall we drop it for a few weeks and try again?"

"No. Nail it down. I want this settled." Hawke felt as he had in high school in the last moments of a basketball game, tense and happy under pressure.

The agent grinned, a fighting spark in his eye. "Okay. Let's see what we can do."

He began to manipulate the two telephones again, alternating courtly English with Ross Hodge and crude bluster with Prince. The performance worked up to a crescendo, and Hawke lost track of what was happening in the rapid spouting of figures and conditions into one receiver and the other. Then, quite suddenly, Lax was laughing and making genial farewells on both lines. He slammed both telephones into their cradles with an artistic crash.

"Well, Mark Twain, there it is. You're free of Prince House. You get six thousand advance from Hodge for this navy yarn of yours, with a contract equal to the best in the business. No percentage of the movie rights to the publisher. None. The book after that is now completely in the clear."

Hawke strode to the desk and held out his hand. The agent shook it calmly, saying, "I don't know. I feel we could have had Jay for less, and then we could have gotten you more. But maybe not. It was the idea of getting all his money back, every cent he'd paid you plus an extra thousand, or so, and clearing his share of the movie money as well, that made him break from cover. I'm afraid Jay is grasping." He blew out his cheeks. "You going back to the studio? I can send you in my car."

"Ferdie," Hawke said, "it's more than I hoped for. More than I could ever have done. I want to thank you for a masterly negotiation."

Lax looked up at him, and just for a moment, on the face of the clever

sleepy parrot, there was the look of a pleased lonesome man. "Well, I have a reputation as a son of a bitch. But I just believe writers should be paid a fair price for their wares, say like shoemakers and whores."

Hawke said, "Now what happens? Can I go back to New York?"

"Are you out of your goddamned mind? You're on an assignment here. Wait till Jay signs the release, at least."

"This job's a nuisance, Ferdie."

"Don't give me that. It's no nuisance to pick up eight hundred a week, mountain boy. Not for you, not yet."

"The thing is I don't understand what's going on. Honest I don't. Ever since this fellow Sy Goodhand moved in we've done nothing, practically, but sit in projection rooms in deep leather chairs, and smoke cigars, and look at old movies. We've put in maybe an hour a day, no more, just discussing what my novel is about. Can you imagine? *What it's about,* I swear! Our secretary has typed up about two hundred pages of this random talk. Do you know Goodhand? Tall, blond, always running off to his analyst with some coy excuse the way a girl goes to the bathroom?"

"I know Goodhand. He paces himself on a job. He'll get down to work when it's time. Don't worry, he's picking your brains while you talk."

Hawke said mulishly, "I don't need the money, and I've got work to do."

"Listen, you took this assignment. If you walk off you'll get a reputation as a temperamental artist. You'll find it very hard to get work in this town."

"I don't expect to write for the movies again."

"That's a mood. You'll bring your pitcher to this well often. It's the one that doesn't run dry. You stay on the job."

"I feel as though I'm stealing their money."

"Oh Jesus, Hawke! That's too much. You think *you're* stealing from *Travis Jablock?* Travis Jablock could steal the tits off a Vassar girl and she wouldn't know it. If in twelve weeks you contribute two good scenes to the picture, or a beginning of a clear story line, you'll have earned your pay. A successful movie can gross *five million dollars, Hawke!* Can't you grasp that? Jablock's gambling a few eight-hundred-dollar checks on you. What is that? He's getting daily reports on you from Sy Goodhand, from your secretary, and probably from the scrubwoman who empties your wastebasket. If he decides you're useless you'll be out before you can look around. Listen, I'm having a dinner party Thursday night, just a few people"—he named half a dozen of the greatest stars in films—"Georges Feydal will be in town with that solo show of his, you know. He's coming over afterward. Will you join us?"

"Sure," Hawke said. "What's the occasion?"

"Nothing special, there's this writer coming out from New York, and I want him to meet a few people. Maybe you've heard of him. Howard Fain."

"I've heard of him," Hawke said ironically. Fain was the twenty-three-year-old monster who had written the war novel that had blanketed the fiction field, and that still stood in prosperous piles in the bookstores. Hawke had sometimes loitered in a shop and seen a stack of the Fain novels disappear in half an hour.

Lax said, "I haven't met him myself yet, just talked to him on the telephone, but I hear he's a hot kid. However, you're my boy. You know that. Next Thursday, sevenish, no black tie or any of that crap unless you feel like it."

2

Next morning he was having coffee by the pool, watching Fay Pulver writhe her shapely self here and there in the water in an utterly transparent pink jersey suit. He was feeling no more personal interest than if she were a dolphin; possibly less. He was worried and irritated at Jeanne's failure to telephone. The night before he had been full of rosy plans for summoning her to California now that he was a Hodge Hathaway author, and enjoying an all-out romance with her which, if it led to marriage, would be quite all right with him! He had called New York, and an answering service had told him that Miss Green was out for the evening. He had left a message for her to call him, no matter when she came in. What was the damned girl doing staying out until all hours? Why had she ignored him? With whom had she been out?

A loudspeaker grated, *Telephone for Mr. Hawke.* He bolted to his villa. "One moment for New York . . . Mrs. Green? Ready with Mr. Hawke. Go ahead, Mrs. Green."

"Hello?" Jeanne's voice: a little raspy as always, but full of sweet warmth.

He said, "*Mrs.?* Tell me it isn't true, Jeanne."

Her laugh, low and intimate: "Hardly. Same bitter old spinster at this end. How are you?"

"Why didn't you call me last night? I left word for you to call me."

"Yes, Mr. Hawke. I didn't get in till four-fifteen and I was in no shape for business conversation. You are talking to the owner of one of New York's historic hangovers. Something I can do for you?"

"What were you doing until four-fifteen?"

"Helling around."

"With whom?"

"None of your business. Karl Fry, since you ask." Jeanne did not mention that Fry had proposed marriage to her, after filling her with champagne at the Empire Room of the Waldorf and then taking her on a

round of night clubs. It did not seem politic to tell this to Hawke, not now and probably never.

"Jeanne, it's all set, my move from Prince to Hodge Hathaway. Did Hodge tell you?"

She said cautiously, "I heard something. I don't know what I am and what I'm not supposed to know any more. Exactly how does it stand, can you tell me?"

He told her the status of negotiations, and made her laugh with a description of Lax's phone-juggling. She said, "Well, I think that's marvellous. I'll believe it when it's really happened on paper."

"Jeanne, I'd like to finish up this book fast so we can publish it in '48. The political novel is begging to get written. It's piling up in my head like a headache. I want you to come out here now. You know Ross Hodge will send you like a shot."

"Oh?" It was not said loud but the word carried a strong female charge. A measurable silence: then, "Are you sure you want that? Maybe you should just gallop ahead and finish. The queries might upset you and slow you up."

"I do want you. This business of working by mail is slow and unsatisfactory. You and I could clear up tons of this stuff working together in a few hours, instead of writing back and forth incessantly. And it would be more fun. Wouldn't it?"

"Well, I mean, but, you know, aren't you coming back to New York in the next few weeks anyway? From your last letter I gathered you're about ready to give up movie writing as a bad job."

"I'm staying on. I have to."

"You seem to be doing a lot of work on your novel. I received that last hundred fifty pages you sent me."

"I wrote fourteen pages last night. After a hard day at the studio."

"Isn't that illegal? Aren't they renting your brains on a twenty-four-hour basis?"

"Yes. What I've been sending you is bootleg literature."

"It's wonderful that you're making such progress."

"My monastic habits."

"Yes, yes," she said, but then the sarcasm faded to wonder, "but you can't be dissipating too much with all this copy you're turning in. How about the starlets? Aren't they beautiful?"

"Can't see them for the smog. And for thinking of you."

"All right," she said like a schoolteacher. "I can't possibly come out there. What's the weather like? Of course I'd get a chance to see my mother, which is long overdue."

The upshot of much fencing was that Jeanne admitted she could perhaps get out there in two weeks; not any sooner. Hawke bargained her

down to a Monday morning ten days away, suspecting that she was being coy. But he could not move her further.

The fact was that Jeanne, as she talked, was in a grand flutter, and was swiftly revising in her head complex plans that included, beyond heavy editing chores, a visit to Karl Fry's two children in St. Louis. She had been out with Fry almost every night in recent weeks. She liked Karl, and admired him. She felt that she could strengthen him and even perhaps help him to new literary success, a revival of his once splendid reputation. She was with him in the office every day. They had become easy joking comrades. He had been lavishing the theatre, the restaurants, and all the multi-colored pleasures of New York on her. In her first wounded weeks after Hawke had gone to The Park Tower, Jeanne had leaned desperately on Karl's quiet devotion, just to get through the days and the nights and now the thing had come this far. Marriage to Karl no longer seemed totally absurd to her, as it once had. Compared to the young doctors, lawyers, government men, and business men who had taken up with her over the years, Karl Fry came off quite well. He was too old, and he was divorced. But he had a sharp intelligence, which was an absolute requirement; she could not endure the thought of marrying a man duller than herself. He was decent, and his sense of humor was superb, and he was deeply in love with her. Her misfortune was that she loved Arthur Hawke. If she could not have Hawke—and during the break over Mrs. Winter she had forced herself to believe she could not—it almost did not matter what became of her, and to look for love like that again was hopeless. All these thoughts whirled in a vortex in Jeanne's mind as Hawke sprang on her this sudden plea to join him in Hollywood. The implications were plain, and dizzying.

Here he was, the big exasperating Southern clown, still arguing in that ridiculous thick accent: "Jeanie, mah *birthday* is the Sunday before that. Sho'ly you can leave Saturday and celebrate mah twenty-eighth birthday with me heah?"

"No, I can't."

"You owe it to me as my editor not to let me face such a milestone in solitude. It would depress me."

"You have friends out there."

"Not one I'll spend my birthday with."

"It's out of the question. I'll be there some time on Monday the twenty-ninth of August, unless I write you otherwise. I'll bring the manuscript. I'll call you at the studio when I arrive. This is all quite exciting, and I'm not at all sure I can arrange it, but I'll try. Anything else?"

"Not that I can think of, Jeanne."

"What do you hear from Mrs. Winter?"

As any other man in the world would have done, he lied, "Not a thing."

"Lovely. Bye, Arthur."

3

Hawke was dressing for the dinner party at which he was going to meet Howard Fain, the young author who had caught the brass ring, slain the dragon, reached the Pole, with his first novel. He felt no rancor toward Fain, and was but mildly jealous of his vast success. This was due to no unusual fund of Christian virtue, but rather to a lunatic serenity that lay under all his moods, a conviction that he too was going to be rich and famous, if not now then a little later. The effect of this eccentric self-confidence was to make him oddly amiable, as writers go.

Lax telephoned while he was at the mirror, worrying over the tightness of his dark suit. "Hawke, I may be throwing you a curve here but I thought I'd better check with you. Do you know that Frieda Winter's coming to my party?"

Hawke's throat tightened, and he cleared it with an effort. "Frieda? I just got a letter from her from New York."

"Well, Feydal is having temperamental fits. Wants to cancel the tour. She came to calm him down. As a matter of fact she and Howard Fain arrived on the same plane last night. Didn't she phone you?"

"No."

"Well, I'm just telling you, she'll be here."

"I'm glad to hear it. She's a delightful woman."

"Look, Hawke, it's none of my goddamned business but Frieda is very much older than you. Not to mention that she's so much smarter than you that it's no contest."

"Ferdie, I barely know Mrs. Winter, but I've always found her conversation agreeable."

"Very good, Hawke. Just stick to that. Stick to conversation with her, in large groups of people, in brightly lit rooms. She can't stay here more than a few days, she's got a big piece of a show trying out in Hartford that's coming in right after Labor Day."

"Thanks, Ferdie."

The piece of information that bothered him most was the fact that she had arrived on the same airplane with Howard Fain. There seemed to be a peculiar, perhaps very unpleasant, significance in that. He finished dressing with much greater care.

Ferdie Lax lived in one of the best houses on one of the best streets of Beverly Hills. Hawke had often prowled those streets in wonder. There were palms all over Los Angeles, but none like the palms of Beverly Hills. Elsewhere the palms had long brown beards of old fronds hanging down sometimes twenty feet; in Beverly Hills each palm was barbered

smooth up to this year's tuft of green. Elsewhere lawns were gray-brown in the drought of summer; here each house had a sweeping soft green lawn watered from buried sprinklers by clockwork. There was no style to the streets. There was a glut of style that erased style. Each block was a museum shelf of model mansions, but because real estate cost so much, the mansions stood cheek by jowl, separated only by cement tracks for automobiles. A French château which needed, to complete it, twenty acres of greensward, stood huddled between a Tudor manor that also cried for a vast park to enable it to breathe, and a Spanish ranch house without its ranch; and so on for long blocks. Nothing testified more to the evanescence of position and wealth in Beverly Hills than its architecture. There was money in abundance to put up the settings of the grand life. But land—the one true mark of stable grandeur—was not to be had. The town was an industrial compound of the temporarily well-paid.

A bowing butler in uniform opened Ferdie's door. The agent stood in the foyer under a Utrillo painting, laughing and joking with the new arrivals; he was holding a cigar in one hand and a huge thick tumbler of whiskey and ice in the other, and his parrot face was gleaming with elation.

"I'm late," Hawke said. It was a quarter to nine.

"Hell no, right on time."

"Frieda here?"

"Not yet. We'll be eating any minute," the agent said, leading him by an elbow into a gigantic brilliantly lit living room. Here Hawke at once recognized five great movie stars, three men and two women, scattered among nobodies, or at least people who seemed nobodies. The men were the dour Western star, the dashing costume movie star, and the charming villain star of the time. The women were the wiggling sex star and the heavy dramatic star. These types are fixed in American films like cabinet posts. The people who hold the posts come and go because of age, or illness, or bad pictures, or a shift in public fancy; but the offices remain, and are seldom long vacant. Lax introduced Hawke to these dazzling men and women; and though he had seen a couple of them before at lunch time in the studio dining room, he was thrilled as a schoolboy to shake their hands. The sex star astounded and delighted him by saying that she had read *Alms for Oblivion* and liked it; she was as gracious as a young queen. Then Lax presented Hawke to two tired insignificant-looking men, and they turned out to be the most famous directors of the day, and to a dozen other people of descending importance, including a once-prominent British novelist who now wrote Hollywood movies.

These people greeted Hawke with pleasant charm, but his arrival caused no change in the party noise, and everybody went on chatting as before once he had passed down the line. At the Prince party eight months ago he had been an unknown quantity, a potential new hero. Now he

was just another young novelist with a poorly selling book; no cause for excitement among these luminaries! Lax took him to a bar in the next room, a library which in size, ornate wood panelling, and sweep of leather-bound volumes, put the Prince library to shame.

"Ferdie, your library is magnificent! Good God, it's the library of a nobleman!"

Lax said, "I just rent this place." He named the owner, a director of fluffy comedies. "He's over in France doing the foreign residence bit."

"What's the foreign residence bit?"

"Something we'll get you on as soon as possible. You don't pay income taxes."

"That's impossible."

"The hell it is. It's the greatest thing since the Emancipation Proclamation. Get a drink."

Hawke sidled into the living room, stood near the library door against the wall, and drank and listened and looked. The room was furnished with heavy dark pieces, Italian or Spanish, he thought. The main colors of drapery and upholstery were plum and gray. Grotesque modern paintings in bold colors flared on the walls. A black concert grand piano was quite inconspicuous in a corner. The immense fireplace of old rough stone looked as though it had been brought stone by stone from Europe, and it was flanked by a colossal hammered copper woodbox of Mexican design.

It had become quiet in the room because the dashing costume star was telling a joke, and he had almost everybody's attention. The joke was long and ribaldly funny. Hawke had never heard it before. What amazed him, accustomed though he was by now to the way Hollywood people talked, was the famous actor's calm, totally unself-conscious use of the foulest obscenities in the presence of the women, and their smiling acceptance of this. In none of the company through which Hawke had drifted—and he had been in fairly salty company sometimes, in his drunken bouts at college, and on shore leave in the Seabees; he had been in whorehouses and at parties of Greenwich Village perverts, and here in Hollywood he had stumbled into several appalling brawls in his rounding with Goodhand—but in none of these places had he encountered anything like this whole indifference of polished and elegant women to supposedly dirty language. A drunken prostitute on the street, Hawke thought, would look arch and at least pretend offense if you spoke to her as the actor was speaking to these grand ladies, two of them internationally worshipped, all of them magnificently and most tastefully dressed, all of them displaying in every gesture the graces of culture and of prestige. An explosion of delighted laughter greeted the end of the story, which turned on sodomy between a woman and a dog. As the laughter started to fade

the heavy dramatic woman star struck in with skill, and began another story, equally obscene.

Hawke was still enough of a Hovey boy to be, not offended, but stupefied. The fault could not be in these people, he thought, so self-confident and so eminent. There was a liberating idea, a piece of cultural knowledge, that they had and he lacked. Into his mental inventory went the note that ordinary standards of talk did not exist for the people of the films; that women, so far as manners went, had no sex.

And as the joke session went on, and he stared at the laughing relaxed film stars, he began almost to feel that he was in a nightmare, in which he had wandered into a waxworks museum where dummies of the stars had come to life and were blabbering at each other in dream language. The scene had the dislocated overreality of a dream, due in part, no doubt, to the stiff drinks he was swallowing one after another in anticipation of encountering Frieda, and to the excitement of being in a room with five world-famous people. His stomach hurt from hunger; it was past ten o'clock; but there was no sign of dinner, and no sign among the other guests that they missed it. They went on and on drinking and swapping jokes, and then all at once, far down the immense room just inside the open arch to the foyer, there she was.

Frieda Winter, in a high-fashion swathe of black that billowed around her hips and tightened to her knees, and a little scarf of black on her brown hair, peering around the room with her head down, and then half-turning her elastic body to say something to the small man who had come in with her, throwing her head a little to one side to laugh—it was she, she and nobody else in the world. She walked down the room, her hand resting on the arm of the man. Most of the people in the room she greeted familiarly, and then introduced her escort. As the guests became aware of the new arrivals the quality of the room noise changed. Random chatter and laughter subsided into the buzz and murmur of a business office. Eyes that had been looking here and there now looked one way. For the young man with Frieda, as Hawke perceived immediately, was Howard Fain. The triumphant author wore a rough blue-and-white checked shirt, a brown corduroy jacket, and unpressed gray trousers; a "novelist's rig" with a vengeance! And a perfect costume for this room full of wealthy, perfectly groomed people; nothing could have answered better. Frieda saw Hawke, and she nodded and smiled from a distance, much as she had been doing to everyone else. He stood where he was, with his back to the wall at the library door. After a while she came, leading the author.

"Well, the only two really important people in the room certainly ought to meet," she said.

Fain's hand was small, rough, and powerful. Though he was so short that he hardly came up to Hawke's shoulders, he did not look

like a little man. He had the handsomeness people speak of as Byronic: strong male features, with a softening trace of sensitivity at the mouth; brilliant blue eyes in a pale face, curly heavy black hair worn long, and shaped with care that contradicted his rough clothes. Hawke thought instantly that Fain was carrying off the "novelist's rig" with an effort, and that Fain, like himself, was overanxious about his appearance.

Hawke said, "Hello. Your novel's a wonderful work. I'm sore as hell at you for blotting me out."

Fain said with a mechanical smile, "Thanks. I'm sorry I haven't read yours. After what Frieda tells me, it's the next book I will read."

"How's Paul, Frieda?" Hawke said. Her perfume was troubling him; it flooded his mind with pictures of their secret love-making. But she was again the New York woman he had first seen: cool, poised, remote as a star, barely smiling.

"Which one, Arthur?"

"Both."

"Both fine. Paul junior's back at school after prolonging his malingering as long as he could." She put her chin almost down to her chest, and squinted at him from under her brows. "Haven't you put on weight?"

"I'm afraid so."

"I have to talk to Ferdie." She slipped away, leaving the two authors in a stance like boxers or roosters sizing each other up for a fight. A waiter passed with drinks. Fain took two large brimming martinis and set one on the piano. "I'm a little behind here." He drank off most of the drink in his hand, and stared around at the people in the room with a bitter, disappointed look. "God, this is a sick town."

"You've been here before?"

"Once, for forty-eight hours, three months ago. I couldn't get on the plane to New York fast enough. In that time I went to three parties like this and I had conferences with two of the grand moguls of the industry. All to the same effect. Wouldn't I consent to changing my story a little bit, just a wee touch here and there—about as wee as having the Nazis win the war, for instance—so they could get Army cooperation in making the goddamned film? One suggestion was that my insane general become a gruff old war correspondent, see, because that took the curse off the military aspect. I told them my book was intended to put a curse on the military aspect. They laughed." Fain took the other martini and glanced up at Hawke, with a trace of disdain on his pale, angry, commanding face. "Frieda says you're working at a studio. How in Christ can you stand it?"

"I'm making a lot of money. I do my writing at night."

"I guess you know what you're doing. It's so appalling," Fain burst out, after pausing to drain the drink, "here is the perfect art form, the synthesis Wagner dreamed of. Music, words, color, spectacle, infinite

pictorial range, the entire Grand Canyon one minute if you need it, and the next minute the whispering intimacy of lovers' faces, all at your command. And yet a good film will never be made in this town. Never, never, never. Because producing a picture here is like making an aircraft carrier. Too many people involved, too much money at stake. It's like trying to write a story with a golden pen forty feet high. These people are all sick from constantly attempting the impossible and knowing they must fail and drudging on and getting rich doing bad work, while their guts sicken over the everlasting failure."

Hawke said, "You're attributing to them your own drive to excel. If that doesn't exist in them your idea is cockeyed."

"In them? Nothing exists in them but energy, and talent ground down to a blunt weapon for fighting through the mob," Fain said. "None of the important people in Hollywood are capable of an ordinary human reaction. They can simulate anything—pleasure, anger, courtesy, amusement, love, hate, fear, grief, humility, awe, graciousness—and in a given situation they'll produce the right reaction. They do so in order not to frighten normal people, in order to get along with them. But their attitudes don't mean anything, any more than the praying of a praying mantis does. Among themselves they have a mantis language, and a peculiar mantis humor, mostly faintly obscene parodies of ordinary human conduct. You should have heard Travis Jablock appealing to my patriotism to get me to change the end of my book. It was heartrending. The two producers and the director in the room with us were loving it. After a while I realized what was actually happening. Jablock was telling a mantis joke to me. In effect he was saying, 'Come on, Fain, you're too talented to be one of *them*, you're a mantis, admit it and let's make a deal.' . . . Say, is this agent Lax as redhot as Frieda says?" Fain shifted in an instant from the far-off burning look of an angry prophet to a guileful grin.

Through this farrago Hawke kept thinking one thing: Was this young man sleeping with Frieda Winter? He had the looks, he talked well, he had the glamour of his triumph; and Hawke recalled with stabbing pain how readily Mrs. Winter could decide to give herself. He had wanted to break with her; he still did; but to lose her like this, to a more successful writer!

He said as calmly as he could, "Haven't you sold your book to the movies yet? You have the biggest smash in years."

"Army cooperation, Hawke! Three million dollars' worth of free scenery and extras! They won't touch my book if it outsells the Bible, at least that's what they say, if they don't get Army cooperation. Can Lax lick that?"

"He's damned good, Fain."

Fain said, "Agents have always struck me as a low form of lice. I've

gotten on very well without one. I brought my book into a publishing office in a satchel and they read it and bought it."

"That's what I did. All the same, you need an agent here, believe me. And in New York too, I'm beginning to think. An agent is an interpreter who talks mantis language, let's say."

The author glanced up at him with a quick, melancholy, extremely winning smile. "That's good. Maybe I'll try Lax."

"I don't know why you should bother, right now," Hawke said. "Haven't you got all the money you can use for the next ten years?"

Fain laughed, biting the nails of one hand. "You know better than that, Hawke. It's all rolling in this year and flooding down the tax toilet. I have the distinguished privilege of pulling the chain. Whatever is left will hardly be enough to divvy up among my needy relatives, who've been around my head like bees since my book was published. I come from a big prolific tribe of congenital paupers. I must take care of all of them. I'm doing it, by God, I'm the Fain who's made money and it's only right. You can anticipate what's happened. I'm hated by ten uncles and cousins who used to like me. They think I'm a stingy lying son of a bitch."

"Where did you meet Mrs. Winter?" Hawke said clumsily, unable to help it.

"God, isn't she a fantastic woman? At a party. If I were ten years older I'd shoot her husband and marry her. What's her husband like? Have you met him?"

"Yes. A man in Wall Street with a white mustache who has made money, who is making money, and who will make money."

Fain laughed. "You and I ought to have a couple of beers some night."

"Let's peel off tonight after the food, if it ever comes."

"Not tonight," Fain said, seeing Frieda come out of the library with Lax, and beckon to him. "Some other time. Excuse me."

Hawke watched Frieda slip her arm through Fain's and walk off between him and Lax, talking earnestly to the author, her head down, her eyes wide. She did not even glance at her lover—or her ex-lover; Hawke had no idea what he was.

4

Dinner was announced. It was a quarter to eleven. Candlelit tables for four or six people filled the dim dining room and spilled out into the garden. Hawke shuffled in to dinner alone. He saw Frieda seat herself at a table with Fain, Lax, the cowboy star and his wife; there was no room for him there, and nobody had invited him anyway. He ended up at a small table out in the garden beside a green-tiled swimming pool. Sunken floodlights brilliantly illuminated the water; he saw a huge

drowned spider, it must have been a tarantula, at the bottom of the pool, standing on its legs as though alive.

One of the famous directors he had met came to his table with the British novelist. They sat, hardly pausing to smile at him, and while they ate they talked of a scheme for turning movie income into capital gains by setting up a Panamanian corporation, exchanging stock with a distributor, and so forth. Hawke tried hard to follow the details but he could not. The novelist described the idea volubly, spreading his long fingers in stiff nervous gestures. The director, grumpy and skeptical, made a dry comment now and then in tough ungrammatical language, with a trace of a European accent. These were men whose work Hawke unreservedly admired. He had read almost all of the Englishman's sardonic books, two of which were famous. The director was an absolute master of the film; he had made dramas, comedies, Bible spectacles, love stories, war epics, and he had won many awards. His name on a film meant almost as much as the name of a star. The two men talked of nothing but money. When for a moment they touched on Fain's novel, the director merely said it would cost a lot to shoot and was a hard one to sell to the movie audience, and the Englishman declared that if the director would pick it up for fifty thousand or so he could easily revise it so that Army cooperation would be forthcoming. They ignored Hawke. But they successfully diverted him from his disturbance over Frieda, and he discovered after a while that he had mechanically helped himself to the food passed on platters by servants, and had eaten a large meal without any real appetite.

He wandered back into the living room to look for Mrs. Winter. A plump young woman in black evening dress, with impressive diamonds at her throat and a sable stole over her arm, stepped in his way and spoke to him. "Hello there! I waved to you before, Mr. Hawke. You didn't see me or you don't remember me."

Her face was not quite strange, but he had to say in embarrassment that he did not know her name. She laughed, unoffended. "When we last met my name was Honor Lesser. I'm married now, and my name's Hauptmann. I'm Anne Karen's daughter."

He recalled now newspaper accounts of her marriage to a wealthy foreigner, and the afternoon in the Waldorf-Astoria when he had seen her in her mother's suite through a fog of fatigue and high fever. Her hands were too plump for a young woman's; small fat white hands. He remembered the hands more than anything else about her. "Of course. I fell in on you out of a blizzard. You saved my life by filling me full of Scotch." She nodded, her eyes bright. He went on, "Is your mother still in India? That's the last Luzzatto told me."

"Oh, yes. She saw a few Indian movies and she has an idea it's going to be the next world center of films. She's there with a battalion of

lawyers buying in on this and that. She'd come back very fast if you finished that script and she liked it."

He told her about Goodhand and she made a disgusted face. "Oh no. Not Sy. He'll just put the withering touch of Hollywood all over it. Why don't you write down the story exactly as you told it to us at the Waldorf? It was wonderful. It gave me the chills."

A burst of music rolled out of the library, sobbing and thunderous. "Ye gods, that sounds like the start of a movie," Hawke said.

"It is," Honor Hauptmann said indifferently. "Movie time. Ferdie has the new Wyler picture, if you want to look at it."

Hawke said, glancing at his watch, "At a quarter to one?"

"That's the after-dinner amusement in this dreary town. A movie, or cards, or bitchy arguing. Are you very annoyed at the fuss everyone's made over Howard Fain tonight? Don't be. People here are impressed only by sales."

"So am I. He wrote a better novel than mine. He's entitled to the fuss."

"Don't be mealy-mouthed," she said sharply. "Yours is a better book and you know it. He'll never write another novel. That one is a freak." She held out her hand. "I've been hanging back to say hello to you. My husband's out getting the car. I hope mother likes your script. You shouldn't really be writing movies."

"I've almost finished a new book."

"Wonderful. I'll have it sent to me. I think you're a great writer."

"Well, bless your heart. The good Lord sent you to this party to say that. Let me shoot my new book to you when it's published. Where do you live?"

An odd shadow passed over her face. "Well, my husband's a Peruvian, but we travel a great deal. It's awfully sweet of you, but please don't bother. I get all the new books from New York by air mail, wherever I am. I read a lot. Goodbye."

5

Frieda was not in the living room among the card players. Nor was she in the library. One broad wood-panelled wall full of leatherbound volumes had vanished, and a railroad train in full color was roaring from one side of the room to the other; then the enormous image of an actor appeared, strolling through the train, to some perky pizzicatto music. This effect of a full-size motion picture in a library was extremely odd, and Hawke now understood better why the room had been made so long and large. It was a camouflaged movie theatre. A shadowy small audience filled the chairs and the sofa. Hawke had not yet shaken

off the yokel thrill at seeing a movie without buying a ticket. He stood in the doorway and watched for a while. The actor's image became much smaller as the camera took the scene from another angle to include a beautiful girl in the train watching him. Then came a closeup of the actor's head, filling the entire wall of the room, as his eyes showed awareness of the beautiful girl. So the film proceeded, and in the strange setting Hawke experienced a raw awareness of the peculiar nature of a movie, as though he were his own great-grandfather seeing this talking moving dissolving play of bright pictures on a wall for the first time. He watched for five minutes, no more, and in that time the film covered events that, in a novel, might have consumed fifty pages. The switching of the camera from one view to another, from night to day, from a city street to a girl's face, might have puzzled his great-grandfather for a few minutes; but so smooth, so palatable, so vivid, so swift was this way of telling a story that surely the old man would have been spellbound. No wonder Hollywood was so full of gold, Hawke thought; it had industrialized storytelling, and freed the eye from the drudging bondage of print . . .

"Youngblood Hawke, my dear fellow," said a marvellously rich voice. He turned, and there was Georges Feydal, slumped on an ottoman near the library door, with a big crystal tumbler of plain whiskey in his hand, blubbery in a shapeless gray suit, his face gray and worn, his thick mouth pouting, his eyes half-closed, his hair rumpled. Beside him in an armchair sat Pierce Carmian, turned out beautifully as always, with gold cufflinks like saucers. The two men had the air of being in the middle of a quarrel. Carmian was chewing the brown knuckles of two slender fingers.

"Do sit down," said Feydal. "Forgive me for not getting up, I'm bone-tired." He held out a thick white manicured hand, and Hawke shook it. "So sorry you had to leave my apartment. Did you enjoy it?"

"Very much," Hawke said. "I think you'll find everything in order."

"You mean Pierce will. You remember Pierce." Carmian barely smiled at Hawke, and Feydal went on in a childish whine, "Unless I can get Frieda to cancel this wretched tour. It's driving me out of my mind, I want to drop it and go back to New York. Frieda has booked me into one sinkhole of a hotel after another, I can't imagine what was on her mind, and these lecture women I have to deal with are masters of incompetence, one town worse than the next. They misspell my name on the playbills, do you know? And would you believe that one of them got up and said before three thousand women in horrible hats in Denver, Colorado, that I would now read from the great Greek dramatist, Molière? If this goes on I shall seriously reconsider my affection for the United States. One should never get too close to what one admires, one begins to see the coarse grain."

He drank all the whiskey in a long swallow. "Now tell me, dear fellow, have you written my play?"

"I'm afraid not."

Carmian said, "Haven't you heard, Georges? Mr. Hawke has succumbed to the fleshpots. He's writing movies."

"Oh, quiet, Pierce, you'd dearly love a pass at the fleshpots yourself, you've tried hard enough to get in. The fleshpots!" The actor smiled at Hawke, his head craftily to one side, and he said with thrilling resonance, " *'We remember when we sat by the fleshpots, the fish which we did eat in Egypt freely, the cucumbers, and the melons, and the leeks, and the onions.'* Mr. Hawke, have you never thought of the Exodus for a play? You write the part of Pharaoh for me—it's the finest villain part in literature except Milton's Satan—and I promise you I'll play Moses off the stage."

"It'll never do, Georges," Carmian said. "Obviously in the Exodus you must play God. That is, if they can build a solid enough Mount Sinai."

Hawke got away from the bickering pair, and went to the garden, where he saw Frieda. But it was impossible to talk to her. She was reclining on a deck chair, her face in shadow, and beside her Howard Fain sat in a yellow garden spotlight, holding forth to a circle of people, including several of the stars, as well as the director and the British novelist. Hawke could tell at once that Fain was drunk, not from a blurriness of speech but by the exaggerated opposite, a stiff precision of words in a rhythmic drawl. Fain was repeating his mantis speech, with some witty embellishments. He was evidently the kind of talker who threw off the best sparks when he had many listeners. Hawke was appalled at Fain's temerity in insulting these Hollywood people to their faces. But then he saw they were prodding him on with questions that were eager and not hostile. They seemed to enjoy the tongue-lashing. They looked at each other, and laughed, and appeared refreshed at nearly two o'clock in the morning. Fain, stimulated more and more, drew superb word pictures of the American cinema that might have been, and that could never be. He was wonderfully good-looking, his thick hair tumbled this way and that as he talked, his negligent commanding looks and gestures dominated this party of rich and powerful people though he was so young, and so pallid, and not big, and dressed like a workman. Hawke strained his eyes to see Frieda's face, but he could not. He could well imagine, however, how she must be basking in Fain's performance.

"Brilliant, isn't he?" Pierce Carmian said at his elbow. He and Feydal had come into the garden together. Carmian leaned against a tree. Feydal slouched on a cushion by the pool, his eyes closed, and he seemed on the verge, now and then, of toppling into the water.

"Damned brilliant," Hawke muttered.

"You'll have uphill work against him. I wouldn't want such competition myself."

Hawke glanced at him angrily, detecting a reference to Frieda. Carmian added with a grin, "I'm glad I'm not a novelist."

The change in the talk came subtly; a slight sharpening of the questions, then a goad or two about best-sellers that had Fain momentarily floundering. As soon as his stride broke the British novelist took up the conversation and praised Fain's candid and merciless analysis of the sordid film industry, for which, in all truth, there was little to be said. While he granted that movies were all artistic failures, he hoped Mr. Fain would agree that at least a few were honorable failures, that the makers had really tried. Fain grudgingly assented to this. Then the Englishman wanted to know, did Fain consider his own best-selling book an artistic success or a failure?

"A failure of course," Fain growled. "A failure that somehow worked. But I'm still young."

"Yes, you are young, Mr. Fain." The way it was said drew a laugh. "Now let's talk about the novel field. Won't you name a few artistic successes for us?"

Fain started to speak; he was clever, he saw the trap, and he stopped; but then he did name several books into the heavy silence. The carnage began. The Englishman tore apart the books Fain had cited, forcing the young man to defend absurd weaknesses in the stories. He caught Fain in errors of fact. He knew the books better than Fain did. He did such a brilliant job on *Moby Dick,* quoting some of the more stilted poetic passages by heart, that he had all the listeners laughing uproariously. Fain became rattled; he withdrew *Moby Dick* from the list of artistic successes. Thereupon the Englishman quickly rounded on him. "On the contrary, that is the one genuine success you did name. Defects and failure are not the same thing." He fired the names of other books at the young man, uncovering the fact that Fain's reading, especially in French and British nineteenth-century novelists, was very weak. He made the young man look so foolish with this—the women were giggling openly— that Fain at last broke out, "What the hell does it matter what I've read or haven't read? An artist should be able to create if nobody ever created before him. That's the privilege of Adam."

"Very good, Mr. Fain. But I think you'll grant that a novelist named John Dos Passos wrote half a dozen excellent novels in the exact style you have chosen, about the time you were born. You say movies are imitative. If Mr. Dos Passos had not done his work—if you had not had him to imitate—how would you have known where to begin?"

All the faces turned to Fain. He looked groggy, and he said nothing at all. He stared at the Englishman and said nothing. Perhaps half a minute went by. The Englishman said kindly, "I think in this case we'll

have to say Mr. Dos Passos was Adam." His face crinkled in mischief. "But we'll certainly grant that you are Abel."

The timing of the play on words, climaxing the rout of the young man, brought a buzz and a laugh, and the director reached over to slap the Englishman's back.

Frieda Winter's voice slashed out of the shadow, clear and sharp. "Philip, you make me sick. Howard Fain has written the most tremendous American novel in years. It's a critical success, and it's going like hell in the bookstores. It's just been published in England, your own home ground, Philip, and it's a smash there too, as you undoubtedly know, if you still take the *Times Literary Supplement* and the *New Statesman*. Howard got his material by being captured in the Battle of the Bulge and spending half a year in a German prison camp. You haven't published anything in nine years. You sat out the war beside your pool in West-wood, adapting tearjerker novels for Lana Turner. I think that sums up the discussion."

After a still moment somebody in the darkness said, "Wow."

Fain said quickly, "Frieda, Philip Widdleston is a superb novelist whose work I've admired for years, and whose style I can't begin to approach."

The Englishman said with a forced laugh, "That's handsome, Mr. Fain. I did think we were just having a bit of fun. I suppose I needn't dwell on the heart condition which prevented my gathering material in the Bulge or on any other battle ground, an opportunity I do envy you." He got up and walked into the house. The conversation broke up into a delighted multiple noise. It was very late, it was almost three, but those who had stayed were agreeing it had been worth it. They had been rewarded not with one cutting to pieces, but with two.

Carmian said to Hawke, as he lit a cigarette, "It would seem perfectly obvious that Mrs. Winter has moved up to the top of the best-seller list."

All the complicated feelings in Hawke's breast, all his sickness over Frieda's revealing spring to Fain's defense, all his rage, all his excitement, all his humiliation, now became resolved in one simple, grand, exhilarating release. He did not stop to think. He scooped up Pierce Carmian by the shoulders and knees in an easy powerful movement, like a vaudeville performer. He took two strides to the side of the pool, and he threw the playwright far out into the middle of the brilliant green water.

It happened so fast, and with so little struggling, that most of the people in the garden were taken by surprise when a towering sparkling splash leaped twenty feet out of the pool; though one or two of them may have heard Carmian's belated "Hey!" when for a moment he was flying through the air. Here was a new treat, a fully-clothed man flailing and gasping out curses in the pool! They swarmed around the edge, stretching hands to Carmian, all talking at once. Georges Feydal, who alone had

seen and heard the entire transaction, sat laughing cross-legged on his cushion like a demented Buddha. "Oh lovely! Oh lovely, lovely! Magnifique!" Hawke was generally ignored for the moment—he had stepped back into shadow—but Frieda was at his side almost at once.

"Now what on earth did you do that for, you big wild ape?"

Hawke, feeling wonderful to his very bones, but also somewhat embarrassed at his unthinking act, said, "Let's go home, Frieda. It's late."

"Go home? What are you talking about? Are you drunk? I'm staying at the Beverly Wilshire."

"Well, let's go there. I have no prejudices."

Carmian had slopped his way to a ladder, and two men were helping him climb out. He was saying shrilly over the din, "My lighter, that's a very valuable gold lighter, does anybody see it?" And a woman shrieked, "There it is, on the bottom. Right by that horrible spider."

Frieda said in a voice like a hiss, "Bloody, why did you throw Pierce in the pool? Now you *tell* me."

Hawke mumbled, abashed, "Said something about you and Fain."

"Oh Christ." She took his hand and led him almost at a run out of the garden, where all the remaining guests at the party were now surrounding the dripping playwright. She plunged into the back of the house and entered a hall which ran past the library, where the huge colored movie was dancing and talking on the wall to an empty room. "There are columnists here, you imbecile," she said. "My God, why did I ever get mixed up with a Jukes out of the hills? Where do you live? Oh, yes, Rainbow's End. Have you got a hat or anything?" Seeing that there was nobody in the living room she darted across it, still dragging him, his big hand in her tight little grip. She whisked a fur out of a hall closet and was outside the house with Hawke in tow, and there was Ferdie Lax, trotting through the car port, grinning broadly. "Leaving so soon, children?"

"Oh God, Ferdie, what a mess," Frieda said. "Where's my car? What the hell was it? I just rented the goddamned thing. Oh yes, green Cadillac, there it is. I hate green cars. Can you still drive, you Neanderthal, or are you too drunk?"

"I'm quite sober," Hawke said as she gave him keys.

Lax said, "It's okay, Frieda. He tripped and fell in the pool. That's what he said, that's the story. He's in my bedroom cleaning up. Hawke, you crazy son of a bitch, thanks a lot. The party was dying a little bit there. That boy Fain didn't last long against Phil Widdleston."

"I think it was disgusting the way those people led the boy on. Get in the car, Arthur!"

Lax said, "Why, Frieda, he was setting Hollywood straight in one easy lesson. You know how eager to learn everybody is out here."

"Yes, well, I wasn't going to let Philip get away with it," Frieda said,

getting into the car. "Phil Widdleston, of all people! Howard Fain is the greatest talent in America right now, except maybe this brainless elephant here . . . What's the matter with you? Start the car!"

"Where does the key go in a Cadillac?" Hawke muttered, fumbling.

"Here, Tarzan," she snapped, taking the key from him, jamming it into the ignition slot, and starting the car with a swift jab of her high-heeled shoe on the gas. The roar of the motor seemed to relax her. She sat back and laughed, and turned to Lax. "You'll take care of Howard? That boy has had far too much to drink. I drove him here."

"I'll put him to bed myself. He's at the Beverly Wilshire, isn't he?"

"Yes. Oh lord, here they come," she exclaimed, as the front door of the house opened and several people streamed through, laughing and shouting. "Take off, Bloody!" Off they went, in a roar and a scrabble of gravel.

6

"*Now* where are you going?" she said after they drove for a few minutes in silence and he made a left turn.

"Beverly Wilshire."

"Then what?"

"I don't know. Nothing. I'm taking you to your hotel."

"You'll never get a cab this time of the morning. You take yourself to Rainbow's End. Then I'll drive on back to my hotel."

"Anything you say. I can walk to Rainbow's End. I walked out here."

"Yes, I know, you're the great philosophic prowler, you've made my feet blister often enough. It's after three. Keep driving."

They were at his place in five minutes. Neither of them had said a word. She sat against the door, her arms folded, the scarf of black lace on her head framing her white face in the passing flares of the street lamps. He pulled the car to the curb and turned off the motor.

"Well, good night," she said.

Hawke said, "How long are you going to be here?"

"Till Sunday."

"Let's have lunch or dinner or something."

"I'd like that very much, but I've got a lot of business to do. We'll see. I don't know whether Georges will even be human to me after you threw Pierce in the pool."

"Why, he loved it, Frieda. He was laughing like a crazy man."

"Yes, that sounds like him. Look, you fool, you didn't have to defend my honor. What exactly did Pierce say?"

"Nothing worth repeating."

"Bloody, what did he say?"

"That you had moved to the top of the best-seller list," Hawke mumbled.

Frieda looked surprised, then she threw back her head and laughed. The scarf dropped from her head. The neon rainbow flashing on and off a few feet from them bathed her face in soft colors. The car smelled very new, and there was Frieda's unchanging scent faint through the new-car odor. She said, "Is that all? It isn't even particularly clever, and it's quite harmless. You ducked poor Pierce for nothing."

"When did you get here, Frieda?"

"About midnight last night."

"Why didn't you call me?"

"Dear, I know that's your hour for the creation of new American prose. I wouldn't have disturbed you for worlds."

Hawke said awkwardly, "This Fain is quite a boy."

"He's wonderful. A Byron out of Staten Island."

Hawke said, "It's bad enough he's got such a smash hit. Why does he have to be so good-looking, and such a brilliant talker to the bargain?"

"Now, Arthur. You've done a bit of talking in your time. This was his night. He paid for it, poor thing."

"You certainly clawed up that Englishman who went for him."

"Don't you think he had it coming?"

"You seem to know Fain pretty well."

"I met him at a party, the way I met you. I put him in touch with Ferdie. That's how this party came about. Ferdie's done such a good job for you, and Howard really needs help. He talks bravely but he's stumbling and he's terribly scared. He can't get his new book started. He needs distraction. A movie job would be excellent for him, just for a while."

"I've almost finished my new book."

"Oh, you, why not? The juggernaut crashing along."

"I haven't had a big success to panic me. That helps."

She said, "Oh, sure. I'll just bet it worries you dreadfully. You and your Nobel Prize. Look, aren't you tired? I am." She yawned, looked slyly at him, and laughed. "What's the cross-examination for? Don't tell me you're jealous of Howard Fain?"

"No. It did strike me that you were ignoring me rather pointedly at that party."

"Come now, my friend! Who did what? Every time I glanced at you, it seemed, you looked away as though I had snakes for hair. I couldn't fathom it, but I figured, well, if that's how our Kentucky genius wants it, all right, I'll survive."

"You seemed so damned thick with Fain. It was news to me, that's all. It's happened mighty fast."

"Now look, Mr. Youngblood Hawke, you and I had the loveliest fare-

well, don't you remember? I behaved like an angel up to the last second. I may have closed the door a bit hard."

"Do you like Fain?"

"Why, I think he's enchanting. Except he makes me feel motherly, and I don't like that. You didn't make me feel motherly . . . You have a frown on that big phiz of yours, Arthur, like an oncoming tornado . . . It was more or less accidental that Howard and I came on the same plane. Georges was sending up distress howls and I had to come anyhow. I knew Howard was on his way out so we came together. Anything wrong with that? He's wonderful company, though it's mostly a monologue, and a little too much about sex. He has rather jejune ideas on the all-importance of sex."

"With which you wholly disagree."

"It has its place. There are more important things."

"For instance?"

"Love. I'm not sure Howard knows much about that. Or you either. Young men generally find out about love after it's slipped through their fingers. Then if they're lucky they get a second chance, but that doesn't happen often enough to make this one big happy world. And that concludes the evening's entertainment. I'm perishing for sleep. Good night. Call me about dinner." She moved as though to shift into the driver's seat, and reached across him to open his door.

He caught her hand. So they sat, the touch of their hands stopping them both in their positions for a moment. What he wanted to know most desperately, of course, was whether Frieda had been sleeping with Howard Fain. But it was impossible for him to put the question direct.

And suppose he found the hardihood to croak out the question, what answer could he hope for? She would get angry, or she would humiliate him further with her slippery mockery. He would never know the truth, never, unless a drunken Fain some day told him, and even then he would have no way to prove it and no sure reason for believing it. Nothing was easier than for a woman to betray a man, nothing was harder than to find it out beyond a doubt. Hawke understood in this moment, for the first time, what the relationship of Frieda to her husband probably was.

He said, "Come in for a drink."

Her eyes opened wide, her brows rose in a satiric arch. Her mouth parted in a slow smile that showed all her teeth. "That, Bloody, my boy, is just exactly what you don't want."

"I do want it."

"Well, I don't. It's hours too late. I'm not thirsty."

"One drink. Just to show there are no hard feelings."

"Well, you did defend my honor, didn't you? And nearly ruined my reputation in the process. I guess I should toast my shining knight of the

Two Left Feet. All right, one drink." He eagerly opened his door and she laid her hand on his arm. "Better pull the car into the lot. All kinds of drunks roar along Sunset Boulevard this time of night, or is it morning? I don't want a wrecked rented Cadillac on my hands."

Obediently he started the motor, his arm a-tingle where she had touched him. "Good old Frieda. Presence of mind, no matter what."

She said, "One drink, exactly that, nothing more."

"One drink, Frieda."

Jeanne was not coming until Monday, he thought. This thing hadn't been planned. It had just happened.

7

Hawke sat at his desk, and Frieda sat near him in an armchair under a reading lamp, sewing buttons on a shirt. A pile of shirts lay on the floor at her feet, a smaller pile on the table beside her. It was after midnight of the following night. They had eaten a tremendous dinner at a Polynesian restaurant, and they had made love, and now Hawke was attending to his work, with perhaps a little less dash than usual, but at the regular rate of four pages an hour. Fay Pulver's heels ticked on the walk outside; ticked and stopped. Looking out from his lamplit desk, Hawke could see the shadowy form of Fay, halted near the window. He was afraid for a moment that the idiot would tap. But obviously she saw Frieda. The ticking began again, and she melted into the dark. Hawke put down the pen and yawned, thinking that perhaps Frieda ought to have met Fay Pulver. It was probably owing to Fay that she was in his villa. Had he not written that long lonesome letter after the flat business in Fay's bedroom, there would have been no opening for Frieda to start working her way back to him.

He still wondered—and he supposed he would always wonder—to what extent Frieda's appearance at the Lax party on the arm of Howard Fain had been a planned provocation. How could he know? She had fallen back into his arms, and now there was no more question of Howard Fain, if there had ever been a question. Now she was mildly hinting at postponing her return to New York for a few days, and he was mildly evading a response. She was leaving Sunday, and Jeanne was coming Monday; a damnable close call as it was. An old rhyme of which his mother was very fond was running in his mind these days:

> It is good to be merry and wise,
> It is good to be honest and true.
> It is good to be off with the old love
> Before you are on with the new.

Frieda was the old love—though not so very old in the elapsed time of their romance!—and in all truth he wanted to be off with her. He had tried. Her incursion into his life now was not really welcome, though their moments of love-making yielded much of the familiar sweetness. The thing had happened. But it had not changed his desire for Jeanne Green. He was absolutely determined that Frieda should leave Sunday as planned.

She saw he had paused in his work. "Will you please tell me why not one of those shirts has a button at the collar? What is this fatal ailment that afflicts your shirts?"

"I have a way of tearing my collar open when I'm working. Look, I can sew on those buttons myself. I was planning to do it Sunday."

"Oh sure. You'd pile up those shirts until you had to back out of this villa and then you'd just go and rent another one and start filling it with dirty shirts minus collar buttons." She had to push a letter on the table aside to make room for a finished shirt. The letter fell to the floor. She picked it up. "Sorry."

"Mama," Hawke said. "I've got to write to her before I turn in."

"Oh? Your mother?" Frieda looked at the envelope with candid curiosity. "Go ahead and read it."

"Oh, may I? I'm a terrible snoop." She snuggled down in the armchair and held the letter close to her eyes. "So, your sister's getting married!" she said after a moment. "You'll go to the wedding, of course."

"Yes. I'm hoping my job here will be done by then, otherwise I'll fly down and fly back."

"She's marrying that strange-looking man she brought to dinner, isn't she? I hope you don't mind my saying he looks strange."

"Not at all. I always expect him to take off his wig and his face and turn out to be Fredric March or somebody. But I guess John will never take off that face."

"Paul was impressed with him, you know. Said he knew something about investments."

"Well, his family runs a small private bank in Ohio somewhere."

"Isn't this nice of your mother!" Frieda exclaimed. She read aloud,

—About inviting friends of yours in New York I don't know, that's up to you. That Mrs. Winter was awfully kind to us and she seems right fond of you and of course we'd love to have her and her husband if she'd come, she's quite the grand lady, maybe she'd get a kick out of seeing a back-country town like Hovey at that—

"Indeed I would," Frieda said. "Are you inviting me?"

"You're invited, but I'm not sure you want to expose yourself to my relatives, Frieda. They're a peculiar lot. Especially on my mother's side. Some of my distant relatives chew tobacco and are handier with a shotgun

than a fountain pen. I have a second cousin who shot an off-duty police-man in a tavern. Proved self-defense and got off with two years, but he did it. He'll be there."

"You're perfectly capable of that yourself." Frieda read on and then said, "Is that this Cousin Glenn that your mother seems to be suing?"

"Oh no, that's the genteel side of my family, my father's side. West Virginia originally, the kind that always goes to college, that has the money and all that. It's a nice point of etiquette mama raises, isn't it? Do you invite a branch of a family to a wedding when you're suing them for cheating you of a million dollars? Is blood thicker than money?"

"A *million dollars?*" Frieda smiled incredulously, still reading.

"It comes to that. That or more. In my mother's mind only, I hasten to add. The whole thing is mad, like most family squabbles, especially in the eastern counties of Kentucky."

"Well now, look here!" Frieda dropped the letter in her lap. "Why on earth didn't you tell me you had a birthday on Sunday?" She took off her glasses. "That's wonderful. The older you get the better I like it."

Hawke had forgotten the last paragraph in the letter, or he would not have allowed Frieda to read it.

She said, "I am going to cook a turkey, right in that kitchen."

"Don't. Birthdays depress me."

"Arthur, you still don't know how well I can cook. Sausages and corn fritters are nothing. I'll show you, my boy, I'll show you something."

"But when does your plane leave? Can you hang around on Sunday long enough to make a dinner?"

She took a fistful of his hair in her hand and yanked his head back and forth. "All right, my scribbling friend, I know I slow you up and you can't wait to get rid of me. Have no fear. There's a terrible flap going on in Hartford, the two leads in the show are threatening to quit, and I have to leave Sunday at five, no matter what, so you've nothing to worry about. Okay?"

"Look, Frieda, I'm all for roast turkey, any time."

She slipped the letter into its envelope and dropped it on his desk. "Now tell me about that lawsuit."

It was one o'clock; he had at least five more pages to write. He gave her a bare, hurried description of the dispute over the mine on French-man's Ridge. Frieda said, "It can't be that simple. You're making your mother out a lunatic."

"Not at all, my mother is clever, a lot cleverer than I am, probably, about money. This is an obsession, it focuses all her family resentments like a boil coming to a head. My only objection is that I'll end up paying the lawyers and spending weeks in court, and all for a fantasy. She hired some ignorant yahoo out of the back hills to start the suit because she said otherwise the statute of limitations would shut her out from ever

collecting. What she's hoping for is that somehow, somewhere, sometime, I'll get a brilliant big-city lawyer who'll come riding into Hovey on a white horse, and bring the rich Hawkes grovelling to their knees, and make the poor Hawkes millionaires. Actually she always wanted me to be a lawyer, and do you know she wrote me two weeks ago that it's not too late for me to go to law school? Writing is an uncertain business, she pointed out. Look how my novel has flopped. When my mother has an obsession in her head there is no blasting it out."

Frieda came to him, smiling, and brushed the hair from his brow. "Has it ever occurred to you that there's something slightly obsessive in sitting up night after night filling long yellow pages with scrawls when you're making eight hundred dollars a week, when you're—what, twenty-seven?—when your whole life is ahead of you?"

"Oh, I readily grant you a writer must be crazy. I'd better return to my obsession unless you want me to get dangerous."

"At the moment I think I would rather like it if you got dangerous," Frieda said. "Sort of dangerous."

The remark did not surprise Hawke; he was getting to know Frieda's little ways. He laid aside his pen and responded readily, if at first a bit dutifully. But then the enchantment was as strong as ever. . . .

She said with mock distress, "I've committed the sin of sins. I've broken into your routine."

He only kissed her. She said, "Now I'm going back to my hotel. Go to sleep, for heaven's sake. Don't drag yourself back to that damned desk. Tomorrow's another day. You'll overtake Balzac in due course."

"All right, Frieda."

"Tomorrow at noon I'll come for you, and we'll go to the Farmer's Market and pick out the best turkey in Los Angeles for your birthday. I'll finish those shirts tomorrow too."

8

The next day, Saturday, they went to the Farmer's Market and Frieda bought food for an hour, and—as Hawke complained—for an army. When they came back to the villa the stuff overflowed the small refrigerator and indeed all but blocked passage in and out of the kitchen. "It doesn't matter," Frieda said. "Between today and tomorrow nothing will spoil. Now get out of here. You can write in the daytime too, can't you? I have about three hours of preliminaries here, then we'll leave everything and go to that dinner party Georges has arranged. It might be fun."

She looked so contented and pretty as she put on an apron and went humming about her task, that Hawke reached out a long arm to embrace her. She knocked it aside with a deft strong chop of her hand. "Out of my

way, masher, I'm busy." So he went to his desk and worked, and after
a while some wonderful smells drifted out of the kitchen. It was near
nightfall when Frieda emerged dishevelled and still humming, her forehead moist. "Well, so much for that. Keep your big hands and your
big nose out of everything. Leave it all as is, until tomorrow. I'm going
back to the hotel for a siesta and a clean-up. I've earned both. Pick me
up about eight. Wear your dark suit, of course. Maybe you should have a
snooze too. It'll probably be a long night. God, I'm sweating like a horse."
She found her purse, gave him a kiss like a commuting husband late for
the train, and left.

The dinner party was at the home of a producer, one of Feydal's
Hollywood friends. He saw many of the same faces he had seen at Ferdie
Lax's party, including Ferdie, and it seemed to him that the agent all at
once looked exceptionally sleepy when he met Hawke and Mrs. Winter
together, though his greeting was affable enough. Howard Fain was not
there; Ferdie told him that he had placed Fain at Paramount, where he
was going to attempt an adaptation of *The Iliad*. "Five thousand a
week," Lax said. "Which is good and bad. At that rate he has to deliver
fast. At eight hundred you can sort of slop along, but of course I couldn't
let a blue chip like Fain go to work for eight hundred. The price of
fame."

Georges Feydal came late to the party, still aglow from the thunderous
ovation of a good Saturday night audience, and minus Pierce Carmian.
Pierce had gone to New York to possess himself of Feydal's apartment.
Whatever Feydal's complaints over the tour, Frieda had smoothed them
all away. After dinner he captured Hawke, took him to the billiard room,
and over a game of pool he improvised an idea for a play, based on the
last hundred pages of *Alms for Oblivion*. It struck Hawke as excellent.
He could see the play in every scene; he was sure he could write it in a
week, and he did not see how it could fail. "Just the aunt's death, dear
fellow," Feydal said. "Just the death, and the scrabble over the money.
It's the whole secret of playwriting, to raise your curtain in the last throes
of a long story, at the very crisis. Just the death."

"I've sold the damned thing to pictures already," Hawke said. "If not
for that—"

"I know you have, Hawke," Feydal said, neatly sinking a two-cushion
shot with a dart of his fat arm. "This is a very complicated industry.
For every hundred scenarios that are written maybe one film is shot, maybe
not even that. Bear in mind what I've told you. Just the death. If you do
write it I want it. I can't play the aunt, alas, which is the jammy part.
But I think I'd make a fair Uncle Theodore, I do the heavy business
pretty well, and I would dearly love to direct it. Just the death."

Frieda came and watched the game. When it was over she led Hawke
off without ceremony. Feydal beamed after them like an old priest.

"It's five past twelve," she said, taking him to a small bar in an anteroom. "You're twenty-seven, my boy. We're not going to make a public fuss of it, but you and I are having a drink on it here and now, then we're leaving."

They went to her hotel. Frieda had a large suite with a balcony that looked over the great flat expanse of the Los Angeles lights. It was a night without smog and without a moon. The stars blazed thickly in the black sky. Because it was, in his own mind, a night of farewell—not only to Frieda, but to his first twenty-seven years, to his stumbling youth, and he hoped to youthful mistakes—he gave himself to the moment without reserve, without a second thought. When a ghostly sliver of the dying moon came up with the dawn, he went back to his villa.

He was actually carrying the steaming turkey from the kitchen to the sideboard the next afternoon, with Frieda behind him telling him not to let the juices drip from the carving plate, when the telephone rang. He set the bird down and answered it.

"Hi there, Youngblood Hawke," Jeanne Green said in his ear. "Happy birthday."

It should not have been such an unexpected thing, that Jeanne should telephone her good wishes, but it staggered him. "Hello, Jeanie, thanks," he said. "Good God, you sound so close. Where are you?"

"I'm pretty close," Jeanne said. "I'm in the office of Rainbow's End."

"*Here?* You're here?" He stood there, astonishment and consternation written all over his face, while she cheerfully explained that she had been unable to get a plane reservation for Monday so she had come a day earlier after all. "So, if you're sunk in the birthday blues maybe I can still help out. I've brought some pretty good news."

"Where will you stay? Have you got a hotel room?"

"Villa Ferrara, a few blocks from here. I drove by here and I just jammed on the brakes to say hello."

At this moment Frieda came out of the kitchen and said quite loud, "Who is it? Is it Georges?"

And Hawke, whose presence of mind was utterly gone—and he had never had too much with women—said without covering the telephone, "It's Jeanie Green, my editor at Hodge Hathaway. She's here, in the lobby."

Jeanne said, "Oh, is somebody there with you?"

Simultaneously Frieda said, "Oh, Jeanne Green! Well, how nice. Tell her to come on over to the villa."

Now Hawke covered the mouthpiece and whispered, though it made no sense to whisper, "Don't be idiotic, Frieda!"

"Don't you be idiotic. There's turkey enough for a regiment. She's a very nice girl. I like her."

Jeanne said, in a somewhat sharper tone, "Hello, Arthur? Are you still there? I seem to have interrupted you, I'm sorry. I'll ring you tomorrow."

The devilish thing about a telephone is that it demands immediate answers. If you are confronting somebody face to face you can smile, you can move around, you can light a cigarette, you can find a dozen ways to stall while you collect your thoughts. The telephone is a pair of black holes; one talks, the other waits. Hawke in the instant before he answered, realized that he was afraid of Jeanne, afraid of letting her see him with Frieda, and in a perverse impulse of defiance he babbled, "What do you mean, tomorrow! God, I'm glad to know you're here, Jeanne. Come on over here and have a drink."

"Are you sure?" Jeanne might better have driven on to her hotel, but her curiosity was aroused.

"Of course. Number 4, to the left. Come on."

"Well, I'd love to say hello, just for a minute. And I do have some news that'll cheer you up. Number 4, you say. Coming."

Hawke hung up, and almost at once heard Jeanne's steps on the concrete walk. He barely had time to think what a catastrophic fool he had been, how easily he could have said he was taking a shower, or working, or anything, anything! Frieda leaned in the doorway of the kitchen, arms folded, a quiet smile on her flushed face. The mountainous brown turkey smoked on the sideboard, and champagne cooled in a bucket beside it. The table was set for two with shrimp cocktails and a great centerpiece of roses. There was a knock at the door. Hawke went to open it. He was in his shirtsleeves.

Jeanne Green, chic and beautiful in a dark blue linen suit, went through the next few shattering minutes exactly as though she were an editor calling on an author. She was all smiles as she greeted Frieda Winter. She exclaimed in admiration over the turkey. She declined Frieda's invitation that she join them at dinner, declined again when Frieda pressed her; then when Hawke added his urging, she directed a short glance at him and accepted—"providing," she said to Frieda, "that I can help."

"By all means," Frieda said, "anything to keep that lumbering ox out of the kitchen. But right now everything's about ready."

"Well, there'll be dishes and things," Jeanne said.

"Oh, of course," Frieda said. "Excuse me, I won't be a minute," and she disappeared into the kitchen.

Jeanne deliberately stripped the gloves off her smooth, slender, beautiful young hands, and lit a cigarette. "Well, if you're interested in good news—" she said.

"Oh yes, the good news. Of course I am. Not that Jay Prince has released me. I knew that when it happened."

"No, not that," Jeanne said. "Ross Hodge has had his sales department making a careful survey all over the country on *Alms for Oblivion.*

Reorders don't always tell the story right away. The real question is about inventories, and rates of sale in the department stores and such. I've been keeping tabs on it, and before I left I talked to our sales manager. Reorders are going to start pouring in about ten days from now. The book has caught. Fred thinks it will go forty thousand or better. Most rental libraries have waiting lists and are adding copies. You see? Even *Alms for Oblivion* is a hit."

"What do you mean, even *Alms for Oblivion?*" Hawke said.

"There's no question about *Chain of Command*," Jeanne said, wondering at her own ability to keep talking through a knotted throat, and to fight back the tears. "It will be one of the greatest successes in publishing history. Especially if I can get you to cut Chapter 47 in its entirety. Good God, how could you write a scene in Heaven, in *Heaven* for Pete's sake, after Iwo Jima?"

"It was meant to be ironic," Hawke said.

"All the irony is in the battle scene. Leave out Heaven, please."

"I'll look at it again. I guess you're right."

Frieda came out of the kitchen and put dishes and cruets on the table. Then she stepped down into the living room. "Dinner's on, birthday boy," she said. "Open the champagne."

"I have one more piece of news," Jeanne said, and this was truly fresh news, perhaps two minutes old. "But this is about me. I'm going to marry Karl Fry."

She had the satisfaction—for whatever it was worth—of seeing that the words struck to Hawke's heart and sickened him. His face visibly went white. "Well, that's great," he mumbled, and he turned away and plodded to the champagne, adding, "we all have a lot to drink to, it seems."

Frieda clucked and twittered about the marriage announcement, overflowing with sweet pleasure at the news, while Hawke opened the wine. Meantime Jeanne was thinking, insofar as she could think at all, that she would have to telephone Karl almost at once to inform him about their marriage.

The three of them stood in the center of the living room, brimming champagne glasses in hand. Frieda said, "Well, shall I propose it? To your birthday, Arthur, and to the happiness of Karl and Jeanne."

Hawke said, looking into Jeanne's eyes, "To your happiness, Jeanne, all your life long."

"To Youngblood Hawke," said Jeanne. She tossed off her wine, and turned to Frieda. "It was so nice of you to ask me to stay. I find I'm terribly hungry, after all. I'm starved."

And the three sat down to dinner. The turkey was superb. Anything Frieda Winter did, she did thoroughly and well.

Part Three
1948–1950

CHAPTER TEN

1

ALMS FOR OBLIVION climbed near the top of best-seller lists, and hung there for months, selling almost fifty thousand copies. Its rise was slow, and nearly a year went by before it was at the peak of its success. Ross Hodge therefore put publication of *Chain of Command* over into the spring of 1949. He expected great things of the Iwo Jima novel, as he called it, and he judged it poor policy to glut the bookstores with two long books by the same author at the same time. Most people only became aware of *Alms for Oblivion* during 1948. It seemed, when the new book came out, as though Youngblood Hawke had composed two enormous novels one right after the other, in the space of a year or so. His achievement was not that spectacular, but it was striking enough. *Chain of Command* became, as Jeanne had predicted, one of the greatest successes in the history of American publishing. It leaped to the top of the lists in five weeks. It stayed there week after week, month after month. Ferdie Lax peddled the movie rights before the novel was published, when a swell of excitement over "the new Hawke" was running through the gossipy entertainment world. He got a hundred and twenty-five thousand dollars.

What was equally astonishing, in view of the popular success of *Chain of Command*, was its excellent reception by the critics. There are curious tides in the literary life, and they are magnified in the United States, a land given to sudden passing extremes of opinion. Perhaps the battering of *Alms for Oblivion* had put the critics in a forgiving mood. Perhaps Quentin Judd's sober advocacy of Hawke in *Midchannel* had made them think twice. Perhaps Hawke's surprising ability to keep working in the face of his bad reviews and to produce a new large novel so quickly woke their admiration, for Americans greatly admire gameness and industry. Most likely, however, *Chain of Command* happened to be a good story which struck the right note at the right time.

Hawke had made two decisions when he started to write the book: first, that the Second World War had been, unlike most wars, a just battle in a good cause, not a senseless waste of life and property; second, that since this was so, it ought to be written up not with the disillusion, dirt, and horror that had been both modish and appropriate for books about

the muddy trench stalemates of World War I, but rather in a bold and exciting narrative vein. What made the book more than anything else was a grand panorama of the invasion of Iwo Jima, almost on the scale of Tolstoy's treatment of the battle of Borodino, which Hawke had intently studied. The novel was masculine, violent, sometimes comic, generally cheerful, and full of diverting incidents, with a last sobering turn into tragedy; on the whole a tremendous effort to entertain, and to declare that the war had been a good war. Jeanne cut the first draft almost in half. The tale bowled along from incident to incident, gathering speed and broadening in scope until it burst into the huge picture of Iwo Jima, and closed with the death in action of the mountaineer hero on the slopes of Suribachi. When it was finished Hawke felt a revulsion against the picaresque tone of the book and its verdict on the war. He thought he had composed a shallow rattle-brained yarn, and in one drunken crisis-argument with Hodge and Jeanne and Karl Fry, which lasted until five in the morning, he argued that he ought not to publish *Chain of Command*, ought to burn it. Hodge assured him that he was experiencing the old morbid melancholy of authors on completion of a big task, much like the depression of a woman after childbirth. Indeed Hawke quickly got over this mood. "At least," he said to Ross Hodge next day on the telephone, "to quote the immortal words of Jay Prince, it's a big goddamned doorstopper of a book that'll sell like hell."

"That it is," Hodge said.

"Well, I want the money. Publish it," Hawke said.

"You couldn't stop me," Hodge said.

Hawke resolved that in The American Comedy, the big master work which lay in the future, he would treat the Second World War as it deserved. The avalanche of money and praise that followed on publication buried his worries about the book. Critics took it quite seriously. The New York *Times* said the novel mirrored the American spirit that had won the war. Yet, though he basked in the good reviews and gloated over the money, he had no feeling that he had written a masterpiece, or even that he had arrived. When an interviewer asked him, "Doesn't it trouble you to know that all your books hereafter will be compared to *Chain of Command?*" Hawke blurted innocently, "But they won't. Ah can raht better than that. Ah'm rahtin' betta raht now." It was an unlucky answer, picked up by a national magazine and run as a caption under a revolting picture of Hawke eating an oyster, so: THE WORLD HIS OYSTER— "Ah'm rahtin' betta raht now." But it could not have been more sincere. He had written *Chain of Command* as he had written his first novel, at a rate of three or four thousand words a night, and when it was published he was already well along in his novel of Kentucky politics, *Will Horne*, working at the same rate.

He went on writing *Will Horne* through all the distractions, all the

dissipations, all the extravagances, all the mistakes, and all the nuisances, that make the life of a new celebrity in the United States something like a long Halloween.

The radio and television appearances, the newspaper interviews, the literary luncheons, the cocktail parties and dinner parties given for him by society people who contrived to meet him, were wearing enough, though flattering and heady. It was the army of organizations that threatened to consume him alive. He had never before known how many organizations there were, or how many good causes. A famous playwright telephoned Hawke, a man so celebrated that at first Hawke thought someone was playing a joke on him, and asked him to become co-chairman of the Council of Artists of the Free World. A great actress cornered him at a dinner, and cooed him into agreeing to speak at a luncheon for her favorite charity, a home for crippled children. This kind of thing went on and on. The causes all seemed worthy; some of them were unquestionably vital and urgent. He did not know how to refuse anybody. He met celebrated and rich people at luncheons, councils, board meetings. He was so many times elected a sponsor, a trustee, a director, a governor, that he lost count. Always he was assured that what was wanted was only the luster of his name, the name of the author of *Chain of Command*, and that his artistic life would be inviolate. But it was seldom long before he was summoned to a budget meeting and asked to contribute, on a scale that staggered his Hovey-bred mind. Beyond these face-to-face levies by eminent people, appeals in the mail piled up. Hawke had his mother's streak of social conscience. One night about six months after publication of his book he went through his accounts and found he had written helter-skelter contribution checks totalling about twenty thousand dollars, and yet he knew he had disappointed everybody!

He threw this perplexity into Frieda's lap. She said, "Okay. There was no point in trying to tell you at first, you wouldn't listen, you were lapping up all that attention. If you keep on the way you're going they'll tear you to pieces, your work will stop, and you'll have contributed nothing to anyone. Let my office handle this. Stop answering the telephone. Send us your mail to be screened. Go over these requests once a month, and figure out who you want to give money to and how much. This business will be with you till you die, it's part of being somebody, but you're not supposed to cave in under it. Stop going to meetings. Stop making speeches. New York's full of people who carry on that work. Of course they like fresh faces, but they were doing fine before you came on the scene. Give them money, that's what they need and they're entitled to it. Stick to your work."

He followed her advice, probably just in time to avert a collapse. Through those first infernal six months he had never stopped writing. Whatever his activity of the day and the evening, midnight had found

him at his desk, and he had seldom laid down the pen before the night turned lilac and the sky showed streaks of pink. He slept between four and five hours in the morning. On this scheme he managed to survive. His mother remarked every time she saw him that he looked like death warmed over. People were always commenting on his pallor and his red eyes. But the words kept rolling, and he did not drop dead. He avoided doctors. He was sure they would tell him to change his ways and he didn't want to. He would not even go to an eye doctor though he was troubled by a growing blurriness of his own handwriting and of the print in books, and by headaches that often pounded behind his eyeballs. He took aspirin instead. In the worst of his slumps the hallucinations of smell would come back—sharpened pencils, smoldering hay, rotting leaves —but he schooled himself to ignore them.

One residue of the first fantastic whirl was a house which he now owned, an old brownstone on East Seventy-third Street, only a few blocks away from the Winter home on Fifth Avenue. Meeting famous people, visiting their elegant homes, he had grown ashamed of the pleasant little three-room apartment in Greenwich Village which Frieda had found and furnished for him on his return from Hollywood. He began to talk to real estate brokers in the fashionable neighborhoods, and to inspect penthouses and duplex apartments. Then he became interested in brownstones. This particular house came suddenly on the market at a distress price, and he bid for it and bought it. He said to Frieda, exultantly showing her the contract of purchase, "That's step number one. Three blocks westward and Ah'm home."

"You're a damned fool. You should have invested that money," Frieda said. He paid thirty-five thousand dollars for the house; and when the remodelling bills passed twenty thousand more, with the house still a wreck full of shouting plumbers and plasterers, its bachelor owner—holed up in two garret rooms—began to suspect that Frieda had been right. All the same he went on with the construction, even discovering ominous pleasure in it.

Hawke had a weakness common to authors; he was a master builder at heart. Used to erecting mansions of air in his tales, he found an inebriating excitement in having a real mansion to reconstruct, and the ready cash to do it with. He rejected Frieda's offer to take the task off his hands. He read every book he could find on the remodelling and redecorating of old houses. One of these books mentioned a New York contractor named Charles Yousseloff, who specialized in this kind of work. Hawke hunted up Yousseloff, and found him an immensely engaging man in his fifties, tall, cadaverous, lantern-jawed, with a rich Russian accent and an endless fund of comic stories of his years as an officer in the Czarist army. He engaged the man to do the job, and was delighted with him. Yousseloff had clever ideas and good taste, or at least taste that Hawke admired.

Yousseloff in turn was full of praise of Hawke's ideas, and especially pleased with the furnishings he bought. Hawke was frequenting auction galleries, buying up chairs, breakfronts, paintings, statuary, old chandeliers, even while the house was a gutted shell dripping old plaster and lathes from roof to cellar. New York City was suddenly an Arabian bazaar full of the most ridiculous bargains, opportunities of a lifetime. He and Yousseloff were making over the house in the style of the Colonial homes in Virginia; so he kept buying antiques, and writing out sizable checks week after week.

Yet so much money was coming in that he was able, at the same time, to make plays in the stock market, and to put a large sum in another building venture of Scotty Hoag's. The garret room in the brownstone where he worked was bare, except for his desk and work tools; the other room was full of papers, books, magazines and clothes piled around an army cot, not unlike the loft room of his days of poverty, but much more cramped. Most of the books and journals in his room dealt not with literature but with Wall Street. He had a three-drawer filing cabinet full of company analyses, market charts, and investment service booklets. He made money steadily in the market; and he kept salting away his gains bit by bit, in tax-free bonds.

Before Frieda's office began screening his mail, he was writing about a hundred letters a week to unknown people. Most of the letters he received praised his book, and the replies to these were easy. But there were many intelligent letters that attacked him for glorifying war. This pricked his own uneasy spot about the book, so he wrote long vehement replies.

Then there were the crank letters by the dozens: religious exhortations, accompanied by tracts; pleas for a loan, sometimes well-written and very upsetting in the details of the writer's misery; accusations of plagiarism; offers to give him a marvellous idea for a novel, and to split the royalties fifty-fifty; rantings to the effect that he must be a Jew, or a communist, or an anti-Semite, or a fascist, or a Catholic, or a Catholic-hater, most often that he was a nigger-lover, because he had a heroic Negro sergeant in the book. For months he agonized over such letters, and wasted countless hours trying to write temperate and decent answers. After Frieda's office started the screening process he saw no more of them.

Frieda's office relieved him of another distraction: flirting letters from strange women. The jacket of *Chain of Command* described him as a bachelor, and the photograph was perhaps the best that was ever taken of him: it showed a hulking young man in deep shadow, leaning in a doorway, with a ray of light falling dramatically across his face, the face of a strong, sensitive brooder, the eyes looking far off, the big mouth compressed in raw egotism, but touched with humor in the corner. The female letters began coming at once; some enclosed photographs, and the pro-

posals in some could not have been blunter. To compound this temptation, Hawke kept meeting women, in his first months as a social lion, whose eyes and whose smiles signalled interest or downright beckoning. He succumbed a few times to the letters and the beckonings. He found himself engaged in lies and deceptions, in multiple telephone calls, sometimes in hairbreadth sneaking around that bordered on French farce.

Each time it happened he swore to himself never to stray again. He was committed to Frieda now, and devoted to her; she satisfied him; what more did he want? But Frieda was often busy or out of New York. After all—he told himself on the brink of each new fornication, with the willing new woman in his arms—Frieda was somebody else's wife, not his. These escapades did his health no good, and complicated a life that was already a blizzard of wild wearing nonsense. But all this happened to Hawke in his twenty-ninth year. Men of twenty-nine are not good at rejecting the advances of pretty women. Had Hawke been married to Jeanne it all might have been different; but then, who can say? Jeanne herself, working closely with him on *Will Horne*, saw more of all this than Hawke realized. She told herself twenty times that she was well rid of her infatuation with him, that she would never have been able to let him out of her sight, that marriage with Youngblood Hawke would have been hell. She told herself this, and she believed it.

2

Jeanne had married Karl Fry, all right; married him two months after she returned from California; married him with Hawke present, looking as though he were at a funeral. The wedding took place in a downtown courthouse. The bride and groom left the offices of Hodge Hathaway to get married in the middle of the business day, in a lashing rain, and Jeanne carried under her arm one of Hawke's red portfolios. Karl Fry noticed this, of course, and the furrows of his thin mouth deepened in amusement, but he said nothing. The judge's chamber was gloomy, small, ringed with dusty books; the one small window was barred. Jeanne's friends at Hodge Hathaway brought two bottles of Scotch. Jeanne's poor mother, the puzzled little dentist's widow who had understood nothing about her pretty, strong-willed, fast-moving daughter since the girl had passed puberty, contributed a wedding cake which she had baked herself and carried across the country on an airplane in her lap. There in the judge's chamber, when the gray man in the black robe had read through the juiceless words of the civil ceremony, the little party, ten people in all, nibbled cake, drank Scotch, and made some routine jokes, and then Jeanne went to live in Karl Fry's apartment. That was her wedding.

Little need be said about Jeanne's initiation into what used to be

called the mysteries of marriage. There was no honeymoon. October is the height of the New York publishing season. Seventy-two hours to put the bride in countenance, and the Frys were back at the office, both looking unchanged, and in good spirits. Jeanne had never done much cooking. Now she bought books and went at it. Karl Fry put on ten pounds in a month, and Jeanne herself became more curvy, which was all to the good; her encounter with Hawke, the eight suspenseful and disastrous months, had left her hollow-faced and gaunt. Everybody said she was blooming. The odd marriage had, in the general opinion at Hodge Hathaway, taken firm healthy root.

After a couple of months of practice at the stove, the first dinner guest Jeanne invited was Youngblood Hawke. It was Thanksgiving, and so she cooked a turkey. The immense bird—browned to cracking juicy perfection, tender as a young chicken, stuffed with some magic substance that included oysters—was surrounded by a parade of smaller perfections in the way of a thick blackish soup flavored with wine, and a salad touched with oil, garlic and cheese as by some French kitchen genius, and airy hot rolls out of the oven, and a cauliflower white and foamy as a wave; and then when Hawke had eaten everything with wild voracity, while Karl Fry beamed proudly, she brought out a smoking mince pie with a hypnotic smell, and he ate a huge slab, groaning, "Jeanne, it's the best turkey dinner I've ever eaten. It may be the last. I'm eating myself to death."

"Are you sure it's the best?" Jeanne said. "We had a pretty good one in Beverly Hills." And she carried off a stack of dishes, leaving Hawke thinking that Jeanne would have been too much for him, really. There was something decidedly bleak about her habit of driving every nail to the board.

Despite Jeanne's marriage, her relationship with Hawke went on much as before. They worked together in the same way, and she was free with the sharp edge of her tongue, especially about Mrs. Winter, whom she openly and inexorably hated. Her attitude toward Hawke did not dry up, did not become busy and externalized as every happy bride's does to all men except the one she has chosen. She and Karl did seem quite happy. Yet Jeanne looked at Hawke as before, out of eyes that sparkled with emotion, and she smiled at him as before, in a way that she seemed to smile at nobody else, and she moved with certain freedoms and graces that a woman uses without thinking when she is with a man who means something to her.

And this was so even though she knew quite well—as indeed everybody else in New York knew, since Youngblood Hawke had become a name worth gossiping about—that the author of *Chain of Command* was conducting an all but public liaison with the beautiful concert manager, Frieda Winter. This had not been the case at first. Mrs. Winter had

begun by keeping her young lover in the shadows. They had gone to movies together, rather than to plays; they had avoided the grand restaurants in favor of the obscure good ones. Hawke had never come to Frieda's office, and had telephoned her there as little as possible.

This pattern dissolved after their return from California, and Jeanne's marriage to Fry. The Italians used to have a term for what Hawke now became; perhaps in the backwaters of their enigmatic society they still use it. He was Frieda Winter's *cavalier servente*, a young man openly attending a married woman with her husband's knowledge. Among the upper-class Italians the social fiction of Platonic love used to make the arrangement workable. The married woman and her admirer were supposed by general courtesy to have minds that harmonized. In a land of pleasure-loving people where divorce was all but impossible, some such formal device probably had to evolve. But even in the United States today divorce does not necessarily suit the parties in an adultery. Certainly Frieda had no intention of divorcing her husband, breaking up her comfortable establishment, and distressing her growing children. Nor, evidently, was Paul Winter thinking of such a thing.

But after California, Hawke and Frieda wanted to be together more and more. Jeanne's marriage was a deep shock to him. He realized once it was done, from the jealous agonies he endured at his first meetings with Jeanne in her new character of Mrs. Karl Fry, that he had loved this girl, whatever his involvement with Mrs. Winter, as he might never love anybody else. But the thing was irrevocable. He clung all the more to Frieda Winter, and since she was a woman who saw everything, she made herself as charming a consolation as possible. That was why she took Hawke into the open, to plays, to parties, to her office, to her country house. He pleased her and made her happy. She wanted to hold him; the more so perhaps as the sun of success began to shine on him, but in fairness to Frieda it must be said that she had been attracted to him when he was nobody, and that she probably would have stayed loyal to him, so long as he pleased her, whatever his luck of the moment in literature.

Frieda never told anybody in so many words that she was Hawke's mistress. Hawke never said he was her lover. It was not inconceivable, after all, that they had a Platonic affinity! And if Plato has too often acted the pimp in adultery, as Byron once acidly pointed out, cynics and gossips were free to say what they pleased about the forty-one-year-old Frieda Winter and the twenty-nine-year-old Youngblood Hawke. Their position was made easy, in fact unassailable, by Mr. Winter's acceptance of the situation. You might see the three of them at a play, or dining together. What Paul Winter actually thought, nobody knew. Hawke found the husband's dry cordial irony unfathomable. Frieda allowed no discussion of the question. Her idea was to take her pleasure and put nothing damag-

ing into the spoken word, and she taught Hawke to play the same game.

Indeed, Frieda was capable of delivering long passionate speeches about love, and fidelity, and loyalty at Hawke, when she caught wind of one of his little amours. She was completely oblivious to any inconsistency in this, and once went for Hawke's face with her nails when he could not suppress a grin in the middle of such a tirade. Hawke became quite familiar with the man he was cuckolding. Winter, heavy-set and gray, with a pouched double chin, was something of a dandy, took steam baths three times a week, played golf on certain unvarying days with the same friends, had a bridge game on Monday nights which dated back to his college years, and wore extremely expensive suits, well-cut, usually of smooth gray cloth, with handsome touches of tailoring—a new variant of lapel, a fresh material, a different setting of the buttons—which Hawke often envied and which he could never quite duplicate, though he tried. Winter specialized in the bonds of European countries, and in the manipulation of foreign currencies. Hawke gathered that during the war and in the years right afterward Winter had much increased his large fortune by complicated switching of Chinese, Latin American, Indian, and Balkan currencies in commodity transactions, and then by a successful major venture in West German bonds. Hawke sometimes questioned Winter about these things on the pretext of wanting to use them in his books. Actually what he hoped for was a few hot tips. Winter answered his questions with long cordial technical lectures that shed no light on what Hawke should do to make some money. Now and then Hawke asked Winter about some of his own stock speculations. Winter always gave him a judicious, predictable opinion.

Once when Scotty Hoag came to New York with a plan for a huge supermarket to be built on the outskirts of Louisville, Hawke brought him to Winter's mahogany-panelled Broad Street office, high in an old building overlooking New York Harbor. Frieda's husband asked Hoag searching questions for an hour or so. He telephoned Hawke that night and said, "Well, Arthur, a situation like that boils down to your confidence in your friend Hoag. From the elements it rates as highly speculative. The insurance company that's putting up the mortgage is well protected, naturally, by the land and building value, and Hoag can hardly go wrong since as the contractor he'll make a sizable fee out of the construction. The risk capital can all be lost if any one of the assumptions proves wrong, or money tightens up, or a couple of those big leases cancel out, or something like that. You can also double what you put in, of course, as Hoag says."

"Well, what do you advise?" Hawke said.

"I don't know this Hoag," Winter said. "And I don't know Louisville, and I can't take the time to investigate. I spend all my time arbitraging a

few percentage points here and there, Arthur, it's nothing spectacular and it's very tedious, but that's about all I know."

"I've made money with Hoag in the past," Hawke said.

"Well then maybe that's your answer. Those propositions can be remarkable money makers when they're well thought out. He talks like a man who knows his business."

Hawke invested thirty thousand dollars. He took the plunge largely on the basis of Winter's judgment, and he eventually made almost twice as much in a capital gain. He was almost as grateful to Winter as to Scotty, for Winter had said the decisive word that had pushed him to invest so heavily with Hoag.

Several times, too, Winter stopped him from going into losing ventures: things like a stock flotation of a new Cuban oil company, and a massive purchase of U.S. government bonds, with a loan of a million dollars from a bank. Hawke came on these propositions in the cocktail party round of New York. He met many men who made their living in the financial world, and he would question them. Most of them were flattered enough by the interest of a successful writer to talk about what they did, and Hawke used a mock manner of absurd Southern innocence that made these men laugh and expand. But they seldom came up with any specific ideas to help Hawke get rich fast. Those who did suggest tips and propositions always turned out to be promoters of a new stock or building syndicate or bond transaction in which they wanted him to put his money.

3

Once Winter and Hawke got rather drunk together. Frieda had to rush off to a sudden crisis at the rehearsal of a play after dinner and the two men were awkwardly left in the living room of the Winter home, playing chess and drinking brandy. Winter perched himself on the couch which Hawke and Frieda had sanctified with their first act of love, and Hawke sat opposite him in an armchair, frowning at the elaborate Chinese chess pieces. Hawke made dashing attacks, and he won the first game; but in the next two games Winter opposed the attacks with one thoughtful move after another until Hawke's position collapsed, whereupon Winter finished him off. They kept talking about finance. At last Winter said, as he replaced the pieces one by one in a box lined with crimson velvet, "Doesn't it strike you, Arthur, that these propositions you keep bringing up are more or less of the same nature? They're the risky ventures of promoters. There's only one way to make big money, and that's by using money. If you haven't got it you have to borrow it. The banks and the insurance companies aren't interested in helping nobodies become somebodies. That's risky. Banks and insurance companies don't have to take

risks, they've arrived. They assume the riskless part of a venture and charge a good fee for the hire of their money. The venture money itself has to come from elsewhere.

"That's where people like you come in, people with a little money who want to make it grow faster than the usual four or five percent a year of sound investment. You're the ones who provide the working money for the promoters. Now mind you, I'm not talking about fakers. I give you credit for enough intelligence to smell the crooks who prey on doting old ladies, confused widows, and for some reason, doctors, doctors have a diseased craving for bad propositions. I'm talking about legitimate promoters. Some of them are clever and lucky and tough, and they're becoming the new millionaires. It seems your friend Hoag is one of those. Some keep fumbling around the fringes and never make it. Some go bankrupt and wipe out a hundred investors at a crack. They play a hard game. The insiders are at least as smart as these outsiders, you see. The obvious and safe channels for making money are all well occupied. The newcomers have to keep probing around the fringes where the risks are high.

"Now you ought to think out what you're doing. Do you really want to go on lending money to promoters, on the basis of confidence and hope? People like this fellow Hoag? I want to make it clear that by choosing the right promoters and analyzing their propositions carefully you may become a millionaire in five years, at the rate you're going. But you can also get in hot water. Why do it? Why waste an artist's brain studying real estate deals and stock market charts? You're a productive and successful writer. Why don't you spend enough to live well, save the surplus—just ten thousand a year, say—and invest it cautiously? In thirty years you won't even be sixty—an age I don't consider advanced any more—and you'll have a few hundred thousand dollars bringing you in fifteen or twenty thousand a year. What more do you want?"

The elderly husband of Frieda kept drinking brandy and puffing on a long cigar as he spoke, and his usually veiled eyes looked direct and bright at the young author, making him uncomfortable. Winter was breaking through the shell of politeness, possibly because of all the brandy, and talking to him like a wise friend, and this caused Hawke to recall that he was the sneaking bed partner of the man's wife. As a rule he was quite oblivious to this embarrassing fact in Winter's presence. The husband was a shadowy, not quite real person even when he was physically there. People committing adultery are oddly gifted with this mental shield. Nobody can be genuinely sweeter and kinder to a wife, for instance, than a woman who is quietly having an affair with her husband. It is the reason why, as people say, the deceived ones are the last to know; and it is really not beyond belief that Winter was not sure that Hawke was sleeping with Frieda, so candid, and innocent, and good-humored, did even this clumsy young

man manage to seem with him. But of course it is unlikely. Winter was a man of the world. He was prominent in charity drives, a member of the board of two museums, and the mainstay of several opera and symphony organizations. He had met and married Frieda through his interest in music, when she was still trying to be a concert pianist. In every way he was a polished and admirable man, but Hawke was cuckolding him, and so could not help despising him. It made Hawke uneasy to receive such sage and warm counsel from this fat old ghost of a man whom he preferred not to believe in, when he thought of him at all.

He covered his embarrassment with a rush of words. How could he be sure that he would go on writing successes like *Chain of Command* every year or two? Now was his chance. The money was in his hands. Taxes would eat away most of it if he didn't act fast. Capital gain was the only kind of income that didn't consist of funny money, fake dollars printed with two honest coupons on them, so far as he was concerned: ten or fifteen real cents for Youngblood Hawke, ten real cents for an agent, and the rest phantom cents written into his checking account and then written away on a tax return. "I'll never save a quarter, let alone ten thousand a year, on that funny money, Paul. I have to look for special situations, tax shelters, dividends that show up as a return of capital, all those queer set-ups that let me keep seventy-five cents out of a dollar. It's the Treasury's hocus pocus, not mine. I didn't invent the system, I don't even wholly understand it, but if I want to achieve independence I must act on it. I don't want independence at fifty-eight. I must have it before I'm forty. I have serious work to do. I want the money problem out of the way by then."

"It would help," said Winter, who had been smiling a little at Hawke's financial jargon, "if you didn't go buying and decorating a house for sixty odd thousand dollars as soon as you get a little ready cash."

"I ought to be allowed some fun too," Hawke said. "Anyway I can get all my money out of that house any time I turn around and sell it. There's no better investment than Manhattan real estate."

Winter said, "You seem to object to paying taxes. They're the price for keeping America in one piece, you know."

Hawke said, "I'm the most loyal American you ever did see. I've simply observed that other fellows get rich under the tax system we've got and I think I can too."

Winter said, "Who does your tax work for you?"

Hawke hesitated, then said with defiance, "Ah do it mah-self."

Winter sat up in surprise, looking at him with eyes that actually popped, and the young man laughed. "Shocking, isn't it? But all I know is in 1947 I used a tax man that Ross Hodge sent me to—first time in my life I ever needed one—a little wizened spider of a man covered with cigarette ashes,

and all he did was give away my money by the fistful. Why, we had a revenue agent who was after my blood, and this accountant, why he just helped him pump it out of my veins when the revenooer got tired. 'We won't argue about that,' he kept saying. When it was all done, why, this little spider he sort of smiled at me and said, 'They don't let you writers get away with much, do they?' That finished me. I made out my own return in 1948 and 1949. There's nothing to a tax return, you just have to read the instructions carefully."

Winter shook his head. "That's ill advised. Taxation is as complicated nowadays as medicine. You need a doctor, not self-dosing, and you need a tax man."

"I'll do better by myself," Hawke said, thrusting out his under lip. "I'll bet you anything. All a tax man does is read the right books and Treasury leaflets. I can read, and I've done it, and I'll keep doing it."

Frieda's husband studied, through the smoke of his cigar, the face of Frieda's lover. He said, pursing his lips, "You might consider the fact that you have one of the finest special situations I'm aware of and you're not doing anything about it."

"What's that?"

"You write the books of Youngblood Hawke."

"Well? Novel royalties are paid in funny money, Paul. I've read every book I could find and talked to four different lawyers, including the big legal brain at Hodge Hathaway. There's no way on earth to turn royalties into capital gain."

"Have you ever thought of publishing your own books?" Now Hawke sat up, and Winter added, after a long puff on his cigar, "It's a premature suggestion, but at some point you ought to look into it. Number one, you stop paying for Hodge Hathaway's tremendous overhead. Those six floors at 660 Madison and all those big salaries come out of nothing but authors' earnings, after all. Number two, and probably number one for you, you move into a corporate structure, a stockholding situation. I'd certainly insist that you attempt it only with a first-rate tax man. But three or four more books like *Chain of Command*, or even half as successful, would make you a millionare, an old-fashioned solid cash millionaire I'm talking about, if you did it right. Moreover instead of gambling on real estate in Louisville and oil in Cuba, things you know nothing about, you'd be taking your chances with the one situation you know about and control from the start—the novels of Youngblood Hawke."

Hawke said slowly, "Why in God's name didn't I think of that? Why hasn't my agent suggested it?"

"Because as I say, there are pitfalls, and it's not common practice. Ordinarily you're much safer sticking to common practice in business, but you insist on pushing into the risk area. Walter Scott and Mark Twain

bankrupted themselves doing their own publishing. On the other hand Dickens made streams of money that way, and I think Shaw's become a millionaire by simply hiring a printer and selling his own books."

"It's the greatest idea I've ever heard," Hawke said.

4

Scott Hoag had gotten his start in life by becoming a rich man's son-in-law; that is to say, he had married his main chance instead of earning it. A man who does that gives himself a character at an early age, and tends to stay in that character. Rich girls can be as attractive as poor ones, and a poor man can certainly fall hard in love with a rich girl. But when his business career rests on that romantic impulse, somehow or other he tends to resemble, in the long run, and as a general rule—and with all the exceptions you please—Scott Hoag.

On the outskirts of Lexington, Kentucky, there was a new residential section called Dog Leg Park. It had smooth old lawns and thick old trees, as well as big new flat modern homes constructed at luxurious intervals, a green acre or two apart. It was the chopped-up remains of a grand estate where blooded horses had until recently been raised by one of Lexington's noblest old families, and it was named for the crooked little trickle, Dog Leg Creek, that ran through it. At the center of the park, the hugest and newest and flattest of the modern homes squatted in the center of three acres, on the thick foundations of the imposing Lightwood mansion, which had been thrown down when the estate was bought out and chopped up. This was the residence of Scotty Hoag, the man who had done the buying out, the throwing down, and the chopping up. Dog Leg Park was one of the most successful developments in Lexington.

The home of the developer, inside and out, was new. It was so crashingly new that there were even some antiques in it, adorning the newness as a beard nowadays adorns the faces of college boys. Except for these antiques the house was all flat roof, flat wood, flat handsome geometric furnishings, exposed flat bricks, beautiful soft carpeting in endless square yards, a fireplace hung in midair in the middle of the living room, and so forth. The house was very comfortable, very wisely designed, very pretty to look at. Under the old oaks that shaded it, however, and that had once shaded the Lightwood mansion, an unmistakable air of the mushroom invested it; and like a mushroom it was to some tastes peculiarly slick and unpleasantly cold.

Ten in the morning, a lovely morning in May, 1950. Scotty was having breakfast in the patio, amid the pleasant scents of blossoming crabapples, in the shade of one of the great oaks, at a table of glass and iron, and he was glancing over a blue-bound operating statement as he ate. He was still

dressed in worn boots and breeches, having just returned from a two-hour ride around another grand estate, Seven Oaks Farm, about a mile or so farther out from Lexington. He was friendly with the family there, and with the horse trainers. He never rode through the estate without thinking quietly about its possibilities, chopped up. He was slowly getting the family less hostile to the idea of converting this beautiful but heavily taxed land into a big chunk of ready cash. It was a project that was several years off, because one of the sons wanted to keep the place as it was till the day he died. Happily he had a taste for bourbon that was rapidly advancing the day.

Scotty's breakfast was a huge one—a ham steak, three eggs, a heaping plate of biscuits and honey—not only because he was hungry after the ride but because he was about to drive up to Hovey. His wife Ellie whined placidly at him from the other side of the table, taking no food at all, merely smoking as Scott ate. Eleanor Hoag, the mother of three children, was a tall slim long-legged handsome young woman. She stayed slim by subsisting on tobacco smoke and cottage cheese. You might meet her ten times without recognizing her the eleventh. Her hair, her paint, her clothes, her talk, were wholly dictated by the magazines out of New York. The Dog Leg Parks all over the United States are full of women like Ellie. Lecturers who hop by air to speak in cities fifteen hundred miles apart sometimes have the eerily flattering feeling that their audience has flown secretly from one place to the other to hear them again. The multitudinous Ellie Hoags have given the land an honest reputation for being full of beautiful women, but they tend to merge into one ubiquitous glossy household item, like the deep freezer, and Ellie did suffer from this General Electric look.

But she was a satisfying wife and mother, strong on culture, and she ran a charming household. Her whine remained to her from her childhood spoiling. It was not an unpleasant whine, but rather a perpetual minor-key recitative, with a faint threat under it of coming down with some dread ailment if she were not pampered. At the moment she was whining about moving to New York. The theme was familiar enough so that Scotty could carry on a perfectly rational conversation, at the same time thinking out the business problems that would come up at the annual board meeting of Hawke Brothers Coal Company in Hovey, even doing arithmetic in his head. "Ellie, honey, the trouble is how would I make a living?" he said, turning the pages of the statement to the balance sheet. "Them sumbitches up in New York too smart for me. Down around here a dumb country boy like me can figure out a deal now and then that can pay off."

"Oh, Scotty, that's just talk. You weren't born in Lexington and you built Dog Leg Park. As long as we left Hovey I don't see why we don't go where the living is best."

Scotty said, mentally dividing the net profit of Hawke Brothers by the

number of shares, and coming out with a very good dividend, "They a lot of things down here I got to keep my eye on. This coal binness—"

They heard chimes at the front door. Urban Webber, Scotty's white-headed attorney, came sauntering through the French doors to the patio. He accepted an invitation to coffee, and unrolled a newspaper flat on the table with something of a flourish. "Seen the big news?"

The photograph of Youngblood Hawke from the book jacket stood out in a two-column feature story in the middle of the front page:

KENTUCKY NOVELIST
WINS PULITZER PRIZE
FOR WAR NOVEL
'CHAIN OF COMMAND'

"Hey! How about that, Ellie! Ole Art, your own cousin! He's not only rolling in money, he won the goddamn Pulitzer Prize!"

The Hoags devoured the article, their heads together over the newspaper. Ellie whined happily, "Honest, when I remember Art at high school! He was just a big gawk who couldn't find a pleasant word to say and his neck was always dirty, and now if he isn't famous."

"Guess you went for the wrong fellow, hon."

"Are you crazy? My own cousin? Anyway, if Art Hawke had ever made a pass at me I'd still be running. All the girls thought he was awful. I mean he could be *sweet* but you couldn't take him seriously, he was so, I don't know, so *immature*. Honest, the way things turn out in life. If we lived in New York I bet we'd meet all the famous people through Art."

"Well, hon, one of these days maybe I'll look into the situation up there. The Pulitzer Prize! Goddamn! Ole Art!"

5

Scotty's Cadillac slid up into the mountains through a pelting rain, taking the steep twisted grades of broken blacktop as though they were a level highway. Urban Webber said, after some desultory chatter about the agenda of the board meeting, "I take it you're pretty friendly with this Youngblood Hawke."

"Ole Art?" Scott kept his eyes on the road. They were entering the stretch where coal trucks thundered down from the western end of Letchworth County to the rail spur at Canton. "Why, we went to U.K. together, and as you know he was in the Clinton Road syndicate, though he backed out of that, and he has a big piece of Bluegrass Shopping Center in Louisville which is coming out real good. Also he's in on a couple of my other jobs. When I was in New York last we had a real good time and killed a hell of a lot of bourbon together. Art's a great fella."

"I'm a little surprised," the lawyer said, "that you haven't been able to settle with Mrs. Hawke through him."

Scotty grinned. "Well, now, Aunt Sarah's a funny woman, got a mind of her own, as you would say. What's the difference? She doesn't have a shadow of a case. So you've repeatedly told me."

"I adhere to that position," Webber said, his blue eyes less merry than usual, his round face drawn in determined lines. "It's my interpretation of the facts. In a lawsuit, though, especially when you go into land titles and mineral titles, you can never be sure how or where you'll come out. It's always better to avoid an action or to settle it."

"Granted," Scotty said, "but I'm afraid Ellie's aunt is what you might call a grasping woman, being a poor relation, more or less. I haven't pushed Art for a settlement. I haven't even raised the subject for a couple of years."

"Well, we're on the calendar of the Circuit Court for June 18," Webber said. "Now might be the time to raise it."

"Why? What's the urgency? That whole Frenchman's Ridge binness happened so long ago I don't hardly remember none of it, but I sure don't see where we could possibly owe Mrs. Hawke anything. Why, the mine showed a loss, didn't it?"

"Let me review the facts for you," said Webber patiently. Scott had a way of playing dumb, and of finding his ideas while the lawyer talked. "Without wanting to cry over spilt milk, I think it was unwise to let Mrs. Hawke's accountant examine the books of the mine."

"That accountant's retired and gone to live in California," Scott said. "Had a coronary last summer."

"I didn't know that. It's just as well that he isn't available. In fact that's a real help." The lawyer smiled at his client's habit of treasuring and then springing useful bits of news. "We're left, all the same, with the fact that we told Mrs. Hawke the mine lost money."

"Well, it did, didn't it? The books of Hawke Brothers are in perfectly good order. I don't remember what we told her and I don't know what her accountant told her, I only know we opened our books to him and I don't see how a binness could be more open and above board than that."

The lawyer said, "It's perfectly true the first mine you dug at Frenchman's Ridge turned out unprofitable. That's what the accountant reported."

"It sure was unprofitable. That was what finished me in the coal binness."

"You also ought to recall that your geologists found the seam branched off in a promising way toward the disputed land. Now for various tax reasons, which we can readily disclose in court because they were bona fide, I recommended that you continue to carry the loss of the first operation in Hawke Brothers and form a new Delaware corporation to continue

the operation, which eventually extended under the land Mrs. Hawke claims."

"Was that the Eleanor Coal Company? It's all very unclear in my mind, I don't know anything about Delaware corporations."

"That was the Eleanor Coal Company," the lawyer said with an amused twist to his mouth. "And let me remind you that Eleanor Company took some five hundred thousand tons of top grade Lazarus number four coal, with a total value at the mine head, at wartime prices, of about one million eight hundred thousand dollars. It paid royalties at five percent to Hawke Brothers."

Scotty said, "Well, I was always confused about that Eleanor Company, it was just a lot of paper shuffling that you recommended. But if it's relevant to this binness why didn't Mrs. Hawke's accountant come across it?"

"Because the royalties that Eleanor Company paid to Hawke Brothers went into general receipts, Scotty," the lawyer said, a shade too patiently. "Hawke Brothers was getting royalties from sixteen or seventeen smaller operators in wartime. Mrs. Hawke's accountant probably should have asked whether any of those general receipts represented royalties on the disputed land. But he didn't."

Scott swung the car into a filling station. "Let's grab a cup of coffee while they fill up."

They lunged through the heavy rain into the tiny diner where two skinny mountaineers in shapeless blue clothes slouched on stools, talking a language that hardly sounded like English. The mountaineers glanced at them through narrowed eyes and went on talking in lowered tones, about a game warden who had either shot somebody or been shot. Scott said, over black bitter coffee, "The way you put it, Mrs. Hawke's suing me because she hired a stupid accountant. I made that offer for her to look at the books in good faith because I thought that would ease her mind about a settlement. I didn't reckon on her taking me up, but I didn't care if she did. Her claim is ridiculous. We owned the mineral rights to that land. You examined the title for Eleanor Coal Company before we commenced mining. Your written opinion approving it is in our file."

The lawyer said, with a slight shift of his eyes toward the miners, "Scotty, I'm sure you'll do very well before a jury if it ever comes to that but there's no jury here."

The mountaineers dropped coins on the counter and went out, and the lawyer watched their departure with relief. The counter man was loudly frying eggs in the kitchen. "You may recall that my title report was the second. Hawke Brothers got an opinion of the disputed parcel from Judge Sparkman. His conclusion was that Mrs. Hawke had title."

"I don't recall that at all and I'm sure you're wrong," Hoag said. "It would have obliged us to offer her royalties. Aunt Sarah never would have

accepted reasonable royalties, she'd have asked for the moon and my left arm. We never would have gone into the land if there was any cloud on our title."

"That's not going to work, Scott, because you were on the board of directors. There are minutes which you signed that show a discussion of that first opinion, and the feasibility of making Mrs. Hawke an offer."

"Are those minutes in a loose-leaf book or a bound book?"

The lawyer wrinkled his whole face. "You're not suggesting that we lose some pages of minutes? It's loose-leaf, as you know well, but a hole in a sequence of minutes is far more damaging in court than—"

"Hold on, Urb. I'm no lawyer but I'm not exactly a goddamn fool. I'm just thinking that many times I haven't been present at a meeting or came in late and had no idea what went on. I've signed minutes as a matter of form without looking at them a year or so after the fact, and then they been inserted in the loose-leaf book. You know how slow they are sometimes at Hawke Brothers bringing records up to date."

The lawyer fell silent. They paid for the coffee, returned to the car, and resumed driving through the rain. Neither spoke for several minutes. Scott reached a hand toward the radio when Webber said rather sharply, "That's all well and good, but I have my own position to consider."

Scott took his hand off the dial and looked into the lawyer's eyes for an instant. "Why, what's the problem, Urb? This the first I know that you worrying about this sumbitch, so help me."

"I must say you'll make a wonderful witness, but let's hope it never gets to that point," Webber said. "I hold to my legal opinion that you and not Mrs. Hawke—by you I mean Hawke Brothers, of course—had title. Mrs. Hawke *thought* she owned the mineral rights because that old illiterate John Crewes sold her a fee simple deed without restrictions. But he'd already sold the coal rights years before. If both our claims simply went back to the common grantor John Crewes you'd be totally in the clear. The trouble is that damned quitclaim she bought in for five dollars on that dead Halphen patent. She did it pro forma, because old Judge Crain told her to. But on one interpretation—the interpretation of the first opinion you got, as a matter of fact—the Halphen patent is the senior line of title."

Scott said, "Are you saying that because Mrs. Hawke signed a paper she paid five dollars for and didn't even understand, she's in a position to collect a whole pot of money? It's ridiculous on the face of it."

"Now Scotty, the price anyone pays for title is irrelevant to land law. You know that. Good God, the whole state of Kentucky could have been bought for a couple of hundred dollars at one point. Huge tracts did change hands over and over at that rate or for even less. But the titles trace back to the sovereign and are good as gold. As for Mrs. Hawke's not knowing what she was doing, half the cases of land law in these counties involve, somewhere along the line, the X marks of illiterates.

"And the thing is, Scotty, Mrs. Hawke's lawyer has based his case on that quitclaim. He's just a young bonehead from Edgefield and his petition is incompetently drawn, it isn't even in good English, but he's nosed out the main point. He's asked for an accounting. If you have to give an accounting in court you'll have to disclose the whole Eleanor Coal operation, Scott, you can't monkey around any more, believe me. It doesn't look good that you didn't disclose it to Mrs. Hawke, and the judge will be unfavorably impressed.

"But that isn't the worst of it. The judge could find against you on the question of title and make Hawke Brothers pay her the amount of the royalties. That would be, depending on the award, between one and two hundred thousand dollars. The bigger risk here is that if the court learns of the first survey—if it knows that you were legally advised from the start that she had title—then even if you did go and get another opinion, he may find that what you did was wilful trespass. Wilful trespass calls for punitive damages equal to the *full market price of the coal*, Scotty, that's nearly two million dollars. You were the president and guiding spirit of Eleanor Coal Company. I can't assure you that you may not be found personally liable for a truly fantastic sum of money.

"Now one more thing. Though as I say I rigidly adhere to the soundness of my title report, it may be considered questionable practice that I conducted it without taking cognizance of the first examination in any way. That was an accommodation to you, and I'm not sorry, but—"

Scott said, "Let me stop you right there, Urb. I'm just a binness man and the fine points of the law are beyond me, but I never asked you or anybody to accommodate me with any act of questionable practice. You're a seasoned lawyer and a hell of a lot older than me and anything you did I had every right to assume was in order and legal. This is a hell of a time to tell me you did something questionable."

"I utterly deny that I did anything questionable, I'm talking about possible interpretations of a circuit court judge. Scott, I'm going to refresh your memory a little more. We were having dinner together at the Gray Meadow Country Club, in the far corner by the statue of Man o' War, just the two of us. I'd just completed the title examination you asked me for, and I had the written opinion with me. You read it right there at the table. You said, 'This is what I want, Urb. Thanks a million. I guess we can go ahead.'

"I said that you had to remember you'd be held responsible for your knowledge of the first opinion."

"You said, 'Urb, who's really got title here?'

"I said, and I remember my exact words, 'If I were sitting on the case in a court I might or might not find for Mrs. Hawke. But this report represents my best judgment at this time.'

"Then here's what you said, Scotty, more or less. You said, 'What can

we lose here by going ahead? Chances are she'll never find out, even if we do have to go under White Branch Section. It's all a lot of black rooms and tunnels under the hill. So far as the mine foremen are concerned there's just another corporate entity taking over the operation and writing the checks. It happens all the time. If she does happen to find out—' "

Scott said, whirling the car out of a skid around a sharp curve, "She wouldn't have found out if she hadn't stumbled on that punch-through, wandering around in the goddamn wilderness. Go on."

"You said, 'If she does find out, what's the difference? We've got title. We show her how old John Crewes skinned her. We make a sympathy settlement for a quitclaim. If she gets tough and sues, knowing Aunt Sarah, why, a lawsuit takes years and thousands of dollars. She may die. She may get tired of shelling out legal fees. Anywhere along the line we can settle, if we have to, for a small fraction of what she'd ask as royalties. She's a grasping woman and if we try to make a deal with her we'll never mine this coal. At the worst, the very worst, we'll lose the case and the court will award her royalties at a lower percentage than she'd hold us up for. I think we're in fine shape.' " The lawyer paused to light a cigarette. "Maybe I've changed a few words here and there but that, Scotty, is the gist of what you said."

"I don't remember a word of that. I don't even remember having dinner with you. I remember getting the title report from you in the mail."

"I gave it to you hand to hand at the country club," Webber said.

"Urb, what's your recommendation here? What action do you want me to take?"

The lawyer said, "If you think you have sufficient influence with Youngblood Hawke, by all means prevail on him to drop the case. The land is really his, the mother holds it in trust for him. They're both plaintiffs, though the mother's pushing the action. If one plaintiff withdraws we probably can get a summary judgment and squash the whole thing."

Scott said, half to himself, "Well, ole Art sort of does have confidence in me, a little bit. He's invested quite a bit with me, you know. I hate to go pressuring him on a thing like this."

Webber said, "I appreciate that a successful author is a fine continuing source of risk capital for you. You have to consider, however, that your possible liability in this lawsuit is really appallingly large."

Scotty heaved a long thick sigh, almost a groan, then shook his head. "I don't know. Art might want to come along. Old Aunt Sarah wouldn't let him. She'd make life such hell for him he'd never withdraw. Why she'd go up to New York and move in with him. She'd never stop talking till he did what she said. Art likes his peace, where his mother is concerned. I don't blame the poor sumbitch."

"Then the only alternative I can see," Webber said, "is to try again to settle. Offer her something substantial. Say ten thousand. She'll leap at it."

Scott laughed. "You one hell of a good lawyer, Urb, but you no binness man. We made only one mistake in this thing so far. When we offered Mrs. Hawke a thousand. I did it, it was all my fault. It made the old lady smell blood. She's gonna follow the trail by the Christ till she finds the body. She means binness. Old Aunt Sarah's okay."

6

The first new business at the meeting in Glenn Hawke's office, after a discussion of the finances, was the election of a new chairman of the board of Hawke Brothers. Scotty casually announced that his building work was interfering too much with his duties, and so he had to step down. The logical man to take his place, he said, was Glenn. He did not mention the real purpose of this move, which he had worked out with Urban Webber; it was to get his brother-in-law out of the presidency. Scott had decided that Glenn's day-to-day management of the firm had been deteriorating badly because of his excessive dissipation, which was becoming something of a scandal in Hovey. The idea was to put the chief mining engineer of Hawke Brothers in Glenn's place.

Glenn was far from stupid, though he was a self-indulgent weakling. He sat slumped in the big red swivel chair under his father's portrait, behind the enormous mahogany desk he had bought himself, and he swung the chair from side to side, glowering at Scotty through puffy filmy eyes. As soon as Scott finished he said, "Who takes on the presidency?"

"Well, that don't hardly matter, does it, Glenn? You'll stay right here, and of course chairman of the board runs the whole works. That's been the trouble here, I been away so much I been falling down on the job. I thought maybe to take the day-to-day mining details off your hands, the unimportant stuff, we might move up Charlie Verban. I mean he's been chief engineer long enough now so he wouldn't foul anything up."

Glenn looked around at the other directors: Urban Webber, and an old retired uncle, his mother's brother, and a bald little attorney from Louisville representing his father's sister who now lived in Florida, and another lawyer who acted for his mother. They all invariably did as Scotty said. In the first year after Mr. Will's death Scott had calmly asserted leadership of the firm and held it, simply by displaying the will power and the business sense to make quick decisions that were usually sound. Glenn said, "You want to kick me upstairs and let Charlie Verban take over. It's unfair. There isn't a company in Letchworth County that's showed a better statement than ours this year. I think I've done a good job."

Scott said, "Hell's bells, Glenn, you be taking over my job. You've told me twenty times, not that I think you're right, that I been bossing the company. I'm handing over to you."

"Would you remain as a director?"

"I got to, fella. Ellie's a big stockholder."

Glenn said, lighting a cigarette that trembled on his lips, "As long as you sit in the meetings it'll be your show."

Urban Webber put in, "Look here, Glenn, the chairman of the board is the top post in any corporate structure. The president's often just a hired hand."

The talk went round and round, Scott Hoag staying silent. All the other directors were for the change. In the end Glenn, confused and overborne, accepted the chairmanship and gave up the presidency. Scott said, "Well, I guess I ought to hand over the gavel with congratulations and we can adjourn. Except there's one little piece of binness we maybe ought to talk about first."

Glenn said, "What about Aunt Sarah's lawsuit? Don't we have to go to court in three weeks or so? What's been done?"

"That's the little piece of binness."

"Little? It's damned serious. I told you five years ago that Aunt Sarah would go to bat if she ever found out about the mining of that land. I guess I wasn't so stupid on that matter. Now what are we going to do?"

Webber said, "Glenn, this is a nuisance claim of the crudest kind. There are dozens of them all the time in the circuit courts of Kentucky. They mean nothing. We never concealed anything from Mrs. Hawke, so your use of the expression 'finding out' is inappropriate. The good lady took it into her head to go walking a piece of wilderness where she owned no mineral rights, and she stumbled on a drainage tunnel of ours and started an utterly hopeless lawsuit."

"Well, maybe that'll sound good to somebody who doesn't know the facts. I sure hope so. We know there's an opinion by Judge Sparkman in our files that says Aunt Sarah has title."

The Lexington lawyer said, "Without meaning any unkindness to the dead, Glenn, that opinion was so totally wrong on the documents and the law that I can only conclude Judge Sparkman was failing in his mind when he prepared it. As you know he died only a few weeks after submitting it."

Scotty said, "Anyway, are you sure it's still in the file?"

Glenn looked at him scornfully. "You mean we should arrange to lose it?"

"All I know is I remember looking through those files when Mrs. Hawke first started cutting up and I couldn't find it. That girl Phyllis Trosper we had there for a while sure fouled up the files of those years. They still aren't right. Probably never will be."

Amused glances went back and forth among the men in the room, and the old uncle winked at Scott. Glenn said, "That won't work. Sparkman's office will have a copy, obviously."

The bald little attorney said, "Well, maybe the widow kept all his old files but it's been seven or eight years. I reckon when they tore down the old Combs building to make the parking lot back of Ittleman's the dead files went by the board. The judge had three rooms full of them."

The old uncle winked again. "I reckon we can count on Mr. Webber and Scotty here to handle this thing all right. I've got a dentist's appointment and—"

Glenn burst out, "Well by God you've just elected me chairman, and by God if that means anything I don't want this meeting adjourned until we decide on a policy. We've been sweeping Aunt Sarah under the rug for two years and now by God we're for it, we've got to go into court and that lawyer up in Edgefield won't allow any more adjournments. We've got to do something. My father was against the whole operation on Frenchman's Ridge, and he only let you go in there, Scotty, because you'd married Ellie and he said you might as well get your feet wet there as anywhere. He told me that. You all know goddamned well that my father would never in a million years have gone for that monkey business of a Delaware corporation, and crossing a property line when there was the slightest doubt as to title. My father didn't work that way, he didn't have to, he got goddamn rich without it, and by God the minutes will show that I was against it, I thought it was a hell of a peculiar maneuver."

Urban Webber said, "You seem to be questioning my competence, Glenn. My opinion was and still is that this company has clear title, that the Halphen patent was moribund and that John Crewes by adverse possession had completely eliminated it from the picture. I don't want to labor legal technicalities here, but—"

"Mr. Webber, I don't question your competence in the least, you're goddamned smart and so is Scotty. But I'm not an imbecile. I know that in such a situation with two conflicting title reports like that, we should have quieted title either by settling with Mrs. Hawke or going to court if necessary before we crossed that line. But my father died, and while I was on my honeymoon you all went ahead with this Delaware corporation, and now by God it's all coming home to roost, and I say we'd better arrive at a policy here, that's all."

Scott Hoag said with a smile, "Glenn, you had twenty percent of the Eleanor Coal Company and your mother had forty percent. You all made a bundle."

"I'm aware of that," Glenn said, chain-lighting a cigarette. "I'm in it up to my ears and that's why I want some action here instead of just drifting along and hoping Aunt Sarah will drop dead. God knows Aunt Sarah has always given me the most tremendous pain in the tail, I've never known a more unreasonable or envious or greedy woman, but by God she's made of iron. And now my cousin Art's a big goddamned novelist, why he just won the Pulitzer Prize, do you know that? Not but what I still think

he's just an overgrown screwball same as he always was, but still he's got money now. He's a plaintiff same as Aunt Sarah. If he comes down here with a smart New York lawyer he can blow this thing sky high. By God, if they get us on wilful trespass here we'd all better make reservations in the poorhouse."

Urban Webber said at once, "Wilful trespass is unthinkable in this case. I'm not afraid of any lawyer, from New York or anywhere else."

But Glenn's outburst had made an impression. The other directors looked anxiously at Hoag. He said without rancor, and in a calm tone all different from the sharp note that Glenn had struck and that Webber was beginning to take, "They always a black side to every picture, Glenn, and you sure giving it to us real brunette, but that kind of thing don't help much when you talking policy. We're in good shape here, if I didn't think so I'd say as much."

Glenn said, "I'm not just talking. I have a policy to offer. It's very simple. We didn't steal anything from Aunt Sarah, it's a case of a dispute with two sides to it. The Eleanor Coal Company paid royalties of about two hundred thousand dollars to Hawke Brothers. I say we ought to split those royalties with her fifty-fifty. We should have done that from the start. I think that's fair and by God if she wants more let's fight her up to the Supreme Court. That gives the woman a hundred thousand dollars and by God she ought to be satisfied."

"Where do we get the hundred thousand?"

"Hawke Brothers treasury, where it was paid in."

"That's a lot of cash money, Glenn."

"We have plenty of cash reserves for this kind of contingency. I think we owe the woman the money."

Scott said seriously, "Well, there we disagree. On the facts I don't feel we owe the woman anything, and I don't think we should give away this firm's funds on account of some legal harassment."

There was a long silence in the room. The old uncle said, "That's a very large settlement."

Webber said, "I would call it at this stage a drastic, if you'll forgive me a panic-stricken settlement. And I doubt she'd be satisfied. It would only give her the idea she was entitled to a million."

Scott said, standing, "Let me make a phone call. Excuse me." He went out.

The handsome bronze clock on Glenn's desk ticked away fifteen minutes while the men talked politics, weather, and sports; all but Glenn, who sat sunk in the big chair, alternately puffing at a cigarette and gnawing at his nails. It was obvious that, with Scott out of the room, business was out of the room too. He came back saying with a grin, "Sorry to keep you all waiting."

Glenn said, "Were you talking to Aunt Sarah?"

"No, I been on the phone to Edgefield. This young fellow Randy Peters, Aunt Sarah's lawyer, agrees to an adjournment until the fall."

Glenn sat back in astonishment. All the men in the room looked surprised and delighted. Webber said, "Good lord, how did you manage that? I was on the phone with that Peters for an hour last Friday. It was hopeless."

Glenn said, "I talked to him too. I never encountered a more ornery little bastard."

"I think you fellows got him wrong," Scott said. "He's pleasant enough, but somebody got his back up on this lawsuit. He's on a contingent fee, of course, and he don't even make office expenses until there's some kind of action. I think he's going to help us reach a settlement. Christ knows he just wants to see some money. He's not thinking of any big sums. Five thousand would be a victory for him. He as much as said so."

Uncle Dave said, laughing, "See, Glenn? You were talking a hundred thousand."

"The whole problem is Aunt Sarah," Glenn said.

"Scott, on what basis did you get an adjournment out of him?" Webber said.

"Well, the funny thing is it turns out I know him. Actually been doing binness with him sort of indirectly. You know I'm in with Sol Haynes on that professional building Sol's putting up in Edgefield. Sol asked me a couple of months ago about an Edgefield lawyer, and it so happened I had Urban's file of the Frenchman's Ridge case on my desk and I picked this young fellow's name out of it. I been on the phone with Sol and he talked to Randy and then I did and it all couldn't have been pleasanter. It always helps when it turns out you know a fellow. Sol is Randy's biggest client right now, Randy's just a kid getting started. Anyway, Urban, you call him any time next week and you'll work out together some basis for an adjournment."

The directors glanced at each other, and the old uncle stood creakily, a fat flushed old man in a white linen suit. "Well, is this meeting over, or should I call my dentist?" he said to Glenn.

Glenn said, "If that's a motion to adjourn—"

"Second," said the bald attorney.

Glenn said, "Okay, adjourned, but we haven't solved anything, Scotty, we've just swept Aunt Sarah back under the rug again."

"Well, no, Glenn, we just needed a little time here to do something constructive. I think I got a pretty good idea. Let's talk about it at dinner."

CHAPTER ELEVEN

1

HAWKE had heard the news about the Pulitzer Prize the day before, about five o'clock in the afternoon. Ross Hodge had warned him that the jury was meeting to vote that day. He had successfully buried his awareness for a while by scribbling at *Will Horne* in the library of his brownstone house, the one room that had been almost completed. But at about three o'clock he was written out, and the carpenters and plasterers on the floor above were making a hideous racket. What to do next, while he waited? It was probably absurd to hope that his novel, of all the hundreds of novels published during the year, was even being considered for the prize. But the Hodge Hathaway office was agog, and their hopes had infected him. He thought of going to a movie; but suppose the call came, if it were coming, while he was out of the house? He telephoned Frieda's office. She was at lunch. Like a backsliding drunkard, after a brief wrestle with his conscience, he called up a young actress whom he had not seen in a month. The girl rather resembled Jeanne Fry in the squarish face and the small blunt hands, and even her name was Jean, Jean Stevenson, but her moral character was something else. She was very much the golden-hearted slut so dear to our playwrights; she could whip off her skirt or her slacks with amazing speed, and with all the casualness of a housewife opening a can of soup. She could also talk in Freudian jargon about novels and plays, and there was something pathetic about her, as about most young actresses in New York. Hawke had taken her home from a party, and thereafter had fooled with her surreptitiously for a few weeks, in one of his less troublesome infidelities-within-an-infidelity, until Frieda had thrown a monumental fit upon learning what was going on; then he had desisted.

But on this tense afternoon it suddenly seemed to him that nothing could kill the hours so effectively as a little fornication, so he summoned the girl. She came as soon as she could, but it took her an hour to clean up and contrive a New York exterior. When she arrived he fell on her like a sailor and demolished her efforts in a few minutes and with no ceremony. Then decency required that he put up with her loving small talk, which branched into a long searching analysis of the newest dramatic success about two mistreated homosexuals, all this to a continuous obbligato of banging, thumping and shouting overhead. The call came; and so it was

that he first shared the news that he had gained the grand distinction of the American literary life with a dishevelled, paint-smeared, half-undressed slattern who somewhat resembled Jeanne Fry.

"What is it?" she said as he put down the telephone. "You look like it's big news."

"I won the Pulitzer Prize," Hawke said.

"You did! Well, how wonderful, honey! I told you you're a wonderful writer. You deserve a great big kiss for that," and she ran to him, a highball splashing in her hand, one rolled-down stocking trailing along the floor, and planted a loose wet whiskey-flavored kiss on his mouth. She was full of gay enthusiasm, and wanted to bestow her favors on him again at once as a reward for his triumph. He managed to disengage himself from her amorous arms. He had to go down to the publisher's office, he said. She spoke wistfully of dinner, of some kind of celebration as she began to dress. She had a date, she said, but she could break it. He evaded the hints with but an ill grace, saying that his publisher had plans for the evening. Easygoing though Jean Stevenson was, he could see that she felt the rejection, and that it hurt her, but she kept a cheerful face. This gallantry in a trivial girl made Hawke feel contemptible. When she left she said to him, smiling, "As long as I live, I'll never forget that I was with you when you found out you won the Pulitzer Prize."

He strode downtown, his long legs carrying him past most pedestrians as though he were running. His mood was a whirling, not exactly pleasant mixture of elation and melancholy. On the one hand there was the glorious releasing sense that his work had won a great decoration, that his name would be printed hereafter in almanacs in a list of famous authors (with some nondescript and forgotten names), that an important jury had judged his work to be something more than a passing amusement. This knowledge made him understand for the first time the phrase "walking on air." It really did seem that airy soft cushions under his heels were bouncing him along, so that he never struck hard pavement. Yet under this floating excitement was a dejection that he traced to Jean Stevenson, to the bedraggled picture she had made, sprawled on his black leather couch in pink underwear when the news had come; and to his own shabby treatment of her afterward. He regretted having sent for her. He wondered at the impulse of lechery that had made him do it; and he realized that if the girl would remember the scene forever, he was not likely to erase it from his mind either. The trouble was, he told himself, that until he was twenty-five all the women in the world had seemed to be in a conspiracy to deprive him of sex; now as he neared thirty and had acquired a name and some money, about half of them seemed to have formed a new conspiracy to provide him with it, personally and individually, one by one. It was a dizzying change and he still could not find his bearings. That was his excuse to himself.

But his dejection had a deeper cause; it came from the prize. Hawke had two views of himself and his work: one, that he was an industrious nobody, a grinder of words, who failed on every page, let alone in every book, to say what was on his mind, and who with great good luck had managed to find a sale for his concoctions; the second, that he belonged in the company of great authors, and that he would show his true stature once he achieved independence from money problems. There was no consistency between the two views. He never tried to reconcile them. He switched from the one to the other with a switch in mood. The prize touched off his emotions in a roiling minute-by-minute alternation. He was a young god of literature at Sixty-fifth Street. By the time he crossed Sixty-fourth Street the award of the prize to an entertainment like *Chain of Command* only proved the corruption of taste, and his own counterfeit worthlessness. He could not get out of his mind the picture of the rumpled, smeared, wounded Jean Stevenson; and there seemed to be an indefinable ill omen, a cancelling mischance, in the fact that it was to her that he had first spoken the words, "I won the Pulitzer Prize."

At the publisher's offices he was caught up in the excitement, happily accepted the congratulations from telephone operators, receptionists, swarming secretaries and sub-editors, threw his arms around Ross Hodge, and then around Karl Fry, hugged and kissed Jeanne (doing his best to ignore the image of Jean Stevenson which she called up), and he even bellowed and capered for a bit. He called his mother from Ross's calm, gloomy oak-panelled office. While he sat chatting with Ross, waiting for the call to go through, Jeanne Fry brought in proofs of an advertisement proclaiming that *Chain of Command* was the prize novel. "This is how sure I was," she said. "I had this ad dummied up last week. It'll pop out all over the country tomorrow."

Hawke looked at his own picture on the proofs, at the still unbelievable announcement, and then at Jeanne. She wore a dress he had not seen before, a form-fitting dark blue silk, not at all a costume for an ordinary business day; her hair was coiffed as though she were fresh from the beauty parlor; she had really gotten herself up for a great day, with sublime confidence. He said, "Jeanie, those juries can do anything. They missed *Main Street, An American Tragedy, Look Homeward, Angel, The Great Gatsby, A Farewell to Arms, The Sound and the Fury*, in fact you name it in recent literature and they missed it."

"I know," she said. "I'm not saying this will be your best book, maybe it wasn't quite good enough for them to miss. I just knew they had no choice this year but Youngblood Hawke." She had the fresh glow of a bride on a honeymoon.

Ross Hodge said, "Yours was by far the best novel of the year and let nobody kid you about that. Sales, if you're interested, just passed a hundred and sixty thousand. We're going back to press with another fifty."

The long-distance operator rang. Hawke took the phone and told his mother the news. She did not know what the Pulitzer Prize was, and asked how much money it meant. When Hawke told her five hundred dollars she sounded disappointed, but then he heard the excited voices of Nancy and her husband in the background, and Mrs. Hawke said, "Well, I declare Nancy and John are dancing around like a pair of crazy people, and her pregnant as a cow. Nancy, you stop that! I guess it's a great honor, son. I'm right proud of you. Don't you think you ought to come home and celebrate? Nancy's due any day— Nancy, you stop cutting up, you'll have that baby right on my parlor rug—"

Hawke said, "Well, we'll see, mama. I just wanted you to know about the prize."

"Art, we go to court on June 18th. You've got to be here for that. You're a plaintiff."

"Not me, mama. That's your little pleasure, that lawsuit. You can have it all. Goodbye, mama. Love to Nancy and John."

"Now look, Art, you come home. I just know you look awful again, you haven't been home for a year. You sound tired."

"Mama, let me know when Nancy goes to the hospital. I'll try to fly down."

Then he called Frieda's office. Jeanne leaned against the window, arms folded, a slight acid smile on her face, as Hawke broke the news to his mistress. The upshot of Frieda's hosannahs was an improvised dinner party—the Frys, the Hodges, the Winters, and Hawke—after which they went to the hit musical show of the moment. Frieda knew the stars, and got house seats, of course. It was a bright entertainment, but Hawke sat glum through it, still on the seesaw, his unstable mood intensified by the rare experience—actually, the first since the California debacle—of being with Frieda and Jeanne at the same time. Each looked lovely in her way— Frieda smarter and more glamorous, perhaps, in a mauve Paris dress, but seeming a bit more wrinkled around the eyes than usual, Hawke thought— and each beside her husband, with Hawke sandwiched between the two couples. His spirits were not helped when in the lobby during the intermission he chanced on Jean Stevenson, accompanied by a handsome charming young Negro. While Jeanne and Frieda listened, he had to force small talk with this girl who had been copulating with him a few hours before. Her amiable remoteness made him grateful and ashamed, and he was pointlessly angry at the cordial Negro, whom she identified as a sculptor. All in all, considering that Hawke had just won the Pulitzer Prize, he was not having much fun that night.

It was so evident that when they were all sitting around a big circular table in the bar room of Number One and Ross Hodge was ordering up champagne and caviar, Mrs. Hodge remarked on the author's quiet, sober air. "Who would guess what had happened to you today?" she said. She

was a handsome graying woman, of an excellent Boston family, and so distant from her husband's publishing trade that it was a thrill for her to be out with a successful author.

Jeanne, still sparkling from the news of the prize, and from the musical show at which she had laughed like a fool—and also, Hawke suspected, from a sense that she showed to advantage tonight against Frieda, Paris dress or no Paris dress—Jeanne observed with a smile that Hawke's demeanor merely showed conceit, the most overweening possible conceit, a conceit so vast that it could swallow a tribute like the prize without being appeased or even given pause.

Oddly enough, Frieda took sides with her. She said, "Oh, him. He's got his eye on the Nobel Prize, nothing less. When he gets it he'll probably be sore because they didn't award it to him ten years sooner. Why, he's capable of turning it down out of sheer pique at the delay."

"Look, I'm happy. What shall I do, walk around on my hands tonight to prove it? I finished *Chain of Command* two years ago. It's work performed."

Jeanne said, "And you haven't even got your million dollars in tax-free securities."

Hodge said, "He ought to be getting there one of these days, if he doesn't build another house."

Karl Fry said, "It's that great unwritten epic that's on his mind. The American Iliad, or whatever."

"You're all being rather hard on Arthur," Paul Winter said, lighting a long cigar with measured gestures. "A young man unspoiled by success is a rarity, and here you are baiting him. He's right. What would you have him do?"

"Act impressed," Jeanne said a little sharply. "It's not easy to win the Pulitzer Prize."

"I hope I've acted grateful, Jeanne," Hawke said. "I don't think I'd have the prize if you hadn't borne down on me. With what you chopped away here and there, we cut a full-length novel out of the manuscript. That made the difference between a readable story and an overstuffed botch."

"Oh, who knows?" Jeanne said. "Maybe you had *War and Peace* in the first draft and I made you gut it to a slick best-seller."

Hodge said, "Maybe we ought to publish that novel you cut out."

"Nobody will ever see a word I discarded," Hawke said. "Only Jeanne knows how badly I can write."

"I have an idea," Fry said. "I saw *Oblivion* in rough draft. I think Jeanne would stab me if I peeked at those yellow pages she brings home, but I don't understand why. I'm a pretty good editor."

A fat heavy hand fell on Hawke's shoulder. "My dear fellow! How fortunate that I can congratulate you on your night of triumph!"

Georges Feydal stood over him, his enormous pink face shining from a fresh removal of stage makeup, his jowls trembling as he nodded gaily. "Yes, dear Hawke, and it's only the beginning! You have the theatre still to conquer, and you will conquer it, too. . . . Dear Frieda!"

Frieda introduced the actor to the party. The publisher's wife went into a flutter and insisted that the great Frenchman join them for supper. He did not need to be pressed. Making room for his bulk, which seemed to have doubled in a year, occasioned much shifting and sliding and scraping of chairs. Waiters descended to help this process, captains began to reset the table, and the commotion occasioned a general stare of all the rich and noted chatterers in the bar, which Feydal took as calmly as a president of the United States.

"How did it go tonight?" Frieda asked as he settled himself into a chair.

"Beautifully. Cheers at the curtain. Half a house, though." He kept settling as he talked, his flesh draping under the stress of gravity around the rim of the chair in folds of blue serge. He shrugged and pursed his lips. "Monday night is always hard on Shakespeare. I'm not at all sure it was wise to revive *Timon of Athens*. It's not a play, you know. It's a monologue two hours long calling the audience dogs, liars, whores, whoremasters, and idiots. All quite true. But what words, what words. . . . So!" He turned to Hawke. "What a night of news for you! You win the grand prize for *Chain of Command*, and *Alms for Oblivion* is in the clear at last to become a play. All at once!" The actor glanced from Hawke to Frieda, and his cheery look dissolved with marvellous slow modulation into a large mask of tragedy. "Surely you know about poor Anne Karen?" They both shook their heads. "Dead, poor woman. Died on the set in India, where she was making some *White Cargo* kind of thing. A stroke, I think. I heard it in my dressing room on the radio during intermission."

Hawke said, astounded, "Are you quite sure? I had a letter from Luzzatto last week. He's set to start shooting in August."

Feydal said, "Boy!" Three elderly waiters and two busboys sprang at him, and he desired them to fetch a morning paper. A *Herald Tribune* came in a moment. He displayed the front page at Hawke with a beaming grin, pointing at the Pulitzer Prize story: "There *you* are, my dear fellow," and then leafed through the paper, looking sad again. "Yes, here's poor Anne. Page five. You see what comes of not working. A few years ago she'd have made page one."

Hawke glanced through the obituary and stared at the lovely photograph of Anne Karen. It was impossible to imagine that this powerful, beautiful woman—whose voice on the telephone was the first he had heard from the peaks of fame, who had swept so regally into the Waldorf living room on the day of the snowstorm—that Anne Karen was lying a corpse in a foreign land. He said, "Is that her daughter's married name? Hauptmann? I thought she'd married a Peruvian."

Feydal said, "That young woman will be as rich as a rajah. Her father was Monroe Lesser, you know, the greatest of the great producers. Hollywood went dark for me when he died. All the time Monroe was a bachelor—and that was the first twelve years that he ran the studio—he lived like a college professor in a small house in Culver City, and put all his money in real estate. Land, land, nothing but land, he kept buying land, anything at all providing it was between Los Angeles and the ocean. Some of it is now producing oil. The rest is prime residential property. We all thought he was crazy. Good God, if I had listened to Monroe—he *begged* me to buy land out there—I wouldn't have to paint my face in my declining years and play the scaramouch on the Broadway stage."

"It's pathetic, isn't it?" Frieda said. "Any day now you may have to sell a half dozen or so of your Renoirs. Maybe even a Seurat."

Feydal blinked at her sidewise, his eyes creasing to slits. "I've bought paintings because I've loved them, Frieda. It's been foolish self-indulgence."

"Yes indeed. Bought them in the depths of the depression, at two cents on the dollar, and they've appreciated exactly like Beverly Hills real estate or better. You and Monroe Lesser were a pair."

"He was the only man of business who ever understood me," Feydal said. "He loved art."

Hawke said, "What will happen to the *Oblivion* movie?"

Feydal made a collapsing gesture with his two hands, and one could see a cathedral tumbling to dust in an earthquake. "But why?" Hawke said. "There are a dozen actresses who could play the part."

Feydal's shoulders heaved. "Movie financing has always been a Rosicrucian mystery to me, dear fellow. I asked Travis Jablock about this movie long ago, because as you well know I've been perishing to have you turn the last hundred pages of that book into a play. Just the death. He put me off with some esoteric jargon about Anne Karen going on the note to the bank for the financing. You see, Hawke, your book is not a conventional movie story. It's what they call off-beat, or down-beat, or some other very objectionable beat. Unless they find another multi-millionaire actress so eager to play the part that she'll in effect guarantee the studio against loss, that script will not be shot. Which puts you in a delicious position. You've collected your money for the movie rights. Yet behold, you can now write a play without fearing that a film will blot out your Broadway audience. It's a dream, and you can't possibly fail to have a smash hit and make another fortune."

"That's what Artie needs at this point," Karl Fry said. "A little success."

"He's in the middle of his new novel," Jeanne said to Feydal. "I don't think he should break off."

Feydal's heavy eyebrows rose at this severe statement from the young pretty woman, and his eyes shifted to Frieda. She said, "Mrs. Fry is

Arthur's editor, Georges. Half her job is being a watchdog, and she's very good at it."

Jeanne said, "Thanks, Mrs. Winter. I try, though I've been caught asleep once or twice."

Frieda said to Hawke, "You might want to talk to Ferdie Lax about this."

"Just the death," Feydal said. "A Broadway smash hit for three weeks' work, most of it mere editing. Just the death."

Paul Winter said, "You'll have to consider your tax situation, Arthur. Theatre royalties right now may consist wholly of what you call funny money, just disappearing numbers in your bank account."

Karl Fry stood. "There, Artie, is the theme of an important tragedy. Tantalus, or the struggling artist under capitalism. I must be in bed by twelve every night, my doctor says. I will therefore kick off one glass slipper and leave. Please don't let it disturb the party." Jeanne started to get up, but he put his hand on her shoulder. "You stay, darling, you may have to bark a bit more at Mr. Feydal."

"It's a very attractive bark," the actor said.

Paul Winter rose across the table. "I'll beg off, too, Ross. Delightful evening. Frieda only gets hungry at midnight. She'll stay, of course." The two husbands went off through the crowded smoky bar room.

Everybody but Feydal had steak sandwiches. The actor, explaining that he never dined before a performance and therefore was somewhat hungry, called for a double order of Little Neck clams, and onion soup, and sole Marguery, and Danish blue cheese and a bowl of fresh fruit. He quaffed a lot of champagne with this snack; and while he ate he described the play of the aunt's death. So clearly and brilliantly did he picture the drama, complete with act divisions and even curtain lines, that Frieda and the Hodges were soon blazing with enthusiasm. Feydal began by addressing Jeanne, saying, "I shall attempt to soothe the watchdog, and persuade her that I am really a friend of the family." He played the entire perform-ance at Jeanne, and after a while Hawke could sense her disapproval melt-ing away, though she said nothing. "I hope you'll agree, dear Cerberus," he said to Jeanne when he finished, "that there's something to what I say, and that I do not deserve to be bitten to death by your three heads— speaking in figures, since your one visible head is not at all doggy, but very human and extraordinarily nice."

Jeanne laughed, flushing a little, and said to Hawke, "I know nothing about the theatre, but I do think it sounds like a good play."

The publisher said, "Nobody's more anxious than I am to see your new novel finished, Arthur. But it would be wonderful if you struck into the theatre now with a success. We publish plays, you know. I think we might do damned well with one of yours."

Mrs. Hodge said, "I've never heard anything more exciting. Maybe you'll win the Pulitzer Prize for drama next year."

"The trouble is he probably will," Frieda said. "Georges, the whole thing is masterly. Of course you should direct it."

"I might play the old lawyer," Feydal said, blinking his heavy lids and tilting his head in a grand pantomime of modesty, "if the author agreed to the casting."

Hawke said, "Well, it won't take me but till next December or January to finish my book. Then, who knows? Maybe I will have a crack at this play."

"Next December or January," Feydal said, in the deep organ tones in which he had spoken of Anne Karen's death. An amazing change came over him. His face went white, his eyes rolled up in his head, the thick lids dropped over them, and his body seemed to settle further in the chair, a vast blue bag of meat without bones. He sat so in silence, his countenance as blank as an egg. Everybody in the party stared at him in alarm, except Mrs. Winter. She said, "Poor Georges. You're a bit tired, aren't you?"

Feydal said without opening his eyes, in a voice from outer space, "Next December or January."

Frieda said, "Well, all right, it means skipping a season, but what's the difference? The seasons fly by."

Feydal's eyes barely rolled open, like a medium's in a trance, and he said, "How many seasons have I left, Frieda? Missing a season! What is it to be next year? Again Shaw? Again Shakespeare? I need a play."

Hawke felt he had created a frightful emergency in the actor's life; he was completely convinced of it. He said, "I suppose it really wouldn't take me more than three weeks. Possibly less."

Feydal's eyes opened a little wider. He turned his head slowly and stiffly, as though it rested on a pillow in a death scene. "I swear to you that for a man of your fecund genius it will take less. Molière wrote original masterpieces in a week. You have a bare editing job to do. You've written the play already."

"Why don't you dramatize it?" Hawke said. "You have it so clearly in mind. I'd grant you permission."

"I should love to," Feydal said. "Alas, as soon as I take any kind of writing instrument in hand—typewriter, pen, pencil—I am stricken from head to foot with agonizing paralysis, as though I had touched an electric eel."

Hawke said to Jeanne, "Look, I have to go home to Hovey any day now because Nancy's having a baby. Would you come with me? I swear I think we could draft out the play while we were up in those hills. I'm planning on a two-week trip."

"Good lord, you don't need me," Jeanne said, crimsoning. "What a crazy idea."

"Jeanne, you're better at pulling the heart out of one of my scenes than I am."

Feydal came to smiling life, and shone on Jeanne with all his might. "Dear Cerberus, do make this young man write this play. He's one of those rare geniuses who commands both narrative and drama—he's a Galsworthy, a Maugham, a Victor Hugo. He has staked out his claim in the novel. Now he must plant his flag on the stage."

"But it's not up to me at all," Jeanne said, flustered by the actor's gross, strong charm, and by the shift of all attention to her, and perhaps most of all by Frieda Winter's cool smiling study of her face. "I have a job, and a husband, just a few trivial details like that, which make it hard for me to go off into the hills with our double-barrelled genius here."

Ross Hodge said, "Of course if Arthur needs you, Jeanne, you can have any reasonable leave of absence."

"Well, it's completely out of the question."

Frieda said, "Is it? Maybe you'll give it some thought."

"If I had not become an actor," Feydal said, "I think I would have been an editor. One loves creative genius. One is not granted it. One can at least have the privilege of ministering to it. You and I, dear Cerberus, serve the same master—I with my leather lungs, and you with your blue pencil. We must do our duty when summoned and where summoned."

"Oh, hell," Jeanne said. "It's just the easiest way to make money I've found. It beats standing behind a counter in Macy's. I have to go home." She gathered up her purse and wrap and made off in an agitated, clumsy haste that left the Hodges, and Hawke, and Frieda looking at each other.

"A formidable young woman," Feydal said, delicately peeling a pear. "And so pretty."

2

"Let's go to your house," Hawke said to Frieda as they settled into the taxicab outside Number One.

"Oh?" Frieda's faint note of surprise blended at once into a matter-of-fact, "By all means."

He took her hand, and they said nothing as the cab rolled up the dark empty avenue. He knew she had expected to be invited to his place for a little sexual celebration of the event; but his mood was bleakly hostile to love-making. It was understood between them that in the Winter home they kept their distance. Their first whirl of sex was far in the past. Now they had a pseudo-marital pattern: indulgence of their passions when both had an appetite for it, little romantic spells when he joined her at a trial of

a play out of town, or when they found a decorous excuse to go on a trip together, otherwise a stable companionship sometimes shaken but never yet broken by quarrels.

He reclined on the sofa in her living room with a big glass of whiskey and ice. That historic piece of furniture had long since lost its special significance. Now and then when they happened to get drunk together they would reminisce about their queer first experience on that faded Christmas Day, their volcanic break into a new life. At the time neither had understood the implications. Hawke had been thunderstruck by his sudden conquest of a brilliant New York woman, and Frieda had been astonished at herself and ashamed, and had put the occurrence out of mind, until his letter months later had called the affair to life. All that was long ago. Hawke would no more have pulled Frieda down on the sofa beside him now than he would have necked with her in Central Park. The sofa was big and soft; a fine place to lie down when he was tired, an obscurely comforting place.

Frieda closed the French doors, then sat at the piano and played Scarlatti and Mozart. The old house had thick walls and ceilings, and she often played for him late at night. She was not at her best in this kind of music; the piano coldly, correctly tinkled as she built up geometric crystals of sound; but it was this music that he liked best. Then she played Chopin, and he came from the sofa and stood beside her. Romantic music was more in Frieda's line. It supplied warmth of its own to her muscular playing; she could rise to the showering fiery cascades of notes, and she played the sentimental parts in a chocolate-rich style.

She smiled at him and broke off. "How's that old feeling of doom?"

"Is it that obvious? Much better, thanks."

"Good. Bring me a drink."

She liked gin with a little tonic water. He mixed it without asking her, and he said, "The gears really slipped tonight, Frieda, about the time Feydal started talking about my conquering the stage. I tell you I took part in the conversation from then on with the greatest effort. That old business of watching a movie and at the same time being part of it and having to shout an answer of some kind at the screen when one of the characters turns to you and says something. Real horror. Not to mention the old nightmare, which has been right strong all evening—strongest during that goddamned silly musical show, where twenty brainless beauties did their best to amuse me by waving their loins at me—the old nightmare of the one true friend I've missed knowing, the one wise book that's on a shelf somewhere that I've never been able to find, the one error in judgment I made long ago, I don't know when or where, the one wrong turn that put me on the wrong road which I keep stumbling along, further and further from the friend I should have met, the book I should have read—and add to that, almost as a trivial afterthought, the conviction that the atomic

bombs which the Russians have brought into New York bit by bit and assembled in cellars all over the city are all set to go off tomorrow—and add to that a headache like a hatchet sunk in my head—"

"Have you taken something for your head?"

"Oh yes. It doesn't hurt, the edge of the hatchet is well wrapped in soft fuzz, it's just there."

"How much sleep have you had lately?"

"The usual. About four hours at a stretch, mostly from dawn or thereabouts to half-past ten."

"How long do you think you can keep that up? Isn't it time you went on a normal regime? These moods you have are nothing but neurasthenia, nerve fatigue."

"Nerve fatigue. I see. Frieda, what is there about my regime that's abnormal, that you would suggest changing? I'm just an average young American with a nice wife and two kids. I couldn't be leading a more normal existence."

"Don't start that." She left the piano stool, walked to the fireplace with her drink and stood with her back to it, her elbows resting on the low red marble mantelpiece. It was a favorite pose of hers during a fight, or when she feared one. "I'm not the one that's consuming your time for sleep lately, lord knows. I don't know who it may be. It just seems to me you should be the happiest young man in New York. Good God, the Pulitzer Prize, an award most writers never get, or if they get it they're grayheaded, and you have it at twenty-nine, and your book is roaring along on the top of the best-seller lists. I'm not saying you have no right to a touch of melancholy. It's a reaction to all the shock of success, and that horrible vortex of charity and publicity foolishness that I had to pull you out of, and this damned house you're remodelling, which by itself would give an ordinary person a nervous breakdown, and then there's all your stock market shenanigans, and on top of all that you keep writing at a new book as though you were a pauper, trying to break in, staying up all night and drinking coffee by the gallon. Why, you're behaving exactly as though you were still in that loft room with the laundry hanging all around. Is it a wonder that you have black spells and start all this old stuff about the friend you should have known and the book you should have read? Arthur, all you have to do now is enjoy what you've become, plan your pleasures, plan your work, take vacations, and live to be a hundred and five. Maybe we should go to Europe, you know? It would do you good to see Europe. We ought to live in Paris for a year. You need civilizing."

"Possibly, but you have a few family obligations that might interfere. Like Jeanie. Jeanie has a husband and a job, so she can't come with me to Hovey. The ladies I know all seem to be terribly involved with husbands."

"Don't worry, Jeanne Fry will go with you to Hovey. I don't know why you need her, but if you do she'll trot along, never fear."

"Are you jealous of Jeanne Fry, too?"

"Why should I be? I wouldn't trust you, but I'd trust her. If she's been in love with you all these years and hasn't done anything about it she's not going to, any more. She married Karl and she's sticking to it. A very upright girl, Jeanne Fry."

"Jeanne isn't in love with me."

"Oh no." She left the fireplace and dropped beside him on the couch, where he slumped frowning. "Arthur, I have a million good reasons for going to Europe. Really, I'd love to. I can arrange my end of it, never fear. I'm thoroughly tired of New York; it's the greatest city on earth but after a while there's just too much repetition, the same faces, the same theatres, the same restaurants, even the same waiters. It seems to me I haven't heard a new joke in a year. Paris is heavenly, and there's London, and Rome, and Florence, and Venice, and all of Switzerland. Honestly, with airplanes nowadays getting around Europe is a joke, it's just one big lovely amusement park with the best paintings and the best music and the best scenery and the most exquisite food and wine and the most amusing people, and the most wonderful shopping and just everything to make the days delicious. All you need is money and now you've got it. We don't have to worry about your dear old Southern manhood any more, we'd go strictly Dutch. Darling, we could have the most memorable, the most glorious time of our lives. There's England. You don't know what beauty on earth is until you've seen the Devon countryside. We could take a house in Widdecombe-on-the-Moor or any of those little storybook villages. There's so much we could do, Art. You wouldn't have a second for the glooms."

He said, "Would I be able to work?"

"Why not? I should think you'd work better there than here. You'd be stimulated, and isolating yourself there for a few hours a day would be so easy. There'd be nobody to bother you, no phone calls, no publicity appearances, nothing but work when you wanted to work and play the rest of the time. I think you'd get on a more normal regime. You might start writing in the daytime."

He was looking more and more thoughtful. "How about the Feydal play? Do you think I should try to do it?"

"Yes. Do it at once and get it out of the way. If you wrote it now Georges could bring it in by September or October and then we'd go to Europe. Perfect timing, just when the schoolteachers and the tourists go home and Europe becomes habitable again."

Hawke grunted, fondling her knee with a big careless hand. "It's funny. My first dream was to be a playwright. I wrote seven plays while I was in the Seabees, and sent them in to New York producers. All I did was

waste about three hundred dollars in air postage. Can it be as easy to have a hit as he says?"

"About the theatre Georges knows everything. If he says it'll work it probably will. I'd produce it like a shot. Though, with one thing and another I guess it would be better if someone else did."

"Why do you want me to go with you to Europe?" He said it with a stray trace of a mountaineer's suspicion.

She bent her head far down, looking at him through wide eyes, then she put the back of her hand to his face in a soft brief brush. "Why, as I say, because it would be good for you. And also—since as you've remarked now and then in a raised voice, I'm the most selfish and calculating cat in existence—why, I want to have Europe with you. Because when I'm with you everything is so new and so sharp and so good. Food tastes wonderful, and music sounds gorgeous, and the colors of paintings seem to shimmer and come alive . . . Boston! Good God, the number of times I've been in Boston and thought it was a gray old city where the service was slow and the hotels sepulchral and it always rained and the notices were bad. Then you came to Boston, and somehow there were marvellous restaurants with darting waiters and I saw the old trees and the beautiful public squares for the first time, and the architecture was funny and lovely, and it was droll that there was a bank on every corner, so much sheer money, and the old hotel suite with the ceilings fifteen feet high and the rusty bath water seemed pricelessly charming. I'm in love with you, you big mutt, that's why I want to go with you to Europe. It's time we had a decent honeymoon."

Hawke said, "If I really thought I could work—you know, I'm suddenly hungry enough to eat anything that moves. I may eat you. Those steak sandwiches at Number One were nothing."

She laughed, sitting up. "Don't eat me, that's killing the goose that lays the golden eggs. I can cook you something." She jumped to her feet, saying gaily, "Let's go look in the icebox—good God! Paul! What are you doing out of bed?"

Hawke turned and saw the thin boy, in blue pajamas, standing in the doorway. Both French doors were wide open. Paul said, rubbing an eye, "I just wanted a drink."

His mother said, "Well why didn't you say something? Imagine, just standing there! Come along. What will you have? Milk? Water? Do you want a soda?"

"I guess I'll have a Coca-Cola."

"Not in the middle of the night you won't. You'll never get back to sleep." She led him toward the pantry, and Hawke followed. "Come on, you'll have some milk."

"I want cake with it."

Hawke was wondering, of course, how long Paul had been standing in

the doorway, and what the boy had heard. But if Frieda was worried she gave no sign of it. She bustled about cheerily, getting milk and cake for Paul. While he sat at the small white pantry table eating and drinking, she began frying eggs and bacon. The boy said, watching her, "Isn't that something you eat for breakfast?"

"Well, Arthur is hungry," his mother said, "and bacon and eggs are good late at night too."

The boy peered at Hawke over the rim of the glass of milk, from under his eyebrows, in a manner comically like Frieda's. After a moment during which nobody said anything, and the only sound was the sputtering of the eggs and the scrape of the frying fork, Paul said to Hawke, "Are you my cousin?"

Caught off guard, Hawke said stupidly, "What?"

"Are you my cousin, Arthur?"

Hawke knew it was wrong to glance at Frieda, but he did and she looked at him, half-embarrassed and half-amused. He said, "What gave you that idea, Paul?"

"Well, are you?"

"No, I'm not."

Frieda said, "I never told you that. Arthur is a very good friend of mine and of Daddy's."

"Daddy's asleep."

"Yes, he's tired."

Paul filled his mouth with cake. His face had changed in two years; the bones had become more prominent, and he had masculine good looks at the age of ten, enhanced by large gray eyes like Frieda's. But he was very thin, and when he turned his head a certain way he could look haunted and cadaverous. He said to Hawke, "We used to have this nurse, Tina. Remember when I was sick all the time a couple of years ago? I asked her once about you. She said you were my cousin. My other cousins are all my own age, so I wondered."

Frieda said, "Tina was stupid in more ways than one. She was mistaken. Finish up and go back to bed."

As Paul left the pantry he said to Hawke, "You haven't told me a story in a long time. You never finished that one about the invisible cat."

"Didn't I? And you still remember it! Well, you're too old for that one now. Next time I'm here I'll tell you one about going to Mars."

"Come tell it to me now."

Frieda said, "At half-past two in the morning? Don't be a fool, Paul. Off with you. You have school tomorrow."

She put the food before Hawke. After a while she said, "Honestly, if you think I know what goes on in that boy's mind, or in the minds of any of my children, you're mistaken. Your own children are the most remote strangers on earth."

"I wouldn't know," Hawke said.

"Imagine!" Frieda said. "That stupid maid telling him a thing like that, and for two years he never mentions it, and then pop! out it comes. Not that it means anything, but it's disconcerting. My daughters are just as bad. The only one that I can communicate with at all is my oldest, Bennett. Now that he's in college he's beginning to show human tendencies. What's the matter? You're not eating. I thought you were so hungry."

"I'm eating."

"Are you going to work tonight?"

"Just for a few hours."

"That's crazy. You ought to go straight to bed. You look frightful. White as paper, and those rings under your eyes. You take everything too hard."

"I'm not going to write anything. I'm going to look at the end of *Alms for Oblivion* and see whether that play of Feydal's is really there."

"You can do that in the morning."

"I can't do anything in the morning. Certainly not in New York. Anyway I got the habit of writing at night in the Seabees and I'm used to it."

"Before you do anything on that play you should talk to Ferdie Lax."

He pushed the plate away with half the food uneaten, and lit a cigar. "I don't know. As soon as I broach the subject to him I'll owe him ten percent. Why do I need him? A contract is written in English. Terrible English, but English. I can read English."

"You're being a little too smart for your own good." She poured steaming coffee for him. "Negotiating is a business, and a tough one."

"You do it all the time. Are you so much tougher than I am, Frieda?"

She laughed. "Arthur, I've been through a lot of it. Anyway the concert business is all different from literary negotiation. I started out by getting my own bookings simply because at that time I thought all the concert managers were incompetent phonies, and I was a peanut attraction. I just sort of stumbled on the bits and pieces of the old Chautauqua circuit, and then I got dates for a few of my friends, and about that time it became clear to me that I probably wasn't going to make it as a concert pianist, mostly I was getting bookings because I was twenty-two and pretty. And then I married Paul, and I guess I went on with the agency to prove I wasn't just a rich man's darling. But even by then I'd had a lot of experience and now, good lord, I know everybody all across the country on that circuit, and what they'll pay, and what their hall capacities are, and all that. And believe me music is a piker's game compared to literary negotiation. Ferdie is very fast on his feet. You'd better stick to him."

"You could advise me on a theatre contract. You've been in a lot of productions."

Frieda ran her fingers through his hair, gripped a handful, and yanked

his head to and fro. "So. You hillbilly skinflint. All you've ever wanted from me, really, is free agency service."

"I can do it myself," Hawke said doggedly.

"You get yourself off to bed," Frieda said, "and you call Ferdie tomorrow. That's my professional advice, and anything more specific will cost you *twenty* percent. That's what we charge in the music business, my boy."

As they walked through the dining room she said, "Didn't you turn the living-room lights off?"

"Yes, I did."

A yellow glow came from the French doors. They went to the doorway and saw Paul supine on the sofa, turning pages of a big picture book of dinosaurs, his folded legs long and bony in the pajamas. Frieda said, "Paul, what the devil's the matter with you?"

"I'm not sleepy," the boy said.

"You get up to your room this minute—nothing doing, leave that book here. The idea! Now you won't be able to drag yourself out of bed in the morning, as usual."

"Good night, Arthur," the boy said, trudging up the gloomy staircase. He stopped and turned at the landing under a Japanese print. "I'm sorry you're not my cousin. I wish you were." And he went out of sight.

Frieda said, "That child strikes me as spooky sometimes." She walked down the marble staircase with Hawke and kissed him at the door. "Congratulations. You think about Europe. And look, you call Ferdie, do you hear?"

3

When Jeanne Fry got home, about half-past one, she was startled to see light slanting out of Karl's bedroom.

They had separate rooms because Karl's doctor wanted him asleep by midnight, whereas Jeanne did most of her manuscript reading in bed, sometimes until dawn. Her habit of coming late to the Hodge Hathaway office in the morning was an old joke, but Jeanne had her privileges, because she carried a large work load, and most of all because Youngblood Hawke relied on her. The gross receipts of *Chain of Command* were passing half a million dollars, and the money was still rolling in; and so Jeanne Fry, who was editing Hawke's next book chapter by chapter, was a fairly free woman in the publishing house.

She thought Karl might have fallen asleep with the light on. But no, there he was sitting up in bed, writing on a pad clipped to a board, and smoking. When he saw her, he crushed the cigarette in a tray full of ashes and butts, beside a water glass half full of dark whiskey. "Guilty on all counts," he said with an abashed grin, letting the pad fall on the blanket.

"Up after curfew, throwing down the booze and smoking, also caught with pencil and paper *in flagrante delicto*. Bring the rolling pin."

"The booze is all right," Jeanne said, "except that you use it to keep going, and what do you need to keep going for? Have you had a blazing inspiration that can't wait until tomorrow?"

"I've never had an inspiration that couldn't wait. No, I had a visitor today, and I'm writing up a little memorandum at his request."

"Oh?" Jeanne said. "That certainly can wait. Put out that light and go to sleep."

"No, I won't," Fry said. "You go get yourself a drink."

Jeanne looked at him for a moment, then went to the kitchen and came back shortly with a highball. She sat in an armchair near the bed.

Karl drank whiskey with the old swooping gesture of arm and head, elbow stuck far out, the determined long swallow of a real drinker. It was a mannerism he had all but dropped since their marriage, as he had dropped his heavy drinking. He said in a roughened voice, "He was a pleasant non-descript fellow. A stoutish man in a gray suit, steel-rimmed glasses, almost never stopped smiling, nice manner, cheap cigars, tie a little too red, you'd swear he sold autos or insurance or real estate. Name is Sam Erskine, and he lives in Forest Hills. He works for the FBI."

Jeanne said as lightly as she could, trying to still the alarm that shot to her fingertips and her toes, "I see. What is it, Karl?"

"Don't worry, now. Sam said I'm in excellent shape, as good as anybody he's had to deal with in this particular situation. He doesn't think it's any more than a formality in my case. Moreover it's strictly on a voluntary basis, and if I don't choose to cooperate that's wholly within my rights, but he sort of feels I will." He finished the whiskey in the glass, and then said through a one-sided grin, "It seems that somewhere along the line in the Hiss case somebody mentioned my name. The bureau is routinely checking all the leads, and it would merely like me to describe in detail—if I feel like it, that is—any connection I may have had with the communist party, and they'll be grateful for any information on the subject that I would care to volunteer."

Jeanne said with the same forced calm, "Well, you told him what you know, I suppose. I'm not aware that you have anything to hide."

Fry sighed noisily, looking off into vacancy, and running a toe here and there under the blanket. Then he faced her. "Well, the old skeleton has sure come capering out of the closet, snapping its bony fingers, hasn't it?"

Jeanne said, "I'm not afraid or ashamed or worried because you were a communist. It's a legal political party. During the depression it seemed the hope of the world to a lot of people. I've always assumed that you never did any passing of secret papers or anything like that. If you had, you would have told me before we got married."

Fry made the huh-huh sound that passed for his laughter. "Are you sure?"

"Yes. You'd have told me of any ailments you had, or any children you'd run over, or any espionage you'd done, just as you told me, without my asking, about your finances."

"Finances, children I'd run over, yes," said Fry. "I'm not at all sure I'd have told you of a successful murder I'd committed and more or less put out of my mind. I haven't told you a great many things, Jeanne. There's a world of things you haven't told me. I think most amiable marriages are built on vast solid slabs of silence laid over a muddy quaking past. One of the things I admire most about you is your capacity for silence."

"Did you do any spying for the communist party, Karl?"

Karl moved his legs to and fro under the blanket, gnawed his lips, glowered at his wife rebelliously, and at last broke into a grin. "No, Jeanne, I didn't."

"Well, all right then." Jeanne was something of a hypochondriac, and each time she passed a physical checkup a weight fell from her heart. She felt now exactly as she did when the doctor told her she was in good health. "There's no problem, then."

Karl said peevishly, "I had no scruples against spying, mind you. Obviously they considered me unsuitable, and obviously they were right. I'd be just as unsuitable to the FBI. My trouble was and still is that I make jokes. There's no room for a want of earnestness in secret work, whatever side you're on. But so far as the right and wrong of it go, I think a communist is in duty bound to pass papers or do whatever else must be done. If he boggles at it, he's just been playing at being an advanced thinker. He hasn't understood what Marxism is all about. I quit the party in order to have a pleasant fag-end of life for myself, and let other people change the world. What with my coronary and my many reprimands for nihilistic joking, I didn't think I was depriving the movement of any appreciable energy. I give the cause what money I can spare, as other people contribute to their community chests, and that's that."

Jeanne now felt as though the doctor had added a casual word to the effect that her blood pressure was dangerously high. She said, "I didn't know about the money, Karl."

"That's my own business, isn't it, what I do with my money? Since as you say it's still a legal party—and since, as the orators like to remind us on the Fourth of July, this is a free country."

Jeanne took a while to answer, and on her forehead, between the eyes, appeared three vertical lines that signalled her attack on a hard editorial problem. She said, in an absent business-like voice. "That's not quite right. You're getting the money from Hodge Hathaway, a major publisher with a conservative public name."

"I get the money for services rendered. After that it's all my own. I can spend it like a Vanderbilt, on anything I please. You're chopping hairs, Jeanie."

"Maybe. Think about Ross Hodge, though. The newspapers, if this ever gets to the newspapers, won't appreciate your fine point about the money being your own."

Fry compressed his lips. "I don't give a good goddamn about the newspapers." He picked up the pad and studied it, his pale face a picture of obstinacy in the side light of the bed lamp, which deepened the lines and shadows around eyes and mouth.

"Anyway," Jeanne said, "you look exhausted. Please turn in."

Fry said, "I'm almost through with this. I'm writing a chronology of my party career, ravelling out my weaved-up follies. It's been quite a jaunt down memory lane. You know, I don't have to do anything at all about this. Sam of the red tie said that if I didn't choose to give any information that would be that. No prosecution, no further harassment, nothing."

"You'd have to tell Ross that you had declined to cooperate with the Department of Justice."

"Why?"

"Because it's the thing to do."

Fry said nothing. He frowned and wrote on his pad.

Jeanne said, "Have you been giving them checks or cash?"

"What's the difference, darling? We've always had separate bank accounts. You're wholly in the clear."

"That's just what was worrying me." Jeanne spoke in a muffled tone. Karl looked up, threw the pad aside, and held out his hand. She came to the bed. He clasped her hand, kissed it, pulled her to him. "All right. I'll go to bed. I think I've been making a play for your sympathy with all this bad-boy stuff. The arrival of Sam, the red tie man, in my life is a bit of a problem, that's all."

"I know, Karl."

"Can I have one more short shot of booze?" He held out the glass to her, grinning. "Be a pal."

"Sure." She brought it to him, and sat beside him.

He kissed her again, and grunted as though he were amused. "Well, to hell with it. What happened with our Pulitzer Prize novelist? Did you win the argument for Artie's soul, or did Feydal?"

Jeanne told him what had passed at the restaurant. "I'll be damned," Fry said. "Feydal's a hypnotic old mastermind, isn't he? I didn't see the faintest possibility of a play in *Alms for Oblivion*."

"You would have if you'd heard him. I couldn't lie, I had to admit it sounded good. Of course Mr. Youngblood Hawke's proposal that I accompany him up into the Kentucky mountains and help him write the play is a new high in egomania, even for him."

"Why? From Artie's point of view it's a logical idea. I'm sure you'd cut his work time in half for him. That's all he really cares about."

"How well I know that," Jeanne said.

Fry said, with a swift look at her over his whiskey glass, "It's far too late to start on that topic though."

"I'm not going to Kentucky with him, so there's nothing to discuss."

"Jeanne, your trouble has always been, so far as Artie is concerned, that you expect him to behave like an ordinary human being, and a pretty straight-laced human being at that. Whereas he's only a poor benign giant, half arrested adolescent and half narrative genius. I do think he's a genius of a sort, I've come around to it after *Chain of Command*, mostly because of the speed and assurance with which he wrote it. It's an immature book but god damn, it shows brilliance and brawn, especially the way he slammed it out right on top of *Oblivion*. He'll write several more big books and one or two of them may be as permanent as, say *An American Tragedy* or *Babbitt*. At least I think so. There isn't an atom of poetry in him so he doesn't belong with the top echelon, with Dostoevsky and Dickens and Twain, but hell, what kind of criticism is that? I think he's better than most people know yet. But darling, the major artist is a monster nine times out of ten. There have been few worse horrors in the world than Goethe or Wagner or Gauguin or Balzac. They were trolls, not people. Actually Artie isn't too bad, he has an overpowering innocence that nothing seems to penetrate, not even associating with an enchanting old thug like Frieda Winter, and his selfishness takes childish rather than evil forms—that ridiculous house, the chippies he keeps sneaking past Frieda—"

Jeanne snapped, "It's getting later and later. You're just talking."

"This is fun," Fry said, sipping his whiskey.

Jeanne said, "I don't think Arthur Hawke is a monster. If he were you could treat him that way and be done with it. I think he knows just what he's doing. I dislike weakness in a man. He has the strength of an elephant, and yet time and again he slouches along the path of least resistance. And since half the time his foolishness backs up to my desk in the form of more work to do and more messes to straighten out, I'm angry at him half the time, and I get still angrier when he makes a preposterous suggestion like the one tonight, that I should trail after him into Kentucky."

Fry did not speak for a while. Then he said, shading his face as he lit a cigarette, "Jeanie, the part you play in Youngblood Hawke's literary career is really your life."

She looked at him, startled. Then she said, meeting his glance directly, her head thrown back, her eyes half-closed, "That's not so. I'm proud that I can be useful to a fine author, but my life is my own. I live it here with you, and I like it very much, therefore please go to sleep and take care of yourself."

Fry said, "I think you ought to go to Kentucky with Artie. That is, if you really think there's a play in that big fat piece of headcheese called *Alms for Oblivion*. You're his editor now, not his critical girl friend. If you wore trousers you'd go. You're entitled to no special emotional reactions

because you happen to fill that blue skirt so beautifully." He said this with a light caress of her hip as she picked up his glass. Then when she was walking out he spoke in a different tone. "Jeanne, what shall I do about Sam, the red tie man?"

She turned, the three lines creasing her forehead, and said slowly, "I think you should finish that memorandum tomorrow and send it in. It's true the communists are a legal party. It's also true that when the Justice Department asks you for help you ought to give it, unless you have a good reason not to. And I think you should either discontinue contributing to the party's causes, or resign from Hodge Hathaway."

"I see." Fry stared at his wife, who stood in the doorway, one leg and hip thrust out. "I fear you would look all too natural in a red tie."

"I'm trying to tell you the truth, Karl."

He said, "I know you won't give me more booze. How about another kiss, or am I in the doghouse?"

"God, no." She kissed him, turned out the light, and returned to her room. She undressed, but did not get into bed. She sat in an armchair in her night gown and smoked. Perhaps a quarter of an hour went by. She quietly walked into Karl's room. He was asleep, with one elbow clumsily resting on the clip board. She slipped the board free and put it on his desk. Back in her room she took a fresh *Alms for Oblivion* from a bookshelf. She arrayed crayons and cigarettes on her bed table, put on her glasses, got into bed, and began reading at a page about two-thirds of the way through. Soon she was making sharp black slashes on page after page.

CHAPTER TWELVE

1

A FEW days before Hawke and Jeanne left New York, he wrote a candid letter to Ferdie Lax, telling him about the play, and also about his growing inclination to pursue Paul Winter's idea that he publish his own books. In effect this was a letter of dismissal. Hawke added, sincerely enough, that he would retain Lax if the agent felt that their handshake three years ago bound him to do so. He expected a protesting letter, or wire, or phone call, but he heard nothing from Lax.

Hawke welcomed the trip to his home town for more reasons than one.

Feydal had fired him with the vision of the play, and with the urge to strike off this theatre piece and win a success in a field which he had thought was closed to him. He liked the idea of spending three or four weeks with Jeanne in a knotty creative task. He was excited at the prospect of the birth of Nancy's baby. And as much as anything, he was glad to get away from his still unfinished house.

The rebuilding of the old brownstone, which had started as such an intoxicating lark, had gradually become a weariness, a burden, a misery. The contractor, George Yousseloff, had promised at first to do the whole job for thirty thousand dollars in three months. Six months later, the day before Hawke went to Hovey, he added up his accounts and found to his stupefaction that his expenditures on the house and its furnishings—beyond its original cost—had already exceeded sixty thousand dollars; and all he had to show for it was a place wrecked and gutted as by a bomb, and some crates of furniture. He had a bellowing showdown with the contractor, who tried in vain to pacify him with the usual pleasantries in his comic Russian accent. Hawke was past being charmed or amused. Yousseloff swore that the job was done, that the last steps went like lightning, that Hawke was aggravating himself without cause, that virtually all expenditures had been made, and that when he came back from the South in three or four weeks he would walk into the exact house he had planned and paid for, finished to the last detail. Yousseloff promised to uncrate the furniture and put everything in place. He said Hawke would find Scotch and bourbon in the bar, ice cubes in the bucket, coffee percolating on the stove; and, he added with a grin, a blonde in his four-poster bed, if he wished, though that would be an extra. Hawke left with relief, not exactly believing Yousseloff's rosy picture, but hoping for the best, and glad to get away from the hammering and the plaster dust.

About three weeks later the author was in one of the Hawke Brothers mines, the big Norma number six mine near the company's old cement office building. Dressed in coveralls and a miner's cap, he was driving a coal-handling machine like an immense iron crocodile, with a loading car for a tail. His face under the miner's cap was smeared black; and his eyes showed white and his grin red as a vaudeville minstrel's, in the eerie yellow light at the mine face. All around him miners in coveralls with electric lamps in their hats were moving about, yelling, or shovelling coal, or hammering at timbers. Several of the iron crocodiles rumbled and clattered here and there, the drivers sunk in seats only an inch or two above the floor, their heads barely clearing the timbered black roof; for the seam here was only about four and a half feet high. Hawke knew several of the miners. They had accepted him among them for the day in rough good fellowship. He was planning to write a novel about the coal industry after finishing *Will Horne*, and he was refreshing his recollections of the mines,

not having been in one since he had tried working as a miner for part of one summer, long ago.

Hawke knew that Lax was on his way up from Lexington. They had an appointment to meet at the office building at three. But he was having great fun, and he had lost all track of time. He was extremely astonished when a train of cars rattled up and the mine foreman came tumbling out of a gondola car followed by the Hollywood agent, who crawled after him on hands and knees through the black puddles, dressed in big flopping coveralls and an oversize miner's cap. The agent's bespectacled bird face looked so peculiarly incongruous in this outfit that Hawke roared with laughter. "Hi, Ferdie! I be god damn, you goin' in for honest work at last?"

Before Lax could answer there was an explosion, and a sound of rattling collapse. Black dust and gray smoke boiled out of one of the branching tunnels. The agent shouted at Hawke, "It's quite safe, I suppose?"

"Well, pretty safe. Vernon here, his uncle got killed last week in that tunnel."

Vernon, Lax's guide, yelled cheerfully that it wasn't blasting that killed his uncle, he was driving roof bolts and the roof fell in on him. Hawke drove the monstrous machine away with giant snortings and rattlings. He returned in a little while, ambling along with his knees up around his chin and his knuckles touching the ground, laughing as he came. "Let's go, Ferdie, let's hop a ride and get back to the sunshine. You're a brave man."

"How the devil did you learn to walk like that?" Lax shouted, following him on his hands and knees. Some of the gondola cars brimmed with coal, others were being loaded, but there was an empty one into which Hawke and the agent tumbled. The loading made such an infernal racket that talk was impossible. Soon a voice bellowed from the darkness, "Hey Art, you okay?"

"Okay, Verne," Hawke howled, and the cars lurched clanging into the tunnel.

Hawke said, his voice shaking with the jolts of the car, "You should have sent word in. I'd have come out. You're an hour early."

"The plane got to Lexington early. I'm glad I came in, it's interesting. A little scary."

"I was having fun running that loader. It's just a low-slung bulldozer, is all. You run a bulldozer you can run anything like that."

"Hawke, I don't think I ever saw you looking so happy. Maybe you're in the wrong business."

The writer threw back his big head and laughed, then yelled in his thickened accent, "Mah trouble is, Ferdie, Ah cain't really believe rahtin' is work. Now what Ah want to know is, what are you doing here? Why the rush? Why did you have to come up into these Godforsaken hills?"

"Well, Hawke, you've kept postponing your return to New York. Roland

Givney has to go to Europe. He finally said the hell with it, let's go see him in Kentucky."

The coal train was making so much noise in the low totally black tunnel —squeals, groans, rattles, clangs—that Lax had to scream this answer twice. Hawke laughed, and gestured at him in the faint lamplight from his hat to stop talking. After a while the cool clammy air grew warmer, and dim twilight appeared ahead. It brightened, they rolled into sunshine, and the noise abated. The cars jerked to a stop on a high wooden tipple above a line of empty trucks. "Come on, before they dump us," Hawke said, blinking in the strong light. They scrambled to the platform, as the bottoms of gondola cars began to flap open, showering coal with a roar into the trucks.

"The thing is," Lax puffed as they went to the shack where they both had gotten the caps and coveralls, "I wanted to talk to you before you meet Givney. I thought maybe we could talk in the mine. I didn't think it'd be so noisy."

"Now who is Givney, again?"

"Roland Givney. People's Library. He's a paperback publisher."

"And he wants to finance me in publishing my own books, is that it?"

"Yes. I just want you to know," Lax said, scraping black muck off his suède shoes on the concrete sill of the shack, "that I buy your letter a hundred percent. Our contract was a handshake. You feel I've served my purpose. That's that. If you do make a deal with him, you owe me nothing."

Hawke stepped out of the coveralls in shiny blue serge trousers and a cheap tan windbreaker. Lax emerged like a butterfly out of a cocoon: gray slacks, a lemon yellow jacket, and a soft cap that looked rather like a large muffin baked of gray tweed.

"You've made a long expensive trip, Ferdie, to get nothing out of it."

"Look, you're a human being and I'm a human being. Paths keep crossing. You may want an agent again some day. I'm glad to do it, and I hope something comes of it."

Hawke stopped at Glenn Hawke's office after cleaning up, to thank him and say goodbye. His cousin said with a bleak effort at being friendly, "Any time, Art. Did you get the dope you were after?"

"Well, it was sort of a refresher. I reckon mines don't change much."

"Not in this county. You taking your Hollywood friends down to Hovey? They won't be impressed." Hawke laughed, and Glenn said, "I'm still not used to having a famous man in the family. How's Nancy? When's she having that baby?"

"Dunno, Glenn. Seems to me if she could get up a good sneeze she'd have it."

Glenn laughed without mirth. "Art, you talked to your mom at all about that goddamned lawsuit? It's a hell of a thing. I mean in a family people ought to be able to get together without having the law in."

"You know my mother, Glenn."

"I sure do. Scotty was on the phone a while ago. I told him you were here in the mine. He asked to talk to you when you came out. Okay?"

"Sure."

Glenn told his secretary over the telephone to call Scott Hoag in Frankfort.

When Scotty came on the line, he was bubbling with optimism about the doctors' and lawyers' building in Frankfort, in which Hawke had invested twenty thousand dollars. "This gonna be the best yet, Art. I'm up here checking it over. It isn't a large project, I mean there's not too much involved, but Jesus it's a sweet one. We all gonna pull out better'n two hundred percent."

"Great."

"Say, Art, I knew you were in Hovey but I heard you were working and I didn't want to disturb you. Also, I hear you got yourself one hell of a redhead tucked away in the General Morgan Hotel. You the talk of eastern Kentucky, Art, you know."

"She's my editor, Scott."

"She is? Then I better start writing books, by the Christ, from what I hear. Haw, haw. Say, Art, something's come up on that Frenchman's Ridge binness that can bust it wide open, if your mama'll be halfway reasonable. We have a chance to sell that whole goddamn ridge, some nineteen hundred odd acres of it, to a West Virginia outfit that wants to take the timber. There's this new chemical process that makes that trashy third and fourth growth up there good for paperboard or something. So they say. We won't get any fortune but it's a chance to clean out the mess. The thing is we can't move while there's litigation going on. If you and this young lawyer up in Edgefield could work out a figure, and get your mom to go along, I think this thing could be settled."

"What do you call a figure, Scotty?"

"Jesus, Art, there you got me. You know the bind we in. We mention any amount of money, and your mom she wants ten times as much."

"Just give me an idea. Five thousand, ten thousand, fifty thousand?"

Scotty burst into rollicking laughter. "Hey, hold on, Art. We just country boys down here. What I mean, if you fellows show up talking somewhere around five, and if you can guarantee your mom'll go along, I think maybe this thing could be worked out. Your mom sort of has us over a barrel. But we'd have to move kind of fast. These people, this timber outfit, they about walked out on us when we had to tell them we got a lawsuit coming up on that land. If they drop out, this is all off."

Glenn was watching Hawke's face with apparent unconcern, dragging deeply on his cigarette every few seconds.

Hawke said, "Well, I'll talk to mama, Scott."

"You do that. I mean this is a dead parcel of land that's given all of us nothing but headaches. I mean you get your mom to talk any kind of sense at all and she'll get a pretty good windfall, because you and I both know Hawke Brothers don't owe her a goddamn quarter, Art."

2

The General John Hunt Morgan Hotel was not much of a hotel, but it was the best that Hovey had to offer: an old gloomy hostelry for travelling salesmen, built of red brick before the first world war, with sagging horsehair sofas and Morris chairs in the tiled lobby, and a few sagging dusty palms in pots, and a deaf clerk in his seventies sagging behind the desk. A syndicate led by Scotty Hoag was building a new motel atop MacDougall Hill, with a view of the Cumberland Mountains in every direction, and the Chamber of Commerce people said that the MacDougall Sky Lodge would be the making of Hovey. Meantime visitors still had to put up at—and with—the General John Hunt Morgan Hotel. Lax checked into this establishment with his party: the plump little paperback publisher, Roland Givney, and a girl named April who was a remarkable facsimile of Fay Pulver, except that she was an inch or two taller. April surveyed the lobby in dismay, while the shirt-sleeved old loafers in the Morris chairs stared at her with lecherous grins. She said to Lax in a tinkling voice, "My uncle ran a hotel just like this in Toledo, where I grew up. My aunt went crazy in the depression and he sold it."

Lax said, "Quiet, April." The old clerk was unable to take his gaze off April, and he peered after her in glassy-eyed shock as the bellboy led Lax, Givney and the girl off to their rooms.

Hawke called Jeanne on the house phone. She had the best accommodation in the hotel, a two-room suite, and fortunately the place struck her as comical, so she was enduring it well enough.

"Did your friends show up?" she said, her voice scratchy from cigarettes.

"Yes. Lax hauled me out of the mine, in fact. I'm having a drink with them, then we'll all have dinner. Want to join us for the drink?"

"Lord, no. I have no clothes on, and I have to do my hair. They must have some real dilly of a proposition if they've tracked you into these hills. Listen, Arthur, I think you've got the third act right. I've been going over it all day. When on earth did you write those new scenes? They're not anywhere in the book."

"I wrote them last night after I left you."

"But you said you were leaving for the mine at dawn. It's practically a new act."

"Well, I didn't sleep much, Jeanie."

"Good God . . . How was the mine?"

"Dark."

Jeanne chuckled. "I'm going to have a bath. You must need one too. And you must be dead. Dinner when?"

Hawke went into a spasm of deep baritone coughing. "Say eight o'clock."

"What's the matter, Arthur?"

"I don't know, it was chilly in that mine. I still haven't warmed up. I need a drink."

"You need a night's sleep. Listen, don't sign anything, do you hear? Just listen."

"Yes, love."

The bar in the hotel was called, for some reason, the Chinese Room. Perhaps it had once had an Oriental décor, but it had undergone the frightful face-lifting that has transformed most American bar rooms since women began to drink publicly. It was all maroon leather, chrome strips, and dim pink neon, and its one Chinese aspect was a steady loud drip in a tin sink behind the bar. Hawke, Givney, and Lax squeezed into a dark wooden cubicle and ordered bourbon, after Givney learned to his regret that no authentic Kentucky moonshine was available.

Hawke had been studying Givney during the automobile ride down to Hovey, which had mostly been filled with April's chatter about the heat and her thirst. This fat small man had odd prim ways with his hands and with his compressed mouth, a manner almost like a high school principal's. His straight pale hair, pince-nez glasses, and narrow features spread and softened to an even sleekness by good feeding, added to this ultra-respectable look. His expression in repose was a happy beam; but when his interest was aroused, as when the car first drove into Hovey, the beam gave way to a look of alertness, his lips disappeared, and all his features sharpened.

After some opening pleasantries Givney said, dancing spread fingers against each other, "I am here to talk about an author named Youngblood Hawke. And I am here to say that what an author like Youngblood Hawke needs is a million dollars. Not as money. Not as a reward. So that he can forget money. So that he can forget rewards. So that he can have an assured income and devote himself with a mind single and clear to the creation of art."

Naturally, Hawke was startled to hear his own long-cherished dream thus thrown back at him; and he was extremely suspicious of Givney. He said, "Well, I think if an author named Youngblood Hawke were here he might agree with you." Givney beamed at Hawke and giggled, and lit a cigarette, which he held and smoked as though it were forbidden. Hawke went on, "But who wants to endow such authors with a million?"

Givney said, "Mr. Hawke, you've just used the right word—an endowment. I understand from Mr. Lax that you want to publish your own books."

"That's true."

"It's a wise thought. The novel today is a mass consumer item—the novels of certain authors, to be sure—and therefore can be big business. I also insist that novels, at least your novels, are art. What I propose is a division of labor. Yours the art, mine the business. You've seen the People's Library on the news stands. I think you'll agree I'm a fairly realistic individual. We publish Westerns. We publish mysteries. We publish silly sex stories with undressed girls on the covers. We've found that the uncultivated reader has certain tastes. If we're to survive and to serve the larger end of nurturing art—and I think our library has nurtured some art, if nothing yet of the standing of the works of an author named Youngblood Hawke—then we must please those tastes. The People's Library has shown a profit since the year it started.

"Now then." He drew from his breast pocket a pad of white paper, and a long pencil sharpened to a needle point. He flourished the pencil, and drew a dark line down the middle of the pad. "Let us call that line the tax structure of the United States. On one side of the line we have an author named Youngblood Hawke." He wrote the name on the pad. "And on the other side we have—" He silently wrote $1,000,000 in sharp neat figures. "My task is to move that sum across the line unscathed, thereby creating our endowment. Correct?"

Givney beamed at Hawke. Lax regarded Givney from under heavy lids. Hawke stared at the sheet with the legend

Youngblood Hawke | $1,000,000

"Damned right," he said. "But there's no way to get the money across the line."

"Why, yes, there are several routes," Givney said. "Let's first consider Spread. That's the commonest device. If there's a large amount of money to be paid, you mustn't collect it in one year, because it goes into the ninety percent bracket and has to be handed straight over to the government. You spread it. In the case of our million, let's say, we would pay it to you at the rate of forty thousand a year over twenty-five years. Of course that cuts down the tax bite. But frankly I dislike this device. Let me show you why."

He began scrawling figures on the pad. He was sitting next to Hawke, and was writing under Hawke's nose, leaning against him and exuding the sweet smell of some hair lotion. "Let's say certain people are willing to put down a million for all the rights in a number of novels by you. They start paying you forty thousand a year.

"Now look here, Mr. Hawke. Any competent stockbroker can take that million and put together a four percent portfolio—utility bonds, high grade rails, blue chip stocks, and so forth. Now four percent of a million dollars is forty thousand a year.

"Mr. Hawke, don't you see that a spread deal like that is all done with

mirrors? All we do is pay you *your own interest*. Of course there are taxes to pay on that interest, but we can find any number of jiggles to offset them. At the end of the twenty-five years we not only keep the original million, the capital sum that rightly belongs to you, but we've actually made money on it, because portfolios go up in value over a quarter of a century, and we get that appreciation. Not to mention further than twenty-five years from now you'll only be fifty-four, at the very crest of your creative powers, and the payments will suddenly stop. Now I call that unfair. I call it ridiculous."

Lax murmured, "It works."

"Who guarantees it?" Givney said sharply. "Who says for sure the Treasury won't turn around some day and throw out every spread deal that's ever been made?"

"Nobody can guarantee that the Treasury won't turn around tomorrow and take everything away from us and give us all numbers and ration cards," the agent said. "We just have to hope that the whole thing won't fall apart for a while."

"That's talk," Givney said. "The United States isn't falling apart. I say there's a criminal lack of imagination in the literary industry. My contention is, when you're doing business, study the masters. Study the oil companies. Study the big electric combines. Study the corporations that hire more tax brains than the Treasury can afford to hire. Their practices are legal, ethical, and inventive. Now, they've demonstrated that there are definite advantages to doing business under a foreign flag—what the shipping companies sometimes call flags of convenience. Of course when you create a foreign corporation you look for tax advantage plus stability. It turns out that Switzerland is a good place for many reasons. If we formed a Swiss corporation to publish your work and sell its subsidiary rights, such as paperback, stage, and film rights it would be a very simple matter to construct the stock picture so that within five years you could take home that million tax-paid at a capital gain rate. I assume you would continue your present rate of writing, and produce at least three important works by Youngblood Hawke in that time."

Hawke said, "What's involved? Would I have to become a Swiss citizen?"

Givney smiled at Lax. The agent said, "Nobody becomes a Swiss, Youngblood. You have to establish residence, but hell, you want to spend some time in Europe anyway, don't you? Switzerland's comfortable, and it's fine. A writer should know Europe."

Hawke went into another spasm of coughing. He had drunk two straight bourbons, but the chill of the mine was still in his bones. He said uneasily, "Look, I'm no patriot. I'll do anything that makes sense, within reason. But this sticks in my craw. I'm not going to change my citizenship or take up a phony residence abroad."

Lax shrugged. "Everybody's doing it."

"I understand you, and I applaud you, Mr. Hawke," said Givney, raising his eyebrows. "There speaks, if I may say so, the voice of the Kentucky hills, the voice one hears in your novels. I respect that, though I don't quite agree. So we rule out a foreign corporation. That leaves the route with the most difficulties, an American company. Still, it can work."

Givney now launched into a description of his scheme, which Hawke found rather hard to follow. He had had almost no sleep in forty-eight hours, and not much food; he had forgotten to take any lunch into the mine, and had gotten by all day on half a ham sandwich and a swallow of coffee given to him by his friend Vernon at the mine face. The two drinks of bourbon had set his head swimming without warming him up. The nub of Givney's idea seemed to be that Hawke would get rid of ordinary income tax rates by dumping all the rights of his next three or four books—publishing, dramatic, film, paperback, and everything else—into a corporation. In return he would be issued some stock, and more stock as he produced the books. "Certain parties," as Givney put it, in the movie and publishing fields, would capitalize the firm at something like a million and a half dollars. Givney had these certain parties lined up and willing. Corporate taxes could be minimized in various ways. In due course Hawke would get the money out as a capital gain. "Let's not forget," said Givney, "that none of this is fanciful, that we're talking soberly about conservative facts. A novel like *Chain of Command*, cascading through bookstores, book clubs, paperbacks, the stage, the films, television, foreign countries, and all the rest, is going to gross many times a million dollars for all the proprietors involved. Ten or fifteen million dollars may be nearer the real figure. And out of all this bonanza, does it make sense for the author to get a mere shred, only to have that shred shredded again by ordinary income tax? It's insane. The sober, the only thing to do is to put all those proprietorships under one roof, Hawke Incorporated, and to make the proprietor the only rightful one—Youngblood Hawke."

Hawke said, "These certain parties of yours will hold stock in the corporation, won't they?"

"Of course."

"How do I assure myself control over what happens to my work? Which I must have, or no scheme is worth anything."

"The stock structure will give you voting control."

"If you do that it's a personal holding company, isn't it? The taxes are even more prohibitive than ordinary income tax."

Givney and Lax exchanged a glance. Lax's sleepy eyes opened wide, and he smiled at Hawke with what seemed to be fatherly approval.

"Very good," Givney said, "except that money from the sale of books isn't personal holding company income, according to the law. We can get bogged in detail here. I'd like to give you the whole picture."

Hawke said, "How do I get the money out of this corporation, once it's in?"

Givney said, "We liquidate the corporation for cash at the right time, and distribute the assets."

"That means I'd sell off my copyrights to strangers and lose all control of my books. And you'd get in a hell of a mess with valuation problems."

The paperback publisher burst out laughing. "You've been doing your homework. I think that's admirable. The very greatest literary artists have all had a keen money sense. Voltaire, Balzac, Twain. Let me assure you that these minor difficulties can be circumvented."

Hawke said, "Even assuming that, all the money from a book piles in during a year or two. What do you do about the undistributed profits tax?"

Lax said with a grin, "No wonder you fired me, Hawke."

Givney smiled primly. "Did you study to be a CPA, by any chance, before you started writing?"

Hawke said, "No. You can find out a good bit in the Forty-second Street Library if you're willing to sit and read. I've done a lot of it. I've gone through this whole business of incorporating myself. I think the Treasury has booby-trapped it out of existence."

"I can only tell you," said Givney, beaming, "that some prudent people —actors, and writers too—have discovered that that isn't so, and as a result they are amazingly well off."

Hawke looked to Lax, who had subsided into his false slumber again. He very much wanted to ask the agent what he thought, but he knew that one such inquiry would bring Lax back in his employ. He was excited, and hungry, and very tired. His hands, he noticed, were still seamed with coal dust in the knuckles and under the nails. He clasped them with the fingers inward. "Well, you're going to have to put your proposal on paper, of course, so that I can study it."

"Of course," Givney said. "Just bear in mind that most of the pitfalls disappear if we do two things. First, if you yourself take some real money risk. Second, if Hawke Incorporated doesn't merely publish your books, but engages in other investment. There are many tax shelters we can find—"

"You mean orange groves, beef herds, oil and gas leases, that kind of thing?" Hawke said.

Givney's beam brightened. "Those are the well-publicized ones. The Forty-second Street Library ones, shall we say. They've been overworked. There are others. We could, for instance, produce the films made from your books ourselves. Many, many possibilities open up as soon as one uses imagination, and gets out of the rut of conventional formulas. Bear in mind, too, that when you're an officer of a corporation, as you will be,

vistas of easier living open up. Expense accounts come into play. An operating item called 'miscellaneous,' sometimes known as petty cash, can make the difference between living luxuriously or meanly—at no extra tax cost." His beam sloped to one side, just short of a wink. "Now, then, I understand you're working on a new novel."

"Yes."

"Is it as good as *Chain of Command?*"

"It's better."

"Can you divulge the subject?"

"I'd rather not. Are you thinking of starting with this book? I owe it to Hodge Hathaway."

"Do you have a written contract?"

"No."

"Then you don't owe it to them. Of course we'd get a major publisher to handle the actual production and selling of the books, for a fee. I was thinking of Prince House."

Startled, Hawke said, "*Prince* House?"

"Mr. Hawke, I've had long talks with Jay Prince and with Waldo Fipps, the editor who introduced you to the world of letters. There is sympathy for Youngblood Hawke in that house. There is admiration. And of course there's a burning desire to have you back."

"It's one-sided. I have no desire to go back."

Givney looked sad, and his lips disappeared. "That's a dash of cold water. I do hope you'll see the merits of using that firm to make and sell the books."

Well, Hawke thought, there goes the streak of red, the fox breaking from cover. Jay Prince! Waldo Fipps! All the talk of a million-dollar endowment was his own drunken conversation with Fipps at Number One, so long ago, played back to him with hardly a change. In a flash he recalled the days at Prince House: the condescending hostility of Fipps; the garrulous warmth of Fanny, a hot sweet sauce poured over solid ice; the hearty fatherliness and the grasping at pennies that characterized Jay. He said, "I won't have Prince House. I gave my word to Ross Hodge that he'd get this new book. I'll keep my word. Does that end the matter?"

There was a pause during which Givney's lips remained out of sight, though he smiled. "Mr. Hawke, with Prince House we're ready to go. I don't think we could interest Ross Hodge. Hodge Hathaway is an old successful house, a conservative house, not interested in imaginative new structures designed to solve modern tax problems."

Hawke said, "Well, I like Hodge Hathaway." He made a move as though to slide out of the cubicle.

Givney laid a plump hand on his windbreaker. "Prince House isn't an absolute must."

Hawke said, "Can we continue this at dinner? I'm hungry. I'll get my editor, and we'll go over to the American Legion Hall. They put out a fair steak sometimes."

Givney said, "About your editor—Mrs. Fry, isn't it?"

"Yes."

"It's well known in the trade how devoted you are to her, and vice-versa. Of course in this new situation she would hold an important post. She could conceivably be your publisher. And there would be a place for Karl Fry too. He's very well thought of at Prince House."

3

It was an awkward dinner they had in the smoky gloom of the Legion dining hall. Givney's offer, after all, was an attempted raid on Hodge Hathaway. With Jeanne at the table the men could not discuss it. At least Givney would not open the subject, so the others didn't. The unexplained visit of a Hollywood agent and a New York paperback publisher to a Kentucky mountain town was heavily absurd. The result of this reticence was a limping conversation, full of forced smiles. Jeanne and April chatted about summer clothes, and for once Lax did not tell his companion to be quiet. It was a relief when Hawke was called to the telephone, and learned that his sister had suddenly gone to the hospital, in labor that promised to be swift. That broke up the dinner. Hawke and Jeanne drove to the hospital, taking Lax with them to drop him at the hotel; April and Givney went in the limousine.

Lax said in the car, "I'm sorry we haven't had a chance to talk. You probably figure if you ask my advice it'll cost you ten percent. I'll volunteer it for nothing. I assume you'll be discussing this with Jeanne, anyway."

Hawke said, "I've told her I've been offered a million dollars. I didn't elaborate."

"What do you think of that?" Lax said from the back seat to Jeanne, who sat beside Hawke.

She said, "It depends on what they want of him. I don't understand the proposition at all."

Lax nodded, "Here's how I feel, Hawke. First of all you're dealing with people who have the money. Or at least can get it. That's important."

Hawke said, "Is Givney really anybody? All that stuff about *nurturing* art." He took his hands off the wheel to caress an invisible globe in the air. "I wanted to feel for my wallet."

"Hollywood's full of guys like that. They think that's the way to talk to writers. I checked on Givney. He came out of nowhere, out of third-

rate pulp magazines, in the last few years. He's made a dent in the paperback market with a cheap line and hard selling. Now he's reaching out for respectability, for class, hence the pitch to Youngblood Hawke. I know the movie people he's got lined up, I'm not at liberty right now to say who they are, but the dough is there. As for Jay Prince, well, you know Jay. I'm surprised at his being in a deal of this magnitude. Givney may be just using him and calling the percentages and the figures. Jay would agree to practically anything that would get you back, short of parting with substantial money. The money will come from Givney and the film people. Everything depends on the contract, and you'd better look it over with a high-powered microscope."

"I take it you're advising against."

"No. If you really want to clear a million dollars tax-paid out of your writings, Hawke—and that seems to be your notion—this kind of thing is the only route. You can live pleasantly on royalties, but that's all. There will never be another author made rich by royalties, fellows like Maugham. Amassing capital these days means getting in with a loophole artist like Givney. Now fellows like him have figured out some remarkable gimmicks in recent years and made big fortunes. Established publishers and old-time movie makers won't give you such deals, they don't like the risks and the complications. You know me, Hawke, I'm the old bird-in-hand man. I'd ask for the million spread over twenty or twenty-five years."

Hawke said, "You heard Givney. All they'd be doing is paying me interest on my own money."

"It would be an assured income for half your life or more," Lax said. "The other thing is a complicated gamble. Your future books will be successful, if you don't go crazy or something, and you seem to have your heart set on becoming a capitalist, so I can't tell you to turn the deal down. I can only tell you to have it scrutinized by the best lawyer you can find."

Hawke stopped the car in front of the hotel. After the refrigerated cold of the dining room the dark street was steamy, and in the red light of the hotel sign he could see that Jeanne's forehead was moist, though she wore only a sleeveless cotton dress. Lax, slumped in the back seat, seemed cool as a turtle on a rock. Hawke said, "I don't know. Maybe you should handle the deal after all."

Lax said, "Either way we'll be the same friends. Just don't rush into anything. I'll be at the St. Regis until Monday. We've decided to roar on back to Lexington tonight, I think maybe we can still make the late plane." He gave Hawke his usual boneless handshake. "I'm sure your sister will be fine. We all came into the world that way. Bye, Jeanne."

Hawke thanked him, and drove off to the hospital. The little agent

entered the hotel, and rode the creaking elevator to the second floor. He hesitated in the dingy corridor for a moment; then, instead of going to his room, he walked to the end of the hall and knocked on the door of Roland Givney.

4

Behind a white folding screen, the doctor was palpating Nancy's abdomen. Hawke caught a glimpse of the balloon-tight white belly marbled with branching blue veins before Nancy, seeing him, flipped a sheet over her naked skin and the doctor's hands. "Go away, Art, you big fool. Hello, Jeanie." Jeanne and Nancy had become good friends.

The doctor, an interne with a crew cut who seemed about sixteen years old, said he was through. Mrs. Hawke and Nancy's husband, seated in armchairs at the foot of the bed, looked at him anxiously. He uttered a spate of medical-school jargon in a South Carolina accent flattened by study at some eastern school. Mrs. Hawke at last said, "Well now, doctor, that's right fine. How's she doing and how long will it be?"

"I'll examine her again in an hour and perhaps we'll have oxygen and blood plasma as stand-by precautions. At the present rate delivery won't occur before two A.M. I'll keep in touch with Dr. Eversill."

The husband stared at the young doctor, his big ugly mouth hanging open, his thick wig askew at the forehead line. "Doctor, is there anything that can be done? Some extra precaution? There's no question of expense."

The doctor said with a pitying little smile, "Well, we'll just see in another hour." He took the stethoscope from his neck with a highly professional gesture, and left.

"It's a funny thing," Weltmann said, "how hard it is to get a straight answer from a doctor."

"Stop fretting, John," Nancy said. She lay back on a mound of pillows, her dark hair spread in disorder around her pale unpainted face, perspiration standing on her forehead and her upper lip. She appeared excited, uncertain, and happy. Hawke thought he had never seen Nancy look so pretty, not even at her wedding, the big mound of her belly under the bedsheet notwithstanding. She held out her hand to her husband. He shambled to the bed, and sat, and they clasped hands. She smiled at Jeanne. "You must be getting pretty tired of Hovey."

"Nancy, I grew up in a small town."

When Nancy's pains began again she sent Hawke out of the room with her husband. The two men sat on a battered sofa in the corridor in gloom, in the smell of disinfectant; from other rooms than Nancy's came now and then sobbing, or a cry, or a buzz for the floor nurse with the

flashing of a red light. The second hand of the electric clock on the wall crawled around and around, seemingly at half the normal speed. Weltmann said, "It's a fine hospital. Much better than one would expect, in Hovey."

Hawke said, "The coal companies had the sense to put it up. One more way of keeping the union out of the county."

He had to force himself to talk. He was haunted by the same thought that was haunting everybody. If the baby were born hairless there would be a year of strain before anyone could know for certain whether it was doomed to be a bald freak like its father.

The youthful doctor came an eternal hour later, looked Nancy over, and departed with more cabalistic mutterings about oxygen, transfusions, dilations, and the fetal bloodstream. The tempo of Nancy's pains quickened. She sent the mother out of the room, and only Jeanne remained with her. Mrs. Hawke's feathers were badly ruffled by this. "Says I make her nervous! Her own mother makes her nervous!" she snapped at Hawke, pacing in the corridor. "Reckon if she prefers the company of that Jewish secretary of yours, that's all right with me." Weltmann was lighting a cigarette. She said, "Give me one of those."

Weltmann swung his heavy head toward her, like an ox who has been unexpectedly kicked. "A cigarette, mother?"

"I guess I can have one if I want to."

The lighting of the cigarette was a tremendous undertaking, the mother snorting out the first few matches Weltmann lit for her. She stood with her back against the wall, puffing at the cigarette defiantly and continuously, holding it as though she were blowing soap bubbles. Hawke was hard put to it not to bellow with laughter for all his tension, or maybe because of it. He had long ago given up trying to persuade his mother that Jeanne's family were all Presbyterians, and that she was an editor. Mrs. Hawke refused to connect the term *editor* with a young woman like Jeanne. She was a secretary, and she was Jewish like everybody in New York. But the mother had taken to her, and often cited Jeanne as a proof that there were some fine Jews.

Dr. Eversill, the old family physician, arrived in his usual bulky slovenly gray suit, from which the Hovey *Gazette* inevitably protruded; casually examined Nancy, yawning, then went off to change his clothes. It was half past two when the wheeled table came, and Nancy was carted off to the delivery room. Hawke followed as far as he could. When he saw the sheeted, bloated form of his sister pass through the double doors into a blinding blue glare from floodlamps, he had a sudden horrible feeling that he would never see her again alive; it was as though she were being fed into the furnace of a crematorium.

Mrs. Hawke was talking a mile a minute, cheery and giggling. "Why pshaw, she's having a much easier time than I had. Twenty-five hours in

labor, and believe you me in those days there were no shots and no pills to make it go easier, and no fine modern hospital like this. I had Nancy right in my own bedroom and Art too. Why, those days one mother out of every three had some kind of serious trouble after, and who hears of such a thing nowadays? Just like rolling off a log. Why, Evalee Blaine only last week in this very hospital had a fine eight-pound boy and there was all this RH business, whatever that is, and they were all ready to pump out the poor baby's blood and pump in different blood and then it was all unnecessary. Why that boy peed right in Doctor Eversill's face the minute he was born and served him right, scaring everybody like that. The trouble is they know too much nowadays. They scare the wits out of you. Having a baby's just as natural as eating a dinner. Nancy'd be better off at home instead of in this place. The smell is enough to depress a body, why, I never walk into a hospital but I smell death." Mrs. Hawke went on in this vein, working around to vehement support of modern medicine and then back to denunciation of it several times. John Weltmann sat on a chair, his head sunk in his hands. Jeanne leaned against the wall under the clock with the slow-crawling second hand, an elbow resting on the back of a fist, smoking and smoking.

The clock read a quarter to four when the wail throbbed in the night air. There were other baby cries in the hospital, but this was different: sharp, angry, protesting, rhythmic, raw. Jeanne, Hawke, and Mrs. Hawke looked at each other. Weltmann slowly raised his head, the wig ridiculously awry, his mouth hanging open, his eyes staring. A nurse walked out of the delivery room, a small thin woman with carroty hair. As she passed by them, going into Nancy's room, she said offhandedly, "It's a boy and everything's all right."

John Weltmann called after her, "My wife? My wife?"

"Fine." The nurse began straightening Nancy's bed. The wheeled table appeared after a while, with Nancy flat on it, her hair in disorder, her face wet, gray and exhausted, her eyes brilliant, the lump at her waistline much reduced. "Did you see him?" she said smiling, and making a feeble gesture with one hand. "He's back there in the cage." Weltmann ran after the table, grasping Nancy's hand. The others hurried down the corridor to the turn where an arrow read "Nursery." Behind a glass wall in a dimly lit room there were baskets on wheeled racks covered with thin white cloths, each basket labelled with a family name in thick black crayon: *Napier, Carter, Holcomb, Caudill.* A masked nurse appeared, pushing along a rack with a basket labelled WELTMANN. She propped it up at the glass window and there was the baby. She smiled and waved at them, and walked off.

The baby was yawning, stretching, and blinking great blue eyes. It was clean, pink, totally and amazingly human, with a square, determined face not unlike Hawke's. He had expected to see a red scrawny monkey-

like creature, but Nancy's baby was beautiful; he thought it the most beautiful thing his eyes had ever seen.

"Well, he's sure got plenty of hair, that's one thing," Mrs. Hawke said. The baby indeed had a thick black thatch of hair.

Hawke said, "It's astounding. I had no idea babies could yawn and stretch."

"What did you think they did?" Jeanne said in a breaking voice. "They're people."

He looked at her and saw that tears were pouring down her cheeks, and she was not wiping them. He touched his handkerchief to the rivulets on her face. "What the devil are you crying about?"

"Who's crying?" Jeanne said.

Weltmann came treading heavily into the nursery, walked up to the window, and looked through the glass at the baby without expression. Its eyes were closed, it was still yawning ferociously, and moving its tiny arms at random. From the neck down it was swathed in a blue blanket.

"Well, John, do you like him?" Mrs. Hawke said. "I'd say he's a pretty good specimen."

Weltmann fell to his knees, his head bowed against the glass. For an instant Hawke thought he had fainted, and reached to support him. Then he heard his brother-in-law saying, "Thank God, thank God." After a silent moment Weltmann stood and looked around at them with a foolish happy look, his eyes red, his mouth loose. "I have to build a church," he said. "I don't know where, I don't suppose they want a Lutheran church in Hovey, but I have to build a church. There's no hurry, I don't have to build it tomorrow, so long as I build it." He looked at the baby. "Did you ever see so much hair?"

5

Hawke drove his mother home, and then took Jeanne to a highway diner framed in gaudy neon, the all-night oasis of the truck drivers. As he whirled into the parking space among the coal trucks and trailer diesels, Jeanne said, "I don't know. I'm not exactly dressed for a diner, am I?" She glanced down at her rumpled frock. "Lord! I look as though I'd been sleeping in the rain."

"This is where everybody goes after a dance or a party. Come on."

There were about a dozen drivers in the brightly lit, white-tiled diner, big cheerful men in tan or blue work clothes, smoking, eating, drinking beer, talking. A wonderful aroma of fresh coffee triumphed over the tobacco and food smells. Hawke and Jeanne sat at a little table, and some of the drivers glanced at Jeanne with friendly appreciative grins. A burly young man in green coveralls said, "Hey Art, you up early or late?"

Hawke said, "Late, Earl. Old Nancy just had herself a boy up to the miner's hospital."

"Hey, a boy! You an uncle, I allow. She'd a had a girl you'd be a aunt." Hawke joined happily in the laugh. "Nancy all right?"

"Just fine." Hawke repeated the news to Dan, the fat red-faced man in a chef's cap who came out of the kitchen, and Dan shook his hand and slapped his back and served two cold beers on the house at once.

Jeanne liked diners, they reminded her of college dances, of the glowing befuddled aftermath of necking, and she particularly liked this one, where Hawke was so much at home. It occurred to her, as he sat before her drinking beer in his tan windbreaker, unshaven and tousle-headed, his knuckles still grimy from mine dust, exchanging repartee with Dan in hill jargon, that he seemed much more like one of the drivers than like Youngblood Hawke, the Pulitzer Prize novelist.

By now Jeanne knew scores of writers. Her early awe of them, which had drawn her to the publishing business, was extinct. She considered them a sorry lot, petty shy incompetent self-pitying egoists, filled with envious hatred of each other. It had been her fortune, or her misfortune, to meet Hawke at the outset: Hawke, who was generous about other authors, who moved through literary parties with awkward good nature and was jovial even with the scribblers of venomous reviews about his books, who came to her time after time alight with enthusiasm about new novels, sometimes the current best sellers and sometimes obscure and difficult European works, who was more widely read than anyone she knew, but hardly ever referred to his reading, who tempered his maniacal self-confidence with a peculiar lack of pride in any of his completed work. She knew he believed at bottom that he was something like a Balzac reborn. If she did not detest him for this it was because she suspected it might almost be true, and also because this opinion of himself was not reflected in conceit or in literary airs, but in obsessive drudgery. Nobody worked like Hawke, nobody at Hodge Hathaway, nobody in the American literary scene, so far as she knew. He sat opposite her, pale, pouchy-eyed, but afire with the excitement of the birth and with gusto for the food Dan set before them. She did not know when he had last closed his eyes in sleep, or for how long. She only knew that he had left her at the hotel near midnight and had gone to the mine at dawn, after depositing at the hotel an envelope containing almost a whole new act of a play, scrawled on forty yellow sheets. During these two weeks in Hovey, when he had been hewing the play out of *Alms for Oblivion*, he had not stopped working on the novel *Will Horne*. "Fellow's got to carry water on both shoulders sometimes," he had told her once, with weary good cheer.

Karl was right, she thought, Arthur was a giant, and this was what a giant was like; bigger than other men, coarser, gentler, in some ways simpler, or even weaker, a careless benign volcano of a man. She had

loved him, she had hated him, she had been repeatedly angry at him, but after all Karl had spoken the truth, the not entirely bitter truth, that her work with Youngblood Hawke was almost her life. This was true though for two years she had been Mrs. Karl Fry, and knew only Karl in the last intimacies that should have been at the center of her life. She fell to eating the scrambled eggs and bacon with all the gay hunger of a girl who has been out all night dancing.

And Hawke—Hawke thought these were the best eggs he had eaten in his life, golden yellow, scrambled in plenty of butter just short of dry, a curly mound of four eggs surrounded with heaps of bacon; Dan always piled on the bacon, and it was always right too, drained of grease, and there was a huge plate of perfect French fried potatoes too, crisp to the teeth but meal-white inside, good truck-driver food, and the new rolls were still warm, and the beer was sharp cold, and Dan's coffee at five in the morning was the best on earth, because Dan scrubbed out that god-damned urn and scalded it before he started coffee again! Dan's coffee had the exalting, the almost sacramental lift to it of the fresh coffee he had drunk at dawn on the beach at Iwo Jima, bulldozing the black sand heaps of the unloading area, with guns popping in the interior of the island, red tracer bullets rising in dotted lines to the green sky, and a plane bursting into a rose of flame and slowly falling and twisting . . . Jeanne, as she ate, was looking at him with an intoxicating light in her eye, a light she had long been suppressing. Hawke laughed out loud, for no reason at all and struck the table with his fist so that all the plates jumped, and said, "By God, isn't this food good?"

She said, "It's wonderful. It's marvellous."

He said, "And am I crazy or is Nancy's baby unusually beautiful? Uncles aren't supposed to be starry-eyed like parents."

Jeanne said, "I've seen a lot of babies. This one beats them all. I don't understand it, he's the image of you and I wouldn't call you beautiful, but that baby is a vision, he makes you believe all the stories of angels dropped from the skies. I could commit murder and steal that baby. Arthur Hawke, for heaven's sake, stop eating like a wolf. Slow down."

"What in hell are you talking about? You've eaten four rolls to my two and you've already finished your bacon and eggs."

"The man only gave me half as much."

"Have some more."

"No, no. Conceivably another beer, if there's another one that cold."

Hawke roared at Dan for more cold beer. He could not understand why the truck drivers kept looking at him and Jeanne, in a friendly amused way. The other aspect of Hawke's extraordinary ability to take in and remember details was an almost incredible obtuseness, sometimes, to plain reality. It did not occur to him that there was anything odd in his sitting in the diner at half-past five in the morning with a pretty

young woman in a pink cotton frock, a woman with New York style, moreover, as conspicuous in Hovey as a polar bear, nor did it strike him that he and she were laughing and looking at each other like lovers. He was genuinely amazed when Earl Fouts, the driver in green coveralls who had grown up with him on High Street, stopped on his way out and slapped him on the shoulder. "Well, you tell Nancy for me nice going, hear? Maybe you two be next in line."

They both rocked with laughter. Nothing, it seemed, could go wrong with this moment; nothing could dim their mood, a single mood that wrapped both of them in a transparent sparkling cloud.

Hawke said, slipping into workman's speech, "Jeanne, these fellows gonna have me believing we married. Mind now you don't let me do nothing absent-minded when I take you to the hotel."

She only laughed louder.

The truck men kept coming and going in the long narrow diner ablaze with white light. From the jukebox a hill singer lamented that the only girl he ever loved was marrying his best friend. To Hawke the scene in the diner had taken on the sharp, light-bathed truth of a painting—the long clean counter of gray plastic and stainless steel, the row of stools, the shining urns, the menus on the wall of white movable letters embedded in black strips, the gaudy jukebox, Dan in his white chef's cap, the brawny drivers in blue jeans and brown windbreakers—all seemed to have fallen into a static composition in a frame, a painting of a scene of his youth. It was as though Jeanne were not there, and yet there too—a lovely memory, or a ghost, because this was Dan's Diner in Hovey, and he was nineteen, and he knew no person named Mrs. Jeanne Fry; but he was buoyantly happy with the knowledge that he was going to do great things some day, and marry the most famous and sought-after beauty in the world.

"You know something, Jeanie?" he said. "I used to think Hovey was the world's capital of ignorance, stupidity, pettiness, and greed, and all I had to do was escape beyond the hills to find the fair world and the fair people of the novels and the movies. I know now that Hovey is simply the place where I first saw human nature, and where I first encountered resistance to my big opinion of myself. That's what ruined it for me. But that would have been true of any place where I grew up. Hovey's a nice place, the air is good and the hills are magnificent, and the people are all right. They haven't had the advantages of the city people and they have their narrow and mean streaks but by Christ they're Americans. There wasn't an able-bodied man or boy walking the streets of Hovey in the war. It was a town of women and children and creeping old men. Except a few miners that got kept on the job, and half of them had a bad arm or a bad leg or something. I'm not saying it's a birthplace of heroes but—I be

goddamn. It's dawn, Jeanne. Look at that sky! My nephew's first day on this screwy planet."

"This is scandalous. Take me to the hotel," Jeanne said.

"Are you sleepy?"

"God, no. I'm vibrating. It's like I used to be in exam week after I'd had four benzedrine pills. But I mean, Arthur, we both need sleep. Especially you!"

A chill wind was blowing outside, and Hawke went into a spasm of deep harsh coughing. Jeanne said anxiously, "You'd better take something for that."

"I'm just tired."

Hawke sang his high school song for her as they drove to the hotel, and she then sang the songs of her school, to much laughter. They both were buoyed along in the same exultant mood, a spirit almost of adolescent dating, a mixture of fatigue and merriment radiant with keen sexual desire that had to remain unfulfilled. It was a great mood, and Hawke at least was having thoughts of going up to Jeanne's room and extracting a few kisses from her. After all! The mood collapsed in an instant for both of them when Jeanne went to the hotel desk to get her key, and the sleepy Negro boy took a yellow telegram out of her box.

She said, ripping it open, "When did they deliver this?"

"Dunno, mum. I came on at midnight. It was in de box."

She read the wire and looked at Hawke with a face from which all gaiety had departed. "When's the first plane out of Lexington today, Arthur?"

"About four in the afternoon on the new schedule. What's the matter?"

"Karl's in Washington. He wants me."

"What's he doing there?"

Jeanne started to talk, then stopped. After a slight pause she said, "That's beside the point. I'd better pack and get right on down to Lexington. Can I rent a car here and drop it off there?"

"Jeanne, go ahead and pack if you want, and then get a few hours' sleep. I'll come for you at half-past twelve and drive you down."

"That's pointless. You'll waste a day."

"The hell it's pointless. You're not driving on that road with those coal trucks roaring both ways. Look, do as I say. I'll make your plane reservation."

"Arthur, I can take care of myself."

"Shut up and go to sleep for a while. If you don't I'll fire you. You're not a good editor anyway, I'm just keeping you on because you're pretty."

Jeanne laughed in a deeply weary, resigned tone. "I hate a bully. I have your play script upstairs, and all—"

"I'll come and get it."

He had entered Jeanne's suite only half a dozen times in the three weeks she had been in Hovey. She had contrived to avoid having him there, and he had not especially wanted to torment himself with isolation that could lead to nothing. He was not going to force Jeanne Fry into adultery; he was not sure the possibility existed, but in any case, the conduct he accepted as normal with Frieda Winter was impossible with Jeanne. Now he went upstairs with her, and they stood in the dowdy, dusty room in the early morning light, and she handed him his pages neatly bound in a red portfolio. Their exhilaration was utterly quenched. The project of snatching kisses seemed boyish folly.

"Jeanne, I'm sorry you have to rocket off like this."

"So am I. But the job's just about done, anyway, and I must go. Dan's Diner is the greatest restaurant on earth. I'll never forget it, Arthur."

When Hawke got home he went upstairs, walking softly to avoid waking his mother, and put himself at the old tiny desk, where yellow pages lay in two squared-off piles: the novel and the play. He sat and stared at the two piles, lacking the will to take the pen in his hand. It was the old pen with which he had written everything since the first night in Kwajalein when he had without forethought begun a play about the Seabees. The rubber tube in the pen had long since rotted; he had replaced it, but the pumping lever no longer worked; he had broken several pen points and inserted others; nothing was really left of the pen he had started with but the black plastic barrel. Yet he would write with nothing else, though he had to dip it in a bottle of ink now after every few lines. Once he grasped the pen his hand started to move across the page; the thing had acquired talismanic force, together with the old watch that always lay beside it.

This time, however, he did not think even that magic could work. Fatigue was so soaked in his bones that breathing seemed to come hard, and he was still coughing. In a space of thirty-six hours or so he had rattled off almost a whole new act of a play, each line of which had felt as correct as a piece of a jigsaw clicking into place; he had been in the mine, revelling in the rough friendly talk of the miners, and the powerful good feel of the big loading machine; he had talked to Givney, exchanged financial cabalisms with him, and he could still see before his eyes the publisher's cunning pencilled legend

Youngblood Hawke | $1,000,000;

he had seen Nancy's baby, a revelation like the first tent evangelist's speech which had sent him running forward to fall on his knees, a boy of eleven, to declare for Christ. His thoughts were little more than pillow fantasies, though he was sitting up: thoughts of recapturing Jeanne from Karl Fry; thoughts of what he would do after collecting Givney's million,

thoughts of abandoning the quest for money, fleeing his present life, and going to England or Italy and Mexico and living like a miser, of dropping the three intervening novels he had planned and starting at once on The American Comedy. The anxious depression that often came with excessive fatigue had him in its grip, and a scary headache ran like a quarter-circle of hot metal from the top of his head down to his right ear.

With all this, he reluctantly stretched out a sweating hand and took the pen and the novel pad. The first few lines he wrote wavered across the ruled paper as though he were sick; then his writing firmed. His mother found him at noon—he had left a note for her to call him then—fast asleep in the chair at his desk, his head on his arms, his right hand and his forehead smeared with ink.

6

The drive to Lexington was a lugubrious one, except when they talked about Hawke's work; then Jeanne managed to rouse herself and speak up in her usual free and sharp way. Otherwise she sat in a frigid calm, looking out at the mountains, at the trees dripping and glistening in the warm rain, and smoking cigarette after cigarette. She rebuffed very shortly one or two questions he put about Karl's trip to Washington. He kept glancing at her as he drove, and her remoteness made her all the more provoking and desirable. Jeanne did not look her best in profile; there was something tough, almost thrusting in the firm lines of her nose and jaw, when they were not softened by the delicious curves of her high cheeks, and the mischievous brightness of her eyes. When she was tense, a muscle at the side of her face rhythmically tightened under her skin; and he could see that muscle working now.

But nothing could lessen her charm for him. From the moment when he had brushed tears from her face as she looked at Nancy's baby, he had broken into a new period in his long and complicated relationship with her. Those tears had signalled for him the unreality of her marriage. It was almost as though time had kindly slipped its cogs and brought him together with her as at the very first. He loved Jeanne. He wanted to marry her. He was haunted by the picture of his ridiculous brother-in-law on his knees, thanking God for the hair on his new baby's head. The realization was strong in him that to go on and on copulating with Mrs. Winter in planned sneaked hours, and to intersperse this indulgence with other casual copulations, was a course that had run itself out. The fascination Frieda had always had for him was far from dead, and he knew he would never forget her, any more than a man forgets his first wife. But he desperately wanted a better existence.

So Hawke ignored all the warning signs that Jeanne's mood was, to say

the least, not attuned to a declaration from him. He was full of his new yearning for a life of virtue with her, and out it had to come, though he was seeing her off to join her husband in some undisclosed emergency. The plane was late; he saw to her bags and her ticket, then took her into the airport coffee shop where they sat in a booth and had sandwiches. And there he blurted coarsely into Jeanne's abstracted silence, "Jeanne, tell me just one thing. Is it absolutely out of the question?"

She had been staring at a woman in another booth wearing a preposterous gray hat with a stuffed purple bird on it. She turned to him, her eyes seemed to focus on him with difficulty, and then she measured him with a long glance, her head tilted back. "Is what absolutely out of the question? What are you talking about?"

"I want you back, Jeanne. I'm sure you know that now. I want you for life. I want you to be my wife." He had an ear for words, at least, and he knew the unintended rhyme was clumsy and made him sound foolish.

"You want me back? What is all this? When did you ever have me?" Her voice was flat, cold, hostile.

"I think you once loved me. I've done many stupid things, but I won't believe they're irreparable. I'm only asking whether we can start again, whether there's the faintest possibility of it, whether there's anything I can hope for." Jeanne shook her head in exasperation and started to talk, but he overrode her. "I know this is a shock, I know it's a hell of a time for me to come out with it, but there'll never be a good time, and once it's said at least it's said, and we can go on from there. I'm telling you what I want. I want to marry you."

"Arthur, you need sleep. This is just wild talk, so stop it right now, and let's both forget it."

"Look, Jeanne, you can say no to me. But don't ascribe what I'm saying to lack of sleep, and don't take it lightly. I have an enormous amount of work to do, and no matter what you think of me, no matter what mistakes I've made, you know that that work is important. I believe I have a chance to get it done if you're with me. I know I have the powers to get my work done if all goes well. And all going well means having you, nothing else."

Jeanne's look was softening. She smiled a little, and something of her usual affectionate look came into her eyes, veiled with an odd ironic secrecy. This gladdened Hawke, but he might not have been so glad had he known what she was thinking.

She was thinking how absurd he was. Hawke had written wonderful scenes of the folly of men in love. In fact, in *Will Horne*, he even now had a situation unfolding of his hero trying to win back his boyhood sweetheart after having made a cynical marriage that he regretted; and he was writing the psychology of the woman, as well as of the man, with remarkable accuracy. Yet here he was, talking away like a worse boob than any in his books. She thought of the fatuous tomcat sex life of Balzac, of the in-

decent and silly involvements of Byron, and her mind jumped to the historic ridiculousness, the Gallic bedroom farce, of Napoleon's amours. Obviously a man might be wise or important or great, but he could not be other than a man in his dealings with women. And when he came fumbling and fawning around a woman who was not in love with him— or in love with him and out of the mood at the moment—nothing could save him from seeming a fool, the more so because in other things he was a person of consequence. So Jeanne thought. She had a streak of unforgiving clarity that bordered on the cruel, and that perhaps had driven herself and Hawke apart as much as his own raw boyish appetite for the forbidden fun offered by Frieda Winter.

But she also thought—all this took only a moment or so to go through her mind, of course, and it lay behind her softening look and the melancholy smile Hawke found so encouraging—that this was a bitter-sweet sort of triumph that had been a long time coming; but that Arthur characteristically could not have chosen a worse time. What he was asking was not unthinkable. She still was in love with him. There were moments in their work together when she came close to worshipping him, so brightly could he blaze with inspiration and energy; and she could not help finding him physically magnetic. She was touched by his appeal. But she could not respond to it. What was all this nonsense? Karl was in trouble, and she was going to him. Karl could be exasperating, really devilish, especially in invalid or drunken spells. Jeanne more than once had had desperate thoughts of divorce, and even daydreams of being recaptured by Hawke in some such development as this strange talk in an airport coffee shop in Kentucky, between squawks of the loudspeaker. All the same, this moment was wrong, Hawke was being a fool, and the thing had to be cut off sharply. A female instinct murmured, far back in her consciousness, that if this wild change was ever meant to come to pass, it would, and nothing could stop it. Meantime she had to act in the common sense of daylight, and in common decency.

She said, "Karl is a wise bird. Sometimes his prescience is irritating, it's so spectacular. Do you know what he said to me this morning on the phone about you?"

"Obviously I don't," Hawke said, disgruntled by her turning the talk to Karl, and by her light tone.

"Well, I'll tell you, word for word. He said, 'How's our hill-born genius doing? Has he been making passes at you, without La Winter to keep him calmed down?'" Jeanne laughed.

"I fail to find that either prescient or funny, and in fact it gets me angry," Hawke said. "It's in bad taste, and it's a little late in the day for Karl to start worrying about you and me being alone together. I hope you told him that I haven't made anything remotely resembling a pass at you."

"Maybe you should have," Jeanne said, lighting a cigarette, feeling mean pleasure in the use of her claws on Hawke.

He looked shocked, shocked as a pastor hearing profanity. "You know that's impossible, Jeanne, you're just talking."

"I don't know anything. For instance I certainly didn't know I was going to get a marriage proposal this afternoon, or I might have screwed myself up into a more romantic mood. You've certainly accomplished nothing here. Maybe if you'd made a pass at me, some real caveman stuff back in my hotel room, I might have succumbed. Women are supposed to eat up such primitive tactics, at least they do in all the frank and boldly realistic novels that go across my desk. Not in yours, I must say. Maybe you don't understand women."

"I understand women. You'd have broken a lamp over my head."

"Most likely. Well then, turn your understanding on me, for God's sake, Arthur. I'm married. I'm not the girl who enjoyed that memorable turkey dinner in the villa at Rainbow's End. I've made a life and I like it. Obviously I love working with you, but any repetition of this kind of talk could put an end to that. Anyway this is all just nervous conversation, it doesn't mean a thing, you'll get back to Mrs. Winter next week and to use Karl's charming phrase, she'll calm you down in short order."

"Fair enough," Hawke said, "not what you're saying, but the fact that you're saying it. You owe me that and a lot more, and no doubt in due course you'll get it all out of your system. But I'm telling you straight out that I want you, Jeanne, and that I need you."

"But for what, Arthur? I'm just another woman. There are millions of them all built more or less alike, and you've already demonstrated that your requirements are, shall we say, flexible? For editing? You've got me for that." The loudspeaker grated out the announcement of Jeanne's plane. She snatched at her purse, her cigarettes, her gloves, and her lighter. "Here I go. Arthur, you'll have to forgive me if I accept Karl's diagnosis rather than your burst of new insight. You're lonely for a woman. Your restlessness will soon be soothed, I feel confident." She got out of the booth.

"You can be a brute, Jeanne."

"I'm not good at lying."

She said in a different tone, pulling on her gloves, as he trudged gloomily beside her to the plane gateway, "Look, you know me. I'm not going to say any of the sweet nice things a cultured young lady is supposed to say when she gets such a decent proposal from such an eminent and desirable man. Thanks, Arthur. It's no good, it's a hell of a mess, but thanks. I have few fears about you. Nancy's baby is divine, the whole trip was worth it just to see that baby yawning behind the glass. I think if you can cut thirty pages out of the first act and fix that long stretch of legal talk in the second act the play might work. As usual I'm amazed at the

amount, and the speed, and the quality of the work you've done. I think Feydal will be pleased, and you'll make another pot of money, which you need so badly. You've got my plane ticket, give it to me."

He handed her the bright-colored envelope. "I must be insane," he said. "You're nothing but a cold sharp over-educated shrew. But I take back nothing I've said, I want you, and now you know that."

She put a white-gloved hand to his face, stood on tiptoe, and kissed his mouth. "A couple of years too late, you son of a bitch," she said. "But you don't need me, you don't need anybody. It might help, just in general, if you got rid of Mrs. Winter. Give her back to Mr. Winter. You've had her."

She strode to the plane and went up into it without looking back.

CHAPTER THIRTEEN

1

WHEN he came back to his house on Seventy-third Street it was late at night. He was worn out from a plane ride through thunderstorms, and in no condition to face what greeted him.

The house appeared to be in exactly the same condition as it had been a month ago, if not worse. It was filled with carpenter's machinery, tumbled piles of cement blocks, heaps of old lathe and plaster, stacks of lumber, tiles, and copper pipes; also huddles of furniture, appliances and fixtures under big paint-stained tarpaulins. Broken walls gaped at him. The pervading smell of paint, sawdust, and new plaster, which he had learned to hate in the interminable months of reconstruction, hung heavier in the air than ever. The dust of the day's plaster-smashing had not settled. It danced in the light of the naked bulbs that Hawke switched on in room after room, rushing through the place in growing rage; it filled his nostrils and made him sneeze; it whirled merrily after him in coiling thin clouds, and his feet made prints in it on the floor. And this was the finished job he had been promised! The formal Colonial home he had planned, in all its austere American elegance, the perfect retreat for an American author in the very heart of the turmoil and the buzz of modern New York; complete to liquor in the bar, coffee on the stove, and a blonde in the bed!

Coming to the attic room where he lived, he found on his cot a manila

folder containing a sheaf of bills, and clipped to these a cheery note on one of the pink memorandum sheets the contractor used. The note said in effect that these bills had to be paid before work could proceed. Hawke glanced through the invoices. They added up to at least fifteen thousand dollars.

He telephoned the contractor at his home in Queens; he dialled several times and let the ringing go on for minutes, but there was no answer. He was too furious to sleep. In the pile of mail on his desk in the library there was a grim dry letter from the Bureau of Internal Revenue summoning him to an examination of his income tax returns for the past two years, the returns he had prepared without an accountant's help. In his excited state this document was a bad shock.

Hawke had plunged almost overnight, it must be remembered, from living on fifteen or twenty dollars a week—from walking miles to save a subway fare in order to be able to buy a frankfurter—into a new existence where money poured at him in tens of thousands of dollars every month. He had undoubtedly done some idiotic things—he was beginning to see that the house was a great idiocy—but he had done careful things, too. He had invested money in cautious increments with Hoag, who several times now had demonstrated that his enterprises were shrewdly conceived and very profitable. He had bought common stocks after much study of the market; and Paul Winter, reviewing his holdings at one point, had remarked with some surprise that his selection showed knowledge and good sense. He had long since discontinued speculating in commodity futures. His net worth, counting the money dumped into the house, was perhaps close to two hundred thousand dollars, an amazing result in a few years for a penniless Seabee. But little of it was free cash. He knew he could not take a severe tax assessment easily. He feared becoming so involved in money troubles that he could no longer write; he feared this much more than returning to long walks to save subway fares.

The fact was that his sudden prosperity had from the first seemed a dream; he had never exactly believed in it though his senses assured him he was waking; and now, sitting in his expensive unfinished ruin of a house, staring at the shocking summons from the tax gatherers, he experienced the physical quake, the fear of falling, that often seizes a man just before he wakes out of a dream. After a brief wrestle with himself, desperate for somebody knowledgeable to talk to, he telephoned Frieda.

Mrs. Winter was at his house in half an hour, magnificent in an orange sari and a necklace of diamonds, radiant and pretty, the powerhouse Frieda, at peak voltage. He had just caught her, she said, five minutes after she had gotten home from a dinner party. She reproached him, not very severely, with failing to write or telephone her often enough from Hovey. She made no mention of Jeanne, and when Hawke said he had

finished the play she clapped her hands, her eyes shone, and she said that all was forgiven.

She put on her glasses and went through the house with him, room by room, asking brief questions, her manner turning businesslike. Mainly she examined the floors, the ceilings, the new molded woodwork, the freshly painted surfaces. "Well, he's doing a superb job," she said at last. "It's going to be one of the most beautiful little places on the east side. A gem. He knows his business."

When Hawke spoke of the cost she made an impatient gesture with one hand. "Oh, look, you'll get no sympathy from me. This is what you wanted to do. You're not a lawyer, you're a crazy writer. Finish it, forget the price, have fun."

"How much more money will it need, Frieda? And how much more time?"

She looked at him with her head bent far down, her gray eyes very wide. "Do you want to be cheered up, dear heart, or do you want the truth?"

"The truth."

"Well, depending on what's already been paid for, you'd better figure another twenty or thirty thousand dollars. And four months."

Hawke uttered an animal howl and began throwing things—boxes, tiles, boards—at the broken walls of the living room. It took Frieda a while to quiet him down. She telephoned The Park Tower, and booked a room for him. "You can't sleep here tonight, you'll go out of your mind," she said. "What a rube you are, to be sure! Don't you know what contractors are?"

"This is a city of liars, of thieves, of bloodsuckers!" Hawke roared.

"New York is just America distilled, my love. You have to watch your money or you'll lose it, here or in dear old Hovey. Come along quietly, and stop making noises like a stabbed elephant. It'll be a beautiful house."

The room at The Park Tower was not quite as high up as Feydal's suite, but it was on the same side and had the old view—the black park webbed with roadway lights, hemmed in four-square by tall black buildings checkered with light; the streams of headlights on the streets, hardly diminished at half-past two; the velvety Hudson River beyond the buildings of the west side, and above the rosy glow of downtown, some dim stars and a bronzed half moon. They could see the Paramount clock, which so often had promised Hawke at ten past five that his New York woman was about to telephone him, and which had equally often warned Frieda at seven to go home to her family for dinner.

Everything that followed that night was familiar, nostalgic and delicious. The warm and silken sweetness of Frieda Winter, when she was in the arms of Arthur Hawke, was not a temptation to be easily resisted.

2

He woke in The Park Tower, in a blaze of sunshine, and he passed several dazed minutes recollecting what point of life he was at, picking up one by one the threads of his predicament. Nothing good faced him. There was the maddening mess of the house to be resolved; there was the summons from Internal Revenue, which he had to answer today; perhaps worst of all, he was supposed to have lunch with Jeanne Fry. After the unexpected night with Frieda, he had as little stomach for a meeting with Jeanne as a mud-caked boy has for an encounter with his parents.

He went to the house. On the street men were carrying lumber in from a truck, and more men were carrying out broken plaster and lathe. Inside the house still more men swarmed through clouds of plaster dust, hammering, sawing, smashing, wheeling, dumping, and burning with blowtorches, all in a screechy uproar. Hawke groped through the noise and filth from room to room, looking for Yousseloff. He found him at last in the library, with blueprints spread out on the desk, yelling instructions at two dusty foremen. He hailed Hawke merrily. "Well, well, so the boss is back! How do you like it? Great, isn't it? Really coming along. Hokay, fellows." He handed the plans to the foremen, who went off with furtive glances at Hawke.

Hawke shouted, "You told me the place would be finished!"

"Why, it is finished. This is the clean-up, every job needs a clean-up, Artie." They had been on a first-name basis from the start. "It's going like lightning now."

"George, this goddamned house won't be habitable for four months!"

The contractor looked hurt. "Artie, it's habitable now."

"You said you'd do the job for thirty thousand dollars. I've spent more than twice as much. Now I have to spend at least that much again."

The contractor said, "Yes, that's how it goes, isn't it?" And he giggled.

Hawke strode up to the desk, put his face an inch from the contractor's —Yousseloff needed a shave, and he had a ragged malodorous cigar in his mouth—and he roared, "Get out! Get out, you hear, and get all these men out! Get your machinery out! Get out! Stop the work! I'm firing you! Get out!"

Not at all upset, Yousseloff replied, "Artie, no client can see when a house is finished. This place is a stage set, I'm telling you, that just needs to be swept and have the lights turned on it. You have a lovely house and it's all done. What's today, Wednesday? You can have your housewarming Saturday. I mean of course next Saturday."

"Get out, I say! Get these men out! Or I'll start throwing them out,

one by one, and you first!" Hawke's Southern accent was thickening, his face was purpling, and he was beginning to stammer with rage.

The contractor said, blandly happy, in his warm voice tinged with a charming Russian accent, "Artie, will you believe me that every job comes to this point, and every client throws a fit like this? And it's just a day or two—at most a week or two—before the job's all done?"

Hawke howled, "You a lyin' sonofabitchin New York crook, and you get your tail out of mah hass before Ah *kick* it out, heah?"

Yousseloff smiled with priestly tolerance, "Artie, I've taken the men off jobs too. I've been through this a hundred times. All they do is come back a day later. If it'll make you feel better I'll send them home, but there's a nine-hundred-dollar payroll under this roof right this minute and they're going to be paid anyway, that's union rules. Don't give way to your emotions. Be mad at me, that's fine, but don't cut off your nose to spite your face."

Hawke seized Yousseloff by his collar and the seat of his pants and danced him out to the head of the stairs. The contractor said, "All right, all right, Artie, you're entitled to throw away your own money. I'll send them home, I'll give them a day's vacation with pay if you insist."

"*You* goin' to pay them, you goddamn vampah, Ah ain't payin' nobody nothin', heah, you gonna sue me to the *soopreme* co't, heah, before you get a cent more from *me!*" Hawke trampled down the stairs waving his arms and trumpeting above the din, "Out, out! E'body out! All you New York bastuds *get out of mah hass!*"

The workmen, not particularly perturbed, seemingly not even surprised, one by one put down their tools, picked up their lunchboxes, and streamed out into the street, chattering amiably. It took a quarter of an hour for Yousseloff and his foremen to flush them out of all the cloudy nooks of the building; they kept pouring out like ants after it seemed to Hawke that a regiment in overalls had departed. Quiet and plaster dust settled through the ruin. Yousseloff lingered in the doorway, a captain on the bridge of a sinking ship. "Artie, in the mood you're in I don't want to press you, but we owe Jackson Plumbing forty-seven hundred dollars, and that's one bill you shouldn't hold off, because . . ."

Hawke picked up a carpenter's bench which, with the vises and power tools clamped to it, must have weighed almost three hundred pounds, and he flourished it over his head, electric cords snaking all around him. Yousseloff said hurriedly, his good-humored grin changing into an opaque stare for the first time, "I see you're a little upset. I'll phone you tomorrow." The iron grill door clanged.

Hawke trudged through the silent house up two flights of dusty stairs to the library, where he telephoned the Bureau of Internal Revenue.

3

Jeanne was also having her troubles. That same morning she sat with Karl in the office of Ross Hodge, waiting for the arrival of the publisher. Hodge was late in returning from a salesmen's meeting. Karl smoked. Jeanne sat stone still, her arms folded. Hodge walked in after a while, pre-occupied, businesslike, taut; he spoke agreeable nothings until Karl Fry opened the real subject.

Karl launched into his story: his trip to Washington, his intention to cooperate with the Department of Justice, his change of heart. Hodge listened, leaning back in his swivel chair, his tanned round face a little drawn, his eyes half-shut. When Karl stopped speaking he glanced at Jeanne, then said, with a characteristic controlled chop of one curved palm, "Well, how do things stand now? I'm not quite clear on that."

Fry said, "Apparently the matter is closed. I'm not going to be prose-cuted. There's nothing they can prosecute me for. They said that from the start. They were friendly enough when I decided not to give them the memorandum or any other information, though they were disappointed. I've exercised my rights of privacy, they have no legal basis for pressing questions on me, and that's that."

Hodge said, "Karl, you told me three years ago that you'd quit the communist party. Was that on the level?"

"Yes, it was."

"Can you tell me why you changed your mind about talking to the FBI?"

Fry, sunk in an armchair with his jacket standing away from his thin neck and making him look shrunken, said "Huh-huh" and lit a cigarette. After puffing deeply several times he said, "Well, I can try, but I think you'd have had to be there in Washington in the room with me, Ross, and with these two fellows who interviewed me. One of them was beefy, an ex-football player gone to fat, said he had six children, not at all stupid. I didn't mind him. It was the small one. When I say small I mean about my size, small by contrast, and sort of wispy and pale. Bristle haircut, collegiate clothes, the manners of an advertising man, half-fawning and half-pushing. Midwestern accent. He was the one who suddenly made me smell the hot pincers. He made me feel that I had sinned, that he knew all my sins, and that he was prepared to make a deal with me for absolution at a price—recantation plus betrayal of my fellow heretics. And he was loving it so, talking this way to a New York editor! The foot-ball player was just trying to do a job that he was suited for, a man of simple loyalties and dogged energy. This other one was scary. The whole thing wasn't conversation in the United States any more, it was very

European, with a present smell of blood and burning flesh. Some of this was my morbid imagination, no doubt. But I was born in St. Louis, Missouri, and you don't talk to me like a ham American movie actor impersonating a Nazi. He would have been totally ridiculous except that he was sitting across a desk from me, speaking for the moment as the voice of the government of the United States of America. That fact struck me. I zipped shut my briefcase with my thirty-page memorandum in it, made my farewells, and left. It was delightful to see young Bristle-head all of a sudden lose his Halloween aspect and turn into a weak American law clerk who was afraid he had loused up an interview and might get hell for it. He was pleading with me to reconsider, in the most jovial tones, when I left. His last words were, 'The latch is always off here, Karl.'"

Hodge said meditatively, "Well, you ran into a stinker. It's too goddamn bad. I think you were right in the first place, when you went to give them the memorandum."

"Maybe."

Jeanne said, "Karl hasn't mentioned one thing. He did quit the party, but he's always felt free to go on contributing to its causes. He and I have disagreed on that."

Fry said promptly, "I'm prepared to resign my job, Ross, if you feel I should put a limit of any kind on what I do with my money after you pay it to me."

Hodge passed a hand over his brow. "Hell, I'm in over my depth here. You're a good mystery editor, Karl, that's all I know."

"Thanks, Ross. I don't want to give up my job. I'm telling you how things are."

The publisher said to Jeanne, "If Karl were to resign would you go too?"

"I wouldn't want to. But if Karl went to work in another city, or something, that's how it might end up."

Hodge took off his glasses and rubbed his eyes. "Well, if it isn't one thing it's another around here. We just had a rotten sales meeting, too. Look, this is absurd. I can't lose two people like you. Karl, do you mind if I get a lawyer in on this?"

"Which lawyer? I've been thinking I probably should have had a lawyer. But the fuddydud who handles my will and my lease would go into convulsions if I mentioned the FBI."

Hodge pondered, his hand on the telephone. "Well, the fellow I'm thinking of may be out of left field. It's just a hunch. He's a tax man, has a Wall Street office and also teaches tax law up at Columbia. We just had him in as a consultant. He did a damn good job setting up that new children's book company of ours, Starlight Press. Saved us a couple of hundred thousand, probably, in tax payout. Damn keen mind."

Karl said, grinning crookedly, "I doubt a Wall Street tax man would care to save an ex-Red from the righteous wrath of the government."

Hodge said with the shade of briskness that showed he was at the end of his patience—he could make decisions quickly, and preferred making them to prolonging discussion—"Well, this is sort of a mess, Karl, you know. I don't want our regular legal staff in on it. Everybody talks in this place. A thing like this will get out to the columnists in a week. If Myra Hathaway reads about you in the papers, there'll be a special board meeting and I'll have to let you go. That's what I'm trying to avoid."

Fry shrugged.

Hodge said into the telephone, "Get me Professor Adam. If he's not at Columbia try his downtown office." He hung up. "Matter of fact, Jeanne, I think you'll find him interesting. He comes from the same part of Kentucky as Hawke—I think he said he's from the same county. Says he remembers Hawke from the University, though he doubts Hawke will remember him."

4

After the high emotional note on which Hawke and Jeanne had parted, he anticipated an awkward lunch with her at best. He was relieved to find her behaving as though his clumsy marriage proposal in the airport had never occurred. He told her about his set-to with the contractor, making it all a wry joke on himself, and she laughed, heartily. They soon settled their business. He told her what he had done with the play. She approved, and undertook to correct the script and see it through the typist. She had one martini while they talked, then another, an unusual indulgence for her at lunch, and she asked for a bottle of white wine with her chicken.

They were at a corner table of the Commons Room. Like Frieda Winter, Jeanne now had her own business corner, and a tame headwaiter who bowed her to it. Ross Hodge considered her the best person on the staff for talking to young authors about their work, especially when it came to cutting out sex scenes, philosophy, luxuriant descriptions of train rides, and dirty words. She signed for hundreds of dollars' worth of lunches each month.

She said when she had finished her food "What do you know about a Professor Adam at Columbia Law School? A tax expert?"

"Nothing at all, except that I damn well could use his services."

"Sure you don't remember an Adam from the University of Kentucky? Ross called him Gus on the phone."

Hawke looked thoughtful, then his face brightened. "No—is that so? It couldn't be Augustus A. Adam, for Christ's sake. Teaching tax law at a northern university! What a hell of an end for him, if it's him."

"You do know him?"

"Well, sort of. There was this fellow came from Brightstar—you know, the town about forty miles up from Hovey on the road to Lexington, Jeanne, where we stopped and had coffee in the drugstore—"

Jeanne laughed. "He's from there? Three stores, a church, and a filling station. Brightstar!"

"That's right. Everybody thought there for a while up at U.K. that that one-horse town had produced a coming governor or president or something. Augustus A. Adam. Tax law at Columbia! Ye gods, how have the mighty fallen. He was one of these oppressive people, Jeanne—good football player, big debater, never got a mark less than an A, president of the student council, and so forth. And all this without sweat, you know, you'd always see Triple-A Adam having a Coke somewhere, or walking with some girl on the grass."

"He is smart, then."

"They didn't come any smarter at U.K. What about him? You having tax troubles, too?"

Jeanne hesitated, sipping her wine, looking at Hawke in an odd way that stirred him. It was strange to be lunching with her again in New York. Their three weeks together in Hovey seemed in retrospect a clean delicious idyll. He remembered her bare arms, her pastel-colored cotton dresses, her free tossing hair. He remembered her in the hospital and in Dan's Diner. Here she was once more in a tailored black suit, a pearl-buttoned shirtwaist, a small black hat, and her wedding ring seemed an enormous yellow wheel on her finger.

She said, "Well, I'm not going to be able to keep this from you much longer, and I hate pussyfooting anyway. Karl's in trouble." She told him the whole story, starting with the visit of the man from the FBI up to the meeting with Hodge that morning. "Ross has had some dealings with this lawyer and seems to think a lot of him. I can't do any more with Karl. I hope Professor Adam is as smart as you say."

"Well, it's a dozen years since I saw him, Jeanne. The last thing I expected was that Triple-A Adam would have become a teacher. I hope he can help."

"Now you know why I ran off to Washington. I found Karl in his hotel room, roaring drunk. He's not allowed to drink like that, it's dangerous for him." She struck the table with her fist. "Why, *why* did this have to happen! He was writing, he was working, we'd saved some money, we were looking for land up around Harrison to build a little house. We were happy."

Hawke said, "I've never understood Karl. I had a red spell in college. I was invited into this little hush-hush group, I guess because I was always ragged and intellectual and needed a haircut, and I had a reputation as a wild character. I read everything they fed me, Marx and Shaw and

Strachey and I don't know what all any more. One thing I can do is read. I got all in a sweat about it. But then when I really studied it out, what it added up to was a well-intentioned dictatorship that was going to wither away on the great getting-up morning. A dictatorship that would wither away sounded to me like a rainstorm that would fall up. Anyway, this stuff they handed out was full of the most disgusting English. You'd think Karl would be offended, too, his ear is better than mine. 'The toiling masses,' and all that. This country has no toiling masses, we have Dan at the diner and Verne in the mine and Jerry in the steel mill and Burdette at the filling station and so on. They don't *toil*, for Christ's sake, they do a day's work and then they go home and have a beer. You can't get them into a mass for anything. If there's a good ball game on TV they won't come out to see the president ride by."

"Well, I learned long ago not to argue with Karl on that subject," Jeanne said. She gestured nervously for the check. "Want to come back and meet Adam? He's due at the office at half-past two. I'd like to know what you think of him."

"Well, sure, I wouldn't miss it."

"You won't be able to stay long, no big University of Kentucky reunion. We have a lot to talk about, and he can only stay an hour."

"I just want to see what he looks like. Old Triple-A Adam. I be damn."

5

Hawke recognized him, though his appearance had much changed. Adam sat at his ease, legs crossed, on a straight-backed chair in Hodge's office, stuffing a pipe out of a folding pouch striped dull red, white, and blue. He was much stouter than he had been at U.K. He still had most of his sandy, somewhat curly hair, and despite the law school and the Wall Street office his color was ruddy, as though he lived mostly outdoors. Hawke had forgotten about the broken nose until the moment he saw Adam; then he remembered the last football game of his freshman year in which Triple-A had been carried from the field unconscious. It was one of the rare cases when a broken nose had not marred a face, perhaps had improved it. Hawke remembered Adam as having a sharp, driving, slightly foxy look. The foxiness had come from the configuration of his very bright but small blue eyes, and a large straight nose. The broken nose was broader—not crooked, but spread and softened. This, with the added flesh, had relaxed the lawyer's face. The eyes were as keen as ever, though shadowed with years and with work.

The lawyer and Hodge stood as Hawke and Jeanne came into the office. Karl remained sunk in an armchair.

"Well!" Adam said to Hawke with a grin, after Hodge introduced him

to Jeanne. "I guess nobody has to introduce you. Do you remember me, by any chance?"

"I sure remember Triple-A Adam, the big wheel on campus, when I was a freshman nobody. I don't know any Professor Adam at Columbia Law School."

Adam laughed. "You weren't a nobody. I still remember those alligator shoes you used to wear. I thought your stuff in the paper was the only really funny writing I'd seen at school in four years. I didn't think you'd turn into a serious novelist, but I kind of thought you'd go somewhere."

Hawke noticed that Adam's Kentucky accent had all but vanished. He spoke like any other cultivated New Yorker; yet Hawke believed that if Adam had been a stranger he would have soon spotted him as a man who came from Letchworth or one of the nearby counties. Adam went on, "I guess it bores you to hear it, but I want to tell you I think your books are excellent. Of course reading *Alms for Oblivion* was like taking a trip back home. The legal material was well done."

Karl said from the depths of his armchair, "Artie, it's good to see you." He addressed the lawyer. "Our Artie is a playwright too. He seems to have written a smash hit during a little vacation down in Old Kentucky."

Ross Hodge said, "Jeanne says you also managed to push ahead on the new novel. I think that's marvellous."

Hawke said, "I'm off to push ahead some more. Professor Adam, I'd like to see you and talk to you some time."

The lawyer beamed. "You name the time and the place. You've been to Letchworth last, you can bring me up to date on who's been shooting whom."

Hawke made his farewells, and left.

The lawyer said to Hodge, dropping into his chair, "I guess I didn't sound enthusiastic enough. It's hard to gush to a man's face. He's a fine writer. He tells a good story, and he tells the truth. That's why his books sell, and I think they may last."

Hodge said, "Gushing is never required."

Adam said, looking around at the Frys, his gaze resting quizzically on Jeanne. "Well, I'm at your service. I'm sorry I have this class to teach at four."

Hodge said, "Karl, I gave Professor Adam the main facts before you came in. The contributions and so forth. Maybe you'd better tell him your Washington experience."

Karl repeated the story of his interview with the two FBI men. Adam smoked, keeping his eyes on Fry, now and then darting a look at the others for their reactions. When Karl finished, Adam looked to Jeanne, puffing at his pipe. His heavy, rather shaggy blond eyebrows raised humorously, and he said to Hodge, "Well, if it's my turn, I appreciate that it's

a very tricky business. It doesn't seem to involve taxation, and my question is, what can I do for you?"

Hodge said, "I suppose I want a more organized, maybe a more legal brain than mine bearing on the problem. I've gone outside the house for obvious reasons." Adam's nod was just perceptible. "I guess I'd like your opinion as to whether I'd better ask Karl to resign, or whether you think I can keep him on, or whether there's some way out that hasn't occurred to me. Karl and Jeanne are two of my best people."

Karl said, "My wife is Youngblood Hawke's editor. He's quite dependent on her. Or he thinks he is, which with writers comes to much the same thing."

Adam turned his gaze to Jeanne, who felt uncomfortable and at a loss for words. She was grateful to Hodge for striking in. "Jeanie edits a lot of authors besides Art Hawke. She's valuable, and Karl's valuable, and good editors are damned hard to find."

"Well." Adam knocked out his pipe into a tray on Hodge's desk, and narrowed his eyes at Jeanne. "Do you share your husband's beliefs, Mrs. Fry, and do you contribute to communist causes too?"

"I've never been a communist, and I don't think it's right for him to make the contributions while he's an editor here."

"I see. Let me ask you one more question. If Mr. Fry resigned, would you continue in your post, editing Youngblood Hawke? And of course, other authors?"

The shade of irony in Adam's added phrase, 'And of course other authors' disconcerted her. The slight pause before she answered was enough to shoot the tension in the room upward. Karl stopped in his cigarette-puffing and stared at her. Ross Hodge was immobile on the edge of his swivel chair, though his face showed nothing. In this moment Jeanne realized that the crux of this matter was not Karl's communist past, nor his contributions, but the profits from the novels of Youngblood Hawke. The lawyer had probed straight to the live nerve. She said, "If Karl goes I'll go."

Hodge said quickly, "You didn't put it that way before, Jeanie."

"I said it might work out that way, Ross. I think it will."

Hodge sank back in his chair. Karl's smile at his wife mingled gratitude and sadness. Jeanne felt a new pulse of affection for him, because she was protecting him.

Hodge said, "The thing is, I have to estimate the effect on our publishing house if Karl's position becomes public knowledge. I frankly don't know whether we could ride it out."

The lawyer shifted lower in his chair, and put the spread tips of his fingers together in his lap, like a clergyman. "There's no question," he said, with a forward thrust of all the fingers, "that today your house would be somewhat embarrassed. It's the Alger Hiss business. That has

sent a tremor all through the United States. We have a moderate red scare going. Nothing like the hysteria after the First World War. The risk here lies in a possible intensification of the red scare. If it comes to the pitch that it did in 1921 and 1922, I think you might get into a boycott by certain people of books bearing your imprint. It could have a real effect on your dollar volume. These things pass. At least they always have in the United States. But the siege could be long."

"We're not in such a situation now," Hodge said.

"No, in my judgment we're not. Not yet," Adam said.

"I'm interested in what to do right now," the publisher said. "Next year's another year."

Karl said, "If I understand you, Professor, you don't feel I'm honor bound to resign. As of now."

Adam said with a grin that, under the arch of his brows, was somewhat mocking, and with a new shade in his speech which reminded Jeanne of Hawke and of Hovey, "Well, Mr. Fry, you're introducing a new element. I thought we were talking business, not honor. In my opinion Mr. Hodge doesn't need your resignation today for business reasons. And we have Mr. Hodge's word that he does need your services—and of course, your wife's."

"I'll buy that," Hodge said. "I don't see running for cover at this point just to avoid a little crackpot criticism. I'm damned grateful to you, Professor Adam. You've cleared my mind."

Karl said, "He hasn't cleared my mind. I'm ready to talk honor. In fact honor is what interests me here. As a matter of business I wouldn't have disclosed anything to you, Ross. I'd have kept my mouth shut and gone on collecting my pay and doing what I pleased with it." Karl glanced to Jeanne for approval.

"Good," the lawyer said. "But the requirements of honor are such a personal matter that the opinion of a lawyer may seem uncalled for."

"Not if I call for it." Karl sat up, his elbows on his knees, his hands clasped.

Adam took his cold pipe from the desk and made measured gestures with it. "All right. You decided at one point as an honorable man to disclose to your government, at its request, the facts of your communist past. You went to Washington with a long written memorandum. There you had a strong emotional reaction. You reversed your view. You decided not only to give the FBI no information, but to persist in supporting communist causes. Also, to confront Mr. Hodge with this decision, and in effect force him to endorse it, or risk losing you and Mrs. Fry."

"You're making it cut-and-dried," Fry broke in. "I've been improvising to meet unexpected events. I've made no calculations. I don't accept your statement that my final stand is emotional. It's true I reacted violently to the smell of Goebbels in Washington. I think that was a sound reac-

tion, an appalling insight gained under pressure as most insights are. I'm standing on it."

"And so is your wife."

"Not at all. Her views are opposite to mine. She's made that clear. We have separate bank accounts. My contributions reflect no discredit on her, and never will, even if the hysteria you're afraid of does come."

"That's thoughtful," Adam said. "Mr. Hodge, however, must either accept your stand right now or your wife, who handles at least one very profitable author, may leave the firm."

Fry said after a moment, "That's her decision."

Jeanne said, "Mr. Adam, if Ross Hodge worried about whether all book buyers approved of the politics of all his editors he'd have to close up shop."

"That's absolutely true," Adam said, nodding to her as to a bright pupil. "The question turns on whether communism is politics within the American use of the term. I guess I've said all I can on the subject of what honor requires here, Mr. Fry. I may have merely muddled things."

"You've made yourself quite clear," Fry said. "You think I'm striking a self-righteous pose behind my wife's skirts, and that I'm only getting away with it because Youngblood Hawke's novels make money." Jeanne saw Karl light a cigarette with the set of gestures that signalled a decision: cigarette jammed in the corner of the mouth, an angry scratch of the match, a jet of smoke from the nose: then would come the daring chess move, or the tumbler of straight whiskey, or the verdict on a manuscript. "Ross, what's today? June twenty-sixth, 1950?"

"It's the twenty-seventh, Karl."

"Okay. You can put it on the record that as of this date I'll make no more contributions either in public or in secret, that can ever embarrass Hodge Hathaway. You have that on my honor, such as it is. Your counsel here may advise you that that's worthless. In that case I'll resign."

Adam said, "Look here, if I've offended you—"

"Good God, Karl, your word's good enough for me, it always has been," Hodge said.

Jeanne said, "Ross hasn't asked you to do this, Karl. I don't think you should jump to such a decision." Karl's quick surrender alarmed her more than his obstinacy.

Fry grinned at her. He looked, all at once, as he had in his worst days after his divorce, when she had first met him—bitter, beaten, cornered, ill, full of humorous self-disgust. "Darling, I said when we came to talk to Ross this morning that the whole thing was fuzzy in my mind. I also said last night that I preferred to let the whole thing lie. You wouldn't have it so. We've talked to Ross. We've uncovered the facts. We have an astute counsellor here who's put them together for all to see. I guess I had some cloudy notion of being at once a free American and a Marxist

sympathizer. In theory, if the American way weren't a romantic dream, that should be possible. Professor, I'm in your hands. What next? Shall I go back to Washington and hand the memorandum to my amateur storm trooper in the Department of Justice? I'll do so if you say so. I want to keep my job, and not by hiding behind my wife's skirts."

The silence in the room was thick with embarrassment. Jeanne looked at her hands, fighting to hold back tears.

Adam at last said in a subdued tone, "I think this decision about the contributions is wise. The memorandum is another problem."

"You're the doctor," Fry snapped. "Let's clean this mess up now and then let's have no more of it. What shall I do about that?"

Adam's fingers crept together, tips braced against tips. He said, almost as though to himself, "A man travels to Washington to offer information about his communist past. That demonstrates good faith. It's an unpleasant thing to do. He's entitled to courtesy. We don't have the written record of that interview. Judging from my meeting with you today— especially your decision in the last few minutes—I'm prepared to believe that you were treated discourteously and stupidly in Washington. Your indignation, in that case, was justified. You now say you're prepared to submit your memorandum at any time upon advice of counsel. Is that correct?"

"I want to get this damned thing out of my hair and my wife's hair, once for all."

"Of course I haven't read your memorandum. Is it a full and frank disclosure?"

"Of my own history, yes. I mentioned no names."

Adam chewed at his pipe. "Oh? Why not?"

"I don't know anybody who was a spy. We were all talkers and scribblers. My viewpoint is information yes, informing no. I'll never change that. I'll resign first, if I must. I'll go to jail too."

Adam nodded. He said to Hodge, "My status here is a bit foggy. I haven't been formally hired by anyone."

Hodge said, "That's no problem. This conference can be recorded and the cost of it met in any way that seems best to you."

"All right." Adam leaned his forehead on a hand, his elbow on the desk, and repeatedly smoothed his heavy eyebrows with two fingers. He pondered so for a couple of quiet minutes. "All right. Speaking as the firm's counsel in this matter then—or as Mr. Fry's counsel—I'm not sure yet how we'll handle this—I recommend that the memorandum be filed away and forgotten." Seeing the astonishment on the three faces confronting him, he shrugged. "Why not? Let Washington make the next move. It's always just as well not to be on the record, in such matters. Maybe it'll all get lost in the shuffle. I'm sure the investigation of Mr. Fry

was routine—just one of thousands. You're under no obligation, Mr. Fry, to reopen it."

"I'll be goddamned," Karl said. "Professor, I wonder if you aren't a secret sympathizer. If ever I heard subversive advice—"

Adam laughed, glanced at his watch, and stood. "Okay," he said in a voice of lighthearted dismissal. "The bell will be ringing at Columbia in twelve minutes." He shook hands all around.

Hodge said, "I can't tell you how grateful I am."

Adam said to Jeanne, making his handshake with her very brief, "I was pleased to meet you, Mrs. Fry. If Youngblood Hawke relies on you, you must be an extremely able editor." He put on a big soft battered hat with the brim pushed unfashionably upward, and walked out.

6

Hawke's old pen had come to a stop. Caked with dry ink, coated with plaster dust, it rested in its stand on the desk in the library, the one nearly finished room in the empty silent wreck of a house. Not war, not illness, not poverty, not love-making, not celebrity, had succeeded in stopping the onward rush of that worn cheap pen. It had poured out more than a million words in half a dozen years. The stream of words had turned into a stream of money. And money had stopped the pen.

Hawke owed the government sixty-four thousand dollars. That was the verdict of the revenue officers. He owed twenty-four thousand dollars in unpaid bills on the house. He had extracted from the contractor, in a long hostile meeting on the sidewalk in the rain, in front of the house—Hawke would not let the villain cross the threshold—a firm estimate for completion of the work: thirty-two thousand dollars more.

The need to produce these large sums should have lashed Hawke into his greatest frenzy of sustained writing yet; or at the very least sent him scurrying to raise the money, to battle the tax assessment, to find some less expensive contractor to finish the house. He did none of these things. He fell into a curious indifference. His drive to write evaporated, and he could hardly believe that he had ever sat at a desk night after night for months and years on end, filling pages with a racing pen. He went to one movie after another, sometimes to three different pictures in a day. He wandered to museums, to concerts, to art galleries. He failed to appear on a television show and was not at home and not to be found when frantic calls went out all over the city. He infuriated two wealthy ladies (with one of whom he had once had a brief affair) by not showing up at dinner parties constructed around him. He committed the unspeakable crime of forgetting an interview with a columnist, so that a poisonous attack on him appeared a day later in the newspaper, which he didn't read. He took long

aimless walks by himself, and he even found excuses to avoid seeing both Frieda and Jeanne. In plain fact he was ashamed of his money troubles, and stunned by them. Also—though he did not discover this for a while— he was walking around with pneumonia. His once blazing vitality was flickering low and blue.

"I have to find a hundred twenty thousand dollars," was the phrase that repeated and repeated in his mind. He went to sleep thinking of the figure. When he woke it flashed before him as though projected on the wall. A hundred twenty thousand dollars! Once he walked to the automat near his old loft room, and sat at his old table in the window, and ate one of the unchanging, stomach-filling beef pies, the smell and taste of which brought back the not distant days of his pennilessness; and he said to himself over and over in idiot wonder, "I have to find a hundred and twenty thousand dollars. Art Hawke has to find a hundred twenty thousand dollars."

The amazing thing was that apparently he could do it. Pencil and paper scribblings, which he repeated many times, showed that if he sold his stocks, and drew his money out of Scott Hoag's building ventures, he would realize almost a hundred thousand. He was still getting royalties from his books, though taxes melted each check to a fraction. One way or another he could certainly make up the remaining twenty thousand. But then where would he be? After his gargantuan labors, and his unbelievable burst into affluence, he would have no savings, no investments; he would have a remodelled mansion on the east side of New York, a folly that gave him griping stomach pains every time he walked into it. As for his dream of living on the income of investments and writing The American Comedy, that was further away than it had been in Guam. Then at least he had had no reason to disbelieve it; and he had been charged with all the boiling young energy that had produced two huge novels in short order. Now he was six years older, very tired, bogged in an adultery, and in love with yet another man's wife. He was disheartened to the bone. He could sell the house, of course, once it was finished. But he had little hope of realizing more than half of what he had sunk into it. And, what then?

His early idea had been that if only he studied Wall Street and slowly, carefully invested his money, all would go well. He had studied Wall Street. His investments had prospered. All his stocks were worth more than he had paid for them. But he had not foreseen his own temperamental lapses. He could not understand how he had made such glaring mistakes, such ill-considered estimates, in the tax returns; he could not fathom the cheerful imbecility with which he had plunged into the house. He knew—he had always known—that the classic disaster of authors was the mansion: Balzac's Les Jardies, Scott's Abbotsford, Jack London's Wolf House. Yet he had taken the contractor's word that the renovation

would cost thirty thousand dollars and had turned loose the wrecking swarm. Why not? Money was pouring in.

"As wealth increases," said the Preacher, "so do its devourers." That was the point of information Hawke was now picking up.

"My dear Hawke, it's marvellous," Feydal said, opening the door of his hotel suite to disclose his hairy naked belly ill-concealed by drooping pajama bottoms. His smile was fat and radiant. He seized the author's hand and pulled him inside. The sight of the striped silk-upholstered couch, the pervading lemon smell of Feydal's pomade, overwhelmed Hawke with remembrance of his early love-making with Frieda. Ye gods, how much time had passed! He felt as though he were growing old by decades while other people aged by years.

Feydal babbled happily about the play, flourishing the orange-bound script in one hand, and drinking a vast martini with the other.

Hawke said, "You do think it'll work?"

"Work! *Work!* It will work like a Rolls-Royce, that's all. You'll never spend the last dollar you'll make from it. Just the death! I told you, didn't I? I did hope you'd do a *little* more with Uncle Theodore. You know I'm not a part-fattener, I detest such foolishness, dear Arthur, only the drama-tist knows whether a part deserves two sides or two hundred, but I'd really look a little silly in a walk-on like that. But it doesn't matter, we'll do the play and we'll roll in money, we'll bathe in it."

Hawke accepted a martini, though he had never become used to the lunchtime alcohol of New York. He was chilly, despite the sultriness of the day. The cough that had been troubling him since his return from Hovey—he believed he had caught it in the mine—was growing worse. He thought the drink might warm him up. But what it did was to deepen his odd detachment. He was neither surprised nor upset when Feydal, after a long speech on the uncertainties of an actor's existence, revealed that he had, while Hawke was in Hovey, accepted a contract to play Pontius Pilate in what he called, "some silly rot about the Crucifixion," a Technicolor movie that would take a year to film. So he could not direct Hawke's play until the season after next, though he was dying to do it and bitterly regretted that he had gotten himself into the Crucifixion. "My dear Hawke, how could I have dreamed that you would take me at my word and write off this brilliant theatre piece in a month? You are an absolute superman."

It never occurred to Hawke to reproach him. In his trance-like state a resigned pessimism filled his spirit. Of course Feydal was not going to put on his play, and probably was too polite to say that he really didn't like it. He left, accompanied to the door by the actor's rhapsodies and regrets. Feydal remarked in farewell that Hawke looked a bit peaked, and he hoped he had not been overworking.

Next Hawke roused himself enough to telephone the man who was so eager in Hovey to press a million dollars on him tax-free. Givney begged him to come over at once, greeted Hawke in his office with joy, ordered in coffee, and issued strict orders to his secretary to leave them undisturbed. The paperback publisher quickly elicited from him that he was in need of money. Their conversation was long and, at least to Hawke, confusing. When the coffee was all drunk up and he disentangled Givney's position about money from the ecstatic talk about literature, it seemed to come to this: Givney was ready to go ahead with the corporate venture at once and to advance something very sizable in the way of cash. It happened that his wife was ill and anxious for something to read, and could Hawke let her see some of his new novel? Hawke explained that the book was an unfinished, mixed-up mass of scrawls on yellow paper, but Givney said that was just fine, Mrs. Givney derived wonderful excitement from reading handwritten scripts however rough and illegible.

Hawke left, allowing Givney to think that he might consider putting together a portion of his book for Mrs. Givney to read. It was too much trouble to argue. But bemused as he was, he had not the slightest intention of exposing his unfinished work to anybody but Jeanne Fry; not for a whole million, let alone an unspecified fraction of it. Money problems were important, they had to be attended to, but they were not a really serious matter, like letting some fool woman read a manuscript in progress.

He walked back to the wrecked house in mid-afternoon, went to the library and lay down on the black leather couch. He was wet with perspiration, yet he felt cold, and he had a pain in his side which he attributed to walking too fast. As he was drifting off to sleep it occurred to him that he ought to call Scotty Hoag and find out whether he could withdraw his money from Scott's various enterprises, for otherwise it was beginning to seem that he was in rather a pickle. He forced his big body off the couch to the desk, and put in a call to Lexington.

Scott answered, and he was all gay jokes until Hawke mentioned money; then the cheerful voice took a decided turn to sobriety. "Art, I'd sure like to oblige you, but this time it's real rough. I'm stretched good and thin myself, between Skytop Lodge and that job in Frankfort, I reckon I bit off a little more than I can chew, damn near. Mortgage money is really murder down here now. Everything's gonna be just fine, boy, we gonna make a potful, but I don't think I can take cash out of one of these things. How urgent is it, boy?"

Hawke said it wasn't urgent at all, he was just asking.

"Well, that's good, Art. Listen, I thought what you were investing was surplus funds. I mean the idea of venture capital is that you tie it up for a while, Art, in order to borrow a hell of a lot more dough from a bank or an insurance company, and build something big and rack up a profit. If

you want to be able to call in your dough any time like this, the answer is guvment bonds, boy."

"I know, Scott."

"If you stuck for ten thousand or so temporarily, Art, I can probably fix it to get you a loan."

"Thanks, Scott, it won't be necessary." He stumbled back to the couch.

Next thing he knew, the ringing of the telephone came like a knife-thrust. He groaned and rose and dragged himself to the desk It was still light outside.

"Darling, I just wanted to remind you to wear a dinner jacket," Frieda's voice was high, merry, and busy.

"For what?"

"Ye gods, for what? The African dancers, and then Phil York's party! It's a good thing I telephoned. Were you up all night writing, or something? It's Thursday, my love."

Hawke dimly remembered now. He noticed with a little curiosity that sweat was dripping from his face to the desk. His side hurt each time he breathed. "Frieda, I'm not sure I can come."

She asked him questions, became alarmed and said she would send her doctor up to look at him. Hawke hated doctors, he knew none in New York; ordinarily he would have resisted her—he often had in the past—but this time he did not.

It was a good thing he did not. He had an advanced pneumonia in both lungs. The doctor said he had probably been walking around with it for ten days. A big grayheaded man with a paunch, a little beard, and a severe permanent knot in his eyebrows, the doctor also volunteered that Hawke seemed on the brink of a nervous breakdown. "You're a fine author, I admire your books and I think a man like you should take better care of himself," the doctor said, brandishing a hypodermic needle full of penicillin, and neatly sliding it into Hawke's arm. "From what Frieda tells me, you lead a disorderly life. Penicillin usually knocks out pneumonia. Otherwise you'd have been a dead man in two days. I'm putting you in a hospital, you can't stay in this messy tomb of a house by yourself."

Hawke had a horror of hospitals, and was certain that if he entered one as a patient he would never leave it alive. Painful as it was to breathe, he argued forcibly until the doctor said, "Well, I'm sending a nurse here to take care of you, at least. Though I don't know how long a nurse will stay in this place. You're damned sick. I don't think you're the most sensible young man I've ever met. If you want to write many more books, you'd better reorganize your thinking and your living."

When the doctor was gone Hawke wandered here and there in the broken house like a solid coughing ghost. He knew he was very sick, but he didn't want to believe it. He trusted nobody in the huge city; he would have trusted Jeanne, but she had Karl Fry to take care of. After a while

he made another long distance call. He sat at the desk with his head down on his arms, and he was dozing when the ring came. He groped for the phone. "Hello? Hello, mama? How's Nancy, mama? And the baby? That's good. Look, mom, do you suppose you could come up here and do for me for a spell? I'm not feeling good."

7

Hawke lay in his bed in the garret room running a high fever, his large frame racked with shivering and sharp coughing, his teeth chattering quite out of control. He remembered little of the events of that night, the day that followed, or the night after that. There was a nurse, and the doctor came and went, and—unless he dreamed it—Frieda in a black dinner dress and pearl choker put an icy hand on his forehead and said "Jesus Christ," and it seemed to him that he had a long acrid fight with Jeanne about his latest chapters, though that probably was pure delirium. He slept, and woke, and slept, submitting half-consciously to the jabs of needles. The pain in his side faded. When he came fully awake again the slant red light of a New York morning lay across his bed, the nurse was gone, and his mother was pottering around the room in a familiar faded purple apron, dusting his books and picking up his scattered clothes. The ceiling of the room sloped like his attic room in the old house in Hovey, and for a moment or two he had the strongest possible delusion that he was back in his Kentucky home, a high school boy recuperating from a grippe, and that his entire career as the author, Youngblood Hawke— the encounters with Frieda and Jeanne, the great successes, the Holly-wood adventures, the Pulitzer Prize, the shower of money, the house disaster, the tax troubles—had all been the fever dream of a night.

His mother saw that his eyes were open. "Well, hi there, my big money maker," she said. "I was beginning to think you'd sleep forever. Aha ha ha. Been a bit poorly, haven't you? I thought you looked awful when you left home last week, but I've given up telling you such things, you just get ornery."

"Where's the nurse?"

"Why, I packed her off. I asked her what she was getting and when she said five dollars an hour I said I reckon I'd do it for half-price. . . . You hungry at all?"

"Well, maybe I could eat a scrambled egg, mom. Mom, I'm glad to see you. Maybe two scrambled eggs. You couldn't make some biscuits, could you?"

Mrs. Hawke smiled, and felt his pulse. "Scrambled eggs and biscuits, hey? I reckon New York hasn't quite killed you off. Though from what that nurse said, it was sure close. Double pneumonia! It's this air, Art, I

don't know how anybody's alive in this town. You'd think they'd all be walking around with gas masks. Why the soot lies along the windowsills here in little black piles. I declare I can *feel* a layer of soot in my lungs already. It tickles when I breathe. I bet when you start coughing up all that stuff in your lungs it'll be black as tar. And all those dollar cigars didn't do you any good either. Money can kill a man, you know, if he lets it."

Hawke said, "Let's see, I don't suppose there are any eggs down in the kitchen."

"There was nothing in that kitchen but some horrible moldy cheese, and cans and cans of beer. I'll say one thing for this crazy town. I went out half-past one in the morning looking for some food and do you know, I found three different groceries open? The men behind the counters looked as green as corpses but they were alive all right. Do you know what they wanted for eggs? A *dollar and a quarter a dozen.* That's more than ten cents an egg! Why, I went to all three stores just to make sure I was hearing right, and the last robber, he wanted a dollar-thirty. How can anybody but millionaires ever eat a square meal in this city?"

"Mom, I'm kind of hungry," Hawke said. "Can you fix those ten-cent eggs?"

She reappeared in short order with a tray of smoking food. "I don't know about the sausages, the doctor would probably have a fit, but I think at this point you need something that'll stick to your ribs. Say, you know that sprout of Nancy's has a head of hair like a man's! As though he was making up for his father. Aha ha ha."

Hawke devoured the food while his mother rattled on, watching him eat and wrinkling her nose each time he took a bite. The sweetest imaginable sensation of well-being flowed out through his whole body. It was better than getting drunk, it was better than making love, this feeling of coming back to life. The telephone rang downstairs. He said with a great yawn, "No matter who it is I don't want to talk to them. In fact you call the telephone company and tell them to disconnect that goddamned thing."

"No, I've got to talk to your doctor now and then. But don't worry, nobody's going to see you or talk to you till you're a whole lot stronger." Mrs. Hawke added as she went out, "It's going to kill me traipsing up and down these stairs. What a place to live, way up here under the roof. We've got to fix you a place below."

The mother did just that. She swept the mounds of rubbish out of the broken-walled space on the second floor that was supposed to become the master bedroom. She moved down the furniture and books from Hawke's garret lair herself, everything but the folding bed in which he lay, a relic of his loft room days. The next time the doctor came he was briskly commanded by the mother to "get aholt of t'other end of that bed, I cain't

get it downstairs myself and Art's weak as a kitten." He dumbly obeyed, and Hawke watched with amusement as the bearded Park Avenue physician tottered into the hall after the mother, carrying the bed, and panting, "Not so fast, madam."

She said, "It's all right, I'm used to this and I reckon you're not, I'll take the downstairs end, only mind you don't let go your end, I can't afford to pay a New York doctor, aha ha ha."

The doctor said after examining him, "Very dramatic response to penicillin. You can thank God for it. Your lungs still sound awful. You're damned sick and you will be for weeks. Don't let the normal temperature and the sense of good health fool you. No smoking, absolute bed rest, no writing for a month and I mean that. I've seldom seen a more exhausted man." Next he added to Mrs. Hawke, "This young fellow may be a genius, but I think he needs looking after by a woman."

"You all do," Mrs. Hawke said.

In his weak, euphoric state, Hawke told his money problems to his mother: the house mess, the tax troubles. His mother took it all cheerfully. The vast sums involved did not dismay her nearly as much as the idea of paying ten cents for an egg. "Well, Art, you can make the money all right, you have the gift, so there's nothing to worry about. Do you have the bills somewhere for what you've spent on the house?"

Hawke told her where the files were, an inconceivable thing for him to have done in a normal frame of mind. He had shut his mother out of his personal affairs since his seventeenth year.

That evening, when he was wolfing a huge bowl of her famous thick soup, which seemed inexpressibly delicious to him, she said, "What's wrong with you? Don't you know any girls?"

"Girls? I know thousands."

"Well none of them cares a rap about you, it seems. There's only two women keep calling and they're both married—Mrs. Winter and Mrs. Fry. A body would think they were both sweet on you."

Frieda and Jeanne seemed far away to Hawke, lying there in the gloomy room with the broken walls, in a snug bed under a floor lamp, talking to his mother over a bowl of her soup, as in childhood days. He was glad that his mother was there to answer the telephone and turn them off. He might have told her about his love life too, but her eyes were a shade too bright and eager as she put the questions. For the moment she came out of the character of the ministering mama and was another inquisitive woman, and that bored him. He said, handing her the empty soup bowl, "I'll have some more. You tell Jeanie Fry next time that I'm okay but I won't be working for a while. That's all she wants to know. As for Mrs. Winter, she can come and pay me a visit any time. She was nice to me when I got sick."

Mrs. Hawke said, "Nobody's visiting you."

"That suits me," Hawke yawned. "Mrs. Winter is a smart old bat, but she talks too much."

The mother brought him more soup. A letter lay on the tray beside the bowl. "Maybe this is from one of your girl friends," she said. "Most of your mail today was bills, but this one smells kind of interesting. Aha ha ha. Real foo-foo."

He picked up the letter languidly: an unknown feminine hand, a Rome postmark. He tossed the letter on the blanket. "I'm more interested in soup."

Mrs. Hawke said, wrinkling her nose as he put the spoon to his mouth, "I reckon you get bushels of fan mail, hey?"

"Not bushels, mama. I'm not a movie actor. I write books. Most people don't read books."

"Why, your books sell by the millions, I thought."

"I get a few letters a week. A lot more right after a book comes out."

He took up the letter when she left. There were six small sheets of air-mail paper, of a curiously marbled texture, covered in an elegant hand, more nearly vertical than most feminine writing. The woman had a habit of leaving out letters, and when a word ended in "ing" there was a mere squiggle. He glanced at the signature; this was no mere fan letter; he knew someone named Honor Hauptmann. In his foggy condition it took him a moment or two to place her as the daughter of Anne Karen, the plump young woman who had married a Peruvian.

Dear Mr. Hawke:

I have just this minute closed *Chain of Command*. It is your second demonstration, and I think a superfluous one, that you stand above your contemporaries. It is a fine entertainment. I suppose entertainment is hard enough to come by in this terrifying time, so the book is probably its own excuse for being. My question is, Mr. Hawke, when are you going to get to work?

This is an impertinence, and I can't stop you from throwing my letter in the wastebasket, but I'm going to have my say anyway. I not only admire you —many do that—I understand you, and it seems to me I have understood you ever since I read the first pages of *Alms for Oblivion*. In fact, if you can possibly take the word in a totally disembodied and abstract sense, I love you. I'm a happily married woman with three children. The third is about four days old and is lying beside me in a hospital basket, fast asleep under gauze. Perhaps it was a bad time for me to read your book, but my husband knows how much I admire you and so he gave it to me. You must know, with your intuitive sympathy, that a woman after childbirth is melancholy, and sensitive, and vulnerable. I felt in reading your book that—for all its crowded excitements and competent love scenes—the author was suffering from the worst loneliness and incompleteness a young man could endure; and that whatever his random pleasures, he had never truly known a woman. Though I write to you across a bottomless gulf, I think I might have given you that knowledge,

had our lives crossed in any significant way. But such things are not decided here below.

Mr. Hawke, you are a genius, a writer of the first magnitude. What you have done so far is nothing but finger exercises before your real work. I read everything. I read four languages. I think I have read all the novels in the world. I was born well off, as you know, and I am married to a man much richer than myself, so that I have absolutely nothing to do nine tenths of the time. Sports have always bored me. I don't drink, and when we're not travelling we live far, far out in the country. I read a couple of books a day. It seems to me that the American novel has sunk to a nadir unequalled in any art in any century. Am I mistaken, or have contraceptives become the chief preoccupation of American novelists? I think that the modern American novel should be called rubber opera. I'm sorry if I seem coarse, women can get a lot coarser than men when they choose and they can give cards and spades any day, believe me, to these writers of rubber opera. Your work juts out of this mass of pretentious dirty rubbish: young, crude, terribly marred by the desire to please and the greed for money—but no more so than much of Dostoevsky, Balzac, and Twain—but alive, masculine, in plain English, about living people, not about walking talking genitals and rubber.

What do you have to care, after *Chain of Command*, about critics and royalties? You'll never go hungry again. If there is one living person who can record this incredible, bloody, and marvellous century, it's you. I tell you what your wife would tell you if you had one, and if she were a true wife.

I can't imagine that you've read this far, and if you have, that you want to answer me. The only answer I'd want would be a new book worthy of you. If you care to let me know that you got this silly scrawl and didn't merely laugh and throw it away, I'll receive a letter sent to American Express, Rome. I won't be long in Rome, and I don't care if I never hear from you. I've come to the end of what I wanted to say.

Honor Hauptmann.

Hawke read the letter twice, indolently and with no strong response. He had received, by this time, much mail from readers; including some acute discussions of his books, and also including several teasing notes from women trying to intrigue him. This one fell somewhere between the two kinds. He liked praise; he even liked it as gross as Mrs. Hauptmann's, but her discussion of American novels struck him as ridiculous. The lady had misread him. He did not require abuse of other authors to make praise of himself pleasant, and his own opinion was that American novel-writing was at a high point of variety and force. Some of his competitors—Howard Fain for one—seemed to have surpassed anything he had yet accomplished, and he believed frankness about sex was all to the good when it was necessary.

Damned expensive note paper, he thought; no engraving of any kind on it, no identifying touch, except for a watermark that might be Japanese. Of course Anne Karen's daughter was very rich indeed. The picture of her in a hospital bed was convincing, and the whole letter, especially the out-

burst about loving him, read like the indiscretion of passing melancholia, the kind of thing women are often at some pains to recall and destroy later.

Among the things his mother had brought down from the garret was a box of his own best stationery: pale silky blue, with YOUNGBLOOD HAWKE engraved in small darker blue letters to one side at the top. He wrote a short reply thanking her for her praise, disclaiming his right to the eminence she would give him, and hoping his next book would strike her as more serious. He expected to go to Europe shortly, as soon as he recovered from a slight illness. Would she still be in Rome, and was there a chance that they might meet?

The idea that he might get out of his New York imbroglio by bolting to Europe was just starting to form in his mind.

8

"Who are those men?" he said to his mother a couple of days later, when she brought him his breakfast. Baritone voices had awakened him, echoing along the stairs, just below his room and now above it.

"They're from the bank. They won't disturb you, I told them not to come in here."

"Bank! What bank? What are they doing here?"

"Why, I don't know but one bank here, Art—yours, where I cash your checks. I just thought I'd ask how much of a mortgage you could get to finish this mess up. I dunno what else you can do, boy. You'll lose a fortune if you try to sell it all wrecked like this."

"Ma, you can't get a mortgage on a torn-up ruin."

"Why, Art, this older fellow here, he's their chief appraiser, he's just been looking at the plans up in the library and saying he thinks the bank might go for about fifty thousand dollars. 'Course they know you're Youngblood Hawke, that makes a difference. They know their money's good."

Hawke stared at his mother, sitting at the foot of the bed in a cheap orange print dress with her knotty hands folded in her lap. Why had a mortgage not occurred to him? It was the obvious answer. There would be no trouble paying it back out of royalties over the years; moreover if he wanted to sell the house—and that was what he did want at this point —it would be easier to do with a bank carrying much of the cash load. He had assumed that no bank would mortgage the broken shell he owned. His mother, assuming nothing, had found the way out of the problem as easily as a cat pushing open a screen door with a paw. "Well, that's a right good idea, ma, if it works."

"What's more Art, I'm pretty sure that contractor of yours has been

stealing you blind. Have you gone through those bills and added up the items? Sand! Why if that man bought all the sand he's charged you for, then you also own a dam he's built somewhere, son. You got to check on these fellows, Art, building contractors by and large are bigger crooks even than butchers. This fellow, he's crooked as a corkscrew or I can't add. I've got three other contractors coming here today to look at the place. You need a few fresh estimates for finishing it."

"Contractors? Where'd you get hold of contractors?"

"Asked the real estate man at the bank. He gave me half a dozen names. You've got to get this thing off your mind, Art. You've fretted yourself sick over it and what's more you've stopped writing. That's the worst of it. That's the only way you'll ever make money, by writing. You ought to get out of this house and come home and rest up, and get back to work. Finish up this mess here the cheapest way possible and sell it. It's just a piece of foolishness, Art, what does a bachelor need a big house for? Anyway it's too dark, it's on the wrong side of the street. I wouldn't live in this city for all the tea in China but if I was forced to I sure wouldn't live any place that didn't face south. Why, all the sunlight you get in here is one thin red sliver just at sunrise. You need the electric light on all day. This is a great house for mushrooms, not people."

This speech, which ordinarily would have rasped Hawke on several tender nerve ends, struck him at this time as both relieving and shrewd. His mother occasionally had the eye and the guts to see the truth and to speak it.

All day he heard through his closed door the brisk sharp questions of his mother and the answering voices of men. It was a comforting feeling, to sit in his bed reading a Walter Scott novel, knowing that someone else was doing something about the accursed house. The thought was growing on him that his mother, tough and suspicious and rustic as she was, might be just the person to leave in charge of the building while he fled New York. He had heard her during his adolescence bargaining over bits of coal land. A New York contractor who tried to get the best of his mother, he figured, would soon wish he were in some other business.

The doctor discharged Hawke—in a fashion. He came and thumped and felt and listened and asked questions. He sat for half a minute, tugging at his beard and looking at Hawke. "All right. You have an amazing constitution. I isolated you more for your nerves than your pneumonia. Your lungs are clear and you seem to be acting normally again, but I don't know. You were drifting in a schizoid state when I first examined you, do you realize that? I think you should have that old brain injury you told me about looked into thoroughly. I'm not a psychiatrist and I don't pretend to know how the artistic personality functions, but I think the next thing you need is some mental therapy."

Hawke said cheerily, "I tell you, doc, I have these slumps off and on. I always come out of them and they don't signify. There's no reason I can't see my editor, is there?"

The doctor shrugged. "So far as your pneumonia goes, you're well."

It was always a little surprising to Hawke to realize how small and slight Jeanne was, after he had not seen her for some time. She arrived in a dripping blue raincoat, underneath which she wore a plain white blouse and an old skirt. Her makeup was sketchily applied and she had a harassed, tired look. It gave him a surge of delight to see her face, press her hand, and hear the gravelly voice say, "Hi. Here you've been yelling at me for years about abusing my lungs, and who gets the pneumonia? For the future, my friend, the way to fend it off is three packs of cigarettes a day. Be sure to inhale. Gad, you look better than you did that first night. Thank heaven."

"You were here, then? I thought I dreamed it."

"Of course I was here. You insisted on my coming. Otherwise you were going to get out of bed and fetch me. You with a hundred and five plus, and this was after midnight. Two doctors here, and a nurse, and Frieda. I must say I felt like an idiot coming here that time of night and what I was really afraid of—oh, well, you're better, that's the main thing, isn't it?" A red flush crept into her white cheeks, and she looked much better all at once, and quite confused.

"What were you afraid of, Jeanne?"

"Well, Arthur, you know, they said you were out of your head. And after that preposterous talk we had in the Lexington airport I didn't know what the hell you might not come out with. But I must say even at death's door you were the writer to the last. All you wanted to do was argue about some cuts I'd made and then discuss the new pages. They told me to humor you so I went through the motions. I hung around most of the night, so did Frieda. She and I had quite a talk in that bombed-out kitchen of yours. You've seen her since, of course?"

"Jeanne, you're about the first person I've seen in a month."

"Really? I'm complimented." She undid her damp red portfolio, bending down her head. "If you're interested I've never seen a woman more upset and frightened than Frieda was. She said many strange things, and maybe the strangest was that if anything happened to you she could never face your mother. I feel quite different about her since that night. It's a pity you two aren't married. Maybe it's still not impossible. Stranger marriages have come off. Is this a get-well visit or are you up to working? I have some things here."

Hawke was taken aback at Jeanne's nervous, indiscreet loquacity. He said they would work, and he watched her while they talked. Her voice quavered, and once or twice she seemed to lose the thread of the conversation. When Mrs. Hawke came in and left them a tray of coffee and cake

he broke off the work, saying he was tired. She told him the late gossip from the publishing business, including a juicy switch of wives between an author and editor who were next-door neighbors in Connecticut. They chatted idly, and her spirits seemed to improve. Then he mentioned that he had decided to abandon the house—finish it up and sell it. She looked startled, her pallor became more marked, and a haunted expression crept over her face. "Are you sure you want to do that? You've put so much thought into it, let alone money."

"I'm sick of it."

"You were so happy over it at first, you had so much fun with the plans."

"Yes, I know. Let someone else live in it."

Jeanne said slowly, "It's eerie. This morning I talked to the real estate agent in Harrison and gave up the piece of land Karl and I had an option on. Such a wonderful piece of land, Arthur, forest and farms and a lake. Forty minutes on the parkway to the office."

"Why did you give it up?"

"Oh, with one thing and another it wasn't practical. We won't be in a position to build for years. Why sink money in land and pay taxes?" She lit a cigarette and said with comic dismalness, "I think you and I are the kind of people who are destined never to build a house."

Hawke said, "You and I could build a house, Jeanie. A good house."

Jeanne's eyes glistened and she put her dry cold hand on his. "None of that, for God's sake. Just because you're convalescing don't take advantage of me. Karl is in Polyclinic Hospital." Hawke sat up, astonished. She straightened her skirt as she stood. "I'm going there from here. My jolly round this morning."

"What's the matter, Jeanne?"

"Heart. Milder this time, which is a comfort, but it's the second. If I seem less than my old bright chirping self I can only tell you I've had quite a month of it. Among other things Karl's oldest son got drafted—imagine me being the stepmother of a soldier, if you can—and promptly came down with jaundice at a camp in Texas and almost died. I don't know whether that did Karl in, or your brilliant friend Gus Adam."

She told Hawke about the meeting in Hodge's office. Adam had driven Karl brutally to the wall, she said. Even though he had convinced Karl to follow the course she herself had wanted, she hated the lawyer for it. "Karl's face was as gray as the carpet when he promised Ross he would stop making the contributions. He never pulled out of it. He was quiet for three days and then one night we were just sitting around listening to music and he took sick."

Hawke said, "Karl couldn't have stayed in his job otherwise very long. Adam spoke the truth."

"Oh, Christ, Arthur, there are more important things than the truth sometimes. Your Adam is a cold clever bastard and I don't trust him. I

don't know why he advised Karl not to go to Washington and clear everything up." She put on her raincoat.

Hawke said, "Jeanie, I'm thinking of going to Europe."

She paused in belting the coat, and looked sharply at him. "With
Frieda? She talked a lot about that."

"Not with Frieda. With nobody, I guess. I was going to do my damnedest to take you with me but that was a sickbed daydream, it appears."

"Trying to run from Frieda again, are you? You'll have to run far and
fast. You tried that once. Next thing I knew we were all eating turkey
together in Beverly Hills."

Hawke said bitterly, "You're the forgiving sort, aren't you?"

Frieda Winter walked into the room at that moment with Hawke's
mother. Mrs. Hawke said, "As long as you're seeing people I figured you'd
like to see Mrs. Winter, she's been so thoughtful and all."

"I can't stay but a minute." Frieda wore no hat. She seemed to have
tried hard to look like a frump: brown low walking shoes, a bagging brown
linen suit, her hair crudely pinned up. Hawke had noticed before that she
had some gray hairs, but the gray seemed to have come out in streaks all
over her head. Had she been dyeing her hair, and decided now to let the
gray come? It was not unattractive; indeed he felt a painful throb of affection, seeing his mistress in this careless state, a frankly aging woman with
a pretty face and a still seductive figure. She walked to the bed and shook
hands with him. "Hello, stranger. I guess you're meant to be hanged,
and nothing else can kill you. God, were you sick! Hello, Jeanne. I heard
about Karl. I'm sorry."

"It's not severe, Frieda. The worst of it is he's back on that regime he
hates, starting with six weeks in bed."

Frieda said, "My husband just got put back on a rice diet. I swear all
the men are falling apart."

"Isn't it the truth?" said Mrs. Hawke. "Any day now they'll face up to
it and put one of us gals in the White House." She guffawed. Hawke had
an irrational spasm of fear, seeing the three women grouped so at the
foot of his bed: the mother laughing inanely, Frieda dishevelled and gray,
Jeanne's face a white mask slashed with lipstick under a shapeless black
poplin hat. Jeanne and Frieda were measuring each other with looks as
the mother giggled. It reminded Hawke of their first confrontation in the
Prince library. With all their added knowledge of each other, with all
that had happened in the passing years, the wary hostility between them
was the same.

"How do you like this hat?" Jeanne said to Frieda, jamming it flatter
on her head. "Just the thing for the chic editor visiting the great author,
isn't it? Or for carrying some peat moss home for the rubber plant."

"Darling, what can you do in the rain?" Frieda said.

"I like your hair that way," Jeanne said. "Goodbye, Arthur."

Frieda stayed only ten minutes. She acted the motherly neighbor looking in on a sick young man to such perfection, gabbling with Mrs. Hawke about symptoms and about diets for convalescents, that he found himself perversely calling up mental pictures of her in moments of abandoned passion. The contrast was unbelievable. He could not help wondering just what his mother made of Frieda. With her ingrained mountaineer suspicion, her readiness to believe the worst of everybody, how could she continue blind to the shrieking fact of his affair? For a moment it appeared that she guessed the truth; she offered, with more than a trace of roguishness, to go down to the kitchen and leave Frieda alone with Hawke. Frieda said briskly, "Nonsense, I have to run along. I just wanted to see for myself how our young genius is coming around. The only sensible thing he's done in the three years I've known him was to send for you to take care of him."

"Well, Mrs. Winter, he saved the price of a nurse that way, that was all."

Frieda laughed as merrily as Mrs. Hawke. The two women went out together, talking about the allergies of Frieda's son Paul. Frieda said in the doorway, "Well now, Arthur, you bring your mother over to dinner when you're up and about. Young Paul keeps asking for you." There was not a hint on the woman's face of anything but bovine jolly middle-aged friendliness.

His mother came back shortly. "Art, you're lucky to have a friend like that."

"I like her, mom, when she isn't too bossy. She has a way of taking over if you let her."

Mrs. Hawke said, "You'd never believe how people will talk and how gossip travels. Do you know that even back in Hovey people have had the nerve to come whispering to Nancy and me about Mrs. Winter, saying God knows what all? They claim they've read it in New York gossip columns. I guess that comes of being well known. The mother of four children, for heaven's sake, and as gray as I am!"

She was looking at him rather keenly, and Hawke said, "Well, I guess I gave them something else to talk about, putting Jeanne up in the General Morgan Hotel for three weeks."

Mrs. Hawke chuckled. "Land, did you ever! People just have nothing better to do, and you know, Art, malice loves a shining mark. 'Course the sooner you find a nice girl and marry her the better off you'll be. If there's a girl somewhere who can hold you. Now, Art, there's all kinds of people been calling these past weeks, you know—newspaper people, radio people, your Hollywood agent, and such like. I never even told you their names. Doctor said I was to keep you quiet."

"If something's urgent they'll call again."

"Do you really know this movie actor Georges Feydal so well? He's

called about ten times. It's always dear Arthur this, dear Arthur that.
Then there's Scott Hoag."

"Scotty been calling from Lexington? That's nice of him."

Mrs. Hawke said with a sniff, "He's right here in New York, at the
Statler. Been calling for a week. Says you told him you needed money
and he's got it for you."

"I'll be damned, did Scott come up here just for that? The Statler, you
say?"

"Art, you stay in that bed. I'll do the phoning—"

"Rats, mama, I'm okay. All I need is to move around and get my blood
stirring."

9

Scotty, genial and sunburned, dressed in his usual horsy clothes, showed
up with a leather portfolio and a gigantic roll of blueprints. He was in
New York to explore the possibility of building a shopping center in the
middle of Long Island, and he was so enthusiastic that he insisted on
spreading the plans on the floor beside Hawke's bed almost at once. Mrs.
Hawke's face froze in disapproval as Scotty talked, but he addressed her
and her son with equal warmth and good humor. "What it is, Miz Hawke,
the New York money's been coming down into Kentucky and buying up
all the choice situations, you know? And some not so choice. It's a sudden
panic in Southern real estate and us poor local boys just don't stand a
show. So I figure turn about is fair play, and Ellie's been talking up New
York for years anyway, she says the schools here beat ours, not that I go
along with her on that. But I tell you something, Art, I swear I think I
can do binness here. Just because I got this Letchworth accent, why,
everybody here thinks I'm ignorant and stupid. Boy, that's one hell of
an advantage if you can hang on to it. You be amazed the lease commitments I got lined up here"—he patted his portfolio—"big New York department stores, big chain stores, and I swear it's because they all think
I'm a hillbilly and I'm giving space away, but the way I've got it figured,
this the biggest thing yet, we'll beat that Bluegrass job in Louisville ten times
over. And you want to know something? Mortgage money is a cinch up
here compared to Kentucky. They used to talking money here. Art, this
is where the big pot is, and don't ever forget it. All the money in the goddamn world is right here in New York. Ellie's done me a favor chasing me
up here."

He talked about the progress of the three construction jobs in which
Hawke's money was tied up: the building for doctors and lawyers in
Frankfort, a shopping center in the outskirts of the same city, and the
Skytop Lodge in Hovey. There had been some difficulties with mortgage

money, but all three were coming along well and were going to throw off at least a one hundred percent return in a year or so. He regretted at length not having been able to grant Hawke's request for cash. "Art, I been in binness ten years and I never seen money so tight as it is in Kentucky right now. That's why this Frenchman's Ridge thing is a windfall, for me even more than for you. A builder can never have enough cash. I tell you I'm gasping a little bit right about now. This is the answer for all of us—for you too, I reckon, Miz Hawke. I'm right glad you here in New York, so I can talk to you both. I think you the binness man in this family." Scotty laughed, rasping open his briefcase, and he passed carbon copies of a long letter to Hawke and his mother. "You just look that over."

The letterhead, recopied by a typist, read, "The William Coffman Development Company," with an address in Wheeling, West Virginia. The gist of the three pages of single-space typewriting was an offer to buy two thousand acres on Frenchman's Ridge owned by Hawke Brothers Coal Company, on a complex basis of cash installments over ten years. Hawke skimmed the foggy arithmetic of the offer and came to this paragraph on the last page:

Our title search showed, finally, that a wedge-shaped parcel within this tract, of some ninety-odd acres, referred to on your map as the White Branch Section, is now the subject of litigation in the Circuit Court of Letchworth County in Kentucky, Sarah Hawke and Arthur Y. Hawke, plaintiffs. You have represented to us that this litigation will shortly be settled. Since it would be much less practicable to develop the tract if this parcel were excluded, since it is the readiest access and roads cannot be run around it due to the added expense, in view of the engineering difficulties of the ravine below, and the vertical cliffs on the north side, our offer is contingent on the settlement of this lawsuit. If this settlement cannot be reached within a 90-day period this offer will be withdrawn since we have other tracts in the same county in mind

The letter was signed Luther Coffman, President.

Hawke said, "We talked on the phone about this, when I was in Hovey."

"That's right, Art. It looks goddamn good to me, the way it's come along. I think this Coffman Company is just fronting for New York money myself, it's an old land speculation outfit that mostly has stuck to West Virginia before this. I got a credit report on them if you want to look at it, Miz Hawke, they a solid outfit."

The mother said, "I reckon you made sure they're solid What do they want the land for?"

"Well, what they say is some new processes make all that trashy second and third growth up there commercial for paperboard. Actually, I think they speculating on coal bouncing back, with plastics coming up like they

are. Right now you read all these New York binness magazines and they all making a big to-do about coal. It's like a fad."

Mrs. Hawke said wisely, "If it's that valuable to them maybe it's even more valuable to us."

"Ma'am, that could be, but I think I dropped enough money in the coal binness to speak with some authority and I say if these New York people have worked up a sudden sweat on coal, then for sweet Jesus' sake I want to unload all I got before they switch to cement or whale oil or something. They keep running around in circles, these New York monkeys, they wound up so tight they can't stop running, always looking for a new investment idea, and I tell you, Miz Hawke, they *loaded*. I tell you the money in this city is something unbelievable."

Hawke said, handing him the letter, "What do you want to do, Scott?"

"Art, we dying to sell. That land's just sitting idle eating up taxes like a horse, and we carrying a quarter of a million in red ink against the Frenchman's Ridge mine." He turned to Mrs. Hawke. "You want to know what Glenn said? He said 'Aunt Sarah's got us over a barrel. Ask her what she'll take to settle, and give it to her.' That's from the chairman of the board."

Mrs. Hawke glanced at her son, triumph and suspicion comically mingling on her face. "I just don't know. Art's getting over pneumonia. Maybe he and I ought to talk it over for a week or so."

Hoag said anxiously, "Miz Hawke, even if we agree on a figure today, it'll take weeks for the lawyers to work it all out. We got a ninety-day deadline. I sort of hope we can settle here and now."

"Suppose my price is too high?"

"Ma'am, we ready to go a mile to your inch."

"Well, but suppose it is?"

Hoag sighed heavily, blowing out his cheeks. He rolled up his blueprints in silence, and doubled a thick rubber band on them with a loud snap. "We gonna go to court with you then, Miz Hawke. I tell you that in all honesty. They won't be any more adjournments. I wish you'd show your case to some experienced land lawyers over to Frankfort or Louisville, instead of that young fellow up in Edgefield. We been bending over backwards because of the awkward family situation, but if you cost us the Coffman deal we got to fight you and clean this up. I just hope Art won't allow it, ma'am, it'll cost you a fortune in legal fees. It don't mean nothing to us, it's another loss we can carry forward into a good year."

Mrs. Hawke said, "Well, I reckon I better talk to my lawyer."

Scott reached into his briefcase. "I got a letter here from him." He handed it to Hawke. The mother came and sat beside Hawke on the bed, and they read it together. The lawyer had investigated the Coffman offer, he wrote, and found it bona fide.

"However," he went on, "This does not affect my client's claims in any way, and she is determined to press them. You will find it difficult to reach a settlement with Mrs. Hawke. I am not prepared even to bring this matter to her attention unless you're thinking in serious terms, perhaps ten thousand dollars. I am not authorized to quote even that figure, or any figure I am merely venturing a guess as to her thinking, and she may want considerably more for granting a release."

Mrs. Hawke laughed. "Well, ten thousand's a sight better than one thousand, which was your last offer, Mr. Hoag."

"Ma'am," Scott said patiently, "at that time we were trying to settle a mixup which was no fault of ours. This offer is a windfall. It changes the picture. If we don't grab it that land can lie on our books as a liability for another ten or fifty years, and as for you and us, we'll just go to court and wrastle around for years and nobody'll get nothing except lawyers' bills. I'm sure that young fellow of yours is on a contingent fee basis but even so you'll have to give him expense money and you'll be just amazed, Miz Hawke, how that mounts up. You'll get a bill for pretty near a thousand dollars for stenography and printing before you've even started."

Mrs. Hawke said, "Art, what do you think?"

Hawke said, "Well, it sounds like a break for everybody. Let's take twenty thousand, mama."

Scott frowned. "Holy cow, Art, I thought you a friend of mine."

"I'm no friend of Hawke Brothers, Scott."

"That's too rough. They'll let the deal fall through."

"That's their business. I don't care one way or the other. You know I've never been hot on mama's lawsuit, but by Christ I'm beginning to think that the thing to do in this world is just put up the goddamnest scream for anything you think you have the slightest claim to, and then grab hold and hang on until you're dead and for three days after that. Twenty thousand dollars, Scott."

Mrs. Hawke patted her son's hand. "I declare, Art, you're getting real hard-hearted."

Once again Scott fished in his briefcase, and this time brought out documents which he passed to Hawke and his mother. "There's a contract of release I brought, hoping you'd sign it and I could take it back with me. The company took your lawyer's letter at its face value. The price it's willing to pay is fantastic, in view of the fact that you have no case at all and any first-class attorney will tell you as much."

The document was opaque legal gibberish except for one typewritten phrase in the middle of a large white space, coming after a series of "whereases"

Therefore, for the sum of . . . . . TEN THOUSAND DOLLARS . . . . . *and other good and valuable consideration, to be paid in full upon execution of said proposed contract of sale with the William Coffman Development Company, or ninety days after the execution of this contract, whichever is sooner.* . . .

Hawke said almost at once, "Does this mean my mother gets paid whether or not the Coffman sale goes through?"

"The company has got to take that chance, Art," Scott said. "Coffman won't sit down with us unless we show a release on White Branch Section. We gotta figure they gonna go through with it, that's all."

"Scott, what is this printed form? I once signed a printed form and got in a hell of a mess."

Scott laughed. "That's a form all the banks and real estate lawyers in Kentucky use for a release. Call up Lexington First National collect, charged to my account, and read it to any one of the managers over the phone."

Mrs. Hawke said, "This says ten. Art wants twenty thousand."

"Is that the price you asking, ma'am?"

"Well, it's Art's price."

Fencing ensued for perhaps ten minutes. Scott kept trying to pin Mrs. Hawke down and she avoided speaking out her price. At last Hawke said, "Mama, tell Scott how much you want, for Christ's sake, or go ahead and sue him, but stop this foolishness."

"Why Art, I been saying all along that you're the man in the family and if that's your price, who am I to argue?"

Scott looked at his wrist watch and stood. "I got to go to La Guardia airport in an hour. Sorry I didn't manage to see you till today, Art, but your mom's been guarding you like a tiger. What do you say, Mrs. Hawke? Would you take twenty thousand?"

"Are you offering it?"

"Here we go again," Hawke said. "Mama, tell him whether or not you'll take twenty thousand dollars."

Mrs. Hawke hesitated, and at last whined, "Well, it may be a lot for a release, but it's nothing to what your company owes me and you know it, Mr. Hoag. I'm tired of fighting, and I've never been able to find a good lawyer to take my case. All right. Twenty thousand dollars is more than I had any hope for, I guess, without a big court case."

Scott sat, opened his briefcase, took out the folder, carefully crossed out the old figure in all three copies of the release and inked in *Twenty thousand dollars.*

"Is that legal?" Mrs. Hawke said.

"Yes, ma'am, if all three of us initial it," Scott said with a shade of exasperation.

There was much fuss over initialling and signing of the documents,

mainly on the mother's part. She scrawled slowly and painfully, as though she were parting with a substantial fraction of two million dollars with each stroke of the pen. She looked extremely relieved when Scott said she only had to sign one copy, and she did it after long hesitation, saying, "Well, let's hope it's for the best."

Scotty shook hands with them, put the folder in his briefcase, and hurried off. Mrs. Hawke sat with her son, folding and refolding the carbon copy of the release which she had kept, saying in a dozen ways that she hoped she had done the right thing, she hoped she hadn't signed away the birthright of her grandchildren the way her grandmother had signed away her own birthright, and so forth. Then she went down to the kitchen. Half an hour later the telephone rang. Hawke heard her answering it. She came into his room in a few moments, saying, "Land sakes, where's my copy of that release?"

"It's in your apron pocket, ma."

"Is it? Well, so it is." She opened the paper, which already looked battered from her constant nervous folding. "I declare, he's right. That's your Mr. Hoag calling from the airport. He says I kept the one copy I signed, and so I did. Now what made me do such a thing?"

Hawke frowned in great annoyance. "Tell him you'll mail it to him, ma."

"Why of course, but I feel like such a fool. I'll mail it later this afternoon when I go shopping. You lie down and sleep Art, you've done too much today."

CHAPTER FOURTEEN

1

HAWKE came out of the gloomy house after nearly a month of stifling entombment, into the kind of glorious day that New York usually produces just when you are about to despair of that monstrous, racking, abominable and magnificent city; as a peevish pretty woman will turn adorable at the exact moment when she has pushed a man to the verge of kicking her out the door for good. The rain was gone; the mugginess was gone; the dirty haze was gone; miraculously, for the first week of July, the heat was gone. It was a sweet crystalline morning. The sunshine poured white through each gap between the buildings; it blazed along the straight

broad north-south avenues. From Central Park a soft breeze carried a morning smell of green dewy leaves. The fumes of the buzzing auto traffic seemed to burn into nothing, almost into perfume, in the clear sunlight. Such was Hawke's impression, anyway. Part of his high spirits no doubt came from the fact that he went straight to the bank with his mother and within a few minutes, just for the signing of his name here and there on half a dozen papers, acquired fifty thousand dollars in his account, a liberal mortgage loan repayable over twenty long years. But there was also the animal pleasure of using his limbs again, of striding along a hard sidewalk in the sunshine, of breathing fresh air, of wearing clothes, of seeing good-looking women swing their hips past in sweetly form-fitting dresses. The main thing was New York itself, the treacherous piercing charm of New York, never stronger than on this day, when he was setting out to arrange to leave it.

His mother returned to the house and he walked into the park. He climbed the big gray outcrop of rock at Sixty-seventh Street and sat on a boulder at the top, feeling his heart pound at his first exertion in a month. He had sat on this rock many a time, in choking summer heat, in the sharp air of autumn, in whirling snowstorms. His thinking walks—that was what he called the long somnambulist strolls during which he invented most of the scenes he wrote off at night—usually took him at last to this perch, where the view of the city was far-reaching. A quarter to eleven. He was alone on the rock. Here he had sat dreaming through the invented dilemmas of his characters, sometimes laughing or weeping aloud like a lunatic, oblivious of the clangorous city around him; and he had sat worrying over the real dilemmas of his own life, too, but then he had been well aware of the towers, the noise, and the weather—hot, cold, stormy, windy, dead gray or clear and perfect like today; nearly always extreme, nearly always given to swift violent change, like the city itself, and like the fortunes of the people in the city.

A few more ends to tie up, and he would be off. He had already reserved his ship passage by telephone, without telling anyone about it. He felt poised for departure; this look at New York was a farewell look. The jagged flat-topped shafts of Fifth Avenue and midtown, and the immense green oblong of the park, remained fair and exciting even now, beyond his boyhood visions. He had read enough books of finance to know that many of the high towers had been the incautious ventures of optimists; that a number of them were monuments to bankruptcy, that the great landmark of them all, the Empire State Building, had for a long time been a half-empty, half-finished ruin like his own house. What did that matter today? The old towers stood, and new towers rose. Some men got rich and others got poor; the talented and the stout-hearted did the work, and the crafty spun the webs of arithmetic; and New York became each year more dazzling, more crowded, more improbable, more

lovely, and more spiky with human striving and achievement. Money could not build such a city, he thought, and the people who called New York the city of money were fools. Money was the mere dirty haze that hung over Manhattan, the burned thin residue of the great combustion of human spirit that had raised the towers, and that filled them night and day with blazing light and incomparable work. It was the world's first city, and it could only be American.

Had he won or lost his yokel's battle with it? Hawke smiled wryly in the clean sunlight on the high rock, and gave himself a shaded draw. He was retreating, all bloodied up and barely escaping death by exhaustion. He had made clumsy slips. The tremendous flailing machine had caught and tumbled and beaten him, marking him for life. With all that, he had become Youngblood Hawke. That had been the stake of the game and he had won it. New York was not impressed with Youngblood Hawke, to be sure. But it was not impressed with royalty or presidents or conquering heroes either. Its idea of a supreme tribute was to empty its wastebaskets from its high towers, and heap a hero's head with shreds of its discarded paperwork. But New York with its hard-bitten arithmetical measures had printed his name for many months at the top of its best-seller lists—and there, as he left the field, his name stood:

"1. *Chain of Command—Youngblood Hawke.*"

It was the one test of an author that New York cared about, despite the lofty chatter in its literary magazines. It left appreciation of a writer's art to the unborn, and wanted to know only whether his books sold. That was all Hovey wanted to know, too; as Frieda had said, New York was just America distilled.

If he wanted to see Gus Adam today, Hawke thought, he had to go and telephone him at once. There was no time for meditation; there seldom was, in New York. Hawke stood, intending to climb down the rock, and then paused irresolute. He did not want to leave this spot, so peopled by the phantoms of *Chain of Command* and *Will Horne.* He hesitated too because he had little desire to unravel for Professor Adam, who had seemed to admire him so much, his tangled stupidities and miscalculations. But he had decided in his sickbed self-analysis that he was a money-waster, a true artist in this if in nothing else, and he needed a steadying hand. Adam had seemed a genius at the university, and he had turned into a most sober-sided tax expert; the very man for him, and he would feel easier with a fellow from Letchworth County than with any New Yorker.

He started down the rock, and he saw on the walk far below him the gross figure of Georges Feydal strolling along in a ludicrous striped seersucker suit like a carnival balloon, in earnest conversation with Pierce Carmian. Hawke wondered whether he should not dodge the encounter,

having last seen the dandy flopping around in Ferdie Lax's swimming pool. But Feydal looked up and exclaimed, "My dear Arthur!" in the voice that could roll across a football stadium without a loudspeaker, and Hawke was caught.

Carmian said with a flash of white teeth, holding out his hand, "Hello. I earned that ducking, I was rude and bitchy, and here's my apology, if you remember the incident." Hawke shook hands clumsily, and Carmian continued, "I hope you don't mind, but Georges let me read your play and I'm on the ceiling about it."

Feydal said, "I must have telephoned you forty times. Are you all better? You haven't given the play to anyone else, have you? I've been sick with worry about you."

Hawke said he had done nothing about the play.

"Marvellous," Feydal said. "Pierce wants to do it. Pierce has been doing some remarkable work in production out of town. That's his métier, you know, not writing. We've decided that."

Carmian said, "I leave the writing to you, Mr. Hawke. I think your play is sensational, I know just how it should be done, and I'm ready to give you a very substantial advance and go into production at once."

This was a strange turn for Hawke. He stared at Carmian, handsome as ever and turned out like a male mannequin, to the last thick sweeps of his black wavy hair. Had anybody thrown him into a pool, he would have wanted the man's blood to his dying day and somehow sometime he would have had it. These New York people seemed to have no continuity in their lives. They were all like Frieda, they lived from situation to situation, from yesterday's gossip to today's gossip. A fresh chance to make love, or to make money, seemed to wipe out all prior commitments and experiences.

He said something about Feydal's being unavailable to direct the play. Feydal quickly replied, "My dear fellow, I believe I will be. They're having an awful time casting the Christ. The whole thing may be put off. Do you know that ridiculous cowboy star Bill Blaydes wanted to do it and almost got it? Imagine Jesus saying shucks and yep and bashfully kicking pebbles! Sheer sacrilege! Those people don't know what taste is, they'd cast a dog as Saint Peter if the dog were box office, and change the part to St. Bernard. You will tell your man of business to get in touch with Pierce, and let him have the play? Ferdie Lax, isn't it? These curious Hollywood names, that one is rather like an impolite patent medicine. But he's a dear chap."

2

Gus Adam's manner was polite, cool, even nonchalant when the author called for him at his law school office. But in the hallway he introduced Hawke to a couple of his colleagues, and it was obvious that he felt good about having a best-selling novelist in tow. Adam took him to the Columbia Faculty Club, and here too Hawke sensed that he made a stir among the graying, wise-looking men who filled the dining room. This deeply flattered him. His cup ran over when an English professor whose name he recognized, because he wrote leading book reviews in the New York newspapers, came and shook his hand, and told him he was probably America's most promising young author.

Hawke found it awkward to talk to Adam at first, though they had university reminiscences and Letchworth County gossip to exchange. It turned out that they both kept up subscriptions to their home town newspapers. They laughed over the continuing mélange of church news, shootings, and local politics that the papers reported. "Do you suppose eastern Kentucky will ever get civilized?" Hawke said.

"Well, I don't know whether I want it to," Adam said. "Of course the conditions in the back hills are impossible in this day and age. But then again, some of the finest people I've ever known are those old-timers up in the hills around Brightstar. When I read of one of them dying I feel terrible, and they're going fast now. Letchworth will be all full of four-lane highways and deep freezers one of these days, no doubt. I wish the people could get the hospitals and education and services without changing too much, but I suppose that's absurd."

They ate without talking for a while. This was more comfortable than making chatter. The lawyer resembled many people Hawke had known back home. "Adam" was one of the widespread family names in that part of Kentucky, like Combs and Horne, and Adam's oval red face and sandy hair appeared with slight variations all through the Cumberland mountains. Hawke was used to the Letchworth manner of sitting or standing or squatting around and not saying much of anything. Adam broke the silence, "How's Mr. Fry? Last I heard he was in the hospital."

"They've moved him home, but he'll be in bed for weeks."

Adam shook his head. "He didn't look good the day we met."

Hawke said, "Jeanne Fry more than half blames you for Karl's attack, you know."

The lawyer's eyes narrowed, his shoulders sank, and he all at once had a wily, watchful look. "Really? It was a very unfortunate business, but I gave the best advice I could."

"Jeanne thought you were brutal to Karl, and she still doesn't understand why you were against his going to Washington."

Adam took out his pipe and the red, white, and blue pouch, and stuffed the bowl automatically as he spoke. "Well! I wish she had called me later and asked me, I think I could have made my reasoning clear. But events have justified my advice, haven't they? If Fry had gone back to Washington, he might now be dead."

Hawke said, "You accused him of shielding his communist activities behind his wife's skirt."

Adam lit his pipe, and squinted at Hawke through a cloud of blue smoke. "You depend a lot on Mrs. Fry's editorial services."

"Quite true."

The lawyer puffed in silence, looking hard at Hawke, who at last blurted out, "And I'm extremely fond of Jeanie, of course, and of Karl, too."

Adam nodded. "Fry's attitude about his communist past is hopeless. He proposes to confess all about himself but to name no names. In Washington that's the way they tell sheep from goats among ex-communists. Ross Hodge knows that. I'm sure he's keeping Fry on because of Mrs. Fry's usefulness to you. I saw that Mrs. Fry was offended when I touched on that point. But if a meeting isn't to be just chit-chat somebody at some point has to say what it's about."

"Why didn't you advise Karl to resign? That might have been more frank."

The lawyer cocked his head and arched his heavy brows. "Why should he resign, so long as Hodge is willing to keep him on? He's a good editor. The government mill grinds slowly. He may have a couple of years' grace before they come around to him again. Or they may never do so. What's lost and who's injured if he just goes about his business?"

"With a sword hanging over his head," Hawke said.

"Hung there by himself," said the lawyer. "He has to make the best of his life. Before the government bothers him again all kinds of things can happen. The panic about communists may subside. Fry may quit editing. Or since he's had two heart attacks he may die. Of course we hope that won't happen, and it's unlikely. People who can solve a lot of problems by simply dying are the ones who hang on and on." He was pouring coffee as he talked. When he said these last words he put down the pot and glanced at Hawke, and Hawke in a flash was reminded of the way Adam had looked on the campus: alert, foxy, and too self-satisfied to be wholly attractive, despite his handsomeness and his heroic prestige.

"I guess what bothers Jeanie, and me too, is that it isn't clear whose side you're on."

"Why, like any lawyer, I'm on the side of whoever pays me."

"Do you think it's right to hound a man out of his job because he was once a communist? Do you think a man who's left the party ought to be forced to name names to the government?"

Adam smiled, wrinkling his eyes to slits. "I'm a tax man, Mr. Hawke. My main work in life is setting up the debt structures of large corporations, especially utilities, so that they pay as little taxes as possible, and my main pleasure, aside from hunting and fishing, is passing on this small brand of wisdom to Columbia law students. I'm not in the moral judgments business." He fell silent, looking at Hawke expectantly.

The author said, "I asked to see you because I've committed certain financial imbecilities. I don't know whether it's because I'm naïve and inexperienced or whether I'm a born fool, but anyway at the moment I need help."

The lawyer chewed on his pipe and his blue eyes gleamed at Hawke. "Any man who's willing to consider the possibility that he's a born fool probably isn't one."

"Let's hope not." Hawke told the lawyer his affairs in a fifteen-minute monologue. The lawyer sat like a physician listening to a recital of symptoms, with a blank and forbidding face now and then lit by a mechanical smile of encouragement. He kept putting his pipe to his mouth and taking it away with slow even gestures. When Hawke stopped talking Adam burst out in an odd boyish laugh, and the lawyer turned into an unsophisticated red-faced man from Letchworth County. "Well, it's fascinating, all this about the literary life, Mr. Hawke, and pretty reassuring. You certainly don't have the problem of starving in a garret. You seem to have a case of financial indigestion, that's all—too much reward too fast. Your immediate problem, at least the one I can do something about, is your tax deficiency. That sounds as though you've been manhandled. But you really asked for it, filing returns without an accountant."

"I'm a suspicious mountain boy, I guess. I don't know a good accountant."

"I know several. You'd better turn over your records to me, and I'll talk to Internal Revenue."

"You will take on my mess?" Hawke said. "What'll it cost me?"

"Quite a bit, I'm afraid. As I said, my field is utilities, mainly. There must be good lawyers in the literary field and if you prefer I can look one up."

"No, Professor Adam, we're both out of U.K. and Letchworth County, and that makes me feel good."

The lawyer laughed. "Acting on sentiment like that is a handsome way to get skinned. I'll charge you my going rates on time and office expense. I hope I'll save you enough on taxes so you come out even, anyway. In

the long run it seems to me you'll need a business manager. You're not going to stop making money."

"Maybe I'll learn how to handle it."

Adam knocked out his pipe and stood. "Of course you will. I've got my afternoon class now."

The elevator was jammed with faculty members chatting in quiet cultivated tones. Hawke heard a snatch of a sentence about Santayana, a fragment of talk about radiation, and he felt nostalgic for the academic life. He had planned to be an English teacher before the war had set him to driving a bulldozer in the South Pacific. It seemed to him that Adam, with his law school post and his Wall Street office, had the best of both worlds.

Adam said as they walked up the lawn to the law school amid the hurrying streams of students, "I suppose what you could use, even more than a manager, is a level-headed wife, but of course that's just a matter of luck. Karl Fry now, is a lucky man. Mrs. Fry struck me as an exceptional woman."

"Are you married?" Hawke said.

Adam halted by the statue of *The Thinker* in front of Philosophy Hall, and squinted at Hawke in the strong sunlight. "I was. My wife died. That's one reason I'm up here among the Yankees."

Hawke said soberly, "I see. I wondered about that. Seems to me you'd have had a clear road to the legislature back home."

"Well, you know Kentucky politics. They play with a hard ball." Adam held out his hand. "You let me have your records, now, and I'll take on Uncle Sam for you. I sort of like the idea of helping Youngblood Hawke clear his mind to do his work. I'm not at all sure that it's equally worth while to save Cape Cod Power Company half a million in taxes by a sale and leaseback of an office building. Luckily, as I say, I'm not in the moral judgments business. Give my best to Mrs. Fry if you see her, and try to convince her I'm not a monster."

3

The loudest noise Youngblood Hawke ever heard in his life was the opening of a door.

It was probably inevitable that his mother should find out sooner or later about his adultery with Frieda Winter. But it was not necessary, and it was a horrible thing, that she should find it out by opening the door of his room at four o'clock in the morning and seeing Frieda undressed in his bed. That was what happened.

Whose fault was it? Frieda's, perhaps; deprived of him for more than

a month, she was brimming with amorousness. His own, perhaps; was it so hard for him to keep his head, knowing that his mother was under the same roof with them? He took the precaution of tiptoeing upstairs to her room, making sure that she was asleep, and closing her door softly. Not softly enough, it may be. Whether he woke her by closing the door, whether she woke by herself—Mrs. Hawke usually slept soundly—why she took it into her head to come downstairs and open his bedroom door; he never found out those things.

He was standing in his maroon dressing gown, lighting a cigar. Frieda lay on the bed in a satisfied torpor, her eyes half-open, her smeared mouth curled in a mischievous lazy smile, her limbs under the sheet loose as a doll's. The knob turned, the latch clicked, the door swung open, and there was Hawke's mother, in hair curlers and the old Hawaiian wrapper, blinking in the light.

At the very instant the noise began Frieda started up like a frightened cat and half-turned in the bed to look at the door, leaning on one thin naked graceful arm, holding the sheet to her breast though she was wearing a peach-colored slip, her thick graying hair tumbling over her shoulders. All three of them seemed to freeze into silence for an hour, but the time that really elapsed before Hawke's mother spoke could hardly have been a dozen seconds. Hawke heard his alarm clock ticking thunderously, and the far-off dying wail of a siren in the street.

"Sorry," Mrs. Hawke said. She closed the door, and they heard her footsteps on the uncarpeted stairs.

"Oh, God," Frieda said. She seemed incapable of moving out of her perfect pose of surprised female guilt; still she leaned on one arm, the sheet pulled to her breast, looking over her shoulder in horror at the closed door, her hair in disorder, a naked thigh jutting pink and round from the pulled-up wrinkled slip where she had yanked away the sheet and exposed herself in trying to cover herself.

Hawke's fresh-lit cigar was dead and charred in his hand. He didn't want it; he threw it into the wastebasket. "I think we both can use a drink," he said, and he reached for the bottle of Scotch.

Frieda flung aside the sheet and leaped from the bed. "I'm going home. Oh, God, what must she think of me? She must think I'm a whore. Why did we have to do it, why didn't you stop? I begged you to stop, I said we'd wake your mother. Oh Christ." Indeed she had said those things, Frieda was fond of putting up verbal resistance as an added sauce to love-making, but her eager acts as she talked had more than matched his. She twisted into her red evening dress and began to pull on her stockings with violent haste, as though she were trying to avoid being caught, as though it had not yet happened.

Hawke said, "Look, Frieda, mama's no fool. I'm sure she's known all

along. And she's not naïve, she's told me some home-town gossip that would curl your hair. It's not serious, have a drink."

"She didn't know, she didn't! There are none so blind as those who won't see. She didn't want to see it and I didn't want her to. Oh, God, she'll think I'm a whore. She thinks in those black-and-white terms, and *you do too*, you hillbilly, in your heart you've always thought of me as a whore and you've treated me like a whore. You treated me like a whore tonight, threw me down on your bed in this tumbledown room and I didn't refuse you because I love you. I love you, that's what makes all the difference, that's what she'll have to understand!" She sprang at him and twined her arms around him. Without her high heels she always seemed pathetically cut-down. His chin was higher than the top of her head. "Tell me that you love me, at least. Say it and mean it."

"I love you, Frieda."

"Then kiss me as though you love me!"

Tears were starting from her eyes. In all the years he had known Frieda, in all their many quarrels, he had never seen her shattered and hysterical like this. He held her close and bent and kissed her, and told her in extravagant words that he loved her. She clung to him strongly and quietly like a child, her face against his chest, listening to him.

"All right," she said at last, "I've got to get out of here at once. You just remember that I love you, and that we belong to each other . . . Oh, Christ, little Paul's birthday party," she exclaimed, halting in the midst of putting on a shoe. "She'll never come now, will she? What will I say to my husband, to the children? It'll look so queer if she doesn't come. Paul made such an issue of inviting just you and your mother, he worships you so! I wanted to make a big thing and invite his school friends, but no, no, he insisted, just Art and his mother and our family for dinner, there was no reasoning with him. He knew exactly what he wanted. Ye gods, what a mess! Do you think she'll come anyway? Can you prevail on her to come? But then how will I face her? What are you going to tell her?"

"Frieda, if I know mama she's not going to mention it. She'll come to the party. My mother is out of the hills and she has her strange ways but she's a grownup."

"I hope so. God, look at that ravaged face of mine, will you? To hell with lipstick, I've got to get out of here at once. I feel as though twenty eyes were looking at me through these goddamned broken walls." She threw herself at him, her hair carelessly pinned up, her usual height restored by spindly shoes, and kissed him hard. "I love you. That's the answer to everything, and you had better love me, do you hear? We have nothing to feel guilty about, nothing! Make her come to Paul's party. I've never felt more awful. Good night."

He went down to the street door with her, trying to reassure her, but

she only shook her head and dashed the back of her hand to her eyes. When he opened the iron-grilled front door, Frieda looked this way and that at the black deserted street. "Good night," she said again. "I'll get a cab on Lexington. I'm exhausted." She slunk down the sidewalk.

4

"Till we meet
Till we meet
Till we meet
At Jesus' feet . . ."

Hawke heard his mother singing in the kitchen as he came downstairs. He had not expected to be greeted on this particular morning by song. "Well, hello there," she said. She was in her old purple house dress, chopping vegetables and tossing them into a colander. "Keeping bankers' hours, aren't we? Want some breakfast, or is it lunch? I'm just putting up my soup. The coffee's hot." She poured a cup before him on the kitchen table, where he sat looking through a pile of mail. "There's another one from your foo-foo lady in Rome. Smells real scrumptious."

He found the gray envelope and involuntarily put it to his nose; then he glanced at his mother, and after a strained moment they both laughed.

Mrs. Hawke's aspect was changed. Hawke had expected her to be angry, disapproving, perhaps sulky, perhaps spoiling for a fight. He had not anticipated the faintly lewd, knowing, cynical look in her eye, and the tart smile. It was not too different from the morning look of some women with whom he had slept; the half-disdainful female acknowledgment that men were eager males in the night, and frowsy neuters looking for coffee and food in the morning. And more, it was his acceptance into the adult world by his mother, as though he had just returned from his honeymoon. Certainly she must have known that he was no virgin; but never before had she been compelled to face the physical fact. Now it was done, and because it had been a shaming accident rather than a formal, politely accepted event like a honeymoon, Mrs. Hawke's ribald awareness of sex—which all women have, however virtuous; the laughter in theatres at sex jokes trills mostly from women's throats—was all the more plainly written on her face. For an instant Hawke had an indecent vision of his old mother and his dead father as lovers; then his mind shut the picture out.

"What'll you have to eat?" she said. "A little or a lot?"

"Anything, ma. I'm hungry." He pulled a letter from Scott Hoag out of the pile.

"You usually are these days. That's the best part of getting over a sickness, the appetite it gives you. What does your Mr. Hoag want now?"

Hawke tore open the thick letter. Two copies of the contract, and a stamped addressed envelope, were attached to Scotty's letter, the third he had written since leaving New York. The signed document that Mrs. Hawke had mailed, or said she had mailed, had never arrived. Scott said the post office must have lost it, and asked Hawke to have his mother sign again and send on the papers as soon as possible. The letter was affable enough, but there was a touch of exasperated urgency in the overblown last sentence. "Of course I know we have a deal, Art, and your word and your mother's word are as good as a signed paper or better as far as I'm concerned, but Glenn and the Coffman people won't move without the release in hand, a verbal commitment isn't enough for them, they're more worried about your mother's real intentions than I am, in view of the previous trouble we've had with her, so please don't hold up on this very long."

Hawke read the letter to his mother over the loud crackle of frying ham and eggs. She snorted, "*My* intentions! What about their intentions? What do they want two signed copies for now? He said I only had to sign one. Maybe it's a trick."

"Good God, mama, what kind of trick? The paper's meaningless unless they give us twenty thousand dollars. Twenty thousand dollars, for Christ's sake, for a worthless piece of Edgefield wilderness!"

"Ha! If it's worthless why do they want to give us that much money for it? Do you believe that Santa Claus business? I declare, your friend Hoag ought to go around with reindeer and a red suit, so people would recognize him."

Hawke was aware of the disadvantage he was under this morning, talking to his mother: the knowing leer, mixed with sour disapproval, was on her face whenever he looked at her. He said, with less irritation than he might have put into his voice otherwise, "Mama, did you mail that contract?"

"Oh, I'm the liar this morning, is that the idea? That's very interesting. Well, maybe there's been some lying around here, but I think you'd better not go accusing me, Art. Maybe it's just as well if it did get lost in the mail. I sure didn't appreciate being rushed into signing that thing. Why, we never even showed it to a lawyer. Now we can do that, at least. How do we know what's behind all those big legal words?"

"It's a standard legal form. If we delay too much that offer will fall through."

"That's talk. If land's worth money today it'll be worth that much or more tomorrow." She put a tremendous platter of ham and eggs before him, and a basket of hot rolls. "Eat your breakfast and read your letter

from the foo-foo lady. I'm busy, I have to put up my soup. Scat, you!"
She slammed Hawke's gray alley-cat, Aunt Bertha, off the counter, where
it was sniffing at the bloody beef bones. It flew across the kitchen and
bounded out of the door with an offended squawk. "Lord, even the cats
don't know how to behave in New York. Though I don't know why they
should at that, when the fanciest people behave like cats."

She took up a large knife and resumed her chopping of the vegetables,
whacking a large green cabbage in two with a stroke like an executioner's,
then cutting and cutting again.

> *"Till we meet*
> *Till we meet*
> *God be with you till we meet again"*

she sang in her thin high kitchen soprano. Hawke began to revise his
first impression that he was going to get off easily this morning. His
mother sang during her cooking, he recalled, either when she was perfectly
at ease or when she was on the edge of an explosion.

He opened the letter from Rome.

Dear Mr. Hawke:
Thank you for taking the trouble to answer me. I must say I'm flattered. I
haven't the faintest recollection of what I wrote you from the hospital. All I
know is I was under sedation and floating six feet off the bed. I'm sure my
letter was absurd and probably most embarrassing, and if you didn't throw it
at once into the wastebasket will you please do so now? I don't want to think it
still exists.

I showed my husband your letter of course and he thinks it would be grand
for us to take you to lunch at the Borghese Gardens or something like that, if
you do come to Rome. At the moment I'm quite the heroine at home for having elicited a letter from Youngblood Hawke. My husband seems to think it's
a greater achievement than giving birth to The Peanut (our temporary revolt-
ingly whimsical name for the new baby).

If you're of my husband's mind and want to lunch with a plump and plain
mother of three and her very handsome and devoted spouse, why okay. I
doubt we'll be in Rome when you get here, we're going home soon and home
is very far from this enchanting city or indeed from any civilized place. I
can't imagine what I'd have to say to an author like you. I'd be afraid all the
time that you were seeing through me like an X-ray, and I'm quite uneasy,
frankly, about that letter I wrote you in my narcotized state. Do get rid of it,
if you haven't, and don't bother any further with me, I'm fat as a house aside
from everything else. Just finish that new book. I'm dying for something
decent to read, and if nothing good comes along soon I may start my fourth
time around in Dickens, which would be a decidedly neurotic act of with-
drawal from modern society.

HONOR H.

Hawke looked up from the letter and saw his mother glancing at him, her mouth in a sarcastic twist. "Does that foo-foo lady write as pretty as she smells?"

He tossed the letter on the table. "You're welcome to read it."

Mrs. Hawke's back straightened, and she resumed her vicious chopping. "Hmf! I'm not the least bit interested in reading your mail, thank you, especially from foo-foo ladies. I think maybe you already know too many of those for your own good, but I reckon that's none of my business, is it, you're thirty years old and a famous writer, and I'm just your stupid old mother from the back hills."

"Okay, mama, okay. Let me have some more coffee."

"Certainly, Mr. Youngblood Hawke. I guess I still come in handy for making you a breakfast or coming down out of the hills and nursing you through a pneumonia that you caught doing God knows what in the big city, then when you're all better I'll go home till the next time I have to come and pick up the pieces and get a few more surprises. Is the coffee hot enough for you?"

"It's great, mama, just great."

"Oh, I don't know, I guess some women you know can make better coffee and please you in some other ways but the good Lord in his wisdom has set limits to the services a mother can perform. The good Lord also has set down some other laws but maybe they were just given to country people, nobody seems to know about them in New York and young men who were brought up knowing them seem to forget them here right fast."

Hawke decided that there was no escape, after all. He said, "Mama, I'm sorry you were embarrassed. I honestly didn't think you'd be surprised. I thought you knew."

"*Knew!* I like that!" She dropped the knife and faced him. "You thought I *knew*, and yet went on treating that woman as though she were a respectable person? Why, I help unfortunate people in Hovey all the time, and I have pets I've adopted, old ladies and just lately a crippled boy of nineteen, and I thought this woman was being kind to you the same way, because you were alone in the city. I could understand that. I thought she was a fine woman, but she sure isn't. There's a word for what she is."

Hawke said, "Don't talk about her, mama."

"What shall I do, pretend everything's just jim-dandy? That woman with her gray hair, her wrinkles, her four children, her hands all knotted like an old carpenter's! What on earth could have gotten into you, Art, what do you see in her? It's horrible, what you're doing, it's evil and I can't even understand how you can enjoy it. Of all the millions of women that go wiggling around this city couldn't you find one your own age, not my age?"

"Christ Almighty mama, Frieda's not your age, she's forty-two."

"I'm fifty-three. She's nearer me than you. Art, you're ruining your life, God doesn't allow things like that just to go on and on How long has it been going on?"

"What's the difference?"

"Well, how long? Was last night the first time?"

"The first time? Mama, I've been in love with Frieda Winter for years."

"In love! You call that being in love? Lord have mercy on us. What next? How about that Jewish secretary of yours, are you in love with her too? She's married but of course that makes no difference to a famous writer, I see that. Are you carrying on with her, too?"

Hawke said drily, clamping down on his anger as best he could, "All right, mama. Shut up."

"Shut up! You're telling your mother to shut up? You've come a long way, Art Hawke."

Hawke slammed down his coffee cup. "I don't expect you to forgive or to understand. Frieda Winter and I fell in love with each other long ago. What's been done can't be undone. You're to drop the subject or pack up and go home, today."

"Art, I'm your mother, I have a right to tell you things for your good and I must. You can hate me all you want for it."

"You won't change anything. I know the thing is impossible, I've known it all along. I plan to go to Europe soon and break it off."

"Europe! She'll just follow you to Europe, boy. Come home if you want to break it off. Thank God you still have that much sense. She won't come to Hovey, that I promise you. She'll never face me."

"I can't go back to Hovey. I'll make damned sure she doesn't follow me. That's all about it, mama, except one thing. You're to come to her house for dinner tonight as though nothing had happened."

"Whaaat! Art, you're out of your mind. Why, ask the wretched woman yourself. She'll beg you not to bring me. She'll sink through the floor at the sight of me."

"She wants you to come. She told me so. You're coming."

"I will not. I won't sit at a table with her. She's a disgusting New York thing, I don't care how much money she has and how smart she is. You can say I'm sick or something. I won't come."

Hawke stood, thrusting back his chair so that it clattered across the room and crashed into the wall. He burst out in a maniacal roar, his eyes starting from his head, "YOU'RE COMING, do you hear? And not another word about it."

His mother shrank back from him, plain terror on her face. "Art, for heaven's sake, you're just out of a sickbed, do you want to have a stroke? God help us, your face is purple. How dare you scream at me like that? I'll come, my God."

"That's settled," Hawke said hoarsely. He scooped up the mail and walked out of the kitchen, feeling the room swim around him. It was an extremely elegant early American kitchen, all copper pans and wooden beams and maple furniture, but the floor was still bumpy raw cement.

5

In panic one usually does the least sensible thing. Frieda Winter was a hard woman to panic, but being found in Hawke's bed by Hawke's mother had knocked apart her self-possession, so she had insisted that Hawke bring his mother to Paul's birthday dinner. Frieda knew only one method of carrying off her life, a method that had served for many years— total bland pretense that nothing wrong was ever going on; and by instinct that was the method she seized on to join together the broken pieces of the adultery which for her had become part of her normal existence, her chief pleasure in a life of pleasure. It was a terrible mistake, and she knew it as soon as Mrs. Hawke walked into her house, but by then nothing could be done.

The Winter family was assembled in the living room, and it occurred to Hawke that this was the first time he had seen them all together except in the painting on the dining-room wall. The least real of the lot was Bennett, the oldest son, a chubby boy of twelve in the painting, and now a junior at Yale. Hawke had met him only two or three times in brief chance encounters. He was fully as tall as Hawke and seemed still to be growing; a lean broad-shouldered youngster, with his father's long jaw; dressed to the perfection of advanced collegiate taste, which at the moment leaned to stringy ties, dark suits, pink shirts with tiny collars, and oversize purplish shoes. Whether from shyness or sullenness he hardly ever spoke to Hawke. Tonight after jumping to his feet for the introduction to Mrs. Hawke he dropped on a hard chair and sat round-shouldered, wringing immense bony hands between bony knees. The fat older daughter seemed to have given up the struggle to shine, between her effulgent mother and her younger sister, who at fifteen had bloomed out with a figure like Frieda's, a sharp puckish manner, and sparkling eyes. The older one was doing the unpainted straight-haired esthete in flat shoes and thick dark stockings.

Frieda's husband pushed himself heavily out of his armchair to greet the guests. His mustache was now completely white, and the bag under his chin was a fat thick pouch sharply marked off at the jaws. The illness that had put him back on a rice diet showed in the bluish tinge of his skin. "Well, how's the wolf of Wall Street?" he said, measuring Hawke as usual with a glance of half-suppressed irony. "You seem to have come around pretty well. Frieda had you at death's door."

"He was mighty sick," Hawke's mother said. "Art needs a wife to take care of him, that's what he needs."

"Ah well, it's an old problem, Mrs. Hawke, domesticating the artist," Winter said. "Typically they don't domesticate, they shake themselves to pieces or burn themselves up with their own excess energy. The Poe and Baudelaire pattern. Of course there are also the mellow old married word-grinders, the Trollopes, the Tennysons, the Thomas Manns. Let's hope that Arthur will settle down some day and become one of those."

Frieda loudly popped a cork and said, "Champagne, everybody!"

Mrs. Hawke would not take a glass despite urging, first by Frieda and then by Hawke, who hardly hid his annoyance. When the toast was drunk to Paul, who sat gravely all alone on the big couch, holding half a glass of wine, Mrs. Hawke stood apart, her hands folded before her, a fixed smile on her face.

Then she would not eat. She hardly broke the crust of the shrimp patty. She did not so much as dip her spoon into her soup; it came, it stood and cooled, and the butler took it away. She sat silent directly under the family portrait, a smiling death's head at the feast. Frieda's two oldest children ate gloomily and voraciously, and the younger daughter and Frieda did their best to keep the atmosphere light with family jokes about excessive girlish talking on the telephone, a new boy friend, and so forth. But it was uphill work.

Winter himself seemed well aware, from the way his eyes kept moving around the table, of the discomfiture of his wife and the young author. Whether or not he guessed the reason, he seemed to be taking pleasure in it, and he was obviously determined not to help matters. After lighting a large cigar and explaining that he had to wait for his main course, a heap of boiled rice, he said not a word. He sat puffing, and observing the scene as though he were at an interesting movie; or more nearly at a prizefight where blood was flowing, to judge from the somewhat cruel look of satisfaction on his wan face.

Only little Paul appeared to be enjoying himself. He sat in the huge blue wing armchair of his father at the head of the table, with his parents on either side. He was served first each time, and Frieda allowed him a couple of small refills of champagne; and the boy presided over the table and accepted the privileges of the evening with the solemn pleasure of a child prince. Hawke sat opposite him, down at the foot, and every now and then the boy looked to him with shy pride, as though to say, "I've always admired you, now don't you admire me?"

The main course was a huge rib roast on a spiked board, with half a dozen vegetable dishes in silver serving plates. The colored butler was carving the meat at a sideboard, and Frieda asked Mrs. Hawke whether she preferred her slice rare or well done.

The mother answered, "Why, if you'll excuse me, Mrs. Winter, I believe I won't have anything more."

Frieda laughed gaily, though everyone else at the table looked startled, and the butler paused in his carving to turn his head and roll prominent brown eyes from the Winters to Hawke's mother. "Nothing at *all*, Mrs. Hawke! No main course? You're not turning vegetarian on us? Perhaps you'll have some vegetables. I cooked the zucchini myself, olive oil and garlic and bread crumbs—"

"Aha ha ha, no, I'm not turning vegetarian, Mrs. Winter. I reckon my tastes are as normal as other people's, or maybe more so. I'm just not hungry tonight. Maybe I've seen too much of New York. I'm out of my element and I reckon I'm losing my appetite."

"The way I've lost mine," Mr. Winter said, speaking for the first time in a quarter of an hour. He pointed to the steaming white heap before him. "Mrs. Hawke, maybe you'd like some of my boiled rice. It seems to be just the thing for stomachs turned by the big city."

Mrs. Hawke looked straight at the old inscrutable cuckold for a second or two and then said, "Why, if there's any to spare I do believe I'll have some boiled rice with you, Mr. Winter."

The blank-faced butler brought a plate of boiled rice to her, and she ate it.

This bizarre act of Hawke's mother crushed any remaining spark of life out of the party. Hawke, for all his convalescent appetite, was hard put to it to go on eating, so grossly unpleasant did the climate at the table become. He forced himself to eat so as not to add to Frieda's embarrassment. The older children gobbled away, their eyes on their plates. Paul's enjoyment of his grandeur faded as a total silence fell in the large room. He kept looking to his usually gay mother, to Hawke, to his father, and to Mrs. Hawke with pathetic puzzlement.

As for Frieda, she had for once run out of face. She sat and ate quickly, making no further effort to speak, to act the hostess, to do anything but get through the dinner. Hawke wanted to find something to say—the silence grew more impossible, more appalling, more unbelievable as it stretched into minutes—but he was actually afraid to open his mouth. He could not trust himself to say the right thing. Years ago when his mother had sat at this table it had seemed to him that a red diagonal of guilt ran across the top from himself to Mrs. Winter, mercifully visible only to his own eyes. Tonight the red diagonal seemed to be slowly coming into sight for everybody, like invisible ink touched with the right chemical. He thought that if the silence went on much longer it would be as damning an occurrence as being caught in copulation with Frieda by her husband and all her children at once; and still the silence persisted, and still it thickened, and Frieda sat with her head down, pushing roast beef into her mouth.

Mercifully the butler broke into the quiet by snapping out the light. The cook marched in with a large pink cake, on which ten candles flamed in a ring, with an extra one for luck at the center. Bennett started singing "Happy Birthday to you" in an awkward bass, the others chimed in one by one, and a laggard effect of gaiety struggled up from under the smother of silence. Paul's face, lit by the flare from the cake set before him, took on renewed wistful delight. "This is a bigger cake than Bennett ever had," he said.

"Much bigger, Paulo," Bennett said.

The boy tried hard to blow out all the candles in a breath, but three remained burning. "Is that bad luck?" he said anxiously.

"Nonsense, there's no such thing as good or bad luck," Frieda said. "You make your own luck." She leaned forward and puffed out the three candles. "Cut the cake."

The butler put on the lights. Paul, wielding the big knife like a religious object, made a gash in the cake with the gravest care. Then the butler took the cake to the sideboard, hacked it up expertly, and began passing it around.

"Please ma'am, have a piece of my cake," Paul said to Mrs. Hawke, when she shook her head at the butler. "Even if you're not hungry. It's my birthday cake. Just a little piece."

Mrs. Hawke looked bleakly from Frieda to her small son. "Why, I reckon my sweet tooth is acting up after all," she said. "I believe I can use a piece of your cake, Paul." The boy kept watching her, and she ate the whole slice.

That was the extent of Mrs. Hawke's unbending. She would not take coffee. Nor would she go on with Hawke, Frieda, and Paul to see *Peter Pan*, though they had a ticket for her. The dinner broke up glumly, the older children scattering off with unconcealed relief to meet their friends, having been dragooned by Frieda into assembling to pay tribute to Paul, and having looked at their wrist watches almost continually as soon as they had consumed all the meat they wanted. Mr. Winter went up to the library, Mrs. Hawke went back to the house; and Hawke and Frieda took Paul to the show. Hawke's mother would not even share the taxicab with them. "Shank's mare's good enough for me," she said. "People in this city forget they've got legs. They forget lots of things. Happy birthday, young fellow, and don't worry about those three candles."

6

Paul sat between them, his face reflecting in the darkness the rosy light of the stage setting, his large eyes agleam. Now and then, as when the crocodile appeared or the Indians burst on stage, he put a small hand on Hawke's sleeve.

It was not hard for Hawke to imagine that he and Frieda were man and wife, that Paul was their one son; and that the other three huge Winter children, especially the nightmarish Bennett, over six feet high—and also the watchful, silent white-mustached husband—were all dim characters in one of his early shelved plays. Paul was the only one of Frieda's family who had ever been wholly tangible to him. From the first moment he had seen Paul, in tears, in yellow pajamas, fending off a glass of milk thrust on him by a Negro nurse, the boy had appealed to Hawke; and Paul in turn had fastened on to him like an orphan. Mr. Winter, Hawke had soon observed, did not treat Paul as he did the others. It crossed Hawke's mind, as he watched Captain Hook and Smee capering in a wild dance, that perhaps Winter was not sure he was Paul's father!

He glanced over at Frieda, feeling a guilty pang at harboring the thought. She sat motionless, as she always did at a play, watching the stage through big black glasses, her eyes narrow in professional appraisal. Frieda was one of those people whose looks are not marred by glasses, and perhaps improved. Certainly she was lovely now. The theatre darkness and the stage glow were kind to her, one saw the charming shape of her features and not the marks of years, and the glasses gave her a thoughtful innocent air. That this elegant woman had spawned in wedlock the bastard of a lover and that this winsome boy between them was that bastard, seemed almost inconceivable. Yet Frieda had admitted to him that their affair was not her first. She never talked about the others, but he had heard shreds of gossip that had poisoned his spirit for days at a time. One famous violinist whom she had managed, and whose signed photograph still hung in the anteroom of her office, had had a long affair with her, if general talk meant anything.

This train of thought so engrossed Hawke that he lost track of the fantasy playing before him. The implications of the act called adultery now seemed to come home to him for the very first time. It meant, quite baldly, that fathers could not be sure who their children were, and that children could not know their fathers. Paul's hand on his sleeve might be a groping for a father who was in truth nonexistent in the child's life. Adultery was the subversion of human identity. Arthur Hawke knew who his father was. His certificate of knowledge was not any document, not any physical evidence, but the character of his mother. She too might have hoisted her skirts for a stranger thirty years ago. She had not. She was an honest woman, though she had perhaps every other fault of woman-kind. Her hatred of Frieda was a mixed emotion—simple jealousy was strong in it—but at bottom it was the contempt of an honest woman for an adulterous one. He could never reproach her for refusing Frieda's food.

When the first-act curtain fell and the lights brightened Hawke sat bemused, staring straight ahead of him. Frieda took off her glasses, squint-

ing at him, and laughed. "Arthur, have you fallen asleep with your eyes open? It's not that dull."

He started. "Hypnotized, I guess. Like it, Paul?"

"Too short," Paul said. "I hope the crocodile comes again. I saw the string that was working the crocodile."

Hawke looked past the boy at Frieda, and returned her affectionate smile as well as he could; fairly well, considering that he had been reaching a decision, when the act ended, that tonight he was looking on Frieda Winter's face for the last time.

7

They were on the couch; the famous couch, the historic couch. It had taken a lot of wear, that couch, in all the entertaining that Frieda did. She had had it re-upholstered twice since the occasion of their first amour. Then it had been green, on the verge of wearing through; next she had tried scarlet, and had been dissatisfied with it for two years; now it was brown. The French doors were shut. The house was very still. Through the open bay windows drifted the hissing of tires and the late-at-night Fifth Avenue smell of green trees and auto fumes. Paul had exhausted his excuses for staying up, and was fast asleep in his room; he had dropped off in the middle of a story Hawke was telling him.

Frieda said, pouring brandy into two goblets, "Well! Are we really and truly alone? I hope you're not sleepy." She drained her glass and poured more. "Did it ever occur to you that *Peter Pan* is a sex nightmare, with symbols all over it thick as fungus on a rotten log? The flying boy who never ages, played by an actress with strapped-down breasts, the father who turns into a sadistic monster with a big hook, plotting to steal the mother of the lost boys, who's really a big sister running around in a teasing nightgown? Honestly, I've never known a psychoanalyst who wasn't two tics and a convulsion away from the booby hatch himself, but *Peter Pan* almost makes me think Freud had something. That's never occurred to me until tonight . . . What's the matter? Drink up. You're sitting there and staring just the way you were doing in the theatre. Did your mother give you hell? God, what lunacy to bring her here! Have you ever been through a ghastlier dinner?"

"You asked me to bring her, Frieda."

"I know, I know I did. It goes to show what foolishness you can be reduced to by guilt feelings. I was just rattled. Start feeling guilty and you're lost, Arthur. It's booze or drugs or the analyst or Marxism or all four. I know plenty of fools who are on all four right now. Good God, what do we have to feel guilty about? *I* don't feel guilty, our love has

been fine and rich and good and I'm proud of it. It was only the way she popped in on us. It was so horrible, those unfinished walls, and that miserable folding cot of yours, it was the *untidiness* of it. I hate untidiness. And my hair, god damn it, of all times to try letting it come in gray, I thought it might look good, but there I was, in your bed and gray as a rat, damned near as gray as her! Ugh!"

Still Hawke sat looking at her, holding his untasted brandy. She said irritably, "Why don't you drink? Are you going to refuse to sully your lips under my roof, too? . . . That's better. She's your mother but I say god damn her bad manners. She's entitled to her moral viewpoint, but I'm entitled to mine too, by Christ. I don't believe in ever doing anything sordid or cruel or ugly. I've never hurt anybody knowingly. I think in my lifetime I've come as close to living by the golden rule as she has, maybe closer. What absolutely infuriates me is this pompous holier-than-thou assumption that her morals are the only right ones and that mine don't exist because they're different. Did she love your father? I don't think she could have. If she had an inkling of what real love is, she couldn't have treated me the way she did. Because whatever may be wrong with me I love you, I've poured out my love to you, and you need love, believe me, when I met you you needed love the way a drowning man needs a rope thrown to him. Do you remember the first time, right here in this room! Do you remember? If you think I *wanted* you then, you're crazy. You were so big and awkward and young, your face was such a mask of pain and longing that if you'd asked me for my head I'd have cut it off and handed it to you. I didn't know what you saw in me but that didn't matter, I couldn't bear to see you unhappy, that was all. And believe me, Arthur, it's been that way more times than you know, than you'll ever know. Some of the times you thought were the happiest and the best I've been out of the mood, or worried about my family, or just plain tired. I love you, and a woman in love wants to make the man she loves happy, no matter what. I don't expect your mother ever to understand about us, but I'll tell you something, just talking this much has relieved me incredibly, I'm suddenly not in the least angry any more. I don't want you to fuss at her for the way she acted tonight, do you hear? Not a word. She's set in her ways, she loves you too, and you and I don't fit into her picture of the old-time religion. Be kind to her, put up with her nagging, and let's not see each other again until she goes home, all right?"

This swift change of front by Frieda disconcerted Hawke. He said that his mother was probably going to stay in New York for a long time, that he meant to ask her to look after the completion of the house.

Frieda's eyes began to glint with the old mockery. "Well, dear, if it goes on too long and you find you can't live without the touch of my hand, why, I suppose we can come to an arrangement. We can meet in disguise now and then in a motel in Hackensack, or something."

Hawke roused himself to get through the ordeal. "Frieda, I'm going to Europe, as soon as I can arrange my affairs."

"Why, that's marvellous! Are you honestly, now? I've been trying to talk you into this for months. You need Europe, Arthur. Your work needs it. You'll be deeply enriched, and you'll have the time of your life. What about your play? Georges told me that Pierce Carmian wants to produce it."

"He does, but that's not a good idea, is it? Carmian, of all people!"

Frieda sipped her brandy, and business wrinkles appeared at the corners of her eyes and mouth. "Carmian came into a fortune last year, you know. His mother finally died, I think she was about a hundred and seven. He's a dilettante and a horror, to be sure, but he did some awfully good things with that repertory theatre he started in Berkeley. Georges is in back of everything he undertakes. If Pierce does your play that's one way to be sure Georges will be around. We can show the script to other producers, but I really think you might let Carmian have a shot at it."

"Well, then, I will, but I'm not going to be around when they put it on. I must finish my book, I've lost months already."

Frieda said, "Perfect! Let Georges do the butchery on the road. Mostly your play is too long. Tinkering with lines won't help, there's the whole novel to draw from if Georges needs a patch here or there. And I can keep an eye on it too. I can come back for a few weeks. Thank heaven for planes, Europe's no further away nowadays than a dinner and a pill and a good night's sleep."

Hawke said, "Are you thinking of coming to Europe with me, Frieda? I don't want you to."

She bent her head far down, and looked at him out of large eyes. "Of course I don't intend to come over on the same boat or plane, dear. That wouldn't be nice. I'll get there, I have plenty to do in Europe. We'll just manage to be in some of the pleasantest places at the same time. Paris is a sizable city, for instance, and there's no reason why we shouldn't both be there at the height of the season, among a couple of hundred thousand other Americans."

"Frieda, my reason for going to Europe is to break away from what I've been doing in New York. I want to make a fresh start, I want to push up my rate of work to twice as many pages a night and I don't want to do anything else."

"What are you trying to say, Arthur? You're using too many words."

"I don't want you with me in Europe."

"Not at all?"

"It's best that way."

"Don't you ever want to see me again?"

Hawke looked her in the face and said, "No."

She was sitting upright on the edge of the couch. She took the blow

with a slow blink of her enormous eyes; sat rigid, then sank back against the couch, not taking her eyes from him. "Fill my glass, please. Fill it nice and full, and hand it to me."

Hawke did as he was told. Frieda drank the brandy off, coughed, and said, "Thank you. Fill it again."

"Come on, Frieda. Don't throw a lot of raw brandy into your stomach."

She sat up and stretched her hand shakily toward the decanter. He filled her glass. She took it, emptied it, and set it down. "Thank you." She sank against the arm of the couch, put her head back, and closed her eyes. Hawke sat mute, at the other end of the long brown couch. So several minutes passed.

Frieda opened her eyes, and lolled her head against the back of the couch, toward him. To his astonishment her expression of melancholy mockery was almost exactly like her habitual first glance at him after an embrace. "Well!" she said huskily, "I have to say that the good Lord's best invention after love was alcohol. I didn't want to cry, and now I'm not going to."

Hawke said warily, "I'm glad you can feel that way." He knew quite well that he was not out of the scene. Frieda was a woman of resource.

She said, "Don't you want to go home? You're only a couple of weeks past a pneumonia. I don't want your mother angry at me for keeping you up too late. That would be a legitimate grievance."

"I feel fine, Frieda. If there's anything more you want to say, say it."

Frieda shrugged. "Well, let me reassure you, we'll skip the tears and reproaches of the woman scorned. You're having an attack of Christian conscience, somewhat delayed, but I can't blame you. The shock of last night made me behave like an imbecile in my own way. What we both have to do is simmer down. I've already said that we shouldn't see each other until your mother leaves, so we're thinking the same way, aren't we? Why don't we let it go at that?"

"Frieda, I decided long before last night that I was going to Europe without you."

"Did you? Then wasn't it cheap of you to make love to me last night after such a grand decision?" She was smiling wryly. She crossed her legs, throwing into relief the beautiful line of her thigh and knee under the narrow blue-gray silk skirt.

"Yes, I think it was. There was something fatal about last night. I won't defend myself, and you're free to dismiss what I'm doing as Christian conscience. There are worse things than Christian conscience. I call it self-preservation."

"I see. You're freeing yourself from Circe."

"You were going to skip the reproaches."

"I seem to remember all this happening before. Next thing I knew I

was dragged into your Hollywood villa and set to cooking a turkey for your birthday, and rendering you certain other attentions."

"That goddamned turkey seems to haunt you and Jeanne Fry both. It was years ago, I was younger, and I had considerably more margin for error."

"Have you been discussing your little love problems with Jeanie, Arthur? Is this dramatic renunciation her idea? It sounds rather like her."

"On the contrary, Jeanne thinks you and I ought to get married."

Frieda lifted her chin in surprise, and laughed out loud. "Does she? Bless her heart, that's always her idea of a solution, isn't it? Like marrying Karl. Jeanne's a fine girl but she's too conventional and far too fond of the quick judgment and the drastic move. That's been her undoing. It's a real weakness not to be able to just sit tight."

Something odd was happening to Hawke. At this unlikely moment he was being swept by desire for this aging mistress of his, as she sat collected at the other end of the couch, in a pose that showed the residual beauty of the body he had so long loved; as she sat there coolly and courageously holding her own in the face of a jilting. Because it was difficult for him, after the words that had passed, to take her in his arms, he wanted to. The words he now spoke broke from him without premeditation. "Would you marry me?"

Frieda peered at him and laughed. "Of course, darling, like a shot if it were possible. I'll regret till the day I die that our timing was so badly off, that we met after I had a grown family."

"I'm serious, Frieda. Will you marry me? Will you get a divorce and marry me?" He stared into her face with the greatest earnestness.

She said uneasily, "God bless you darling, I love you, but why all these drastic proposals? You don't have to give me up and you don't have to lead me to the altar, either. Everything's fine the way it is except that your poor mother opened the wrong door last night on the way to get a glass of water or something. It was quite a little shock, but I'm over it and you'll soon be over it, and I suspect she will be, too, sooner than you think. There's no need for melodramatics."

But Hawke felt as though he had stumbled out of a cave into the sunlight, or as though he had suddenly caught on to a game that had baffled him for years. It had never really occurred to him before—except as a fugitive fancy—to try to marry Frieda. Now it struck him that this was the very core of his problem. "Frieda, why not? *Why not?* The difference in our ages? What do I care? The scandal? What scandal, in this day and age? You can just go to Reno and get a divorce, can't you? Maybe he'll let you have Paul. He doesn't like Paul. If we could have Paul, Frieda, and if we could live together like people, it's all I'd ask. I'd forget Europe. I'd settle down and work like a steam engine."

"Look, my love, it's late. Let's leave it that you've renounced me like

a good repentant Christian, all right? Go home and let's both sleep on it. Let's both digest this dramatic situation for a few weeks. You telephone me if you feel like it. I won't bother you."

Hawke said bitterly. "It's beneath discussion, eh? It's the money, after all, isn't it? You like your comforts. His money makes you very comfortable. A writer can't possibly earn enough to keep a real New York woman in style. Even Sinclair Lewis didn't earn that much."

Frieda crackled out a filthy word. Then she laughed. "Sorry. It never ceases to amaze me, when I contrast the human understanding in your books and the utter childishness of the things you sometimes say and do. You can't be trying to insult me. You're really blurting these things out as you think them. Arthur, for God's sake, I have four big children, two of them unmarried daughters, a complicated household, a husband I'm devoted to, and if there's a God I think He understands that that's true. Ten years from now I'll be a shrunken crone. You won't be able to bear the sight of me. You'll be a man in your prime."

Her voice was unsteady. Hawke had known Frieda for more than three years, and now for the first time he felt that he had unexpectedly, in an unforeseen turn of words, gotten the upper hand of her. He bore in with vehemence. "You're younger and more beautiful now than most women of twenty-five that I know. Why should that change in ten years? We can still make a life together. We've done it in a crippled way already, haven't we? We're knotted to each other. Why can't we live like other people? We might even have a child."

"Oh yes. Wouldn't that be precious! It's happened all too often in my family, our goddamn hormones never quit. My grandmother had one at forty-seven and it damn near killed her. Can't you picture how utterly ridiculous I would look with a new infant?"

"You would look wonderful to me if it were mine."

"That's preposterous, Arthur. I want you to drop it right now. You're just talking. It's a nasty cheap trick to put me on the defensive, and I won't have it, do you hear?"

Hawke's exhilaration was mounting. He was out in open water, all guns firing. Whether she married him or whether she did not, this was *it*. If she persisted in refusing, he was free. If she accepted him, he was really ready to marry her. He still wanted her, that was the hell of his predicament. She had forced the desire for her into his bloodstream, and if his fate was a queer marriage to an older divorcée, let it be that! Jeanne was lost, there was no one else, and at least he would put an end to this sneaking half-life.

"Having children would be up to you, Frieda. You've told me a thousand times you love me. I love you. People in love should get married."

"Stop it! Shut up, do you hear? Go home."

"All right."

They both stood, facing each other. Frieda said, "I'm sorry to put you out, but you're behaving atrociously. I've got a headache and you've made my stomach knot into cramps. It's a cruel and disgusting business, this utterly wild and insincere talk of marriage, of having children. Good God, after all these years, Arthur, this brilliant and virtuous brainstorm—"

"I'm absolutely sincere, Frieda."

"You are not! And if you are you're mad! I hate you for what you said about my husband's money. I have plenty of money of my own, believe you me! Maybe that's what you'd like to do, hey, live off my money while you write that great phantom masterpiece of yours?"

"Well, that's a pleasant suggestion."

"You deserve worse. What kind of lunacy is all this, anyway? One minute you don't want to see me any more, next minute you want to marry me. Why don't you make up your mind?"

"You make up your mind, Frieda. I want one or the other."

"I'm damned if you'll get either, see? Did it ever occur to you that I might die trying to have a child after forty? Even Paul was an accident, and I had a fearful time with him, believe me. You men ought to try having a baby or putting together a home some time. You wouldn't be so goddamn free with your ideas of having babies or breaking up homes, just as it suits your wild impulse of the moment."

"What kind of accident was Paul?" Hawke said.

Frieda seemed not to grasp his words for a moment. She peered at him foggily. "What did you say?"

And Hawke, with a reckless and strong sensation of bringing down the axe, replied, "I asked you what kind of accident Paul was, Frieda. You never talk about these things, but now you've brought it up."

Frieda's face worked into a horrid glare. She swung an arm clumsily to slap his face. He caught her elbow, so that the slap hardly grazed him, but she tumbled against him, he caught her in his arms, and they fell to the couch, tangled together. She braced away from him, both hands on his chest, looking into his eyes with pure hatred. She hoarsely whispered, "I'm sick. You don't know how sick I am. Let me go, get up, and get out my house. Don't ever come back. To hell with you."

Hawke released her and walked out of the room without a backward glance. He went down the red marble staircase and let himself out into the street. He stood on the moonlit sidewalk of Fifth Avenue, exhausted and shaken, sniffing the air and looking at the great downtown towers in a dazed way, as though he had just tunnelled up out of a prison.

8

Arthur Hawke had come to New York toward the end of 1945, an unknown huge Southerner in a rear seat of a crowded Greyhound bus, dressed in a patched old suit that was too tight and a duffle coat that squeezed him miserably in the narrow bus chair; a penniless young man with no possessions beyond the clothes he wore and a cracking suitcase containing linen, books, and a bundle of dog-eared pages of a half-written novel; and with no ready way to earn his keep except the low-grade skill of driving a bulldozer.

Five years later, in August 1950, he was leaving New York as the novelist Youngblood Hawke, in a luxury suite of the steamship *Nieuw Amsterdam,* dressed from head to foot in clothes from the best Fifth Avenue shops, but still disorderly in his aspect and still needing a haircut; as pale as he had been on his arrival, stouter, his hair a bit receded at the forehead, his bewildered resolute air of 1945 changed to a weary, worldly, dogged look, that yet retained a ghostly trace of the innocent and hopeful yokel. If the besieging antics of the ship reporters and photographers were any measure, he was the star celebrity sailing on that day. They were waiting for him at the gangway. They followed him into the thick of the milling farewell party in his suite. They dragged in another celebrity, a movie actress with a copy of *Chain of Command* under her arm, and took pictures of her simpering over his shoulder while he autographed the book. Then, with thirty people eating and drinking and smoking and chattering elbow to elbow around him, they pressed him for his views on the evils of television, the state of American literature, and the chances of nuclear war; until it occurred to him to suggest that they join the party, whereupon they dropped these urgent topics, put up their pads and pencils, and fell on Ross Hodge's cold meats and champagne.

Arthur Hawke was not only celebrated, he was well-to-do. By the standards he had brought to New York from the Kentucky hills he was rich. The nightmare of looming bankruptcy, which had overwhelmed him when he was walking around with pneumonia, the spectral figure of $120,000, had dissolved. The contractor hired by his mother was finishing up the house at a smart pace, using the mortgage money. Real estate agents were bringing in prospective buyers; and it appeared that Hawke was going to sell the house without much trouble and without great loss. Gus Adam was negotiating a settlement with the tax gatherers which cut their claim almost in half. Adam was in the suite aboard the ship when Hawke arrived: he had a mysterious green government form for the author to sign, and Hawke scrawled his name without a glance at the contents.

Hawke had also received from Scotty Hoag a few days before sailing, in a long sorrowful letter bemoaning the fact that the company had decided to go ahead and crush his mother in court, a check for forty thousand dollars: double the money he had invested in the Frankfort doctors' and lawyers' building. His royalty accounts both at Prince House and Hodge Hathaway were heavy with payments due. The moving picture companies were haunting Ferdie Lax with inquiries about the new novel, *Will Horne,* and offering substantial sums for an option on the work. Ferdie had flown from California to attend the party, and he was trying his best in snatches of talk to persuade Hawke to let him sell the film rights of the unfinished work now.

Mr. Givney, the paperback publisher, was at the party, too. He managed to press on Hawke, for his leisurely perusal at sea, a thick typewritten brochure labelled *The Hawke Press, Incorporated: A Revised Proposal for A New Publishing House.* Givney was at some pains to make sure that Hawke tucked the document out of sight of his host, Ross Hodge.

Jay and Fanny Prince were there. Jay found occasion to whisper to Hawke that he could not help thinking of himself as Hawke's publisher forever, and that Hawke could come back to Prince House at any time on terms which, he hinted, would be practically a crime against the publishing business. Fanny was all over Hawke and his mother at first, chic and pretty and odorous as ever, bubbling that she looked on "darling Hoke" as a son; whereupon Mrs. Hawke gave the woman such a freezing snub that she wandered through the party, champagne in hand, looking angry and dazed.

Feydal and Carmian were there, agog over the stage production of *Alms for Oblivion,* which had begun to snowball into swift actuality with the signing of the great Irene Perry, an actress eminent enough to have a theatre named after her, to play Aunt Bertha. Carmian fizzed and sparkled with money talk. He would play the show on the road for eight months and come into New York invulnerable to the critics, with a huge profit in the bag! Feydal, consuming a whole roast chicken and two bottles of champagne at a slow sure pace, disclosed to Hawke that his study of the script had convinced him that the play was really a macabre comedy, a grisly wonderful joke about death and money: "It's *Le Malade Imaginaire,* my dear Hawke, with a grim stab of truth at the end, and you'll just have to face the fact that you may be the new Molière."

All these rewards and promises and compliments had come to Arthur Hawke within five years. He had even gained some formal literary dignity. The ship's newspaper which had been handed to him at the gangway called him "the eminent Pulitzer Prize novelist." The five-year transformation had seemed long in the doing. But now, as Hawke stood in the middle of his jammed ornate first-class cabin, surrounded with attention, with flattery, and with talk of money, his mind harked back to his arrival in the

city on the Greyhound bus, and his new identity seemed as suddenly acquired, as glittering, and as likely to be swept away by the tolling of a bell, as Cinderella's ball gown.

Americans are supposed to be Philistines, indifferent to their artists; this idea hangs on although for more than a hundred years they have showered money and praise on the writers who have pleased them, from Mark Twain to Ernest Hemingway; have never allowed a Blake or a Gissing to starve; and today support American composers, painters, and writers in a great mass, either by buying their works or by appointing them to university posts and to fellowships. Certainly Arthur Hawke was not suffering at this time from a lack of appreciation! Yet the work he had done was but a fragment of a serious literary output. The critics who did not like Hawke—and they were numerous and influential—cited the fact that the public read what he wrote as proof of its low quality, since they held to the view that the common American reader was a vulgar boob. Hawke did not share that view, but he set no great store by the books he had written; he thought his important work lay ahead. It was for this reason that this gay and rich farewell party, this orgy of adulation troubled him more than it pleased him.

What had he really done so far? He had completed two books and started a third. He had been various kinds of a damned fool; he had been very ill; the involvement with Frieda Winter had damaged his life; but he was in one piece, after all, and that was what mattered. The night before he boarded the *Nieuw Amsterdam*, amid all the mess of packing in the torn-up house, he had written a chapter of *Will Horne*. The manuscript, with his watch, his dictionary, his thesaurus, his old pen, he had carried aboard in his own hand, in the worn brown satchel reserved for work in progress; and once the ship left New York, he intended to write two thousand words a day. One of the reporters had asked him the banal question: "Aren't you afraid you'll never write another success like *Chain of Command?*" And another reporter had popped out with his old answer, which had become a standing joke about Youngblood Hawke, "Why, he's rahtin' betta raht now." Hawke had joined readily in the laughter. Despite the day-to-day agony of composition, his literary future held no terrors for him, or rather only one, that he might waste his life somehow and not get to his main task. Some invincible naïveté, or, some egotism beyond imagining, saved him from any worry that he would run dry, or do poor work. He knew enough literary history to realize that he might fall out of favor, like a politician, and publish books that would fail, so that all the aura of success would fade away; and perhaps he should have been afraid of that, but in fact all he feared was premature death.

Fanny Prince managed to slip an arm through his elbow and drag him into a corner of the bedroom of his suite. She said in a chanteuse's tones of sexy conspiracy, "Vare is Frieda, my dear Hoke? Surely you invited her."

"It's Ross Hodge's party, Fanny."

"Ach, nonsense. How long vill you two behave like children? She's suffering terribly. I've known her twenty years and she's never been like this. She's going to pieces."

Hawke glanced around at the reporters, a couple of whom presented the too-disinterested profiles and focussed ears of eavesdroppers. "Fanny, I'd better get back to the guests."

Fanny whispered, "Let me telephone Frieda to come. It's an hour yet till the boat sails. Let me tell her you *vant* her to come. Be human."

"Did she ask you to speak to me?"

"Frieda? She hasn't mentioned you in a month. My darling Hoke, New York is the smallest town in the vorld. Who doesn't know you've had a fight?"

"But it's not so, Fanny. Frieda and I are the best of friends. She's been busy with the Shakespeare festival, that's all."

Fanny Prince raised her eyebrows and curled her mouth in scorn but she released her firm lock on his elbow. Hawke plunged back to the other room, glad to be out of Fanny's heavy cloud of rose perfume.

He saw that his mother, radiant in a new pink dress and a three-orchid corsage, had backed Gus Adam against a porthole, and was talking to him at great rate. Hawke could not hear what she was saying over the general din, but the lawyer wore a pained smile, and seemed in need of rescue. Hawke shouldered his way to them, begging off for the moment when Ferdie Lax tried to fasten on to him for a decision on the motion picture rights.

"The thing is, Mrs. Hawke, I'm in no position to try a case in Kentucky, even if I knew land law, which I don't," Adam was saying patiently, sloshing ice around in a tall drink.

"Pshaw, I'll bet you know plenty. They've made you a professor in a New York law college, haven't they? Anyway I'll take a chance on you . . . You Art, why didn't you tell me you've got a lawyer who comes from Brightstar, for heaven's sake, from our own county? Why, he's related by marriage to Rose Barlow, did you know that, who married my cousin Sol Caudill? You were at that wedding! What's the matter with you?"

Hawke grinned at Adam. "Are you supposed to recover the Hawke millions, now?"

The lawyer said, "It's out of the question, Art. Quite aside from my university schedule, I've never been a trial lawyer, and—"

Mrs. Hawke said, "But don't you realize how much money is in this?

We'd split with you fair and square. You'd never have to teach at college again."

"Madam, I like to teach."

Hawke took his mother by the arm. "Now, mama, you've got a fine lawyer. You don't need Gus Adam."

"Why, Art, how you talk! That lawyer I've got doesn't have any brains at all. He wanted me to settle for five thousand dollars, for ten, and now they're up to twenty thousand."

"They were, mama. Now they're offering nothing and you've got a lawsuit to fight down in Hovey, and Gus Adam lives in New York and that's that."

Adam said, "I'd be glad to recommend some lawyers I know in Louisville, Mrs. Hawke, who are excellent on land law."

"I want you," said Mrs. Hawke. "You seem smart to me. I've been looking for a smart lawyer all my life. If my husband had known one, I'd be rich. I even wanted to send Art to law school though I reckon that was a mistake, artists seem to be more or less nincompoops about serious matters."

Adam burst out laughing, his red face growing redder. Then he said with sudden seriousness, "That's an unfair generalization. In some ways, quite aside from his fine writing, your son is unusually astute."

Hawke saw a blue pillbox hat that belonged to Jeanne Fry near the door of the suite, swaying here and there as though the wearer were being buffeted. He pushed through to Jeanne, once again shaking off Ferdie Lax on the way, promising to talk to the agent in a moment. Flushed and breathless, Jeanne looked extraordinarily pretty. Quentin Judd was at her elbow. She said, "Oh, *there* you are," and handed Hawke a red portfolio. "I thought for a while we weren't going to make it, and you'd sail without these precious pages. I'm afraid Mr. Judd and I stayed too long at lunch."

Judd said, "I hope you don't mind my having come along to wish you bon voyage."

"I'm very glad. You're practically my favorite critic."

Judd looked up at him, blinking the glassy yellowish eyes with the startling blue pupils. "So far," he said. "I suppose there's a bar going here."

"Come along," Hawke said with a deference that he could not help.

Quentin Judd remained a fearsome creature to him, though the critic had reviewed both his books with calm measured praise. Judd had in the meantime also performed expert slaughter on some of the other new writers. It was generally said that the young novelist who was in a mental hospital had been driven there by Quentin Judd's precise and masterly assassination in *The Dandy* of his second book. It was always unnerving to Hawke, anyway, to see the critic in the flesh. This small dumpling of a

fellow, this malignant and doughy little Pickwick with the broomstick arms and legs, was so utterly opposite to the literary image his writing evoked, the tall, haughty, handsome, astringent man about town, that Hawke was inclined to regard the critic himself as the less real of the two.

Judd drank off a martini in a single continuation of the arm movement with which he had accepted it, and handed the glass to the bartender for refilling. "I'm going into competition with you, Hawke," he said. "Mrs. Fry's blown the dust off my half-finished novel and read it, and she wants me to complete it. I can see why you value her. She's full of ideas and she's most persuasive. Do you agree with her that a novel ought to have a plot?"

"I think it helps," Hawke said carefully, not knowing what wrong word might anger the tarantula.

"It would appear that what I've written so far resembles certain tropical jellyfish," Judd said, drinking his second martini down. "Brilliantly colored, and giving off a sort of phosphorescent light, but alas, a mere formless blob."

Jeanne laughed. "I never said that. I said the story is lost in the conversations and the side comments, but that they're so brilliant it doesn't matter."

"You also said the audience for such plotless novels was limited."

"Well, I believe that's true. An author ought to know what to expect."

"She's a tough cookie," Judd said. Judd was fond of studding his writing and his talk with fragments of slang. "I like that. She's the first editor who's ever spoken up to me. They all try to kiss my behind, which is a mistake. Despite a formidable body of opinion to the contrary, I don't write criticism with my behind. I'd like as many readers as possible for my novel, so I'm going to take the lady's comment to heart and put in a plot. That shouldn't be too hard, should it, Hawke? You ought to know."

This was a meaningless question to Hawke. Either a novel had a story or it had not. There were some impressive novels without stories, like Virginia Woolf's intricate prose poems and Peacock's iridescent charades, but Jeanne was quite right that only the cultivated few read them. Hawke said, "Well, if your book's half written, its nature probably can't be changed."

"That's what I said," Jeanne observed.

Hawke went on, "But I'm sure it shouldn't be. I'd give a great deal to be able to write like you."

"Thank you, but at the moment I'd give a great deal to get a fraction of your audience, having just built a vast and beautiful house in Connecticut that I can't in the least afford. I mean to have a shot at the common reader. You don't mind, do you? I mean there's room for both of us, I trust."

"Lord, yes," Hawke said. "The more the merrier. People read a book in two days."

Judd accepted another drink from the bartender, and in his abrupt manner turned and walked off.

Hawke took Jeanne's arm, and led her out of the bedroom and through the maze of passageways into a humid glare of August sunshine on the deck. They leaned on the rail in the slant shade of a lifeboat, looking down the towering iron wall of the ship at dirty sloshing water. Gulls squawked and swooped below them, plunging at garbage. Hawke said, "What on earth are you doing with Quentin Judd, Jeanie?"

"He pounced on me at a Book and Author luncheon last week. I couldn't think of a graceful way to duck reading his book. It's wonderful, what there is of it, but it's all pure Judd, the characters are just different names that keep spouting his opinions. And now I'm to help him put a plot into it! The whole idea gives me the horrors."

"Dump him on some other editor."

"He wants me. He thinks I'm the secret of your success. Mostly we talked about you. He cross-examined me about the way you and I work like, I don't know, like a jealous husband." Jeanne shuddered.

Hawke was looking at Jeanne with nostalgic regret and affection. The river smells were bringing back sharply the day of their sightseeing trip around Manhattan; so long ago, so irretrievably on the far side of the events that had forced them apart.

She startled him by saying, "Remember that boat ride we took around Manhattan, some fifteen million years ago?"

"I remember."

"I still have those tired violets you gave me, pressed in the *Oblivion* you autographed—that is, if they haven't crumbled to powder. The book's up on a high shelf out of reach." After a moment she said, "Meaning no disloyalty to absent friends, I kind of wish I were going with you."

"Meaning every disloyalty, the living room of my suite is the most wonderful accommodation I ever saw for a woman. Did you notice that huge blonde wood vanity table? How much guts have you got?"

"Guts enough to ignore your silly talk. I have a nice husband and he needs looking after. Anyway, isn't Frieda joining you over there?"

"No."

Jeanne's mouth wrinkled in a smile of disbelief.

Hawke said, "All right, you may as well know this. It's the last turn of the saga, I think. Shortly after I got better, I took your advice and asked Frieda to marry me. She got furious and threw me out of her house. I haven't talked to her since. It's over."

Jeanne looked at Hawke, taking in this news with a strange look on her face. "I see. I'd heard chatter, of course. I wasn't going to ask you any

questions. That's a different version—the marriage proposal—from the talk that's going around. I daresay it's the truth."

"That's it, Jeanne, believe me."

She shook her head in wonder. "Frieda is a woman who really wants things her way, isn't she? I keep putting myself in her place, and so I always guess wrong. Well! Then is the eminent Pulitzer Prize novelist— as they say—really on the loose, and up for grabs?"

"Pretty much."

"It's a hard idea to get used to. It hasn't been true, actually, since I've known you." Jeanne turned her back to the rail and leaned her elbows on it. She arched herself in a decidedly coquettish motion, kicking out one slim ankle. "If that's really the case, Arthur my lad, maybe you and I should—"

Ferdie Lax chose that moment to come stumbling and blinking out of the passageway. "Oh, there you are, Hawke. I wondered where the hell you'd run off to." He adjusted his hat, which had almost fallen off when he tripped. It was a bright blue almost brimless object, not unlike Jeanne's except that it was made of soft velvet. "Can't we talk for a minute?"

"Of course, Ferdie," Hawke said grumpily, thinking that the agent looked curiously incomplete unaccompanied by a beautiful girl a head taller than himself.

"Well, then, two things," Lax said.

He described a recent stampede in Hollywood toward the purchasing of novels. There was no reason for it except that lately two or three pictures adapted from books had been very successful. All at once, he said, fiction was pure uranium again. "Those guys out there are a lot of lemmings, Hawke. But that's how it is and my job is to tell you these things. I gather you're cold on that million-dollar proposition of Givney, which always had too many strings dangling on it to suit me. In that case you ought to let me try to sell *Horne*. I think I can get you some real money."

Hawke said, "I don't want to show an unfinished manuscript."

"Let me have an outline, for Christ's sake, something the bastards can read and pretend they like. They don't know anything, it's just that this is the season for handing out big prices for a book. Especially the new Hawke."

"All right, I'll send you an outline from Paris."

"The other thing is, how long do you intend to stay in Europe?"

"I want to finish this book and write the next one. Probably two years." Hawke saw that Jeanne looked astonished, and downcast.

"In that case," Lax said, "you're absolutely insane if you don't do the foreign residence bit. I *know* I can get you a screenplay job. A salary you earn as a foreign resident is free of U.S. taxes. That's why Hollywood's turning into a ghost town. They're all over in Liechtenstein and France

and Italy and Switzerland doing the foreign residence bit. And now Yugoslavia's opening up. Travis Jablock is dying to do a Yugoslavia thing. Yugoslavia is fresh. I can sell Youngblood Hawke and Yugoslavia to Travis Jablock over the phone, for Christ's sake. Shall I take a shot at it?"

"Ferdie, I'd love to do the foreign residence bit in Switzerland, but I have all this work to do, you see."

"What's the matter with you? This would be work! The kind of speed merchant you are, you could write three pictures in that time and set yourself up for twenty years. No taxes, Hawke! *No taxes!*"

"Ferdie, I better do my work and pay the taxes."

Lax blinked sleepily at him. "Well, you lose me there, but okay. You may be the only American living in Europe who isn't doing the foreign residence bit. Except for soldiers and fliers." Lax put out his hand. "You send me that outline, now. The time to sell is when they're buying. Bon voyage. Nice seeing you, Mrs. Fry."

As the agent disappeared into the black hole of the passageway Jeanne said softly, "Two years?"

"It's a sentence to the rockpile, Jeanne. I want to hole up somewhere— probably England—finish this book and write two others, a long one and a short one by the end of 1952. Then I can take a deep breath and look around."

"But—two years!"

"I count on you to come over a couple of times—with Karl, I daresay— whenever I've got a whole manuscript to shake together."

"That seems most unlikely. How can I leave my work? How can Karl? Won't you be returning at all? Not for two years?"

"No. The *Oblivion* play would kill six months or a year if I got mixed up in it. Also my mother's starting a lawsuit. I want a broad ocean between me and her while that's going on. I want the Atlantic separating me from Frieda, too."

"Frieda can cross the ocean."

"She won't stay long if she comes. Frieda likes the comforts of her home. She made that clear."

Jeanne stared out at the Palisades, clasping and unclasping her hands on the rail. "What's the long book—the labor story? You haven't said much about it."

"Yes, I thought of the title while I was sick. It's *Boone County*."

He began to talk about the next book, describing it as though it were already written. Its theme was the invasion of a coal county like his own Letchworth by a labor union. He intended to draw a picture of the battle between the old American way of life, the free, unorganized existence of which his home was one of the last surviving pockets, and the new industrial America spearheaded by the union. The force of the picture lay in the fact that both sides were right, that the conflict was generated

by a dislocation in time. The battle would end in riots, murders, and a bitter empty victory for the union, because at the union wage scale coal mining would no longer be profitable in Boone County. The whole marginal industry would wither and most of the miners would leave the county with their families for the factories across the Ohio River around Cincinnati. And Boone County would slump yet more into its character of a bypassed land, a pocket of lost time, a near wilderness of abandoned coal pits, dwindling towns, and trash timber; that would be the end of the trail blazed by Daniel Boone.

Jeanne said, thoughtfully, "That is a long book. And a tough one. I wonder if you're doing a wise thing. Europe is a very diverting place, Arthur. And the European women are notorious—or shall we say celebrated?—for favoring literary men."

"Quite so. But I won't fall in love, and that's what eats up time and spirit."

"What makes you so sure you won't fall in love?"

Hawke looked her in the face and said, "Because I am in love, Jeanne, and it's not going to change and since I can do nothing about it right now but wait, that's what I'm going to do. Meantime there's the rockpile."

Color crept up Jeanne's neck and covered her entire face. Avoiding his eyes, she said, "The rockpile! The lap of luxury, you mean, and a rapidly changing harem, and a pen that gathers cobwebs, or I miss my guess."

"Don't you think I'm serious?"

"You'll be terribly alone. When I said maybe you should marry Frieda, I was thinking that at any price you had to have a base, a home. That's all you were striving for, don't you see, with that absurd house you were building, and that even more absurd talk we had in the Lexington airport? And now you'll be on the loose, worse than ever, in strange lands. However, it's done. You always do what you want to do in the end. You just bull ahead. So God bless you."

Hawke said gravely, "You think I'm making a mistake."

She lifted her downcast face. "How can I tell? I don't know. You've left her, which is rather remarkable. I used to think you were indestructible. But I've seen you sick, and I'm still a little scared, if you want to know." Her voice wavered, and she put out a hand to stop his movement toward her. "I'll kill you if you try to kiss me, Arthur. I've had enough. I'll come to Europe whenever you need me."

Mrs. Hawke popped out of the passageway, tripping over the coaming just as Lax had, and losing most of the champagne in the glass she held. "Now, now what's all this? Big party, and no birthday boy! You come on back and have some of this champagne, Art. You can write this pretty secretary of yours a long letter once the ship sails." She giggled. Her hat was tilted too far over one eye. "Oops, lost all my champagne, did I?

Well, there's lots more. I declare, I'm discovering champagne a little too late in life, but it's just as well, I might have to revise my principles, aha ha ha. Come along, now, Art."

Hawke shrugged at Jeanne, and they walked to the passageway. Mrs. Hawke said, taking Jeanne's arm, "Seems to me you need a little champagne, Jeanie. You're awful down in the mouth. Jeanie, I want you to know Nancy and John think the world of you, and I sure do too. Why, you've changed all my ideas about the Jews. People are just people, and that's a great truth."

The ship was scheduled to sail at two. At five minutes to two Hawke left his suite, where he had been unpacking while two stewards cleared away the debris of the party. Hawke had drunk a lot of champagne after his talk with Jeanne, and he was feeling dizzy and gay, and the end of his nose was numb; something that usually happened only when he was very drunk. He found a place at the crowded rail amidships, and looked up and down the wharf until he saw the splotch of pink which was his mother, and with her Jeanne, and Ross Hodge, and to his surprise, Gus Adam. The lawyer had told him half an hour earlier that he was late for a faculty conference, yet there he was, deep in conversation with Jeanne. Hawke's emotions were all on edge; he had a swift pang of jealousy, and then he laughed out loud at himself, so that the passengers on either side of him glanced at the burly laughing man uneasily. He waved both hands in the air and bellowed, "Hey, ma! Hey, Jeanne! Ma! *Ma!*"

His mother heard, and looked up, searching for him. "Right here, ma! Up here! The big money maker!"

She saw him, and eagerly waved. She pointed him out to the others, who waved too. The ship's whistle blasted several times. The *Nieuw Amsterdam* began to move. He waved and waved. Was Jeanne touching a handkerchief to her eyes? It was hard to see her clearly.

A woman standing beside him at the rail said, "Aren't you Youngblood Hawke?" She wore a fetching white linen suit; she was blonde, perhaps thirty, well-groomed, pretty and her smile was inviting.

"Yes, ma'am, Ah am."

"You've given me many hours of pleasure. I just wanted to tell you that." She fluttered her eyelashes at him.

Lifted yet on the foam of the champagne, Hawke had the impulse to pick up the thrown rose. The woman was not bad-looking at all; she had a small-boned figure like Frieda's. It was a momentary flare of the self that he hoped he was leaving behind. "Ah'm glad, ma'am. Ah appreciate your telling me. Excuse me."

He went to his cabin, got the working pad out of the old brown satchel, and resumed work on page one thousand, five hundred and eighty-four of his new book.

CHAPTER FIFTEEN

1

AMONG Jeanne Fry's old friends in California and Washington she had become a legend. She was the girl who had made good, the glitterer of the crowd, the one who had gone to New York and carved for herself, while yet in her twenties, the career of an editor in the great publishing house of Hodge Hathaway. But Jeanne had not come to New York to seek a career. She had drifted into publishing in order to support herself, while she waited for her destiny, probably in the form of a man. In retrospect her fate seemed to have been fixed by the flimsiest chain of accidents—the encounter at a dreary Greenwich Village party with a girl who had just left a job in the styling department of Prince House to get married; her own stab at the job, which had been a lucky hit; then after months of tedious drudgery the illness of one of the older copy editors, which had resulted in her finding on her desk the enormous messy manuscript of *Alms for Oblivion*; and then—and then Arthur Hawke, blasting through her life like a typhoon and somehow leaving her married to Karl Fry, in a dismal piled wreckage of emotions and dreams. All those decisive events had gone so fast, so terribly fast! She had acted hastily, had said and done many wrong things, and had capped her blunders by striking at Hawke with the only weapon she could find to hand, marriage to another man. Some sure instinct had told her that, whatever Hawke's entanglement with Frieda, it would hurt him if she married Karl; and blinded with rage and frustration, she had done it, and so had stamped a shape on her whole life.

Thinking back on it Jeanne had long since concluded—perhaps in order to be able to keep her sanity—that marriage was all luck. Girls at a marriageable age were emotion-ridden nervous ignorant harried fools. Prudent marriages fell apart; mad marriages turned out beautifully; it was all luck, all luck! Why, even her marriage with Karl had worked, in a fashion! She was fond of him, and on the whole they jog-trotted through the days amiably enough. Jeanne could never decide once for all whether she should or should not have tried harder to marry Hawke, whether she should have been more patient with him, whether other tactics might not have worked better, and whether life with him would have been a glory

or a horror. Of one thing she was certain: she could not have tolerated the casual infidelities that Frieda put up with.

The Frys now lived quietly in the small apartment in the Sixties east of Lexington Avenue where Karl had first taken her years ago, to feed her martinis and commence his tenacious and respectful wooing. They each had a small dark bedroom, and an L-shaped main room of fair size which was library, sitting room, and dining room in one. The furniture was old, dowdy, and comfortable. Nothing was impressive in the place except the walls and walls of books. It was the reverse of luxurious, and when old friends visited her they were surprised, having expected a couple of Hodge Hathaway editors to live in an apartment such as one sees in movies of Manhattan high life: spacious, ultra-modern, with sweeping views of the downtown towers and the rivers. But this small gloomy place was about what they could afford. The rent was fixed by law at a fraction of the prices for new apartments. Salaries of editors are modest, and too much of Karl's earnings still went in alimony. From this apartment they could walk to the offices of Hodge Hathaway in good weather, and on Lexington Avenue there were shops that served the wealthy residents of Park and Fifth Avenues. They could enjoy the amenities of these shops. They ate in restaurants much of the time; but Jeanne could also insert herself into the tiny kitchenette, revolve here and there for an hour or so in a great clatter, and emerge hot and dishevelled with a fine dinner when she chose. Even to the people who knew them fairly well, the Frys appeared to be a happy couple.

At Hodge Hathaway, Jeanne and Karl had two desks in an office by themselves, and they shared a secretary. On the organization chart they were the mysteries department, and they had built up a good list of writers of murder puzzles. But there was not enough work in that for both of them. Karl did most of it. To Jeanne's desk also came a variety of manuscripts, usually first novels or translations of little-known Europeans.

Her relationship with the major novelist Youngblood Hawke, which gave her special status, was most unusual. He had fastened on to her from the first, he had developed an immediate and total trust in her, and he had turned off approaches by senior editors of the firm, who were not too pleased at seeing a money maker like Hawke in the hands of this young woman. Jeanne and Hawke had talked of these approaches, and they suspected that Ross Hodge was behind them. The latest had occurred shortly after the painful meeting of Hodge and the Frys with the lawyer Adam. But Hawke had made it clear that nobody but Jeanne could hope to touch his copy.

Aside from this curious distinction of Jeanne's she was rated as an able and conscientious editor, with certain faults: too intolerant and caustic in her judgments, insensitive to richly poetic prose, inclined to impatience with allegory or symbolism, a ruthless slasher of manuscripts once she was

given the authority to slash, prudish about foul language, violently con-
temptuous of imitations, and decidedly old-fashioned in her emphasis
on plotting. On the other hand, she had an excellent instinct for picking
out promising new books and authors. When she liked a book, she was
effective at suggesting revisions and story changes that could transform
a confused and dubious effort into a success; and her tact and persuasive-
ness in getting weary authors to keep at their tasks, or to undertake new
ambitious ones, were valuable traits. It was always a mistake to give her a
manuscript by a homosexual. There had been some wild blowups as a
result, and Hodge Hathaway had lost one very talented young sodomite
from Canada who was now a critics' darling and a best-seller besides. But
Jeanne Fry had never withdrawn her opinion that his writing reminded
her of soiled nylon underwear.

Her acid judgments had made her enemies, of course. Hawke's fantastic
success had made yet more enemies for her, as well as for him. It was a
widespread bit of gossip in the trade that she was his mistress. People
believed this, despite the fact that Hawke's long affair with Frieda Winter
was the next thing to common knowledge in New York. There was another whisper that also had much circulation: the books of Youngblood
Hawke had "really" been written by Jeanne Fry!

One would think that the professional people who passed this rumor
around would have been the first to laugh at the folly of it. If Jeanne
really had written the books, why had she not published them as hers?
What was gained by pretending that they were written by a man named
Hawke? Yet the rumor held its ground. Publishing is competitive enough
in the United States, though it is not, as in some lands, a snarling whirl
of starved dogs. Hawke's great success called forth in the business the
itch to tear him down. It was not enough that some little magazines and
college teachers berated his books. That was a routine thing; it happened
to all successful novelists. But if he had not "really" written his books, if
an obscure young woman had written them, or had collaborated in the
writing of them, that was wonderful news. It detracted from Hawke, and
somehow added no special lustre to Jeanne. They were a pair of forgers,
and Hawke's popular books were nothing but concocted fakes. When it
soothes people's vanities to believe something, it will go hard but they
will believe it. Jeanne and Hawke knew of this rumor. When Hawke first
heard it he had flown into a bellowing rage. Jeanne thought it was a joke.
Yet a man as astute as Quentin Judd had begun his questions about her
work methods during their lunch by asking how much truth there was
to the story.

In point of fact, Jeanne contributed to Youngblood Hawke's books,
beyond technical editing, about as much invention, criticism, and help
as some authors' wives do. Of course no two authors are alike in their
methods, or in their marriages. There have been famous novelists whose

wives never looked at their books, even after they were printed. But often the wife of a writer serves him as copyist, sounding board, research assistant, day-to-day critic, encourager of his strong points and suppressor of his failings; all this in addition to her household labors, and the special task of being custodian of a creative person, who is usually one sort or another of a cranky fool when he is not burning with his flame. Jeanne seemed born to be an author's wife; perhaps to be Hawke's wife. Had she been married to him the rumors that she was his collaborator or his ghost could not possibly have gotten started. The trouble was that she rendered him these wifely services without being his wife, outside the privacy of wedlock, in which most authors hide the contribution of their wives, taking all the credit to themselves. You might say that Hawke had been sleeping with Frieda Winter, and using Jeanne Fry as a wife in his art. But the way it came out, to the public view, he was an author who depended too much on his editor, and who—on the evaluation of malice—could not exist without her.

2

His first letters to her were wonderful patches of brightness in an exceptionally gray and miserable September.

Never had there been such damp heat, such pouring rain, and such exasperation at home and in the office. Karl was bedridden. The weather was plain hell. She seldom got to the office in the morning without being drenched; if not by rain, then by perspiration. To get a taxicab was next to impossible; when she did manage to halt one, like as not some burly ferocious woman would dart through the streaming rain, seize the door handle, bare her teeth at Jeanne and take the cab; in the unending New York fight for taxis Jeanne was a perpetual loser. She would trudge through the rain to Hodge Hathaway, where the clammy air-conditioning after the steambath of the streets made her sneeze and shiver. She had an unshakable cold, and her voice was down to a rasp.

In her office nothing seemed to await her but bad manuscripts, offended authors, and short stiff notes from Ross Hodge. In the aftermath of the summer demoralization of routine, books were being printed full of mistakes; art work on jackets was coming out all wrong; five thousand copies of one travel book emerged from the binder with illustrations upside down; and so forth. She was doing most of Karl's work as well as her own. Her secretary inconsiderately got pregnant and quit. Nothing was selling, and the fall list was the weakest in years. In fact it seemed to be raining inside the Hodge Hathaway offices as well as in the black streets. The wind howled down Madison Avenue, the thunder crashed and echoed

all day long, and purple cracks of lightning seemed to have replaced daylight as the ordinary illumination of New York City.

Karl was a restless patient at best, and at this time he became a real devil. His two weapons were sarcasm and martyrdom. Of the two she preferred the sarcasm; if it stung, it was sometimes amusing. His white-faced lapses into silence, his too-patient smiles, his averted eyes whenever she returned a short answer, were unendurable, mostly because she knew she was wrong to be impatient with him. It was a beastly trap he was in, a hot bed in a dark room, week after week. He peevishly refused to try an air conditioner, saying that when he was a corpse, which would not be long at the present rate, it would be time enough to refrigerate him. As his health mended and the last weeks of his confinement began to seem a mere medical formality, he grew more trying. They had an appalling squabble over some eggs she scrambled for his breakfast which he thought were too loose, and they did not talk for twenty-four hours, and then his self-abasing apology did not clear the air. A new quarrel broke out when she had lunch with Adam and did not first tell Karl about it.

This happened about two weeks after Hawke sailed. At the farewell party the lawyer had asked for a chance to meet with her and explain his reasons for advising Karl as he had. It was a delicate business, a little like talking things over with a doctor behind the patient's back, but Jeanne had decided to do it, and she was glad she had. Adam's ideas about Karl's predicament made sense to her once he spelled them out. She had to admit that he had probably saved Karl's life by discouraging him from returning to Washington. The lawyer remained an enigma to her—she could not tell whether his politics were liberal or very reactionary, even after talking to him for two hours about communism—and his slightly patronizing self-assurance still irritated her, but she became convinced that he meant well to Karl. Also it was clear that he thought her mightily attractive, and a woman will forgive a man much when she discerns that. But she made the mistake of disclosing the lunch to Karl that night and the effect on her invalid husband really alarmed her. She stopped answering his bitter accusations—which went as far as a remark that men from the back counties of Kentucky seemed to have a fatal fascination for her—because she began to think he might have another heart attack. He got out of the bed, and took several drinks of forbidden whiskey and a sleeping pill. Next day he said nothing about the fight, nor did he ever refer to it again. But it left a further residue of unhappiness in the hot, hot, dark, small apartment.

Into all this petty misery Hawke's letters came like rays of April sunlight. When she saw one at the door in the morning she all but fell on it. He carelessly typed three or four sheets at a time, full of cheery news and irradiated with affection for her. Everything seemed to be going as well as possible. The trip to Europe was beginning to look like

the most fortunate decision of his life. First of all, he was piling up pages of *Will Horne*, and he was doing it with no more than three hours of work a day, three hours before dawn rigidly scheduled and rigidly held to, whatever his hours the night before. His old energy had come back. He could sightsee all day, sleep four or five hours, write off his pages, and tear away to sightsee again. Apparently the solution to all his woes had been to get away from New York and Frieda. He wrote in his first letter, which he mailed from London, that his personal rule for fame, fortune, and good health would henceforth be half a dozen words in the Book of Proverbs: "Give not thy strength to women." He was holding to that rule without any exertion of will power, he claimed, despite the numbers of attractive and unattached women aboard the ship, and at the hotels where he was staying.

If you'll believe me, what decides me against women in the end is the time they take. Nothing more moral or praiseworthy is involved. It's impossible to tell you how much I relish my freedom. I'm reading a book a day, the way I used to before I came to New York. I just got through Kant's *Critique of Pure Reason* in a week; it took me a month in the Seabees, the first time around, but I've read a lot of philosophy since then. If I'm not mistaken the *Critique* is a huge gloomy Gothic labyrinth of words, at the center of which you find a bright red box of crackerjacks. I used to be diffident about such impressions until I read the other philosophers, who all hint that Kant was an idiot compared to them.

This letter then went into ecstatic praise of Devon and Cornwall. He was certainly going to settle down in a small English country town once he had "done" Paris and Rome, and maybe Venice. And he would never stop hoping that she would appear one day, and they would revel together in the magic green picturebook that was England.

I can't tell you what it's like. Just imagine driving into and through a series of dissolving Constable landscapes, like Alice going through a lot of looking glasses one after the other, and you'll have a vague notion of it, maybe. England is heaven, that's all. You've got to come when I finish the book, if not sooner.

His letter from Rome was mainly a narrative of his encounter with the Hauptmanns. Hawke was not inclined to dwell on famous sights:

Saw St. Peter's and the Vatican. St. Peter's a little too much, the Pantheon stuck on top of the Parthenon, Michelangelo trying to prove that the Christian Renaissance had it all over the Greeks and only succeeding in being titanically vulgar to my ignorant taste, like a woman wearing two Paris hats one on top of the other. The chic effect is *not* doubled. The Vatican has a clutter of bad paintings and statuary, too, at least what I saw, besides some good things. Best thing I've seen in Rome, far and away, is Michelangelo's Moses, stuck off in some small church. No point letting that old Jew into the

first-class hotels, I guess they figure, and they're probably right. He's embarrassing.

The Roman food! People talk about Paris but I don't see how any food on earth can touch what I've been eating. I've been lucky in a way, I've been doing Rome with a colossally rich and very pleasant couple who know Rome the way I know Hovey. The woman is the daughter of Anne Karen. You remember, Karen was supposed to play Aunt Bertha in the *Oblivion* movie and then she up and died in India and the movie collapsed. Anyway, her daughter, a Mrs. Hauptmann, once wrote me a letter about *Chain of Command* from Rome. That's how I happened to look her up.

I had only the faintest recollection of her. That was the time I drove from Hovey to New York in a blizzard, you remember, and I must have been plumb delirious when I showed up at the Waldorf-Astoria. I hardly remember anything that happened. But if you'll forgive me, the episode seems to have been one of the most impressive experiences of this woman's life. She describes it with amazing vividness. It seems I fell into Anne Karen's suite in a greasy duffle coat caked with snow, two-day growth of beard, face white as paper, eyes like burning coals, and I proceeded to down a whole quart of whiskey without the slightest effect, and to sweep Anne Karen off her feet—and the daughter too—with the most magnificent narration of a story either of them had ever heard. I promise you I don't remember a particle of this. I know I met with Karen and Luzzatto and they decided to buy the book, but I have no impression of the daughter as she was. All I remember is Anne Karen, sitting on the floor in a puddle of green silk, dazzlingly beautiful though she must have been fifty.

Anyway her daughter now is a too-plump woman of thirty or so with especially fat little hands, but if she were unattached I might be inclined to overlook all that because she must be one of the rich women of the world, and she obviously thinks the world of A. Youngblood Hawke. Her father was Monroe Lesser, and evidently Lesser and Karen between them were two of the cleverest people who ever came to Hollywood. They put all their earnings into Los Angeles real estate—in the depression! Can you picture it, buying in a couple of million dollars' worth of that land *at 1930 prices?* To top it all some of the land is now producing oil! Honor Hauptmann's wealth almost passes calculation. She must be worth twenty million dollars in her own right, yet nobody's ever heard of her. Christ, Jeanne, there are *rich* people in this world, that's one thing I'm learning! I mean *rich.* The Winters are pikers compared to the Hauptmanns and the set they move in, the South American crowd. Because mind you, Honor's husband has even more money than she has! Manuel Hauptmann is a Peruvian. Obviously his family was once German but now they're thoroughly Latinized and they own nearly all the sugar in Peru. It seems that's about half the sugar in the world, which was also news to me. He's a very genteel and manly little man, Teutonic, blondish; he doesn't look exactly Latin and yet his speech and his manners are wholly South American: soft, elegant, fantastically polite. It's an interesting mixture. He goes for racing cars, flies his own plane, has his own yacht, and all that. I

have no idea how Honor Lesser came to marry a Peruvian. I gather they met in Rome about four years ago. Now they have twins three years old and a new baby, but it doesn't keep them from barrelling all over Europe. The kids live with about ninety servants in a villa outside Florence overlooking the Arno. Anyway I've been a protégé of the Hauptmanns ever since I came to Rome. I've met some of the fanciest people, here and in Florence, Italian admirals and generals and marchesas as well as these South American plutocrats—good lord, those Latin millionaires seem to comb the world for the best-looking women! The wives are absolute staggerers, and oh Jeanne, their clothes, their manners, their chic! The effect is to make me firmer than ever in my celibacy, I swear. Why bother with women unless you can have one of those? And I can't. Those cost more money than I now have or probably will ever have. The only other kind of woman worth having is one you love heart and soul, and I have no available candidates in sight, have I? I half wish Honor Lesser had let me know *before* she got married how fascinated she was by the unshaven feverish literary scarecrow who fell in on her out of a blizzard. If Shaw could live off a millionairess, why not Hawke? However, it's just as well, the fact is the slightest trace of excess fat on a woman disgusts me and Honor is too fat. She eats like a pig. A woman should never, never, never have fat hands.

(Here Jeanne stopped reading to take a long look at her hands, turning them here and there. She knew Hawke loved her hands, and indeed they were one of her good points, small, blunt, yet graceful, the skin smooth and translucent, the fingers thin but rounded; strong pretty hands. A lot of good they had done her!)

Then in this long letter he described the magnificence of some of the Italian homes in Rome and Florence that the Hauptmanns had taken him to.

These people live in actual museums, Jeanne, honestly! The paintings and statues I saw in the Rizzoti home, just in the main gallery and the library (I never got into the bedrooms), would be enough to start a museum in Louisville or Trenton. There are dozens of homes like it, maybe hundreds, in Rome and Florence. Yet these people sit and talk and smoke and drink among these stunning million-dollar masterpieces, and eat, and make love, and go to the bathroom, and all that. It's a revelation to me that this way of life exists. I'd never have had a glimpse of it, in all likelihood, if not for the curious chance that Honor Hauptmann has had a long crush on me. However once in the charmed group, I must say I'm treated well. These people are very bored because they've had everything since birth, and I'm a sort of talking bear on a chain I guess. My French is coming in handy though I'm dead in Italian. You never know when conscientiousness will pay off. When I got going on Balzac and Victor Hugo out at sea, during the war, I made the decision never to read any French writer except in French. My dictionary fell apart from eking out my lousy University of Kentucky French, and my accent strains the amazing politeness of these people, I know, yet I get along.

There was more in this vein, including a few references to the "remote and tantalizing" loveliness of the upper-class Italian women, which Jeanne could have done without. But he ended with a handsome paragraph about how much he missed her, and with the new page count of *Will Horne*, which if true was almost beyond belief.

His first letter from Paris was in quite another vein. Nothing about Paris was good. The weather was an unending warm drizzle, the hotel prices were astronomical, and the Parisians were in a general conspiracy to make Americans feel ill-at-ease and inferior.

By Christ, I'm beginning to understand here how a colored man must feel in Alabama. I swear it would probably help if I were colored. I've seen some Negroes in the restaurants and theatres squiring around the most spectacular Frenchwomen in sight (though believe me not one of them compares to the Italian killers I met or to those heartrending collectors' items that the South American nabobs marry!). When I talk French here to a taxidriver or desk clerk I'm like as not met with a sneer and an answer in disgusting zis-and-zat English. So to hell with them, I now talk nothing but English and I lay on Kentucky too. I make these French bastards work to understand me.

I can't imagine where the rumor got started that the French are gay and frivolous. I have never seen people more glum at their pleasures. They eat elaborate lavish meals with dead-pan solemn faces, Jeanne, as though they were ritualistically eating their own fathers. They sit in their naughty night clubs and stare at the drooping files of bare titties parading in front of them, and for all the frivolity they show they might be at a guillotining. The Americans in the crowd get infected with the gloom, they get boisterously drunk in self-defense or they just sit looking as if they'd just heard that their party lost the election. Take my word for it, Paris is ghastly.

He had met Howard Fain, and the encounter had sealed his depression. He saw in the disintegrated young novelist an image of his own future, or at least a threat that was hanging over him. They had the same literary agent in France, a woman who was Ferdie Lax's Paris representative, and she had brought them together for dinner. Then Fain had taken him to a café frequented by the existentialists,

all with the ceremonial dirty trench coat, Jeanie, and the ceremonial cigarette, and the ceremonial thick glasses, and the ceremonial sweater. The French like their priesthoods to dress so they can be recognized at a glance, by God.

Jeanne, I wish you'd been with us in that café as we proceeded to get drunk on brandy and Fain started to let his hair down. In the first place Fain looks so frightful! He must be on drugs. Nothing else would account for the unfocussed glitter in his eyes and a sort of watery, tallowy softness that's spread over his entire body. You met him in 1947, didn't you, when he was the new king of the novelists, the Hemingway of World War II that they'd all been waiting for? My God, how handsome he was! A strong young poet's face, a face like Byron's or Rupert Brooke's, a squat powerful tapering body

and an air of truly noble command. I remember once he walked into a roomful of stars in Hollywood and upstaged them all. Suddenly the man in the room was Howard Fain. (He arrived with Frieda, goddamn her soul, but that's another story and I'll say nothing about *that*.)

He is a physical wreck. He is a gross slob, a red-faced fat little fellow with purple veins in his nose. He wears a dirty shirt without a tie, and the café vestments, trench coat and all. How could this happen to such a handsome and wonderful youth in three or four years? His talk is as brilliant as ever, or more so. I thought I'd read a lot, and I guess I have, but Fain has really been working at it, he's turned into an unbelievably encyclopedic reader. He's becoming like James Joyce, or Edmund Wilson, or Ezra Pound. He's read almost *everything*. But what good has it done him? He's drowned in the Paris brand of existentialism. As I understand the creed, you do what you goddamn please, you chase women and money and drive fast cars and eat rich food like any other Frenchman. The thing is, you do all this with sad irony, and that makes it existentialism. Because life is meaningless and communism is inevitable but will not restore God to the empty heavens, you see. And so you face the absurd universe with defiant courage and take from life, wearily and without illusion, the crumbs it offers. Before the onrushing end comes, the thermonuclear deluge of fire that erases Europe, Russia, and America, ushering in the final and everlasting rule of the Marxist Chinese. I may be simplifying the picture, but not much. Howard presents it with terrible eloquence in a solid monologue an hour long, fueled by brandy. I think he could go home and make a fortune doing it for the ladies' clubs. It is a fantastic chilling horror act, and American club women love nothing like getting scared out of their drawers.

That's Fain the Jeremiah. He has an absolutely different second self, that's even more scary to me—Fain the shrewd angle man, the financial wizard, the international manipulator, the man who's beaten the tax rap and is getting unbelievably rich on movie money and soaking every quarter away. Why? He says to buy himself an estate in Tasmania one year before the calculated blowup. This side of Fain horrifies me because I have my own spasms of greed for money, God knows. In every way he seems the ghost of Christmas-yet-to-come, and he gives me the cold shudders.

It's impossible to tell when he's being serious, or how much he's saying is true. He just talks on and on, his eyes glassy, chain-smoking. But I've seen one or two of his spy movies, they're damned good, full of real European atmosphere and sharp invention, and I'm sure he must be getting rich. Howard speculates in international currencies. To hear him tell it, he has made a couple of killings on wide swings in the franc, due to political events that he's been tipped off on in advance by his pessimistic philosophical friends, who know some big government wheels. These profits are just one more sad existential pleasure they all take with courage and dignity if without hope in this absurd universe, I gather.

Howard is most ominous about my own future as a writer. I told him the story of the new one. He said that I seem to be trying a little harder to be serious this time, but it doesn't matter, I must prepare myself for a bloodbath. "They will be waiting for you this time with cleavers," he said. "Do you

suppose that any critic in the United States is going to forgive you for a smash hit like *Chain of Command* plus the Pulitzer Prize? Your first novel was a freak delayed hit of sorts and somehow didn't count. With *Chain of Command* you entered the circle of success. The iron rule now, on the next book, is that you must go through the ordeal. That is the literary religion in America. It must all be derived from the Aztecs. They raise you high, Hawke, to an exalted pinnacle, to the top of the sacrificial pyramid and there, where all eyes can see you, when you publish your next book, they strip you naked, flourish glittering knives and begin to hack pieces of living meat from your body. Your smoking blood pours out of you, your own flesh lies in gobbets at your feet, and you are required to stand in silence, to offer no resistance, *and to smile!* If you faint, if you wince, if you protest, if you cry out in pain, your disgrace is immediate and permanent. If you die, the ordeal proves that you never belonged in the circle in the first place." (I'm giving you almost his exact words, Jeanne. It really spouted out of him, like blood. His hands shook so the brandy spilled, his eyes glared.) "Who is left in the circle today?" he said. "Three or four mutilated horrors who somehow survived this ordeal, crawling feebly around, Hemingway, Faulkner, Steinbeck, Marquand, all of them scarred like air crash victims, all of them numb and stunned and unwilling to utter a word about literature or literary criticism, pretending to be sports fans or farmers or business men or *anything* but artists.

"Hawke," he said, "I think you're next. You can't escape the ordeal, nobody can, and I'm sure you're going to get it on this book."

It was mighty cheery stuff, Jeanne. I've always thought that if you couldn't take criticism, fair or unfair, you ought to find some other way of paying your bills than writing. I wanted to tell Fain this but I was interrupted, which may have been a good thing. I was interrupted by the arrival of his girl friend, a beautiful small shy French girl in a shabby dress and scarf and the compulsory trench coat, no hat, a dancer in some ballet company, with enormous brown eyes like an animal's, obviously insane about Howard. He acknowledged her arrival with a grunt, didn't get up or pull out her chair. But he bought her a couple of brandies, and our conversation languished. After a while they went off together, and if the looks she kept casting at him meant anything, it was for a long night's exercise of making the beast with two backs.

Well, there you are, Jeanne. I'm writing this letter after scrawling four thousand red-hot words of *Horne*. Went to work right after I got back from the café, didn't even lie down for a nap, just wrote as if all the devils in hell had broken out and were after me. The sun has long since come up. The city looks lovely today from my hotel window, all like a soft etching printed in blue ink, the Paris I once knew from reading about it and seeing pictures of it. But I want no part of it. I want to flee Europe, and go back and bury myself in the most American town in America—St. Louis, Dallas, even Hovey. Paris repels me. Its final wisdom is vulgar and joyless self-indulgence, justified by a lot of learned double-talk. I mean, if all this doom chatter in the cafés is real, why do they behave as they do? They write and talk in the threatening note of the Hebrew prophets, but did Jeremiah after thundering out one of

his denunciations tank up on brandy and spend the night horsing with a ballet girl? Did Ezekiel orate about the valley of dry bones and then pull off a hell of a smart coup in Babylonian currency?

Howard tried to high-hat me at first on the assumption that I hadn't read Marx or the existentialists. I guess he took me as some kind of peasant story-monger. All my long hours on my behind in the Forty-second Street Library came in handy, and I took pleasure in rocking him with some of the Germans who haven't even been translated except in fragments. Among other things I try to keep up with the philosophical journals. I believe if you want to describe a scene at a political rally accurately you have to know what the best contemporary brains are thinking about matter and God, but that it's none of the reader's business. Howard's mistake in his second book was to fill it with existentialist talk, which is exactly like shining your spot lights into the audience's face instead of concealing them and aiming them to bathe the stage. He should have studied the big money maker of the lot, Camus, more carefully. He sure masks his lighting. You'd never know, reading L'Étranger, that this was a man who also writes dense philosophical tracts.

Jeanne, I want to tell you one thing. Put this letter away, and if I die young and fail to do my work read what follows over me instead of allowing anybody to deliver a eulogy. Howard Fain said 'they' had tried to destroy him, 'they' did not respect the creative spirit in America, he would steamroller 'them' with his big masterpiece. What I want to say is this: 'They' do not exist! Critics are only men with wives and children and dogs and mortgages, trying to get along with what skills they have. The creative gift doesn't exempt a man from the struggle of existence. It makes the struggle harsher. The man who presumes to create is setting himself above the captains and the kings. He offers himself as the voice next to God's and he must expect the severest kind of challenge. If Dickens, Balzac and Tolstoy endured this ordeal, why should Howard Fain and Arthur Hawke be spared?

I intend to give them—Howard Fain's nonexistent 'them'—one hell of a run for their money, and in fact, at this nadir, I still think I'm going to make it. Just seeing Fain depressed me. You can understand that.

One last word. I don't think we're going to lose out to the Marxist Chinese.

3

This letter came a couple of days after Karl was released from his bed by the doctor, and allowed to go back to work. Jeanne had been up very late the night before; she did not wake till ten, and Karl had already gone to the office. She read the letter over and over, alone in the small apartment, and she found herself thinking in a fairly matter-of-fact way about divorcing Karl and marrying Hawke.

The choice had only been open to her for a short while. When Hawke had first proposed to her in Lexington, he had been wholly tangled with Frieda. She had confronted Frieda over the delirious author's bed on

the wild crisis night of his pneumonia. She still found it hard to believe that he had shaken Mrs. Winter off for good. But she could no longer deny that he intended to and was trying to. If ever she was going to rally to him, now was probably the time. He had always been in love with her, but now he knew it, and now he wanted nobody but her. She was ready to believe all this at last, and it filled her with hope so extravagant, so shot through with rainbows, that she had to exert strong will power to keep a grip on herself.

Jeanne wondered how other women went about divorcing their husbands. For her it was an unnatural, almost an unimaginable act. If Hawke had ever forced her to come to bed with him, that would probably have solved the matter, she thought. To prove she was not a whore, if nothing else, her one course would have been to give up the man she had betrayed and do her best to marry the man who had prevailed with her. But in her present situation, she could not picture herself calmly announcing to Karl that she was through with him and was going to Hawke. That meant reneging in cold blood on the most serious commitment of her life. Moreover, she was still extremely fond of Karl—one does not shrug off years of married intimacy—and she knew he needed her, perhaps in order to survive at all, certainly to continue in his career. She was in a worse knot with Karl Fry than Hawke had ever been with Frieda; and she did not yet see how she could extricate herself. But after this letter of Hawke's, a large part of Jeanne Fry's daytime thoughts began to go to the question of cancelling three years of her life and starting over with Arthur Hawke.

Then another letter came. Hawke was bubbling again, the book was roaring along, and he took back everything he had said about Paris. It was a city of pure enchantment, the fairyland of the civilized world, and the French were an elegant and admirable people, a little reserved but soaked through with culture and wisdom.

It was just Fain and that disgusting trench coat café crowd that put me off. I should have remembered that Balzac described the scribbling rabble of Paris in *Lost Illusions* once for all. They haven't changed an iota, they've just found a few new rubber words and ideas to stretch and bounce and play with and try to pass off as creative thought. And they've put on trench coats. But I've since met some ordinary Parisians and some genuine aristocrats, and believe me they're all wonderful.

Honor and Manuel Hauptmann, it appeared, had come to Paris and taken Hawke in tow again, and the aspect of the city had quite changed.

Also the author had had a satisfying meeting with his French publisher; satisfying because he had crushed the editor-in-chief, a gray and bitter-faced little man, himself a novelist, and obviously used to making other novelists crawl. The three men had met in the publisher's office, a

minute cubbyhole in a sort of blind alley full of bookshops and publishers' signs. The editor had opened the meeting by saying that *Chain of Command* would have to be revised for the French reader. He had proceeded for ten minutes to describe the plot and character changes he demanded.

I didn't say a word till he was finished, Jeanne. Then I just turned to the publisher and told him that I was convinced the book wasn't publishable by these high standards and so I was withdrawing it and would offer it to some other house. The publisher—a genteel little millionaire who must publish as a hobby, he owns a big château we visited later—turned on the editor and spat out a short burst of French that I couldn't follow. The effect, however, was quite visible. The editor curled up and I'd swear he charred all over. The publisher and I then went to lunch at Le Tour d'Argent, leaving this editor in his chair, a crumpled cinder with staring eyes, and a cigarette burning in paralyzed fingers. This little incident, you'll understand, in itself reconciled me to Paris. The city's been getting better and better ever since.

However, Hawke wrote, he was beginning to feel the strain of living as a tourist and also writing full-time. He was having trouble falling asleep and his headaches were coming back; so he was cutting his Paris stay short and returning to England to look for quarters somewhere in the countryside. He was also getting a little tired of the Hauptmanns.

I wasn't born sociable. I'm aware that my manners are crude. When I'm in high-toned company I'm always working at it. I mean *working*. I perspire. It usually crosses my mind at some point in an evening that I really don't give a good goddamn *what* Madame de Snootvisage, descended from one of the finest French families and living in a cold elaborate Parisian town house, thinks of Monsieur Auk. (That's me.) I get tired of constantly translating my small talk into stumbling French that obliterates whatever little point I'm making. And I remind myself that all these people, Honor Hauptmann included, are bothering with the big ape Art Hawke from Hovey not because he can wear clothes with an air, or exchange persiflage out of a Marivaux play, but because the coarse sweaty vulgarian writes big books that sell lots of copies, and that for all they know may even be art, since Monsieur Auk has won *le prix Pulitzer*. Then I tell myself it's high time I got my tail out of Paris and into some quiet place where I don't have to work at making myself understood, and where I can finish this endless stupid *Horne* and get on to a really good book.

So yo ho for the white cliffs of Dover. If you don't hear from me for a while I'll be roaming England looking for a place to hole up.

I need a conference with you badly.

Your loving,
MONSIEUR AUK.

She did not hear from him for several weeks after that, weeks that were momentous in her life. To any outer view, even to her husband's, Jeanne Fry was going about her business as always. Within her spirit,

however, all was hurricane, earthquake, and tidal wave. She decided that she was going to set her affairs at Hodge Hathaway in order, and then cross the ocean to join Hawke. Once with him she was going to offer to marry him; she was going to put herself wholly in his hands, for better or worse. The decision did not fill her with happiness; fears, doubts, and conscience pangs haunted her, and she spent more nights without closing her eyes than Karl knew. Nevertheless the decision was taken, and she was sure it was irrevocable. But before she even received another letter from Hawke, the one thing that she utterly failed to anticipate—that she no more expected than the arrival of the Messiah in the middle of a business day—happened. She found that she was pregnant.

Like most young women before the first pregnancy, she had had her fears that there might be something wrong with her. The barrenness of her marriage, however, she had been inclined to ascribe to Karl, though he had had children. Jeanne had—somehow—never cared enough about her childlessness to make any medical investigation, or perhaps she had been afraid to. Nor had Karl pressed the matter. They had scarcely spoken of it. Karl was fond of saying that a successful marriage rested on seven pillars of silence, or words to that effect, and his reticence in such things amounted to a blackout. But when a man and woman live together in marriage, whether on terms of great love, or mutual fondness, or mere inertia, they will find themselves in the same bed; and if this part of Jeanne's marriage was not something she set great store by, she had of course accepted it. Nothing had resulted from it for three years. Now nature had worked its most commonplace and least understandable wonder with Jeanne, and she was pregnant.

Her decision to go to Hawke was blasted to atoms by the first words that the doctor spoke on the telephone, reporting the results of the test. It was as though she had been wakened from a sweet dream by a clap of thunder. She was all Mrs. Karl Fry again when she hung up the receiver; Mrs. Karl Fry, dazedly starting to make plans for having her baby.

4

The Mulberries
Haworth, Yorkshire,
England.
January the first, 1951
12:03 A.M.

Dearest Jeanie:

Happy New Year to you and yours, including that little unborn rascal who has loused up what was once a good working relationship. I'm glad to hear that everything is going normally so far. It will all go normally to the last, so stop worrying. There are more than two billion people in the world, Jeanne.

You have every reason to believe that this curious process works. There aren't enough able-bodied storks around to justify the other theory.

I wasn't going to write you tonight. I didn't want to burden you with my blue johnnies. But do you know what just happened? I wrote "1951" in the middle of a blank page in my diary, at the stroke of midnight, just when the church clock finished the twelfth "clong." I turned the page to start the first entry of the new year, and the page tore completely in half in my hand!! Now this is a damned dirty practical joke for a supposedly meaningless universe to play on a superstitious mountain boy, all alone in an old house four thousand miles from home, in a roaring snowstorm. It finished me for diary writing, and I'm afraid you're for it, my love. However, you get paid to put up with me.

I've been making a wretched mistake in the past two days, Jeanie, I've been reading *Will Horne*. I know I should have waited to hear from you about the last hundred and fifty pages, but the stuff came from the typist, and there was the whole pile, and I couldn't resist. I started at page one and read my new novel.

Jeanie, is *Will Horne* a publishable book? If you were ever honest in your life I want you to be honest this time. I know there are good parts in it—I have powers, and they haven't quite deserted me—but isn't the whole thing a catastrophic botch? Is it *alive?* Is it *endurable?* Who is going to read a thick book about an ice-cold scheming bastard like Willard W. Horne? I guess I never realized, in the middle of all that long drudgery, the full monstrosity of this man I've called out of nowhere to go through the antics of a political career. If the portrait isn't truthful then I can't write, and I may as well give up. I think it's all true. The fatal mistake I seem to have made at the very start was to imagine you could write a long book about a leper. You can, of course. You can write a book about anything. But why should an intelligent person slog through a novel about a thoroughly dastardly subject? Jeanie, tell me the truth.

The only sequence that seems really well managed to me is the investigation of the highway contract. It says everything that has to be said about a man like Will Horne. It has a beginning, a middle, and an end. Maybe I should just lift that out and publish it, a short study in corruption like *Death in Venice*. Tell me the truth, Jeanie. I will not say another word in this letter about the sprawling unreadable horror called *Will Horne*.

My low spirits are not due to that alone. I have on my desk a very long letter from a rather well-known New York woman by the name of Frieda Winter. I'm sure you've seen her name in the columns. She does a little of everything in the arts, including sympathetic encouragement of young writers. This is the first word I've had from the lady (whom I once knew slightly) in a half a year or so. She wrote it on Christmas Day in the morning. Christmas Day, I must tell you, had in the past some slight sentimental association for Mrs. Winter and myself. Mrs. Winter writes very vividly and persuasively. If by any chance you read in the New York papers that she has killed herself—I imagine the suicide of such an eminent lady would rate some newspaper space—please send me the clippings, as I will be interested in the details, for old times' sake. However, I imagine you will read that she has been seen as usual at various concerts, first-nights, charity balls, and the like, having a high old time. Mrs.

Winter is a lady who has been far too careful in the construction of her life, and in the planning of her pleasures, to shuffle off this mortal coil on a sentimental impulse, even on Christmas Day in the morning. Please understand me, she didn't threaten suicide, she's too subtle for that. I believe I was supposed to read her last farewell between the lines, and telephone her or cable her or hop a plane home or all three. I did nothing. I would lay a reasonably large sum that she is alive and well. I can be coarsely facetious about it to you, but her letter gave me a frightful couple of nights; nights in which I am sure she had eight full hours of refreshing and undisturbed slumber. The real hell of it is that I haven't forgotten Frieda and that I'll never forget her, although I hope to God I'll find a love some day, some how, that will transform the thought of Mrs. Winter from an agony to a memory. You could have done it, but you're too busy having Karl's babies, and I can't blame you. I am no great bargain.

I'm not likely to find this love in Haworth (pronounced Horth, in case I never told you). My monkish regime continues, nor are the village maidens apt to upset it. When I go up to London, as I do occasionally, I buy the books or clothes I need, see a couple of shows, and retreat hastily to Haworth, leaving the temptations of the great city untasted. It reminds me too much of New York.

Haworth is the discovery of my life. I wonder whether I could get away with ending my days here? I really think I'd like to buy this old place I'm renting— it belongs to some admiral's widow who lives in Majorca and I'm sure I could get it for about fifteen thousand dollars—and just stay on and on in this gnarled, hilly, small Yorkshire town where two great novelists once lived as a pair of old maid sisters in a tiny parsonage. I can't tell you what fascinates me so about this place. It isn't just the Brontës, though I'll admit I hang around that dollhouse parsonage and the graveyard like a ghost. There's something about the moors, and the deep green pastures with the black stone fences, and the distant mountains—it has a little of the feeling of Hovey. But the people are not Hovey people, thank Heaven. It's as though they had a tradition of the proper way to treat novelists; which is, exactly like anyone else, with a little extra kindness because we have big egos and bad nerves. Anyway I've been able to work here like a lunatic, and I've read up whole libraries, and I've taken long walks and auto drives, and I'm getting pretty good at galloping across the moor on horseback, too. Jeanie, this is the life! My one reservation is that any woman I marry—if one will ever have me—is not likely to share my pleasure in being buried out here in the rustic English nineteenth century like this, in this horrible weather. If she doesn't want New York or Paris, she'll want the south of France, or the Italian Riviera, or some other warm place full of palm trees and idle drunken idiots, and she won't let me stay in Haworth. Will she?

Anyway, at the moment it all seems a pathetic dream. I wrote to Gus Adam to ask about the tax angle of making my home in Britain. I'm that serious about it. He sent me back a twenty-page memorandum, the nub of which was that if I don't get the hell out of England by October, I may be liable to British taxes on my royalties—and these British rates are truly backbreaking—and *American taxes TOO!* Getting credit for paying foreign taxes

is a big mess, and to be on the safe side I'm on notice to get my overgrown carcass out of England by September!

Now how about that, Jeanne?

God knows I believe in paying my fair share of the cost of maintaining civilization, particularly with all those Marxist Chinese hammering at the gates, as Howard Fain said, but doesn't it strike you that there seems to be built into existing tax systems a determination to hound writers from land to land and from one counsel of desperation to another until the last tax notice flutters down on the unresponding mud of a new grave?

But I've given this a lot of thought, and I've decided that such an impression is self-pitying nonsense. The problem is amazingly simple in essence. An artist is half an entrepreneur and half a laborer. But he's taxed as a laborer only. Nevertheless if he's lucky he makes the great gains of an entrepreneur now and then. Whenever he does, his laborer's tax rates shoot up through the roof, and he's left with little or nothing. Now you can call it an injustice and rant and rave but that's all foolishness. Writers are damned lucky to get paid at all for doing what they are forced to do anyway, out of sheer inability to do something more useful and sane.

No, it's simply a technical problem. The artist, in the tax structure, is a duck-billed platypus. He fits neatly into no category, so the decision is to cook him and eat him and otherwise ignore him. In self-defense he must figure out ways to get classified as an entrepreneur, not as a duck-billed platypus. The magic words are "capital gains." These are the earnings of an entrepreneur. The tax systems all treat them with the greatest respect and take only a polite nibble. Or nothing at all if the entrepreneur follows wise courses.

Here in the isolation of Haworth I've had the time to do some solid analysis of this problem. I am going to lick it via two routes. One concerns you and one does not. There's no better way to start the new year than to put this program for my liberation on paper. I'll dispose of the part that doesn't concern you very briefly.

You know, of course, that I've been investing in Kentucky construction ventures with an old friend named Scotty Hoag, ever since I started making money. They've all paid off, every one of them. In fact I think I told you that Scott was my physical model for Willard Horne. I used a lot of his mannerisms too. Scotty is much the same kind of jovial cool rascal, but on a smaller, milder scale. Unlike Will, Scotty is not up to deep long-planned skulduggery. My mother, bless her heart, is sure he's the greatest villain in the world, the way she's sure you're a Jew. You remember that lawsuit she kept jawing about? She sued the coal firm which Scotty more or less runs, for two million dollars, on the assumption that Scott had concocted a devilish plot to steal some land of hers and mine it. The case came to court last month, by the way, and mama got thrown out. After years of delay the whole thing was over in a couple of hours. Scott's lawyer moved for a summary judgment and got it. She never had a leg to stand on. End of mama's chimeras. For everybody but mama, that is. She's entered an appeal for a new trial, but even her own lawyer won't take the case any further, and I think she'll calm down and forget about it. Scott's been damned decent about it, he's offered her generous settlements

any number of times, but for mama it was two million or nothing, and so I guess it's nothing. Moral: one mustn't be a hog.

This lesson hasn't been lost on me. The mistake is excessive greed. One shouldn't try to dodge taxes. It can't be done. What can be done is a cool, slow, careful transformation of one's earnings from one category to another. Scotty is now starting to build a terrific shopping complex in the heart of Long Island. He calls it Paumanok Plaza, which I kind of like. Remember your Whitman? That's the old Indian name for Long Island. I've seen the plans and studied the whole financial structure and there isn't the slightest doubt that Paumanok Plaza is going to be a success. Money invested in Paumanok Plaza is going to pay off at three or four to one. Now if the *Oblivion* play is halfway as big a hit in New York as it seems to be on the road—did you see those glittery notices from New Orleans and St. Louis?—I'm going to be getting a flood of cash in 1951 and 1952. Ordinarily I would simply endorse those play royalty checks over to the U. S. Treasury. There wouldn't even be any point in cashing them, hardly. *But* if I form a corporation with Scotty to build Paumanok Plaza, and put in the play copyright in return for stock, all that money can be put to use, *and can be transformed into capital gains!* At least Scott says so, and everything he's told me has proven out right so far. I've got Gus Adams working on this right now. He seems skeptical but Scotty will convince him, I feel sure.

But I have to be severely realistic. This venture may fail. Speculation is speculation. So now I come to the second idea.

It concerns you. It's a new method for publishing my books. Right from the start I assure you that any such plan just about stands or falls on your participation. I daresay I could go on writing books without you, Jeanie. I'd hate to admit that I couldn't. But there's no reason for me to do so, any more than there is for me to start learning to write with my left hand while my right is still good.

This new plan I've worked out in a long exchange of letters with Roland Givney of the People's Library, but now please don't go throwing one of *your* fits. This is all different from that grandiose foolishness about a million dollars tax-free. He just over-reached himself that time trying to impress Youngblood Hawke. This one doesn't involve the movies. What's more our mutual friend Triple-A Adam has read the prospectus and he approves of it. He says that without question there are solid advantages in this plan and it's all legitimate. I gather from one or two remarks in your letters that you've revised your first impression of Gus A., so maybe his opinion will dispose you more kindly to the scheme. You're free to discuss it with him if you want to.

The gist of it is that a new publishing house will be formed to publish my books and also a few books by other writers, so as to eliminate any question of its being a mere tax dodge. That last wrinkle was my idea and Gus is really impressed with it and with me, he says it's the crux of the plan. I have to take a genuine financial risk, put up some real cash to finance the printing of the books. Givney will do the managing, and the stock structure will be worked out so that someone I trust, like Gus Adam, will hold the deciding vote. In effect I'll have complete control and yet it won't be a personal holding com-

pany, which is a terrible sin in our tax theology and the penance is practically every nickel you make. This plan is sound.

The result is simple to see. In addition to getting paid royalties, I'll also get most of the profits of my books! Givney will handle various real estate investments and so forth in the publishing company in such a way that the bulk of these profits will eventually come through as capital gains. When the kitty gets big enough I can either dissolve the company and take out the cash, or it may be that I'll just keep the company going as my main capital structure, a sure base of financial stability. I'm deliberately not giving you details here, I know financial talk confuses and even irritates you, but Adam will answer any questions you have.

The real problem of course is you, and Hodge Hathaway. If Ross will agree to *distribute* the books which this new company will publish, all our ways of working can remain the same. Hodge Hathaway can even design the jackets and the books as before. Gus Adam is quite clear on that point. It comes down to a percentage of the price of each book to be paid Hodge for distribution. It's not unusual for a publisher to act merely as distributor of another company's books for a flat fee. That's my proposal. If you can induce Ross to accept this idea in principle I promise you we can work out a fair deal.

If Ross balks, he had better have some excellent reasons for balking, that's all I can say. His profits on *Chain of Command* must already be close to half a million dollars. He'll have to yield some of the fat from my new books under this plan, true. But Givney tells me that the distributor fees are always put high enough in these set-ups so that everybody does well. I'll listen soberly to any reasonable objections Ross may have. But I'm not going to have patience, I warn you, with a mere desire on his part to go on making all the profits that my books earn. The rule against being a hog has to work both ways. If he is simply intransigeant I think you should be on my side, and perhaps a little more receptive to the idea of leaving HH and heading the new firm.

I readily grant that a publisher takes heavy risks with an unknown writer and is entitled to extra rewards. But candidly, what risk exists on a book of mine now? Appalled as I am by the mistakes in *Horne*, and worried though I am about the whole book, I still think Ross can't possibly lose money on it, and he'll almost surely make a lot. There are entertaining and exciting scenes in it, and people are so starved for an interesting story that they'll probably read *Will Horne* no matter what the critics say about it.

But I'm not proposing to start the new company with *Horne*. I signed a contract with Ross under our old arrangement and I'll honor it. If the book is a success he'll make another killing and he will then be left without any decent reason to refuse this new arrangement on later books.

This is turning into another one of my ten-page efforts. It seems to me the typewriter's been clattering for hours, and all I started out to do was wish you a happy new year and moan a bit about *Horne* which truly does worry me, Jeanne. I'm going to be waiting anxiously for your comment.

Darling, just remember that it took Hugo eighteen years to write *Les Miserables*, and Balzac a whole lifetime to do his *Comedy*. My sober estimate of my own *Comedy* is that it will take fifteen to twenty years of steady

temperate work—about fifteen volumes, one or two years per volume. Surely you must see that I can't risk running out of money during that time, I must have *capital*, a large fund of capital (if not *quite* a million dollars) on which I can live. Royalties are meaningless, they have a horrible way of dissolving in my hands—a tax deficiency, a few extra expenses, and suddenly my back is to the wall again. I can and I must and I will put myself on a sound basis of *capital*.

The last logs in the fireplace just caved in and I'm damned if I'm going out in this snow to fetch more from the shed. I don't much like the thought of plodding upstairs and sliding between the icy sheets of the admiral's old four-poster bed, I'd much rather just sit here in this fuddy-duddy little parlor by the fireplace and go on talking to you on paper. But for now goodnight, and the best of new years, to you, and Karl, and the little one, from me and the Brontë sisters.

Tomorrow I start writing a new book. I won't get any more talented by waiting six months. The sooner I get these preliminary jobs out of the way the better. It won't be *Boone County* however. That'll come after this new one, and *Boone* will be the last book before the *Comedy*.

The new one? A surprise. I'm not talking yet. I'll tell you this. If it comes off nobody will believe that the author of big sloppy epics like *Chain of Command* and *Alms for Oblivion* could have written it.

This was a tender missive, wasn't it? All sentiment and not a breath about money. Well, that's my new year mood, and anyway you've always known I'm just an impractical dreamer.

Ever yours,
Arthur.

5

Hodge Hathaway, Inc.
660 Madison Ave.
N.Y.C.
January 28, 1951

Dear Arthur:

Taking things in the order of their importance: Your weather in "Horth" can't be worse than ours. New York is outdoing itself: snow, rain, slush, wind, hail, darkness. We are momentarily expecting blood and frogs. We all wish we were dead, and in fact we are dying off in great numbers.

The baby is all right. Mine, I mean. I am becoming enormous. I won't plague you with *my* blue johnnies, I'm more considerate than you are. I'll just tell you that I've been taken off cigarettes and liquor. You can picture the rest.

Your baby is all right too. *Will Horne*, that is. Let me remind you with just a shade of weariness that Ross Hodge, Karl, and I spent the better part of one disorderly night convincing you not to burn *Chain of Command*. Considering your deep respect for money, if not for your own narrative art and for literary prizes, I think you might agree at this point that we were right.

Arthur, the new book is excellent and it will be a very great success. Now at what length will you have your praise, by the foot, by the yard? I've told you twenty times that this book was good. The writing is deeper than in the other books. You rely less on cliff-hanging tricks and coincidences. It is almost a wholly realistic work. You've performed your usual miracle of creating a believable world out of nothing, and how you did this with politics, about which you know so little, I can't imagine, but I guess you were wise to stick to Kentucky. Anyway, the book is more than alive and convincing. It is hallucinatory.

As you know, I am not a passionate advocate of pure realism. When I first made the immortally unlucky comparison of your work to O. Henry's—which I believe ended all hope of true love between us—I meant it as a compliment. I think a novel or play begins as entertainment, and only beyond that should carry what wisdom or poetry the writer is capable of. This has been the rule of the masters up to Shakespeare and Dostoevsky. *Lear* and *Karamazov* are in the first instance amusements. I don't believe one bit in "serious writing" as the current pundits define it; that is, as writing untainted by the intent to amuse. I think this definition of serious writing was developed by thoughtful and solemn folks who wanted to put their thoughts into the glamorous forms of novels and plays but lacked the power to entertain. While it may comfort them, this silly distortion has never touched the common reader at all, and thank Heaven you remain impenetrable to it. Under the realistic surface *Will Horne* has several legendary characters in a yarn that gathers weight and power like a train rushing downhill. I agree that the highway investigation is the most fascinating part—in fact I think you'll probably lift it out and make a play of it—but it's also the nearest thing to your first vein of slam-bang dramatics, it's a lot like Aunt Bertha's death, and the young crippled senator who beats Will is a little too good to be true. It doesn't matter at all, though.

Will himself is far from a leper! If he's a leper then America is one big leprosarium, Arthur. Who hasn't encountered Will Horne, in publishing, or in the army, or in the textile business, or in any walk of American life? Why, the man who is out to get his, and to hell with anyone else, is the essential American hero; remember the slogan, "free enterprise?" We believe, rightly or wrongly, that all the uninhibited individual pushing adds up to one big push that is more productive than a five-year-plan pushed from above at bayonet point. Of course Will goes over the red line. He's a crook, and most Americans aren't crooks. Being a crook he gets caught, which is also true, they mostly do get caught. His destruction is satisfying, as is also his rather satanic courage as his star falls. You yourself *admire* Will, Arthur. I fear we all do. Maybe that's a flaw in our way of life.

But the point is, if you get assaulted for this book, and you almost surely will be, I imagine they'll complain that you've made him too attractive, and that you've portrayed our politics as a sewer of selfish power plays without becoming sufficiently indignant about it. The little magazines are going to scold at you worse than ever, of course. They will till you die, for your unspeakable crime of having the power to entertain. However, I also think some of the judicious heavyweights may roll over you. You're due for it, Fain was

right about that, and you're too candid in this one and not preachy enough. Moreover your portrayal of the adultery is far too sympathetic. There, if I may say so, *I* don't too much like what you've done, but let's not go into that, hey dear?

In short, if you want reassurance, here it is. The book is in every way worthy of you. It may well turn out to be a durable work (we'll know for sure when we're all dead). Meantime it is without question going to sell like a son of a bitch—as I believe Charlotte Brontë said to Emily about *Wuthering Heights*.

Under separate cover you'll get a mass of comments I've been dictating for a week. As usual, you can throw most of them out, but I'll fight for the ones I've double-starred.

I wish I could be as enthusiastic and as reassuring about the rest of your New Year's communication.

Just to make the business part clear first: Ross is willing to do as you ask. He isn't pleased to death over it, naturally. We had a four-way meeting: Ross, Givney, Adam, and myself: day before yesterday. I was waiting for the result of that meeting before answering you. Ross and Givney have to work out a great many details, and above all they still have to settle on the distribution figure, before the thing can go forward. But you asked for Ross's agreement in principle. You've got it.

Therefore, still talking business, you've got mine too, since I just work here and take Ross Hodge's orders.

But if I were your wife instead of your editor, I'm damned if you would have my agreement. You would be having hell at home. You would be getting cold coffee and overdone chops, there would be frost in the bedroom, there would be crabbing and complaining such as you've never heard, you would not be able to find your shirts and socks and I wouldn't help you, and when you found them they'd be overstarched or mismatched, and I'd lie awake nights thinking of new ways to make you wish you'd never seen me.

You sneer at your mother. Does it never occur to you that you're worse? She never had any hope of riches except in her silly coal land. You've been granted the privilege of living by art. Nothing will do but you must also make a killing in Long Island real estate, and publish your own books, and master the stock market—and what else, in God's name, what else?

Gus Adam showed me the letter on Givney he sent you. What happens to you when you read such letters? Do you put on special glasses that let through only the sentences that suit you? He did say that Givney's plan had tax advantages and would probably survive a test at law. He also spent an *entire page* telling you that in his judgment you ran the risk of losing more than you gained, because involvement in business might slow or stop your work. He pointed out that the money risks you would undertake would be all too real and serious.

As for Paumanok Plaza, he says it's a speculation for professionals, that the liabilities can run into the millions. He did also say—I'm willing to be more candid than you—that the prospectus seems well thought out and can be fabulously profitable. Nevertheless you're *not* a builder, are you? If you go into it, it's nothing more or less than a confidence transaction. Your

confidence in this man Hoag is based on the fact that you've made money in several of his ventures. Does luck in real estate always run one way? This is a man, after all, who's just defeated your mother in a lawsuit. I consider it highly ominous that he was your model for Willard Horne. I trust your unconscious creative intelligence much more than I do your daylight judgment.

Your letter was a real blow to me, a worse blow than you can imagine. I was beginning to have such high hopes! The trip to Europe seemed to have worked on you like penicillin, clearing away all the febrile follies that had infected you in New York, restoring your strength and your will power. You seemed to be making a real second start in life. Your rate of production on the last half of the novel was, even for you, incredible, and—as you could tell by the drop-off in my memoranda—your discipline and control actually improved even at that speed. I believed, and I still believe, your reports of your new monkish ways. It's impossible for me to tell you what an effect *that* has had on me. Perhaps you can guess. I may be a bloated pregnant monster but I still have my feelings. Arthur, it was all so promising—so wonderful!—and then came your damned letter!—this catastrophic relapse into what I can only call your money malaria. I hope with all my heart that you're going to think better of all this. Maybe your new year's letter was just a mood. God knows that night was a morbid one for me too. If I'd sat up writing you a letter, and if I'd mailed it, it would have jolted you much more than your letter did me. I think it would have jolted you more than Frieda's letter did.

As you see, I'm giving no room whatever to the possibility that these projects may prove tremendously profitable—a concession Gus Adam does make. I'm reacting like a woman.

Arthur, you will *not* go eighteen years without publishing a book, and there is *no rational basis whatever* for your desire to amass capital. If you have the desire for capital, okay, you have it, that's all. It's a common American ailment. Don't try to justify it to me with literary reasons. If you do start a huge work of fifteen volumes, the nature of that form dictates a series of stories more or less complete in themselves. Like Proust, like du Gard, like Balzac himself, you'll publish in parts. I'm not promising that those parts will have the success of your present work. There's a certain portentous solemnity about your planned *Comedy* that's always scared me, though there I may be totally wrong, I do trust your creative instinct much more than my own judgment. All I'm getting at is this: you will always have, at the very worst, enough income from your books to live on, and probably to go on living well, taxes or no taxes, providing only that you stay out of debt. Therefore I can only regard both the "Hovey Press" (Givney's idiotic latest name for your tax-dodging abortion) and Paumanok Plaza as unwarranted risks.

Well, from this cheery disquisition I turn to another equally welcome task. Quentin Judd will be arriving in the office in ten minutes and I have the pleasant task of telling him that his attempt to "put a plot" into his novel is a failure. You wouldn't believe how wooden, how trite, how shaky, how empty our thundering Jove became as soon as he tried to tell a story.

He just can't, that's all, any more than I can. My one defense against his wrath will have to be that I never encouraged him to do it. I wish I'd never touched his work, but the trouble was he kept asking for my help and I did the best I could, which wasn't much. Finally he disappeared for two months and then turned up with a finished book. The question is what to do with it now. The awful "plot" casts a pall over all the wonderful conversation and description. What he had, and what possibly I can convince him to rescue, was a sort of formless comic symposium in Hell. Hell was a luxury hotel in the Caribbean in which everybody was quarantined by an outbreak of bubonic plague—an old gambit, but the writing was golden in its brilliance, and really there were irreverent things about Marx and Freud and T. S. Eliot, about music and painting, that were priceless. As a destroyer there is no touching Quentin Judd, and his viewpoint is austere and sane if deadly cold.

I must stop. You've got me on pins and needles about your new work but I'll ask no questions. Really you're entitled to a couple of weeks at Monte Carlo or something, are you sure you don't want a breather? I hope you're not abandoning *Boone County*. That sounded like one of the big ones.

I'm supposed to report your further pleasure on "Hovey Press" (ugh) to Ross. I'm authorized to tell you that he's ready to discuss more conventional improvements in your contracts instead of that scheme. He offers to come to England to talk to you. Of course Ross's prime concern is the profits of Hodge Hathaway. I honestly think he's also worried about your getting involved in publishing. It happens that my personal feelings in the matter are all on my employer's side and against your bright ideas. You're free to believe that I'm just playing Ross's game.

Love,
JEANNE.

6

Upon receiving Jeanne's letter, Hawke stopped negotiations on both the publishing house and on Paumanok Plaza, and he invited Ross Hodge to come to England.

Hodge told Jeanne afterward that he did not recognize Hawke for a moment when the author came striding into the lobby of Claridge's, partly because his face was so ruddy and partly because he wore a British raincoat and driving cap which completely altered his appearance. But when he pulled off his cap and the hair fell into his face, there was Youngblood Hawke again, looking leaner, healthier, and much happier, though much older. Hodge said he seemed to have aged years in months. He was full of ribald jokes. His clear brown eyes sparkled. Once they were out of London, he drove his low powerful red car at maniacal speed through the misty green countryside, and kept up a boiling breathless conversation

all the way. He talked like a man who had just been found on a desert island: an exhilarated gabble of jumping questions and disconnected vehement opinions. He kept saying how glad he was to see Hodge, and a dozen times he jarred the publisher with slaps on the back. He pestered Hodge for the smallest details of Jeanne's pregnancy, and of the work she was doing. When Hodge told him that Quentin Judd had taken his book to another publisher in a great huff, Hawke roared with laughter. All his reactions were excessive. He was very angry, very amused, very depressed, very excited, by turns, and he seemed never to run out of breath or words.

England was an old story to Hodge, and he was hard put to it to share Hawke's towering enthusiasm for the lukewarm ale and heavy bread and cheese which was their lunch in an old inn on the road outside Nottingham. Hodge had little appetite; his stomach was in a hard ball because of Hawke's driving, and he took his seat in the car again with dread, the more so because of the four pots of ale Hawke had tossed off. Their effect was not to slow the writer down; if anything he swept around the trucks on the winding two-lane road with even more exuberance, never pausing in his rattling description of Howard Fain, or the house he was living in, or his opinion of the current best-seller. Once when Hodge mildly protested, he explained that he had a sixth sense for this kind of thing, developed in his years of driving coal trucks on the Hovey road, and that Hodge was as safe as if he were asleep in a hotel in London. For a fact, he got into no narrow misses, though trucks came roaring the other way every few minutes.

Hawke raved so much about the charm, beauty, and comfort of "The Mulberries," the house he was renting in Haworth, that the place was a real disappointment to the publisher when at last they arrived. It was a small old gray stone house, surrounded by a moss-crusted black stone fence about eight feet high, which enclosed a small garden containing half a dozen tall old trees. The ceilings in the house were oppressively low. The tall author hardly cleared them, and he really had to stoop each time he went through a doorway. There was a dining room to one side of the worm-eaten front door, a study on the other side—both with bay windows—and a few steps then led down to a sitting room that seemed too full of old dingy furniture to admit any people. All of it was so tiny! Hawke took him upstairs to a clammy little bedroom with a sharply sloped ceiling, and left him there to wash up, cheerfully pointing to an old brass basin and pitcher. Hawke said that for some reason he slept best in a bedroom with a sloped ceiling, and he hoped Hodge would, too. As Hodge unpacked he heard the sound of an axe, and glancing out of the narrow window he saw the author in a sweater and cap chopping thick round sections of a log into firewood, in a grassy back yard where snow lay in patches. His strokes were so loose and free that Hodge half-

expected him to cut a foot off, but the axe hit true each time and the wood splintered clean.

It occurred to Hodge, as he watched Hawke, that "The Mulberries," at least the interior, remarkably resembled Jeanne Fry's description of Mrs. Hawke's old house on High Street in Hovey. Moreover Hawke's house-keeper turned out not too unlike his mother in appearance, and in her surly patronizing familiar tone with the famous author. She was a Mrs. Williams, a little shapeless woman in baggy black with a green apron, and her chief characteristic beyond gray hair and a snappy manner was the falsest set of false teeth Hodge had ever seen, two perfect yellow rows like a horse's in her round wrinkled face. She kept the place clean, and the dinner she made for them had its good points; the thick peppery soup was hot, the leg of lamb was juicy and smoking, and if the vegetables were British in their sad boiled limpness, they were hot too. Hawke had taught her to make American coffee. She poured it for Hodge with a self-conscious flourish, as though she were serving a baked alaska. They had two bottles of red wine with the dinner, and afterward they had brandy by the log fire in the sitting room—not without some grumbling by Mrs. Williams, as she brought them more coffee, that burning wood in a coal grate was a dirty, wasteful, foolish American idea—and Hodge began to see why Hawke was happy in Haworth, and in The Mulberries. Mrs. Williams' irascible and fussy presence, together with that of a huge sleepy gray tomcat, purring by the fire, completed the cosiness.

They did not talk much business that night. As Hodge reported their conversation to Jeanne, it was mostly philosophical meandering by Hawke, who stretched his length across the whole room on an armchair and foot-stool, while he smoked two enormous Havana cigars that filled the air with wreathing layers of blue-gray fog. What struck the publisher most was the strange detachment with which Hawke spoke of himself. He was well aware, he said, that he had stumbled on a dream retreat in The Mulberries which couldn't last. Tax problems or some other disturbance would force him out soon enough, and all he hoped was that he could stay long enough to finish the new book, about which he would say nothing. Hodge did not press him. Instead he gave him in detail the cheerful news of the advance orders for *Will Horne* and the enthusiastic comments of the salesmen and book dealers who had read the mimeographed promotion copies. The book clearly was going to be another best-seller. Hodge ventured to say that it was Hawke's best work so far. The author listened, nodding and smiling in a melancholy way. He warned Hodge that the book would get a bad reception by the critics, and he proceeded to offer him consolation as though the event had already occurred, and as though their roles were completely reversed.

Hodge would have to remember when the bad notices came, Hawke said, that the literary life resembled politics, that at bottom it was a con-

test of gifted men for popular favor and perhaps for a name in history; and that every bid for high place, such as he was making, had to call forth strong counterattacks. It was an inevitable process, and it was wisely ordered, for many men could write well and only violent opposition could narrow the field down to the best ones. Having broken into public notice with *Chain of Command,* he now had to undergo the assaults aimed at a candidate in the heat of an election. All his faults would be stated forcibly, and overstated too. Perhaps they were enough to eliminate him. His own idea was that *Will Horne,* though it represented two years of the heaviest work, was merely one of his last technical exercises, and would not count in the final verdict on his main work, which lay far in the future. If it turned out a financial success, so much the better, but Hodge ought not to hope for anything more.

All this was strange stuff coming from an author not yet thirty-two years old, and the autumnal serenity with which Hawke delivered it made an unbelievable contrast to his bouncing, boyish manner during the drive to Haworth. Hodge had known dozens of authors, most of them unimportant, a few eminent. Hawke had much in common with all writers, but there was something different about him too, something that had always put off Hodge and even awed him a little. It was a subtle remoteness, a thick cloak of solitude that he seemed never to cast off even at a party, even when he was drunk and chattering; and tonight, as he talked in this quiet slow way, his face settled into the drawn, mature lines of a man past forty-five, and his remoteness somehow filled Hodge with a sadness and a foreboding that had little to do with the prospect of bad notices for *Will Horne.* The publisher slept poorly that night in the chilly slope-ceilinged bedroom.

The next day when Hodge came downstairs at seven he found Hawke at work in the tiny smoke-filled study, slouched in an armchair with a writing pad on a purple wool comforter spread over his knees. The author said he would be finished at eleven. Hodge ate Mrs. Williams' eggs and kippers alone at the polished old oak table, and then he went out in the cold mist and wandered uphill through the small town, coming at last on the Brontë parsonage. An old lady posted there as a guide sold him a brochure and took him through the house, which was rather like The Mulberries, except that all the furniture was very old and the place had the false neatness and the empty frigidity of a human dwelling turned museum. He mentioned that he was Hawke's publisher and the old lady said, "Ah, yes, our American writer. He comes here often. He doesn't write much like the Brontës, does he?"

After lunch the two men got down to business, sitting by the fire while rain poured outside. Hawke seemed animated and young again—sharp,

even playful as he cross-examined Hodge. The publisher was astonished at the knowledge that Hawke had picked up. He knew to the penny the likely breakdown of costs of a five-dollar book: plates, paper, binding, publisher's overhead, advertising, jobber's markup, booksellers' markup, and percentages to be saved by large printings. He talked like a man of business, and was equal to any turn in the conversation. Hodge conceded early that the author would make more money under the Givney scheme than in any royalty contract a publisher could offer him. He had come prepared to dispute this with some equivocal statistics, but Hawke was too knowledgeable, and Hodge soon decided that his one hope lay in candor.

So he came out with the proposal which he had crossed the Atlantic to be able to make face to face. It was an offer to subsidize Hawke for fifteen or twenty years by paying a tremendous advance against all his future work in guaranteed annual installments, something like twenty-five thousand dollars a year. The striking feature of the offer was an absence of any proviso compelling Hawke to produce books. It was possible for Hawke to sign this contract, live in idle ease while it ran, and never bring anything to the publisher to print; the one limit was that what he did write during those years, only Hodge Hathaway would publish. Hodge said he believed Hawke was a dedicated writer and so the company ran no risk of his failing to write books; and they were willing to gamble that his production during the years of the contract would earn back the immense advance. The offer included generous royalty percentages and an unprecedented split of income from subsidiary rights. Hodge said he knew of no contract to equal it in the field of American publishing. He added that he would negotiate the details, including the total sum of the advance, with Ferdie Lax, if Hawke preferred; he was also prepared to work out the contract with the author himself now, and to execute it at once. Summing up, Hodge said that this was a frank bid to shut out once for all attempts like Givney's to capture Youngblood Hawke away from his firm. He was basing the proposal on Jeanne's information that Hawke planned an extremely long work, and wanted freedom from money problems while writing it.

Hodge was a rich and a busy man, and he had not flown to England to make chit-chat with his author; he had come to stun him. Hawke was stunned. The casual, humorous assurance he had displayed in their first sparring gave way to sober attention, then to open surprise, as the publisher talked on. When he finished the author sat for a long while in silence, looking youthful, confused, flattered, and at a loss. At last he said, "Well, Ross, you do seem to think Ah kin raht novels."

Hodge said, "I have very little doubt that you can write lasting novels. I think possibly you've already written one or two. For the purposes of

this conversation, however, the point is that I think your books can make a lot of money. If you publish them yourself it may be that you'll pull more cash out of each book. I myself think that you'll write fewer and poorer books, though."

"The goose and the golden eggs," Hawke said.

"That's exactly it. I'm backing that judgment with this offer. It's all I can do."

Hawke said, after a pause, "Ah'll have to think it over. Ah'm sure grateful to you, Ross. It's one hell of an offer . . . hey, the rain's quit, hasn't it? Let's walk out on the moor. Ah'll give you some overshoes. It's mucky as hell out there."

He said no more about the proposal that day, nor did he refer to it at dinner, nor thereafter during the long evening. But his manner was so warm and cordial that Hodge went to bed convinced that he had gained his aim. Next morning Hawke insisted on driving him down to the London airport, though Hodge tried to avoid another hair-raising ride by saying he didn't want to interfere with the author's work. Hawke said not a word about business on the way. He talked aimlessly about books and plays.

At the airport, when the loudspeakers announced Hodge's flight, and the publisher was loading himself with his hand luggage, Hawke asked him whether he had seen Frieda Winter at all in recent months. Hodge said that he had encountered Mrs. Winter at the theatre, and perhaps at a party, he was not sure; but yes, he had seen her several times.

"How does she look?" Hawke asked.

"Just the same. In fact very well."

"No doubt," Hawke said.

They managed a cumbrous handshake, and then the author suddenly threw his arms around Hodge. "Thanks for coming, Ross. One way or another, you'll go on publishing my books," he said.

"I hope so, Arthur," Hodge said. "You'll make money for us under almost any arrangement. And if you'll believe me, publishing your work is my first source of pride these days, and I think it may be my one eventual claim to fame."

Hawke grinned at him like a farm hand of seventeen, and he said, "Now, hell, Ross, you *know* all you and Ah care about is the money. You give Jeanne all my love, now."

And so Hodge flew back to the United States.

7

These are extracts from a letter Hawke wrote to Jeanne about three weeks later:

. . . I don't understand Ross's disappointment at my unwillingness to sign right now. I've stated my gratitude and my interest. I don't think he could have made a better offer. It has certain limitations, though. His proposal is a sort of mammoth fellowship, isn't it? It'll expire when I'm about fifty. A project like Givney's for amassing capital would also provide for my old age, which this doesn't do at all. Maybe you think I'm an idiot to be worrying about my old age at thirty-two. But Ross's contract would tie up the main body of my work in my best years. It's true that if the books earn more than the "fellowship" I get the surplus too, but I get it as ordinary income, and it'll melt away as usual like snow on a hot stove; not to mention that twenty years from now the taxes will probably be even higher. However, Ross's argument about the goose and the golden eggs, together with your implacable opposition, have given me great pause, and so I've decided to do nothing for a while. That's a victory for Ross, whether he thinks so or not . . .

. . . I'm sombrely pleased that the book club wants *Horne*. Your cable was a bit too ecstatic, however, and you'll have to forgive me for not shooting back a thrilled acceptance. You must realize that a club cuts the royalty for the author on each copy to a few cents. The guarantee sounds big, but that's because they send out such a huge number of books. In effect a book club selection is nothing but a big cut-rate remaindering by mail at the start of a book's run instead of at the end, accompanied by a lot of hoopla. It's main value is not the money they pay but the sprinkling of the book all over the country, so that talk starts up. The life or death of a book is not in criticism but in talk, Jeanie; in the slight passing comments over cocktails and at dinner tables, to fill up pauses in the chatter. I think they'll tell each other to read it, so let's go ahead with the book club.

I've been wondering how Emily and Charlotte Brontë would have fared in the America of the 1950s, where art means big money, where the airy dreams of the storyteller are rolled out on colossal presses and rushed by the freight car load all over a continent, and turned into queer shadow plays called films that earn millions of dollars, and at last cascaded down into cheap editions that sell in the tons. Of course those girls could never have existed now, they were forced growths whose essential nourishment was utter isolation. That isolation exists nowhere in the United States, not even in Hovey. I'm afraid Charlotte would have been one of those social workers with no makeup on and Emily—well, nothing good would have come of Emily. I guess the big Victorians like Dickens and Trollope would have been right at home, they just would have raked in the dough on an even larger scale than they did then. I've done a great amount of reading of authors' letters recently. It's amazing how the artiest of them—I mean George Elliot, Joyce, V. Woolf,

and of course *any* Frenchman—write about almost nothing but money. It makes me less self-conscious about these grubby epistles I keep sending you. I don't have to prove in my letters, any more than they did, that my heart's blood is in art, such as I can achieve. My stories prove that; or they prove that I'm a barren entertainer, if the opposition is right, as it may well be.

Good news: the new book's rolling, and I think I'll have something for you to see soon. I feel wonderful, and Jeanne, April in England is an enchantment that does much to explain how Shakespeare came to exist. You walk down a green English lane on a sunny April morning after a shower, and you see the yellow flowers and hear the bird songs and you feel that if you rush straight home and do a solid afternoon's work you'll write Romeo and Juliet. It's a delusion, but only because you lack the powers. He had them, and he had this land to inspire him. I don't think the United States will ever inspire anything important but novels—at the high reach, slapdash bursts of greatness like *Huckleberry Finn* and *An American Tragedy*, things like that. We'll never have poetry; we're a prose civilization. Whitman merely wrote prose faked up into poetry. My housekeeper speaks more natural poetry in a day than any American ever wrote. You can tell Karl I said so. I like his satiric things, but the serious stuff that he and the other Americans are writing is jagged dry bony nonsense, because they can't draw any poetry out of the ground they're walking on. "Hog butcher to the world" indeed!

> . . . the isle is full of noises,
> Sounds and sweet airs, that give delight and hurt not . . .

That's England.

. . . The revenooers are after me again. It seems that when Ferdie Lax sold *Chain of Command* to the movies, his lawyer wrote a very unfortunate clause into the contract which enabled me to collect all the installment payments in one year if I wanted to. He was only trying to protect me, his claim now is. The Feds say that means I really got the whole sum in 1949, and so I owe them some eighty thousand dollars, plus interest!

Adam is very gloomy about this, though he's going to fight it. Ferdie Lax came through here last week, on his way to try to get Thomas Mann to write a movie based on the Book of Esther. Mann's holed up in Switzerland, very sick, but of course Ferdie will get into the oxygen tent with him if the deal is big enough. Ferdie acknowledges that my contract was badly drawn and he's since gotten another lawyer. I'm not even surprised at this new plague, let alone upset. I believe flaws will eventually be found in everything I did before I met canny Gus A., and like Joe Louis I'll end up owing the government a staggering fortune, just one more country boy who stumbled into the big money overnight by using his fists or his pen, and piled up an obligation almost as big as a steel company's while still glorying in being able to own three suits. I guess they'll get around to protecting such innocents some day, but not in time to redeem my follies. All the more reason for me to go the way of Paumanok and Givney. But I'm still thinking about that . . .

I suppose the worst news from your point of view—and mine—is that Frieda Winter has risen from the past, and is most eager to rejoin me. She's

coming to France on business, she says, in July, and can't we meet again, for old times' sake? Her approach is quite worthy of her. She says all she is now is a dried-up old woman, the emotions and tensions between us are burned out, and why shouldn't we be great friends? I can only tell you that the one thing that could force me to leave England tomorrow would be the prospect of seeing Frieda. I don't believe a word of what she says. If you suddenly hear that I've enlisted in the Navy again and gone to Korea—a plunge that tempts me on many a drizzly afternoon when I read over the pages I've written— you'll know it's because I decided there was no other sure way to dodge Mrs. Winter . . .

8

Jeanne was sitting up in bed having her breakfast, a bit of pampering to which she was no longer entitled, for her baby son was a month old. She was perfectly well; had in fact been going to the office for over a week. But she had gotten used to this luxury, and was determined not to forego it. It was a quarter past nine. The baby, Jim, gurgled and snorted idiotically in the bassinet near her bed, waving his arms and legs. Jeanne had gone through the mail—no letter from Hawke—had poured her first steaming cup of coffee, and was opening the New York *News* with relish to the spicy fourth page. The *Times* lay chastely beside the bed tray, with no headline wider than one column; no new international horror, then, to absorb with sick heart and short breath; she would in due course read the *Times* through, after coffee and eggs. On the whole Jeanne Fry was about as happy as she had ever been.

She recognized Hawke's picture at once, but it was such a shock to see it on that fatal page that she blinked stupidly for several seconds before her mind took in the headline underneath:

*PULITZER PRIZE NOVELIST
ARRESTED IN VENICE*

The picture was a standard Hodge Hathaway publicity photo. The story, she noticed with dismay, came from a wire service.

Arthur Youngblood Hawke, 32, famous author of the Pulitzer Prize novel *Chain of Command*, as well as the current controversial best seller *Will Horne* and other works, was arrested by the Venice police late last night on a charge of disturbing the peace and wilfully damaging property.

The complaint was lodged against the novelist by William Quint, American proprietor of the Expatriates Bar, a popular café frequented by American tourists. Quint charged that Hawke created a violent scene that drove patrons from his bar. According to Quint, the six-foot-two author, a native of eastern Kentucky, broke several articles of furniture and a large mirror,

threatened the proprietor and a Negro pianist appearing at the café with bodily harm, and threw two lightweight pianos into the canal.

Hawke admitted the charges and declared to the police that he was willing to pay for the damages he had caused. He offered no explanation for his disorderly conduct. The police record indicated that Mr. Hawke was sober when arrested. He was released without bail when surety for his appearance in court was given over the telephone by a prominent Venetian official who was not publicly identified. The author then returned to the Royal Danieli hotel, where he refused to speak to reporters, and cut off his telephone.

Inquiry among patrons of the bar brought out conflicting stories. One version was that an altercation had arisen between Hawke and the pianist over a woman, but this could not be confirmed.

Youngblood Hawke blazed to prominence five years ago with his first novel, *Alms for Oblivion*, a long turbulent book written in his early twenties while he was a Seabee in the Pacific during World War II. His dramatization of this novel, which is due to open in two weeks in New York, has been enjoying a triumphal road tour. At the same time his latest novel—

The telephone rang. It was Ross Hodge; he had just come to his office and found the clipping on his desk, and he wanted to know if Jeanne had any further information. They decided to put a call through to Hawke immediately. Hodge asked Jeanne to do this and report back to him.

Jeanne was only half dressed when the long insistent rings of the overseas operator brought her scampering from the bathroom, and also unluckily roused up the dozing Jim, who decided he was hungry again and began roaring. Jeanne could not hear a word on the phone until the nurse hurriedly hauled Jim off to Karl's room and shut the door. The muffled cries continued.

Hawke's voice was clear and loud. "I'm asking you who's calling me from overseas?"

An Italian operator gabbled in broken English. Jeanne struck in and shouted, "Arthur, it's me, it's Jeanne."

"Jeanie! Hi! All right, operator, I'll take the call, get off the line please . . . Jeanie, how are you, darling? To what do I owe this honor?"

"Arthur, are you all right?"

"All right? Why, I'm fine. You never saw such a disciplined artist. I'm sitting here scrawling silly yellow pages, the sun's getting low over the lagoon outside and all the tourists are sliding by in gondolas. What makes you think I'm not all right?"

"That bar fight you got into, the police—"

She heard him burst out laughing. "Ye gods, how do you know about that? That was nothing, it happened night before last, it's all forgotten."

Jeanne could not help marvelling at the clarity of his voice. The beginnings and ends of his sentences were chopped off by some telephonic process, otherwise he might have been at his house on Seventy-third

Street. She said, "You're all over the New York newspapers this morning. Probably all over the country. The Associated Press got the story."

"Oh, Christ. That must have been the big red-headed woman who kept bothering me. Why, the whole thing was dropped, Jeanie. These Venetians are charming people, it was just that silly American faggot who ran the bar, he made such a soprano fuss, and my Italian is so bad, that the police ran me in before I could tell them who I was or get word to di Strozzi—that's my Italian publisher, he's here in Venice with me. As soon as he talked to the police it was all over. I never said a word to this horse-faced woman reporter who showed up, I knew better than that— Jeanie, how are you? How's Jim?"

"I'm fine. Jim's a monster, all he does is eat, sleep, yell, and throw up."

"Who does he look like?"

"He bears the most remarkable resemblance to Ross Hodge. I'm ashamed to have anyone up to look at him, and Karl's getting more irritable every day."

Hawke laughed. "God, it's wonderful to talk to you, Jeanne. Look, how important is this motherhood business? Could you get on a plane and come over here today or tomorrow, for instance? Just for a week or two?"

"Oh, Arthur, are you crazy? It's utterly impossible."

"Why? Venice is real interesting, Jeanne. It's a lot like Coney Island."

"Well, that sounds divine, but I can't leave Jim. He's howling his simple head off in the next room right now. He doesn't like anyone to feed him but me, and he eats about fourteen times a day."

"Are you breast-feeding him?"

"None of your goddamned business! Honestly! This is an idiotic conversation at twenty dollars a minute or whatever. Why did you wreck that bar? Did you really throw two pianos into the canal?"

"They were sort of miniature pianos. You could have done it, Jeanne. There was nothing to it."

"Why did you do it? What's been happening to you? Why are you in Venice, anyway? I thought you were still in Haworth."

"Didn't you get my letter from Paris?"

"I haven't had a letter in almost a month."

"Christ, I wrote you a twenty-page letter, Jeanne. I'm sure I mailed it . . . hey, you know what? I'll bet Frieda collared it. Nothing is beyond that woman, nothing."

"Frieda?" Jeanne said—feeling, after all the years, Jim or no Jim, the old old sick turning of her stomach. "Are you with Frieda Winter again, Arthur?"

"Not any more. I can't tell you the saga at twenty dollars a minute or whatever the price was you quoted. She's gone. The episode in the bar finished her, as I intended it should. We had a short wild and totally un-

satisfactory reunion, or maybe I should say the stag and the hound briefly tangled and the stag got away again, somewhat mauled and bloody. The hound has got a few antler gashes, though. I'll tell you all about it. Please come over, Jeanne. I'm just finishing the book. I'll be through in three or four days."

"It's absolutely out of the question. Why don't you come to New York for the opening night of your play, Arthur? Bring the manuscript with you. I'm dying to see it."

"I'm not interested in the play. Anyway Frieda must be in New York by now."

"Send the book to me."

"I won't let it go out of my hands, not even to you. Have there been any more of those charming reviews of Horne? Any of the magazines that failed to blast me a month ago?"

"A few more."

"All just as bad?"

"Arthur, the reviews haven't been all bad, why do you talk like that? Some of them were superb."

"Send the new ones to me."

"I won't. I shouldn't have sent you the others. You should be beyond reading reviews. You're grown up. The Times shows you number three next Sunday and the Tribune number two, but you know how slow they both are. You've been number one in the bookstores since a week before publication."

"I'm glad to hear it. Did you read Jerome Brann in the Midwestern Spectator, Jeanie? 'Anybody who buys a copy of a book by Youngblood Hawke performs an act of cultural sabotage equal to setting fire to a public library. The injury to American culture is identical.'"

"Oh, hell, Arthur, can't you let the Jerome Branns have their little tantrums in peace? How would you feel if you were Brann and saw one copy of your new book stuck off in a corner of any bookstore you walked into, and Will Hornes stacked in the windows and on the counters and on the floor like shells in an ammunition dump?"

"Does it never occur to you, Jeanne, that critics may have other motives than envy? That their criticism may be the plain truth? I've been reading over Horne and—" The quality of Hawke's voice changed, it became cracked and shrill and the words lost definition. For a moment she thought he had flown into a hysterical rage, then she realized, as he faded, that the telephone connection had gone bad. In the short time that passed before she could understand him again, Jeanne had a vision of the vast span of ocean and land over which they had been talking, and the picture of Venice rose in her mind: the alluring, romantic city of crumbling marble palaces and dark canals, of the long sunset perspectives of Canaletto, the

place where immortal art was as common as wallpaper. Of all the cities on earth she wanted to see, Venice stood first, and Arthur was there, at the other end of this tenuous telephone connection! The receiver popped painfully in her ear and Hawke was talking again. "Jeanne? Jeanne? Goddammit, can't you hear me?"

"Here I am, Arthur. You faded out about a minute ago."

The nurse came tiptoeing into the room, carrying Jim, who was still sucking noisily at a bottle, his eyes closed. Jeanne gestured at the nurse to give her the baby; and she skillfully juggled baby, bottle and telephone receiver so that she missed none of Hawke's words while she settled Jim beside her, with a feeling of wondrous pleasure which had not yet dimmed at all.

Hawke was saying, "You missed all the most important things I had to tell you. Can't you possibly come over here, Jeanne? I need you right now, truly I do. I'd have called you in a day or two if you hadn't called me."

Jeanne cradled the baby against her side with one arm, and pitched her voice as low as she could. "Arthur, I can't leave Jim. You may not understand that, but he's the one person in the world who's more important to me than you." Jeanne realized as she said it that it was a slip to place Hawke second, but it was the truth, and she was past caring about these niceties; Karl's baby stood first, if Karl did not.

Hawke said, "Look, I understand. I'm the man who had to wipe off your wet silly face when you first saw my sister's baby. Okay, Jeanne. I'm glad about Jim."

"Arthur, please send me your book."

"Well, maybe. I'll think of something. *Horne's* really selling, though?"

"We just went back to press with fifty thousand."

"God, think of all the public libraries burning down. Why, I'm the greatest cultural scourge since Attila the Hun. Jeanne darling, are you okay? I mean, having Jim and all, how did you come through? How do you look?"

"Shapeless, with a face like a pie, thank you. I'm living on carrots and Ry-Krisp, I'll soon look human again. I came through fine. It was very painful. I'd like to have about seven more babies."

"That's okay, as long as you never retire as my editor."

"Not till you fire me."

"That's never. I think we've spent enough of Hodge Hathaway's money. I'll hang up and write you a letter about as long as *Gulliver's Travels*. Goodbye, darling."

"Goodbye, Arthur."

She heard the noise he made hanging up the receiver on the other side of the Atlantic, in the magic city where the sun was setting, while here it

was ten in the morning. Jim stirred against her, and bubbles gurgled in the bottle. There was a traffic jam in the street outside her window; automobile horns were snarling at each other in a violent mounting din. She telephoned Ross Hodge.

Part Four
1951

CHAPTER SIXTEEN

1

ONE of the striking rituals of North American life, in these middle years of our phantasmagoric twentieth century, is the Broadway first night. Like any truly living ritual, it does not seem strange to the people who take part in it. It seems a normal, indeed a privileged, way to behave; a colorful heightening of ordinary hours; a solemnity that calls for special dress, special manners, prescribed things to say; an event that gives all who are there a sense of partaking in a moment vibrant with life or death, with the urgency of first and last things.

Art is the one avenue to the supernatural, or at least to special grace, that most Western minds of the moment recognize; and since the theatre at its rare best is perhaps the highest art, the people who attend the bedizened ceremony of a Broadway first night, all complicated with the odor of money and the possible apotheosis or death of a reputation, are right to hope for a thrill they can get here and no where else, outside the houses of worship which for them are dead piles of stone. Once in a great while they do get the thrill they came for. Usually, as with most rituals, they go through the forms and the flame does not descend; but just the forms are exciting and pleasant.

Frieda Winter had attended as many first nights as anyone in New York over a period of twenty years. The excitement had never staled for her. She found each detail of a first night richly satisfying: the long beauty treatment beforehand, the new dress, the hurried early dinner, the laughing tense crowd of slickly groomed people in the theatre lobby, the nourishing sweep down the aisle into two of the best seats in the orchestra; the quick glances around at her celebrated friends in the rows before and behind, the hand waves and the light jokes of the insiders; perhaps the encounter with the pallid author or the falsely cheerful producer; these things, for Frieda, were ever-bubbling champagne.

And she knew the subtle shades of the first-night ritual. She knew which openings were the great events; which were the shaky, evenly balanced gambles; which were the forlorn attempts, almost foredoomed, of the fringe producers and writers. She never made the mistake of wearing high fashion to a third-class opening, nor did she fail of the brightest

splendor on the big nights. Her husband had little to say about her out-
lays for clothes and jewels. Frieda possessed, as she had truthfully told
Hawke, plenty of money of her own. A canny theatre bettor, she was far
ahead of that game; and her concert management bureau, though small,
was very profitable.

The opening of *Alms for Oblivion* in the second week of October had
long promised to be the first electric night of the 1951 season. As the
September openings went by in the usual failures or dull half-acceptances,
Hawke's play like a magnet began to attract to itself all the unexpended
excitement of the long theatre dearth of the summer. Even if the author
had not been her lover in a long, almost public liaison, Frieda would
have arrayed herself in court brilliance for the New York premiere of
Alms for Oblivion. The show had been rolling across the country for
months in triumph; the notices of the fussy Boston critics had been good,
if a bit tentative; the play was bringing a beloved star back to Broadway
after a four-year absence; the playwright was a towering literary wonder
whose latest novel, like his others, was rapidly climbing the best-seller
lists, despite violent critical attacks; and as a final touch of glamor, it was
widely known that the author had recently been arrested in Venice in a
scene of unexplained violence, and that he was remaining in Italy to work
on his new book, and was not even troubling to come to New York for
the opening of his first produced play! All these things made the premiere
very big news indeed in the opinion of the New York newspaper columnists, and they kept increasing the excitement with reports of huge advance
sales of tickets, of long lines at the box-office in Boston, of new explanations of Hawke's arrest in Venice, and even of Hawke's rumored presence
in New York.

Frieda, the only person in America who knew why Hawke had wrecked
the Expatriates Bar, had said not a word to anybody, of course. With her
genius for blotting out what she did not wish to think of, she had virtually
cut the whole episode from her memory, though her body still bore fading
greenish bruises where Hawke had gripped or struck her. Her luck had
held, her name had not gotten into any of the printed stories, or even
into the cocktail party talk. For Frieda, what people did not know did not,
for practical purposes, exist.

Frieda felt not the faintest shred of embarrassment about appearing
with her husband at this public debut of a work of her former lover. She
was so far from being embarrassed that she anticipated carrying herself
more or less as the queen of the evening, almost like the widow of a dead
playwright. Frieda never had spoken out in so many words the fact that
she had been the mistress of Youngblood Hawke. But she was decidedly proud of the general knowledge of it, as mistresses of French
kings used to be of their illicit status. Even if Hawke had been planning

to come to the opening Frieda would have gone, and would have revelled in the drama and the whispers.

From her point of view, she was responsible for the existence of this play. She had brought Hawke and Feydal together. She had pounced on the idea when Feydal had suggested it at the supper table in Number One, on the night Hawke had won the Pulitzer Prize. She had even pricked Jeanne Fry into accompanying Hawke to Hovey—at least that was how she chose to remember it—and so the play had been born. Moreover she had put up one quarter of the money for the production. If there could be a proprietary right in a great first night equal to the author's, Frieda felt she had such a right in this event. She was adorning herself accordingly: a new dress, of course, in her favorite blue-gray, a queenly stiff swathe of silk to the floor with severe styling, designed for her by a Hollywood pederast who was her good friend; also a diamond tiara, representing quite a plunge of cash. She set aside four hours in the afternoon for the dressing of her hair, which was a soft youthful brown again. She had restored this color more than a year earlier, shortly after having been found in Hawke's bed by his mother.

Twenty minutes to seven in the evening, Frieda stood in her dressing room, in the angle between two full length mirrors—one on the wall, one on the open door to her bath—inspecting herself with the hard unfriendly look that women of fashion give themselves in a last-minute scrutiny of a toilette; imagining themselves, perhaps, in the place of their worst enemies and looking for flaws. There came the hesitant tap at the door which could only be her husband. Such an intrusion was unusual. She did not like to be seen on such an evening until she was quite ready.

"Yes?" she said in a business voice. She was vexed with her hair. Now that it was done it seemed a shade girlish and affected, especially against the adult magnificence of the dress and the tiara.

"If you're decent I'd like to talk to you."

She opened the door. Winter stood there in his dinner jacket, holding a long white envelope. With an admiring glance, and a sidewise twist of his bushy white mustache, he said, "Well, I call this rising to an occasion, Frieda."

"I'm in a fury over my hair. I don't know what came over Charles. I look like a Seventh Avenue model who's reached retirement age."

"You look beautiful, and your hair is fine. I just found this on my desk. I guess it came while I was showering."

Frieda took the special delivery letter with the return address of the Devon School on it. "Is Paul ill?"

"No."

Frieda sat carefully at her dressing table, spreading her stiff skirt, and read the letter. Her husband looked idly at the pictures of her clients and friends, and the various family photographs, that filled all the walls of the

little room in gilt frames from floor to ceiling. Frieda said after a while, "This doesn't seem serious. It's more or less to be expected, his first time away from home."

"Well, I don't mind about the work. Paul's bright and he ought to come around. I do think crying spells in a boy of twelve are out of line."

Frieda shook her head, dropped the letter on the marble top of her vanity table in the clutter of perfumes and beauty tools, and looked this way and that at her hair in the round mirror. "He's always been the difficult one, hasn't he? Worse than the girls."

The father said, "He gave us a very bad time while you were in Europe. I think we were a little fooled when you returned. He was so overjoyed to have you back that he seemed to come out of it. This letter makes me wonder whether he has."

She said, "It's strange. Bennett just cruised through Devon, and Paul's smarter than he is. It's not a severe school."

"Well, Frieda, I'm sure aptitude isn't the problem. You know how little I think of psychiatrists, but this summer I was close to hauling Paul off to one."

Frieda smiled. "He wouldn't tell him anything, and he'd end up analyzing the analyst."

"I daresay. The question is"—the father tapped the envelope against his palm—"whether we ought to do something."

"The letter is quite clear, dear. They don't want us to do anything. They're just trying to forestall a weepy letter or phone call from him. . . . If I had the time I'd take this hair down and do it all over, but I haven't the time." Becoming aware of the silence behind her, she looked around at her husband, who stood in his usual somewhat stooped pose, with one hand in a jacket pocket. "I mean what certainly isn't indicated is that we go up there and see him, is it? That's what he's bidding for. If we yield we may as well take him out of Devon and put him in a school here in the city—which I thought we both decided would be wrong."

Winter shrugged. "I thought possibly you could telephone him tonight before we left, to see how he's doing."

"I'd love to talk to him. I'm not sure it's the wisest thing to do, but I will. In a little while."

"No hurry. It's a pity in a way he's not here tonight," Winter said. "He's always had such a case of hero-worship for Arthur. I'd gladly give him my ticket."

"How absurd, Paul. On a school night?"

"Well, I've read *Alms for Oblivion*, you know. And anyway something's happened to me, so far as Broadway goes. All the plays and all the actors are beginning to seem alike. Or the variations are too small to matter. It's like seeing plays put on at a high school. The pretense doesn't hold, it's just my friends Tom and Harry and Susie dressed up differently on dif-

ferent nights, saying different words they've just memorized. The ravages of age." He picked the letter off her table. "This goes in the Paul, Junior, file, a somewhat sad dossier, Frieda, so far."

She said, "I guess it's the fate of the youngest one to be petted too much and neglected too much. Paul's suffered from both."

"Well, maybe he'll be president some day. He's much the brightest of the lot. I found him reading *Anna Karenina* during the summer. He was in the middle of it. He shut the book as though I'd caught him reading something dirty."

"Please tell Anne we'll have dinner in fifteen minutes."

"All right." Winter tapped the folded letter on his hand. "I'll never get over feeling a bit guilty toward Paul. A man shouldn't have a son at fifty-five, should he? However flattering it is to his ego." Frieda looked straight in the mirror, touching her hair, and said nothing. Her husband went out.

2

The city of New York has a way of honoring its big events with an outburst of foul weather; quite as though the rain, wind and snow were under the control of the mayor, and were considered more spectacular and less costly than fireworks. For the opening of *Alms for Oblivion*, the rainstorm provided by the city was of a routine cats-and-dogs variety, but a cold east wind with gusts up to fifty miles an hour showed some sense of occasion. It rendered almost insoluble the problem of getting ladies in their complex finery and fragile coiffures across the few feet of open air between apartment house entrances and taxi doors, and then the second, far worse patch, worse because it was on a side street—the side streets in mid-town New York are narrow east-west wind tunnels that step up the wind speed by half—between the taxi and the theatre lobby. Once arriving at the theatre the ladies, dressed only for slow stately promenading, had to summon up their courage, scramble somehow out of sunken taxi seats, and make an undignified scramble across the terrible howling wet waste of the sidewalk under the marquee. The marquee did not help. Nothing helped except waiting for a lull in the wind. These lulls came, but not frequently enough. As a result, some celebrated ladies were blown into the theatre with wet dresses, tumbled hair, and ruined dispositions, and taxicabs and limousines piled up in Forty-fifth Street all the way across the town from Broadway to Third Avenue. There they stood in the drumming rain, in the foggy red glare from neon signs of cheap hotels, crawling forward a foot or so every minute. Windshield wipers danced, the wind howled and rumbled, horns blew senselessly and endlessly, tempers grew short and the time before the early curtain grew shorter; and

still the vast line of cars across the town—funeral cortege or victory procession, nobody yet knew which—continued to inch toward the theatre, its rate of progress wholly tied to the courage of each well-dressed lady who had to bolt across the hellish few feet of streaming tempest-swept slippery pavement into the dry heaven of the lobby full of the starers and the stared-at.

Ferdie Lax glanced at his watch and said, "We may as well stop worrying. They'll hold the curtain. They've got to on a night like this." The taxi he was sharing with the Princes and a tall beautiful girl had just crossed Fifth Avenue; two and a half blocks to go, and it was five minutes to eight. Hundreds of cars stretched ahead to the theatre, not moving.

Fanny Prince peered out at the rain and shuddered, pulling her chinchilla wrap close around her. "It's disgusting. I planned for the rain, didn't I? Ve sat down to eat quarter past six, and still look at us!"

Jay said, "How can they hold the curtain? Don't the critics have to run at half past ten no matter what, to get their reviews into the morning papers?"

The agent took off his hat, a very flat black pork-pie, and rested it on his knees. "I talked to Carmian last week in Boston. They've actually got a two-hour show. Feydal's really cut it to the bone. They can go up as late as eight twenty-five tonight."

The tall girl said, "I don't understand how they can cut a play when the author is in Italy. Is that allowed?"

Ferdie took her left hand, on which a colossal pear-shaped diamond ring glowed above a platinum wedding ring, and he mumbled the long white fingers affectionately. "Darling, it varies from author to author. This one is smart, he lets the theatre people mess around while he goes ahead and writes something new that he can sell."

"You mean that you can sell," said the girl, withdrawing her jewelled hand long enough to give him an arch little slap, and then suffering Lax to resume his gnawing. This girl was Mrs. Ferdinand Lax. For reasons unknown to anybody but the agent, and totally invisible to the naked eye, he had found her different from the others, had married her, and was almost suburban in his submissiveness to her. This development was the wonder of New York and Hollywood. Her name was Geraldine.

Fanny was embarrassed by the newlywed foolishness. "Tell me, Ferdie, vill it really be a hit?"

"No contest," Lax said between his wife's fingers. "The advance is half a million right now."

"I once had money in a show that had an advance of half a million," Prince said. "I never saw the money back."

"Well, that's the theatre," Lax said, distracted from his love-play and letting the hand drop, "but you've got to figure the star, the author, eight

months of success on the road, a sellout in Boston. This show is a goddamn juggernaut."

"The critics can kill it," Fanny said. "Two critics can kill it, the *Times* and the *Tribune*. New York is New York."

"This show will roll over the *Times* and *Tribune* like an army tank over ants," Lax said.

"Of course we're rooting for it," Prince said.

Fanny said, "I can't vait to see what Frieda vill be wearing." She sighed. "It's a long, long time since I introduced her to Hoke at our Christmas party, you know? Sometimes I vonder, did I do him a favor? Or her?"

"I've never met Frieda Winter," Geraldine said. "Is it really true about her and Youngblood Hawke, Ferdie?"

Lax said, "A very deep platonic attachment, Geraldine, darling," and began chomping on her hand again.

The sign on the roof of the theatre proclaimed blurrily through the rain, in old-fashioned letters formed of yellow electric bulbs

IRENE PERRY
ALMS FOR OBLIVION

The signs on New York playhouses are small and laconic; to enlarge them, to make them clearer or more informative, would be to descend to the vulgar level of movie houses. Dowdiness plus money is the ready mark of aristocracy. But Hawke's sister Nancy, catching sight of the sign beyond the glare of Broadway, through the windshield of the limousine hired by Ross Hodge, exclaimed, "Look at that tiny sign, ma! They haven't even got Art's name on it! Just that actress's name and the play title. What nerve!"

Mrs. Hawke craned her neck to peer down the street. "Well, that comes of calling himself Youngblood Hawke. If he'd called himself Art Hawke, I reckon he'd have fitted on the sign."

Nancy's husband, John Weltmann, who sat uncomfortably on one of the jump seats—Gus Adam was on the other—said, "It's a question of what brings in the money. In the theatre the star brings in the money."

The lawyer said, "They've treated Arthur well. His name is on the marquee. All the painted signs and window cards read 'Youngblood Hawke's *Alms for Oblivion*.' His name brings in money too."

"The name of Irene Perry brings in more money," said Weltmann.

"Naturally," said Adam.

A loosening of the traffic allowed their car to lurch forward to Broadway, where a policeman stopped them though the light was green. The street beyond the intersection was filled to the avenue's edge with cars.

Mrs. Hawke said, "Why do they put a big show like this in a dinky side-street theatre? Why not one of these decent-size theatres right here on Broadway?"

Adam said something about the peculiarities of New York real estate which had forced stage plays into the side streets. "This theatre is far from dinky, Mrs. Hawke. It's probably the single most desirable house for a drama in New York."

John Weltmann slowly nodded his fat heavy head. He had acquired noticeable hanging jowls since his marriage, and he had not managed to find a more becoming or less false-looking wig. Yet for all his repulsive look, he had hit it off well with the lawyer at the early buffet dinner which Ross Hodge had arranged for the Hawke family and some Hodge Hathaway people. Weltmann said, "That is correct. This theatre has a large orchestra, mother, a small balcony, and no second balcony. The proportion of expensive seats is therefore higher. Forty-fifth Street is the most desirable street. The theatre named after Irene Perry is on Forty-first Street. Irene Perry would probably not play in the Irene Perry Theatre. Risky productions are booked in there. In this theatre are booked plays which probably will be hits."

The lawyer smiled and pulled at his broad sunburned nose. Hawke's mother said, "Where on earth do you find out these things, John?"

Nancy said, "Oh, John can find out anything that has to do with money."

Weltmann grinned the peculiar frog grin which seemed to break his face almost in half, and adjusted his thick glasses. "Facts are usually available. Getting them is boring. You have to be interested in facts. I was offered a syndication of the Irene Perry Theatre, so I had to look into the facts of the New York theatre district. I did not go into the syndication."

Adam's eyes narrowed at the fat grotesque man, who spoke in this plodding way, with a German cadence but without an accent. "You were offered that syndication down in Hovey?"

"I have an agent in New York who sends me propositions," Weltmann said. "Also in a few other places. I have a little money to invest, so I have to manage it the best way I can."

"Don't let him fool you, he's right sharp," Mrs. Hawke said to the lawyer. "I'm still angry at him for not taking an interest when my case came to court. If you'd have looked into the facts there, John, I'd be rich and there'd be a million for you to invest."

Weltmann said, "I never expected to be married. When I found myself getting married I made a rule. I would help my new relations with money to my utmost power if ever they needed it, but I would never take any direct part in their financial affairs. I think this makes for peace at home."

The lawyer said, "It's one of the wisest rules I ever heard."

"Yes, but it leaves me out in the cold," said Mrs. Hawke. "I don't need

money, I need a man to fight for my rights. I still need one. And with Art gallivanting around Europe—"

Nancy said, as the limousine started across Broadway, "Here we go. We're almost there. For God's sake, mama, no lawsuit talk tonight, of all nights. I expect it to be the biggest night of my life and I don't want it spoiled."

Weltmann said, "Just remember, Nancy, the show may fail. Arthur's reputation does not hang on this show."

The mother said to Adam, "Can it really fail? With all the whoop-de-do over Art, and this Irene Perry?"

Adam said, "The critics can stop it in its tracks."

Mrs. Hawke said, "Why can't people make up their own minds about a play? Who are these critics, anyway? They sure can't hurt a book. Why, the things they been saying about *Will Horne* are just terrible, yet it's selling like a house afire."

Weltmann said, "Critics can't destroy a book. They can destroy a play. These are known facts. When you add the high cost of putting on a play compared to the low cost of printing a book, it becomes inadvisable to write plays if you can write books. Arthur is conducting his profession sensibly from that viewpoint."

"Ah, but there's nothing like a play!" Nancy said, her eyes shining in the glow of the marquee as the taxi drew up at last in front of the theatre. "Look at this crowd! My God, look at them marching down the street through the wind and rain just to see Art's play!"

The mother said, "Lot of fools getting their feet wet because they've got nothing better to do. Art was smart to stay in Italy. What does he care? He's a great author, and he makes lots of money. You be careful now, Nancy."

Weltmann stood in the wind beside the chauffeur, helping Nancy out of the car. She moved with the awkwardness of a heavily pregnant woman. "Oh, you're crazy, mama! Art should have come. He'll regret it as long as he lives."

From Gus Adam's blank expression, it would have been very hard to guess that he had spent the day with Youngblood Hawke in his Wall Street office, executing legal documents.

3

There are few more exciting noises in the world than the growl of a gathering audience, heard through a theatre curtain by the actors on stage. When it is a first-night audience, the growl has a special quality in it, quite unmistakable: it is gayer, louder, more eager, and the note of menace is stronger.

The cast of *Alms for Oblivion* was gathered on the stage for last-minute comments by Georges Feydal and Pierce Carmian; but the actors were listening less to them than to the growl, and they all looked ill at ease and dejected. An assistant stage manager, in his shirt sleeves, strangely pale among the painted actors, came hurrying to Feydal and whispered in his ear. The fat actor showed extreme amazement. "Excuse me, won't you? Pierce will carry on. I'll return in a moment," he said to the cast, and he ambled swiftly off the set.

Arthur Hawke stood just inside the stage door in a dripping gray raincoat of a loose British cut, holding a cap that ran water. His hair was long and disorderly, his face white.

"My dear Hawke, what an absolutely electrifying surprise! Why damn you, how wonderful! What an entrance! You've upstaged us all! How are you, old cock?" Feydal threw his thick arms around the author.

"Tired," Hawke said hoarsely, in a Southern accent which seemed to have thickened in Europe. "Dog tah'd. Ah had to flah back on urgent business, so Ah thought Ah ought to drop in on the play."

"Hawke, you've been sent from Heaven. Will you talk to the cast?"

"My God, no."

"Listen to me, they need it badly, they're terribly stale. They're in panic. Coming into New York after eight months of pushover road audiences is very hard. In Boston the critics turned ominous. We've had two ghastly previews and they desperately need a shot in the arm, desperately."

"I have nothing to say."

"The sight of you will be enough. Come along, I beg of you. Dear Hawke, the first half hour of this play can sink it out of sight if the actors aren't at their best. Please do as I tell you, it's frightfully important. What a fellow you are, to be sure, showing up like this!"

"Well," Hawke said, and he allowed Feydal to lead him on the stage. The growl from behind the curtain was clamorous, frightening to him.

"Ladies and gentlemen of the *Alms for Oblivion* company," Feydal said, as the actors sitting here and there on the furniture of the setting stared in wonder at the huge wet apparition with whom he had linked arms, "Here is the author of our play, Mr. Youngblood Hawke, come from Italy to see tonight's performance."

With a common impulse, their faces lighting with excitement, the actors and actresses rose to their feet and applauded. Carmian plunged at Hawke and embraced him. "God bless you Hawke! Welcome! What an utterly mad and marvellous man you are!"

Hawke glanced around at the cast, all looking to him expectantly, and wondered what on earth to say. He had not slept on the plane at all. His throat burned and ached; the chill damp of New York, and the oven-dry steam heat, had attacked him at once. It was nightmarish to find him-

self in this extremely shallow, squeezed-flat, make-believe room which bore a shadowy resemblance to his mother's parlor in Hovey, and to find himself confronted by this array of people painted and dressed like the characters in his first novel. Behind his back, beyond the curtain, the audience growled like a cage full of playing tigers.

He said, in the gravelly tone of a man with a sore throat, "First of all, speaking as a dedicated artist to other dedicated artists, thanks for the large bundle of cash you've already earned for me on the road."

They all laughed a little uncertainly; and Irene Perry, who had sat again in an armchair, in a regal attitude, blew him a kiss. She did not look much like the Aunt Bertha he had imagined, she looked very much like Irene Perry despite the paint, the cane, and the white wig, but she was an arresting presence.

"I'm serious," Hawke said. "I hope we know each other too well, though this is the first time we meet in the flesh, to go through silly pretenses. What we want from those people making that thrilling noise behind me is praise and cash. You've won praise and cash from audiences everywhere for nearly a year with this play. Tonight won't be any different. But I venture that you, like me, want those rewards of success mainly so that we can know that our work has been well done. I feel at home with you because your art is addressed wholly to audiences of plain people, and so is mine. I've never understood art for art's sake, or art for the finicky few. Or rather I do understand it. I admire Joyce and Meredith, but I worship Balzac and Twain.

"This theatre art is yours, not mine. I don't understand the theatre. I think it belongs to players. The best plays have been written by play-actors, like Molière and Shakespeare. I know Shaw never got on a stage, but then he never got off the stage, he never did anything in his life but play-act. This play is really the inspiration of a play-actor, Georges Feydal, and so it works, though it was written by a novelist.

"The whole idea of art, yours or mine, is to tell the truth in a fresh, penetrating, and pleasing way, isn't it? That's all I ever try to do. Tell them the truth tonight, that's all I can say. They're clever and formidable New Yorkers, but they're only people, and their hearts must respond with gratitude, like any human hearts, to the truth beautifully told.

"I'm afraid I'm maundering, but I'm tired. I've come a long way to thank you. Your art is the creating of illusions. Thank you for successfully carrying off the greatest possible illusion, that Youngblood Hawke can write a play."

Hawke did not know actors; he imagined they were jaded sophisticates incapable of being impressed by words, and he was astounded at their eager eyes, their shining faces, and their patter of warm applause when he finished. The noise from behind the curtain was becoming a roar. Irene Perry looked almost ready to cry. Feydal commanded instant silence on

stage with a wave of his hand. "We're too close to curtain time for speeches. I cheerfully acknowledge that I invented all the characters and composed every single speech in this sublime play." He only allowed a ripple of laughter, then his authoritative voice cut through. "I knew Shaw well. He never did a better job of play-acting in his life than Youngblood Hawke has just done, last-minute entrance and all. If that's really the test then you're all looking at America's greatest young playwright—as if you didn't know."

Irene Perry rose and stepped forward in the excited laughter and applause. "May I respond for the cast? We've all heard the word we've been needing for several weeks. Our job is to tell the truth. Nothing else. We are going to tell the truth tonight, Mr. Hawke, the truth you've put in our mouths to speak, and we're going to do our best to please. Pierce, we're ready for the curtain any time you are."

4

The lights in the smoky lobby blinked. Celebrities and nobodies took last puffs on their cigarettes and began to move into the theatre. But some of the nobodies lingered, because limousines and taxis were still disgorging people. A blonde movie star blew in, clutching her wrap and hair in a glittering spatter of rain, accompanied by a notorious homosexual novelist about five feet tall, with a peculiarly gray face. The next few arrivals looked like mere millionaires with their wives—arrogant in bearing and most elegantly dressed, but not recognizable. Then an old United States senator appeared, with a frail aristocratic wife in a black velvet cloak on his arm. More rich well-dressed nonentities trickled in—actually the Princes and the Laxes, followed by six very tall men and women jovially cursing the New York weather in Texas accents—and then, for the diehard starers, came a first-class thrill: out of a black limousine, in a dead fall of the wind, stepped Mrs. Frieda Winter, her face alive with self confidence and pleasure, her eyes wide and shining, her tiara like a coronet. Over her sweeping dress she wore a coat of the same blue-gray silk trimmed with dark fur. The noise in the lobby died down before her, as the wind had died down. She joked with the company manager at the door while her husband brought the tickets out of his pocket. Then she swept into the theatre.

The wave of talking and head-turning occasioned in the orchestra by the arrival of the blonde movie star was just subsiding. Now came a slow rise in the noise, and a general turn of heads toward Frieda as she entered the aisle and sauntered down toward the stage. Her bearing was proud and casual, her smiles and handwaves were like a queen's at a lawn party. It took her only a minute or so to walk past seventeen rows to her seat,

but this minute justified all her hours and hours of grooming, and all her lavish outlay on dress and gems.

Jeanne Fry, sitting among the Hodge Hathaway people in the fourteenth row of the theatre, well back of the fashionable section, said to Karl as Frieda paced past, "What's gone wrong? The band isn't playing 'Hail to the Chief.'"

Four rows down, barely within the insiders' limits, irritated at sitting amid people she did not recognize, Fanny Prince said to Ferdie Lax, "My God, that tiara! How is it the diamonds don't spell out 'Youngblood Hoke slept here?'"

Among the hundreds of faces turned toward Frieda there were perhaps twenty that would have been recognized in a newspaper photograph by any ordinary American. There were about a hundred more people whose names were well-known if their faces were not. These luminaries were at the bright core of the seating plan in the first eight rows, mainly in the center section. From there outward the importance of the faces and the lustre of the reputations gradually dimmed. But few people in that whole orchestra did not have either notoriety, or a connection with the play (like the Hodge Hathaway contingent), or a lot of money. There were even some persons of minor consequence in the first two rows of the balcony, which was otherwise filled by nondescript humans. Nearly all these spectators, famous and anonymous alike, witnessing Frieda Winter's arrival, had something excited or jocular to say to one another. The buzz at her entrance swelled, and became the buzz of the evening; it was, indeed, the rising roar that Hawke heard from behind the curtain at the moment that he finished addressing the players. Frieda had not underrated her place in the evening's ceremonies. To say that she enjoyed the sensation she created would hardly be enough. It was probably the pleasantest and most thrilling moment of her life. She had attended hundreds of first nights; the ritual was second nature to her, and for that reason all its nuances were both familiar and momentous. She had never hoped to sweep first-nighters into a mighty buzz like an actress or a president; but thanks to her open adultery with Youngblood Hawke she achieved, on this night, the grand accolade of fashionable New York.

By a stroke of luck she was even able to prolong the moment and the sensation after she reached her seat. A handsome small swarthy man with blondish hair, in an Italian dinner jacket, rose from the adjoining seat to greet her, so that Frieda remained standing with the eyes of all the audience upon her, while she smiled and nodded and shook hands with the man and with the woman beside him. Then she sank into her seat, accepting an opened program from her husband without looking around at him, still talking to the neighboring couple.

They were Manuel and Honor Hauptmann. She had met them at parties given by movie people, and of course she had known Honor for

years as a quenched saturnine girl drifting in the wake of the brilliant Anne Karen. Honor looked all different now: plump, creamy, ablaze with diamonds on neck and arms, her bosom overflowing a black dress recognizable to Frieda as a Paris original. Yet Honor still retained a trace of the peevish look with which she had once followed her mother about. Her double chin and her fat hands bespoke a woman who could not stop herself from eating pastries and chocolates. Frieda knew that Hawke had struck up an acquaintance with the Hauptmanns in Europe, so she was not surprised to hear Honor say that they had flown up from Peru for this opening. People like the Hauptmanns could and did fly across an ocean to attend an amusing party. The two women were still talking about Hawke, with Manuel Hauptmann sitting smiling and silent between them, when the footlights cast a roseate glow on the curtain, the house lights went down, and the audience noise died.

5

The curtain had only been up a few seconds when Hawke entered the theatre and dropped into a side seat in the last row, vacated for him by the company manager. The author was startled at the lifelike beauty of the setting, seen under lights from the dark auditorium. The flattened, crudely painted fake room was now eerily like the parlor of his youth. He watched the play unfold with almost the same curiosity as any other spectator. He did not know what Feydal had done with it. The actor's first suggested revisions, a long time ago, had plunged him into two days of melancholy rage. He had resolved to put the play out of his mind, leaving it to the theatre butchers for good or ill, and he had done so.

Feydal had, he now saw, cleverly opened the play with a snippet from the very end of the book: a fight between the handy man and the maid, after the aunt's death, over a kitchen table that both wanted to steal. By the change of a few words the scene now comically foreshadowed the greedy battles of the family over the aunt's property, and established her failing health. Hawke wondered why he had not thought of this trick himself; Shakespeare and Shaw loved to start their plays with a quarrel of minor characters.

This scene went well, but then the heavy lump came, the summary of the first four hundred pages of his book, which Hawke had put into a scene between the family lawyer and a nephew facing bankruptcy. There was no help for it, the facts of the plot had to be explained. This was the first-act problem of all the plays he had ever studied, and he had done his best. It was a long, long, tedious scene, despite the violent flinging-about of the nephew. Feydal had directed the actor to rant so as to keep up an illusion of drama during the laborious recital, but without avail. Coughs

rose from the orchestra. Hawke saw people lean their heads together and whisper, or glance at their programs. In the seat in front of him a young man in dark gray flannel with a close-cropped head said in a heavy New York accent to the beautiful girl beside him, "Christ, this thing is a bomb."

In the documents Hawke had signed that afternoon, which gave him a half interest in Paumanok Plaza in exchange for all his rights in this play, the probable total royalty income—based on the assumption that the show would be a smash hit, with road companies—had been calculated at two hundred fifty thousand dollars. He had undertaken to make up the difference in cash if the play earned less than that. He had flown back from Europe to execute those papers; and already the whole scheme seemed to be going glimmering! He wondered whether Scott would let him out of the contract if the show proved a disaster. He was terribly tense.

Irene Perry staggered on stage, clutching her side. The audience roused itself into applause. She timed her stumbling so as to allow for a long pause dead center stage, where she wavered, leaning on her stick, gasping, and clawing at the air, until the clapping subsided. She finished her beautiful stagger to a couch at the far end of the stage, fell on it, and exclaimed in a voice of rich power, "Ah am dying. Call the family. Call Judge Thompson." The show was on.

Hawke became caught up as though he had written neither the book nor the play. *Alms for Oblivion* was distant to him, he had written three books since, more than a million words. It struck him for the first time how much his huge complicated first novel owed to Mark Twain's brief story, *The Man That Corrupted Hadleyburg*. As the members of the family one after the other bared their characters under the gravitational pull of the aunt's wealth, and one by one fell into dishonesty, lying, and treachery, a real coarse picture took shape of small-town American life with its various crisscrossing stresses, all traceable at last to the need or the greed for money. The scene that closed the first act, in which the aunt learned from the doctor that her old game had become reality, and that she really was dying, was very good. It was straight out of the book. Irene Perry faded in a few moments from a happily malignant crone, glorying in her mischievous vitality, into a terror-stricken old woman; she was appealing in her helplessness and fear, and she brought the spectre of death visibly to the stage. When she stiffened into an acceptance of her fate, and went to the telephone to call her lawyer, she became grand. Applause burst from the audience before the curtain began to fall; and when the house lights came on the young man with the bristly head yawned, stretched, and said to his companion, "Smash."

This young fellow was a boor. Smart New Yorkers do not venture a verdict during the intermissions of a first night. They chatter as loudly and brightly as they can about everything but the play, unless they know

each other extremely well. Husbands may express sotto voce opinions to their wives, for instance. But many a polished New York husband fears his wife's disdain too much to stick his neck out, even in connubial confidence, before the critics have spoken. Of course the ordinary people from the balcony, and the rich but gross out-of-towners in the orchestra, will argue out loud as to whether what they are witnessing is a hit or a flop. In so doing they betray themselves as surely as if they had come to the premiere in greasy blue overalls. To the New York view, talking of the success or failure of a play in the hour of its agony is an error of taste. Fear of being caught out in a wrong opinion is not given as the objection.

Hawke came slouching through a side door at a far end of the lobby and leaned against the wall in his raincoat, with his cap pulled down. He wanted to see Jeanne, and his mother and sister; he knew that the word of his presence at the theatre would spread from backstage, if it had not already done so. Accoutred as he was, standing as he did against the wall, he passed as a shabby oversized intellectual from the balcony. Nobody gave him a second glance as he peered here and there. Outside the wind seemed to have stopped, but rain cascaded from the marquee like a waterfall.

In the center of the lobby Frieda shone, greeting people as they wandered by, turning from one to another with a handshake, a laugh, a joke. Her eyes were unnaturally wide and agleam, her smile was exaggerated, her movements were very quick, everything about her trumpeted modishness, self-satisfaction, triumph. Paul Winter stood beside her with one hand in his jacket pocket, smoking the kind of small thin cigar he always lit up in an intermission. Hawke could not hear Frieda, of course, over the lobby din, but he did not have to. He had accompanied her to dozens of first nights, sometimes with the husband and just as often without. He knew the flip irrelevant chatter by heart. Tonight, of all nights, she would surely say nothing about the play. He did not care what she thought of it. It surprised him a little to note how indifferent he had become to Frieda, and indeed to the ways and the opinions of New York.

This scene in the lobby was quite foreign to him, and faintly unreal, perhaps because he had plunged back into his old milieu too suddenly. The thronging bare white shoulders of women, the costly dresses in the queer swathes, drapes and twists of high fashion, the twinkling jewels, the supercilious looks of the young beauties and the strained haughty smiles of the older women, the strutting men in evening clothes with eyes a-roll for pretty girls or for men better known or richer than themselves—once such pictures had been exciting and novel to him; then they had become commonplace with repetition; tonight this living parade of self-conscious New Yorkers before his eyes seemed almost a hallucination, a satiric description of high society in an old book come to life in modern

dress. It was almost as though these people were acting a loud determined parody. How could they possibly be taking themselves, their dress, their gestures, their talk seriously, when they must know they were all familiar extras, mere background figures, in a dusty chapter of *Lost Illusions* or *Vanity Fair?*

Frieda Winter was no background figure, she commanded the scene. She was, he thought, as beautiful as she had been at the Prince party so long ago; a little older, perhaps, but still vivid with the provoking charm, the sophisticated gleam, which had once made her seem the most desirable woman on earth. He had possessed his heart's desire, he had tasted ashes, and it was over. Her opinions, and New York's opinions, did not matter to him any more except insofar as they affected his chances of making money from this play.

He saw Ross Hodge, who was taller than most of the people in the noisy smoke-filled lobby, far down at the other end. Surmising that Jeanne would be with him, and probably Nancy and his mother, he started to make his way through the crowd. Then it was that Frieda— who had seen him wearing these same clothes in Venice—recognized him, before anyone else. "My God," she said to her husband, "It's Arthur. There's Arthur!"

"You're seeing things," Winter said, but Frieda had already started away from him. She said impatiently over her shoulder, "Don't you suppose I know him? He's come home. Arthur! Arthur!" She headed straight for him, with an excited wave of her hand.

It did not occur to her that she was making a mistake. She was riding the crest of glory. She had quite put out of mind the misadventure in Venice. After all, they had had many quarrels! Serenely confident, her face glowing with gaiety and assurance, she drove toward him through the crowd of chattering playgoers—who fell away from her, indeed, since they were all well aware of who she was. A lane opened before her to the huge man in the gray raglan raincoat and tweed cap.

"Arthur!" she said, holding out her hand and coming up to him. "You couldn't resist, could you? How wonderful! Welcome home, dear."

He took her hand and briefly shook it. "Hello, Frieda," he said. He walked past her through the lane that she had just created. "Hey, Ross. Ross! Mah folks theah with you?"

Frieda stood stunned for only a second or two, still smiling, as he walked off. That moment of shocked immobility, with that frozen smile, was enough to give her away to any alert person who was watching. There were dozens. Hawke had not cut her, exactly. It was impossible to find fault with what he had done. Yet he had shown an indifference to her which surpassed contempt. She might have been someone he had once known in college. Frieda pulled herself together as the lobby noise in-

creased, turned on her heel, and rejoined her husband, laughing. "Poor fellow, he's in a daze. He probably hasn't slept in a week."

Winter said, "You know him, dear, but I'm not sure he knows you."

Fanny Prince, who had been standing and talking to the Winters— and to whom this moment was one of the sweetest of her life, though Frieda was as good a friend as she had—said, "A playwright on opening night isn't human. He's getting handsomer all the time, though, isn't he? He ought to get married."

Nobody in the large knot of people around Ross Hodge had an inkling that Hawke was back in the United States, except Gus Adam. For a couple of minutes after the author came shouldering through the theatre crowd in his bizarre coat and cap, whirling the clouds of tobacco smoke, all was delighted confusion at that end of the lobby. The mother and sister embraced him, he shook a dozen hands without knowing whose they were, curiosity seekers sidled up and thickened into a ring, and through this ring pushed more acquaintances to shake his hand. Nancy, after remarking that he looked terrible and would have to come back to Hovey for a long rest, guilelessly proclaimed that the play was absolutely wonderful, a sure smash hit. The mother said that it looked to her like another right smart money maker. Ross Hodge, since the subject was started, stoutly ventured that Hawke had tackled a new art form and knocked the ball right out of the park; and the writer retained enough of his peculiar remoteness to be amused at the mixing of images. His brother-in-law, Weltmann, who seemed to have gotten twice as fat and ugly since he had last seen him, stated in solemn tones that the play had started very slowly but was picking up, and there was a good chance that it might make money, depending on the next act. Karl Fry said nothing could stop it, Hawke had the Midas touch, and he fully expected him to come up next with a volume of excellent sonnets, damn his soul.

Jeanne Fry said nothing. She did not offer to shake his hand. She stood beside her husband, half hidden from Hawke by another Hodge Hathaway editor. She seemed pleased to be hidden. The look she gave him was peculiarly shy and timorous. Hawke at last stepped past the man between them. "Hello, Jeanie. How are you?"

She said in the grainy voice he liked so well, "Oh, you recognize me! Thank heaven for that, most of my friends don't." She wore a low-cut black dress that flared widely at the waist; he could see that she had put on a lot of weight. Her face was quite round, the angular thrust of her jaw was gone. Her neck and shoulders were much prettier with the boniness softened. He said, "Why, I think you're looking wonderful."

Jeanne said, "My face bears a strong resemblance to the harvest moon."

Karl said, "She won't believe me that a little weight is becoming."

"I really came back from Europe just to see Jim, Jeanie. How is he?"

"Revolting. Nobody can see him till he sheds his tail."

Ross Hodge said, laughing, "He's the prettiest baby you ever saw, Arthur."

More and more people pressed in on Hawke, though ringing bells and blinking lights heralded the end of the intermission: Lax, Givney, a couple of newspaper columnists. Scotty Hoag pushed through the on-lookers and delivered himself of half a dozen "sumbitches," while asserting that the play was a gold mine. Scotty had lost almost all the hair on top of his head, and to compensate was allowing the fringe hair to grow in thick. At Adam's office that afternoon, where they had spent several hours signing contracts, Scotty had needed a shave and a haircut badly, but now he was barbered smooth and pink. He wanted Hawke to come to a little party after the show. So did a dozen other people, including Ferdie Lax, Roland Givney, and several of the rich women he had met in his first days of being lionized for *Chain of Command*. Hawke knew the manners of New Yorkers at first-night intermissions well enough to perceive that his show looked like a hit. Authors were avoided in the lobby at a failure as though they were covered with the pustules of smallpox. When the verdict seemed uncertain people were polite and hearty, but constrained. The kind of cordial excitement that was swirling about him now was the old honey-seeking buzz of knowledgeable flies—the buzz he had first heard at the Princes' Christmas party years ago, when he had been an unknown clodhopper in a brown suit.

Through the press around him he caught sight of Frieda with her husband and the Princes, still standing in the center of the lobby. There was no busy little knot of people around them now, and Frieda was not hailing and joking and chattering in her usual way. Playgoers were stream-ing past her into the theatre. She was looking straight at him. Her tiara was like a party hat after the party is over, excessively bright and a little sad. He felt sorry for her, but in truth he had no awareness that he had snubbed her or been mean to her. In view of the way they had parted in Venice, his manner of greeting her had been natural and unpremeditated; he could not have done otherwise. He saw her turn and say something to her husband, and then she walked with her old resolute stride into the theatre.

6

The play was almost over. Irene Perry lay majestically dead in the gloom of the sickroom, lit by four tall candles. The bankrupt nephew had broken into her desk and was rummaging through her papers, casting a horrible furtive glance now and then at the corpse. Still to come were the raucous invasion of the whole family, the ghastly wrangle in the presence of the dead body and the stunning denouement of the aunt's

will. The audience was hushed and unmoving. Nobody had coughed for perhaps a quarter of an hour. Though it was a first night, though these playgoers had come to enjoy the cruel glittering circus of the premiere and not to see a drama, though during most of the evening they had been preoccupied with trying to guess whether they were seeing a hit or a flop, the miracle of the theatre had at last conquered them. They had forgotten themselves. They believed what they were seeing. They hungered like children to know, not whether the show was a money maker, but how the story would come out. Hawke's tale, and the art of Georges Feydal and Irene Perry, had cast the old sublime spell over these New Yorkers; for as Hawke had said they were only people, after all, and their hearts had to respond to the truth well told.

Even Frieda Winter was caught, for the theatre experience is a mass hypnosis. She knew the story to weariness, she had seen rehearsals, out-of-town performances, and a preview; yet she was watching the play with rigid attention, and so, for all his expressed disenchantment, was her husband.

It was therefore a real shock when she felt a hand on her shoulder. It was like being waked out of sleep, but worse; it was a grotesque surprise, totally unexpected and strange. She shivered and looked around incredulously. The person who had touched her was a theatre usherette, a gray-haired woman with an embarrassed, frightened look, whose glasses glittered spectrally in the light from the stage. "I'm terribly sorry, Mrs. Winter," the woman whispered. "There's a telephone call for you."

Frieda collected herself with difficulty. "Who is it? Can't it wait?" All around her the people were turning to stare, angry at the shattering of the stage illusion.

"I'm sorry, they say it's urgent. It's from the Devon School."

Frieda and her husband exchanged a glance. She said, "I never did call. It got so late—" He shrugged, his face blank as a dead man's. They rose, slipped past the august critic beside them, and walked up the aisle after the usherette.

It sometimes happens that critics leave a play before it ends. That is an ominous sign indeed. Most of the playgoers who saw the two people get up and leave thought at first that this was a critic and his companion, but then many of them recognized the Winters. The interruption was hard on the play. There was some whispering, and a barrage of coughs. Hawke was decidedly annoyed when he saw that it was Frieda and her husband who were causing the commotion. His first thought was that Frieda was going out of her way to be dramatic and ungracious. Then in a little while he felt a stir of uneasiness. It penetrated to his attention that the Winters had not walked out by themselves; there had been three figures in the gloom, one of them an usherette. He recalled that he had seen the usherette moving down the aisle alone before the Winters had left. These

puzzling circumstances worked around in his mind. He got out of his seat and went to the lobby. It was empty. He saw a chauffeur closing the door of a limousine on the Winters, who were talking excitedly. He hesitated for a few moments, then ran out into the street exclaiming "Frieda!" The limousine drove off into thick rain suffused with the red and yellow glow from Broadway.

7

After the cheers and the repeated curtain calls, and Irene Perry's low curtsey which brought a tempest of handclapping, and Feydal's incongruous sidling on stage in his bulging dinner jacket to the applause of the cast, Hawke was surprised at the speed with which the theatre emptied. The triumph—as it seemed to be—went by so fast! A few rises and falls of the curtain, a couple of minutes of enthusiastic noise, and then people were rushing past, hardly pausing to look at him, full of their own concerns. Then he recalled that he had himself behaved just this way at other premieres; in fact he had often dived for an exit after the first curtain in order to summon Frieda's limousine or to snare a taxi. The city's erratic transportation, the after-theatre crush in the smart restaurants, the hurry of New Yorkers to get on to the next pleasure—all these things made for the dreamlike speed with which the cheering audience all at once dissolved, leaving usherettes in black moving glumly through barren rows, picking programs off the floor and pushing up the seats with a melancholy slap-slap, while the curtain rose again on a set exposed in its fakiness by a single naked electric light.

Only his mother, his sister, and his brother-in-law remained in the deserted orchestra, lingering because he lingered. He took them backstage, where he found a mood of cautious optimism among the actors and their visitors. In various stages of undress and paint-removing, the players greeted his family charmingly, and seemed grateful for Nancy's gushing compliments, and Mrs. Hawke's assurances that the show was a big success. Weltmann said nothing, apparently quite overwhelmed by the perfume and the glare of backstage, and by the glimpses of actresses darting around in flimsy flying bathrobes. Feydal and Carmian fell on Hawke. The young producer, unlike the others, was exulting recklessly. Handsome as ever, foppish as ever in a curiously frilled shirt and perfect dinner jacket, his teeth flashing, his eyes glittering, his hands fluttering, Carmian hugged Hawke wildly and then he kissed Mrs. Hawke and Nancy. It was hard for Hawke to imagine that there had once been such a vast loathing between himself and this fellow that he had pitched Carmian into a swimming pool. Carmian said to Mrs. Hawke, "How does it feel to be the

mother of America's greatest writer, bar none! A man who produces big best-sellers and smash hit plays at the turn of a crank?"

"Why, it feels right good," said Mrs. Hawke, who evidently enjoyed being cuddled by the incredibly good-looking young man. "So does this, aha ha ha."

Feydal said, beaming, "Pierce, dear lad, the seven little gray men have not yet spoken."

"Damn the seven little gray men," said Carmian, his arm still around Mrs. Hawke. "Forgive my language, mother, but are we afraid of the seven little gray men?"

"Why, they can't hurt my Art. I say damn the seven little gray men, too."

Carmian was so explosively amused at this that he all but flew apart. "I'm going to adopt you, mother. A man can adopt a mother, can't he?"

Irene Perry was sitting at her light-ringed mirror, wiping her pale glistening face with a towel, talking to half a dozen people, when Feydal conducted the Hawkes into her spacious dressing room. Feydal told her who Mrs. Hawke was. The star gravely rose and held out her hand. "I'm honored. How proud, Mrs. Hawke, how very proud you must be of your son."

When they left her room the mother said, "There's the first genuine lady I've met in this city. The greater they are, the finer they are. It's that simple." Hawke thought it as well not to mention that the star had been through four divorces, had twice attempted suicide, and was now carrying on a curious kind of affair with the ingenue of the company.

"Well, now for a bite to eat, eh?" said Feydal. "While we wait for the seven little gray men to decide whether we've done well or ill."

Hawke said, "I'm going back to my hotel and do some writing. Then I'm going to sleep. I can look at the notices in the morning."

Feydal turned on him, his face a huge fat mask of satire, his eyes crinkled to merry inverted v's. "Now, now, my dear Hawke. We're all firmly convinced that you're Superman. It's really not necessary for you to spread your cloak and spring to the top of the Empire State Building. Just come along. Of course your family will join us too in a bite of supper."

Nancy said, "Oh, how marvellous."

Mrs. Hawke said, "Art, it's your night, make the most of it. Your eyes are bloodshot and you're croaking like an old crow. You're not going to work tonight."

Hawke did not want to appear at the restaurant in the character of a playwright on tenterhooks but he was too tired to argue and he went along. He did not feel on tenterhooks. The bullet had left the gun, and it was either going to hit or miss. A few steps through rainy gloom lanced by electric lights and horrid with the horn blasts of automobiles, and they entered the famous theatre restaurant. Georges Feydal made a way like a

snowplow through the jam of anonymous well-dressed bodies around the headwaiter; people turned in annoyance at his push and then fell away awed.

At the first big round table, inside the entrance, the table of tables, sat the columnist Phil York, the blonde movie star, her small friend with the ashy face, Mr. and Mrs. Ferdie Lax, and Jay and Fanny Prince. The agent leaped at the author out of a chorus of congratulations from the table. "No contest! God damn it, no contest, Hawke! And to think Luzzatto got the film rights for thirty-five thousand! I don't care how downbeat the story is, I wouldn't take three hundred grand for it right this minute. I feel awful. I could cry."

Hawke said, "Dry your tears, Ferdie, a few hours from now it may not be worth thirty-five thousand." People all over the restaurant were craning their necks at him and Feydal, and there were a few handclaps.

"No contest, I say! Those seven bastards are going to roll over on their backs with their legs up in the air, kicking feebly. I got a carbon of the *Hollywood Reporter*, it just went out on the teletype." He pulled folded yellow sheets from his pocket. "Want a look? It foams. It's an epileptic fit."

Feydal, who was exchanging pleasantries with the blonde and the tiny gray-faced man, plucked the sheets from Lax's hand and keenly scanned them.

The gray-faced man said to Hawke in a tinkling voice, "If you're going to take over the theatre as well as the best-seller list, how are the rest of us going to eat? You're not a man, Hawke, you're a cartel."

Hawke saw the columnist smile and make a scribble in a notebook on the table. He laughed and walked on. Trading gibes with the gray-faced man, he had long ago learned, was not wise.

There were two elongated tables for parties in the rear of the restaurant. Some players from *Alms for Oblivion* were already at one of them, drinking and making nervous jokes. The Hodge Hathaway people were ranged around the other, and they all called congratulations to Hawke. He waved; and beyond the publisher's table, he saw Honor Hauptmann beckoning to him from an obscure corner. On opening nights, the lines of precedence in this restaurant grew taut; and talent took place over money. After he saw his family to Feydal's table, Hawke went and chatted with the Hauptmanns. They sat with two other magnificently dressed couples, one British and one Latin American, who congratulated Hawke with the somewhat respectful condescension that the very rich use to artists. He promised the Hauptmanns to have dinner with them at the Waldorf before he went back to Italy. He found Honor's flirtatious, slightly possessive manner toward him embarrassing as always. But the husband obviously tolerated it as a harmless foible of his wife. Hawke thought Honor Hauptmann very unattractive, and decidedly neurotic;

the peculiar letters she had written him were never far from his mind when he was with her. But the Hauptmanns had been generous and hospitable to him in Europe. Here was his chance to reward them by sitting at their table for a while. He did not understand why people with so much money should plume themselves on being friends with a writer, but he knew they did. So he paid his respects, and escaped from their company as soon as he could.

Irene Perry arrived a half hour after the rest of the cast, dressed in purple velvet, with elbow-length purple gloves and a startling diamond choker. Applause rose from all over the restaurant. Some patrons stood, either out of respect for the star, or to get a better peek at her. It was the climax of the evening in the dining room. Once the actress was at her table, people began to get up and leave. Several clocks, prominent on the walls, showed twenty minutes to one.

Now began the vigil. Out of what Feydal called "the seven little gray men," four wrote in morning newspapers. It was these four notices that the cast was awaiting. The early morning editions were already on the streets, but from hour to hour the editions changed as news came in; and of course a drama review was important news. The critics scurried from the theatre to their offices—they had not much more than an hour to form and rattle off their verdicts—and then the fateful words on typing paper were fed into the gigantic waiting presses and rolled out in repetitious millions of newsprint columns. The play's future was publicly sealed three hours after the curtain fell; the evening papers seldom changed the judgment. It was a technical miracle of communication, whatever it may have lacked of due judicial process. New York wanted the verdict fast, and got it fast. So used to this marvel were the theatre people who hung on in the restaurant, that the usual thing was to complain of the disgusting delay.

The complaints at the cast table began as the clock hands crawled past one o'clock. The crowd in the restaurant was thinning. The Hodge Hathaway delegation at the other big table became silent and sleepy-looking; at last Ross Hodge called over to Hawke that he was going home, the show was a smash and why lose a night's rest? This signal scattered the publisher's party. Hawke jumped up and caught Jeanne and Karl, begging them to sit with him. This occasioned some talk about Jim's two o'clock bottle and six o'clock bottle, and in the end Karl went home and Jeanne stayed.

The cast ran out of small talk and sat, smoking and drinking. The waiters kept cleaning ashtrays and taking away empty champagne bottles. Irene Perry announced that she was overdue at a party, and she left; this gave courage to some of the other players to go off where they could brood or drink in private. Carmian alternately drank champagne and gnawed his long brown fingers. Feydal alone, at the head of the half-

empty table, kept a serene face, carrying on a bright aimless conversation with Hawke's mother. If he was restless there was no sign of it; he sat like a smiling Buddha.

A small, dark, good-looking man of about thirty, accompanied by what was obviously a wife in an expensive dress and expensive jewelry, came up to Hawke and said, "My wife and I want to say how much we admired your play. Your mother may remember me."

Mrs. Hawke peered at him. "Why, you're Mr. Hirsch, aren't you?"

"That's right."

"Art, that's Mr. and Mrs. Lawrence Hirsch. He's the man who bought your house."

"Well!" Hawke said, shaking hands, "I hope you're enjoying it."

"It's wonderful," the wife said. "Really you have marvellous taste, Mr. Hawke, the way you did that house over. We hardly had to change a thing. We just moved in."

The man said, "I tell everybody I live in the house that Youngblood Hawke built. I think there'll be a bronze plaque on it one day."

"If it were up to Larry," said the wife, "he'd put the plaque up now."

The man laughed and gave Hawke a card. "If you ever feel like looking at the house we'd be honored to have you up for a drink."

"Your play was wonderful," the wife said. "The first half hour was slow, that's all. Good luck!"

The Hirsches walked off. The actors looked at each other and at the producer and director. Feydal said, "Mrs. Hirsch seems to be a charming lady. I hope that when she steps outside she is run over by a large delivery truck."

Hawke said, "The first half hour was slow. Damned slow. All my fault."

Nancy said, "It was not. It was fascinating, every word."

Her husband spoke; so far as Hawke could remember, for the first time since the fall of the curtain. "Nancy, it's always better to look at the facts. The play is a good play, and it will make money. The beginning was slow."

Jeanne Fry said, looking over her shoulder toward the door of the restaurant, "There come the papers."

The headwaiter and a captain were carrying armloads of newspapers among the tables, distributing them to outstretched hands. A waiter came straight to the cast with a large pile, which he placed before Feydal. The actor said sharply, "That's just the *Trib* and the *News*. Where's the *Times?*"

"Late tonight, sir," said the waiter.

Mrs. Hawke said to her son as he opened them one after the other and scanned the columns, "Is it a hit?"

"It seems to be, mama."

"It's a thundering goddamned colossal smash hit, mother!" said Carmian,

giggling insanely over the papers spread before him. "That's all it is, mother. The biggest bloody smash in years! Isn't it, Georges?"

Feydal said, scrutinizing the papers with wise intensity, "I would guess that it worked, Pierce, yes."

Both reviews were outbursts of golden praise, hailing the play as Irene Perry's finest triumph, and Hawke as a major new dramatist. The critics seemed grateful for the chance to use superlatives. Hawke had long since observed that New York theatre reviews tended to be all rhapsody or all scorn. Reading over these hosannahs, these gray columns that the actors had been fearing and anticipating for a year, visible and unchangeable at last, Hawke shared some of the relief of the players, and some of their pleasure. His deal with Scott Hoag was safe, that was the main thing. He was no longer exposed to a heavy call for cash. The *Tribune* review was quite long, and it had good words for nearly every member of the cast. The actors read bits aloud to each other, laughing like children. Nancy sobbed happily over the *Tribune*.

"Listen to this." Carmian was gloating over the *News*. "'*Maybe what the theatre needs is a few more amateurs. Pierce Carmian has never before produced a Broadway play, and Youngblood Hawke has never written one. Between them they have lit up this gloomy season at last with a skyrocketing smash hit.*' A skyrocketing smash hit! That's our lead line for the ads, Georges, by God!"

"I wish we had the *Times*," Feydal said.

Carmian was declaiming the *Tribune* paragraph about Feydal's direction when Phil York came hurrying to the table in a wet overcoat, waving a smudged proof sheet. Several newspapers were folded under the columnist's arm. He thrust the proof at Hawke. "In case you're interested, there's the *Mirror*. I talked to my spy in the *Times* composing room. Rave! Moreover, you're three out of three on the evening papers. I know them all. You're home, Hawke."

Hawke glanced at the proof and passed it to Feydal. It was as frantically approving as the others.

York said, "And by the way, I picked this up while I was at the *Times*." From his sheaf of newspapers he pulled an advance copy of the Sunday book supplement. "Look at the best-seller list, Hawke."

His novel had been hovering in third or fourth place for weeks, though Ross Hodge claimed it was outselling every book in the business. Hawke flipped the supplement open, and there it was:

Will Horne. Hawke.　1

He showed the list to Jeanne. She said, yawning, "Well, good for them. They found out."

"Let me see," Nancy said, clutching for the supplement.

The columnist threw his overcoat on a chair, and pulled another chair

beside Hawke. "So far as I know," he said, "this is an event in literary history. I don't believe any American writer has ever reached number one on the best-seller list and opened a Broadway smash hit in the same week. Who's ever done it? Lewis, Hemingway, Dreiser, Steinbeck? Nobody. It's never happened before. It's the hat trick. You've done it, Youngblood Hawke. How does it feel?"

Hawke smiled at the shrewd, eager, probing look on the columnist's lean face. In his long trotting at Frieda's side around Broadway he had come to know York well, and to like him. He admired the enthusiasm with which the columnist kept at his job. York not only scoured New York night after night, year after year; he circled the world almost every year. He wrote about Moscow, Johannesburg, Cairo, about people like Churchill and Nehru, whom he really knew quite well, and he made all the rest of the earth sound a little like a Broadway show having trouble out of town. Hawke said, "Is this an interview?"

"Hell, yes," York said. "You're major news tonight."

He said, "Phil, these are both old jobs I finished long ago."

The columnist laughed. "Don't tell me you have no reaction to the fact that you stand at the absolute peak of your profession. Come on, talk."

Hawke glanced around at the table, embarrassed. Everyone was looking at him: the players, his own family, Carmian, Feydal: even Jeanne was fixing him with sharp eyes, an enigmatic, rather sad little smile playing at the corners of her mouth. It made him think of the way she had looked at him at the Prince party, watching him flirt with Frieda Winter.

He said, "Oh, Christ, Phil, haven't you seen the reviews of *Will Horne?* What kind of peak is that? And as for this play, what is it but a sausage made of scraps of an old novel? They're my scraps so I'm entitled to the money. So far as serious work goes, I'm just getting started—"

"Here's the *Times!*" The restaurant proprietor rushed up with half a dozen newspapers and handed them around. They smelled strongly of ink; Hawke's fingers blackened as he turned the heavy damp pages. Before he found the theatre section he heard Feydal say flatly, "Oh my God. Oh my God." He felt a little sick on the instant with an old sickness. He found the review.

Since Youngblood Hawke is a big man, in talent and in stature, one expects big things of him. Mr. Hawke may be too big for the theatre. For it cramps his style. After a stupefying first act he has managed to recapture in his *Alms for Oblivion* play some of the flaring excitements of his huge melodramatic novel, but the evening will come alive too late for certain restless theatregoers.

Nobody can say that Irene Perry and a fine company, under the silken direction of Georges Feydal, have not made a neat and expert evening of *Alms*

for Oblivion, once the chloroform of the beginning has been shaken off. We have heard great rumors of this show, and on the whole the plaudits are not undeserved, but . . .

So the review went. Hawke's eye skipped over the details of the plot and the generous praise of the acting to the concluding lines:

It may be that Youngblood Hawke will always be more at home in the large loose spaces of the novel, but one hopes he will return to the theatre. His vitality is a strong antidote to the chronic anemia of Broadway. For his play does have a rough Kentucky vitality, in its good moments. Perhaps he has already learned the first lesson of the drama: unlike fiction, it permits almost no margin for error. In the playhouse it can prove fatal to be even briefly boring.

Hawke's mother said, "Let me see that paper, Art." Hawke handed it to her. There was no laughter and no reading aloud now. Feydal was studying the review through heavy glasses. Carmian tossed his newspaper contemptuously on the stained cloth, lit a cigarette, and watched Feydal. The actors looked over each other's shoulders at a couple of copies of the review, their faces drawn. Nancy and her husband each held one side of a newspaper, reading eagerly. Hawke saw people at other tables, copies of the *Times* in hand, peering over at the cast party to see how the victims were reacting. No waiters came near. It was a while before anyone spoke.

Feydal removed his glasses and sighed aloud. "Well! I call it bad luck that of all the seven dwarfs, we fell foul of Dopey. He's the one that counts."

Carmian said, "I don't think it's bad. I think it's a money notice."

"I agree," said Phil York.

The fat old actor passed a handkerchief over his brow. He had gone quite pale, but he appeared calm and genial as ever. "My dear Pierce, he opens with the word *stupefying* and he closes with *boring.* What goes between does not matter. Our show is a success and will make money. Our run has been cut in half."

Mrs. Hawke exclaimed, still reading the review, "Why, this fellow's just a nasty old fool. What's he so mad about?"

Carmian snapped, "He's mad, mother, because we came into town with a goddamned steamrolling triumph that wasn't going to live or die by his nod. Even so, he had to admit we have a tremendous show. There are ten marvellous quotes in that revolting mess of vomit, and by God I'll use them."

Hawke said, "I think it's the most accurate appraisal of my play." He was thinking ruefully that if the run was cut in half, he would end with a very large cash debt to Paumanok Plaza.

"Why, it's nothing but pure venom," said Nancy.

Feydal smiled at Hawke like a man on his deathbed forgiving all his enemies. "It's quite true, old cock, that he takes note of the weakness which the others overlooked. It's a question of tone. He could have noted for the record, or to destroy. He noted to destroy. This is your first play. We must fault Dopey for ill-using you."

"We won't lose a day of the run," Carmian said. "That notice means nothing."

Feydal said, "Pierce, we had two years in the bag. Possibly three if you could have persuaded Irene to stay on. Now we'll close in the summer."

"Oh, stop talking like that, it's bad for the company morale, and there's not a word of truth in it," said Carmian. "Unless the whole world grovels at your feet you always think the end has come. You're being a hysterical old woman."

Feydal stared at the handsome producer, and to Hawke's astonishment tears welled from his eyes and dripped on his fat cheeks. He got up and strode away from the table and out of the restaurant.

Carmian giggled in the shocked silence. "Georges and his sweeping gestures," he said. "He's just tired, so he turns on the gloom and doom. He's been wanting to go home to bed for an hour. I know the signs. I'd better telephone Irene. She probably has the *Times* by now."

York said when Carmian was gone, "Those two have a running battle royal, don't they?" He tapped the *Times* on the table before Hawke. "You take my word for it. That's a money review."

Hawke said, "I hope so, Phil. Come on, mama, bedtime. Come Jeanie, I'll take you home."

CHAPTER SEVENTEEN

1

LIKE airplane crashes, schoolboy suicides seem to come in the news in clusters. Paul Winter had undoubtedly read about the ones that had occurred in the past two weeks, since he read everything he could put his hands on; whether the stories had influenced him, it was impossible to say. The fact was that, while his mother and father were watching the premiere of Youngblood Hawke's play, Paul had tried to hang himself in his dormitory room at the Devon School.

He had succeeded to the extent that when his roommate found him

he was dangling unconscious from a taut twisting necktie knotted on the rack of a clothes closet, with a pile of books tumbled at his faintly twitching feet. When the corridor master, summoned by twenty boys' yells, cut him down, he still had a pulse, and he began drawing agonized sobbing breaths, his eyes closed, his mouth foaming blood. What followed was a series of mistakes and misfortunes. The corridor master sent a boy for the school nurse. He then telephoned the headmaster and stammered a long tale, trying to explain how it was that Paul had been alone after lights out. Paul's roommate, he said, had gone to an illicit spread in another room, to which Paul had not been invited. The corridor master was in the middle of his self-justifying frightened chatter when Paul's roommate began to shout at him that Paul had stopped breathing. He blurted this to the headmaster in panic, and the headmaster hung up on him and telephoned the police.

It was past ten o'clock at night. The Devon School was four miles outside a small town named Sag Hollow in the Hudson Valley, fifteen miles from the nearest hospital in Peekskill, seventy miles from New York City. The Sag Hollow police did not have a pulmotor, but the fire department did. The man who knew how to operate the pulmotor was at the movies. With all this, the pulmotor and its operator were at the Devon School about twenty minutes after the headmaster called the police. At just about the same time the nurse appeared. The boy who had been sent after her had run here and there witlessly for a quarter of an hour; she had been visiting one of the faculty wives. Ten minutes after that another pulmotor arrived from the Peekskill hospital in a screaming ambulance, with a doctor and two internes.

Minutes count in such events. The human body can go through good times and bad for seventy or ninety years, but it cannot do without air for more than a couple of minutes. Artificial breathing applied in time will often start the body working again. Oxygen and adrenalin may help. The Peekskill internes tried both; and when the headmaster managed to track down Frieda at the *Alms for Oblivion* premiere, they were still working on the boy. He was quite warm, the oxygen-enriched air was going rhythmically in and out of his lungs, and the hospital doctor had not given up hope. Nobody really knew whether Paul could be called alive or dead.

The headmaster's predicament was not enviable. He told Frieda that Paul had had a serious accident, and that she ought to come to the school at once. Frieda pressed him to tell her what the accident had been. The headmaster evaded her questions. At last the husband seized the telephone; it was in the pay booth of the dim empty theatre lounge, and they could faintly hear the lines of Hawke's play echoing from above. Winter said, "What's the matter with my boy, Dr. Finch?"

"As I told Mrs. Winter, he's had a very bad accident. We have a doctor

here from the Peekskill hospital. Everything that's possible is being done for him, but I feel you should come."

"How serious is this? Is the boy's life in danger?"

The headmaster said desperately, "We can't be sure. He's receiving every attention. It's extremely serious."

"We're coming at once. It'll take us an hour and a half at least to get there. What happened to him?"

"He had a bad fall." The headmaster was past sixty, and he could not utter the statement that a Devon boy had tried to commit suicide. He was hoping that Paul would revive and that the episode would be covered up.

Winter said, "There's no question of money, you understand. Do anything that is necessary. Maybe a New York doctor—"

"We will do everything."

When they were leaving, Winter saw Youngblood Hawke rush out of the lobby and wave; Frieda did not, Winter said nothing about it, and the limousine rolled away from the theatre.

It was a hired Cadillac—the Winters did not like to keep their man on duty at night—luxuriously upholstered, comfortable, and well-heated. The black-clad chauffeur showed no surprise at the queer order to drive to Peekskill as fast as possible; he nodded and set off, maneuvering the huge machine with skill through the traffic to the highway along the Hudson. There Winter told him not to worry about traffic police, because it was an emergency. The man nodded again and the limousine leaped off into dwindling black rain at ninety miles an hour.

The boy's parents sat in opposite corners of the wide limousine seat, separated by a thick arm rest. Winter lit a long cigar and smoked it in regular gestures. Frieda fell into the lizard-like immobility that she could command. Hands folded in her lap, face composed, eyes dry and bright and looking straight ahead, she sat in all her lavish finery, the tiara glinting in the parkway lights. She might have been speeding to a late dance. Signs flashed past: curve warnings, exits, town limits, county lines. They passed through one toll collection booth and another. Their first burst of talking subsided, and they sat with their own thoughts. Winter broke a very long silence to say, "One advantage of a city school is that the best doctors are on hand in case anything goes wrong."

Frieda said in an easy low voice, "You don't plan for serious accidents."

"That's true enough."

"Bennett went through Devon. He was in and out of the infirmary a dozen times. They took excellent care of him."

Winter said, "Still, if Paul's all right, as I assume he will be, we ought to consider transferring him to a New York school. I keep thinking how lonesome he must be up there now, how lonesome he must have been right along. He seemed lonesome enough even at home."

Frieda said, "We talked about that. The whole idea was to toughen him up a little and get him used to being on his own. I still think it was right. Accidents prove nothing."

Winter stared at his wife. He had seen her pass through many emotions and moods in one night. He knew her tricks of look and gesture well; this pleasant immobility, this low slow voice, was Frieda at the most extreme strain. She felt his glance and faced him. "Yes?"

"We might have talked about Paul a little more, Frieda."

His wife's eyes wavered in an unusual manner. For a moment she had a lonesome look like Paul's; and like the little boy, she seemed on the verge of pouring out a flood of strange confidences. Then her expression steadied into the self-reliant cool brightness she had displayed at twenty-two; and like the boy's confidences, whatever she had to say went unexpressed. "Let's find out what's the matter with him first."

2

The car drove through the stone gate of the Devon School shortly after midnight. Here it was not raining; a misty bluish moon lit the broad flat lawns and the buildings.

"Look, there's an ambulance," Winter said. "It's at the dormitory. They didn't have to take him away, after all. That's something. That's where we want to go, driver."

Frieda said, "I feel like a fool in these clothes." She took off the tiara and leaned forward to the chauffeur. "Please hold this for me, until we go back."

"Yes, ma'am."

Paul did not look bad at all. He lay on his own bed in the dormitory room, in his maroon bathrobe and blue pajamas, his eyes closed and his chin down on his chest, as he often looked when he fell asleep reading. His face had a blue tinge, as though he was cold, and it had the lonesome, sad look usual to him in repose. His mouth was a little pulled down, as though in disappointment. The only unusual thing was the purple bruise around his neck.

The policeman who met the Winters at the entrance to the dormitory said only, "I'm sorry, it's not good." But the Peekskill doctor, who was writing up a certificate at Paul's desk when they came into the room, stood and said sadly, "We did everything we could. Your boy was beyond recovery. I'm terribly sorry."

"He's—good God, he's *gone!*" the father said.

"Yes, he's gone," the doctor said.

"What happened? *What happened?*"

Nobody answered. The headmaster, the housemaster, a policeman, the

school nurse and the two white-coated internes were also in the room, so that it seemed very crowded. They all had the same look of sickened embarrassment. The internes were packing away a machine of cylinders and rubber tubing, with exhausted gestures. Frieda sat beside her dead son, too shocked for any normal reaction, and caressed his face. How long his legs were! She could not help thinking of him as a baby, though he was over twelve. He was cool, but he had sometimes felt this cold after a swim. The immobility of his chest, and a very faint odor of death, told the story. She looked at her husband and held out her hand; he took it, and stood close beside her. The men in the room kept a respectful distance from the beautiful woman in the splendid blue-gray dress and coat and the stooping, white-mustached man in the overcoat with a black velvet collar.

Frieda ran her fingers along the bruise on Paul's neck. "Is this what happened when he fell? He doesn't seem too badly hurt, but—" Her hold on her husband's hand tightened and she pulled herself to her feet. Her eyes widened and rolled like a terrorized animal's. She said stridently, "What happened to my Paul, Dr. Finch?"

Dr. Finch, a corpulent man in a red dressing gown, his gray face sagging, his eyes red as blood, said hoarsely, "Mrs. Winter, we're sure it was an accident, a prank that went tragically awry. His roommate found Paul hanging by a necktie in the clothes closet. Obviously he was just playing a prank, trying to frighten—" The man's voice failed.

The parents stood hand in hand, staring at Dr. Finch. Then the corridor master, a tall skinny man whose throat kept moving convulsively, said, "It was long after lights out. I had definitely seen them both in bed asleep. I checked twice. His roommate sneaked out for a while, against all regulations, and when he returned—"

Winter said dazedly, waving both hands, "Can we be alone with him?"

The others walked quickly out of the room, the internes carrying their apparatus. The headmaster closed the thick dark oak door.

No sound came from behind the door for perhaps five minutes. Then it opened. The father leaned against the doorway, crying, looking as though he might fall. The man in police uniform at once took his elbow. Frieda stepped past her husband, upright and very pale. She had washed her face and wiped away most of her paint with the towel. There were droplets of water on her neck. The lines around her eyes and mouth were much more visible. She asked the headmaster if any arrangements had been made, and talked calmly of what she wanted done. She had picked out the clothes in which Paul was to be buried, and they were on a chair beside his bed. The upshot of the disorganized conversation among the doctors, the policeman, the masters, and the dead boy's mother was that Paul would be taken to a funeral parlor in Peekskill; that she would go back to New York with her husband, and return later in the day to ac-

company the body to New York after going through the legal formalities. While they talked Winter stood leaning on the policeman, now and then making an incoherent suggestion.

She said to her husband, "All right, that's that. Now the doctor will give us both something and we'll go back to New York."

He said, "But who's going to stay with the boy?"

She said, "We can't stay. Neither of us has proper clothes. Dr. Finch will see to everything. We'll have a lot to do in New York. I'm coming back in the morning."

"All right, Frieda, if that's how it is." But when they were halfway down the hall he broke away and ran clumsily back to Paul's room. They found him kneeling by the bed, his hands clasped on the dead boy's feet. He came along with docility when the doctors picked him up and led him away, his red contorted face streaming tears, his thick mustache matted dark and wet.

He was being helped into the limousine. Frieda stood on the gravel of the driveway, watching. She heard a loud peculiar whisper, "Mrs. Winter! Mrs. Winter!" from behind her. The tall corridor master stood under the yellow light of the dormitory entrance, beckoning at her with a bony finger, grimacing in a way that showed all his big teeth. She went up the steps and followed him into his small book-lined room. He shut the door and confronted her, skinny and awkward, an ugly long-nosed young man with protruding teeth and sandy hair, in a state of hysterical fear. His mouth worked for a few seconds before he managed to say in a high voice, "I feel the way I did when my mother died. It's awful. He was a fine boy, Mrs. Winter, and he would have done very well. None of his problems were serious, he was well-liked, it's utterly incomprehensible. I'm sure he just meant to scare his roommate, and his foot slipped. It's the kind of trick boys play all the time. It's a frightful tragedy." He spoke in a muffled slurring way as though he were drunk.

Frieda said, "I appreciate that it was undoubtedly an accident, and I thank you for your sympathy." She made a move toward the door.

He plunged his hand into a side pocket of his baggy tweed jacket and kept it there. "I don't know whether I've done the right thing. At first of course I was sure Paul would come to, so this seemed to be nobody's business. It's really been driving me crazy, I didn't know whether to speak to Dr. Finch about it, or to the police. I think the right thing is to let you have the responsibility." He jerked his hand out of the pocket. It clutched a wrinkled envelope. "I'm afraid I've messed it inadvertently, through nervousness. But I do think I've followed Paul's wishes, and that was the right thing after all. I found this on his desk when I first came in. None of the boys saw it, I'm sure of that. I'll never say anything about it unless you do. I have no idea what's in it. It's yours to decide about."

He held the letter out to her. His arm seemed monstrously long. She

took the envelope, which was warm and moist from the sweat of his hand, and firmly sealed. On the wrinkled front was a line in Paul's jagged childish hand:

For my mother ONLY—nobody else!

"Thank you," she said. "You did exactly the right thing." She put the letter in her sequined blue silk purse.

"I hope so. I guess I was violating the law. Certainly I took it into my own hands. I've never been in such a situation and I had to follow my instincts."

"Of course. Goodbye."

He seemed reluctant to open the door, but he did, and she walked out. Dr. Finch handed her into the limousine. Winter was slumped in a corner of the back seat. In one hand he held a cigar and in the other the cellophane wrapper. He looked at her vacantly.

"Paul, how do you feel?"

"That was quite a capsule the doctor gave me. I'm sleepy."

"Good. Try to get some rest, it'll be a long drive."

The doctors, the headmaster, the policeman spoke a jumble of regrets to her through the limousine window. Dr. Finch said in a choked tone, "Everything will be in order when you come back, Mrs. Winter, I can promise you that. It's the least the school can do for you."

"All right. I'll try to be back by noon."

"Mrs. Winter, I'm shattered—I've been a headmaster for twenty years and this is the first—all the boys in this school are like my own children—"

"Yes, Dr. Finch." She nodded at the driver, who was watching her, and he drove off. When they came to the stone gate he stopped. "Madam, the police told me what it was, and I want to say I'm sorry." He tipped his black chauffeur's cap, picked something off the seat beside him and extended it to her. It was the tiara. Frieda stared at the jewelled circlet, blinking, for a moment, then she took it and her hand fell into her lap with it.

The limousine cruised down a black asphalt road in the moonlight and came to the parkway. By that time Winter was fast asleep, his broken efforts to talk faded into silence. He had never lit the cigar. She removed it from his limp hand. She looked at his white aged face, which hardly swayed as the car rolled smoothly toward New York. She took Paul's letter from her purse, switched on the reading light of the back seat, and tore open the envelope.

The letter was two pages long. She had hardly begun it when she started, held the letter against her chest, and darted a glance at her husband. Her face wore the same look of dismayed surprise that had come over it when Mrs. Hawke had opened the door and found her in Hawke's bed. She squinted at her husband and shook him gently, but he was insensible. She finished reading the letter. She read it again. She read it a

third time. She let it fall in her lap, where it lay beside the tiara. Frieda switched off the light and sat staring in the gloom at the road rolling past.

And now Frieda Winter began to cry, with her handkerchief stuffed against her mouth so that she made no sound. Her face crumpled into a wounded unbelieving look like a little girl's when she has been struck by an indulgent father. Her eyes opened very wide, and tears ran from them. She cried until the limousine came into the city, but she never made a sound.

When the car stopped for a red light at Central Park West, she asked the driver to step out to the news stand and get her the morning papers. The General Motors sign, high and foggy against a black sky, proclaimed the time: twenty minutes past five. She snapped on the reading light, and as the car drove between the curving stone walls of the Sixty-sixth Street transverse she scanned the notices for *Alms for Oblivion*, though her eyes were so swollen that she could hardly focus them on the print.

The first thing she did after coming home and arousing the household was to put her drugged, bewildered old husband to bed, with the help of the shocked and grieving servants, who had all liked Paul very much despite his queer ways. Her next act was to write a short note to Hawke, which she sealed into an envelope together with the letter from Paul that the corridor master had given her. She went out and mailed this herself. Dawn was dusting the highest towers of Manhattan with patches of pink.

3

Some hours before dawn, Hawke had taken Jeanne home and settled down on the sofa in the living room, quite as in the old days, minus his shoes, his jacket, and his tie. He was as near total exhaustion as he had ever been in his life. His head throbbed, his stomach ached emptily, and he felt shaky all over. But he was cheerful, because he was with Jeanne; and ravenous. He was idly leafing through a large typewritten manuscript, labelled:

Evelyn Biggers
A Novel by
Youngblood Hawke

From the kitchenette came the brisk noises of Jeanne's short-order cookery, and a wonderful smell of corn meal frying in oil. The door leading to the bedrooms was closed. Jeanne poked her head into the room. "I forget how you like your tacos. Lots of hot sauce, or a little bit?"

Hawke said, "Half a bottle per taco."

"Of course. It's Karl who can't take hot sauce . . . Reading your own book?"

"Well, looking at it. I see a million disgusting mistakes in English."

"No doubt. That's what happens at the peak of the profession. Beer?"

"Jeanne, stop pretending we're strangers."

She laughed. "Well, it's been nearly two years. What makes you think your little tastes are so memorable to me?"

In a few minutes she came out with a tray of tacos and two bottles of beer. "All for you," she said. "None for Jolly Jeanne, sweetheart of the freak show, four hundred pounds of quivering female pulchritude."

"Sit down and eat with me. Stop being a fool."

"Arthur, you can't imagine how I hate being fat. I look in the mirror and cry."

He wolfed one taco and took another. "Marvellous. I haven't felt like eating for weeks. Where the devil did you learn Mexican cooking, anyway?"

"Dear, those are sold like hot dogs in California. There's nothing to it, you just fry up tortillas and fold in the meat and vegetables."

Hawke said with his mouth full, "This is the way you always make them best, too, with chicken— What the hell are you grinning about? I can't help being hungry."

Jeanne said, "It's not chicken, honey. It's turkey. From Karl's birthday party last Sunday."

"Christ, when is turkey going to stop being a dirty word between you and me? Jeanne, take a taco and some beer or I'll go home."

"Well, I'll eat one. Didn't Frieda look magnificent at the theatre?"

"She looked the same as always."

"Arthur, she had on a beautiful tiara I've never seen before, and neither have you, I'll bet."

"I didn't notice. She didn't have a tiara in Europe. I don't think she did. We went to the opera once."

"Didn't you treat her shabbily tonight? In the lobby, during intermission?"

"I was very polite to her."

"Exactly, dear."

Hawke was on his third taco. He picked up a bottle of beer and drained it. "Good. Very cold."

Jeanne went to the kitchen and brought him another. She sat beside him, and said casually, "Whatever happened in Venice, it seems to have been cataclysmic."

"Not at all. Don't worry, I'll tell you about it. Just let me eat first."

"Arthur, I'm not trying to pump you."

"Not much! It was a dismal business, and it's soon told." He drank half his beer, looking off wryly and absently at a wall. "She got me to meet her in London, you know. Never mind how, Frieda is an ingenious woman. This was back in August. Then we went to Paris, then after a

while we went to Venice. Frieda's purpose of course, for all her talk of friendship, was to fan the embers. The trouble was that I couldn't do the adoring mountain boy of twenty-six any more, for many obvious reasons. It was all pretty unsatisfactory. Fanned embers, Jeanie, are not fresh logs. In Venice she began to get annoyed. I was just drifting along. I'd finished *Evelyn* and I was in the semi-comatose state I fall into sometimes, really an acute depression stemming from a sense of failure, but it took the form of a certain, shall we say, masculine indifference? Frieda doesn't like that. I guess she decided to try some strong medicine. We were in this bar where this extremely good-looking and talented colored pianist was—I'm sure he'll come over here some day and make a sensation, he's from the French West Indies and he's the kind that makes silly white women breathe hard and giggle nervously—and aside from that he plays and sings good jazz. There were these two little pianos in the bar, back to back. The idea is that amateurs come and play at the other piano, and he improvises along and makes them look good. You can imagine how this wows the sissies with bleached hair who haunt the bar. Well, what happened was that my beloved Frieda started to play a jazz duet with the colored man, flirting with him over the top of the piano as she played, to see if she could strike some sparks out of me. Or maybe she just enjoyed doing it. I've never pretended to fathom her mind. She sat down at the second piano, anyway, and started to go. Have you ever heard Frieda play jazz?"

"I don't think so. Only Christmas carols."

"Well, believe me she plays jazz, as she does everything else, with enormous competence—and when she's in the mood, with something more. That Negro's eyes all but fell out of his head when Frieda sat and slammed out four chords. Then he grinned a mouthful of piano keys and hopped aboard.

"It was something. Somebody should have made a tape recording of that performance. Or better yet a color movie—that smoky dingy bar with its chrome and beige leather for the American trade, and the faggots in their skimpy Italian suits twittering and clustering around those two toy pianos, drinks in hand, and Frieda in a low cut green dress with no sleeves smashing away with those thin strong arms of hers and spider fingers, and the Negro in a red sports jacket grinning and rolling with sweat and pounding his little box till it danced and the angled mirror over his head shook. And of course the big oafish American who had brought this *divine* woman, sitting glowering alone at a table and getting drunker and drunker. Let's not forget that comical slob.

"After they roared through twenty minutes of fast numbers and boogie-woogie they played a couple of slow ones. That was something to hear. They didn't have to flirt with grins and winks any more. They brushed each other with little tendrils of notes. I swear to God Jeanie, that's the

way to make love if you can do it, on two pianos, there's so much more room for nuances of tenderness and passion than in the comical gymnastics of the real thing. Believe me, I couldn't help appreciating the beauty of it, but at the same time it irritated the hell out of me, of course. Especially when this crowd of pretty boys began glancing at me and nudging each other. Imagine being cuckolded in public on two pianos! That was about the size of it. It just went on and on. They began to play fast again. Frieda really got caught up. She was perspiring like this Negro. The homos began to utter little shrieks of carnal delight. I finally walked up to her and said, 'Let's go, Frieda.' She said, 'Oh, go on to bed if you're tired. I'm having fun!' And she went right on banging away, looking the Negro in the eyes over the piano tops. I got squeaks and titters and amused looks from the fairies. It was smash up the place or leave."

Jeanne said, "So you smashed it up."

"No. I'm a good citizen. I walked out. I went back to our suite at the Royal Danieli, but of course I couldn't sleep. I waited one hour, two hours, three hours, four hours, five hours, watching the clock and watching the entrance of the hotel. I watched the sky grow light and the sun come up. It was after eight when Frieda came chugging up in a motorboat taxi. The Negro helped her get out and I heard him shout goodbye to her and laugh.

"Well, then, here comes Frieda into our sitting room, see, humming cheerily, fresh as a buttercup, obviously much the better for a shower and a new makeup job, and altogether in a glow. 'What?' she chirrups. 'Up already, dear? I thought you were so tired.'"

Jeanne raised her palm to silence Hawke. A loud whimpering came from the back of the apartment. She glanced at her watch. "That little devil! He's not due to eat again for hours. Go ahead, maybe he'll shut up."

The baby, as though answering her, uttered a protesting howl. She shrugged and stood. When she opened the door to the bedrooms Karl called sleepily, "Jeanne?"

"Yes, I'll get him."

"Thanks. I gave the greedy bastard a bottle and a half at two."

Hawke heard Jeanne say, "Arthur's here." Fry replied, "Good. How are the notices?" Jeanne said, "It's a smash hit." Her husband replied, "Well, tell him congratulations, and if he wants to adopt a baby I think we can do business."

Jeanne reappeared with Jim wrapped in a blue blanket. "Here. Hold him while I warm the bottle. He likes men."

Hawke said, looking dubiously at the small pink-faced creature, "How do you hold a baby?"

"Easy." Jeanne firmly placed the baby in his arms. "Jim, you keep your

yap shut now, this man won the Pulitzer Prize and he's at the peak of his profession."

The baby and Hawke inspected each other. Jim was an extremely handsome baby, with a square jaw and wide mouth like Jeanne's, and gigantic blue eyes. He blinked at Hawke, and his face folded in a toothless grin. Hawke called into the kitchen, "Jeanne, this thing is smiling at me."

"Better smiling than yelling. Don't panic if he throws up, just let him do it. He often throws up after smiling." Jeanne came in with a saucepan of steaming water in which a nursing bottle stood. "Good lord, you hold him as though he were a rattlesnake. Let me have him. What do you think of him?"

"Well, he's a baby," Hawke said.

"He sure is," Jeanne said, settling on the sofa with Jim in her arms. "I really did it. I couldn't have been more surprised. I never thought I'd produce anything but inter-office memos."

"He's beautiful, Jeanne. If you can call a fellow beautiful."

Jeanne gave him a shy smile, and ran her fingers along the baby's cheek. Jim yawned. She looked at Hawke expectantly. "Well?"

"Well, what? I'll go home and leave you with Jim. Thanks for the tacos and the beer, Jeanie."

"Arthur Hawke, don't you dare, you sit right there and finish that story, for God's sake." She shook water off the bottle and inserted the nipple in Jim's mouth.

Hawke studied Jeanne as she sat placidly in her black evening dress, holding the bottle to the mouth of the blue-wrapped baby cradled in an arm. The calm sweetness of her face made him feel at once sad and exhilarated. "I don't know. It hardly seems a fit topic to pursue in the presence of the madonna and child. Some other time."

"Oh, cut it out, it's delicious for a trapped cow like me to hear how the carefree wicked live. It's better than a movie. Frieda has just walked in at an ungodly hour long after sunrise, having apparently had herself one hell of a time."

"Yes, well, you can imagine what my mood was," Hawke said reluctantly. "I'm afraid I sort of manhandled her. I'd feel worse about that if I didn't know—if I didn't perceive even at the time with complete clarity —that she was bent on provoking just such a reaction. It worked, to be sure. We had a full-fledged lovers' quarrel spiced by physical violence, with the usual aftermath. What Frieda wanted was the aftermath. She got it, but the price was too high. I didn't believe her story, you see, though she stuck to it through some roughhouse that damned near shook the teeth out of her head. Her story was that when the joint closed at four a bunch of them, including the piano player and herself, adjourned to a palazzo rented by some fat old sodomite with red-dyed hair whom

I'd seen in the bar. She said he was a tremendously rich Englishman, but she couldn't remember his name and she was vague on where the palazzo was, too. Claimed they all piled hilariously into gondolas and just went there. She said there was a grand piano, and she played and the colored man played and they had herb omelettes and caviar and champagne, and pretty soon it was sunrise, so she took a shower and came back to the hotel. It was a plausible enough story but there was something that prevented me from believing it, and if you want to know, it was the way I'd seen her walk half a dozen steps from the boat into the hotel. I know Frieda's various gaits, or I think I do. I told her I didn't believe her, and for all the red-hot reconciliation after the fight I didn't. I left her sleeping and went to the bar to ask some questions but of course it was closed, it wasn't even noon.

"I spent the day wandering around Venice in a daze. I can't describe to you how sick I was. I'll never be that sick at heart again. You can only go through that kind of agony once, Jeanne, then something in your heart gives way for good."

Hawke did not see the spasm that crossed Jeanne's face, followed by a shadowy melancholy smile. He was staring at the empty air.

"What seemed to bother me most was that I had gone through the physical act of reconciliation with her. I felt as though my body were coated with some dirty grease that I would never get off. All this, mind you, was whirling around in my head while I walked in St. Mark's Cathedral, and the Doge's Palace, and half a dozen churches and museums. I'm a conscientious boy, I'd been meaning to do the sights for a week, but between Frieda and my publisher I'd mainly been eating tremendous elegant lunches and dinners at the luxury restaurants and going to long chatterbox parties of very flossy Venetians and Britishers.

"Jeanne, Venice is unspeakably enchanting. The water is dirty and stinks and the gondolas are just a prop for tourists now—you take a motor boat if you want to get somewhere—but you have no idea how much art, how much architectural treasure, how much incredible manmade beauty there is mouldering away in Venice. There is more art in any one street of old Venice—dying, blackening, crumbling great art— than there is in the whole United States, in the whole Western Hemisphere. An obscure stairway in an old palazzo, not one of the great ones, will be covered with paintings and lined with sculptures, all masterpieces. And it goes on and on, there's no end to it, one treasure trove more breathtaking than the next. Yet here we had been for a week in this shrine of glory, this great monument to the dignity and wit of the human race, and all our trip had come down to—despite Frieda's prattle of art and beauty, and she really knows a hell of a lot more about painting and architecture than I ever will—all it had come down to, I say, was a lot of

rich stuffing and guzzling and snobbish chit-chat, and at last a nigger pianist in a lousy pseudo-American bar full of fairies."

Jeanne said, "I was waiting for you to say that word."

"What word?"

"Nigger. That's the whole point of the story, isn't it? What else had Frieda done, or what else did you suspect her of doing, that was new to you?"

Hawke nodded slowly. "I've had that thought, of course. You don't get the South out of your bones by reading liberal books and going to New York parties where there are clever and charming colored people. But I think the crude public way she set about putting the screws on me, just to squeeze out a few last drops of an old passion, was the thing—not the colored man."

Jeanne smiled skeptically, turning the bottle in the baby's mouth so that it burbled.

"Be that as it may, I got back to the hotel and found my beloved singing like a lark and putting an extra special golden polish on herself, because we were going to dine at the palace of a duchess. This was di Strozzi's doing. He's my Italian publisher, you know, a mild smooth little man with beautiful thick gray hair, from a terrific old family, with manners like October sunlight, cool and warm at once, and charming in his every gesture, he lights a cigarette for a woman and you hear an invisible violin break into a minuet. A delightful sweet fellow, cultured to the marrow, unbelievably rich, and absolutely nothing interests him but money. My books sell like hell in Italy, you know. *Oblivion* did better there than even in West Germany. Carlo di Strozzi can't do enough for me, and anyway I amuse him.

"He, by the way, was far less impressed with Frieda than most New Yorkers are. He seemed to take stock of her at a glance. The measured politeness Carlo doled out to her with a tincture of disapproval one tenth of one percent short of contempt, was really something to behold. Frieda knocked herself out to look well and to watch her company manners whenever we were with di Strozzi. We went to this palace on one of the side canals, not a grandiose building but my God, Jeanne, the wealth, the wealth! We ate off gold plates, each one engraved with different pictures. The ceiling was covered with frescoes that looked like Tintorettos and may well have been. I should have asked but I thought it would be vulgar. The duchess was a magnificent gloomy old bat in black dragging silk, with a black wiggy-looking wig. There were several other people there, Italian and British, all with the offhand cream-of-the-cream manners and the subtle eye signals of the very rich. Now I get by in such situations because I so obviously don't belong, and I've learned long ago to overdo the bull in the china shop, the note of fresh air, and so make them laugh and feel superior and at the same time in good company. Once a British

noblewoman, Lady Somethingdale, said to me in flirting tones, 'I do so like Creative.' Not creative *people*, mind you. She said, 'I like Creative,' the way you would say you like Wedgwood. That's how I pass in those circles.

"But Frieda really doesn't, you know. I once thought Frieda was an aristocrat. She's sort of middle-crust for New York, but in Italy believe me she's nobody. Not that I give a damn for European aristocrats, either. God knows they're all playing the last cards of a losing hand, and all they have really is their creature comforts, their self-importance, and a life of fear."

Hawke coughed. His voice was hardly more than a grating whisper; it had been steadily weakening. "I don't know how I can drivel on like this. I haven't slept in days but that food gave me a new lease on life. Since Frieda left Venice I've done very little eating."

"How about some hot coffee?" Jeanne said.

"No. I've got to go to the hotel and get some rest. I have several business conferences tomorrow and—Christ, it's half-past four, Jeanne!"

"I know."

Hawke stretched, and began to put on his shoes. "Well, you can guess the rest, can't you? When we finally shook free of the duchess and di Strozzi around midnight, I headed straight for the Expatriates Bar with Frieda. She didn't want to go, Lord she really didn't, she seemed to sense what would happen, said she'd had it, once was fun but a second time would be boring and so forth. But I dragged her there, all right. The faggots all burst into applause when they saw her come in. The pianist was belting away, but he stopped and grinned from ear to ear and shouted, 'Hi Frieda honey, wheah you been? One drink and you on!'

"This bar is small and cramped, Jeanne, and the only free tables were near the piano. We ordered stingers and the pianist kept winking and beckoning to Frieda, and she wouldn't budge. He played the slow thing that he and she had made into a sort of long dirty *Liebestod* the night before, giving her real languorous looks. The fairies were giggling and calling encouragement to Frieda, and she just sat there looking embarrassed and cross. She hadn't enjoyed the dinner, all those wealthy zombies had snubbed her terribly, and this Negro player's manner to her was far too familiar any way you could possibly look at it.

"Well, at one point he called over to her, 'Frieda, honey, you can't do this to me. That empty piano's ruining the show.' That's when I got up and said, 'You're absolutely right. We can't let an empty piano spoil the show, can we? Let me fix that.' I picked up the piano—it wasn't terribly heavy, they must make those cabaret jobs out of aluminum or something —and I carried it outside and threw it in the canal. It made surprisingly little splash, just went down with a big bubble. I was calm, but everybody else got into an amazing uproar. You should have heard the noise

in that bar. It was as though a garter snake had gotten loose in a sorority house. I came in and got Frieda. She was ready enough to go, she ran outside, but the owner of the place, a pleasant fellow ordinarily but very upset at this point, blocked my way and stamped his foot and shrieked, 'How *could* you throw my piano into the canal? How *could* you, how *could* you?' From here on I think I got out of line. I said, 'It wasn't hard, here's how I did it,' and I picked up the other piano, carried it out and threw *it* into the canal. Then I came back into the bar. By now I was feeling pretty good. The pianist was backed into a corner, he had on a purple jacket this night and he looked very frightened, but I wasn't going to do anything to him. I felt no resentment against him, and anyway with mah Kentucky accent and all, Jeanne"—Hawke thickened his accent to vaudeville—"Ah didn't want mah honest moral indignation to be mistaken fo' race prijidice. It was all these chirping and screeching faggots who annoyed me, anyway, it wasn't the pianist. Somehow it seemed to me that they had caused all the trouble. I'm afraid I went behind the bar and shoved it over on them in a great crash of Scotch sours and brandy Alexanders and crème de menthe frappés, and then, and I guess there was no excuse for this, I threw a chair at the angled mirror over the place where the pianos had been and broke it to pieces. That was all I did. I didn't *wreck* the place, as the papers said. I hated the mirror because the night before in that same mirror I had watched Frieda's passionate and sweaty face for an hour or so as she worked herself up.

"The rest I told you on the overseas telephone. I was really amazed, you know, to hear from you. Di Strozzi had smoothed the whole thing over with bland efficiency. I thought it had sunk without a trace, the entire little to-do, into the muddy and malodorous lagoon of the long Venetian past."

Jeanne shook her head at him, then looked down at her baby. "He's finished." She carried Jim inside and bedded him down. When she returned to the living room Hawke had on his baggy gray raincoat and was holding his cap. He said, "When do you think you'll get a chance to read *Evelyn?*"

"I'll do nothing else from now on till I finish it. I should get a few hours' sleep, but I'm not at all sleepy . . . That's quite a story, your Venetian adventure."

"Maybe I made it sound good in the telling. It was a squalid episode. I behaved like a college boy. The worst of it was that I thoroughly enjoyed the destruction. When I broke that mirror I broke with Frieda— I think forever. I went back to the hotel after the police court business without an emotion left in me. Frieda, who had beat it up there long before, was awake and waiting for me. I had nothing to say to her. She might have been a talkative chambermaid. She kept trying to start a conversation but I just undressed and went to sleep. I think she became

frightened at the way the reporters were trying to reach me, because she left Venice on the first plane she could get in the morning. The next time I saw her was a few hours ago, in the lobby at the theatre."

Jeanne said, "You're a great one for throwing things or people around, aren't you? The first time we were ever together, in my Sixty-fifth Street apartment, you threw a man down the stairs."

"Jeanne, I've had only four or five fist fights in my life. I've won them, but I hate the feeling of hitting a man. A good heave is harmless and relieves the feelings. Why, I once threw Pierce Carmian in a swimming pool and apparently I endeared myself to him for life."

Jeanne picked up the manuscript of *Evelyn Biggers* and hefted it. "Feels more like a Waugh than a Hawke."

"It's short for a Hawke, but it was much the hardest yet to write."

"Why didn't you let me see any of it before?"

"You'll know when you read it."

"I'll telephone you the minute I finish it. Some time tomorrow, I'd guess."

"Good. If I'm not at the Plaza try Gus Adam's office."

Jeanne walked out to the automatic elevator with him. "What's going to be doing at Adam's office?"

"I got into a real estate deal that was based on the assumption *Oblivion* would be a smash hit. In view of the *Times* notice I think we may have to call it off."

"Oh, that shopping center in Long Island." Jeanne made a wry face. "You went ahead with that, eh?"

"That's why I flew back, Jeanne, to execute the papers."

"And where to after this?"

"I'm not sure." He grinned at her in a boorish, guilty way. "I sort of left a girl in Venice. Nothing serious, but—"

The elevator arrived and the doors rolled open. Jeanne was scowling fiercely. Hawke put on his cap. "You disapprove?"

"Not at all. From what you tell me of Venice, I should be glad to hear it's a girl."

"I'll stay in New York, Jeanie. Say the word."

"What word? Who am I? I'll call you about *Evelyn*. Good night." Jeanne abruptly went into her apartment and shut the door.

4

The offices of Tulking and Adam, attorneys-at-law, hung some five hundred feet above solid earth in an old tower commanding magnificent views of the city, of the thronging ships in its harbors and rivers, of its surrounding miles and miles of flat gray homes and factories, and even

of a rim of green Jersey hills far to the west. The tower rose out of the money ganglion of the world, the downtown financial district, amid many other towers spiking up around it. Gus Adam's office looked toward the green Statue of Liberty, far out among the hooting ships. Adam was glad he had this office, though it was the smaller of the two executive rooms, because he could see the statue. Mr. Tulking as senior partner of course had the northern office, twice as large and with its own washroom.

Hawke had only seen Tulking two or three times: a small man with a rather hobbling gait, a mottled skin, and veiled eyes that seemed to hold behind them all the evil tired wisdom of old Egypt. Tulking was supposed to know more American tax law than anybody. Corporations worth less than twenty-five million dollars did not attempt to retain him. Tulking disapproved of Adam's troubling himself with the affairs of a person like Youngblood Hawke; he thought it a self-indulgent waste of time, like practicing golf swings during office hours. This was true though he had read Hawke's books and greatly admired them. The sums of money involved in an author's business—even of a famous and successful author —were simply not significant and did not require the attention of Tulking and Adam. Tulking regarded Adam's teaching at Columbia with more favor, that added prestige to the firm, and moreover contributed to the continuity of society and the stability of the law. The senior partner had himself taught in his younger years, before becoming one of the oracular authorities of the land on the mysteries of money.

His mottled face creased in a dry forgiving smile when he looked into Adam's office and saw the author sitting in one armchair and Scotty Hoag in another; it was as though he had caught Adam kissing a secretary. Adam sat in his shirtsleeves, in a swivel chair behind the desk, his arms clasped behind his head. Tulking said, "Good afternoon, Mr. Hawke. Gus, the El Paso people are in my office."

Adam nodded. "Can you start it rolling, Abe? I'll check in, say, in about ten minutes? The first thing is the holes in the prospectus."

"All right. I thought you would present that part, but it makes no difference." Tulking looked at Hawke, blinking his heavy eyelids. "I'm sorry to see the *Times* didn't like your play. I thought it was a fine play, and I want to thank you for the tickets."

Adam said, "The rest of the critics loved it. It's a success."

"I hope it is. It's just that so many people who go to the theatre read the *Times*." Tulking left.

The three men glanced at each other. Scotty scratched his balding pink head and laughed. "Doggone it, Gus, if I didn't think you an honest type I'd say you put your partner up to that."

Adam said, "He spoke right on cue, didn't he?"

"I dunno, I just can't believe New Yorkers are gonna be all that crazy,

to pass up such a show. Why, it's the finest show I've ever seen. My wife says the same."

"Scotty, they're not passing it up," Hawke said. "The box office reports that the window sale is fair and there's a line. But these treasurers can feel the difference between a smash hit and a show that's just going to run out the season."

Hoag said, "I be goddamn if I can see how anybody can tell yet. Sometimes these things get stronger as they go along, don't they?"

Hawke looked to Adam, who glanced at his watch and began stuffing a pipe. The lawyer said, "I'm afraid we're talking in circles here. I've got to beg off in a few minutes. Let me remind you, Scotty, that Art flew here from Venice to sign the papers before the opening for the exact reason that until a show is reviewed in New York the money value of the author's royalty contract is X. It can be worth a quarter of a million dollars or more, as we were hoping, or it can be worth little or nothing. This element of the unknown made the exchange of Art's contract for your Paumanok Center stock somewhat more likely to stand up as a mutual risk deal. As you know I've always had the most serious reservations about this transaction, I think the Treasury will probably rule against it and declare Arthur liable for ordinary income taxes on all the royalties earned even though Paumanok Center Inc. now owns his contract. That, by the way, is also Tulking's opinion, offhand but extremely definite. All the same, until today I had hoped—"

Hoag broke in, "Gus, you forget we gonna be in and out of this sumbitch by January, 1953. Art'll get his money back with what I reckon right now will be a hundred and twenty percent profit before the Treasury ever gets around to his return. We been through five deals now, Art. Have I ever steered you wrong?" Hawke shook his head and Hoag continued earnestly, "Let's say the Treasury rules against Art. I don't think they gonna, not with a smart Letchworth County brain like you on his side"— Adam, lighting his pipe, merely ducked his head at the compliment— "but let's say they do. All right, the worst that can happen is that Art hands them over all the money they askin' for plus six percent interest. That's all the guv'ment charges for the use of that money, Gus, so long as there's been an honest difference of opinion, six percent. That's goddamn cheap rates for a quarter of a million dollars' worth of investment capital on no security, no nothing. Art'll be home free with his profit, less a little interest—probably two hundred thousand dollars or more clear gain. What's wrong with that?"

Adam puffed his pipe. "That's always been your real pitch here, hasn't it, Scotty? The deal gives Art a colorable reason to put off paying a very large sum in taxes for a couple of years, and during that period of delay he turns the money over quickly for an immense speculative profit."

"Now I wouldn't call it a pitch, Gus, I haven't tried to sell Art nothing.

We made a deal, Gus, a complicated deal, a deal we been working on for months, and it don't make binness sense to call it off because some old lady on the New York *Times* didn't enjoy Art's show."

Hawke was looking intently from one man to the other. Now he said, "Scotty, we had an understanding that the deal could be called off if the notices weren't good enough."

"But they *great*, Art. You guys both in a sumbitchin' panic, why you talk like goddamn New Yorkers, just blow sky high if everything isn't all roses."

Adam sat up with a squeak of his chair. His face was dark red. "I don't like to be talked to like a child or an idiot, Scotty. You claim you'll have Paumanok Plaza finished and sold fourteen months from now. That's going like greased lightning in construction, nowadays, and you know it. Bad weather alone can hold you up six months to a year. If you strike water digging the foundations there's no foreseeing how much time you can lose and how your costs can shoot up. There are several competitive centers being built or planned. I have far less confidence than you in a tremendously profitable sale. The collapsible corporation provision presents many hazards, and I'm not sure you can get around them without waiting three full years before selling out. This transaction has always been a risky one. I gave my reluctant consent on your word that if the show was anything but a smash we'd call it off. If you hold Art to the contract now you'll be acting in bad faith and corruptly."

Hawke expected Adam's harsh language and rough manner to bring an explosive reaction from Hoag. He was surprised by Hoag's placid nodding and by the kindly injured tone he took. "I don't think you being reasonable, Gus. I don't think you sayin' what Art really wants. Art still wants to convert royalty dollars, ghost dollars that don't mean a goddamn thing, into real money he can hang on to. He's an artist and if he has to keep bothering his head about money some important American literature isn't going to get written. I think you ignoring my record. Art's trusted me five times and he's made a pile out of it."

"He's never gone in on this scale, with this kind of liability," said the lawyer. "When the show seemed a sure smash it appeared worth while though I freely expressed my doubts—to divert the royalties to a quick turn on the real estate wheel instead of handing them over in taxes. Now the deal is absolutely out of the question."

Hoag turned to the author, who sat sunk in a deep leather armchair, pale and weary. "Art, this thing is good as gold. That show of yours isn't closing tomorrow, it's a hit. You gonna own half of Paumanok Plaza without putting up a cent of cash. Hell, if the unexpected happens and the show closes a little early, I'm not goin' to press you for cash. I just don't see panicking out of a deal that's great for both of us. I've made a lot of commitments for building materials. The bulldozers will be on

the land next Monday. I think it's a hell of a note to put me to financing the thing all over. I think it's ridiculous."

The telephone rang. Adam picked it up, and in a moment said to Hawke, "Frieda Winter's office is asking for you." Hawke shook his head. Adam said, "They say it's extremely urgent, and do we know any place that you can be reached?" Hawke once more shook his head, compressing his lips. Adam said, "Sally, tell them we just don't know where he is."

Hawke said to Hoag, "Scotty, I think we'd better act on facts and not on hopes. I'm sorry to pull out, but Gus is right. I have to."

Scotty Hoag shrugged, and spread his arms. "I'll do my best. It's like trying to stop an express train going a hundred miles an hour, but I'll do it if it's humanly possible."

Adam said, "That's no answer at all. The deal is off and we're going to liquidate the corporation at once and distribute the royalty contract back to Arthur. Do you agree?"

Scotty laughed. "Gus, ole Art has his lawyer with him in this room. I haven't. To me contracts are just pieces of paper, I've always operated on a word and a handshake, and if Art's taking back his word and handshake, I have to tell Urban Webber to get going on the paper work, that's all. But gosh, Art, you better take time and reconsider. This sumbitch can set you up for life, Art, it's real security."

Adam glanced at his watch and stood. "I'll expect to hear from Webber some time today on the liquidation. Is that correct?"

"I reckon so, if I can track him down. Today or tomorrow. What's doing in El Paso, Gus? Oil business?"

"A utility bond issue," Adam said, straightening his tie and putting on his jacket.

"Big stuff, hey?"

"Well, it's a large issue. There are a lot of wrinkles in Federal and Texas law to work out, Scotty, that's the main problem." Adam's manner suddenly became quite pleasant and conversational. He and Hoag were like two boxers chatting after a bloody round. Scotty urged Adam and Hawke to have dinner with him; accepted a promise that Hawke would call him in a day or two, and left. Adam closed the door of the office on Hoag and went straight to the telephone. "Sally, ask Abe if I can have five minutes more here . . . very good." He dropped back into his swivel chair, puffed on his pipe, and regarded Hawke amiably. "Arthur, do you have any of the documents in your mother's lawsuit against Scott Hoag?"

"Christ, no. Why?"

"Have you ever looked into the facts of the suit?"

"Yes. It's a nutty fantasy of my mother's, quite harmless. It's given her a chronic grievance, which she seems to need for her health."

"How does it stand now? Is it all over?"

"No. I think she's appealing for a new trial. Why do you ask?"

Adam said thoughtfully, "I'm not sure yet whether your friend Scott Hoag is a slob or a bad boy. It may be he's just a slob. Either way it might pay you to look into that lawsuit. As I understood your mother, it involved a couple of million dollars." .

"Gus, she got tossed out of court on a summary judgment. Her claim is utterly silly."

The lawyer said, "If she's asking for a new trial there may be a defect in the summary judgment."

"What bothers you about Scotty?"

"His evasiveness. And his folksiness. Watch out for jolly good fellows in business deals."

"Scott agreed to call the thing off."

"Did he? If we had a tape recording of that conversation you could play it a dozen times and I don't think you could figure out what he actually did or didn't agree to." He picked up the ringing telephone. "Yes? Of course, put her on. Hello, Jeanie." The lawyer's ruddy face relaxed in an affectionate beam. "How are you? How's our friend Jim? Yes, I guess I do hear him. Why don't you feed the child sometime?" He laughed. "Just a moment. Art, are you available for Jeanne Fry?"

Hawke jumped up. Adam said, "Here's our great novelist, playwright, and piano mover, Jeanne. What? No, I wouldn't worry about that yet. Tell Karl to forget it. I'm going down to Washington Monday. I hope we won't have to bring Karl down there at all. Here's Arthur."

Hawke took the telephone. Adam stood chewing on his pipe, looking out of the window at the Statue of Liberty. "Hello, Jeanie . . . What, so fast? Didn't you get any sleep? Well, what do you think?" Adam glanced at the author and saw his face grow tense and disturbed. "Of course I want to talk to you. Well, any time. The office? My hotel in half an hour? Okay, but Jeanie, that's a whole half hour. No verdict at all?" He laughed uncertainly, and there was a tremor in his voice. "Well, that's a little more like it. Good God, just listen to that baby bellow. Has he been reading the book too? . . . All right, Jeanne." He hung up and said to Adam, "Jeanne sat up all night—I left her at half-past four—reading my new novel. She finished it a few minutes ago."

"Does she like it?"

"I can't tell."

"I'm sure it's excellent."

"I'm not. What were you saying about Karl? More communist trouble in Washington?"

"Yes. It can be extremely serious at this point. The climate in the country's gotten worse."

Hawke said, "You think so, too? I thought it was just the shock of com-

ing back from Venice into the New York atmosphere. It hit me as soon as I left the airport."

"Oh, there's been a change."

"Change! There seems to be a miasma of terror and panic here. Smartly dressed people in droves rushing here and there in huge glittering new cars all colors of the rainbow on colossal highways, or scampering around the streets and hotel lobbies of the city, their faces as drawn and driven—even the beautiful women—as if the siren has gone off for the atomic war."

"Well, there speaks the literary man," said the lawyer. They stood in a dark corridor lined from floor to ceiling with brown legal volumes. "New Yorkers have always looked pretty frantic and driven. No, it's this Senator McCarthy. He's doing some damage."

"Is he anything?" Hawke said. "In Europe they think he's the coming American dictator."

Adam laughed. "Well, no, he doesn't draw that kind of water. I don't think he does. But for a while things are going to be narrow for people like Karl Fry."

5

Coming into the hotel lobby, he saw Jeanne stand with the old smile and toss of her head, and he was reminded with a pang of the many many times he had seen this welcoming gesture, this shy mannerism of a girl meeting a date, when she had been Jeanne Green. She said in the elevator, "This feels real raffish, an afternoon rendezvous in a hotel room."

And when he opened the door of the small room, which seemed to be all double bed and window, she hung back, then went in ahead of him. "Raffisher and raffisher! Isn't this a modest accommodation for the darling of two continents?"

Hawke closed the door. "Europe spoiled me. I now know what luxury is. I'm going to have luxury or else live like a careful Hovey boy, I don't much want anything in between."

He came to her and took her coat. She slipped out of it with a shrug that was charming and familiar, saying, "You had it on Seventy-third Street, and you sold out."

He said, "I had no right to it, I wasn't secure. The whole thing was parvenu foolishness."

"It's a nice view of the park," she said, stepping to the window and adjusting the black leather belt of her dress. Perhaps because of the all-dominating bed and the hotel odors, Jeanne's movements were as inno-

cently provocative to Hawke as a newlywed bride's. He said, "You don't look as though you've had no sleep."

"Well dear, pancake makeup plus exhilaration can do a lot."

He stood beside her, looking out at Central Park, a bushy carpet of autumn color blocked in by gray buildings. The wind whined at the closed casement. He said, "There's no fit habitation in New York that doesn't have this view, you know. Also a view of downtown, with at least one river."

"Really? About seven million of us live in unfit habitations."

"Yes, you do."

They stood for a little while, saying nothing. He enjoyed her nearness like sunshine falling on him. Her arms were folded, and she looked pensively out at the park, as though she were enjoying the silent isolation with him too. It was all different, not having Karl Fry asleep close by, and Karl Fry's baby; the fearful wall of time and events between them seemed to dissolve. But when she turned her rounded matured face up to him, and a sarcastic little smile flickered on her mouth, the wall reappeared. "Did you have a quick shortcut to luxury in mind, Arthur, when you wrote *Evelyn Biggers?*"

Hawke said, "That's an unpromising beginning."

Jeanne went to the bureau and picked up the typescript. "I always have to worry about the sensitivity of authors, they're a pitiable race. But I'll be damned if I'll worry about your sensitivity. I never have. Why did you write this story, Arthur?"

He threw off his jacket and dropped on the bed, loosening his tie. "Jeanie, I picked up the pen to start *Boone County* and instead it began writing *Evelyn*. After a while I stopped fighting. It was a ghastly undertaking, I had no heart for it, unlike all my other work it was brutal cold-iron drudgery from the first word to the last. I don't even know whether it's publishable. Maybe I was possessed by the ghost of one of the Brontës."

Jeanne sat in an armchair, crossing her legs. "I felt self-conscious and embarrassed reading it, to tell you the truth. Your women have always been good, but this story seems to have been written by a woman. I felt as though you'd been reading my mind, or heard me talking in my sleep. We don't like to have all our petty secrets seen through by a man and written up in this way, Arthur. Or rather we do and we don't. Your book is a very strange experience. It's far and away your best writing. There's almost nothing for me to do."

Hawke was hanging on her words, which were still short of a verdict. He said, "Well, careless outpouring wasn't going to work. It was hell being imprisoned inside that not very bright woman's mind. I hope I never get another idea like it. I tell myself now that I was exercising myself in brevity because the critics say I'm just a spouter, and I also tell

myself that I needed this work to get my hand in for the dozens of women in the *Comedy*. Anyway, it's done. Is it going to sell?"

Jeanne took a long time to answer, looking at him with her head thrown back, her eyes narrowed. She wore a flowing aquamarine silk dress that minimized the fullness of her hips and bust. "I don't know. I speak with less than my usual annoying assurance, but I think the Hawke audience will be jarred and disappointed. Anything with your name on it must sell at first. But it may stop dead. Men aren't going to like it. Until now you've been one of the few serious novelists who has pleased the men."

"Shall I publish it? I can shelve the book."

Jeanne sat up straight. "Are you crazy? Of course you must publish it. That miserable woman living in the Los Angeles hills on the very fringe of the movie world, and as far from true glamour as though she were on Mars, is a lasting picture of the American woman. She's your sister Nancy, more or less, isn't she? I kept thinking of Nancy."

Hawke nodded. "The whole story is the skeleton in our family closet. Nancy had her Charlie Bick, only he was a manager in the bank where she once worked, but the same kind of smooth illusionist. And of course Nancy had a happy ending, but that was just her dumb luck. She should have ended like Evelyn."

Jeanne said, "This is a very hard one to figure. The critics may up and cheer you for a fresh and difficult change of pace. But my guess is they'll pounce like a dog pack and rip the book to shreds. They'll see it as a sign that you're weakening and beginning to pay attention to them."

"How big a first printing, Jeanne?"

"About thirty thousand," she said promptly, "but that may well be it."

"*Horne* has already sold what? A hundred twenty?"

"More. And going like mad. But *Horne* is a familiar Youngblood Hawke novel. *Evelyn Biggers* is a strange little work of art—at least that's how it strikes me—and it may be received as an unwelcome curiosity."

"That raises the question," Hawke said, "as to the wisdom of starting to publish my own work with this one."

The telephone rang. Hawke had found on his doorknob a festoon of four messages asking him to call Frieda Winter's office; he hesitated, letting it ring. It did not stop. He said to Jeanne, "Will you answer it? Impersonate a public stenographer or something. I don't want to talk to Frieda."

Jeanne took the telephone. "Hello? I'm sorry, he's not in—yes, I suppose I can take a message." A horrified look sprang into her face. "I beg your pardon? Five o'clock when? *Today?*" She glanced at her watch, and then at Hawke, her eyes glassy and wild.

Hawke said, "What on earth is it, Jeanne?"

"It's a man speaking. He says Paul Winter's funeral will be in an hour from now!"

Hawke seized the telephone. "Hello? This is Arthur Hawke. What is it?"

"Oh, thank heaven, Mr. Hawke. It's Lloyd," said the simpering voice of Frieda's male secretary. "I've tried and tried and tried to get you. I'm terribly sorry to tell you, but Paul died very suddenly of pneumonia, and Frieda said I was to be sure to hunt you down and tell you about the funeral. I've been trying for hours and hours. It's at the Wilson Funeral Home at Seventy-third and Lexington, it's scheduled for five."

"Paul?" Hawke said. "You mean Mr. Winter?"

"No. Little Paul. He died at school."

"I see. I'll be there." Hawke put down the telephone. He stared at Jeanne in stupefaction, then he began to cry. Jeanne had never seen him cry before.

CHAPTER EIGHTEEN

1

THE STORY, then, at least for the moment, was pneumonia. The funeral was modern and hasty. Frieda had notified only the closest members of the family and a few friends. The service for Paul took place in one of the smallest rooms of the undertaking establishment, and even so Hawke saw rows of empty benches when he came in, and only a straggling knot of people clustered up front near the coffin. He and Jeanne slipped into an empty pew and sat. A man in clerical vestments of black frilled with white was speaking. He quoted a letter of Longfellow about "the early blossoms which sweeten the air in falling." It was a short practiced speech, delivered in easy rhythms like an old song, and Hawke could tell that it was the man's standard performance over a dead child, probably taken from a book of funeral talks for all occasions. The only insertions were the names of the family. "Dear Frieda and Paul, give ear to the consolations of faith . . ." From where he sat Hawke could barely see the boy's still hands and chest in the coffin. His mind wandered from the canned eulogy and he thought painfully about the first time he had seen Paul, in yellow pajamas, fending off a glass of milk in a black nurse's hand; about his pitiful thirst for stories, about his strange and silent watchfulness,

about his grave dignity when he cut his birthday cake. He wanted to make amends to the dead boy, in some way, as we all want to make amends to the dead when they lie before us. He wished he could rise and say something kind and true about Paul. But of course it was unthinkable that he should utter a word at a funeral of this family; he had misgivings about the propriety of his appearing here at all, and that was why he had asked Jeanne to come with him.

The talking ended. The people in the pews filed forward to look at the boy. Hawke was stared at as he came up to the coffin. Paul lay in a heavy casket of chocolate-brown wood, in a creamy froth of white silk and velvet; the horrid thought went through Hawke's mind that it was a little like burying the boy in a rich long birthday cake. He thought too that a child like Paul ought to lie in a coffin on his side, with one hand under his cheek, as though he had fallen asleep. The flat-on-the-back pose with the hands folded was unnatural. Paul was dressed in a dark gray suit, with a blue tie. He was a dead little boy, with no expression, glowing with applied undertaker health under a recessed ceiling light. An organ purred sympathetically. Still Hawke looked, until Jeanne's tug at his elbow made him come away.

He saw the Winter family in the first bench: Frieda in black, her face obscured by a black veil, Mr. Winter beside her, shrunken and vacant, the older brother enormous in brown tweed, bursting with vitality, embarrassed, the two girls also in black, red-nosed and weepy. Hawke remembered the family portrait in the dining room, with the bright-eyed baby on Frieda's knee. He had never looked at that portrait, in all his years of familiarity in the Winter household, without feeling a twinge of discomfort, if not of guilt. The guilt was strong on him now; and he could scarcely connect in his mind the bowed woman in black in the first row with the excited shiny-eyed Frieda of a few weeks ago, pounding the little piano in the Expatriates Bar in her sleeveless green dress, flirting with the piano player; the Frieda who had been his abandoned, tormenting, self-righteous, wily mistress for five long years.

Jeanne had to lead him out of the funeral home as though he were a blind man. He obstinately halted on the sidewalk in front of the place, and waited until the coffin was carried out and slid into a hearse. The hearse drove off and thick traffic swallowed it. In the cold twilight all the electric signs on the avenue were winking and dancing. "Isn't anyone going to the cemetery with him? Christ, I'll go," Hawke said.

Jeanne said, "The family must be following. Be quiet. You're not to go."

He saw Bennett helping his enfeebled father into the first of three black limousines at the curb. Frieda came out and stood on the sidewalk amid a group of people, her veil thrown back, apparently giving instructions on the funeral arrangements. She saw Hawke, walked up to him,

and said without smiling, "Paul would have wanted you to come, more than anybody."

"I know, Frieda."

Jeanne said, "It's frightful. I'm sorry."

Frieda briefly pressed her hand with a hand that was strong and cold. She said to Hawke, "Did you get my letter?"

"No, I didn't."

"It should have been at your hotel today. I sent it special delivery. Anyway, Lloyd found you in time." She went and got into the limousine where her husband sat slumped.

Hawke stood on the sidewalk in a daze while the limousines one by one drove away. Jeanne said, "I'm terribly chilly."

He looked at her as though coming out of anesthesia. "What?"

"There's no point in standing here, Arthur."

Hawke looked around at the chapel, and the shops of the avenue. "Do you know what it is?" he said. "What makes this so strange? This corner is so familiar to me! I've walked past this funeral home hundreds of times. There's the barber I used to go to. That's my house, you know, the fourth one in from the corner. I see they went ahead and remodelled the entrance the way I planned it. It looks better that way, doesn't it, with the little arch?"

"Yes, it does," Jeanne said. She put her arm through his elbow. "It might be a good idea if you took me somewhere and bought me a drink."

Hawke said, "Why don't we drop in on the Hirsches and cadge drinks from them? I'd like to see my house."

"Arthur, you just don't do that. You don't drop in on people in this city. You know that."

"Oh, no? Well, I'm going to see my house. They can always throw me out if I'm not welcome. Do you want to go home, Jeanne? I guess we've finished our business. Or we can talk tomorrow."

Jeanne said lightly, "You're not shaking me off. Karl's got an author for dinner and I have nobody to feed me." She was concerned about him. He was falling into the quiet, remote, gentle manner that had preceded his illness.

Hawke sent a card in with a maidservant, and soon Hirsch came bounding out, tassels flying on the belt of his maroon satin smoking jacket. "Good lord, this is wonderful! You really took me up! Come on in! This is marvellous. You're just in time for a drink. Isn't it great about your play! Nothing but raves."

Hawke introduced Jeanne, and Hirsch seemed just as excited to meet her, and said she was far too beautiful to be an editor. As they walked inside and up the stairs, Hawke observed with wry pleasure—and with a certain sense of continuing nightmare, too—how orderly and elegant the house was, and how well his ideas had turned out. The Japanese grass

paper of the stairwell, black with glints of gold, made a perfect background for the series of small colored prints of the American Revolution along the staircase. The old glass and gilt chandelier, bought after much search and at high cost, made the hallway charming, and set the note of the entire house. The curving cherry wood balustrade which had been carpentered to order from his sketch—the contractor had said it could be done for four hundred dollars, and the bill had come to over three thousand—was beautiful. He only glimpsed the kitchen, but its flowered wallpaper, maple cabinets and copper pans, with the polished broad planking of the floor, looked perfect. The molded wooden archway into the living room, the dark green carpeting and walls, the marble fireplace, the arched bookcases, the cream-colored molded trim—all of it was handsome, all exactly as he had pictured it.

Mrs. Hirsch appeared in a yellow silk housecoat, her hair piled in braids on her head, flushed and laughing, carrying a baby. "What a nice surprise! I've just been bathing the youngest inhabitant of the Youngblood Hawke house, if you're interested in infants."

"Sure I am," Hawke said.

The mother exhibited her child to Hawke and Jeanne. Lawrence Hirsch said, "Let Mr. Hawke take him, Anne. Then Harry can tell his grandchildren some day that the famous author once held him."

Mrs. Hirsch said coquettishly to Hawke, "Oh, you don't want to hold the baby."

Hawke said, "Well, if you'll trust me, I'd like to."

The mother carefully handed Harry Hirsch in his white sleeping bag to Hawke. The author stood in the middle of the room he had designed but never lived in, and made a friendly grimace at the baby, who smelled very powdery. He was nothing like Jeanne's Jim, he was all yawns and red wrinkles, a highly characterless standard baby. But the parents were exploding with pride over him. Hirsch said, "Maybe some of your talent will rub off on him. I'm superstitious, I think such things can happen." Harry was carried off by the maid, and then the young father said, "I think I'm behaving very well. I'm a camera fiend and it was with the greatest will power that I didn't get out all my paraphernalia and record that moment for history."

The Hirsches believed in enormous globular martinis full of ice. Hawke drank one like water and took another. He was touched, and a little embarrassed, by the frank animated admiration of the Hirsches. They had his three novels, bound in blue leather, on a separate table between large brass bookends. After the second drink Hirsch brought out a blue leather portfolio from a drawer and carefully opened it. Hawke saw his own handwriting: four yellow discarded sheets from an early chapter of *Will Horne.* "The workmen came on these in the cleanup," Hirsch said. "They're not my property and I've always meant to return them to you."

Hawke signed each sheet, and told Hirsch to keep them as a gift. The man stammered in gratitude.

They led him and Jeanne on a tour of the house. Only one room did they leave shut, the bedroom where the baby was sleeping, now done over as a nursery; and Hawke was not sorry to pass it by, since this was the room where his mother had surprised him with Frieda. The garret room, the lair where he had written a good part of *Will Horne,* was now the maid's room. Hawke was astonished to see how tiny it was; he remembered it as a comfortable enough space.

When they came outside it had turned very cold, and a cutting wind blew down Seventy-third Street. Hawke stood in the lamplight, looking up at the façade of the Hirsches' home. "It's not a bad house, you know," he said. "It's a pretty good house, Jeanne, even if it does face north, as my mother pointed out."

"It's a glorious house," Jeanne said. "I must add interior decoration to your talents. I never believed it would turn out like that. It looked absolutely horrible when you left."

"Where do you suppose they'll put the plaque?" he said. "*This house not lived in by Youngblood Hawke.*"

"Arthur, you can do it again any time you want to."

"Can I? You once said that you and I are the kind of people who are destined never to build a house."

"Oh, I just talk. You were too restless then to settle down."

"No, I think maybe houses are for ladies' pocketbook makers like Larry Hirsch, and similar useful people. I'm dying of hunger. I got fearfully hungry at the funeral—why should that be?—and those sublime Hirsch martinis—taxi! Don't you like the Hirsches?"

"Very much."

Hawke helped her into the cab. "I don't think that baby will ever be a writer. Your Jim looks more the type. I thought I saw a gleam of insanity in those blue eyes."

They drank so much red wine with their dinner that they had to order a second large bottle. The Italian food was rich and delicious, though the restaurant, tucked in a crooked byway of the Village near Eighth Avenue, was a dim and vulgar room, with plastic table tops, large soft drink signs, and a jukebox. The other diners were mostly morose young couples, who had the look of living together out of wedlock and growing tired of it, the young men tending to beards and the girls to boredom. "This place makes me feel very young," Hawke said. "It dates to the era when Frieda and I were still skulking, mostly because I was so self-con-

scious. Come to think of it, I could swear it was Karl who first introduced me to it, way back when I first got to New York. Hasn't he ever brought you here?"

"No, Karl avoids the Village."

Hawke said, "Karl's the only leopard I know who's actually changed his spots."

"Oh, Karl has his spots, he just wears them under sheep's clothing. That's quite an antipasto of metaphors. Martinis plus chianti. This spaghetti is extraordinary."

"I'm very grateful to martinis plus chianti. To the Jews and the Italians. I'm coming out of it nobly. Here's to the Hirsches, and may they enjoy my house for fifty happy years. Didn't they seem happy? Married to the teeth, and mad for it. Look about you, Jeanie, and see how stupid sin can get to be."

Jeanne said, "If you don't even believe it's sin, it becomes really dreary. All the devilishness vanishes, and you're just being a slob."

After dinner they were walking toward the red neon glow of Eighth Avenue when they saw a well-dressed stout little man sitting in the gutter under a street lamp. He wore a bowler hat and a rolled umbrella lay beside him, and he did not seem in any distress, except that he was sitting in the gutter. Few cars came through the crooked street, so he was in no immediate danger, but Hawke thought he should probably be helped. He went to the man and lifted him by an arm. The man came up readily, saying in a fuzzy high voice, "You're very kind. I dropped my cigarette lighter, and I retrieved it, but then my legs didn't seem to be working quite as they should."

Hawke was himself too full of chianti to be more than mildly surprised at finding that he had picked the fearsome Quentin Judd out of the gutter. "Well, hello, Mr. Judd," he said, recognizing him in the lamplight.

The critic peered at him out of heavily filmed eyes, in which the spots of bright blue stood out clear and scary as ever. "I'll be damned. Our Kentucky Dickens." He squinted at Jeanne on the sidewalk nearby. "And of course, his Agnes. How are you, Jeanne?"

"Just fine, Quentin."

Judd said to Hawke, "I think I'm quite all right, thank you." He disengaged himself and took a few tottering steps. "Yes, I'm fine. I live just a few doors from here, so thank you very much."

"We'll walk with you," Jeanne said.

"Better yet, come up and have a drink."

He lived in a renovated Village apartment house, with a clean lobby and a new automatic elevator. His flat was a model of order, decorated in cool blues and greens, with some excellent antiques and a large array of African sculpture. Judd touched a match to a fire that was already laid,

and brought brandy and glasses. Once in his own home he seemed to steady up; he did not stumble against furniture, and he poured the brandy with a controlled hand. He said, settling into an armchair by the fire opposite the sofa where Hawke and Jeanne sat, "You wrote a pretty good play, and I'm going to say so in the *Dandy* next week."

"Well, you told me once never to thank a critic, so I won't," Hawke said.

Judd nodded, and parted his lips in a short smile at Jeanne. "Novelist's memory. I never remember anything."

There was a silence, and then Judd said archly, "Well, now, shall I show you *my* new baby? Don't worry, Jeanne, it's not another novel. I'm cured, though I'll always hate you for being so right about it."

Jeanne said, "It's an editor's job to tell an author what to expect."

"Very good. And critics and editors will always earn nothing but hatred for telling the truth. That's how the world wags, Jeanie, you're a hard woman, just as I'm a hard man."

"I'm a frightened doe inside," Jeanne said.

Judd giggled. "Well, since I have to leave the novel field to our clumsy but irresistible strong man, I'm off on another tack, and that's why I lured you two up here." He pushed himself carefully out of his chair, took from a bookshelf a bundle of thick cardboards tied with tape, and laid the bundle on the coffee table before them. "This is still top secret, but the word will be out soon."

He turned the boards one by one. It was a paste-up dummy of a proposed new magazine, called *The New York Rambler*; a severe journal of solid columns of small print on coarse paper, almost of newspaper size, without photographs, or cartoons, or advertising, much on the European style of intellectual reviews. The leading article, a statement of purpose, was by Judd: he had written a couple of other pieces; and there were many blank columns with headings for articles about books, painting, and music by celebrated composers and novelists as well as critics. Jeanne said, "Gosh, that's an exciting list."

"It would be more exciting if I could add Youngblood Hawke to it."

Hawke said, "I can't write literary criticism. A target isn't supposed to come alive and start shooting back."

Judd giggled. "That's cute, but it's just an Americanism. The theory of my *Rambler* is that we're going to have some civilized discourse in this town, at least in my modest journal. The people who know most about the arts are going to start writing about them. I think the vein of weary hard-to-please superiority is about worked out. The *Dandy* is choked in fat, one can't read the copy for the ads, and to tell the truth the ads are often a hell of a lot brighter than the copy. I'm bored, I'm *bored*. Moreover I'm tired of getting paid small fees for my work while the *Dandy*

advertising office takes in huge sums and forks the cash over to various stupid bastards who happen to have inherited the stock of the magazine. We won't take advertisements in the *Rambler* at first. But of course if the agencies come pounding at our doors—and I think they will after a while —why, we'll damn well accept the money. But *we'll* give it to our writers. How does it sound?"

"Wonderful," Jeanne said. "When's the first issue?"

"When I find fifteen thousand dollars. Getting started is the problem. I've raised thirty-five so far, putting up most of it myself. I believe in this thing."

"So do I," said Hawke, turning the cardboards. "Can I be counted in for five thousand?"

The critic swung his head at Hawke and squinted suspiciously. "Are you serious?"

"Sure."

"But I don't want money from you, I want copy. You're a hell of a name, however much my colleagues abuse you."

Hawke said, "I don't think I can write for you, but this city can use the *Rambler*. I'd be willing to put money in it. I want to be one of the stupid bastards who own stock."

Jeanne was furrowing her brow at him.

"Well good lord, you're in," said Judd. "Let's have a brandy on it and then I think I'll go out and roll in the gutter again. That's obviously the way to get backers."

He gave Hawke the prospectus of the magazine, and pressed them to stay with him and talk, but Jeanne declared that she had to get home to her baby. When the elevator door closed she said, "Why in God's name did you do that?"

"I don't know. I think I wanted to get out of his apartment quickly."

"Do you realize that you're in a money tangle now with Quentin Judd? Why didn't you go up to the zoo instead and crawl in with the cobras?"

"What money tangle? At worst I'll lose five thousand dollars. It'll be mostly tax money. Anyway I think the *Rambler* may work. It looked fresh, and Judd's the most brilliant man around for that kind of thing."

3

When he opened the door of his hotel room, Frieda's letter with its special delivery stamps lay just inside on the carpet: a thick packet in her small blue-gray stationery, engraved with her Fifth Avenue address. Hawke picked it up and stared at it. "It would probably be an excellent idea if I tore this up without reading it."

"Probably."

He threw the letter on the bed, and as he hung up their coats she saw his eyes move again and again to the envelope, which seemed to glare on the brown bedspread. "Tear it up," she said. "You know what's in it. The boy died."

"Why is it so thick?" Hawke said. "She wouldn't have had time to write a long letter. I'll read it later. Let's go to work. Shall I get out my typewriter and make notes?"

"If you want to," Jeanne said, but she was not surprised when he went to the bed and picked up the letter.

He said, "Get it over with," ripped open the envelope, and pulled out one sheet of blue paper. Two doubled-over lined sheets of white loose-leaf paper, with holes for ring binders, fell to the bed. He glanced at Frieda's letter and his face contorted. His fingers trembled as he picked up the white sheets.

"Arthur, what does she say?"

Jeanne might not have spoken. He read Paul's letter through. The suffering written on his face filled her with alarm. "What is it, darling? What is it?"

He handed the two letters to her and dropped on the bed, burying his face in the crook of an arm. The first words she saw in Frieda's letter sent a red-hot stinging through her body.

Dear Arthur:

Paul hanged himself at school last night. They called us at the theatre, that was why we left. When we got there he was dead.

He left this letter. Very fortunately the corridor master kept it unopened, and nobody has seen it but me. You must see it. After that do with it what you will.

Paul loved you very much. I know that, though he was so inscrutable. I know that you loved him, too. His memory must be a tie between us as long as we live. I'm going back up there now to bring his body home, and my office will let you know about the funeral. We're going to say it was pneumonia. The children at the school will talk, of course, but I think it won't get into the newspapers. Thank God nobody read his letter. My husband has collapsed and I must do everything.

I love you,
Frieda

Jeanne managed to say, "Arthur, am I to read Paul's letter?"

He mumbled, face down, "Of course, go ahead."

Jeanne straightened out the creased sheets. Paul's handwriting was oddly neat and small for a boy's, with as many words as possible crowded into each line:

Dear Mother:

The other fellows including my roommate Charlie Carmel are having a spread in Room 7. I wasn't invited. A few days ago I heard some fellows talking and fooling around in the corridor. I guess they didn't know I was in my room. They were talking about me and about you, saying that my mother was a famous celebrity and all that. Then I heard my roommate Charlie say, "There's only one thing wrong with Paul Winter's mother, she's Youngblood Hawke's whore and I don't like whores." Charlie is always being a big shot, saying that famous movie stars and stage actresses are whores. All the fellows laughed. I wanted to run out into the corridor and smash him one even though he's a lot heavier than me, but I didn't. I just let it go by. I got real sick when I heard Charlie say that especially since he's my roommate and I thought we were friends. Charlie said something to me tonight at dinner about he wished he could see Youngblood Hawke's new play tonight, with a big sneer. I wanted to smash his rotten face with a plate or something. I feel so sick and tired of everything. I have so many demerits I'll never work them off. It won't be different at any other school. Bennett got through this school all right. It's just me. I'm no good for anything, and I can't stand the way they talk. I even dream about it sometimes. Maybe I'm just a coward but I can't fight a whole school. The masters won't even let me telephone home. I hope Arthur's play is a hit. I'm sorry about this.

Love,
PAUL

The handwriting grew less distinct on the last page, wavering across the ruled lines in a scarcely legible scrawl.

Hawke rolled over and sat up, his face pasty and creased. "Well?"

"It's pitiful. The boy was extremely sick before he ever went to the school."

"I killed him."

Jeanne said sharply, "That's a lie! You're never to say it again or to think it. The masters were completely to blame. They should have seen his condition and sent him home."

Hawke said in a toneless tired voice, his shoulders sagging as he sat on the edge of the bed, "Darling, Paul was very hard to figure out. He was bright, very very bright. He made a career of being impassive and stoical. I'll bet his roommate never had the faintest notion that Paul had anything against him." Hawke rubbed his eyes, went to his work valise and pulled out a bottle of whiskey. He poured half a water glass full, drank it off as though he were taking a pill, and did not offer Jeanne any. He set the glass down quite hard on the table top. It broke, and blood welled from his hand. Jeanne jumped off the bed and came to him. He was sponging his hand with a handkerchief saying, "It's nothing, it's a scratch," but the handkerchief was crimson. He had a deep gash at the base of his thumb. She got a first-aid kit from his work valise and bandaged his hand in the bathroom. Blood dripped on the white tiles.

She said, "Are you going to do any more imbecilic things like this?"

"It was an accident, Jeanne."

"I mean I can't very well stay with you all night, Arthur, but I'm not sure you should be left alone."

Hawke laughed in a terribly melancholy way. "My darling, do you suppose I'm going to cast myself out of the window? I'm not little Paul. I have a lot of work to do. I'm a hundred and twenty pages into *Boone County* and if I can't sleep, which I undoubtedly can't, I'll work through the night. It'll be no service to Paul for me to damage myself any further. He's dead and buried." He sat at his desk and pulled the work pad to him. Jeanne went to the closet for her coat, watching him anxiously all the while. He began to write like an automaton.

She said, "I'm glad to hear you're that far along into *Boone County*."

"Yes, I expect I'll have something to show you before I leave."

"How is it going?"

He made a wry face. "As it always has, darling. Good days and suicidal days."

"All the same, I suspect it will be your best book."

"I think so. Before the main job. I'm grateful that you were with me today."

"I was glad I was with you. I'd hang around some more but it doesn't make sense, does it?"

"Of course not. Go home. Jim's probably shrieking for his seventeenth bottle."

She lingered in the doorway, hesitating to leave the small room. The two letters lay scattered on the broad wrinkled bed, the whiskey bottle stood on the bureau. She saw him take up the pen again with his bandaged hand. She said, "It's a pity you had to cut your right hand."

"Oh, I bleed, but I heal real fast. Go home, Jeanne. I swear I'm okay."

"All right, Arthur."

Still she stood in the doorway. He stared at her; put down the pen, came to her, shut the door behind her with his foot, and there at the doorway took her in his arms. She could not fight him. She did not want to. They kissed with hard passion, many times. He swept her in a powerful gesture, his arm around her slight shoulders, back into the room. There on the brown cover of the bed lay Frieda's blue sheet and Paul's creased white loose-leaf papers. He halted, and she felt his arm stiffen.

He said in a voice like an animal's growl, "Christ Almighty, this is a big contribution, isn't it?"

"I don't know. Do what you want."

"You're not a candidate for the vacant office of Youngblood Hawke's whore, are you?"

"No, I don't want to be your whore. I give good service as your editor."

He let her go. "Jeanie, won't you leave Karl and marry me? Won't you let me hope for it? Don't you want to?"

Jeanne stood with her hands in her coat pockets—in their frantic burst of caressing she had not taken it off—and she stared at him, her face flushed and wretched. "What's all this? You're off to Venice to another one of your doxies, last I heard."

"She's nothing, nothing. I told you that."

"Arthur, you're in a fearful spin, it's no time to talk like this. We're both in atrocious shape. Put me out of your room, won't you? Put me out."

"All right."

She said, "Karl is in deep trouble. Gus Adam hasn't told him, but he's told me. And Jim, what about Jim?"

Hawke said, "I love you."

She said, "I know you do. I've been in love with you since the moment you got angry at me for comparing you to O. Henry, which was about two minutes after we met. You've always known it, and it's not going to change, it'll be there tomorrow and the next day and the next year. Tumbling into bed isn't going to help matters, it'll make everything a hundred times worse, so will you throw me the hell out?"

Hawke took her gently by the arm, led her to his door and opened it. "It's been a good session," he said, "and I'll see what I can make of your suggestions."

"Are you angry at me? Don't be angry at me, for God's sake. I can't bear it."

"Jeanne, darling, I should have married you when I could have, that's all."

She said, "There's time, there's all kinds of time, Arthur, there's years. Where in God's name are the elevators in this horrible hotel?"

"You're looking straight at the elevator. Right there. Good night, my darling."

She darted from him and pressed the button.

4

He could not sleep. Night after night he could not. Paul's letter lay in his desk; he could neither destroy it nor look at it again. He cancelled his plane reservation for his return to Venice, and sent a dry cable to the British film actress who was waiting there for him. The shocks of his return to New York had killed his lukewarm desire for her; he could scarcely believe in her existence. Venice itself was a fading dream. He was back in New York, the only half-home of his homeless spirit; New York, with

its bloated frenzied newspapers trumpeting doom daily around the clock in headlines of a dozen changing editions, while the advertisements inside screamed of overabundance and frivolity; New York, where main thoroughfares lay torn open, exposing huge steaming municipal entrails, and forty skyscrapers were going up in a shattering racket, and hordes of people went rushing through the streets day and night, as though panics were breaking out in every quarter of the city; New York, where Jeanne Fry was.

He had enough to keep him busy by day, and in the nights he wrote in the tiny hotel room, sometimes sleeping a few broken hours after dawn.

In his career all was good news and wassail. Ferdie Lax called him from Hollywood. Travis Jablock had exhumed his old screenplay of *Alms for Oblivion*, and wanted Hawke to come out and revise it, at a kingly fee. The movie of *Chain of Command* had just been completed, and Lax said it was going to be one of the greatest money makers of all time; he bitterly regretted having sold the property short. In Hollywood, Lax said, the name of Youngblood Hawke was being uttered in religious tones. All this was mere pleasant noise to Hawke, like far-off parade music. The new book he was writing was beginning to stir with its own life, after the wheezing drudgery of the opening chapters. It was the only effective antidote to his horror over Paul.

Pleasant noises also came from Feydal and Carmian. He visited his play several times and always found the house full. The two men, cooing like turtle doves, assured him that they had survived the *Times* torpedo. Tickets were selling into March. This news took the sting out of the disturbing fact that Hoag's lawyer had balked at cancelling the Paumanok Plaza deal, throwing up endless legal difficulties. Hawke had a spell of fury when he found this out, and a bellowing long-distance conversation with Scotty, who pleaded helplessness in "all this lawyer stuff." Gus Adam was angry too in a cold way that alarmed Hawke, and made him think that he would not care to have Adam as an enemy. But with the strength that the play was showing, the urgency of the cancellation decreased. At last Adam telephoned Carmian to send the author's royalty checks to Paumanok Plaza Incorporated. "We have little choice, Arthur," he said. "A court fight over a tax avoidance scheme is unthinkable. Let's hope Scotty comes through. Paumanok Plaza looks good, I'll say that."

The most pleasant noise of all—harps, flutes, lutes, and dulcimers—came from Roland Givney, who had read the typescript of *Evelyn Biggers* and was in raptures. It was the most electrifying change of pace any major novelist had shown within his memory; without question it would be Hawke's greatest success, and probably the biggest book he, Givney, had ever been associated with. Hawke had written *Everywoman!* Adam

and Ross Hodge also read the book; the lawyer professed ignorance about its prospects, but he thought the writing was fine. Hodge's reaction was almost as enthusiastic as Givney's, though expressed with less celestial music. Having these two publishers' judgments to balance against Jeanne's dubious opinion, and being in a state of mind where mere activity, mere decisions and conferences, were an anodyne, Hawke suddenly decided to go ahead and launch his own publishing house, with Hodge Hathaway as distributor. Gus Adam cautioned him that Hodge's offer of a twenty-year drawing account was far safer and quite generous. But Hawke pressed him to admit that with "Haworth House"—the name he had struck upon—he could reap some of the trade profits of his books as well as his royalties; that he could transform much of the money into capital gains; and that in fact, if he had put his first three books through such a process, he would now probably be a millionaire. Adam admitted these things, and Hawke took the plunge.

He saw Jeanne for the first time after their strained scene in his hotel room at a private dinner party in the St. Regis Hotel, which Givney conjured up to seal the founding of Haworth House. He thought she and Karl both looked terrible; Karl was greenish-gray in the face again and Jeanne, hollow-eyed, haggard, overpainted, seemed to have been sleeping even less than Hawke. The Frys arrived with Gus Adam and stood in a corner of the room with the lawyer for a long time, talking earnestly in low tones over glasses of champagne.

Givney was the very essence of blooming jollity. His party was elegant: caviar, champagne, old French wines, a flower-banked table, white orchids for the ladies, even two wandering musicians with accordion and violin, filling the room with serenades. Hawke's family had stayed on in New York to shop, and Givney flirted with Mrs. Hawke, he made Nancy and even her stolid husband laugh with his bouncy puns, he bantered with the musicians, and he called for more and more champagne. Hawke's mother, who had developed a decided weakness for champagne, was quite captivated by the paperback publisher, and loved her orchid, and was generally having a whale of a time. Nevertheless the party baffled her. She cornered Hawke just before they sat down to dinner, and said that as near as she could figure it out, Givney was stealing him from Hodge, and if that was so why were the Frys and Hodge at the celebration? Gus Adam, who was standing with Hawke at the moment, burst out laughing. Mrs. Hawke turned on the lawyer and asked him if Art was making a smart move. The lawyer soberly answered that if all went well, Hawke would make more money out of his books by this method. The mother said that she guessed if Adam was for it, it was all right; and she began trying again to recruit Adam to fight her second trial against Scott Hoag and Hawke Brothers. To Hawke's surprise Adam asked her a number of questions about the

case, instead of turning her off; he took her in to dinner, and was deep in conversation with her during the meal.

Hawke sat between Jeanne and his sister. They gabbled across him about babies. Jeanne was as casually bright with him as it was proper for an editor to be. It struck him that—a little like Frieda—Jeanne had her own vein of duplicity; and that possibly no woman could quite do without it. He no longer felt at his ease, sitting beside her. They had said too much to each other. He was irritated by her prattle about Jim, yet he sensed that what she was doing was avoiding conversation with him, out of a discomfort like his own. He observed that Karl Fry ate nothing; not the shrimps, not the onion soup, not the filet mignon. He drank vast quantities of wine, and his color became a little better. It was obvious to Hawke that Karl's communist problem had taken a very bad turn. Though Hawke loved Karl's wife, he felt no jealousy toward the editor, and wished him no misfortune. On the contrary, his deepest hope was that Adam would somehow get Fry out of his mess; for he knew Jeanne would not change her life while the man she had married was in trouble.

Givney opened the ceremonies when the coffee and brandy came by rising to propose a toast to Haworth House. He called it a milestone in the nurturing of American literature, and he carried on about the virtues of Ross Hodge as a publisher, and Jeanne Fry as an editor, and Youngblood Hawke as a creator of monuments more durable than brass. Hodge and Hawke responded briefly; Hodge was especially arid. Jeanne said nothing. Karl rose, saying he would speak for her, and capped the party with a mordant speech about Hawke's terrible financial distress which had compelled the formation of Haworth House; about Ross Hodge's joy in the event; about Givney's wonderful disinterested love of literature. The men who were poked at worst laughed the loudest; it was a refreshing note. "A better day is coming," Karl said, "when the lion will lie down with the lamb, and art may even lie down with money. Meantime art is art and money is money and seldom the twain shall meet; except in the case of Youngblood Hawke, where we have the happy miracle that Art *is* money." Everybody had had enough brandy to cheer as he sat down.

Hawke managed a few moments with Jeanne as the party was breaking up in a cascade of Viennese waltzes. "How long am I under the ban?" he said quietly.

"What ban? Are you all right, Arthur?"

"I'm working hard."

"Have you heard from Frieda?"

"No."

Jeanne said, glancing toward Fry and Adam, who stood in their over-coats talking, "Karl's going into a black tunnel. It may be weeks, it may be months, before we see daylight."

Hawke said, "Don't you want to see me at all while it's going on?"

The look she gave him, the candor in her eyes, stirred him like a kiss. She said, "I'll do any work you want of me, but I'd say no Italian restaurants and no hotel rooms for a while. Good luck with Haworth House. It's done now." Karl was beckoning to her, and she left him.

5

He could not refuse to talk to Frieda when she telephoned him from her office about ten days after the funeral. She sounded much the same as always. There might have been a tremor in her business-like tones, or it might have been his imagining. She dropped her voice to speak of Paul's letter. She wanted it back, but she didn't want him to mail it. Would he meet her for just a moment, any place at his convenience, and give it to her? Though he dreaded an encounter with her he said, "Of course, Frieda. Anywhere you say."

Frieda said, "Are you busy right now?" It was ten minutes past eleven. Hawke was at his desk in the St. Moritz, by the whining window that looked out on the bleak park, making some changes in the mimeographed typescript of *Evelyn Biggers*. Jeanne's copy of the script, pencilled with her comments, lay open before him.

Hawke said, "I can meet you now." He added a swift lie. "I have a lunch appointment at one."

"So have I," she said quickly. There was a silence, then she said, "I'd rather it wasn't at your hotel or a bar. Is there anything wrong with meeting at the lion's cage, the way we did once?"

"Nothing. Except it seems pretty cold outside."

"I'm dressed warmly. In fifteen minutes?"

"All right, Frieda."

She was not in sight when he walked through the cold deserted plaza of the zoo to the lion's cage. His breath smoked. So quiet was the park on this gray day of premature winter, that he could hear the scraping noise of a park attendant raking dead leaves in front of the monkey house. Yellow and brown leaves scuttled and eddied on the pavement before him. The benches were empty, save for a few old people crouching muffled to the ears. He was embarrassed and worried by Frieda's choice of this place to meet. He could not doubt that what was in store was a sentimental assault. He did not want to hurt the bereaved woman, but nothing would induce him, he thought, to simulate affection that was gone. Paul's letter was in his breast pocket, and it seemed to hang there palpable and heavy as though written on sheets of lead.

When he saw Frieda coming, his incongruous thought was that skirts had shortened in five years. One of the strongest pictures in his memory was that of Frieda approaching him at that first meeting, striding in the

sunshine through the crowd of baby carriages and young lovers. Here she was coming again along the empty walk, with the same purposeful gait, a blue purse tucked under one arm, the other arm pumping with vigor. The color of her tailored suit was nearly the same, her favorite bluish-gray, but in his mental picture of the other meeting the skirt came halfway to her ankles and today the hem was near her knees. Her shoulders were wrapped in fur. Her head was bent far down, as though she were walking into a strong wind, but there was little wind. She saw him, her head came up, and she smiled and waved.

"Well, we've got the park to ourselves this time," she said, drawing near.

"Just about."

"And there won't be any cherry blossoms. However, you look better than you did then, Arthur." She took his hand and pressed it warmly.

"You look lovely, Frieda."

She scanned his face, smiling. "Thank you, dearest." She peered at the empty cage. "What's this? Too cold outside for the lion?"

"I suppose so. Or maybe he's dead. I guess with the air they have to breathe in this town, there's a fast turnover of lions."

"You've had a long run as a lion," she said. She was still clinging to his hand.

"Frieda, I'm heartbroken about Paul. How is your family?"

Frieda tucked his arm under hers, and walked with him to an empty bench, where they sat. "It's curious how it works," she said brightly. "The men are broken up, the women are more or less all right. My husband is the same now as he was on the first day. He doesn't go to business, he wanders around the house, he doesn't eat, and he begins to cry without any provocation, even in the daytime. I'm seriously worried about him. Bennett didn't go back to school for a week. I knew he was fond of Paul, but I never knew the depth of it. We couldn't get him out of Paul's room for days. He slept there. The girls cried for a couple of days and then went about their work. Of course our house is like a tomb and I don't think it will ever be any different. We all keep seeing Paul coming around corners. I don't think I can prevent the household from breaking up. It was coming anyway, with the girls about to go off to college and Bennett pushing on into engineering. My husband's been talking for years about moving to Jamaica, and I've tried to start that topic again, but I can't interest him. I can't hold his attention at all."

"He'll come out of it."

"I hope so. He's sixty-seven. You don't have the strength at that age."

Pigeons fluttered to the gray pavement at their feet and strutted about, looking for peanuts or crumbs, but the granite was dusty and bare, except for dead leaves. Hawke and Frieda watched the birds. Hawke said, "I have the letter."

Frieda nodded. "Did it distress you?"

"I'm sick over it. I always will be."

"That's wrong. Take my word for it, Arthur, Paul *never intended to kill himself*." She put her blue-gloved hand on his arm for emphasis. "It was completely beyond him. He wasn't that sick or disturbed. He was the greatest little play-actor you ever saw. He was play-acting for his own satisfaction when it happened, writing the note and all. I'm sure he heard that stupid remark, and of course it upset him, but I think he was more upset by not being invited to that spread. I had a long talk with this boy Charlie Carmel, you know. He said the reason they didn't invite Paul was that he already had thirty demerits and they didn't think Paul should risk getting in any more trouble. I absolutely believe him, and I also believe that he was terribly fond of Paul, and that all the other boys in the corridor were, too. Charlie made that remark just to show how sophisticated he was. Don't you remember what you were like at thirteen?" She glanced at Hawke and went on hurriedly, "Paul was a great newspaper reader, he's been reading the *Times* and the *News* cover to cover since he was ten, and I'm sure he read about this new wave of hangings in the colleges. You know there have been three or four in the past month, one almost always generates another. God, I remember Paul would turn his room into a pirate's cave by hanging blankets around and making cardboard skulls and bones and taking my jewelry to heap on the floor, and you couldn't get him to come to meals. When he got going on a fantasy he really went all out. I'm positive he just got to feeling sorry for himself and played out the whole thing. He was standing on a stack of books in the closet. They were still all tumbled on the floor when we got there. He slipped, that's all, he slipped, poor fantastic little rascal—books are a poor support." Frieda's matter-of-fact voice shook. She turned to Hawke and smiled, her eyes glistening. "It's very important for you to understand that it was an accident, Arthur. That's what the coroner in Peekskill decided."

"I'm sure it's true," Hawke said, "and I'm glad that's how the record will read."

Frieda said with vexation, "There you are! Why is it that you understand so readily, and my husband won't? I've told him all this ten times. He just stares at me empty-eyed, when he doesn't get up and walk away while I'm talking. He means no discourtesy, at least I hope he doesn't, but it's as though I don't exist, almost. When he does act aware of me he's pathetically courteous, as though I were some strange woman. I frankly think our situation is hopeless. It isn't just Paul's death that's bothering him, you know, it's guilt."

"Good God, why should *he* feel guilty?"

"He should, believe me, he *should*." Frieda pounded a gloved hand on the iron armrest of the bench. "All Paul's peculiarities were due to the way he treated the boy! He'd suddenly give him a ton of toys or he'd

ignore him for weeks, there was never anything in between, no normal acts of a father." Frieda lit a cigarette, cupping her gloved hands around her golden lighter. "You and I have got to come to an understanding about one thing, Arthur. The night you left me, the night of that ghastly birthday dinner, you said something that made me hate you for a year. I think I'd have stabbed you instead of slapping you if something sharp had been at hand. You hinted that Paul wasn't my husband's child."

"Frieda, it's all gone, the boy's dead—"

"I'm alive and so are you. He was as much Paul's child as any of the others. The exact truth is that I had been having an affair then with Leon"—this was the name of the violinist, Hawke's predecessor; Frieda tossed it off without any self-consciousness—"but there was nothing surreptitious about it. As a matter of fact my husband at the time was going through his phase of tall blonde young mistresses, so it was even-steven on any basis, even by your mother's strict measuring rods I dare say. Sauce for the gander and all that. But of course I took the usual precautions, there wasn't the faintest chance of my becoming pregnant with Leon. It happened that my husband and I went away for the New Year to Jamaica with the children, that's always been our favorite place, and the rum was flowing free and we got very sentimental, and so we had a sort of romantic reunion. It only went on for a week or so and it didn't really go very deep. Once we got back to New York we both fell into the old routines. But it was *in Jamaica* that I got pregnant and Paul damned well knows it! As a matter of fact when it became obvious that I was pregnant I stopped seeing Leon, I didn't see him until long after Paul was born, and it wasn't the same and didn't last much longer. I never loved Leon, Arthur, not the way I loved you and still love you. It was utterly different. He was jolly company and an excellent lover but really he was an ice-cold customer, he cared about nothing but his career and sex and good food. And of course he loves music, I'll say that, and he's a glorious player, playing duets with him was grand fun. But he wasn't *alive* like you, Arthur. He wasn't sweet and real and—if you'll forgive me, wholesome." She smiled at him. "The word probably embarrasses you but I mean it, it's the chief thing about you and your work.

"What I'm getting at is that my husband never had any ground for his hostile attitude to the boy, and now he must realize it, and it's eating his guts out. It was perfectly obvious what he thought at the time. He thought I'd gotten pregnant by Leon and then deliberately provoked that rum-and-gardenia second honeymoon in Jamaica so as to pass Paul off as his. He never said it then, he's never said it in so many words to this day, but oh, God, the little hints! You don't know my husband. He's as deep as poor Paul was. He does the tolerant autumnal business beautifully but there's a terrible revengeful streak underneath, and I'll just tell you this, if he ever advised you to buy any stocks or get into any other

business venture you'd better examine your commitment very, very carefully, Arthur. I think the one thing that could give him pleasure at this point, the only information that could even get through to him, would be the news that his advice had somehow destroyed you. He put Leon into a thing, a short sale on inside information, that all but bankrupted him. Of course Leon was to blame for his own greed, and a lot of smart professionals also got burned in that one. My husband didn't, though."

Hawke had long ago sensed Winter's impotent hostility behind his good manners. Still he shuddered, perhaps because they were sitting in such raw air, and his mind flickered across all his main commitments with a touch of worry. There was nothing in his situation traceable to the guidance of Frieda's husband.

Frieda's tawdry self-defense about Paul disgusted him to his core, this detailed argument to prove that Paul's tragic little life had started in one man's bed and not another's. But Frieda had cheered up in the telling, and clearly felt that she had scored a great point. She peered at him twice, as she usually did after making a subtle joke, to be sure he appreciated her words. "So much for that, Arthur. The main question is the future. We've all been through a smashup, but the world hasn't ended, we've got to go on living. I have to make a confession, and it's not easy. I hope you won't think I'm crawling. I'm not." She looked down at her hands and glanced at him sidewise, shy and abashed, like a naughty attractive girl confident of being forgiven for misbehaving. He thought how pretty and young her thin mouth still was. Hawke expected her to say something about the Negro pianist in Venice. What Frieda came out with absolutely stunned him.

"Arthur, when you asked me that night to marry you, I should have accepted. If I had, Paul would be alive now. That thought keeps haunting me, and that's where my own guilt lies. I know he looked on you as a sort of father, and I know you loved him. I made a fearful mistake. I wasn't thinking clearly, your mother's behavior had shattered me and put me on a bristling defensive. But I want to be candid about this, it's important, and I have to admit that I would have said no anyway. Not on account of Paul's money, though. You should never have said that, Arthur. It may be that that one unfortunate remark wrecked everything.

"I've told you often that I have money, but I've never told you how much. I'm a millionaire a couple of times over, dear. My father left me a good deal. I was an only child. Paul invested it well for me, way at the bottom of the depression, and it's doubled and redoubled. My concert bureau has brought in a lot, I haven't had a losing year since I opened it, and in my Broadway ventures I'm way, way ahead. I've guessed right on several big musicals. Now mind you I'm *not* talking about the trusts and the real estate Paul has settled on me and the children to avoid the

inheritance tax, though all that is mine by right too and there's no reason
for me to give up any of it whatever happens. I'm talking about my own
resources. The rest is in addition. So you can understand, can't you, how
you infuriated me, how you completely misunderstood me, when you
accused me of refusing you because of Paul's money?

"All the same I confess that I wasn't thinking clearly. I thought my
life was fine just as it was. I dreaded the upheaval, mainly on account of
my children. And then you surprised me so, you came out with it so
abruptly, so ungraciously, on such a blatant put-up-or-shut-up basis, when
just the night before there'd been the horror of your mother, bless her
heart, opening the door on us. It was all wrong, the way it happened, it
couldn't have been more badly timed, and anyway my darling how
could I help thinking of the most banal and obvious fact of all, that I'm
fourteen years older than you? It takes a lot of bold thinking to rise above
such a fact, and to decide to accept it because more precious things are
at stake.

"I haven't thought of much else, Arthur, since we buried Paul. If you
still love me, and I'm sure you do, I'm ready to marry you. I think we can
have many, many years of the deepest happiness together. I think my
children will look up to you and love you. I think you'll be able to do your
greatest work with your mind freed forever from any thoughts of money.
And I think it's the one thing you and I can still do about Paul. I don't
know what goes on in the grave and beyond it, nobody knows, but I
think Paul would want us to be together. I think his death ought to unite
us and take away the shame that he foolishly felt. Our love has been great
and fine, it's been the one great thing in my life, and I want to give the
rest of my life wholly to it—if you'll have me." She said these last words
with her peculiarly innocent smile, opening her eyes wide at him, her
face transfigured into a most appealing softness.

Hawke had been quite prepared for an attempt by Frieda to restore
their old intimacy; but this sudden acceptance of a marriage proposal a
year and a half old—and never formally withdrawn—left him for a moment without words.

Frieda Winter was still a desirable woman in the eyes of Arthur Hawke.
Despite her age perhaps it was a depravity in him—he felt still that he
would delight in taking her to bed and renewing well-remembered joys.
Nor was he unshaken by Frieda's bald statement about her money. It
was like Frieda to drive to the point that way. He could picture most
vividly the wonder of a life where tax conferences and Paumanok Plazas
and Haworth Houses would fade like the grisly stupid repetitious farces
they were, and he could simply do his work, so many pages a day, like
Bernard Shaw coddled by his millionairess, perhaps like Shaw in a little
working studio in a garden of their home, perhaps in warm ever-green
Jamaica. The children—well, they were almost grown; Frieda would at-

tend to them and he could be friends with them. The whole thing was far from impossible.

But Frieda was not the woman he had loved, any more. That was the trouble. She was like an identical twin of the clever, elegant, sensuous New Yorker who had enraptured him at twenty-six. There was no visible difference, and in fact she was not an identical twin but the same individual, yet Frieda herself was gone. Events had erased her. To marry this forty-four-year-old person with three grown children and a boy newly buried would be a bizarre and meaningless thing to do, except for the money. He did not love her, though she looked desirable to him. Many women in hotel elevators looked desirable to him.

Since there was no good answer to return, he spoke the truth that came to his tongue. "Frieda, I'm in love with Jeanie Fry, and if she'll leave Karl I'm going to marry her."

"Oh?" Her look remained kind and winning. "Is she going to leave him? That would surprise me. Even before their baby came, you two could never work it out."

"She hasn't said she would leave him."

"Darling, since Jeanne Fry was such an obvious choice for you from the start, and since you've never been able to come together, doesn't it occur to you that you actually don't want each other? I swear I'm not being a cat. Don't you think that Jeanne is afraid of you because she's a prude and you're a wild man; and don't you think she bores you a teeny bit as a woman because she's both predictable and not strong enough? She had you, and she came on us having a bit of a boozle in Beverly Hills, and she petulantly let you go and married Karl. That was a mistake, but certain mistakes define a person."

"She and I both made mistakes."

Frieda said, "You don't love me any more?" He did not answer. "You don't desire me?"

"You known damned well you're desirable. Everything's changed, that's all."

"I haven't changed. What things have happened? You're not thinking of that pianist in Venice?"

"Not just that."

She said, "I went too far in tormenting you—especially with you being a Southerner—but you were being a devil to me, you know. Arthur, if you'll take me right now to the cemetery I'll swear on Paul's grave that that man never touched me. He was very unattractive, the kind of egotistic nobody of a musician that I detest most, I used him to swat you with as I would have used a baseball bat. As I live, as I loved Paul, as I love you, that man never touched me."

They looked each other full in the face. The cold wind stirred the fur against her chin. She was older, certainly older, but lovely as ever. He

said, "I believe you, Frieda," thinking that perhaps she was telling the truth this time, that he could never know, and that after all it made little difference.

She sighed with relief. "Then *that* isn't between us any more."

"No."

"Good. I'm not asking you for an answer, Arthur. I know this must be a startling idea and will take some getting used to. I want you to know how I feel." She adjusted her furs as though to stand.

Hawke said, "Frieda, I won't marry you. I can't let you leave thinking that there's a possibility."

Her eyes narrowed. "Are you going to be as quick and as flat and as final as that? After five years? After you yourself laid down those terms and I've accepted them?"

Hawke said, "You've had a fearful blow, Frieda, you're under a great strain, and I don't want to add to your trouble. Cut the thought from your heart. We're not going to get married. You must plan your future. That isn't it, there isn't a chance of it."

She said, sitting immobile, her voice becoming a little higher and weaker, as it did when she was at the far stretch, "Do you know that there'll never be anyone else for you? I tell you that. Older though I am, and smashed as I am—and I haven't made the slightest plea for sympathy —I'll recover and find someone else before you will."

"That's possible."

"Jeanne Fry is a delusion you've salved your backwoods conscience with for years, the good old-fashioned girl just like the girl who married dear old dad, who you were going to come back to after you'd helled around all you wanted. She isn't available. If you do attain her it'll mean misery for both of you."

"Frieda, what can I say except that whatever happens I can't marry you?"

She rose from the bench and began to walk toward Fifty-ninth Street. He was at her side in a moment. She said calmly enough, taking vigorous strides, "We both have lunch dates. I have to get on to mine."

Sentences of comfort, of compassion, of apology, crowded to Hawke's mind and found no utterance. After a silence in which they walked side by side he said, "Almost the first thing you said to me was 'Never apologize.'"

She glanced at him, with a flash of her old humor under the look of an aging woman hurt to the heart. "It's still a good rule. Don't."

He said, "I haven't given you Paul's letter."

"That's right. You haven't."

She halted. He reached into his breast pocket and pulled out the two folded sheets of theme paper with ragged holes where they had been torn from the loose-leaf book. A wave of pain crossed Frieda's face as he held

them out to her. She stared at the letter and said in a high voice, "What can I do with it? Where can I put it? It hurts my eyes to see it." She looked around wildly, as though she were in a trap. They stood on the walk lined with benches leading to Fifty-ninth Street. A man in brown coveralls was burning a high heap of leaves, red and yellow and brown, not far from them, turning the heap with his rake. She said, "That's the only thing to do," pointing to the fire.

"Are you sure?"

"Arthur, think! What can I possibly do with Paul's letter? With the things that are in it?"

They walked to the burning leaves together. Hawke unfolded the sheets so that they fluttered in the mild breeze; he saw the boy's cramped handwriting. He hesitated, glancing at Frieda. The park workman looked at them dully. She nodded with impatience. Hawke might have protested, but the workman embarrassed him. "Okay?" he said to the workman, holding the papers over the fire.

The man shrugged. "Suit yourself. Paper burns."

Hawke dropped the pages into the glowing center of the pile, where pale flames ate into them at once and curled them to sheets of black ash. The man brought down his rake on the ashes and broke them. "That's that," he said.

Frieda walked off swiftly. Hawke had to take long strides to catch her. She was pulling a handkerchief out of her purse, and she wiped her eyes as she went.

"Frieda," Hawke said, touching her elbow.

She turned a stunned, horror-stricken face to him. "He died," she said. "My baby died. Let me alone, Arthur. Goodbye." She hurried away, touching the handkerchief to her bowed face.

Hawke walked to the hotel, went into the bar, and ordered a double whiskey. He felt spent and broken, and he was shaking. As he sat waiting for his whiskey his mind went back over the scene, one of the worst experiences of his life. It occurred to him, with an unpleasant thrill in his nerves, that Frieda's husband had, long ago, made two business recommendations to him: that he should continue investing with Scotty Hoag, and that he should publish his own books.

Part Five
1952

CHAPTER NINETEEN

1

ON A bright steamy day in September, almost a year later, Karl Fry, his wife, and Gus Adam were riding in a taxicab from the Washington airport to the Senate Office Building. The parks were lush green. The hot damp air streaming through the open windows smelled of foliage newly washed by rain, and the waters of the last thundershower still ran in the streets. Jeanne, dressed in a black linen suit and a large flat black hat, looking quite thin again, said, "Gad, my misspent youth is blowing in through these windows. The smell of Washington, after a thunderstorm that hasn't cooled anything off! My lost ambitions, my withered dreams."

As they went by the Washington monument, Fry stared glumly out of the window, craning his neck to see the top of the great white shaft. "I think it's faintly ironical," he said, "that the tallest structure in this city, the trademark by which the world knows it, is a monument to a subversive. Let's not forget that father George led an armed revolt to overthrow his lawful government by force and violence."

Adam said, "You know the answer to that old gambit. Washington fought to gain freedom, not to abolish it."

"I know that answer. I'm surprised that you would throw such a leaky beanbag," Fry said. "Washington fought to gain a free hand in money making for a small commercial middle class, mostly slave owners like himself. The British monarchy abolished slavery long before the United States did. Marxism fights to abolish the subtler forms of slavery that still exist."

"Yes it's well known that Soviet Russia is the land of perfect freedom," Adam said. "To avoid a sleepy golden monotony, there is the periodic chatter of firing squads."

Jeanne said, "I seem to have heard all this before."

"Soviet Russia is a besieged citadel of the new order, living under martial law in self-defense," said Fry. "You're quite right, Jeanne, God knows I don't want to bicker at this point, I feel pretty awful."

Adam said, "The thing is I thought we were agreed on tactics. Your witty musing about the Washington monument makes me wonder."

Fry started to answer, then saw Adam make a small warning gesture, the mere lifting of a finger from the briefcase he held on his knees, to

point at the taxidriver, a stout bald man in shirtsleeves, who had a protruding red ear cocked for their conversation. The three people smiled at each other—Jeanne's smile was rather nervous—and they fell silent.

Karl and the lawyer got out at the Senate Building. Squinting in the strong sunshine, Karl said to Jeanne through the open door, "I'll telephone you at the hotel in an hour or so."

"All right. Don't sound off about George Washington's subversion to Senator Traynor, please. Do as Gus says."

"Yes, dear. Just one wisecrack on the way to the guillotine, the touch of gallantry, you know."

Jeanne said, "The question is, shall I register and get the bags taken up, or what? I'm hoping we can go home this afternoon. I don't want to stay in this town."

The lawyer said, "Well, chasing a couple of Senators down can be difficult, even though we do have appointments. I'd say wait till you hear from Karl."

"I'll be in the lobby," Jeanne said to her husband. "Tell them to look for the lady with no nails. Good luck, darling—Franklin Hotel, please."

She left the luggage piled at the bell captain's desk, and walked to the hotel news stand. Most unexpectedly, Hawke's novel leaped at her eye out of a row of best-sellers over the magazine rack. She had spent enough time staring at the expensive dust jacket Hawke had chosen, and disliking it, to recognize it at a hundred yards. She said to the man at the counter, "I didn't know Youngblood Hawke had a new novel out."

"Oh yes," the man said. "*Evelyn Biggers*. It's just been published. I recommend it highly."

"I haven't seen any reviews."

"Sometimes they're slow in coming, you know." The man emerged from behind the counter, took the book down and put it in her hand. "Care to look at it?"

Well, thought Jeanne, forty percent of four dollars is a dollar sixty. One couldn't blame these people. He was a small dough-colored man with weary eyes. She looked at the volume with distaste, remembering all the arguments she had lost: about the withered tea-rose corsage, the motif of the jacket, which had made it a four-color job and which she considered obvious and garish; about the excessively heavy paper, the wide margins, the large type, Givney's whole scheme for passing off a medium length novel worth three dollars as another of Hawke's grandiose tales, worth four. Givney had never once mentioned the higher price as his motive. No, *Evelyn Biggers* was literature, a work that would become an immediate and enduring classic, a book to own, and therefore the first printing must have the physical dignity of a classic: thus Givney, in the final, somewhat acrid meeting on manufacture. Ross Hodge had been annoyingly neutral. It was Hawke's money that was going to be spent. What did

Ross care? She had talked against Givney, but Jeanne lacked the vocabulary and the toughness for an outright business discussion, and anyway it was hard to accuse Givney to his face of planning to bilk the public. Hawke had disappointed but scarcely surprised her by approving the volume she now held in her hand. At lunch after that meeting she had attacked him with the waspishness of an irritated wife when she gets her husband alone. Hawke's reply had been that if the people wanted to read his story they'd read it for four dollars as well as for three; moreover expenses of setting up the Haworth House offices had been unexpectedly heavy, and so forth. Now here was the fat, fraudulent four-dollar volume, on sale in Washington three weeks before publication.

She handed the book back to the man. "I'm afraid I'm a spy. I'm Mr. Hawke's editor. I was wondering why you broke publication date, that's all."

The man's look of surprise changed to one of childlike cunning. He crinkled his eyes, put out his tongue sidewise, and winked. "Well, it's a pleasure to meet you. The shipment came in only yesterday and it's almost gone. You don't really mind my putting it out, do you? Sales are sales. They're doing it at the airport."

Jeanne said, "It doesn't really matter. How many did you order?"

"Ten. I have to be careful, books move slowly here. Of course the name Youngblood Hawke is bound to sell copies. We did beautifully with *Will Horne*. Naturally, that was politics, and in this town—" The man turned the thick book here and there in his hands. "I don't know about this one."

"Have you read it?"

"I tried. I couldn't get interested. It seems to be a woman's book. Why did Mr. Hawke write this kind of story?"

"I suppose because he wanted to."

"Well, I guess he figured women do most of the book buying. He's right about that, but—it really isn't very long, is it? It *looks* like a big book, but it's the heavy paper and the large type." The tongue and the wink again. "Publisher's tricks. Say, why not, if they can get away with it? The things people get away with in *this* town!" He put the book back on the shelf. Jeanne took a couple of news magazines and gave him a five-dollar bill. The man said, "Has he really become his own publisher, the way it said in *Booksellers Weekly*? I notice the imprint is Haworth House. I've never heard of Haworth House."

"Well, Hodge Hathaway is the distributor. Mr. Hawke does own Haworth House."

The man's eyes disappeared in crinkles, and he treated Jeanne to the tongue and the wink, still holding her five-dollar bill. "Tax dodge. I should think he'd be a millionaire by now, with his plays and movies and all, but listen, more power to him. The way things are nowadays, you've got

to grab while the grabbing's good, and I say a man's entitled to do anything that's legal. I'm sure a man like Youngblood Hawke has a battery
of high-priced lawyers."

"May I have my change, please?"

The man punched the cash register. "No, if you ask me this one isn't
another *Will Horne*. I took a copy home to my wife. She read it in a few
hours but she said it was depressing. My wife seldom guesses wrong on
books." At last he handed Jeanne her change. "I hope he's working on
another of his big stories. That's what he's good at. Lots of people, lots
of action. We need books like that."

Jeanne went to an armchair in the busy lobby and leafed through the
magazines. She had a tendency to anxiety and gloom in the best of times,
but on this day a dark ring seemed to be closing in on her. Men who
walked by her looked at this pale redhead in a black linen suit and
looked again. She was too elegant and forbidding to be approached, that
much could be seen, but her near-panic was not visible. Her hands poured
perspiration into her twisted handkerchief, her heart thumped hard, but
she sat quietly turning pages.

It was only part of Jeanne's misery that her husband was cornered and
would have to testify tomorrow, unless Adam worked a wonder at the
Senate Building. She had not been separated from her baby before, and
last night Jim had developed a temperature and had pawed pathetically
at his ear, saying "Hurt, hurt." She had decided in the morning to go with
Karl only after a struggle, though the baby's temperature was down and
he was playful. The Irish nurse, Elizabeth, who had become part of their
household, had assured her that she could go. When Jim turned really ill
it was Elizabeth who did the dosing and telephoned the doctor. Jeanne
knew that Jim must be all right. If she had been in a less morbid state
she would have telephoned Elizabeth, but now she was fending off all
gestures of fear, and so she didn't.

Washington stirred old sad memories in her. This very lobby did. The
Franklin bar had been a favorite of the crowd she had run with. Ghosts of
lost days were all around her. The smell of the lobby, the sight of its old
marble pillars, woke in her the ache of early flirtations, which she had
mistaken for love, all mixed up with her pain over Karl and her anxiety
for the baby. By what malignant fate had she come to marry a Marxist?
Now, to cap her troubles, there was this encounter with the newsstand
man. Jeanne had grown to be superstitious about the very first wholly
random comment she heard on a new book. Remarkably often it predicted the book's career. She was most pessimistic about the prospects for
Evelyn Biggers. The tremendous advance sales—the figure now stood at
sixty-four thousand—seemed sufficient proof that she was wrong. Hawke
had at the start paid some attention to her, ordering a first printing of only
twenty thousand. But with advance sales mounting, and with Givney's

encouragement, he had increased and increased the order, until he had at last gone to press with a first run of a hundred twenty-five thousand copies. It was, of course, smart business to do this, providing that all the copies eventually sold. He was saving a lot of money by such a large-scale run. But the risk was that if the sales stopped suddenly—and Jeanne had seen this happen to novels with large advance sales; indeed it had happened to *Alms for Oblivion* before its surprising second spurt—if this happened, Hawke might lose forty or fifty thousand dollars on the unsold inventory. Having plunged with such a big printing, he had further increased his risks by taking on a large advertising campaign. This was one of the things she had feared when she had fought against the Haworth House venture. No author ever thought his books were advertised enough, but in fact the book industry threw away millions every year in over-advertising. If *Evelyn Biggers* sold like his other books, Hawke was going to reap a fortune from it. If not, he already stood to lose as much as a hundred thousand dollars.

And this figure did not include his extravagant spending on his offices! The first idea, that Haworth House would merely be a desk in Givney's paperback firm, had quickly gone by the board. Hawke had rented a brownstone next to Givney's building, and his old decorating mania had broken loose. The offices were splendid—who would not like to have white leather walls, mahogany trim, and antique furnishings?—but the costs had run up so high and so fast that Hawke himself had taken alarm. His plans as usual had been most plausible at first; he would *live* in the offices, and on hotel bills alone he would save several thousand a year, and besides, all these costs were tax-deductible, et cetera, et cetera—but in the end he had squandered so much money that he had rented a car and driven out west to remove himself from the temptation to spend more. Moreover Adam had dropped disquieting hints that Hawke's heavy investment in a Long Island shopping center was not going well. There had been talk of a three-hundred-thousand-dollar second mortgage which Hawke had personally guaranteed. Such figures frightened Jeanne.

It seemed inconceivable to her that Youngblood Hawke could ever really crash. But from what she knew, from what she feared, from what she could surmise, his financial position was perilous, despite all the money he had made. Jeanne knew that great authors had gone bankrupt, following the courses that Hawke was in. Had the damned newsstand man told her he liked the book, she would have seized the excuse to telephone Hawke in Hollywood, just to hear the rough yet gentle voice that could always fill her with pleasure. As it was she could only sit and pretend to read a magazine in this haunted, icy hotel lobby, while a cloud of foreboding thickened around her. So a wretched hour and ten minutes passed, as she watched the clock hands crawl. Then the page came through the lobby, calling her name.

Karl told her on the telephone to go ahead and register. He sounded cheerful. Everything was taking very long, he said, and they might as well plan to stay the night. He had no news, or at least would tell her none. She checked in, and went up to her rooms. The number of the suite was 913. So bad were her nerves that she felt a little dismay at moving into a room with a "13" on the door. But she was not equal to changing it. The bellboy opened the door and stood aside, picking up the bags. What she saw through the open door was the ordinary dingy furniture of an old hotel. It was an effort to walk through the doorway; and when she did, it was as though she stepped through a sheet of glass that broke without a sound.

2

The first thing Karl and his lawyer did in the Senate Building was what most people do who go to government offices on business: wait. The junior Senator from Kentucky appeared after about three-quarters of an hour, all jovial apology and cordial greeting; a tall, heavy, black-haired man not yet forty, in a smooth blue suit, with the full-fleshed jaws and easy manner of one who has had early success. He looked like the former football player that he was. His attitude toward Karl Fry was very gracious. He mentioned two of his mysteries by name and said he wished Fry would write more. Then he took Adam into his inner chamber, leaving Fry sunk in his chair, looking tense and unwell.

"Gus, this is kind of a funny one," he said, after an exchange of news about their families and school friends. He was settled with Adam on a brown leather couch in his large and handsomely furnished chamber lined with law books and framed photographs. "The lawyers we get in these situations are usually way out left, if they're not commies."

"Not with cooperative witnesses, surely."

"Is your man going to cooperate?"

"He'll tell you whatever you want to know about his communist past. I've got here a ten page narrative that he'll read under oath, and answer questions on. It contains some interesting disclosures. He won't name other people, however." Senator Breckinridge grunted, and shook his head. Adam went on, "He says he knew no spies or saboteurs then or now. If he did he'd name them. He doesn't want to injure innocent people."

Breckinridge said, "Gus, your fellow wants to get married but he doesn't want to say 'I do.' We run into it all the time. I'm low man on the committee, but I can tell you that Jack Traynor won't accept that."

"Why not? This isn't a criminal proceeding. Fry retains his privileges as a citizen in giving your committee information."

The Senator said with good nature, "Old stuff, Gus. A citizen owes

Congress candid truthful answers to any questions put to him, otherwise he's in contempt."

Adam said, "Not quite. The questions have to be relevant to new legislation, or the working of existing laws, or some other clear concern of Congress."

"Sure, but this sub-committee's been functioning for ten years. The validity of what it's doing is well established. Your man won't be injuring innocent people by naming them, if they're actually innocent."

Adam tilted his head, arched his thick brows, and danced his fingertips together. "Now, Tom, you know perfectly well that in the present climate to be named as a communist or ex-communist is to incur substantial character damage at once, and probable financial damage. Maybe former communists deserve that damage. I don't know. I'm not arguing now about what your committee does. I have a very limited objective. I want Fry relieved from testifying, or if he does testify I want a stipulation that he isn't going to be asked to name people."

The Senator shook his head again. "Such a stipulation would set an impossible precedent. It's been asked for often and always turned down."

"I'm not interested in setting a precedent. An informal understanding will do. It can be between you and me, Tom, and I'll take your word for it."

The Senator said, "Gus, I'd like to go to bat for you, but I really don't know what I could say to Jack Traynor. It's his decision. Anyway, nobody can guarantee that the minority members would go along. It's a real tough one."

Adam said, "Well, Traynor runs this show. Can't he just quash the subpoena? Look here. This naming of names isn't required of all witnesses, you know that. It's a device you use to pin down uncooperative ones who may still be communists today. It's also a rehabilitation process for ex-communists in fields like government and the movies, where it becomes a test for keeping a job or getting it back.

"That's not the case with Fry, Tom. Hodge Hathaway will keep him as an editor if he doesn't testify. They're satisfied he's out of the party. He's a good editor and they'd rather not lose him. I can vouch for the fact that he broke with the party six years ago. He has no names that you haven't heard before in this inquiry of yours into the publishing field. Those are the facts, and therefore getting him down here and forcing him to name people is useless harassment, I think."

Senator Breckinridge stood and walked up and down his office. "Gus, who are you representing here? Hodge Hathaway?"

"I'm Fry's attorney."

"I mean that's a big, conservative firm, and if I could say you're speaking for them—"

"No, Tom. They've put Fry on his own."

Breckinridge said, "You're asking the committee to let Fry off, though he's been named several times, simply on your assurance that he's a good American now. I can try, Gus, but I don't think I'm going to get anywhere. Traynor will want from him a conclusive demonstration that he's broken with communism, just as he's getting it from others. The one thing communists will never do is name names."

Adam was looking up at Breckinridge, his eyes narrowed, his head sidewise. "There's one more thing you could tell Traynor. Fry is prepared to make a court fight, and to take it to the Supreme Court."

Breckinridge whistled, and dropped on the sofa, sprawling his legs. "He's awfully set on having his way, isn't he?"

"He's a harmless, quiet man, very keen, not in good health, but apt to go to extremes on a point of principle."

"What would be the basis of his appeal?"

"The first amendment."

Breckinridge laughed. "Gus, you know that won't work, or you ought to. It was thrashed out up to the Supreme Court by the Hollywood fellows. They went to jail for a year."

Adam began stuffing his pipe. "The first amendment was my idea, Tom. I think it might work, though of course I hope we won't go to court." He lit his pipe in measured puffs, keeping his eyes on the Senator. "The Hollywood situation was different—puff—those birds stood on a total refusal to discuss their communism, past or present. It amounted to a—puff puff—open defensive maneuver of the communist party itself, a test case. At that they lost a close split decision.

"Now in Karl Fry you've got a different man. He broke with the party years ago. He remains a frank Marxist, which sits a little better than all this crawling, Tom, no matter how wrong-headed you think he is. He's ready to tell what he knows about party discipline and tactics, because that's what drove him out. He has plenty to tell. He sticks at naming people he thinks are innocent, that's all. The American climate is still against informing. Karl Fry could become a sort of hero if his stand turns into a test case. When you go after publishing, remember, you're nudging freedom of the press, which means the newspapers. It's all different from the State Department or Hollywood. Just incidentally Fry has a beautiful and brilliant wife, thoroughly anti-communist, also a new baby. I can't put the baby on the stand, but I can use the wife in the lower courts effectively."

Senator Breckinridge's brow wrinkled more and more as he listened. Now he scratched his head and said, "Gus, I thought you'd become a nice conservative tax man."

"That's what I am."

"The hell you say. This sounds to me like the old fourth-quarter try that got you your busted nose."

Adam grinned and passed the back of his hand across his broad nose. "The thing is, Tom, I've never had a case involving a constitutional test before. It's an interesting technical problem."

"Can a fellow like Karl Fry afford the expense?"

Adam puffed on his pipe. "I wouldn't press him for payment. He and his wife earn excellent salaries. She's an editor too, she edits Youngblood Hawke's books among others. They'd be good for the money."

Breckinridge stared at Adam's impassive face. The telephone rang. It was Traynor's office, calling to say that the Senator was ready to meet with Fry and his lawyer.

Breckinridge said, hanging up, "I don't know, maybe I ought to talk to Jack alone first."

"That's exactly what I want, Tom. You always ran good interference."

The Senator from Kentucky held up a hand in protest. "I'm not running interference. I don't see why your man should get any preferential treatment here. I honestly don't. I can tell Jack you're a mean bastard to get into a fight with, because it's the truth."

Adam said, "Let's be clear here. I'm not looking for a constitutional test. I'm not in the least interested in setting up the first amendment as a shield for communists who won't talk. I want relief for my client. Nobody cares whether your committee calls one witness more or less. Let them think Fry talked in closed session, or to the FBI, the way so many do."

Breckinridge walked to the door, and stood with his hand on it. "Wait here."

"Okay."

"Gus, I can't say I understand you, exactly. Putting this kind of muscle behind a man like Fry."

"Why not? He's been my client for years. He's in trouble, and I'm trying to get him out of it."

The Senator said, "This beautiful and brilliant wife—" he paused, looking straight at Adam. The pause became long.

Adam puffed his pipe. "Yes," he said at last, "what about her?"

"Where is she, right now?"

"At the Franklin."

"Is she really all that beautiful?"

"Well, I think so."

"All right, Gus," said the Senator, with a little smile. "I won't be long."

Adam called in Fry and recounted the gist of the meeting. It was at this point that Fry telephoned Jeanne and told her to register.

3

Breckinridge's shapely office girl came into the chamber, all smiles and swirling white skirt. "Ah'm to show you to Senatuh Traynuh's office." They went out into the high-ceilinged gloomy corridor, lined with tall brown doors that dwindled sharply in the long perspective, and followed the girl's ticking heels to a rotunda and down another corridor. Fry grew more nervous with each step. Senator Traynor had been the chief name in Senate anti-communist investigations long before McCarthy had burst on the scene with his wild antics. The editor had signed many a petition and newspaper advertisement against the Traynor committee. He had never seen the man, but knew his features from a hundred political cartoons and newspaper pictures.

He was startled at the appearance of Traynor in the flesh, standing behind his desk in a shaft of sunshine from a broad window that looked out on the Capitol dome. The cartoonists emphasized the Senator's small round nose, jowls, and curly white hair to give him the look of a bulldog, usually a snarling and slavering bulldog, often dripping black gore from his fangs. But in fact John W. Traynor was a rumpled, handsome man of fifty-five or so, in a pepper and salt suit, with twinkling blue eyes, a rosy complexion, and a charming smile. His handshake with Fry was hearty, even a bit fatherly. There was a photograph of him on the desk taken with his wife, and several children of assorted sizes, and three collies. Also framed on the desk was a cartoon of himself as a bulldog with fangs sunk in the bleeding throat of a prostrate and dying Statue of Liberty. Traynor saw Fry's glance wander to the cartoon, and he laughed. "Take your choice, Mr. Fry. There are two portraits of me. I claim they can't be the same man, one of them's wrong." He introduced Adam and Fry to two men: the chief investigator of his committee, Harold Weller, a sallow young man with heavy, watchful eyes, and the committee's counsellor, Charlie Flagg, a much older person, sandy-haired, big and benevolent in manner. The Senator said, motioning Fry and Adam to seats on a couch with a courtly gesture, "Tom had to run along, Mr. Adam. How's Abe Tulking?"

"He's fine, Senator."

"Brilliant tax mind. Many's the time he's come down here and given us ignoramuses on the finance committee a hand. When you come here flying the flags of Tom Breckinridge and Abe Tulking, Mr. Adam, the latch is off." He turned to Fry and smiled. "I have a great regard for your reputation, both as a writer and as an editor. Tom Breckinridge tells us that though you've broken with the communist party you remain a Marxist."

Fry started to talk, stopped, and cleared his throat. "Senator, the word Marxist has many shades. I believe the revolution predicted by Marx will in time come throughout the world. I can't help believing it. It's what my common sense tells me. On a great many points I disagree with the so-called Marxists." Fry stammered through much of this. The eyes of the silent investigator and counsel, sitting in armchairs on either side of the couch, made him extremely edgy. Charles Flagg, the committee counsel, was the villain of all the hearings Fry had read about, the man who bore in with the cold remorseless questions that forced you to the wall. Yet there he sat, arms folded, legs crossed, a little paunchy, looking benign as an old cat; benign, but alert.

Senator Traynor said, "Now that's a candid statement that I can appreciate. I've said a thousand times—I don't know why people go on misrepresenting me—that any American has a right to believe in the doctrines of Karl Marx. You can't show a single instance where I or my committee have either hurt or persecuted such a man. However"—the Senator's finger swooped in an upward curve and halted in mid-air—"I don't think good Americans should conspire in a secret society to gain a political overthrow of our institutions by force that they can't achieve at the ballotbox, and I don't think Marxists should spread their ideas, which I consider wrong and dangerous—I'm entitled to my view just as you're entitled to yours—in the guise of innocent-seeming movies and plays and books. As you know, sir, art is more persuasive than argument. If I were a great author I could do more to combat communism than I am doing with my present humble efforts. Unfortunately all too many of our fine authors today seem to be on the wrong side."

The other men in the room seemed to be waiting for Fry to answer. He glanced at his lawyer, who gave the briefest nod, gnawing at his pipe. Fry said, "Senator, doesn't that indicate to you that these ideas have strength? They've already swept half the world. They're not obscenity and they're not lunacy. Marx predicted a new order of society. I wish I could believe he was wrong. Perhaps the life we have now in the United States is pleasanter for people like myself than socialism will be. But I think democratic capitalism is a primitive, temporary arrangement that can't survive very far into the industrial age. I think the ideas of Jefferson are uninformed and romantic for our time. Now I and other Marxists, including the communists, could be utterly mistaken. How can we be proven mistaken except by a free exchange of ideas? Why shouldn't Marxists spread their ideas in any form they can devise? If the ideas are weak they'll fall, if they're strong they'll prevail."

"The trouble is," said the Senator pleasantly, "if they prevail our form of government will be overthrown, and I swore an oath to uphold it."

"But if they prevail they become the will of the people, sir," Fry said.

The Senator said, "It's unthinkable. No people has ever freely voted in Marxism."

Adam interposed, "The thing you might consider, Senator, is that our nation seems to be very inept in countering Marxist ideas in the open arena of the world. We've developed a sort of pious anti-communism that seems mere mush when we try to take it outside our borders. Possibly we need more communist propaganda to sink our teeth into, not less of it."

"You're talking theory, sir," said the Senator amiably, "and the theory is fine. But there's the hard practical fact that not everybody's mind is as mature as yours, as able to distinguish subtle lies from the truth, and specious ideas from sound ones. Our advertisers and movie makers address themselves to a fourteen-year-old mind, as you well know, with continuous success. Don't you think such a mind needs some elementary protection from surreptitious poisoning?"

Adam said, "We trust the public mind to elect senators and presidents, don't we? If you believe in the theory of the fourteen-year-old mind, aren't you despairing of democracy much as Mr. Fry has? The advertisers and the movie makers are mountebanks, sir. Mountebanks always capture attention by extravagance and childishness. You yourself can be amused by a cowboy movie and bored by a Sophocles play, Senator, but that doesn't mean you have a fourteen-year-old mind when you come to work on legislation."

"I trust not," the Senator said a shade less amiably, but still smiling, and taking a watch from his vest pocket.

The young man named Weller leaned forward, waving a bony finger. "Professor Adam—that's how I think of you, sir, because when I went to law school I had occasion to sit in on a couple of your lectures at Columbia, and I've never heard a more brilliant discussion of state tax law"— Adam barely smiled—"I can show you pamphlets, put out by recognized subversive fronts, which defend communist propaganda with the same arguments you're putting forward, almost in the same words. Maybe the danger of their methods is greater than you realize, when a man like you can become, I won't say a dupe, but an unwitting transmitter of such ideas."

Adam said, "Why, Mr. Weller, if you'll let me lay aside the character of a professor, I don't give a good god damn whether communists agree or disagree with ideas of mine. Don't you think it's idiotic that theirs should be almost the only voices raised in this country today for freedom of ideas when their open policy all over the world is to crush that freedom? Yet that's the ridiculous pass we've come to. If it's right for Mr. Fry to name his former associates he ought to do it. If it's wrong he ought not to do it. It doesn't matter what line the communists take."

"Now you're talking turkey," said Senator Traynor. "I have to be off to

a meeting, gentlemen, so let me speak my piece and then Harry and Charlie can carry on. Mr. Fry, I frankly want to appeal to you to change your mind and answer any questions Charlie puts to you at the hearing tomorrow, relying on us to treat you with all due courtesy. You know perfectly well that there are other outfits in this Congress who can make a circus of an investigation and really hurt people right and left. You know that. I have not and I will not be a party to anything like that. I moved into the publishing field, I'll tell you candidly, mainly to forestall such a disaster to an industry where freedom of the press is involved and we're dealing with some of our finest minds. But Mr. Fry, we have substantial evidence that there are communists, ex-communists, and crypto-communists in publishing today. Their power to influence the kind of books America reads is enormous."

Fry said, "Senator, that isn't so. An editor who keeps picking dull Marxist books and passing up good non-communist books will soon be out of a job. Our job is making money."

"Well, that depends how far up the conspiracy extends. We have reason to believe that here and there it goes pretty far up. The point I'm making is, if we begin coddling witnesses in this field, Mr. Fry, these other investigators are simply going to come at you after we're done. I perfectly understand your reluctance to name people. Unfortunately in your younger years you obtained information that the United States Congress now needs. We ask you to give it to us. If you wish we can hear you in executive session, behind closed doors. That's a courtesy we're glad to extend."

Fry said hoarsely, "Whatever I do, I'll do in the open."

"Then I only hope you'll do the right thing, sir."

"Senator, I don't even like disclosing my own past, when I've committed no crimes, but as a law-abiding man I'm willing to give Congress that information. I don't believe I owe you a duty of hurting other people."

Charles Flagg uncrossed his legs and spoke for the first time in a rich, relaxed voice. "Mr. Fry, you can plead the fifth amendment, avoid all questions, and be in and out tomorrow in five minutes."

Adam said, "I'm sorry, I can't allow him to do that. In the present climate that labels him a traitor at large. He may lose his job. He's an excellent editor. He's not a communist, and he's not afraid of self-incrimination."

Weller said, slouching in his chair, his eyes half-closed. "May I throw in an idea? Mr. Fry can answer our questions up to the point of naming other people. Then, if after thinking over Senator Traynor's plea—and I hope he'll give it real thought—if he still won't name them, maybe he'll decide to take the privilege of the fifth amendment at that point. I'm not recommending that, of course, I recommend full disclosure."

Adam raised his eyebrows and glanced at the Senator and then at Flagg. Neither spoke, and neither had any facial expression beyond benign waiting. Adam said, "Mr. Weller, you haven't been out of law school that long. Once he answers questions about his own past he waives the fifth amendment. The course you're describing would be indefensible contempt of Congress. If he held to it he'd go to prison. I can't believe your suggestion is made in good faith."

Weller reddened. The Senator and Flagg exchanged a quizzical look, and the Senator laughed and stood. "They'll be yelling for me in the interior committee—"

Weller said incisively. "Since the question of good faith has come up, Professor Adam, may I ask if you know one Milton Davis?"

"Yes, of course. He clerks in my office."

"Do you know anything more about him?"

Adam smiled. "If you mean his past communist affiliations, yes. Why?"

"Well, it may have some relevance to your good faith that you come here talking anti-communism but you employ highly questionable characters in your office. Now, Mr. Fry, when do you claim you left the communist party?"

"April, 1947," said Fry, staring apprehensively at the flushed young man, who was weaving back and forth in his chair.

"Have you ever heard of the Conference for Civil Freedoms?"

"Yes."

"Do you know that it's on the Attorney General's list of subversive organizations?"

"It may well be."

"Did you contribute to that organization three hundred dollars in 1947, seven hundred in 1948, and four hundred in 1949, long after you assert you broke with the party?" Fry stared at him mutely. Weller went on, "Senator Breckinridge said you claim your wife has been consistently anti-communist. Have you ever heard of a man named Robert Alvert, with whom she was intimately associated as far back as 1945, here in Washington?"

Charles Flagg said, "All right, Harry, the Senator has to leave."

Weller turned on him. "I don't like having my good faith questioned."

Senator Traynor came out from behind his desk and put an arm around Weller. "You come with me, Harry, I want to talk to you." He held out a hand to Fry. The editor rose, his face dead white, and the Senator shook his hand cordially. "Mr. Fry, I hope you'll believe that I'm as sincere in my views as you are in yours. Tom Breckinridge said something about a court fight. I'll leave Charlie here with you to talk that one out. I'm sure we're not going to court, but if we must, well, the Congress of the United States has pretty broad shoulders. Mr. Adam—" he pumped

the lawyer's hand, "you give my best to Abe Tulking, now. We're all soldiers, Mr. Adam, soldiers in a time of great national danger, doing our duty as we understand it. I hope you work things out with Charlie. None of us want any trouble that we can avoid."

4

Charles Flagg stood, took the phone, and ordered coffee for three. He half-sat on the edge of the Senator's desk, and grinned at Adam. "You riled Harry there, a bit." His speech had a Western tinge.

"Well, his suggestion was preposterous," Adam said cheerfully. "Doesn't he think I know the Rogers case?"

Flagg blew out an audible breath. "Harry just came with us last year. He still likes the cops-and-robbers part of it, and he delights in cute tricks. But he works very hard. Mr. Fry, I apologize for the reference to your wife. You have my word that no such reference will be made in the hearing, not even if your wife for any reason testifies. Harry's a great little researcher, but short on common sense."

Fry said, dropping heavily in a chair, "Thanks, I appreciate that. There was a man like Weller at my first FBI interview. That's why I walked out."

Flagg said, "Well, one has to guard against the sense of power that an investigation post can give. I guess I committed plenty of sins when I started this work twelve years ago. I've gotten around to realizing that I work for the people, including the people I'm investigating, too. You're actually my employer, Mr. Fry, you know?"

"I am? You're fired," Fry said. The two other men laughed out loud; Fry said, "huh-huh" several times, and color came back in two spots on his cheeks. An office girl entered with a tray.

"Doughnuts, by God," said Flagg. "Why, we're living like kings. Coffee and sinkers on the government. Don't tell the Senator, but I like his chair." He sank into the big chair behind the desk, with a sigh of luxury, and dipped a doughnut in coffee. "Well, isn't this living?" he said, squinting in the sunlight. "Twelve years ago I started with this committee. That's right. I passed up an appointment to the supreme court of the State of Nevada to do this.

"Mr. Fry, I want to tell you a story, and it's God's truth. About four years ago we were investigating a government agency. We ran into this reluctance to name people—we do all the time, of course—in a man who unlike yourself had utterly broken with Marxism. He was rabidly anticommunist, but also rabidly opposed to naming names. I think he'd have gone to jail for ten years on the point. But we had a talk, and somehow he changed his mind. He named no people we hadn't heard about before. In naming one man, he did mention a couple of circumstances that were

new to us. We followed up the leads. They went through the family of the brother-in-law of the man he named. Eventually what we learned was so important it couldn't be brought out in open hearings. We gave it to the FBI. They got two spies out of an atomic installation in Oregon, sent them to jail, and broke up a Russian espionage structure on the west coast. Now that's a true story."

Fry sat looking over Flagg's head at the Capitol dome in the sunshine. "It sounds too pointed to be true. A little moral fable for holdouts like me. The contingency is remote, and the damage done by naming people is immediate and sure."

"I swear to God it happened," Flagg said, very earnestly. "Just as I told it to you, and we're proud of our achievement, which we couldn't publicize. The contingency is remote but it touches on the survival of the United States. Now if as a Marxist you're content to see our country go down I can't reach you and that's that. I'm talking to you as a dissident American, but I hope as an American."

Gus Adam said, "I get a different moral from your story. Our counter-espionage in that area is so feeble that some amateur detective work by staff members of a Congressional committee accidentally saved our country. In that case everybody in counterespionage who was responsible for the failure should be fired, and our professional counterintelligence should be enormously strengthened."

Flagg said, softly bringing a fist down on the table three times, "The constitution requires Congress to act for the common defense and the general welfare. Exposure of communists in places of public trust—in which I include the publishing field, Mr. Fry—is a direct discharge of that duty. You made a joke when I said before that you're my employer but it's so. Congress is a lot of nobodies who come down here for a term of years and then go home. They haven't an ounce of power that the people don't give them. The people are the sovereign. Any Congressman who doesn't do what they want goes into some other line of business pretty fast. Now Congress has voted over and over to give money to this committee and others like it. They've voted it to a man for years, because the people are worried about communism. The people sent you the subpoena, Mr. Fry, and the people want you to tell them what you know. Even Marxists believe in the will of the people."

Fry said, twisting his mouth, "They don't define it, I'm afraid, as the will of Charlie Flagg. They may be too dense to follow an irrefutable line of reasoning, but they don't."

"I know how I'm pictured in the press," Flagg said, "and I don't like it, but I believe in what I'm doing or I'd be back home in Nevada where my grandchildren are, putting on a black robe a couple of hours a day and otherwise enjoying life. I'm disturbed, believe me, by the split between the ideas of the intellectuals and the will of the American people the way

Congress expresses it, and I don't enjoy being known as a horrible Grand Inquisitor, but by God, Mr. Fry, it's Russia or the United States, the game is on, and it's for keeps. That's the one thing I know."

Gus Adam stood, putting his pipe in his pocket, and paced the room as he talked. "You're making a good case for cooperating with the committee. It's true that you speak for the sovereign, and that the sovereign is the people. The sovereign may be ill-informed. It may err in approving of your committee's work, or your committee may be making constitutional errors. There's no reasonable doubt, at least in my mind, that what you do is a serious abridgement of liberty. You're pleading national danger as the reason for the abridgement. You may be right. Then you get into Fry's contention, that our free way of life is a primitive arrangement that can't work under twentieth-century pressures. It's a large question. We won't solve it in this room. If you want to take it up to the Supreme Court my client and I are ready. We might perform a public service on both sides."

The committee counsel laughed, and lit a cigar. "We get these threats of a Supreme Court fight all the time. If we paid attention to them we'd just shut up shop here. They seldom materialize."

Adam said, "I wouldn't call it a threat. But in this case it will materialize."

Flagg and the lawyer exchanged a measured glance. Flagg rolled the cigar in his mouth. "Well, let's see how things work out tomorrow. We don't examine every witness with the same rigid procedure. We never waste the committee's time, we're too far behind as it is. However, we don't yield to threats, and we don't make deals. We follow our own needs." He stood and held out his hand to Adam. "Senator Breckinridge referred to you as an ornery son of a bitch in a fight, but I've enjoyed this. And I've enjoyed talking to you, Mr. Fry. Maybe we've all learned something."

They were in the taxi, driving to the hotel, before Fry spoke. "What do you think?" he said abruptly.

Adam said, "Well, we lost the first round."

5

Hawke sat in his shirtsleeves scrawling at a vast antique desk with a green leather top, a desk of the size Hitler or Mussolini would have fancied. It stood in the middle of a broad stark room that had two walls of roughhewn blue stone, two walls of glass, and a colossal white bearskin in front of the desk on the marble floor. The bear's bright dead glass eyes

looked out on a dizzy plunging canyon covered with the brownish green scrub of Southern California.

A hollow voice came out of nowhere, echoing on the hard surfaces of the room. "I beg your pardon, Mr. Hawke."

The racing pen slowed and stopped. Hawke spoke into the empty air. "Yes, Gordon? What is it?"

"Mrs. Honor Hauptmann is here, sir."

"Christ, is it lunch time already?" Hawke picked up the old cheap watch that he had won in high school. "Where has the time gone to? Tell her I'll be down right away."

"Very well, sir."

Then a woman's voice: "I'm coming up."

"Hello, Honor. Look, I'm not shaved, I'm a real mess. Give me a minute."

"Nonsense, I think you look best unshaven. Remember the Waldorf?"

Hawke sat back in the enormous swivel chair, put his hands up to rub his eyes, and was surprised to strike the eyeglasses. He had been wearing them less than a month, and was not yet used to them. He took them off and squinted at the page he had been writing, hoping that the diagnosis was foolish after all, that he didn't really need glasses. He was still making these tests. But the lines he saw on the yellow page were certainly vaguer now than before.

When the doctor had first forced the glasses on him Hawke had been astounded by the new hard clarity of print, of movies, of street signs, of his own handwriting. The headaches had much diminished, though they still came on now and then. The doctor had scolded him for having had no physical examination in so many years, and after some ominous talk about the trembling of his hand and the hallucinations of smell during long writing sessions—he had mentioned possible brain damage from Hawke's accident at nineteen—the man had given him capsules which had cleared up that trouble. Hawke was certain nothing was wrong with him but overwork. He had been driving at *Boone County* ferociously, and was proud to have almost two hundred thousand words in hand before his previous book, *Evelyn Biggers*, was even being reviewed. He was used to overworking, and he did not intend to slow down on his longest and best novel because of a Hollywood doctor, or even because of the brain specialist who had been called in, and who had been equally grave and scary. Hawke had had headache and eyestrain and tremors before. Once he finished a book, a week or two of rest and hard drinking usually quieted down the symptoms.

There was a rap at the door.

"Honor? Come in."

He had not seen her since the opening night of *Alms for Oblivion*. She wore a sleeveless navy blue dress, no hat, and no jewelry. Iron corset-

ing gave her an acceptable if stiff shape, but her sunburned face was fatter than before. She said, "Hello there. Did I break in on a deathless page?" She strode up to him and offered her cheek, kissing the air with her painted lips. "What in God's name are you doing in Travis Jablock's house? I almost died when Ferdie told me you were here. My father sold Travis this land long long ago."

Hawke said, "You look mighty elegant. I've ordered lunch here but we can go out if you'd rather."

"God, no. There isn't a restaurant in this town I don't know and loathe, and the food's wonderful too. It's the faces. Can we have a big big martini and talk first? My, you *are* unshaven! What's this, Arthur? Eyeglasses? You? The world's most perfect man?" She picked the glasses off the desk and held them to the light.

He said, "Temporary, I hope. Too much night work." He pressed a button on the desk and ordered drinks.

Honor Hauptmann dropped on an immense divan covered with furry white material. On the stone wall behind her was a Modigliani, a woman with an eggshaped head aslant on a long snaky neck. Honor's pose amply displayed her legs, which were almost as beautiful as her mother's had been. "It's years since I've been in Travis's eyrie. Doesn't it give you the creeps, sort of like the platform on the Eiffel Tower? Unless you have an ego like Travis's, you're bound to feel you're on the edge of a plunge to your doom. It's built that way. I think he modelled it after Berchtesgaden. He was invited to Berchtesgaden, you know, back in 1937. The son of a bitch actually went. My father wouldn't talk to him for years."

Hawke said, "It's a good place to work. Quiet."

"Oh, it's that, all right. You're not *renting* it, are you? I can't imagine Travis renting this abomination."

"No, I'm his guest. The whole thing is most peculiar." He told her how he had driven from New York across the country, stopping at motels and writing at night, sometimes staying in one place a week or more. He admitted that he had been running away from his orgy of squandering money on the Haworth House offices. Honor was amused, and said it served him right for being so damned greedy; he belonged in a garret and that was where he would end. The butler came with martinis, his manners and his speech so like a movie butler's that Hawke grinned at Honor behind his back. "I have to fight with myself not to call him Jeeves," Hawke said, when he left. "I've been here three weeks and I'm still not used to him, nor to anything about this monstrous house. I don't know why Jablock pressed it on me. He came to the party that Ferdie Lax threw for me at Romanoff's when I got here. That, by the way, was an occasion I'll never forget. Do you know that when I came into the room Dane Garnett walked up to me, fell on his knees and kissed my hand? He did. He kissed my hand, down on both knees. And everybody else reacted

in almost the same way. I couldn't have caused more excitement, more awe if I'd been the Queen of England or the Pope. And the people there were stars, Honor, big directors, millionaires."

"Arthur, the movie of *Chain of Command* has been number one at the box office for how long? Sixteen weeks? Ferdie says it's going to gross ten million, domestic. Dane Garnett is going to get an Academy Award for playing the hillbilly marine as sure as I'm sitting here. In this town you're awesome, dear. You're holy."

Hawke said, "The last time Travis Jablock spoke to me, before I saw him at this party, was six years ago. I was walking on the studio grounds with another screen writer. He said, 'Hey you! The tall one!' He claims now he doesn't even remember what I looked like then. He owns the movie rights to *Oblivion*, Luzzatto had them cross-collateralized some way and Jablock bagged them. He's making the picture, naturally, now that *Oblivion* is a Broadway success."

Honor finished her martini and held out her glass. Hawke refilled it from a dripping pitcher. She said, "The one thing you must know about Travis Jablock is this—never trust him, and never believe him. He lies the way you breathe. He's very good at playing dumb. Mainly because he is dumb, dumb as a dog, but terribly cunning. My father used to say that you're helpless in the movies until you learn that great stupidity and great cunning can go together. Is that what you're doing in this house, for God's sake, writing a screenplay for Jablock? *You?*"

"Hell no, I'm almost halfway into my new book. Jablock told me to stay here as long as I pleased. He said it's better to have someone in the house than to give his staff the run of it. He's in Cannes."

"I know he is, Manuel wrote me that he went with Travis to Monte Carlo."

"What's Manuel doing in Cannes?"

"Skin-diving. He struck up a friendship with a loathesome lunatic we met in Marseilles, one of these bearded skinny boat bums who's crossed the Atlantic alone in a sailboat and all that. They skitter around the Mediterranean diving for Roman pottery and swimming through sunken wrecks and whatnot. It's asinine and it's dangerous, those people are always getting drowned, and it gives me the horrors just to think of it. But Manuel's wild for it, and he couldn't care less about my feelings, as usual." She stood. "Arthur, you don't look well. You look about the way you did when you fell into the Waldorf a hundred years ago, except you're not dripping snow. You're not feverish, are you?"

"No, I've been up since before dawn and my eyes get red, that's all." He went to the bathroom. Honor followed him and leaned in the open doorway, sipping her drink while he took off his shirt and lathered his face. He was a little uneasy at being so isolated with her in Jablock's huge

house. She said, glancing at his broad bared chest and shoulders, "How do you stay in such shape? You don't exercise, do you?"

"No. I haven't been eating much."

"Maybe that's why you have that haggard expression. But it doesn't matter. You certainly don't have the physique of an esthete, do you? You look as though you'd been carved out of brown marble."

Hawke said in embarrassment, scraping the razor down his jaw, "What's brought you to Hollywood, Honor?"

"What brings everybody here," Honor said. "One of my father's old corporations is being bought by an independent—you know the way Hollywood's dissolving into new shapes, more disgusting than the old ones. The trust my father left me is the chief stockholder and the lawyers wanted me here. It's a great nuisance. I'm flying back home tomorrow. I can't wait to leave. Of course stumbling on you has made it worth while."

The hollow voice spoke from the other room, "Mr. Morris Fuld is on the telephone, sir. He wants to know if he can come by at three today."

"One moment," Hawke said. "Honor, what are you doing after lunch?"

"I don't know. Shop, I guess. Unless you want to cheer up a depressed old friend and take me driving."

Hawke called, "Gordon, I can't see him today. Tell him tomorrow at ten."

Honor poured herself another martini. "What does little Morrie Fuld want of you?"

"He's doing the *Oblivion* screenplay. Jablock asked me just before he went to Europe whether I'd be available to answer Fuld's questions now and then. I said yes, of course. It's turned into a script conference twice a week."

"For which you're getting how much?"

"Well, nothing."

"Oh God." Honor laughed heartily. "*That's* why Travis gave you this house, of course. There had to be something. And you fell for it? You should be getting fifty thousand dollars, as a consultant, you fool."

"Well, I know, Ferdie threw a big paroxysm when he found out, but Christ, Honor, I'm glad to talk to Fuld about the picture. Maybe it'll turn out less of a comic strip than the *Chain of Command* movie is."

Honor shook her head. "I said you're greedy, but you don't know what greed is, really. You just go through the motions. You're not disciplined about money. You're an inattentive slob. I bet I could manage you and make a millionaire of you in no time."

"Probably so."

They had lunch in a patio extravagantly planted up with tropical vegetation, where two Japanese gardeners moved to and fro trimming and weeding. Honor only picked at the trout, but she drank most of the

bottle of Chablis, and she gobbled her dessert, a large biscuit tortoni, and asked for another; and after downing that she glanced at him slyly, licking her lips, and asked whether he'd think her too awful if she ate a third. Honor Hauptmann was the only woman Hawke knew who habitually ate more than one dessert; her sweet tooth was one of her least attractive traits. She was both penetrating and tough in her judgments, a trait she no doubt had from her father, but she seemed to have inherited little of her mother's charm, and there was a spoiled, aggrieved, whining manner about her that sat ill on a young woman whose wealth was almost beyond his own imagining. There she sat, this incredibly affluent young woman, in her sleeveless Paris linen dress that perhaps cost more than the ordinary American woman spent on all her wardrobe for a year, stuffing herself with nut-sprinkled ice cream like an adolescent, and maundering about Hollywood and her father.

"The great tragedy of my father's life was that he was a Jew," she said. "He did nothing about it of course, he believed nothing, he observed no holidays, and he liked to eat things like rattlesnake and octopus, but he couldn't have been more Jewish, more intensely and obsessively Jewish, if he'd been a rabbi with a beard down to his knees. He was horribly sensitive on the subject. My mother in her charming way stabbed at that sensitivity when it suited her. We had a terrible home, and yet they loved each other and as far as I know were even faithful to each other, though who can say what goes on in this vile sink of a town? But when the three of us sat at breakfast the atmosphere was usually as cold and clammy as a morgue. They both had too much on their minds. My father was a great man and a very sad man, and—"

The butler was hovering at the patio doors, holding a thick newspaper. Hawke said, "There's today's New York *Times*. Want a look at it?"

"God, yes. These moronic papers out here, five hundred pages a day and nothing in them but advertisements and rapes!" Hawke beckoned to the butler. Honor said, "I'd go out of my mind down home if I didn't have the *Times*. I don't get the air edition, I get the paper itself flown from New York at a dollar a copy. Cheap at the price. I like to see the department store ads. Thank you."

Honor said after a little silence, in which they both rustled pages, "You must know this Karl Fry."

"What about him?" Hawke reached impulsively for the paper. Honor's finger pointed at the headline:

HODGE HATHAWAY EDITOR BALKS
AT TRAYNOR COMMITTEE HEARING

It was a long story, continuing to an inside page, where there was a picture of Jeanne in glasses and a big black hat, looking gaunt and anxious:

Mrs. Karl Fry, also an editor at Hodge Hathaway, hears her husband testify.

Flagg had asked Fry to name his associates in the Marxist discussion group, after Fry had described its workings. Fry had refused. Legal wrangling had ensued among Flagg, Gus Adam, Senator Traynor and Fry, to clarify the exact basis on which the editor was declining to answer. The session had ended in this disorderly and indecisive exchange; and Senator Traynor had directed Fry to appear at the next hearing prepared to name his associates or to be cited for contempt of Congress.

Hawke returned the paper to Honor and rested his face in his hands. "Poor Jeanie," he murmured.

"She's your editor, isn't she?" Honor looked at Jeanne's picture critically. "I'm sorry I've never met her. She seems quite pretty for an editor."

"Why should an editor be a beast? Anyway she doesn't look pretty there, she looks shocking. That picture's made me sick. What a trap, what a damnable foulup!"

Honor said, "He's a fool. He should plead the fifth amendment and be done with it. Why talk to those old bastards in Congress at all?"

Hawke threw his cigar into the shrubbery. "Shall we go for a drive?"

"Of course. You seem terribly upset."

"I like them both."

"Was she ever a communist?"

"Jeanne? No!"

Honor wrinkled her nose at Jeanne's picture and put the paper aside. "Communism is coming, Arthur, and damned fast, everywhere in the world but here. And then how long can we hold out?"

"Well, I think you're wrong, but I'm not up to that argument just now."

When they were settled in Jablock's red Italian roadster, swooping down the deserted canyon road, Honor said, her voice pitched high over the wind, "How's Frieda Winter?"

"All right, I guess. I hear she's in Jamaica."

"You hear? Don't you write to each other?"

"No."

"Is it really over, then? That's what the talk's been."

"Yes, it's over."

"You had some bad luck, Arthur."

"Frieda once told a son of hers, the little boy who died, that you make your own luck. I think it's true."

"Did that boy really kill himself? I heard that, too."

"No, it's a lie. He had pneumonia and they couldn't catch it in time. God damn people and their flapping mouths, can't they let a child of twelve lie quietly in his grave?"

Honor stopped talking for a while.

Hawke was going eighty miles an hour down a straight stretch at the bottom of bleak canyon walls. She put her hands to her streaming hair. "Ye gods, you drive like Manuel does back home, but there nobody will arrest him."

"There's no one ever on this road."

"Look, Arthur, if you want a peaceful place to work, for heaven's sake come down and stay at our place for a while. It's the most beautiful country in the world, you've never seen such mountains, and the air and the climate are heavenly. Believe me, there are no distractions! I speak with authority. There isn't a damned thing to do but ride horseback and read. You'd finish your book in half the time."

"I doubt Manuel would like that."

"Manuel!" She twisted her shoulders and flipped her hand in a sudden odd Latin gesture. "He's suggested it himself more than once. You should spend time in South America, Arthur, then you'd see why I say communism is coming. Manuel and his crowd! They roar up and down in their Cadillacs past villages where the Indians live in caves, real caves in the rock, thousands of them, eating nothing but corn meal and bitter roots, and they think that's the way things should be. I have spells of real horror sometimes, Arthur. Do you know we live behind an electrified fence? The Indians have brains, some of them are very wise, and it doesn't take much knowledge to shortcircuit an electric fence. I get visions of waking up and finding the throats of my children cut. The Indians are patient, wonderfully patient, and they're *good*. That's been the salvation of Manuel's crowd, but they don't understand. They think they're the natural lords of creation, born to drive Cadillacs and fly to Europe and guzzle champagne and whore around with models and ballet dancers and American divorcees."

She sounded so bitter that Hawke glanced at her. She sat looking straight ahead, arms folded, hair flying, her plump face a mask of sulkiness. Seen in profile her heavy double chin made her seem almost forty, yet she was younger than Hawke. He said, "It was a drastic change for you, marrying a South American. Maybe you're not quite used to it yet."

"Damn right I'm not. Come down and see. It's another planet, or rather the same planet in another century. Take away a few of those ghastly modernistic excrescences in Lima, those apartments and office buildings where they twist and arch the concrete like spun sugar, and believe me Pizzarro would be quite at home if he got out of his grave. He'd just exchange his horse for a Cadillac. You can't imagine what it's like to be a woman there. The richest woman in Peru has fewer rights and less freedom than the lowest male Indian shovelling manure in the stables, and what's more he knows it and looks down on her. I'm a pariah, of course. I behave and talk like an American woman and nothing and

nobody can stop me. I was seen having dinner at a hotel in Lima with a harmless Italian ambassador when Manuel was in Paris. The fuss his family raised, and the talk that went around! All this time, mind you, Manuel was assumed to be sleeping with every available poule in Paris, on both banks of the Seine. They're not even aware of the inconsistency. Well, I could go on forever, but the thing is for you to come down and see for yourself. You'll get the material for your greatest novel."

They drove down to the shore and out past the grand houses of Malibu to a deserted stretch of waterfront without a fence. Honor was peculiarly excited. "Stop the car!" She ran out on the coarse brown sand, kicked off her shoes, lifted her skirt and whipped down her wispy stockings. Then she bounded to the water's edge and went in to her ankles. "My God, how *cold* it is, it's so cold it burns," she cried, as he walked up to her. "Take your shoes off, you cream puff."

"No, thanks."

"Do you save all your romance for your books?"

"Beaches have never struck me as romantic. Too gritty."

Honor laughed, and strolled along the water, plopping her naked feet in the washing edge of the waves, making dark stains on her blue skirt. "You're wrong. I once became engaged on this beach, not too far from this very spot. It was hopeless, all he wanted was to get a job with my father, as papa pointed out to me rather cruelly—in fact that was the story of my youth, pretty much—but I'll never, never forget those moments on the beach, kissing in the sunset with the waves sloshing around our bare feet when I was seventeen. He was as tall as you, and he had bright blue eyes. He's in television now, a nobody. Do you understand why I married Manuel? He had no interest in movies and his family had more money than mine. And Peru seemed terribly romantic when I visited it with him. I wanted to escape from here, and I did, Heaven knows I did. . . . The question is whether I found a better 'ole . . . Arthur, what's the matter? You're a million miles from here. Is this boring you? I've had my paddle, let's go."

He laughed guiltily. "Sorry, Honor. I'm worried about Karl and Jeanne. I'm wondering whether I could fly to Washington tonight and get there in time for the hearing tomorrow."

Honor said, "There ought to be planes. Don't stew about it. Telephone and find out." She ran up the beach, retrieved her shoes and stockings, and walked barefoot to the car. "Thanks for letting me wade in my past," she said when he got in beside her. "It's not such a good idea. Terribly cold. And now that you mention it, quite gritty. If you do fly to Washington, can I come with you?"

Hawke said uncertainly, starting up the car, "Of course, but why should you?"

"Well, it's a chance to see one of these hearings. I'd never go alone."

Hawke shrugged. Honor would be an encumbrance and an embarrassment, but how could he possibly tell her so? "By all means, if there's a plane, come along."

CHAPTER TWENTY

1

JEANNE was awakened by the clatter of a typewriter. She started up in horror, finding herself in a strange bed in a strange room, with the frightful awareness that her baby was not there. It took her several moments—pulling herself out of a wild dream of being in an airplane which had lost a wing but was still flying in a groaning, shivering way—to recall that she was in Suite 913 of the Franklin Hotel in Washington, and that she was waking from a baseless bad dream into the real bad dream of Karl's predicament. She went to the door of the bedroom and opened it, blinking. "Karl, what in God's name are you doing? It's four o'clock."

Karl sat in wrinkled gray pajamas, slouched over his portable typewriter at the writing desk. Scrawled sheets of hotel stationery lay all over the desk, the ashtrays overflowed with butts, and a bottle of vodka stood beside the typewriter. "Sorry, darling. I did close the door. I've got to type this up, the committee's rules are that you must file a copy of a statement with them before they'll let you read it."

"But you and Gus prepared the statement yesterday. It's all done."

"I know. It's a fine job, Gus is a hell of a lawyer, but it's not exactly what I want to say. All the chips are down. I may as well speak for myself."

"Have you changed it much?"

"I wrote a new one."

"Good lord, how long have you been awake?"

"I never went to sleep, Jeanie. Just played possum until you passed out. You look very fetching. French postcard effect."

Jeanne moved away from the reading lamp that was illuminating her gown, and dropped in an armchair. "This isn't good, Karl. You have to get up again in a few hours."

"It's amazing how spry I feel. I think I've struck off quite a piece of prose. It may go down with Vanzetti's letter from the death house."

Jeanne passed a hand over her brow. "Maybe it's as well you got it off

your chest, but I think you'll end up reading Gus's statement. Vanzetti's letter didn't help him much. How much longer before you come to sleep?"

"I'll be in bed in half an hour."

"See that you are. How much vodka have you had?"

"Small nips for fuel. I'm totally sober." Indeed Fry seemed quite sober; weary, determined, yet placid. Many of the tension lines were out of his face. But he looked shrunken and frail. He offered the bottle to her.

"No thanks. I'm quite in the mood to start on raw spirits, and then I'd never stop. Finish up and get some sleep, please."

"I will, I promise."

She lay in bed in the dark. The clattering went on and on, then stopped. In a few moments, much to her surprise, her husband slipped into the narrow twin bed beside her, a compliment that had all but vanished from their lives since the birth of Jim. "No evil intent," he said, putting his arms around her. "Just friendship. We're still friends, aren't we? Despite this bog I've got you into?"

"Oh, for Pete's sake, Karl." She embraced and kissed him. He reeked of cigarette ashes.

He said, "Jim is a cantankerous little beggar, but it's strange how I miss him tonight. I wish he were in the next room bellowing. I'd like to see him."

"Well, we'll see him soon enough. One way or another it'll all be over tomorrow. I guess I mean today. There are streaks of pink in the sky. Look."

"The dawn of a new day," Karl murmured, "with liberty and justice for all." He sank on the pillow and fell asleep almost at once. There was hardly room for both of them in the bed. Jeanne went into the sitting room, and read the new statement, three copies of which lay neatly clipped beside the typewriter. Then she reread Adam's statement. It was quite true that the new one sounded just like Karl, and the other did not. She sat in an armchair, smoking, staring, the tears standing in her eyes, while the sun came up gloriously over Washington.

2

Adam met them for breakfast in the hotel coffee shop. He looked ruddy as a farmboy, and his curly blond hair was in tangles. He had walked a mile and a half from his hotel, he said, the weather had turned brisk and windy, and he was feeling in great form. He ordered an extra large breakfast of meat, eggs and grits, and put the food away with dispatch. Over the coffee he read Karl's statement, his face falling into a severe cast. Once or twice his clownish eyebrows went up as high as they could go. "Well!"

he said, handing the sheets back to Fry and lighting his pipe. "I don't think they're bargaining for that kind of thing." Jeanne and Karl were regarding him anxiously. He smoked for a while. "You know something? I'm half tempted to try it."

Jeanne said, "Is it as strong as yours legally? I don't think so."

Adam said, "Jeanie, the legalities here are cloudy and shaky on both sides. Legally I don't think the committee should be doing a lot of things it does. Legally Karl shouldn't balk, perhaps. American law hasn't digested communism yet, that's the long and short of it. The founding fathers didn't foresee people conspiring to destroy a free society because of some queer philosophical doctrine. They took it as a finality of history that men wanted above all to be free. It's a new constitutional problem. I like Karl's statement because it goes to those points. It gives Traynor a rather original reason for climbing down gracefully. It could work! They're not happy, you know. They've shifted to the big caucus room today because of the newspapers. Tom Breckinridge called me last night to press the idea of a closed-door session."

Fry said, "To hell with closed doors. I'm not skulking behind any closed doors."

Adam puffed meditatively, surrounding his face with a blue cloud. "Karl, if you prefer to make that statement, go ahead. We can always fall back on the legal ground."

"You mean the Supreme Court fight."

"Yes."

Fry was turning a fork over and over. "I'm starting to wonder whether I'm up to being this year's Dred Scott."

The lawyer smiled. "It's a long way to the Supreme Court. These things often kick around and get lost."

"But once in it I've got to see it through. I talked to the legal staff at Hodge Hathaway, you know, before we came here, just to check. They said the tab might come to twenty-five thousand dollars."

"If it goes all the way it might."

"I can't afford it."

Adam nodded, and kept nodding in silence. Then he said, "I've been thinking that over, too. Last night I phoned Abe Tulking. Our office is prepared to conduct this case without cost to you, Karl, from start to finish, if you stand on the first amendment."

Jeanne and Fry looked at each other. Fry said, "That's most generous of you. I don't think I could accept it. Why should you do it?"

"Well, Abe agrees with me that the situation needs clarifying. He's a hard-shell, gold standard Republican, but he thinks investigations like Traynor's may be weakening the fibre of the law. He compares the situation to prohibition. The whole country thought it wanted prohibition and then found out it didn't. He says the investigating power of Congress

is very precious, and should be spelled out so that the whole country can be for it. Right now it's become an issue between the yahoos and the intellectuals. Abe thinks it's unhealthy that the intellectuals should be against Congress. So do I. Congressional investigation is the best tool we have for uncovering corruption in the executive branch, the armed forces, and the country itself. It seems a far cry from that to forcing you to name in public all the dismal wretches you saw at a Marxist parlor meeting twelve years ago. The thing should be straightened out. I'm ready to do it if you are. It's interesting. If it hadn't meant so much pain for you and Jeanne, I'd say I've been enjoying it."

Jeanne got up abruptly. "It's unbelievably good of you, Gus, and don't try to put another face on it." Her tone was dry and rough. "Am I being too optimistic, or can I go up and pack?"

Adam said, "Why, whatever happens, I should think we'd be going back tonight."

Jeanne hurried away.

Fry, who had eaten nothing, poured what was left of Jeanne's pot of coffee into his cup. "That's what troubles me, Gus. Jeanie. This kind of abominable ordeal going on and on—"

"She's for it, isn't she?"

"She once said she's for my keeping my self-respect. That's as far as she's gone. Jeanne has amazing powers of shutting up, for a woman."

The lawyer said, "I think she's for the court fight, if you want it."

Fry grinned in a crooked way at Adam. "Your gallant offer is to Jeanne, as much as to me."

Adam said after a pause, "Yes. I admire Jeanne."

"I don't blame you." Fry gave the lawyer a keen, long sidewise scrutiny. "Do you know that she married me on the rebound from Artie Hawke? I daresay you've surmised that long ago, what with your general clairvoyance."

The lawyer cautiously nodded. "Well, of course, I barged into the middle of a situation, but it soon became clear that to you and Jeanne he was more than just a successful author."

Fry said, "She got irked at his shenanigans with Frieda Winter and suddenly accepted my forlorn overtures. She and Artie were both a little young then. I grabbed her. Maybe I did her a disservice."

The lawyer said, "Don't misunderstand me, but I think any man who'd pass up Jeanne on almost any terms would be an idiot."

Fry grunted and drank coffee. "I don't know why I'm falling into this vein. The drowning man, I suppose."

"We won't let you drown. I'm sorry we couldn't talk them out of making you testify, but that was a long shot."

Fry lit a cigarette with the peculiar swift gesture, and the jet of smoke

from his nose, that signalled a decision. "Gus, is Artie Hawke going to go bankrupt?"

The lawyer blinked, and raised his eyebrows high. "That's an odd question."

"I'm not asking idly. I know he's up to his neck in this Long Island shopping center, the goddamned fool, and from what I hear about Haworth House, that can go very sour unless *Evelyn Biggers* is a runaway best-seller. Jeanne and I don't think it will be."

Adam said, "Well—in general, I'd say Hawke has put himself into a risky position. At the moment neither of his big ventures looks safe. He may be exposed to a very serious setback. His earning power is so enormous, however, that I don't think an actual bankruptcy's in the picture." He suddenly grinned and waved both hands upward. "*And* of course everything can turn rosy overnight and he can end up inside of a year with the million in hand tax-paid that he's always talked about."

Fry twisted his lips. "A worthy aim for an artist, isn't it?"

"Well, Karl, it's a general American aim."

Fry said, "Sure. Not that I want to rehash our differences, but in the Soviet Union all these disgusting shifts and dodges he's gotten into would be both outlawed and meaningless. A writer of his talent would have an assured excellent living, all the luxury the country offers—which isn't too much for anybody, and I happen to think that's a good thing— and a place of high honor."

"That's true," Adam said. "It's the city dog and the country dog. He'd wear a collar there. Hawke's the country dog, free to write and act as he pleases, and also free to make a thundering ass of himself, something artists have always been very good at, in any society. Why are you asking me about Hawke's affairs? Haven't you enough on your mind?"

"Hawke's on my mind." Fry shredded the butt of his cigarette, staring at it. "I've had a few white nights lately, as you can imagine. With two coronaries under my belt I do find myself wondering what would become of Jeanne and Jim if somewhere along the line in a court fight I goofed out. Artie's still around. After all I've put Jeanne through, it'd be hard lines if her next tour of duty was with a dizzy bankrupt, however gifted."

Adam looked at his watch. "Well! Those are real midnight thoughts, aren't they? Nothing like that's going to happen. It's about that time, Karl."

Fry got out of his chair heavily. "Let's go, counsellor."

3

Jeanne was more surprised by Hawke's eyeglasses than by the fact that he was in Washington. There he sat in a light gray suit, in one of the front rows of folding chairs in the great high-ceilinged room, towering over the other spectators, talking to a beautifully dressed plump woman whom Jeanne had seen somewhere before. The glasses were most incongruous on Hawke's face; it was as though he were wearing them for a joke. "Look, Arthur's here," she said to Karl, as they walked to seats kept for them in the front row. Adam was outside, having been stopped at the door by Senator Breckinridge.

Karl said absently, "He is? Where?" Jeanne pointed, and at that moment Hawke saw them, waved, and made his way out of the row. He came to them and shook hands. A photographer's bulb flashed. There was only a scattering of spectators, but the two lateral banks of chairs for the press on either side of the room flanking the small witness table and for the long table of the committee, were filled up. Nobody was at the committee table yet but Flagg and Weller, whispering together over papers. Heads turned when the bulb flashed; the reporters buzzed among themselves, obviously identifying Hawke, and made notes.

"Karl, this may sound ridiculous," Hawke said, "but if there's any possible way I can help—character witness, money, I don't know what—anything I can do, I'm here to do it."

Fry said, "Why, Artie, all you know about my character is that I got your first novel published, a hell of a subversive move against American literature." With a twisted, tired grin he put his hand on Hawke's arm. "I think everything's under control. Thanks."

Jeanne said, "Glasses, Arthur?"

Hawke smiled self-consciously, and removed them. "I always forget I have them on. The beginning of the end, Jeanne."

She said, "I hope not, I've worn glasses since I was sixteen."

Senator Traynor walked in behind the long table, followed by Breckinridge and four other men. "Here we go," Fry said. "It's a long way from Hollywood, Artie. I appreciate your coming."

"Good luck, Karl."

The Senators sat behind their name plates. Each had a microphone before him. Traynor and Flagg spoke in low tones to each other at the center of the table, while Weller walked along passing mimeographed sheets to the Senators. Gus Adam came and sat beside Karl and Jeanne. "There goes your statement, I think," he said. "Don't take this too seriously yet, but my guess is it shook up Flagg and Traynor. Breckinridge

just told me Traynor's going to make a compromise offer, and begs you to take it, because that's *it*. He wouldn't say what it was."

"Oh, God," Jeanne said.

Karl said, very hoarsely, "Don't tell me I've written my way out of this box. It's incredible. It'll change every idea I've ever had."

With few preliminaries Fry's name rang out. He stepped to the lonely witness table and sat between two microphones, directly facing Traynor. Around him was a broad empty space; beside him, another chair for his lawyer. Adam, however, was still sitting with Jeanne. Traynor and Flagg continued to whisper while Fry sat mute, smoking. The other Senators were reading the mimeographed sheets Weller had passed to them.

Hawke was glad he had brought his glasses. Without them the faces of the Senators were pink blurs; but he put them on and saw the six men plainly. He said to Honor, "The strangest thing about those Senators is how ordinary they look. They're just half a dozen decently dressed guys. You'd think they'd been elected by shaking up names in a hat and pulling a few out."

"That might be a better system," Honor said.

Hawke said, "Look at Traynor. Joe Blow, vice-president of the Hovey Chamber of Commerce."

"This is terribly exciting," Honor said, "I'm perishing for sleep but I wouldn't have missed it for worlds. It's like a bullfight, except it's a man." She sat on the edge of her chair, craning her neck to see Fry, her eyes shiny.

Hawke glanced down at her with distaste. "I understand if Karl does talk, they award Traynor his ear."

Honor looked at him, a little abashed. "Well, I didn't mean it that way."

Breckinridge was walking from one Senator to another, whispering to them. Jeanne said to Adam, "They're so damned *casual* about everything, aren't they?"

"They're elected for six years. It's relaxing," Adam said, glancing around at the empty rows stretching far back into the oblong room. "They could have kept this in the other chamber. People aren't interested in publishing. Now if Karl were a movie actor—"

Senator Traynor rapped his gavel, and the talk in the room faded. Karl Fry sat up in his chair, resting both elbows on the table, his face gray and skeletal between the two microphones.

"Mr. Fry, at the last session of this hearing, committee counsel put a question to you which you declined to answer." The Senator's voice was pleasant and firm, and he was smiling. "You offered some ill-defined ground of moral scruple which was unacceptable by the rules of procedure of this committee, or any Congressional committee I know of. If witnesses could withhold information from Congress at will, on a plea of moral

scruple, the investigative power of Congress would cease to exist overnight. The damage to this country's welfare would be terrific."

He paused as Flagg put a hand on his shoulder and whispered to him.
Traynor nodded a little impatiently and went on, "This committee recog-
nizes that up to that point you were a cooperative witness. You frankly
described your experiences in your communist days including the tragic
story of your forced recanting of a book review. You gave us valuable insights, and in that way acted like a patriotic American. While we can't
accept any vague plea of moral scruple, because it would create a bad
precedent, we want to cooperate with you in turn.

"The committee has decided to excuse you without further questioning, therefore, because of your previous cooperation." A buzz rose in the
press section. The Senator's finger swooped upward in a curve and stopped
in mid-air, and silence fell again. "We ask only one thing from you in
return—that you now state to this committee your willingness to meet
with the Federal Bureau of Investigation, only if the bureau thinks it
desirable of course—and there answer, in the privacy of a confidential
discussion, and not under oath, the questions they may see fit to ask you
concerning this situation. If you will give us this token of your good faith,
you're excused."

Fry sat motionless for perhaps a full minute, a cigarette burning in his
fingers. Then he spoke in a grave, measured voice. "Mr. Chairman, may
I consult with my counsel?"

"By all means."

Adam dropped into the chair beside Fry, and covered one microphone
with a cupped palm. Fry covered the other, and said, "What is this, Gus?"

Adam said, more excited than Fry had ever seen him, "Karl, it's an
open door out of this room. They don't want to play."

"Why? What's happened?"

"Well, everything's begun to work, I guess. They take the court fight
seriously, after all. I also think they don't like your statement."

"What shall I do?"

"I'd say grab it! It's just a face-saving formula for them."

"But doesn't this commit me to name people to the FBI?"

"Only if and when they call you. That's another fight, Karl. Meantime
both you and Traynor slide off this particular hook."

"I don't know. This puts me right back where I was three years ago,
except I'm on record that I'll talk to the FBI. I'll get out of here, but I'll
be crawling out."

"Not necessarily. It's a grandstand play of Traynor to the press. It's
very unusual, I don't know that it's been done before, but it's clever. Let
me try to clarify this."

"Go ahead."

Adam spoke into the microphone. "Senator, I think we all understand

that if Mr. Fry made the statement you ask for, he would not be limiting any of his rights as a citizen in talking to the FBI. Is that correct?"

It was the turn of Traynor and Flagg to confer over choked-off microphones. Breckinridge from one end of the table, and Weller from the other, hurried to the center and joined the colloquy. Weller seemed the most vehement of all. After a minute or so, Charlie Flagg spoke. "Ah, Mr. Adam, I think we all agree nobody can take Mr. Fry's rights as a citizen away, unless he goes to jail for a year and forfeits some of them."

Fry spoke out hurriedly, blurring Flagg's last words. "Mr. Chairman, in plain English are you asking me to state here that I'll name people to the FBI?"

Senator Traynor said, still smiling, "Mr. Fry, I think I can stand on what I said to you, it's clear enough. We have a long agenda this morning and we're ready to excuse you."

"Mr. Chairman, I have no information on treason, espionage or sabotage to give the FBI, and so my attitude would be the same there as it is here."

Adam started to put his hand on Fry's arm, then let it drop. Traynor and Flagg shrugged. The Senator glanced unhappily around at the press section and at the committee, and sighed, "Well, I hope those present will agree that we've gone all the way trying to show consideration for your scruples. In view of what you say I regret I have no choice but to ask committee counsel to put the question to you again, and I must direct you to answer to avoid incurring the penalties for contempt of Congress."

Flagg said, reading from a paper in a thick folder, "*Did the first meeting of this discussion group which you attended take place in the home of Arnold Bingham, of the firm of Prince House?*"

Fry fumbled in his breast pocket and pulled out papers with a crackle that the microphones amplified all over the room. "Mr. Chairman, may I make a statement in connection with that question before answering it?"

Traynor said shortly, "The rules of this committee exclude vague philosophical discussions and statements that attack the committee's function. They waste the time of the elected representatives of the people of the United States. Unfortunately we've found that the press is often more interested in excluded statements than in the most revealing testimony, and we can't stop you from releasing the statement. We're willing to enter your statement in the record, and now will you be good enough to respond to the question?"

Karl Fry said, reverting to the strange grave tone he had used at first, "Mr. Chairman, this moment is the turning point of my life, and I respectfully ask for leave to read my statement."

Flagg and Traynor whispered. Flagg said drily, "Okay, read your statement, Mr. Fry."

Traynor said, "I wish the press would report that there's no suppression of free speech here, though I'm not too hopeful that they will."

Fry lit a cigarette, and spread the sheets on the table. Adam leaned back in his chair, his palms over his eyes. A sigh and a rustle passed through the room.

4

Fry began in an even, resonant tone tinged with fatigue:

"Mr. Chairman, a man doesn't find himself in a predicament like the one I'm in right now without doing some soul-searching. I've learned a lot about myself in the past few days. I've learned, for instance, my real reason for leaving the communist party.

"I've always said and believed that I left because I couldn't take discipline, and because I selfishly desired to enjoy the remaining years of my life, instead of giving my energy to a political cause. But I now know that the reason was deeper.

"My trouble has been that while I'm convinced that communism is going to triumph in the world—and that it ought to triumph because it's the one wise and just way to maintain an orderly industrial society on a crowded planet—while I believe that, I really love the United States just as it is. That's what I've found out. I love this do-as-you-please country, for all its inequalities, its follies, its logical contradictions, and its exploitation of the workers. I have no honest love for the severe order that must replace it to bring and enforce social justice. I could never, even in my early days in the party, work up the religious fervor for the new day that is part of being a good communist. For better or worse, I couldn't take leave of my critical intelligence. My refuge was always in sarcasm and joking. Those are poor traits in a Marxist, or in any movement requiring zeal, self-sacrifice, and total conviction. I at last allowed my divided attitude to creep into a book review, as I've testified here. I was ordered to write another review recanting what I had said. I obeyed the order, but after that I was dead to the party, and for a long time I was dead to myself. My leaving the party two years later was a formality. In spirit I left it the day I submitted that second review.

"Mr. Chairman, allow me a moment to tell you how I differ from my former party comrades about Marxism. To me, the 'dictatorship of the proletariat' is a long clumsy euphemism for Plato's Republic, which is the benevolent forcible rule of the many by the intelligent few. Plato called these few the guardians of the state, or the philosopher-kings. I'm certain that the Republic is at hand, that in an industrial world the many cannot rule themselves, that they must drift into ever greater sloth, indifference,

anarchy, self-seeking, dreaminess, and moral decay. Power flows to the cunning, and the rule of the many becomes the rule of money.

"I think America as it exists today is a laboratory specimen of the process, far advanced. Our peculiar squandering, our fantastic luxuries, our silly television dream world, our wild Wall Street plunging, are merely the rouge and lipstick that heighten the sick look of a dying society. The Marxists already rule half the world, sir, and I believe they will soon rule the rest of it. In every backward land the intelligent few will seize power and join hands with them. Modern society is too complicated and dangerous a machine to be left to people like you and me, Mr. Chairman, and to the loose vagaries of a liberal constitution written by eighteenth-century Deists. A tough elimination process in the communist party brings forward the best men of talent and will, who can run the social machine for the good of the people. The ideas of a classless society, and of a state that will wither away, are the golden myths that Plato prescribed to keep the many happy while their wise masters rule. All this I believe. It isn't orthodox communism at all, but it's what my brain tells me. I know no answer to it.

"But all the same, sir—and this is what my ordeal here has taught me —it is a wonderful thing to be free. It was wonderful that I could walk out of the party unchallenged and untouched six years ago. It has been wonderful ever since to go about my business, and do as I please, and make my own mistakes, and spend my money foolishly or wisely, and consult nothing and nobody but my conscience and my wife. You can't appreciate that feeling of freedom as I can, Mr. Chairman, because you've never been in the party. I have. I believe American freedom is an idyll that must pass, a brief rainbow episode in the long iron-gray history of compulsory human order. But I love it, though I think it is doomed.

"Now what I ask of you in all earnestness is this: can I possibly be wrong?

"I wasn't surprised, sir, when first the FBI and then your committee summoned me. Not at all. I understand a compelled and directed society. It's what I myself believe in. It has always seemed inevitable to me that as the United States began to skid faster on the downward slope, it would begin to clutch here and there in panic, and would begin abandoning freedom early, but clumsily, incoherently, without plan and without effect. I think I'm here at this moment because America is in panic.

"Sir, I appear before you now as a conscientious objector to your own abandonment of the ideas of the American constitution. I'm not a dangerous man. You know that. You want from me the formal gesture of recanting which you exact from other ex-communists. I'm a boorish, recalcitrant, inconsistent, anarchic, freedom-loving Marxist. I have no names to give you that you haven't heard before. You know that, too. I once recanted because the communist party ordered me to. Must I now

recant because the sovereign Congress of the United States wants me to? Is there no room left in the United States for the conscientious disobedience of Thoreau? Are you that far down the slope?

"I've written this statement late at night, Mr. Chairman, hastily and in anguish of spirit, throwing aside the legalities my counsel prepared for me to speak. I have no heart for legalities. The founding of the United States was an act of defiance to all the weary wisdom of the world's political logic. If you now let me go, you'll be indulging in the same kind of brave defiance of old wisdom. Your act may loom small against the massive arguments of Marx and Lenin for a forcibly ordered society. It may go unnoticed as a piece of quixotic clemency in a congressional committee. But it will plant in my heart at least, and perhaps in some others, the hope—the most unexpected seed of hope—that there's some mysterious eccentric cog in the American spirit that makes a free society possible after all, even in the terrible age of machines, and that Marxism may not be inevitable."

Fry pushed the sheets aside, and his impassioned voice fell to a wry conversational note. "I've talked much too long, sir, and you've been incredibly patient. I thank you most respectfully and humbly."

5

The Senators of the subcommittee followed Fry's statement on their mimeographed sheets at first; but Jeanne saw that one by one they laid the papers aside and fastened their eyes on her husband, their expressions serious and far from hostile. His hollow, grave, declamatory reading, much like his manner at the rare times when he read his own poetry aloud, was gripping. By the time he ended, everyone at the long table was listening intently except Harry Weller, who was buzzing in Flagg's ear. The young man had been moving along the table all during the reading, passing a note here, whispering there. In her entire life Jeanne never conceived a deeper hate for anybody than she did for this sallow scuttling little person, whose name she did not even know. It gave her immense satisfaction to see Senator Breckinridge at one point wave Weller off like a fly, keeping his gaze on the witness.

Honor Hauptmann said to Hawke in the moment after Fry finished, when the Senators were whispering back and forth and a murmur rose from the press tables, "I've never heard anything more touching. He's done it. He's going to walk out free without giving the names. They can't possibly do anything else."

Hawke's face had a stunned faraway look. "It was wonderful," he muttered, half to himself. "I disbelieve everything Karl said about this

country and about the future. If I live, I'll write a book to answer him. But it was wonderful."

The rapping of Traynor's gavel stilled the din. The Senator seemed surprised by the swift descent of silence. He hesitated, then spoke with a certain solemnity, though he smiled. "Mr. Fry, that's quite a statement, as a piece of writing. It's a display of talent worthy of a better cause. I've often said that it's a national disaster that at this turn of history some of our finest minds are either indifferent to the future of our free system, or hostile to it. You're more eloquent than I am, sir, and what I have to say will be an anticlimax. I have a responsibility I can't escape, as chairman of this subcommittee, to find out all that can be found out about the penetration of subversives into our communications industries. You're not a subversive, sir, you're what I would call a misguided idealist. These are chaotic times and I don't know all the answers any more than the next fellow, I—all I can do is—" The Senator paused, seeming to lose the thread of what he was saying. "Your statement boils down to the old plea of moral scruples, Mr. Fry, doesn't it? Only you call it conscientious objection. As for the philosopher-kings, I'm not going into all that, but I believe that all people prefer to be free, just as you do, and I think America can stay free if we exercise the necessary vigilance. And as long as we're free, these bloody tyrants with their execution squads and their jabber of social justice aren't going to rule the world.

"Speaking as an individual, Mr. Fry, I'd be happy to end your interrogation at this point. I think the security of the United States can easily survive your unwillingness to answer this committee's questions. But the precedent of moral scruple that you want to set up would be a blank check to subversive activity in this country, sir, and make it invulnerable to the scrutiny of Congress. Having heard your statement patiently, the subcommittee is with me in directing you to answer. Mr. Flagg, will you repeat the question, for the last time?"

The committee counsel, who looked tired and old, opened the thick folder and intoned, *"Did the first meeting of this discussion group which you attended take place in the home of Arnold Bingham, of the firm of Prince House?"*

"May I confer with my counsel?"

"Certainly." Charlie Flagg mopped his brow, though the room was chilly.

Fry covered the microphone and turned to Adam. His sickly face was exhilarated, his whisper surprisingly cheerful. "Well? Is this it?"

Adam said, "Yes, this is it."

"What do I do? What are my alternatives?"

"Well, Karl, I think you can still accept that FBI formula. That's the most practical out. Otherwise this becomes the kickoff, and you'd better answer formally. Here's the response."

Adam had been folding and refolding the paper in his hand. He now laid it before Fry. The editor scanned it, his hand over the microphone, muttering the words.

Mr. Chairman, with the greatest respect for the authority of this committee, I am now advised by my counsel to decline to answer the question on these constitutional grounds.

First, freedom of speech and of assembly are guaranteed by the constitution, even, and especially, to the holders of unpopular opinions. Forcing the public disclosure of the names of people who have assembled to discuss a very unpopular political doctrine constitutes an abridgement of those rights, if not the destruction of them, since it must discourage future assemblies and discussions by dissidents.

Second, this inquiry is beyond the scope of your committee's powers, and the authorization given it by Congress. The first amendment guarantees freedom of the press. You are trying to find out here the political affiliations of people in the publishing field. But any statute that attempted to regulate or limit the political convictions of publishers or their employees would be in violation of the first amendment, and therefore void. Since no other kind of statute can develop out of this inquiry, the question you have put to me is beyond your committee's authority.

Because of these rights guaranteed by the first amendment, sir, I most respectfully decline to answer the question.

Karl said softly, pursing his lips over the sheet, "It doesn't sound like me."

Adam said, "When you're heading for the Supreme Court, Karl, personal style is not the question. You lay a groundwork of legal formulas."

Jeanne was watching this colloquy with desperate attention, though of course she could not hear a word. As it happened, she was touching a handkerchief to her eyes when her husband suddenly turned full around in his chair and looked at her. She dropped the handkerchief to her lap and smiled as cheerfully as she could. He shook his head, made a gesture of drying tears, and wagged his finger in mock reproach, grinning. Then she saw him do a strange thing. He threw his arm around Adam, gave him a brief hug, and clasped his hand, saying something that, from the look on his face, was a wisecrack. She heard his voice on the loudspeaker, firm and a little shrill. "Mr. Chairman."

"Yes?" said Traynor, in the silence that fell at once.

"Mr. Chairman, the meeting was at the home of Arnold Bingham."

Shocked as she herself was, Jeanne saw Adam sit bolt upright in amazement. All along the committee table there were expressions of surprise. Senator Breckinridge looked a little dismayed. Traynor sat holding the gavel, staring at the witness, his mouth open in a comic picture of a man caught unawares.

Flagg said, stammering, "Of the firm—of the firm of Prince House?"

"I think Arnold was working for Jay Prince then. I'm not sure."

Flagg exhaled a heavy breath. The microphone carried the sound like a groan, all through the vaulted room. "Will you name the other people who were present at that meeting?"

"Well, it's been twelve years. There was Philip Byrne, of course, he brought me there."

"Spell that name, please."

"Yes, sir." Karl's voice was becoming lower and heavier. "B-y-r-n-e."

There was rising noise at the press tables. A few reporters were walking out. Traynor banged his gavel. "This witness is entitled to the courtesy of all present, and I especially mean the gentlemen of the press!"

Flagg said, "Mr. Fry, does your recollection extend to any other people at that meeting?"

Karl said hollowly, "Evelyn Ringle, of course, the kind lady who named us all here two weeks ago."

"Evelyn Ringle of Cardiff Books?"

"Yes."

"Spell her last name, please."

Fry was sagging low in his chair. He spoke each letter like the tolling of a bell. "R-i-n-g-l-e."

"Do you recall anyone else?"

In this manner Flagg drew Fry to pronounce and to spell fifteen names. It became a sad and sombre litany between the two grim men. Then Flagg closed his folder wearily, and whispered to Senator Traynor.

The Senator cleared his throat. "Mr. Fry, I think the committee can now excuse you. You have found yourself in a moral dilemma here. I speak for the Senate of the United States in thanking you for making the difficult, the patriotic choice. You have set an example which I hope others will emulate. Men of your intellectual stature should not be harassed. We need you in the fight for freedom. I have every hope that you will yet make even greater contributions to that fight than you have today."

Fry said in the same sepulchral voice, with a ghastly smile, "Mr. Chairman, it's bad enough to die once. I haven't enjoyed dying twice. I lack the strength to fight for freedom, or I would have made the patriotic choice. I have done the Congress a disservice by answering those questions. You can't beat the communist party at its game, sir, and by abandoning your own game you're throwing in your hand. I've always thought it was a losing hand. But I leave here filled with irrational grief because I no longer think freedom will die in this land, I know it will. However, everything has its season and dies. Am I excused, sir?"

"You're excused," said Senator Traynor.

6

Reporters clustering at the door of the caucus room surrounded Fry when he came out with his wife, his lawyer, Hawke, and Honor Haupt-mann. A man poked a stick-microphone at the end of a long black cord into Fry's path, saying, "Mr. Fry, sir, I'm William Callaghan of Station WGW Washington. We've been carrying this morning's proceedings and I wonder if you care to add a word now that it's all over."

"Two words. Thank God," Fry said.

The announcer laughed. "Would you care to expand on that, sir?"

Fry smiled wearily and shook his head.

"What are you going to do now, sir?"

"Sleep and eat for a week or so. I haven't done much of either lately."

Gus Adam said, "This has been a gruelling business and I think you'd better excuse us. We have a car waiting—"

A reporter interjected, "Mr. Fry, why didn't you take Senator Traynor's offer?"

"I don't know."

"Do you now feel your decision was wise?" the radio announcer said, thrusting the stick up to Fry's mouth.

"Well, my lawyer told me this morning that it's an American privilege to make an ass of yourself. I guess I availed myself of my birthright."

Jeanne said, "Come, Karl," and pulled at his elbow, but he seemed in no hurry to leave, he looked around the circle of faces with a weary, defiant, dazed grin.

A reporter said, "Wouldn't it have been preferable, sir, to naming those people at an open hearing? I think everyone was surprised at your sudden abandonment of your position."

"Well, call it pride of authorship. I'd written this statement and maybe I just wanted to read it. Try sitting in that chair some time and making quick decisions."

Hawke stepped beside Fry, put his arm around him, and said, "Let's go, Karl." He was a full head taller than Fry and he looked like a bespectacled colossus, embracing the frail thin-faced editor. He started to move with Fry through the press of men, when one of the reporters stepped directly into Hawke's way: a burly young fellow in a very short raincoat and checked collegiate cap, with a beaked nose protruding out of a fat white face. "Mr. Hawke, I'm Ira Borso, New York *Star*. What do you think of Mr. Fry's action today?"

"I think the hearing was a tragedy for everybody concerned. Now we've got to be going—"

"Sir, on another topic, are you going to make a public reply to Quentin

Judd's accusation?" The reporter stood his ground, his sharp nose thrust upward straight into Hawke's face.

Hawke said, "Accusation? What accusation? I don't know what you're talking about."

"Haven't you seen the new *Rambler?* Judd says you didn't write your latest novel."

Despite himself Hawke blurted, "What? Who does he think wrote it?"

"Oh, he's quite definite about that, sir. He says it was written by this lady here, Mrs. Karl Fry."

Jeanne exclaimed, "Nothing could be more ridiculous, neither of us has seen the article but we both know Quentin Judd well and he couldn't possibly—"

"Mrs. Fry, would you or Mr. Hawke care to glance at the *Rambler?* I have it with me." The man turned his thrusting nose on Jeanne and pulled a magazine from his raincoat pocket. "It's just out today, I picked it up at La Guardia. Maybe it hasn't been delivered to Washington yet." He proffered the wrinkled gray journal to Jeanne and then to Hawke. The other reporters crowded in around him, their faces alight with interest.

Hawke brushed the reporter's hand aside. "I don't know what Quentin said. I consider Mrs. Fry the best editor in the United States, but I write my own books and Quentin Judd knows that as well as I do." A chorus of questions broke from the ring of reporters. Hawke said, "Sorry, now we go," and ploughed through them, his protecting arm around Fry.

Mrs. Hauptmann had a hired Cadillac waiting outside, and she offered to take the Frys to their hotel. Karl Fry looked at the immensely long car and the bowing chauffeur with a childlike smile. "Well, well, this is the way a Marxist gets to leave the Senate Building, after making the patriotic decision. Most appropriate. Thank you, Mrs. Hauptmann."

As they drove off, he said that mostly what he wanted to do was sleep. He felt amazingly good, twenty years younger, and if he could only nap for an hour or two he would be ready to start a new life. He made no comment on the reporter's startling news about Judd; he seemed not to have heard it. Jeanne said she would make new plane reservations for the evening, after dinner. Karl said, yawning, that he had always heard there was a great seafood restaurant in Washington, and they might as well get a good dinner out of this dreary expedition. After a little talk all five agreed to meet for cocktails at the Franklin Hotel and then to have dinner together.

Honor said, "Mr. Fry, you probably don't want to talk about what's just happened, but I want you to know that your statement was the most brilliant thing I've ever heard. It will live when all these senators have been forgotten."

"Thank you," Fry said. "I'll be happy if it lives long enough to appear in tomorrow's papers. I doubt that it will. Submission isn't news. As a

matter of fact I don't think I want to look at tomorrow's newspapers." He put his hand on the arm of Gus Adam, who sat on a folding seat before him. "Gus, I hope you don't mind my spoiling your fun. You'd probably have taken them to the Supreme Court and licked them."

Adam shrugged. "I don't know. The composition of the court's changed since the Hollywood decision, but the climate's still bad. You certainly did a reasonable thing in dropping the fight. And in point of fact you didn't injure anybody, they'd all been named."

Fry said, "I know that. The issue had importance only in my own mind. It's strange how trivial, how forgotten it all seems already. We've only driven half a dozen blocks, and it's as though the hearing happened a year ago." He turned to Jeanne. "Were you surprised?"

"A little, dear."

"Well, I saw you crying and I decided—kind of suddenly, I grant you— that I was being heroic at your expense, and Jim's, not to mention Gus Adam's. Don Quixote should be a bachelor, with an independent income. That's how Cervantes described him."

Jeanne said, "I wasn't crying."

"Weren't you? Something in your eye, no doubt. Well, it's all over, we're not facing a year of court fights and publicity, and I couldn't be happier." Karl's eyes were closing, and he leaned against his wife. "Jeanie, you have hard shoulders," he muttered. The others stopped talking as he dozed.

When the limousine halted in front of the Franklin Hotel he sat up with a start, blinked and grinned. "Wow. I feel better already. An afternoon's nap and you'll see a man reborn."

Hawke stepped to the sidewalk to make way for the Frys. Karl came out and offered him his hand. "My boy, I hope the scene was worth a trip from Hollywood."

Hawke said, "You acted wisely, Karl. I'll never forget a moment of it."

Fry peered up at him, his thin mouth warped in the old grin. "Artie, you going to put me in a book one day?"

"If I live, I guess so, Karl."

"Be sure you do live. Absent thee from felicity a while. And be sure to make the point that in this harsh world Don Quixote should be a bachelor with money. We'll get good and plastered tonight, won't we? Thanks for the ride, Mrs. Hauptmann."

Jeanne and Hawke exchanged a strained look, and Jeanne went into the hotel with her husband.

Hawke said as he got back into the limousine, "Honor, can we run out to the airport? They'll have the *Rambler* there if it's anywhere."

"Of course."

The chauffeur nodded, and started the car.

Adam said, "I'll come along. What the reporter said sounded serious."

Honor said, "Why, it's inconceivable."

Hawke said, "There's something odd about this. Quent Judd telephoned me a month ago in Hollywood, just after I got there, and asked for galleys. He wanted to do a good job on the book, he said, and the *Rambler* went to press so far in advance that he'd rather not wait for review copies. Givney had just mailed me the first book off the press. I told Quent I could airmail it to him. He was most grateful, and promised to read and return it in a couple of days. The last thing he said was, 'I read terribly fast.' I never heard from him again."

Gus Adam said, "Well, at worst the *Rambler's* circulation is tiny."

Hawke read the Judd article not only with the sinking feelings that any bad notice caused, but with an added vertigo such as one experiences in an earthquake. He sat between Adam and Honor on a couch in the booming, racketing waiting room of the airport, which faced out through towering glass walls at a constant roaring crisscross of airplanes. He had bought three copies of the gray dull-looking journal, and they were all reading at once. It took Hawke only a minute or so to absorb the two closely printed columns on the front page, and the two columns inside; and to realize that he had encountered a disaster of a magnitude that could not readily be measured.

Honor spoke first. "This is beyond belief. What in God's name made him do it?"

Adam said, turning the page, "It's pretty bad so far."

"It gets no better," Hawke said.

Honor said, "It isn't a review. It's a libel, a brutal criminal libel. You have to issue a statement denying it, at once, Arthur. I don't see how you can avoid suing him. What alternative have you?"

"Oddly enough, I'd be suing myself. It would cost all the stockholders money if I won."

The lawyer said, still reading, "Suing a critic is usually futile. The privilege of the press is very broad. Besides, he's done this adroitly. I'm not sure there's an actionable statement in it."

"I couldn't possibly sue Quentin Judd, Gus. I'd be the laughingstock of the United States."

Honor said, "Arthur, besides the personal attack on you and all you've written, he as much as says that you've palmed off a book written by Jeanne Fry as your own."

Adam folded the journal and slipped it into his pocket. "That's the impression it conveys. It's malignant, neatly written, and from a legal standpoint, very clever. Arthur, have you had a quarrel with this man?"

"I thought we were on the best of terms. As much as you can be with such a fellow," Hawke said. "I found him drunk in a gutter one night

and helped him home. That's how he happened to recruit me to put money in the *Rambler*. He seemed grateful, then and ever since then. I'm staggered, Gus."

Adam nodded. "That may have been your mistake. There's a striking bitterness in this. Maybe he thought you were trying to buy good reviews from him." The lawyer smiled, and his eyebrows arched high. "Was the thought wholly absent from some dim corner of your mind, Arthur? Why should you back a magazine?"

"Jeanne was furious at me for doing it. Jeanne has an exasperating way of being right."

Honor said, "It's impossible to ignore it, Arthur, absolutely impossible."

Adam said, "Well, it needs thought. You may have to take some action, Arthur, as much for Jeanne as for yourself."

Hawke stepped to a wastebasket and thrust his copy inside with a bang of the swinging tin lid. "I don't want Jeanne or Karl to see this tonight. They've been through enough for one day."

"Certainly not," Adam said. "They'll find out soon enough."

7

Honor had booked herself a suite in one of the new hotels, though she had planned to go on to New York without sleeping in it. She now went there, after leaving Adam at his hotel, and insisted that Hawke come up with her. "You didn't have any more sleep in that plane than I did. You can stretch out on the sofa. Come along. I'm just going to sleep until cocktail time."

Hawke came, but uneasily. He was sure Honor's offhand manner with him was a pose. He remembered her gushing letters. He also remembered moments in Italy and France—her way of pressing close to him in a motor car, occasional glances she gave him after drinking a lot of champagne, her way of dancing with him, like a college girl trying to captivate a quarterback. He had always avoided occasions of being alone with her. But he had no place to go, and he was in a whirl of thoughts about the Judd onslaught, so he followed her into the hotel.

She ordered a light lunch with champagne sent up to the suite. They ate in the broad sitting room, by a curved corner window with a view of the White House, the Capitol, and the monuments. Honor became gay after a glass or two of wine. "This city is thrilling, there's nothing to touch it except New York. Do you know that tears came to my eyes and blinded me when Fry said, 'I love the United States just as it is?' I do, too, Arthur. I love this silly vulgar tremendous marvellous country, with all its faults. It seems as though I just realized it today. Believe me, as soon as the children are old enough for school, Manuel's in for the fight of his life.

I'm going to take them to New York. He can come or not as he pleases. I'm going to get the loveliest apartment with the highest and best view in New York, I don't care what it costs, and I'm going to furnish it like a palazzo in Venice, and I'm going to *live*. I was a fool to run away. My mother's shadow doesn't haunt me any more. I've seen her movies on television. Her hairdo and make up look funny and her acting style is dated. I'm not her daughter, I'm me, and I intend to make a delightful career out of being me. I can paint pretty well, you know, and don't faint, but I think I can write. Will you read my first novel and criticize it? I've actually got a plot all worked out in my mind."

"Of course I will, Honor."

She had ordered a plate of French pastries and was eating them one after the other. "Of course I'm not going into competition with you, nobody can, you're up on Everest all by yourself. When am I going to read this new book, by the way?"

"I airmailed you a copy to Peru."

"Oh, *that* blasted postal system. I may see it next July." She looked at him slyly. "Arthur, is there any shred of truth to what Judd says? I know it's ridiculous and horrible, but—"

"Jeanne Fry did a lot of editing of my other three books, Honor. She was especially good on *Chain of Command*. I poured out a flood of war reminiscences and she cut it to the bone of the story, and probably made it the success it was. It happens that she did almost nothing on the new book. I wrote it in Europe. When I sent it to her she said I should print it as written. Judd couldn't be further off the mark."

Honor said, "Are you sure that what she's done has been good? You remember I've objected to a certain obviousness in your books. Maybe that's been her doing. I think creative outpouring is sacred. Who is Jeanne Fry or anyone else to cut a line that Youngblood Hawke has written?"

He said, "Look, Youngblood Hawke is just a scribbler trying to get at the truth. Do you know how many drafts the good novelists have written of their books? Jeanie has saved me maybe half a year of drudgery on each of those novels. I edited *Evelyn Biggers* myself, and I know."

Honor said abruptly, "Tell me about this lawyer Adam. Who is he? What is he? Where does he stand on anything? He strikes me as a very puzzling customer."

Hawke described Adam's background, from the University of Kentucky onward, and mentioned the tax difficulties that Adam had cleared up for him. "He's very able, that's for sure. I've never known a man less prone to coming out with what he thinks. You have to judge by his actions. Conservation is his big interest, outside his work. He's on the board of a wildlife society, and a national park association, that kind of thing, and he goes off in the woods for weeks at a time when you need him most.

That's why he looks so good. He looks ten years younger than I do and he's four or five years older. I don't know his exact age."

"He does not look younger than you. I don't much care for his looks. I never did like pink sandy men. Is he married?"

"He was. His wife's dead."

"Are you aware that he's in love with Mrs. Fry?"

Hawke said at once, "You're crazy."

Honor's eyes narrowed at him. "And you're supposed to be the observer. Did you hear Fry say that the court fight would have been at Adam's expense? Didn't you notice Adam's tone when he talked to Mrs. Fry? Why should a tax lawyer go to this kind of trouble for a balky Marxist?"

"Well, I think Gus is a nut on principle. He saw this as an important constitutional problem."

"He's a nut on something. Forgive me a feminine interpretation. Ready for your snooze?"

"God, yes."

He was almost asleep on the sofa when she called from the bedroom. "Arthur?"

"Hmmm?"

"Come and talk to me for a minute, or are you passing out? I'm reasonably decent."

She sat at a dressing table in a beautiful white slip, a sheath of silk and lace, combing her hair. "Hi. We're old pals, don't mind me. I'm sitting here wondering whether I ought to tell you something."

Hawke dropped in a chair. Honor was naked under the slip, her body bulged candidly where the fat was piled, yet she looked a bit exciting like this; a Turk's dream.

She said, "Do you know that the day you came to mama's suite and told the story of *Alms for Oblivion,* I fell for you like a madwoman, though you were a total stranger and looked absolutely frightful. I mean it was wholly a physical reaction, even before you told your novel so brilliantly. I was hard put to it not to track you down after you left. I actually called Prince House for your address! Then I got cold feet and slammed down the receiver. I'd felt this way when I was younger about an elevator boy in the Beverly Hills Hotel, and if you'll believe me, about my father's Filipino chauffeur, briefly. Anyway, what I'm sitting here and wondering is, whether a lot of lives wouldn't have been vastly different if I'd followed my impulse and hunted you up?"

Hawke said, "I have a better one, Honor. How many angels can dance on the head of a pin?"

Honor came and sat on the arm of his chair. "I'm not discussing angels."

After the years of Frieda Winter, Hawke had a real horror of adultery; and though Honor had somehow gained a sexual aura for the moment

by the obvious expedient of discarding her clothes and showing her bare fat body under a veil of lace and silk, he wanted no part of her. There being no polite alternative, he put his arm around her. She yielded to the touch, and there they were kissing in the chair. Her bare flesh in his hands felt like warm dough; any excitement he had experienced died away with his first contact. She kissed him heartily for a while, then leaned back and uttered a low pleased laugh. "You're being a gentleman. I've wanted to kiss you for years. Anything more would be a catastrophe and couldn't possibly lead anywhere. On this small sample, I'd say I should have tracked you down from the Waldorf, Arthur."

"Well, Honor, I wish you had, and it's charming of you to say all these things, but here we are."

Honor said, lolling happily on him, her thighs mashed flat and broad, her cheek against his, "It's interesting though. Youngblood Hawke hugs and kisses, et cetera, like any man of flesh and blood. No doubt Dickens did too."

Hawke said, "He had to do something about having those ten children, or Mrs. Dickens would be more famous than he is."

Honor laughed, jumped off his lap, and pirouetted clumsily to the dressing table. "All right, all right. Go have your snooze."

8

When Hawke telephoned Room 913 from the lobby of the Franklin Hotel, it was a long time before anyone answered. Jeanne came on at last, her voice high, vague, and soft. "Hello? Who is it?"

"It's Arthur. I'm here with Mrs. Hauptmann."

"Oh." Jeanne laughed. "Hello, darling. I mean—well, yes, hello darling. What time is it, for heaven's sake?"

"Half-past five."

"Lordie. Arthur, Karl's sleeping like a baby and I seem to have passed out over a detective story. I feel so silly."

He said, "Maybe you should both just sleep on."

"No, no, he's looking forward to this dinner. He ate no lunch, he's had five straight hours in bed. I'll roust him out and put on a face and so forth."

"Shall we wait down here?"

"No, come on up. The door will be open."

The suite had none of the elegance of the one he and Honor had just left. The sitting room was small and angular, the purple wallpaper was water-streaked, and the furniture seemed grayed by dust. As they came in Jeanne looked out of the bedroom with a nervous smile. Her face had no

paint on it. "Hello, please make yourselves at home. Sorry we're late." She closed the door hard.

Honor and Hawke hardly had time to sit, both puzzled by her abruptness, when the bedroom door opened again. Jeanne said, with the same mirthless quick smile at Mrs. Hauptmann, "I'm sorry. Arthur, please come in here."

Her tone made him jump from his chair and cross the room in a few strides. Jeanne closed the door behind her. The shades of the bedroom were drawn. Karl lay in gray pajamas in the gloom, in the bed near the window. Jeanne said, "I hope I'm not in panic. He's a heavy sleeper, but now I can't wake him. I've really tried."

Hawke went straight to the bed, touched Karl's shoulder, touched his perspiring face, then shook him—at first gently, then harder. "Come on, Karl, let's get those martinis and that seafood dinner."

The loose inertness of Karl's head as he pushed the shoulder scared Hawke. "Karl?" He sat beside him and lifted him to a sitting position. Fry's head rolled forward to his chest, his eyes closed.

Hawke said, "Bring me a glass of whiskey if you've got any and call the hotel doctor."

"I've called him."

He tried to make Fry drink from the brimming glass of vodka that Jeanne brought, but the liquid ran down Karl's chin and trickled coldly along Hawke's hand. Jeanne stood with her hands clutched together before her, watching. Gus Adam came into the room. He stood in the doorway for a moment, snapped on the bright overhead lights, and came to the bed. "Let's see, Arthur." He felt Fry's pulse and pushed open his eyes, which stared flatly. He went to the telephone.

Jeanne said, "The doctor's on his way up."

Adam said, "Operator, which is the nearest hospital?— All right. A man in Room 913 has had a heart attack. He's unconscious. Please call for an ambulance. Thank you."

Hawke was still holding Fry. Jeanne came beside him and lifted Fry's head with both her hands. "Karl," she said. "Karl!"

The door was opened by a stout man with a gray mustache, carrying a black leather bag. Hawke made way for him, resting Karl back on the pillow. The doctor sat on the bed and opened Fry's pajama shirt without a word.

Hawke went to the other room and found Honor Hauptmann standing by the window at the furthest end, her face twisted in fright. "What's the matter in there, Arthur?"

Hawke told her. She made peculiar little motions with her hands as though his words were insects that she was fending off. She said, "Well, dinner's out of the question, then, I suppose?"

"Dinner? God, yes!"

She said, "Arthur, is it all right if I just leave? Won't that be best? I mean you'll tell Mrs. Fry how sorry I am, and that I hope everything will be all right?" She darted for the door, stopped with her hand on the knob, and turned to him, her face working. "I'm sorry, I have an uncontrollable horror of illness and death. I've always had it. I'm no use at all here, I'll just make things worse for everybody. You'll give my apologies to her, won't you?"

He said, "Well, sure, Honor, go ahead."

"Don't think I'm behaving badly, Arthur. It's something I can't control. If you want the limousine or anything—"

"No, no."

"When will I see you? I mean will you still be taking that plane tonight? Will we go to New York together?"

"Honor, I haven't the slightest idea. I think Karl Fry has died, don't you see?"

She said shrilly, "I'll write you. I'll be at the Waldorf tonight if you come to New York. I'm leaving from Idlewild in the morning." She lunged to him and planted a smeary kiss on his mouth. "Please don't think I'm behaving badly. I'm sorry, Arthur. I can't help this." She turned and ran out, leaving the door open. Hawke closed it, and returned to the bedroom, wiping purplish-red lipstick streaks on his handkerchief.

The doctor was talking on the telephone, a stethoscope dangling on his chest. Karl lay with his head rolled sideways on the pillow, his chest uncovered. On the other bed sat Jeanne, crying softly into her handkerchief. Gus Adam sat beside her, his arm around her. Jeanne was saying in a clear but broken voice, "He didn't want to live after this morning. I knew that. He didn't want to live, so he died. Just like him."

Adam said, "That's about it, Jeanne."

"I knew we'd never get out of this hotel room without something fearful happening," Jeanne said. "But I thought it had happened this morning. I thought we were in the clear." She became aware of Hawke. "What about your friend, Arthur? Mrs. Hauptmann?"

"She went."

Jeanne nodded. It seemed to Hawke that he had never seen Jeanne so beautiful—her face drawn and gray, her lips pallid, her eyes glittering with tears. The beauty was in the strength of her expression, the resolute look of a woman mastering great pain. There was something girlish about her too, as she sat there beside her husband's dead body. It was as though the years had all at once rolled back, cancelling her marriage.

He wanted to help her, to comfort her, but no words came to him; anyway, Gus Adam already had his arm around her.

9

Long Island is the place where both the dead and the living are piling up faster than anywhere else in the United States, because this fish-shaped piece of flat land contains New York City's main cemeteries, as well as its main suburbs. People who escape from the city's grinding punishment, either by buying a little house in the country or by dying, tend to go to Long Island. So it was that Karl Fry was laid to rest in a spot only twenty minutes by car from Scotty Hoag's huge Paumanok Plaza shopping center, built at a hub of three highways clustered with new developments and housing projects. Gus Adam telephoned Hawke early on the morning of the funeral and said that they had better plan to go straight from the interment to the Plaza; because Scotty was back in town for an emergency meeting at the construction site.

Fry's dramatic death a few hours after his capitulation to Senator Traynor had been an important news story, on television as well as in the papers. The curiosity seekers and the people from the publishing industry overflowed the largest chapel in the funeral home on Lexington Avenue near the Fry apartment. They jammed its hallways, and made a crowd in the street despite the heavy rain.

Jeanne had asked Hawke to deliver the eulogy, abruptly and almost as an afterthought, when he had visited her in the Fry apartment the morning after Karl's death. It was the only mark of attention she gave him. The apartment was full of strangers: Jeanne's mother, a gray and shapeless little woman with a squarish face like Jeanne's, western and rustic in her talk and manner; and Karl's six-foot son in an army uniform, and Karl's father, a withered gray caricature of Karl; and a nurse, and an undertaker, and several men and women who were never identified; and Gus Adam with one of his clerks in the midst of the turmoil making phone calls and decisions, and giving Jeanne papers to sign. Through all this, dazed by sedatives, Jeanne drifted in a gray house dress, unpainted and sorrowful, holding her baby, who cried loudly most of the time, scowling at the new faces.

Hawke had consented to eulogize Karl, of course. When he mounted to the lectern in the amber-lit, flower-filled funeral chapel and looked out over the closed coffin at the crowd, he saw the eager faces of people at a book-and-author luncheon, awaiting the words of a celebrity. All the visible grief was in the front row, where Jeanne sat among the relatives. She wore no veil. She was in black; the drawn white face was turned up to Hawke with an empty look.

Hawke spoke incoherently about Karl's talent, integrity, and tart humor. He was unable to say anything about Karl's reticent love for his wife and

baby, though he had meant to. The room was so full of prying outsiders! And on the faces of some of the people from the publishing business he thought he saw a knowing ironic awareness of the Judd review, and of his own love for the dead man's wife. In truth he spoke very badly, until he found himself blurting a few sentences that he had not had in mind at all:

"and so he's gone. . . . Nobody can say that Karl laid down his life for his country, but he did lay down his conscience. We now have to ask ourselves whether this is a sacrifice the United States ought to require of a man. You may think Karl's conscience was anarchic and bizarre. But a man whose heart can break when he violates his conscience seems to belong to some fresher era than ours. Karl was certainly no hero. He's been called a fool. He saw through Marxism but he didn't believe freedom could work any more. It's hard to name and to judge what he was, but you might call him a born dissenter. Dissenters founded the United States. Now this nation is the world's most complicated and powerful machine, but it has dangerous foes. Karl Fry asks us in death, is there room left in the beleaguered machine for dissent? He loved to walk out of a room or an argument, leaving a puzzling challenge behind. Now he's walked out of life that way."

Hawke stared out at the expectant audience. He could think of no more words. He stepped down from the platform.

He and Adam were pallbearers. When the casket was bestowed in the hearse, they both made their way through the vacuous onlookers, standing under umbrellas in the thick rain, to the car Hawke had hired. The two men settled into the car, both of them heavily spattered with rain. They did not speak for a while. Hawke was jealous of the intimacy Adam had achieved with Jeanne by taking over the funeral arrangements and handling the legal problems of the death. Honor's suggestion that Adam was in love with her haunted Hawke.

The college began to form up and follow the hearse through the midtown traffic. Adam broke the awkward silence once the car was in motion. "You spoke well. I think you comforted Jeanne, as much as anyone could."

"It seems to me I babbled. At the end I half-said something that might have made sense if I'd put it properly."

"You put it properly. The nub of this thing was its inconclusiveness. I agree with you that nothing could be more characteristic of Karl."

After a long silence, Hawke spoke again. "There was one more thing I wanted to say. Somehow I couldn't bring it out. It didn't seem to fit in a eulogy. Yet it's the point that mattered most to me in Washington."

"What was that?"

"I don't believe this country is dying because Karl talked, though that's how he left it."

The lawyer made a sardonic sound, not quite a laugh. "More likely Karl talked because he was dying."

Hawke said, "You think he'd have died like that, even if he hadn't knuckled under?"

Adam said nothing. Hawke glanced away from the wheel and saw the lawyer, who looked quite odd with a new large black hat covering his thick hair, staring at the dancing windshield wiper, his ruddy face frozen in an angry expression. Adam caught the glance. "Sorry. Funerals set me back, especially one like this. Would he have died the way he did? Who knows? Karl wasn't well. If you want to know, I'm feeling uncomfortably guilty right now. I feel I made a botch of Karl's affairs. He and Jeanne trusted me. I advised him years ago not to go to the FBI. I believed him when he said he wouldn't name people. I figured it was best to put this ordeal off as long as possible. But I seem to have misjudged my man. Maybe it would have been best to have had it out then, either plead the Fifth Amendment, or go through the naming, and be done with it. Pleading the amendment would have cost Karl his job. It would have put Jeanne in a cruel dilemma, because editing your work means so much to her. How could she stay on in the firm that fired her husband? This way they did have some years of peaceful work together, and they were happy. There was always the chance that he'd never be called. Do you think I did the right thing?"

This was a strange note from Adam. In the years Hawke had known the lawyer, Adam had never before come out of his shell of ironic, mock-modest omniscience. Hawke shrugged.

Adam said, "I also feel guilty about encouraging him to make the court fight. I may have given him support he didn't really want and pushed him into an exposed position. Telling him to put up or shut up, as it were. I hope this is nothing but the glooms brought on by a friend's funeral in the rain. I haven't felt like this since my wife died."

Hawke said, "Well, reading Karl's mind was impossible. Jeanne told me often that she never knew what he was thinking, but my guess would be he was ready for the fight and intended to make it, until the very last second."

Adam said, "I'd like to think so."

"Would you have won?"

The lawyer shook his head. "Who can say? I think we had a chance, but we'll never know." He picked up a briefcase on the seat and slid open the fastener. "Would it be inappropriate if we talked a little business? I mean no disrespect to Karl but it's a long way to the cemetery, and several things are going to require your immediate attention. If you hadn't come back I'd have called you in Hollywood and asked you to make a trip to New York."

The sound of the slide fastener on Gus Adam's briefcase had become

ominous to Hawke. He said, "Well, after what's happened no news can seem very bad or serious. Troubles, no doubt?"

"I'm afraid so," Adam said. He took out a folder marked HAWKE in blue crayon, filled with white documents and yellow scratch paper, and lit his pipe.

"Bad?"

"Well, so far not very. The main thing is Paumanok Plaza. You'll recall that back in April when Scotty had to get the second mortgage, Newton Leffer insisted that you and Scotty personally guarantee the loan."

Hawke said, "Last April. That was when I was up to my ears in Haworth House, and also writing all night. Who's Newton Leffer again?"

"Newton's my friend, the lawyer for the Swiss people who put up the three hundred thousand for the mortgage."

Hawke nodded. "The little man with the purple growth on his forehead?"

Adam laughed. "That's Newton. Except he's since had the thing removed. Now Newton's a perfectly decent fellow and a very competent lawyer. Scotty got the three hundred thousand from him—from these Swiss people he represents—on a short term basis. It's supposed to be repaid in four equal installments, of $75,000 every six months. The first installment was due Wednesday before last. You remember Scotty told us he'd take care of this second mortgage and we could just forget about it."

Hawke said, "I remember that, all right."

The line of cars following the hearse was entering the midtown tunnel, and the drumming of the rain on the metal roof gave way to the louder noise of echoing motor roars in the white-tiled tube. Adam said, pitching his voice louder, "Well, Newton didn't get the check. Scott asked for a week's grace because he was involved in a large refinancing situation down in Kentucky, and of course Newton gave it to him. Newton is sitting pretty, with your two personal guarantees. Even if Scotty isn't good for the money, which seems rather unthinkable, he assumes that you are.

"I wouldn't be concerned about any of this, Arthur, except for two things. Scotty's made a special trip up here and asked for a meeting with me and Newton today. He told me not to bother you, but of course he didn't know then that you were coming east. I don't like the request for a meeting. What concerns me more is that there's an acceleration clause in the mortgage. That's a common practice, and what it means is that as soon as one payment is missed the whole loan falls due. Scotty's already ten days behind on the first payment. In theory you're personally liable right now to repay three hundred thousand dollars if Newton chooses to press you. I'm putting it in its blackest terms."

"Black is right," Hawke said. "It would bankrupt me."

The lawyer took out of the folder a white sheet of typed figures. "I don't think so. I had the accountant draw up your balance sheet again. Unless

you've done something in the last couple of weeks that I don't know about, you could muster in an extremity almost a hundred fifty thousand in cash. I'm talking about the market value of your stocks, real estate and so forth, and the bank balances as of September first. Then there's your new book coming out. We have every reason to hope for a paperback sale and a movie sale of the usual size, more or less, in addition to the trade sales. You'd be left with some tax problems—of which you have a few as it is, and I'm coming to them in a moment—but I think by one means or another, you could actually meet a sudden cash call of three hundred thousand dollars." The lawyer grinned. "Which is quite a thing to say about anyone, let alone a literary artist not much past thirty, and an amazing tribute to the quality and quantity of your writings."

Hawke said, "It would strip me to the skin. I'd have to borrow heavily, and mortgage my whole future."

"Yes," Adam said, "but you could do it, that's the impressive thing."

Hawke said, "Well, what other good cheer have you for me?"

The car rolled out into a whipping rain that obscured even the garish billboards at the tunnel exit. Adam said, "I thought you ought to know about the shopping center situation. We can let the rest go for now."

"No no," Hawke said. "For God's sake, this is the time for lugubrious news. Karl's up ahead there in a box, and I'm alive and well. I defy you to depress me."

Adam said, "Well, frankly, there's nobody I know who has more reason than you to look to the future with confidence, and even with joy. Money troubles shouldn't penetrate an inch below the surface in a life such as yours is, or is undoubtedly going to be." The lawyer's tone in these last words caused Hawke to look at him. Adam was leafing through the papers in the folder, puffing on his pipe. Hawke felt that the lawyer had referred to Jeanne. He wondered whether Jeanne, with Karl still unburied, could have said something to Adam to give rise to that dry twanging hint. The lawyer said, "Well, if you've got the stomach for more bad news, here it is. We've had two tax defeats. You'll recall that we appealed to Washington on the movie contract of *Chain of Command* which was so badly worded that it seemed to throw all the money into one year. The afternoon that Karl died I was up at the Treasury checking on that one. We're going to get turned down."

"Which will cost me what?" Hawke said. "That came to about eighty thousand plus interest, didn't it?"

"Yes, but we're a long way from paying. The Treasury still has to write us a formal letter, giving us 90 days to pay the deficiency. I'll appeal it to the tax court, if you approve."

Hawke said, "What are my chances?"

Adam said, "The man who wrote the contract was an idiot. Your legal position is not all it should be. I think the intent of the contract is clear,

and the recent cases have tended to support this kind of spread fee. I'm also hoping that the courts will see the essential predicament of a writer getting a lot of money in one year, and maybe no income the next. But nobody's going to shed tears of pity for Youngblood Hawke, I fear. It's worth a try. If we lose I won't charge you much. If we win I'll take a reasonable percentage of what I've saved you."

"All right, let's fight."

"I think so. That's what the tax courts are for. The other thing is a little disturbing. Maybe that same revenue agent put out a general alarm on you. They've pounced on last year's return already, and that seems very early. It's the deal with Scotty, of course. They want to know where all the income from your play is. I produced the documents in the Paumanok Plaza transaction. They say it's a subterfuge and you owe income tax on all the royalties. As you know, the play paid in about a hundred twenty thousand dollars to Paumanok before it closed."

"I never collected the royalties. How can I pay taxes on them?"

"That, of course, is your problem. This result doesn't surprise me, Arthur, I think you'll recall that I predicted it, but the theory was we'd be out of this venture with a profit before they ever examined your return."

Hawke said, "What's the status of the center? Is it finished?"

"You'll see it. It's virtually finished, some of the tenants are already beginning to move in. Scotty did a good construction job, it's a fine center. The finances are another matter. He didn't bring it in for a million six, he spent almost two million dollars. It may well be worth the money and I even think you may end with a capital gain. But right now—"

The cortege piled up in an approach to a parkway, and the two men sat in the stopped car, looking through the blurry swathes of the windshield wipers at long unmoving lines of automobiles, a motley string of beetle shapes in a dirty wet day. They could not open a window, so heavy was the rain; it drummed on the car with a sound like hail. Adam's pipe smoke wreathed in the stagnant air and wisped out of an angled glass vent.

Hawke said very calmly, after a long silence, "I'm no longer sure that we can look for much help from my new novel. I suppose I've gotten into the habit of success, and anything else seems unnatural. But you know, the movie people shied away from the book. Ferdie Lax went through one of his elaborate melodramas with a single typewritten copy a month or so ago, letting several of them read it under a pledge of secrecy with a forty-eight-hour limit, swearing he was betraying me by showing it before publication, and so forth. It's amazing that the Hollywood people should fall for the cloak-and-dagger claptrap that they've pretty much invented themselves, but Ferdie's scored some big sales that way. He ran into a wall with *Evelyn Biggers*. They all want to wait for the reviews. The one review so far is Quentin Judd's."

The lawyer said, "Well, that's a highly peculiar reaction. What about the paperback sale? Givney was talking in terms of a hundred thousand dollars, as I recall, which he was prepared to give you any time you wanted it."

Hawke said, "Givney is so mad about this novel that he can't speak of it without turning soprano. He feels, however—I quote him—that a paperback sale before publication, since he's a stockholder in Haworth House, would smack of collusion and might be questionable taxwise."

"That's utter gibberish," Adam said.

"I know," Hawke said. "Put into English, he wants to wait for the reviews."

"Has a book club taken it?"

"Yes. The wrong club. Little cachet and a small advance. The big club reported to Ross that they'd chosen too many novels lately with a similar theme. Maybe the rain and the funeral are getting me down, too, Gus, but so far all signs point one way. I seem to have picked the wrong book for starting my career as a publisher."

Adam said, "What about the one you're working on now?"

"*Boone County?* That's different. Crowds, gunfire and money again. There's not the slightest doubt, at least in my mind, that it will be my most popular book. Jeanne concurs. But, even working as hard as I possibly can, I'm a year away from finishing it. It's very long."

"Has Jeanne read any of it?"

"No. I'm stacking up the first half and then I'll turn it over to her."

Adam nodded. "In view of the Judd article, you may want to reconsider that. Perhaps even dissociate yourself from Hodge Hathaway entirely, for this book."

"To hell with Quentin Judd," Hawke said. "I need Jeanne."

"That was Judd's point," Adam said. "It's a very serious charge. What you mean is, it's more convenient and practical to have Jeanne, which is different."

Neither man said another word until they reached the graveyard. The cemetery, or the undertaker, had gone to some pains to soften the harsh facts of burial. The piles of dirt beside the hole were covered with mats of artificial grass, of a bright window-dressing green that made the real rain-soaked grass all around the grave seem quite dull and dismal. There was no shovelling of earth, no hollow strike of dirt on wood. Once the coffin sank gently out of sight on guide ropes, attendants laid boards across the brown hole—a little brown was inevitably visible for a few moments—and stretched more false grass across the opening; and then there was nothing but a small angry area of bright green, humped here and there, surrounded by the grass and tombstones of the graveyard. Jeanne walked a little apart from the knot of people at the service, and stood alone in the rain, looking down at the gay green mats. Hawke saw

tears dripping from her eyes, though her sombre expression did not change. She straightened up after a while, and passed a handkerchief over her face; looked around as though she were coming awake, and strode toward him.

She said in a voice roughened with pain, "Thanks for what you said about Karl."

"It wasn't enough, Jeanne, I ran dry, I'm sorry."

"No, I think Karl would have passed it, and you know how hard he was on you."

Karl's son came beside her, an army trench coat over his uniform, and took her arm. She said with a faded smile to Hawke, "It wasn't so long ago I thought a twenty-two-year-old army lieutenant was a heavy date. Now I'm a stepmother to one and it seems quite natural, somehow. It all goes fast."

Adam said, "Shall we go back with you, Jeanne? Do you want anything?"

She shook her head and patted the soldier's arm. "Nicholas takes good care of me. And I've got mama. I just want to go home to the baby. I'm so full of dope I'll probably sleep for eighteen hours." Jeanne turned to Hawke. "I feel as though I've been out of the world for six months. Have you had any news on your book?"

"Nothing, Jeanne. Nothing at all."

Jeanne smiled again, the mournful dim smile. "Imagine me talking business here. Karl would understand. Editors have no hearts. Goodbye, Gus. Goodbye, Arthur."

Hawke and Adam drove to Paumanok Plaza.

Part Six
1952–1953

CHAPTER TWENTY-ONE

1

THE shopping center was not exactly finished, but Hawke was staggered by what he saw. The architect's pleasing little sketch had become a stupendously large real thing, a two-storied U-shaped edifice of concrete, aluminum and glass, three city blocks wide and two deep, enclosing a ropy lake of liquid yellow mud that bubbled in the thick rain. The most striking feature of the scene at the moment was a gargantuan silver trailer truck in the very center of the morass, sunk in the mud to the tops of its wheels, slanting dangerously, squealing and groaning and shuddering, for all the world like a dinosaur of the horror movies caught in quicksand and going down. Workmen stood in hip boots around the trapped monster, bawling suggestions, thrusting planks at the wheels, and dodging showers of mud and splintered wood that the truck threw up in its roaring agony. Standing well clear of the mess, on a long path of rough planking that stretched across the yellow bog from the edge of the highway to the paved strip in front of the building, was Scotty Hoag, bareheaded, arms akimbo, with a transparent plastic raincoat over his green tweed jacket and gray slacks. He stood alone. At this distance he looked surprisingly old: a bald man, bulging at the middle. But when he noticed Hawke and Adam getting out of the car, and came trotting toward them, waving and smiling, Hawke could see again the Scotty of his college years, the pleasant, good-looking campus politician, not too much changed except for the loss of hair.

"Art, y'ole sumbitch! I thought you were in Hollywood. I *told* Gus he didn't have to disturb you about this."

Hawke explained that he had had to come east anyway.

"I see. Well, it's great to see you, Art, absolutely great." Scotty swept an arm toward the shopping center, his face animated with pride. "What do you think? Made a little progress since that hole you saw in February, hey? Be honest, Art, did you think we'd ever get out of that hole?"

Hawke said, "Well, it was a hell of a hole, and it's a hell of a building."

Scott said, "You don't know the half of it. Wait till I show you around. It's fabulous. Fabulous. And on schedule, by the Christ."

A chorus of yells and cheers rose from the workmen as the truck lurched out of its trap with maddened roars, and slithered and writhed a

couple of yards; then the clamor died as it floundered to a splashing stop, sunk worse than before. "How about that?" Scott said. "I *told* him not to try to cross the lot in a deluge like this. We'll be three days draining off. The sewers on this island are no goddamn good, just like the politicians that built 'em. You spill a glass of water within five miles of this goddamn intersection and it rolls and rolls and settles right smack in the middle of our lot and nowhere else. And we got underground rivers and every other goddamn thing, I tell you we could water the whole state of Arizona right out of our parking lot here. 'Course when we pave we got it all worked out with culverts and conduits so this whole lot will be bone dry in an hour even after a sumbitchin' hurricane. We gonna start paving next week, Art. That's always the last."

Adam said, "What's in that truck, Scotty?"

"That's what so ridiculous, Gus, it's fixtures and stock for a lousy kiddie shop off at the north end. They could have brought that stuff in a month from now, nobody's gonna be doing binness here till we pave. But sometimes a silly sumbitch like that truck driver just insists on getting into trouble and you got to let him go ahead and burn out his bearings. Look, let's not stand around in this rain, come on in the shack, there's coffee going. Christ, you look great, Art. Where's Newt, Gus?"

"He'll be along. I talked to him this morning."

"Well, great. I got everything under control." He was leading them along the plank path to a square plywood shed at the end of a short branch-off of the planks, midway in the slough. The planks made squirting bubbling noises as the men walked, and several sank beneath the surface under Hawke's weight, inundating his shoes with yellow muck. Scotty looked back at Hawke and laughed. "Art, you go in the building binness you gonna get mud on your shoes, that's for sure." He paused at the door of the shed, beaming around at the great expanse of soaped shop windows and concrete pillars. "Not a bad job for a couple of Letchworth County hillbillies, hey, Art? We got the goddamnedest electric sign you ever saw going up next week. I sort of wish we'd called it Kentucky Plaza. This is the last job I ever do on Long Island, though. They got the worst goddamn weather outside the north pole."

The tin-roofed shed was lit by naked bluish fluorescent rods that made everyone inside look bilious. Men in overalls and battered wet hats stood at a long high table, arguing over unrolled blueprints. At steel desks piled high with ledgers and papers a couple of men worked adding machines, and a woman in a green smock drummed on an electric typewriter. Scotty took them to the other end of the shed, where he had a cluttered desk and a swivel chair beside a red-glowing heater. "Long Island damp gets in my bones," he said. He gave them coffee in tin cups out of a Silex on the desk, and began to show Hawke and Adam an array of documents, which on his interpretation made an extremely rosy picture.

The shopping center was geared to show a profit if only sixty percent of its space was occupied. Adam had verified this fact for Hawke long before. Scotty displayed signed leases for seventy percent of the space. Most of the tenants were well-known chain shops. The occupancy diagram showed only one unshaded area, a big white rectangle in the center of the plan, designed as a suburban branch for a New York department store. Scotty produced two files of correspondence with the A. C. Mehlman store, one of the four largest in Manhattan. Inspecting the letters, Hawke saw that they mainly dealt with minor details of construction; the correspondence took quite for granted that A. C. Mehlman was going to move into Paumanok Plaza.

Scotty told them, raising his voice above the rattle of the rain on the corrugated tin roof, that he would sign the Mehlman lease at the end of the week. With a hundred percent occupancy thus assured, he had lined up two buyers for the Plaza, professional syndicators, who were talking in the area of two and a half million dollars, and slowly bidding each other up. He named the buyers and their attorneys, and suggested that Adam talk to the lawyers to verify this. Adam knew all the people he mentioned.

The one real problem, Scotty declared, was when to sell and take the tremendous profit. If they held on for three years they would have a solid capital gain. If they sold sooner than that they would be a "collapsible corporation," and would have to go through a complicated liquidation that would cut down the final pot of after-tax profits. It was an embarrassment of riches. Their decision would have to be either to grab the bird in hand, or wait and gamble that a depression would not reduce the value of the property in three years. Scotty was confident that the price would go up and up the longer they held on.

He moved easily to the matter of the second mortgage, and the delayed payment of seventy-five thousand dollars. He gave Adam the latest weekly balance sheet on the job, which showed a surplus of cash over debts of a hundred thirty thousand dollars. He explained that these funds were allotted for paving the lot and finishing the interior of the building. He had to have the cash to meet the weekly payrolls and material costs, so it wasn't available to repay Newton Leffer. Scotty's story was that his time table had been thrown off by one piece of bad luck, otherwise no problem would exist. The man in the Mehlman organization who had been negotiating the department store lease, the president of the company, had died of a stroke three weeks ago. (Adam nodded to confirm this.) The closing of the lease had been scheduled for the very day after he died. Had the lease been signed, Scotty said, he would have been able to borrow the money to pay the installment without the slightest difficulty. Moreover in ordinary circumstances he would simply have paid it out of his own pocket. But it happened that he had just swung the biggest deal of his life, the purchase of Seven Oaks, one of the great old horse farms outside Lexing-

ton, which he was going to develop as a luxury residential area that would outshine his own Dogleg Park and indeed any exclusive section in the country, including Bel-Air in Hollywood. He had had to move fast on the transaction—the story he told was very long, all about an eccentric old lady in St. Petersburg, Florida, who was the key to the property—and he had used all the cash he had and all he could borrow to buy the farm. Here again, Scotty said, he could resell this famous piece of real estate tomorrow and make a profit, but he didn't want to do that. Seven Oaks Farm was going to be his crowning venture, he intended to do it alone instead of syndicating it, reserving ten of the choicest acres for his own horse farm, and thereafter he was going to live, as he put it, "like one of the quality, and to hell with it all."

In short, said Scotty, if ole Art happened to have the seventy-five thousand and it wasn't an embarrassment, it would probably be simplest if he paid this installment. Scotty would personally guarantee him in writing to pay the remaining installments himself as they fell due, either out of corporation funds or out of his own money, and also to return Art's loan—because that was what it would be, a loan, and he wouldn't hear of treating it any other way—within three months at six percent interest. If it was inconvenient he was pretty sure Newton Leffer would appreciate the situation and agree to accept $150,000 six months hence, two installments paid at once. It was all a question of timing.

Adam had listened in silence, except for an occasional question about the papers Scotty showed him, for the better part of an hour. He now said, "Well, Scotty, it's a good picture and indeed a very healthy one, especially if you get that Mehlman lease signed. But I warn you Newton will want his seventy-five thousand today."

Scotty turned to Hawke and said cheerfully, "Well, how about it, Art? Ellie and I saw that *Chain of Command* movie. Boy, that's the best sumbitchin' picture ever made and I want to tell you Ellie and I clapped like fools when your name flashed on that old screen. I know it's cleaning up all over the country, they still standing in line outside Radio City Music Hall every night. D'you think you could spare the seventy-five?"

At that moment the woman in the green smock came to Scotty and said, "There's a Mr. Leffer wandering around the main building looking for you, Mr. Hoag."

Scotty jumped up. "Well, great, let's show old Newt around. Come on, Art, take a look at your property. It's still kind of messy but just remember it's a goddamn big success just as it stands. We're *in*."

2

Many people in the business world—accountants, lawyers, bank managers, real estate men, stock brokers, and the like—were utterly unimpressed to find themselves dealing with the famous Youngblood Hawke. Not a few of them showed the condescension and even contempt that practical fellows naturally feel for artists; though in recent years, because of the mountains of money Hawke was rumored to be piling up, these practical fellows sometimes used a certain puzzled caution in talking to him. On the other hand, he encountered a number who had read his books and who allowed literary admiration to tinge their manners. Newton Leffer was one of these.

They found him in the enormous pink-plastered space in the center of the Plaza reserved for the department store, a slight little gentleman almost without shoulders, in a pin-striped black suit and gray tie, leaning on a rolled umbrella in the middle of the echoing vault, where grimy stalwart plasterers, electricians and plumbers were shuttling, shouting, hammering, burning, and drilling. His worried face brightened when he saw Hawke. He came toward the author with little bounds. "Well, this is an unexpected treat, Mr. Hawke. I thought I was in for just another business meeting. Hello, Gus. Hello, Mr. Hoag." He shook Hawke's hand. "Well, aren't we taking you away from something important? I'm sure you're working on something new. You're so prolific." A puckered red scar marked the place over his nose where the purple growth had been.

Scotty threw his arm around Leffer's frail shoulders. "Newt, you ole sumbitch, I'm glad we finally got you out here. Come on, don't you want to look around and see what this property is? You fellows sit on your cans down in Wall Street, for Christ's sake, and just shuffle a lot of papers. You never see the real things that your money creates. This is a goddamn exciting job."

Leffer glanced around, still in Scotty's hug. "Well, it's very promising, very impressive, but in the end it all comes down to the facts and figures you know."

Scotty took them on a tour of the Plaza, pointing out the excellence of the materials, some tricks of construction that had cut costs and increased space, and so forth. Most of what he said was technical jargon; but his enthusiasm did add an aura of excitement and success to the empty shell. In many places there were no walls, only bare wooden studding and a forest of pipes and wires, but the two lawyers appeared satisfied with the progress of the building. Leffer's one recurring question, as they went from space to space and Scotty mentioned the well-known

shops that would occupy them, was, "Have they signed the lease?" And Scotty would answer with a shade of amusement, "All signed, you'll see the file in a minute, Newt." So they traversed the big edifice from one end to the other amid new-construction smells of plaster, glue, sawed wood, paint and raw cement. The roof leaked, and they had to walk around murky ponds on the rough floor, but Scotty explained that a bonded subcontractor had done the roof and would have to get it water-tight at his own expense.

Next they went to the shed. Scott repeated for Newton Leffer his optimistic picture of the finances. When Leffer saw the leases signed for seventy percent of the space—he made little notes in a leather pocket-book as he examined each lease—and the balance sheet showing the cash on hand, his attitude toward Hoag began to thaw. At one point he uttered a small laugh through pursed lips and said, "Well, if it all works out the way it appears here, somebody's going to be making quite a fortune." He glanced waggishly at Hawke and gave him a furtive little poke with an elbow. "I hope you won't stop writing books, Mr. Hawke."

He congealed again when Scotty began to explain that he didn't have seventy-five thousand dollars for him just at that moment. He heard Scott through without a word. His narrow face got longer and longer and his mouth smaller and smaller; his shoulders seemed to slope more and more. When Scotty halted, Leffer looked around at Hawke and Adam, then said through a tight rosebud of a mouth, "I'm not sure I understand, Mr. Hoag. Surely you're not saying that the corporation's going to default on the first installment. That's unthinkable."

Hoag said genially, "Jesus, Newt, default? I'm talking about next week. Probably next Tuesday, if we get the Mehlman lease signed Friday, as scheduled. You know I can take that lease to any factor and get seventy-five thousand overnight, the condition this sumbitch is in now."

"That may be, but those are all your problems. I've had three cables from my clients this week. I took quite a responsibility on myself, giving you the grace period I did. I can't let the thing slide another day." There was a moment's silence among the four men, while the business machines clattered at the other end of the shed. Leffer said to Adam rather plain-tively, "Gus, you know a second mortgage is a straight money proposition. This kind of thing is wholly out of line. I'd have to cable for permission to hold off even another twenty-four hours."

Hoag laughed and poured more coffee into Leffer's tin cup. "Now shucks, Newt, these people of yours are the biggest goddamn textile operators in Switzerland, from what I'm told. They can't be pressing you all that hard, they've got millions."

"Yes, they have, and they're very interested in good American second mortgages, and very insistent on mortgage payments when due. I recom-

mended this mortgage. My own relationship with them is involved. You have a cash surplus and I'm really going to require that you pay today."

Scott said, "Newt, I've got to keep that cash on hand to get my paving contractor to bring his equipment in here tomorrow, and also to meet my payrolls for the next four weeks. If I'm sitting here with a couple of acres of yellow gunk out front when the Mehlman people come out Friday, and no sign of a paving job underway, it's going to be kind of embarrassing. They figuring on opening up here right after Thanksgiving for the Christmas trade."

There was more of this inconclusive arguing. Then Leffer said, "Well, I suppose that's what the personal guarantees were put into this deal for. Everything you tell me about your construction problems, your leases, your ventures in southern real estate, may make excellent sense. However, my people want their money. I have your signature and Mr. Hawke's on a six-month note. It's past due and I'm presenting it to you for payment." With that Leffer took the leather book from his inside pocket, undid the rubber band and pulled out a blue slip of paper. He laid it on the desk in front of Hoag. Hawke could see his own signature under Scotty's, one of a dozen he had scrawled during the boring paper work of the second mortgage closing, back in April; and he could also see plainly the figure, $75,000.00.

Scott stared at the note and shrugged. "Newt, I can't pay you today. I've told you why. Even if you want to get legal about this, I'll have the money for you long before you can start an action, so what purpose does this serve?"

Leffer said, "There are two signatures on that note." He turned to Hawke with an apologetic smile. "I realize that you're very much a silent partner here, Mr. Hawke, and that construction and finance aren't your métier. Seventy-five thousand dollars undoubtedly doesn't mean much to you. I wouldn't press you if I didn't have an obligation to my clients."

Adam struck in. "I think you could give Scotty till next Tuesday, Newton. That's all he's asking for. It's five business days."

Leffer said, "Yes, but suppose next Tuesday comes and there's another hitch? I'm not questioning anybody's good faith but Mr. Hoag hasn't got that Mehlman lease at the moment and his affairs seem a little complicated. Suppose I stick my neck out as far as it can go and a little farther, and carry this matter till next Tuesday? Will Mr. Hawke give me his word to pay seventy-five thousand dollars on that day if Mr. Hoag doesn't?"

Hawke found the three men looking at him: Leffer solemnly, Scott with a little smile, Adam with bushy eyebrows arched as high as they would go.

As he hesitated, Leffer added, "I'd feel very awkward about this if your earnings weren't common knowledge. Your guarantee, Mr. Hawke, was what decided both myself and my clients in favor of this mortgage. It's the real security we counted on, the security of your earning power and your personal reputation. My people are admirers of yours, they read you in German."

Hawke said, "That's very pleasant. The common knowledge of my earnings is exaggerated. I've made a lot of money and spent a lot, and I have a couple of sizable unresolved disputes with the U. S. Treasury."

Leffer smiled a tiny rosebud of a smile. "With Gus Adam as your doctor that shouldn't be a serious ailment."

Adam said, "I've lost a few patients."

Leffer said to Hawke, "Will you give me your word that you'll meet the note on Tuesday, if Mr. Hoag doesn't? If you make the commitment and then fail to keep it, I'll be in trouble with my most important client."

"Newt y'ole bastard," Scotty said cheerfully, "you'll have the seventy-five Tuesday morning or before that."

"I'm asking for Mr. Hawke's commitment," Leffer said.

Hawke said nothing.

Hoag said, "Now look, I told Art that this second mortgage would be of no concern to him. I'll give you my personal written undertaking, Newt, to pay a penalty of $1000 a day for every day after Tuesday that I don't meet that note. If I run as much as ten days over, why you can foreclose on this goddamn job because I'll be dead or something. This job is a sumbitchin' gold mine, you've seen the letters from Steiner Associates and Lou Falkman, for Jesus' sake, talking in terms of two and a half million to purchase on January first, and this niggling over seventy-five thousand dollars is ridiculous, why it's fantastic. It's a lot of New York foolishness. We don't do binness in Kentucky that way."

Leffer's rabbit-like face became bleak, and his eyes took on a slaty look. "I've done business in Kentucky. I haven't noticed any difference." He turned to Hawke. "What do you say?"

Hawke said, "That's my signature you've got there. If Scott doesn't pay by Tuesday I will."

Scotty said, "Art, that's unnecessary, but if it makes Newt feel better, okay."

Leffer offered Hawke his hand, and Hawke shook it. The little man rose, smiling. "Well! How do I get back to Wall Street, from this magnificent mudhole?"

"Hell, I'll drive you, Newt." Scott jumped up. "Got to see the Mehlman crowd at three anyway."

"Well, I'll appreciate that, Scotty. No, no more coffee, thanks a lot."

The animosity between the two men was all gone. They were making

jokes about the weather as they left the shed side by side, followed by Hawke and Adam. The rain was still falling heavily. The trailer truck lay silent and abandoned, sunk aslant to its wheel tops, in the muck of Paumanok Plaza.

3

Jeanne drifted to the desk in her apartment one morning, a few days after the funeral, to glance through the piled-up mail. Sorting out the letters and the magazines, she was putting aside the rolled-up *Rambler* when she recalled the reporter's questions in Washington, in the dim time before the death of her husband. She tore off the wrapper and spread the gray journal on her desk. There in the center of the front page was the startling heading:

> *EVELYN BIGGERS*
> *by Youngblood Hawke?*

She read the review with alarm that gradually became horror.

At one point in this peculiar new production from the pen of Youngblood Hawke, the author causes the heroine to say to her seducer, "I hate you for allowing me to hope. It's the worst thing you did to me." That is a pretty fair statement of this reviewer's present feelings toward Mr. Youngblood Hawke.

The publication seven years ago of *Alms for Oblivion*, his sloppy but undeniably powerful first novel, gave real grounds for hope that a new Jack London or Theodore Dreiser was trying to struggle up out of the abominable miseducation and obscurantist criticism that make the writing of serious American fiction just about out of the question today. Naturally he was attacked at once by the learned boneheads who carry on current literary discussion. These priests have consistently opposed Mr. Hawke not because he writes badly, as indeed he does, very badly, but because they need mysteries. There's not much sacerdotal dignity in telling the public that books are good when the public already likes those books; dignity consists in pointing out that the peasants are buying brass and ignoring gold. But the history of criticism shows that the common reader is wiser than the priests. The thing is that much of the time there isn't any gold around, and then people settle for the shiniest brass. They like to read stories.

Mr. Hawke's legion of foes will make gory holiday out of the carving-up of this novel, a weak, listless, and remarkably silly little work by an author who, whatever his glaring faults, has been carrying all before him until now with his unusual energy. I am sorry to see this catastrophe of a promising if

limited talent. The one purpose in dwelling on it is to try to derive, if one can, from the spectacular spin-in of Youngblood Hawke, some general truths about the low present state of American fiction.

Let us look at his new story, to begin with.

Here Judd described the plot and characters of the novel with his usual derisive technique, a mixture of solemn plodding accuracy and bursts of savage slang. The result was amusing and lethal; Jeanne found herself wincing and smiling at the same time. Then Judd proceeded:

. . . One would like to dismiss this gray and damp anecdote as an experimental failure, a laudable if mistaken attempt by the author to extend his range by writing a short honest character study of a dreary woman: an American *Eugenie Grandet*, let us say. But a closer look at the package brings to light disturbing details that bode no good for Mr. Hawke's creative future, or for the art of fiction in the United States.

I have called *Evelyn Biggers* a little book. It *is* little. A word count probably would not exceed seventy thousand. Mr. Hawke's previous behemoths have weighed in with Victorian amplitude at three to four hundred thousand words. However, when this volume comes to hand it does not look little. It is a big thick book. Set it on the shelf beside *Alms for Oblivion*, *Chain of Command* and *Will Horne*, Mr. Hawke's popular successes, and it seems a worthy successor in bulk, if nothing else. But then one reads through the tale—if one can stay interested in Mr. Hawke's lugubrious nuisance of a heroine—in perhaps an hour and a half. How is this possible? The answer is simple. Fat margins, fat type, fat paper, fat binding, every imaginable kind of artificial publishers' fat, have gone into the book, with only one conceivable purpose: to raise the price. A butcher can go to jail for selling fat as meat. An author seems to be beyond the reach of that just ordinance.

The publisher of this work is "Haworth House," an imprint nobody has ever seen before. It is no secret in the book trade that "Haworth House" is Youngblood Hawke himself, and that he has bludgeoned this device out of his actual publishers, Hodge Hathaway, in order to get a larger share of the book's earnings. As an old hand at the writing racket, let me say that I hope the arrangement works. My hat is off to Mr. Hawke for pioneering along new paths away from the crowded literary poor-house. It was not my impression, however, that destitution was threatening to overtake Youngblood Hawke. He cannot have earned less than a million dollars since his career began in 1946; probably he has earned more. That is not hay to most starveling word-mongers.

Why "Haworth House," then? Why these greasy layers of false blubber in the new book? What on earth is Mr. Hawke up to? One is almost forced to conclude that success in American fiction today, by flooding a young man with sudden big money from all the mechanical sources of mass revenue—the movies, the book clubs, the paperbacks—simply drives him cuckoo. Instead of standing apart from the endemic American money insanity that may yet

destroy us all, and indicting it with the voice of art, he himself succumbs. Out roll the next books; each slicker, more calculated, emptier than the last. If he happens to grind out a skimpy flop along the way, an *Evelyn Biggers*, what of that? He has the brand name by now. The one problem is to pad up the package.

With the arrival of Mr. Hawke at this abysmal stage, it becomes important, and in a sense necessary, to examine certain curious facts about his publishing career. Ordinarily, it is true, criticism addresses itself to printed texts, and an author's personal life and business practices are—or should be—irrelevant to literary judgments. However, the case of Youngblood Hawke is no ordinary one.

For we now have in hand a strange and revealing statement on the dedication page of *Evelyn Biggers*:

> *To*
> *Mrs. Jeanne Fry*
> *who has helped me in all my work*
> *far more than I had better admit,*
> *with deepest affection*
> *and gratitude*

Mrs. Fry is the Hodge Hathaway editor who has seen all of Mr. Hawke's books to the press; including *Evelyn Biggers*, notwithstanding the fiscal abracadabra of "Haworth House." The dependence on Mrs. Fry that Youngblood Hawke now publicly confesses is not news to anybody in the book business. When she left Prince House five years ago and went to Hodge Hathaway, Mr. Hawke at once followed her. Hodge Hathaway has on its staff some of the most distinguished editors in the United States. Mr. Hawke could have had his choice among them. But from the first day he came to the house, no editor but this little-known young woman has been permitted to work on a Hawke manuscript, or even to read it, until it has left her hands and gone to the typist. What Mr. Hawke contributes, what Mrs. Fry adds or subtracts, nobody knows.

This kind of loyalty of an author to an editor is commendable. It is also rare. I have had the opportunity, as it happens, to work with Mrs. Fry. She has qualities which are praiseworthy. She also has very narrow limits. She holds strong opinions, her will power is awesome, her analytic comments on character are good, and her sense for plot is serviceable. Her preoccupation with plot may be her chief fault, for she is ruthless in subordinating all other values in fiction to the story. One would gather from Mrs. Fry that the evolution of fiction came to a stop at Robert Louis Stevenson. She has little interest in the present state of the fiction art, or in modern thought generally. I do not imagine she knows Herman Hesse from Herman Talmadge. And she has a powerful, single-minded devotion to the heavily plotted best-seller. One sees at once the affinity of Mr. Hawke for an editor with such a Philistine view. It is actually not an unsound view at the moment. The next renascence of American fiction may well come in a swing from the present overtwisted and overworked vein of romantic pessimism and symbolism to the classic three-decker naturalism of Trollope and Fielding. It is not that one side is more

right than the other in this long dialogue of the fiction art. It is merely that, as the politicians say, it's time for a change.

In fact, Mr. Hawke's instinctive seizing on old techniques in *Alms for Oblivion* was my chief reason for hoping at first that he was headed somewhere. The overlay of Dos Passos and Joyce-Faulkner could be dismissed as the placental material that apparently must accompany the birth of a novelist nowadays; under this messy business was a strong, well-controlled, Trollopian story, and most important, a broad convincing fresco of a Kentucky mountain town. Mr. Hawke wrote this novel before encountering Mrs. Fry. Since then it has been all downhill for him, at toboggan velocity.

The critic now discussed each of Hawke's four novels, carefully tracing in them a growing mechanical cynicism and lack of honesty. His long methodical assault on *Chain of Command* astounded Jeanne, because he had given the novel a favorable notice when it first appeared. He made no apology for his earlier review, and did not refer to it. *Chain of Command*, in short, was commercial trash, derivative to begin with, and shocking in its "Rover Boy attitude to the horrors of modern warfare." *Will Horne* was even worse,

. . . the most tired caper of today's lending library fiction, the triumphant heel who gets his comeuppance on the next to the last page, after a protracted glorious riot in elevator-boy fantasies of wealth and sex. This literary form was invented by Defoe, of course, and saw sturdy service for centuries thereafter, rising to its high mark in serious fiction in *The Financier* and *The Titan*; but once Hollywood took it over, the form passed out of artistic usage; as a beauty celebrated in her youth is no longer welcome in good society after she has become a drunken old bag. Mr. Hawke, undismayed by this fact, ground out *Will Horne* and collected his heavy booty and his thrashing by the book reviewers with no visible pangs.

After completing his studied dissection of the four novels, Quentin Judd went on:

In the publishing trade, it has long been whispered that Mrs. Jeanne Fry "really" writes the novels of Youngblood Hawke. This gossip will gain swifter circulation after *Evelyn Biggers*, because the book is so frankly feminine in outlook, and so weak and slight in execution. Nobody has ever answered the question, if Mrs. Fry writes the novels, why doesn't she put her name to them? And what are we to do with the imposing presence of Mr. Youngblood Hawke himself?

I would like to venture an answer. It now seems clear to me that Mr. Hawke is that too-common figure in modern American letters, the one-book novelist, done in by the onslaught of success, of sudden fame and sudden money. Any one of us would love to have such troubles, no doubt. But the destructive effect of the process exists, all the same, and it has resulted not only in artistic collapses like Mr. Hawke's, but in a number of suicides.

Three of the best writers to appear in the United States since the Second World War have died by their own hands, and several more have become mental cases. It is true that successful authors in every era have had to cope with this transition, but the strain of it has been fearfully multiplied by the money magnitudes and the publicity glare of mass culture.

What Mrs. Fry has done for Youngblood Hawke, then, may have been an act of rescue. Apparently she has kept him at work, and that is something. All this is guesswork; but we may suppose that ever since the delayed but explosive success of *Alms for Oblivion*, she has set him one synthetic narrative task after another and to an unknown extent has helped him to execute them. If so, she has rendered good service to Hodge Hathaway, for the job of an editor in our society is to bring in the best-sellers; and she has indeed given Youngblood Hawke "far more help than he had better admit."

For in all fairness to Mr. Hawke, he has certainly done a lot of hard work, he has sedulously ground out words by the metric ton, and he has provided many people with ephemeral amusement in a grisly era. The trouble with *Evelyn Biggers* is that it is not amusing. Perhaps Mrs. Fry has indeed had more of a hand in this book than in the others, or perhaps Mr. Hawke's dogged energy has finally given out. It doesn't much matter. If Mr. Hawke has not developed into a serious writer, I think one can blame the times, and not the man. It may be that he will yet recapture the possibilities that were in him. He is not yet thirty-five. But he will have to find his salvation in his own inner resources, if they survive, and not in the strong-minded guidance or collaboration of a commercial editor, however loyal and clever. Mr. Hawke should forget about being a money maker, in short, and make one last try, against all the odds, to become a writer. The chips are down.

Ordinarily Jeanne could hear her son whimpering, even through the drugged sleep that had been her only rest since Karl's sudden death; but the Judd review so hypnotized her that when she finished reading it she heard the wails of the child all at once, as though a radio had been turned on. The baby was hungry, and Elizabeth was clattering together his breakfast in the kitchen. She went and talked to Jim, until his food came. Then she telephoned Hawke.

He answered at the first ring. He was at his desk he said, having been up since three in the morning working at *Boone County*.

She said, "Arthur, I've just read Quentin Judd's review."

He said, "Oh." Then after a pause, "I'm sorry, it must be a nuisance to you. How are you, Jeanne?"

"I'm all right. A nuisance to me, indeed! Arthur, it's a violent attempt to destroy you."

Hawke said with weary good humor, "It is kind of rough. We're holding a council of war at noon. Gus, Ross Hodge, Givney, and me. Can you come?"

"Sure I will. I'm an interested party, to say the least. At your place?"

"Yes."

"I'll come early. I want to talk to you."

"Good. You sound better, Jeanie."

"I'm beginning to pick up the pieces."

She went through the old hair and makeup rituals with care. As she painted her face, for the first time in over a week, she seemed to be painting color back into her existence.

4

HAWORTH HOUSE, read an austere bronze plaque on the wall of the brownstone house, newly sandblasted to an angry pinkish color. Hawke's organization consisted of a secretary-receptionist and an editor-business manager: not a large staff, but it meant twenty thousand a year in overhead, and much social security paperwork and other accounting annoyance. Givney had not exactly taken these things off his hands after all; forms, documents, contracts, bills, checks to sign came at him in thick piles quite regularly.

The receptionist sat just inside the street door, a fat Wellesley girl clad in purple fuzz, clearly disenchanted with her stagnant little place in the publishing world. "He's in his apartment, Mrs. Fry," she said to Jeanne, with a malicious flash in her eyes that spelled Judd.

Jeanne rode up in the tiny elevator installed by Hawke. The estimate for the job had been ten thousand dollars. She had been present at Hawke's insane outburst when the bill for twenty-three thousand had come to his desk. It had been the last straw; he had left for the west the next day.

From the elevator she stepped straight into the enormous slope-roofed room where he worked and slept. He had had all the partitions of the old servants' quarters knocked out, and the room was as long and as wide as the house itself. Before it could be decorated, he had cut off all expenditures on Haworth House, so it was unfinished and barren; indeed not unlike the loft room where he had worked on *Alms for Oblivion*. There was no laundry hanging around, but books and magazines stood in untidy piles on the dusty floor, a refrigerator jutted from a corner between a small electric stove and two steel file cabinets, and a broad unmade bed was at the other end of the room. Hawke sat at the same old cheap desk, in his shirtsleeves, scrawling. He glanced up at her, and again the glasses surprised her. "Jeanie, can I finish one paragraph before it melts away?"

"Of course." She skinned off her black gloves and sat on the one chair at this end of the room, thinking how odd it was that despite all the money Arthur had poured into this building, he had in the end merely spun the old shabby cocoon for himself again. He had done it before in

the garret of the Seventy-third Street house; had lived in exactly this squalid manner for a year under a sloping roof while beneath him the workmen had been creating a costly mansion. Here in the floor below was a handsome bachelor's apartment done in Colonial style: living room, dining room, kitchen were all finished, and there was an excellent antique desk under a tall north window. Yet this grubby lair, originally intended for his bedroom, was where he lived, and apparently where he chose to work.

He thrust his pen into the holder, took off his glasses and rubbed his eyes. "Well, there you are. Eight and a half solid hours of ephemeral entertaining. Say what you will about Mr. Hawke, he works hard." He came toward her with long lunging strides, holding out an ink-stained hand. "Hello, Jeanie."

She took his hand in hers, but resisted the slight tug to pull her to her feet. "Hello, Arthur."

So they remained for a moment, she in the chair, he towering over her, looking into each other's eyes, holding hands, both aware of the emptiness where the barrier of Karl Fry had been. Hawke said, "How's Jim?"

"Thank God for him. He's just fine."

"You look good, Jeanie."

"I'm a ghost under the art work, dear, and I've lost eleven pounds, which I guess is a good thing as far as it goes. Anger is the best restorative. I'm full of fight. I want to find a way to exterminate Quentin Judd."

Hawke laughed, dropped her hand, and sat on the bed. "You'll have to stand in line, Jeanne. There are a large number of people in this city who want to exterminate Quentin. Some of them have great seniority. I'll tell you something strange. When I was out at Guam, sitting on my bunk in a Quonset hut, writing *Oblivion* by a flashlight before reveille, I used to wonder how Quentin Judd would go about tearing apart what I was doing. I used to love reading a full-dress Judd annihilation. He did a piece on Eugene O'Neill that was funnier and much more venomous than this job on me. I tell you, the first time I actually met Judd, at Fanny's party, it was a bit like meeting Hitler. But now, to me, Quentin's a little fat man who comes to life very entertainingly when he does an axe job, and that's about it. It was my turn, I guess, and I'll have to endure it."

Jeanne said, "You're making fine stoical noises. Most of the article is malignant and very damaging falsehood—not only about my doing your work, but about the nature of your books. What does Gus say? Aren't you compelled to sue him for libel?"

"That's what today's meeting is supposed to settle. Gus has a few other Hawke problems. I think at the moment I'm taxing that vast brain more than any three light and power companies."

He lurched to the refrigerator and peered inside. "I ought to eat some-

thing." He pulled out a large object, unwrapped the aluminum foil, and gnawed a bite of red meat off the greasy bones of a rib roast. "Got this from a Jewish delicatessen a couple of days ago. Pretty good."

"Is that your breakfast, Arthur?"

"What? I just eat when I'm hungry." He ripped a bone off the ragged mass. "Have a bone?"

She shook her head. "Don't you want me to warm it up for you? You've got a stove there."

"Darling, I've eaten more damned cold beef bones. I like it just as it is." He carefully wrapped the remains of the roast in the foil and shut the refrigerator. "I'll tell you what," he said, pacing the floor and chewing at the bone, "any good axe job stands on truth. You take a tone of pained condescension, you play up the bad and ignore the good. It's a rigid formula. Twain and Shaw did it better than Quentin, when they set out to destroy somebody." He marched here and there, almost seeming to talk to himself, speaking sometimes with the bone in his teeth. "You see, Judd is right about the padding of the book. He's right about Haworth House. The padding was dishonest. I thought Givney knew more about making money out of publishing than I did. Ross, after all, didn't object. You threw one of your fits, true, but it's an old story that your moral tone's a little higher than mine, and this time I thought you were being a naïve prude about clever business practice. You'll admit you're not much of a business woman."

"The world's worst," Jeanne said.

Hawke said, "I don't know, we might even have gotten away with it, if Quent hadn't blown the whistle. But he's caused an enormous stir among the insiders. Ross's spies report that reviews will dwell to some extent on you and me, but there's going to be a pretty general attack on the padding job. Do you know, Jeanne, that doesn't bother me nearly as much as the fact that I let Givney do it. It was a corrupt thing to do. Not world-shaking, but then putting out a novel isn't world-shaking. In publishing a book that was about as corrupt as you could get. My family have always been honest people, and I've tried to write good books. Tax-dodging is a game as old as governments and I won't think ill of myself for that. Haworth House was ill-conceived and grasping, maybe, but not corrupt. The padding of the book was corrupt. I wonder what happened to me."

"Don't take on," Jeanne said. "You got greedy, or rather Givney did. As for corruption, what about Quentin Judd, accepting your money to get out his magazine and then using it to try to smash you?"

Hawke paused, wrinkling his brow, then gestured with the bone. "I've thought about that. I think I put the money in his magazine to bribe him, really. That's what it came to."

Jeanne nodded. "He took the bribe."

"Yes, he did. And then to prove that he couldn't be bribed, he wrote

this article. I think that explains the whole strange business. It explains his eagerness to get an early copy and to come out with this blast weeks before publication date. He wanted to do me the greatest possible damage. I offended him to the soul, but he needed my money, and this is how he solved his dilemma. It's complicated behavior, but it's not corrupt. He didn't pay off on the bribe, and I own my shares of the *Rambler*." Hawke tossed the clean-gnawed bone into a waste can, and looked at his watch. "The others'll be here right away. I've been talking as though I'm the one with troubles, Jeanne. Sorry."

She said, "I don't have troubles. I have a burden, but it's not to be changed by any action. You're the one who has to act. You've been defamed."

He came to her, and took her hand, and though she resisted again, he brought her gently to her feet. She looked at him with saddened, mistrustful eyes. It was not an encouraging look. She said, "What's happened with all these other troubles Gus is working on? How about Paumanok Plaza?"

"I'm not sure yet. Gus will have news on that too." He added in a light tone, "I think possibly the stag's down."

"The stag isn't down. I don't believe it and I won't."

"Well, if I am, I'll get up and shake them off."

"Indeed you will."

But it was an unlucky blurt, the remark about the stag. It brought Karl into the room. For both of them it awakened the memory of their meeting at the Prince party, and a vision of the long unhappy curve of time between that point and the present moment. They stood looking at each other, with this awareness in their eyes, the young woman in black and the huge, tired, bedevilled man who at thirty-two was beginning to look middle-aged, and who yet kept something boyish about him, a petulant wilfulness, and a readiness to smile suddenly in a whole-hearted way, without any adult caution constraining his mouth.

The telephone summoned them downstairs.

5

Givney and Ross Hodge were waiting in Hawke's office on the second floor, below his apartment. Jeanne was the target of a long speech of condolence by Givney, who described Karl as a great poet, a great editor, a great human being, and a martyr. She hardly listened. She hated this lavish office with its leather-covered walls, Swedish furniture, and antique gilded sunburst chandelier, its bookcase full of old leather-bound editions of the masters, and its enormous unused barren desk that summed up in one concrete image the whole fake of Haworth House. Nor could she

stand Givney, who grew more buttery by the year, and who always looked to her, despite his superb black Italian suits, his faultlessly brushed hair, his gleaming nails, his jewelled cufflinks, as though he should be selling patented can openers on a street corner, with one eye out for the policeman.

The eulogy over, Givney began to bubble. So far as he was concerned, the Judd article was a wonderful break. Nobody in the book trade was talking about anything now except the new Hawke novel. It was an iron rule of publishing that controversy could put over even a bad book, let alone a masterpiece like *Evelyn Biggers*. He had spent the morning with the editor of the Sunday *Times* Book Review, and he was bringing thrilling news. The editor had committed himself to give a whole page to Hawke to defend himself from the Judd charges, and to explain his exact working relationship with Mrs. Fry! There was one stipulation. Hawke would have to wait until the *Times* reviewed the book. "I saw the review," Givney said cheerfully. "Philip Backer of Cornell wrote it. It's another blast like Judd's, except that he also turns on Judd and defends the critics. The whole thing's becoming a Donneybrook, and that means sales, Youngblood, sales!"

Hawke said with a melancholy smile, "It's as bad as Quentin?"

"Oh, worse, because Backer's an unsuccessful novelist, you know, it's just a lot of professorial abuse. But they're giving it the front page. Display is what counts, Youngblood, attention! I think we're in marvellous shape and you can start writing your answer now. They'll also be interested in half a page from you and half a page from Mrs. Fry, if you prefer to do it that way."

Jeanne said at once, "That's a monstrous notion, giving me equal space with Arthur. It plays right into their hands. I'm nobody, absolutely nobody, and that's what he'll have to make clear."

Hawke said, with a boyish little smile at her, lapsing jocosely into thicker Southern cadences than usual, "Wha Jeanie, Ah cain't hardly do that. It isn't gentlemanly. It also isn't true. Ah hardly know what Ah'd put in such an article. Ah might make things worse because by God Ah'd have to tell the world what you've actually done."

"Arthur, I did nothing on this book."

"Twenty pages of notes, a good editor's usual job. You didn't do the manuscript cleanup on this one, but how do I explain such fine differences? The more I'd say about it the better you'd come out."

Ross Hodge was sitting up straight in an armchair, smoking one cigarette after another, his tan skin stretched taut over his cheekbones. He broke in, "Arthur, you may not have a choice here. I appreciate Roland's desire to be optimistic, but you've got an acute crisis not only in your artistic career but in the selling of this book. Controversy doesn't necessarily sell copies, not when the issue is whether the book's a fraud. Talk

of fraud can stop sales dead. There have been big books that wilted and died in a couple of weeks that way."

Givney said, "This isn't a charge of fraud."

Hodge said, with an unusually rude edge in his voice, "What the hell do you call it? Our salesmen haven't written an order on *Evelyn Biggers* in a week. The Judd thing has spread like wildfire. It's amazing, he can't have a circulation of ten thousand, but you'd think it was *Life* magazine that had attacked Art."

Hawke said, "What's the advance now?"

"Sixty-two. We've had cancellations."

Hawke said to Jeanne, "It begins to seem we may have overprinted."

Givney said, "The *Times* wants to know right away whether you'll do the page."

"I think not."

Givney said, "Youngblood, the Manson printing people have been on the phone with me every day since the Judd piece came out. Originally they agreed to hold off their bill for the manufacturing so we could pay in installments out of sales income, but that was just a verbal understanding. Now they're worried and they want their money. I told them half an hour ago about this page in the *Times*. Ben Manson jumped for joy over the telephone and said if that were really true he'd hold off until then."

"What's the bill?" Hawke said.

"About seventy-three thousand dollars. As you know, Youngblood, we have no cash balance in Haworth House, and we have bills of over eight thousand dollars."

Gus Adam came into the office, with weary apologies for being late. His ruddy color was faded to a pale pink, and he seemed so dim and preoccupied, as Givney repeated the main points of the meeting for him, that Hawke thought he might be ill. At one point Adam took a cigarette from Givney's package and lit it. Neither Hawke nor Jeanne had seen Adam smoke a cigarette before. He smoked it with the quick gestures and deep drags of an addict.

"Well!" he said, zipping open his briefcase when Givney finished, "I managed to do a few things between classes today. Unfortunately this is my heavy morning at school." He pulled out a file scrawled in the usual blue crayon, *Hawke—Rambler Corporation*, and spread it open on the desk. "I've been inclining to Jeanne's idea of legal action. The legal ground is weak. The common law, at least in this country, gives great latitude to a critic. I think Judd could suggest in that clever ambiguous technique of his that Arthur recently committed incest with his grandmother and it's affected his writing, and he'd get away with it. But we may have some cards to play. This morning I spoke on the telephone with most of the stockholders of the *Rambler*. Nearly all of them are

shocked by the attack on you, Arthur, partly because you're a stockholder too and partly because of the uncalled-for savagery of it. I told them we may start a damage suit to force a retraction. I think we could marshall a solid majority on our side if it came to a stockholders vote."

Hodge said, "Quentin Judd will never write a retraction. He'll commit suicide first. I'm perfectly serious about that."

Adam nodded, lighting another cigarette. "I expect you're right. A lawsuit might end in Judd being fired, or in a retraction printed by the corporation over Judd's protest. Or it might mean the end of the *Rambler*. The journal's been a steady moneyloser, you know—though this issue's been a shot in the arm, it's all sold out—and there's not much enthusiasm among these people for keeping it going."

Jeanne said, "It would be something to knock out Judd or destroy the *Rambler*."

"I don't see why that would interfere with the page in the *Times*," Givney said. "The more ammunition we can fire off here the better."

"I'm not going to write the *Times* page," Hawke said. "I'd better tell them so." He put out a hand for the bronze-plated telephone.

Givney slid it along the desk out of his reach. "Youngblood, I told Ben Manson that this page was set, that you were already writing it. He was in a panic. Somehow this calmed him. If you don't agree to do it, he'll find out and I'm certain he'll press for full payment on the printing bill, right now."

"Then we'll pay it," Hawke said.

"As I told you, there's no cash in the corporation, there's a deficit."

"I'll advance the money."

Adam said, "How much is the printing bill?"

Hawke said, "Seventy-three thousand dollars. I can manage it easily." He stood and took the telephone out of Givney's hands.

The lawyer said, "Well, Arthur, I'd hold off on that, just for the moment. We have other matters to discuss."

Total silence clamped down in the room. Jeanne in her black suit in an armchair, Ross rigid in another armchair, Givney at the desk, Hawke standing immobile holding the telephone, all looked at Adam, who kept his eyes on the file, turning papers.

The telephone rang in Hawke's hands.

Hawke said, "Yes? *What?*" He glanced at the others and said, "I'll be damned. She says Howard Fain's here, he's leaving for Europe tomorrow, and he's got to talk to me at once about Judd . . . Put him on . . . Hello, Fain. Listen, it's great that you're here, can we have lunch or something? I'm in a heavy powwow right this minute. Yes, the Judd article, what else? Oh, sure, my lawyer, my publishers, my editor." He laughed. "Yes, the lady who writes my books. Oh Christ, I guess so, yes. Come on up." He said to Jeanne, "He wants to meet you. He sounds stewed."

Givney said, "There's a literary tragedy, a great talent disintegrated to nothing."

Hawke said, "He writes damned good films."

"Films!" said Givney with deep moral indignation.

Fain burst through the door, dressed in a loud hound's tooth jacket of brown, white and green. He had gotten extremely fat, and his doughy pallor had given way to the permanent streaked red flush of the wine drinker and rich feeder. His eyes sparkled and he looked gay and content. He made for Hawke, seized his hand and clapped his back. "Why, you big uncouth Kentucky bastard, who ever told you you could write books? *Evelyn Biggers*, indeed!" He turned to Jeanne, and his tone changed. "You're Mrs. Fry."

"Yes, I am. How do you do?"

"I met Karl a few times. I thought he was a hell of a guy and I knew all his poems by heart when I was a kid. I'm very sorry." Jeanne nodded an acknowledgment. "Look, how would you like to write a few novels under my name? I'll give you a better deal than Hawke does."

Jeanne smiled. "You can't afford it."

Hawke introduced him to the other men. Fain said, "I suppose you're trying to work out a policy on Judd?"

Ross Hodge said, "That's right, and if you have any ideas they're welcome."

Fain said, "I know precisely what you should do. I would take a short Scotch and soda if there's one on the premises." Hawke called the receptionist and ordered the drink. Fain said, "We exiles who do the eighteen-month bit are allowed no more than so much time on our native soil in any one calendar year. I always stay a little fried when I'm here. The only place I love on the face of the earth is New York, and I can't stay and must screw along or pay a walloping tax bill. Hawke, how come you don't get on the eighteen-month thing? It's the only way to breathe. Twenty thousand tax free and the next twenty thousand starts in the zero bracket. I support an army of well-fed relatives, and despite that I'll soon be independent . . . Ah, thank you, I'm very grateful," he said to the girl in purple wool, who blinked at him flirtatiously and went out. He sipped the drink. "Hawke, god damn you, how could you write a book like *Biggers* after those tremendous sloppy jobs you were turning out?"

"You've read it?"

"Read it? I cried over it, you bastard, I cried over Evelyn herself and I cried because you wrote it. Christ, I looked over all the competition in 1947 and I didn't see anybody in sight. I thought you were utterly insignificant. Well, I blew it, but that's another story. How the hell did you write *Biggers*, honestly now? Did you study *Une Vie* and *Cranford* and all those? It's a beautiful job."

Givney said, "I've insisted from the first that it's a major work of art,

and I'm very glad, Mr. Fain, that you're saying what you're saying. It ought to dispel some of the pessimism we've been running into here—"

Fain said, "Oh, don't misunderstand me, it's not going to sell. You're going to get slaughtered on all sides." He said to Hawke, "One of the things I've admired you for is your thick hide. You can take this pounding that's coming, can't you? The book is good and it'll hang on, they'll be reading it long after the dust settles. How'd you come to write it?"

"I don't know. I think I was dissatisfied with the women in the other books, they were written too easily. This one made me work."

Fain nodded. "Very good. The women in your other books were rather sketchy, except that crazy aunt. Listen, are you writing a new one?"

"I'm half through."

"Good?"

"This is the first good one, Fain. I've got this one under control."

"Long?"

"The longest. Union warfare in the coal country where I was born. Families, money, shooting."

"Oh, Jesus. That sounds like it. That sounds like big casino. All right. That's what I wanted to know. Now, shall I tell you what to do about Judd?"

"God, yes."

Fain drained his drink, set the glass down with a thump, and said, "NOTHING. Not a god damned thing. That's what you're going to do about Quentin Judd's review and all the others, do you hear, Hawke? *Nothing!*" He glared up at Hawke, with both fists planted on the desk.

His vehemence took everyone unawares. It was a few seconds before Givney said, "Well, that's pretty easy to say, and a little negative. Youngblood Hawke has been unfairly attacked and—"

"OF COURSE he's been unfairly attacked," Fain roared at Givney, his face taking on scarlet tones. "Are you telling me anything new? This is his ordeal. He must do two things: keep absolute silence, and *finish his next book.* What d'you want him to do? Write letters, write articles, start lawsuits, go on TV and radio and lecture platforms to defend himself? I did all those things, I did every one of them. If I have a single regret in my whole life it's about the way I chickened out after my second book. Why, damn your soul, Hawke, you've written *Evelyn Biggers!* There it stands. Nothing can change it. Suppose you did fake a publishing house and pad up the book? Since when is an artist supposed to be St. Francis of Assisi? You were out for a fast buck, like everybody else in this screwy country, including Judd with his *Rambler,* and why should you be different? That's just the holier-than-thou horsemanure of a critic out to murder you. But he can't touch you, Hawke. You've written four serious efforts in seven years. You've won an audience. You had the wonderful luck to come down out of the hills. All the competition are big city boys like me, we

have no nerves, no ground to stand on, no sense of the country. I've been through analysis, Marxism, Trotskyism, existentialism, I had the Buddhist phase, for Christ's sake, all those nets of words, nets of words to catch some self-esteem, some sense of dignity, some sense of fitting in to a scheme of things, a *scene*, a *scene!* You, you lucky bastard, you belong square in the United States scene, Christ, you belong like an old Mack truck bowling along Highway 66. You're vulnerable, you have terrible defects as a writer. I've said nastier things about you from time to time in public and in private than anything Judd wrote, for the simple reason that you sell too god damned many books. Judd's attack on you filled me with fierce pleasure when I read it. I write good movies, it's a difficult craft and I've accepted my enjoyable life. I'm not looking for any new fancy word games, I live well with myself at last, but all the same, you bastard, I'm writing pictures and you're making it, and would you deny me the delight of enjoying Judd's review? But even while I gloated I felt what you must be feeling, the horror all came back, and I had to see you. I'm returning to exile tomorrow. I've come here to tell you just one thing. Do NOTHING about Judd, absolutely nothing, do you hear? Finish your book. It sounds to me like the one that will put you in place." He held out his hand to Hawke. "I'm an intruder, and I'm plastered, and I get mean and snotty when I start arguing, so I'm now going to walk out. I think I've been surpassingly noble here. I've given you the single best piece of advice you'll have in your whole life. In fact I've given you a transfusion of my own heart's blood. No charge. Good day, gentlemen. Mrs. Fry, if you allow this big talented rube to acknowledge the Judd attack in any way, I'll believe you wrote *Evelyn Biggers*. Goodbye."

He went as he had come, with a plunge at the doorway, and a slam of the door.

Jeanne was the first to speak after a moment of general astonishment. "I withdraw my vote for legal action."

Givney said, "Well, that was a melodramatic presentation, but as a matter of cold business—"

Jeanne rode over him. "I was personally hurt and I wanted to strike back. It's a natural reaction, but the wrong one for Arthur. Fain said it all, and I'm for ignoring Judd."

Adam said, "Are you prepared to take the embarrassment of the charges if Arthur doesn't answer them?"

"The charge that I write his books is too stupid to be taken notice of. If I could write *Evelyn Biggers* I'd leave Hodge Hathaway *and* Arthur and set up shop as a novelist. That's so obvious that people must eventually say it themselves, or our saying it won't help. Keep silence and finish the next book. That's my vote, and it won't change."

Ross Hodge said, "Then you're giving up the fight on *Evelyn Biggers*, Jeanne."

Jeanne said, "You can't increase sales by answering critics. I think the dead stop in the advance is a coincidence. Book sellers have read it by now and realized that it isn't the usual Hawke merchandise. Arthur overprinted. It happens all too often, even at Hodge Hathaway."

Hawke sat back in the swivel chair, puffing on a long cigar, still in his shirtsleeves, glancing at each person who spoke. He looked unworried, but very haggard.

Adam was smoking another cigarette. It effected an odd change in his whole personality; the sedate air had given way to a tense foxy wariness. He said, "Well, Fain carried me. Mostly because he was making an extraordinary personal gesture. Such truth comes hard. I think he gave us the truth."

Givney said, "Well, before this meeting stampedes may I just have a word here? I don't bring the emotional charge of Mr. Fain nor the excitement of alcohol, but from a pure business standpoint he was talking like a boy, and this immaturity is probably what has sapped his work. We need quick dramatic action before the reading public. The *Times* page is the answer, it can absolutely turn the tide. Youngblood has to rise to the occasion and write a magnificent credo, a statement of the artist's integrity, yes, a Gettysburg address of literature. I know he can do it, the situation cries for it—"

Hawke said without rancor, "Rollo, you mean that we can stall Ben Manson for a while if I write the damned thing."

"That's discussing the matter on its lowest level, but all right, I should think that ought to concern you too, since I gather from your attorney that you can't meet the bill."

Adam interposed, "I didn't say that."

Givney said, "It seems very strange to me that of all the people in this room I'm the only one who hasn't lost faith in *Evelyn Biggers*." He turned on Gus Adam. "I think we should act on the facts here. Can Youngblood pay a seventy-three-thousand-dollar printing bill if it comes in today?"

Adam hesitated and Hawke struck in. "I've got a better idea, Rollo. You've always talked of the paperback rights in terms of a hundred twenty-five thousand dollars or more. You pay that printing bill and you've got the paperback rights. Okay?"

Givney laughed, and threw up his hands. "There, you see what the atmosphere is in this room? Panic and fire sales. Why should you cheat yourself like that?"

"To clean up a problem, that's all, since I've got several. I'll be glad to make the deal, Rollo, honestly. This is a firm formal offer of the paperback rights to *Evelyn Biggers* for seventy-three thousand dollars. Will you take it?"

All eyes were on Givney now. He said, "I'll grab that, Youngblood, subject of course to the approval of my board of directors. I don't have the authority to buy any one book on my own for more than fifteen thousand. They don't meet until the tenth of next month, so that's not much help in this crisis."

Adam said, "I'm sure a special meeting could be easily arranged."

"Not so easily," Givney said.

Hawke said, "As a matter of fact, Rollo, you round up this board of yours and make this deal and I'll write the piece for the *Times*, how's that?"

"You mean you won't do it to affirm your artistic integrity but you'll do it for money? That's not very admirable."

Hawke said cheerfully, "No, not very, but I'm in sort of a jam. Is it a deal, Rollo?"

Givney did not answer for a moment. He endured everybody's stare, twirling a sharp pencil round and round in one fist on the desk. The usual jollity of his face faded away, leaving stiff lines at the ends of his thin mouth, an outthrust jaw, and drooping eyes. He said, "I can't arrange a special meeting of my board. I can buy the paperback rights to *Evelyn Biggers* for fifteen thousand dollars. I assume you're not interested."

Hawke said, "No, I'm not, Rollo, but thanks."

Ross Hodge cut into the heavy stillness. "Well, then, if the idea is to do nothing about Judd I'm for that, and can I run along? It's seldom a mistake to ignore a critic."

Hawke said, "That's the decision. I just have to wipe the pie off my face and carry on. Meeting's over." They were talking as though Givney were not there. He sat smiling primly and smoking.

Ross stood. "Arthur, I'm sorry you're in a jam. I don't want to know details, but Hodge Hathaway will give you a fifty-thousand-dollar advance any time, sight unseen, on your next book, if that will be a help."

Hawke looked abashed. He said in a low tired tone, "Ross, it isn't half done and it might turn out another *Evelyn* or worse."

Hodge nodded. "That's the risk. My job is taking risks, Arthur. My objection to Haworth House always was your involvement in risk. I can't write books. Nobody can write Hawke novels but you. I hope you don't mind my saying one more thing. I'd have published this book in two hundred pages and sold it for three dollars. If you decide you want the advance, just tell Jeanne." He put out his hand in his curious stiff way, shook hands, and left.

Adam rasped his briefcase shut. "If that's it, Arthur, you and I have to go to the St. Regis to see Scotty, in a hell of a hurry. We're half an hour late."

CHAPTER TWENTY-TWO

1

JEANNE, Hawke and Adam piled into a taxi. It stopped first in front of the tall office building on Park Avenue, all glass and bronze facing, where Hodge Hathaway had its new offices. When Hawke stepped out and offered his hand, Jeanne hesitated. "If only people would skip the condolences," she said shakily, "and if only there hadn't been this Judd mess! I'm going to be a two-headed calf around here, for God knows how long. Well—I can't retire to a convent." She took his hand, slid to the door, and with a prim quick move she was on the sidewalk. "So long. The decision about Judd was right. I think Roland Givney is a beautiful human being—if that's what he is." She looked up at Hawke as though she wanted to kiss him, then she laughed. "Ye gods, let's not be seen together like this in public, eh? The female Svengali giving Youngblood Hawke his next plot in a sidewalk conference." She turned and strode into the building, her youthful black-clad figure disappearing at once into a waiting elevator.

Meanwhile Adam emerged from the cab, saying, "We may as well walk to the St. Regis." As he stepped out, Jeanne's black kid gloves fell from the cab to the gutter. He picked them up and brushed them off, grinning. "Wouldn't Karl have growled about this! It was his favorite joke, the way she loses gloves."

Hawke nodded. "I once heard him say if she'd give up wearing gloves for a year they'd be able to buy their country home."

"Well," Adam said, holding the gloves rather gingerly, "who's going to be seeing her first?"

"I don't know," Hawke said. After an awkward moment, the lawyer offered Hawke the gloves. Hawke took them and put them in his pocket. The two men started to walk up the avenue.

Hawke said, "What do I have to know for this meeting?"

"Well, this is the showdown with Newton Leffer, Arthur. Scotty got one more day of grace by saying that he was signing the Mehlman lease this morning. Scotty's become very hard to locate in the past few days. You have to telephone a dozen times to catch him once. That kind of thing. Newton's had the same trouble. I finally nailed him yesterday."

Hawke said anxiously, "Can't you dig up any reliable information on the department store lease?"

"I've tried. It's hard to get solid answers out of the law firm that represents the Mehlman family. They're very stuffy high-button-shoes Philadelphians. And you can't pin down Scotty. He'd better have the answer today, that's all."

Newton Leffer sat alone on a couch in the hotel lobby, stiff and wrathful, umbrella between his knees, black Homburg on his lap. He said he had been waiting for forty-five minutes. No sign of Hoag, no telephone message; and he had begun to think that Adam and Hawke were avoiding him too.

Leffer had unearthed an extremely discouraging fact that morning, he said, by telephoning three of the firms which had signed leases in the Plaza. None of these were really firm commitments! Scott had signed separate letters of agreement with these three shops, stipulating that if he failed to get the Mehlman department store lease, these other leases were cancelled. Leffer sternly asked Hawke and Adam whether they had known of these letters. He appeared convinced by their dismayed denials, but his anger did not decrease.

"I think your Mr. Hoag is a little free with facts," Leffer said, looking up at Hawke with formidable iciness. "His behavior in avoiding my telephone calls, and his failure to show up today, are pretty well explained. He may have no leases at all! I don't know whether or not the Mehlman lease has been signed. I can't find out, and I'm rapidly losing interest. Here's how matters stand. If before five o'clock today you, or Mr. Hoag, or Gus, appears at my office with the Mehlman lease, *and* a representative of the department store who will confirm that there are no hidden wrinkles or escape agreements, I'll accept seventy-five thousand dollars as the first payment of this mortgage, now seventeen days overdue. Otherwise I'm going to invoke the acceleration clause, tomorrow at nine in the morning, and hold you personally liable, Mr. Hawke, to pay me three hundred thousand dollars at once."

Adam exclaimed, "Newton, for Pete's sake! You have every right to be annoyed and distressed, but good lord! Arthur can and will meet the first payment, but three hundred thousand dollars in cash at a crack is rough for anybody."

"I know that, Gus. I presume Mr. Hawke knew it when he signed a note promising to pay that amount if there was a default. We have his signature, I recommended the loan on his signature, and he must make it good."

Adam started to speak of appraisals he could show Leffer, which proved that the shopping center would be worth close to three million dollars when completed and occupied. The little man waved this aside with a short jerk of the umbrella handle. "I have my own appraisals in the file. Unless my terms are met today, my clients are getting out of this situation. In effect Mr. Hawke will be buying the second mortgage from us. He's

welcome to it, with all the eventual gains." He stood. "You know quite well, Gus, that if you were in my place this is the action you'd take. It's just what Abe Tulking did on the second mortgage of the West End housing project. There's only one way with people like Mr. Hoag. I'm not going to pursue him by telephone or wait for him any more. I'm very glad I got Mr. Hawke's guarantee, but that was the basis on which we proceeded, as you know." He turned to Hawke, putting on his hat and giving the umbrella a little flourish. "You have the most remarkable knowledge of human nature, Mr. Hawke, judging from your books, but I think it deserted you in the choice of this business partner. Money does cloud the best judgments sometimes. Heaven knows I've made my mistakes. There's nothing personal in this. —Gus, I'll be in my office till five."

"All right, Newton."

The little man squared his almost non-existent shoulders, somewhat lessening the angle of their slope, and stalked out through the revolving door.

Hawke said ruefully, "Well done."

Adam said, "Oh, Newt's a competent lawyer. He's quite right, he's doing exactly what I'd do." He got out of his chair, and it struck Hawke that his movement was a tired, sagging one. "Let me make a couple of phone calls. The best thing for you is to sit right there and watch the door for Scotty."

"Okay," Hawke said. He sat and watched the door while a variety of people went in and out: ugly men, handsome men, beautiful women in extreme clothes trailing clouds of perfume, stately old women, men in groups arguing and laughing, foreigners chattering in their languages. They all bore themselves as though they had a lot of money. But he wondered how many of them could meet two simultaneous calls for seventy-three thousand dollars and three hundred thousand dollars in cash.

Adam returned after fifteen minutes, stripping cellophane off a package of cigarettes. Hawke said, "Gus, since when have you taken to nails?"

Adam said, "I'm having a lapse. I'll quit again. No sign of our wandering boy, eh? Let's give him till three o'clock. He's not punctual at best." He dropped on the sofa beside Hawke, and regarded him with a melancholy grin, head cocked sidewise. "My bill *is* going to be a big one, some day. I never knew what I was letting myself in for when I took on Youngblood Hawke. I thought literary legal problems would be a refreshing change. Now I'm beginning to feel like one of those fifth-act messengers in Shakespeare, who keep galloping onstage with more bad news."

"What now?" Hawke said, with a twinge of dread, and yet with a certain awakening in him of nervous exultation, as when a sailor learns he is in for a hurricane and braces himself to do what he can to come out of it alive.

Adam lit a cigarette and drew on it so that the end glowed down for a

quarter of an inch. "Well, one of those conversations was with Internal Revenue down town. Let's skip that for the moment because I then called Washington and some wheels are still turning. I thought I'd better call Scotty's Lexington lawyer, that Urban Webber fellow, because he really knows Scott's affairs. I had quite a talk with him. I can't tell how much of what he said is true, but it's certainly the position Scotty's going to take. He puts it that Scotty's worse off than you for meeting a cash call, in fact he has no cash whatever and his credit is stretched as far as it can go. It's all on ventures like the Plaza. Scotty has about five of these things coming along in various stages, though the Plaza's the biggest. He's a plunger, he's been in tighter spots than this, Webber says, and he's always come out richer than before. Webber asserts—and indeed I think it may be true— that in the end the Plaza's going to be a money maker for both of you. The trouble is that before one gets to the end of a thing like this somebody can be very badly burned, if there's a cash squeeze."

"Gus, it's a lie about Scott not having money. Hawke Brothers is the biggest coal mining operation in Letchworth County, it's one of the big ones in eastern Kentucky, and Scott runs it."

Adam blew out a thick cloud of gray smoke from the depths of his lungs. "Well, Arthur, I've found out a good bit about that, checking into your mother's lawsuit. Actually I have a young cousin in Brightstar, a lawyer, who's doing most of the legwork. I'm not sure your mother's prospects are too good, but meantime there's some interesting stuff about Scotty. Your Uncle William left the stock of Hawke Brothers in trust for his children. Scotty represents his wife on the board, he draws a good salary, but the wealth is hers, he can't touch it, and what's more important his creditors can't. I'm sure he's delighted to have that coal property in his wife's name and wouldn't dream of changing it if he could. It's his whole base of operation. He's borrowed freely from Hawke Brothers and drawn a lot of salary over the years, and yet it's invulnerable. His airfield behind the Yalu River, you might say. I gather though—this is Urban Webber again, being very candid, which is sometimes the best smokescreen, but anyway—that there's bad blood between Scott and your cousin Glenn because Scott has borrowed far too much venture capital from Hawke Brothers, and so that tap has been completely shut off."

"What it comes to," Hawke said, "is that I'll have to pay Newton Leffer."

Adam said, "Inside of a great cloud of words, that's the message. With the cheerful postscript that this second mortgage is going to turn out to be very valuable, and Scotty's going to give you a nice bonus in the end for taking on the payment at this somewhat embarrassing turn."

Just then Scotty came into the lobby, followed by the doorman and a bellboy carrying packages with the large ribbony M trademark of the

Mehlman department store. Scotty hailed Hawke and Adam with the greatest cheerfulness, and insisted that they come up to his suite for a drink. He was late, he said, because he had been with the Mehlman managers and lawyers until ten minutes ago, hammering out the lease. Everything was in good shape, and they were out of the woods at last. He tipped the doorman a dollar, gave the bellboy who carried up the packages in the elevator another dollar, and told him to bring setups for drinks. "Christ, I'm starving. We talked straight through lunch time," he said. "Those people sent out for some goddamn chicken sandwiches. New York chicken sandwiches, you know, all bread and mayonnaise and a teeny thin something in the middle that could be chicken or a sheet of toilet paper, it's always a good idea to check the chicken for a row of holes in this town. Chicken sandwiches!" He called room service and ordered a lobster cocktail, a filet mignon, ice cream and coffee. Adam and Hawke declined any food and Adam, saying he would have to leave shortly, told Scott of Newton Leffer's angry ultimatum.

Scotty seemed amused. "Good old Newt, he gets real fierce, don't he? He's a good guy and I think he'll give us a little more leeway, it's the only course that makes sense at this point." Whereupon he launched into his account of how the department store lease now stood.

The death of the president of the company remained the one difficulty, because Scott had dealt mainly with him. He was a man who had worked up to the presidency of the firm from floorwalker. The Mehlman family and their Philadelphia attorneys had always disliked him, but had advanced him because of his efficiency; however he had never been more than an employee. Since his death the family had been looking into rumors that he had enriched himself by juggling inventory, by taking bribes from the salesmen of large accounts, and so forth. They had as yet uncovered nothing, but they were reviewing every contract he had been negotiating at the time of his death, including the Paumanok Plaza lease.

"They'll never find anything on old Phil," said Scott. "Phil was a smart fellow and a damn fine administrator. He was in to me for about five thousand, but he wasn't a crook or anything, you just want to take care of a man who brings you a big lease like that. Those are the things I never charge you for, Art, they've got to come out of my own pocket because they can't show in the books, and Christ, they add up. Now in all fairness was I expected to anticipate that the poor sumbitch would drop dead? Newt's being unreasonable."

Scotty added that he had successfully survived a severe cross-examination on the lease by the attorneys. The only remaining snag was that another shopping center near Mineola had been bidding from the start for the big lease; and since "Phil's" death its builders had swarmed in on the

attorneys and the Mehlman family, confusing the picture. The verdict of the attorneys at the meeting today had been that the Paumanok lease looked excellent, but they intended to order a whole new comparative analysis of the two centers, and Scotty would hear from them again in about four weeks.

The waiter was wheeling in Hoag's food on a table agleam with silver dish covers on a snowy cloth, brightened by fresh roses in a cut-glass vase. Scotty dropped this catastrophic news with the utmost nonchalance, at the same time lifting a dish cover and exclaiming at the appetizing look of the steak.

Hawke said, "Scott, for God's sake, do you know the implications of this? If Leffer calls the entire note tomorrow can you pay it? I can't. I can't begin to."

Scott sat and fell to with gusto on his lobster cocktail. He said gaily that Newton was just talking, that a sudden call like this was unheard of and would do Leffer no good. Why, they had nothing to fear from the Mineola competition! That center was badly built, badly located, and their terms actually were higher. The Mehlman lease was in the bag. There was just this four-week delay. Then he repeated Urban Webber's picture of his own affairs. "Hell, Art, I'm so cash-poor I'm travelling and living on Ellie's household money right now. These binds come along for any binness man. They temporary and they don't mean nothing." Six months hence, he said, all his jobs would be cleared up except Seven Oaks Farm, and he expected to have nearly a million dollars in cash. That was how it went. He was sure, he said (starting to devour the steak), that Leffer would gladly accept seventy-five thousand tomorrow, and if ole Art would just pay this installment Scott would give him his note for eighty thousand dollars plus six percent interest, payable on the first of January.

Scotty's blandness stupefied Hawke. He was slow to anger, and short of picking Scott up by the collar and punching him all over the luxurious suite, he had no idea how he could break through his good cheer and make this man acknowledge that he was pushing him to the edge of a major financial disaster if not actual bankruptcy.

Adam said harshly, "I've got to go. Scott, will you come with me to see Leffer at five and tell all this to him?"

"Why, sure," Scott said. "Be glad to. I'd like a little snooze first. Been going since dawn."

Adam said, "I'll be here in a cab at half-past four. I strongly advise you not to disappear again. You be in the lobby, waiting for me."

"Course, Gus, sorry I been so rushed. Art, you take my word for it, it's darkest before the dawn and you gonna clear half a million tax paid out of Paumanok Plaza."

Adam said at the door, "You'd better have some convincing explanation for Newton of those separate letters of agreement."

"What explanation?" Scott said. "Now goddamn it, that gets me a little sore, Gus. That's common binness practice! Don't Newton know that a lease next to a Mehlman branch is worth three times an ordinary lease? How does he think I got those high rentals? I be a sumbitch if I ever get into New York financing again. Bunch of nervous old ladies." He spoke these indignant words without heat, chewing on steak all the while.

Adam's hand was on the doorknob. "Scotty, by the way, what was the purpose of the Eleanor Coal Company?"

A large red chunk of steak, travelling on a fork toward Scott's mouth, halted in midair and dripped. Scott looked at Adam with an open countenance and said pleasantly, "The what?"

"The Eleanor Coal Company."

Scott shrugged. "I guess you got me. What's the Eleanor Coal Company?" He ate the piece of steak.

"Well, you know that Mrs. Hawke gave me her Frenchman's Ridge lawsuit to look over."

"Oh, *that* binness. No. Did she? That's a waste of time, Gus, the court took all of three hours to throw her case out."

"Well, I'm just wondering why you had to set up a separate Delaware corporation to mine that ridge."

"Oh, Jesus, Gus, that was years ago. Who can remember? The whole thing was a big bust, that's all I know. I never can follow Urban Webber's paper shuffling anyway, but you can ask him." He looked at Hawke and grinned. "Christ, I admire your mom, I swear. She never gives up, does she?"

2

Adam said in the elevator, "Ride up with me to my place. We can talk a little more."

"Sure," Hawke said. In all the time he had known Adam he had never visited the lawyer's apartment, and even the disasters crowding on him could not quench his writer's curiosity.

The lawyer sank into a corner of the cab seat, lit his pipe, and went into some kind of trance behind blue wreaths of smoke. "Business—or what our friend calls binness—is a rough game," he said at last, taking a peculiar professorial tone, as though he were facing a class. "Most business men who hold the leading places are like Ross Hodge—cold and tough, and out for their own profit, but honest. That's because fair dealing in the long run tends to pay off. Then there are the crooks, who keep popping

up and going to jail. Then there's the twilight area of sharp practice where you find the Hoags and the Givneys. What bothers me is that the twilight zone seems to be broadening lately." He raised his thick eyebrows in a grin at Hawke and said in a drop to a conversational note, "Maybe that's because I've gotten so involved in your affairs, eh?"

Hawke said, "I do seem to have dragged you into a kind of freak show."

Adam said, "I wonder. You won't accept your pleasant fate as a distinguished artist. You keep looking for special deals, clever advantages, and inevitably I suppose you attract the twilight creatures. A first-rate builder doesn't need an author as a partner, and a solid publisher doesn't go about starting phony new houses. I don't say this in reproach, but as some guide to the future." Adam moved forward to the edge of the seat and stared at Hawke rather forbiddingly. "Now Arthur, you once asked me about bankruptcy. When we get home I'm going to give you some stuff to read. Don't get alarmed, I just want you to be a bit more informed in case we have to make some fast moves in the next couple of days. I'm confident we'll get through this knothole without a bankruptcy, if we have any kind of decent luck. You have to be clear, first of all, on the difference between insolvency and bankruptcy. If Newton Leffer calls the whole loan tomorrow and puts the burden on you, there's no doubt you'll be insolvent. You don't have the money, that's all, and you can't raise it right now. Bankruptcy is something else. It's a legal status. Everybody who's in love doesn't necessarily get married, and everybody's who's insolvent doesn't go bankrupt, not by a long shot. There are two main reasons for a bankruptcy—either a man despairs of paying his debts and seeks relief, or his creditors lose confidence in him and force bankruptcy on him. The court takes his affairs out of his hands and divides up all he's got as fairly as possible among the creditors. Bankruptcy washes him clean, so to speak, and he can start over. Hence the twilight types call it taking a bath, and some of them are very blithe about filing voluntary petitions."

Hawke said, "There's no question of my going bankrupt voluntarily. I can earn the money to pay off every debt in sight. I will, whatever happens, and however long it takes me."

Adam nodded, approval glinting in his eyes. "Very good. Very sensible. Setting aside the moral disgrace, if one cares about that, bankruptcy is a scar that never comes off. It marks you as a fool or a shoddy dealer. I'm afraid Mark Twain and Walter Scott—whose cases I've been looking up, by the bye—have to be called fools about money. Both of them fell into unlimited personal liability for large companies with many creditors. You're in nothing like such a pickle. The problem here is convincing one big creditor, Newton Leffer, to give you time to pay in full, if the worst

comes to the worst. I'm hopeful we can do that. I'm assuming, Arthur, that I know all your affairs."

While the taxi bounced and groaned along a torn-up section of midtown Broadway, the lawyer asked Hawke a number of questions about his expenditures in recent weeks.

He lived in an old house on a hilly side street between Riverside Drive and Columbia University, in a dark apartment on the ground floor. Two boys in collegiate costume complete to dirty white shoes rose to their feet as Adam led Hawke through the living room. The furniture was exceedingly dowdy and ancient, and all the walls were solid with old books. He took Hawke into a tiny dark room, hardly more than a large closet of books with a desk in it, switched on a bright yellow lamp, and closed the door. The light brought to view a startling life-size oil painting of a beautiful girl in riding clothes, which took up most of one wall.

"Who's that?" Hawke said at once.

"That's Louise. My wife," Adam said. "This is a musty hole of an apartment but I like it. I rented it years ago from the widow of a philosophy professor, furniture, books, housekeeper and all, and it's worked out fine. She lives in Florida on the rent I pay her. Now where's that booklet on bankruptcy? I know it's in here." He stooped and peered around at the shelves.

Hawke was staring at the lovely dead wife of Adam, trying to connect her with the lawyer and this bookish-smelling little room, and finding it hard to do. She was painted in too vivid colors in a poor photographic style; a very tall girl in her twenties, brown-haired, with large piercing greenish eyes, and a subtle smile. "Are those really law students out there?" he said.

"Second year. Why?"

"They're children, Gus. I'd place them in high school."

Adam said, "A symptom of advancing age, my friend. Ah, here we are." He pulled a thin green paper-backed book from a lower shelf and handed it to Hawke. "Tonight's assignment."

The booklet, the sight of the title, the feel of it in his hands, gave Hawke an unpleasant turn. *Insolvency and Bankruptcy, A General Discussion. by Everett A. Wollas.* Adam said, "Ev teaches at NYU. It's not very complete, but he writes well and you'll be able to get through it."

"Well, mama always wanted me to study law," Hawke said. "I reckon she wins. But I put up a hell of a fight."

"I'm sure you weren't cut out for the law, Arthur," Adam said, laughing. "Wrong temperament. Anyway there are lots of good lawyers and there's only one Youngblood Hawke. My wife was interested in writing," he added, glancing at the portrait. "She might have done something, too."

"What happened to her, Gus?"

Adam dropped into the chair behind the desk and began emptying his briefcase into the drawers. "Well, strangely enough you see her almost exactly as she looked just before she died. It was a riding accident. She was a fine rider, she'd ridden since childhood, but this horse bolted and fractured her skull against the top beam of the stable door. We think she was dead before she hit the ground."

"Good God," Hawke murmured.

"Yes, it was incredible, the sheer suddenness of it. To tell the truth I don't think I've ever wholly gotten over the surprise, I live in a state of slight shock, and if I've ever seemed absent or remote that's the reason. We'd been married less than two years. You once asked me why I never went into Kentucky politics. I don't think I'd have made a good politician, but in any case I couldn't go back to Louisville after that. When my army service was over I came north quite on purpose." Adam smiled up at Hawke, who stood awkwardly holding the green bankruptcy booklet, glancing from the lawyer to the portrait. "I even took a speech course to smooth out some of the Letchworth, because people here are disinclined to take a Southerner seriously. They think we're cute."

Hawke said, "She was beautiful, Gus."

The lawyer said, "There's no use my telling you how bright she was, too. Jeanie Fry reminds me of her, the tough-minded intelligence plus the honesty and the absence of faking. Not too common among the ladies. Well, so I went into tax law, and then Abe Tulking said I'd enjoy teaching so I tried that, and there's the story. You now know all you need to know to put me into a book, Arthur, if you can ever use such a stodgy character." He stood. "I've got to dispose of these lads and get after Scotty again. I'll talk to you tonight. Do your homework on bankruptcy meantime, but don't fret about it. We're preparing to lick it, that's all."

3

The nursemaid let Hawke into Jeanne's apartment. He could hear Jeanne shouting in her strident key, the register of anger and frustration which she had risen to more than once in arguing with him, "Jim, you eat this soup! It's good and you need it! Eat it, I say! Stop that! Oh, you little *fiend!*"

He hurried into the kitchen. Jeanne stood glaring at the little fiend, who sat on a high chair in tears, with red soup running down his chin into his bib. She was dabbing at her stained black silk dress. "Hello!" she barked. "This wretched monster knocked the spoon aside with his

hand, he's drenched me with this goddamned tomato soup from head to foot!"

"Jeanne, let Elizabeth feed him. Come have a drink."

"Elizabeth can't get anything down him. This child has eaten nothing in a *week*, Arthur. Jim, what am I going to do with you? You must eat or you'll die! You must eat!"

Jim had grown to have a strong boyish face that yet retained the shape of his mother's, and his eyes were enormous, clever, and very blue. Weeping silently as he was, the face was uncontorted; he was a charming child, though he looked hungry and wan. He now reached out a little paw to her, stained with tomato soup, a plea for forgiveness and comfort from the person he loved, the very one who was harrying him. Jeanne seized the hand and kissed it. "Great disciplinarian I am," she choked.

The Irish maid, looking on restlessly in the doorway said, "Mrs. Fry, he might eat a bit of bacon. It's his favorite. Let me make some."

"Oh, all *right!*" Jeanne said peevishly. She added to Hawke, "And will you mix about twenty gallons of martinis, please? You know where everything is. I can't entertain a great author for dinner when I'm all splattered with tomato soup."

Later she said, having downed a large martini and poured another, "That was quite a display. Sorry. You've always called me a shrew, so you shouldn't be surprised." They were sitting on the sofa in the L-shaped living and dining room. On the mantelpiece the photograph of Karl, which had always been a trivial detail of the room, now seemed ringed in red neon.

"Jeanie, Jim isn't eating for the same reason that you were yelling at him. You must give him time."

"I know, I know, Arthur, I should be all sweet reasonableness. I'm not in good shape. I overestimated my strength today, obviously. Hodge Hathaway was hell. I don't know if I can ever go back there."

It had been bad enough, she said, to confront Karl's heaped desk in the office they had shared, so full of memories: things he had said, private jokes they had had, scribbled notes in his handwriting, the smell of the Turkish cigarettes he had been smoking in the past year. But there was also the damned Judd review! One after another the people of the staff had come in to talk about it as word spread that Jeanne Fry was back. Within an hour she had had three calls from literary columnists, demanding interviews and probing at her. She had fled, leaving both desks in total disorder. "I've never left a desk looking the way mine did in all my life," she said, "but I was on the verge of a screaming fit, and it seemed the better part of wisdom to pull out." She glanced shyly at him. "I don't know if this will surprise you, or what. I've been thinking that I ought to pick up and go home for a while. Just take Jim and stay with mama in the

California sunshine through the worst of the winter, and sort of pull myself together. What do you think?"

Hawke was startled and cast down, but he said as cheerfully as he could, "Whatever you think best, Jeanie."

She was eager to explain. The words began to tumble out. "I'm utterly shot, my dear, that's the plain fact. I realized it for the first time today. I guess you just saw a small proof of it. It's out of the question for me to go back to work at the office, for months anyway. This apartment gives me the horrors. Jim does very poorly in this foul New York winter, always an earache or a sore throat, fevers spiking up to a hundred and five, midnight doctor visits and so forth. They've always passed off, but oh God, Arthur, they're fearful while they last, and I'm in no condition to endure another siege of them. I don't know what'll become of me if I see him in convulsions again, the way he was last February. It almost drove me crazy even then, when I was feeling fine. And with the disgusting Judd business, Arthur, it really does seem to me the best service I can render you right now is to disappear. Just vanish until the tempest dies down, so that nobody can corner me and make me say something idiotic." She peered at him, her face lovely and searching. "Would you mind so very much? It's you I'm worrying about. I'll do anything you say. It just seems to me I need a little time and peace to grow some skin. I'm one raw wound, no good for anybody or anything."

Hawke was thinking, as she talked, how impossible it was to foresee real events before they were upon you. He had thought many times of the possible death of Karl Fry. His mind had always moved straight from the death to a picture of Jeanne in his arms at last, black-clad and tearful, but happy, united with him forever after the long mischances. Instead, this was the way it was working out; and he thought ruefully that God was always the best at realism. He knew that Jeanne loved him and wanted him; he had not realized that when a man died he did not disappear, but took on a last burst of importance that he might even have lacked in life, before he faded to invisibility. Jeanne was having a private agony over Karl's death to which he would never be admitted. Until it was over, the marriage remained a bar between them, even more than in Karl's lifetime.

It would be no great matter, Hawke sensed, to isolate Jeanne with himself and make her come to bed. She was shattered and defenseless, and she loved him. But it would be a peculiarly grisly form of adultery while she was in this state. Having had to wait for his wife so long, he now had to wait a bit longer. That was all.

He said slowly, "Jeanne, I'm sure that's the best thing you can do."

Her face lit up with relief. "Do you honestly think so? You're not just agreeing with a shaky drunk?"

He said, "I'll miss you, I don't have to say how much, but it's sensible, it's the answer right now."

"Thank heaven!" She drained her glass. "If you knew how I dreaded saying this to you! It looks as though I'm running away from you when you're in trouble, but it isn't that. I'm absolutely yours to command, you know it, Arthur."

"Where does your mother live, again?"

"Oh, you've never heard of it, it's called Bell, it's one of the ten million flat suburbs south of Los Angeles. The smog's never too bad there, and mama has this fenced back yard where Jim can run around on the grass in the sun, and there's a dog and four cats—"

"How far is it from Beverly Hills?"

"A terrible drive, two hours or so, why?"

"Well, it occurs to me that Travis Jablock isn't returning until April. I can still go back to his place to work, and drive over to see you now and then, and sort of get to know Jim, and your mother too, a little better. And we could see each other, Jeanne, go swimming and to restaurants and such, without the New York columnists carrying along the Judd fantasy." He smiled. "That doesn't sound too bad, does it?"

Her eyes were shining. "It sounds unbelievably wonderful. Will you really do it?"

"Sure I will."

She jumped to her feet. "I'm going to fry up those tacos. I'm suddenly ravenous." She turned back at the kitchen doorway. "It's chicken, I'm afraid. We're fresh out of turkey." And at this ancient secret joke, so like the standard joke of a long-married couple, both of them laughed in tones not untinged with sadness. She hummed as she moved here and there in the tiny kitchen, pulling out utensils and food with swift sure motions. "How about a beer while I do this? I'd like one."

"Sure."

"In the freezer," she said, gesturing over her shoulder with a knife she was using to shred lettuce. "By the way," she added very casually, as he punched open the icy cans, "whatever did become of Frieda Winter?"

"I believe she's in Jamaica."

"You believe? Don't you know?"

"Ferdie Lax told me he saw her there around Christmas time."

"When did you last hear from her?"

"I saw her for the last time, Jeanne, when I gave her back that letter of Paul's. It must have been a week or so after the funeral."

"And she doesn't write, and you don't write? Nothing?"

"Nothing."

She glanced at him over the rim of her conical beer glass, a flash of the old mischief in her eyes. "Well, it was a long siege."

Hawke said, "A spiking fever, you might say."

"Yes indeed. A very bad case of the New York crud. I often thought it would be the death of you. Well, stand clear for the spatter of frying oil and the like."

They were eating tacos and salad in the dining room when the phone rang. Jeanne answered it. "Hello? Oh, hello, Gus. Why I'm fine. Yes, he's here. Good guess." She held out the receiver to Hawke. "The legal mind."

Adam sounded very hoarse and tired. "Hello, Arthur. I've just finished with Newton Leffer."

Hawke looked at his watch. It was a quarter past nine. He said, "Long session."

"Yes. A long session."

"How do we stand?"

"Well, it could be worse. We have to talk right away. I'm sorry to disturb you and Jeanne."

"You want to meet tonight?"

"Right now."

"Where?"

"Any place you say."

The telephone was on a little table at the bend of the L into the living room. Jeanne said, "Does Gus want to talk about your finances?"

"Yes, Jeanne."

"Tell him to come up here."

Hawke looked doubtful. He said to Adam, "Jeanne wants us to talk here, at her place."

There was such a long silence that Hawke said, "Gus, are you there?"

The lawyer said in a strained tone, "I'm here. As a matter of fact, if she isn't too tired, I imagine it would be a wise thing to include Jeanne."

4

Soon the lawyer sat in the living room in his shirtsleeves at Jeanne's insistence, his tie off, eating tacos from a tray. He needed a shave, and his hair was unkempt. Hawke noticed that the bristles on his face were reddish rather than blond. He looked more tired than Hawke had ever seen him, but the food and the beer brought him to quickly. "Why, these things are marvellous! What do you call them, Jeanne, tacos? I've never eaten anything like this. Delicious! Is there a restaurant in town where I can order these?"

She said, pleased, "Well, if you can find a lowbrow enough Mexican joint they'll probably have tacos, but I wouldn't endorse the contents, Gus. Better ask me, when you feel like having them again. They're easy to make."

"Why, I'll certainly take you up on that. Thank you."

Hawke felt a twinge of jealousy, to see Gus Adam eating Jeanne's tacos in a chair under the picture of Karl Fry. These little hot fried corn meal pouches of chili-soaked meat and vegetables were part of his own long romance with her, and for the moment Adam seemed a most unwanted intruder. But the swollen briefcase was Adam's passport into the scene. It lay on the floor beside his armchair like a ticking bomb.

Adam said, "Well! Thank you, Jeanne, that was a real treat, and I needed it." He began to fill his pipe. "Unfortunately, Arthur, our deadline for action is tomorrow morning at nine, so we'll have to keep going."

"By all means."

Jeanne sat on an ottoman, hugging her knees, glancing from Hawke to the lawyer, her eyes sharp and bright once more. The traffic noises were loud in the street as Adam lit his pipe: honks, motor roars, and squeals of brakes. The room was lit a warm amber by two floor lamps, and seemed very peaceful. Karl's picture glowed in the upward flare of the lamp beside Adam.

He said, "To begin with, Arthur, did you read the booklet?"

"Yes. It looks to me like I'm a Chapter Eleven type rather than a bankrupt, at worst." At this a small grin wrinkled the lawyer's mouth, and his eyebrows arched. Hawke went on, "Except I guess if Newt wants to get technical, my paying ten thousand dollars to the advertising people day before yesterday was an act of bankruptcy. I sure was insolvent, and on notice that Newton wanted his money. But hell, Gus, that bill was due."

"Very good Arthur, really! A plus. Technically that payment probably was a preference, and Newton could file on that basis. But if all goes well he's not going to file, and there won't be any need for Chapter Eleven. That's the aim here, let's be clear, to keep Youngblood Hawke out of bankruptcy court entirely. The damage to your prestige would be fearful, and I don't care if Twain survived it, the fact is he never was the same afterward. I'm going to recommend some drastic steps here, so let's never forget that aim."

Jeanne said, "Bankruptcy court! Are things that bad?"

Hawke said, "I'm not sure."

Adam's face turned sober. He picked up his briefcase, set it on his knees and rasped it open. "Well. Let's go." He pulled out the HAWKE folder and deliberately removed from a sheaf of papers in a fastener two government forms, one of ordinary size and one a short slip. Without a word he passed them to Hawke, who sat forward, elbows on knees, and looked at them in the light of the floor lamp. Jeanne scanned Hawke's face nervously. His expression did not change. He studied the papers for a minute or two. Then he glanced up at Adam, and an ironic smile suppressed his broad mouth. "If I understand what I'm reading, Gus, this is it. This puts me under."

"Well, now does it? That's what we have to figure out. I don't think so. I believe you can still squeak through."

Hawke shook his head. "No. Another ninety-three thousand dollars! I just don't know where it can come from."

"What are those papers?" Jeanne said.

The lawyer said, "It's a jeopardy assessment, Jeanne, an Internal Revenue instrument, and a rough one." He stood and paced, talking about the documents that Hawke was holding. He had known the assessment was coming for a week, and had been fighting it off up to high Washington levels. Internal Revenue had the power, he said, to decide that a man's finances were deteriorating very badly, and that it must protect the government's tax claims by taking quick action. The bureau could proceed without further ado to seize all his property, or enough to satisfy the claim.

The agents looking into Hawke's recent tax returns, Adam said, had scanned the Paumanok Plaza financing and had reported to the district director that Hawke was exposed to huge impending losses. The director —Adam knew him well—had called the lawyer in, questioned him severely about Hawke's financial picture, and at last said he was going to make a jeopardy assessment of the $80,000 deficiency from the movie sale of *Chain of Command*, plus $13,000 interest; and another jeopardy assessment for the deficiency arising from the contract which had put the royalties of the *Oblivion* play into Scotty's shopping center. Adam had argued with him for days, had telephoned all the high officials he knew in Washington over and over, and had at last won the concession that only the first assessment would be made now. The District Director felt that this was an extraordinarily soft-hearted decision, and would not budge further. "He admires you personally, Arthur," Adam said, "but of course the New York districts have had a lot of bad experiences with actors, writers, and such. Speaking fiscally, he said, artists are confirmed tax-dodgers, squanderers, and potential bankrupts."

Hawke said, "Speaking fiscally, I'd call that a reasonable description."

"So, he feels that his responsibility is to grab while the grabbing's good," Adam said. "The jeopardy assessment is a formidable thing. Its force is absolute. You can't appeal from it. I know of no recourse in law against it, neither an injunction nor any other stay. The government seizes your property. Then you go to court. If we win—I think we have a good chance of winning both disputes, as I've told you—the bureau hands back the money and says, 'So sorry.' That's how it works."

"God Almighty," said Jeanne, "I didn't know such a thing existed."

"It's a sad day for anybody who has to be informed that it does," the lawyer said.

"Amen," said Hawke, staring at the forms.

Jeanne said, "Karl ought to be alive. We'd have another lecture on the status of the artist in Russia."

Adam said, "Well, I'll admit the jeopardy assessment smells of confiscation without due process, it's the heavy hand of government at its heaviest, and I have some abstract doubts about its morality. But it's obvious why it exists. The government is a very slow and bumbling legal mover. When you deal with frauds and bankrupts—against whom this procedure is typically used—fast motion is the one thing you need. Grab first, argue later. I think the use of it against Arthur at this point is not only unlucky but punitive. However, there it is, and the question is, what next?"

Hawke said, "Is this all the bad news, now, Gus?"

"All that I know of," Adam said. "I'm coming to my deal with Newton, but that's not a fresh obligation."

Hawke said thoughtfully, "I own about a hundred fifty thousand in stocks and bonds, don't I? Money that I can immediately lay my hands on. There's the fifty thousand Ross offered me today, that makes two hundred. I have about forty thousand in real estate syndication units, but those damned things can't be turned into cash. I might be able to borrow something on them, not much. The printing bill, the other Haworth House bills, this assessment, and the Leffer note add up to nearly half a million dollars. I don't see how I can close the gap by borrowing, Gus, and I don't think even the earnings of my next book will get me clear. If Leffer really calls that whole note, I go down."

"I managed to convince Newton of that," Adam said. "If you agree to certain conditions, he's not going to call the note. The conditions are stiff."

"All right," Hawke said. "Let's hear them."

Adam again carefully removed from the folder three sets of clipped sheets in blurry carbon-copy typing, and handed a set to Hawke, and another to Jeanne. *Memorandum of Proposed Agreement Between Y. Hawke and von Fisken Fabrik, Incorporated,* was the heading on the first page. Jeanne found the legal language hard going, but she saw Hawke turn the sheets rapidly. Then he said, calmly enough but with an edge in his voice that hurt her, "Well, this is kind of stiff, at that. On the whole I guess it's acceptable."

Adam said, "It's not unlike a Chapter Eleven arrangement, Arthur. Of course we're going to have to clear your other debts before we go into this. A special arrangement with one creditor while you're insolvent is a statutory act of bankruptcy."

"Well, then, Gus, I don't see daylight. If I pay the printer and the jeopardy assessment that more than cleans me of cash. I haven't got the seventy-five thousand for Newton that this calls for."

The lawyer said, "I think you can muster it. There's Hodge's advance of fifty thousand. Of course you'll have to pay taxes on that eventually. But we're fighting for oxygen at the moment. Always remember that you have a large stake in Paumanok Plaza, and its potential is good. You have

to survive until Scotty pulls it through. Scotty is a cheerful fraud, but he knows this business and his interest lies in finishing that shopping center and selling it. He'll do it sooner or later."

Meantime Jeanne was beginning to puzzle out the memorandum. These four flimsy sheets of paper, she perceived with dismay, were the four stone walls of a jail with heavy bars, in which Hawke would live shackled until the debt was paid. He was even limited in his personal spending money! She flung the papers to the floor with a crackle, midway through the third page. "My God, Gus, is this the best you could do? Arthur, you can't sign this. Why, you're bound hand and foot as though you were a convicted embezzler!"

The lawyer said, expelling a long breath, "You may be getting a little too upset at a lot of legal boiler plate. Have you ever read an ordinary mortgage instrument?" He waved his spread loose fingers at the tumbled papers on the floor, a typical Adam gesture. "In effect Arthur will just have to go on writing at top speed, which he's doing anyway, and not engage in other business activities, which is a damned good idea, and not spend large sums without consulting Newton, which is also a good idea right now. It's a humiliating instrument, I grant you, but Arthur's posture at the moment is not one that will support your indignation."

Jeanne sensed that her nerves were giving way again, but she could not stop herself, and she snapped shrilly, "Where's your indignation? That's what I want to know. The man who's responsible for the debt is that crook Hoag, nobody else, and you seem to have gone to great pains to hobble Arthur, if not to destroy him, and to let Hoag off!"

Adam shot back, "I realize you're tired, Jeanne, and we all are, but you don't know what the devil you're talking about. Withhold your verdict till you find out a little more."

Hawke said, "Here, here. All hands take an even strain."

Jeanne and the lawyer lit cigarettes with irritated gestures that were so nearly alike as to make a comic mirror effect. Adam spoke first after a pause. "Sorry, Jeanne."

"Oh, it's all right. I guess I should go to bed. I'm not contributing anything here but female noise."

The lawyer stood and paced. "No. This thing must be thrashed out. Somebody should talk against it. Arthur as usual doesn't really give a damn about anything but his work."

"Fiscal idiots, us artists," said Hawke. "The thing is, Jeanne, when a man signs a note and it falls due he ought to pay it. If I can't pay I have to take the terms I can get."

Adam said, walking back and forth, "The alternative here is an involuntary bankruptcy proceeding against Youngblood Hawke that Newton Leffer will start tomorrow morning. I sat in his office while he talked on the transatlantic telephone with his Swiss principals for twenty minutes.

Those are his instructions. These Swiss fellows are professional money-lenders, specializing in second mortgages, putting down a quarter of a million here, a hundred thousand there, all over the world, the way you'd put chips on a roulette board. Their procedures are cut and dried. When there's a default they apply the pressure where it'll hurt most. It couldn't be more abstract. The most sensitive point in this picture is Youngblood Hawke's public standing. That's always been their ace in the hole, and they're playing it." He stopped in front of Jeanne and spoke straight to her. "I'll win a bankruptcy proceeding, Jeanne, I'll get it dismissed. Arthur's assets, when you add in the continuing royalties from past work, and the book that's half finished, and the book he's publishing, and the real estate he's frozen into—including Hoag's venture—are considerable. He's in a murderous cash bind, that's all. Of course Hoag's responsible, and in a court his responsibility would come out."

Jeanne said, "These Swiss people are blackmailing Arthur because he's prominent, that's what you're saying."

Hawke said, "Except that it isn't blackmail because I signed the note and owe them the money."

"Why did you let him sign the note?" Jeanne said to Adam.

Hawke struck in, "Well you see, Jeanne, it happened to be my twenty-first birthday that day. Gus couldn't stop me."

Adam looked at Hawke, and his eyebrows went up in the clown look. "Thanks, Arthur," he said, and he dropped in his chair.

The two men did pencil and paper work for a while, and determined that Hawke was about twenty thousand dollars short of what he needed to clear all his debts and pay the first Leffer installment. Adam said that wasn't going to be a problem; he could arrange a twenty-thousand-dollar loan. Jeanne began to press him suspiciously; if Hawke's situation was as bad as Adam said, who would lend the money, and on what security? At last the lawyer said that he intended to put up some stocks of his own as collateral. They were just lying in a bank vault, and it made no difference to him. Hawke protested, saying he'd go to Hodge for a higher advance or even sell the paperback rights of *Evelyn* to Givney for fifteen thousand dollars.

"That's silly," Adam said. "I'm being purely selfish here. Once you're out of this hole I intend to hit you with one of the biggest legal fees on record. I'm protecting my investment."

"I see," Hawke said. "You're a greedy vulture, and that's why you want to secure a note of mine that nobody in his right mind would touch at the moment."

"Exactly."

There was quiet in the room while Jeanne picked off the floor the sheets she had thrown down. She said to Adam, "Arthur has known all along that I'm a shrew, and now you do."

Adam said, "Well, I hope I gave as good as I got."

"All right," Hawke said. "Before we close with a benediction, there are two things in the agreement that are out of the question. They must be changed or Leffer can take me to bankruptcy court."

Adam picked up his copy of the agreement. "Shoot."

Hawke said, "Page three paragraph 15 sub A. '*Hawke agrees to complete his new novel, Boone County, within six months.*' I can't do it."

Adam nodded. "I asked for a year. I told Newt there might be trouble on that one. What's your earliest possible date?"

Hawke lay back in the armchair with a hand over his eyes, lolling wearily. After a while the antique clock on the mantelpiece broke the silence by striking midnight, in long slow tolling bell-sounds. He sat up. "If I go on the emergency routine, and if I have a reasonable escape clause for serious illness and so forth, I can and I will deliver this novel on the fifteenth of June. Eight months."

"You can't," Jeanne said. "Not from what you've told me. You're working now as fast as you possibly can, and the end's a year away."

Hawke smiled at her. "Now? Now I'm coasting. I wrote the second two hundred thousand words of *Oblivion* in five months, and I did some bulldozing too, for grocery money. The real problem's the revision. After the Judd review I think I'm bound to do this one all alone, Jeanie, for your sake as well as mine."

"Oh, God, to hell with Judd."

"No, I'll do this one alone. Ross will publish exactly what I turn in. That will take care of that."

Adam made a note on his sheet. "June fifteenth. We'll get that point, since we have to. What else?"

"This provision here that I give my manuscript now to Leffer, and send him more pages as I write them. I've never let an incomplete manuscript out of my hands in my life, except to Jeanie. I can't agree to that."

"That's an absolute must, straight from Switzerland. Physical possession of the manuscript."

"Christ, they've got every cent it can possibly earn tied up, Gus! Isn't that enough?"

"No. To put it bluntly, Arthur, in case you die the unfinished last manuscript of Youngblood Hawke will be a valuable property. They don't want merely a legal claim on it. They want possession of it. The deal will break on that point."

Hawke looked to Jeanne. "I have to give them the manuscript," he said wonderingly. "How will I work?"

Adam said, "Newton suggests you photostat what you've got and then either keep carbon copies or photostats of the rest as you write it."

Hawke said, "I guess I can work from photostats. Do you know, Gus, if I had a wife it would be no harder for me to deliver her to the bed of

another man than it's going to be to give Leffer my yellow pages of *Boone County?*"

"Well, you speak as a bachelor. This has to be, Arthur."

"Yes, I speak as a bachelor." Hawke slumped in his chair, and for the first time that evening he looked like a fighter who was losing.

Adam stood and began putting papers away in his briefcase. "We all need sleep badly. Don't ever forget, Arthur, that this is a temporary thing, a counsel of desperation, coming out of a run of very bad luck. If that rascal Scotty gets the big lease and refinances the second mortgage, or if your *Evelyn Biggers* becomes a real success, as I still think it may, or any event comes along that gives you cash relief, we'll wash this thing out and you'll be free as air. And you'll get back the manuscript."

"Just tell little Newton," said Hawke, "that if anything happens to my manuscript while it's in his possession, small as he is, I'll beat him into raspberry jam."

Adam put on his tie and jacket, and took up his briefcase. "Well, Jeanne, thanks again for those tacos." He looked at her, head cocked to a side. She slouched on the ottoman, her face clouded. "Are you satisfied, now? I'm not the world's best lawyer. If I tell Newton tomorrow that Arthur's getting another lawyer to negotiate a different settlement, I imagine he'll grant a week's grace for that."

Hawke said, "Don't be ridiculous, Gus. I'll be at Leffer's office at nine." He walked with Adam to the elevator.

When he returned Jeanne was splashing whiskey into two glasses. She said, "Have a slug for a nightcap? It's routine for me. I'm trying to get by without the sleeping pills."

They sat side by side on the couch, drinking straight whiskey. Jeanne had turned out the lamp that illumined the picture of Karl, and the room was restfully dim. Hawke said after a while, "Here we are, more or less back where we were that first Christmas Eve, after the Prince party. Remember?"

"I remember. A few things have intervened."

Hawke said, "Time for the man to show up hammering at the door for his prostitute."

Jeanne laughed sombrely.

Hawke said, "I think he damn near ruined two lives, you know? I'm glad I threw him down the stairs, and I'm only sorry I didn't kill him."

"He didn't ruin anything. If I couldn't win you away from an old vamp like Frieda there was something wrong with me, or you, or both of us, at the time." She drank. "What are you going to do? Will you still come to California?"

Hawke sat with his elbows on his knees, pondering. "No, I hardly think so. Not now. The emergency routine is tight. It requires isolation.

I think my answer's going to be the same as yours, after all. Home to mama."

Jeanne said desolately, "Hovey?"

Hawke nodded. "The old upstairs room in mama's house. This is a regime that turns night into day, Jeanne. It's a torpedo run, you commit yourself to it and you must keep going. Hovey's the only place. I'm just old Art Hawke there, and all this business about my writing books is sort of a joke. As for mama, she leaves me alone except at meals, and then her drivelling is sort of peaceful, like the babble of a brook."

Jeanne could not help laughing. "Well, but this is awful. You mean we're not to see each other until—when? June? My God."

"Jeanie, darling, I wish we could get married tomorrow and never leave each other's sight again. But a man trying to scribble his way out of a bankruptcy is no fit bridegroom, and anyway—"

She said softly, "Wait, wait. Hold on now. That was a big leap. Who was talking about marriage? I never said a word about marriage."

He said, "I didn't intend to. It's the wrong time to talk about it, the wrong place, the wrong everything, but we will get married, won't we? As soon as we can? As soon as we've both dug out of our cave-ins?"

She looked at him for a long time, with a strange stern expression that at last softened into a faint smile. "Well, don't keel over with astonishment, but I'm going to accept that beautiful proposal. Only on an abstract basis. Like your agreement with the Swiss moneylenders. Don't kiss me or anything. I'm not up to any more emotions, joyful or sad."

"What's there to kiss about?" Hawke said.

Jeanne yawned luxuriously. "Do you know something? I'm going to sleep tonight without a pill. I can feel it. Go home."

"Sure." Hawke downed his drink and put on his jacket.

"This isn't goodbye, is it?" she said through another yawn. "I mean you won't be going to Hovey for a few days, will you?"

"Certainly not."

She walked with him to the door, holding his hand. "I feel awful about this ordeal you're plunging into, this eight-month sentence to your mother's upstairs bedroom. Isn't it possible that you'll send for me once or twice? For an editorial conference?"

"Yes, more than twice." He leaned in the doorway. "Jeanne, all this is for the best. We're going to live in a small house with a small car having small expenses all our lives, while I write the Comedy. I don't care if money pours in like a deluge. No real estate. Not even one share of A T and T. Cash in the bank, government bonds, and you're going to handle all the accounts."

"Well, fine. I'll make us both rich. I have an exciting tip right now on a shopping center."

"Jeanne," he said, "I love you."

She stood on tiptoe and kissed his lips, briefly and sweetly, like a girl at her door after a school dance. "Now go home," she said, and he left.

When he got back to the garret room at Haworth House he went to the desk, brought the Leffer agreement out of his pocket, and read it straight through, though fatigue, and the effect of the last helping of whiskey, made the words jerk and slide about. He impaled it on a spike. He pulled open a desk drawer, took out the unfinished manuscript of *Boone County*, and put it in a neat yellow stack before him, a stack about a foot high. He stared at the manuscript—just sat and stared—until his eyes began to droop and his head to nod. He sighed, pillowed his head on the manuscript, and fell fast asleep in the lamplight, with his long arms circled around the thick heap of yellow pages.

CHAPTER TWENTY-THREE

1

Gus Adam quite understood Jeanne's anger at the Leffer deal. But he could not answer her by telling her the real truth—which was that he had avoided the bankruptcy suit by the merest hair.

One of the things the Swiss moneylenders had wanted was a life insurance policy on Hawke for $300,000, to be taken out and carried by the author until the note was all paid. Adam had laughed at this as an indignity to Hawke—a very bull of a young man, he pointed out— and a totally unnecessary expense. He had maneuvered this demand into the narrowing number of matters still at issue at the end of the bargaining, and he had managed to trade it off for another of Leffer's points. Adam suspected that Hawke could not pass an insurance examination; and he was sure that if the Swiss people ever found out the author was a questionable health risk, they would lunge to throw him into bankruptcy.

Adam knew few definite facts about the author's health. Hawke was closemouthed about this, as about nearly everything else. But Hawke's spells of trembling, his red-banded white capsules, his complaints of headaches, gave Adam concern. More alarming were Hawke's sporadic disclosures of hallucinatory symptoms when he was unusually tired. Several times he had asked the lawyer whether he was carrying any freshly sharpened pencils. This disorder of smell haunted him; it had gotten to be a morbid joke. Hawke during a conference would say, "I'm smelling

those goddamned pencils again. Let's knock off for a while." He had also spoken of the smell of damp, smoldering hay and of dizzy spells.

Adam had once asked him what the capsules were, and Hawke had said they were dilantin sodium, a sedative. Checking with his own doctor, Adam found out that this was a medication for epileptics. He told the doctor everything he knew about Hawke, and the doctor guessed that Hawke had sustained some brain damage, resulting in the formation of scar tissue, from his trucking accident at the age of nineteen; and that lately stress or fatigue had been bringing on either the aura of a convulsion, or perhaps an actual convulsion or two. The disturbances of smell fitted the picture. The doctor told Adam that while Hawke could live to ninety with proper care and medication, he dwelt on an edge of danger; and he had volunteered the remark that such a man was a poor insurance risk. Adam had gone into the Leffer negotiation with this knowledge. Sidetracking the insurance demand, which he had done in the most casual way and almost as an afterthought, had been a skilled victory for which he could never claim credit. Because there was something about Hawke that forbade, at least for Adam, any talk of his possible infirmity.

Adam had little doubt of Hawke's eventual recovery of health and prosperity, once he got through this narrow time. The lawyer was reconciled to the fact that Hawke would sooner or later marry Jeanne, and he knew this would be the author's salvation. Adam had been instantly and violently attracted to Jeanne Fry at their first meeting, and she was the only woman who had so affected him since the death of his wife. But he had been compelled to veil his infatuation; and not merely because she was married. He had quickly discerned that beyond the barrier of her husband lay the famous author, to whom Jeanne was tied in a peculiar and inextricable way.

A promising turn in Mrs. Hawke's lawsuit made Adam decide to pay a visit to Hovey during the Christmas recess of the law school. She had been granted a new trial; as Adam had guessed, the circuit court had made a reversible error of law in its summary judgment against her. This did not mean, of course, that she had any better chance of winning a second trial. Adam was not interested in catering to an old woman's obsession, but the more he looked into the case, the more he began to suspect that Mrs. Hawke might recover some money; especially as he became familiar with Scotty Hoag's character. Adam's young cousin Fred in Brightstar, who had just started the practice of law, had won the reversal with only scant supervision of the appeal by the older lawyer. Now Adam thought—or rather had a hunch—that he himself ought to make a fishing expedition to Hovey for some facts. Also, he wanted to see how Hawke was bearing up.

He had no good news to bring Hawke for Christmas, three months

after the crash of the author's fortunes. Scotty had failed to get the Mehlman lease; it had gone to the Mineola shopping center. Paumanok Plaza was about thirty percent occupied. It had a gaping space with enormous soaped windows where the department store should have been, and an air of failure hung about it, but Scotty was negotiating with other big stores on reduced terms. Even on those terms Adam calculated the center could become a money maker, if Scotty could stave off the collapse of the corporation. Otherwise, if the bank took over on its first mortgage, the three hundred thousand dollars Hawke was paying for the second mortgage would perhaps melt irrecoverably into air. Scotty had a big cash stake in the Plaza. He was putting in more cash month by month to keep it going, and Adam expected that he would pull it through out of pure self-interest, and in so doing save Hawke's investment. But at the moment this was just a hope.

For the rest, *Evelyn Biggers* was the failure nearly everyone had predicted; thirty-five thousand copies sold, and returns starting to drift back. Such a sale, for another author, would have meant success, but Hawke's launching of the book had cost more than the profits on those copies. The critics had been strangely divided. Many had followed Judd's lead in denouncing the book, the printing job, and the author, but some influential ones had called it Hawke's best work, and a marked advance in his powers. Nevertheless it had died in the shops, the big pyramids in the windows dwindling quickly to a couple of dust-gathering copies on rear racks, eclipsed by new pyramids of the season's fiction success, a vast book about the gold rush in Alaska, well laced with gory death and sexual intercourse.

Adam had wound up the disaster of Haworth House by sub-leasing the ornate offices to a fashion designer. His remaining worry was taxes. He was appealing in the tax court both from the jeopardy assessment and the ruling that Hawke's diversion of the play money into the shopping center was "constructive receipt," the Treasury's dry term for a dodge that wouldn't work. There was a horrendous possibility that Hawke might not only lose all the income he had thus fed into Paumanok Plaza (besides the three hundred thousand he was paying for the second mortgage), but might have to meet heavy taxes on the money he had lost! Adam saw no point in harassing Hawke with this threat until a decision came. He had persuaded the district director to withhold a jeopardy assessment for this second amount by flatly warning that it would destroy the author financially and mentally. He suggested that Internal Revenue would be wise to give Youngblood Hawke a chance to recover and pay large taxes another day. The director, an amiable family man and not in the least an ogre, had seen the sense in this; all the same he was trying in tax court to fix the debt on Hawke. Adam couldn't blame him.

These problems of the author were grist for the legal mill, familiar messes,

interesting only because a famous man was caught in them. Adam devolved most of the actual legal work on junior attorneys in his firm. His guidance of the author's affairs was half a hobby. It gave him pride and satisfaction to help a personage like Youngblood Hawke through this crisis of his career; and he also found a melancholy pleasure in serving Jeanne Fry by trying to rescue the author. His efforts for Karl Fry had really been efforts for Jeanne's happiness; and in a way he was still doing the same thing.

2

Hawke was at the gate to the plane, a solitary figure on the snow-swept Lexington airfield, in a bulky red and black checked lumberjacket, shapeless blue jeans, and a black wool cap pulled over his ears. "Welcome to the old country," Hawke roared over the whine of the wind and the plane motors, seizing the lawyer's hand in a great grip and pounding his back. "How the hell are you, Gus?"

The lawyer held his hand and gave him a keen scrutiny. "Well! You look thoroughly rusticated."

"I'm a goddamn hillbilly again and I love it. I never should have been anything else." He pried the briefcase from the lawyer. "Got all kinds of horrors cooking for me in here, hey?"

"No horrors, Arthur. Everything's under control."

"Great. So's everything at this end."

The lawyer thought Hawke looked better: fresh color, eyes clear and unusually bright. There was something wild and uncouth in his look and his hearty manner, almost as if he had turned hermit. He smelled of whiskey, though it was only a little past noon.

They drove up into the mountains in Mrs. Hawke's old green Chevrolet, which Hawke pushed along at seventy miles an hour, and Adam talked about finances as they went. Hawke listened in silence, watching the road and whipping around trucks. He said at last, "Gosh, things don't sound too bad. If that weasel Scotty really pulls through, I'll be back on my feet."

Adam asked cautious questions about Hawke's health, about the tremors, the headaches, the smell of sharpened pencils. Much, much better, Hawke replied; practically all better. The doctor who had brought him into the world was still practicing in Hovey, though he was nearing eighty, and he had told Hawke that it was all a lot of nonsense, nothing but nerves.

Adam asked about the capsules. Yes, Hawke was still taking them. Old Doc Eversill had said they could do no harm. If they helped him get over the shakes they were as good as anything else; probably the effect was mostly mental but what was the difference, as long as they worked? Hawke

said he would take an old country doctor any day against these fancy Hollywood quacks. Doc Eversill had treated every ill known to man for fifty years. He knew the human body.

That evening, at dinner with the Hawke family, Adam made the mistake of praising the mother's soup. He thereupon had to down three bowls of it, to the accompaniment of Mrs. Hawke's great soup soliloquy. Nancy's husband fell fast asleep during the performance, his big bewigged head dropping heavily on his chest, and Nancy had to jab him hard with an elbow. When they moved into the parlor after coffee, Mrs. Hawke made a grand ceremony of urging the guest to sit in the poisonously green armchair, which she called "the new chair," though it was now six or seven years old. Many a time she had growled at Hawke for slouching in soiled work clothes and drinking beer in "the new chair." Adam packed his pipe, and said, "Well! Quite a meal. It seems almost a shame to talk business after that."

Mrs. Hawke said, "Well, I reckon you didn't travel a thousand miles just to eat my soup. Though some folks have said they would," and she laughed uproariously. Hawke was used to his mother's ways, but in the presence of a newcomer they were jarring, and he wondered whether she were not slowly turning senile. She looked the same as ever, perhaps a little grayer, with deeper shadows around the eyes, and she worked as hard as always—she had persistently disdained his and Nancy's efforts to get her a maidservant—but her garrulity and her cackling seemed much worse.

Adam said, "I'm here to do a little fact-finding, Mrs. Hawke, that's all. There's no change in the picture yet, no hope of recovering millions of dollars, I'm sorry to say."

"That'll come," said the mother placidly. "Now that I've got a smart lawyer."

John Weltmann, who was still drinking coffee rather noisily, held up a fat hand. "Excuse me. You are going to discuss the lawsuit against the Hawke Brothers Coal Company. I will go out for a walk and smoke a cigar."

Hawke's sister said, "Oh, don't be ridiculous, John, it's all in the family."

Weltmann said to the lawyer in his heavy Germanic manner, "In the Hovey Savings and Loan Association, in which I am an investment manager, Hawke Brothers is a substantial depositor and stockholder. This is what happens in a small town. Interests tend to overlap and crisscross." And the fat grotesque man rose heavily and waddled out.

Adam started by remarking that Mrs. Hawke really seemed to have no case. "Here's a major coal mining company," he said, "with what appears to be a clear line of title to the mineral rights of a piece of land. Without question, Mrs. Hawke, you were bilked by that old man who sold you the land and didn't tell you he'd disposed of the mineral rights years earlier. Hawke Brothers mined, and they lost money. Or they say they did, and

your accountant confirmed it. Years later you popped up, having stumbled on an abandoned tunnel in the wilderness, and claimed old Mr. Crewes had sold you that land. All they could do was sympathize. They had documents of record showing that John Crewes had sold them the mineral rights first."

"That old rascal signed his name with an X to his dying day. He was just as dishonest as he was ignorant," said Mrs. Hawke.

The lawyer opened his briefcase and pulled out a folder. "There was, of course, the quitclaim Judge Crain had bought for you for five dollars, on a moribund senior patent, but the title report of their lawyer indicated this had no legal standing since Crewes had perfected his title under the junior patent by adverse possession."

Mrs. Hawke, wrinkling her nose and her forehead, said, "I always get lost when you lawyers start using language like that. Is it important for me to understand it?"

The lawyer laughed. "Not very. All I'm getting at is that their case seemed foolproof, Mrs. Hawke, and your claim just one of these very commonplace nuisance things, if you'll forgive me, just a family grudge." Mrs. Hawke tossed her head and sniffed. "But once I got to know Scott Hoag, a couple of things began to puzzle me. First of all, he did offer you, at the very outset, a thousand dollars. That was a decent and generous thing to do. The trouble is, Scotty is neither decent nor generous. He's a manipulator. Such people don't part with money except for compelling reasons. Generosity has no meaning for them, it's just a useful pose sometimes. The question is, why did Hoag need to strike that pose, when he already had a sound legal case?"

"I told you!" Mrs. Hawke shouted at her son, shaking her finger under his nose. "I *told* you, when that Lexington lawyer said Scott Hoag was being Santa Claus, that there was something fishy. Mr. Adam, I hope to die if I wouldn't have taken that thousand dollars, if that fellow hadn't said what he did about Santa Claus. *Santa Claus!*"

Adam said that the second peculiar fact was the offer, three years later, of twenty thousand dollars to settle the lawsuit, in order to clear the title on the whole ridge, for a sale to a West Virginia land investment company. Again, he said, this might have been a wise thing to do, except that Scotty Hoag was most unlikely to pay out that kind of money. Adam's assistant, checking back on the offer through a lawyer with whom he corresponded in West Virginia, had learned that, at the time the offer was made, Hoag had been a partner in the building of a motor court outside Wheeling. One of the other partners had been a man named Coffman, the same man who had written the letter offering to buy all of Frenchman's Ridge if the lawsuit with Mrs. Hawke could be settled.

"Ha!" said Mrs. Hawke to her son. "I smelled *that* rat, too, didn't I?

That offer was a fake! You remember how riled you got when I wouldn't mail him that contract? Why, you were ready to tear me to pieces!"

Adam said, "Mrs. Hawke, I don't know that the offer wasn't bona fide. Coffman might have learned about Frenchman's Ridge through meeting Scotty in that deal."

"It was a fake," said Mrs. Hawke. "Fake as a wax apple."

The lawyer said he was trying to learn all he could about the Eleanor Coal Company, and about the accounting Mrs. Hawke had received which showed that the mine had lost money. He had come to Hovey just to see what he could stumble on. He was going back to Lexington tomorrow night to meet with Webber, although he was losing hope that he would get information that way.

Mrs. Hawke said, "They'll tell you nothing. They're a pack of bad men with bad consciences, and that white-headed old liar in Lexington is the worst of the lot, except Scotty Hoag. Santa Claus!"

Nancy said, "If Mr. Adam wants to dig around for dirt on Hawke Brothers, mama, maybe Phyllis Trosper is somebody he should talk to."

The mother nodded. "It's a thought."

Adam said, "I see. And who is Phyllis Trosper?"

Mrs. Hawke simpered ridiculously at her son. "Maybe Art would like to tell you. Hey, Art? Or is the wound still fresh?"

"Ye gods, ma!" Hawke turned to the lawyer. "Phyllis Trosper was Phyllis Hicks, the belle of Hovey High, Gus, the girl I was mad for. I kept sending lousy sonnets to her, until I finally realized she was showing them around for laughs. God, she was beautiful. She's a matron with three chins. I see her hauling kids and groceries around town."

Mrs. Hawke said, "Yes, and she's complained many a time to me about the way you high-hat your old friends. That's no way, Art, just because you're a famous writer."

"Ma, I've got work to do, Phyllis ought to understand that."

Adam broke in patiently, "May I ask what the belle of Hovey High has to do with Hawke Brothers?"

Mrs. Hawke said, "Oh, why, she was Will Hawke's secretary for years, that's all, and when Scotty Hoag and Glenn took over she left, and she was sore as a boil for some reason. Claimed she wasn't treated fair."

Nancy said, "Actually she was having babies one after another, and they were right to let her go. Phyllis is sort of a pill."

At this moment John Weltmann came plodding heavily in, and the conversation stopped. He looked around and said, "If I am interrupting I will go out."

Adam shrugged. "I'm finished. We're just chatting."

Weltmann dropped into a chair with a loud creak of old wood. The two women went to do the dishes. Nancy whispered at the men, turning with a mad gleam as she followed her mother out, "Millions! Millions!"

Weltmann glanced after them to the kitchen, and dropped his voice. "As I say, I don't mix in the family's affairs. But as long as your attorney is here, Arthur, let me make an exception and ask a question. In this town there's been a rumor that the New York papers say you're in financial trouble, maybe bankrupt. Is there any truth in it?"

Hawke frowned sullenly at his brother-in-law and at Adam. The lawyer said, "Arthur is overextended in investments. He's had to retrench. I believe that he's not in any long-range trouble."

Weltmann nodded. His big head kept nodding as though he lacked the power to stop it. Then it did stop with a jerk. He grinned at Hawke, a wide-mouthed idiotic grin, and said with an emphatic downward move of his extended fat thumb and forefinger, "I am interested in buying the second mortage of the Paumanok Plaza Shopping Center in Floral Gardens, Long Island."

The very sound of the name was startling. This was the first time anybody in the family had referred to Hawke's grand disaster. He had never talked about his investments with any of them. He said, "What do you know about it, John?"

It developed that Weltmann knew a great deal about it. He was a steady investor in real estate syndicates, and corresponded all the time with brokers and syndicators around the country. His favorite areas, he said, were California, Arizona, and the New York suburbs. Scott Hoag had approached him on several deals, but he had investigated and steered clear of the man. He considered Hoag a clever fellow and a fair builder, but slovenly and reckless in financing, and not exactly reliable in his statements. Hawke and Adam both smiled at the description. Hawke said, "What you mean is, John, Scotty's the biggest liar that ever came out of the state of Kentucky."

Weltmann said earnestly, "Well, that is a statement that takes in a lot of liars." When they both roared with laughter he seemed astonished, and grinned like a frog, and added, "But Kentucky is no different from the other states. It is merely bigger than some."

Hawke said, "What do you want with that second mortgage? It's a straight Scott Hoag venture, that plaza, and right now it's losing money."

"I believe the mortgage will be good."

"It's for three hundred thousand dollars."

"I am aware of the amount."

Hawke studied his ugly brother-in-law, the pasty, jowly, heavy-eyed man with the preposterous rich brown wig that stopped short at a line of white hairless skin. The Weltmanns lived in an old frame house two blocks away, not much larger than his mother's and very sparely furnished, and the man wore a cheap shapeless old gray suit. "John, since we're nosing into each other's affairs, *can* you swing three hundred thousand dollars in cash?"

The brother-in-law said, "As I told you when I proposed to Nancy, my net worth was then seventy-eight thousand dollars. It is now five hundred forty-seven thousand dollars, most of it in negotiable securities. I also have some real estate. I have been fortunate in real estate."

Hawke said, "Fortunate! For Christ's sake! What have you been in?"

Weltmann said, nodding, "Shopping centers, garages, private hospitals, garden apartments, motor courts, the usual things. I am offered many deals. I once figured that I participate in one deal out of about fifty. But I analyze every deal to the bottom. My arithmetic is good. I have been burned several times, but I'm willing to dig for the facts. It takes a lot of time and it's stupid work, I suppose, but it's what I do."

Adam said to Hawke, "You see, he doesn't waste time writing novels."

The brother-in-law slowly grinned at the lawyer, his mouth widening until his head seemed about to split horizontally. "That is true. I don't waste time writing novels. That is a very good joke."

Hawke said, "You've undoubtedly analyzed Paumanok Plaza, then, and you know it's shaky, and the second mortgage may not be worth anything at all."

"Paumanok Plaza is good," Weltmann said. "It may take as much as a year or two, but it's good."

Hawke said, "Obviously you know I'm stuck with that mortgage. That's what this is all about. Would you offer to buy it otherwise? As a straight investment?"

Weltmann paused for a long time. "We were making jokes about novels. Nancy and I are proud of you. You are writing this new one under difficulties. Your mother and Nancy and I all think you are working too hard. It would give me pleasure to stop worrying about you. As I say, I think the mortgage is good." He laughed irrelevantly and foolishly, looking from the author to the lawyer. "Too much mental work too fast is hard on a man's health."

Hawke had to clear his throat before he could answer. "John, I'll be goddamned if I'll let go of this juicy, gilt-edged prize of a second mortgage. I know a good thing and I'm hanging on to it."

Weltmann's big head bobbed. "I thought I ought to make the offer. I mean it, and it stands. Nancy and mama don't know about it. I see no point in mentioning it to them." He grinned again. "Your mother would be sure I'm trying to skin you."

3

When Phyllis Trosper opened her front door next morning at nine-thirty, she wore a low-cut black velvet dress, she was corsetted and rouged as though for a dance, and her hair was done up in pretty sweeps and

whirls. She was quite transformed from the fat small-town slattern Hawke had been absently greeting on Main Street, to a plump living ghost of the high school beauty she had been; her eyes sparkled, and she was in a gay flutter. Her home had the look of having been flattened by a hurricane of housekeeping; it was all impossibly neat, and a great bunch of yellow chrysanthemums overflowed a vase in the parlor. She pressed cake and coffee on the two men, mentioning that it was her own cake, and regretting that she couldn't really bake at all. The cake was superb. She threw Hawke a languishing schoolgirl ogle over her coffee cup and said, "How is it you've never married, Arthur? Too busy becoming famous?"

"Bad luck, Phyllis. I'm hoping to get married next summer if all goes well."

"Oh? Anybody I know?"

"Well, she visited here a few years ago. She's my editor. I don't think you met her."

"Oh," said Mrs. Trosper shortly. "That small red-headed woman who stayed at the hotel."

"Yes, the small red-headed woman."

"I suppose she's from New York."

"Well, she's actually from a small town like this, in California."

Mrs. Trosper bridled. "I suppose she's very clever, if she's an editor, but —my, you went far afield, Arthur. There were an awful lot of nice girls around here who liked you."

"Well, Phyllis, to tell the truth I never got that impression."

"Ha! You should hear some of the talk at the hen parties these days. Of course, now you're Youngblood Hawke. That makes all the difference. Honestly, it seems you were really in love with nine-tenths of these girls, and they could all have had you, too, but you were just too shy to speak up, and they weren't going to make the first move."

Hawke said, "They all were spared a horrible fate, then. Actually, Phyllis, you were the only one who had such a narrow escape."

She laughed and blushed, glancing at Gus Adam, who sat smoking with slow gestures. "Well, you're gallant to say so, now that you know it's safe, but I'll never repeat *that*, I'd die if my husband ever heard it." She spoke to Adam in a quick change of tone, "It's been several years since I left Hawke Brothers, but I'll be glad to tell you anything I can."

He asked about the Eleanor Coal Company. She looked blank. She recalled the name, and also seemed to recollect that there had been separate stationery with that heading, on which she had typed a few letters. Hawke Brothers had had many subsidiaries over the years. Nor did she recall anything about the accounting Mrs. Hawke had obtained.

Adam said, "You do know, of course, that Mrs. Hawke is suing the company over some mining at Frenchman's Ridge, west of Edgefield."

The woman smiled. "This is a small town. Anne Maggard already had

my job when that business started. I just don't know much about it, except gossip."

Adam shrugged and smiled. "Just a shot in the dark." He knocked out his pipe.

She said, "The funny thing is I think Frenchman's Ridge may have cost me my job. I had a run-in with Mr. Hoag about the files, and somehow I was never too popular with him afterward."

Adam said, "What sort of run-in?"

"Well, it was just that he was going through the Frenchman's Ridge files, bringing them up to date, and throwing out reams of stuff—they had gotten awful unwieldy and full of deadwood, he was right about that— but I happened to come into his office and see a title report in the waste-basket. I fished it out and gave it back to him, but he said it had been superseded, and tossed it away again. I mean, I suppose it was wrong of me to argue with him, but I was feeling on the defensive about the files, they really were in a mess. I had far too much work piled on me in that office, they've had three girls doing my work ever since, but anyway what I said was true, Mr. Will was a fanatic about not throwing away records and correspondence, no matter how old and out-of-date, and we had some words. He said Mr. Will had been a fine man but he wasn't running the office now. And I sort of resented that, but—" the woman shrugged and laughed. "Here I am getting mad, and it all happened a million years ago."

Adam said, "This wouldn't be Mr. Webber's title opinion?"

"Mr. Webber? No, it was one of Judge Sparkman's, it had the brown cover he always used. Judge Sparkman did all our title work until Mr. Will died, and for a while after that, actually I guess until he died too."

Adam nodded, looking rather disappointed. "Well, if you know anything that can help us in this situation—I gather you're friendly with Mrs. Hawke—"

Mrs. Trosper glanced roguishly at Hawke. "I guess I've always been on fair terms with the whole family. I just can't think of anything. Frankly I never could stand Mr. Hoag, but I think he's an honest man, I don't know anything against him, and there's nothing wrong with Glenn but liquor and women. I hope Mrs. Hawke gets something out of this, of course. A lot of people do. She's a fine woman and she does a lot of good in this town."

The men took their leave. Mrs. Trosper said at the doorway to Hawke, with a last flare of archness, "You tell your red-headed lady she's got a sincere friend in Hovey named Phyllis Trosper. Hear?"

Adam said in the car, as Hawke started it up, "Well, your belle has a lot of her charm left. I understand about the sonnets."

"Do you? To me Phyllis is like a haunted house, just scary and depressing. She was a flower, Gus, an angel, the girl who turned into that."

"How long ago did this Judge Sparkman die?"

"Years ago."

"Is his widow alive?"

"Yes. She lives in Lexington now. Mrs. Bertel Sparkman." Hawke glanced at the lawyer. "Why? Is there anything in what Phyllis said?"

"Well, if Hawke Brothers got an earlier opinion on the title to that land, I ought to look at it. Maybe she still has his files. I'll be in Lexington tomorrow anyway, I'll try to call her. Wait, where are you going, Art? You may as well take me straight to the hotel. The bus leaves at eleven."

"Let's go by the house for a minute. There's about two hundred pages you can take back to Leffer. I hate sending my manuscript through the mail."

"Sure enough."

On the sidewalk in front of Mrs. Hawke's house, Adam paused, sniffing the air, glancing up and down the steep hill at the old ramshackle wooden houses. It was a gray raw day, filled with the smell of the rotten brown leaves that lay all over the roofs, the front yards and the street gutters. "I don't know," he said. "Maybe I should have stayed in Kentucky myself. I had my Phyllis Trosper too, in Brightstar High. Smell this air!"

"Ye gods!" he exclaimed when Hawke took him upstairs into his bedroom. "Is *this* where you work?" There was barely space for the two men to stand in, and Hawke, crowded toward the sloping ceiling, had to stoop over his desk, which was piled high with gray thick photostat pages.

"Why, it suits me fine," Hawke said, laughing. "I sort of hate to leave it, but I'm thinking of renting a cabin up the road. Mama means no harm, but I just can't take the drivel."

Adam was troubled by the half-empty bottle of whiskey on the desk beside the stack of photostats, and the wooden case of whiskey under the bed. "Do you drink when you write?"

"Just now and then. Want a snort?"

"No, thank you."

Hawke took a glass from the washbasin, poured about three fingers of bourbon, and drank it off. "Doctor's orders," he said. "Great healer, Dr. Eversill. Small town tragedy. Mute inglorious Milton." He stood a wooden yard ruler beside the pile. "Of course photostats are much thicker than plain paper, but still, sixteen inches of solid story! That's something, hey? I calculate *Boone County* will be almost exactly two feet high. Here are the pages for Leffer. Guard them with your life."

Adam was staring at the crumpled black gloves on the desk which Hawke had uncovered by picking up the manila folder of pages. Hawke laughed. "Yes, they're the same ones. The ones you picked out of the gutter. They still have a trace of her perfume, d'you know?"

"What do you hear from her, Arthur?"

"Her letters get more cheerful all the time. She says she's turned into

a vegetable and is seriously thinking of staying one. Jim's gaining weight and is all brown. California was obviously a good idea."

"Well, with that talisman before you I'm sure you're writing a great novel," Adam said, carefully putting away the manuscript in his briefcase, "My last word to you is, easy on the booze. Dr. Eversill may be an unsung genius, but I'm not sure John Barleycorn is a novelist's best collaborator."

A winning, faintly desperate, smile passed over Hawke's face. "It's an emergency, Gus, don't you see? I don't expect to burn alcohol ever again, but I'm going to deliver this novel on the fifteenth of June. Tell that to Leffer. I'm right on schedule, and despite everything it's going to be the best book I've ever written."

4

Mrs. Hawke's second trial came on early in May. Adam rescheduled a couple of seminars so as to allow himself two days in Hovey. He was more concerned about Youngblood Hawke's condition than about the lawsuit, which he felt his cousin Fred could probably handle well enough. Hawke's letters had been getting fewer and shorter all winter. The last one had come late in March: half a dozen drunkenly scrawled lines on a yellow sheet, saying that the novel was rolling along too fast to be interrupted by letter-writing. Adam flew down the night before the trial was to begin, drove from Lexington to Hovey in a rented Chevrolet, and presented himself at Mrs. Hawke's door at nine o'clock in the morning. She greeted him with a combative spark in her eye; she was dressed in a good-looking black suit she had bought in New York, and her best jewelry. He talked a bit about the trial with her, refused the breakfast she tried to press on him, and asked her to take him to Hawke's cabin.

"Who, me? Not on your life," said Mrs. Hawke. "Why, that boy's like a bear with a sore nose these days. It's worth my life to show my face around that hovel. When he happens to think of coming home I feed him, and that's about all the good I am to him. You want to see him, you just drive on out Indian Creek road, that's right straight out Main Street to the south, keep going, and you'll see this cabin in the woods on the left. He's got this old Pontiac painted a horrible yellow out by the road, you can't miss it. If you can make your way through the whiskey bottles and the beer cans, there he'll be, the big money maker."

The yellow car blazed like a beacon, pulled up off the road under the trees beside a pile of household coal dumped on the grass. The cabin was on a steep hillside across a ravine that fell away from the highway. Adam went down the meandering dirt footpath to the creek, crossed the stepping stones and climbed to the cabin. It was an unpainted brown shack, surrounded by high grass and ragged weeds, with a refrigerator and

a washtub on the front porch. An orange cat nursing half a dozen kittens under the washtub stand gave the lawyer an unfriendly meow as he approached through the litter of whiskey bottles and beer cans; there were empty food cans too, sardines, pork and beans, tomato soup and the like, in a buzzing cloud of flies. Adam heard an alarm clock go off inside the cabin as he mounted the shaky porch steps. His wrist watch showed half-past nine. He rapped at the door, and elicited a groan and a sleepy hoarse voice, "That you, Patchy? Half a minute."

"It's Gus Adam."

"Hey, Gus! Is this Wednesday already? I lose track of the goddamn days." Adam heard heavy trampling about, and in a few moments Hawke flung open the door. He was barefoot, buttoning blue jeans over a red wool shirt, and the sight of him gave Adam a real start, because he had grown a bushy brown beard streaked at the chin with gray. Since his brow and cheeks were so broad the beard made him appear very fat. His eyes had a tired, burning look, and all in all he was a savage dirty object at first glance. "Gus, I didn't know whether you were arriving today or tomorrow. Come on in, for Christ's sake." He closed the door, stumbled to an iron-bellied stove and threw a match into a mass of crumpled paper. There was a flare, a roar, and an instant blast of heat. "Gloomy, chilly little hole, isn't it?" Hawke said, lighting a green-shaded desk lamp, and pulling on thick mud-caked shoes. "Home, sweet home, though. Wrong side of the ravine. Don't get the sun but about an hour a day. How about that stove, hey? One day's issue of the New York *Times*, boy, makes this place comfortable in a couple of minutes. I've almost stopped burning coal, it's getting on to May. But *this* is what takes off the chill like nothing else." He splashed bourbon from the bottle on his desk into a glass. "Have an eye-opener, or do my depraved ways disturb you? Doctor's orders."

"No, thanks, Arthur."

The bewhiskered author tossed down the bourbon, grinned at Adam, then lumbered to a corner and got the yardstick. "This is what you came to see, isn't it, Gus?" He set the ruler beside the towering pile of gray photostats in manila folders stacked on the desk. "Twenty-two sonofa-bitching inches, Gus! By God, I called it! Three or four inches to go. Four big scenes, all laid out in my head, and *Boone County* will be written!" He flung the ruler into the corner. "Did I eat supper last night? I guess not, I'm hungry as a wolf. How about some bacon and eggs, Art Hawke style? That's drowned in chili."

"Sounds good, Arthur. I don't have to be in court until half-past ten."

Hawke went out, brought food from the refrigerator, and began cooking on a kerosene stove. He never stopped talking as he moved clumsily about. The book was going well, very well indeed. He was proud of it. He was sorry Adam had arrived on a Tuesday, because Wednesday was when this Negro boy Patchy came and cleaned up the place, so there was a

week's junk around. In the main room of the cabin Hawke had created once more his usual environment of piled books, flung clothes, scattered papers, steel cabinets, and a strangely neat, orderly desk. There was the smell in the room of a big man who was neglecting to wash, although the wonderful breakfast odors of bacon and coffee were obliterating it. Adam saw Jeanne's black gloves beside the author's desk watch, and a new large photograph of Jeanne in a leather frame on the desk; a pensive pose, the back of her hand under her chin, a faint melancholy smile softening her mouth.

He said, "Jeanne wrote me she was coming here at the end of April. What happened?"

Hawke shot him a sly look. "Well, the fact is the mountain's going to go to Mohammed instead, and don't ask me to unriddle that dark saying till we've had some chow. She was coming in February and Jim got the mumps. She was all set for March fifteenth and there was that goddamn airplane strike. I talk to her on the phone twice a week. If Leffer doesn't like it he can sue me. I'm living on about twelve bucks a week here."

"How is she?"

"Wonderful. I think she's all right, Gus. She's full of pep. Hodge Hathaway's been sending her some manuscripts to edit again.— Chow down. The desk is also the dining table, so pull over your chair and let's go."

He ate voraciously, spilling egg and chili sauce on his beard. Wiping himself with a paper napkin, he laughed, his teeth showing big and white in the frame of hair. "How about this beard? Do you want me in court today? I've been planning to whack it off anyway, sooner or later, and I can do it this morning."

"We won't need you today, Arthur. Tomorrow, possibly. Maybe not at all."

"Is mama going to win me a couple of million dollars after all, Gus? It sure would help at this point."

"Well, Arthur, it's not inconceivable that she'll recover some money, depending on the verdict and the accounting."

Hawke said, soaking up egg and chili sauce with a broken roll, "But I shouldn't count on that money in making my plans for the next sixty or ninety days, I gather."

"You can't count on it at all, as I've told you often. One never knows how long a circuit court will take to hand down a verdict, or what it'll be in a land dispute."

Hawke nodded, pushed away his plate, and poured himself more bourbon. "Gus, there's bad news about the book. I can't make it."

"I'm sorry to hear that."

Hawke glared at the lawyer like a mountaineer confronting a revenue officer, all white-rimmed eyes and ragged whiskers. "I've done my damnedest, and my conscience is clear. Not Balzac, not Trollope, not Scott, not

Dostoevsky, *nobody* has ever worked harder with a pen in hand than I have on *Boone County*. I'll finish by the fifteenth of June, all right. My miscalculation was on the revision. I thought I could revise the old scenes and work ahead on the new at the same time. I couldn't. I've poured out this book. It's excellent. This is my best story, Gus, it's going to be extremely successful, and I'll tell you something, even the English is pretty good! The college professors are going to start to fall in line on this one. I've really proved to my own satisfaction that I belong in this wretched trade. But I can't deliver it by June fifteenth. It would be criminal to publish the book in this form. It's all disfigured with repetition, extraneous scenes, the scaffolding that has to be knocked away. I must give it four more months of labor. There's only one thing more important to me than honoring my signature on that goddamned note, Gus, and that is not cheating on my writing. Because that's honoring my signature too, honoring it to the people who buy my books because they're by Youngblood Hawke. Even if it means a bankruptcy proceeding, I'm crawfishing on the June fifteenth date. The new date is October fifteenth. You're going to have to get it from Leffer."

"That's rough, Arthur. I don't think I can."

"Not even if I pay him seventy-five thousand dollars on June fifteenth, in lieu of giving the manuscript to the publishers?"

Adam's eyebrows shot up. "That's different. I'm fairly sure we could do business then. It's two months past the due date"—Adam was half talking to himself—"it changes several points in the agreement, we'd have to revise the liens and—well! The point is I think we can negotiate a respite on such a basis. But this is a very cheerful piece of news, that you have the seventy-five thousand dollars to give."

"I know where to get it."

"Will you borrow it from your brother-in-law? That would make excellent sense—"

Hawke jumped up with such suddenness that his chair crashed to the floor, and he slammed his fist on the desk so that the dishes rattled and the lamp danced. "*Get* that idea out of your head, Gus!" he roared, and he began to pace around like a madman. "I'll be everlastingly damned if I'm going to ask him or anybody else on God's green earth for help, do you hear me? I'm not paralyzed, I'm not sick, I'm a grown man, I've been a fantastic money maker, I think I'm going to be a great writer, and by the living Christ I'm going to be one artist who went to his grave without sponging on any man or woman! I'm not going to borrow from John Weltmann. I'm not going to borrow from Frieda Winter, either, though she sent me a sweet-as-sugar letter saying that she heard I was having money troubles and all I had to do was say the word. I'm not down, and I don't need rescue." Hawke halted in his pacing, and stood with his legs planted apart, facing the lawyer with haggard defiance. He

spoke more calmly. "Ferdie Lax is flying here tomorrow to talk about a screenplay deal for me. I telephoned him last week. I told him I didn't care what the job was, providing I got seventy-five thousand dollars on or before the fifteenth of June."

The outburst took Adam aback because of the raggedness of nerves it disclosed. He said with purposeful calm, "That's a sensible thought. I hope it works out. You understand you'll eventually have to pay taxes on that seventy-five thousand too—"

Hawke laughed, "Gus, I'm well aware that I may be half my life digging out of the tax hole. As you said seven months ago, right now I need oxygen."

"Won't you have to stop work on your book?"

"Hell no, and I'm not selling my soul or any of that foolishness. I have a real regard for movie storytelling, it has some artistic advantages over fiction though it's more limited in the long pull—at least I think so—but anyway it's the director's art, not mine. The screenplay is just one of his tools like the scenery, the actors, the cameraman. I'm a storyteller and I can cobble up a screenplay. Happily Hollywood pays large sums on occasion to an experienced storyteller. I'll revise *Boone* by night and write the screenplay by day. I couldn't do this back in September. I was barely past the middle of the book, grinding uphill. I couldn't risk the least distraction. Now it's got a thundering momentum, and I can pile pages under any conditions. It's a wonderful book, Gus." He dropped into a chair, with a melancholy chuckle. "You know something? I felt terrible last week when I read about poor Quentin Judd. For two reasons. It's awful to think of any man you've known actually killing himself. But so help me, as *Boone County* has been taking shape I've begun to look forward to Quent's review of it. I think he would have taken it all back, truly I do. He was a venomous man, but he had a sharp mind, and he did admire good writing. He put up a real fight for it all his life. *Evelyn* was a peculiar book, and not his cup of tea. He'd have loved this one. Now Judd will never take it back."

Adam said, "I happened to be in Ross Hodge's office when the news came. It caused quite a stir. Somebody said it was the scorpion stinging itself to death, and someone else said that all publishing houses ought to declare a half holiday, and distribute free champagne."

Hawke scratched at his whiskers, leaning back in his tilted chair. "It's a sign of advancing age, I guess. I've taken to looking at the obituaries first thing when I get the paper. It's a hell of a note, in my early thirties, but it's the truth. Do you know something? The same day Judd did himself in, my first editor died, Waldo Fipps of Prince House. He only got half a column, and no picture. Difference between heart attack and suicide, I reckon. There's the first man I ever told about the Comedy, Gus, the first professional who handled my work. Would you believe that he conceived

a hate for me the moment he laid eyes on me? It's true. He barely troubled to conceal it. I seem to inspire violent feelings, and yet I'm a peaceable enough man, even a little on the meek side, if people stay off my toes."

"Meek is not quite the word, but— You were talking about the Comedy that long ago?"

"I've had it in mind since I started writing during the war. Of course it's come more into focus with the years, Gus. All my experiences have been streaming into it. Karl's appearance in Washington was crucial. So was this money crack-up I've been through, in fact the head doctors would hint that I forced myself into it because I needed the information about financial catastrophe, it's such a pervading bass note in American life. I'm ready to go, just give me a breather after *Boone*, just a little honeymoon for two, and I'll be off."

The two drinks of whiskey had quieted the author and put him in a sudden genial mood. Lighting a cigar—Adam noted that it was a long rich Havana—he began to talk in detail about the series of books he called the Comedy. He had never confided any details to Adam before. He talked and talked, with the greatest clarity and concentration, and the lawyer, for all his habitual coolness, gradually became hypnotized. At first he was troubled by what seemed a heavy philosophical preamble; the breadth of Hawke's reading in philosophy, economics, and religion surprised him; but soon the vision of the United States that Hawke was describing caught his imagination. He followed the author's words in growing excitement. He did not interrupt once. In this gloomy, ill-smelling wooden cabin in the Kentucky hills, listening to this big hairy-faced man in a mountaineer's grimy clothes talking in rolling brilliant sentences at a great rate, pacing back and forth, his eyes alight and looking far off, only now and then resting on the lawyer as he made some emphatic or comic point—sitting and listening to Hawke's incandescent harangue, Adam realized that this was a once-in-a-lifetime experience. When the author turned his back in pacing the lawyer sometimes glanced at his watch, and saw that he was late for the trial; but it didn't really matter, his assistant was scheduled to open the case; and anyway he could not have left. Hawke held him in a spell like the Ancient Mariner's. He would have made notes if he had dared, but he sensed that the author would stop talking if he did so. He resolved to write a memorandum that night of everything he could remember out of all this. Adam felt on this morning, that Youngblood Hawke was almost certainly a great man, for all of his extravagant weaknesses, and he even understood why Hawke was used to speaking slightingly of his "early" novels, the books he had written so far. The lawyer's habitual frigid skepticism did not desert him; he was aware that many men could spin glorious dreams in talk that they could never put on

paper; but he knew what Hawke's powers were. If the author actually executed the grand design he was painting now in this torrent of speech—

Hawke broke off, stopped in his pacing, and studied the lawyer's face with a weary, ironic grin; but his look still had in it some of the wild exultation of his discourse, which had lasted almost three quarters of an hour. "Well, there you are. I've left out several of the panels, but that's the main idea, and I could talk about it all day, but I seem to be talked out at this moment, and no doubt you're very grateful. That's what I'm going to do with the rest of my life, Gus, if the good Lord lets me live, and that's what I'm going to be judged by."

The lawyer said, after a moment, "I don't quite know what to say. I don't overwhelm easily, but I guess I'm overwhelmed, Arthur. I hope to God you set about writing these books as soon as you can."

Hawke said, falling into his chair in the loose collapsing way he had, "All right, Gus. This will help you to understand why, with the best will in the world, I can't pay too much attention to anything else. It's an effort for me even to take my obligation to Leffer seriously, if you want to know. I think I've done so mainly because so many artists claim the right to live without conscience. I'll be a dirty son of a bitch if I'll be known as one of those. I've been a racketing dog in my time, God knows, and I've committed many idiocies, but I was young. That's all over. Now I'm going to pay my just debts by my own exertions, I'm going to marry my love, and then I'm going to get down to business."

"Which I'd better do right now, myself," the lawyer said, standing. "That trial's been on for half an hour."

Hawke hitched his chair to the desk, shoved aside the dirty dishes, pulled the yellow pad in front of him, and took his old pen out of the holder. "Each man to his trade," he said. "Call me when you need me."

Adam could not help seeing the terrible tremor of the author's hand as he took up the pen. He decided to pay a visit that same day to Dr. Eversill.

5

Land law disputes offer few openings for courtroom drama. Both sides usually "stipulate"—that is, agree on in advance—the documents and many of the facts. What they want from the court is a judgment as to what the documents prove. The judge has to decide which jumbles of words on which old pieces of paper come nearest to describing the truth of tiresome transactions dimmed and fogged by time. Often the cases are decided on the merits of the papers, and nobody testifies. Adam, however, was planning to bring in some testimony.

He had recovered from Judge Sparkman's widow a copy of the title

opinion the judge had prepared for Hawke Brothers years before. The old judge had worded his findings cautiously and cloudily, but as Adam understood the yellowed document, it gave Mrs. Hawke the better of the dispute. That was Adam's view of the conflicting titles too. Together with Scotty's action in removing the opinion from the company's files, this raised the possibility that Hawke Brothers had committed wilful trespass. In that case Mrs. Hawke might win punitive damages up to the full market value of the coal! Nobody disputed that hundreds of thousands of tons of coal, valued at four dollars a ton in wartime, had been mined from the land; so at this point, Mrs. Hawke's dream of millions was something slightly more substantial than an old woman's folly. But there was a long ladder of "ifs" leading to such a victory and Adam had small hope for it. He did expect that the increased risk of a verdict of wilful trespass might force a swift and generous offer of settlement out of the defendants. He was prepared to seize on this, if he could make Mrs. Hawke listen to reason.

He found his young cousin from Brightstar, in proper dark flannel with narrow lapels, and a collegian's striped tie, droning competently through a direct examination of the old foreman who had been in charge of the mine at Frenchman's Ridge. The foreman was standing at a large mine map crisscrossed in solid sections of red, blue, and yellow, using a long wooden pointer. In the spacious square courtroom there were rows of empty brown seats, and an empty jury box. A fat gray-headed judge in a brown sack suit slouched on the raised bench, in front of a dusty American flag, his chin on his hand, not looking at the map. There was nobody else in the room beside the clerk and the attendant, Mrs. Hawke, Glenn Hawke, and Urban Webber and his assistant. The miner's nasal voice echoed in the nearly empty chamber.

When Webber saw Adam he rose and beckoned to him. They went to the hall outside, which had the slight urinal smell of so many public buildings. Webber said jovially, his blue eyes twinkling, "I don't know about you, Adam, but I'd like to wind all this up today and get on home. I'm calling no witnesses, I'm standing on our stipulated facts, and I wonder if we can't further agree on the points you're trying to make here and have your witnesses excused."

"Suits me," Adam said. The purpose of the mine foreman's testimony, he told Webber, was to establish the change from Hawke Brothers to the Eleanor Company in the middle of the mining work.

"That's no problem, we never concealed it and we'll stipulate that." Webber smoothed the silvery hair at the back of his head.

Adam said, "There was no mention of it in the record of the first trial."

Webber said, "It was irrelevant. Your lady had no claim to the land and still doesn't on the documents, and there's no need to go behind them."

They talked about the testimony of Mrs. Hawke and Phyllis Trosper, but could strike no bargain on them. Webber said, "Well, then, we run over

into tomorrow. Let's get rid of this old duffer and his map, anyway. He can go on all day."

The two attorneys returned to the courtroom, and Urban Webber interrupted the examination. Defense would concede, he said, that beginning on a certain date the pay checks, the mine bulletins, and all the rest of the paper work bore the name of the Eleanor Coal Company instead of Hawke Brothers. He described the tax advantages that had been gained by the change. The judge with some show of pleasure dismissed the foreman and recessed for lunch.

In the afternoon Mrs. Hawke, after seven years of battling, at last had her hour in court. Adam was sorry that he hadn't asked Hawke to come to the trial, because the old lady's performance was fine. The lawyer had feared that she might rant and ramble and fling accusations from the witness chair, but nothing like that happened. When her name was called the little woman in black rose and walked to the witness stand like a queen—a queen who had been wrongfully deposed, and was now mounting her throne after long suffering. She told her side clearly and simply, sitting straight in the chair: her first purchase of the land, the buying of the quitclaim on the other patent for five dollars, her discovery of the tunnel, the meeting at which Scott Hoag had offered her a thousand dollars as a settlement.

Adam said, "What did you think of that offer?"

"Well, my lawyer and my son Art seemed to think it was all right, and I'm just a woman so—I guess I'd have taken it if Mr. Webber there hadn't said that Mr. Hoag was being Santa Claus. I figured Santa Claus wouldn't get far in the Kentucky coal business these days, and Mr. Hoag was doing all right. So I thought maybe I'd better look into it a bit more."

Adam saw the somnolent judge faintly smile at this. He said, "And did Santa Claus ever come again, Mrs. Hawke?"

"Oh yes, with a right smart big bag of new toys." And she told about the twenty-thousand-dollar offer Hoag had made in New York.

Urban Webber was genteel in his cross-examination, as though sensing that Mrs. Hawke had favorably impressed the judge. She made a sympathetic figure, indeed; small, upright, gray, with motherly steel-rimmed glasses, in a simple black suit, facing him with a courageous smile. Still, the Lexington lawyer went straight to his task: to show up Mrs. Hawke as a greedy, ignorant, and irresponsible litigant, suing an important company which had clear title to its land, out of the vague hope, common to petty speculators, that a worthless claim might somehow turn into a lot of money.

He made her admit that her son, a famous and highly intelligent author, was the real owner of whatever claim she was pressing in court; that her son had advised her to take both settlement offers; that she had gone to law against his wishes. The first offer, Webber suggested, had been

a mere gesture of sympathy, had it not, to console her for her disappointment at finding out that old John Crewes had cheated her?

"Well, you said it was a present from Santa Claus," Mrs. Hawke replied, with a glance at the judge.

Webber said, beaming, "I do recall that the meeting took place during
the Christmas season, so that a jesting reference to Father Christmas was
in place. But was there the slightest suggestion that Hawke Brothers was
offering to clear a cloud on its title?"

"Well, I reckon you fellows know better than to admit such a thing."

Webber passed to the second offer made in New York, of twenty thousand dollars. That had been an effort, had it not, to clear up nuisance
litigation on this small parcel in a hurry, in order to make a profitable
sale of the whole huge ridge?

Mrs. Hawke said, "Well, that's how Mr. Hoag put it. I had my doubts."

"Your lawyer investigated that land deal, did he not? And reported it
as bona fide?"

"Well, not the lawyer I've got now. I think I made a healthy change."
The judge smiled again, behind his hand.

Webber went into the matter of the juggled copies of the contract of
sale in New York. She had pretended to give Hoag the signed paper, and
then had never mailed it to him. "You in effect accepted an offer, made
an agreement, signed a contract, then deceived Mr. Hoag by switching
papers, and failing to hand him the signed contract. Was this acting in
good faith, Mrs. Hawke?"

"They say a woman has a right to change her mind."

Webber said with animation, "You do admit then, Mrs. Hawke, that
this substitution of papers was no accident, but a deliberate piece of
fraudulent deception?"

Adam stood and objected that he was asking the witness to recall her
state of mind in an event long in the past, but the judge allowed the
question. Mrs. Hawke said quickly, "Why no, it was an accident, but it
gave me time to think it over, luckily. That fellow Hoag put on this rush
act, upsetting my son Art, who was sick in bed, not even giving us a
chance to speak to our lawyer or anything. I never understood what he
asked me to sign, why it was all in tiny print, these four-dollar legal words.
He's sure one high pressure salesman, he'd sell a body the Brooklyn Bridge.
I reckon he's sold my son a couple of considerable lemons."

Webber asked the judge to strike out the entire comment about Hoag,
and the judge sustained him, smiling.

Next Webber led her to describe her speculations in coal land over the
years, and asked her to list her present holdings. Adam objected, but
Urban replied that this question too bore on the contention of the defense
that this was a nuisance lawsuit typical of small amateur speculators. The
judge overruled Adam. When Mrs. Hawke finished her tale of the twenty

or so little parcels she held, Webber said in his kindliest manner, "And you've been trading such bits of land back and forth all your life, Mrs. Hawke, in the hope of hitting the jackpot some day. Isn't that right?"

"I've always thought coal land's a good investment. I reckon this trial will prove I'm right."

"Just so. You're determined to get the reward for your lifelong coal gambling out of the hide of Hawke Brothers one way or another, aren't you?"

"Well, better them than someone else. My husband was one of those two brothers, and my family has nothing to show for it."

"Exactly." Webber nodded, and turned to the judge with a tolerant smile that appealed to their long mutual experience with such women and such claims. "I believe I'm through with this witness, Your Honor."

The judge recessed until the morning.

6

Dr. Eversill answered his front door bell with the yawning tousled look of a man aroused from a nap. He was of middle size; he had the prolapsed belly of the very old; his face and neck were pink bundles of freckled cords, and his hands were shrivelled and spotted. He wore an undershirt yellow from bad laundering, and his unpressed trousers were more open than not. He ushered Adam through a little parlor where the dust and disorder showed that he was a widower, into a minute office stacked with medical magazines. The narrow open window looked out on a wild tangle of yellow forsythia that breathed a springtime tang into the room.

The doctor settled into a decaying swivel chair. "So. You're Art Hawke's lawyer. What's the matter? Wouldn't Art talk to you about his physical condition?"

Adam said, "I don't think it's a good idea to question him too closely about it."

Regarding him through drooping eyes, the white dishevelled head to one side, Dr. Eversill said, "What are you disturbed about? Art's a big strong young fellow."

The lawyer described the symptoms that worried him.

Dr. Eversill uttered a grumpy little laugh. "I know all about that. Art went to a young smart-aleck out in Hollywood who brought in another young smart-aleck, a brain surgeon, and between them they did their best to scare Art into status epilepticus. Talking about front-lobe damage, and cortical lesions, and brain tumors, and cancer, and what all, to a fellow like Art! Art don't scare easy, but even if they didn't know he's a famous author they should have realized just by talking to him for five minutes that he's an imaginative, anxious type, an artist. What you say to such a

patient, and the way you say it, is as important as the medication. A sight more important."

Adam said, "What exactly is wrong with him?"

The old man stared at him, turning over and over on his desk, with one shaky spotted hand, a blackened brass letter opener shaped like the Empire State Building, marked *Souvenir, New York World's Fair 1939.* "All that's wrong with Art is that he broke his head when he was a young fellow and was unconscious for a whole day and night, and you don't get off free from such a banging-up. He comes from excellent stock, and there's no reason he can't go on to a ripe old age. His father sort of lost the will to live there in the depression when everything went bad for him, or he'd still be around. His mother's going to live to be as old as Methusaleh, and then somebody's going to have to shoot her. I've known Art since he was born, I delivered the famous Mr. Youngblood Hawke into this vale of tears, and by the time he was five I knew he was going to do remarkable things. That child had the willpower of a grown man, and he was so fine strung that he'd shake all over if he thought he was being badly treated or lied to, you couldn't lie to him, not to that child, no sir. Yet he was gentle, you'd give him a true reason for hurting him and he'd hold still better than a grownup. Yes, Art was quite a child." The doctor seemed to catch himself rambling; he threw a self-conscious glance at Adam and grunted. "Art's got a couple of bruises there inside his cranium, one on the left side of the brain and one in back. He's been living too hard, he's got all these money worries, he's been making great demands on himself, and that tissue has been acting up. He's been having auras, and I think out west he may have had an actual mild motor seizure or two, from the way he tells it. They gave him the right medication. That stuff's a blessing as long as you keep up the level of it in the blood. And that's what's wrong with the famous Mr. Youngblood Hawke."

"Is alcohol good for him?"

"No, it isn't good. Lowers the threshold of cortical irritation."

"He says you prescribed whiskey."

"I did."

Adam peered at the doctor, who looked straight at him with his aged yellowish eyes. There was a silence. Then Dr. Eversill said. "Those Hollywood boobs told him not to touch it. That scared Art more than anything. He's not a booze hound but he uses whiskey to get himself going, and also to slack off after a hard session. He never gets drunk, and his consumption is pretty stable. My judgment is that it does more good than harm to let him drink right now. The whole idea is to keep his spirit up. You keep Art Hawke's spirit up and he'll last a long time and write greater books than what he's done, even. I manage to see him once every couple of weeks or so. He looks pretty fierce with that beard he's sprouted, but I think he's doing all right."

Adam stood. "Well, that's what I came to find out. Are there any serious risks in his condition? Anything that can go suddenly wrong?"

Dr. Eversill's thin faded lips trembled in a little smile before he answered. He was missing several teeth. "Brain injury always carries risk. I think any further increase of stress should certainly be avoided. But as I often tell people, it's a damn risky thing to be born, and the prognosis is a hundred percent bad." He held out his hand without rising, in the soft, easy gesture of an old man, and shook hands weakly. "I'm keeping an eye on Art. We think a lot of him here."

7

That night Gus Adam sat at a desk in a dingy room of the General John Hunt Morgan Hotel and wrote this memorandum on several sheets of the hotel's cheap oversize stationery.

Hovey, Kentucky
May 3, 1953.

I am impelled to try to set down the substance of a conversation I had today with Youngblood Hawke about his ambitious literary project, "The American Comedy," on which, so he asserts, he will commence work within the year.

Hawke proposes a series of some fifteen to twenty novels, which he repeatedly calls "panels." The number will vary, depending on how much material he gets into each panel. Unlike his previous works, these books will be of conventional length, about three or four hundred pages each; for, as he points out, they really add up to one vast book. He expects to spend a year on each panel.

In comparison with other literary works of this kind his work will range wider in time than any, and the aim will be different. Those other works (Proust, Balzac, Dos Passos) all had the same purpose, he said: to draw a full picture of an existing society, the society in which the author was living. Originally he had the same intention. But he is now convinced that describing the United States at one point of time, however fully, would be an artistic blunder, because this country can only be understood in its unfolding. He says his model will be the Bible narrative describing the story of the Hebrew people by means of the life histories of certain master personalities, covering a long stretch of time and showing a striking evolution of a national character which yet remains at bottom the same. Hawke has a vision of the American people as a people with a destiny. He proposes to show the country at its worst and at its best from the time of the Revolution to the present day. The great historical persons will be offstage in the books, except in a few panels devoted to politics and to the workings of justice.

There is a heavy content of amateur philosophy in Hawke's conception. He has done an unusual amount of reading in the field. Hawke believes that

modern times truly begin with David Hume (whom I have not read) though the modern note can be found in earlier authors. Skeptical inquiry by a free mind, he says is the note; and the failure of European civilization is its inability to sustain a true skeptical attitude. If they rejected the dogmas of Roman Catholicism, it was to embrace the equally rigid dogmas of positivism, or Marxism or Fascism, with all the old hard narrow certainty. He said the dirtiest word in the world was *ideology*; that it summed up the curse that Europe lay under, and that America had freed itself of. The United States was the land of genuine skepticism, the one land of the naturally open mind; not necessarily well-informed, or cultured, or mature, but open; and this was the meaning of the freedom slogan, more than our political structure. It was a new thing under the sun. The two-party system was an inspired idea of skeptical politics in which all ideologies were dissolved. He talked about the presidential nominating conventions. The circus atmosphere and the clowning were part of the instinctive American urge to deride the solemnities of power and keep their rulers in check, and the hazing every four years of the two men who wanted to be president, the long grinding humiliation of the campaigns, was a ceremonial ordeal that went to the heart of the American view of power.

He said the Americans, to preserve their freedom, had learned to "keep power in solution" in two ways; in representative government, and in the money system. The communists in talking of "Wall Street" as our rulers had hold of a distorted shred of truth, but the money system was so designed that power kept circulating among persons and organizations and never piled up anywhere in the quantity and for the length of time necessary to establish a stable ruling class, a compulsory order, that is, a despotism. America is the first wholly successful experiment in history, he said, to establish and keep national order without compulsion and it is based on a new view of human nature. Our order is shaky, but it is holding. Traditional political wisdom assumes that men cannot govern themselves, and have to be led by an elite monopolizing the wealth and the means of force. This was the politics of Egypt, of Greece (except for the brief failure of Athens), of Rome, of all European monarchies and Asiatic tyrannies. Communism is the restatement of that old wisdom in a fake vocabulary of freedom. The inside-out language of communism is forced by the existence of the United States, which gives the lie to the old axiom that freedom can not work.

Hawke says the theme of his Comedy is two words: "Freedom works." He will demonstrate it mainly by showing all the abuses and inconsistencies that have existed and still exist in the country: the profiteering in the Revolution, the near-anarchy before the Civil War, slavery, chronic political corruption, the narrow greed of the nineteenth-century capitalists, and the great sag at the present time in decency and probity, which will take up perhaps half the work. His work will be regarded as a violent and despairing attack on the United States until it is all finished, and even then what it says will perhaps not emerge in critical discussion for a while, but he believes ordinary readers will understand him from the start.

Hawke talked for three quarters of an hour without interruption, and evoked a glow, I will say a blaze, of excitement that of course is missing in

what I have put down. I have actually left out most of what he said. There was a great deal about American Christianity, for example, to which he attaches great importance, but his notion of it is tied in with Tolstoy's version of the gospels and other writings which I know nothing about. I have probably garbled Hawke's ideas in part, since philosophy has never been a subject that interested me.

His narrative method will be spare and old-fashioned, nearer to *Evelyn Biggers* than to his other books, which suffer from his tendency to cram in too much. The enormous space of his design will allow each novel to be written in clarity and in proposition. Each will stand by itself as a story, and he will publish them one by one.

Hawke's health at the moment is precarious due to an old head injury, and excessive strain. He is aware of it, and is burying the knowledge because he must finish *Boone County* in order to extricate himself from his financial difficulties. It seemed to me that this outburst, this immensely long description of his future work, was an overwrought and erratic performance, however enthralling; and quite uncharacteristic of him, for he is very secretive. He looked feverish and ill in the telling. I have the assurance of the local physician taking care of him that he is in no present danger.

I believe that all those associated with him, myself as much as anybody, have a duty to see him through this difficult period safely. If "The American Comedy" is written I believe it can be valuable literature.

In Hawke's marriage lies the main chance for the realization of what is now only a grandiose and fascinating dream in one man's brain.

8

The yellow Pontiac glared in the slant morning sunlight outside the courthouse. Mrs. Hawke said to Adam as they drove up, "Art beat us to it. There! Will you look at him hunkering around with those loafers? Sometimes he'll spend the whole day here just a-whittling and a-jawing, for all his talk of working his head off."

The author was squatting on his heels, one knee a little forward of the other, amid half a dozen men in work clothes, all in the same posture, on the green lawn in front of the courthouse. Like the others, he was whittling at a long stick with a jack knife. He looked odd among them, what with his shiny blue city suit, his extravagant size, his overgrown hair and his irregular, ragged whiskers, which he hadn't taken off after all. Nor was he chewing tobacco and spitting, as the others were. The fatter and less limber old timers sat on wooden benches nearby in the sunshine, also whittling and talking and spitting. The scene was a familiar one to Adam; the only noteworthy touch was the presence of an internationally known writer among the courthouse idlers. The lawyer could see as he approached with Mrs. Hawke along the sidewalk, and mounted the steps to the lawn, that Hawke was quite accepted in the circle. The talk, whatever it was

about, was flowing naturally, and the big fellow in the blue suit threw in a word now and then like anyone else.

He noticed his mother and Adam and jumped up. "Hey! Scotty and his henchmen are in there already. You better hurry, ma, they'll be buying off the judge."

Adam said, "Well! So Webber brought Scotty down after all. At least he's taking us seriously."

Hawke said, "You made up your mind whether you're going to call me? I can run over to the barber and get these whiskers off."

"Praise be!" said Mrs. Hawke. "Tell him to do it. I've been after him about that for months. If he don't look like the wild man of Borneo."

Adam said, "Unless Scott takes the stand and tells some real whoppers I don't know that I'll need you. I daresay the judge has seen whiskers before."

The lawyer and Mrs. Hawke passed between the tall white wooden pillars of the porch into the old brick courthouse, and Hawke squatted among the men again. He came into the courtroom about a quarter of an hour later, just as Phyllis Trosper was being sworn, and sat with his mother in the first row of seats. A wide aisle split these rows in the middle, and across the aisle, in the same row, Scott Hoag was whispering with Glenn Hawke and two other directors of Hawke Brothers. Scott glanced up at Hawke with a small wave and a slight grin. Hawke made no acknowledgment.

He had not seen Hoag since the afternoon in the St. Regis Hotel when the builder had told him, while cheerfully devouring a steak, the news about the department store lease which had destroyed his fortunes. Scotty looked just the same: sportily dressed, jovial and plump, balder than ever, and completely unworried; unlike Glenn Hawke, whose face was puffy, drawn, and angry as though he were enduring a bad hangover.

The sight of Scotty gave Hawke a twinge of annoyance, an echo of the sinking feelings of the catastrophe itself. Since then he had walked away from the crash; had accepted it as an event, and gone on with his work. He held no real grudge against Scott Hoag. Scott couldn't help his nature, and so the thing had happened. Peculiarly enough, when Scott grinned at him Hawke could still feel the old attractive warmth that had made the fellow so plausible. As he took his place beside his mother, she put her rough hand on his. "Now we're going to give it to them." she said. "And high time."

A few of the idlers came drifting in and sat here and there in the vacant rows during the first minutes of Mrs. Trosper's testimony, with an instinct for the time when a good show promised. Phyllis Trosper, composed and faintly self-righteous, plumply attractive in a white and red print dress, answered up to Adam's opening questions with good voice. Urban Webber rose to his feet with his first objection as soon as Adam asked her to

identify Mr. Scott Hoag, and Phyllis pointed to Scott, saying dramatically, "That's the man."

Webber said in a tone of injured reasonableness, "Your Honor, this is a dispute over a land title, not a criminal trial. Defense is quite ready to stipulate that this lady was an office employee of Hawke Brothers, a rather disgruntled one most of the time, that she knew all the officers, that she left its employ with a violent display of ill-feeling and an abusive letter of resignation which we'll be happy to produce for the record. I would be grateful if Mr. Adam would get to the point with this witness, if he has any."

The judge said yawning to Adam, "There's no jury in the room."

Adam said, "Do you recall an occasion when Mr. Hoag asked you to give him all the files of the Frenchman's Ridge mining operation?"

Mrs. Trosper hardly managed to say "Yes" before Webber was on his feet again, protesting that none of this could possibly bear on the questions of law involved in this case. Adam replied that it would bear on the issue of wilful trespass. The lawyers argued back and forth until Adam pulled out from a file on his table a legal document in a faded brown paper binding, studded with tarnished fasteners. The judge at once wanted to know what it was. Adam identified it as Judge Sparkman's title opinion, obtained from the judge's widow. Thereupon Webber flew into an expert courtroom rage.

He had been practicing law in the State of Kentucky for forty-odd years! He had been at one time or another counsel for the plaintiff, counsel for the defense, amicus curiae, and legal consultant in hundreds of land, timber, mineral and water disputes! He had never in all his experience seen anything like this attempt to introduce a meaningless piece of paper, not legally competent, not legally relevant, mere rubbish from somebody's wastebasket or attic, as serious legal evidence! If this was the notion of documentary evidence in the State of New York, where plaintiff's counsel now resided, he thanked Heaven it wasn't Kentucky law. Webber orated in this vein for several minutes, becoming quite red in the face, and ended by demanding that this waste paper be excluded from the record and that the witness be dismissed if plaintiff's counsel had nothing else to question her about.

The judge listened with what seemed to be appreciation for Webber's voice and gestures. Then he said, in exactly the bored tone he had used before, "There's no jury in the room." He turned to Adam and asked him what the purpose was in offering the document. Adam said that the existence of a title opinion earlier in date than Mr. Webber's, prepared for Hawke Brothers by a local legal expert, and coming to the conclusion that Mrs. Hawke had title, was a controlling piece of evidence on the issue of wilful trespass.

Another angry outburst came from Urban Webber against this chain of

preposterous, false, bald assertions. He demanded to see the document. He took it from Adam's hand as though it were something slimy, riffled through the pages, and tossed it on Adam's table with vast contempt. Why, there was absolutely no way to prove that Judge Sparkman had even prepared this survey! There was no signature on it, just a typed name! It might have been typed yesterday, he didn't know by whom and he didn't care.

Adam said, "If defense counsel wishes, I'll take the stand and testify under oath that I obtained this document from Judge Sparkman's widow and that I haven't tampered with it or substituted any pages, though the condition of the paper is clear enough evidence of that. If defense counsel further wishes we can subpoena Mrs. Sparkman to testify that she took it from the judge's files and gave it to me."

"Say, Urb! Excuse me, Your Honor." Scott Hoag was on his feet, smiling, leaning on the wooden rail separating the seats from the attorney's tables. The judge, who was beginning to peer over his glasses at Webber with some irritation, flipped his hand at the defense attorney. Webber wheeled about, strode to Hoag, and began a furious whispered exchange in which Glenn Hawke joined.

"The crooks are caught," Mrs. Hawke said to her son, who wondered whether it might not be true. Until this very moment it had seemed impossible to him that his mother would win this case. Scott Hoag was a manipulator, true; was he really a thief on a million-dollar scale? Could he have misread a man's character so far? He didn't exactly follow the play over the Sparkman opinion, but it seemed clear that Webber was trumpeting distress.

But here was Webber again, turning to the court as Scott and Glenn sank back in their seats. "If it please the court," he said in a total change to his gentle, smiling manner, "defense is casting no doubt on the able counsel's good faith or on the veracity of a fine lady, Mrs. Bertel Sparkman. We will stipulate that Mr. Adam obtained the document in its present form from Mrs. Sparkman, and that she got it from the files of the deceased. What we don't concede, of course, is that it was ever delivered to Hawke Brothers. We'll introduce some testimony on that point. I'd like to point out that even if it had been delivered, it would be as legal advice, and therefore it couldn't be admitted as evidence. It would be a privileged communication between attorney and client. There is no basis whatever, therefore, for admitting this material. It should be excluded and the witness should be excused."

The judge glanced at Adam, with a sober look. Adam said, "It certainly was legal advice given to Hawke Brothers, no doubt of that, and my witness's testimony establishes that they did receive it. However it was advice based wholly on information from public records, not upon

information obtained from Hawke Brothers. As such I can't see how it's privileged. It's admissible and important evidence."

The judge hesitated for a moment, then said he was going to overrule Webber and admit the document. A heated discussion ensued, but the judge did not change his mind. Webber took acrid exception, saying that he thought it was an error that would lead to a third trial, and that the case would drag on until doomsday. Mrs. Trosper identified the document as a copy of the one she had seen, and the clerk took it and marked it as an exhibit.

Webber began his cross-examination of Mrs. Trosper by producing her letter of resignation. He had it entered as an exhibit, and asked her to read it. The shrill, injured note of the words written years ago infused Mrs. Trosper's voice after a paragraph or two.

Webber said, taking the typewritten sheets from her. "You did write this letter?"

"Indeed I did."

"Mrs. Trosper, what did you mean by this closing sentence here, 'Some day Hawke Brothers will be sorry for forcing me to leave my job?'"

"Well, Mr. Hoag had brought in this Anne Maggard who knew almost nothing, a pretty enough young thing but fresh out of business school, and—"

"You weren't threatening them to take reprisals as a hostile witness in any lawsuit, such as this one, that might arise?"

"I wasn't making any threat."

The attorney pressed her to describe the incident of Hoag and the files. He drew her to admit that Hoag had candidly asked her for the folders; that he had discarded a basketful of papers besides the brown-bound document; that he had made no effort to conceal what he was doing, but had gone through the files in her presence, while several other people passed in and out of the office.

"Mrs. Trosper, if Mr. Hoag had been destroying legal evidence, wouldn't it have been extremely stupid of him to do so in the presence of witnesses? Wouldn't it have been much smarter, and just as easy, to do it on the quiet, some Sunday morning when nobody was in the office?"

"I'm not saying he was stupid or smart, I'm saying what I saw. Mr. Will once said to me very early on that Scott struck him as pretty stupid."

The lawyer asked that the response be stricken from the record and the judge sustained him.

Never dropping his kindly manner, in fact emphasizing it the more he bore down on the woman, Webber led her to contradict herself on the Sparkman document. At first she said that the brown binding was what identified it in her mind. He forced her to admit that such bindings were available in the Hovey ten-cent store, and that she herself had used similar brown bindings on her own office papers. He said, "Then this document

that Mr. Hoag discarded might have been one you fastened up yourself, and not one from Judge Sparkman at all, mightn't it?"

The woman stammered for a few seconds, and then said, "Well, I remember now how I knew what it was. I saw on the cover, when I picked it out of the wastebasket, that it was something from Judge Sparkman. His name's on the cover."

With a little smile at the judge, Webber asked her to recall the exact date of the incident. She refused to name a day. It was in 1941, not earlier, she said, because it happened the same year she left her job. And it couldn't have been much later than March, because the ground outside had been knee high in snow and Mr. Hoag had been wearing galoshes. She stuck to this detail of the snow, though Webber tried hard to shake her. Webber said, "If I understand you, then the date of this document could be some day in March, 1941."

"Ha. I never said that! It's probably way earlier. I said that's when Mr. Hoag threw it away."

"Couldn't it be dated later than that?"

"How could it? That's when he threw it away and it had been in the files a good while."

The defense attorney then picked up the Sparkman survey, turned to the last page, and read the date of it to her: July 15, 1941. He showed her the page. The woman leaned forward in the witness chair, staring with wide disbelieving eyes.

"Have I read the date correctly?"

Mrs. Trosper barely nodded.

"Then by your own testimony the document Mr. Hoag threw away couldn't possibly have been a copy of this survey. Now could it, Mrs. Trosper?"

Mrs. Trosper's eyes began to redden. She said directly to the judge, "It must have been some other time that I saw Mr. Hoag wearing galoshes. He went over the files a lot that first year when they made him chairman."

Webber said very kindly, "Now Mrs. Trosper, you're under oath and of course sometimes we think we remember things and we really don't. In view of this development, do you now wish to change your previous testimony?"

"I was wrong about the snow, that's all. The rest was God's truth."

"Don't you think your memory may be equally faulty in the matter of that document? Did you really and truly see Judge Sparkman's name on it? Or do you just somehow think you did?"

"I'm not a liar and I'm not crazy." The woman's face wrinkled as she gave this hoarse answer, and she seemed ready to cry.

Webber said gently, "Nobody's accusing you of being either, Mrs.

Trosper, and I believe I can safely leave it to the court to evaluate your remembrance of this episode. No further questions."

Webber sat, smiling at the judge, who dismissed Mrs. Trosper, after Adam indicated that he had no more questions. She stalked straight up the middle aisle and out of the courtroom. The scattering of onlookers glanced after her and whispered.

Adam strolled to the rail and said in a low voice to Hawke and his mother, "That's our case."

"That's all?" said Mrs. Hawke, very disappointed. "Aren't you going to get those crooks on the stand, Glenn Hawke and that awful Hoag?"

"They're defendants, Mrs. Hawke. If Webber puts them on I can cross-examine."

Hawke said, "He made a hash of poor Phyllis."

"Well, that was stuff for a jury. We got the Sparkman opinion in the record. Do you have any strong desire to testify? You can verify some of the things your mother said. That's about all."

"Use your own judgment."

Adam squinted until his eyes were almost shut. "Oh, hell. Let's see what Webber does." He turned to the judge and announced that the plaintiff rested.

Webber at once rose, and said that he had not planned to call any witnesses, but in view of the testimony of Mrs. Trosper, he was going to ask Mr. Hoag to set the record straight in the matter of the Sparkman opinion. Scotty took the stand with composure, and sat with legs close together, his hands spread loosely on the knees.

Scott somehow looked to Hawke like a stranger, sitting in the witness chair. His face had a different cast, serious and somewhat grim, under the genial smile, which did not depart. He seemed very eager to talk. Webber's first questions started him on long rambling answers, and twice the judge had to caution him to stick to the question. Scott turned to the judge and said with a helpless upward gesture of one palm, and an easy grin, "Your Honor, I'm a binness man and I reckon I'm not up on all this legal procedure. This is a simple narrative and all I'm trying to do is tell it in the best way I can."

He did not remember, he said, ever reading the Sparkman opinion. There was no copy of it in the Hawke Brothers files. In the summer of 1941 Judge Sparkman had been in feeble health, mentally and physically. He had in fact died in September. He had done the title abstracts and reports for Hawke Brothers for many years, but the officers had decided that they could not rely on the judge's work any more, and so they had ordered a title opinion of the land in dispute from Urban Webber's firm. Hoag definitely did recall that Judge Sparkman had dropped into the Hawke Brothers office one day when this parcel had been under discussion. The old man had offered to prepare an opinion. There was no

kindly way to turn him off, and they had told him to do so. That was all he recalled of the matter. Perhaps the judge had fallen into his last illness and died without sending on his report to Hawke Brothers. Perhaps they had received it and discarded it, since they had already ordered Urban Webber's report. He had certainly not removed the document from a file. He had no remembrance of the incident Mrs. Trosper described, "not with snow outside and not with goldenrod outside." He had indeed spent much of his first year as chairman going through the important files, which had fallen into a deplorable state, throwing out deadwood and insisting on a better filing system.

Scott's manner of telling this story was so open, so cheerful, so good-humored that Hawke found it hard to disbelieve him, even knowing the man's mendacity as he did. Hawke was certain that the judge would take Scott's word, and he himself wasn't sure what the truth was. His mother had no such doubts. She muttered to him at one point, "Did you ever in your born days see such a liar?"

Adam's first question in cross-examining was, "Mr. Hoag, the Eleanor Coal Company made a great deal of money, didn't it?"

Urban Webber was on his feet objecting before all the words were out of Adam's mouth. Direct examination had dealt only with the question of the Sparkman opinion. Counsel had to limit himself to that topic. The plaintiffs were suing for an accounting and weren't entitled to one until the court awarded it to them, and here was counsel trying to get his accounting in a cross-examination in open court.

Adam mildly replied that the testimony on the Sparkman report went to the issue of wilful trespass, and he was seeking to establish the motive of the trespass. The judge hesitated and then overruled Webber, who took exception sharply.

Scotty replied that he had been in perhaps a hundred complicated business transactions since 1943 and didn't carry the balance sheets of all of them in his head.

Adam said, "You've called yourself a business man. You don't have any recollection of the outcome of an operation involving the mining of several hundred thousand tons of coal?"

"Well, this Eleanor Coal Company was just some kind of bookkeeping arrangement as I recall it, that Urb Webber there dreamed up, just a legitimate way of lowering taxes on officials' salaries or something. I'm not a paper shuffler and never have been, I leave all that to you legal gentlemen."

"Did it lose money?"

"I just don't know offhand. You'd have to unscramble all the figures. It's an accounting job and like my attorney said I'm not prepared to give you one here and now, I'm sorry."

Adam said to the judge, "I believe the witness is being evasive."

The judge leaned forward, clasping his hands before him. "Mr. Hoag, if you know whether or not this Eleanor Coal Company was a profitable operation, answer the question." The voice was business-like and quite dry.

Scotty glanced at the judge's face. "Well, to my best recollection it ended in the black, Your Honor."

Adam said, "You told Mrs. Hawke and Mr. Arthur Hawke that Hawke Brothers lost a fortune on the Frenchman's Ridge mine, didn't you?"

"We did. We ended a quarter of a million in the hole."

"Oh. You're very clear on that particular recollection."

"A binness man don't forget a licking like that. Maybe a lawyer would."

"You didn't mention to them, did you, that another company of yours took over the operation, mined a vast amount of coal, and ended up in the black?"

"I don't know offhand at what point the bookkeeping shifted over to this Eleanor binness. These folks are trying to claim a small pie-shaped parcel on that ridge. There was no question ever in our minds that we owned all the mineral rights to the rest of the ridge and that parcel too. We had title and it never crossed my mind to go into a whole story to them about our bookkeeping that I wasn't even too clear on myself. You'd have to go in those old tunnels or get out all the old maps and figure out just where Eleanor bookkeeping did begin to apply."

"Did you ever tell Mrs. Hawke or Mr. Arthur Hawke about the Eleanor Coal Company? Just answer that question."

"No." Scotty's face was flushing, though the cheerful smile remained.

"Did you offer Mrs. Hawke a settlement of one thousand dollars?"

"Yes."

"When the Eleanor Coal Company or Hawke Brothers, or both, had taken several hundred thousand tons of first-grade coal from the land she was claiming, and the Eleanor Company had ended in the black— you told them that the operation had been a dead loss, is that correct?"

"I said Hawke Brothers had lost money, and it did."

"Did you think a thousand dollars was a fair settlement to this old widow," Adam said, raising his voice and filling it with open contempt, "for a claim for royalties on perhaps a quarter of a million tons of coal or more?"

"Yes, I thought it was fair," Scotty replied in a sudden harsh tone, "because we weren't prepared to admit that we owed her anything."

Hawke stared at Scotty Hoag as the man sat forward in the witness chair, his hands clenching his knees, regarding Adam with a spirited little smile. He recalled Scott's easy offhand charm in that first meeting so many years ago; the kindly, tolerant way in which he had made the thousand-dollar offer, his frank assurances that the mine had lost money. He remembered his mother's suspicions, which had seemed preposterous in

the face of Scott's convincing words and manner, and he remembered his own unquestioning belief in Scott. All at once Hawke seemed to grasp that there really were such people as Scott Hoag, and that he himself had an unchangeable streak of childish innocence.

He had known about the Hoags of the world, written about them, encountered them in business; Givney was one, and there had been many others; but here was one naked and wholly exposed in a courtroom, and Hawke found himself surprised and a little shocked, even at this late date.

Adam was going on, "Did you think the offer was generous?"

"In the circumstances, considering we had title and she had nothing but a nuisance claim and the real owner of it, her son, didn't even want to press it, I thought it was quite a generous offer, yes."

"Did you think you were being Santa Claus?"

Scott turned to the judge with his old affable grin. "I want to cooperate here, Your Honor, but really—"

Adam said, "It's a facetious question and I withdraw it. That's all."

Webber said the defense rested. The judge told the attorneys to submit written briefs; there was some talk about the time needed to prepare them, and then he left the bench. The courtroom emptied. Webber gathered up his papers and walked through the swinging gate in the rail without a glance at Adam. Hoag and Glenn Hawke followed him up the middle aisle, the three men whispering as they went.

Mrs. Hawke said to Adam in a disappointed tone, "Is it over?"

"That's it. Of course the real heart of the case is still in the documents and the law. It's up to the judge now." Adam and his assistant were stacking papers, and the assistant left with two bulging briefcases.

"Well, anyway, you sure made mincemeat of that crook Hoag."

Adam grunted. "That didn't mean much, Mrs. Hawke. I don't like Scott and I took the opportunity to make him squirm a bit." He grinned at Hawke. "I think the judge was quite wrong to allow my question on the Eleanor Coal Company's profits and everything that followed. It had no bearing on the legal issues. But it's not a reversible error. I think he just got curious himself."

Mrs. Hawke said, "We'll win for sure now." She seemed downcast, and anxious for reassurance."

Hawke said, "I don't know. I thought Scott handled himself damn well, considering."

"Oh, yes. I think our friend Scotty once again showed himself to be what he likes to call a binness man. I'm glad I went into the law instead of binness. Shall we get some lunch?"

As they stepped out into the white sunshine of noon on the high-pillared porch of the courthouse, Hawke saw Hoag and the others talking together in a little knot, in the shadow of one of the broad round pillars. Bad men with bad consciences, his mother had called them, and that was

what they looked like; there was something furtive about the lot of them.

"Hey, Art! Can I talk to you a second?" Scotty detached himself from the group and came toward him, waving and smiling. Hawke was already going down the steps with Adam and his mother, who said, "Don't stop to talk to that trash, hear?"

But Hawke turned and came up on the porch. Scott said, "Art, you look right literary with them whiskers. I didn't want to bother you, fella, I know you busy with your book, or I'd have written you about the Plaza. Looks like we getting Gimbels lined up. That's gonna put us over with a real bang."

Hawke said nothing. Scott said, "I'm sorry as hell about Newt Leffer, Art. I never been in such a cash bind in my life, I really feel goddamn bad about that mortgage and when this plaza pays off I'm going to hand you one goddamn big bonus."

Hawke said, "Can you pay the second installment on June fifteenth?"

"Art, I been throwing in ten, fifteen thousand a month just for repairs and maintenance and improvements. I gotta keep doing that or the whole thing'll sink and the bank'll take over, and you and I will lose everything we got in it, fella. You be patient three, four more months and I think we gonna be home with a bundle, boy. Say, Art." Scotty dropped his voice. "This binness here, this trial has been goddamn silly, it never should have gone to court and I still think you and I can settle it. The whole problem always has been your mother, how to make her be reasonable. That claim's really yours, you know. Why don't we try to do a little binness, just you and me?"

Hawke said, "What do you call a settlement, Scotty?" Adam and his mother were waiting for him down on the sidewalk, and his mother was making impatient gestures.

"Well, fella, listen." Hoag slipped his arm into Hawke's elbow, an old mannerism of his when talking about money. "Art, you got no case. I swear to God you haven't. Ask Gus Adam on the level if you have! Urban Webber is dead against settling for one red cent but old Glenn there is getting a little nervous and that's what's working for us. Me, I'm delighted that there's this excuse to get some dough out of the company's treasury for you, boy. Why, the miserable sumbitches, they've shut off the water on me too. That's the only reason I can't handle Newt's mortgage, Art. I need capital right now but bad, and their treasury's loaded, and I can't get a quarter from them, not even at fifteen percent I can't. And me a member of the board! I'm goddamn sore and by the Christ nothing would please me more than to hand you fifty grand of theirs on a silver platter, Art. I swear I think Glenn would go for fifty right this minute. Maybe not tomorrow, but right this minute I swear I think I could swing it."

"Nothing doing, Scott. Sorry." He attempted to free his arm.

But Hoag only hugged him closer. "Art, this is the psychological moment, so help me God. Glenn is nervous enough today to do it, you can have a check this afternoon. Tomorrow may be too late. Fifty thousand, Art." He brought his face close to Hawke's. "I don't think there'll be a cent of tax to pay the way we can work it out."

Scotty's breath was foul. His clinging touch disgusted Hawke. "Forget it, Scott," he said, and shook his arm to free himself. But in his revulsion, he shook Hoag off much too hard. Scotty staggered away from him, tripped on the top step, tried to regain his balance, and began a toppling, staggering fall down the flight of stone stairs in the sunshine, crying, "Hey! Hey!" His flailing gestures reminded Hawke in a flash of the dirty drunkard who had pounded on Jeanne's door bawling for a whore, and whom he had thrown down the staircase. Scotty managed to stay on his feet, with wilder downward staggers, until he was halfway to the bottom of the steps, then he fell and tumbled and rolled until he landed on the lawn in a sprawled, dazed sitting posture.

The whittlers stopped whittling and talking. They stared. Hawke came down the steps, his heavy shoes thumping loud. Scott sat where he was, looking up at the huge approaching bewhiskered man, apparently not sure whether he might not be in for a beating. He was smiling, in a strange way that showed his upper gums.

Hawke stopped and looked down at him for a moment, at the grinning bald man in the green sport jacket sprawled on the grass. "It was an accident, Scott. I'm sorry," he said. The look of sudden relief on the man's face was comical. Hawke walked off to join his mother and the lawyer.

"What was all that?" Adam said.

"Scotty wanted to talk about a settlement."

The lawyer said drily, "I gather you declined."

Scotty had picked himself up and was dusting himself off, while the other Hawke Brothers officers came down the stairs and clustered around him.

Mrs. Hawke said, "How much did he offer you?"

"Fifty thousand dollars," Hawke said. "Tax free."

Adam pulled down his mouth and widened his eyes, showing that he was impressed.

"Umph!" said Mrs. Hawke, tossing her head. "Chicken feed."

Part Seven
1953

CHAPTER TWENTY-FOUR

1

THERE was a telegram from Ferdie Lax at Mrs. Hawke's house:

HAVE VERY EXCITING PROPOSITION INVOLVING JABLOCK FEYDAL
JOCK MAAS. ARRIVING LEXINGTON SIX-THIRTY PLANE TONIGHT. MUST
ATTEND IMPORTANT MEETING TOMORROW NEW YORK NINE AM.
PLEASE MEET ME CAMPBELL HOUSE LEXINGTON SO I CAN GO BACK
ELEVEN PM PLANE. REGARDS LAX.

Hawke showed the telegram to Adam. "Well!" the lawyer said. "That's my plane at eleven o'clock. Maybe I can get to know Mr. Lax a little better."

Ferdie Lax had hired a suite in the Lexington hotel, just for their meeting, and had ordered up a dinner for two, which he immediately changed to a dinner for three when Hawke appeared with his lawyer, around six in the evening. He made the expected jokes about Hawke's beard. The little agent looked sleek, fat, and extremely married; the first thing he did was to show Hawke and Adam a dozen colored photographs of his firstborn son, who seemed to be carrying on the parrot strain in full purity. The wife appeared in some of the pictures. For the life of him, Hawke thought, he could not have picked her out of a line of the tall brunettes Lax had squired down the years; love was a wonderful thing.

When Ferdie broached the subject of his visit, over the shrimp cocktails, Hawke at first could not believe what he was hearing. According to the agent, there was a sudden wild wave of excitement in Broadway and Hollywood over a forgotten early scrawl of his, a farce called *The Lady from Letchworth*. This was one of the seven plays he had written at sea during the war, a crazy antic in which he had imagined his mother striking it rich in her coal gamblings and attempting to enter New York society. It had been a cold-blooded exercise, a deliberate imitation of *The Bourgeois Gentleman*, and it had convinced him that the writing of farce was not one of his gifts. Shortly after the *Alms for Oblivion* novel had turned into a success Lax had read over all Hawke's early writings, and had had a burst of enthusiasm for *The Lady from Letchworth*,

which had evaporated when two Broadway producers had turned the play down. Since then the single existing copy had been moldering in Lax's files.

Lax now said that upon receiving Hawke's call a week ago he had tried hard to find him a screenplay job. Hawke's name was as revered in Hollywood as ever—it was amazing how the flop of *Evelyn Biggers* had failed to tarnish it—but high-paying jobs for original screenplays were becoming non-existent. The present big-money stampede in Hollywood was for books and plays. Lax had bethought himself of *The Lady from Letchworth*, because of an event that was the talk of Hollywood and Broadway.

The partnership of Georges Feydal and Pierce Carmian, after several successful productions, had just blown up with a world-shaking blast, in the course of preparing for a new show starring Irene Perry. Feydal was now suing Carmian; Carmian was suing Feydal; they were both being sued by a theatre booking agency; they had come to blows and rolled on the floor in the bar of Number One, and Feydal, having the better of the weights, had rolled on Carmian's arm and broken it in two places. This splendid quarrel had greatly brightened a dismal spring in the New York theatre world.

Carmian owned the rights to the play they were producing. Irene Perry sided with Feydal in the dispute, but she wanted above all to do another national tour like her successful one with *Alms for Oblivion*, and Feydal's sole chance of getting her away from Carmian—which he had publicly vowed to do—lay in finding another play for her in a hurry. Lax had pulled *The Lady from Letchworth* out of the files and had kept three stenographers up one entire night typing copies. Feydal had now read the play and was delirious over it. Irene Perry loved it and was especially pleased that the play was by Youngblood Hawke. Travis Jablock had read it. Once it opened out of town he would make a pre-production movie deal, with a seventy-five-thousand-dollar down payment. Feydal had taken on Jock Maas as a managing partner to replace Carmian, since Maas happened to be free; and they were even willing to hand over to Hawke their producer's share of the down payment and recoup it later, so sure were they that the play would be a smash hit!

But the greatest haste was imperative. Irene Perry wanted to open not later than the first week of July in Philadelphia, where a summer subscription festival of the performing arts was being planned. Irene Perry's new show led the list of possible main attractions. The subscriptions meant three guaranteed weeks of full houses in a huge auditorium.

This tumble of news dizzied Hawke. He had been quite out of the world for the better part of a year. He had missed the story in the New York *Times*, if there had been one, of the break-up of Feydal and Carmian. Had anybody but Ferdie Lax been telling him these things he would have been extremely suspicious. But Lax, of all the strange people Hawke

had encountered in his Sinbad career through the American publishing and entertainment fields, had proven to be perhaps the most reliable, under his fantastic surface. He had never lied to Hawke. He had gotten him great amounts of money. He had made one or two bad deals, but his performance in sum had been excellent. Hawke saw that Gus Adam listened to Lax with respectful attention.

The fatigued harried author tried to keep down the gladness surging in him as Lax talked. Why, if this were true—if there were nothing more to it than this—he was home at last. There wasn't even any work to do, the play was all written! The grim deadline of the second mortgage installment could be met without bonding himself to Hollywood. After that the completion of *Boone County* would take off the pressure and probably solve all his problems. To be rescued like this, almost in the last extremity, by one of his early forgotten playscripts! It was like finding seventy-five thousand dollars in the pockets of an old suit.

He said abruptly to Adam, "Gus, what do you think of all this?" They had finished the dinner during Lax's long harangue, and were sitting in armchairs drinking coffee.

Adam said, "Well! This is quite a business you're in. If one can call it a business. It makes my head spin sometimes. What about this old play of yours? Do *you* think it has possibilities?"

"Christ, Gus, *I* don't know. It was funny enough as I remember it, but good lord, I was just learning how to write, and I knew nothing of New York. The thing's a wild vaudeville."

"I tell you it's sidesplitting," Lax said, "and if you remember, I've always thought so. The important thing is, Irene thinks so. And Travis."

Adam got up and paced the room. "Let's remember, Arthur, that the inducement here, the goal, is that seventy-five thousand dollars from the movies. You'd do it because you need that money right now. Anything the play itself earned would be a windfall."

"That's right."

"You'd get into rehearsals and rewriting. That would interfere with the finishing of your book. It's not like *Alms for Oblivion*, where Feydal had a huge novel to draw new scenes from . . ." Adam screwed his face up. "It's risky and nebulous. I wish we could sound out this movie man and see how strong his interest actually is."

"Travis Jablock? Nothing easier," Lax said, going to the telephone. He put the call in to Hollywood, and got Jablock almost at once. "Trav? Ferdie," he said. "I'm in Lexington, Kentucky, Trav. I'm sitting here with one of the world's great authors, our mutual friend Youngblood Hawke. He's grown a beard a foot long. Doing the Shaw bit. Now he wants to talk to you about *The Lady from Letchworth*. Trav, Hawke's lawyer is here, a very able gentleman from New York named Gus Adam, and I'm putting him on our extension, okay?"

He handed the telephone to Hawke and motioned Adam to the bedroom extension. Jablock exchanged pleasantries with Hawke in his curt piping voice, calling him "Youngblood" as most Hollywood people did. He said he was dying to read Hawke's new novel the moment he finished it. The word all over Hollywood was that it was a vast masterpiece.

Hawke said, "Travis, you've read this old farce of mine, *The Lady from Letchworth?*"

"Sure, very funny and charming little script. Not at all what people expect from Youngblood Hawke, but that's an exciting switch."

"You're interested in it for a picture?"

"Definitely, once you get the production on. With Georges Feydal, Irene Perry, and the Youngblood Hawke name, I don't think you can miss."

The lawyer said, "Adam speaking. You understand that Arthur is preoccupied with completing this new novel. A play production would seriously break into his schedule."

"Well, Youngblood's always been a bear for work. I'm sure he'll breeze through rehearsals and keep writing his book too."

"I don't think he should take it on unless he has a tangible inducement," Adam said. "Ferdie Lax spoke of a first payment of seventy-five thousand against an escalator arrangement tied to the run of the play."

"Yes, that's what we've talked about."

"If you'll pay the seventy-five thousand dollars at this point I'll advise Arthur to go ahead. Otherwise I'll be against it."

"No can do, Mr. Adam," Jablock said gaily. "I'd like nothing better, but I have the bank to answer to. All the banks who do movie financing these days are insisting on what they call guaranteed acceptance. They'll go for it as soon as we have the first out-of-town notices in hand, especially with Youngblood's name, but until then I can't move. Sorry."

Hawke said, "You do think the play'll work, Travis?"

"Why shouldn't it? Terribly funny little script. I fell out of bed laughing. You're a versatile bastard, Youngblood."

Adam tried to argue further with Jablock. The movie producer said over and over that he liked the play, and would buy it now on his own responsibility for say, thirty thousand dollars; but that an old unproduced farce—even by an author as eminent as Hawke—simply could not command the kind of deal Lax was asking for. Once any kind of public acceptance was proved, the whole picture would change.

"You know what it is?" Hawke said to Lax, as he hung up, "I can't bring myself to believe that that play is really worth anything. Why, I haven't even read it in six or seven years. I don't remember the names of the characters."

The little agent said, "Well, maybe the next thing is for you to talk to Feydal. You trust his judgment, don't you?"

"As much as anybody's."

Lax glanced at his watch. "The hours Georges keeps, he may be just getting up. He's in New York. Let's try him."

Feydal's rich, magnificent voice was shaking with laughter, as though he were in the middle of reading the play, when Lax handed Hawke the telephone. "My dear fellow, it's wonderful. Is there anything you can't do? It's supremely funny and deeply touching, and it says something. You can't help saying something in all your work, even in the light things, the *soties*, can you?"

"Georges, I wrote the bloody thing when I was a kid in the Seabees."

"Dear Hawke, I know that, and it's by no means *Oedipus Rex*, though I wouldn't be surprised if you come up with that next, but it's unspeakably funny, and it will *work*. Irene is insane about it. You will let me have this wildly funny little play, won't you? I *want* it. Now I'm sitting up to my chin in a hot bath, talking to you, and I have a horrid fear I'm going to electrocute myself and I'll never get to do that play."

"I'll call you tomorrow, Georges, or Ferdie Lax will."

"Lovely."

Hawke said wonderingly to the agent, "I'll be goddamned. I think you've pulled the rabbit out of the hat, Ferdie, so help me."

"You're the man behind the curtain who slipped the rabbit into the hat," the agent said. "I just remembered it was there."

"I'm going to think about this overnight," Hawke said. "But there's something you've got to do for me right away."

2

The next day around noon a messenger boy arrived at a little house outside Los Angeles bearing a thick large envelope from the Ferdinand Lax Agency, marked with the quill pen and antique ink pot which was Ferdie's heraldic device for an agency that traded in writers and their works.

Jeanne Fry was sitting in a yard in a lounge chair watching Jim play with her mother's cat under an orange tree. She wore a brief yellow sun suit, and the warm up-and-down glance of the pimpled messenger endorsed her own notion that she was looking good again. She drew the script out of the envelope.

THE LADY FROM LETCHWORTH
A *Farce Comedy* by
Youngblood Hawke.

Until last night she had been unaware of the existence of this play. Hawke had once mentioned to her the seven plays he had written during the war, calling them worthless exercises which had served merely to

prove to him that he had better try fiction instead. She opened the play to the first page, after a glance at Jim. He lay on his stomach, in the shade, making grabs at the cat's tail. The cat, a fat tabby, was pretending Jim was a kitten, and teasing him with swift flips of the tail out of his reach.

Her mother found her in a fit of laughter when she came to offer her lunch. Jeanne declined to eat, and asked her mother to feed Jim and put him to bed for a nap. Dropping the script on the grass about an hour later, Jeanne sat in the sun, smoking and pondering. Then she went inside and telephoned Hawke in Hovey. He had told her he would wait for her call in his mother's house.

He sounded less strained than he had the night before. His voice in that conversation had alarmed her with its weary sags and strident bursts of words.

"Arthur, it certainly is funny," she said. "I've been laughing like a fool. Mrs. Caudill was sort of an early sketch of Aunt Bertha, wasn't she?"

"I guess so, though I didn't know it then. What do you think, Jeanne?"

"Well, Broadway has always baffled me, dear. The plot and the characters are quite shallow, you must know that."

"Of course I do. I'm wondering how much that matters."

Jeanne said, "The play is a curiosity, really. The value of it is in the light it sheds on your books, the faint traces of your later ideas. Even if you can't produce it I think we ought to publish it some day, maybe a volume of those early pieces."

"That's another question. The immediate question is, Jeanne, do you think I should go ahead with Maas and Feydal?"

"What does Gus say?"

"Well, like both of us, Gus finds the theatre a puzzling place. He hasn't read the play but he says it wouldn't help if he did."

"Arthur, this play can't increase your reputation. You have to face that fact. But who knows? It's hilarious. Maybe it's just the thing for Broadway."

Hawke said, "I have to come to a decision today."

"Wow! They're not giving you much time."

"No. This thing's blown up like a cyclone. It'll blow away just that fast if I don't decide to ride it. Irene Perry's got to jump one way or the other by tomorrow. She's ready to do my play."

Jeanne took a resolve and spoke. "Well, for what my opinion's worth, you shouldn't do it. Not unless you're in the direst financial straits. It's bound to be a distraction. If you think it's the only way out there's no choice, really. I do think it could make money. On your finances, Gus is the one to talk to."

"I talked to him half an hour ago. He tried to get the second mortgage payment deferred and the lawyer became hysterical. They'll start suing

me on June sixteenth if I don't deliver the book or make the second payment."

"Good lord, Arthur."

"I'm not scared or worried, Jeanne. But speaking of dire straits, I believe the spot I'm in qualifies."

Jeanne said, "Well then, if there's absolutely no other way out I suppose you should try this. I'm a little afraid Feydal may just be using you as a club to beat his ex-partner with."

Hawke said after a moment, "Leave it to you to think of that. You may be right. Feydal is a wonderful artist, the finest that I've known, all in all. I can't believe he'd lie to me in a professional judgment. But then, I'm perpetually being surprised by the lying that goes on in this wicked world. I'm a goddamned mountain boy and I never will be anything else. I'll have to trust Feydal and Lax and Irene Perry and go ahead."

"Gosh, then you'll be returning to New York very soon, won't you?"

"Pretty damned soon, if this thing is really on."

"Arthur, in that case I'll come back myself. I'm getting tired of sitting around contemplating mama's oranges. Ross Hodge has been after me, too."

"Marvellous. God, just that will make it all worth doing, Jeanie darling. Come as soon as you can."

3

An amazing amount of successful work has been done in mapping the brain. Thrust the needle into one spot, and you touch the gray blob of tissue that sorts out odors; into another, and you prick the flaccid little place where chemical reactions in the eye turn to colored pictures. Here words form; there one feels sorrow. All this can be proved by experiments. The brain surgeon will tell you that his ignorance of how the brain works much exceeds his knowledge. Still, he can cut up a dead brain with an expert analytic lecture, and he can do marvels of healing on a live brain, to show that he knows what he is talking about.

Arthur Hawke suffered from two afflictions in the mysterious domain of the mind. One was his old brain injury, which Dr. Eversill had properly located and diagnosed, and for which Hawke was taking the right medicine. But for his other trouble, which for want of a better word might be called neurasthenia, there was no effective medicine; there never has been.

The symptoms were pictured perfectly in Burton's *Anatomy of Melancholy* centuries ago, tied to an obsolete medical theory of humors, which may have to make space in the lumber room some day for theories we today assume to be true. There are descriptions of the identical symptoms in the books of Greece and Rome, in the Bible, in the old

scrolls of Asia, and on the baked mud tablets of Mesopotamia. Alexander the Great was a pronounced neurasthenic. So was Shakespeare, on the evidence of the sonnets. Perhaps it comes of attempting more than a man can achieve. That would explain why it is an old affliction of artists. The man who proportions reach to grasp is a craftsman. The artist is the ridiculous fellow who takes on God as his creative rival. Sometimes God smiles at the effort, leans down, and contributes a vital touch here and there, which we call inspiration; and so a new work of art comes to exist. Neurasthenia, or anxiety neurosis, or melancholy, then seems a small price to pay.

Hawke had endured spells of it ever since he had started to write. But his constitution was strong, and so was his small-town upbringing, on the whole. He had learned to suffer the affliction without becoming an alcoholic, or a lecher, or a runaway, or a sex deviate, or a drug addict, or a gambler, or a chronic liar and beggar, as some artists do. Not all of them do. That is a popular mistake, which perhaps holds its ground because people both dislike artists and enjoy romanticizing them. There is the bill-dodging Balzac, and there is the Walter Scott, dying pen in hand to pay off the debts of a bankruptcy forced on him by the mistakes of other men. There is the wife-stealing Wagner, and there is the impeccable paterfamilias, Bach. The penalties of art: the hypochondria, the forebodings, the irritability, the passing phobias, the spells of exhaustion, the recurring sense of doom: all these miseries Hawke had come to accept as other people do chronic asthma or rheumatic pains, and he sought no compensation for them beyond the pleasure of his work, and the earnings it brought. He flogged himself through the bad spells, allowing himself no mercy, and after a while they would lift. At least they always had before the writing of *Boone County*.

He had been most reluctant to believe that the new symptoms—the tremors, the headaches, the tingling of his arm, the multiplying hallucinations of smell—were any more than some new squeaks and rattles of the creative machine under stress. His idea was to drive through the book and then indulge in a long rest. He was confident that all the symptoms would at once subside. He continued to take the capsules that the Hollywood doctors had given him, since Dr. Eversill had approved of them, but in his heart he thought it was all nonsense. Underneath the chronic forebodings of disaster, he had a dogged faith that he was going to survive to a great age and execute an enduring body of work. The severity of his sufferings during the writing of *Boone County*, and the new symptoms, he ascribed quite naturally to the extreme demands of the work itself, to the pressing deadline, and to his money problems. Nothing could have induced him to stop working. Dr. Eversill had discerned that, and so had not tried.

Hawke called Gus Adam immediately after talking to Jeanne, and told him to execute the contracts. This decision, once taken, gave him a great lift, fatigued and shaky though he was. He had committed himself to an interesting and unexpected run of events, with freedom from his money tangle as a visible goal only six or seven weeks away. He went to the barber; and with the beard, with the great clumps of hair falling to the old blue linoleum floor, he felt he was shedding the black melancholy that had been with him through his long ordeal in the mountain cabin. His cheerfulness increased as he saw his face emerge from the mask of hair. How young he looked, after all; how young he really was! He had seen himself in this same mirror as a boy and a youth, and the same barber, old Fred Perkins, had cut his hair then; but meantime he had written and published successful books, and the world knew his name. He had lost a lot of weight, and in his pale face the bones stood out, the square resolute jawbones of his mother, the broad brow of his book-loving father. He appeared in his own eyes to be twenty-seven again, and at the start of things. Old Fred, sweeping away the heaps of hair on the linoleum floor, said, "Well, Art, you're not only talented, by gosh, you're a handsome young fellow under all that spinach. You just need a little sun." Hawke walked out into Main Street as though there were springs in his heels.

He went to his cabin and helped the Negro boy to tidy it up. He left his books and the stack of photostats as they were. He planned to come back in a couple of months to revise the novel, and the rent was so small that there was no need to move out. After the boy left, Hawke sat at his desk, staring around at this chilly hovel where he had endured such a long nerve-wracking vigil. The water-streaked plasterboard walls seemed peopled by the hundred phantoms who were the characters in *Boone County*. He had been as happy in this cabin, he thought, in an existence below the standard of even the poor in the United States, as he had been in The Park Tower, or in Travis Jablock's Hollywood mansion, or in the Royal Danieli Hotel in Venice. Driven, anxious, sometimes wrung by spasms of muscles and bowels, often sick, often deathly lonely, he had been happy in the steady dry whisper of the pen and the unfolding of his tale. He had lacked nothing but Jeanne.

He now did something he had never done before, even in the trough of the worst depression. He took a sheet of yellow paper and in three short paragraphs wrote his will, feeling sheepish as he did so, but unable to resist. Sealing it up in a long white envelope, he scrawled on the face, *Not to be opened except in case of my death*—A. *Hawke*, and laid the envelope on top of the pile of photostats under the bronze medal from the University of Kentucky, awarded to him after the publication of *Will Horne*, which he used as a paperweight. He expected to come back in two

months and burn the will in the stove; it was just a gesture of anxious folly. He locked the cabin with a heavy padlock, and went all around the outside trying the windows. As mountain cabins went, it was secure. Thieves were welcome to whatever was inside, except the photostats, and why would they want those stiff gray heavy sheets filled with his scrawls?

He was very merry at dinner that night with his mother, sister and brother-in-law. There was a great to-do over the improvement in his looks with the removal of his beard. He made so many jokes and kept them laughing so hard that the mother gasped at last, "I declare, Art, I can see now why you're going to New York to put on a comedy. You sure are in the mood." He insisted on walking to the Weltmann home afterward and playing with his nephew and niece. He tossed them in the air, squealing and whooping just as the children did; he rode them on his back; he told them funny animal stories. Both children loved this monstrous comical uncle, and they complained and clung to him when he said he had to go back to work. He threw an arm around his foolishly grinning brother-in-law, and said he was glad one prolific male had come into the family; for Nancy was once more pregnant.

She walked back to the mother's house with him in the moonlight. "Well, so you're escaping from Hovey again," she said.

"Nancy, you can escape any time you want to."

"I know. I used to have a devious long plot to make John move to New York. It wouldn't be too hard. But after all I think I'll stick it out here."

At the mother's gate she said suddenly, "Are you okay?"

"Sure, why?"

"I haven't seen you this gay for a long time. I just wondered. John's concerned about your going off to do a play when you haven't finished your book. He thinks you were pushing too hard without that."

"John is a stuffy investment manager. I'm a sensitive artist. He doesn't understand me."

"Look, Arthur, if you get married up there this time, none of this elopement. You ask mama and John and me to come up. Hear?"

"It's a promise."

She said, "I love Jeanne. You should have married her years ago. I love you, too. And I forgive you for writing *Evelyn Biggers* with my heart's blood."

Hawke's gaiety vanished. "Writers are all vampires, Nancy."

"So I've learned. I don't mind any more, though I was shocked at first. At least Evelyn is my memorial. I won't die and disappear."

Next morning, packing up his working valise, he realized that he had left Jeanne's gloves on his desk in the cabin. He would have driven out there to get them, but there was no time, if he wanted to catch the plane for New York. He accepted the oversight as a good omen. The gloves would draw him back in a very short time, bringing Jeanne.

4

"Many lights," said Jim, pointing with forefinger and straight thumb at the blaze of night-time New York through the window of the bumping airplane.

"Yes, darling, lots and lots of lights." Jeanne was watching his face nervously for the sweaty forehead and the sudden pallor that meant he would throw up, but Jim seemed happy, and fascinated by the descent.

Indeed the lights were something to see. It was about an hour after sundown. The clear starry shell of the sky still held a purplish glow of twilight, arching over the golden radiance of the city; and set low in the shell there was a crescent moon, and one bright planet. Surely this was the best time to come back to New York, and the best way! How beautiful this immense black and gold carpet was under the moon, with lights winking in the dark places like diamonds as the plane soared along, and crooked rivers of headlights flowing on the main streets and highways, and fantastic towers of black studded with gold standing out against the purple sky! It was really her childhood vision of New York, the magic place where fortunes lay piled for the taking and all the handsome, beautiful, clever people lived and did grand things, the race of graceful demigods who resembled her small-town neighbors only in their human form. The vision had its truth, Jeanne thought, though the truth was partial. New York was a dirty and murderous place, but it was golden too. She had been through too much in the city, she had rejected or violently edited too many second-rate manuscripts about its slum miseries, and too many trivial books about its decadent upper-crust luxuries, to be able to view the sight with a fresh eye, even after an absence of almost a year. Let Jim enjoy the lights. She settled back for a last cigarette before the warning signal.

Hawke and Adam saw her awkwardly come down the steps of the plane, with Jim on one arm and a swinging leather hatbox in the other hand. Jim seemed twice as big as before, a boy quite old enough to walk off a plane with those long legs, but Jeanne staggered along with him and the hatbox. She was dressed in green wool, slim and looking very sunburned even in the dismal light of the ramp. They both called to her, and Jeanne's face brightened with her peculiar smile, at once sweet and somewhat tartly mischievous, which Hawke had never seen on any other woman's face, and which he thought the loveliest smile there could be.

"Hi, Gus!" she cried. "You here too? Great."

She put down Jim and the box and embraced Hawke heartily and swiftly, kissing his mouth. "Hello, darling. Gad, it's warmer here than in California." She shook hands with Adam, and with a little hesitation and

a swift peck, kissed his cheek. She dived at Jim, who was rapidly walking off in the crowd. "Come back here, you! Honestly, thirty seconds and he's out of sight."

Hawke said she looked marvellous. With a keen glance at him she said he looked all right, but not exactly as though he were on vacation. He laughed. "Just putting on a Broadway show and finishing a novel at the same time," he said. "Nothing strenuous like taking care of Jim."

Driving in from the airport, Hawke explained that he had asked Adam to come along and settle her into her apartment. He had to go straight to the theatre, due to a major crisis. "Something about casting," he said wearily. "Don't ask for details. How wise I was to dodge the *Alms for Oblivion* production! It went on without me and did very well. This one has four crises per day that will prove insurmountable and will sink the whole show if the author fails to come at once. That's aside from the rewriting."

Adam said, "The play was perfect as it stood, I thought."

Hawke laughed.

They left him at the stage door of a theatre on Forty-fifth Street. He said he would come to Jeanne's apartment as soon as he could. Looking after Hawke until the door closed on his tall stooped figure, Jeanne said, "Gus, he looks absolutely appalling. Is he well?" The gay manner she had maintained with Hawke instantly evaporated.

"I don't think he's ill, Jeanne. He's driving himself too hard but I don't know that there's anything anyone can do about it." The lawyer told her of his conversation with Dr. Eversill in Hovey.

While Adam unloaded her bags from the taxi Jeanne took Jim up in the self-service elevator, which seemed to have become much dingier, smaller and squeakier in her absence. A mixture of emotions assailed her as she put the key in the lock of Karl's apartment and opened the door. The lights inside were blazing. The Irish nurse Elizabeth came into the hall, exclaiming, "Mrs. Fry, is it? And Jim? God bless you both!" It was a complete surprise. She had written to the nurse and gotten no answer. The two women embraced, and then the nurse confronted Jim. "You don't remember me at all, do you, James Fry? Glory be, how big you are!" He inspected her warily, keeping his distance. Then a smile slowly illumined his face. "Lispet," he said, pointing at her with forefinger and thumb. The nurse seized him and laughed and burst into tears.

Adam explained as he brought in the bags that he had tracked the nurse through the agency, and found her taking care of a paralytic woman in Scarsdale. He hadn't told Jeanne because he thought she would enjoy the surprise. The apartment was freshly cleaned, the beds were made, there were flowers in every room, the refrigerator and the pantry were stocked, and the bar had a row of fresh bottles and a bucket of ice. Jeanne's relief

and pleasure were beyond words. She had anticipated coming to a dark empty apartment left in a mess by the subtenants, and having to start up a household late at night with a tired hungry boy on her hands. Instead there was nothing to do but hand Jim over to the exulting Elizabeth for a bath and his supper, and then sink on the old sofa and ask Adam how on earth all this had been managed.

"Well, getting Elizabeth was most of it. She's very good. I've lived alone a long time, you know, and I'm familiar with the routine. There are services that come in and do almost everything. It amounted to a few phone calls."

Jeanne looked at this puzzling man, red-faced and with thick curly sandy hair, with the mobile thick eyebrows and the odd expression at once stern and a bit ironic and foxy. She felt very shy with him. "It took a lot more than that, and I'm grateful."

"Would you like a drink?"

"Oh, gosh. A drink? It would set me on my ear. I haven't had one in months. It upset mama to see me mix a martini and drink it, she still thinks only bad women drink. The smoking's hard enough on her. I didn't seem to need the booze when I got out there, and I just stopped. Frankly, after seeing Arthur I think I can use one. I'm terribly disturbed."

"Scotch and soda?"

"Okay."

Adam said, "Arthur's situation is disturbing, and it's tantalizing too. His earning power is remarkable, he's made so much money, he will make so much, yet he's in this fearful spot now. Of course these last two ventures, the publishing house and the shopping center, were really catastrophic—when you add it up they drained him of about half a million dollars—though he may have a good recovery some day from the center, but that's no help now."

Jeanne said, "It was the jeopardy tax assessment that was the worst. I won't forget that night as long as I live."

The lawyer handed her a tinkling drink. "I think you ought to know that another tax judgment has come in against him."

"Oh God. No."

"It's the Paumanok deal, which always was on shaky ground. I'm appealing, so I thought it best not to tell him right now. It'll be months before we have a final determination."

"Gus, you were right. Don't tell him until you absolutely must. How much this time?"

"Eighty-six thousand dollars. Plus interest."

Jeanne put her hand over her eyes. She sat up straight and set her glass down. "They're harrying him to death."

Adam looked sidewise at her, his eyes almost shut. "Well, I'll have to

risk another outburst at me like your last one. The tax people are doing their duty under the law. Arthur had some bad advice and went into some questionable situations. It's that simple."

Jeanne said, "I won't break out at you, but I think it's a hellish state of affairs."

Adam said, "I just want you to remember hereafter—because I know he'll listen to you when you're married—that the hazard is not the tax laws but his temperament. I trust that he's been cured of speculating, or if he isn't, that you'll rein him in. That's the real answer to his problem."

"I couldn't rein him in before. Heaven knows I tried. Maybe he's acquired some respect for my batting average as a predicter of misfortune."

"I'm sure he has."

Jeanne added with a wicked little grin, "Of course the nagging power of a wife will be a formidable new weapon. It's probably the edge I've always needed." She glanced at her drink. "This tastes funny. Exquisite, but funny. Can it be that I'm going to like New York again?"

"I hope you will, since I'm stuck here, and I hope to see you and Arthur—and Jim—reasonably frequently in the coming years."

Jeanne glanced at him with instinctive coquetry. "How well you look! If Arthur only looked one tenth as well!"

The lawyer laughed and stood. "I do a humdrum day's work, seldom sleep less than eight hours, and usually spend one or two days out of seven in the wilds. Arthur's schedule is a little different."

Jeanne bathed, perfumed herself, made up with care, and dressed in a clinging green and gold Chinese silk housecoat. Her mirror told her that she looked more desirable than she ever had in her life, but worried. She relaxed the frown between her eyes with an effort.

Shortly before midnight the doorbell rang, and Hawke came stumbling in with heavy footfalls, like a man falling downstairs. "Hello, my love. It took forever and ever and I'm sorry, and it was all about absolutely nothing." He grasped her by the shoulders, looked at her haggardly and crushed her to him. Still holding her, he raised his head and sniffed. "Well, this is a tender gesture, I must say, after an all-day plane trip and everything else. Thank you, darling."

"What is?" She thought he was talking about her array and her perfume.

"You're cooking tacos, aren't you? I could smell them clear down in the elevator. It's a perfect cloud in here."

She knew about his smell hallucinations and felt a thrill of alarm, but she said with a light laugh, "That's all you can think of when you're around me. I'm not, but if Elizabeth thought to buy canned tortillas I will. Let me go look."

He caught her. "No, no. I'm not hungry. My smeller is out of whack. Doesn't mean anything. You look irresistible. Where did you get this slinky green thing? Ye gods, my only reason for ever liking you was that you were so smart. Now you've turned beautiful. Let's sit down somewhere and neck."

"I'm not that kind of girl," she said, moving as fast as he did to the couch.

They kissed furiously for a while. Hawke said, "When will we get married?"

"Any time."

"Have you any bourbon?"

"Sure."

"Plain. No ice. And a bottle of beer."

"Right."

It struck her that he was acting and talking in a daze. He was rational enough, yet he had taken no notice of the extraordinary condition of the apartment, and he was ordering her about as though they had been married for years, with no slightest attempt to bridge the gap of the months since they had seen each other. When she came in with the bourbon and beer he sat slumped with his legs thrust out and his head on the back of the couch, eyes closed. His nose stood out like a beak, and his white cheeks were sunken. It was an upsetting sight. She thought he might be asleep, but he opened his eyes, sat up and smiled at her with the sudden innocent pleasure of a boy. "You look so lovely," he said. "You're such a beautiful woman. You smell so good and you feel so good and you look so attractive. This is just wonderful."

She asked him about the progress of the book. He downed the bourbon and sipped at the beer. He had not stopped working on it for a single day, he said. He had done a long stint on the plane to New York. His writing hours were midnight to ten in the morning; then he managed a few hours' sleep before the theatre business started up. The last chapters had stretched out, but he believed he'd finish the raw manuscript about the time *The Lady from Letchworth* opened in Philadelphia. "After that I think we should get married," he said, "win, lose, or draw. Until then, darling, you'd just be a kissless bride."

"You need sleep more than a bride right now."

He said, "I want to talk to you. There's so much to say. I can't exactly pull myself together. Can I lie down for half an hour? Then get me up and we'll talk, and then I'll go back to work."

"That's a good idea."

He closed his eyes, stretching his big frame the length of the couch with a pitiful groan. "A half hour, you hear? No more. That's all I need."

"Yes, Arthur."

He fell asleep instantly. She brought an old quilted comforter out of a bedroom closet and covered him, after loosening his tie and slipping off his shoes. Hawke slept on the couch straight through until noon of the next day, not moving.

5

In the first week of rehearsal Jeanne's hopes rose as she watched Feydal and the actors go about their work. The pains they took to map out each move and gesture, the gradual painting of life and intelligence into the lines, the improvisations of comic business, the script changes Hawke made on the spot to meet little difficulties, the new lines (some of them very funny) which he would bring out of a half-hour's isolation in a dressing room with a typewriter, the astute suggestions of Irene Perry—all these things impressed her. She began to think that Feydal had made a wise commercial judgment, and that this old play was a rediscovered treasure that was going to ransom Hawke. But she was alarmed at the physical cost to him. He was writing at his book all night and spending most of the day at the theatre. He put in the long hours cheerfully, but each day that she saw him he looked worse. A cup of coffee shook and spilled in his hand. Once when she remonstrated he said, "I'm in it now, Jeanne. It's only two more weeks at this pace. I'd feel like a dog if I didn't pitch in. It's their livelihood too, you know, and I'm not working harder than any of them. It's just that I'm doing another job at the same time. That's my own affair."

"*Alms for Oblivion* was produced without you."

"A comedy is different. Anyway, to be honest, I find the whole thing interesting. I never want to do it again, but it's a thing to go through, like a death or a war."

"Then stop working on your book."

"I can't."

Adam would come in the afternoon, and sit with Jeanne in the orchestra, watching the rehearsal. He shared her concern for Hawke, and a lack of sympathy with the entire theatre process. The transparent vanity of the actors, their long elaborate character analyses leading always to a plea for more lines; the popinjay airs and temper tantrums of Jock Maas; the thick sugary flattery which Feydal used on Hawke, to get the writer to change scenes or write new ones—Jeanne and Adam watched such commonplace rehearsal events with satiric disdain. Hawke would glance around and see them whispering or laughing together in a rear row. He would wave at them and grin, acknowledging that he was caught up in a dance of folly, and turn again with weary patience to the nagging little crisis at hand, whatever it was.

It would have taken clairvoyance on the part of Jeanne or the lawyer to guess that they were feeding Hawke's private nightmare and sapping his remaining mental strength as much as the importunate actors and director. The fact was that—whatever the source of that mysterious human property called nervous strength—Hawke had about come to the end of his.

He had serious causes enough for anxiety in his financial predicament, his physical condition, and the uncertain value of this play he was putting on. But he kept these fears suppressed, and the bottled-up anxiety was breaking forth in the wild and groundless fantasy that Jeanne was falling in love with Gus Adam! Hawke in more normal times, and even now in his lucid hours, knew not only that Jeanne loved him, but that she had loved him from their first meeting and had never stopped loving him. He was ashamed of his nightmare. He knew it for what it was, and so could not give voice to it; but all the same it haunted him, and was haunting him more and more as the days went by, as the pressures on him mounted, and as his last reserves of strength began to give out.

It had started at the airport when Jeanne, walking away from the airplane, had called out to Adam first, instead of to him, "Hi, Gus! You here too? Great!" This had struck Hawke as a peculiar thing for her to do, and jealousy had flashed into his mind though he himself had brought Adam to the plane. The hesitant swift kiss she had given Adam had also offended him. Jeanne and Adam in their wildest imaginings could not have discerned that during the taxi ride to the city Hawke had, while keeping up a normal conversation, constructed a complete fantasy, which was this: Jeanne had long since tired of his eccentricities and follies. The sober, reliable, clever Adam was far more to her taste. Adam was the sort of man she truly wanted and needed. She might or might not be aware of this; most likely she was. At any rate he, Hawke, observing small telltale things she did and said, had seen through to the truth.

As Hawke spun this stuff in his mind, another side of him remained unmoved by it, recognizing it for the silly anxious daydream it was. But he could not dismiss it. When he came to the apartment that first night and saw the pains that Adam had taken for Jeanne's comfort, his reaction again was fiercely jealous. He resented the fact that the lawyer had the leisure to do this kind of wooing and he had not; and his refuge was to say nothing about it. Even when they had necked on the couch Hawke had bitterly sensed that Jeanne was working at pleasing him, instead of feeling real passion. There was this much truth in it, that Jeanne was dog-tired, and worried about Hawke, and also that she did not want to start sleeping with him in this apartment, certainly not with Elizabeth there; nevertheless she had loved being in his arms and had

experienced in those moments the first true flickers of happiness she had known in years. When Hawke woke after his twelve-hour sleep and had breakfast with Jeanne, he remembered his imaginings as one dimly recalls a horrible fever dream. He had been tempted to recount them to her so that they could laugh together over his idiocy and forget it. But he was unable to bring the crazy notion out in the daylight. By night-time it was rising in his mind again as he sat through the unending tedium of casting. In the days that followed the delusion came and went like a malaria fit, like his delusions of smell, and he tried to live with this new aberration in the same way, promising himself that it was a ghost conjured up by exhaustion, which would vanish with rest. He was in this unreasonable vein only for short periods. Sanity would return, and he would be filled with love for Jeanne and grateful friendship for Adam, and he would resolve to choke off the next fit when it came.

The first run-through of a play can be decisive to a knowledgeable onlooker. Often it is better than the finished performance. The players are fresh to the task and still struggling with it. This adds vibrancy to the acting. The absence of the heavy literal sets and costumes of Broadway permits the imagination to go to work. Hawke had high hopes for *The Lady from Letchworth* during the early scenes of the run-through, as the cumulative impact of theatre make-believe enlivened his words. But as the rehearsal went on he became less sure. He resolved to be silent and to listen to what others said. There was a sprinkling of spectators at the rehearsal: backers, staff assistants of Maas and Feydal, understudies, costume and scene designers, and the handful of anonymous Broadway people who are always present when anything serious is happening in the theatre. This was the first run-through of a new play linking three radiant celebrities who had had a success together not long ago: Youngblood Hawke, Georges Feydal, and Irene Perry. There was almost continuous laughter from the sparse audience.

When the performance ended excited chatter broke out both in the orchestra and on the stage. Maas was off in one corner of the theatre making jubilant noises to smiling backers. Feydal on stage had summoned the actors into a semicircle, and was exchanging animated comments with them. Lax was exulting to Hawke that it was no contest, that he was flying back to Hollywood at once to tell Trav Jablock that if he wanted this play for a seventy-five-thousand-dollar down payment he'd better come east and see a rehearsal and make a deal; after the opening in Philadelphia the down payment was going to be a hundred fifty thousand! Even Adam was cheerful. He said the theatre would never cease to amaze him. From everything he had heard of this play, from everything he had seen at rehearsal, he had been pessimistic; but tonight the

comedy had sprung to life for him, and he believed it had a good chance for success. In Adam's measured and cautious vocabulary this was wild raving.

Jeanne said nothing.

Hawke and Jeanne escaped after a while, and darted to Sardi's through a rain that sparkled white and gold in the theatre lights. He said to Jeanne over their first drink, "Well, it's just *The Lady from Letchworth* after all, isn't it?"

She said, "That's what I thought."

He said, "We're right. The others were just talking."

"However, Arthur, all those people were laughing, Lord knows. Even Gus! Gosh, if old Blackstone himself is amused maybe there's hope."

Her reference to Adam gave Hawke a twinge of sickness, but he suppressed the jealousy with a grim effort, as though he were forcing down a tough spring with his hand. He was not going to give way to that craziness any more!

He said, "It's a lesson, isn't it? All that labor, all the invention of Feydal and the actors, all my rewriting, all the genius of Irene Perry—did you ever see a woman who could do more with the rise and fall of her voice, or a gesture with a purse?—all it comes to, in the end, is the silly farce that I wrote in 1943 on a Kaiser liberty ship going from San Francisco to Guadalcanal, twenty-seven days at ten knots without seeing land, living on dehydrated potatoes and fried spam, cold spam, spam salad. That's it, you see, Jeanie. Do what you will with spam, it remains spam. And all the theatrical geniuses in the world can't rise above the level of the play they're doing."

Jeanne said, "Still, it may make money."

"I guess it may. Christ, I have to hope so. There's some fun in it. . . . Say, Georges! Looking for Molière? Table number four."

Feydal sailed over to them, unmindful of the stares of everybody in the restaurant, and sat, beaming. He had a copy of the next day's *Times* under his arm. "Victor Hugo, more nearly, my dear Hawke. Master of all forms. Good evening, Cerberus, you look dazzling, hang you. I'll have a double gimlet, extremely dry," he said to the waiter. His merry face turned tragic. He passed the *Times* to Hawke. "I'm shattered about this. Really, I could strangle my agent. They're all alike. There isn't one with the tact of a charging rhinoceros. Imagine breaking such a story when we're ten days from opening! The morale of the cast is going to plummet."

The paper was unfolded to the drama section. The headline over the movie news read:

FEYDAL WILL STAR
IN LIFE OF BALZAC

and the story disclosed that shooting of the movie would begin on the sixth of July. It was quite true, Feydal said. He had actually signed the contract weeks ago but had demanded that the news be suppressed until the Philadelphia opening of the Hawke play. "One had no choice, dear boy, the money is fantastic and the part is lovely. One must keep one's bills paid. The cast expects me to wetnurse them across the country for weeks and really it makes no sense. The play will be what it will be when it opens in Philadelphia, after which I'll leave. Nothing will matter much after that. Of course I'll fly out from time to time and check the performances."

Hawke said, "Don't you think the play may need work after it opens?"

"Jock Maas is very capable, truly he is. He'll take over very well."

"Maas is a lunatic, Georges."

"Dear boy, a touch of lunacy is helpful in the theatre. Just be sure you don't let him fatten up that tall blonde's part, what's her name? I presume she has a name, but how can one remember it? He keeps pushing, you know, because he's sleeping with her, isn't it dull of him? A television girl twenty-one years old. So insipid. I should think Jock would prefer stronger cheese."

"I didn't know about that."

The moon face turned crafty and ironic. "One soon learns the signs, dear Hawke. We have three red-hot affairs going in the company at the moment. The motto of a play company in rehearsal is the cry of old Lear, 'Let copulation thrive.' It releases tensions, and after all, one should have a little jam with all that dry bread, hm? All that tedious repetition?"

While consuming a vast platter of spaghetti with clam sauce, Feydal discussed the run-through. Despite the optimistic talk he wasn't quite satisfied. He felt that the yellow script had lost some of the first freshness of the black script, even of the red script. Moreover there were some good things in the green script that they might put back. He felt he should spend a whole day with Hawke scissoring together the best things of all the versions, and he had ideas for one or two new scenes. He said with a sly glance at Jeanne, "You see I haven't even asked Cerberus what she thought of the run-through. I could hear all three heads barking back in the theatre."

Jeanne, figuring she had nothing to lose, said, "I'm wondering if it's fair of you to get Arthur into a play production by saying the script was excellent, then persuading him to do a new version every week, then walking off before the job's done. He's in this thing because he believes in you."

"You're a terrible woman, my dear," said Feydal. "Under that dear sweet American surface there is the steel of Saint Joan. I am absolutely terrified of you. I can only say that this man's writing so hypnotizes me that

I thought the play was perfect and I said so. One finds things out in rehearsal, my love, just as one strikes rock or clay or water in digging a building's foundation, and then one must adjust one's blueprints a bit." He turned to Hawke. "You know I wouldn't leave you in the lurch, dear Hawke. You know I wouldn't do that, don't you? I promise you that I'll give my heart's blood to this job between here and Philadelphia, my heart's blood, and there'll be nothing left in me thereafter to contribute, anyway. I'll be wrung out like a dishrag, I swear to you. I have a late appointment with that idiotic monster, my agent, clear on the other side of town. Do forgive me. Cerberus, you're far too severe, and I abominate you, but as women go you have few peers and I've known them all."

She said when he was gone, "He wanted your play to pry Irene Perry loose from Carmian. That's done. He can't wait to be off."

Hawke said wearily, with no trace of surprise or anger, leafing through the *Times* to the obituary page, "I guess so. Sainthood is in short supply these days, Jeanne. I settle for talent and honest workmanship. He's working hard— My *God!* Manuel Hauptmann drowned!"

"Who? Who drowned?" she said, startled.

"Manuel Hauptmann!" Hawke's glance was racing down the page. "You remember that sort of fat dark woman who came with me to Washington, Jeanne, Anne Karen's daughter, it's her husband. He drowned skindiving. In Tangiers, of all places!" After a moment he said with vexation, "This is a very vague and stupid story, they don't have any facts about what happened, but Christ, he's dead, all right. There was a French movie actress on the boat too. This is a hell of a mixed-up story for the New York *Times*."

"Is that the woman who wrote you the letters? And then was so nice to you in Europe?"

"Yes. They both were nice to me, Jeanne. This little Manuel had the manners of a prince, he was a small man but God, he was strong and courageous. How the devil could he drown? He swam like a porpoise. Poor Honor!"

"Do they have children?"

"Several. And millions of dollars. Really millions. Manuel's family is one of the tremendous landholders in Peru."

He reminisced sadly over his brandy about his adventures with the Hauptmanns in Italy and France. "And now Manuel's dead!" he kept saying. At one point he wrinkled his face like his mother, and said with a peculiar exhausted grin, "You know, it's queer that it never crossed my mind to try to borrow money from them. They're far and away the richest people I know, and I know them quite well."

"I doubt they'd have lent it to you. Rich people stay rich by hanging on to their money."

"Manuel might have lent seventy-five thousand dollars to me. Honor wouldn't. She's a frustrated business man, actually, with a grip on a dollar that even my mother would respect. Yet she could lend me seventy-five thousand with as much ease, and feel it as little, as the Chase Manhattan Bank, damned near."

"Yes, well don't go borrowing money from any woman. I speak as a woman."

"I'm not borrowing money from anybody."

"Let's go, Arthur, shall we? Gus is coming to see me early in the morning."

"What about?" Hawke said, instantly alert and annoyed.

"Oh, papers to sign about the estate, and this and that. He's not the most convenient lawyer to have, between the law school hours and his office routine. You have to see him when you can. But he's good."

"Damned good," Hawke said drily. He paid the check and took Jeanne home. She invited him to come up for a drink, but he refused. It was past his time to start writing, he said. She attributed his short manner to disappointment over the play, or perhaps to shock over Hauptmann's death; but it upset her.

6

There was no diminution of his drive, or of the clarity and fertility of his imagination, when he sat down to his nightly work on *Boone County*. He would read over the pages of the previous night, scarcely remembering them, with gratitude for this inspiration that was coming to him from a source apparently outside his tired, emptied self. He would hardly feel fatigue at the end of many hours of driving labor. But the moment he lay down in the broad daylight he would fall asleep, and sleep like a stone; thanks perhaps to the bourbon that he nipped on a carefully rationed schedule through the long dark hours.

He was scrawling away, oblivious to the grimy hotel room in which he sat, and the cacophonous noises and motley neon blaze of Broadway outside the window, when a knock at his door startled him. The watch beside his writing pad showed ten minutes to three.

"Who is it?"

"Jock Maas. Your goddamn telephone operator's asleep."

The producer walked in, dapper and fresh in gray tweed, with the friendly and yet somehow appalling lipless grin that curved up near his ears. "I trust I'm not interrupting anything important, Youngblood. I know you're a night bird like me."

"I work on my book at night, Jock."

Hawke tried his best to keep distaste out of his voice. One of the

real drawbacks of this theatre venture, in Hawke's mind, was the presence of Jock Maas. He could not forget that Frieda Winter had come into his life on the arm of this man. The sight of the long, sallow, rather skull-like face, the mirthless smile, the slicked black hair, the sound of Maas's oddly weak, whispery voice, brought back unwelcome memories of his young days, and often gave Hawke the strong sensation of smelling Frieda's wildflower perfume.

"Ah yes. Well, my boy, a play in rehearsal is a ship in a hurricane. Sometimes our little routines must give way. We have no show, you know. The run-through was a disaster. And now we're losing Georges in ten days. You know about that?"

"Yes."

Maas helped himself generously to Hawke's bourbon and took a cigar. "Why on earth are you staying in this dump? Can't you afford a decent hotel?"

"It's near the theatre. I want to simplify things. I'm trying to do two jobs at once."

Maas settled comfortably in an armchair, kicking off his shoes. "Yes, we're in real trouble. You must be prepared to tear your play to pieces."

"I'll be glad to discuss it with you in the morning."

"This play is important to some thirty-five people, Hawke, including backers who've put up a hundred thousand dollars, counting on the good faith of the playwright, among other things. You can't give us crumbs of your spare time ten days from the opening, even if you are Mr. Youngblood Hawke, the busy novelist."

Hawke wearily took off his glasses and rubbed his eyes. "Very well. What's on your mind?"

"A change that's not hard to make, a change in approach that'll spark the whole comedy and transform the flop we've got right now into a solid smash hit. You can execute it in one honest day's work. I'll be glad to help you."

"Let's hear it." Hawke settled on the sofa, yawning.

Starting far back in the lives of the characters, Maas began to narrate a heavy, involved emotional chronicle behind the events of the farce. He jumped from his chair and walked the room in his stocking feet, mincing, prancing, thundering, whispering, giggling, popping his eyes, imitating all the actors one by one, and in effect doing a capsule one-man performance of the entire play, with his new material inserted. It was an interesting feat. The suggested change was more of the pseudo-Freudian reconstruction that Hawke heard all the time from the actors, delivered this time with the authority of an archbishop, as the sure way out of damnation into salvation.

"What do you think?" Maas said, pirouetting to a stop under the glaring dirty chandelier of the sitting room.

"Well, it adds a lot of new scenes for that tall blonde girl. I'm not sure what else it does."

"You're crazy. You have no conception of the theatre," snapped Maas. "This isn't a goddamn novel ten million pages long, Hawke, you desperately need an emotional line, I tell you, you must paint it in with bold deft strokes exactly as I've done. Otherwise the whole play's nothing, I assure you. It's an empty tissue of old-hat humor."

Hawke said mildly, "You're quite wrong. It's a great comedy and a sure smash hit just as it stands. Georges Feydal and Jock Maas told me so."

Maas looked astonished, then he began to squawk obscenities. Hawke got a little tired of it, stood, and suddenly roared out at Maas with some far rougher language from the Seabees and the Letchworth miners. The producer was quite taken aback. He shut up, and after a moment the weird grin slid up his cadaverous face.

"Why, that's pretty good, Youngblood. I thought you were one of these modest backwoods boys who never cussed."

Hawke picked up Maas's shoes and thrust them into his hands. "I'll see you tomorrow. If you ever break in on me again when I'm working on my book I'll punch the teeth out of your head."

"Bless me, what's happened to our gentle giant? I guess we're all a trifle edgy." Maas stepped into his shoes, and walked to the door. "Think it over, Youngblood. Unless you do exactly as I say, your play is doomed." He glared at Hawke like Death. Then the grin pulled up his features, and he left.

Hawke tried to get back to work. But Maas had dumped muck on the fire of his imagination; it was out. This angered and upset him more than the stupid conversation and the lost time. Writing through the night at so many pages per hour had become a compulsion. The discharge relieved his nerves, and enabled him to get through the next day. He knew well enough that he was on the edge of a breakdown. So far he had staved it off. He believed that if he held to his regime he would get past the magic date, the opening of *The Lady from Letchworth* in Philadelphia on the fifth of July. Adam had extracted an absolutely final postponement from Newton Leffer of his demands until that date. Beyond it lay deliverance, or disgrace, or—Hawke was past caring what lay beyond. That date represented the end of his effort and his strength. It was a black curtain in the calendar.

He paced the room trying to decide between a sleeping pill, a tremendous jolt of whiskey, or perhaps a foray to one of the all-night eating places on Broadway. He then bethought himself of Honor Hauptmann. Why not write a letter of condolence to her? The newspaper had mentioned that she was at her home in Peru. It wouldn't be hard, it was a kindly act, and the flow of words might start his brain functioning.

He wrote the letter. It was awkward at first to find words of condolence

that weren't trite and stale. But he broke into a sympathetic recollection of Manuel's character and of the good times the three of them had shared in Europe, and soon he had covered five pages. He added another page of acid humor on his Broadway imbroglio, thinking it might cheer Honor a bit. When he read over the letter it was disconcertingly warm and intimate; too much so. But then he thought that she was a distraught widow, and a warm letter from a man she admired was true charity just now. It also occurred to him, but in a shadowy hinting way, that beyond the black curtain of July fifth Honor Hauptmann might somehow be a last resort, if all else foundered.

7

Jeanne was buying nothing for her trousseau. Her idea was that when the nightmare of the farce production came to an end in Philadelphia— whatever that end might be—she was going to force Hawke to enter a clinic. She was certain that, even if no serious damage were found, he would be ordered to a sanitarium. Had she dared, she would have made the fight for this step now, but she knew that there was no dealing with the careening author until the play went on and he finished *Boone County*. She usually found him at the theatre in his shirtsleeves, unshaven and hollow-eyed, making the endless little changes or arguing against them with the enduring plodding patience of a donkey slogging its way through a thunderstorm. Jeanne had come to hate, to hate deeply, the vague per-fumed smell of a Broadway playhouse, and the gloomy rows of empty seats. She would not have gone to the theatre at all except that she worried about Hawke and wanted to watch over him. She resented Hawke's good-natured tolerance, his conscientious willingness to listen to long foolishness, his complaisant sitting at a typewriter over and over and over to write a few jokes or change a few sentences or write some new speeches, which like as not would be discarded the next day. It was plain to her that all this drudgery was to no avail. Nothing could change *The Lady from Letchworth*. It was what it was. The number would either come up red or black at the opening in Philadelphia. When she said all this to Hawke he agreed with a sad grin. "I will never do this again. I believed Feydal, and here I am, on a toboggan with a lot of people, halfway down a steep icy slide. It would be dirty play to jump off now. And who knows? I still think the goddamned thing will make money."

A couple of days before dress rehearsal, he had a late breakfast at her apartment and played with Jim on the floor for an hour, so absorbed in the little boy and so happy with him that Jeanne let it go on and on. When they arrived at the theatre the rehearsal was under way. They sat together in a back row. After a few minutes Hawke said, "What the hell?

I never wrote those words." He strode down the aisle. "Hold it, please."
As he vaulted on the stage, Maas rose from the front row and climbed over
the footlights after him.

The new scenes, it developed, were the ones Maas had suggested to
Hawke in his night visit. He had written them out and showed them to
Irene Perry who thought they were worth trying. Feydal said placatingly
to Hawke, "Just walking through them, dear fellow, pending your arrival.
You *were* late getting here, you know. We're only four days from opening."

"I know. Sorry I was late." He turned to the tall blonde, who was a
spectacular object in black tights and a bright green pullover. "May I see
those scenes please?"

She handed him the pages. He tore them in half and let them fall
fluttering to the dusty stage. "Sorry, Georges. There will be no words in
the play that I haven't written. I think we'd better lock up now and do
the play we've got." With this he walked to a table at the side of the stage
where there was a jug of coffee, and poured himself a paper cup full.
Maas directed a burst of loud abuse at the author's back. Jeanne was
astounded at the language—several young actresses and the grand Irene
Perry were looking on—but the ladies did not seem offended or surprised.
The whole cast was watching the incident with lively pleasure.

Hawke drank up the coffee, then turned and walked toward Maas, who
was still berating him. Maas stood his ground, quivering with anger, his
long sallow face drawn up in a grinning scowl. Hawke came close and
halted. He was a head taller, and twice as broad, as the producer. Maas
glared up at him and shrilled, "All right, big as you are, let's see you start
something, you unreasonable ————!" It was the dirtiest epithet that current English affords. It brought a horrid hush, and pained glances among
the actresses. Hawke looked down at Maas for a long moment or two.
With a sudden swoop of a long arm he placed his empty coffee cup upside
down on the producer's slicked head; then he walked away, leaped the
footlights, and strode back up the aisle to Jeanne.

Maas stood transfixed with surprise, the little red paper cup balanced
on his head, dregs of coffee trickling down. His face was all wrinkled, and
he looked something like a startled organ grinder's monkey. After a moment there was an explosion of laughter from the players. The guffawing
Feydal, with old theatre generalship, started a round of handclapping in
which the entire cast joined except the tall blonde. Maas shook off the
cup and darted into the wings through the laughter and applause, shouting
something indistinguishable.

Hawke said as he came back to Jeanne, "I didn't know what else to
do. He's too small to hit."

Jeanne said, "That was inspired. You're in better shape than I
thought."

This *coup de théâtre* of Hawke's cleared the air in the company. There

had been much bickering and nerves over the continuing alterations, and a rising quarrelsomeness that came from a sense that Feydal would soon be leaving them in the hands of Maas. But the coffee cup had snuffed Maas out like a candle. He did not appear again at the theatre until the dress rehearsal, when he conspicuously ignored Hawke and Feydal, glowering from a rear row.

The incident also reassured Jeanne about Hawke. It was such a solid display of self-command that she wondered whether her vigilance might not be, not only misplaced, but annoying to this man she loved. He had been treating her with a curiously remote affection all through this period, irreproachable in any detail, but mystifying and distressing to her. She decided to stop watching him so closely; to stay away from the theatre, and let him get through the mess in his own way.

Jeanne was not the first person to be deceived by someone in bad mental condition. When Hawke put down Maas so neatly, he was far gone. Standing over the little producer on the stage, he had heard the epithet shouted at him as from the bottom of a well; and Maas himself had appeared tiny, as though seen through the wrong end of a telescope. Putting the cup on Maas's head was a dreamy, slightly mad action that occurred to him instead of the natural response of knocking the producer down. It was probably a misfortune that it happened to be so successful.

The dress rehearsal gave no new indication of the play's chances. The production itself was beautiful. Whatever Maas's drawbacks, he did know how to mount a play. The setting of an improbable penthouse on the East River was a glittering bitter joke about New York taste. The costumes added to the grotesque caricature of Manhattan, being overdone to a point just this side of absurdity. Hawke thought the production showed Broadway's best face, the dedicated attention to detail, the gleaming technical polish. But his concern about the outcome was fading into a hazy euphoria. All through the dress rehearsal, sitting between Adam and Jeanne, Hawke kept fondling a secret thought, as a child in a classroom will fondle the dime that means an ice cream soda once school lets out. It was the thought of Honor Hauptmann, the widow with millions in Peru. He had in his breast pocket a thick airmail letter which she had shot back to him, much longer than his own, an outpouring of confidences and indiscretions in the warmest possible language. She was unable to mourn for Manuel though she wanted to. He had wrecked her life. The French actress who had been on the boat with Manuel had been his mistress in a blatant public liaison. Honor's surroundings had become horrible to her. She was being bedevilled by the family and its lawyers. She could hardly bear to hear Spanish or to speak it any more, and she grew angry at her children and struck them if they forgot to talk English in her presence. She had to flee Peru, she intended never to return, but she was

in the grip of a terrible inertia. She badly needed a rescuer. Did he know any knights with white horses? She wrote a biting page about his folly in stumbling into the Broadway mire. He deserved everything that was happening to him. How could he need money that badly, after all his grandiose success? And if he had encountered some dismal luck why hadn't he called on his friends?

And Hawke—physically and mentally unwell, his powers drained by the drive on *Boone County* and on top of it the ordeal of his gamble on a Broadway farce; his nights, long lonely vigils of desperate writing under an electric lamp; his days a plague of theatre fretting—Hawke was drifting into daydreams that Honor Hauptmann not only would lend him all the money he needed, but might be his millionairess, after all. Why, look at Shaw! Shaw had taken a millionairess to himself in a sterile marriage, and the great author had done his work thereafter without ever having to think about money. And he had piled up a grand fortune of his own with his pen.

Hawke had these thoughts with Jeanne at his side, as the actors chirruped through his farce in the nearly empty theatre. And he thought that, far from hurting or jilting Jeanne, he might be planning exactly the course she herself ardently desired: some decent and final way to break off their romance so that she might find happiness with the man most suited for her, the cool commanding intelligence who never slipped into wild follies, old Triple-A Adam, the red-faced human rock.

8

The company left New York by train for Philadelphia at ten in the morning, the day before the premiere, and Hawke went with them. Nobody seemed aware that it was the Fourth of July, and the national holiday had made no change in the schedule. A theatre venture about to open knows neither calendar nor clock; there is only one date, that of the opening, and there is only one time, curtain time. Jeanne, following her new policy of not dogging Hawke's every move, had suggested that she come down the following day with Adam, in time for the performance. With a distant smile, Hawke had agreed that was very sensible. His manner disturbed her. She offered to come with him instead, if he preferred. "Of course not," Hawke said. "You'd only be bored. Just more dress rehearsals and line rehearsals." He changed the subject. It was an unsatisfactory little scene, but Jeanne was afraid to press him, and let the decision go that way.

The actors were in wonderful spirits on the train, joking, playing pranks, passing Scotch around in paper cups. The excitement and tension of the

trip to Philadelphia reminded Hawke of bus rides with the basketball team of Hovey High on the way to a big game, and of the nervous joking of a ship's crew bringing his Seabee group to a beach under fire. The theatre people might be all the things Jeanne and Gus said they were, but they were gallant, Hawke thought, they laughed going into battle and they were charming. Jeanne lacked tolerance. Here was Randy Sissell, for instance, the fat-faced, white-headed mountebank who played the tax collector in the farce, sitting beside Hawke and shouting over the train rumbles a long account of his acting triumphs. The man was a stupid, preposterous egotist, and he was committing adultery with one of the young married actresses in the cast. But Randy was one of the best minor comic actors on Broadway, he read lines cleanly, he used no cheap tricks, and audiences loved him. He was perfect for the part, and Hawke could not help liking the bawdy old fool. Jeanne abhorred him.

This strictness of Jeanne's, her unwillingness to suffer fools or sinners, the blue pencil with which she kept slashing at life and people, was her own peculiar weakness, he thought. Anyway, she would find nothing to condemn or blue-pencil in Augustus A. Adam! They were a well-matched pair of austere and high-minded souls. So all his thoughts kept meandering back to his obsession.

Jeanne arrived in Philadelphia next day early in the afternoon. She rapped at his door and there she was, in a black flat hat and a black suit with a white collar, looking beautiful, and saying with a puckish grin, "Well? Is there any hope?"

He stood in his shirtsleeves holding the door open, the writing pad under his arm, and he said, or rather stammered, "Wha—where's Gus?"

"Coming on the last possible train. I decided I couldn't wait."

The lovely sight of her there in the doorway, the look in her eyes, her coming without the lawyer, shook Hawke out of his sickly frame of mind. He pulled her inside, took off her hat and threw it across the room, and embraced her passionately. She responded with unmistakable eagerness, and so they kissed and kissed. She leaned back in his arms. "Well! I was beginning to think you were mad at me or something. I've been trying for days to figure what I've done wrong."

"You haven't done anything wrong. You can't. I love you." Hawke could no more have told her now of his suspicions about Adam than he could have struck her. His morbid imaginings were too shameful and baseless, when she was in his arms, to be dignified with words. What was the matter with him? He said, "Today's July fifth. Ten days ought to be enough time. Will you arrange for us to get married on July fifteenth, my beloved, while I finish up this miserable book?"

"All right," she said cautiously. She still planned to have him undergo a medical check-up first. He looked very ill, and his endearments, though

sweet and pleasing to her, had frightened her a little. He had been shockingly rough and coarse at first, though he had quieted down, and he had never stopped shaking as though he had a fever. "How are you feeling, Arthur, with the great night at hand?"

"To hell with the great night. The main thing is the book, Jeanne, I don't think I have more than three solid sessions left. I'm doing the burying and the marrying, that's all."

"Well, you bury and marry away. I haven't even registered yet. I came straight up, I was so anxious to see you."

"Why register at all? Stay here with me."

Jeanne cocked her head at him. Her eyes dropped half-shut and she slowly smiled. "Is that what you want?"

He gathered her to him again, with tenderness and great strength, and laughed. "Don't misunderstand me, you're the world's most appetizing woman, but I'm damned if after all these years my honeymoon is going to be interrupted by that baboon Maas pounding at the door, or Feydal on the telephone. He calls forty times a day. God knows we've waited long enough. Half the cast is happily fornicating somewhere in this hotel at the moment, the five o'clock tumble, and let's leave it to them. Go get yourself unpacked. We eat at half-past six. The curtain's at eight-fifteen."

9

The premiere in Philadelphia started weakly. The auditorium was a huge one, unsuited to comedy, and the audience was full of starchily dressed old Philadelphians, strong for culture and slow to lose their gravity. But the laughs began at last, and mounted to roars at the first act curtain. Hawke stayed backstage, he was too conspicuous a figure to wander around in the lobby and listen to comments, but Jeanne did, and came back to report.

"Mostly what they talk about is whether or not it'll be a hit on Broadway. They all seem afraid to commit themselves. I must have heard twenty people say, 'Well, I like it, but you know those New York critics—'"

At the end of the last act she posted herself at the main exit, eavesdropping on the departing audience. Mostly they talked about their transportation or where they were going next, with an occasional remark that the play was fun, or a good laugh, and now and then a comment of wonder that Youngblood Hawke had written such a light comic piece. Backstage the actors were subdued and nervous as they took off their grease paint. Maas prowled here and there, his face tight in a congealed grin. Feydal was gone. Hawke seemed more cheerful than anybody.

"Well," he said to Jeanne, "we've put in the quarter and pulled the handle. Tomorrow we'll know whether it's to be cherries or lemons."

Ferdie Lax, who was standing with him, said, "Three bars. The whole goddamn jackpot, I tell you. No contest."

Lax had the best suite in the hotel, and the next day at noon Hawke, Jeanne and Adam were there for the fateful telephone call to Travis Jablock. Jeanne and Adam sat together on a sofa, Lax was at the telephone with the notices spread out before him on a coffee table, and Hawke stood in the bedroom doorway holding the other telephone. Lax said, glancing at his watch, "Trav's always in the office by nine. Here goes." He put the call through.

Jablock's reedy voice was full of energy and good spirits. "Hi, Ferdie. How did it come off?"

"Trav, it was real good. A million laughs. You'd think they'd been playing it for years. Irene was miraculous. The people were falling out of their chairs. I've never seen such an audience show. They loved it."

"Really? That's marvellous!"

"It's a bloody big hit, Trav. It's going to run two, three years on Broadway. You've got yourself one hell of a bargain."

"Terrific! How were the notices, Ferdie?"

"Very good, Trav. Solid money notices, every one."

"Do you have them there?"

"I've got a few, yes. Just a second."

Lax put his hand over the mouthpiece, and said to Hawke, "Trav's playing games. He's got the notices off the teletype, right on his desk . . . Hello, Trav? Now I said these were money notices. I didn't say they were raves. I'm levelling with you here. They don't understand farce in Philadelphia, you know, unless it's *Charley's Aunt*. Anyway, listen to these. I'll just give you the highlights." He read the best paragraphs from the notices, all of which said in one way or another that the audience had laughed a lot. But one critic had excoriated Hawke, Feydal, and Irene Perry for wasting their time on such vapid stuff; one had guessed that Youngblood Hawke had dashed off this frail piece to pay the income taxes on his novels; a third had treated the enterprise forgivingly, and said that if a ticket buyer didn't look at the author's name, he might have a gay enough evening at *The Lady from Letchworth*.

Travis Jablock punctuated Lax's readings of the good morsels with exclamations of delight. "Marvellous . . . wonderful . . . couldn't ask for anything better . . . Great!" When Lax finished, he said, "The only thing is, Ferdie, I had a quick look at the teletype sheets on the way in and, as I recall, they sort of expressed some reservations, too."

"They did, Trav. I said these notices are not raves. They report the

truth, that the audience laughed like maniacs for two solid hours. What else matters? It's a comedy."

Jablock said, "I have the *Hollywood Reporter* here." He read the entire notice. It declared in movie argot that the enterprise was a disaster which should be closed at once to spare the reputations of the eminent people involved, and added that this ridiculous failure, coming on top of *Evelyn Biggers*, indicated that Youngblood Hawke, one of America's best writers, was cracking up badly.

Lax said, "Trav, I don't have to remind you how many times the *Reporter* has muffed, especially out of town."

"Well, sure, Ferdie. I have no doubt they're all wrong. The thing is— what town do you play next, and when?"

"They jump to Pittsburgh, Trav, in three weeks."

"Pittsburgh, eh? Well, let's let the thing hang till then, okay? I'll only get a turn-down from the bank, Ferdie, at this point. Those ignorant bastards believe the *Hollywood Reporter* more than the New York *Times*."

Lax glanced toward Hawke, whose face was expressionless. "Now, none of that, Trav. We had a deal, at a fire-sale price. You don't grab it now I'm taking this property down the street, and I mean this afternoon. What's more I'll sell it."

"Of course you will, Ferdie. I urge you to do just that. I'll withdraw here and now. It's a damned funny little script. I personally couldn't care less about Philadelphia critics and the *Reporter*. It's these bank vice-presidents. All they go by is the goddamn printed word, they have no show business instincts."

"Just a second, Trav." Lax said to Hawke, covering the telephone, "He's stone cold. That bank talk is an out. Got any ideas?"

Hawke said hoarsely, "Think you can peddle it elsewhere?"

"Not unless you build up some raves on the road. The *Reporter* notice is fatal."

"I'll talk to him . . . Hello, Trav? This is Hawke."

"Hey! Youngblood! How's America's finest novelist? Got that big new book ready for me to read yet? I lie awake nights thinking about it."

"It's all but finished, Trav. I guess Ferdie's told you I'm in a bind for seventy-five thousand dollars. I need it right away."

"Well, no, he didn't." Jablock dropped his voice as though discussing a death. "Tax foul-up, Youngblood?"

"Among other things. Trav, will you buy the movie rights to my new novel sight unseen for seventy-five thousand?"

Lax at once spoke into the phone, "Wait a second, Trav. I didn't authorize that offer and it's absurd, this is Art's biggest work, it'll be worth half a million when it's done—"

"Shut up, Ferdie," Hawke said. "This is a distress offer, Travis. It's a better book than *Chain of Command* and will make a bigger movie."

Jablock said, "I believe you," and there was a brisk new note in his voice, "Seventy-five, hey? That's rough, sight unseen, Youngblood. Isn't there anything you can let me read? An outline or something?"

"There's no outline."

"Would you fly out here and tell the story to me?"

Hawke looked around at the long faces in the room. Lax sat in a defeated slump, the telephone to his ear, and he shrugged at Hawke. "Jeanne, he wants me to fly to Hollywood and tell him the story of *Boone County*."

"Don't you dare. Let him come here."

Adam said, "Arthur, I'd wait before taking such a step. It's an important work. I'm sure it's worth far more money than that."

Hawke said, "That may be, Gus, but I'm in default on a note, you know . . . Hello, Travis? Will you give me seventy-five thousand dollars at once if you like what you hear?"

Jablock paused before saying, "Well, all this is kind of sudden, Youngblood. I think I could promise you twenty-five now against seventy-five down when I read the script. I think for taking such a long chance I ought to get an exclusive first reading of your next book too."

Lax said angrily, "Trav, go to hell. Get off the line, Art. You're talking about the biggest property in sight. Trav, do you want the play or not?"

"I sure want to hear Hawke tell that new book, Ferdie. I really do. I'll pay a substantial price for the privilege and I call twenty-five substantial. Not seventy-five. Not for a story conference. I can't justify that."

Hawke said, "I'll take any screenplay assignment that's available, Travis."

"Youngblood, we're at a standstill here. I'm sorry, I'd be proud to have you on a screenplay, you know that."

Lax said, "How about *The Lady from Letchworth*, Travis?"

"Ferdie, feel free to offer it anywhere you please. I have to withdraw."

Lax and Hawke hung up, and in a long moment of silent gloom the four people looked at each other. Hawke sat down on the floor in the middle of the room, folded his long legs Buddha-fashion and grinned like a tired boy. "Well, so much for *The Lady from Letchworth*. It was a nice try." He turned to the lawyer. "What happens now?"

"I can't say, Arthur. If Newton isn't bluffing, and I don't think he is, he'll take us to court at once. The process will consume some time. Till then we can hang on and hope. The sooner you finish your book the better."

"Yes, indeed." Hawke's voice had a faraway sound.

Lax sighed. "It's just too goddamn bad, coming right on top of that tax jolt, Art. It's a hell of a time for your luck to go sour. That goddamn *Hollywood Reporter—*"

Hawke smiled sadly. "The jeopardy assessment? I paid that off a year ago. I don't even think of it any more."

Lax said, "No, I don't mean my *Chain of Command* deal, though that was horrible enough. I mean this slug you got on your Long Island real estate deal—you know, the play contract . . ." The agent's voice faltered, and he glanced at Adam and Jeanne, both of whom appeared stricken. "Look, I heard about this weeks ago, Gus, from the same stupid son of a bitch who wrote the *Chain of Command* contract for me. He's been working with your office on the appeal, and someone there told him about this big new assessment—I'm sorry if I've got it all wrong, I hope I have—"

Hawke said, "It's news to me." He turned on Jeanne and Adam sitting side by side on the sofa. "Is it true, Gus?"

The lawyer said hesitantly, "We got an adverse ruling, yes. I've appealed it. I saw no point in worrying you with it meantime, since—"

Hawke broke in, "Jeanne, did you know about this?"

Jeanne, who would have given much for the power to carry off a lie said, "Yes, I knew. I told Gus he was right not to tell you. Arthur, you've been under a killing strain and—"

Hawke said to Adam, "How much is it this time?"

The lawyer compressed his lips and hesitated. "Ninety-three thousand dollars."

Hawke uttered a jolly laugh.

Adam went on, "Arthur, I beg you to remember that this ruling can be reversed, that we can still win our appeal on the other assessment too, and that Paumanok Plaza may pay off. The picture is far from black. In fact I have a letter from Scotty in my room, that I wanted to show you, it's highly encouraging—"

"Scotty!" Hawke said. "The original source of good and reliable tidings." He got off the floor and confronted Adam and Jeanne, his face stern. "I'm just wondering, is there any other bad news you two are withholding from the poor overburdened artist? Where can I get the truth if not from you two? Whom can I trust? Where do I stand? What comes next? If you're taking over my affairs and don't think I'm competent to face them, why don't you have me put in an institution?"

Jeanne tried to speak, but he raised his voice in anger, and she put her hands over her face.

"Jesus *Christ!* Don't you think I'm a man? Have I flinched from anything that's happened yet? Tell me whatever you've got to tell me, both of you! Either of you! Talk! See if I turn a hair! Just don't lie to me! Don't treat me like an infant or a lunatic! I'm *Youngblood Hawke,* do you recognize the name? I came to New York alone, I got to the top of the writing heap, I made a fortune, I lost it, and I'll make another fortune, do you hear? This is what I needed, by the living God, this is hitting bottom. I don't mean losing the gamble on my stupid farce, that couldn't matter

less. I mean being treated by you two as a child. Now watch me come back, alone! Without either of you! Just watch me!"

Adam stood and put his hand on Hawke's shirtsleeve. The author flung it away. Jeanne sat staring at Hawke, tears running down her face. Adam said, "Arthur, nobody on earth has more confidence in you than Jeanne and I. I'm sorry this disclosure came in an awkward way. I thought it would serve no useful purpose to add to your worries."

Hawke said to Jeanne, "Dry your eyes. Crying is no contribution."

She said, putting a handkerchief to her face, "You're quite right."

He said, "Okay, I'm sorry I blew up. It seems to justify this business of babying me. I hope you understand that nothing can be more infuriating to a man. I know I'm tired, but I'm making it, Jeanne, I'm almost through this tunnel. My book's all but done. It'll earn tremendous sums. You can edit it while I rest up. I don't give a damn any more about poor Judd's review, it's as dead as he is."

Jeanne brightened up. "Now you're talking! Arthur, the thing is you're not very well, don't you know that? I was scared when I first saw you at the airport, and since then you've been through a grind that would put an ordinary man in a hospital."

Hawke was pacing the room in lunging strides, glancing now and then at Jeanne and Adam. "All right. This is all there is to tell me, right? I'm in the hole for another hundred thousand, more or less. This is the worst. There's no more hidden bad news you two are saving up for a time when I can take it better, eh?"

Adam said, "None, Arthur. None that I know of."

Jeanne said, "What else can there be? What are you driving at?"

"God knows," Hawke said. "I'm trying to collect myself here, that's all. I don't want any more shocks. I'm not in the best shape for taking them with a gallant grin. Okay. I have to go to a pep rally for the cast this afternoon, and then out of decency to the actors I ought to attend tonight's performance. I'm then going to disappear into a different New York hotel so that Maas can't trace me, and I won't leave it till I finish *Boone County*. After that we'll pick up the pieces as best we may. It'll take me less than a week. I must do it."

Lax said, "That makes sense. Don't write off this comedy, either. They may love it in the next few towns, and we can still pick up a healthy hunk of change, before it even gets to Broadway. It's funny as hell."

"It's rubbish," Hawke said. "I did my level best, but there's a natural law about silk purses and sows' ears. If it pays off it'll be luck. The script should have stayed in your file, Ferdie. However, I made a wrong decision, and that's that."

10

It was a melancholy meal they had in the huge ornate dining room, the more so because it was only half-past twelve and most of the tables were empty. Hawke ordered a steak but ate only a couple of bites of it. Adam kept looking at his watch and finally said he'd have to leave on the next train to attend a late afternoon seminar at the law school. Hawke said there was no reason for him not to leave at once. "I suppose you'll go with him," he said to Jeanne.

"If you don't mind," she said timidly, "I'd rather stay here with you."

"Suit yourself. There'll be nothing for you to do. I'll be busy in post-mortems all afternoon. After the performance—which I'm sure you don't want to see—I'll take the first train out of here that I can catch. It'll probably be late at night."

Alarmed by his tone, Jeanne said with a forced laugh, "Well, if my hanging around comes under the head of babying you, Arthur, which seems to be the big crime at the moment—"

"I think perhaps it does. I'm not going to kill myself. Not with a good novel almost finished. Go ahead, go back with Gus. I'll telephone you as soon as I get to New York."

"No matter what time it is?" Jeanne was completely at sea, and full of dread, and above all she did not want to anger him further. His tirade in Lax's suite had shattered her.

"The minute I get in."

Jeanne had to decide on the spur of the moment, her mind was in a whirl, and she feared Arthur's displeasure above everything. "All right, then, I'll go now. Whatever you think best."

"That's best," Hawke said.

A little while later, when Hawke closed the taxicab door and said through the open window, "So long, Gus. See you later, Jeanne," she had a sickening sense that she was making a mistake. There was an unnatural wide stare that went with his cordial smile.

She said, "Look, darling, call me at dinner time, won't you?"

"Why?"

"I—well, I just want to be sure there's no change in plans."

"All right, I'll call you at dinner time." The taxi drove off.

Lax was waiting in Hawke's room when he came up. "Did they get off all right?"

"Sure."

"I wouldn't want the professor to miss his class."

"The professor misses nothing, and makes no mistakes. The professor is a very perfect gentle knight."

The agent said uneasily, "I'm sorry I threw the curve about the tax ruling."

"Better so. You wanted to talk to me, you said?"

"Just a little thing," Lax said, "then I'm off to the airport. I'm suing our mutual friend Roland Givney, and at some point my New York lawyer may ask you for a statement. You won't have to testify or anything. Just an affidavit."

Hawke said, throwing off his jacket and slumping into a chair, his head in his hands, "An affidavit? What about?"

"Well, you remember when I brought him to you for the proposal about the publishing house, in Kentucky? When I fetched you out of the mine?"

Hawke glanced up and smiled wearily. "Way back then? Yes."

"Well, I had a letter of agreement with him. I was to use my good offices to bring you together. If a publishing house resulted my fee was to be five thousand dollars. I mean it's not a fortune, but I don't like welshers, and he's refusing to pay. He says your Haworth House setup was a whole new negotiation. My lawyer says that's irrelevant, by the terms of the letter he clearly owes me the five grand, and I may as well collect it."

Hawke was so deep in his own thoughts that he hardly heard all this. "What? What does Givney owe you money for?"

Lax explained again. Hawke began to look at him with the same cordial wide-eyed smile that had upset Jeanne. "Ferdie, didn't you make a great point then that you expected no compensation for bringing Givney to me? You were doing it because you thought it might be a good thing for me."

"That's right. I expected no compensation from you, Art. I didn't see how I could get ten percent of an indefinite thing like tax savings. It was reasonable to get my compensation from Givney. He stood to be the big gainer if he tied in with Youngblood Hawke."

Hawke said in a tone of melancholy amusement, "You were selling Givney your connection with me."

"Now hell, Art, what a thing to say! The man made the proposal to me. He was a reputable publisher. I saw where you might do very well in such a setup—too bad it never worked out—and I didn't want to charge you, but I think my time was worth something. It usually is."

"Why didn't you tell me at the time that he was paying you, Ferdie?"

The agent blinked and slumped, and his head fell to one side. After a moment he said slowly, "If you think I was off base just forget the whole thing. I'll drop the suit."

"Not at all," Hawke said. "You're a business man. You've been a good agent, too. Tell your lawyer to send me the affidavit, and I'll sign it."

Lax said, "I mean the world doesn't run on charity, Art." He stood, and put on his hat, a gray straw thing shaped like Robin Hood's cap, without the feather. "Well, good luck. You just finish up that *Boone*

County. We'll make a tremendous killing, I feel it in my bones, and that'll clear up all your worries." Lax held out his hand. Hawke perceptibly hesitated, then shook it. The agent noticed the hesitation, and blinked; but he said no more, and left, jamming on the hat without a feather.

CHAPTER TWENTY-FIVE

1

HAWKE did not appear at the theatre at four o'clock, when the meeting of the company was supposed to start. The players sat around the stage in their sharply stylish street clothes, defeated, deflated, muttering to each other, with now and then a bitter laugh rising over the funereal buzz. Feydal and Maas arrived together. The stage manager planted chairs for them in the middle of the fake flattened penthouse living room lit by one white bulb on a standing pole. Feydal ordered the lights thrown on and the bath of pink and amber rays immediately cheered things up. Soon Feydal had the cast laughing with jokes about his own mistakes in directing the play, and with anecdotes of out-of-town failures that had turned into smash hits. The fat Frenchman was beaming, buoyant, charged with optimistic energy. *The Lady from Letchworth* was going to fight on, no mistake about that! Maas interrupted him, when an assistant brought a scribbled slip of paper, to announce that there had been a line at the box office all day, and the treasurer had taken in, as of this moment, over eight hundred dollars! The actors cheered and clapped their hands, and slapped each other's backs. One after another they began to offer comments on the performance, and to suggest changes in the script. The meeting turned lively, in fact gay. Agreement emerged that all the show really needed was some rewriting, mainly an injection of more plot and about thirty good jokes. Nearly everybody had an idea for the author to work on. A clamor for Hawke arose. How could he be so late for such a decisive and fruitful conference? Maas left the stage to telephone the author, and returned a few minutes later looking stunned. Youngblood Hawke had checked out of his hotel, leaving no forwarding address! He had abandoned the company to its fate and vanished!

Feydal stilled the panicky reaction of the actors. In a voice rolling like thunder, he said he could not believe it. Hawke was the most stable, reliable, cooperative playwright he had ever known. Youngblood Hawke

was a truly great author. There was some misunderstanding, some crossing of signals. He would call New York and straighten the matter out. He recessed the meeting, went to a backstage telephone, and called Gus Adam's office; but the lawyer was not there. He then called Jeanne Fry.

Jeanne, who had arrived at her apartment only a short while earlier, was getting Jim ready for a walk in Central Park. She heard Feydal's news with a stab of dismay, a sharp real pain. No, she told Feydal, she did not know where Hawke could be. She remembered his plan to go to an un-named hotel in New York, and—without telling it to Feydal—she hoped that this was what he had done. But Hawke had said he would attend the meeting first, and stay in Philadelphia for the performance. This action was unlike him. He had drudged faithfully through the last weeks of the ordeal the farce venture had become, largely out of loyalty to the actors. She promised Feydal to notify Maas in Philadelphia as soon as she heard from Hawke. Feydal said he himself was flying off to Hollywood in an hour.

"Dear Cerberus, do tell our dear lad that this is no time to bow out. Jock Maas will begin rewriting the script, he has no conscience what-ever, and he'll make a hideous hash of it. Really, my love, utter catastrophe is days away unless Hawke returns."

Jeanne said, "I'm afraid the catastrophe occurred when Arthur gave you the play to do."

"Nonsense, my dear. Courage in adversity! One doesn't abandon ship at the first bit of heavy weather. It's not like Hawke and I'm sure there's some simple explanation of his disappearance." Then came the famous chuckle that the whole world had smiled at in movies. "And I'm not at all sure you don't know the secret. You're a deep one, Cerberus. Produce your author, I tell you, or all is lost. Ta ta."

She took Jim to the park, unable to face a vigil at the telephone. Walk-ing in the hot, dusty zoo from one animal cage to another amid the pushing afternoon crowds, she endured torments of fear. She prolonged her stay as long as she could. When she came home, Elizabeth told her that there had been no calls. Jeanne could not eat. She would have liked to get drunk, but she feared that a crisis might be gathering that would demand a clear head. She would not even allow herself her evening martini. At seven she telephoned Adam. The lawyer was as startled as she had been. He said he would call the Philadelphia hotel and then try some of the more likely New York hotels.

He came to Jeanne's apartment at nine, looking sombre. He kept staring at the floor, puffing on his pipe, his red face sharpened by worry lines. It was almost hopeless, he said, to try to track the author down among the hundreds of Manhattan hotels. Who could say that he had not slipped off to Brooklyn or Newark instead, or even to another hotel in Philadelphia? Notifying the police was unthinkable. A missing-person alarm for Young-

blood Hawke would be a damaging news story, especially linked to Newton Leffer's lawsuit, which was going to start next week unless some
deliverance came to pass. There was nothing to do but sit tight and hope
that Hawke himself would soon appear. He was opposed to checking the
Philadelphia hospitals; that might start rumors which could get into the
newspapers. If something had happened to the writer he would be readily
identified at any hospital, and Jeanne would hear about it. However, the
talk about hospitals made him decide to call Dr. Eversill in Hovey.

It took some time to get through to the mountain town. The old man,
awakened from his sleep, said nothing but grumpy "Uh-huhs" for a while,
and Adam could hear him yawning. Then Eversill asked the lawyer
pointed questions about Hawke's recent behavior. Adam told him about
the wild outburst over Lax's disclosure of the new tax assessment.

Eversill said, "I can't blame him. Seems to me you people up there
been hunting Art Hawke to death like an animal. He's a good boy. He's
conscientious, that's most of his trouble, he's too blame conscientious.
He's been a fool too, getting himself in the hands of moneylenders and
Broadway nuts and all. New York's no place for a mountain boy. I think
Art's going to show up one place or another pretty soon, maybe Philadelphia, maybe New York, maybe even back here. If he does show there, you
put him to bed right away, no matter how fine he seems, d'you hear? And
call me right away, and I'll decide what to do next, but get him to bed."

Adam said, "Why, what do you think is wrong with him?"

"I hope nothing. This taking off without telling anybody sounds like
epileptic behavior. He may need treatment right away. If he's all right
and he's just disappeared for a while to get the lot of you out of his hair
I can find that out pretty quickly, but you do as I say."

Adam took Jeanne out to a restaurant. After a couple of cocktails they
both ruefully agreed that they weren't hungry, and there was no point in
ordering food. Jeanne consented to go to a movie, to create a stretch of
blank time in which Hawke might call. The colored shadows jigged and
dissolved without meaning on the screen for two hours, while she sat
scared in the darkness. When she got home there had been no calls from
Hawke, but three from Maas in Philadelphia, demanding news of the
author's whereabouts.

She did not close her eyes that night. She was afraid to take a sleeping
pill, in case news should come. At two in the morning she gave up the
tortured tossing in hot gloom, got up, made herself a cheese sandwich,
and spent the rest of the night in the living room on the sofa, working
over a trashy Civil War novel that Ross Hodge had given her, and comparing this dreary task, with a sick heart, to the brilliant excitement of
having a new Hawke manuscript in her hands.

The next day was perhaps the longest and most anguished in her life.
Morning blazed into noon, noon sloped into a sultry afternoon, night

came on, and still there was no word from Hawke. Jeanne paced her apartment, went out and shopped, spent two hours at the Hodge Hathaway office, killed two more hours at the hairdresser, calling her apartment often. Twice she telephoned the theatre in Philadelphia. Adam came again in the evening; and since one becomes used to anything, even the rack of uncertainty, this night they ate and drank. Adam was wavering about notifying the police. Another forty-eight hours at most, he said, and they would have no other course.

Jeanne's doorbell rang at about eleven-thirty the next day, when she was expecting nobody. She rushed to the door, and there stood a fat pale perspiring postman, who smiled and showed two rows of big teeth that seemed frightening. He held a thick manila envelope plastered with stamps. "Airmail special delivery registered, ma'am," he said, giving her a yellow register slip to sign. She could see Hawke's writing on the envelope. She scurried to her bedroom with the package and tore it open raggedly, breaking a nail so that her finger bled.

The contents were a sheaf of Hawke's long manuscript pages clipped together. Inserted in the clip were several smaller sheets of an airline's flimsy bluish stationery. She fell on her bed and read Hawke's letter.

Jeanie, my love—

I've done it. These are the last pages of *Boone County*. I've just finished the book on a Pan Am plane to Miami, bumping through a thunderstorm, so some of the sheets may be a bit harder to decipher. But I've finished it, Jeanie. I've finished my biggest and best book. I think I deserve a few points for effort, because I've finished it against odds.

I can't tell for sure what its fate will be. I should think it would be a widely read book for all its tragedy, because it's full of truth and the storytelling, unless I'm much mistaken, is as good as anybody can do who is alive now. Of course I'm nowhere for symbolism or poetry or the despair of civilization business. That side of the street has to be worked by other hands, but for the plain tale told by the daylight of Cervantes, without fancy figureskating, I think *Boone County* will stand for a while, maybe. I also feel as though I've used the last drop of gas in a drying tank to cough and shudder to the last page. But I've done it.

Now, Jeanne, when you edit this one be careful about slashing out the somewhat long dollars-and-cents stuff on how the coal business works in Letchworth (Boone), and the occasional paragraphs where I talk straight to the reader. I know this technique is a high crime nowadays but I've never conformed to the current fads of the English teachers. I'm a nineteenth-century novelist, as Quentin Judd rightly said. I think that century holds the main vein of the art. Beyond a certain apprentice period a man should stop paying attention to critics and write as he pleases. I've done that in this book from start to finish for the first time. I wrote *Evelyn* to please the critics and you saw what happened; though I still love *Evelyn* and think she'll hang around for a few years, too.

I'm sure Mr. Leffer will give you the mss. so you can get to work on it without delay. It's to his interest to see that the book gets to the press fast. But if he makes legal difficulties you'll find a stack of photostats in the cabin in Hovey where I wrote most of *Boone*. There you'll also find your black gloves, and my will.

I wrote the will in one of my anxious spells. I'm having another one right now; I'm drenched in sweat though this plane is chilly. Writers are sad animals. This business of creating people and events out of thin air drains some vital fluid out of you and leaves you a prey to ridiculous and pitiful melancholia, if not worse. I think this entitles us scribblers to a certain— not moral latitude, I'll die without conceding that an artist is entitled to behave less decently or honorably than a plumber—but a certain forgiveness for our follies, our mistakes, and our extravagances.

I'm sorry about Frieda, Jeanie. If she hadn't been at the Prince party I think you and I would be a settled happily married pair with God knows how many children. My work would be further along, I'd have avoided most of the disasters that have befallen me—because you'd have stopped me—and generally I'd be a healthy author charging through the American Comedy, instead of the weary fleeing beast I am at the moment. But let me say that Karl, God rest his soul, was wrong about one thing. I have been my own worst pursuer, and nobody else is to blame. I have always sounded the horn for the hounds myself. I have made fearful mistakes. Frieda was the worst.

I can plead the old plea, I was a young yokel in the big city. I think maybe we can also fault Frieda a bit for being so totally devoted to her own pleasure, so utterly incapable of considering that you can't suck up five years of a young man's life without irreparably altering that life. But I was well over twenty-one! The choice was mine. I guess I wanted to eat my turkey and have it. Frieda was all too ready to serve the turkey with all the trimmings.

Nor can I blame you for marrying Karl, though in low moments I often have. You're not as compassionate and long-suffering as you might be; you're a bit deficient in charity, but that's the fault of your virtue, a strong back-bone. Anyway, Jim Fry had to be born. He may turn out to be more im-portant than all of us. The long and the short of it must be what our mutual nemesis Frieda once said—"some mistakes define a person's char-acter." There's no going back and doing it over, but I want you to know that of all my mistakes I regret that one most, and would give much never to have laid eyes on Mrs. Winter.

I should apologize for the ink spurts and blotches that come from writing with a fountain pen at eighteen thousand feet, but on the whole I'm sur-prised by the clarity of the words I'm putting down. I'm really saying what I want to say to you. This must be the very last cough of the engine that produced *Boone County*. You know, Jeanne, a very curious thing has been happening to me in recent weeks. Some day I ought to write it up. It's really interesting. It's as though all my vital force, all my remaining brain energy has shrunk by some self-preserving instinct into my hours of writing. You'll see that these last scenes of *Boone* are excellent, perhaps the best stretch of sustained work I've ever done. Yet I can assure you that each day, from the moment I laid down the pen until the next time I took it up,

I've been living in a baffling fog full of screechy noises and red flares, a whirling dizzy onrush through darkness something like a tunnel ride in an amusement park. The only saving thing about it has been the dreaminess of it. I stopped "believing" in *The Lady from Letchworth* and all its attendant foolishness long ago. It was all a scary Coney Island ride full of bobbing cardboard devils, and I'd emerge into daylight sooner or later, or at least into an ordinary night time of hot dog stands and lamplit carousels, all I had to do was grit my teeth and hang on.

Of course I knew it was real, another mistake of mine and one of the worst. It's no excuse that Feydal and Maas encouraged me to try to market this old trash of mine. Why did I agree to do it? Money pressure. I'm well served. I'm sorry to think of the play going on even for another few weeks, to think of people buying tickets because my name is on the playbill. I have never deceived my audience but this once. The sooner the show closes the better. I feel no guilt at leaving it to perish, or to be pulled to pieces by that poor jackanapes Maas. I sympathize with the actors, but all it comes to is that they, like me, unwisely gambled time on a bad venture. It's a risk of their profession.

Jeanie, darling, I'm sorry I blasted you and Gus. You must take my word for it that my reserves are gone. I can't trust myself to produce normal conduct any more. It's a hell of a horrible feeling. You find yourself struggling to say things that will fit accepted standards, all the time fearing that anything can come out of your mouth—a stream of obscenity, or even insane gabbling! I have found out what it's like to be crazy. It is to stand apart and observe ordinary life all around you with the panic of an actor on stage who has forgotten his lines and his business. What one doesn't realize in ordinary mental health is that daily life is a *show*. You have to put on a right costume, to improvise right speeches, to do right actions, and all this isn't automatic, it takes concentration and work and a simply amazing degree of control!

The money pressure has eroded that control from my mind. What I'd give for the insouciance of Balzac, who let half the bill collectors in Paris search for him with bankruptcy judgments while he cheerfully ran up fresh bills in new shops under assumed names! I'm a goddamned Hovey boy, that's my trouble. To be beholden to any man on earth for anything, let alone a large sum of money, is an intolerable burden, a degradation like slavery, a poison that eats out the heart and soul. It must be gotten rid of at any cost.

Don't let this letter alarm you. I've been feeling better and better ever since I left Philadelphia. It's as though I've lanced a boil; but it'll be a long time draining, and I can't trust myself with you or Gus or anybody, and above all I must stay beyond the reach of the *Lady from Letchworth* company in its last thrashing agonies. I know that if the cries for help got through to me I wouldn't be able to resist, I'd plunge back into that doomed picking and picking and picking at the witless empty play I wrote as an ignoramus of twenty-two. If there is any experience short of physical torture, or the death of someone you love, that is worse than trying to dredge jokes out of an exhausted and sick spirit, I can't imagine it.

To free you from the responsibility—because I know they must be hounding you for my whereabouts—I'll tell you nothing of where I'm going, what I'm doing, or when I'll be back. You'll hear from me again, I don't know just when or how. Gus Adam is a great guy and I know things will never get out of control as long as he's in charge. I may say I'm in a state of extreme confusion regarding certain things, including just where I stand with you. When I asked you the other night in Philadelphia to make the arrangements for our wedding on the fifteenth you said "All right" with a very peculiar slow caution. I don't know why, and I prefer not to dwell on it. Frankly I've been aware for some time that I haven't been quite well and I haven't trusted myself to start discussions I might not be able to endure. I don't know whether I'll be back by the fifteenth but anyway you and I obviously have a great deal of frank talking to do before we proceed further. Or maybe you have only a frank sentence or two to utter.

Anyway, everything can wait. Everything can wait. I finished my book. I did that, and here are the last pages.

Hawke appeared to have run out of ink, for the page was only half written on, and the next sheet was pencilled in a hurried and peculiarly cramped hand.

I never loved anybody but you. Even in all the years I was stewing in the bed of Frieda Winter, I loved you, Jeanne. I pictured you before I met you, I recognized you when we met, except that you were too short and smoked too much and had too sharp a tongue, but still I knew who you were. No matter what happens, whether this plane crashes (as I'm dead certain it will, in my present frame of mind) or I live to ninety and commit a thousand follies far worse than anything I've done yet, you will always be my one love, the arms that should have embraced me, the lips that should have kissed me, the body that should have joined with mine. Maybe it will still come to pass. Maybe I'll fly safely through this storm. I love you, and in my heart I'm not scared. It's just that I'm worn out.

ARTHUR.

Jeanne sobbed over the last scribbled blue page. But she pulled herself together and telephoned Adam. Within the hour she presented herself at his office, looking as woebegone, Adam thought, as she had after Fry's death. She had the airmail package with her. The lawyer carefully put aside the yellow manuscript, and read the letter, puffing at his pipe, and glancing at Jeanne now and then from under his eyebrows. She noticed that he suddenly stopped reading at the next to last page and put the sheets on his desk.

"Well!" he said. "That's not too good. But it's something. Is there any further information in those last personal lines?"

"Nothing about where he is. I have an idea," Jeanne said. "I don't know how to follow it up."

"Where do you think he is?"

Jeanne told him of the evening when Hawke had learned of the death of Manuel Hauptmann, and of his oblique suggestion that Mrs. Hauptmann might solve his money problem. "I called my travel agent to find out how you get to Peru. The flight goes via Miami. This is just a hunch, Gus, but I think it's possible he's gone to borrow money from Mrs. Hauptmann. It's the only way Miami in July makes any sense. His mental state is not normal and I think this may have suddenly seemed to him the simple solution to everything. The main thing was, it involved running away three or four thousand miles. Good God, I know all about that urge to run away!"

Adam nodded several times, half-shutting his eyes, canting his head far to one side, and dancing his spread fingers against each other. "It's something to explore, and we shouldn't lose any time. Let me talk to Abe Tulking, he's done a lot of work for the Cerro de Pasco companies."

"All right," he said, returning to the office in a few minutes, fastening his tie. "Let's go to the Peruvian consulate. It's up in Rockefeller Center. By the time we get there Abe will have cleared the way."

In the cab he said after a long silence, with a keen look and the foxy smile that he tended to show in tight moments, "You know, if that's what Arthur's done he may not be so crazy. This woman is immensely wealthy. The amount of money Arthur needs is insignificant to her, especially as there's no question whatever of her being repaid in time. She's a long-standing admirer of his work. It may be a way out."

Jeanne said, "Oh hell, Gus, you know that the richer anybody is the more significant any sum of money is to them. I spend money more freely than Ross Hodge does. I doubt that he'll get it from her, and if he does he'll be damned sorry."

Adam grunted and said no more.

They had to wait a few minutes on the hard bench in the main room of the consulate, staring at the handsome posters of titanic Inca ruins and rugged snow-capped Andes peaks, while typewriters clattered at the many desks and half a dozen Spanish conversations went on among the staff. The consul appeared in the doorway of his inner office, shaking hands with a departing visitor.

"Meester Adam? Meesus Fry? Come in, please." The consul's little inviting gesture was full of grace. He was a fat-cheeked short man of fifty or so, with clever brown eyes, and thick black hair laced with gray. "So," he said, following them in, and motioning them to armchairs. "It is most interesting! Meester Youngblood Hawke's books are popular in Peru. *Will Horne* is my favorite. Politics in Kentucky, politics in Peru—not too much different!" He sat in his swivel chair, clasping his hands on his desk, displaying a heavy gold ring. "Well. I have spoken to Mr. Tulking, whom I know well, and I am at your service." He glanced from Adam to Jeanne,

with the narrowed eyes and kind smile of a man whose main task was to
size people up at short notice.

Adam said, "Have you found out yet whether Mr. Hawke got a visa in
this office recently?"

"Tourist card. A visa is not necessary." The consul slipped on heavy
black-rimmed glasses, picked up a paper on his desk, and looked it up and
down in a practiced way. "Yes. The card was issued ten days ago. Mr.
Hawke wrote that the purpose of his visit was business." The consul
pointed with his glasses at the paper, and sank back in his chair, waiting,
his eyes shifting from Jeanne to the lawyer and back, his ringed hand
drumming the desk.

Adam said after a little silence, "We're going to have to speak to you in
confidence. Youngblood Hawke has been under a severe mental strain
lately. He went off on a trip suddenly, day before yesterday, without
notifying Mrs. Fry, to whom he is engaged, or any of his associates. We
believe he's not quite well. He may need medical care when he reaches
Peru, if that's where he's gone."

The consul nodded, his expression not changing. "It isn't hard to find
out whether he came through the Limatambo Airport in the past few
days, or if he's booked to arrive there soon. And we could check the main
tourist hotels, and trace him. Have you no idea of his possible destination
in my country? None at all?"

Adam looked at Jeanne, who sat impassively on the edge of her seat,
hands clasped in her lap. He said, "Are you acquainted with the Hauptmann family?"

The consul's control slipped; he was not equal to this surprise, and his
face became alive with the zest for news. "Very well, of course. All three
brothers are my close friends. I mean, of course—you know, Manuel recently died. The oldest one, Bernard, and I went to school in Switzerland
together."

Adam said, "Manuel and Honor Hauptmann were good friends of Mr.
Hawke. There's a chance that he may be visiting Mrs. Hauptmann."

The consul nodded slowly three times, his face coming back under
control, a faint smile lingering around his eyes. In the three nods was a
world of Latin appreciation of the picture in all its luscious possibilities,
the famous novelist, the rich American widow of the dead Hauptmann
brother . . . He said with exaggerated calm, "It might be an idea to telephone or cable Mrs. Hauptmann, then."

Adam said, "I've thought of that, and that's probably the next step."

"Do you know her? I'll be glad to put the call through and explain
what the situation is, if you prefer," the consul said briskly.

Adam said, "Mrs. Fry and I have both met Mrs. Hauptmann. You
might have better luck than we would, though, trying to telephone Peru."

The consul laughed. "We have our troubles, too." He took the tele-

phone and spoke in commanding tones in Spanish, mentioning the Hauptmann name and the word "Miraflores" several times. He said to Adam and Jeanne with a smile, "Manuel built a charming place, rather palatial, in Miraflores, it's a beautiful district just south of Lima proper, and I don't think he ever slept half a dozen nights in it, poor fellow. I imagine Mrs. Hauptmann will be there. She prefers Lima to the country. Everybody does. Of course the hacienda up north is magnificent, but—" he shrugged eloquently. "Sugar cane as far as the eye can see, hm?"

He answered the ringing telephone, and after a short exchange in Spanish said to Adam and Jeanne, "The circuits are busy. We can talk to Lima at a quarter past two. Would you care to have your lunch and return here? I shall not be leaving."

Adam and Jeanne made their way to the French restaurant of Rockefeller Plaza through the underground tunnels, because a cloudburst was showering the streets in a dark gray slanting curtain. It was still raining when they had both glumly consumed their brook trouts with a glass or two of wine, so back through the tunnels they went and up to the Peruvian consulate—which, when they re-entered it, seemed as familiar to Jeanne, posters and all, as though she had been working there for a year. A girl showed them at once into the inner office.

The consul greeted them like an old friend, his first wariness quite gone. He was smiling and excited. "Ah, what a pity. They put us through to Mrs. Hauptmann not fifteen minutes ago. She was up at the hacienda, after all, which is near Trujillo, about three hundred miles to the north. Getting another connection with her would have been very chancy. I took the liberty of discussing the matter. I don't think it's five minutes since I hung up. I did try to prolong it. I'm so sorry."

Jeanne said, "Is Arthur there?"

"No, he isn't, Mrs. Fry, but— Sit down, please. Sit down, Mr. Adam." The consul savored the pause as they sat looking at him anxiously. Runaway novelists were not the usual fare in his repetitious days. He clasped his hands, pursed his lips, and at last spoke. "I would say I have very good news. Your famous Mr. Hawke is located. He is indeed on his way to visit Mrs. Hauptmann. He would be in Peru now except that his flight was held up in Miami by bad weather. He should be en route now, and should be landing at Limatambo Airport this evening."

Adam glanced at Jeanne. "Good hunch."

Jeanne said to the consul, "Has she talked to him by telephone? Does she know anything about his condition?"

The consul suppressed a small masculine smile. "Mrs. Honor Hauptmann has talked to Mr. Youngblood Hawke by telephone twice in the past three days, Mrs. Fry—once from Philadelphia, once from Miami. She was astounded when I mentioned, as delicately as I could, that Mr. Hawke's attorney was somewhat concerned about his—mental serenity.

She says he has sounded in good spirits, full of jokes and energy, his old self in every way. Mr. Hawke has just opened a play in Philadelphia, and he has purposely told nobody where he was going—this is what he said to Mrs. Hauptmann—because he wanted to be sure of an uninterrupted vacation. She was quite surprised that anyone had found out he was on his way there, and very relieved when I said the inquiry came from Mr. Adam."

Jeanne said, "Did she mention how long he plans to stay?"

The consul said with the same faint smile, "Apparently for a little while, Mrs. Fry, because she spoke of taking him sight-seeing, and if he goes to see all the places she mentioned it will take a couple of weeks." He grinned at Adam. "There is much to see in my country. I made it clear to Mrs. Hauptmann that the belief here was that he might need some medical attention. She is quite incredulous, but we left it this way. She will telephone or cable you, Mr. Adam, without his knowledge, as soon as she has seen him and formed an impression of his—his well-being."

"Very good." Adam glanced at Jeanne, who made a despairing little gesture with both hands. Adam stood, shook hands with the consul, and thanked him. The consul said he only regretted that Mr. Hawke had chosen July to make a trip to Peru, because it was winter there now and the weather tended to be gloomy. He had perhaps been presumptuous in suggesting to Mrs. Hauptmann that Mr. Hawke might be induced to honor the San Marcos University by giving a little lecture there. "It isn't every day that we have a person like Youngblood Hawke in our country," said the consul. "It might give him pleasure to lecture at the oldest university in the Western Hemisphere. Goodbye, Mrs. Fry. I feel that there is very little to worry about."

Jeanne said to Adam as they walked down the corridor, "The consul has Arthur throwing me over for Honor Hauptmann. He finds the whole mess rather delightful. I'm glad somebody's amused."

Adam said, "That's a little far-fetched. We're in much better shape now than when we came here, Jeanne. We know where he is and we have some indication that he's all right."

"We're in as good shape as Arthur is," Jeanne said. "It seems we won't know how good that is for a while. I'm open for an invitation to get drunk tonight."

"I happen to be free," said the lawyer.

2

Running away is, in certain circumstances, a delicious sensation, however illusory and short-lived the delight may prove to be. To cut one's ties, to leave no forwarding address and no telephone number, to tear free of

one's web of commitments and communications, to drop suddenly the things everyone supposes you are going to do, the people you unquestionably are supposed to stay in touch with, to vanish into the broad buzzing anonymity of an industrial civilization—it can be the very balm of Gilead to a harassed spirit. Hawke felt, in the exultation of his train ride out of Philadelphia into thin air, that he all at once understood the criminal mind. He wondered why he had not thought of this grand surcease before. Buoyed along in this intoxication he checked into one of the shabbiest hotels in the side streets of midtown Broadway, signing the register *Anthony Trollope*, with the address 1040 Twain Street, Dreiser, New Jersey. The fat waxen-faced clerk gave him a key, glancing at him with a tinge of bleary suspicion; probably, Hawke thought, because he was too well-dressed to be checking into this place without a whore. The grimy little mildew-smelling room, with its ragged carpet, its torn washed-out bedspread, the window facing directly into the glaring red neon letters HOTE—, gave him a sense of calm snug peace like a monk's cell, for all the traffic noise and radio jazz that filled the air. He felt a twisted pleasure in staring at the greasy black telephone and not calling Jeanne, or Adam, or anyone else. He was escaping from Jeanne, he thought, as much as from anybody. Jeanne would rush him to a doctor. He was damned if he needed a doctor! He was fine! These were his thoughts as he downed a second and third slug of bourbon out of a bathroom glass. It even crossed his mind to go out and ask the depraved-looking elevator man to provide him with a prostitute. How long it had been since he had even had such an impulse! Why, he felt as full of zip as a college boy! But then he wrinkled his nose in disgust, took another heavy drink and fell asleep with his clothes on.

It depressed him next morning to have to doff the cloak of anonymity at the bank and at the airline office, but he reflected that after all he wasn't a fugitive, there was no alarm out yet for him. He went back to the dirty hotel room and scrawled through the day at the last scenes of his book until it was time to go to the airport, still enjoying very much the perverse pleasure of not telephoning anybody. His happy mood did not begin to evaporate until he went through the gate and saw the airplane, big, stiff and ugly in the raw dusk, with its four round propeller engines bulging out of the wing, and its eager long silvery snout seeming to strain to leap into the storm clouds. Hawke had the sudden strong premonition that this machine had been built to carry him to his death. It had a menacing, historic look about it as it straddled there on its wheeled legs. In his mind's eye he saw it scattered in flaming broken pieces even as he was carried along in the push of the passengers through the gate through the rain up the movable staircase to the black oval door. But he dismissed these neurasthenic imaginings. He had his workpad in a brief-case, and as soon as he belted himself into a seat he began to write, ignor-

ing the curious glances of the gray-headed woman beside him. The plane was on the ground for over an hour before it took off, and he wrote ceaselessly. He had reached that inspiring point in a manuscript where the last moments, the last words, were clear to him, and nothing remained but to cut his way to them through thirty or forty pages. He paused only for the jolting of the take-off and the rough climb through the clouds. When the plane levelled off above white cottony clouds under the stars and a glittering moon he bent to his task again. He had seldom written so much so quickly; but whatever the weakening of his judgment in other things, it was in sharp focus as he glanced over his pages. The work was good. The English was clear and spare. The long long tale was nearing its last grand chord. His pen raced forward. The plane almost faded from his consciousness. His spirit was in the small Kentucky town where his last scene was unfolding—it was Hovey, of course, he could never write at his best except about Hovey—and he was quite startled when his seat began to buck and toss, and lightning blazed along the wings, and the captain droned some reassuring garbled words over the loudspeaker. They had been in the air nearly four hours. He was only a few pages from the end. He steadied the pad as well as he could, scrawled on in straggles of words that danced above and below the ruled lines of the pages—and at last, came the exalting moment when he printed

THE END

En-Route New York–Miami
7 July 1953.

He had nobody with whom to share his pleasure, his overpowering sense of achievement and of deliverance. The gray-headed lady beside him sat clutching her chair arms, eyes wide in fear. He asked the stewardess as she stumbled by with airsickness bags to bring him some letter paper. The haggard girl looked astonished, but she did so. Meanwhile he became all too aware of the storm, and aware too of the immense drain that the writing spurt had been. His head hurt abominably, and all his limbs were shaky. Still, he wrote the letter to Jeanne.

Finishing the book gave him a flash of clarity about his trip. What in God's name was he doing flying to Peru? Why was he in the air, in a storm over Florida? Why wasn't he with Jeanne, cracking a bottle of champagne? What kind of insane course was he in? By the time he ended the letter he had all but resolved to turn back from Miami—and not only that, but to return by train, and to give himself into the hands of doctors when he got back to New York. When the descending plane jolted out of the blackness at last and he saw the lights of Miami not far below in a

golden mist, his mood improved, and when the plane bounced to a landing and taxied to a normal quiet stop he felt a little ashamed of his spell
of dismay. All the same, the impulse to turn back remained strong. It
carried him to the desk of the airline, where he saw the posted notice
that his connecting flight to Lima had been put off twelve hours. This
was a relief. He would get some sleep, he decided, and see how he felt
in the morning.

He went to an expensive hotel in Miami Beach, checked in under
his own name, and ordered a quart of champagne and some caviar and
crackers. The icy air conditioning of the bleak big room, all glass and
fluorescent lighting and metal tube furniture, was a welcome change
from the wet choking July heat of Miami. He celebrated the completion
of his novel by drinking up the champagne himself and eating the
caviar, toasting his glum solitary image in a mirror.

In the daylight next morning he felt silly at the notion of returning
to New York. Taking the train was too womanish to be thought of. Really,
however, he did want to turn back. The charm of running away was
fading. He missed Jeanne. He was troubled to think how puzzled and
upset she must be. Against all this, turning back would be an admission of
mental disturbance. It was impossible to explain as normal—or even as
normally quixotic in an artist—deciding to fly to Peru, getting as far as
Miami, and then reversing his track. Besides, his trip was not a deranged
flight! Honor Hauptmann had offered over the telephone, when he had
called her from Philadelphia, to lift from his neck the millstone of debt
which threatened to drown him in an unjust bankruptcy. By pressing on
to Peru he would prove that the trip was a thoughtful act, not an impulse
of psychoneurosis.

And yet he dreaded going on. He felt ill. Sleep had not helped him.
His skull was horribly tight, as though he were wearing an iron cap that
was slowly being compressed by the turning of a screw. Random aches
and stabs of pain came and went over his body, none of them lasting or
definable, but each bringing on a cold thrill of fear. Much of this was
acute hypochondria, he knew; but he could not recall ever feeling so close
to the edge of dissolution.

In the end, after sitting in his pajamas on the edge of his bed with his
hand on the telephone for perhaps ten minutes, a picture of paralyzed
irresolution, he put a call through to Honor, telling himself that if he
could not reach her he would take it as a "sign" that he should turn back—
a sign from whom or from what, he did not specify. The sign was not
forthcoming. It was only half-past seven, and the call went through. Hearing Honor's voice, he roused himself to make jokes about the delay and
the weather, and gave her his new arrival time. She was very gay and
chatty. She would send someone to meet him and bring him up to the
hacienda, and she was counting the hours. Lima was an impossible small

town, her life would be unendurable if she were seen there with him, especially if she met him at the airport. He hung up, breaking the connection with a voice thousands of miles away in the lower hemisphere of the world, and set about going to his fate, whatever it was.

In his depressed and confused state of mind, he forgot to do something he had been so anxious to do that he had written himself a note the night before, fixing it on the bathroom mirror with Scotch tape: BUY D-S. He had run out of his red-barred white capsules in Philadelphia. He had intended to renew the prescription in New York, and then had forgotten, in the drive to finish his book. He had meant to go to a drugstore as soon as he arrived in Miami—the capsules were called dilantin sodium, and could be had anywhere—but again other preoccupations crowded the medicine from his mind. He read the note on the bathroom mirror; but he was on the airplane and it was taking off before he remembered that once again he had forgotten to get the capsules. He figured that in a big city like Lima he would be able to have the prescription filled. Hawke felt no ill effect from not having taken the stuff for several days; in fact he was not as wretched physically as he had been in the last days of the rehearsals. In his heart he hated being dependent on a medicine. There was something unmanly about it. He even thought that half his ills might be due to the continuing saturation of his bloodstream with a foreign substance. But Dr. Eversill had been emphatic in ordering him to keep up the medication, so of course he would do it. One was never wholly one's own man nowadays, he thought, as the plane soared southward in brilliant morning light. Any American adult was half in the hands of his lawyer and his doctor.

3

A week later, Adam was at his office in the law school, conferring with a student, but finding it hard to concentrate on the young fellow's explanation of his failure to hand in a theme paper on time. He was thinking about Hawke. Five days had gone by since the Peruvian consul had called to read him a night cable from Honor Hauptmann, asserting that Hawke was in good health, in wonderful spirits; and that he had charmed everybody at the dinner party at the hacienda the evening after his arrival. She said the author planned a day or two of rest, and then some leisurely sight-seeing, and there was nothing whatever to worry about. Since then Adam had heard no more. All day the lawyer had had a feeling that a break in the situation was imminent.

And indeed the secretary of his Wall Street office telephoned him while this student was still talking to him. "There's a cable from Mr. Hawke," she said. "I thought you'd like to know right away."

"*Yes!* Read it."

"Okay. *Returning tomorrow. Please ask Doctor Eversill come up to New York. Not exactly ill but need checking over. Have arranged loan meet payment. Tell Leffer. Love to Jeanne. Don't alarm her. Hawke.*"

Adam said, "I see. Look, call the Peruvian consulate right away, will you? The consul's name is Galvez. Ask him for the cable address of Mrs. Honor Hauptmann. She has two addresses, one in Miraflores, the other in some district up north. You'll have to say you're calling for Youngblood Hawke's attorney. Let me know when you have them."

He got rid of the student, and put in a call to the doctor in Kentucky, wondering wryly at the author's unchanging suspicious nature. With all the doctors to choose from in New York, the medical center of the world, Arthur Hawke still wanted his old Hovey doctor, the man who had treated him for his childhood fevers.

Jeanne was back at Hodge Hathaway, putting in a full day's work. Adam went there without telephoning her. In these days of crisis he often dropped by in the late afternoon and took her out for cocktails and a review of the situation. He found her in her windowless editor's cubicle, dankly air-conditioned, the four walls lined with new Hodge Hathaway books in a rainbow display of stiff unsoiled jackets. On her desk was a pile of four cardboard cartons. A fifth was in her lap, and she slouched over it, holding a sheaf of pages high in one hand, laughing at what she read. "Oh, hi," she said, peering up at him through owlish round glasses. "You know, it's kind of eerie, but some kid from Seattle has sent in a manuscript which is remarkably like Arthur's early work. Even these boxes are what Arthur used for *Alms for Oblivion,* his emptied cartons of typewriter paper. He's obviously imitating Arthur, but he has his own vein and it's good. He's Irish, his name's O'Connell, and he's only twenty-four."

"Well, that's impressive," the lawyer said. "Arthur's become a model already, and so far as he's concerned his real work hasn't begun."

Jeanne took off her glasses and put the carton aside, marking the page she had been reading. Adam went on, "I have a cable from him, Jeanne."

Her relaxation vanished. Lines of concern and fear sprang into her face. "Yes?"

"He's coming home tomorrow."

"Is he all right?"

"Apparently. He says he's arranged the loan."

"Oh. He has." Jeanne's tone was cold and flat. She lit a cigarette with fumbling gestures.

Then Adam told her of Hawke's request for Dr. Eversill. Jeanne took the news stolidly. Adam said he had telephoned the old Kentucky physician, and Eversill had agreed to fly to New York that night.

Jeanne said, "Something must have happened down there. Something more than arranging a loan."

"He specifically says he isn't ill."

"What plane is he coming on? We'd better meet him."

"He didn't mention a flight number or an airline."

Jeanne's hand stopped in the act of tapping ash off her cigarette. She looked the lawyer in the eye for a long moment. "He's coming with the woman."

"He didn't say so."

"Anything else in this cable?"

"No. 'Love to Jeanne' were the last words."

Jeanne said drily, "Bless his heart." She struck the pile of cartons in front of her with a fist. "I pity the girl who gets involved with this one, that's all."

"Jeanne, we're in an unfortunate spot because of timing. I'm about sure Arthur won't need that loan. You know Hoag's been claiming for a month that he was about to sign Gimbels for his shopping center. I've kept in touch with Gimbels' lawyers. They're terribly cautious but this morning they told me that the closing of the lease will probably take place Friday. I called Newton Leffer. He says if I show him a signed Gimbels' lease he'll release Arthur from the agreement. Arthur probably should know this."

"Well, he will tomorrow, it seems."

Adam said, "Possibly we were remiss in not cabling him about the decision on the jeopardy assessment, but there too I only have the word of a man in Washington for it. I hate to raise Arthur's hopes only to dash them again, when he's taken such a battering. I'm thinking I might still cable him about these things, and about the closing of the show. It would improve his spirits, and maybe he wouldn't have to escort Mrs. Hauptmann back here, if that's what he's thinking of doing."

Jeanne pondered this. "Well, there's no harm in trying, though I suspect things have gone too far and are beyond our control. He'll have to stay somewhere, unless the doctor admits him to a hospital. Do you suppose we should make a hotel reservation?"

"I did. I booked Dr. Eversill and Arthur into the Plaza. He has a horror of hospitals."

Jeanne began clearing her desk. "Well, well. I had an appointment to marry Mr. Youngblood Hawke on July fifteenth, you may recall. It's never been officially cancelled. Do you suppose I should rush around assembling a trousseau?"

"I don't see why you shouldn't buy some things, Jeanne. A lot will depend on his condition."

"If that's what it depends on—" She rammed her drawers shut and locked the desk. "He used to come to my apartment almost every night

when he was writing *Chain of Command*. This was before—before Mrs. Winter. I never knew until he got there whether I should be dressed for a work session or for dinner at the Colony. And believe me, he would roar with impatience if I so much as changed my dress, let alone did my face. How young and stupid I was! I put up with this nonsense for almost a year. I suppose it was this talent for keeping me guessing that enslaved me to him. To this hour I don't know what the devil to expect next from him. Me, I've always been as predictable as a milkman."

Adam stood. "I think you surprised him a little by marrying Karl."

Jeanne looked up at him sharply, eyes gleaming. "Served him right, the miserable wretch."

"Cocktail hour," said Adam. "But first I'm going to cable Arthur, if you concur."

Jeanne pushed the telephone across the desk to him.

4

Hawke did not receive Adam's cable. When he arrived in New York he had no idea of the improvement in his fortunes. His spirit was at a black ebb. He was taking dilantin sodium capsules again, but his physical condition was disturbing, if not alarming. He had had a fall, and some kind of mild convulsion, while sight-seeing in the Andes; he had fallen on a stone terrace of the Inca ghost city, Machu Picchu, and had been unconscious for about five minutes. The Indian guide had brought him to, and had dismissed the seizure as a touch of the *soroche*, the altitude sickness, an affliction that struck many foreigners who refused—as Hawke had—to heed the warnings of the tourist books, and to take long rests at these heights. What troubled Hawke most was that he remembered absolutely nothing about the fall.

All of his time in Peru was a wild whirling phantasmagoria in his memory: the parties at the huge house of the Hauptmanns in a Lima suburb, and the huger hacienda in the north, the weird brown deserts through which they had driven, the queer chill drizzle that had never stopped falling in Lima, the heavy low gray sky that had never let through a bar of sunlight all the time he was there; the amazing steep gorges of the Andes that they had either flown over, sucking oxygen from tubes, or rode through on rickety trains crawling along breath-stopping chasms; the museums full of monstrosities of solid gold, the extravagant Spanish churches, the awesome Inca ruins built of stone blocks each as big as a railroad car, fitted together without plaster like mosaic work; the strange little sweetmeats individually wrapped in gold foil, which were the favored dessert; none of these impressions were sorted out in his mind, he could not have said which day he had driven up the coastal desert and

which day he had flown to Cuzco, but at least he remembered that he had experienced these things. About his fall he could recollect absolutely nothing. He did remember leaving the hotel and walking to the ruins. The next thing he could recall was sitting in the hotel bar about an hour later drinking a highball and arguing mulishly against being put to bed. Honor had described all the circumstances of his seizure, but his mind remained blank about that stretch of time. Honor's physician in Lima had examined him and had tried hard to make him enter a hospital for brain tests. Hawke had insisted, with loud stubbornness not far from panic, that he was going home; and he had sent off the cabled request for Dr. Eversill.

Then had come Honor's peculiar last-minute decision to travel with him. That too, had dismayed him. Honor's behavior throughout his visit had been baffling, and very wearing on his already spent nerves. She had never once mentioned the question of the money, until he had said he was returning to New York; then in a few quick dry sentences she had offered to come with him so as to arrange the loan with her New York lawyers. Until then she had turned in an exasperating performance of the merry widow, flirtatious and coy, hot and cold, by turns. The only clear thing about her conduct was that she revelled in having Youngblood Hawke trailing around after her. She had exhibited him to as many Peruvians and foreign diplomats as possible in a series of dinner parties. None of this had been good for Hawke's mental or physical well-being, though he had worked hard at being the gracious and amusing American author, in order to please her. After all, he wanted money from her!

He dreaded the effect on Jeanne of his returning in Honor's company, but what could he do? There was no discerning Honor Hauptmann's intentions. Was she planning to have an affair with him as the price of the loan—his skin crawled at the idea—or did she have some notion of developing their relationship into a marriage, or was she merely following caprice without any long thoughts? Her ways of thinking were utterly foreign to him. She had too much money. He had put himself in her power and he had to ride out the event. On the information he had, she was saving him from a scandalous lawsuit, and perhaps a bankruptcy.

The most frightening thing of all happened on the plane a few hours before they reached New York. Just when dawn began to show pink in the east, making rosy gleams on the plane's wing, he had a muscular attack. First he noticed that the thumb of the hand with which he was holding his paperback detective story began to twitch. This was not new, fatigue or nerves sometimes brought it on. But the twitching was stronger than ever before, and soon spread to his whole hand, so that he had to drop the book. Then the convulsive jerking marched up his wrist, to his forearm and then to his elbow while he watched with horror his own body going more and more out of control. All this time Honor was beside

him sleeping off nembutal, which he had also taken, but without effect. By some desperate instinct Hawke seized his shaking left arm in the firm grip of his right hand and held it rigid for several minutes, arresting the motion. After a while he felt the jerks in the muscles subside, and when he cautiously let the arm go he found it was obeying him again, though it was shaky and somewhat numbed.

He did not mention the experience to Honor when she awoke much later, all cheery, refreshed and ready to polish off the scrambled eggs brought by the stewardess. Hawke did not eat, and he was hard put to it to respond to Honor's affectionate good humor. The nearer they got to New York the more intimate she became. He found her blandishments oppressive; he much preferred her in her hard-boiled moods; but he had made the trip to get seventy-five thousand dollars from her, and the mission now was about to succeed. He was already falling into a sense of obligation and subservience. What could he do but be pleasant to the woman?

A limousine long and black as a hearse took them into the city. Hawke felt a brief pulse of good cheer when he saw the towers of Manhattan rising beyond the flat square apartment houses of Queens, beyond the twisting highway and the rivers of snorting automobiles. It was one of the rare days that can come in July after a night of wild electric storms, when the New York air is clear and springlike, and there is even a tang of the sea in it; though within a few hours the hot summer miasma of smoke, dust and steam darkens all once more. Honor chattered like a bird. This was the only city in the world! She intended to spend six months a year here at the very least, it was the one place for clothes, for talk, for people, for gaiety, for food, for fun, for the latest word. All the big European cities were soft overripe fruits compared to this enchanted tough spiky town; and she and Hawke were going to have the time of their lives for a few weeks!

The limousine stopped at the side street entrance of Imperial House on Fifth Avenue, near the plaza, a huge apartment-hotel that had been prominent in the view from Feydal's apartment, with a tower that rose higher than the others nearby, capped with an incongruous mansard roof sheathed in green copper. "Come along," said Honor. "I want you to see my place. It's kind of nice."

Hawke followed her into the lobby, done in black marble and tarnished gilding, giving the effect, he thought, of an Italian tomb; the effect being heightened by the grave hush after the noise of the street. There were a few silent old ladies in costly black clothes sitting here and there in the lobby, and one startling huge African man in brilliant robes. The elevator went up and up and up. "Do you have the penthouse?" he said.

"One of them. Actually Manuel's brothers shared the cost. Whoever

happens to be in New York uses it. And our business friends sometimes. The President of Peru once stayed here. It's quite comfortable."

She let herself in, opening a black door set with a circular Chinese ornament of green stone. "The hotel sometimes rents it out by the week. People pay incredible prices. Diplomats, Hollywood stars, and such. It ends up costing us surprisingly little."

The height-horror that had often overcome him in the Andes prickled in Hawke's nerves as he walked into the living room. One wall was nothing but glass, looking past a narrow railed terrace across empty space to the downtown skyscraper clusters. The wrought-iron rails of the terrace were a comforting break in the view.

Honor said, "I think this Chinese modern was a mistake, to me the whole place looks like an oversize powder room, but Manuel saw an apartment like this in Rome and was mad for it."

With an effort, Hawke pulled his gaze away from the abysmal downtown view and looked dizzily around the room. It was a rectangular expanse of black and white, with white walls and black mirrors, an improbably rich white carpet like the massed pelts of a thousand ermines, a black couch as long as the side of a subway car, big black armchairs, and Chinese screens, jars, Buddhas, and dragons blooming here and there in blotches of wild color.

"Well, it's quite a place," he managed to say. "Quite a view."

"Oh, the view is in the bedroom. Come here."

The bed was circular, covered in purple, and big enough for six people. There was little else in the room beside more of the furry white carpeting and one gigantic black urn streaked with purple. Picture windows opened north, west, and south, with no rails to bar the view. It was a sight of New York such as an airplane pilot might enjoy. To the left the downtown windows glittered in the towers; to the right the rich green trees of the park stretched off to the distance, lined by the opulent broken wall of Fifth Avenue; straight ahead were the high hotels of Central Park South, and beyond them the Hudson and the Palisades, and the unseen three thousand miles of a more prosaic United States.

"As views of New York go, I call this a view," said Honor. "This room was what sold Manuel on the apartment. Until then he was muttering about owning a brownstone in the east sixties. Well? What do you think of it?"

"Beats anything I've ever seen." To quell his vertigo he was staring at The Park Tower, trying to pick out the window where he had often stood with his naked mistress, looking at Central Park.

"Well, good, I'll have them bring up your luggage," Honor said, and she picked up a white telephone on a bedside table.

"What? What the devil are you talking about, Honor?"

"Hello? This is Mrs. Hauptmann. Will you please get Mr. Hawke's

luggage from the black Lincoln at the side entrance? The chauffeur knows which is which. Yes, and deliver it to P 3, please. Thank you."

"Honor, don't be absurd. This is your apartment, I can't stay here and I don't want to."

A sly grin animated her chubby face. "If you're worried about the proprieties, dear, my suite is already reserved at the Waldorf. It's the suite my mother always used. Remember?"

"It isn't that. I mean—well, it's terrifically kind of you, but—it's out of the question, really it is." He was stammering because he could not utter his real objections: first, that the height sickened him, and second and more important, that the situation was taking on a nightmare resemblance to his early sparring with Frieda Winter.

While they were arguing, the ministerial elevator man brought in Hawke's bags. "Good heavens, you can use it till you find something more permanent, can't you?" Honor was saying. "I *want* you to have it. I can't stay here, don't you realize that! Manuel pops out at me wherever I look."

"Honor, I'm not used to living like this, that's all, I feel uncomfortable and silly here, an impostor—"

Honor's face hardened, and she said in her bank manager tone, "Arthur, is there any substantial reason why you can't accept my hospitality for a few days? Or why you don't want to? If there is out with it, and stop all this talk."

This was a slice of the knife to the bone of the problem, which was Jeanne. Hawke hesitated. Fatigue, lassitude, mortal defeat and depression dropped over him, a mantle of smothering sackcloth. "Well, for a few days, till I get myself a place, I guess I can stay," he said. "I seem to be in at this point, bag and baggage, don't I? Thank you, Honor, it's very gracious of you."

She put her hand on his arm and gave him a slithering lipstick kiss on the mouth. "Now I'm getting out of here. You look tired and I think you should sleep. I have a couple of appointments scheduled. That loan should be all lined up by tonight. Suppose you come and have dinner with me at the Waldorf about seven, okay? And I'll tell you how things stand."

"All right, Honor."

"What I would really like," she said, "is for it to be snowing like all hell outside tonight, and for you to fall in with bloodshot eyes and a three-day beard, in a greasy sheepskin coat with snowflakes still on the collar. I'd pour Scotch for you by the glassful, and we could turn back the clock and start there again, and cancel whatever has happened in between."

He said with a pallid, exhausted smile, "There are four books I'd rather not write all over."

She laughed. "No, no, and there are three children I'd rather not bear all over. We'll keep the books and the children, okay? And blot out the rest. Get some sleep, my dear. Pull the shades and sleep. You're done in."

When she was gone Hawke paced the elegant penthouse like a prisoner in a cell, trying not to look out of the windows, trying to fight off a growing sense that he was coming to his end. The smell of Frieda Winter's perfume pervaded the place. When he threw open a window and it streamed in thickly on the breeze, he realized he was having an exceptionally strong hallucination. He strode around senselessly. The place had a luxurious kitchen, four luxurious baths with golden fixtures, each with a luxurious dressing room. He saw his haunted face everywhere in elegant dark mirrors. The penthouse was in every touch the dream of shopgirls and mountain boys come true, and it was probably his for the asking if he could bring himself to woo Mrs. Hauptmann. It was the America that Hollywood had been portraying to the world for decades, it was the most spectacular possible view of New York, it was the very top of the world. It filled him with loathing. Why had he not defied Honor? How could he call Jeanne now and tell her he was staying in Honor Hauptmann's apartment? Yet he wanted to call Jeanne, he was desperate to see her, he needed help badly and quickly and aside from his mother she was the one person in the world he could lean on. And Dr. Eversill, he wanted to see him but to do that he had to call Gus Adam, and he could not call Gus before he called Jeanne, the implications were too wounding. As his panic mounted and his mind misted, one thing only seemed to come into focus clearly—that his suspicion of Jeanne, his notion that she was in love with Gus Adam, had been a self-destroying mad lapse. He was at the end of his rope. He had to call her at once and put himself in her hands.

He could not help looking out of the windows as he paced wildly, and each time he looked at the gulf of air and the park and the towers his giddiness and illness increased. He began to wonder whether he could make a coherent telephone call.

He was in the bedroom, facing down town, and the great spire of the Empire State Building made him think of the time he had stood with Jock Maas on the observation platform, an ignorant boor from Kentucky, shouting against the shriek of the wind that he would lick this city! And almost at the same instant he remembered everything about his fall at Machu Picchu—everything, the climb up the stairs to the terrace, the overwhelming terror at the green gulfs opening before him, the flash of religious exaltation, and he remembered going down and striking the cold stone with his forehead.

He stumbled to the telephone and seized it.

Jeanne's phone rang at her desk in the Hodge Hathaway offices. The

sound of Hawke's voice, the ghastly tone of it, shocked her. "Jeanne, is it you?"

"Yes. Darling, where are you?"

"Jeanne, I'm not well. Is Dr. Eversill here?"

"Yes. He is at the Plaza. Where are you, Arthur?"

His shaky, sepulchral, hurried voice replied, "Look, I think I'll make it till you get here but if anything happens I don't want to go to a hospital, do you hear! Get my mother and she can take care of me."

"Arthur, for God's sake *where are you?* What's the matter?"

"I'm at Imperial House in the penthouse, I think P 3. Yes, P 3. I'm all alone. I'm just not well, Jeanne. Come right away. I'll try to call the hotel doctor meantime, maybe he can give me something. Are you coming?"

"This minute, darling."

"I love you, Jeanne. Hurry, please. I'm really not well."

She called Dr. Eversill at once. It was almost half an hour before she could get a taxi and it could crawl through the midday traffic to the hotel. Eversill was in the lobby when she arrived, bent, white-headed, red-eyed, carrying his doctor's bag. He said, "He didn't answer the door and he doesn't answer the telephone. They're getting a passkey."

She could not speak.

A pink jolly-looking clerk came out of an office with a bunch of keys. It seemed to Jeanne that the upward ride of the elevator took half an hour, and she thought that they might not be moving, there was no building in the world as tall as this. Then the car jolted to a stop, and the jolly pink clerk opened the black door to penthouse P 3.

"Arthur!" she shouted, her voice echoing as she dashed inside. "Arthur, are you all right?"

She halted so suddenly that Dr. Eversill ran into her. She drew her breath in sharply, with a loud grating sound, and screamed.

Youngblood Hawke lay in the middle of the glorious white carpet, his big arms and legs sprawled awkwardly as a corpse's. He was writhing feebly, and his blue face was covered with a bloody foam.

CHAPTER TWENTY-SIX

1

THE news that the author of *Chain of Command* had been struck down by a possibly fatal illness made a wide public stir, almost as though he were a movie star or a baseball hero. It was an item on the evening radio and television news. The New York *Times* began the story next day in a small box on the front page, and carried it over to a whole column on the book page, in effect a discreet tentative obituary. Hawke had not fared too well in the reviews the *Times* had given his works one by one as they came out, but here he was acknowledged as a careless and coarse but powerful realistic storyteller who might eventually hold a place like Theodore Dreiser's. The worst thing the anonymous writer said of him was that he lacked the sombre poetry of Southern authors like Wolfe and Faulkner. In the other newspapers more was made of the gargantuan sums of money he had earned and dissipated, for by now it had become general New York gossip that Hawke was about to go bankrupt. The tabloids managed to mention his long friendship with the beautiful concert manager and theatrical producer, Mrs. Frieda Winter. On the whole, and except in the sober *Times*, it was clear that Hawke was newsworthy in good part because he had wielded his gifts like a conquistador to re-enact the American dream—log cabin to White House, Kentucky mountain boy to millionaire Pulitzer Prize author—and it added to his romance that he had plunged and lost his quick-won fortune. His career had height and depth, light and shadow, and it glittered with money, and it trailed the perfume of lovely conquered New York women.

Beyond all that he was newsworthy because so many people had read his stories. His trade sales in the hundreds of thousands, his paperback and book club distributions in the millions, had spread his name through the land; and every person who had closed a copy of *Chain of Command* or *Will Horne* with a satisfied sigh, and had studied his massive face on the dust jacket for a little while, to see what manner of man this was who had conjured up a bright non-existent world, had become in a sense his friend.

Jeanne was concerned about what his reaction would be when he woke and found himself in a hospital. Dr. Eversill assured her that it was no problem; and the staff brain specialist Dr. Rivkin, told her the same.

"He'll be too dull and weak to care at first," said Dr. Rivkin, a short lively man with grizzled hair and very bright and humorous brown eyes, "and then when the drugs wear off he'll be too glad he's alive to think of much else."

Still Jeanne worried. She sat by the bedside of the inert author all night.

Mrs. Hawke arrived early in the morning on the day following Hawke's collapse. Dr. Eversill had explained the gravity of the case to her on the telephone, and she had hied herself forthwith to Lexington in time to catch the night plane to New York. When she first walked into the hospital room and saw her famous son lying still, his body bulking large under a sheet, his yellow-gray face turned to one side on a pile of pillows, his tumbled hair black and clotted with perspiration, she halted and her countenance was tragic. But then she went to his bedside, put her hand to his head, felt his pulse, and turned to Eversill with a brave little smile, and with dry eyes only a bit brighter and wider than usual. "Why pshaw, Henry, he's cool and he's breathing all right. His pulse is good."

Eversill said, "He's doing well. Right now he's just sleeping off the heavy sedation. He's always been a strong boy."

Mrs. Hawke said, "I reckon this is the only thing that would ever make him take a vacation. You'll see, it'll all be for the best."

She tried to get Jeanne to go home and sleep, but Jeanne said she wasn't at all tired; she would leave a little later. The two women chatted there, in armchairs near the window, about Mrs. Hawke's plane trip and the weather, until the nurse walked out. Then the mother began asking questions. She was stupefied by the story of his dash to Peru. "Lord have mercy!" she said. "And him so worn he was ready to drop before he even left Hovey! And then all that horrible Broadway business on top of it, and then a trip to *Peru!* Why, you know, Jeanne, I reckon they drove this boy a little out of his head."

Jeanne explained Hawke's financial emergency, and told her that Hawke had obtained a promise of a loan from Mrs. Hauptmann, so that the trip was not a mere aberration. Mrs. Hawke shook her head. "Plumb foolish," she said. "Why, John would have loaned him twice that much. He offered to. I tell you, Jeanne, I'll be glad when you two are married because Art never is going to have any sense, and you'll have to supply the sense for two, just as I did. Where is this woman now, this Mrs. What's-her-name from Peru? She been here in the hospital at all?"

Jeanne told her of a telephone conversation she had had with Honor Hauptmann the night before. Honor had sounded terrified at the thought that somebody might expect her to put in an appearance at Hawke's bedside. She had an uncontrollable fear of these things, she had explained, but if money was needed Jeanne could call on her. She was sick over

what had happened and would probably go back to Peru in a day or so. Jeanne said the woman had talked hysterically.

Mrs. Hawke wrinkled her nose. "Humph! Her hysterical! What's *she* got to be hysterical about? Who is *she?* Sounds like another Mrs. Winter. Art won't need her money, I'll darn well see he doesn't, and she can just go on back to Peru! Peru! Plain out of his head!"

As they talked on Jeanne gave voice to a thought that had been gnawing at her. The whole calamity was her fault, she said. She had failed Arthur by running off to California at the time of his financial crack-up. She should have stayed with him, taken care of him, seen him through the writing of *Boone County*. Mrs. Hawke said, "Why pshaw, Jeanne, you had just lost your husband! You can't go from one man to another like you're changing your dress, at least a woman who's worth anything can't. I'm not talking about your Mrs. Winters, I reckon they can go to four different men in one night if it suits their pleasure. There are only two kinds of women. You're the kind that had to go away for a while, it was altogether the decent and proper thing to do."

Jeanne said, "He seemed all right whenever I talked to him, and anyway I figured you were there. Still I meant to come twice. I was all set, and each time—"

Mrs. Hawke said, "Now look, you can tear yourself to pieces with that kind of nonsense and it's silly, there's Art resting comfortably, he's going to be fine, and this time next year you'll be married and this will all be just a bad dream. Art's had a breakdown from overwork, that's all, and if he weren't strong as an elephant he'd have had it long ago, and it had to happen to convince him he's made of flesh and blood."

Hawke began to move and murmur. The two women went and stood beside him. It was a little past eleven in the morning. His eyes opened. He looked at Jeanne and blinked, then his glance shifted to his mother, and he smiled. "Hello, mama." His voice was clear but feeble.

"Hi there, son."

"How's Nancy, ma?"

"Why, she's fine. How are *you,* Art?"

"Not so hot."

"Well, you'll be okay."

"All right, ma. I'll have another bowl of soup."

Mrs. Hawke smiled uncertainly, and glanced at Jeanne, whose face was taut. "What's that, Art?"

Hawke said distinctly, and with petulance, "I said I'll have another bowl of soup."

The mother stammered, "I see. Well, let me see what I can do about that—" but even as she spoke Hawke's eyes drooped shut and his chest rose and fell regularly as before.

They called the nurse, who brought an interne to the room. The young

man was not particularly interested in the news, but said he would report it to Dr. Rivkin. Hawke might do this several times before really coming to, he said. There was nothing alarming about it, he had been talking in his sleep.

Hawke slept on and on, and after a while Jeanne dozed in her chair, determined not to leave until some definite change took place. She was awakened by Hawke's voice. "Hello, Jeanne darling." He was sitting up a little and looking at her. He was fearfully pale but the expression on his face was alert and sadly smiling. Both doctors were in the room, and Mrs. Hawke stood by the bed.

"Gosh, hello. You're awake."

"A lot more than you, I'd say." He glanced around at the massed bouquets. "Who sent all the flowers?"

Dr. Rivkin said, "We've given some to your neighbors, otherwise we'd have had to move you out."

A nurse brought a tray of toast and tea, and Hawke ate and drank. Jeanne saw that the doctors looked at each other with satisfaction. Rivkin said, "Well, he's swallowing nicely. We'll go to oral medication."

Hawke said to Eversill with a mouthful of toast, "I'm in a hospital, after all, hey?"

"Damn right, Art," said the doctor. "You're sick as a dog. Now you listen to me, I'm a suspicious hillbilly like you. So you take my word for this, hear? Dr. Rivkin is one of the best brain men in the United States, and he's the man who's giving the orders."

Hawke frowned. "You're going home?"

"Shucks, no, I'll be here as long as you want me."

The author nodded and looked at Dr. Rivkin. "What's the matter with me?"

Rivkin gave him a straightforward account of what had occurred, of the perils following such a seizure and the brain damage it implied. He said Hawke must consider himself in danger, though he had started making a good recovery; that he must reconcile himself to a course of medication and a stay in the hospital, the length depending on the character of his improvement. After a while would come the tests to evaluate more precisely what his condition was. The seizure had undoubtedly been caused, he said, by the old injury, the depressed skull fracture he had sustained at nineteen, when he had been unconscious for a day and a half. Hawke's irregular life and the various pressures on him had caused a flare-up in the irritability of the brain surrounding the scar tissue. The week-long lapse in taking dilantin sodium had come at the worst possible time. Hawke had had plenty of warnings, and now he had sustained a full-fledged multiple epileptic attack of the severest kind, which went by the name of status epilepticus. His recovery chances were

good, but the brain damage he had received would require that he live more carefully for the rest of his days. Hawke's piercing expressive eyes never left the little doctor's face.

He said, "Will I ever be able to write again?"

"Not at the breakneck pace Dr. Eversill has told me about."

"Will I be able to write, though? Will my mind work? Will I be able to start writing my next book some day, even on an easygoing schedule?"

"I see no reason why not," said the doctor, "but that is a long way off."

Hawke said, "Because if I can't write again I don't especially want to leave this room alive, you see."

"Oh, shut up, Art," his mother said.

Dr. Rivkin said firmly, "You know that Dostoevsky was an epileptic. Our knowledge of how these things affect creativity is nil. My job is to get you well and to tell you what you must do to stay well. Then your life is all yours again."

"My right arm and leg feel weak. I can hardly move them."

"Yes. That's a result of your attack, it has a fancy name but all you have to know is that it'll clear up as your general condition improves."

Hawke said to Eversill, "I like this doctor."

Eversill said, "That's good. This is no job for an old G.P. from Hovey, Kentucky."

Rivkin's eyes sparkled at Eversill. "You're the important fellows." He turned to Hawke and his face was serious and kind. "Do we understand each other? It's a question of your life. Your chances now are good, but any temperamental conduct is out of the question."

Hawke managed one of his old boyish grins. "I'm not really a crazy artist, Doctor. I've just been in the damnedest hole somehow, ever since I struck it rich."

The nurse gave Hawke a capsule and a glass of water. "You'll be taking a lot of that for a while," Rivkin said as Hawke gulped the medicine, "and mostly you'll sleep for the next few days."

"Sounds great."

Mrs. Hawke said, "How about company?"

"No visitors." Dr. Rivkin gave the mother an appraising look. "Do you cheer him up or aggravate him?"

"Aggravate him when he's going strong, cheer him up when he's flat on his back," Mrs. Hawke said. Hawke laughed and nodded, yawning.

"Standard mother," said Rivkin. "Well, stay around, but keep talking to a minimum." His glance rested on Jeanne.

Hawke said, "I'm going to marry her if I ever get out of here, if she'll still have me. She can stay, can't she?"

Rivkin said, "By all means."

The author's eyes were growing heavy. He reached out and took Mrs. Hawke's hand. "Sorry, mom," he said. "I've been a trouble to you right along."

"Well, that may be," she said, "but I'm Youngblood Hawke's mother."

2

The doctors said he was improving. His appetite began to return. They tapered off the sedation, and four days after the seizure they said he could receive visitors. Ross Hodge was the first. He and Gus Adam had been telephoning several times a day, and the publisher was at Hawke's bedside a half hour after Jeanne called him, spruce and brisk as ever, the taut skin glowing with a reddish tan on his round face, the lapels of his London-cut gray suit flaring handsomely. "I just want to tell you a couple of things and then I'll get out of here, Arthur," he said. "The first is that I've read the hundred twenty-five pages of *Boone* that Jeanne's gotten to the typist so far. It'll probably annoy you if I pass judgment on the basis of such a fragment, but I think it's not only your best book, it's your first great one."

Hawke was sitting propped on pillows in a gray hospital gown. He held out his hand to Hodge. "Even if you're saying that to cheer up your ailing prize bull, you've said the right thing. Thank you, Ross."

The publisher shook his hand, noting with surprise—which he did not allow to show in his face—the clammy weakness of Hawke's grip. "The next thing is about money and I'll be brief. Jeanne's been telling me your financial problems are more or less clearing up. Still, on the basis of what I've now read of *Boone* you can draw another fifty-thousand advance on it if you want to. I'll also give you just about any contract you ask for on the next book, here and now, short of handing over the firm to you."

"I tried publishing," Hawke said. "It's not my game. I'm grateful, Ross, and to show I am, I'll instruct my lawyer to hold you up for every last nickel you've got."

Hodge reached into his pocket. "Now at the latest count about four or five hundred get-well letters, wires, and cables have piled up for you at the office. I've never seen such an outpouring. They're from celebrities and from people you never heard of, and they've come from everywhere. There's one from Australia and another from Pakistan, to give you an idea. We'll acknowledge them with a card, if that's all right with you. I thought you'd like to see a few."

He handed Hawke a sheaf of letters and telegraph forms clipped together. The author read several, and Jeanne noticed that his hand began to tremble and his big lower lip to quiver. She came to him nonchalantly and took the sheaf. "Let me look too, dear."

Hawke said to the publisher in a shaky voice, "It's the greatest privilege in the world, the power to give people pleasure with stories. I never did anything to acquire it. I just discovered I had it. All I can claim is I've tried to use it diligently. And I tell you, Ross, what I've done is nothing compared to what I will do."

"I know that," said the publisher. "Just get well, now."

When he was gone Hawke sat looking straight ahead, his eyes far away, his expression drawn and melancholy. Jeanne pretended to read the letters, but she was watching him anxiously.

Hawke said after a while, "Where would you like to live, Jeanne, after—after all this?"

"Most anywhere, darling."

"I'm thinking of a university town in the Southwest—New Mexico, Arizona, some place like that. You see, Jeanne, first of all I want sunshine. I want it to pour sunshine where I live, all the year round. And I pretty well have to have a good library at hand for the Comedy."

"Sounds grand," she said. "I'm from Southern California, you know. I'll just be going home."

He said, "Maybe that's what we'll do on our honeymoon, eh? Drive around, real easy, through the Southwest, looking at the college and university towns. When we find one we like, why, we'll just rent or buy a little house and set up shop. You'll cook and I'll scribble." He grinned. "'We'll build our own little nest, out there in the West'—right? How many kids?"

She laughed. "To begin with, four. Then we'll see." He seemed to be getting drowsy. She wanted to break off the conversation without irritating him.

He said, "You won't feel cheated if we don't go to Europe? I never want to leave the soil of this country again. Not for years and years, anyhow. Foreign soil drains something out of me, as though it had the wrong kind of electricity in it. You know? You get a little charge with every step you take on your own land, and you lose a little charge into foreign soil with every step. That's just a silly fancy, I suppose. But it's very vivid to me just now."

"Did Ross's visit tire you, Arthur?"

"A little. You see, I'll need a library because so far I've just been writing from my own experience, spending my capital, but *Boone County* cleaned me out. I've got to start faking and inventing, like Balzac and Dumas and all the rest who did a large volume of work. Research is the tool." He lifted a languid hand to look at his wrist watch. "This arm's getting better, just as Rivkin said it would. Give me my red pill and I'll take a snooze."

He settled down and closed his eyes. Then he opened them. "It's amazing how tired I am, now that I've given way to it. Did you ever overwind a

watch and then all at once it wound as easy as you please but you weren't winding anything any more? That's the way I feel. Not bad, but loose, you know, and stopped."

Jeanne said, "You wrote five books in seven years, and four of them were about as long as *Anna Karenina*. You'll never have to work like that again, thank God."

"I'll tell you something," murmured Hawke, his eyes closing again, "I was never truly happy except when I was doing that."

He woke in the late afternoon, demanding a rare steak, a big baked potato, a dish of scallions, and a bottle of beer. Mrs. Hawke and Jeanne were both there when he woke, and they delightedly sent for Dr. Rivkin. Hawke was more nearly himself than at any time since the attack. He teased his mother about the weight she was putting on, and told Jeanne he wanted paper and a pen, to start writing immediately after his meal.

The doctor came and looked him over with obvious pleasure. He vetoed the beer, but allowed the rest of the meal, and laughed when Jeanne mentioned the request for pen and paper. "He's welcome to try, but nothing'll come of it." He agreed that Hawke could have another visitor. Gus Adam had been telephoning all afternoon saying he had news that would improve Hawke's spirits. "Just throw the man out after ten minutes or so," Rivkin said to Mrs. Hawke.

Hawke began to tear into his steak with something of his old gusto, while Mrs. Hawke stood over him, wrinkling her nose in delight at every mouthful he took. "All this boy needs is some nourishment that'll stick to his ribs. I wish they'd let me into that kitchen to make some soup for him."

It was a big slab of meat and he soon slowed down. "I don't know," he said, looking at the big red chunk, "if he'd have allowed me that beer I'd have made it. You can't eat steak without beer."

"Never you mind, you've had plenty and he's one smart doctor," said Mrs. Hawke. "And a right nice fellow, too, for a Jew." She glanced at Jeanne. "Meaning no offense, dear."

Jeanne shrugged. She was quite reconciled to being an Israelite to her mother-in-law forever.

Adam came in like a gust of mountain air, red-faced and tousled and unusually gay of mien. It was half-past five. Thick bars of yellow sunshine lay across Hawke's bed. "Well, young fellow," he said, grasping Hawke's hand, "what seems to be the trouble?"

Hawke said, "One hell of a hangover."

The lawyer burst out laughing, and looked around at the two women. "Some especially potent native brew in Peru, no doubt." Hawke grinned sheepishly. Adam said, "Speaking of which, I had a call from Mrs. Honor Hauptmann's lawyer a little while ago. The lady left for Peru at noon. She sent her fondest regards and best wishes for a rapid recovery, and the

lawyer would be willing to meet with me to discuss a certain loan. I told him to forget it."

"Good," said Mrs. Hawke.

Hawke said, "Can we afford to forget it?"

"I think so. Of course Jeanne's told you about Gimbels, and the informal reversal of the jeopardy assessment."

Hawke said, "Did Gimbels sign?"

"The closing's now set for next Tuesday. Newton Leffer knows the Gimbels' attorneys pretty well. He told me yesterday that he's not proceeding with the lawsuit, and in fact he was rather abjectly apologetic, in view of your illness and all. There's nothing new on the tax thing, Arthur, beyond the talk I had with the Washington people, but I hope we'll have a written ruling in a week or two."

Hawke said dreamily, "Am I actually out of the woods, then? It seems so hard to believe."

The lawyer dropped into a chair. "Well, all I can tell you is, Scotty Hoag—if you'll forgive my using such dirty language—is negotiating again with the syndicates that bowed out when the Mehlman lease fell through. At the prices they're discussing you could even meet both the tax assessments and come out ahead. Remember, the money from the Plaza will all be return of capital—no tax at all—or capital gain. You have better than two hundred thousand dollars in that venture, Arthur. I never did believe it would go up in smoke, you know, and I said so. It appears you're going to recover it with a profit."

Hawke smiled wearily, as though he were hearing an amusing story of distant places. "Well, fine. Jeanne said you had good news."

"That's not the good news." Adam started to fill his pipe in an elaborate display of calmness. "At noon I had a call from Brightstar, from my cousin Fred Adam, the young fellow who did so much of the trial work in the suit against Hawke Brothers. The decision was handed down this morning. We won. That's my news. It's a complete victory. Hawke Brothers committed wilful trespass on your land. That's the verdict."

Mrs. Hawke jumped up, clapped her hands, and uttered a "Ha! Ha!" of warlike triumph, like the horse in the Book of Job. "We won, hey?" she cried. "We really beat those robbers! We won! Hear that, Art?"

Adam went on, "We've got everything we sued for. Costs, an accounting, and an award for the full market value of the coal."

Hawke stared at the lawyer in mute stupefaction, his head sunk in the pillow, his eye sockets deeply shadowed in the slant sunlight.

Adam said, "I've been the messenger bringing the bad news all too long. This is a very pleasant change of roles for me, Arthur. You had a tide of terrible luck, but you've ridden it out, and it's turned."

Mrs. Hawke said, "Yes, it has. Praise God." She marched to the lawyer,

put her arm around his neck, and planted a hearty kiss on his cheek. "Why, thank you, Mrs. Hawke. That's all the reward I ask."

"Ha, fat chance! You'll charge us a murderous fee, I've got your number. But you're entitled to it. I wrote Arthur the very day I came on that hole in the hill—didn't I, Art?—that all we needed was a smart lawyer. I *smelled* it. It was pure robbery. There are still laws in this country!"

Hawke said, in a waning tone that caught Jeanne's attention, "How much money is involved, Gus?"

Jeanne said, "Maybe you can talk about it some more tomorrow."

"Jeanie, he hasn't been here five minutes. I feel fine."

The lawyer said, "That's part of the dispute, Arthur. The question is just where their tunnels did cross under your land. Our own informal survey before the trial showed that a verdict of wilful trespass might mean an award of well over a million dollars. Some of the tunnels are fallen in, and there'll be problems. They're going to appeal, of course. We don't have the money yet by a long shot."

"Well over *a million dollars?*" murmured Hawke.

Mrs. Hawke said, "Let them appeal, let them. Ha ha! The robbers were caught and they're going to pay. More than a million dollars, Art! Hey? How about your crazy old mother now?"

Hawke sat straight up and stared at Adam, shaking his head. "Gus, what kind of cuckoo system do we live under? Fifteen years ago mama bought a legal paper she didn't even understand, for five dollars. By what logic does that entitle us to this staggering fortune? It's fantastic. It's absurd. It makes *money*, money itself, seem ridiculous and unreal."

Adam said, "Art, that's one reason there's a steady traffic in land quitclaims. Nobody made the land or the coal, God put it there. Either the government owns land or some private party does, and the law now says that you own this parcel. You have clear title going back to the sovereign commonwealth of Kentucky which granted the senior patent that your mother bought into, and that's that."

Mrs. Hawke said, "Glory be, what I'd give to see some faces in Lexington and Hovey. Glenn Hawke, Scotty Hoag, and that rotten lawyer with his Santa Claus talk. Santa Claus! Ha, ha!"

Adam said to Jeanne, "I confess I feel pretty good about it, because the decision comes down on all fours on the main points in my brief. I had very little doubt that title rested in Arthur, once I studied the documents of record, but courts don't always read the law and the documents properly." He turned to the mother, laughing, clearly enjoying his triumph. "By the way, I telephoned your Mr. Santa Claus as soon as I heard the news, Mrs. Hawke. He was breathing fire, of course, but amid the smoke and flames, there was also a faint suggestion of a settlement."

"Settlement! Ha! No settlement! Let them appeal!"

"Arthur!" Jeanne said, and then more sharply, "*Arthur!*"

He was lying back with his eyes closed. Jeanne started up, but he turned his head and opened his lids slowly. "I'm here, honey. I'm just digesting it. I'm just thinking. I'm thinking that when you come right down to it, I was really a millionaire back in 1947, before I even started to try to make a million dollars. All I had to do was listen to mama and get a good lawyer. It's interesting, when you think about it."

Adam said, "It never was that simple. If you want to give credit, I think we have to assign top place to your mother for her tenacity, and I might say, her low opinion of human nature, which certainly fitted friend Hoag. Scotty had a good scheme. It should have worked. At worst he should have gotten off with a settlement of a few thousand dollars somewhere along the line. Indeed he almost did, but your mother's resolve to fight made this verdict."

"I knew they were all crooks," Mrs. Hawke said. "It was that simple. I knew it."

"Well, I wasn't sure we'd get a determination of wilful trespass, Mrs. Hawke. That's a fearfully punitive result. But the fact is Scotty damned well knew he was trespassing. The law has to be rough on such acts when they're detected, or all mineral titles would be in chaos. It's a messy enough area of the law as it is."

"You're absolutely right," Hawke spoke from the bed in a ghostly far-off voice, not looking at anyone. "All I needed was a good lawyer. I had my million before I started."

The cheerfulness faded from Adam's face. He glanced at Hawke and at the two women, then rose. "Well, Arthur, I don't want to tire you. The point is, whatever troubles you may have, money isn't one of them any more."

Hawke held out his hand in a slow soft gesture. "You're all right, Gus. It's a funny feeling, not having money worries. I guess I'll get used to it again. I didn't have any when I ran a non-union bulldozer for two dollars an hour." His voice was dwindling to a whisper. Adam shook hands silently and left. Hawke settled down to sleep. He spoke in a trailing tone, "Okay mama. You were right about Scott Hoag. Let's see you write a novel."

3

"Frieda Winter!"

He heard the name spoken in a tone of anger and disgust. The sound slashed into a dream of swooping in a black Cadillac through the bad lands of Peru under a lurid purplish sky, and in the dream Honor's chauffeur turned around and spat the name at him, grinning like a skeleton. But the voice was a woman's, not a man's. The dream misted away and

he was in his hospital bed. He heard his mother saying, "Tell her he can't see visitors."

Then Jeanne's voice, harsh and cold, "Possibly he would want to see her."

And his mother, "All the more reason to keep her away, if he's that big a fool."

He opened his eyes, not knowing whether he would see day or night. It was day. He tried to speak. To his dazed surprise no sound came. It was like trying to talk in a dream, but Hawke knew that this was reality. He had been passing often enough between dreams and life in the past days to know the difference. This was the stable coherent drab world of truth; the sheets of the hospital bed were sweaty, the coarse gray gown was cutting under his chin, his head hurt, and he needed a shave so badly that the bent bristles on his face were sticking him. But his throat, lips and tongue would not obey him.

The nurse in the doorway said, "She's terribly insistent. She says she's one of his oldest and dearest friends."

"Let her go to the devil," said Mrs. Hawke.

He tried to talk again and out came a croak, "I'll see Frieda, ma."

The two women turned and came to him. The mother said, "There! She woke him up."

Jeanne said, "How are you, Arthur?" and she put a cool dry hand on his head.

"Dopey, and thirsty," he said, finding his vocal apparatus responding a little better. "What time is it? What day is it?"

It was the morning of the day after Adam's visit, they told him. He had been sleeping almost continuously for sixteen hours.

He said to the nurse, "I'll see Mrs. Winter, if she'll wait a while."

Mrs. Hawke said, "Art, I don't want to argue, but what is there to say to the woman?"

"She must have come a long way, ma. Last I heard she was in Jamaica." He turned to Jeanne. "Do you mind, darling? I'll send her away if you mind."

Jeanne said, "Suit yourself." She wore a new dark red dress with a crisp little white collar and white cuffs, her hair was carefully piled in the style he liked, and she looked unusually fetching.

Hawke said, "If she's brought a turkey sandwich we can always throw her out."

Jeanne faintly and acridly smiled.

The nurse said, "In half an hour, perhaps?"

"In an hour," Hawke said. "I want to get cleaned up. I'm hungry, too."

Later he heard the rapid click of Frieda's walk in the corridor and recognized the old no-nonsense stride. No other woman walked quite like Frieda. When she came in she found Mrs. Hawke and Jeanne standing

on either side of the bed, a pair of sphinxes at the entrance to a temple, grim and unsmiling to her polite greetings. Nothing daunted, she strode to the foot of the bed. "It was sweet of you to see me, Arthur. I won't stay long."

"It's nice to see you, Frieda, and it was nice of you to come."

This exchange of banalities, the first words they had spoken to each other since the parting at the zoo almost two years earlier, seemed to exhaust the situation. She stood looking at him in a silence that grew long, and he lay propped on the pillows, observing her, and also observing his own feelings about her, with the recording faculty which never died in him.

She wore her favorite blue-gray, a soft summer dress belted with a blue sash, and a gray hat with a blue feather. Her hair, now a lustrous light brown, was rolled and coiled charmingly. Frieda was fresh from the beauty salon, polished in every detail, but she was quite old. It shocked Hawke a little to see how old she was. The skin was crinkling beyond all art on her neck and around her eyes, and her tropic tan gave her face a coarsened look. The determined lines at her mouth and nose were carved deep and dark. She had always had a little down on her upper lip, but now at the extremities of her mouth the hair was visible enough to give an unpleasant hint of a mustache, and he wondered why on earth she did not have it removed. The features that were lasting best were her gray eyes, still huge and brilliant, set off by her tan, and the handsome bony outline of her face. She had a package under her arm, wrapped with a blue gift ribbon.

He said finally, "You look grand, Frieda."

She smiled in a way at once grateful and ironic. "Yes, I grow younger every day, don't I? I'm sorry they got you down, Arthur. I never thought they could."

"Well, several things sort of hit at once, you know?"

"They can't keep you down. Nobody can."

"That's right, Frieda. I'll be up and at them again."

"You'll leave them all behind next time. For good."

"I intend to try."

What a conversation, he thought, conducted under the scrutiny of these two sentinels, frozen-faced as Soviet diplomats. There was something familiar and ominous about the presence of these three women at the foot of his bed. He remembered now that he had seen them grouped so at his bedside during his illness in the unfinished house on Seventy-third Street; that Jeanne and Frieda had been wearing raincoats then, and that Frieda's hair had been heavily shot with gray; and he remembered too that the sight of them standing so had filled him with dread.

Frieda said, with a flicker of her glance at the other women, "You

know, Arthur, anyone as prominent as you is going to be talked about even though the talk may be nonsense. I wrote you from Jamaica because I'd heard the same thing from half a dozen people. If there's any truth to it, what I said still goes. You can have any kind of loan you need, it's barbaric and abominable that an artist like you should ever have to think twice about money—" she added in a raised tone as Hawke started to speak, "just let me finish. It won't involve our seeing each other or even corresponding, the attorneys can handle everything. I know you and Jeanne are going to be married and I know you're going to be marvellously happy. I hope you'll both be able to think of me as a friend because that's what I want to be, even if it's the sort of friend you never see." She turned to the mother. "I would like to think you could regard me as a friend, too, Mrs. Hawke."

The mother looked at her, hands folded primly, face blank.

Hawke said, "Frieda, everything has cleared up, I don't need help, but I appreciate your offer. How is your family?"

Her resolutely cheerful look darkened. "Paul isn't well. He's had a couple of strokes and—he pretty much has to be taken care of, Arthur, twenty-four hours a day."

"I'm sorry."

"Well—" Her smile returned. "Bennett's grand, he's going into the air force, the girls are in college, and I've turned village idiot, I just sit in the sun by the side of the pool."

"You like Jamaica?"

"Paul has always loved it, and now—it wouldn't be fair to move him. Jamaica's all right, but I'm only alive in New York."

Silence; the two sentinels unmoving and unsmiling; the sick man looking at the former mistress with eyes uncomfortably analytic and cool. Frieda, for all her ability to carry off almost any situation with an innocent and gay air, began to shift her feet and glance here and there, smiling uncertainly. She remembered the box under her arm, snatched it and held it out toward Hawke as though it were an identity card that proved her right to be in the room. "Well, I guess I'll be off, Arthur. I brought this for you. I hope you'll like it."

He stretched forward a long gray-clad arm. "A book, Frieda? As the funny men say, I have a book. Right now I can't concentrate well enough to read." He smiled kindly at her. "But I'll get to it. Thanks a lot."

"Well, I just wanted to bring something. Goodbye, Arthur, get well soon. God bless you."

"Goodbye, Frieda."

She turned to Jeanne. "With all my heart, I wish you happiness, Jeanne."

"Thank you."

"Goodbye, Mrs. Hawke. I'm glad to see your son is still in the best possible hands—yours." Not waiting for a reply, not looking at the mother,

she darted out of the room and her heels clicked away in the corridor. The fan stirred faint eddies of her perfume in the room for a moment, then the scent faded.

"Good riddance to bad rubbish," said Mrs. Hawke.

Jeanne heaved an audible sigh. "That's that. I'm going below for lunch. I conceivably will have a martini or so first if hospital lunch counters serve martinis. Otherwise I may slip over to the corner saloon and have one with the boys."

"Bootleg one in for me," Hawke said.

"What would you need one for?" she said, and walked out.

A fat hairy-faced nurse appeared, fed Hawke a capsule, and sat in an armchair with a movie magazine. Mrs. Hawke left to chat with other patients on the floor; she had fallen almost at once into her old practice of visiting the sick, and was already great friends with some of Hawke's hospital neighbors. Hawke opened Frieda's gift, mildly curious to see which current best-seller she had thought he might enjoy reading. Stripping off the paper, he found a rich red leather box. He undid a heavy gold clasp, raised the lid, and started with surprise. Inside the box was *Alms for Oblivion*, an early copy with the stupid blue jacket design of a tiny young man shaking his fist amid towering mountains; Prince House had changed the cover as soon as the book had started to sell. This dust jacket was in perfect condition. He lifted out the book with care. Underneath it was a folded letter in a cheap yellowing envelope. He recognized on the envelope his old loft room address, rubber-stamped in purple, and he knew what Frieda's parting gift was.

He opened the book. There was his inscription, with the flourishing signature of his early years, that had long since given way to the plain small letters with which he now signed his name.

> To Mrs. Frieda Winter,
> recalling with gratitude her
> kindness to a young man alone
> in the city,
>   This first copy off the press
> of the first fruits of my pen,
> with sincere admiration
>   that can never change—
>   Arthur Youngblood Hawke

The ink of that inscription was faded. Beneath it was another inscription, in fresh bright blue ink, in Frieda's firm hurried hand:

> For Arthur,
> as a get-well present, the most precious thing
> I own or shall ever own,

and I give it without regret, without tears,
with the single wish for your enduring happiness,
and with love that cannot change though it can
be silent—
        Frieda

His hand trembled as he took his letter out of the envelope and read it, astonished to see that he had typed it on coarse yellow second sheets, now brown and cracking at the edges. How could he have typed a love letter? And on yellow paper! What a boor he had been! Then the callow, proud, pleading words embarrassed him and at the same time brought tears to his eyes. God in Heaven, he thought, had he been this ignorant, this vulnerable, this over-sensitive even at twenty-six, even after writing *Alms for Oblivion?* A youth of seventeen might have written this letter, a romantic youth crammed with reading and as ignorant of women as of banking. That was the appeal of the letter—that, linked to the fact that the writer of it had just published a book. Knowing Frieda as he now did, he understood that the temptation to take up with him must have been irresistible. It had been a fatal encounter.

Everything came back in a flood, as when one hears an old song of the time of one's first love affair. He remembered sitting in his loft room in drenching heat, writing this letter over and over, correcting it, making insertions, crossing them out, until all natural flow was erased and this stilted absurd composition emerged. He remembered typing it and hovering near a mailbox in the rain for twenty minutes before dropping in the book package. He remembered what she had looked like, swinging her arm as she strode through the crowd in the zoo. He remembered the pressure of her arms, the touch of her hands, the way that she kissed, the look of her body in moments of disrobing. He felt once more the forgotten ache, the thick sweet pain, of a young man famished for love and for sex, and the wild delight of having that hunger satisfied by a skilled, eager, glamorous, beautiful woman. God, she had been beautiful to him! Whatever life held in store for him, the sweetness of that time was gone. He had spent it in the piercing pleasures of an adultery. Nothing was left of all that passionate love-making, nothing; no child, no home, no friendships; nothing at all had come of it, except that a boy had died; it had been a long spilling waste of love; the residue was this book in a red box and the disintegrating letter, and Frieda had returned these to him knowing to the last just how to reach him most nearly, just how to hit him the hardest.

He put aside the box with the letter and the book, and lay back, staring at the nurse, whose mustached face reminded him grotesquely of the hair he had seen on Frieda's lip. A dark wave of illness passed through him, and his breath came hard.

4

There was an anteroom in the hospital lobby where mournful, worried, or sobbing people could usually be seen at any hour of the day or night, slumped on heavy old-fashioned furniture, bearing as best they could their share of the load of grief that rolls down the years across the shoulders of the living, now pressing here, now crushing there. Young people often do not know or care that this rolling burden exists and must come their way at last; old people hold their backs stooped and ready for it. Jeanne Fry had a working familiarity with that wheel, and she tended to quicken her step when she walked past the sad room, but on this day she saw the blue-gray dress out of the corner of her eye and she halted.

Frieda sat in an armchair, with an elbow on a small table, her head bowed in her hand. Jeanne could see nothing of her face, only the gray hat and the blue feather. Jeanne hesitated a long moment but her kindness of heart prevailed. She went to the woman and touched her shoulder. "Frieda. Are you all right?"

Mrs. Winter raised her head. Her expression was one of suffering, her eyes were bleared. "Oh, sure," she said in a hollow voice. "I put some drops in my eyes just before I went upstairs because they looked so red and disgusting—an extra strong dose, I admit—and they're kicking back in a strange way. I'll have to ask my doctor about it. I guess I'll be okay in a minute, but right now I see nothing but a lot of bright wiggling worms. Maybe I'm just falling apart. It's high time, isn't it, Jeanne?"

Jeanne said, "Is there something I can do for you?"

"No, thanks. My eyes are an old story. I guess if I were going blind I'd have done so before now." She peered up at Jeanne. "Tell me the truth, Jeanne, what do the doctors say about Arthur? Can he possibly live? He looks so awful, so absolutely awful."

Jeanne said, "He's in danger, but they think he'll be all right. Or that there's a very good chance of it. He looks much better than he did four days ago."

"How's it possible? He's a shell, Jeanne, nothing but a shell, he's lost a hundred pounds, his face is gray as a dead man's. What in God's name has he been through since I saw him last?"

"A little too much," Jeanne said, with a sickening at her heart. "If I can't be of help to you, Frieda—"

Mrs. Winter's hand darted out and fastened on her arm. "I'll tell you what," she said, "will you just walk outside with me and put me in a cab? I could probably make it myself, the worms are fading, but I don't want to bump into any incoming pregnant women or anything."

"Of course," Jeanne said, and so the two women walked arm in arm out of the hospital into the sunlight of the street. Frieda squinted and put a hand up to her eyes. Jeanne signalled to one of the waiting taxicabs, and escorted Frieda to the door, which the driver threw open.

Mrs. Winter released her arm. "Thank you. I'm sure it's no treat for you to be kind to me. I wonder—will I ever see you again? Not that I see you too well just now, though you're coming into focus a bit. I really want to be your friend."

Jeanne said nothing.

Frieda touched her arm. "Please don't hate me. I never meant to harm either of you, and I loved him. You must know that. Goodbye, Jeanne." She climbed into the taxicab, and as it pulled away she wriggled her fingers perkily at Jeanne.

The floor nurse gave Jeanne a large brown Hodge Hathaway envelope when she returned from lunch. Ross Hodge's signature was scrawled over the trademark. Inside was a bundle of press cuttings, still tagged with the pink slips of the clipping bureau. Ross had written a note with the bundle: *Jeanie, if you think these'll cheer our man up, show them to him. I selected the best.* Glancing at the articles, she thought she heard Hawke's voice raised as though in anger. The door of his room was closed. She hurried to it and went in, quickly shutting the door again, because Hawke was shouting at his mother. His face had a terrible purplish tinge.

"That's goddamn well why papa *made* you put the land in *mah name!* Because he hated this money insanity of yours!"

Jeanne said, "Arthur, for pity's sake, there are sick people all around you on this floor."

He glared at her, his eyes starting from his head. "What?"

Mrs. Hawke stood at the foot of the bed, clutching the enamelled rail with both hands. "Well, I guess he's getting better, he's beginning to holler at his old mother again."

"It's so goddamned infuriating, Jeanne," Hawke said, with less violence. "I made a purely casual remark, but it happened to be on the subject of money—"

"Casual remark? Jeanne, he said that when we got the money from Hawke Brothers we ought to give it all to the State of Kentucky to build libraries with. All I said was, and I meant it as a joke, that with him just escaping from bankruptcy maybe he should think twice about giving any money away—and merciful Heavens, how he started to roar!"

Jeanne put into Hawke's hands the envelope of clippings. "Here. These may amuse you." She walked out with the mother and closed the door behind her. "Good God, how can you quarrel with him?" she whispered.

Mrs. Hawke said plaintively, "I didn't start it, Jeanne. Gracious, I'm not an idiot. But really isn't that idea preposterous? Libraries! Of all the land I ever bought this was the one parcel that brought in the fortune,

and he wants to give it all away! Before we've even got it! What do you do with a man like that?"

"Mrs. Hawke, where's your sense? Until he's out of this hospital you must *agree* with him, surely you understand that, calm him, cheer him up, do everything his way. I think you might tell the floor nurse to call Dr. Rivkin and have him look at Arthur. He seems very ill to me."

"He seems just the same to me, in fact when he tore into me he sure was his old ornery self again. But I'll ask for the doctor."

Hawke was smiling over the clippings, Jeanne was glad to see, though his face still appeared sunken. He said to her, waving the bundle, "I don't know, Jeanne. Maybe I ought to quit while I'm ahead. Dickens! Dreiser! Howells! Zola! One woman mentions *Tolstoy*, did you see that?"

"I thought you'd be amused."

"God, yes. It's great fun reading your own obituaries. Obviously they have these things all written up and ready to go. The thing is to fool them by having a narrow squeak. I feel sort of as though I'd sneaked into a movie without paying."

"Did you notice the *Times*?"

"I sure did. The front page, by God! Just a little box, but still—"

Jeanne said, "Once in Philadelphia you said that right now you'd rate two columns and a picture on the *Times* obituary page. You sold yourself short. You made page one just by getting sick."

"I know," he said. "I'm most absurdly pleased with myself. I think I could make real headlines by cutting my throat." He put the clippings aside and glanced at her with a hangdog grin. "I know I shouldn't have let go at mama. She infuriates me more than anybody on earth—Scotty, Feydal, Givney, Prince, none of them ever came close to getting me as mad as mama can. Yet I love her, Jeanne, truly I do."

"I know you do, Arthur."

"Anyway, Jeanie, don't *you* think the libraries are a good idea? Memorials to my father? He bought that piece of land, after all. Reading was what he loved. There aren't half enough libraries in those coal counties. Let the goddamn coal do the people some good for once."

"I think it's a grand idea," Jeanne said.

When Mrs. Hawke returned a little later she was all smiles. "Art, I'm a narrow-minded nobody and I don't know how I ever gave birth to a great author. I think you're dead right about the libraries, I honestly do, and it's all decided."

Hawke's eyes widened in astonishment, and he glanced at Jeanne. "The devil's turning Christian."

"Don't you believe me?" said Mrs. Hawke, laughing.

"Well, I'd sure like to, ma."

"Art, I just passed a joking remark and you exploded and never let me

explain myself. I'm proud that you have the spirit to think in those terms. I admit I can't." She went to one of the armchairs, where she kept her big black patent leather reticule. "You know, when I heard you were sick I went up to that mountain cabin of yours before I left Hovey. I don't know why I went, just a hunch." She was fumbling in the bag. "I had a time prying the padlock loose, but I did it." She pulled out of the bag the envelope in which Hawke had sealed and labelled his will. She also produced Jeanne's black gloves. "I thought, I thought it was just possible, that I ought to bring these things along. Now I guess it's time to give them to you."

Hawke accepted the sealed will and the dusty gloves from his mother with a melancholy smile. "Were those photostats still piled four feet high on the table?"

"Well, no, they'd slithered all over the floor, it was an awful mess. The rats had been at everything, in fact how you lived all those months in that horrible hovel I'll never know."

Hawke said to Jeanne, "Want your gloves?" and he waved them at her.

"No. I'll only lose them. They might be good for driving around in the Southwest."

"Just so, Jeanie." He pulled open a drawer of the bed table, and she saw him drop the gloves on top of a red-leather box. He slid the drawer shut and picked up his will. "I sure was in a morbid state of mind when I wrote this thing. I don't even know if it's legal."

"Well, I just thought, son," Mrs. Hawke said, "if you want to put in your will about the libraries that's all right with me. I want you to know I mean it."

His glance at her was full of resigned, wistful affection. "Come and give me a kiss, mama."

She did so. "My, you're soaking wet, Art."

He tossed the will aside. "To hell with this. I'm not dying yet."

Dr. Rivkin came in with a cheery greeting, but when he looked at Hawke his face became business-like. He ordered the women outside and asked them to send in the floor nurse.

Ten minutes later he emerged from the room, closing the door carefully. Jeanne and Mrs. Hawke were sitting on a sofa in the corridor. He came to them and said, "Has he had many visitors today?"

Jeanne said, "Just one."

"He's not as good as he was," Dr. Rivkin's expression was calm but serious. "These things have their ups and downs. We have to walk a fine line between overtiring him, on the one hand, and depressing him by depriving him of company, on the other. I think visits should be discontinued and conversations kept brief. I've put him to sleep. I'll examine him again tonight."

5

The telephone startled Jeanne out of her sleep in the dead of night. She was wide awake on the instant as she picked up the receiver. Her alarm clock showed half-past three.

It was Mrs. Hawke, and she sounded full of cheer, she even laughed now and then. "Jeanne, don't be alarmed, I'm calling you because Dr. Eversill says I should but I know my Art, and it's all bosh. He's had a little setback, but he's more than holding his own. He has a heart of iron. It's one of those things, it's darkest before the dawn and I don't blame everybody for being concerned—what, Henry?—well, I am telling her—Jeanne, I'm saying he's going to be all right, I know God's going to let Art live, he's a good boy and he's got everything to live for—what? Well, all right, tell her yourself, then, I'm doing my best. Jeanne, Arthur will be all right, I tell you. Here's Dr. Eversill."

Then the old man's voice, coarse and rheumy: "Mrs. Fry, Arthur's called for you a couple of times, he's a little delirious and it might be well if you're at hand. There's no cause for real alarm yet."

Jeanne said painfully, "Is it another attack?"

"He had a bad attack about half-past eight. These things can just happen. The real trouble was that it hit him very soon after dinner and he vomited. He aspirated the stuff into his lungs, and we're dealing now with an acute onset of pneumonia." He sounded tired and sad.

"I'm coming," Jeanne said.

Mrs. Hawke was sitting on the sofa in the dim red-lit corridor outside Hawke's sickroom. She greeted Jeanne with a dry brief smile. "They've put me out, so I guess they won't let you in," she said. "But you can try."

"How is he?"

The mother laughed. "They're saying he has a fifty-fifty chance. Imagine! They don't know Art. He's got the constitution of my family. He'll pull through, with God's help. I've prayed and I'm still praying."

A large sign printed in black letters hung on the closed door: NO ADMITTANCE. Underneath it was the inked card in a brass slot: A. Hawke. Jeanne hesitated, with her hand on the knob. She said to the mother, "It's happened so fast! So terribly fast!"

Mrs. Hawke sniffed. "Well, they say it's pneumonia. I've seen pneumonia carry a strong man off in six hours, but that was before all these wonder drugs. They've shot him full of so many things I only hope they haven't interfered too much with nature. Nature is still the best doctor. Nature and a good heritage. That's what I'm counting on."

The door creaked as Jeanne pushed it open. Before she could step into the room the hairy-faced nurse was barring her way. "Oh, it's you," she

whispered. Hawke's bed was hidden by a tall white folding screen. She laid her finger on her lips and beckoned Jeanne to follow her.

Beyond the screen the familiar room had turned to a scene of terror. There was terror in the grisly looking oxygen machine over Arthur's head, terror in its regular wheezing noise, terror in the quickness of his breath and the brick-red color of his face; terror in the crowd of three doctors and the two nurses with doleful looks hovering over the bed; terror in the long needles stuck in his arms and the snaky brown tubes; terror in the sick ugly smells. Everything was changed around the bed of Arthur Hawke. Death was in the room, and the big man with the broad dark red face was fighting it off, pouring sweat in the struggle for his life. His eyes were closed. He was breathing as though he had run a mile, in sobbing gasps. The other two doctors barely glanced at her, but Eversill came to her side and put his thin arm stiffly around her shoulders. He allowed her to watch Hawke in his agony for perhaps half a minute, then he led her outside.

Mrs. Hawke said at once, "Any change?"

Eversill shook his head.

Jeanne said, "I thought the new drugs knocked pneumonia out. They do, don't they?"

The old man said, "He has that filth in his lungs, and his resistance is very low. That's the trouble. He's a strong boy and he's fighting hard."

"He'll walk out of this hospital," said Mrs. Hawke. "You'll see. His lungs are weak, that's all, this is his second pneumonia, and I'm going to make him swear never to smoke those big awful cigars again. He'll do anything for me that I really want."

Jeanne said, "Is he conscious?"

Eversill said, "Off and on. The anesthesiologist is watching the thing carefully. Art needs sedation because of the attack, but too much will dampen his remaining vitality, which is what he needs to keep fighting. It's a ticklish business. They've given him everything, they're doing all the right things, and the rest is up to him."

"I think they've given him too much. Is that oxygen any better than good fresh air from an open window?" said Mrs. Hawke. "Won't it burn his lungs?"

"Sarah," said the old doctor, "this is one of the best hospitals in the world, and Arthur is in the best hands you can find anywhere."

"He's in God's hands," said Mrs. Hawke. "That's why I have confidence."

Jeanne sat beside her. The doctor went back into the room and the two women endured a silent vigil for half an hour. Then the door opened and the fat nurse beckoned to them.

Hawke was awake. The oxygen machine was pushed aside. He stretched out a hand to his mother. The long needle in his arm wavered and the

rubber tube writhed. The anesthesiologist, a young bald man with a chalky face, jumped to steady the needle. "Mama!" Hawke said in a choked voice, grasping her hand. "Everything hurts like hell. It sticks me every time I breathe."

"I know, son. You're having a bad night, but the morning's coming and you'll be better."

Hawke looked up at Dr. Rivkin, his eyes rolling whitely. "I'm not going to die, am I?"

"You're doing all right, Arthur," the doctor said calmly. "The drugs need a few hours to catch hold. You just hang on and you'll be fine."

"Where's Jeanne? Did Jeanne come?" The light was shining in his face, and he could not see her at the foot of the bed. Jeanne came into the cone of light and seized the hand he held out. "Hi, darling," he said. His hand was slippery and cold, but when she touched her palm to his cheek the burning of his skin frightened her. He gasped, "I've been thinking about driving through the West and settling there. It's a great idea, you know, sweetheart? For the Comedy. I don't know the West at all, and so many of the panels have scenes that—"

Rivkin said, "Save your breath, Arthur."

Hawke rolled his head from side to side, looking from Jeanne to his mother. His fiery face wrinkled in a pathetic simulacrum of his old boyish smile. "So help me mama, Jeanne isn't Jewish," he said. "Not that it would matter, you know— Ah!" All his features contorted. "God, Doctor, that hurts when I breathe. It's like a knife stuck in my side."

"All right, Arthur. It's better not to talk. Let's let your ma and Jeanne go for a while."

Hawke tightened his hold on their hands. "I love you both. God, I have so much work to do! I've just gotten started."

"You'll do all the work God means you to do, Art," his mother said.

Hawke looked at Jeanne. "More time. That's all I ask for. Nothing else. I hope God will give me more time. More time! I have so much to do."

Dr. Rivkin gently broke Hawke's grip on her hand. "Rest now, Arthur. Go outside, Jeanne. Go outside, mother."

"Jeanne!" Hawke called as she was walking out. She came back to the foot of the bed. He stared straight at her with glittering eyes. "Are you there? I can't see you."

"I'm here, darling."

"Jeanne, I'm sorry about Frieda."

She pushed past the doctors, put her arms around his shoulders in the sweat-soaked gown, and kissed his cracking wet lips. "I love you, Arthur, I've never loved another man, and I'll love you until I die," she said. "Now do what they tell you and get well. We have a life to start living."

He nodded, smiled, and closed his eyes.

His big powerful frame fought on for a day and a night, long after he had passed into a coma, long after the doctors had showed in their faces and their actions, though they never spoke the words, that hope was gone. The two women did not leave the hospital for thirty hours. When the last day was dawning, the terrible huge breaths began to come further and further apart; his face took on the green of death; a trickle of bloody spittle came from his mouth, but still he fought. When he was quite still, and Dr. Rivkin turned to the mother and said that it was over, Hawke gasped in one more tremendous gulp of air. Then the big body lay inert and the head lolled to one side, the eyes shut.

"Is he truly gone?" Mrs. Hawke said to Rivkin. Her face was bathed in tears but she was calm. She was utterly exhausted.

The doctor, embarrassed by the last unexpected gasp of Hawke, checked the body here and there. "Yes, I'm terribly sorry. Your son is gone. He fought magnificently right to the last, but there was too much against him."

Mrs. Hawke got slowly out of her chair, went to the bed, sat beside her son, and took the heavy lifeless head in her arms. She rocked him against her bosom. "All right, Art," she said. "I'll take you home now. It's all over, and I can take you home. You worked so hard, and now you can rest. Home, Art, home, son. I'll take you home."

Jeanne was bowed in an armchair. She had been crying for a long time, but new grief welled up in her, seeing the lover whom she had never embraced, and now never would, dead in his mother's arms. He was the same Arthur, he did not look worse than he had many times in the past awful year, but he was gone. His body belonged to his mother. It had never belonged to her. She had no right to fall on it like a wife, and to cry her heart out. They had never even been formally engaged. She had no ring.

Jeanne rose and went to the bedside table, where a nurse was beginning to clear away bottles, needles and instruments. "Excuse me," she said. She opened a lower drawer, and there were the black gloves on top of the red-leather box, and the envelope containing Hawke's will. Jeanne had surmised at her first glimpse that the box was Frieda Winter's parting gift to Hawke. She looked at the dead man's face, resting against his mother's gray print dress, and she had no desire to open the box. She took the gloves and shut the drawer.

"Mother," she said, "I have to go home to my boy for a while. Can I come to Hovey with you? With Arthur?"

Mrs. Hawke, clutching her huge lifeless son to her breast as though he were an infant, said, "We'll all go home together. Art loved you and you would have made him happy. We're going home, Art, home."

Jeanne nodded, and dashed the last tears from her eyes with a handker-

chief. She kissed Mrs. Hawke, and then she kissed the warm, still perspiring face of the dead man once on the lips. She drew on the black gloves, and walked out of the room of death.

The reporters in the lobby startled her, pouncing on her as she emerged from the elevator. There seemed to be a dozen of them, and they crowded around her with questions. She passed through them like a sleepwalker, out into a busy street, a hot cloudy day, out among pedestrians and grimy brick buildings and noisy automobiles. The death of the famous author had made no change in the look or the pace of New York.

A reporter put his face to the window of the taxicab door as she pulled it shut. "Mrs. Fry, do you think his works will live?"

The question somehow penetrated to her. "Yes," she said. "I think the books will live. But he's gone, and there will never be another Youngblood Hawke."

EPILOGUE

1

FERDIE LAX missed the funeral, being detained at his desk in Hollywood in a tense three-way bidding contest for the film rights of the new fiction success about sex misconduct in an Ohio town; a battle of wits so complex, and involving so much rumor, welshing, and playing off of rich suspicious men against each other, that it strained even Ferdie's remarkable ability to talk on several telephones at once. He wired a gigantic offering of flowers to Hovey.

After that he had no further occasion to see Jeanne for several years. Now and then he talked to her on the telephone or corresponded with her about subsidiary rights to the Hawke works, and about new authors whose books she edited.

When he heard of her marriage to the lawyer Adam, about a year after Youngblood Hawke's death, he was not surprised. The lawyer and the pretty though somewhat acerb editor had always struck Lax as a congenial and intimate pair. On the whole Lax thought Jeanne was much better off with that tough, smart, solid lawyer than she would have been with a wild man like Hawke, who had killed himself by a senseless sudden dash to South America when he was gravely ill. That was the version of Hawke's death which had passed into general acceptance; though Dr. Rivkin had told Jeanne, for whatever comfort there was in it, that Hawke might well have died when he did, no matter what kind of life he had led. With the brain injury, he had always dwelled on a brink of peril.

His reason for going to Peru had never become public knowledge. Lax himself was not aware of it. As for Honor Hauptmann, she shunned the topic of Youngblood Hawke forever after. Even when she visited Hollywood nobody could get her to talk about the author. In the public mind, then—and even in the poor and tasteless biography of Hawke that appeared six years after his death, written by a publisher's hack who appeared not to like Hawke much, but to be enamored of Mrs. Winter—the verdict was that the author, in the climax of an insensate drive to make money, had gone clean out of his mind and had in effect committed suicide by roaring off on an exhausting purposeless trip while suffering from a dangerous brain condition.

Though Hawke was dead, he continued to be one of Lax's most im-

portant clients. The negotiation for the film rights to *Boone County* was one of the most spectacular of the agent's career, and the price paid at last was enough to make little Jim Fry independent for life, quite aside from the other large revenues of the book; for Hawke's will, scribbled in the mountain cabin, had left all his property and all his works to his mother, except the copyright of *Boone County*, which he had willed in trust, in its entirety, to Jeanne's son.

New ways of exploiting the Hawke copyrights kept cropping up. Television opened a fresh market. Lax managed to get twenty thousand dollars for a TV performance of *The Lady from Letchworth*, which won Irene Perry a broadcasting award; whereupon Lax dug out all of the author's early plays and began selling them to television, one by one. The author's name on any property meant a major negotiation, as the popularity of his books continued, and they began passing to the stable audience generated by high school and college reading lists. *Boone County* soon took a place as required reading, though there was no agreement among critics as to Hawke's rank in serious literature, and a few denied him any at all. The posthumous novel was an enormous document of the struggle between capital and labor as it was fought in Kentucky in the 1930s. For high school and college purposes, its main virtue was that the most indifferent and sluggish student was likely to get caught up in the story, and to read through a seven-hundred-page novel of American life which had little to do with sex in its natural or aberrant forms, and teachers did not have many books of this kind to choose from. *Chain of Command* was also widely read in schools, the other books less so.

But a new and growing academic coterie began to assert, some years after he died, that the only good book Youngblood Hawke had ever written was *Evelyn Biggers*. It was this late-blooming vogue for Hawke's one failure that caused Lax to pay a visit to Jeanne Adam, late in October of 1961.

He arrived about four in the afternoon at the old apartment house on Riverside Drive near Columbia University where she lived, and rode to the top floor in a dilapidated and creaky elevator manned by a surly thug in shirtsleeves. She opened the door to him. The little fat agent stood and blinked at her, then said hesitantly, "Is this Jeanne?"

"It might be her mother, I know," she said, laughing. "But it's Jeanne. Come in."

"On the contrary, I was thinking you might have a younger sister staying with you. You've changed so little." But she had changed much, and he had actually been a little unsure when he first saw her. Different clothes —she was wearing slacks—and a short haircut made some of the difference, but the main alteration was in her face. The tense, bitter, brooding expression he had often seen in her was gone; also the girlish, incompleted

look which had marked her even in the years of her marriage to Fry. This was a mature busy woman at home, a bit plump, a bit worn, a bit untidy. In the middle of the large living room, which had sweeping curved windows looking out on the Hudson River, a baby in a bright green sleeping bag sat in a play pen, tearing up a picture book with amused gurgles.

Jeanne said, "That's Arthur. It's a little silly having a new baby at my age, but Gus and I wanted a boy and it took four tries and three sisters. Arthur, this is Ferdie Lax, who lives off writers, like mama, only he makes a better thing of it."

The baby said something that sounded like violent language and threw scraps of the book at Lax, grinning charmingly all the while. He had shocking red hair. Jeanne went to a desk, put paper weights on piles of galleys, and took off her glasses. "Well," she said. "At your service, Ferdie. Too early for a drink?"

"For me, yes. I want to give you the pitch before we meet Bob Luzzatto, Jeanne. I have two more appointments between now and dinner time, so—"

"Okay. Let's talk. Arthur is the soul of discretion." Jeanne motioned Lax to sit with her on the couch.

"Good, because this is confidential. It's also big, and let me get right at it. One of the great Hollywood stars has been reading some of this literary magazine carrying on about *Evelyn Biggers*. She's got the message that Evelyn is the American female incarnate. She wants to play Evelyn in pictures. A commitment of this woman to appear in a movie, Jeanne— any movie—means an immediate million-dollar bank loan. Join her with a Youngblood Hawke book and you're talking about a two-million-dollar loan just to start production."

"Who is it?" said Jeanne.

"Sorry, I can't say. I'm not supposed to know. This is top secret hush hush firing-squad information, Jeanne. But it's the key to what's happening. Now is the time to sell *Evelyn Biggers*, if it's ever to be sold."

"It can only be Taylor, Monroe, or Hepburn," said Jeanne inquisitively. "Or is Garbo rising out of the sarcophagus for one more?"

"Don't pump me. I wrote to Mrs. Hawke, I've talked to her on the phone, and she doesn't or she won't understand. I can't disclose to her what I've told you. She says Hollywood ruined *Boone County* and Evelyn Biggers is really her own daughter Nancy and we can all go to hell."

"They did ruin *Boone County*."

"Eleven million domestic, Jeanne," said Lax solemnly.

"I don't care."

"Well, all right, they corned it up with that phony happy ending. Now the man who would write and direct *Evelyn*—you'll meet him tonight— would preserve the integrity of this book." He named a famous young director, whose films Jeanne had seen and admired.

She nodded. "He might at that. I'll tell you, Ferdie, if you mentioned a large enough sum of money to Mrs. Hawke she'd probably turn polite. She's quite a business woman."

Lax shook his head. "I tried it."

The front door opened and a boy and a girl entered with school books, wrangling. They dropped the satchels in the hallway and came tumbling into the living room demanding food, but they turned quiet when they saw Lax. Jim smiled very pleasantly, shaking hands with the agent. He was about eleven, weedy and clever-looking. The girl, a red-faced dumpling of six or so, began playing with the baby, glancing impishly at Lax. Jeanne ordered them off to have chocolate cake and milk, but they both busied themselves with Arthur, who was crowing with delight at seeing them. Meantime an elderly woman with an Irish accent came in leading two more small girls, both squealing and clutching lollypops. A burst of racing around and showing off ensued. It seemed to Lax that the apartment was boiling with children and that all further business talk was hopeless. But Jeanne got up, rapped out commands, and with the maid's help herded her five children out of sight, picking up Arthur herself. The noises died off as various far doors slammed shut. Jeanne returned, tidying her hair and grinning self-consciously at the agent.

"Now you know why we live in this grisly old house. Nine big rent-controlled rooms with thick walls. On the East Side a place like this would cost fifteen thousand a year. And of course Gus walks home from the law school in two minutes."

Lax said, "Makes sense."

"I don't have three dozen children, it just seems so when they all get in one room. Visitors stimulate them."

"I'm wondering how you also manage to hold down a big job at Hodge Hathaway."

"Well, as you see I do a lot at home. Ross got used to my irregular ways long ago." Jeanne sat at her desk and played with her glasses. "If Mrs. Hawke has turned you down, why this meeting tonight?"

"The last time I talked to her, I asked whether it would make any difference if Jeanne and Gus Adam were for it. That woman said if you were for it, she'd do it."

Jeanne slowly smiled. "That doesn't mean she would."

"Well, Jeanne, think about it this way." Lax leaned forward, elbows on his knees. "We're talking here about a transaction of maybe three or four hundred thousand dollars ahead of the line, with sliding percentages of the gross that could run up maybe to eight hundred thousand dollars. It's a brilliant deal for this property. And it all hangs on the whim of a star who might read some other goddamn novel next month and go stone cold on *Evelyn Biggers*, which between you and me is a difficult work with a limited audience. This vogue it's having is a temporary thing

among the highbrows, and the fact that this actress has become infected is like lightning striking. It will never happen again to this book."

Jeanne said, "That may be."

Lax said, "I'm in the peculiar situation of having to persuade not the buyer but the seller. This sometimes happens to properties tied up in estates. I've failed to sell Mrs. Hawke myself. If you'll help me to sell her—and I don't want you to do so, of course, until you meet the director tonight and convince yourself that he can create a film of integrity that will befit Arthur's memory and stature—but if you will help me, I'll split my commission with you."

"I see." Jeanne lit a cigarette with an expert flip of a lighter, not taking her eyes from Lax's face.

"And to be absolutely frank with you," Lax said, "my chief interest here is to get this star what she wants, because I have other and bigger transactions that involve her. The business nowadays is totally at the feet of the stars. They call the tune. Now that's the pitch, Jeanne."

"Well, you're talking business," Jeanne said.

Lax appraised her through nearly closed eyes, slapped his knees with both hands and stood. "I know you'll want to talk it over with Gus. If you're willing I think the idea is for all of us—you and Gus and myself, with Luzzatto and the director—to make a flying trip over the weekend to Hovey. There's a jet to Lexington now so it's nothing to go and come in a day."

Jeanne walked with him to the door, and handed him his coat and hat. "I've got the pitch. We meet at Hadrian's Villa when—seven?"

"Right." Lax absently kissed Jeanne's hand—a newly evolved bit of Hollywood courtliness—and left.

2

Hadrian's Villa was the restaurant which had recently put Number One in the shade. Fancy restaurants in New York have runs like shows, lasting ten years or so. At the end they do not close but turn into tourist places and the cognoscenti, whom the tourists come to see, flee elsewhere. The hounds now occupied Number One, and the hares were in Hadrian's Villa. It was part of Jeanne's business to entertain best-selling authors at Hadrian's Villa, and she was not floored by the vistas of red and ivory velvet, the gilded scrollwork molding, the paintings of Roman ruins, and the Lucullan menu two feet high and two hundred epicurean items long. She knew that the old faces from Number One were all here, and that these faces mainly consumed steak, potatoes, and martinis, as always.

Lax and Adam had not seen each other since the time in Philadelphia when Hawke had gone nearly berserk with rage, after the call to Travis

Jablock. They took each other in with equal sharpness, shaking hands. Adam noted how fat and bald Lax was getting, and Lax noted the academic gravity that was settling in strong lines in the lawyer's face. Roberto Luzzatto, Jeanne observed, had become extremely gross, and he was swarthily tanned as ever. This was a man who went through bankruptcies, she thought, as other men went through summer showers. One threatened bankruptcy had poisoned Arthur's last years.

The young director dominated the dinner. He knew he was there to do a selling job, and he did it. His name was Fred Mannes, he spoke volubly and well with a slight Hungarian accent, and he presented the favored surface at the moment of a Hollywood director—the closest possible simulation of a scientist at the Institute for Advanced Study in Princeton. He was slender, his clothes were sombrely collegiate, his glasses were thick-rimmed, and though he was only twenty-nine his close-cut hair was sprinkled with gray. His persuasive hand gestures, his smooth flow of talk, his easy jokes, his occasional hard-boiled references to money, were not the manners of a scientist. Jeanne liked him despite the Hollywood sheen. Mannes had read all Arthur's books and had understood them. His indignation at the film botch of *Boone County* was a hard professional verdict of silly waste. He claimed that a good picture would have earned twice as much, and he did not expect *Evelyn Biggers* to do nearly as well. But he thought he could make a fine picture; and as he talked exuberantly of his vision of the film, with Luzzatto beaming at him fatly, and Lax and her husband watching the young man like poker players, Jeanne decided that he was all right, and that she ought to recommend this deal to Mrs. Hawke. Mannes made no pretense that he was trying to do anything but win Jeanne over, and she liked this; she even liked the slightly flirtatious manner he took with her.

In point of fact Mannes, an impressionable young man, was excited at meeting the well-known Mrs. Jeanne Adam, and he was shrewd enough to give his excitement rein. He was a real partisan of Hawke's works, he thought Hawke was a great American writer—an opinion more common in Europe than in the United States—and he knew the story of Hawke's unfortunate loves, of course. Mannes was thrilled to meet the woman who had been so close to Youngblood Hawke, who had almost married him, and who had been at his deathbed. Her appearance and her conversation did not disappoint him. He saw a well-groomed Manhattan woman, calmly affectionate to her keen-eyed scholarly husband, quick in humorous repartee, business-like as soon as business was the topic, attractive to look at and radiating a motherly warmth. But he saw more. Painting was his hobby, and he thought he would like some day to paint this small lively red-headed woman, and capture if he could the essential thing he saw: a sadness buried in intense living, in good humor and in work, a sadness with roots striking down to old secrets beyond all probes.

The dinner ended without any decision being made. Jeanne said to her husband in the taxicab, "Do you suppose Elizabeth can manage those five monsters unaided for a whole day Saturday?"

Adam did not show surprise. "Why not? Jim is self-operating. The girls are easy enough, and Arthur's pretty harmless." He waited, then said, "Your answer's going to be yes?"

"Gosh, Gus, I think so," Jeanne drawled, in her usual tone announcing a business decision. "This looks like the best chance for *Evelyn* to be a decent movie, and to give Mrs. Hawke some substantial money."

"She needs it," Adam said. Jeanne merely laughed. Adam went on, "Well, I happen to agree with you. Mannes is brilliant. Now and then he shows a little of the fire Arthur used to flash. And he does know what the book says. I'm wondering, though, why I have to go. Mrs. Hawke will do whatever you recommend. You can just tell her you have my vote."

Jeanne shot a strange glance at him. "I won't go to Hovey without you."

Adam sighed. "It means calling off a faculty meeting. I daresay the walls of the law school won't fall in."

Jeanne now told Adam of Lax's offer to split his commission with her. Until this moment she had not mentioned it. Adam listened with a trace of the old foxy look that he seldom displayed any more, since he had left his Wall Street office to give all his time to teaching.

"Well!" he said. "That could mean as much as forty thousand dollars for you! Quite a killing. You'll have to edit a lot of books to make that much."

"We could buy a new apartment on Lexington or Third Avenue," said Jeanne, "and get out of the Casbah."

"Jeanne, we can do that whenever we want to. We're living very conservatively, and it's mainly your idea."

"With three girls to marry off I think it's a good idea," Jeanne said.

Adam stared at his wife. The cab came to a stop in front of their apartment house. "You're thinking of accepting Ferdie's offer?" he said, helping her out.

"It's only business," Jeanne said.

3

Mrs. Hawke was a little slower, a little grayer, a little heavier in her movements, but otherwise unchanged, and she apparently was making a career of keeping the old house on High Street, where she still lived, unchanged. Jeanne had not been back to Hovey since the funeral, and the sameness of the home seemed eerie to her. Even the smell was exactly the same—though that might be merely Mrs. Hawke's famous soup sim-

mering on the stove—none of the furniture was different, and the same old mildewed best-sellers of the 1920s filled the bookshelves of the parlor, slumping, it seemed to Jeanne, at the same angles. Surely *The Story of Philosophy* had been askew in just that way, in just that corner, eight years ago! It was as though time had stopped in this house on the day of Arthur's funeral.

But the very studied sameness was the true change. The house was a museum now, she quickly realized, and Mrs. Hawke was curator and guide. The mother chatted for a while in a friendly way with Jeanne and Adam, but she was restlessly conscious of the Hollywood visitors, and soon she asked them whether they wouldn't like to see where her son had lived and worked. Of course they eagerly said they would. Thereupon Mrs. Hawke conducted them to the front hall, asked them to sign a fat register, and gave to each of them—even to Jeanne and her husband, with a coy laugh—a little printed leaflet labelled *Home of Arthur Youngblood Hawke, Hovey, Kentucky*. It contained a little summary of his life and work, and photographs of the rooms in the house, of Hawke, and of his mother. "It's just amazing, the people who've come here lately," she said. "There's more every year. When you consider what an out-of-the-way one-horse town Hovey is, after all— You just look at that register later! India, New Zealand, Germany, Canada—oh, lots from Canada—and I don't know where all, and the schoolteachers! Lord, Arthur really put old Hovey on the map, and don't think the people here don't know it, though sometimes when it suits their purpose they pretend different."

She had a great grievance against the town, about which she rattled on as she conducted the party through the house, interspersing her natural flow of words with the routine comments of a guide—"Now this is where my son ate most of his meals. He was a kitchen eater, like most good Americans, ha ha, and his favorite foods were steak, and pork chops, and of course my vegetable soup, he never could get enough of that soup, why even after he was a world-famous author, he'd come back to Hovey and his joke was that he just wanted a decent plate of soup— now up this staircase are the bedrooms, that one at the head of the stairway is where Youngblood Hawke was born, just step inside please, if you will, and I'll tell you all about it—" during this, and while the visitors were looking about, Mrs. Hawke in asides to Jeanne complained bitterly of the lack of cooperation she was getting from the Hovey officials. Jeanne already knew that the mother had offered to leave the house to Hovey in her will, as a monument to her famous son; but she had insisted that the town put up a fund of fifty thousand dollars for the maintenance of the place, and the town officials wanted her to deed them the money as well. "Imagine the nerve of them! And I'm getting nowhere, Jeanne. Only yesterday I had it out with the mayor and he tried to tell *me* how rich I was. Well, I told him a thing or two! I had him down crawling

on the rug, but still the best he'd offer was fifteen thousand, and I'm supposed to give the other thirty-five! Well, I told him where I'd see him first, and it wasn't Miami, Florida, I can tell *you*, but a place that's a lot hotter— Now here is Youngblood Hawke's bedroom, gentlemen, and it may seem tiny, but that's just where he grew up, and that's where he wrote a lot of *Boone County*, and"—here she dramatically threw open the door—"there is his desk, and his chair. No one has ever sat there since. That's the desk on which my son wrote. Everybody seems to want to see my son's desk."

The scarred, ink-streaked desk, in the cubbyhole room with the steeply slanted ceiling, looked like a piece of doll furniture. The bed was made up, but the blue cover was faded and sunken, and there was a dusty, stale smell in the room. Jeanne broke away and hurried down the stairs.

After the visitors had made a lunch on Mrs. Hawke's immortal soup, crammed in the tiny dining room like subway riders, and after they had duly begged for more and exalted the soup beyond all praise, they went to the parlor for the business of the day, Mannes' presentation of his ideas on *Evelyn Biggers*. Nancy and John Weltmann appeared at this point. Jeanne and Gus were used to seeing them when they came to New York, so their greetings were easy and offhand. The Hollywood visitors, young Mannes especially, inspected with some curiosity the fat middle-aged woman who was Youngblood Hawke's sister, and who, in the upper part of her face, bore a ghostly resemblance to his photographs; who appeared, further, to have the ugliest husband in the world, a frog-faced grinning old imbecile in a wig and thick glasses. They knew, however, from the Hawke biography, that Weltmann was a millionaire.

After a slow, cautious start Mannes talked about *Evelyn Biggers* for an hour, warming to eloquence, striding around the parlor, acting snatches of scenes. At one touching moment Nancy burst into tears and rushed from the room. Jeanne went out and comforted her, and after a while brought her back. From then on the room was charged with the strong emotion that is the bread and butter of movie directors, and the young man rode out his narrative with victorious spirit. Still, Mrs. Hawke was not one to be carried away. She smoothed her skirt, and put a handkerchief to her eyes, and thanked Mr. Mannes kindly; and now, she said, if everybody else would withdraw for half an hour or so, she wanted to talk things over just with John and Nancy.

Jeanne and Gus left the others, who proposed to walk around the town "for atmosphere"; Luzzatto also expressed some interest in finding the nearest bar. The Adams took a cab to the Ira Hawke Memorial Library, which stood on the crown of another hill, in a pretty park full of tall trees ablaze with autumn color. Jeanne and Gus walked on a carpet of fallen leaves to the wide low brick building. There was nobody inside the library but one young woman behind a desk, who went into a grand

flurry when Jeanne identified herself. Nobody was using the library at the moment, she explained, because the whole town was at the high school football game; Saturday afternoons in the fall were always bad. Jeanne noted that the long rows of books along the walls had a somewhat pristine and undisturbed look, under the rosy fluorescent lights. It was not surprising, she thought, that the young inhabitants of Hovey were less interested in devouring literature than Arthur had been. If one new Arthur came along in ten years, it was still well that the library should stand and wait for him, and meantime now and then somebody in Hovey might want a book!

The librarian said that of course Mr. and Mrs. Adam would want to see the Youngblood Hawke collection. As she fussed in her desk for keys she gabbled about the other two Hawke memorial libraries in county seat towns, and the mobile library jeep-trucks that went up into the mountain areas. Of course the other libraries were smaller than this one, and had no Youngblood Hawke exhibit, but it was only fair that Hovey should have received the best building.

When the librarian opened the door into the exhibit room Jeanne was shaken by the huge picture of Arthur that confronted them from the far wall. She had never seen it before. It was his high school graduation picture, blown up beyond life size. The broad head, the unruly hair thicker than she had ever seen it, the big lower lip compressed in pugnacious, self-conscious resolve over the upper one, the brilliant alert eyes were all like the Arthur she had known. But how heartbreakingly young he was! She looked away, and walked among the glass cases with her husband; the librarian discreetly withdrew. There were Arthur's manuscripts, some with her own pencilled comments in the margins; there were the wonderful letters he had received from Marquand and Faulkner; there were his honorary degrees, his prizes, his medals. One wall section was filled with all the editions of his works, American and foreign, more than a hundred volumes of every color and size, in hard covers and paper covers, that had proliferated from the five novels. Behind a locked glass door was a leather-bound row of first editions. Another wall was a solid mosaic of photographs. There were several snapshots of herself standing with Hawke. She halted and stared at these.

"God in Heaven," she murmured to Adam, "how young I was, Gus, when it all happened! How young he was!"

Adam said, "It gets to seem that way."

She said, "No more of this." But at the door she stopped and looked back at the picture of the high school boy.

The cab was waiting for them. She said drily to her husband, "I'll never come back to Hovey again. Let's go to the cemetery. All right?"

Adam said, "I thought we would."

The cab driver said, "Oh sure. Youngblood Hawke's grave. Lots of

people go there. Yes, I knew Art Hawke. He was a right pleasant fellow. Never put on any airs." He reminisced about Hawke all the way to the cemetery.

At the grave, as she stood with her head down and the wind whipping her skirt, with red and yellow leaves tumbling and whirling all around her, Jeanne's face wrinkled and tears fell from her eyes. Adam walked apart. Soon she came to him, drying her eyes, and leaned against him, contemplating the stone, which read:

> Arthur Youngblood Hawke
> HOVEY, 1920—NEW YORK, 1953
> *Death is only a sadness. Tragedy lies in waste.*
>   —CHAIN OF COMMAND

Jeanne said in a harsh voice, "They're all flourishing like the green bay tree, aren't they? Givney is the biggest man in the paperback business, Hoag goes on as before, Feydal just won an Academy award, and Frieda has a new young husband who seems to suit her just fine. Only Arthur is dead."

Adam said, "Well, Hoag was forced out of Hawke Brothers, but I'm afraid he's prospered since, so you can't call that retribution. They weren't villains, Jeanne, they're people who acted according to their nature."

"They were villains," Jeanne said. "Arthur didn't always punish his villains. He told the truth."

"Nobody's story is over," Adam said, "except his."

Jeanne fell silent.

When the taxicab drove out of the cemetery gate she said suddenly, "Do you think he would have written the American Comedy if he'd lived? Or is it true that the artists who are fated to die young sense it, and work insanely in the short time they have?"

Adam said, "Jeanne, I'm not sure—I don't believe anybody can be sure yet—but I think maybe he wrote the American Comedy."

Jeanne stared at him, and a gleam of affection broke through her black mood. "You," she said softly. "The man with the answers."

The three men from Hollywood stood outside the Hawke home, the low roof of which was deep in autumn leaves, drifted among a number of yellow rolled-up newspapers. Luzzatto said, exhaling a strong odor of Scotch, "We thought it would be smarter if we all went in together."

As they came inside, the evidence in the parlor suggested that the mission had been a success. Mrs. Hawke, Weltmann and Nancy were laughing, and a bottle of whiskey and a tray of soda crackers had appeared on the round center table. The mother, obviously enjoying the suspense, asked them all to be seated. Before giving her opinion, she said,

she wanted to hear from Jeanne and Gus, whom she trusted above anybody else where her son's work was concerned.

Jeanne glanced toward Lax, who blinked sleepily at her. She said, "Well, in the fewest possible words, I say take it."

The mother nodded, and looked to Adam. The lawyer said, "Of course I'll want to see the contract, and I'm not clear on some details of the escalator clauses. If those things work out, I'll be for it."

Mrs. Hawke said to Weltmann, "John?"

Hawke's brother-in-law grinned, touched his wig, and shrugged his thick shoulders. "As I've said, *Evelyn Biggers* was a failure. A film success would be a fine way to recoup. The money is good."

The mother turned to Nancy, who said, "Maybe the movie will make people read the book. That's all I care about. It was Arthur's best. Nobody appreciated it."

Mrs. Hawke cleared her throat. "That's what I think. I think a good movie is all that's needed to make that book sell in the millions. It's a great book. My trouble is I'm just sentimental. I guess that's what has decided me. Mr. Luzzatto bought Arthur's first book, and it's so nice that now he wants *Evelyn Biggers*. So it's yours, Mr. Luzzatto—providing of course you satisfy Mr. Adam as he says on all the details of the contract."

Jeanne's voice cut sharply into the jubilation and the congratulations. "*Mrs. Hawke!*" Her tone commanded silence, and everyone looked at her. "I have some good news for you. Mr. Lax has already told me that, if this deal works out, he'll give half his commission to the town of Hovey for the preservation of your house. There's every reason to think that it'll amount to at least thirty-five thousand dollars or more."

Mrs. Hawke exclaimed, "My, how perfectly wonderful! Thank you, Mr. Lax!" She jumped up and seized the whiskey bottle. "Now *that* calls for a drink all around."

Ferdie Lax, possibly for the first and only time in a lifetime of discussing money, looked surprised. So did the other two movie men. Then the agent lowered his eyes reverently. "It's the least I can do, Mrs. Hawke. Your son was a great man."

Hawke's mother stood in the doorway of the little house, as the party piled into the car which was to return them to Lexington. Her arms were folded, she was smiling, and holding her head high—and as she smiled, Jeanne saw her lower lip curl over the upper one in triumph. The mother's face, at that instant, seemed to dissolve into Arthur's.

"You just watch what happens, Jeanne," she called. "Art will have the last laugh on them all yet. That book is going to turn out to be the big money maker!"

Jeanne waved once, and with the same hand covered her eyes. As the car rolled down the hill, the curtains of the years parted. She saw Arthur's face as she had seen it in their last hour together. She felt his

perspiring cracking lips on hers, and she heard her own voice say, "I love you, Arthur. I've never loved another man, and I'll love you until I die."

It was just for a moment. Then the merciful curtains closed, and she was back in the crowded automobile, in the present day, beside her husband, going home to her children.

4

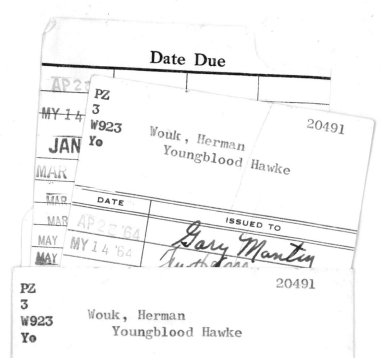